ALEXANDER CORDELL'S NOVELS OF WALES

Book One
The Fire People

THE FIRE PEOPLE was inspired by, and climaxes in, the inglorious Merthyr Tydfil riots of 1831 and the hanging of Dic Penderyn, the first Welsh martyr of the working class.

It is a novel of great power and vividness, peopled by a host of fascinating characters – Irish immigrants, European refugees, Welsh foundryworkers, whores, soldiers, miners, preachers, policemen – all lending to a backcloth that is alarming and appealing at one and the same time.

But most important is the story of Dic Penderyn – his warmth, his understanding, his dignity, his love for his wife, his loyalty to his friends, his courage in the face of helpless adversity.

ALEXANDER CORDELL'S NOVELS OF WALES

Book Two
Land of my Fathers

LAND OF MY FATHERS begins in Amlwch in North Wales in the 1830s, a copper town ruled harshly by Cornish experts in the pay of the Marquis of Anglesey, who, like the ironmasters in the south, owned everything, including the people. We follow Taliesin Roberts, the youthful son of the widely respected Gwyn, through the years of his childhood — mostly hard, but often idyllic — into manhood and eventual conflict with authority. This lures him south in escape to Dowlais and Sir John and Lady Charlotte Guest, who take him into their employ.

With the approach of the Chartist rebellion, Wales, under the spell of the euphoric Unions, was at that time a hot-bed or intrigue and espionage. Both Taliesin and his father, now an escapee from the transportation hulks, became inextricably entangled in the web. And it is against this tapestry of earthy realism and adventure that we watch the love Taliesin holds for Rhiannon flower into fulfilment ... and the hopeless devotion which Poll, Tal's cousin, bears him.

ALEXANDER CORDELL'S NOVELS OF WALES

Book Three
This Sweet and Bitter Earth

Toby Davies joined the men who worked the quarries in the north of Wales at the beginning of the century as a young boy. He was to share their dangerous, unhealthy, underpaid lives and join the bitter struggle for their Workers' Combination, to set their rights against the Owners' conditions. He was to learn about the dignity of man: before the hearth, and in the riotous communion of the streets. He was to learn love – from Bron, and Nanwen O'Hara.

And when he came south, to the Rhondda Valley, to work with coal, he found no easier future: dust had given way to soot, the slate caverns to dark tunnels where he crawled to hack away the coal, and above ground poverty, held ruthlessly to ransom by the Coalmasters, was rampant. Toby was there, at the notorious Tonypandy riots of 1910, their aftermath of police suppression, and the eventual military occupation of the Rhonnda – on the orders of the Home Secretary, Winston Churchill. He was there with Bron, and Nanwen, among the people whose town was robbed of its manhood, living in the shadow of the hated Universal pit.

**Also by the same author,
and available in Coronet Books:**

The Fire People
Hosts Of Rebecca
Land Of My Fathers
Peerless Jim
Rape Of The Fair Country
Rogues March
Song Of The Earth
This Sweet And Bitter Earth
The Welsh Trilogy
   (Rape Of The Fair Country
   Host Of Rebecca
   Song Of The Earth
   in one volume)

Alexander Cordell's Novels of Wales

THE FIRE PEOPLE
LAND OF MY FATHERS
THIS SWEET AND BITTER EARTH

Alexander Cordell

CORONET BOOKS
Hodder and Stoughton

First published in three separate volumes:

The Fire People © 1972 by Alexander Cordell
First published in Great Britain in 1972 by Hodder and Stoughton Ltd
Coronet edition 1973
Land Of My Fathers © 1983 by Alexander Cordell
First published in Great Britain in 1983 by Hodder and Stoughton Ltd
Coronet edition 1985
This Sweet And Bitter Earth © 1977 by Alexander Cordell
First published in Great Britain in 1977 by Hodder and Stoughton Ltd
Coronet edition 1979

This edition 1987

British Library C.I.P.

Cordell, Alexander
Alexander Cordell's novels of Wales: The fire people:
Land of my fathers: This sweet and bitter earth.
Rn: George Alexander Graber   I. Title
II. Cordell, Alexander. The fire people.
III. Cordell, Alexander. Land of my fathers
IV. Cordell, Alexander. This sweet and bitter earth
823'.914[F]   PR6053.067

ISBN 0-340-40790-5

Printed and bound in Great Britain for
Hodder and Stoughton Paperbacks, a
division of Hodder and Stoughton Ltd.,
Mill Road, Dunton Green, Sevenoaks,
Kent (Editorial Office: 47 Bedford
Square, London WC1B 3DP) by
Richard Clay Ltd, Bungay, Suffolk

For Richard Lewis, who they
called Dic Penderyn, unjustly hanged.

Book One

THE FIRE PEOPLE

I am indebted to Mr. John Collett, F.L.A., and Mr. Michael Elliott, F.L.A., both of Newport Public Library, for making available to me numerous books of research and rare documents. To Mr. Tom Whitney of Merthyr Tydfil Library I am grateful for nineteenth-century maps and other references, and to Miss M. E. Elsas, the Glamorgan County Archivist, for assistance in historical locations. To these, as to Mr. A. Leslie Evans and other historians, I offer my thanks.

Certain vital papers have come to light during my research which, lost for a hundred and forty years, are valuable evidence concerning the life and times of Dic Penderyn; these new facts have a direct bearing on the Merthyr Rising and are important enough to be included as an appendix to the book.

I wish to acknowledge the assistance given by the Departmental Record Officer of the Home Office in tracing these documents.

. . . As to the men I accuse, I do not know them, I have never seen them, I have no resentment or animosity towards them. They are for me merely entities, spirits of social maleficence. And the act which I perform here is only a revolutionary means of hastening the revelation of truth and justice. I have but one passion — that of light. This I crave for the sake of humanity, which has suffered so much . . .

Zola

1

THERE was more commotion going on than a Tipperary bath night.

Big Bonce was clogging around with Lady Godiva; Curly Hayloft, as bald as an egg, was doing a bull-fight with Tilly; Skin-Crone, the cook, was beating time to the shriek of the fiddle, and the navvy hut was alive with dancers of Kerry and County Mayo.

And as Gideon played he saw in his near-blind stare the twenty beds, the labour-dead sleepers straight off shift and the dark eyes of the Welsh girl who watched him from a seat in the corner. Someone turned up the lamps and he now saw more clearly as he fiddled out the old Irish reel: the coloured waistcoats of the navvies he saw, the violent disorder of the blankets, the mud-stained jerkins and hobnail boots, the soaked dresses of the wives hung up to dry: all this he saw partly by vision and partly by memory, from the days before he was blind. And he knew that in a shadow by the table old Peg Jarrotty, the wake corpse, would be hanging by a rope under his arm-pits, a broom under his chin, and a pint of home-brew slopping in his fist. Hooked on his chest would be the coffin plate—'Peg Jarrotty, Wexford: died June 14th, 1830.'

'There's me wee darling!' cried Tilly, dancing up in a sweeping of skirts. 'Won't you raise us a smile, Peg Jarrotty, for the look on your face makes me miserable to death!' and she tipped him under the chin.

Vaguely, Gideon wondered if it was respectful to the dead, but he played on, smiling: this is what they wanted, he reflected; this was their religion.

Belcher Big Tum came up, all sixteen stones of him. 'Sure, hasn't he drained that pint yet? It's the same stuff he used to sink down the Somerset Arms, isn't it?'

'It is not!' shouted Lady Godiva. 'He never touched that dish-water without a two-inch livener, isn't that right, me lovely dead fella? Shall I lace it up with a drop o' hard stuff?' And she stroked his face.

'Can't you show some respect for the dead?' asked Jobina, the Welsh girl in the corner, and she rose, her dark eyes sweeping around the dancers.

Gideon lowered his fiddle; the noise of the hut faded.

Jobina said: 'I can stand the randies and the heathen language, but I can't abide the wakes. Do you have to act like animals?'

'She's asking for a filling up again,' said Moll Maguire.

'You leave the Irish to the Irish, woman!' shouted Tilly.

'And the Welsh to the Welsh, and remember it!' Jobina put her hands on her hips. 'Irish, you call yourselves? Dancing around a corpse, and him hanging from the ceiling with a broom under his chin? Don't tell me they do that in Kerry.' She strolled the room, looking them up and down. 'You've got him like a pig on hooks. Have him down tonight before I'm back off shift or I'm taking it to Foreman. It's bad enough having to eat with live Irish without sleeping with dead ones.'

'Heavens above!' gasped Tilly. 'Did you hear that? She's asking for a doin' . . .'

'Ach,' said Belcher testily, 'we're not after woman-fighting. If the wee Welsh bitch wants old Jarrotty down, I say let's give it.'

'Why give her anything? She's a foreigner here,' cried Tilly, breasting up.

'You're the foreigners,' replied Jobina, 'or isn't this the county of Glamorgan?'

Big Bonce swung to Gideon, crying, 'What do you say, fiddler—you're Welsh, too, aren't you?'

'The fella's as Irish as me, aren't ye, son?' Moll Maguire now, with her arm around Gideon's waist; she was tall for a woman, yet only inches above his shoulder. Gideon smiled

12

with slow charm, saying:

'It's no odds to me, Irish—I'm only the fiddler, and you pay well.'

'You should be ashamed of yourself!' said Jobina, turning away.

'And why should he?' demanded Skin-Crone, the cook from the other end of the hut: she was sitting astride a chair stirring up a cauldron for the midnight supper, and the steam was going up like a witch's brew. 'When are we putting wee Jarrotty down, then?' she asked.

'He's having a decent Catholic service the moment we find his leg.'

'Haven't ye found it yet, then? Wasn't it buried under the fall?'

'How did it happen?' asked Gideon, and Belcher said:

'He was barrowing the big stuff on the dram-road slope, with the mule wagging along the line as if tomorrow would do, but little Jarrotty slipped, ye see, and the dram came down. The dram came down, then the mule and then the muck, and he was under six tons of the stuff when we dug him out.'

'And he'd only got one leg,' said Moll.

'Where did the other one get to?' asked Lady Godiva, scratching.

'Search me—the mule must have eaten it.'

The talk went on, the drinking was heavy. Gideon leaned against the hut wall and imagined the stars above Taibach, for this was his country. The wind moved over the heath and he smelled the heather and a tang of sulphur from the works, and he raised his face instantly to the salt of the sea-drift, which he loved.

'Here's your pay, fiddler, the dancing's stopped,' said Belcher, and pressed a shilling into his hand; Gideon took it, and did not reply. Instead, he lifted his head higher to taste the sea-drift, and Jobina followed his sightless gaze to the open window, threw her red shawl over her shoulders for the cropping and wandered towards him.

'What's your name?'

He straightened to her. 'Gideon Davies.'

13

Bending, she pulled at a red stocking. 'What the hell are ye doing in a place like this?'

'What are any of us doing?' he asked.

'You local?'

He said evenly: 'I used to be—Taibach.'

'Welsh, eh?'

He smiled at her, and she added: 'It's a pleasure to be civilised, even if ye have to live with the heathen.'

'They're not so bad,' he said. 'Give me Irish in preference to the foreigners.'

Beyond the vision of her unseen face he saw the windows of Aberafon winking at the moon, the square thatch of Rhigos where he stole from the orchard: he smelled again the sulphur of the night wind coming up from Briton Ferry and saw the baying brilliance of the night when the molten iron flashed on the bungs of Dowlais. The white-hot bucketings of Skewen and Swansea were in his bedroom of childhood, and he would lie awake listening to the cries of the mules under the whips in the stack-yards and along the dram-roads of Morriston. There was the black shine of the cassocks in the C. of E. the bearded thunderings of Ianto Nonconform in the little red-brick chapel off the Vernon Arms, and the brown arms in summer of the girl he knew but whose name he had forgotten.

'You play good,' said the Welsh girl, watching him.

'Thanks.'

'Where did you catch it, then?'

'Taibach Copper Works.'

'That bloody place, cauldrons and chopped colliers.'

The navvies had stopped carousing now and were feeding on the bench: the pot Skin-Crone was serving from contained many different foods: vegetables which she had stolen from Taibach market made the slush. The meats were attached by strings, and each portion she pulled out with care and gave it to the owner: half a hare for Belcher, a born poacher; two pig's trotters tied together for Curly Hayloft, a sheep's head between Mercy Merriman and Betsy Paul, Dick of the Iron Hand's woman, who was visiting. Crone and Moll shared an ox-tail they had blackmailed from a butcher with two wives;

14

Blackbird feasted on a pound of ribs of beef, which he had bought, being honest. All had wooden spoons, and these they dipped excitedly into the pot, blowing and gasping at the steam and elbowing each other for room.

'B'ant you eating, fiddler?' asked Belcher.

'No, I'm just off to Mamie Goldie,' replied Gideon.

'Who's Mamie Goldie?' asked Moll. 'She don't sound decent.'

'She is clean,' said Gideon instantly.

'By God, that's a change. You lodge with her?' asked the Welsh girl.

He nodded and she looked again into his face, seeing the telltale tattoo of the furnace grit, yet his eyes appeared untouched by the blast: bright blue, they shone in his brown face.

'How did you collect it?'

He could have gone into the detail, but the wounds were too new to his soul. He could have told her how the copper exploded in a damp mould; that Mike Halloran had just come into the casting-house and stopped for a ladle in front of him, so he took most of it. Also, Popo Hopkin, aged seventy, due to retire in three weeks, took some, too; and screamed and went in circles with his body on fire as the copper bit deep. Halloran died in shrieks they heard as far up as the Brombil dram-road. Strangely, for all his age, Popo did not die, but lived on the black shadows of his forge-sided cottage, nurtured by Company respectability—come in, boys, see what we're doing for Popo Hopkin. Maintained by a devoted wife on four and six a week pension, Popo lived where the children could not see him. And a disability like this do have a bit of compensation—apart from the four and six—he used to say to the Quakers who visited, faces averted—for you can't appear shocking in a two-ale bar and you eat that much less with only half a mouth.

In his two years of blindness Gideon had bred great shafts of hope that wounded despair. The comradeship of ear and nose had constructed a new world in his darkness: and touch, a vital sense left to him, completed the resurrection from self-pity. Now he said lightly:

'There is nothing to tell—the mould was wet, and it spat.'

The navvies quarrelled at the table in good-natured banter and oaths, and Betsy Paul shouted: 'You'm a fine fiddle, boy. You tried us up in Pontstorehouse?'

'He do not play in cellars,' said Jobina.

'The money's right in Merthyr, mind—we got fiddlers and organ-grinders, and my Dick Llaw-Haearn is right fond of music. You like to play for silver some time?' She tore at the sheep's head, grinning above it with strong white teeth, and swept back her matted hair with a greasy hand.

'Some time,' said Gideon. 'But it's a Derry fiddle and it sings that much sweeter to the Irish.'

'You Irish?' asked Jobina. 'You said you were Welsh.'

'Welsh parents and born in Galway.'

'It makes no difference, there's still the business of eating. I'm cropping night shift up on Brombil—you going that way?'

Gideon nodded. 'Miners' Row.'

'Bloody good for you—right on top of the mill.'

'I am not there all the time,' he said.

Reaching the door of the hut, he turned and bowed to the room. The navvies, now clustered around the wake of Jarrotty, shouted rough goodbyes.

'The heathen lot of bastards,' said Jobina.

Gideon touched his hair. 'Good night, and thank you.'

'You pay 'em too much respect,' said she.

As she opened the door the night swept in; the wake candles fluttered and the room was alight with the flashing of the Taibach vents. In the sulphurous stink that enveloped them, Gideon said reflectively, 'Once, in a hall in Tredegar, I played first violin in *Judas Maccabaeus*, and I bowed to people then.'

'Who's Judas Maccabaeus?'

He smiled as they went down the steps of the hut. 'It doesn't matter now.'

'You staying on here?' asked Jobina.

'No. I'm on the road in the morning.'

'And you blind . . . ?'

'It makes no difference. Every year I do the round to Merthyr and the Top Towns—on the fiddle with political

16

pamphlets.'

'God! An agitator! You do this all the year?'

'Chiefly in summer—too cold on the mountains in winter.'

'Where you bound tomorrow then?' she asked.

'I won't get far above Mynydd Margam.'

'We'll be at Maesteg this time tomorrow—that's strange.'

'I thought you were cropping at Brombil all summer,' said Gideon.

'Ach, no—there's no bread in it. If I'm bedding with the navvies I might as well work with them, and the Nipper Tandy gang is on the Maesteg dram-road in the morning—might see more of you?'

'I doubt it,' said Gideon.

THE Welsh girl left Gideon at the company shop and took the Constant Incline up to Brombil.

'You be all right, fiddler?'

'Of course.'

'I'll hand ye down to Miners' if you want it.'

'I can manage.'

'Good night to ye, then.'

'Good night.'

With his fiddle under his arm Gideon began to tap his way down the dram-road which brought the works coal from The Side, and he knew exactly where he was for the thunder of the drams was behind him, singing on the incline; before him, flashing on his open eyes, the vents of the copper works glowed and flared against dull banks of sulphurous clouds. Here, as a child, he had known this place from Granny's Hole up to The Green where the soldiers paraded. He was at home here, and he knew the blackened trees and the carnage of a burned land. But even in his time he could also remember the clear beauty of the Rhanallt stream where he used to fish for trout with his fingers. Often he had grimly considered the advantages of blindness as row after row of workers' cottages were flung up across the bright fields of his youth. And there still lived in his ears the chinking *tribannau* of the breast-ploughing: the steaming, straining oxen, six abreast and led by a horse was a treasured vision of his past, with his clothes dusted white with the lime-carting from Cornelly quarries. His father, long dead, used to hire himself out at the fairs of Swansea for fifteen sovereigns a year, and by this means came to Taibach and the

Groeswen cottage where Gideon was born. There was home-brewed ale for weddings and cider for harvesting; bread was baked in an earth oven in the garden—and neighbours came for miles for its service—barley bread for weekdays, pure wheat loaves for Sabbaths, all brown and crusty on the top, and his mouth watered now at the thought of the rich yellow-churned butter of the fat wives on the stalls at Taibach market. Then, on *Calan Gaeaf*, the first day of November, a pig would be slaughtered, salted and stored in oatmeal. The girls, he remembered, were gay in poke-bonnets and giggles and mostly dark-haired. But one whose name was Angharad Jones was fair, and it was she whom he had kissed in a lane near Rhigos one Whit Sunday: her lips, he remembered, tasted of bitterness, for they had been picking wild sloes.

He awoke from his reflections as Dai End-On, going to the Somerset Arms, hawked deep and spat at his feet. He did not speak, but Gideon knew him by hop smell.

'Good night, blind man.' A young tramping Welshman with a bundle on a stick passed him at the top of Miners'. He was rolling a little in his gait; there was about him a happy, tipsy charm.

'Good night,' said Gideon.

The red flashes of the casting-house guided Gideon with the accuracy of a lighthouse beam to a ship in an ocean waste, for, by some inexplicable chemistry the vicious light imposed its brilliance on the half-dead retinae of his sight, bringing visions that momentarily exposed panoramas of the blackened landscape. The labouring night shift of Cotton Row and Miners' bellowed his childhood's music with a new ferocity, for a big order had come in from Spain. Dram-wheels grated to a stop on the road behind him and Gideon leaped away with astonishing alacrity.

'You mind your back, Gid!' cried Randy, Mamie's boy. 'You damn near took it that time, remember!'

'You run me down and you will answer to Mamie,' said Gideon, smiling, and waited while the dram went past, pushed by two, for another was there; young Blod Irish, by the sound of her, for he heard the soprano in her gasps.

'You fiddlin' at the Jarrotty wake tonight, then?' called Randy over his shoulder: imp-black and in rags was he, and Blod, aged sixteen, with her body as straight as a bar on the dram beside him; hauliers both, and the coal was heaped high, for Randy, to his credit, never pushed easy.

'Yes,' called Gideon back, 'how did you know?'

'Met a friend of yours—get about a bit for a musician, eh?'

A group of men were talking about the benefit clubs as he tapped down Miners'. The copper vents mushroomed with flame then, and he saw his door. Opening it quickly, he entered the room that was shared by Little Randy and Dai End-On. Here flashes of the works did not enter, and he was blind again. Like others in Miners' Row, this was a company cottage, three up, two down; owned by the English Copper Company who owned everything of value in the district, including the population. Yet there existed a paternal benevolence among the masters that allowed them rare acts of generosity, and Nine Miners' Row was one example. In the tenancy rules signed by her husband, deceased six years ago after passing through ten-ton rollers, Mamie Goldie was allowed to continue tenancy on the undertaking that she did not take in lodgers. But there were two lodgers in Nine Miners'. There was Zimmerman, a Pole of doubtful origin, who shared with Gideon in the upstairs front, and it was generally agreed to be one of the best upstairs in Taibach: Mamie herself shared the downstairs back with Dai End-On and Little Randy, her son, who was there to keep it proper, for the neighbours can be buggers where a virgin lady is involved, as Mamie used to say.

'That you, Gid?' she called now.

'Yes, Mamie.'

'You done the navvy?'

'Yes, the wake is nearly over.'

'Pity about him, isn't it?'

'Ay, a good little man was Peg Jarrotty.'

The silence beat about them after a bedlam of snores from the three Irish brothers Tim, Mike and Joe, Mrs. Billa Jam's lodgers next door. Lately come in from Fishguard from yet another Irish famine, they had seen people grazing in the fields like cattle up in County Mayo, though it sounds a tall one to me, said Mamie Goldie, for we don't have the molars for grazin'.

'Astonishin', it is, how Mary's Children always snore in unison,' she said to Gideon once. 'The Welsh, on the other hand, snore in harmony: queer, isn't it?'

It was not queer, it was a fact. Often, when he could not sleep Gideon would wander the deserted streets of Taibach and listen to this phenomenon.

'It's lyin' on their backs that does it,' said Mamie, 'and there's better choral singing done unconscious than swimming the River Jordan in the back pews of Swansea Calfaria upright, and I do mean Swansea, for this lot don't know a crotchet from tonic sol-fa. You all right, Gid?'

She peered up at him now, clutching at the front of her faded nightgown.

'Fine, Mamie,' he said, moving past her.

'You eaten?'

'I ate with the Nipper Tandy gang,' he lied.

The mill roared obscenely between them, and Gideon sensed the warmth of her humanity. Strangely, although he was nearly twenty-six he had never known a woman's love, nor Mamie the gentleness of a man such as he. He was big, she thought; until now, standing close to him, she had never realised the size of him; and he was made even bigger in her eyes by his unusual gentleness. The men Mamie had known were those of fists and ale, with an eye filled up at the very first argument. Their talk was of the copper vats and iron-pudding, with fighting most Saturdays down at the Oddfellows Lodge of loyal brothers, and the lot of them put together as loyal as a bag of biblical serpents, then some, said Mrs. Billa Jam next door. Gideon, for his part, saw in Mamie Goldie the mother he had lost to the Old Cholera when he was ten years old: always in her presence he smelled again the heavy scent of funeral flowers, and saw in a window a candle flickering on polished oak.

'You heard about Merve—Billa's lad next door?'

21

Mamie loved and nurtured Mervyn Jam, aged nine, and his twin, Saul.

'No, what has happened?' Gideon paused at the stairs.

'Collected a backside of buck-shot from that old devil up on Rhigos.'

'Mr. Evans?'

'Mr. Waxey Evans—I'll give him cobbling, shooting at the boys—far too handy with that blunderbuss, he is.' She belched and pardoned. 'All fair to young Merve, he told the truth. Him and Willie Taibach laying night-lines in Rhigos pond and the old beggar comes out and lets fly—got Merve in both cheeks, and one is still in—pellets, I mean. Another two inches and it would 'ave been through his watchercallit. Ain't good enough, I say—might have laid him up for life.'

'Is he really hurt?'

'He was when I was getting 'em out—and Billa nearly fainting off. Daren't tell his da, of course—not that he'd care—oiling his apple down at the Lodge . . .'

'There are still some pellets left in?'

'Only one, and I'm after that now—just slipped out for a tot of gin to send the little soul off . . .' She smiled, coming closer, breathing gin all over him. 'Buck-shot in lads is nothing—it's the men's the trouble. If God had a heart for women He'd have let nothing in trousers live beyond the age o' thirteen.' She added: 'You seen my Randy boy?'

Gideon nodded.

Mamie said: 'Were Blod Irish with him?'

'I . . . I think so.'

'And Dai . . . ?'

'He just passed me, and . . .'

'And took his ticket for the Somerset Arms.' She bowed her head. 'I see him; parting his whiskers and pouring in a pewter without so much as a swallow.' Raising her face, she said: 'You see what me life is, Gid? A randy and a drunkard. Did me boy smell clean?'

'Like a pear drop—neither ale nor short on him.'

'Ay, but he's havin' it off with that Blod Irish as soon as I'd take me life. But that don't keep me tossing awake, lad—it's

22

the ale. If he loosens one in her he can always walk her up to God, but it's the drinking that's drowning me—just the same as his father.'

He wanted to go to bed but she retained him with ease, such was her music.

'An' me a Jew-Welsh from London—a fool he is to get mixed up with the Irish.' She turned away. 'God smooth your dream,' said she. 'By the way—Zimmy's in.'

The works flared again as the copper boiled and in its redness she watched him climb the stairs. When he reached the landing and turned from her sight, Mamie leaned against the door of her kitchen, clasped her hands and stared up with clenched eyes through the roof to the stars.

On the first-floor landing Gideon stopped, his hand outstretched for the door, but he did not touch it. There came in a draught beneath it a faint scent of pine and fire; then he heard a step within the room.

'That you, Zimmerman?' He asked this as he entered, but he knew it was not the Pole, for the step was too light for the heavy-footed Zim: also, women breathe in faint sighs when fearful, sounds that only the blind can hear, and he knew that the room window was open for the mill hammers were sharper, the roller-whining keener. Entering swiftly, Gideon shut the door behind him, turned the key and dropped it into his pocket.

Trapped behind the bed the girl glared at him in the flashing of the works, and the smell of her rags, the crushed hay of her rough sleeping came to Gideon's nostrils. Gaining the window, he slammed it shut; the girl made an inarticulate sound when he moved towards her; she backed away.

'No nearer,' she said. 'One move and I'm swipin' ye.'

Gideon knew she was young, and smiled; he preferred this ragged aggressor to a fawning servility; and he was wondering what she could be stealing, unless it was something of Zimmerman's, for he himself owned nothing. Then he realised that he had bought bread and cheese from the Shop that morning. With an agility that amazed him she suddenly leaped across the bed and ran to the door, rattling the handle.

'It is locked,' he said, and approached her, gripping her arm as she slid away, and she beat her fists about his face as he pulled her against him, controlling her, and the door rattled from the fight. Mamie stirred downstairs.

'You all right, Gid?' she called.

The mill was momentarily silent. Panting, they clung to each other; light flared in the window and the girl knew him for blind. Mamie shouted; 'You bumped yourself again, Gid?'

The girl in his arms groaned quietly to the pain of his fingers, Gideon cried at the door: 'Yes, I'm all right, Mamie.'

'Then tell that Zim to stop kicking about.'

Outside in the Row a man was singing drunkenly. Breathing heavily, Gideon and the girl listened automatically, and she no longer struggled. Nor did she move away when he released her.

'What have you taken?'

She hugged the food against her.

'Give it to me,' he commanded.

She made a sweet lamenting noise, and said: 'I'm bloody starving, mister.'

'Give it to me.'

He was impatient of her now. Soon Zimmerman would be back from the Oddfellows, and for all his talk that property was theft, for all his idealistic theories he would hand this one over to the Military because theft was a major crime: property in Taibach was inviolate and the less one possessed the more it was sacrosanct: the child would go to transportation for sure.

Taking the bread from her hands Gideon broke it in half, did the same with the cheese and returned to her a portion of each.

'Blind, aren't ye.' It was a statement, not a question.

Gideon said: 'Now get out before somebody catches you in here.' He opened the door, adding softly, 'Next time don't steal—ask for food.'

'Ach, ye get nothing at all for the asking, for I bloody tried it.'

24

To him it was pleasant that she was so young—perhaps only about fifteen, he thought. His life since blindness had been the blousy, golden-hearted scitterers of the doorsteps, or the bawdy fish-women of the Old Bar. His mind reached back to the kisses of Angharad Jones, and he wanted this girl to stay. Sometimes Zimmerman, for all his talk of morality and social justice, would bring home a woman. And Gideon would be forced to lie in his blindness while Zimmerman denied him the right to other senses.

'Go now,' he said, 'and do not make a noise.'

She did not speak again and he heard her descend the stairs with a burglar quiet, open the street door and softly close it. The night air touched his lips from the window: he knew he had not done with her. Vagrants such as these haunted good-will; they could not afford otherwise. Yes, he thought, she would be back. Men, unlike mules, stand skinning twice.

He listened to the smooth, satin clamour of her bare feet racing down the Row.

Zimmerman, his room-mate, came in hours after midnight: Gideon turned in sleep, opening blind eyes to the light of the candle.

'It is I,' announced Zimmerman, and began to undress.

'It was a good Oddfellows?'

'It was not a meeting of the Oddfellows,' said the Pole. 'Sit up, for I have something to say.'

'It is a damned good time of night.'

'It is not night,' said Zimmerman, 'it is nearly morning. Are you listening?'

Gideon nodded, silently cursing him. This was typical of Zim; everything was dramatic, and if it was not already dramatic, he made it so. Heavy-footed, the big man sat down on the bed.

'I have been speaking with an agent of the Friendly Association.'

Gideon sat up. 'The Lancashire people?'

'Also Doherty of the Cotton Spinners. You hear he has opened an office in London?'

'For the protection of labour?'

'For the drawing together of all trade unions—resistance to wage reductions—even to apply for wage increases...'

'*Increases?* That is ridiculous!'

'He is not too ambitious,' said Zimmerman, and lit his pipe, puffing out smoke. 'One day it will come. More, there is to be a meeting of colliers of Staffordshire, Yorkshire, Scotland and Wales—to be held at the Bolton Authority Lodge. Meanwhile, we are to test the pulse—you call it that?—of the Welsh.'

'We aren't ready for full Unionism yet,' said Gideon, sitting up. 'We'd be lucky if we got support for the Benefits.'

Zimmerman said: 'Wales must be got ready, she cannot lag behind. I told the agents—I am always telling the agents—when the trouble comes it will begin in Wales: these people are like mine, of fire. Up in Bolton they all seem half asleep.'

Gideon said: 'Sometimes I wonder if we are working for Unionism or rebellion...'

'Are these not one and the same?'

'Of course not.'

'But how can you have Unionism without rebellion? The employers will fight tooth and claw; they will not part with a sovereign unless you eradicate them.'

'It will take time,' said Gideon blankly.

'That is where we differ.' Zimmerman rose and walked about the room. 'You may have the time, but I have not.'

'It can be done,' came the reply. 'There is no need for blood.' The copper works mushroomed flame, the night became white with incandescent fire; immediately in the line of his sight, Gideon saw the Pole quite clearly, then the vision died.

'I am leaving for Merthyr in the morning,' said Zimmerman. 'The population is big—nearly thirty thousand. I am told, too, that unrest is present and that it is likely to grow. You know they have a temporary Union branch there?'

'I did not know.'

'You should read the pamphlets, Gid.'

'I'd be delighted to.'

Zimmerman grunted. 'I apologise to you. Sometimes I am

26

particularly stupid.'

'You are being particularly stupid if you think you can organise a riot in Wales.'

'You should read your history,' replied the Pole. 'They are an aggressive little people; they have been organising riots since the digging of Offa's Dyke, or must I also teach you history?'

Gideon lay back on the pillow again. Zimmerman possessed the ability to anger him: often he had wondered at the possibility of them continuing to work together, for the clash of their personalities was inhibiting the bond of their common ideals. The Pole's vague antecedents did not particularly worry Gideon; at times Zimmerman talked of Krakow, his birthplace, and the fight of his people for decency in the face of an appalling oppression; and there were occasions when Gideon wondered why Zimmerman was not fighting for them instead of advancing his radical ideas in Britain. But one thing was sure, he had done a lot for Wales; the opening of five benefit clubs and three Union branches, mainly in the north, was no small achievement.

'And I wonder what the Coal-Miners' Union would say about that?' asked Zimmerman, undressing by his bed.

'Say about what?'

'My theory that you cannot have Unionism without rebellion?'

'Little, I expect. It's a theory that's been done to death. Doherty didn't spill any blood forming the Spinners, did he? The same can be said of the Friendly Association.'

'It is you who is speaking of blood, not I,' said Zimmerman.

'I thought riot meant blood, or perhaps I'm mistaken.'

The Pole got into bed and blew out the candle; the mist about Gideon darkened, and the other said; 'Sometimes I think we talk a different language, Gideon Davies. People like Doherty and William Twiss and the Bolton representatives are scratching the surface. When I talk of riot I mean rebellion that leads from riot: if I ever talk of blood I mean a nation in revolt. The natural outcome of such an event would be to

27

decimate this generation in sacrifice for the next; wash the hands clean of it, and start all over again. Often I think that Unionism is stillborn. Its embryo died because it could not exist in a society of thieves.'

'It's an attractive theory,' said Gideon, turning over. 'You should mention it to the Authority Lodge next time you are in Bolton.'

'Perhaps I will do that. By the way—how did you get on with the navigators today?'

'They had their wake, they had the ale and their women, but they were not much concerned with politics.'

'Exactly. Sometimes I think we are wasting our efforts with this generation of workers; this was the point I was trying to make.'

'Let's march on London and have a blood bath,' said Gideon.

'Merthyr first, London later. Good night, my moral force friend,' said Zimmerman.

3

MAVIS SAMUEL, wife of Lemuel Samuel of the Company shop in Taibach, was having her first in that month of June, and I expected she'd have a going-over, said Mamie Goldie, for very big in the head is Lemuel, same as his da.

'Eh dear, love you,' said Lemuel, beloved spouse behind the curtains, while Mervyn Jam hammered the counter in the Shop.

'A ha'porth o' bulls-eyes!' cried Merve. 'Shop, shop, Lemuel Samuel!'

'Who is that?' whispered Mavis, twisting.

'Only one of the kids—that brat Jam by the sounds of him.'

'You there, Lemuel Samuel?' called Merve. 'What about some bulls-eye, then?'

'Coming!'

Gaunt as a pile of haunches and shinbones is Lemuel the Shop, official of the English Copper Works at twenty-two shillings a week, and only Company tokens taken, remember, if the customers are Company employees, and half a crown a week stopped for the rent. And here is my Mavis having her first, God help her, and the first is always a bit of a squeeze, they tell me. A son and heir for Lemuel Samuel, another hand behind the counter, preferably in the butchery department where I have filed off the numbers on the weights.

'What shall we call him, love?' asked Lemuel.

'I know what I'll call him,' replied Mavis groaning. 'You can have the next one. For the love of God, go and fetch Eunice Night-Time.'

'She sleeps in the day, my lovely,' said Lemuel. 'Besides,

seven and six she charged Mrs. Billa Jam Tart for an assisted delivery, and that was her ninth—fairly slipped out. But Mamie Goldie's been sent for, rest assured.' Patting her head as he proceeded into the shop.

' 'Morning, Mr. Samuel,' said Merve.

'Good morning, Mervyn Jam.'

'Ha'porth of bulls-eyes, please, Mr. Samuel.'

Bright-faced and quiffed is Merve, aged nine and well soaped behind the ears by Mamie, who practically kept him, although he was the boy next door, and she always hoses me down first thing in the morning, said Merve. Up on tip-toe now, he examined the scales, for Lemuel Samuel had a name for sleight of hand; a trick so astonishing that gum-drops had been known to vanish up his sleeve. With the flourish of a high priest Lemuel dropped in eight to a halfpenny and Merve subsided with a grin.

'Oh, God!' gasped Mavis from behind the curtains.

'Mrs. Samuel don't sound too good,' said Merve, peering.

'Suffering, as you can hear, my son,' said Lemuel. 'Got a slight touch of the colic.'

'Oh, ay?' said Merve, 'I thought she was nine months gone.'

'There are various interpretations of the state,' said Lemuel severely. 'And for boys of nine the colic will suffice. Incidentally, is it true that you were recently involved in a shooting incident, Mervyn Jam?'

'Ay, sir—got me breeches heated with buck-shot. Four in me left cheek, two in me right.'

'And how might that have happened, Mervyn Jam?'

'Poaching down at Rhigos with Willie Taibach, Mr. Samuel, but don't tell nobody.'

'And Mr. Waxey Evans the gentry cobbler the fortunate eye behind the gun?'

'Ay, ay. And fair peppered us, he did, the old basket. Willie got off but I got it proper. Haven't told anybody else, see, for Waxey still don't know it was us on them night-lines...' and Lemuel Samuel interjected:

'Then let the punishment fit the crime, Mervyn Jam,' and he lifted out two bulls-eyes and dropped them back into the jar, saying, 'Never let it be said that I would inform on a customer. Where, by the way, is Mamie Goldie?'

'Down Taibach market, Mr. Samuel,' said Merve, glum.

'Excellent, and when might she be back?'

'Not till tonight, Mr. Samuel.' He added: 'You want her for Mrs. Samuel, Mr. Samuel?'

'Certainly not. If I need medical attention I will send for the expert, Eunice Night-Time. Good day to you,' and he shut the door.

Mavis stiffened on the bed. 'Was that Mervyn Jam?'

'It was, my lovely—how did you know?'

'I dreamed it,' she gasped. 'Send him for Mamie, Lem—she's a midwife, too, and she only charges half a crown.'

'That is just what I've done, my precious—she'll be with you under the hour.'

'Oh, God—an hour!' whispered Mavis Samuel, and bit at her fingers.

In the sweating sighs and prayers of Mavis, beloved spouse, Lemuel Samuel of the company shop sat in a dream of sonship —one, two, three, four—five big lusty sons—two in the butchery, two in the groceries and one in the drapes—good old Mavis: in a dream of profit he sat amid red garters for girls, crêpe for funerals, lace for weddings; tiger-nuts and liquorice all-sorts, also Glyn Neath horse tonic, which was excellent for morning sickness, said Mrs. Billa Jam, the expert.

'Oh, God! Oh, God!' gasped Mavis, twisting on the bed.

'I tell you Mamie's coming, girl—I've sent the half a crown. Hush you, for heaven's sake—it's very bad for trade.'

Mavis Samuel died at half past ten that night.

'Poor wee soul, he was cut up dreadful,' said Billie Jam Tart.

The morning was all over bright and merry with June when Gideon took the road to the mountains.

'You comin' back for dinner, Gid?' Mamie screwed at her hands.

'Of course not, Mamie, I'm taking the road.' He did a strange thing: bending, he kissed her face and she raised her hand to it and stared as if he had struck her.

'When the leaves turn I'll be back,' he said, and she lowered her head.

'Goodbye, Gid. God guide your feet.'

She stood at the door watching him tapping with his stick up the Row towards the mountain, and Mrs. Billa Jam next door came out wiping her hands on her apron, and said: 'The fella wants his head hooking out—leaving your cooking.'

'And mind the new ditch up The Side, Gid!' called Mamie. She wept then.

'Doesn't know when he's doing well, that one,' said Billa.

'May the Rabbi bless and keep ye, Gid,' whispered Mamie in sobs, and Billa said:

'I always said he wasn't a full pound. Ach, it's a queer thing—a man like that shootin' off at this time o' the morning.'

'You get ye face behind that door before I stove it!' cried Mamie. 'And cease your lewd remarks about a decent working man!' She shouted into the sun. 'Mind ye feet in the drams, Gid. And if there's a sickness in you—send for Mamie!'

He waved his stick against the sunny sky, and took the middle of the Brombil dram-road for Constant, and the mountain was waiting for him, blowing live and free in the wind.

Mamie wept, and would not be comforted.

Little Randy and Blod Irish, the ones in love, were spragging the coal drams up the Constant Incline past the Balance Pond, with Randy stripped to the waist and belted and buckled up to show her his muscles, and find me the man who can stick ten rounds with me and he's yours, girl. Down with three drams of Brombil coal and up with five empties before dusk, then home to Mamie and her ox-tail stew.

'Oh, Mam—Blod's a fine one—she's all right, I tell ye!'

'She's bad through and through, and I won't abide her!' cried Mamie. 'This is a decent, God-fearing house, and ...'

'Decent?' cried Randy. 'Decent, ye call it, with you and Dai End-On ...'

'How dare you!'

32

'But Mam...'

'Don't you mam me, ye good for nothing ... accusing your own mother of shananikins—and with Dai End-On—what the devil d'ye take me for?'

'But I thought...!'

'Well, stop thinking, for ye haven't the brain. Me and Dai End-On, indeed! Never heard the likes of it. The fella's a lodger like any other of 'em.'

'I'm sorry, Mam.'

'You'd better be, ye wee devil. And lay some odds on this—that Blod Irish is never stepping foot in this house, understand? One day you'll learn, me son, that ye can always stoop to pick up trash—and that's what Blod Irish is—rubbish!'

'But ... but won't you just talk to her—Mam, just once ...?'

'Don't tempt me,' cried Mamie. 'Talk to her—I'll brain her, for she's the sweepings of an Irish gutter. Here you are surrounded wi' decent Welsh women and ye have to pick...!'

'All right, all right!'

'Oh, Randy, now ye pa's gone you're the only decent thing I've got!'

The empty dram inched up the incline for The Side, with Blod and Randy heaving like horses, their fine slim bodies tight to the load and their bare arms like rods as they braced to the sleepers.

'Och, ye Dai Dafto!' cried Blod, her black hair flying, 'ye'll do yeself an injury, man—give it to the mare!' Laughing was she, in gasps, her head back, eyes shut to the sun, her sack dress ragged about her breast.

'Then stand clear and watch this particular one!' Randy wiped his hair with his hand and the sweat flew in diamonds of light. 'Missus, you don't know nothin'! *Hei up!*' He heaved the dram upward with sheer strength, and the wheels grated on the gradient.

'Gi' it the horse, man—don't be daft!' She ran beside him with the excitement of a child, laughing at the sky, and her teeth were white against the red curves of her lips, and she was

33

beautiful in her rags, her voice tinkling out above the thunder of the drams. And she found a stick and danced around him, making mock swipes at his rear. 'Whooah, *whooah* there!'

'You watch it, woman—marry me and you're marryin' a stallion! For there's no two fellas in Taibach can move this dram up Constant!' and he heaved and gasped and the sweat sprayed from his face and shone on his muscles.

'Dear me,' said Mrs. Moocher, half-way out of her top window of Two Constant, 'don't it drop the tone of the neighbourhood.'

'Oh, I love you, Randy!' cried Blod, her face alight, and she flung her arms round his waist and kissed him.

'Reporting it, I am!' cried Mrs. Moocher, and she leaned over the sill with her hair in crackers. 'Worse than that Perky Polly over in Blaina, then some.' She shouted down at Randy, 'You hear that—reporting you—disporting yourselves in daylight!'

'But we were only kissing, missus,' cried Blod, laughing up.

'Ay, but one thing leads to another—got the morals of a hen-run, the pair of you!'

'What bush did they fish you out from under, then?' asked Randy, grinning up, smudged with coal.

'*Well!*'

'Ay, bloody *well*, woman—what you want of us, just misery? A blutty old hen you are, and no eggs for broody.'

'Randy, do not lower yourself,' said Blod, sad.

'Then tell us what you want from us,' shouted Randy, hands on hips. 'What d'you need of us, you blutty old cockerel?'

'Nothin'—just nothing!' Mrs. Moocher waved her chemise and lost the stitches. 'Just eatin', sleeping and work—that's all your kind are entitled to.'

'See, we got nothing but each other,' said Blod, face lowered.

'Aw, dunna cry, my little honey. You'm so pretty laughing.'

'She's an old bag,' said Blod.

'Ay, with no tops or bottoms,' said Randy, and he put his arm about her. 'You got everything and I've got everything—

34

we got you and me.'

'Even your mam do not count for me,' said Blod.

'She will one day, my lovely girl. One day she'll sit you on a knee—you hear that, little chicken?' he shouted up. 'Marrying we are, Blod Irish and me.'

'And not before time, strikes me,' cried Moocher.

It is night: the June moon is flashing, the mackerel gleaming silver in the surging harbour of the Old Bar: doves are whimpering in the woods of Dinas where the sulphur has not stained the trees.

'Oh, Randy!'

'Hush you now, my pretty little Welsh ...'

'Don't be daft, man—I'm bog-Irish ...'

The ghosts of the otters are calling from Avan; the rotting fish of Goytre stink on the blackened banks of the rains of Duffryn Mill.

'Oh, come on, ye darlin' thing!'

'Och, no, Randy me soul. What d'ye take me for?'

Humping and heaving is Randy and I should have known better getting mixed up with you.

'Och, me sweet lovin' boy, I'd die for ye, but would ye have me the way they make me in Taibach ...?'

The moon was in her face, brightening the high cheeks, undertaking shadows deep around her mouth, and her lips were black in the strange light: the leaves rustled to her bare arms.

'Oh, Gawd,' whispered Randy.

A baby cried from Eight Miners' Row, Billa Jam's ninth, and Blod heard it and closed her eyes while about her sang the tainted wind of the works. And even while Randy kissed her again she heard the sobs of Mavis who died.

'You scared, then?'

'Ach, no! Didn't God make me for babies?' She shoved in disgust.

'I'll do right for ye, girl.'

She saw the pennied eyes of Jarrotty of the wake and heard the rumble of the drams coming down from Brombil. She heard the shriek of the Mayo women aboard the *King of Ire-*

land when the boiler burst on the no-return ticket from the Connemara famine; she begged again along the road from Fishguard and drank in the lanes the oatmeal broth from the cauldrons of the Quakers. Through a rift in his hair she saw the moon and she smelled again the tang of copper as she came over the mountain to Taibach.

'Ach, Blod, come alive!'

He drew away from her and thought she was sleeping. For a moment, indeed, he thought she was dead.

But she was thinking, in the clenched darkness of her eyes, of Mill Yard Row that ran along the English Copper Works where they took her in at half a crown a week, and of Mrs. Halloran, where she first lodged. Plump as a wheat-pigeon was Mrs. Halloran but demented with thoughts of rising prices, and as clean as a new pin, with her breast and stomach all in one, tied with a little white apron.

'You married, Mrs. Halloran?' she had asked.

'In the soul, girl, but not in the body, if you get me,' said Mrs. Halloran. 'Two and sixpence a week suit you, Blod Murphy?'

'Do fine, Mrs. Halloran.'

'Leaves ye sixpence a week for the essentials, ye see.'

'Thank you, Mrs. Halloran.'

'It's the economics, see, Blod Murphy,' said Mrs. Halloran. 'You can't have copper without talk of economics, and it's these economical things that keep prices up, according to Lemuel Samuel, the Shop.'

'You got a husband now, Mrs. Halloran?'

'Ay, but he's been on shift these past two years, so I dunna see hide nor hair of him.'

'A two-year shift, Mrs. Halloran?'

'Och, I've known longer. Do ye recall when Popo Hopkin collected it and the fiddler Gideon Davies was blinded?'

'Sure, I've only been in the place a fortnight, Mrs. Halloran.'

'Ay, yes—well, my man Mike caught it then, an' died.'

'Whee, I'm terrible sorry, Mrs. Halloran.'

'But it's all right, girl, it's all right now. The mould spat, ye

36

see, and the shed caught fire. They got the fiddler and Popo Hopkin out, but all they got from my Mike was copper dust.'

'Copper dust, Mrs. Halloran?'

'Ay, no flesh nor bone—just copper dust.'

Blod's eyes were like saucers in that red mill light.

And now, through the patterned moonlight of the woods of Dinas, she saw the face of Randy above her: his eyes were filled with a glaze of copper and his head was bald where the fire had taken him, and she saw in his cheeks a calcined whiteness, and between his teeth where the lips had melted was a finger with a splintered bone.

'*Randy!*' She shrieked and fought to escape him, but he had arms that bulged with the heave of the drams, and he pinned her beneath him while she stared in horror.

'What ails ye, woman, what's wrong with ye? I'm only asking for the lovin' of ye, nobody's going to eat ye!'

'Didn't ... didn't they find Mr. Halloran, Mrs. Halloran?' asked Blod, dreaming.

'But I told ye, love,' and she patted and preened at her hair. 'They got him in copper dust. A pound and three-quarters—weighed him meself.' Mrs. Halloran sighed. 'Hope you'll be happy here with the two of us—got him in the tea-caddy, see—a real gentry tea-caddy—can't afford tea, of course.' She fetched it down. 'Like to have a look at him sitting on the shelf?'

'Oh, God,' whispered Blod.

'Aw, hell!' exclaimed Randy, sitting up and shouldering.

Blod clung to him, sobbing without sound, and she cried:

'Promise me, Randy, oh, promise me—never take a job in the casting-house!'

'Mark, Mary and Joseph!' said Randy. 'What the hell has the casting-house got to do with a time like this?'

She sobbed on, rocking herself. 'If ye love me, man, will ye promise?'

'Ay, promise I will, woman—to kill a pair o' quarts. I'm away down to the Somerset to lie me under a barrel for I'm wasting me entire future sittin' up by here.'

Ashes to ashes, dust to dust, said Mrs. Halloran—'you listening, Blod, my love? But he is luckier than most, being buried in the kitchen, so to speak, for the nights are cold up in the bone-yard. But don't get your tins mixed up, girl—that's all I ask. This is the tin for my man Mike, this is the one for salt. Don't clean your teeth with 'im like the last girl did.

Diminutive, a hair on the chin of the mountain, Gideon walked north.

The Irish immigrants were pouring in from Kenfig Sands: in their hundreds they came, the men scarecrowed with hunger, the tattered women with their skeleton babies lurching on their backs.

'Irish, Irish!' The cry of alarm rose above Taibach.

Since the little winter famines they had been coming, striking the Welsh coast in their rotting boats, begging their way, like Blod Murphy, to the new Welsh industries of iron and copper. What began as a trickle grew into a flood of humanity that choked the Welsh lanes: they filled the barns, stole from the orchards, rifled larders: they ate their way from barren Connemara, giving birth in the frozen fields, finding graves in wayside ditches. The churches and chapels were filled with keening women and rebellious men: these, the descendants of the heroic 1798 Rebellion, whose fathers had forged their pikes for a promised land, now deserted crucified Ireland for promises of food in a country of brothers, all Celts under the skin; for the Welsh, they were told, were only Irish who had never learned how to swim. They came in droves across the sands of Kenfig and Margam and the industrialists cornered them and signed them on at starvation wages in furnaces of Merthyr to Swansea, Aberdare to Blaenafon: they put their crosses on the books of the company shops for the horrors of truck: they housed themselves twelve to a room and five to a bed, naked at times, to make more room. And the iron and copper-masters packed them in like herrings in a barrel; the dram-road sub-contractors bedded them in culverts and water-pipes, and bricked up bridge-arches for rooms, with tin chimneys going up through the sleepers where the drams rumbled overhead.

38

'Irish! Irish!'

The cry flushed like a forest fire through Taibach Copper Town: doors came open on chains up Constant, windows were slammed down along The Side. Up the Conk the dram-road navvies like Belcher and Blackbird leaned on their shovels and stared down into the valley at the crawling black snake of immigrants from Kenfig Sands where the boats were unloading. Fights began in the streets, with bottles going up and heads going down and it was raining Irish confetti between Colliers' Row and Granny's Hole, and half of Cotton Row lost its glass according to Mamie Goldie.

All this Gideon heard in the wind driving up the mountain, and he smelled the familiar tang of clothes drenched with salt water and sea-sickness. The invading, tattered Irish—Mary's Children, as Taibach called them, had been coming in for as long as he could remember.

Behind him, not fifty paces distance, the thief Sun Heron walked, and her bare feet were noiseless on the mountain grass.

Gideon knew exactly where he was and the direction he was taking, for these were the tracks of his childhood. This took him up the dram-road and past the Balance Pond to The Conk, Pillows Mound and Brombil Pit. Remembering Mavis Samuel, he stopped, turning in the early sunlight to face down on Taibach, which he loved. Even death, in this particular town, had its humour, he reflected: only in beloved Taibach could Mamie Goldie's flowered hat be buried as a floral tribute. And he recalled with a sudden, impatient joy the colliers thronging down the narrow streets of Pyle, and the hostile crags of Kenfig Castle outlined against the stars.

Taking a deep breath he slowly turned to face the sun.

The red surge of light illuminated the blood of his eyelids and he saw crimson: a spectrum of diverting colours flashed and gleamed. Deliberately, he momentarily opened his eyes to the glare until the tears ran down his cheeks, but he was smiling. It was as if a light was beginning to grow within his head: gradually, he saw a great canopy of gold and misted images of racing blue and purple as the mountain grew into shape about

39

him. Out of the astonishing brightness, fraught with pain, there slowly painted on the retinae of his eyes faint colours of green, and this was the heather. Then he stared down on Taibach, seeing a flowing maze of crammed houses: the crazy, winding streets fed slowly out before him with a new, conspicuous clarity, and he could have cried aloud with the joy that he could momentarily see. Then the vision faded: blackness fell with obliterating speed. Dropping to his knees, Gideon put his hands over his face and waited for the surging pain. Had he opened his eyes above the red coals of a forge and struck white-hot iron the sparks could have caused no less agony, and as he knelt enduring the penalty for momentary sight the tears welled through his fingers and ran in hot streams down his throat, but he endured this pain in silence. There grew within him then an almost ungovernable elation as he rose; he could have shouted aloud with joy. Not only had he seen the mountains this time, but the streets, too. For a long time he stood with closed eyes, allowing the wind to dry his face, then he put his fiddle under his arm and his bundle over his shoulder and took the track through Quarry Dip to Mynydd Margam, and the wind changed with his new direction. Instantly, he knew he was being followed.

If it was a man, he was particularly light upon his feet, Gideon reflected.

After walking for over an hour Gideon rested, assured that his follower had gone. He took a track on the northern slope of Mynydd Margam to a ruined barn and tapped with his white stick along its entrance. With the sun low overhead he sat in the shelter of a wall and ate some bread and cheese Mamie had given him, then made a swaying path down to a stream near a tumulus of trees.

Sitting with her back to a boulder not a hundred yards away Sun Heron put her elbows on her knees and her chin in her hands and watched Gideon take off his clothes. In the graceless poise of the slattern she sat while he waded into the stream, arms outstretched for balance. A fox watched him from a bush: Gideon sniffed the wind, nodding. When he came out of the water his hair was comically tufted, and Sun

Heron smiled, hugging herself; then managed to stop herself laughing aloud as he suddenly lay flat on the grass of the bank, rolling over and over as a dog dries itself. She had seen men naked before and the sight had induced in her disgust. Once she had seen fifty dram-road navvies disporting themselves on the banks of the Nedd, playing leap-frog like little boys, and their chunky antics had defiled the day. The body of this man was different: it possessed in its lithe strength an almost feminine beauty. She stiffened imperceptibly when Gideon began slowly to walk towards her. Fear grew in her as he approached: it was as if, in his blindness, he was attached to her with an invisible string and was winding himself to her very feet. She did not know that the fox had left the bush; that Gideon could now smell her.

Standing before her, he said: 'I would not have done it to you,' and, turning, walked up the hill to the barn.

Because it was lonely sitting by herself in the sun, she got up and followed him.

When she reached the entrance to the barn Sun Heron waited, for Gideon was still dressing. Squatting in an ungainly posture she watched him collect sticks for a fire, and did not offer to help. There was a fascination in watching him do these things as accurately as a man with sight. His hands, she noticed, were long and slim, the fingers tapered, the nails cut square. Going deep within the barn he returned with an iron tripod and a boiling-can: this he suspended over the sticks, then brought out an earthenware jar and rose to fetch water.

'I'll get it, mister,' she said, and took it from his hand.

Breathless, she returned and knelt, facing him, offering the jar: he did not move, so she placed it against his knee. She did not offer to fill the boiling-can, and for this he was thankful. Filling it, he fumbled for matches, and struck one: the sticks flared into life.

'You got a good fire there, mister.'

'Why are you following me?' He spoke for the first time.

'For food.'

'And you think I will feed you again?'

41

'God help us, what's a bit o' bread?'

Sighing, he reached behind him and hooked in his bundle: the girl watched him unwrap it: a trickle of saliva ran from her mouth.

'Christ,' she said, 'cheese. You givin' me some?'

'I will give you what I can spare,' he said, 'then you must go.'

She wiped her mouth, watching as he broke the bread and cheese: he offered this and she snatched it from his hands across the fire.

'Oh, Christ,' she said, tearing it with her teeth.

'Please do not swear,' said Gideon.

'Who's swearin'?'

'You are.'

'I didn't!'

'You blasphemed; it is the same thing.'

She stopped chewing, staring at him. 'You a minister, or something?'

He said evenly: 'It is ridiculous to do it; it is nothing but a waste of breath.'

'Saints preserve us . . .' She swept back her hair.

'They might if you don't blaspheme.' He paused, listening to the simmering of the can. 'What is your name?'

'Sun.'

He peered at her, and she said, swallowing: 'Sun Heron.'

'Is that your real name?'

'No. Me ma called me Mari.' She put the rest of the bread into her mouth, chewing and gasping with hunger.

'How old are you?' asked Gideon.

'Eighteen.'

They sat silently, listening to the water.

Suddenly it boiled in noisy spurts and he took the can off the chain. The tea died in a sigh of agony.

'You never burn yourself?' she asked.

'Often.'

She spoke again but he did not reply because her presence was beginning to disturb him.

'You givin' me some tea?' she asked.

Gideon nodded.

'You got milk?'

'We will have it without milk.'

'I passed a cow down in the farm. Sure, if ye want some I'll milk the bugger.'

He sighed. 'There is only one mug—you drink first.' He swept the earth floor behind him, found his mug and filled it from the pot. Taking it, she sipped, blowing at the steam.

'You looked good with no clothes on.'

'I'm obliged,' said Gideon.

'But you anna the first man I seen without clothes on, though.'

'No doubt.' Rising, he went into the barn, and she called:

'I saw the navvies washing in the cut down Resolven way once, when I was twelve.'

He did not reply. There was a straw bed within the barn and Gideon knelt beside it, sweeping it rough with his arms. Tonight he would stay here, but first he must get rid of the girl: he was wondering how to do this when she said, coming to the doorway: 'An' I saw Dai Docker with his clothes off when I were five.'

'You started young.' His back was to her.

'You know Sker Rocks at low tide?'

He nodded, still on his knees: there was a stub of a candle somewhere; he was trying to find it.

'Dai Docker and his missus took me down the rocks after cockles, wi' a donkey ...' She sat at the doorway, cupping the mug against her and looked down the hill to the brook. 'The sweet virtue of the cocklin' was in them, an' they took me because I cried, I reckon. She was a fancy piece was Dai's gipsy missus, they said, but she worked good and carried me on her back in a shawl, like the Irish back home. You say ye know Sker?'

Gideon got to his feet; there was in her a new melody, and he was intrigued. She said: 'When the tide goes out at Sker on the flats there's white bones growin' out of the mud and antlers they grow on stags, all white and shinin' in the sun, like a burned-up forest. Folks say they come from when the world

43

was ice, but Dai Docker said that were daft.' She suddenly laughed at the sky. 'His gipsy missus carried me while they cockled and cockled and the bloody donkey was fair up to his belly wi' the weight of them when Dai led him back to the shore. He took his clothes off to cockle deeper, I remember, and the gipsy missus said, "Have ye no thought for the wee one, ye dirty old thing?" and he said, "to hell wi' the wee one for there was nothin' in nakedness, and she'd best learn young, anyway ..." ' She looked into the barn. 'Are ye listenin'?'

'Yes.'

'Then the missus carried me in her arms and there was macassar oil on her hair, I remember, for it was shining bright black in the sun. Dai led the donkey an' the woman was chewin' tobacco and kept holding me off and spitting, an' the spit hung on the top of a bone, and the sun made it bright and beaded in the drips, like diamonds—you ever seen that?'

He was standing close to her now for her voice was quiet. 'So we went on, the three of us and the moke, wi' the gipsy chewin' and spitting and Dai in his birthdays up in front, an' I saw the muscles of his behind all bulging and shining wi' the sweat, an' mud was on him, but I never saw his front because his missus said it weren't decent for the child, an' put ye trews on before we get to the rocks, ye tuppenny thing. An' then she started swearin' and cursing to raise Satan, an' when the poor old moke got deeped in the mud she kept reaching out and thumping it wi' her fist. Can you see that?'

'Every bit of it,' answered Gideon.

'It were savage,' said Sun, and started to drink the tea.

A silence came: the wind whispered between them. Gideon said:

'When ... when did you come here?'

'Taibach? About three days ago.'

'With the other Irish?'

'Ay, out of Stallcourt Barn. You know Blod Irish, Randy's piece?'

'Yes.'

'I come over with her first, with me ma on the *King of Ireland*—that was a hundred years back, but we starved, so Ma took me back for she couldn't get no work up in Merthyr and suckle me, too, for I was two and needed feeding. Blod Irish came back, too—we knew her back home in Wexford County. Then me ma died and Blod came again an' brought me wi' her—the fare was a penny on the *King of Ireland* for she had holes in her decks ye could put ye feet in. She pitched five overboard outside Carnsore, an' though it was summer we were freezing solid on the decks, and some people hugged round the boiler, an' the damn thing burst just off Fishguard and people were scalding an' some jumping off with their clothes alight an' screaming blue murder, an' ye've never heard such a commotion since they lowered the gang-plank on the Ark.'

'And then?' Gideon sat before her.

'Ach, the pair of us walked and ate on the Quakers—you ever seen Quakers?'

'Yes.'

'We come up The Top first, to Blaenafon, but they didn't need women, d'ye see? Then we tried for Merthyr and Aberdare on coal-cropping, but it was bad in the groin wi' me, said Blod, an' ye've got to consider the childer ... A fella gave us sixpence for nothing on Cardiff dock and took us on a coaster, for I think he fancied Blod. But he got nowhere wi' that one—ye realise her?'

'I do.'

'That Randy's lucky—she's firm on the point.'

'So I understand.'

'And last Monday we come in on Kenfig.'

Gideon said: 'There must be a mistake here. I know for certain that Blod Irish has been here a fortnight.'

'Is that so?'

'It is. You could never have come over with Blod Irish.'

She rose, giving him the mug. 'It's near enough,' she replied. 'It'd be a queer old world if ye got the truth all the time.'

'So you've been telling me lies?'

'*Arrah!* Not lies, they're only imaginings.' She got up, wandering about on tip-toe, smiling at the sky.

Gideon said: 'I happen to know that Blod Irish doesn't come from Wexford, anyway—she hails from Mayo.'

'Is that a fact?'

'It is. Now tell me when you first came to Wales.'

'Yesterday, with the Kenfig Irish.' She paused, staring down at him. 'But you're not the first fella I've seen wi' no clothes on—I swear it. As we came past Giant's Grave on the coaster I saw the navvies up the Nedd River ...'

'And all that about Dai Docker and the cockle gipsy—that was all lies, too?'

'Ach, what's the odds? Sure to God, you've got to mix the gold wi' the dross, as me ma used to say, and ye must admit it made a wonderful story.'

'Good God,' said Gideon.

THAT afternoon Gideon rested, awaking at dusk free of pain in the barn straw. Astonishingly, in that sepulchral light he could see even better after the punishment of the sun glare: this was unusual, he considered. Previously, as if in revenge for momentary sight, his darkness lasted many days.

Lying motionless he listened to the rhythmic breathing of Sun Heron on the other side of the barn. He was surprised to find her sleeping.

Rising, Gideon went to the barn entrance and stared into the dusk. He saw, with a leaping excitement, the glare of the ironworks of Aberafon and Bryn flickering in his curtain of blindess, mere pin-points of red glow that brightened and died in faint rainbows of crimson and white.

Hearing him, the girl sat up. 'You there, Gid Davies?'

Gideon did not reply: already he was sick of her presence. She was a liar and he hated lies. The obscenities of the taverns touched him less than lies.

'That you, Gid?'

He wondered how she had discovered his name, and hated the familiarity. Scrambling out of the manger Sun joined him at the door.

'We going now, then?'

'I am going. You're staying here.'

'Here—alone?' Fear was in her voice.

'You are not coming with me,' he retorted. 'You will be quite safe here. In the morning you can go back to Taibach.'

'Why can't I come with you? God love us, I'm doin' no harm!'

'I am not your keeper and you are not following me around.'

'I'm only wanting for friends!'

Gideon said evenly, as to a child; 'Look ... it's all I can do to feed myself. I don't earn enough to feed you, too.'

'I anna going to eat much back in Taibach.'

'Yes you will. I can get you a job.'

'You'm a hard bugger,' she said.

'Hard? Ever since you came here you've been a pest to me. You thieve from my room—food at that. If Zimmerman had been there you'd have finished up in Swansea. I've fed you once today and you're getting no more. Now, out! It's the wrong way round—you ought to be keeping me.'

'You let me, Gid Davies, an' I'll do that,' she replied.

'*Out!*' he cried, and seized her arm but she twisted away into the barn, and he shouted: 'Come on, out of it. You're not even clean, woman, I can smell you from here!' He walked into the barn, hands outstretched, feeling for her, following the slurring of her feet on the earth.

'That's a cruel, damn wicked thing to say!'

'It's true. You're nothing but a thief and a slut . . .'

Suddenly, to his astonishment, she ceased to evade him and began to cry.

'Oh, for God's sake, don't start that!'

She wept on, slipping down to her knees against the wall, rocking herself and beginning the Irish keening. Gideon turned away in disgust, mainly with himself.

'I anna a slut,' she said brokenly. 'Don't you ever call me that ag'in, Gid Davies—I anna a slut.'

'Are ye even Irish?' Turning, he yelled it at her.

'As the bogs, for I'm Connemara!'

'A couple of hours back you were County Wexford and you don't even talk like an Irish to me . . . !'

'I see ye once an' I'm made for ye, Gideon Davies,' she said. 'I could have got food from the chapel, or even up Constant where the folks were out, for I tried the doors. But I got it from you because I've been wantin' ye—from the moment I saw ye down on the Bar three days back when I come in from Kenfig. And I followed ye every moment: I see you at the

48

Somerset an' I watched ye playing in the Jarrotty wake and come out wi' that fancy piece in the navvies' hut, for I looked through the window and a lad told me who you were.' Suddenly reaching up, she gripped his arms and drew him closer, whispering, 'I'll be no pest to you—I'm arming ye this once but never again, till ye bid it—if ye'll let me stay, for I'm empty without ye.'

Gideon turned away. She watched him as he knelt on his bed. Tying up his bundle he reached for his fiddle case and rose.

'Because of that fancy navvy, isn't it?' said Sun Heron.

'I am going now,' said Gideon. 'Stay here tonight. In the morning go back to Taibach. Go to Nine Miners' Row and ask for Mamie Goldie. Say I sent you, and she will take you in. Blod and Randy will get you a job on the drams, Mamie will give you a bed. Here, take this shilling.'

'Bloody keep it.'

As he went through the barn door into the dusk, Sun said; 'Jobina, eh? You ask my opinion and I'd say she's a tart.'

'How old did you say you were?' asked Gideon.

'Eighteen.'

He grinned despite his thoughts, rubbing his chin.

The moon was a glass marble when he reached Maesteg.

Light, smoke and hops struck him in the face as he opened the door of the Maesteg Old Swan Inn, and there exploded from momentary silence the roar of men and the shrieks of women.

'Love ye soul, Gid, come you in!'

They were the customers of the Jarrotty wake, from Taibach, and they thronged about him: there was Belcher, the hut foreman who stopped picking a fight with Curly Hayloft over Mercy Merriman: Skin-Crone, the cook was there with Tilly, and Big Bonce dragged Lady Godiva and Moll across by the hands. And they badgered and shouted about Gideon as he shouldered his way to the light, and the bar. He knew Dai Posh still kept the place because of the smell of his macassar oil: Sid Blump Boxer was there, too, for Gideon heard him as he shadow-boxed and snorted in a corner: Shoni Melody, the hare-lip tenor he instantly indentified, and the presence of Jobina he sensed. She, from a chair in a corner, watched Gideon enter and straightened imperceptibly.

'And isn't it time you showed yourself, man?' cried Lady Godiva. She fluffed up, hands on hips, breasting through the men and her teeth shone white under the lantern. 'Where's Blackbird?'

'I'm here, me darlin' thing!' cried he.

'Tell him now, Blackie—weren't ye breezing it over Mynydd Margam and see him splicin' it with a wee Irish maid from Taibach?'

'As sure as Fate, I saw him,' Blackbird, chirping.

'You did not,' shouted Gideon. He elbowed his way to the counter, and Jobina sat unmoving, her fingers playing with the cross at her throat, her eyes glowing in her dark face.

'Is it a quart, Gid?' asked Dai Posh.

'Make it a pint.'

'Is it true, then?' asked Tilly, all five foot of her, fussing up on tip-toe. 'Come on now, fiddler, you can tell ye heart to Tilly!'

'Tell Tilly and ye tell the country,' said Skin-Crone. 'You keep your own counsel, Gid. What's ailing you, ye daft numbskull, bandying wi' toy women?'

The amber brew flooded over his mouth and he saw through drowning gold, and the room was submerged in hops and gurgles, cold to the throat after the dusty mountain. Gasping, he wiped his mouth with his hand.

'Is it right, Gid, boyo?'

'She was a child,' he replied.

'She dunna look much like a babe on the breast to me,' remarked Blackbird in his queer falsetto.

'Depends what you call a child,' said Jobina, but nobody heard.

They elbowed and pushed in the raucous vapouring of the near-drunk: they had come off at dusk and the shift was hard, with four-ton boulders levering out and stone sleepers going in, and the culverts were three feet diameter and the men were

50

stained with sweat to their yorks, and the skirts of the navvy women painted yellow a foot up the hems with the bright clay of the vats. Soon the embankments would be sloped and the cuttings cleared and the mule-drams would take over for the end-on laying, with the long-handled barrow drams taking down, which was the way Jarrotty died, for they took six tons. The work was safe in the early stages, but it was hard. Spills and accidents would come later.

'But he always comes back home,' cried Big Bonce, swaying, 'for he's sweet on our wee Jobbie. Isn't it true he carries a reel o' cotton in his pocket and winds his way back to her skirt?'

'Not this time he didn't,' said Jobina, and sipped her small-beer.

'What's the odds, woman?' cried Moll. 'The man's here, isn't he?'

'Will you give us a tune, fiddler?'

'If you pay,' said Gideon.

'Have you eaten proper, Gid?' This from Dai Posh, flat-faced, smoothing his parting.

'I'm rumbling for pounce-thunder, but I'll last,' and Gideon opened his case on the bar: then he deliberately turned to face Jobina, lifted his pewter and drank steadily: smiling, he imagined the toss of her head and the pout of her lips in profile. Amid the bawling of the room he called:

'She was a child, girl; a child.'

'And how old is that?'

'Eighteen, so she said.' He smiled at his thoughts.

'Oh, ay? Blackie said he wouldn't trust her with his latest son, and he was two years old last Sunday.'

Shoni Melody, the hare-lip singer, took the middle of the room and the navvies backed away to give respect: he cupped his hand over his mouth to hide his deformity and made a sweet consoling sound, listening for the key.

Jobina said: 'You're nothing to me, fiddler—what makes you think it?'

'I just hoped you would be pleased I came to Maesteg.'

Shoni Melody began to sing, a beautiful counter-tenor, and

51

the tune was *David of the White Rock*: the navvies, though Irish, listened in a fumble of ale and tears. Jobina wandered over to Gideon, mug in hand.

'Where is she now, then?'

Gideon said: 'I sent her to Mamie Goldie...'

'Irish, is she?'

'You cannot trust anything she says.'

'Good for you, and I'll tell you something else. I'm Welsh, and have an eye for you. So if she crosses me with her fancy tarts I'll put one on her ear that'll land her back in County Cork.'

The hare-lip tenor sang on, even when the door went back on its hinges and the colliers of Morfa Pit flooded in, grimy with coal, and noisy with banter. And they thronged through the Irish navvies, pushing them aside and hammering the counter for quarts, with the dram-lads stumbling around their thighs begging for half-pints to settle the gob and Dai Posh going demented with the mugs: the home-brew flooded over the counter.

Jobina said to Gideon: 'Where you bound for now, then?'

'Merthyr.'

'You settling there, then?'

'It's a town of real people and the place is alive. It's the music I am after.'

'Music! In Merthyr?' she laughed.

'In the people,' said Gideon. 'You've never seen such people.'

'If you come at the right time you'll be following me around.'

'You bound there, too?'

'Within the month. Nipper Tandy's sub-contracting us on canal dredging—the Old Cyfarthfa. Anything's a change from the dram-roads—there's not much life under a two-ton boulder, but you can't drown properly in ten inches of water.'

'But it's hard,' said Gideon.

The noise of the room beat about them: Belcher was doing a clog-dance with Sid Blump and the Welsh colliers were clapping the time; a cock-fight was beginning in the sawdust, the birds being groomed, their feathers flashing, their spurs like jewels in the lamplight and the pitch-and-toss dram-lads leaped to the new excitement.

Gideon said: 'You wait for me in Merthyr, Welsh girl?'

Jobina's eyes lifted to his face. 'Once I might have done, but these days I'm not anybody's woman.'

'Nobody said you were.'

'Hey, Gid, gi' us a tune for the dancing!' cried Moll.

'You heave off,' said Jobina, pushing her away.

Gideon said: 'I didn't ask you to live with me, only wait for me.'

'*Aw*, fiddler, come on!' cried Tilly, dragging at him.

Gideon held Tilly's wrist: 'Merthyr, then—in the fall?'

Jobina got up, smiling over her shoulder. 'Autumn? Good God, man, the gang of us could be six foot down long before then.'

'Gid, Gid, *Gid*!' the Irish navvies began the chant, and he reached for his fiddle, calling to Jobina, 'But you'll be there?'

'Ay,' answered Jobina, 'more fool me, for I've been had before.'

Despite the feathering shriek of the birds, Shoni Melody was still singing, his lovely counter-tenor sweeping over the heads of the milling, roistering crowd: with averted face he sang, his hand shielding his strung mouth, that it might not sully the beauty of his throat. And Gideon took up the air, playing above him a descant carefully phrased; a silence fell over the room; even the cock-fight was stilled. Here the flushed faces of ale, bulbous and nosed: the gin-parlour faces of a dozen bawdy towns; humped and brutalised stood the navvies, the colliers Welsh dark with tattooed cheeks and head-bumps of coal: Moll stared with bright blue eyes from the obesity of her blowzy face: Skin-Crone of the dram-lined mouth, yawned; the prancing buccaneering Belcher leered: Dai Posh was stilled in a pout of soap and macassar, impatient of a clientele drinking music. And Jobina, her slanted eyes shining, watched Gideon. The lanterns flickered, the only movement: Shoni Melody sang on, his shoulder against a wall, his face cast down, and Gideon played, his dark hair falling over his brow. Lady Godiva, one breast bare in her rags, wept soundlessly into Belcher's coat: Mercy Merriman was nibbling at cheese with the furtive appreciation of a mouse.

The duet stopped abruptly: all heads turned to the door, which went back on its hinges.

The girl Sun Heron was standing there: smoothing her red hair from her face she looked around the room.

It was astonishing, thought Gideon afterwards, that he instantly knew she was there, for neither smell nor sound assisted him: he saw her in his head, standing in brightness. Straight and white were her legs below the hem of her ragged dress and her feet were bare.

'Gid...' she said.

Gideon pushed through the men towards her. 'I sent you to Mamie Goldie. Why didn't you go?'

Sun Heron's eyes were on Jobina. 'Because no gunk of a man's tellin' me what to do.' She came down the step into the room, pushing people aside. Expectant, the men went back, giving her the floor.

'So you're the fancy piece he talks about,' she said to Jobina.

'Ay,' said Jobina, getting up. 'And you're a cuckoo in the nest, girl, and he's pledged. So out.'

'Jobina, for God's sake...!' whispered Gideon, and struggled through the men.

Sun Heron said, smiling, 'Make a ring, boys, she's the clout I'm after.'

'Now, now!' cried Dai Posh. 'No woman fights in here!'

'This won't be a fight, mister, this'll be a slaughter.'

The Welsh colliers backed away to the walls, their bass shouts and falsetto derision battering the room. The navvies, riding the navvy rule of best woman win, made a circle around the tap, while two stood guard by the door. The event was not unusual: the women of their compounds fought for their men with the same ferocity of the navvies for their women. Jobina, also, had fought before, when she was nineteen, before she

54

wore a cross, but this was an event with the Welsh: it was a trick she had learned from the dram-road Irish. Up in an Aberdare tunnel she had lived with a North Country ticket-navvy—a travelling newspaper from Wigan—and his wife came down on a coach and claimed him. Jobina had fought then for him, her first man: she had intended taking a stick to him afterwards because he had told her he was single, but she fought for him first in a spitting claw of a fight that ended rolling in the yellow mud of the tunnel in a tangle of hair and skirts, and the navvies pulling her off a wife in rags. But the man, whose name was Clarence, went back with his wife just the same, prodded on the end of a Wigan knobkerry all the way to the coach. Now Jobina rose from the table and finished her small-beer, tied back her hair and tightened the big cro-belt at her waist, her eyes glowing at the prospect of a fight, and amid Gideon's agonised protests as the men held him, Dai Posh shouted, up on the counter:

'For shame, Jobbie Morgan! And you taken the cloth! She's scarce out o' her napkins!'

'She will be when I've done with her,' said Jobina, and Gideon cried:

'Belcher, Blackbird, stop this! Bonce, Bonce...!'

'Make a ring!'

'Fives on the Welsh—I take fives!'

'Two to one against the Irish!'

Gideon shouted, trying to shake off the men who held him:

'Godiva! Tilly, Moll—in the name of God!'

Jobina took off her little crucifix and dropped it on the table.

'Belcher!' Gideon ducked and fought with the colliers, but they held him, laughing at the ceiling.

'I would if I could, Gid,' shouted Belcher, 'for I'd die in respect of ye. But this is women—would ye have me hanging on hooks?'

'See to her, Jobbie, the wee slut,' whispered Skin-Crone, her skinny hands twisting, and Sun Heron smiled wide at this and whirled up her hair and tied it in a top-knot, then stepped aside with the grace of a dancer as Jobina rushed. Held off by colliers, Jobina turned: Sun took a last pull at the knot and stooped, hands out, feet splayed. 'Right you,' she said.

'Jobina!' Gideon's voice rang through the silence of Sun's slithering feet as she circled.

'You go to hell,' whispered Jobina, and her heavy navvy boots clumped on the boards.

'Sun Heron! Sun Heron!' gasped Gideon.

'Ach, don't bother yourself, me sweet thing,' said Sun, and wiped her mouth with the back of her hand, and feinted, going left, then twisted to the right and Jobina reeled away before her astonishing speed as the girl stooped with sweeping hands and fastened on to her dress. The pull sent Jobina's head back, then her shoulders, and her nailed boots skidded in the sawdust, the men opening behind her with wild shouts. Jobina slipped to the floor and Sun Heron ran around her, spinning her with the pull; the skirt ripped below the cro-belt, splitting up to the waist. And the moment she was upright, arms waving for balance Sun came in again, her darting hands seeking another hold, but Jobina braced her body and clutched her, wheeling her around with her back to the counter. Trapped, Sun went limp, threw up her arms, slipped through the grip to her knees and clutched Jobina's legs and rose, taking her feet from under her. And as her adversary fell Sun danced across her, one hand reaching to snatch at her bodice: on this she flung her weight and the rough cloth tore a yard down to the cro-belt. Jobina shrieked, and hung on to the sagging bodice: Sun leaped clear, and the force of her spun the Welsh girl. Jobina got up. Her hair was already down. She backed away, holding the torn dress high against her throat. A man said softly:

'By hell, she's a quick 'un!'

'Do her, girl!'

'Into her, Jobbie! What are ye gapin' for?' Tilly's plea was shrill. But Jobina, her face white, stumbled backwards in the clogs that were hindering her and Sun Heron followed, smiling.

Gideon was standing in the arms of the men, head bowed, and there was in him a sickness.

'Twos on the youngster!' A navvy bawled it, his silver held high: Jobina retreated still, trying to gather up her tattered dress, and Sun followed her, her feet noiseless in the thumping of the clogs.

'I'll give threes!'

'Taken!'

'Watch it, Skewen, she anna done yet...'

Deliberately, Sun Heron turned her back: Jobina leaped at her in a shriek of anger, and her rush carried her over for the trip: she fell, sprawling, and in a moment the girl was astride her, her fingers clawing deep into her petticoat. Legs braced, she straightened, heaving in gasps; the red flannel held first, then ripped in zigzags from neck to cro-belt, and in the instant before Jobina turned on the floor, her assailant snatched at the seam below the belt and flung her body backwards in a drape of red cloth: Jobina shrieked at the speed of it, and Godiva cried:

'Watch it, Jobbie, the thing's undressing ye!'

Jobina turned on the floor, and prised off her boots. Disdainful of her approaching nakedness, she flung her hair over her bare shoulder and rose, gasping.

'Come on, then, ye navvy heathen,' said Sun Heron.

The men shouted, backing away as the fighters tore into each other with clawing hands: locked together at last, they fell, gasping, rolling, with Sun underneath. But as Jobina pounced for her face she twisted away with the litheness of a cat, coming back instantly for wild snatches at Jobina's clothes; then the backward lunges, and retreat. It was a pattern unfolding more surely every moment: outwitted, outspeeded by the amazing agility of the younger, Jobina floundered before one attack after another, forced in the last resort to protect herself from nakedness. All this Gideon saw in the terror of his mind: garnering the progress of the fight by the shouted obscenities of the men and the hysterical shrieking of the women: the scuffling bare feet of the fighters, their gasping breaths beat into and branded him, and he felt unclean. Again and again he heard the ripping of Jobina's clothes, and he screwed up his hands as she began to cry aloud in her

57

distress as Sun Heron, soundless, darted in and out with snatching fingers, never for once seeking combat with Jobina's outflung arms; never, like Jobina, seeking to scratch. But with each lithe attack by lunge, run or isolated snatch, she came away with a little more of her opponent's dangling rags.

'Let 'em drop, woman—who cares?' cried Lady Godiva. 'What ails ye, ye stupid Taff!'

The crowd was roaring now as Jobina's clothing ripped and tore, and Gideon, in sudden fury, beat about him with his fists and broke from the ring of colliers: some were struck but none struck back as he hit out wildly and gained the middle of the ring. Colliding with Jobina, he gripped and held her.

'Leave her!' he commanded.

But Sun Heron came sneaking past him for what was left of Jobina's petticoat as she slipped and fell. Gideon knelt, gathering her into his arms.

'What ails ye, man—leave them! It's woman-fighting— leave 'em or we haul ye off!' This from a big North Country man with a cropped head.

'Merriman, Moll, Tilly!' shouted Gideon, and rocked Jobina against him.

'We're here, ye honour!' shouted Godiva.

'Get a hold on the girl!'

'You touch me,' gasped Sun Heron, backing away from their hands, 'an' I'll not be responsible!'

'Would you tear her to pieces, then?' cried Gideon from the floor.

'Ay, in strips, if she comes between me and you.'

'You stupid bitch,' whispered Gideon. 'Get out. You mean nothing to me.'

'Do we up-end her, then, Gid—will ye make up your mind?' said Moll.

'Let her go,' he commanded. 'One of you give me a shawl,' and Tilly obeyed.

'If you put that round her,' said Sun behind him, 'it's about the only thing she'll be wearing...'

'I told you to get out!'

Money chinked about him: the colliers grumbled deep, like

58

bulls nosing an empty manger.

'Heaven above,' said Tilly, 'rather Jobbie than me—the thing anna human, is it, ducks?' and she lifted Sun Heron under the chin.

Sun said: 'I fought fair an' decent. I didn't use a nail on her, an' just look at me face . . .'

'She's scraped bad, Gid,' whispered Mercy Merriman.

'The kid's gone on ye, fiddler,' said a voice.

'Gawd,' said Godiva, 'our Jobbie's fainted . . .'

'She skinned a wench and found herself a lynx,' said Belcher.

Gideon rose with Jobina in his arms. 'Will somebody lead me to the kitchen?' He was worried; he could feel her heart thumping against his chest.

'In by here, fiddler,' said Dai Posh.

After they had gone Sun Heron tied back her hair and smoothed down her dress in a circle of the men, and none spoke but all watched her.

'You'd best go before Gid gets back, child,' said a woman.

She smiled at them, tightening the girdle around her waist, and a collier said lightly, 'No odds to her, *fach*—won't you stay awhile and drink with the Welsh? The night's young for a tot or two of gin, and . . .'

But Sun was at the door. 'And share the likes of you? Hell's alight, man, I'm choosey where I do me drinking.'

'Yet you fight for the likes of the fiddler—half a man.'

She opened the door and looked round the room. 'Ay, for there's not a fella in here comes up to his shoulder.'

The stars were bright over Mynydd Margam as Sun Heron went out into the night; the wind was chill for June, and she pulled the rag dress closer about her. 'Dear me,' she said at the moon, 'there's an ache deep in me for you, Gid Davies.'

Faintly, as she climbed the hill out of Maesteg she heard the full, sweet voice of Shoni Melody singing a tenor aria from *Judas Maccabaeus* and although she did not know it, she thought it was beautiful.

Kneeling by a brook she washed the blood from her face and dried herself with her hair. Later, on the bank of the Avan she

59

met a cow clear of the farm, and milked it, drinking from a cupped hand.

The young Welshman who had greeted Gideon in Taibach was sitting cross-legged on the bank, eating from his bundle. He gave her a happy grin in the light of the moon as Sun, suddenly aware of a presence, looked up.

'I'd try that myself if they milked home-brew,' he said. 'What's your name?'

Sun did not reply; she was tying back her hair.

The young man said: 'I'll walk you if you like, missus. You on the iron for Tredegar?'

'If I tell ye that you'll be as wise as me, boyo,' said Sun, and left him.

She struck east along the old pack-horse trails, making for a great redness in the sky that outshone all others, and beneath this redness was the town of Merthyr.

GIDEON walked slowly through Pontypridd, making his way
to the market in sunshine so brilliant that he, too, could see it.
For the last week he had been playing in the inns of Gower,
Kenfig Hill and Cymmer, and the rising industrial towns and
villages had greeted him with song. The Staffordshire specialists of Neath had welcomed him, dancing in the taverns to
his fiddle in round North Country oaths. The Welsh colliers
of Resolven had sung to the hymns of his youth—Robert
Edwards' *Caersalem* ... Smart's *Bethany*, *Rhuddlan* and *Ar
Hyd Y Nos* the Welsh traditional. Fresh in their grime along
the River Afan they had sat at the benches with closed eyes
and roared their harmonies at the tap-room ceilings. And
Shoni Melody, who travelled with him as far as Tonna, sang
with a shielded mouth. In Clydach, after he had sung *Bethlehem*
the colliers went to his corner and drank from the mug from
which he had drunk with his deformed lip, and passed it
slowly round the company for each man there to sip, while
Gideon stood, his head bowed. Here he had preached Reform
and the aims of the young Union, and they had been avid
pupils, cheering him, and distributing his political tracts. It was
south of Clydach that he had played to the Spaniards; a rushing Tarantella in which the Italian labourers had joined with
tambourines; one black-haired gipsy girl from Catania dancing
in her red shawl and buckled shoes, acting the death-spider in
the rhythm of her castanets, and Gideon had longed for sight
as dancer after dancer succumbed to her bite. In the inns of the
pack-horse trails he had fiddled out the tramping songs of the
drovers, whom he hated: expressionless to their bawled ob-

scenities, he had played, and strangely they paid best, though wanting nothing of his political speeches. But his pamphlets were being read; his placards crying for Parliamentary Reform were pinned up like a white snake over the mountains. He was coming into Pontypridd one sunny morning, wondering how Zimmerman was getting on in Merthyr, when he met Mrs. Duck Evans, once of Aberdare, with whom he had lodged.

'Good God! Gid Davies.'

He stood before her, beaming, his hat removed.

Mrs. Duck Evans was so named by her neighbours when her husband was arraigned at the Sessions for the theft of a duck. The punishment ranged from between two years hard labour in the House of Correction to seven years transportation to the Colonies: Mr. Evans got off with a flogging and eighteen months.

'*Diawch!*' she cried. 'You on the road again, Gid?'

'Ay, this past week or so.'

'Good pickings?'

He nodded. He imagined her correctly, thinner than when he lodged with her, but still fat and cherubic; her chattering greeting to everyone a part of the repayment for social misdeed, but he sensed that behind her cheerful ingratiation lay the crucified features of her soul. Her days were shot with disdain when she lived in Aberdare, her nights were haunted by fat ducks and thin ducks, ducks feathered and plucked, perching on the window-sill, easing their feet on her bed-rail; roosting on the brass knobs, hanging from the sampler, their red beaks and gory eyes floating in her nightmare of the public whipping and the shrieks of Mr. E., with a king duck sitting on the bench with a wig on its head, and the stolen duck a squawking first witness.

'Good weather we are having, isn't it, man?' She turned up her face to Gideon.

'It is a beautiful July, Mrs. Evans.'

She touched his hand in mute appeal as they stood there with the people pushing around them: bowed her head as Mrs. Windy Jones went past them with her nose up: next door but one in Aberdare until twelve months ago, and very good friends until ducks came into it.

'You see that, Gid?' said Mrs. Duck Evans. 'Won't speak, see . . .'

'Are these people necessary to your happiness?'

The drovers came, beating the calves past them to the pens where the butchers were waiting with red hands and knives: the dust at their feet was beaded with saliva.

'How is he?' asked Gideon.

'As well as can be expected on bread and water, an' his poor back that cut with the whip.' Tears were in her throat.

'I know, I know.'

'Not . . . not fair, I reckon. Never did anything like it before —eighteen months hard and a whipping in public. Just tempted, you see—saw the blutty thing and picked it up, and he's got a soul as white as a bedsheet—very gentle with me, you understand . . . ?'

Gideon nodded.

'No lust nor sloth in him—sidesman at the Ebenezer. And there's a few buggers I know you'd 'ave to pull up a chimney for a clean.' She blew and wiped on a rag.

'Do not hang your life on a duck, Mrs. Evans. There are people in this country stealing souls.'

Distant fumes moved on the wind; Gideon felt physically sick; it reminded him of Taibach where there was no escape from the appalling garlic stink where the land had died under the tawny orange deposits that stained the roofs and laid waste the people who expired prematurely from chronic bronchial complaints, and a halfpenny a week was deducted from the 'long pay' towards defraying the cost of a white pine coffin made at the Company saw-mill.

'Ah, well,' said Mrs. Evans, 'I expect I've got to go. Me an' the kids are on our way to Merthyr—nobody knows us there, you see.'

Discovering her hand he pressed two shillings into it: the people jostled them in market chatter and smells of hot cloth.

'No, Gid, no . . . !'

'Once you helped me—take it for the children.'

'Not badly off, you know.'

'You are now. Please...'

She screwed the coins in her hand. 'God grant ye sight,' she said.

He bowed to her.

'You come across our girls in your travels, Gideon Davies?'

It was Mrs. Afron Hewers at the market vegetable stalls, wife to the limestone cutter. Gideon paused, smiling into the sun: he recognised them by smell. Gran Lloyd was there, too, in her carbolic; Mrs. Hewers was onions.

'Megsie Lloyd, and Anne Hewers?'

He always mixed up the latter with Annie Fewers of Taibach, recently married, thank God, said her da: the Hewers and Fewers, he reflected, had one thing in common—their daughters were wild. Gideon shook his head.

'Been out all night, see, Mr. Davies,' said Gran. 'God knows what will happen when my man comes home—granddaughters is very difficult, mind.'

'And my fella,' added Mrs. Hewers, gaunt and sallow and five feet ten. 'He raised lumps on my Annie last time it happened—drew blood: she got the buckle not the belt.'

'It is not what they take out that matters,' interjected Gran Lloyd. 'It's what they're inclined to bring home, see—that's the problem. My Megsie will 'ave to sort it out, though, and so will Annie. If they burn their backsides they'll 'ave to sit on the blisters.'

Gideon had always pitied Megsie and Annie; for years he had been coming to Pontypridd on the circuit, and watched them grow up. Now, about sixteen, they were the unhired mothers of their mothers' children, the nurse-maids, unloved, of a new generation of squallers, bawlers and sobbers. In the thunder of Ponty they changed, bottled and babied from dawn to dusk: neither could read nor write, both took in washing.

'Can't do more than bring them up decent, can you?' asked Gran Lloyd.

'Had better chances than we had, mind,' said Mrs. Hewers. 'Taking after her grancher on my husband's side, is Annie.

And the pair of them not too prominent in the head but very passionate, if ye get me—very, very passionate.' She tied a bundle of carrots and tossed them on the side.

Gideon smiled. Earlier, coming down from Hafod, he had heard Annie Hewers and Megsie Lloyd laughing gaily as they took the road to Merthyr.

'Oh, Gideon Davies, do not tell on us—promise ye will not tell!'

Mrs. Hewers said now, counting eggs, 'Don't forget, Gid Davies—don't forget, if ye see 'em . . . ?'

'Not on your life,' said Gideon.

On the corner of High near Pneumonia Alley a little dog accosted him, and he stooped, fondling it. Once he had possessed a dog and it had begun to serve him, but then it died, and he had sworn to himself never again to bring such a scourge to his affections.

'Away, now,' he said to this one, pushing it off: tapping with his stick he entered the sweet shop: the mongrel watched him, scratching in the sun.

'Good morning, Miss Thrush,' He removed his hat; the door-bell jangled behind him.

'Good morning, Mr. Davies,' said Miss Thrush, 'and a pleasant day it is for sure.'

Gideon had never been able to formulate a shape for Miss Thrush the Sweets, so named because she had a sister called Miss Thrush Hen who kept chickens six doors down.

'Last person in the world I expected to see,' said Miss Thrush.

'I am usually in this valley at this time of year,' replied Gideon.

She knew it, to the day: often, wandering in town she would casually enquire about him from the drovers, and marked his progress towards Pontypridd with the accuracy of a steersman plotting a course by the stars.

'What can I do for ye, then?' Her voice was broad North Country: she would scream, she thought, if this year of endless waiting for him ended in a request for laces.

Her hands, her arms ached for him.

'A pair of laces, if you please, Miss Thrush. Nowhere can I buy the laces I get in Pontypridd.'

Earlier she had seen him coming to the shop, and had rushed behind the trays of sweets to the cracked mirror of her parlour, and there smoothed away the lines under her eyes, patted her hair, tightened the white, lace-fringed bodice over her breasts and closed her eyes to the panic of his step, forgetting in her haste, that he could not see. Sometimes, when he played his fiddle in the Market Tavern she would walk up and down outside, listening in the dark despite her fear of men.

'Are you well, Miss Thrush?' He took the laces and paid the money, not noticing the trembling of her hand.

'As well as can be expected. One thing's sure—I've only myself to think about.'

Gideon smiled and she clutched at her hands. His teeth, she thought, were incredibly white, his face burned brown by the sun and wind. His eyes, too, were beautiful: no man, she reflected, had the right to be blind, yet so handsome. It induced in a woman an unbearable pity to add to the unbearable desire: once, in winter, he had called to buy and their hands had touched. He was shivering, and his fingers were blue with cold. Had he but asked he could have warmed them between her breasts.

'Somebody in here asking about you a few days back,' she said, eyes closed.

Gideon paused on the doorstep. 'Asking about me?'

'A navvy woman on her way to Merthyr.'

He nodded. 'That would be Jobina. Poor Jobina.'

'Didn't look poor to me—fancy boots and scarf—scarlet stockings: saw what she was the moment she came over the step. It's the same with 'em all, Mr. Davies—like that Annie Hewers and Megsie Lloyd—very hot below the waist, if you'll pardon it. Don't hold with it, cheapening yourself.'

'Thank you, Miss Thrush.' Gideon paused at the door.

'Men are all the same, too—never met one different—not one, you understand?'

'I understand.'

'Big, useless oafs, swillin' their stomachs with ale on pay nights, and fightin' like animals. Take decent women like they take their dinners—no respect for person or privilege, don't give a nod to the community.'

'Goodbye.' But he did not move, being captured by her vehemence.

'Wouldn't give 'em house room. If I was fool enough to treat one decent I'd do it and die of shame. Drink-sodden bunch of randies. I wouldn't raise a finger to point one the way.'

The bell clanged as Gideon opened the door wider.

'No, *wait*!'

He said at the street. 'Yes, Miss Thrush?'

She lowered her face. 'It ... it don't matter, Mr. Davies. Goodbye, Mr. Davies.'

'Goodbye.'

The slam of the door pole-axed her dreams for another twelve months. Miss Thrush made a mental note to order more leather laces and size nine boots. After a few moments she wiped her eyes on her apron. Going outside she watched him tapping along the railings, the little white dog trotting at his heels.

'Oh well,' she said aloud, 'time soon passes. Thank God he's got company.'

Doing it while she remembered it, she hurried inside to order the boots. The first thing she noticed on the drapery tray was a pair of scarlet stockings, and she picked them up.

Vaguely, she wondered as she stared through the window, if he was on his way to Merthyr ... ?

'IT is my proud boast that no soul in need is turned from my door,' said Mrs. Nancy Thomas of the Somerset Arms Inn, Taibach.

'Then for the love of heaven, woman, have pity,' cried Mr. Waxey Evans, gentleman, of Rhigos Farm.

'Dear me, there is nothing so touching as threadbare good breeding. All right, fella, but when you going to pay?'

'I have a rich relation with ten thousand acres in Hereford; I know a London merchant who can stand bond!'

'I'd rather have the deeds of Rhigos, Mr. Evans.'

'But it has been in my family for three hundred years—what will Grandfather say?'

'What would Grandfather say about one thousand six hundred pints, eighteen cases of whisky, thirty-five bottles of rum and twenty-four cases of dandelion and burdock, Mr. Evans?'

'Madam, I beg you!'

'Assist him off the premises,' said Mrs. Nancy Thomas, and posted the deeds of Rhigos down the front of her.

'Gadarene swine!' yelled Waxey Evans. 'May you rot in the pit of hell, Mrs. Nancy Thomas. May you be pestered in the loins by your own iniquities and a scourge of scorpions plague your guts!'

'Dear me,' said Mrs. Thomas, 'Grandpa wouldn't like that. A bucket of pig-wash ought to shift him, boys.'

And Mr. Evans, late of Rhigos Farm, left, leaving behind him the heritage of Grandpa.

Miss Grieve, more than a bit above the neighbours, sat in

the empty window of Number One, Brick Row, and wrote in her diary:

'Lemuel Samuel failed in business; his dog ate the letters as fast as they arrived.'

'Mrs. Goldie's new hat was buried as a floral tribute last Wednesday.'

'That Polly Perks called Perky Polly is a very tarty piece.'

'Saw Aunty Sally Sara hiding behind the clothes-horse when the rent man came.'

'Joy sings within me at your touch, Ianto. By the strangest coincidence Mr. Waxey Evans, heir to the Herefordshire estate, is also moving to Merthyr ...'

Done up and polished in his best tunic and hunting trews, resplendent in brown leggings and chapel boots, Mr. Evans, his hair smarmed down with goose fat, waited outside Number One, Brick Row, Taibach, and every neighbour in the street was either hanging out her washing or sewing her nose to the glass.

''Morning, Mr. Evans!' cried Merve Jam, his face bright with sun.

Said Waxey: 'What the hell are you doing here?'

'Only helping Miss Grieve to pack, Mr. Evans. That right you sharing her trap to Merthyr, Mr. Evans?'

Waxey bowed low again, his cap sweeping the gutter as Miss Grieve appeared. Dressed in black was she; dark and lovely in expectancy of ten thousand acres in Herefordshire: stately as a maharanee to a funeral pyre she came.

'Dear me,' said Billa Jam, 'don't they look lovely together? One thing about the gentry, they always do things different, ye know.'

'Can't say I've noticed it, mind,' said Pru Knock Twice, fluffing up her hair. 'Give me a collier when it comes down to the essentials, dearie.'

Merve said, excitedly, 'Eh, Mamie Goldie was right, Mr. Evans. You and Miss Sarah Grieve seem very suited to each other, you don't mind my saying? You got a penny for me, Mr. Evans? For holding the 'orse's head, Mr. Evans?'

'But you had a penny for that, you darling child!' said Miss Grieve, and bent to kiss his grimy face. Her serene beauty, the very softness of her seemed to call him within her embrace. Miss Grieve's perfume swept his nostrils, and he would have gone to her then had he not remembered his mother, Billa Jam: to kiss another would seem like infidelity, but he closed his eyes and held his face, beaming with pleasure. Reaching out Miss Grieve caressed his hair, smiling beautifully.

'Get going, you little runt,' she said.

'Aw, Randy, for the love of God stay and tell her—don't write!' whispered Blod Irish.

'Are you light in your top?' asked Randy. 'If I stay to ask she'll fetter and bind me, and I'll not get away to Merthyr this side of ninety.'

'But it'll wound her sore, just going off and leaving a note.'

He sighed on the rack of decency. 'Ay, all right, then—but you keep out of it—you keep away or you'll get her jaw. Where will ye be?'

'A hundred yards up from the Somerset with me bundle.'

He smiled at her in the dusk. 'Ye love me, Blod?'

They fought in whispers of breath and kisses.

'Wait, then,' and he was gone.

Blod Irish looked up and down the dark streets: redness was flickering along the vents of the copper works.

Mr. Billy Jam turned the end of Miners' at that moment with his donkey and cart, and his voice was shrill:

'Old iron, cans and pegs, rags, bones, pots!'

The door came open in Number Eight and Mrs. Billa Jam came out, her head shawled black. 'That you, Billy Jam?'

'Ah, dear wife!' Stopping the donkey he bowed low to her.

'Gawd, are ye drunk already?' she peered at him in the flickering light of the copper vents.

'How dare you!' Outraged, he stared back at her, staggering.

'Oh, God in heaven,' cried Mrs. Billa Jam, bringing up her apron. 'Oh, God, what's to become of us? There's scarce a penny in the house an' you're swilling your belly with quarts.

And we got ten kids need feeding and on tick at the Shop! Oh, God!'

The children came out then, wailing around Mrs. Jam and tugging at her skirts; but she wept in dishevelled wetness, and the night echoed her sobs in the garlic reek of the copper while Mr. Billy Jam did an Irish reel in the road in a drunken, staggering beat of hobnails.

Then Mike McTigue came out, one of their three Irish lodgers, and he took Billa's hand.

'Don't cry, girl,' he said. 'Please don't cry . . .'

Blod Irish watched.

Randy went into the kitchen of Nine Miners', sat down by the glimmering lamp and licked the stub of a pencil: in a big round hand, he wrote:

Dear Ma. Me and Blod Irish do love each other and we are away off to Merthyr after the iron, for marrying decent. I'll do good for you if ever you come. Love from Randy, and Blod.

He looked around the faded walls, the earth floor: standing in a corner was a crate piled with washing: on the table Mamie's ironed sheets were piled high. A faint, savoury smell touched his nostrils and he knelt, opening the oven. A bowl of Irish stew was within, and he remembered then that he was supposed to light the fire. This he did, kneeling and staring into the flames, remembering the days of his childhood before the obscenity of Dai End-On. He saw a clean man sitting at the table, a man of few words and who carried a candle-tack and a bottle of cold tea: in the dance of the flames Randy saw the red glow of the fire on this man's back and Mamie kneeling beside him, swabbing, swabbing, and he heard the hiss of the hob and there were black hairs on the man's chest, and his shoulders, streaked with coal and suds, were wide. Snow lay thick on the sill and rimed the man's eye-lashes and brows when he came off shift from the casting-house. Then one day he did not come and Mamie cried. He had never since

71

seen anyone cry like Mamie, in a blueness of face, a slobbering grief. The man had been caught in the copper works rollers between the cog and the line, with only his foot sticking out. His boot, the only thing left, was still upstairs in Zimmerman's old room. Randy reflected: it had been lying there ever since he could remember. On a sudden impulse he rose from the fire and ran upstairs three at a time. Opening the wardrobe he took out the boot: downstairs now, he stuffed it into his bundle. Once more he looked around the kitchen, sniffed, and ran his fingers through his hair.

'Goodbye, Ma,' he said.

Blod was awaiting him up near the Somerset.

'You told her, boy?'

'Ay.'

'You explained as to how there was nothin' left to do?'

'Ay.'

She looked at him and he lowered his face before her. Blod said, 'Randy, you got ... you got to say goodbye to your ma!'

'How can I say goodbye to her if she anna there.'

'Hei now, me sweet boy, listen to me.' She clutched him against her. 'For me, Randy—for me, trace back ye steps, find her, and say goodbye to your ma. For me, will ye?' She stared into his pale face.

'Leave me alone, ye set bitch,' he said.

'Randy!'

He strode away and she hurried beside him, tearful, her hands beseeching along the road that led to Merthyr.

EAST of Tir-Phil the old Gitos Farm squatted black and shapeless in a covey clear of the drovers' track, its square thatch flashing at the moon. In a derelict coach by the barn Gideon rested, sinking back gratefully on to the ripped upholstery. Weariness began to sweep over him after the plundering heat of the day. Not even bothering to eat the last of his bread and cheese from the shoulder bundle, he lay staring through the window at the extraordinary brilliance of the night; in growing excitement he examined the phenomena that threatened to consume him; it was a realisation of increasing sight that forbade movement. Not since the screams and dousing buckets of the copper works had he been able to see so well, and he allowed the full light of the moon to merge into shape and growing brilliance.

Drifting into the buoyant haze between nod and sleep Gideon listened to the songs of the farm; the bass grunting of the sow, the snorting of piglets. Cattle muttered; feathered images of moonlight barged each other on perches in cluck, clack and an easing of feet. From the open top window of the tumbling farmhouse came the snores of humans. These were the last sounds Gideon heard before the drovers came through.

They came from the mountain farms abounding between the little town of Cardiff and the thriving iron centre of Newport, from the packed cattle pens of Caerphilly, Pontypridd and Risca. Ten deep over the mountain road came the cattle, seeking the track of ancient Sarn Helen and the Midland towns. And they came in a whisper of sound that later grew in power, bringing Gideon upright in the coach, and longing for sight. Sun Heron, lying on her stomach in the cover of a nearby thicket, also watched. In the reviling shouts of the drovers the cattle ran; bucking, shouldering, leaping upon one another in a mêlée of flying bodies and dust. And their hooves beat a rhythmic thunder on the flinted road to an accompaniment of cracking whips and a shrieking of cow and heifer. Barging, leaning, horning, the mad pack came, and the night was filled with the agony of the passage: whips curled and flashed against the moon: men stood at out-stations with braced legs and cracked their flails in the faces of the beasts to maintain the herd; Welsh collies raced through the bordering heather, barking and snapping at their heels, others lay like quivering arrows in the grass, waiting for the command that would send them into battle. And the drovers, bow-legged and heavy with ale, bawled their obscenities and raucous oaths to keep the mob in being, fists thumping into the faces of oncoming heifers, boots swinging to maintain the line. Six hundred head of cattle were streaming over the breast of Old Pantlattyn, heading for the slaughterhouses of Hereford, Welshpool, Chester and Liverpool. And after the cattle came sheep and these numbered more than two thousand; a crawling, maggotty mass that blanketted the common. Fringed with racing dogs and shepherds, they followed the mad stampede of the cattle at a slower pace, thronging the pens of the wayside inns in a cacophony of bleating and baa-ing, and from their sweating bodies there rose a billow of heat and breath shot brown with dust. Carrying on their backs the wool for the factories of Cheshire, these were the packets of walking meat bound for the knives and killing-boards of the west. In the vanguard ran the fittest, in the middle the majority flock, and at the end of the heaving mass fell the foot-rot stragglers, the old ewes, the blind rams baa-ing pitifully in their limping, staggering pace, for to fall meant death: this they knew by instinct. And the killing shepherds walked in file behind them with blood-stained crooks and gullet knives, and behind them was a donkey-cart filled with carcasses for market sale or eating at the next inn down.

'Get up there!'

The night was filled with shrieks and the cracking of whips.
'Keep 'em going, Bounder! Keep at 'un, Nell...!'
'Hey-whey-*up*! Hey-whey-*up*!' The cattle stock-flails
flourished against the stars and cracked down over the heaving
backs. Dust billowed as a heifer went down, instantly trampled
under the milling hooves.

'Get 'un on his cheeses, Towzer, me lad! On 'is tail, me
lucky lad! Up, up. Where the blutty hell is you, Dai Downer?
Ye get up front afore I shift ye! Up front, *up front*!'

Gideon heard the innocents crying under the thumps of men
called human: this, the stinking refuse of the tramping trails—
North Countrymen mostly, but their numbers swollen with
brutal Welsh, the prize fighters and vagrants of the Welsh
gutters, the sweepings of the dissolute inns; old soldiers from
the French wars, still wearing the uniforms of their discharge;
the tattered dregs of the ironworks, burned out in eyes and
brains twenty years before their time. These were the drovers
of industrial Wales; murderers who had escaped the rope,
thieves who had swum from the transportation hulks—the
Leviathan of Portsmouth, the convict ship which lost shackled
prisoners by crew corruption; the *Captivity* lying at Devon-
port, whose captain sold felons at a guinea a time and took
their wives to the brothels of the East.

'*Hey-whey-up!*' The stock-whips rose and cracked in
shrieks. An old ewe fell; pause, kneel, slit her throat, and she
is flung up in a blood-shower. The trampled heifer bellowed to
the slash of the knife; two drovers on her threshing legs and
stained in gory disembowelling. Of these, thought Gideon, a
romance will be woven for new generations. Their songs will
be told as the songs of the road, and the old drovers' tracks
will snake into history, revered in lilt and doggerel. He bowed
his head as the procession of torture passed him, making north.
And behind it were trails of blood. Once, when he was young,
he had seen the drovers pass, and wept. The bedlam grew
fainter as the cortège took twin paths to lower ground; the
night was murmuring in sadness to three thousand fainter
throats; now all was silent save for the distant cracking of the
whips. Then the handle of the coach door turned in a faint

squeak that few but Gideon would have heard. The wind moved, bringing the stench of urine and the droppings of bowels turned to water: had he sight he would have seen the multitudinous tracks of saliva criss-crossed in silver on the moonlit road.

'You there, Gid?'

He stiffened imperceptibly, then sighed, running his fingers through his hair.

Sun Heron said: 'Are ye hogging both seats in there, or is one going free?'

He did not reply, so she entered, closing the door softly behind her. And sat on the seat opposite him with her hands between her knees, smiling into his face.

'How are ye?' she said.

Gideon was not surprised that she had come, he had been expecting her. Strangely, too, there was solace in her presence after the appalling cruelty of the droving.

'I waited for ye for a bit after doin' the navvy, but you didn't come,' she said.

The warmth of her crossed the coach and touched him; also, she smelled clean for once, and this pleased him. Anticipating his thought, she said: 'I was in the farm pond washing meself when the cattle come by: there's neither dirt nor scum on me, for I hooked a bit o' soap off a stall in Ponty and I washed meself twice since then—here, smell me hair ... I cut off a hank and sold it for a shillin'—in case you're short o' money.' She bent towards him. 'See, I'm all scented and washed—I'm as bright as a steel bodkin.'

Gideon did not reply, and she said: 'You shirty with me?'

'No.'

'The night's hot and I'd be weathering it outside, but I'm afrit of the Cefn boys.'

'There are no Cefn boys round here.'

'Ay, there is! I heard tell on the road that they got a church fella near Blackwood—and he pick-a-backed seven o' them till he fell, and they cut him cruel with the sticks, an' his legs black and blue, poor sod.'

76

'Blackwood is a long way south from here,' said Gideon.

'Ay? Well I'm frit o' them, for if they catch me I'm lucky if I'm pick-a-backing, for they do a terrible offence, dear me.'

Despite himself, he had to smile. She said: 'You let me stay by here?'

'If you please.'

Her voice lowered. 'Then I sit like travelling baggage? Or do I come over there beside you?'

Gideon moved over on the seat and they sat together, unspeaking.

There was growing in him a need of her; it was a new and startling emotion that dried his throat. The dog was panting under his hand and he could feel the beating of its heart.

Sun Heron said: 'You going to Merthyr, Gid?'

'Of course; you know that.'

'You doing your politics there, then, and handing out the pamphlets, and fiddling?'

'Ay.'

'What's the politics, Gid?'

'You wouldn't understand.'

'But I would!' She turned, speaking into his face. 'Ye treat me like a kid, but I'm not a kid—I'm turned eighteen and fending for myself. Didn't I act like a woman when I did that Jobina?'

'It's men's business, Sun.'

She interjected happily, 'You said me name! *Well!* I've been waitin' for that—just to hear ye say me name. Ach, come on, don't that stand next door to a kiss? Aw, kiss me, Gid Davies.'

In seconds it happened.

She was suddenly against him, her arms about him, and he heard the convulsive sobbing of her throat, and her strength beat about him in vigorous beauty. He held her, kissing her, but his need was spitted with bitterness, because he did not truly know her age. Pushing her away he got up and leaned, head bowed, on the door, his hands gripping the glass.

'Aw, be a sport, what ails ye, Gid?'

From the corner of the seat she examined him, her legs

77

crossed, trying not to giggle, while he stood in a brooding quiet, ashamed. Anger and need, tempestuous and rioting, were burning within him.

She said: 'Mind, it's a pretty shame after ye've done it, but the mood soon passes. Billy Ugmore had a word for it—like a rogue elephant was Billy, but he made a radiant woman out o' a girl just off me father's knee. Ach, come on, Gid Davies!'

'You are evil,' he said.

'An' that's for truth!' She threw back her head in elfin laughter. 'I'm upright and daisy, because I'm alive. But you're dead, fella! Sure to God, I thought if I smartened meself up you'd have an eye for me, for I've a sweet little leg on me and a yearning for wickedness. Can ye see out o' that window?'

Gideon raised his head and saw the light of the moon. She cried, gaily. 'Ye taking it all too fearsome, man, and it anna that important. And if it isn't now it'll be later, for ye need me deep in your breast. Look at me pretty legs—come on now— shall I give ye ease, for that's what you're wanting.'

'For God's sake leave me alone,' he said.

'I will not, for you're set on me. I'd be thick in the head if I didn't know that. The moon's got a hunter's polish on him, boy, and he's fair for kissing and loving . . . ?'

He sighed, eyes closed, like a candle going out, for he was one with her in his mind but his body was standing by the window; the thought of her nearness rose hot within him, and he turned. Instantly he was in her arms, her kisses eager on his mouth. Mute and clasped within himself, he held her while her gay joy beat about him: he was experiencing a strange in-difference that was making him selective and apart from the demand. Also, there was about her a sort of bastard rudeness that eased the wanting: rather more than love-making, hers was an assault on dignity: in the very gust of her breathing he saw a smile, and stood removed from the panic of her loving. Presently she went limp in his arms and began to cry, and the crying broke into a wild disorder of sobbing, and she sank back on to the seat and beat her fists upon it.

'For God's sake hush,' he said, 'you'll have the farmer out!'

'An' bloody good luck to him!'

'Be quiet, Sun!'

'I wanna!'

'*Whist!* Or I'll turn you out!'

'You try!'

He sat beside her, holding her hands. Dolefully she said: 'Billy Ugmore was a right good fella. More'n once he leathered me, but he never turned me down.'

'Nor have I,' said Gideon. 'Please do not cry.'

She said: 'You turned me down, you blutty turned me down, Gid Davies.' She raised a tearful face to his. 'An' I washed special for you.'

'Stop shouting! You're making too much noise!'

'I'll shout when I like!' Her voice rose in defiance. 'You'm a belt an' braces man, Gid Davies—you'm too careful.' She pulled her hair over her face and loosened her tears. 'Beyond my damned exertions, you are—you a preacher, or somethin'?'

He shook his head wearily: now that the wish had left him all he wanted was peace. She said, bitterly, 'Well, you dunna give much away, Gid Davies. I reckon they weren't all born in Jerusalem.'

'You are a child and I am trying to be a man,' he said softly.

'I'm eighteen—ain't that old enough?'

He turned away, and she said bitterly, 'I canna help meself with ye. A night out wi' some high-stepping girl would have cost ye a fortune, but it all comes free with me.'

'Perhaps that is the trouble.'

She sighed and put her hands over her face. 'Dear me,' she whispered, 'that were a close one: somebody's been gnawing at me with no teeth.'

'It will pass,' said Gideon, sitting down beside her.

As if to herself she said: 'You'm not like Billy Ugmore, though. A woman didn't ask twice off him, though he had no time for dark behaviour...' She stared at Gideon, her eyes moving over his face. 'An' he had no time for the preachers, neither. Pious brains they do have, said Billy, but no minds. You understand that?'

'I expect so.'

Warming to him she fluffed up and prided, hooking her arm through his and nudging on the seat. 'Ah, well,' she said brightly, 'got to make the best of it, like Billy Ugmore says...'

Gideon interjected: 'I am becoming a little tired of Billy Ugmore.'

She settled back. 'In time you'll come to it, Gid. Then shave off your eyebrows and I'll eat ye alive. Dear me, boiling oil's too good for me. A painful and troublesome day it's been, me lovely boy, so we'll say good night to it. But before we sleep—are ye sure you won't change your mind, now I'm all scented and clean?'

'I doubt it,' said Gideon.

'Dear me,' she said, hugging herself. 'Grow your hair, Samson, and we'll have the roof down on the pair of us. Good night to ye.'

Gideon stared sightlessly at her in the cold-breathing air, then lay down opposite her, and slept; to awake almost instantly, it seemed, to a garrulous argument of courting hedgehogs beneath the coach.

Then the scent of a wood fire struck his nostrils and he raised himself to the window; Sun joined him, staring out. At the foot of a tree not fifty yards away a fire was burning and beside it, stirring a cook-pot, was the young Welshman she had seen outside the Swan, Maesteg. He was on his way to Merthyr from Pyle, and the cottage *Penderyn* where he was born.

Now he began to whistle a quaint, happy tune.

'Who is it?' whispered Gideon.

'Ach—some gunk I passed on the way—like as not he's bound for Merthyr.' Cupping her hands to her mouth, she yelled, 'Will ye stop the birdies so decent people can get to sleep, ye noisy fella? D'you realise it's past midnight?'

Gideon hauled her back. 'Hush, you'll raise the farmer!'

The whistling ceased.

The moon was full on her face, and as she settled down again Gideon leaned closer to her, for the brightness had given her shape. Taking off his coat he put it over her, smiling.

'Good night to ye,' he said.

Annie Hewers and Megsie Lloyd, late of Pontypridd, arrived in Merthyr two days after Gideon had met them on the road; they came down through Georgetown in Sunday best and as large as life, and thank God we are finished with babies, bottle and bottoms, and is there work in the biggest town in Wales for two lusty girls?

Down Dynefor Street they came and along the canal, bonnet streamers blowing, and the brickfield women were chattering on the doorsteps and look what is coming down now, good God; the burned-out miners of an earlier generation of Crawshays stared through red-rimmed eyes and champed their toothless jaws on clays, remembering their lost youth and the legion of their lovers.

'Dear me,' whispered Megsie, gathering her shawl about her.

'Looks pretty savage, don't it?' said Annie, and on they went, bowing left and right to the grimy refuse of the Ynysfach ironworks that leaned on the corners of Bridgefield Terrace. On the cobbles outside the Miners' Arms the off-shift colliers of Lefal were sitting on their hunkers winking above their quarts, and Shan Shonko, the big-nosed puddler from Carmarthen was crossing her thick legs and waving a scarlet shawl and whooping like a Sioux Indian. Bedraggled, ragged children who had escaped the ravages of the early cholera in Georgetown and Williamstown, played aimlessly in the gutters amid the cracking of the mule-whips and clattering hooves. Shafting through the squalor rode the stately barges of the Glamorgan Canal loaded with the iron of Cyfarthfa, gliding for Newport and the ports of the world. And all around rose the cinder tips: the hot-drops of Ynys were glowing and filling the air with the acrid stink of sulphur: the straggling dramroads wound in and out of the alleys and working compounds like black vipers on the burned tumps.

'Where you bound for, girls?' This from an old crone; up to Megsie's shoulder was she, with a black shawl scragged round her head and her heavy-lidded eyes drooping in the folds of her broken face.

'Come for work,' said Annie.

'Have ye now, me little ones. And have ye an appointment with Crawshay, so to speak?'

'We just arrived,' said Megsie.

'Ay? And can I ask where from, me lovely?'

'Pontypridd.'

'Well, then, you can take ye pick. You can mine iron on the tumps out on Hirwaun Common or coal-crop on the Old Glamorgan levels—are ye scared of healthy work, ladies?'

'That is what we are here for,' said Annie.

'Then the world's wide open for ye in Merthyr, for it's a town of work, heaven and the devil. Is it quick money you're after?'

'Quicker than that, for we've got to eat.'

'Well now, that's unfortunate, for the belly's the enemy, ye understand? With a full belly ye can pick and choose, but with an empty one you've got to take what's going, you see. Do you fancy going underground in the Cyfarthfa pits, for the fellas are always after dram-fillers at six shillings a week.'

'She's weak in the chest,' said Annie.

'Then you go below and she crops on top—sure that's a fine arrangement.'

'We're not being parted,' said Annie.

'Would ye like to have a word to Aunty Popi Davey in the Lodgings?'

'Who's she?'

'She sees to all the new female labour coming in, me darlings. And she'll fix ye up decent, with a good shift and a bed for a penny in the shilling.'

'You work here, missus?' asked Megsie.

The sunlight shafted between them, a sword of fire blading through the smoke-pall of Ynysfach. The old woman said, 'Well, not nowadays, for I've given me best, ye see, now I'm nearly thirty. But I worked for the old beggar up in Cyfarthfa when I was seven—come over from Old Ireland on the ticket —and I filled the drams down the Lefal with me pa. When I was ten I was shovelling on the levels, and after I was fifteen Crawshay had me on the face, but the screws took me when I was twenty, being wet working, ye understand.' She sighed and grinned and her yellow teeth rolled drunkenly in her mouth. 'Now I work for Aunty Popi Davey in the Lodgings—don't ask much now—just a bit o' bread and a do on the gin when things come delicate in the limbs, see, me lovelies?'

'Aunty Popi Davey?' asked Annie, looking about her. The flame-hot chimneys of Ynysfach she saw and heard beneath her feet the rumble of the shot-firing underground: she saw the pit-wheels revolving in the swirling smoke: women were quarrelling beyond the steps of the Miners' Arms, their voices shrill. At her side, beyond her as far as she could see the land was upturned, the fields laid waste in blackened upheaval as if by the cannon of an invading army: bright flashes lit the sky above Cyfarthfa Works where the molten iron was pouring from the cauldrons.

'You on, Megsie?'

'Ay.'

Annie shrugged. 'We got to do something.'

'That's it, girls. Come on, we're away to see Aunty Popi Davey. You stick to her and she'll fix you right,' said Old Wag.

Madoc Williams, top Cyfarthfa puddler, stood on the corner of Bridgefield; off shift, he watched Megsie and Annie go by. He saw Annie first because she was bigger, and smiled. Like a princess she went, with her black Abergavenny shawl akimbo over her arms and her bright hair falling over her shoulders; she had a neat swing on her hips, he thought, and her breasts were firm and high. Megsie he saw drooping in the delicate beauty of the consumptive adolescent, aged sixteen; her eyes, round and bright in the pallor of her cheeks, seemed to rove within his soul; once he knew a girl like this drooping one, and she had coughed out her lungs on a bed of rags in the Irish cellars up at Pontmorlais. Dobi, his ladler, had a sister like her well-set friend going with Old Wag up to the Aunty Popi Davey Lodgings, and she ended as one of Sgubor Fawr's molls on the Iron Bridge, touting the drunks coming off shift on pay nights, until they found her face down in the Taff one winter morning. Rumour said an agent had her first for a sovereign

83

and her father got a shilling a week rise on the limestone hauling, but he never had the proof of it.

Shrugging, he turned away, caught Shan Shonko's hands in
passing and wheeled her in a circle to the shrieks of the squatting colliers, then, pulling her drum-hat over her eyes, he went
within the Miners' and hammered the counter for a pint. He
was due to meet Bron Babbie, his wife, but he had forgotten
this.

Miss Thrush the Sweets, looking younger than her forty
years, cried to the waiting coach:

'I will not be a moment, Mrs. Taibach. Tell Mr. Note that I
am just coming.' Outside on the cobbles of High Street the
coach for Merthyr, with Mr. Bottom Note's harmonium strapped on the back, stamped and lurched with expectancy: Willie
Bach Genius, his violin case under his arm, cried nervously
around the door of the shop:

'Got to get going, see, Miss Thrush. Mr. Note's got a revolution coming off in Merthyr: he don't like being kept waiting.'

'The revolution will wait another five minutes, Willie Bach;
it will be that much more effective if Mr. Note keeps calm.'
Before the cracked mirror on the wall, the sole furnishing of an
otherwise empty shop, Miss Thrush patted her well-groomed
hair and smoothed her hands over her body: now turning in
profile to flicker a wink at the glass, while her sister, Miss
Agnes Thrush cried in wet misery:

'I don't know what's got into you, I just don't. If our ma
was alive it'd drive her lunatic, and me feyther must be sittin'
upright in his grave this moment. Woman, see sense—you
can't just sell up at forty and land yourself in Merthyr un-
escorted—you know what'll happen don't ye?'

'Stand aside, sister.' Miss Thrush took Willie's arm.
'Kindly escort me to the coach like a gentleman, Willie.'

This Willie did, and held the coach door wide for Miss
Thrush to ascend, while his mother, sitting beside a fuming
Mr. Note, nodded and beamed her approval.

'Good morning, Mrs. Taibach,' cried Miss Thrush. 'Good
morning, Mr. Note. Let us pray for a safe journey and thank

84

you for suggesting I should share the coach and the cost.'

And Miss Thrush, late of the The Sweets on High Street, steadied her broad-brimmed hat with one hand; with the other she drew high her voluminous black skirt, exposing to Willie's delighted gaze a long, shapely leg from bright buckled shoe to suspender as she stepped up. According to Willie later, even the horse looked round.

And in the doorway of the empty shop with its notice 'Sold' on the window, Miss Agnes Thrush clasped her kerchief to her throat in growing panic, and cried:

'Save us! She's got nought on! Why, ye scarlet huzzy, Milly Thrush. And to Merthyr, in scarlet stockings . . . !'

Percy Bottom Note, commanding a good view of the ascent, rose from his seat with a shivering smile and bowed low. 'Pray enter, good lady, pray enter . . . !' Vigorously he dusted the seat with a red handkerchief, crying, 'I must say, Miss Thrush, although I have seen you many times before, I never dreamed . . . pray, pray be seated.'

As Willie Bach Genius observed afterwards, a couple of inches of Milly Thrush thigh and they stop the revolution.

'Welcome, I'm sure,' said Mrs. Taibach, and hooked Willie beside her, abdicating his look of awe. 'You sit by here, and I'll know where you are.'

In this fashion, with Willie Taibach Genius staring at his idol in utter disbelief, they took the road to iron, and Merthyr.

WITH the listless demeanour of a woman lost, Jobina walked down Plymouth Street past Maerdy Gardens where the big oaks stood, fighting their everlasting battle against the encrusting residue of coke, their boles gleaming with sparkle-mine under the July moon. Outside Dark House she rested against a wall and bathed her feet in a gutter with water piped from the works into the nearby Taff. An urchin watched her from the shadows, one of many who had followed her in from Plymouth Works where the Nipper Tandy gang were building a dram-road culvert. Belcher and Big Bonce were working there, also Skin-Crone and Godiva, and Curly Hayloft who was nursing his grief for Tilly, who was dead. Merthyr had not been kind to the Nipper Tandy and the new Plymouth dram-road. Working for the navvy contractor Peto the Baptist, whose tentacles ranged from Darlington to Newport, they had contracted for the culvert on piece-work; twelve hour shifts at two pounds a foot, and hit the rock strata north of Mae Level on the William Davies land, and this meant blasting. Belcher went in with the drills and Big Bonce followed with powder, and they charged the bore-holes in wet working up to their arm-pits, said Lady Godiva.

'Where's me Tilly?' asked Curly Hayloft, and they said she was on top.

'Has anybody seen me darling girl?' Curly asked again. 'Will you hold that match, Belch, until I discover me woman?' but Belcher had lost an ear-drum on the Stockton barrow runs, and his side to Curly was deaf.

'Away to go!' he cried, and fired the fuse. 'Take cover, me

lovelies, for it's two pounds a foot, and this should fix it!' and he scrambled behind a rock.

'In the name of God, where's Tilly?' shrieked Curly, and he stared down the hill while Tilly, whistling with her face up to the sun, went into the tunnel with the nose-bags.

'Tilly!' shrieked Moll. 'Tilly, Tilly!' screamed Godiva.

The tunnel barked fire like the muzzle of a gun: the morning sang with the whine of boulders: black smoke billowed and blinded the sun. They found Tilly in the mouth under a six-ton rock, and Curly went on all fours like a dog, burrowing in the drift, then lay beside her on the blood-stained ground and reached into a fissure and touched the tips of her fingers.

Tilly died in the tongue of Wigan, where she was born, and only Curly understood when she spoke from her tomb, though he was from the south.

'There's nought but you in a mile o' dinners,' she said. 'An' I threw the nose-bags clear as I come in, Curly. Are you with me, lad?'

'Ay, me sweet one.'

'Ye'll do well by me ma back home, Curly?'

'I will that,' he said. 'I'll skin me fingers for her, since she touched me with a good woman.'

'Eh, me chap, it's comin' awful dark,' she said, and died.

Now Jobina looked through the smoke at the moon, and the memory of Tilly was like cutting the stitches of a partly healed wound. It took Blackbird and Skin-Crone, Moll Maguire and Mercy Merriman to pull Curly off Belcher when he got him by the throat, and Jobina helped with a pick-handle.

'I'll give her one thing, she saved the dinners,' said Betsy Paul, collecting them up.

Now there was in Jobina an emptiness as she wandered, looking for Gideon, and as she went past the Angel into Court Street the children followed, though none saw them: these, the orphans of Cyfarthfa, Penydarren and Dowlais, lived in the disused workings of an earlier age. By theft they lived, for they lacked food. Denied poor relief or parish help, they had banded together for the common good, living like animals on the tumps by day, the ragged outcasts of an era of wealth and privilege: by night, in summer, they slept on the mountains. In winter, with the practised skill of trained soldiers, with lookouts in the vanguard and spies at the rear, they slept beside the coke ovens of Thompson, Ynysfach and Cyfarthfa until beaten out into the frost by the special constables. Within the shadow of the rope or cell, the transportation hulks or treadmill, they followed the easier prey like lame tigers: weakened by starvation, slowed by disease, they found strength in numbers. Aged from nine to sixteen, they roved in bands: twenty-four who lived in the old workings on the Meyrick and Davies land, were now following Jobina beyond the gates of the Unitarian where the Thompson agents were inside on their knees, and up the dram-road to Adulum Fields.

With her shoes in her hands Jobina wandered, wondering if Gideon would have come in on the Dowlais road: if he had, she reflected, he would likely be lodging in the Pontmorlais area, for he loved the Irish. So intent were her thoughts that she did not see the shadows moving about her, or hear the whisperings and the brushing of bare feet among the trees: for the Thompson works went into blast at ten o'clock and the world seemed to tremble, and a pillar of flame rose from the furnaces like a blow-torch fusing the stars. The red light played on the watching faces about her as she wandered, eyes half closed now to the sobbing of Curly. Then, realising that she was too far east, she stopped and rested. She was sitting there quietly in the shadows of the road when a hand brushed grass, a foot slithered on a stone behind her. The night was suddenly incredibly quiet: even the Cyfarthfa night-shift seemed to have died in sleep; the soil beneath her rumbled to the underground workings and the sprag of a dram five hundred feet below. A threat in moving hands and switching eyes grew from the darkness and the moon faded in a billow of smoke from Thompson. A finger of ice seemed to touch her brain, and Jobina slowly rose from the ditch, and turned, looking about her.

The ring of small faces were motionless above the grass of the berm.

Staring at them, she put her hands to her face and backed across the road, then turned and fled, weeping aloud as she went past the Independent and she heard them gasping in their swift pursuit. She shrieked as they came abreast of her on the edge of the new burial ground, the fleetest in the van: here Jobina stopped in prayers of incoherent terror as they closed the ring around her, and pulled her down.

'Ach, dear me,' said Blod. 'rest your wee self, Randy, me love, it's a tryin' time for the pair of us.'

Humping and heaving was Randy, with his fine body sweating in the straw of the barn and his eyes on sticks, and if there's one thing that drives a fella berserk it's a gorgeous filly like you diving around and never in one place long enough to pin ye.

'Listen, have you no pity? I could take me pick of the wenches from Merthyr to Aberafon, and here I am punching around in the dark and getting nowhere. Won't ye give a fella an outing?'

'I will not!' Upright and shocked was Blod, her head an inch from the barn roof, and he saw her eyes like diamonds in her face and the smudged shadows of her cheeks: golden as the straw was her hair tumbling in thick swathes over her shoulders and her skin was stained brown by the sun, her mouth shining with kisses: and he thought he had never seen so lovely a creature in a march from Merthyr to Penarth where the weekend coasters came in from France. Every Saturday night they came and anchored off the jetties in deep water, and the onion men from Breton would row ashore in their little sharp currachs with the Spanish immigrant women for the industries, and these they would land along the little stone quays, and he had never seen the likes of them either. For they were beauties from the eastern coast of Spain, many being of pure gipsy blood, the Gitano who fled inland from the persecutions of Gascony and Rousillon. They were hot women, this he knew, with siesta sun in their veins and their hair was black, their eyes slanted; their bodies were beautifully proportioned, and he saw them again in the sawdust of the Welsh inns, and heard the rattle of their castanets and the high shriek of their *tella tella hoi*! And he heard in the throat of Blod Irish the whispers of a girl called Marajeala, who said yes, yes, yes. She was sixteen, he remembered. Now he moved in the barn straw.

'No,' said Blod. 'No, no, *no*!'

'Aw, woman, gi' it a rest!' He sighed deep. 'Yes for a change, is it?'

'No,' said Blod Irish. 'If you want a girl for midnight sport you can seek her elsewhere. I'm standing before the priest or nothin'—didn't I tell you that before we left for Merthyr? When I'm wife to you and mither o' your children, could ye look me in the eye and call me decent if ye had me in barn straw?'

'Gawd help us,' said Randy, 'with speeches like that, and me setting fire to meself.'

'Aw, you poor little soul,' whispered Blod, 'tutty down here on me,' and she pulled his head down to her breast, but up went Randy like something scalded.

'Would you drive me deranged, girl? That's the last place in the world I can sleep.'

'What's the matter now, fella?'

'I'm off to the next door barn,' said Randy.

'Please yourself, I'm sure,' said Blod. '*Arrah!* If this is the start of it, what will be the end of it? The man's a heathen, a most temperamental creature.'

On her back, with her eyes closed at the roof, Blod listened to him going down the ladder; but he was back in seconds bending above her.

'No, no, no!' said Blod.

'Och, dry up, woman,' said he. 'Hush up, and listen.'

'God bless the Pope,' said Blod, peering down the road. 'Just look what's coming ... !'

Mamie Goldie and Billa Jam, Moke Donkey and the children were coming down Fishpond Street with the cart: Moke was walking behind with Merve and Saul pushing, the rest of the children were asleep on the cart with twin donkeys, and Mamie and Billa were harnessed in the shafts.

90

'Didn't I tell ye that moke was carrying for twins?' said Blod.

'Has the old girl been producing, then?'

'Like as not she's birthed on the road. There'll be hell to pay rent to when Mr. Jam finds that donkey kidnapped.'

Randy rubbed his face, saying, 'Will the damned woman never let me be? Will you tell me why I canna start a new life without her chasing me up with kids and donkeys?'

'It's a powerful love she bears you, Randy.'

'Och, go to sleep,' said he. 'I'm sick to death of females, anyway—the likes of you and mothers in particular.' He heaved over away from her and thumped the straw for a pillow. 'If I went down there what would it be? The same old tongue pie, the same old mythering, with you getting the sharp end of it as a good for nothing Irish quick-wit snatching at the first fine son that comes along—is that what you want?'

'You'll never change Mamie, that's for sure,' said Blod.

'Then why do you stand for her when she gives you nothing but jaw?'

'Because she's your ma, boy. And I've never yet come across an apology of a son who could bed himself down for the night while his mother does the work of a donkey—ach, you make me sick, Randy Goldie. Did you hear that—ye make me sick!'

Randy sat up and clutched himself; with flickering eyes, Blod watched.

'The big fat thing,' he said. 'She's not worth a second look. She's done nothing but moddle and coddle me, so I'm making the break. D'you hear me, Mamie Goldie? I'm done with ye—I've cut the strings for good.'

Blod waited, breath pent.

'Are you asleep, girl?' Randy leaned above her: through half-closed eyes Blod saw the sweat of his face, and breathed on with the rhythm of one asleep.

'Och, holy God,' whispered Randy, knuckling his mouth. 'Ma,' he said, and Blod watched him.

The hoof-beats of Moke began to fade.

'Ma,' he said again, 'eh dear . . . Ma!' and he leaped up and vaulted ten feet down to the floor of the barn: Blod rose in the straw watching him tearing through the moonlight up Fish-pond, and his voice came to her in flushes of the wind:

'Ma! Ma!'

Smiling, she looked at the stars.

Strident in her grief with Percy Bottom Note slipping away under her nose, Mrs. Taibach sat upright in the swaying coach and her soul snorted its fierce anger. In the vicious encounters of her mind, she clutched the libertine robes of Miss Thrush and tore them, shrieking, from her body, while Miss Thrush, done up in Sunday braveries, rocked on Mr. Note's shoulder like a captive butterfly: she swayed and bowed to the bucking coach and the drumming of hooves in a piratical dream. With the furnace glare flashing on her sleeping face and the stars of Dowlais Top spying in a rent of smoke, she nuzzled closer to Mr. Note in the comforting hollow between shoulder and starched collar. And she saw him not as one tattered in soul and frayed at sleeve but as a chevalier of high nobility.

'I'll blutty give it you,' whispered Mrs. Bach Taibach.

Mr. Note, Corresponding Member for the Merthyr Union Branch, nodded and dreamed in his plans for Miss Thrush the Sweets. Adrift from his ideals of property reform, the repeal of the Corn Laws and dissolution of the slave trade, he sat in a wicked, bare-legged crow of a dream. In a buccaneer pursuit of Milly Thrush, casting off a demand for higher wages, anti-shopocracy and pro-democracy, he exchanged the tub-thumped trumpetings of youth for a hunt along a palm-fringed beach while Miss Thrush, attired in red stockings, went in mecurial flight, arms up, her long hair flying. Removed from his castigation of the mine-owners, abandoning his resentment against Truck and the revenue of the Crown, the Poor Law coming, and parish relief, he cornered and caught her in a tangle of ribbons, bringing her down in shrieks of girlish laughter. And he heard Miss Thrush's cry as one of submission, a finale for the last chord of his new Gun Symphony, and he raised his fist high and brought it down, crying:

'*Diawch!*'

Miss Thrush awoke, gathering her things about her and easing her head off Mr. Note's collar with a smile of surprise at Mrs. Taibach and Willie, while Mr. Note blew his nose violently into a big red handkerchief.

'You 'aving nightmares, Mr. Note?' asked Willie, brightly.

Sonorously, Mr. Note replied: 'As a matter of fact I was conducting the last movement of my new Gun Symphony...' He twiddled his thumbs with delight.

'I'll give him Gun Symphony,' whispered Mrs. Bach Tai-bach.

The coach braked then, its locked wheels slithering along the rutted road opposite Adulam Fields: Willie peered out of the window. The gravestones of the new burial ground were standing white against the moon.

'We there, then?' asked Miss Thrush.

'We are not,' said Mr. Note, bass, and put his head out of the window. 'What ails us, coachman? What is wrong?'

The lights of Merthyr glowed in the valley; the furnaces of Cyfarthfa simmered on the night air. The coachman clambered down from his seat and came to the door.

'Been an accident, it appears,' said he.

'An accident!' Mrs. Taibach clutched at her throat.

'Kind of, beggin' your pardon, sir,' said the coachman to Mr. Note. 'Some poor vagrant found dead on the road. I suggest the ladies turn their fair 'eads as I take us past the gambo, for the sexton has got 'er.'

'Kindly proceed when convenient,' said Mr. Note.

As they lurched past the gambo Mrs. Taibach averted her head and pressed Willie's face into the folds of her coat: even Mr. Note lowered his eyes in respect. But Miss Thrush, impelled by some dreadful curiosity, looked out on to the road.

Jobina was lying on the gambo and her face was upturned in a drive of the moon.

The sexton wrung his hands and stared up at Miss Thrush, his great eyes brilliant in his cavernous face. 'Can't think how it happened; neither scratch nor bite on 'er, and beads and bodice intact, an' two shillings in money in her purse ... her heart must 'ave stopped, poor soul.'

'Oh, God,' said Miss Thrush, and bowed her head. For unmistakably, as she had suspected, projecting from beneath the tied-down skirt were the buckled boots of the navvy and the calves of two red stockings.

THE sun was nearly overhead when Gideon and Sun reached the outskirts of Pentre next day, and here rested in a ditch clear of the Merthyr road, and the mail coach for Cardiff passed them in a swaying gallop and horn-blast from a clowning postillion; the manes of the four big chestnuts were flying in the wind, their nostrils dilating red under the whip, their eyes wild.

Gideon eased himself up. 'Come on,' he commanded. 'I want to be in Merthyr before the sun goes down.'

'And me poor spags that blistered!' In the middle of the road she squatted, examining her feet. 'Man alive, you're as cussed as Moses with the tablets—we've got all day.'

Gideon did not reply but walked on, for there had come to him an unaccountable premonition of distaster; obedient to the warning, he strode on, while Sun followed, protesting. But now, the limp gone, she ran on tip-toe about him, crossing her feet in the manner of the Desmond gipsies and singing in a high soprano. Of a sudden, the mood of fear left him and he grinned and knelt, pulling out his fiddle, and played for her a merry Mayo reel.

'Are you dancing?' But he knew she was dancing, and played on, changing to a higher key and raising the tempo, and still she danced, madly pirouetting, and the dust rose to her feet. Then she stopped, and stared at the hedgerows. Gideon was still playing when the *Caro ar Cefn* appeared.

They rose slowly from behind the hedges: their game was at its height: six of them, and they approached slowly, their hands deep in their rags. Theirs was the sport of pick-a-back riding; and their prey was turned from human into a horse.

Gideon lowered the fiddle. 'What is it?'

'The *Caro ar Cefn*,' said Sun, clutching his arm.

The leader of the Riders smiled.

These were the hooligans of the Taibach industry, the refuse of the ironworks, pits and quarries who begged their way from one short-job to another, mixing humour and cruelty in their highway robbery; the pick-a-back riff-raff of the bawdy inns of Pyle and Kenfig Hill, who had drifted north when a victim died.

'How are you?' They ringed Gideon and Sun in the road. Dishevelled from rough sleeping and drink, they grinned, tossing a gin flask from hand to hand. The leader drank last, gasped, and wiped his mouth, saying, 'Dear me, we wink at the sky and the manna drops. A travelling fiddler and his prancer, is it? And pockets filled with gold?'

'You're a long way north, Rider,' said Gideon.

'You know us, and you blind?'

'I can smell you.' The dog began to whine at his feet and he stooped, picking it up. 'And what gold I have stays on me, but you're welcome to it if you can get it. Let us pass.'

'Have you right of way?' It was the age-old shout of the drovers, who fought for it for fun.

'The roads are metalled; the right is established,' said Gideon.

'If you shift us, blind man.' They ranged across it, barring the way.

Gideon said: 'I'll lay you this, Cefn Rider—you don't know who you're stopping. Stumble one of us and I'll come back with men who will tie you to trees and take blood from your backs.'

One shouted with laughter; the eyes of the leader danced in his face.

A dwarf of a man pushed to the front. 'Did you hear that, Iolo? The chap's going to cripple us!'

'The brutal fella!'

The Rider said: 'Well, there's nothing I like better than a bucking blind fiddler—down on your knees, boyo.'

'You are getting no lifts from me,' said Gideon.

'Then your missus might oblige?' They ringed about them, nearer. Another shouted: 'Ask natural and polite, Bando, and she might give you a lift of another kind.'

They laughed full-throated at this, stamping about. Gideon said, head averted, 'Run for it, run for it.'

'An' leave ye with these hooligans?' Sun shrieked at the men, 'Have ye no common decency—and him blind?'

Another cried. 'He's a fine set-up fella, missus. He don't need eyes to hand us poor weary travellers a ride!'

A big one, stark Irish, called: 'Is it too much to ask—a lift for a few of us—just a couple o' hundred yards?'

'Take his money but leave him in peace. Have ye no souls?' she yelled it into their faces as they advanced, drawing their short ash canes from their belts and swishing them in the air. Sun backed away, pulling Gideon after her.

'In the name of God, look, I'm begging ye! Leave him!'

'Ach, what's the odds? We're only after improving the manners of the community, don't ye see? If he takes the big ones and you picky-up the little ones we'll be half-way up the road to Merthyr without even swishing a cane—are ye on?' The Irishman was in the forefront now, the Welsh leader snatched at Sun's wrist, but she twisted free.

'God grant me sight,' said Gideon, and leaped, striking by sound. It was an astonishing blow and the Irishman took it square in the face, and sighed, slipping to the ground: with direction lost, Gideon flailed and swung, crouching and hooking vicious blows which the Riders avoided with laughing ease: Sun shrieked, fighting herself free of the leader in a tangle of hair and skirts.

'Ay, wang 'em Gid, the hairy bastards!'

'Get down the road, woman—run, run!' Gideon dived among them, caught one and clubbed him to his knees.

'Hey, Nevan, Will—give me a hand with this wild-cat!'

The men ran in a circle, taking Gideon from behind, tripping and bringing him down and they fought in grunts to secure him. He heard the cries of Sun Heron.

'Have ye got him?'

97

'Aye, an' settle his hash.' Face down, they held him.

'For pity's sake, Evan, can ye strike a cripple?'

'I can—look at me face!'

Gideon raised his head and his voice rang out from the struggles and oaths of the men above him: 'Sun Heron, run, *run*!'

The redness of the morning was fading in his eyes and there was a weariness in him; the blows and curses were dying in his ears. And he heard a scream, loud and clearly he heard it, then silence. They hauled him on to his feet, pinioned from behind. He said: 'In the name of Jesus, let the child go. I'll carry you, I'll give my money, but let her go.'

'Who's for harming her?' This from the Irishman, square and strong but still staggering from Gideon's blow. 'If ye'd come peaceful you'd not be on the end of a hammering now. Now settle yourself and enjoy the gallop. Are ye ready, for it's only a question of a morning trot, seeing you're delicate.'

Held by four of them, Gideon, inches the taller, raised his head. 'Sun Heron! Sun Heron!' he shouted. The woods echoed.

'Settle yourself, me son,' said the Irishman. 'She's in the very best of hands.'

'Just act easy with us, that's all we ask. Everybody's always after belting us, d'ye see, and us just polite travellers begging a lift on the way. Act civil, man, an' I'll speak for your wildcat.'

'Down on your knees, fella.'

'Hold him steady, Daio!'

'Kneel, ye big mare—how can I mount ye standing—sure to God, the thing must be all o' fifteen hands!'

'Down, blind man, or it'll come worse for your filly!'

Gideon knelt in the road, eyes closed.

'Ah, that's better, eh, Will?'

'You on first, Bando boy, and give him one in the shanks if he don't behave.'

'Open your chops for the bridle, girl.'

They twisted a rope between Gideon's teeth: the man on his back now cried: 'Up, up! *Aw*, that's the daisy! Wheeah,

98

there, she's a spirited mare. Are you steady, fella?'

On his feet now, with the man on his back, Gideon waited, holding the rider's legs.

'Right, away!'

They neighed at the sky, three of them dancing about in the manner of children playing at horses: the fourth man, on Gideon's back, lashed at his legs with the cane.

'Right, girl—gallop!'

With his head held back to the strain of the gag, Gideon broke into a swaying, staggering run with the Cefn Rider pick-a-back and the three pursuers thrashing at his calves, crying falsetto and urging him to greater speed. In this manner he went, brushing the hedgerows in his blindness while the rider heaved on the bridle yelling with joy. A boulder in his path and Gideon tripped, falling headlong, and the rider was on his back the moment he rose and the beating started again, but he did not feel the pain nor even the weight of the man upon him. There was growing in Gideon a fury that reached into the depth of his soul: it was all-consuming; a paroxysm of wrath that brought to him a new, vehement strength; crying aloud, he went headlong so that the rider fell: scrambling around, Gideon found him, caught his clothes and pulled him close, sought his throat and clutched; and to escape the blows of his tormentors he rolled over and over in the road, gasping with the effort to cut off his adversary's breath. In choking snarls and gasps they rolled to the verge and collapsed in waving legs into the roadside ditch. Gideon was underneath with the face of the choking man hard against his own, his whole being thrust-ing every moment of his strength into the cramping grip of his fingers. And although the fists of the other riders beat upon his head he still maintained the hold on the other's throat, pulling him higher as a shield, concentrating all his fading effort into the tips of his fingers: the body of the Cefn Rider began to stiffen and a trembling began, and Gideon heard the rumblings of his chest: his arms began to flail the air, impeding the efforts of the others who tried to haul him off. But even as they raised him out of the ditch so Gideon came too, stitched to his victim with a strength that made them one. Then he heard a shout, and thumping footsteps; cries of alarm began to beat about him and the blows of the Riders stopped; the man he held began faintly to gasp, weakly waving his arms as if in protest at the approach of death, and at that moment he was pulled from Gideon's grasp.

Sun came back to the edge of the road when the Cefn Riders left her, to face the new attack. With her hands pressed to her face she watched the young Welshman, recognising him instantly as the one who greeted her outside the Swan when she fought Jobina. With his bundle at his feet he was into the big Irishman first, fighting with the silent intent of the professional, and the man sagged before the sweeping hooks and swings, dropping to his knees as the Welshman left him, to bend and seize the bearded leader, pulled him over his shoulder; the man hit the road face down, and as two more Riders came storming in, the young man wheeled to face them; seeing Sun, he yelled, 'Don't stand there, woman, come on in!' He ducked a cane slash, took another on his shoulder and hooked a man solid, then backed away, tripped over the leader and fell headlong, but bringing down a third Rider as he went: they rolled, striking.

'*Arrah!* I'm comin', fella!' Sun shrieked, and stooped, picking up a stone. Gideon was on his feet now, seeking combat with sweeping hands, staring into the sun for sight. And through the vicious rays he saw the outline of fighting shapes and cried aloud, crouching towards them.

'That's the boy, Gid. Boot 'em, wang 'em, the big oafs!' and Sun stooped and cracked a Rider with a stone as he staggered up, and ran around the Welsh boy who had another on his back and stoned this one, too. Gideon had found the big Irishman now, a swaying shape against the sun, and struck, missed and struck again, and the man took it square, and dropped, motionless: one was running, another was trying to take the Welshman by the legs until Sun got him from behind; freed, the boy straightened the Welsh leader with a left as he rose and pulled down his hands. The punch that felled the man travelled but a few inches; his feet came off the road, his shoulders followed, he hit the berm of the road and lay still,

100

eyes closed. Now Gideon was swaying towards them, seeking a new target for his aimless swings and hooks, tripped over a Rider, and stumbled blindly.

'*Bayo!* Gid, it's over!' shrieked Sun, and dragged the Welsh boy out of Gideon's lunging path. 'That's done 'em! Three down and two runnin'! *Hei wei!* Slow up, fella!'

The Welshman was gasping, leaning on Sun, but he was grinning.

'Ay now,' he said, going double, 'that was a good one!' He licked his knuckles.

'Good? Bedamn, I've never had such a fight since Derry and Billy Ugmore! Are ye hurt, Gid?' She reached him, turning him to face her. 'Ach, the dirty gobs—you've an eye fillin' up, man—look what they've done to ye!'

'Are you all right?' gasped Gideon.

'Just about! The young chap here beat them to it. Och, it was a joy to see ye doin' 'em—where are you from?'

'Aberafon.' He stared about him. 'By God, these Riders are a long way north!'

Two of the men were getting up now, and she shrieked at them, 'Ye pesky snakes, have done wi' ye!' and she raised her stone, but Gideon caught her, dragging her back.

'Leave them, leave them!' he said. He turned to the Welshman. 'We can find no words to thank you.'

'It's little enough. I heard the shouting, but I'd seen the Riders earlier, and slowed me down. It was the woman I was worried for—where you bound?'

'Merthyr,' said Gideon. 'What's your name?'

'Dic Penderyn.'

The man on the bank stirred, groaning; the one by the ditch had gone.

'Dic Penderyn, eh?' Sun looked him over, smiling. 'Sure, there's the sound of a bird in that.'

The young man said: 'I saw you in Maesteg, and again at Gitos Farm. You travelling together?'

The dog was whining at Gideon's feet; stooping, he lifted it against him. 'I'm for Merthyr, but I don't know about you?' He looked at Sun. To his astonishment, and joy, he could see her quite clearly.

'Ach, one place is as good as another.'

'One thing's sure,' said Gideon, 'with the Riders this far north it would be safer to travel together, do you mind?'

The Welshman was wondering about them; he had seen Gideon in Taibach; Sun he had first met in Maesteg; outside Tir-Phil he had seen them sharing the coach. The girl was ragged, and he judged her age at sixteen; the blind man was well dressed for a man on the road, and at least ten years older; also, he was educated, and the girl was not.

'Aw, ye poor thing, Gid—they've broken your fiddle!' Sun picked it up, cherishing it against her. 'Now, if there's money in that fella's pockets he's goin' to pay for it.' She turned. 'D'you realise the little one lifted your purse?'

'Both can be replaced,' said Gideon. 'Leave the man be—enough evil for one day, child.' He put out his hand to her.

'Can I take another wang at that fat Irishman 'afore I leave, then?'

'You can't—come on!' Gideon pushed her in front of him. 'Merthyr.'

'Ay,' said Penderyn, 'Merthyr.'

Gideon, Sun Heron and Dic Penderyn came through the cellars of Pontmorlais where the labouring Irish lived when the sun was going down. Earlier, they had come down the Penydarren dram-road past the works, and here the setting sun was dimmed by the incandescent flashes of iron. The labourers of the slopes and inclines were outlined against a sky of scarlet; the barrel-loaders tipping their limestone, coal and ore into the furnace maws, brought to pygmy size by the fire-shot smoke of the open hearths, and the ground shook to the shot-firing. Now, farther down the hill, they saw the twin glows of Cyfarthfa and Ynys Works, and heard the roar of ironmaking, the air buffeting their faces as if from the velocity of surface explosions.

'The old Cyfarthfa stink,' said Dic Penderyn.

Yellow smoke filled with sulphuretted gases was billowing upwards from the roasting mine; shafts of fire pinned the dusking sky, and from the inferno of light and smoke there came the hiss and venting of pistons, the clanging of bells and the whine of the mills. Here, with an almost total disregard for the human condition, the violation called Merthyr sent its finished iron to the ports of the world, its economics tuned to rate and price. Men were mutilated here, eyes put out, children worked in the pits here or laboured in their hundreds on the Hirwaun open-mining in all weathers; women gave birth at the face, youth was old at ten, and the expectation of life was the age of twenty. Here was no sanitation, no water supply save from polluted wells; here the cottages—a legacy of Bacon the Pig, an earlier iron master—leaned in their ricketty confusion along tortuous courts and alleys; a criss-cross, crazy mass of leaning roofs and hovels which, at their worst, compared to the slums of India according to distinguished travellers. Down the hill the cobbles were piled high with garbage, the gutters crammed with rubbish, and excrement spilled searching fingers for the lower ground. And there rose a smell so offensive that Sun had to cover her mouth; Taibach was as nothing compared to this destitution. Here ill-clad children played and ragged people watched from doors; old men with the quaking pallor of the prematurely aged, followed them with hollowed eyes as they passed; beggars cried shrilly to them for alms; dogs and cats picked over rubbish with furtive apprehension.

'God alive, Gid,' said Sun, 'is this your beloved Merthyr?'

Yet, through the little cobbled streets that rose to higher ground she could see lines of washing out to dry despite the smoke, and from behind the neatly curtained windows of the tradesmen came the unmistakable gleam of brass and the flickering of homely fires.

'What address you going for, blind man?' asked Dic.

'Eighteen Cross, you know it?'

'We pass it on my way home.' Dic glanced from one to the other. 'Are you both bound there?'

'Not me,' said Sun, 'I'm on me own.'

'I will speak to Zimmerman,' said Gideon. 'He will know what to do.'

'Nobody's asking favours,' said she tartly. 'I told ye before

—I'll see to meself.'

'A bed for the night at least, woman; please do not be stupid.'

A gentry brougham passed them and drew up at the entrance of the Castle Inn as they turned into High Street.

Here the workers were flooding in from the open-cast mining of Hirwaun Common: men, women and children, Irish mostly—scrabbling on the heath for the furnace food of iron mine; and they were happy in their banter on a shilling a day, brown-faced and chattering, for it was summer. Later they would work with frozen bodies in the icy winds of Aberdare mountain, labouring under the sights of the little brass cannon of the Crawshay tower, in the name of benevolence.

Dic Penderyn said as they pushed through the crowd to Cross Street, 'If it's only a bed for the night you're after, I expect my mam could do it.'

'It's two beds, make no mistake on it,' said Sun.

They turned right past the Lamb public and Dic stopped at a door.

'This is Number Eighteen Cross Street, blind man.'

'We owe you hospitality—this is my friend's house, please come in.'

'You owe me nothing, man—I'd have done it for anyone.'

'You work here?' asked Gideon, knocking on the door.

'Ay, hauling, mainly—but the last month or so in the Ynys compound, under a rodder.' He smiled down at Sun. 'Is it work you're after?'

'That's the last thing she's after,' said Gideon.

Sun jerked her thumb. 'D'ye hear that? He's always slandering me. I'll be getting work when I'm good and ready, but I'm not going back to Taibach, for I'm sick to me stomach of the place. Can ye coin it here, man?'

'You can earn your keep—you can pick ore on Hirwaun, and that's all right now, in summer, for a shilling a day, but it's hard. Or you can stack under Liz Treharne down the Ynys Compound, and that's one-and-six a day, but it's murder.'

'You work there, you say?'

'Ay, ay.'

'And you live where?'

'Round the corner in Islyn Court with my mam and dad.'

Sun smiled at him. There was about him a native charm; he was not handsome as Gideon was handsome, and his strength was uncultured, as was his speech. But his youth called to her tempestuous nature, possessing as he did the same boisterous arrogance. With his hands deep in his pockets he flickered a wink at her as they waited for the answer to Gideon's knock, and she slid her eyes over him so that he grinned of a sudden.

Gideon, for his part, was astonished that the Bolton Authority Lodge should trust Zimmerman with anything, let alone the South Wales circuit. To site the Union branch here, in Cross Street, was typical of the man's inordinate lack of care; it was rather like booking a hotel room next to an iron master: even from here he could hear the high-pitched voices of the gentry arriving outside the Castle Inn. Then the door opened before him, and Zimmerman cried, reaching for Gideon's arm:

'Ah, my old friend, you are here—and in such charming company!'

'Don't overdo it,' murmured Gideon.

'You will come in?'

'The young man, too,' said Gideon.

'It is nearly a regiment.' Zimmerman opened the door wider, and they entered; immediately they were within he turned and locked it, saying, 'Good God, man, what the devil is happening? I thought we were acting alone?'

'We are. Both these young people are workers—they will know of our existence sooner or later.'

'The man I do not mind, but the woman ...'

'Had my young friend not guided me I doubt I'd arrived at all.'

'Right,' said the Pole, turning to Sun. 'Now goodbye, young friend.'

'Oh, no, Zim—she stays.'

'But you, of all people!' Zimmerman smiled faintly. 'And you admonished me when I brought home women!'

'They were in my room,' said Gideon blandly, 'it's a rather

different matter. The child needs a bed—give me a guinea!'

'God alive, Davies—didn't you earn on the road?'

'We met the *Caro ar Cefn*—come, it's a long story—give me the sovereign.'

'Och, he can keep that,' exclaimed Sun, eyeing it.

'Take it,' said Gideon, 'and don't be a fool. Penderyn, did you say you had a bed?'

'With my mother, but I'll have to ask...'

'Good. You see the trouble of her staying here?'

'It's damned good, isn't it!' said Sun. 'I'm not five minutes in the place and you're dumping me.'

'It is safer you go, so please,' said Zimmerman. 'You cannot stay here. In Tredegar the man Donovan kept a woman for cooking and mending, and she talked. Women are all right for the table and the bed, but not for the politics.'

'The politics again, is it? I might have guessed,' said Sun.

Gideon said: 'Paste on the door that this is the Branch Union and Merthyr itself will know—are you off your head, Zim?'

'She must go!'

A silence came between them. Deliberately, Dic Penderyn reached out and took the sovereign from Gideon's fingers and spun it up in Zimmerman's face, who snatched it.

'We don't charge for the beds in Islyn Court,' he said. 'Come on, girl, away out of it.'

Hand in hand they went down Cross and through the arch into *China*. Dim lights were burning in the cottage windows and there was a flicker of firelight and the gleam of bare shoulders, for the colliers had come off the day-shift from Winchfawr, Cwmglo and Penheol where out of seventy men employed half were on parish relief. The older miners were squatting on their hunkers and women talking on the doorsteps, and look what Dic Penderyn is bringing home, good God, and it is funny where they collect them for she don't look like Merthyr pits to me. But some of the men got up as they approached and the women dropped curtseys.

' 'Evening, Dic, boy!'

'God help her,' said Bron Babbie, shifting her latest on to the other. 'She do not know what is coming to her, eh, Dico? Seen my Madoc, have you?'

'Outside the Wheatsheaf, but coming now just, I think.'

'Ach, a devil he is, but good otherwise, mind.'

'Good night, Bron!'

'Good night to you, boy, for you're going to need it. You wait till the minister catches you with that in your hand!'

Dic took a deep breath and opened the door of Islyn Court. His father was reading *The Cambrian*, off shift from Ynys; his mother turned at the hob.

'I've got a lodger, Mam.'

His mother's look of expectancy changed to fear. She said, 'But we haven't the room, lad . . .' She turned to her husband. 'Dada, we haven't the room, have we? I mean, when Gwen, Morgan and the children come . . .'

'Is it a female?'

'Ay, Dad, and Irish—her name's Sun Heron.'

'Time you was settled. Time you took to a girl and gave up the politics, me lad.' His father turned in his chair. 'Bring her in and let's have a look at her.' Removing his pipe he looked Sun up and down. 'With a wash she'd come prettier—Irish, ye say?'

'Welsh, and my name's Mari Beynon, though me mother called me Sun.'

'Ay, she's winsome, Welsh or Irish. Bring her in. You're not the first, young woman, and like as not you won't be the last . . .'

'But Dada, we haven't the room . . .' protested his wife.

'*Diawch*, it's only for the night, Mam,' said Dic.

'Settle him down, woman,' said Dic's father, 'and we'll get more babies and less politics: I'd pay a king's ransom to ye woman, if ye just settle him down.' Rising, he took Sun's arm and led her within.

SID BLUMP, lately removed from the apartments of Dai Posh of the Old Swan, Maesteg, to follow the iron, was engaged in deep discussion with Jump Jackson, the one-legged landlord of the Wellington.

'You see this thumb?' asked Sid Blump, holding it up.

'I do,' said the landlord.

'Give me a gallon of best home-brew and I'll chop it off.'

Sid Blump, glassy with hop contentment, fixed Jump Jackson with a stare, seeing through the lined, cavernous face of the landlord the white porcelain jars of his youth; the gilt-lettered *Rum*, the funereal black inscription *Port* and the dignified Roman imprint *Whisky*, and these called to him down the lost legions of the years when the bouts were easy, the purses good and gin was a penny a time. Beyond the banded stomachs of the forty-gallon casks stamped *Hopkins Ale*, *Tanyard*, he saw, too, the hate-lined faces of four hundred opponents imaged on the mirrors of his soul; a soul in black tights and hobnails, a cauliflowered deformity of head-bumps, a flattened nose, and the criss-cross cuts of its pounded youth. In a confusion of ale and pain Sid Blump, mountain-fighter, mouthed back the threat of Knocker Pyle of Ponty and Tancy Boy of Newport, the one who hit him when he was down.

'You all right, fighter?'

'You bugger off,' said Sid Blump.

In a ruptured, blood-streaked brain made egg-shaped by the head smashes of men five stones larger, he remembered the sweat and white bodies, the leaping ropes, the douse of the reviving buckets, and the baying crowds on the tumps. In his little gobbles of ears beaten out of his skull he heard again the mountain wind and the thump of hobnail boots on turf. In his mouth was the taste of blood.

Dic Penderyn came in. His dark eyes switched from Sid Blump to Jump Jackson, the landlord.

'Old fighter,' said Jump. 'Quart as usual?'

'Ay.' Dic put down a penny.

Bleary, his fat face puckered up, Sid Blump raised his thumb. 'You see this, boyo?'

Dic nodded.

'For a gallon of home-brew I'll chop it off.'

'You'll chop it off?'

'I'll chop it off and eat a basin. You know Bull Skewen?'

Dic shook his head.

'I beat him up on Llanthony mountain—hit hell out of him. You done any, son?'

The landlord said: 'Watch who you're talking to, fighter—he's done a lot.'

'Ach, hush!'

'Is that a fact?' asked Sid Blump with puckered joy.

'Just with my mates.'

'Well now!' Sid Blump regarded him with the warm eyes of friendship; Dic winked at him over his jug. The old fighter said: 'Then you must have heard of Bull Skewen.'

'I have not.'

'But everybody's heard of Bull Skewen—the heavyweight Welsh?'

'Not me.'

'Before his time, I expect,' said the landlord.

Furnace flashes were playing on the window, staining red on the sawdust of the bar. Three men entered and the smell of iron came in with their rags. Two were ballers from Cyfarthfa, the other a rodder of Ynysfach furnaces: the right side of his face was burned scarlet by the dandy-fires, a growth.

'Three up, Jumpo,' said one. ' 'Evening, Dic lad!'

' 'Evening,' said Sid Blump.

They nodded briefly. The old fighter waited while they lifted their pewters and drank.

'My old pals,' said Sid Blump. 'Another quart, landlord.'

One wiped the froth from his mouth. 'You heard he's dropping ironstone again, Dico?'

'By how much?'

'Two shillings a week.'

'There'll be bloody trouble.'

'There will be if I don't get another quart,' said Sid Blump.

'I told you before,' said the landlord, 'you can't drink on the slate.'

'Down in Taibach we drink on the gate.'

'The gate?' Dic's eyes were shining.

'Down in the Burgess—now, there's a pub—not like this one hop sawdust. Old Nana, she was, and worked it on pints.' He raised his voice and shouted Irish, ' "Me foine fellas, me hairy handsome men, ye can drink five bars for the rate o' one, but when Nana crosses 'em out, that's the diagonal, and then ye pays ..." Christ, she was a landlord!'

Jump Jackson said to the furnace men: 'And what are the Oddfellows doing about the cut, then?'

'The Oddfellows never saw me short of a pint,' said Sid Blump.

'You think they'll call us out?' asked the baller.

'Not me, man, my missus says we can't afford it—got one and tenpence in the caddy a week before pay.'

'None of us can afford it, but we come out just the same. You heard about John Hughes, Bethel Street?'

'What about him?'

'Got his furniture restrained.'

'He won't be the last.'

'And they took Wil Goff's bed from under him a week last Friday.'

'They didn't!'

'They bloody did.'

'You see this thumb?' asked Sid Blump.

'Court of Requests?'

'Coffin's Court—they just rolled up with a cart and donkey and a paper from the beadle, and took it—near drove his missus demented.'

'And that Crawshay's worth hundreds of thousands!'

'One day we'll have that blutty court down,' said the rodder with the burned face. 'My missus reckons it's a scandal.'

'It's a scandal that you put up with it,' said Dic, looking into his mug.

'What you say, boyo?'

'I said it's a scandal you put up with it. Union representatives have been down from London and gone back without a hearing . . .'

'God, listen to it! Pin up your napkin, son, and leave it to your elders. If we listened to you we'd finish up at Monmouth.'

'Better that than sitting here whining!' said Dic. 'Twice this week Mason's been speaking at the Miners' and six turned up to hear him. If ye want the Court of Requests down you'll do it by collective action and in public; if you want your furniture back you'll get nowhere sitting on your backsides whining in private.'

'Crawshay has outlawed the Union, lad. Talk sense.'

'He wasn't so keen on the Benefit, but he's got one. God Almighty, if you're going to ask Crawshay every time you move he'll have another quarter of a million and you'll not handle a loaf.'

'Words, words, and they get you nowhere,' said the rodder. 'My dinner's in the oven; I'm off,' but he did not go.

The door went back and the day-shift furnace men of Cyfarthfa crowded in, sullen with the twelve-hour shift, and their shirts were stained with sweat; some had their arms tied with grimy bandages from old burns, two had scalds on their faces from furnace blow-backs: these were Jump Jackson's best customers, drinking the half-strength Hopkins malt ale that replaced in their dried limbs the loss through sweat. They were rangey men, and gaunt, hostile in their silence.

'You're just in time,' said the landlord.

'For what?'

'To see the old fighter eat a basin and cut off his thumb.'

The men did not speak, reaching for their jugs: one said, 'Where's the catch, Boxer?'

'I want a gallon of Hopkins.'

'It's a price to pay for that bloody stuff—are ye sane?'

'Sane as a judge, look at his ears,' said the landlord.

Dic said: 'There's a meeting at the Bridge tonight—at ten—Mason, the Union man is speaking again. Are you coming?'

'Watch him,' said the landlord, 'he's touting round the publics, and it ain't healthy. Don't mix drinking with politics, I say.'

'But the lad's right,' said a refiner. 'We ought to support the Union.'

'He's an Englishman and I dunna trust the foreigners.'

'He's a Union man and the last hope you've got,' said Dic.

'What about me thumb, then?' asked Blump, holding it up.

'God help us, fighter, give it a rest.'

'Join the Union and you get thrown out of chapel now—you heard?' a man asked.

'The Reverend Morgan Howells?'

'Calvinistic Methodist, and he's not the only one.'

'There's a bloody loss—thrown out of chapel. I'd take it as a compliment.'

'Not me, not with my missus. Anything frightens me it's the Streams of Loveliness: put the fear of God in me, they do, and she's a life member. She reckons our minister's God.'

'Black magic, and the Church is against us, too, mind.'

'And the Chapels. And in their spare time the parsons go rook-shooting. God alive, what a country!'

'Not the Unitarians, though—be fair, they're behind us, and old Tom Cothi.'

'Talk about the blossoms of Gethsemane. *Women!* A lot of shrieking banshees, I call 'em. They're either wearing out their knees or bowing and scraping in High Street—I'm always telling mine—you take a furnace shift, girl—do you good; a sod, she is.' He spat in the sawdust. 'Airs and bloody graces...'

'Not mine,' said another. 'If Merthyr rises she'll be up front with pitchforks. Very benevolent.'

'You'm damned lucky, Daio.'

'Though she can be a hot one for the fellas, mind, when me back's turned.'

112

'That's all part of the benevolence.'

'Be human, Daio, she's half your age.'

'Ay, ay, but she's bound to draw the line, I say. She don't go up to Cyfarthfa just to clean her teeth.'

They pushed, they spluttered in their ale, and one cried: 'Is it just young Francis she's entertaining, *bach*?'

'Nineteen, is he? God knows what he'll be like when he's ninety!'

'Ach, live an' let live, Daio man—the stallions have to learn on someone to find out tricks for the gentry fillies!'

The baller with the burned face said: 'Oh, ay? Well, I've got three daughters, and if they try their tricks on them I'll be up to see their father—come fair, he don't hold with it—the old man plays it decent—he'd give him Francis.'

A rodder said: 'Ay, well don't count my girl in wi' Daio's skirt, for I got a good one. We got eleven lodgers in one room and six kids in the other, an' she gets sick in her stomach because she can't expose herself—there's always somebody lookin'. Night time I take her up the mountain, an' then she can't go. And it's the same up and down our Row, poor bitches. Unions, ye say? I'd give my arm for a four-inch drain pipe.'

'Ay, and I bet the agents don't walk a mile for a bucket o' water,' cried another. 'What you say, Dico—will ye Union grant us sanitary and clean drinking?'

Dic said earnestly: 'You'll get all these things once you've got a Lodge. Trouble's coming, and you'll have to get a Lodge to speak for you. And it's not only in Merthyr, mind. The foresters in the Dean are on a meal a day. Some of them haven't seen meat in years and the stuff's flying round them—gentry game; everything belongs to the squire. Tread on a partridge egg and you're booked for transportation. The country's mad. Every time the price of iron goes up people like Guest make a fortune in the Shops. They tell me he's looking for a country seat at half a million pounds—no bloody wonder.'

'And another half million for its art treasures while Dowlais children starve.'

'No truck in Merthyr, give Crawshay credit, remember.'

'Ay, no,' said a furnace man, 'but what about the reductions —you heard there's another one coming for ironstone?'

'Twenty per cent,' said Dic.

'Don't be blutty daft!' A man spat.

'I got it inside—it's true, and I'm telling you. This time next year he'll be dishing them four shillings in the pound.'

'When that happens I'm marching on Cyfarthfa Castle,' said a rollerman.

'By the time that happens it'll be too late,' said Dic. 'Look, can't ye see the sense of it ... ye *must* have a Union!'

'I'll do it now, if you like,' said Sid Blump.

'You're not making a mess in here,' replied the landlord. 'I'm a one-legged chap and I jump off Jackson's Bridge every Saturday night for a wager, but I don't hold with performances that mess up people's property. That's why I don't hold with politics and riots.'

'You'd riot with the rest of us if you worked for Crawshay, Jump.'

'Perhaps. Meanwhile I pour ale for brutal gunks like you. Now will somebody give me a hand to ease this silly old bastard out of here?' He gripped Sid Blump's collar, pulling him along the counter. The old boxer steadied, palmed his face and leaned over the counter, hitting short. The landlord sighed, and disappeared; there was no sound but his heavy breathing. Dic looked over the counter.

'Now you've done it, Boxer—that was the blutty landlord.'

'He's only got one leg, you know,' said the rodder, peering.

'He's got none now,' said the baller.

'All I wanted was to chop off me thumb,' protested Sid Blump.

The colliers were thronging down from Lucy Thomas and the Tasker which served the nine-foot seam, and from the Lefal the colliers came out riding on the drams, sitting in blackened, disconsolate groups on their way down the dram-road from Dynefor. The horses pulled with the lethargy of near exhaustion, mouths skimming the stone sleepers. Dic

114

vaulted on to the back of the last dram down.

'You there, Hopkin?' He peered through the grimy men.

'Right, you!'

'Down the Bridge tonight?'

'You'll get us all blutty hung, you will, Penderyn,' said a man.

'Brecon Barracks will be spinning special hemp to dangle you agitators, when the old man calls 'em out.'

Dic Penderyn said earnestly: 'Look, lads, Mason's speaking at Bridgefield tonight. The Bolton Authority Lodge is sending down a representative . . .'

'That's taking a chance, isn't it? Supposing we're raided . . .'

'If you want a Union you've got to take chances, and if you want basic wages—without cuts every time world rates go down—you've got to have a Union. There's a dozen branches up in the Midlands—why can't we have them in Wales?'

'Because we've got Guest, Sam Homfray and Crawshay.'

'Don't talk soft. There's worse than them in Lancashire.'

'Ay, ay? Well, count me out, I want no black-list. My brother's been on it these past two months and all he wanted was a Benefit.'

'If he'd got a Union he wouldn't need a Benefit, but it's the men we're after, not the blutty mice—who's on?'

An old miner said: 'Your trouble is that ye talk too much, Penderyn, and you go too fast. If you buttoned up a bit and made less damn noise you might get takers. If I'm going to swing I'll do it in me own time, not yours. Take my word on it, son—they'll 'ave you one day.'

Dic said: 'If we did everything in your time, Grancher, we'd never get a Union. You lot have sat on your backsides too long.'

'How much will it cost us?' asked another.

Dic groaned and ran his fingers through his hair. 'God alive!' he whispered. 'Listen, lad, we can start on a penny a week like we started the Benefit. Now come on, make up your minds. Who's with me? Who'll be there?'

'Not me, boyo,' said a smith, 'I'm staying in one piece.'

'And the devil take the hindmost?'

'Ay, if you like. I've got six kids and I'm on fifteen a week. My missus says I can't afford to be transported.'

The dram swayed on, passing the cottages down Dynefor: here the doors were open for the men coming off shift; shawled women were feeding their babies on the fronts, children playing hop-scotch on the line, jumping from sleeper to sleeper. In old wooden chairs sat the grandfathers of Georgetown, the torn and mufflered relics of the old pits and levels; the worked-out scrap of an earlier generation of Crawshays and Anthony Hill of Plymouth Works, of whom heat and cold had taken their toll. These were the withered sticks of humans parched by the fire-boxes of Cyfarthfa, Ynys and Hirwaun; the red-blinking near-blind who had stared too long at the open hearths. And they moved their dried joints to ease them as the younger men went by, waving heavy greeting; champing with naked mouths at a new generation employed by William the Second, for the earlier Crawshay was an absentee iron master in London. They, the ghosts of Canaid Dingle and a dozen other drifts, mines and pits that had emptied trouser-legs and sleeves, gossiped at night about the Great Wheel and output, firm in the pride that they had made good iron and dug good coal under a meteoric master of the mountains, a man they feared but of whom they boasted. These were the tradesmen who had built the Farewell Rock upon which the industrial greatness of Wales was to stand, and Merthyr, to them, was the finest town on earth.

'Count me in, Penderyn, for I've had a gut-full,' said a collier now. He was young and his face was gaunt. He added. 'I lost my grandpa down bloody Cwmglo last month, remember?'

'That bloody slaughterhouse, eh?' said Dic. 'One day she'll give us a thumping.'

'He's only another grancher,' said the man Hopkin, 'they don't come no different.'

'Maybe, but he was mine, an' he shouldn't have been there at all. I was working short 'cause me woman was ill. So he strikes a tinder for a candle-tack, the old way, God help him— in the Cwmglo and she's chock full of gas. The fire went

116

round the face an' it took him full. They said he was the only one in the stall, but he wasn't, for when I went down with a sack to fetch him back up I found three hands, an' Grandpa only had two, as I remember: the other was small, like a boy's, but none claimed it.'

'Weren't he on the books?'

'Ay, but alone. Yet he must have had a boy because he'd got two drams.'

'And never mentioned it?'

'Never a word, for he swore to me missus he was only filling one, poor old bugger. Took him up to Adulum a week last Monday.'

'God rest him.'

'And God rest bloody Merthyr,' said the man. 'What time you say that meeting was?'

'Sharp ten o'clock—the Iron Bridge Inn.'

'Count me there, boyo—me an' my son.'

'It stinks,' murmured Hopkin in a sudden silence of the dram.

'So does the whole bloody country,' said Dic, getting off the dram.

As he walked home he began to think about Sun Heron. He liked her red hair and the way she screwed up her eyes when she smiled.

Dic took another pint at the Horseshoes, then walked slowly along Bridgefield where Ynysfach ironworks was belching smoke and soot at the sun, and over the narrow road that led to *China*, the slum of Merthyr's slums. Below him the black Taff brooded and sulked in her dirt-swims and dead cats; old washings from the great engines of Cyfarthfa stained her banks where once the trout and grayling fought their way up to their spawning beds in the mountains. Now all was dead. Momentarily, Dic paused, staring down at the Crawshay sewer: then, raising his eyes, he saw great flushes of ragwort and a redness of poppies along the banks, fighting for life, and he likened the colour to a stain of blood. Turning away, he grinned, hands on his hips, for Shan Shonko and Old Wag, the bully women of

117

the prostitutes were squatting against the trestles, their clays cocked up in their shattered faces, and four molls from the Aunty Popi Davey lodgings were whistling up the colliers as they came in file off Ynys shift. Seeing Dic, they barred the way and he lowereed his head, frowning up, weaving and sparring with his fists, threatening them.

'*Arrah*, Molly, here comes a fine big handsome fella, be God.'

He smiled with slow grace, putting his arms across their shoulders as they walked beside him.

'Aw, Dic, lad, haven't ye a kiss for wee Maurie here? And her pining to death for ye!'

'And no pay-day since four weeks Friday? Am I made of money?'

'Ach, man, give us the womanly grace—you're fair loaded wi' it!' cried Shonko, clambering to her feet. 'Is it true he keeps it under his bed?'

'Aw, Dic, me lovely fella, come on!'

Molly Caulara cried in mock weeping: 'Is there no pity for you, and me and Kath by here just dying for a big healthy collier.'

'How's your ma?' asked Dic, grinning still.

'Och, you're wasting your time here, Molly, the fella's incapable, and I got the personal proof of it.'

Leaning over he made a backward swipe at her and she ducked, flouncing along behind them in a lifting of her skirts, laughing at the sun.

'Mind, girls, he'd collect a leathering if his Elizabeth Gwen found out.' She added: 'She's home, ye know—the minister's brought her to visit.'

'Easy on his sister!' cried Old Wag. 'Leave his sister be!'

He laughed, but he was angry, and he was glad that they were not Welsh, though there were Welsh girls in plenty in the Aunty Popi Davey lodgings. James Abbott, the High Street barber, came over the bridge then, face turned up amid the clamour of the women: with his top hat firmly on his head and his stock arching proudly, he evinced the air of a man who was not to be tampered with, and the girl Kath cried, sauntering along beside him:

'Sure to God, it's the hair-cut man. Is it true, fella, you've nothing to do wi' the females?'

'Not your sort,' said Abbott.

'Dear me, we're the same as all the others, man, if ye care to look close enough.'

'Oh, don't waste your time, Kath!' shouted Shan Shonko, as the girls barred Abbott's way, stepping left and right before him, and Old Wag cried to shrieks of laughter: 'Will you gi' us a hair-cut, fello, or treat us decent, like young Penderyn do?'

'Scum should mix with scum,' said Abbott, and pushed the women aside.

'You mind your tongue or Shoni Sgubor Fawr and Dai Cantw'r will 'ave you, mind!'

'Leave him, leave him, girls,' said Dic over his shoulder, and he marched along with his arm around Molly Caulara.

'Is it true you've brought a woman home, Dico?' she asked.

He shrugged. 'Ay, she's come in with a friend o' mine—the lodging's convenient.'

'She's right pretty, I hear say—five feet an' with bright red hair.'

'Can't say I've noticed—ach, you're a wench for other people's business, Molly Caulara!'

'Sure, your dear sister Gwen'll be making it hers, too, an' all.'

He was faintly annoyed that she should even mention his sister's name, for there was within him a deep and abiding love for Gwen, who, before her marriage to the Reverend Morgan Howells of Newport, had mothered and brought him up.

'What you thinking about, Dico?' asked Molly Caulara.

He knew these Popi Davey women as few men did, for he had been crossing the Iron Bridge since he was eleven. Indeed, he had learned of womanhood from Molly Caulara when he was sixteen. Now, six years later, there was growing in her face the sullying alleys of Merthyr, and he pitied her.

'You got a kiss for me, boy?'

'If it's for free,' he answered.

A faint hurt touched her face, but she smiled. 'It's always free to you.'

He winked. 'Me ma's expecting me and there's bacon for tea if they caught the pig. Can I trifle here with you when the fine minister from Newport's visiting with me sister?' He imitated her Irish accent.

'Ye don't like him, do you?'

'Ay, sure, but he worries me with his talk of hell.'

She cried: 'Ach, boyo, but it isn't every day o' the week that a *China* family have a minister the size o' that one come to visit. And he's a fine fella, say I, though he's off the Pope.' She crossed herself. Do you know what he says to me once? "Molly Caulara," he says, "ye ought to be ashamed of yourself. Did God give you that lovely bit o' workmanship to sell over the counter like ribs of beef?" "Ay, but it's all right for the likes of you, Minister," says I, "for yer world's fat and dandy." "Ay, ay," he says, "and so's yours, if ye let God come in with the sun. In any case, have you realised you're selling yourself short? If you bought a kerchief for a penny, would you sell it for a farthing?"'

Dic laughed. 'Did he say that?'

'He did indeed! "Molly Caulara," he said, "I can go down the Shambles and buy meself a five-pound loin for a penny a pound, an' that means I'm paying out fivepence ..." Then he stands back and weighs me up for size, so to speak, and says, "Molly Caulara, I reckon you weigh a hundred pounds or more. Even at a penny a pound you should be charging eight shillings minimum, do ye realise that?"'

'Eight shillings!' Dic gasped.

'Ay—eight shillings for me—anna I valuable? That's what the minister told me. "Molly, me girl," says he, "you're going over the blanket for less than the price of meat, do you realise that?" So I asked him should I put up me rates. Do you know what he comes back with?'

'I can guess.'

'Just this—he says to me, "There's a price on every tag, there's a rate for every piece of goods, and there's a rate for you. I'd weigh ye in rare jewels, pay a sovereign a strand for

120

your hair and a king's ransom for your love. No gold can buy ye, Molly Caulara; you're priceless in the sight of God." '

A silence came. Dic said: 'The minister's right, Molly.'

'Like as not, does it make any difference? You started me, remember?' She drew herself up; there came a coldness; he dared not speak.

He walked away. Looking back once he saw her standing against the rail of the bridge, ignoring the commanding shouts of Old Wag and Shonko, for the Spanish tub-men were coming in from the Old Glamorgan since this was the night of the six weeks pay. Later there would be drinking and fighting in the taverns. Molly did not turn to the shouts of Old Wag and Shan Shonko, but stood there smoothing back her hair.

'Fool that I were, you had me free, Dic Penderyn, and I was worth eight shillings.'

The furnace smoke drifted between them.

Dic went through the arch and into *China*. The alleys were crowded with workers from Ynys and Cyfarthfa. Wizened faces too old to die stared down from cracked windows as he passed: half-starved children, the waste of iron, stared up from crowded doorsteps. A beggar jeered at him, waving his stumps, Dai No Arms who wouldn't go through the rollers. A Catholic priest, rotund and neat in his black cloth, was washing the face of a woman in labour, and he smiled as Dic went by. All around was the incredible stink that was a part of Merthyr's *China*, the mud of the road stained yellow. But the air became cleaner as he walked, and as he neared Jacksons Bridge a little wind blew from the iron master's park, bringing the tang of Hopkins Brewery: the British Tip reared up before him and at its burned base new harebell was growing in astonishing profusion amid the usual cat's-ears and dandelion. Bending, he picked a flower, looking about him at the squatting cottages, the sagging roofs, the confusion of slamming doors and shouting humans. The ground trembled about him and faintly he heard the drop-hammers of Cyfarthfa.

Bron Babbie Williams, aged twenty, was scrubbing her doorstep; three behind her and one at the breast, and she sat

121

on her haunches and spread her fingers on the thighs of her sack apron. 'Oi Oi!'

He pulled her hair as he passed.

'Meeting tonight, Dic?' She wiped the sweat from her face.

He nodded. 'Is Madoc coming?'

'That he is, or I will want to know. But he takes the politics gentle, like. A regular prophet of woe, he is these days. Nothin' like his da, see? Nor me, I'd have Cyfarthfa Castle down—give 'em damn stick, Dico. Wages, is it?'

'Unions mainly,' he replied.

'You got visitors, you know?' She winked. 'You also got a red-head.'

He grinned at her. The chemistry of youth moved between them. Suddenly Bron said: 'My Yorri's got a stye coming, you see it?' She reached behind her and brought up a child all feeder and bubbles. 'He do get 'em—one after the other.'

'You tried the wedding ring on it, Bron?'

She said: 'My little brother had a strawberry nose and my mam licked it every morning before eating, and it went away —it's the sleeping spit that does it, they say. You think it might work on this eye?'

'You could try it.'

'He won't go blind, or nothing?'

'Of course not, you're his mother.'

She put her finger to her cheek and looked at the sky. 'I never thought of that,' she said.

He saw in her face the early ravages of children, and Madoc, her puddler husband. Madoc Williams earned good wages up at Cyfarthfa, but she didn't know where he was from minute to minute. There was a claim made by the masters that good wages brought drinking and idleness, he reflected: often he wondered if there was something in this. It transgressed his every ideal but it was a startling revelation—when things got better the drinking got worse: Madoc was a stay-at-home man when Crawshay had a cut, and a high-stepper when the rates were returned.

Bron said: 'You try to get Madoc home reasonable tonight after the Lodge?'

'I'll watch him.'

'I got to handle him, see.'

He nodded.

'And Dic—any chance of laying me on at Ynys compound?'

'Working?' He frowned at her. 'What about the kids?'

'I could get 'em off on to Grancher—very good with 'em, he is.'

'Only rail-stacking, and you're not up to that.'

'Good God, fella, I'm as strong as a horse! Things are a bit delicate in the larder, ye understand . . . ?'

It was ridiculous: Madoc Williams was on top puddling rates; he would rarely bring home less than thirty-five shillings a week. Rocking the baby against her now Bron smiled up. 'Do me good, I reckon—nothing but kids, kids, kids round by here.'

'Come tomorrow—first shift, and I'll try. The stacking foreman's needing new horses—Liz Treharne of Pendydarren —you know her? She's lent by Homfray.'

Bron shook her head, and he added: 'She's a tough 'un, mind.'

'So am I,' said Bron. Unaccountably, he gave her the flower, crossed the alley, took a deep breath and went into the back of Islyn Court. His father and mother were there, so was the minister, but the only one he really saw was Gwen, his sister.

'Ay, ay.' He nodded, and went out the back to wash.

He had changed his shirt when he returned, for Gwen.

' 'Evening, Minister.'

Always there was the air of expectancy when Gwen and her husband called: it was as if at any moment the silence might break by everybody talking at once, yet it never did. His father, as usual, was sitting by the grate; his mother, plump and cherubic, toiled patiently at the hob, smiling to herself in peace.

'What time did you come, then?' Dic asked, sittting down at the table.

'After you left this morning,' said Gwen. Strain had banished the usual serenity of her eyes. 'You . . . you had a good day?'

He lifted his head from his plate, meeting the minister's stare.

Nothing had yet bridged the silent antagonism between them in the four years of Gwen's marriage. Although outspoken in the pulpit on the subject of Reform and fearless in his condemnation of the masters, Morgan Howells did nothing to hide his hatred of militancy and the coming Union in particular. Small of stature, possessing the pallor of a man constantly ill, his massive intellect seemed to fill the room. To Dic the ranting *hwyl* that held the congregation on the tips of his fingers was an art that could be done without in the face of the squalor that possessed the towns; and Morgan Howells' constant cry for peace was too high a price to pay in flesh and blood: and the fact that Dic never entered a chapel although he was Wesleyan, did nothing to strengthen the bond of relationship. Yet, astonishingly, Gwen, whom he loved, was happy with this man; they lived over a bakery in Newport Stow Hill; soon Morgan Howells would be full-time minister of the famous Hope Chapel. Two children had been born to them, but Dic rarely saw them.

'How's Ebenezer?' he asked, breaking bread: this was Gwen's son.

'Not too good.' She sat opposite him, and her eyes were smiling into his: there was about her a calm and distinctive beauty he had known in no other woman; and there existed between them a love that survived despite the complications of family and distance.

His father said, removing his clay: 'They got more discharges today, down Tasker—you heard?'

'Ay.'

'Bill Tender's off—you see him lately?'

Dic shook his head.

'Folks say he's gone over to Nantyglo for Crawshay Bailey, then he'll have to work.'

'And Hope?' Dic raised his face to Gwen, as if he had not heard.

Gwen's eyes danced. 'Oh, she's wonderful. If Ebbie had half her vitality he'd be up and about—we left him with Mrs.

Evan Jones, the Swansea girl.'

As he ate in the silence he wished desperately that Morgan Howells would go and leave Gwen at home—if only for the night; he never saw her these days and he wanted desperately to walk with her, to engage her in talk of the coming Union, the new clubs for sick benefit, the chances of getting a hospital. The clock was ticking away on the mantelpiece, the sun was setting in the window. He said, swallowing hard. 'Are ... are you all right, Morgan?'

'Perfectly.' The reply came instantly; the elfin face puckered up and the minister peered at Dic as if suddenly aware of his presence. Dic's mother clattered at the hob, his father cleared his throat noisily, rustling the newspaper, squinting over the top of his glasses.

Gwen said hurriedly: 'She's a nice girl, Dico! She's ... she's rough but she's nice.'

He beamed at her. 'Sun? Ay, I'd almost forgotten her— where is she?'

'Out scrubbing at Cross, but she's been down the compound,' replied his mother.

'For loading? She's too small for that!'

'She can load, lad,' said his father, 'she eats enough.'

'Got pretty hair,' said Gwen. 'You know, Morgan, she's the image of that Olwen Rees in Hope...' she nudged her husband, '... young Maldwyn's wife, remember?'

The minister said, lowering his cup, 'You're wasting your time, you know that, don't you?' His eyes were full on Dic's face. 'Never in this world will you get a Union ...'

Gwen said immediately, getting up, 'Ah well, Mam, I think we'd better be going...'

She kissed Dic in passing; he momentarily gripped her hand. She whispered into his face, 'Please, Dic, please...?'

He took a deep breath. 'Ay...' he said.

11

THE iron was coming out at Ynysfach.

In a scene of beauty the iron came out at dusk. The drams were coming in from Tramroadside with mine already roasted in the ovens of Cyfarthfa and limestone from Penymeol, and the loaders seized and turned them on the tops, filling the long-handled barrows at half a ton a time, and the hauliers took them: these, the giants of the furnace-filling, wheeled them up the barrow-roads above the Miners' Cottages, their sweating bodies, bare to the belt, made pygmy in the heat and flash of the furnace mouths: and tipped, one after the other, into the white-hot maws. In the shouted commands of tellers and overmen more came, and the furnaces belched and moaned, alternatively simmering in hiss and billowing smoke, now blazing red as the gases ignited, wallowing up at the clouds the incandescent lighting that was Ynysfach, competing with the giant Cyfarthfa, her sister iron for heat.

'Tap 'un! Tap 'un. Rodders out!'

'Hopkin, you there?'

'Comin', gaffer!'

'Rod 'un, and lively! You ready, Goff?'

And Wil Goff, whose furniture was in Coffin's Court, spat on his hands and took the bright rod and wiped sweat from his eyes. The furnace brewed then; Number One, they said it was, for they had coked her high and she was moaning and sighing like a cow in labour. And she flashed then, bright at the plug as Tom Llewellyn slid up and hit out the stone.

'Hold filling up top!'

'You up there, Hughes?'

'Ay, Over.'

'Right, you—stand clear. Rodders, rodders—take 'un!' The overman stood barrel-chested against the blackened hearths, fists on hips, his bull chest jutting and his eyes alive with the fire, and there was a taste of rust in him, which is the taste of iron, the first boiling of the ore. The furnaces were bubbling now, impatient for the sow and the nuzzling piglets waiting at her teats for their suckling of the molten iron. And behind Llewellyn worked the drams; the hauliers, the streaky Irish, grunting out their song as the drams moved up for the loading of the pig. Before them the white lanes of the sand-moulds, clear and cool, awaited the deluge of fire.

'Number Two up, Llewellyn?'

'Lazy by her looks, Over . . .'

'Give her door, Hopkin—air she wants—give it her . . .'

The firebox swung back: Number Two, feverish with her choked vents, bayed white fire at the dusk, and the men went back, hands to their eyes, but the foreman stood his ground, and the simmering grew to a hiss and the hissing into a wreath of smoke that rolled from under her belly instead of from her throat, then she boiled of a sudden and spurted flame, and the red cinders shot skyward. There came to the compound a merry song of the iron bubbling, spraying up a geyser of calcining whiteness and a billion sparks.

'She don't look good to me,' said Dic.

'Best blutty furnace this side of Tredegar, an' I calls them furnaces,' said the overman. He bellowed then with cupped hands. 'Right, rodders again—up, up. You ready, tappers?'

'Ay, ay!'

'Skip drams up—boys ready. Where the bloody 'ell's them boys?'

'Here, here, Over!'

'Right, plug her out—One first, Goff!'

'She looks dandy,' said Dic. He turned to Sun. 'You stand quiet, now, and watch the iron, and you don't see it like this in Taibach.'

As if a blanketing hand with spread fingers had descended on Ynys furnace compound, the activity ceased; drams rolled to a stop; gasping, sweating, the hauliers leaned their grimed faces on the iron rims; the cokers stopped, drooping on their shovels; the barrow-men, the scrapers, the mould-fillers, the women labourers of the coke and mine-breaking, all paused, lowering their hammers to watch the miracle of the liquid iron. And Sun Heron narrowed her eyes to the white flashing of the aenus when Wil Goff crouched with the fifteen-foot rod and hit out the plug, and Number One, as if anticipating her release from a bellyful of molten iron, belched within, instantly agitated by the blow. Slowly, reluctantly, the water-iron moved at the hole, the excrement of the mix, and pus gathered in huge globules, cauterised by the cold air. The overman took a ladle and, stooping, reached for the scum and seared it off. Behind it was the bright gleam of the grate, the incandescent mass of the iron. A bubbling began deep within.

'Touch her up, Penderyn!' and Dic moved up, eyes screwed to points against the astonishing glare, and rodded deep into the stomach of the furnace and his rod came out in glowing whiteness, the iron on fire.

'Watch your eyes. Back, back. Stand back, there!'

For the watching workers, who had seen it all a hundred times before, were pushing in a mass around the shimmering moulds. Sun Heron looked about her at the expectant faces. These, the ragged, sweating specialists were the brothers and sisters of bigger Cyfarthfa, and they sent their finished iron to the ports of the world: Irish, Welsh, North Country stackers and men of the Cornish tin, all were here, their lean faces backed by Italian and Spaniards of the Spanish Row over in Ynysgau. In their seared faces and blistered eyes she saw the tragedy of a generation, yet a task well done, for these were the best iron-makers of their time, and they knew it: this, and this alone, kept them to their task when lesser workmen would have foundered: hammered by fluctuations of wages, for the rates rose and fell according to the prices of world iron, they lived out their lives in the squalor of the drainless, waterless houses, the putrid springs: within the shadow of Crawshay's Castle, built for thirty thousand pounds at a time of high employment; denied by their masters the Union representation that

128

would put a bargain on their labour, harassed by threats of discharge and action by the civil power, they laboured under a system of paternal dictatorship that bled them white and chained them to a dynasty of masters whose succession served only to increase their workers' anger, if not dilute their respect. Trouble was coming: even the stranger, Sun Heron, knew this. The banquets and shooting parties of the Crawshays, the elegant assemblies and brilliant wealth in the midst of the sewer-poverty of Pontmorlais and *China*, where the shift beds of the workers never grew cold, stained Merthyr beyond the confines of its boundaries: bringing, in later years, only the literary apologists to fawn on a management that combined greed and force to make a fortune of millions from the labour of men, women and children of a dozen different nationalities.

The iron was pouring from the bungs now in cadent whoops of rainbow gold and red in the dusking sky, now smouldering, now flashing again with seething brightness in a volcano of sparks and fire: down, down, filling the giant pig-mould to the brim as the tappers and rodders stirred, now reaching out fingers into the sand-moulds, each beaming in gaudy scintillation, each bed merging and blending with the mother sow into a giant, smoke-swept conflagration. And still the liquid iron descended, a writhing globule of light hissing at the plug. The furrow of the pigs was filled, the sand-moulds steamed with their first damp breath of night.

'Right, plug on. And Two!' The overman bellowed and his command split the gathering darkness as the fires died along the moulds. The fireboxes spurted reproach as the bungs were stopped; smoke rolled over the compound; one fine, purple flame enveloped the base of Number One and shot up into the darkness, lighting Ynysfach with a torch that faded and instantly died; the town was torn by dusk. Dic cleaned his firing-rods amid the bellowed commands of Liz Treharne, the six-foot woman overseer just come down from Penydarren: hands on hips she stood, a giant of strength, taller than a man with her hair plaited high and the women stackers scurried about her on the cinders, their half-naked bodies shining with sweat in the dying light of the moulds.

'Right, you Biddies, lever out, shake it, shake it!'

'They'm not cold, missus!'

'They're cold enough for shift—out wi' them!'

'You come and try, Liz—frying hot down 'ere.'

'Ach, ye tarts! Stand clear, and I'll take 'em!' And she gripped a lever and straddled a mould and levered low, her bare arms bulging muscle, and the dull hot pig-legs came up. 'Pincer 'em—come on, come on, we ain't got all night. Bess Jenks, Phyll Wright, Bron Williams—forward—pincer, pincer!'

' 'Tis a four-woman load, girl!'

'Three while I'm around—come on, shift it—lose Crawshay a penny an hour an' he'll bleed to death—move, *move*!'

Bron Babbie came up to Dic's shoulder. 'Christ,' she said, 'she's a tough 'un. Back to the kids with me if this is iron stacking.'

He grinned over his shoulder. 'Well, you asked for it.'

'Got womb trouble, an' it's wearying...'

'God alive!' He swung to her. 'What are you doin' here, then?'

'Och, it'll dry.'

'You got womb trouble you get back home to Madoc.'

'Perhaps I come too early after having Nick, me last.'

She leaned on him and he sensed her weakness, and saw in the faint glow of the moulds the worn lines of her face and the dull shifting of her eyes, and he shouted: 'Liz, girl, this one's out for a bit.'

The big overseer sauntered over to them. 'If she is she's out for good.'

'Ach, be reasonable, woman—her old man's a toss of mine, and she's sore in the middle with her last.'

'So am I, an' I had twins.' Over her shoulder she shouted: 'Joe Gab, leave that woman alone or I'll take the ladle to ye!' Turning to Dic and Bron, she said, 'Listen, this is consignment, an' if it isn't off tonight Crawshay'll have a heart attack. In this cinder you're either in or out—take pick.'

'*Jawch*, be human—she's only needing an hour.'

'You frig off,' said Bron, 'I can speak for myself.'

130

'Well, give her ten minutes.'

'Just a breather, Liz,' said Bron, leaning on the iron, 'for I need the loot.'

'And your fella puddling on the bouncer rate? God alive—if he was mine I'd have him under the handle and tie him to the bed-post—all right, then—I'll gi' you an hour.'

'Down by here,' said Dic, and patted the cinders. 'Make a hole for your hip and sleep it out.'

'And put your legs up,' said Liz Treharne, and Dic gave her a glance as he settled Bron down under the iron, weighing her in at something over fourteen stones: down at Jackson's on a Saturday night she fought like a man with her chest banded and sacked, and anything under six feet was frightened to death of her. Bull Skewen reckoned he had seen her stripped for the pump once, breaking the ice in winter, and he laid a bet that she had hair on her chest, though nobody got the proof of it, for since she courted Abod of Penydarren, the strongest navvy in the valley it would have been hard to find out, but either Abod loved her as wife or he was too frit to say, said Bull. A year after the altar, she had a child—a sickly four-pound girl who died a week after the birth: the labour of it nearly killed her, said Abod. Now the woman smiled, her teeth appearing white and strong in her smoke-grimed face, and her eyes were good.

'An hour, remember, then you're up and into it, or out.'

'You're a hard bugger, Liz,' said Dic.

The other women were still heaving on the levers along the moulds, others hauling up the drams for the loading on to the canal, and Dic shouted a rough but respectful banter at them, handing out slaps for haunches as he passed the gangs, laughing at their shrieked insults. In a drift of coke drams just come down from the main works he found Sun bucket-washing, flinging the water high and swilling it over her face and chest in clenched eyes and bubblings, with her long brown arms caressing the sky as he stalked up behind her: with his hands on her waist he steadied and held her, and over her wet shoulder kissed her face.

'You anna decent, you fella,' she said, not turning.

'You coming home with me, missus?'

'Are ye friendly?'

'Ay for sure—don't ye even care who's kissing you?'

'Not as long as it's a man. And he's a rare one for the liberties—and me hardly dressed—can I raise me bodice?'

'If ye ask proper off Dico Italian?'

'The new macaroni from Pescara, is it?'

He put his face in the wet hair about her neck. 'That's him, and he's a devil with the women. You love-spoon with me, Irish girl?'

'Enough of that, ye foreigner, I'm Welsh.'

'You don't sound Welsh to me.'

They stood together and he did not turn her in his arms or look upon her, and the night wind was cold on their bodies.

'You scarce know me, Penderyn,' said Sun, her voice low.

'Who cares? You have to take 'em as they come today, for there's not a lot of choice.'

'You ever had other women?'

'Ay.'

'Like that little Molly Caulara from the Aunty Popi Davey?'

'Ay.'

'But not now?'

'Not now—long before you come. A man gets hot about women and Unions, I reckon. Then along comes one who takes his eye and he doesn't lay a finger on her, not even when she stands like this, half naked.'

'Put your hands about me if you like, Dic Penderyn.' She raised her face.

'Ach, no, I'm saving it for Christmas.'

She said at the dusking sky, 'You treat me respectful, but you don't know nothing about me ...' Pulling up her ragged petticoat she turned in his arms and he saw her eyes large and beautiful in her blackened face. 'Since I known you there come a difference inside me, you understand?' She held herself. 'And perhaps there's a lot about this woman you ought to know before you treat me decent, like this, and not like that Molly Caulara, a woman of the pave ...'

He said, softly, 'I just aren't interested, girl.'

Sun saw him in the light of the moon; his face was smudged, too; on him a smell of sweat and the tobacco he chewed and spat at the furnace hauling to keep the wetness on his throat. When he smiled at her she saw his teeth appear like magic in the grime of his face and he bent to kiss her, but she put her fingers on his mouth and held him off an inch, and he heard a whisper he did not understand, until she said:

'*Arrah*, me sweet one, Dic Penderyn.'

'You love me, Sun?'

'Ah!'

Breathless they stood enwrapped, and the drams rang and bellowed obscenely about them; panting, he held her away. ' 'Tis daft, Sun! It's no more'n a fortnight, and the devils are after us...'

'The devil take them!'

'The big man's coming tonight for Gwen. He'll be asking us to table soon, for the Welsh are ones for rumours, and we're in the news.'

Said she: 'Are we beholden to the churches and chapels?'

'You are when you're living in our house, with Morgan Howells, the minister, arriving.'

'Am I? Think again, fella—I'd spit in his eye soon as look at him.'

He quietened her with a gesture, but she cried: 'I can tell by his mood that he doesn't approve of me, and your pa's half the same. Say nothing for your mother, and I only keep me a still tongue because of your Elizabeth Gwen.'

'Then keep it happy for her, Sun—keep it happy for Gwen.'

She went tall and frisky, bothering her shoulders and Dic lowered his hands.

'If the old fella thinks I'm a whore, why doesn't he say?'

'The minister doesn't think that, Sun.'

'He damned near said it night before last!'

'He said no such thing. He only said that the soul was famished without the food of God, and asked you to come to the Calvinistic with him and Gwen.'

'And me attached to the Pope?'

'Are you religious, then?'

'No, but the Pope will do to keep the other fellas off.'

'So you don't believe in God?'

'Not in Merthyr,' she replied, and hooked her arm about his waist; together they went over the Iron Bridge: Annie Hewers and Megsie Lloyd were talking to a group of puddlers; vaguely Dic wondered where he had seen them before.

'I tell you what,' cried Sun. 'Let's go into the town to see the illuminations, for the little minister will be hogging it back in the house—it'll give him a chance to get off.'

The stars were big over Dowlais Top for the smoke of the Ynys tapping had cleared; the ragged workers of the pits and drifts were thronging in down the dram-roads, shouting their banter at the coming night.

Dic said: 'Shall we take a spell up round Castle Street for a peep at the gentry and the letters coming in?'

'And the agents booking in Brecon Bank wi' the loot from Penydarren! Sure, I love seeing the silk and lace of 'em, and the spotted pudding dogs an' blackamoors!'

Laughing, they pushed through the crowds jamming the arch by the Lamb. The boozies were already at it in there, parting whiskers and tossing the pots: the big drays were stamping on the cobbles outside the post office on the corner of Cross and the agents heaving bags of Crawshay money into the bank. On the end of Thomas Street the moody relics of the old Welsh fraternity went with measured tread into the Wesleyan, mournful with their love, their brass-bound bibles under their arms.

' 'Evening, holy Father!' cried Sun, and a Catholic priest, buttoned and booted in black, bowed over his beads on his way to the keening Irish in the cellars of Pontmorlais. Unmindful of the tipsy long-shift workers spilling out of the Wheatsheaf and Star went the Quakers with their soup-carts, trundling for Bridge Street where two thirds of the workers were on parish relief, discharged because of a drop in world rates of iron. High-stepping were the pony-traps of the agents along Graham, Front Street and Thomas Street, and the elegant broughams of the incoming gentry grinding behind their frisky

134

greys past the doorstep chatter of the out-of-work Welsh and Irish: women, shawled and babied at the breast or in the stomach watched Dic and Sun go by with expressionless eyes; the men, standing aimlessly with the moody indifference of the long discharge watched also, following the paths of the stuffed over-rich with resignation.

'How long you been out?' asked Dic, reaching a group.

'Nigh two weeks.'

'Tasker?'

One said: 'No, Cwmglo—this fella's Tasker.'

'What's the rate there?'

'About half and half—six in ten on poor relief in Lefal.'

A woman said: 'It's a bloody scandal, mind—not a crust of bread in the house, and my three begging up by Canaid Brook.'

'Like as not we'll be took on Wednesday, according to the agent.'

'That damned Crawshay—they said that last Wednesday. It's a stink, man.'

'It's a stink and it must stop,' said another.

'You getting Benefit money?' asked Dic.

'Don't talk to me about Benefit!' An old man spat.

'A shilling a week is better 'n nothing.'

'A shilling a week! What the hell are we—blutty animals?'

'You take the Oddfellows' oath and you'll get benefit club money—free bread on the quiet and free burial, remember.'

'What about free living, then?'

'You'll get that when you get a Union,' said Dic, moving away.

'Ach, talk sense, man—would Crawshay stand for a Union?'

'He didn't stand for the Benefits, but he's got them,' said Dic, 'and he might act easier than most.'

Beggars were crying shrilly in the gutters up by Quarry, and the Tanyard specialists were sinking it in noisy banter along the rails: wizened girl-mothers were coming down from Cyfarthfa, the mine-breakers of the Yards, their kerchiefs tight round their starved faces: amazons from the stone-grading, straight of carriage and comely, passed them with the treble shrieks of girls at play: emaciated children from Sulleri played *Devil at the Window*, darting between the moving drams along Tramroadside and *Touch me Last* down Iron Lane where the brass and china dogs of the well-paid puddlers gleamed in the lamplight.

'Good God,' exclaimed Sun, 'would you believe it?' For on the slopes of the Trevor tips six lay preachers declared their joy of belief to nobody in particular, giving it out from Genesis to Revelation, all bearded and smoking with the fire of hell's damnation. Fists clenched and shaking, the political tubthumpers of a new awakening denounced clergy, masters and workers alike, surrounded by apathetic groups of ragged Irish labour. And up High and down Clive the workers of the six weeks' long-pay flooded into the shops where collared grocers of the new shopocracy were weighing and scaling, shortchanging and overcharging, and Abbott the Barber was cutthroating the customers in a flapping of sheets and suds; next door but three Jones Draper was doing good business in Abergavenny waistcoats and new woollens from the Penyrheol factory, Chartist design; socks long and short, non-tickle vests for under stays, belly-binders for colic babies.

'Wait a bit while I get some macassar,' said Dic.

'I'll come, too,' said Sun, and followed him into the Abbott shop.

Swarthy and thick was James Abbott, the barber, and he turned idly from a shaving and get that bloody tart out of here, and quick.

'Who's he addressing?' asked Sun, peering.

The man put down his razor, and said softly, 'You've a mite of cheek, Penderyn, to bring the Old Wag molls into a decent establishment. Shift her.'

'Who are you talking about?' asked Dic, and Abbott pointed at Sun. 'That Molly Caulara, for I saw her frisky on the Taff bridge with you not a fortnight back; now move her before I get my boot.'

Dic ducked low, frowned up, hit short, and the barber took it full on the chin, going backwards over the chair and the

136

customer was upended in shrieks and suds with *The Cambrian*
going up and the colliers roaring their excitement; but one,
Shoni Crydd, the cobbler boxer, came from the back.

'Watch him!' shrieked Sun, and Dic turned, feinted as the
man came lumbering in, hooked to the body and switched the
same hand to the throat, and the man croaked with the pain
of it, falling clumsily: one moment peace, next a palaver, with
women collecting in the barber's entrance and shrieking, hat
pins coming out and boots going in, and the colliers and
miners sparring up, delighted. And in the middle of it Dic
paused to swing a left at Shoni Crydd as he got up, and down
he went again on top of Abbott in a tangle of legs, customers
and sheets.

'Run for it!' cried Sun, dragging at him.

But they couldn't get out of the door for customers, and
Abbott, big and powerful, rose, flinging people aside. Laughing, Dic squared to meet him, but Sun barged out backwards
through the door, dragging him after her. Abbott reached them
in the road and swung a left at Dic, who ducked, feinted, and
hooked hard. The barber took it full and went over, boots
waving. He said from the ground while the people ringed
them:

'By God, Penderyn, one day I'll be up with thee!'

'Then you'll have to move faster than this, Abbott.'

Now the illumination crowds were flooding down from the
Bush and the special constables were running in from Cross
Keys. Sun cried, snatching Dic's hand, 'Come on, boyo—run
for it!' Hand in hand they skidded past the Castle Inn and
under the Arches into *China*. Gasping, she cried:

'Och, ye stuffed him! Jebers, did ye hit that fella!'

'Ay, well he had it coming to him.' Dic licked his knuckles.

'But he'll be up wi' you—you'll have to watch him—did ye
hear what he said?'

David Rees, the puddler preacher, came up then, laughing,
and said: 'The wee woman's right, Dico—you watch that
Abbott, or sure as fate he'll take you to task.'

Dic straightened. 'He asked for it, Mr. Rees.'

137

The man nodded, walking away. 'He might have, but you watch him.'

'Who was the moll he took me for, anyway?' asked Sun after Rees had gone.

'A friend of mine.'

'That fresh Molly Caulara, would it be?'

'It is,' he said, breathless still, 'and she isn't a moll.'

'But she's one of the Aunty Popi Davey girls, isn't she?'

'She might be, but she still isn't a moll.' Angry, he glared at her.

Sun shrugged. 'Ay, well I suppose there's more'n one name for a kidney pudding. You realise, don't you, that the second fella you hit out was a special constable?'

He grinned. '*Diawl*, there's no law against hitting out special constables—it's a hobby round these parts.'

'And he'll make it a hobby to see to you proper one day—take my word on it.'

'Enough trouble for tonight, girl: we'll see to special constables tomorrow—home to Islyn now, eh?'

'Let's hope it's quieter up by there,' said Sun.

'One thing's for sure,' said Dic. 'Gwen's chap will be gone.'

'Best make sure,' said Sun. 'Shall we take another turn round town to cool him, for I couldn't stomach the man just now.'

Dic kissed her, and she did not expect it: what began as a caress of friendship ended with hard arms and quick breathing, till she pushed him away. 'You're not clinching Abbott the Barber,' said she. 'A walk in the night might cool you. Away!'

Outside the Aunty Popi Davey lodgings Miss Milly Thrush, the new shopkeeper, was serving black shag to Wil Thomas and chewings to Little Dusty Wilkins, who was four feet six, and hundreds of thousands to the pop-eyed urchins with tear-streaked faces from Pen Yard: just come in from Taibach was she, according to rumour, and paid twenty pounds goodwill to Mrs. Rees the Lollipop of Cross Keys, and God knows what is going on behind the scenes with that Mr. Note the musician hitting up Handel and Willie Taibach on the fiddle and his ma on the hob.

'Ounce of Tanyard Light, please,' said Dic, and Miss Thrush fluttered her eyes and Sun hooked him out saying she could swear she had seen her before but couldn't think where.

'Good evening, sir,' said Dic, and bowed, for old Iolo Morgan-Rees was labouring up Bridge Street on a child's arm, spectacles on the end of his nose, stopping betimes to gaze at the stars, as fragile as his poetry. Bull-chested and surly, Shoni Sgubor, the giant Emperor of *China* before Redman Coleman, was strutting up Thomas with his retinue of women and mountain fighters, breasting a path through the colliers coming in from Cyfarthfa, And, up in the castle of the Crawshays light blazed, fingering golden shafts on the lawns, and the giant chandeliers beamed on the rhododendron clusters purple and white, shimmering on the parkland lake where the great trout lazed under the mushrooming redness of the works, for the night shift had come on and the furnaces were roaring again and the sky above Merthyr was exploding anew in showering sparks. Organ-grinders were rasping out their garish music on Jackson's, monkeys climbed sticks and did acrobatics along the parapets; one-legged Jackson was gathering bets for his Saturday night jump off the bridge. And the whole Top from Aberdare to Blaenafon was coming alight as on a signal; the whole cacophony of life bursting in the narrow streets and alleys as Dic and Sun pushed through them hand in hand: this, the Saturday night illuminations and revelry of the biggest town in Wales, with the Jews and hucksters pouring in for the market, the tipsters and touters, the priests and prostitutes and pimps; and the salvationists bellowing the harmonies of their pamphlet hymns, The chapels were full for special services to keep the congregation out of the publics, blending their voices into Tans'ur's *Bangor* and Giardini's *Moscow* and vying with the bawdy choruses from the Patriot, Wheatsheaf, Dynefor and Crown where a dozen men, stripped to the belts, were fighting bare-fist along the pavement: there was cock-throwing going on at Glebeland and tip-tap betting and Bandy being played on the tumps: as they passed Biddle's foundry old Snelling was at it, adding to the commotion with shoeing and hammer-

139

ing, for the chaise was up from the Castle Inn and the gentry were abroad for fishing over at Langorse with the Crawshays.

'Good night, Mrs. Evans!' cried Dic.

'Good night, Dic Penderyn, how's your Gwen?'

'Dandy, she is, Mrs. Evans.'

Fat and merry was Mrs. Evans, wife of Evan Evans who hoped for a dowry of a cow and a half from Six Bells when he married, and received her and the offspring, and that is the equivalent, think yourself lucky, said her dada.

'Your Gwen very lucky, eh, married to the famous minister of Hope, Newport! Best preacher in the circuit, they do say.'

'Ay, ay.'

'But mind your step, Dic lad—strong against the Unions—cast you out as soon as look at you!'

On, on, with Sun dropping curtseys, and they went down to Cross Keys Gaol where Mr. Stinkin Shenkins, brother to the beadle, was wriggling in the stocks for inebriation and bad language to the clergy: piled high with garbage was he and singing at the sky in his blue ruin doldrums, and serve the old soak right, said Mr. Steffan Shenkins to Dic as they passed: what the devil is he up to, with me a deacon—brother to Barrabas, I am. And in the black hole they call a prison sits the bowed and broken form of Mr. Duck Evans, just released on family request from the Swansea House of Correction, and due out next Friday and Mrs. Duck Evans, on all fours, is whispering down the grating:

'Oh, my love, do not take it hard—it is only another few days!'

'Woman, in God's name,' said Dic, and lifted her up, but she fought clear and knelt again, whispering:

'Do not cry, Mr. E. Things are better now. I got the kids in an attic up in Pontmorlais—taking in washing with old Nanny Humphries, and I earn a shilling a day. And you are being discharged here, ye know—that's fine, see—nobody knows us here, and that gossipy Mrs. Windy Jones is still in Pontypridd. Oh, Mr. Evans, give me a glance ... ?'

She raised her voice saying this because Mr. Shenkins was

140

singing, his drumstick arms akimbo, his cackle of a mouth vapouring neat gin, 'There was a little maid and she loved a little man, hooray, me love, Abendigo! And he was a little ram and she took herself to bed...'

'Look at me, my love ... Oh, Mr. Evans ...'

'... instead of gettin' wed, hooray, me love, Abendigo, an' she didn't give a damn ...' Mr. Stinkin Shenkins subsided in slurps and bubbles as Dic pushed fruit into his mouth, and knelt again to Mrs. Duck Evans.

'Home, missus,' he said. 'Home if you love him, eh?'

'Oh, God, I cannot bear it,' said Mrs. Evans, and wept.

Blind Dick and Hugh Pughe the harpist were playing and singing outside the Boot, and Shoni Melody, the hare-lip counter-tenor was there, too, and Sun saw him and leaped to him, seizing his arm. Smiling at the sky, with his face alight, Blind Dick sang with the gaiety of his soul, and the pure, feminine voice of Shoni swept above him in the descant, and Hugh Pughe's thick fingers, the nimblest in Wales, swept the strings and it was beautiful with the lovely strains of Edwards' *Caersalem* soaring up into the night, and the publics came open and the rowdies tumbled out, with the ragged children of the cottages squatting on the cinders and the colliers, rodders, ballers and puddlers standing with their women ten deep, letting the godliness of it enter them. Out with the pamphlets then, with urchins selling them at a penny a time, and they went like Welsh bakestones—Blind Dick's latest composition, and if ever we have a workhouse up in Glebeland I will sing God Save William the Fourth at the Abergavenny Eisteddfod and damn my soul to everlasting fire, and who is dining on silver plate with Crawshay now, not the Whigs, by God, but Lord Reform...

'Home?' asked Dic.

Sun nodded and he took her hand and drew her through the gathering crowd of the Boot, and the words of Blind Dick's chorus grew in beauty and power, for the sopranos had come and the treble children had joined in with the pit tenors, and the great sound grew into a crescendo, sitting on contralto and bass, and they sang:

O, Thou Who rides a chariot of glory,
Bring us to peace in the valley of coal.
Light in the eyes of Thy broken people
A rebellious flame of a stubborn goal.
Cry out! Cry out, Thou great Jehovah! ...

The stars were at their brightest over Dowlais Top, said Dic, as they went up Bridge Street and through the arch into *China*.

12

ASA aged six and Adam aged two were playing on the dram-road and running off on a last across as the drams went by up to Cyfarthfa: up Dynefor came the drams that day, but coming from Ynys and heaped high with the glowing furnace slag, with the old horse plodding along in front with a wet sack over his rear to stop him blistering, and you could fry an egg on the doorstep when they were emptying the hearths, said Billa Jam, who was settled with Mamie in Number Five, and it isn't good enough and what the hell do they think they're up to? If I had my way I'd have Mrs. Crawshay coming down here to dolly up the sheets—what about my blutty washing, then—all smuts, just look at it: agents' sheets, too, mind, and nobody washes whiter than Mamie Goldie and me. Some got tapestries on 'em—you ever seen lace on sheets? Spit on the iron, girl, send up the steam—bedsheets for Ynys, tablecloths for Penydarren—scrub, scrub, scrub—working our fingers to the bone: eleven kids now, just produced my Joab, the latest—spit and image of Mr. Jam, too, he is. Here, hand me that dolly, woman—slash 'em on the stones. How you doing, Mamie?—can't see ye for steam. And just when we got going that morning along come these blutty drams, soot and all, smuts an' all—oh, hell, Randy—look at my washing ... Hey there, Merve—mind you don't fall in that canal, and watch the kids on the drams—where's Asa?'

'Under my feet,' sang Mamie, scrubbing.

'Long as he anna under mine. You got Abiah, Randy?'

'Abiah's on the pot, Billa?'

'Like as not, then we know where he is?' She added: 'The

143

drams're coming.'

'Dear me,' said Mamie, 'I got the sheet from under the Reverend John D. Ellison, bet that anna seen much fun: got a face like a turnip that Reverend Ellison, but then, being Church of England. *Diawch*, look at the soots comin' in. Seen who, Billa?' She sang tunelessly at the cracked ceiling of Number Five as the drams thundered by, for they were rodding out Three at Ynys, and she was choked with slag—should have been done a month back, said Foreman. 'As long as I never dunna see my old man. You miss yours, Billa?'

'He was here a minute back,' said Randy.

'Who?' asked Blod, washing under the tap, and her long hair was stranding her face and shoulders.

'By God, you look lovely,' said Randy.

'Ay, as long as you got him, then,' said Billa, scrubbing.

'Got who?' asked Blod, pushing Randy off.

'My little Adam,' said Billa, humming.

'He isn't by here, mind,' said Blod.

'He was a minute back, girl.'

'Who?'

'Adam.'

Mamie sang, pegging things out. 'Is that little one out there with you, Billa? You seen Adam, Billa?'

'God no! I've been asking!'

'Watch him on the drams!' shrieked Mamie, and as she said it the sprags went down: the brakes went on and the wheels whistled; up went the horse on his shanks and the glowing slag spilled into the backs.

'Oh, Christ!' cried Randy, and Blod covered her face. 'Oh, Christ!'

Billa said, swaying against the door, 'Get him out, Randy, in the name of God, get him out...'

The spraggers came running into the heat, knocking up the links of the one at the back, and they pulled it clear with scorching hands while Randy heaved with Blod at the back, and they opened the line and found him: Adam, aged two, crying for Billa outside Number Ten with his legs side by side outside Number Nine. And Randy went full length between

144

the rails and clutched his thighs, one in each hand.

They got a doctor from Cyfarthfa, for the Company surgeon of Ynys was out with the cholera up in Ponty with the Irish.

'There's a boy,' said Randy. 'There's me lovely little Adam.'

'I want my mam,' said Adam.

'Don't faint, Billa,' whispered Mamie, holding her. 'For God's sake don't faint, Billa.'

'What happened?' asked the surgeon, kneeling on the cinders.

'He was sitting on the rail,' said Randy.

'Where's his mother?'

'I'm his mother,' said Billa.

The surgeon was young; his handsome eyes flashed up. 'What the devil are you doing letting your children run wild?'

'He was here a second ago, sir,' said Mamie, screwing her apron.

'You damned Welsh! If you thought as much about your children as you do about your ale ... Can you hold him, lad?'

'Yes, sir,' said Randy.

'Then don't move him: I'll trim him where he lies.' He glanced at Billa's stomach. 'Are you in milk?'

'Yes, sir.'"

'Then bare and feed him; he knows no pain yet. *Drammer!*'

A spragger came running with his whip.

'Drop that thing and collect those legs. I want everything cindered and washed down the moment I've finished. And you ... !'

'Yes, sir,' said Mamie.

'I want clean clothes, and water—but plenty of clean cloth —and clean, you understand?'

'She washes very white, sir,' said Blod, weeping.

So they stood in a circle, did the people of Ynys, and Billa Jam sat on the rail with Adam at her breast while the surgeon trimmed and tied him. And the bed-sheet that enwrapped them like a shroud had tassels on, belonging to the agent, stained red in widening blotches; and the one they tore into strips was the one belonging to the Reverend John Ellison.

145

'He was a good little fella,' said Billa afterwards, 'he never made a sound. I just breasted him and he suckled and fed.'

'I'm sorry,' said the young surgeon, touching her face. 'He lost too much; your baby is dead.'

'An' that's how it happened,' said Mamie later. 'Now she's got ten.'

'Never mind, Mam, you always got me,' said Merve, aged nine.

'*Uffern Dan!*' exclaimed Zeke Solomon, next door. 'Everything happens to Billa Jam Tart: she scrubbed the next two months to pay for those sheets.'

Randy and Blod got married that September, the dear little souls, said Mamie Goldie. 'I could look the whole world over and never find such a daughter-in-law—gained a dear relative, I have.'

'Something to approve of your daughter-in-law, mind,' observed Billa.

'Wouldn't have her a mite different, wouldn't hear a word against her,' said Mamie. 'The day I set eyes on that girl, I said, "Mamie Goldie, fancy is as fancy does, but this dear girl comes different." Virtue is its own reward, as I told Randy, and there's nothing like a mixing of the blood to put some froth into the new generation. Like the Good Book says, "Look not upon me, because I am black, because the sun hath looked upon me," and what's good enough for Solomon is good enough for us.'

'Dear me,' said Billa. 'One thing about you, girl, you never bloody vary.'

'Wouldn't put a foot in their way, wouldn't raise a finger to impede 'em, so to speak. Irish, of course, but a handsome one, is that—full in the breast and narrow in the haunch, and shouldn't be surprised if she didn't milk well, bless her, too. You there, Blod, my love?'

'Coming, Mamie!'

'There now, my little lovely! All ready for the Rabbi, are you?'

'All ready for the priest, Mamie.'

Even Billa Jam, who saw her through tears, said she was beautiful.

'Oh, well,' said Mamie, patting her, 'we can't have everything, can we? Even the gentiles are equal in the sight of the Lord. Virgins and virtue do collect the just reward, I say.' She peered at Blod Irish.

'Yes, Mamie,' said she, peering back. 'You can be sure o' that.'

'God bless ye for the pure upstanding creature that you are, then,' said Mamie. 'And thank God for the foresight that I chose you for me son.'

She wept then and Billa handed her a cloth.

And so, with the big spiders doing night-shifts along the hedges of Vaynor and the mist of the Beacons weaving its patterns over the Glebe, Randy Goldie, haulier of Ynys but late of Taibach, married Blodwen Irish late of Derry, and God grant them the same happy marriage as me, said Mamie, in tears.

'Salvation to you and may God forgive ye, Mamie,' said Billa, and she raised her lost Adam up against the stars, and kissed him. 'Good night, my precious,' she said.

The furnaces were weeping over Ynys that night, they said, in the sheet of the rain, and the hiss.

'You there, my beautiful?' whispered Randy in the dark.

'Unless someone's lifted me,' said Blod.

Outside in the rain the roofs of *China* shone wetness and the moon over Brecon dripped and waned; the dram-roads lay in viper snakes among the tumps and cinders of Cyfarthfa. A lone light shone in the window of the castle: a lone lamp burned in the curved flats of the Iron Bridge, and the Black Taff groaned in his basin of cholera, seeping for the lowlands and the cleansing sea of Cardiff.

'Where you got to, then?' asked Randy, keen.

'Over by here, man,' said Blod. 'All waiting and expectant.'

The furnaces were simmering in Ynys, the puddling pits steaming in Cyfarthfa: Gideon lay in his bed by the window up in Eighteen Cross Street, enwrapped in the bellowing snores of Zimmerman, and he was thinking of Jobina. Day after day he had hunted for her, questioned the navvies, caught Belcher by the coat and shook him to rattle.

'No sign of her, man, and that's the truth—no hide nor hair of her since the day wee Tilly caught it—we reckoned she was upping out Merthyr lookin' for you.'

The rain was washing down the window of Five Ynys Row: the vagrants were huddled for shelter under the dram-arches, the destitute Irish sheltering from the rain beside the warm coke-ovens, the agents bedding the feather-down mattresses in a haze of sleep and accounts, the masters under the canopied velvets and curtained gilts. Miss Thrush lay dreaming in a sleep of fauns with Gideon beside her on a bed of gossamer, and his lips were soft on her face. Down below stairs Mrs. Taibach was driving them home, with Willie the other side of the bolster up among the trebles: bass and booming was Percy Bottom Note, peeping over the top of his dream like King David at Bathsheba, gathering up the brass for the last, strident fanfare that would tear down the walls of Jericho, trumpeting from sleep an amorous Miss Thrush.

'You are not yourself tonight, that's for sure,' said Blod.

'Oh, dear me,' said Randy.

'What's come over you, mon?'

'Don't ask me,' said Randy.

In the cellar under the Crown in High Street Annie Hewers awoke, lit her candle and got out of her side of the bed, and her eyes were like rubies in the wavering light, her bright hair was tousled, the plaits tied with red ribbon. For a moment only she sat there and listened to the hoarse breathing of Megsie in the bed beside her. Dim moonlight was filtering into the cellar from a pavement grating overhead as she tucked her nightgown around her thighs and stepped into a foot of water. Holding on to the brass balls of the bedstead, she waded slowly to the grating and looked up at the misted night; rain instantly spotted her face and she wiped it away with her hair. It was a sheeting downpour of a night, with the wind whistling down from the Beacons and whining like witches among the crippled chimneys of the moon.

'You all right, Megsie?'

Megsie Lloyd stirred in sleep, and opened her eyes at the ceiling.

'Ay, what's up?'

'We got water coming in.'

Megsie sat up. 'Where's it coming from, then—through the grating?'

'Up from the floor.'

'Can't be.'

'*Diawl!* It is—only spots coming down the grating. You all right?'

'I just said so,' said Megsie. She looked over the rail. '*Jawch!* It's worse than Noah's flood ...' She coughed holding her chest.

'You got any pain, then?' asked Annie.

'No.'

'You must have pain, you've been moaning and sobbing all night.'

'You're hearing things. What are we doing about this water?'

'Can't bale it. If it comes any higher we'll be floating. Look, it's up me shins. Bloody hell.'

'No good cursing it,' said Megsie. 'It's like Old Wag said— that's why the rent is a shilling a week. You seen it up by the Star?'

'Can be five foot up in the cellar there, they reckon. Must have washed Lady Hamilton out of bed—bet that cooled old Horatio. Comes out of the graveyard, they say, after washing up the corpses.'

'God, no!' whispered Megsie.

'Ay, it do—they got Knights of the Garter up there doing the breaststroke.'

There was a silence broken only by the howl of the wind, metallic plops and the hissing of water.

'It's only two inches under the mattress,' said Annie, looking under with the candle. 'What we want is a barge, not a blutty bed.'

149

'I saw Gid Davies yesterday,' said Megsie at nothing.

'Who?'

'Gideon Davies—you know, the Taibach fiddler.'

Annie sat on the bed beside her. 'What about him, then?'

'Seems he's staying in town. " 'Morning, Gid Davies," I said, but he didn't hear at first so I shouted again. "Well, me one-legged aunt," says he, "if it isn't Megsie Lloyd! How long you been in Merthyr, then?" So I told him. I left a few things out, of course—what the ear don't catch the heart don't grieve for—I reckon he forgot how he saw us on the road: one thing's sure, he never told my Gran.'

'Nor my mam—or me dad would have been up by 'ere with Bibles and belts. Could never understand my dad, see,' said Annie. 'Used to read me a chapter on the Provocation of David and then hit hell out of me—got all this religion in his knees, my da.'

'Expect he meant well,' remarked Megsie. She shivered and folded her hands over her knees. 'Eh, midear, sometimes I think o' the good times we had in Ponty.'

'Whee, it's shivering cold with this water,' said Annie. 'Back into bed with me, is it?'

'Ay,' said Megsie, 'and mind your head on the ceiling.'

The candle guttered: outside in the night the wind began to whimper like a sleepless child.

Megsie said softly: 'You awake, Annie?'

'I'm floating, woman. Look, we got our own lake. First thing tomorrow I'm up to Mrs. Crawshay to borrow her paddles.'

'You reckon we're doing it right, Annie?'

'Depends, don't it?'

'No, it don't depend,' said Megsie. 'I told Gid Davies we were coal-cropping. He asked me where, an' I said up at the levels serving Cyfarthfa Yard, but if he looks up there he'll not find neither of us.'

'That were daft,' said Annie. 'They've got no cropping girls up there.'

'Up till now I always kept decent . . .'

'Mr. Duck Evans is coming out of Cross Keys Gaol tomorrow, they say.'

'My mam would turn in 'er grave...'

'It seems they shifted him up here from Swansea because Mrs. Evans moved up from Ponty, poor soul. Doing all right, too—taking in washing with old Nannie Humphreys, I heard.'

'Perhaps that's what we ought to do—take in washing.'

'Poor soul, he just sits and looks. Aunt Popi Davey says he's had the brains beat out of him—poor soul—all for a duck.'

'Oh, God, make me clean,' said Megsie.

'You all right, girl?' Annie peered at her, holding high the candle.

Her face was flushed with the fever, her eyes large and sparkling, and there was in her a strange, unhappy radiance that lacked a smile: her hair was black and smoothed either side of her cheeks, which were stretched tight over the high bones of her face: her lips were crimson, her throat smooth and white against the rag of her vest. Annie said, shaking her head:

'Dear me, you look gorgeous—like Aunty Popi Davey said —it would be a crying waste to the customers to see you coalcropping or pulling on the drams or filling at the face. No wonder they always ask for you, Megsie. You all right, kid?'

Megsie nodded, her eyes closed.

'Sleep now, is it?'

'Ay, sleep,' said Megsie.

'You got no chest pains, or nothing?'

'No.'

'Nor blood?'

'No blood now,' said Megsie. 'I never felt better—must be the rain.'

'That's the girl.' Annie huffed down under the blankets. 'It's another day tomorrow—call me if the corpses come in, throw out the lifebelts.'

'It's none too warm,' said Megsie.

'What will ye do when winter comes?' asked Annie, and turned, reaching out. 'Come down by here, kid, tutty up with aunty...'

The Reverend Morgan Howells, minister of the Calvinistic Methodist, lay flat on his back in his bed in Islyn Court, and breathed with the sonorous serenity of the godly just: in the brass gleam of the room, with his black trews over the bed rail and his frock coat over a chair, his boots under the bed, toecaps kissing, and his knee-length socks airing in the the window, he lay in a black starch of a dream mainly concerned with redemption and obedience, solemnities and benedictions. Horizontal in the Big Seat he floated on a mattress of Bach oratorio amid a great surge of Welsh choirs, gathering about him all the princes of Israel and the priests and the Levites, Chronicles 1:23.

And from the mist of this glory, watched by the sampler *My God and King* above the bed, there rose in his vision a woman of beauty whose name was Elizabeth Gwen Penderyn; and bringing her refinement this woman came to him and knelt before him and when he raised her face, she said:

'I sat down under his shadow with great delight, and his fruit was sweet to my taste. I charge you, O ye daughters of Jerusalem, that ye stir not up, nor awake my love, till he pleases...'

'Oh, Christ, Mamie,' said Billa Jam as Randy picked her Adam up from between the rails outside Ynys Row, 'Oh, Christ, Mamie—look, he's got no legs...'

And the Reverend Morgan Howells, bass in sleep, lay on his back with his spade beard staining the sheet, and said at the ceiling: 'Come with me from Lebanon, my fair Elizabeth Gwendoline, my spouse: how fair is thy love; how much better is thy love than wine!'

'That Bron Babbie, the silly bitch,' said Liz Treharne, the Pendydarren stacker, 'that Mrs. Bronwen Williams—begging your pardon, Mr. Coroner—don't know a smelting compound from a nursery. As God's me judge, I warned her, sir. She was actually walking backwards in a furnace area, sir, with the iron being tapped, ye worship—ye understand, sir? Take my word for it—the moulds were being filled and the blutty fool starts walking about. I shouted to them all for standing still—it's the rules, ye see, sir—beg your pardon for the language, sir, but they gets me hot, ye see. The rules stand firm an' clear—the agents has 'em pinned up in the compound—everybody but the tappers stand still when the furnaces are tapped, but not Bron Babbie, and she walked backwards over a ladle, and trips and falls—there was a pain in her stomach, ye see—had a hard time with her fourth, ye worship, and the milk fever was on her, too, poor sod, beg ye pardon: an' she falls and put out her hands and the sand-moulds take her just as the puddlers were creaming off the sludge. Well, ye can imagine, sir, can't you? This is molten iron, and, naturally, there's only one lot supposed to be stirring that with their fingers, and even they use ten-foot ladles. I remember much the same thing happened when I was stacking for old Homfray up in Penydarren, your honour. There was a woman called Morris—come down with her people from Cardie; she was a wanderer, too—never could keep still . . .'

The coroner said: 'Please confine yourself to the facts of this case, Mrs. Treharne—the inquest on the woman Mrs. Bronwen Williams of Ynysgau.'

'Ay, well as I was saying, sir, she trips over the ladle and falls backwards over the sand-moulds just as the pig is filling and running into the moulds, and she sort of turns over in fallin' and lands in the moulds . . .'

'The pig, the pig . . . ? Make yourself clear, woman.'

'The sow taking the trickle of the molten iron, your worship: when it fills up it overflows into the little pigs—it's the piglets milking on the sow, as we say in the trade . . .'

'I understand; please continue.'

'Well, she puts her right arm in one mould and a hand in the other—Christ, you can imagine, can't you? I couldn't believe it when she got up. She got up and just stood there for a second with one arm burned off and the other arm on fire at the elbow, and her bodice going up in flames, and she were screaming. Oh, God, your worship, you should have heard that woman screaming . . . she made more noise than a gentry hunt. Did our best, of course, that's natural . . .'

'Death by misadventure,' said the coroner, and entered it accordingly.

The rain was lashing the roofs of Merthyr, filling the Irish cellars of Pontstorehouse where the Spaniards lived, running down the embattled windows of the castle where the Crawshays lived: little James Crawshay aged four, who died aged eight, was asleep in his lace cot, his breathing whispering down the ornate corridors where generations of Crawshays walked under the splendid chandeliers: Selina Williams, aged one, daughter of Bron Babbie Williams who lately died of fire, the silly bitch—Selina Williams fumbled for the breast of Bron on her bed of wood and rags and her bawling kept the colliers awake as far up as Iron Lane and the lodgers of the Popi Davey, and I wish they'd gag that bloody kid, said Percy Bottom Note, getting out of bed and going head first over Willie's violin and I'll brain that Willie first thing in the morning: bellowing kids and woofing dogs do send me demented.

'Ach, get back to sleep,' said Mrs. Taibach.

'*Heisht, heisht*, my little Selina,' whispered Mr. Madoc Williams, husband of Bron, and he held his baby against his empty breast.

'*Diawch!*' said Mr. Note, wandering the room. 'Hours and hours that blutty kid has been at it!'

'Dear me, dear me,' whispered Madoc Williams. 'As God's my judge, I will never touch another drop. Oh, my love, my poor little Bron...'

And Selina bawled on, fumbling at his chest.

'Hark at it—just hark at it!' cried Mr. Note.

Mrs. Taibach sat up. 'Soon you will have my Willie up, you old fool. Get back into bed—his opinion do count a lot for me, remember. Disgraceful, it is, absolutely disgraceful, heaven forgive me.'

'Thy lips drop as the honeycomb,' said the Reverend Morgan Howells in the bed in Islyn, and, although he did not know it, an old vagrant in rags was wandering along the swilling gutter of his dream, his shining puddle of a face rising above the floods of Shenir and Hermon of a modern world of crucifixions. Thunder bellowed and reverberated among the great Van Rocks and around the fortifications of Brechain where an ancient woman was slain, and her name was *Tydfil*, the daughter of a Brecon King who once ruled Merthyr. And Merthyr, under a king of commerce, slept in filth and tears and silver plate and laughter; a new land of promise, a Canaan of gorging sewers and cholera, the tapestries of Hebron and the damask-robed priests of Zion: and down in Morlais and the cellars of Ynysgau the Irish huddled four to a bed on mattresses that never grew cold.

'What's wrong with you tonight, then?' asked Blod, sitting up in bed.

'*Diawl*,' exclaimed Randy, sitting up beside her.

She giggled then, did Blod, thumping the pillow.

'A fella can come too keen, mind,' said Randy, delicate.

'Whee jakes! I'd never have believed it. When I were single I was galloping for me life: now I'm signed for, sealed and ready to be delivered, nobody wants me.'

'Nothing to laugh about, mind,' said Randy, glum. 'It could happen to anyone.'

'*Jawch!*' said Blod, rubbing it in. 'Here is your flower of desire all ringed up and respectable, the bride of your heart, and the groom's gone cold. *Jawch!*'

'You'm a rotten dog, Blod,' said Randy.

And Blod put her face down into the pillow to stifle her laughter and clenched her hands and thumped and thumped, and presently she tossed over on her back and pealed her laughter at the ceiling, and every neighbour from there to Court Street sat up in bed and listened, and Mamie Goldie, knitting downstairs with Billa Jam, said:

'You know, Billa, for happy newlyweds that pair upstairs are acting queer. First nights is no laughing matter, as far as I remember.'

But Billa Jam did not reply for the ghost of Adam was in her arms.

'You reckon I've caught a chill or something?' asked Randy, vacant.

'Could be,' replied Blod, spluttering. 'I'll have ye examined first thing in the morning.' She kissed him then. 'Good night, lad, don't take it hard.'

'I anna myself, that's for sure,' said Randy, and Blod, in the

155

act of turning over, fell out of bed and landed with a thump.

'That sounds more healthy, mind,' said Mamie, pausing in her knitting.

The moon flooded the wall of Blod's bedroom then, and as she climbed back in beside Randy she saw his face: it was pale, and she no longer laughed. Also, there was in him a silence she had not heard before, and a look in his eyes of a man lost.

'You all right, boy?' she whispered.

'Ay,' said Randy.

He was looking into a corner where the shadows were dark, and he was not in the bed with Blod, his wife. Unaccountably, he was standing in the rolling house of the Taibach Copper Works, aged ten, just as they stopped the ten-ton rollers and got his father out.

'You can have this, son,' the smelting foreman said, and gave him the boot.

So now he was not within the warmth of Blod Irish but sitting on the rag-bolts of the casting-house in Taibach with the smashed boot in his hand; and in his nostrils was not the perfume of Blod's hair but the smell of torn leather, and under his hands was not the satin smoothness of her body but the rough of his father's boot.

His eyes were fixed to the shadows of the corner where it lay wrapped in brown paper, and he remembered the foreman's voice, the bloody sawdust and the dripping rollers.

'They'm mighty quiet again, mind,' said Mamie at her knitting.

'You go on with you, you old thing,' said Billa, mending.

Blod Irish held Randy in the bed and stared at him, and he drew away from her, for her arms, round and white, were like the arms of one they were cutting free, and her face was a mask of blood in his sight; her breast he saw riven with the bolts, and the hands she raised to him were smashed. And he screamed, shrinking away from her on the pillows.

'That anna normal, ye know,' said Mamie. 'Noises like that just anna normal for a first night,' and Billa lowered the mending in her lap, listening.

Later, the rain stopped and the moon came out and flooded Merthyr with light, and Blod held her husband, and he slept.

'*Heisht* you, me little boy,' she said.

And Mr. Madoc Williams, teetotaller, held his Selina, too, and she no longer cried for Bron Babbie, her mam. The town was quiet under the rain-washed stars; the Taff River lay silent, smiling at the moon.

'About time, too,' said Percy Bottom Note, getting back into bed.

THE mist was wreathing the Penderyn woods outside Merthyr and the trees clustered in green moss amid the refuse of their lonely autumns. Field bindweed was opening its cups to the sun as Dic and Sun went hand in hand, singing up the lane for Tafern Uchaf and the church. From here the valley of the Penderyn quarries that served the trade was white with mist, but a smoke cloud hung over distant Merthyr, and Aberdare was sending flame-shot cinders into a bright September sky.

'Did you know lots of chaps before me, then?'

'Nearly a few—about two thousand.'

'Serious, though.'

She said, stopping him: 'If you keep talking about it, mon, you'll barge into a tantrum.' Going on tip-toe, she kissed him and he tried to hold her but she slipped out of his arms and ran through the trees.

'I've got to know, Sun,' he said catching her.

'Right, you asked for it; sit down by there.'

They sat in the leaves and stared at each other over the yards between them.

'Can you hear me, Dic Penderyn?'

He grinned, folding his arms about his legs, resting his chin on his knees: full length lay Sun, and turned on her back, tracing the pattern of overhanging branches against a bright sky. He could not see her face, only the homespun dress stretched tightly over her shoulders, and her hair, which was spare and tufted, bright red against the green.

'You after tying me up, Penderyn?'

'You know it.'

'Then you best know I'm a bad beggar, if you're serious.' She heard him move in the leaves, and added; 'No, you stay there and hear me out. You chase me through these woods, that's one thing, Dic, but you talk of crippling me for life, that's another. You know Gid Davies well?'

'Only met him twice.'

'He knows you and me are sparkin'—and he never mentioned a fella called Billy Ugmore?'

'No, never.'

'Not once—you swear?'

'No, not once.'

'Ach,' said she, 'he's a right handy one is Gid. You reckon I'm pretty?'

'Prettiest I've seen in Merthyr.'

'That's outside. Inside I'm black as thunder. Give you three guesses what happened between me and Billy Ugmore.'

'Same as what happened between Molly Caulara and me, I expect,' he said. 'That makes us quits.'

'Oh, no it don't. Six weeks I was on the Derry roads with Billy, doing the tinkering cans; knocking on the doors by day wi' the pegs and poles, and four weeks of that I was his woman.'

She heard him move again, and called: 'No, don't come, Dic; you hear me out. When you buy a waistcoat at Merthyr market you're entitled to know what wool you're getting. There were a sailor from Bantry off the cutters, a fella from Dublin working the inns wi' a squeeze-box, and another called Windy—you ever heard a chap called Windy? And there was a wee oyster-catcher come in with the tide on Waterford Head—he were just sixteen, though I never knew his name.'

'You got around,' said Dic, his eyes low.

'But no, that were the trouble—they got round me, and there's a difference—you understand?'

'Not much.' He plucked a blade of grass and put it between his teeth.

'It's the difference between a woman and a man—but I

159

din't love none of 'em, except perhaps little Billy Ugmore—
you want to hear about him?'

'No.'

The wind whispered in the wood: a hare watched them
under trembling ears, its ball eyes glistening in the filtering
sun of the wood.

'You gone off me now, Dic?'

'What about Gid Davies, then?' he raised his face and she
swung over on her stomach, and called:

'Ay, what about him?'

'Did he ever have his way with you?'

She sat up, appalled. 'The devil wi' you! What the hell
d'you take me for? You sit there accusin' me of shananikins
with a man like Gid Davies? You'm got a nasty mind, Dic
Penderyn!'

'I'm sorry.'

'And ye should be, bedamn!' Her anger swept between
them. 'You sit there dancing me up on that blutty Molly Caulara from the Aunty Popi Davey, and then accuse me and Gid
Davies of a fine insinuation—you're not fit to clean the fella's
boots!'

'*Did* ye!' He leaned towards her, and her laughter pealed
about him as she rolled in the grass again and flung the leaves
high in a shower.

'*Arrah!* I did not, but it weren't for the want of trying. I'd
have managed it likely if I'd got him outside a quart or two o'
porter!'

'You're wicked to the devil, Sun Heron, and I'm finished
with you!'

'Och, don't be angry, Dico—if you ask daft questions you'll
collect hot answers.'

'Not true, then?'

'Of course not! Gid Davies is married to a Union—anyway,
why bother yourself? Isn't it more important to know who I've
loved than who I've mated?' She added, sitting up in the
leaves: 'And you're not exactly a monk yourself.'

'But you loved that Billy Ugmore, didn't you?'

'Ay, but only his tongue, for it were golden. But the difference between you and him is that I love all of you. You listening?'

He lit his pipe and the smoke drifted among the leaves and touched her nostrils.

'I'm listening,' said Dic.

'You play an Irish love game with me, Penderyn?'

He gave her a sigh of disapproval.

She knelt then, put her hands together as if in prayer and lowered her head in mock shyness, saying: 'If I swear to being true, will ye kneel a yard closer, Dic Penderyn?'

He pocketed the pipe, remembering the Irish game of the Merthyr streets: linking his fingers behind his back, he moved towards her on his knees, and she said:

'And if I wash me body white for you and put sugar on me lips, will you come a yard closer, Dic Penderyn?'

He obeyed, shuffling nearer. The hare watched, an ear cocked in the distant spinney: a badger grunted and shouldered from his earth, waddling in heavy swerves among the late butterwort of a thicket. Sun said:

'And not to smile to break the pledge: if I cook red beef without a burn, nor soup to scald—will ye come a bit closer, Dic Penderyn?'

The badger heard him move, and turned, listening.

'And take ye in my arms and never touch another, save me mother—will you come a foot closer, Dic Penderyn?' This he did, and put out his hands to her, and she reached also, but their fingers did not touch, so she said:

'Kiss me this once, and fill me with childer. Will you kiss this body, Dic Penderyn?'

Raising her head she opened her arms to him and he came to her and held her: the hare scampered in a rustling of dead leaves; the badger lumbered into his earth: a dog fox barked from the covies of the common and the sun burned down.

'For I love you better than a gipsy from Derry, Dic Penderyn.'

He held her: astonishingly, she had tears in her eyes when he kissed her.

'And no more Billy Ugmores?' he said.

'I swear it.' She kissed his face, his hair.

'No Bantry sailors, nor oyster-catchers on Waterford Head?'

'None no more, nor Molly Caularas, and you swear, too.'

'I'll do me best,' he said.

'Right for me. Will you be me chap, Dic?'

For answer he leaned her back in the leaves and the boles of the big trees shone green with sun and lichen, their roots garlanded with bittersweet, and in their nostrils was the wood scent of the hawkweed and rampion flowering yellow and blue, and the bees hummed about the wavering harebells in the wind. From the distant road to Brecon came the faint clanking of cavalry, and Sun felt him stiffen momentarily, eyes switching.

'Ach, to hell with them,' she said, 'this is ours.'

The Hirwaun Works were thumping and the earth-trembling entered them.

'I love you, Sun.'

There was no sound now but their breathing, and a rustling of leaves. There was no reward for custom: his strength astonished her and she twisted away her face, gasping.

'Will ye ease up—I'm only five foot.'

A man shouted with laughter from Tafern Uchaf: faintly clanged the gate of the church and the trees were suddenly alive with a chattering of birds above the vaulted graves.

'You realise you're lying on your skirt, woman?'

'I anna forgot.'

'But I love you. Who's to know?'

The hare raised steepled ears above the gorse, peering.

'I shall,' said Sun, and heaved him off. 'You promised me decent, an' you're not lining me up for a Molly Caulara.'

The metallic clash of hobnails savaged the road and the voices of men came on the still air; rising, Sun brushed herself down, saying, 'If you're half as hot as me you're melting, but I'm away for me night shift and it's time for your meeting.' She suddenly clung to him. 'There's an ache in me for you, Penderyn, and I felt the strength in you. But keep us clean, is it?'

162

He held her away, smiling. Pushing clear she ran to the edge of the clearing, then turned, waving. 'Give me love to Gid Davies.'

Picking up his hat Dic beat it against his thigh, smiling as he watched her running with her dress held up to her knees, swerving through the trees, ducking overhanging branches.

With his hat on the back of his head, his clay cocked up in his mouth, he took the track through the Penderyn woods to Tafern Uchaf.

Most of the Oddfellows Lodge were already seated in the Long Room above the bar when he arrived and he helped Wil Goff Half Pint, whose furniture was in Coffin's Court for debt: staggering under a tray of a dozen quarts was Wil, and them's thirsty sods they are upstairs, this is the third bloody time I've been down. The landlord winked at Dic as he took the tray and shouldered little Wil aside. With the tray poised he climbed the stairs to the Long Room and booted the door. A dozen faces swung down each side of the ceremonial table as he entered.

'Hoi hoi, Dico, me lovely!' cried a man: others bawled greeting, banging their mugs and he grinned wide as the bedlam beat about him and elbowed Wil Goff aside and set the tray on the table, crying, 'I took this off the five-foot boy on the stairs—ye'll be twisting off his rollickers with this bloody lot—who's for tan and who's on blue ruin?'

Gideon, the chairman, rose. 'Easy with the language, Dic.'

The greetings died to a whisper: Dic frowned at the woman at the end of the table. 'Och, no, Chairman—not bloody women!'

'Watch that tongue, Penderyn.' Zimmerman got up beside her, running his fingers awkwardly through his mop-gold hair: his large, bald eyes blinked with apprehension: the Long Room tinkled with silence and breathing. Dic eyed the girl: rarely had he seen a woman so beautiful. Her black dress trimmed with white lace enhanced the fine upward sweep of her bodice, but it was her eyes ... they held his with a piercing awareness, and her face in its sweep of dark, plaited hair was

163

pale and lifted with a hint of questioning and challenge. The big man the other side of Gideon raised his eyes at the ceiling, fearful of an onslaught.

'Ay, well sorry, missus,' said Dic. 'No women, see—this is a Lodge.'

'You keep order, Penderyn,' said Zimmerman softly, 'or you're out.'

'I'm out on the vote of members not by you, foreigner.' Picking up a pewter from the tray he went to the door. 'Speakers from Blaenafon, you said, Gid Davies—not the Streams of Loveliness—is she a member?'

'Of course not, but . . .'

'If she's not a member how the hell can she attend?'

Zimmerman shouted. 'She is here with Mr. Bennet by the special request of the Lancashire Association . . .'

'I don't care if she's here by the express wish of Mr. William bloody Crawshay—this is a Lodge meeting, not an annual outing, and we don't brook women.'

The shouting of the men died when the woman rose. She said softly: 'But you brook them hauling drams—you take them on the cropping and you sign them on the pig-stacking . . .' He drank deep at the door, watching her. She continued: 'You work them on the ore and hauling on the ladders; you pay them under the rate—and Christ knows yours is low enough—you put them on their knees with chains through their legs like bloody animals and you work them on a twelve-hour shift, then haul them off to the hob and the bed. By God, Penderyn—whatever they call you, you're a cheeky swine for voting them out of a second-rate Lodge.'

He held the pot against his chest, and grinned.

'She talks like a man, I give her that,' he said.

'You've had it easy,' said the man called Bennet, 'wait till she gets going.'

The men whispered laughter at this: Dic said:

'English, eh?'

'Ay, and I'll trip you up north to the mill-owners, son, then you can thank God you're Welsh.'

'I am Welsh,' said the woman, sitting down, 'though God

164

knows at times I doubt it and God knows at times I'm ashamed.' She looked around their staring faces. 'You've got ten thousand working out their guts for the greediest masters on The Top and you can't produce more than twenty for an Oddfellow Lodge—do you call this Benefit? Do you call this the Union?' She pointed at the window. 'Over there is Blaenafon, which is my town—one of the smallest—she turns out a tenth of your iron but she's got ten times your soul.'

'Mind your words, woman,' said a man.

'Words are nothing, boyo—they spit on the air. Mind my words, indeed—who the hell are you talking to? Are we in this together for plain words and fair arguments? Or do we sit and wrangle among ourselves while the masters coin the profits—you, Penderyn ...' and she pointed, 'will ye give me aloud the Four Points of the Charter—you're handy with your mouth—now we'll try your politics—come on—the Four Points.'

'Six,' said Zimmerman, softly, 'all unpublished.'

'*Four!* And Lovett's—the other two are coming.' She put her hands on her hips and stared at Dic.

'Leave it, Morfydd,' said the big man beside her.

She shouted: 'Can ye tell me one—just one, then? Any of ye here? By God, if Wales is dependent on the likes of you, then heaven help Cobbett and Fergus O'Connor. Is ale and Lodge rules the only thing you have to offer? And Thursday night at the Benefit at twopence a week for the amputated and nothing for the scalded? Is this what you want? You listen here, Penderyn—don't you speak of iron masters and me in the same breath or it'll be the worse for you, and don't you talk of voting me out for a woman until you've crawled coal under the Coity—I've got the nephew, remember—I get paid by Crawshay Bailey.'

Dic pulled up a chair and sat astride it. 'Count me in, then, but don't call it a Lodge.'

'That's the last thing I'd call it,' said the man called Bennet.

'And tell that witch to put a peg on her tongue for she don't know the length of it.' He gave her a happy grin and elbowed Wil Goff. 'Slip down to the bar and fetch her a gin.'

The girl said: 'I'll drink with you when you've got a

wheeled stretcher in Cyfarthfa and you know the difference between Reform and the Reformation.'

Gideon Davies rose. 'Lodge meeting cancelled—the ayes first, please.'

Dic drank steadily, watching the girl over the brim of his pewter. Someone counted the hands.

'Thirteen—majority. Lodge meeting cancelled—Mr. Secretary, kindly note that in the minutes: political meeting begins —Tafern Uchaf, September the first, 1830—does that suit you, Dic Penderyn?'

'It suits me,' said Zimmerman, heavily, 'and that's all that matters. Guest speaker is Mr. Richard Bennet of the Workingmen's Association. I introduce his friend, Mistress Mortymer, of the Blaenafon Benefit—your chairman is present, I believe —Mr. Idris Foreman: greetings to new members as follows: Mr. Lewis Lewis, known as Lewsyn *yr Heliwr* of Penderyn, Mr. R. Goldie and Mr. John Hughes of Forge Side...'

The names droned on: Randy lifted his face and watched Dic Penderyn and the new man Lewis Lewis; and Madoc Williams, his eyes still swollen with weeping for Bron Babbie, watched the woman, Morfydd Mortymer, and saw in her form the mist of another. Dick Llaw-Haearn of the Iron Hand was there from the shambles they called Silluri also Will Johns, who later ran, and condemned his friend ... Abednego Jones, aged fourteen who said he was older, sat beside Mervyn Jam in a corner and watched with smouldering eyes. Hancock called Han, and Richards the draper and Parry of the Penydarren grocery and Owen Davis who went mad through riot and finished with the lunatics of Llandisilio: all were there, together with others who later said, in evidence, that they were not, and Rowland Thomas who was afterwards shot dead for picking up a soldier's hat—he was also present (the jury called it *Excusable Homicide*). Strangely, Mr. Thomas Rowland, meek as always, sat beside him: he who later went in chains for seven years forced labour in Botany Bay (which needed colonising) for stealing a sixpenny bonnet, while David Morgan, who was not present, went to prison for two years for the rape of a little girl. Both men, according to *The Cambrian*, as

166

feckless as ever, were tried by the same jury: the value of a bloodstained child being worth something less than sixpence.

'Gentlemen,' said Gideon, getting to his feet, 'we are living in a terrible period of Welsh history. In a century from now they will try to excuse our treatment by saying that those who terrorise us are children of their time. But the forces of justice are organising against this evil. It is on this subject that our colleagues will address you...' The room fell to silence. Gideon said: 'It is true that the world price of iron is dropping; it is also true that the masters of the ironworks are standing in the heaven of an economic piety: the translation of the term is simple; economic piety exists among men when they possess private and industrial assets of round about a quarter of a million pounds and make rather less than the normal standard of profit.' He smiled, his blind eyes, brilliant with an inner fire, moved over the room. 'Owing to the generosity of friends in high places I am able to give you examples of how the piety of our iron masters is expressed, and from this you will be able to deduce the degree of paternal benevolence which they claim they shower upon us—the workers, the object of their affections...'

The men laughed; the woman Mortymer bowed her head, and Dic watched her intently; it was as if she was undergoing a private crucifixion. Gideon said: 'My source of information says that in the year 1815—twelve months before the last big riots in Merthyr—William Crawshay the First held in the Cyfarthfa Works a capital investment of ninety-five thousand pounds; a year later—the actual year of the riots—this figure increased to a hundred thousand pounds—a sum also returned for 1817, which was a year *after* the riots.' He smiled. 'And so, if the bank espionage is correct, and I am assured that it is, it would appear that this paternal master lost nothing in profit at a time of his workers' distress. In fact, and I wish to stress this point, his son wrote to Josiah John Guest of Dowlais, who extracts fortunes from his workmen by illegal Truck ... his son wrote this letter on October 16th, 1816, in which he admits to the hunger which the workmen themselves claimed as their reason for the riot.' Gideon paused. 'At last, it appears,

167

we have an admission of hunger from a dynasty of death that lives on the lie of paternal benevolence: if this is benevolence then let us have tyranny. But let this bit be read so that we fully recognise the forces of greed which encompass us ... can the Welsh speakers understand?'

'Ay, but take it slow,' mumbled Lewis Lewis, and Dic glanced at the man. Dark-haired and surly, he sat glowering in his corner, with one clenched hand pounding gently against the other. Gideon raised the letter, and Zimmerman read:

'The enemy is in too great a strength to oppose with any probability of success; have possessed themselves of all our works and wholly stopped them. They are yet exulting in their victory and are about to proceed to Pennydarren and Dowlais. My spies tell me that they threaten hard your Shop, for they are hungry...

Should anything more serious threaten you, I shall be glad to hear from you, as I would gladly do anything in my power to assist you, but the enemy have not yet evacuated their possessions here.'

Gideon said blandly, 'I ask you particularly to note the term "enemy". This is the manner in which our masters think of us; this is the paternal benevolence of the gaoler to the prisoner and the hangman to his victim. I ask this company to stand in memory of Aaron Williams who was hanged for his part in this riot, though he caused no injury to any person; also, to remember the earlier martyr, the collier Samuel Hill, hanged in the knowledge of Richard Crawshay, the church-goer, for leading riots against starvation sixteen years before.'

The men stood, removing their hats: the woman Mortymer did not rise, but sat with her face in her hands. When the company was seated again, Gideon said:

'And how stand we now? The economic piety continues, the paternal benevolence streams unabated from Cyfarthfa Castle; wages continue to slide to maintain profits, and hunger and degradation stalks the slums: the expectation of life is round about the age of twenty-two—half our children die before the age of five: include these murderous figures and the life expectation of the average worker is reduced further. The facts are indisputable; later, when the Medical Board publishes findings, the indictment of this barbarity will be there for future generations to read for themselves. Give me Crawshay Bailey, I say, if I have to have the Crawshays, for at least he is honest. He spreads no words of benevolence, he brooks no charity towards his Nantyglo slaves: instead, he builds embattlements to protect him from the people he employs—knowing them to be his enemies, and accepting them as such: he keeps his thugs he calls his Workmen's Volunteers in a barracks to defend him from the Scotch Cattle, who are the heroes of the coming Union. But the masters of Cyfarthfa and Nantyglo are one and the same: they have the bone and flesh of those of Penydarren and Dowlais, Tredegar and Pontypool; Hill of Plymouth and Uncle Willie Tait, Fothergill of Aberdare, God forgive him, and the rest of the miserable train, who, surely to God, will find no seat in heaven. *Listen!* You know the terms, you know the consequences—need they be repeated? From the grain riots of Beaufort to the stink we call the iron towns of today, it has been a story of privation, disease, degradation—and miserly wage rates, too, from these pirates of industry, and the reductions are increasing. We are prepared to assess the state of the trade, but not to bow to these decreases without good reason. And there is no good reason when minor Windsors like Cyfarthfa Castle can be built at a cost of thirty thousand and Hensol Castle bought on a whim!'

'By God, blind man,' shouted Lewis Lewis, 'one day they'll hang you!'

'You lead us, Gid Davies!' bawled another, 'and we'll follow!'

Gideon said quietly: 'There can be no leaders in this fight —the people themselves are the leaders. And if I hang—if any here hang—let our names be as unknown in a hundred years as Sam Hill's is today, for we are but the few who speak in the name of thousands. And when the history of our time is told, let the hero be the hungry man, and his mistress Merthyr Town: let it not raise the unimportant one or two, as most

169

stories do, but the whole condition of our society that longs for change—the idealist and the drunk, the atheist and ranter, the refiner and the humble digger—let no man stand an inch above another.' He straightened, smiling. 'Now back to the facts—give me the names of the distrained of Coffin's Court.'

Wil Goff got up, and read from a paper: Lewis Lewis, by 'ere . . .' He indicated the haulier beside him. 'One chest and a bed; two chairs and a framed picture, the kitchen table and pots and pans—value six pound ten. Robert Jones . . . lost his bed and mirror, his grancher's armchair and a clock—collected and auctioned by the beadle at the court and bought by the mother of David Williams, Front Street: taken in debt for groceries—three pound eleven and fourpence—is the fella here?'

'He is,' mumbled the man Jones, 'and he'll get back every stick, mind.'

Wil Goff read: 'Tom Rees and Mr. Vaughan—he caught a tartar—you here, Vaughan, lad.'

'Here!'

'A bed belonging to Vaughan's mother and a stool and two framed pictures—one of the *Ascent of Venus* and the other of the *Whipping in the Temple*, also a commode for a nursing mother, two breast phials and a cloak; the hat and stick of the man Rees's uncle, while visiting, and two china dogs: taken on the eighth of August in recovery of a five pound debt due to two shopkeepers and one saddler for stirrup leathers: auctioned by the beadle of the Court of Requests and bought by Mary Phillips.'

'Last week I met her in *China*,' said the man Rees. 'Me and Tom Vaughan met her and walked her side by side, and I asked her if she'd heard of the Court of Conscience: we'll have that Court down, mark me, and Mr. Coffin wi' it. My missus don't stop weeping for them two little dogs.'

'Left her by her grancher, see,' said the man Vaughan, his glasses on the end of his nose.

Richard Bennet said: 'What are you all talking about? What is this Court of Requests?'

'My God,' cried Dic instantly, 'and they send him into

170

Wales to instruct the Welsh—get back up north where you come from man!'

'Not so fast,' shouted the woman. 'He's arranged the return of debts and fought for parish relief from here to Glasgow, so a little less old tongue, unless you know the inside of a Lancashire prison, for he's just come out of one.'

Gideon rose and said: 'It is quite simple, Bennet. The Court of Requests, administered by a certain Mr. Coffin, of Merthyr, has the power under the local magistracy to seize workmen's furniture and effects and auction these articles to repay private debts—usually groceries—and ale: be fair, they are not without their faults.'

'My God,' said Bennet.

'In depressed times like this,' added Gideon, 'half the furniture of the town is changing hands every month, and you cannot get through the streets for the carts and gambos ...'

'So what happens?'

'We sleep on the floor and eat off bloody boxes, man,' shouted Lewis, 'that's what happens. My missus got tired of sitting on the step in an empty house, so she ups and offs to her gran in Brecon wi' the children, while I sleep rough in Penderyn woods.'

There was a silence. The woman said, her fists on the table: 'So what are you going to do about it?'

'We're having it down, missus, that's what!'

'And Coffin with it!'

'An' hang that damn beadle from a rafter!'

The boy Abednego Jones said, though none heard him in the ensuing shouts: 'My mam got moved back to Carmarthen by the parish, and she's breaking stones in Llandovery to repay.'

'You seen the transportation lists?'

'Hey, Bennet—you follow the hunt?'

'My old woman lifted a door handle down Duke, and they got her in the Swansea Correction ...'

'And I got a girl of ten—working at the face under Cyfarthfa—that's what, you cheeky buggers—what we going to do about it, then, ye brass fools ... ?'

'Order, order!' shouted Gideon, his hands raised high. 'Try

171

not to get excited.'

'Excited? You blind idiot! You give us lectures on the luck of the masters and that clown don't know the Court of Requests? You got an Englishman up there, an' you got a Pole—will ye tell me when the hell we're going to get some Welsh?'

'I told you before,' shouted the woman Mortymer, 'you've got one here. Will you tell me what use a meeting is if it can't be run with order? Don't you know what will happen if you lay a finger on that court, or Coffin?' Silenced by her shriek they subsided, grumbling deep, and nudging, and she looked them over in their sullen anger and rags. 'You move too soon, you crowd down here in Merthyr, and the gaffer will be delighted.' She shook her fist in their faces. 'You raise one finger in Merthyr town and he'll bring the Military in...'

'Let him, an' we'll bloody show them how!'

Dic watched the raving anger of the man Lewis Lewis.

'With the redcoats on a six-hour tap from Brecon barracks —talk sense, ye gunk!' cried the girl. 'What chance have ye got against the forces of the Crown? You're prepared to go to street barricades for a few loads of furniture?'

'I lost a kid last month, missus, so mind...'

'And I saw ten die up The Top last week, man, and not by cholera!' She rose. 'Do you think you and yours are the only ones starving? Fourteen years back Sarah Hopkins built a school in my town, and taught in it, and she and her old Sam the Welsh were the best masters of the day. But the kids still die in Blaenafon, like they die in Ponty and Tredegar and up in Nanty under Bailey, where I work the Coity. But you can't expect to move before your time, d'you hear me? I came here with Richard Bennet to talk of the new Union, but you're not ready in this town for a Union of workers: you're not even ready for a decent Benefit, for you are nothing like the standard we're running on the Eastern. Before you talk of action, before you shout for blood and burning this and hanging that, you've got to organise. Christ, I was up with the Dowlais puddlers the night 'afore last and I thought them bad enough. Don't you remember what happened to the Luddites? Or don't you even know who the Luddites are? What the hell have you been doing these past fourteen years since they hanged Aaron Williams? Can half of you even tell me who Aaron Williams was? He raised a flag and ye dropped it in the dust, like Samuel Hill before him, but you lot let it ride: you let it ride because times were reasonable—they dropped pennies in the good times and you scrambled for the pickings: now you howl on the doorstep when they distrain your goods, you go to the beerhouse when they drop your wages, you moan to your minister when they lengthen the shifts. And all in ten minutes you're shouting for blood. What are you planning to do—march on London?'

'It can be done,' said Zimmerman.

They heard Tom Rowlands breathing, but he was weak in the chest.

Gideon said: 'Not now, Zim, in the name of God,' and Randy Goldie shouted: 'You see this paper parcel? I got a boot in this paper parcel—all they gave me was me father's boot.'

'Shut your snivelling! What's the Pole saying?'

'Here, Wil—fetch another round to moisten things up—ay, put it on the five-bar, the landlord's all right.'

'I asked you what the foreigner said,' shouted Lewis Lewis, up on a chair, and Dic watched him, sipping from his mug; and knew in this man an affinity he had known with no other, like a forging together in a fire.

'My missus has gone, do you know that?' cried Madoc Williams. He wept aloud, the only drunkard not drinking, and shivered his fist in the air. 'She were on iron stacking, and, and . . .' He covered his face.

'Hush, Madoc,' said Dic Penderyn, pulling him down, and the commotion of the men thundered about them, some bawling for the Pole to speak, others demanding to throw him out for a foreigner when the door came open and Sid Blump came in, and Belcher, and Big Bonce with Lady Godiva on his arm, also Peg-Moll and Crone and Curly Hayloft, balder still, his face low and griving for Tilly. And the customers from the bar downstairs came in with shouts and splashing mugs, raising a song of Reform that hit the rafters, and the landlord cried,

173

banging on a gong:

'Gid Davies, Gid Davies!'

'Ay?'

'Boy just run in—says a redcoat troop are going past the Lamb—down on the Brecon road—you hear me?'

'I hear you,' shouted Gideon and brought down a clay flagon, banging it on the table for silence. The room swayed with faces; whispers died and there was a shifting of boots on the boards. Gideon said:

'My God, I weep for Merthyr. A vote of thanks, then, for the London speaker who never got a hearing. But he will be back, for unless you're senseless you'll have to raise a Union. If it's the last thing I do in this town, I'll raise a Union—we must have a negotiating body to meet the new Reform. Away now, and quietly. Keep clear of the Brecon road or they'll be among you with sabres.'

'When's the next Oddfellows, Gid?'

'I'll let you know.'

'How?'

'By word. What do you expect me to do—pin it on the works? Mistress Mortymer . . . are you there?'

'Yes, Mr. Davies.' And she took his arm.

Dic was still standing by the door, the mug dangling from his hand, watching her. He thought she was the most beautiful woman he had ever seen. Pausing before him she lifted her eyes to his face.

'Good for you, missus,' he said. Then Lewis Lewis pushed up, and the woman moved on with Gideon and Zimmerman. Lewis Lewis said:

'You come from round here?'

'No, from Pyle—parish of Aberafon.'

'Then why call you Penderyn—like these woods?'

'Because the cottage that raised me was called Penderyn.'

The man grunted: hair from his chest, Dic noticed, was sprouting out of his collar; his arms were thick to the broad shoulders, and he looked drunk with strength. 'What's your real name, then?'

'Dic Lewis.'

'Same name as me.'

'Ay,' said Dic, 'that's the trouble with the country—too many blutty Lewises.'

'You reckon you could take me, then? I saw you looking more'n twice.'

Dic grinned. 'No real reason, but I like your style.'

'You ever sink a loose quart come Saturdays?'

'Sunday, too, if I get the chance.'

'Wellington?'

'By Jackson's—Merthyr?'

'That's it—old Jumpo's place. It's poison, but it's cheap.'

'Some time, mate—we'll see how it goes,' said Dic.

'And you fancy a swing for the fun of it—say a guinea?'

'If I swing you for fancy, Lewis, you won't need a guinea.'

The man grinned wide, and made a fist of his hand and put it on Dic's chin. 'Saturday night, then—we'll give them Merthyr.'

When Dic got back to the tap Gideon Davies, Bennet and the Mortymer woman were going down the hill beyond Tafern Uchaf. It was a pity, he thought, for he would have liked to talk to Gideon Davies about Sun Heron; also, he would have liked to have been nearer the woman ... He remembered Sun then, and her smile; the way her red hair tufted up under his hands and the laughing freshness of her, all over fizzy like parsnip wine: and he remembered again the mature and dark beauty of the woman he had seen; the slow lift of her eyes at the end of the table. Undefinably he knew that his destiny was linked with hers; the thought was more a sensation, and eerie. Smiling, he said softly:

'Paid member of Parliament, Secret Vote ... No property qualifications...' he paused, scratching his ear. She had been right, he thought; he couldn't even name four points of the new Charter everybody was talking about. Then he remembered Lewis Lewis and next Saturday night at the Wellington, and he wandered back into the Tafern tap-room and slapped down a penny.

'Quart of the best.'

He looked around the little room. A few aged men sat in

solitary dejection, staring into their mugs, and he knew them for the generation that had been hammered on the anvil of economic piety, burned out by one agent after another: personally, he blamed the agents more than the Crawshays—anyone, he reflected, could blame the masters for they were vulnerable: blame was a commodity one could slice up and apportion just where the mood took you, and Gideon Davies, in his opinion was as bad as any when it came to this. He drank the ale slowly, wondering about this, and grinned to himself. He didn't like the Crawshays better than anyone else in Merthyr, but it always amazed him that when the mob burned anybody in effigy, they always chose the masters; the real enemies, he thought, were much lower down the scale ... The landlord's voice shattered his inner silence:

'Thank God that lot's gone. Get me bloody hung, they will —but he's all right, mind, that Gid Davies.'

'Ay.' Dic drank again; amazingly, he could hear the sound of the woman's voice still.

'But fella! Did ye see that beauty he brought over from Blaenafon?'

'Ay,' Dic drank again: her eyes, he thought, were the most beautiful he had ever seen.

'Like polar bears, I say—ought to be chained up: enough to drive a lad demented, and I'm nigh sixty.'

'I'd rather be in her than in the Union.'

'What did you say—you want to join the Union?'

Dic put down his mug and went out into the sunlight.

With his hands deep in his trews and whistling to have his teeth out, he went down to the Lamb. There he drank steadily, staring into his mug. The memory of the Mortymer woman of Blaenafon had completely obliterated his thoughts of Sun...

GWEN, Dic's sister, gave Morgan Howells his third child when the leaves were falling on the old church up at Vaynor, and the country was russet and the trees of Penderyn woods were tracing the skies with tapestries of black. The cold hand of winter laid its spell on workers and masters alike, and there came to Merthyr and the trade a vice of stagnation. The bitter winds of depression howled down the ricketty streets; ice grew in the windows and shone on the boards, the skies darkened over the Beacons and the leaves gusted along the alleys of Graham and High. With the coming of the snow—five feet drifted up Chapel Street and choking the gutters of the Wesleyan—the Irish huddled in the cellars of Pontstorehouse and Sulleri and sought warmth in the blessing of their priests. The ice-breakers were heading the barges along the cut, which was frozen from the Old Cyfarthfa canal right down to Cardiff, the water was solid in the polluted wells. But the Quakers under Tregelles Price sent in their little donkey soup-carts and the gentry in their screened pews sent up prayers for the distressed poor. From Staffordshire to Newport, Swansea to Blaina the furnaces simmered and died, the weakest masters going first to the wall: the great iron stocks lay rusting along the docklands in hundreds of thousands of tons from Cardiff to Gower, the naked cranes and hoists raked the empty sky. But the Tommy shops, made illegal by the Act of 1820, were flourishing as the masters bolstered their fading profits by raising the prices of goods: the old truck shop of Guest of Dowlais which once tied his workers to him hand and foot, was reopened in the face of legal prosecution: all the workers had fought for—the removal of the hated Truck—was swept aside in the free-for-all that swept the valleys of Monmouthshire and Glamorgan. But the Crawshays, to their credit, followed the policy of the founder Richard, and no truck shops existed in Merthyr, though, for convenience (but not profit), they paid in their own printed money. And the shopkeepers, the great middle-class of the town, seized on this loophole for personal benefit: price rises began which decimated the pay packets of the Merthyr workers: a new tyranny arose; a shopocracy that enriched the few at the expense of the many. The paupers increased and thronged the roads from Merthyr, lined the frosted pavements from Cyfarthfa to Dowlais Top, or lay in destitution around the furnace area of Ynys and Penderyn. Hunger and cold walked the empty streets of Merthyr: no longer the children played hopscotch along Thomas and Duke, no longer the women chattered over the garden walls with their black Welsh shawls over their heads and shoulders. The old ironstone miners, the sallow colliers of an earlier generation, took to their beds for warmth, babies wailed from the tight-shut cottages. With the works of Cyfarthfa and Ynys running at a loss, the shivering sale-coal colliers stood in dejected groups on the pneumonia corners and beat themselves for warmth. The trade of iron, falling since the boom of 1825, slid down the graph to rock bottom. The publics were empty; even Jump Jackson was down to a barrel in the Wellington, it was said. But the chandeliers of Crawshay's castle still blazed over the eighteen acres of park land: still the parties gathered on the lawns, still the guests arrived. While over the wasted land the little black processions grew into a processional hymn of death, the carriages of the gentry and the new merchant princes clattered along the deserted streets of The Top towns on Sundays. And the older workers, who remembered the lavish and amorous escapades of George and Richard, the high flyer of a new era, watched with burning eyes this show of blatant wealth in the midst of their poverty.

Trouble was coming. It was whispered down the alleys, it moved in motions at the secret Lodge and Union meetings: many workers left the district, evicted for non-payment of rent, more were tracked down and sentenced to the Usk tread-mill for leaving their place of employment: others went to the houses of correction for debt, other for theft; some to the scaffold or transportation, for robbery in the face of hunger. To support the losses of trade rates of wages were cut again; stoppages, as eight years before, were instantly punished; the employers withholding from the workmen all wages due previous to the stoppage on the grounds of illegal combinations. Ringleaders were summarily arrested, their families left to starve. Troops were at hand in Brecon Barracks to quell all disturbances. Starvation produces wonders, this was the Clydach cry. A few weeks on the black-list when none of the masters in the iron masters' union would employ them, and the most determined leaders of the new benefit clubs and embryo Unions were begging for five shillings of work to feed their pallid children. And in the midst of these tears the new middle-class shopkeepers flourished on The Top; in Merthyr a new Crawshay, Robert Thompson aged thirteen, drove with his father in the fly down the dingy streets; he who was later to lie in Vaynor churchyard with *God Forgive Me* on his grave.

Yet, despite these indignities, Merthyr retained her soul. Every Sunday, and for many of the weekdays, the churches and chapels were filled; and if the inns and taverns were filled, too, and the bawdy shouts of ale vied with songs of praise, this confict existed in a melting-pot of thirty thousand people, the biggest town in Wales: a town which possessed but the nucleus of an ancient community of peace and law. For Merthyr was then the crucible of half a dozen different nationalities, and more—Spanish, Italian and the coloured populations; Hebrew and Scandinavian, some French and Dutch; English from almost every county flooded in under the magic carpet of 'following the iron'. And the Irish never ceased to come, cramming into the cellars of Pontstorehouse and Sulleri, bringing their new religion and the conflicts of their beliefs.

Gigantic problems, social, religious and economic, beset the masters of iron, who were indicted for every injustice.

Dic and Sun Heron, whom some called Mari Beynon, were

married in the Wesleyan by the Reverend Edmund Evans on the last day of September, before the coming of the cold. They went to live in Seven Ynysfach next door but one to Mamie and Billa, once the cottage of Joe and Marion Morgan, evicted for a relapse in the rent. But it was more'n a relapse, said Billa, it were practically a death, for Joe's missus hit the rent collector with her grancher's Irish shillelagh.

'She never did!' said Sun, on the doorstep.

'She did,' said Billa, changing Asa, 'for I saw her. And his 'ead had a hole in it.'

'Ay, but that weren't done by Marion,' said Blod, hanging out.

'It were—I saw it.'

'You didn't,' said Mamie. 'That was done by the Spaniard in Number Ten—don't hold with Spaniards, mind,' she said to Sun. 'Paying the rent wi' a dog spike can be a very dangerous thing, but it's all you can expect of a foreigner. You Welsh?'

'Ay,' said Sun, 'and proud of it, missus.'

'You don't sound like one,' said Blod.

'Chiefly come from Ireland an' the bogs, but me da was as Welsh as a leek, and me real name's Mari.'

'Mari what?' asked Blod with pegs in her teeth.

'Mari Lewis, but I expect they'll call me Penderyn, like Dic.'

'The handsome fella with the big blue eyes?' asked Blod, coming alive.

'Ay, ay, though it's me that's saying it, girl.'

'Does he treat you good?' asked Mamie, ' 'Cause I saw him coming out o' the Miners' night before last and there weren't a leg under him.'

'Ach, he's fine and sweet, and he don't lay a hand on me—and he's on good money, despite the slump. You got fellas?'

'I have,' sang Blod. 'He's only little, see, but he's winsome, ain't he, Mamie ma?'

'You got husbands, Mrs. Goldie—you and Mrs. Jam?'

'One apiece—down in Taibach, but it ain't far enough away —we wish it were Japan, don't we, Billa?'

And Billa Jam looked beyond the dram-road and its rusted rails and wrung her hands with cold. 'I don't know. Sometimes I miss my little fat old chap . . .'

'Got to go,' said Sun, and she buttoned up her cloak and pulled tighter her shawl. 'Mustn't be late: got a good little job up in Cross, and it helps things out—scrubbing and cooking for Gideon Davies—you know him?'

'Know him, girl—he's me property,' said Mamie. 'He lodged with me down in Taibach, and if there was room in by here with Billa's tribe of Israel, I'd put him a bed down to-morrow.' She sighed deep, closing her eyes. 'Ah, a good, fine fella is my big Gid Davies.'

'Give him my love,' cried Billa, her arms full of washing.

'And mine!' sang Blod, fetching more out of the copper.

'Tell him we're all right,' called Mamie, and peered round the wall at Mrs. Zeke Solomon in Number Four. 'You want anything, Solomon?'

'No, Mrs. Goldie. Only passing the time of day, so to speak.'

'O, ay? Lend me your ear and I'll pin it to the door.' She sighed. 'Blutty shocking, it is—no privies and no privacy. You put your head back in there or I'll land ye one—rabbi or no rabbi.'

'No offence intended, Mrs. Goldie.'

'None taken,' said Mamie, 'now vanish.' She waved, then, her breath steaming in the early mist. 'Goodbye, Mrs. Penderyn—do us right by Gid Davies, mind.'

'There's one thing about it,' said Billa in passing, 'with those Crawshay drams gone cold at least you can pin out the washing.'

'The trouble is that the washing don't keep ten, do it?'

'Thank God I fed my Joab, and thank God my little Adam is in peace, I say,' said Billa, wringing out the mangle. 'Moke Donkey and her twins brought six-pounds-five, but that's nearly gone. Break my old man's heart, mind, when he finds out I sold Moke.'

'We'll manage,' said Mamie.

'We won't,' said Blod. 'Randy keeps us but the washing don't keep you lot and we're all in it together, so I'm going down the pit.'

'In your condition? Don't be daft!' said Billa.

'Effie Brown the Lancashire went down yesterday, and she's five months gone.'

'The Union will be after you—no women down while the men are off, they say,' observed Mamie.

'The Union doesn't mind,' replied Blod. 'Randy's been a paid up member with Gid Davies ever since he started.'

'Thank God for the Union,' said Mamie. 'Soon we'll be eating coal.'

'One day for Randy and one for the baby,' said Blod. 'And there's no real sweat to the job—opening a few doors—I can get on wi' me knitting.'

'What a blutty state we're in,' said Mamie, and pushed in more sheets, crying, 'Will you keep off, Asa—you'll burn your backside backing on to that copper...'

Miss Grieve, sitting in the bay window of Ianto House, bulging with woollens, headscarfed and ear-muffed, with her Abergavenny blanket over her knees, wrote with a black, mittened hand in her diary:

'In the last two months I have seen the following in Merthyr: Mamie Goldie and Billa Jam Tart with her ten small boys—they have left that Dai End-On and Billy Jam; there is no love in the marriages of the working classes, as is widely known in gentry circles. Saw Mrs. Duck Evans go past today; her husband was convicted of the theft of a duck; she looked like a woman with something on her conscience. Yesterday, passing Number One, Ynys Row, I noticed an astonishing thing. Miss Blossom Thomas was sitting in the window nursing a baby, but when I looked closer, I saw that it was only a rag doll; which is very strange behaviour.

Last week I saw Lemuel Samuel begging in the gutter down Front Street and throwing stones at passing dogs: this is understandable, the way those things have treated him.'

Miss Grieve sighed deeply, and wrote in her book:

'Oh, Ianto Phillips, do you forgive me for my flight from the path of virtue? The shares in Fothergill's you left me have gone down twopence because of the avarice of the workers—recently they looted his company shop. Just heard that Willie Bach is going down the pit; he is a big boy for eleven, and the pit is the place for him. O, Ianto, do not think I have trespassed our love just because I am sleeping with Mr. Waxey Evans. Only the other night I sighed your name in a kiss, but he is not very sharp. This house, these possessions, the six thousand pounds you left me is insufficient for my station in life, and with ten thousand acres in Hereford it is safe to say he is a good proposition; Merthyr, you'd agree, is a soft-cornered old place to live—everybody with black faces, and choke and smoke are brothers; better to cry in health than sickness. Nothing is clean here; even the walls are stained with idleness where the colliers lounge. But the mansion in Hereford has red plush chairs in the parlour, says Waxey. Met that horrid little Mervyn Jam with Mrs. Goldie last Tuesday; his face, I would say, had a suspicion of acne. Did you like the winter flowers I scattered on your grave last Sunday? I feign death when Waxey Evans comes to me, though he is a morsel lower than himself day by day ... the physic is safe, if inclined to be slow in action... If fortune is kind to me, soon I will be in Hereford...'

Miss Grieve snapped the book shut as Waxey appeared in the parlour: top-hatted and frocked was he, brushed up against the pile and polished, with his corsets tight and a gold-knobbed cane in his hand, and half a pint of blue ruin inside him at ten o'clock in the morning.

'Are you there, my love?'

'Yes, here, my darling!' called Miss Grieve.

Entering the ornate room, he kissed her forehead. 'I am wondering ... would it be possible...? The prices are up in town, as you know—a few sovereigns these days does not go very far.'

'Another twenty, shall we say?'

'Thirty would be handier, mind,' said Waxey. 'For all is signed and sealed, and in your name, is it not? Soon you will be in Hereford.'

Miss Grieve smiled. The coffin lid opened, and shut.

Sun said, 'Make in me a little one, a little Dic Penderyn. . .?'

The moon was putting his fist through the window, icicles were tinkling down the crooked streets of Sulleri where the miners coughed deep in their chests from the sale-coal pit: Mr. Madoc Williams, puddler bereaved, spouse to Mrs. Bronwren Williams, gathered his four in his arms in the brass-knobbed bed of Islyn and watched the stars fall out of the sky; and the children breathed softly against him, their cheeks lashed heavy in the pallor of sleep. Madoc opened wide his eyes and shouted at the ceiling:

'Bron! Bron!'

Sun said: 'Ach, boy, do not worry, we will be able to keep him. And I shall feed him at six and two and seven o'clock, and his name will be Richard Jay, which, like yours, has the flight of a bird: if it is a girl I will call her Joy, which is the name of your touch. Lie deep to me, my boy . . .'

'Oh, God,' said Dic.

In the hot-head, madcap essence of the dream; in all the lost visions of the loves that never happened, he drew deep to her in the bed, and there was in her a tumult he had never heard before; a beauty removed from the skittish laughter of the half-tart girls of his rollicking adolescence: no submission was this, for she claimed him in a fury of love, and in her was made a hand, an arm and ten fingers, and her body was smooth under his hands.

'Oh, God,' said Dic.

'Jesus, forgive me,' said Mr. Madoc Williams, bereaved.

'You all right, Dada?' asked Olwen, aged eight, sitting up in bed.

184

'Oh, Bron, my little Bron,' said Madoc.

'No good shouting for our mam, Dada,' said Meg, aged six, 'for our mam's dead.'

And Dic drew from his wife in Number Seven, Ynys, and saw in her dark face the face of Gwen, who mothered him: and the moon cocked an eye in the glazed ice of the window, smiling at her breasts so strangely like the breasts of Molly Caulara, but with no hay-seed upon them, for she was loved in a field: the mouth of Sun was then the mouth of Gwen, his sister, so he did not kiss it, but leaned his cheek against its wetness; then turned his face and kissed the lips of Molly, and these were the lips of Sun Heron: he smelled in her red hair the rust of the iron and the hands that smoothed his shoulders were calloused with the stacking.

'Do not leave me,' she said.

'What you up to, Dada?' asked Olwen Williams, aged eight, the daughter of Madoc.

Sun said: 'Do not go, Dic; please do not leave me.'

Outside in the street the night watchman was singing the hymn they had sung together in the Wesleyan on the day of their wedding, though the Reverend Morgan Howells did not come, nor Gwen, his sister ... Dic had wept for this, but Sun did not know ...

And there came to him then the face of the woman called Mortymer: even in the tumult of Sun's breath he heard this woman's voice, and her lips were full and red and her teeth shining and white; it was as if she lay in the bed beside them, so clearly did he see her, and she spoke to him, and he heard her say; 'Die hard, Dic Penderyn, die hard, Dic Penderyn.'

And Olwen Williams, aged eight, the eldest daughter of Mrs. Bron Babbie Williams who died by fire ... Olwen smoothed back her Welsh-dark hair in the bed of her father in Islyn Court, and put her arms around her possessions, which were a baby brother and twin sisters; and opened wide her eyes in terror.

185

'No, Dada,' she said, 'Oh, no...!' and opened her lips for the scream.

But Sun Heron, bride to Dic Penderyn of Number Seven, Ynys Row, smiled at the man possessing her and narrowed her eyes in love and reaching up, she drew him down into her soul and there ravished him, while in her he knew joy. And there was about this man a great host of men with coloured banners and pennants which were streams of fire. Presently he sighed and was as clay in the hands of the woman, and there came from her then a sound that others before her had made; the sound from a throat that was not her own, but one this man had fashioned beneath her breast.

A scream chilled the bed and they tensed, then listened to the watchman who was singing along the streets of Islyn Court; his voice was bass and pure in the icicled wind:

'Let not Thy worship blind us to the claims of love;
but let Thy manna lead us to the feast above ...'

Hearing this, Mr. Madoc Williams, husband of Babbie who died by fire, peered with shining eyes through the ice-glazed window of Islyn Court, and rubbed off the frost with a razored fist.

And the children behind him bled to death.

MAMIE GOLDIE said, 'I reckon God knew He couldn't be everywhere at once so that's why He dished up mothers.'

'And we fell for it,' said Billa Jam, taking a swipe at Abiah. 'Where you off to, Randy, son?'

'Got a meeting at the Lodge.'

'What about your dinner, then?'

'Give it to Blod, she's the one working.'

'But she's just polished one.'

'Then give her another. Feeling like a mule, she is.' He swaggered to the door, his trews tight over his slim buttocks, his waist no bigger than Molly Caulara's and there was tightness in him.

Mamie said: 'And I cooked it special—scrag end o' horse, but it's red meat, and good.' She looked at him with large, wet eyes. 'You'm a collier, Randy—you got to eat.'

'I'm half a blutty collier now I'm on Relief.'

Billa Jam came up then with Saul on her back and Caradoc under her arm and hooked in Asa with a foot, and she said, bothered: 'Don't reckon it's right having Lodge meetings on a Sunday—even Ynys only simmers. What you up to at these meetings—putting everything right?'

'Finding out where it's wrong.'

'Oho, hoity-toity, eh? Kiss them under the Coity, eh? You'm wasting your time at those Gid Davies meetings, Randy Goldie.'

He swaggered to the door and there was in him bitterness. 'Not now, Billa Jam, though I've wasted too much before.' He opened the door. ' 'Bye, Mam.'

'You kiss me, boy?'

The lines of obesity had thinned into drags and the flesh hung loose on her pin-bone cheeks. But she stood with her face up, waiting and he slowly came back and stood closer, then bent and kissed her.

'You'm a blutty good one,' he said.

'How about me?' asked Billa Jam, coming up, eyes shut, lips pursed. 'Got one for aunty?'

'You bugger off,' said Randy and slammed the door and went out into the weak, December sunshine.

They were still making iron at Ynys and Cyfarthfa, thanks to Crawshay, but the output was low.

'I'll bloody kill somebody if I get my hands on 'em,' said Randy as he went up Cross.

Tap tap on the door of Number Seven.

'Come in!' sang Sun.

Welsh cakes for my Dic, sizzle them on the stone, flap-jack, black-jack, brown on the bottoms and sugared on the tops and sweat 'em over the griddle: got a good fella to live with, neither lip nor fist from him, not like that swine Billy Ugmore: Gawd, I'd give him Billy Ugmore if I saw him now. Rainbow in his head, indeed? Can't think what got into me, ought to be ashamed of meself, should have had me head looked in: should have kept meself free for me big, strong Dic. She sang then, her voice like an angel: 'I got a big chap and his name is Dic, *Whee-hoi-hoi*, Abednigo! But it's a pity he drinks so much—got a gullet like a horse. Never mind, girl, can't have everything...'

Bang bang on the back.

'I said come in!' yelled Sun, wiping her hands on her apron.

Bang bang ... and she swung the door wide to heat its hinges.

Dai End-On and Mr. Billy Jam of Taibach were standing on the step. Side by side were they, done up in Sunday best, hats on ears, alpaca suits, boots to shave in, starched collars under their whiskers, and smelling of peppermint, and never a quart had passed their lips.

''Morning, missus,' said Dai End-On, screwing at his fingers.

''Morning,' said Billy Jam, taking off his hat.

'Ay, and what can I do for ye?' asked Sun.

'Well,' said Dai, 'me and me friend—that is, Mr. Billy Jam by 'ere have been recommended to come to ye...'

'You've got the wrong house,' said Sun, 'you want the Popi Davey.'

'Actual,' said Dai, 'we called on Gid Davies, but he is out, so the big Pole Zimmerman sent us down to you.'

'Did he now, and what ails ye?'

'We want you to speak for us, missus,' said Billy Jam.

'To speak for you—who do you belong to, then?'

'Me lawful wife is next door but one,' said Dai, stuffy in the nose.

'And mine,' said Billy. 'Mrs. Billa Jam.'

Sun rubbed her chin, looking them over: repentant schoolboys, they lowered their eyes before her strict, unsavoury stare.

'I've heard of you two,' said she.

'Ay,' mumbled Dai End-On, broken.

Under the floor a mouse was in tears.

'And you, too,' said Sun.

Billy wiped his nose with the back of his hand. 'She left me months back, and she took me moke,' said he.

'Is it your moke you're after, then, or your missus?'

'Oh, ma'am!'

'And you're off the glass?'

'As God's me judge,' said Dai. 'Strike me dead, may I never move from here...'

'Not a drop, not a smell,' said Billy. 'I tell you this...'

'All right, all right. I'm daft, but I'll speak for ye. Wait by here.'

Taking off her apron Sun patted her hair, which was smooth to her head and bright red, tightened the scarf at her throat and went next door but one.

Returning in minutes she put her hands on her hips and breasted up to them, showing her teeth, her eyes bright with success.

'You're back,' she said, simply.

Incredulity struck Billy Jam. 'She's taking me back, woman?'

'I spoke well for ye, mind—I made a few promises—no ale from now on, no Lodge, no hammerings.'

'Ach, God bless ye soul,' said Dai, and kissed her hand. 'You're the loveliest sinner I've seen for a mile. An' Mamie, too?'

'And Mamie, too,' said Sun, 'you're in!'

Dai removed his hat in an act of reverence. 'Och, to hell, she's a wonderful woman. And she cooks the best blutty ox-tail that's gone past me lips this last five months.'

'Dear me,' said Billy, 'I'm all of a fumble. Are the kids there, too, girl?'

'All lined up and waiting,' said Sun, and tip-toed up to them. 'Smell your breath—ay, that's as sweet as honeysuckle.' She tightened Dai's muffler and smoothed Billy's hair, spitting on her fingers. 'All groomed up and dandy, there's a couple of handsome fellas. Next but one down then, and act respectful, tap on the door, lads, not too loud.'

'Eh, by Tanyard Light!' said Billy, 'you're a beautiful little lady,' and they marched out. And within ten seconds they were going down the dram-road with Mamie and Billa Jam Tart after them with the Irish confetti, and the kids hurling everything from cinders to fire-bricks. Quite fast went Dai End-On and Billy and they did not stop until the range lengthened, and there was a lump on Mr. Billy's head like a walnut, and sparking.

'Well, I never,' said he, rubbing. 'I never ever had that one before—that were the handle off the mangle.'

Mamie Goldie wiped her hands on her apron, disgusted. 'The pair of heathens! Of all the blutty cheek! What do they take us for—getting folks to speak for 'em, indeed!' She yelled: 'Out, out, Dai End-On. You brute for treating a decent woman so! If my Randy were here he'd hand you an outing!' Turning, she stared at Billa Jam Tart. 'What's wrong wi' you, then?'

'You hit him,' said Billa, glum. 'You hit my Mr. Jam on his 'ead.'

'On his head? I'll blutty decapitate him. The sauce of it!'

Disconsolate, rubbing, Dai and Billy mooched off to the Wellington via the Popi Davey: with the children clustered about their skirts Mamie and Billa went back to Number Five and every neighbour in the Row was either hanging out washing or scrubbing the doorsteps. Even Old Papa Tomo Thomas came down to dig the garden and he'd been abed five years with rheumatics.

Mamie shouted for all to hear: 'Pesterin' virgin women, indeed—I'll take 'em to law, eh, Billa?'

But Billa Jam Tart did not reply.

Things were not tight with Dic and Sun. He was working full shifts up on Two Cyfarthfa, and though the rates had been dropped by some twenty per cent and the streets were crowded with people on parish relief, his wage was good—twenty-two shillings on a full shift, sixteen and fourpence on a thin one, and Sun thrived. Good hauliers, as usual, were at a premium, and he gradually furnished Number Seven, being careful at the auctions not to bid for sticks impounded by Coffin's Court from others less fortunate.

'But others are not so choosey, mind,' said Mrs. Taibach.

'I know, I know, ma'am,' replied Mrs. Duck Evans. 'They've taken everything of mine except the bed.'

'Ought to be hung,' said Mrs. Taibach. 'Enough to make a woman go into Purdah, it is.'

'Where's that, love?' asked Annie Hewers, passing.

'If you don't know girl, it do not matter,' said Mrs. Taibach, and shouted, 'Mr. Note, kindly raise off your backside and sweep out the back. Appalling, it is, these harmonious musicians laying about—and me working my fingers to the bone.'

'That's what my little Megsie says,' said Annie, vacant, and her face was thin and pale. 'It do not matter—nothing matters any more, says my Megsie.' She smiled at Molly Caulara coming up.

'A blutty scandal, it is,' said Molly Caulara 'The rates are down in every trade; most of the furniture is being bought by the upper class while the working class sits on the floor—cannibals, we are—living off each other. The shopkeepers are rising the prices—a penny on this, a halfpenny on that, and the Government don't care—I can't find a name for these blutty shopkeepers—they don't give a damn for their customers.'

'One day they will,' said Annie, quietly. 'One day we'll have those shops down, and their keepers.'

'Nothing like a good company shop, I always say,' said Mrs. Penderyn, Dic's man. 'It would cut their profits, mind, if Mr. Crawshay opened a Shop.'

'Don't talk daft, woman!' cried Mrs. Taibach. 'D'ye want the same as Guest hands them in Dowlais? Get in debt wi' him and he pulls the blankets off the bed, an' his prices are even higher than the private shops. We had a Shop in Taibach —everything from a pin to a coffin and prices up fifty per cent when copper went down. Give Crawshay credit for once— everybody singes the poor so-and-so.'

Annie Hewers said at the winter sky: 'It don't really matter, though. Could you spare a bit for my Megsie, Mrs. Taibach?'

'Spare ye? Woman, what do ye take me for? I'm down to my blutty uppers.'

'I got some,' said Mrs. Duck Evans. 'All the time I got a loaf you can have a bit for Megsie—poorly, is she?'

'Christ,' said Annie. 'She do nothing but cough.'

'And my fella does nothing but starve. Never very strong in the constitution, mind, and it's skinny on the parish. Ah well, things will get worse till they get better—look on the bright side. You hungry, Annie Hewers?'

'No.' She smiled, holding her stomach.

'You'd be best back home with your da in Pontypridd, mind. Got good times in Ponty, they do say—copper's staying up well, according.'

'Ain't going home,' said Annie. 'Me and Megsie ain't never going home to be leathered.'

'She's poorly, remember.'

192

'Ay, but she's all I've got—I ain't never going to see her leathered.'

'Come from the wilderness,' said Mrs. Duck Evans. 'Like I say to my old man—come out of the wilderness and smile like Jesus my Lord, and it will all come right—come home with me for the bread?' Looking at the sky, she said in silent prayer:

'Oh, God, Oh, God, help me to get out of Merthyr.'

Arm in arm, scragging their shawls round their faces, they went over Iron Bridge and down to the Dynefor Doss.

'Are you ready, then?' asked Gwen Morgan Howells, smiling on the doorstep of Number Seven, Ynys Row. And her eyes danced brightly under her blue poke-bonnet.

'You look beautiful this morning, Mrs. Gwen Morgan Howells,' said Sun, closing the door behind her. 'You don't mind my saying?' She clutched Dic's arm, on tip-toe to his face. 'You agree, Dic—don't your sister look beautiful?'

He winked.

'Marriage to the minister do suit her, eh?'

Gwen took Dic's other arm. 'He is a fine man and a splendid husband.'

'He might be, but he doesn't like the Unions,' said Dic.

'Aw, stop it, Dico!' cried Sun. Three abreast they walked down Castle on their way to the Methodist. 'You're coming, you said, so don't spoil it . . .'

'I'm only coming to please you.'

Gwen bowed to the doors of Ynys Row. 'Good morning, Mrs. Goldie, good morning, Mrs. Jam!'

' 'Mornin', missus!'

Blod came out with a pile of washing in her arms and stopped to curtsey to the minister's wife.

Dic said: 'One thing, you raise the tone of the place. I've never noticed that one curtsey to me. Poor old Blod. Four months away and she's still down Cwmglo. If she keeps her first she'll be lucky, with Randy out. Now you tell me, Gwen, why your old man stands against a Union.'

'Now, if you start that again, I anna coming,' said Sun,

angrily. 'We are going to the Methodist after a kind invitation from the minister, so be kind to your Gwen.'

'Just this once, boy—for me?' asked Gwen. 'And I know it would delight Morgan...'

They went together past the Castle Inn where the Gentry broughhams and flys were standing, the horses stamping impatiently. Alderman Thompson, owner of the Penydarren works, paused in the act of picking up a piece of coal, and raised his hat to Gwen; Hill, over from the Plymouth, bowed. Even old Sam Homfray smiled from his trap.

'God's teeth, we're going up in the world,' said Dic, bowing back.

'And none o' that, ye skillet!' whispered Sun.

'Anyway, I'm Wesleyan.' He elbowed Sun. 'And you belong to the Pope.'

'Methodist this time, just for me,' said Gwen.

A procession of worshippers was coming down the street in the Calvinistic Methodist: Gideon Davies was tapping with his stick along the railings of High, smiling into the January sunlight; behind him came Mrs. Bach Taibach holding Willie's hand, and for God's sake watch out, Mam, lest my mates do see me; and these were overtaken by Miss Milly Thrush who was pursuing Gideon. Nobody seemed to notice Lemuel Samuel in the gutter, nor the passing, inoffensive mongrel he assisted along with his boot.

'Mr. Davies ...!'

Gideon turned, instantly recognising Miss Thrush's voice.

'Why, good morning, Miss Thrush! Whatever are you doing in Merthyr?'

Unseen, Shoni Sgubor Fawr, pugilist, the Emperor of *China*, went by in rolling strength with his tenor friend Dai Cantw'r, and Dai was singing in a sad, minor key unsuited to the morning. Milly Thrush curtseyed, also unseen, and said: 'Got a shop on River Side, Mr. Davies—didn't you know? I've been expecting to see you ...'

'And you sell the same things? Is it a good shop, Miss Thrush?'

'Ay, fair wonderful!' She warmed to him in the passing glances of her customers: women were eyeing him secretly from under bonnets: the dark eyes of a young gentry girl lifted and narrowed, and Miss Thrush was pleased; it came naturally to believe him her personal property. Swallowing down the heated bumping of her heart, she said: 'Ay, business is fine. I've ... I've sort of been expecting you. I sell sweets and drapery—really, I took over from the Lollipop Woman, but I've extended, if ye understand—men's wear, mainly underclothes, and razors, boots, laces ...' Her voice faded, and she raised her face to his and closed her eyes, swallowing dry in the throat.

'But ... but where is the shop, Miss Thrush?'

'Outside the Popi Davey lodgings—River Side. I share the rooms above with Mrs. Taibach and her Willie ...'

'Are they in Merthyr, too?' He was astonished.

'Came in with me—and Mr. Note of Taibach—they say they have been looking for you, like me ...'

'I ... I spend a long time away, Miss Thrush.'

'So do they,' said she, instantly. 'Mr. Note and Mrs. Taibach and Willie spend a lot o' time away—mainly with relatives back down south...' she began to twist her gloved fingers. A passing child stopped to stare at her. Miss Thrush said: 'I ... I'm on my own a lot, so if ... if ... if you'd ever care to ...' She wilted, head bowed.

Reaching out he gripped her hand. 'Are you going to chapel, ma'am?'

Her face brightened. 'Ay, for the big Morgan Howells!'

'Calvinistic? So am I. The pavement is difficult, would you help me, please?' Staring momentarily, she peeled off a glove in a frenzy.

Her hand burned in his. The urchin child watched. Hand-in-hand they went down High. She began to tremble; the trembling began to control her and she fought it away; she wanted to cry with joy.

Mrs. Bach Taibach stopped on the other side of the road on her way with Willie to Ynysgau Chapel.

'Well, I'll be damned,' she whispered. 'An' holding his

195

hand, the sneaky little bitch!'

'Who's a sneaky little bitch, Mam?' asked Willie.

'Never you mind!' Turtling up and breasty was Mrs. Taibach.

'Here comes Mr. Note, Mam,' cried Willie.

Among the passing crowds on their way to a destitute God Mr. Percy Note drooped head and shoulders like a fractured oboe, following the lavender of Miss Milly Thrush like a hound follows aniseed, automatically nosing up the steps of the Methodist till jerked on the leash of Mrs. Taibach's command.

'Mr. Note!'

Collared, he retraced his steps amid the bellowing, harmonium strains of Wesley's *Heathland* and beg-pardoned his way across the street. 'Yes, my love.'

'Are you or are you not Wesleyan, man?'

'Yes, Mrs. Taibach.'

'Then what takes you into the Calvinistic?'

'Miss Thrush just gone in there, Mam,' piped Willie. 'Miss Thrush...'

'Anywhere you like, then,' said Mr. Note, broken. He had been racked on the ardour of the Taibach widowhood; his new Gun Symphony had died to a whisper in a savage boudoir that had put paid to an earlier spouse.

'Right, you,' said Mrs. Taibach, gripping her Willie, 'we will all go into Calvinistic.'

And as they climbed the steps Willie looked into the eyes of Mr. Note, and said: 'No more music lessons, Mr. Note?'

Percy Bottom Note shook his head.

Willie's eyes clouded. 'But what about the Revolution?'

'No,' said Mr. Note.

Willie clutched him, bouncing the latecomers entering in a hurry. 'But you must, Mr. Bottom Note. You promised, you promised...!'

'No, my son. No more revolutions.' He lowered his eyes from Willie's face.

'But property is theft—you said so, Mr. Note...' whispered Willie.

'Come on, *come on*,' said Mrs. Taibach.

'It is finished,' said Mr. Note, and turned away.

Blod went down Cwmglo Pit on the morning shift, though it was a Sunday, for you can't have everybody praying, said she, and Randy's got to eat.

''Morning, Goldie,' said the overman.

''Morning, sir,' said Blod, going down in the cage. 'You got a decent dram for me today?' The cage descended with a whine and crash.

'You're down here for the doors—Six Stall, anna ye?'

'Ay, but I could do with a dram, Mr. Overman. Me fella's still off, you see.'

'He told me no drams, mind—he told me you were on the doors.'

'An' me as strong as a dray, then some—come on, Overman!'

The overman rubbed his chin. 'You need the money—I'll see what I can do—meanwhile they're lining up on the vents, so move.' He pushed his way through the colliers coming out of the cage, and Blod followed with her bottle and candle-tack of clay, carried in the press of their half-naked bodies down the gallery: stripped to the waist went the colliers in a clanking of picks and shovels.

'Ay, ay, missus!' Big Ned Tranter, the collier from Wigan elbowed her in the crush, pushing a path for the young labour; Merve Jam, for one, walked with May Harries, aged six, who was on Two Vent Door, with her hair either side of her face in coal curls.

'You seen my doll?' asked May Harries.

'Ach, no,' replied Merve, pushing it away. 'Blutty rags and bones it is.'

'It is not!' cried May, indignant, and she folded her candle-tack under her arm and held her doll high among the barging shoulders of the colliers. 'Look now—she has real hair from my gran and leather boots, see?'

'So's me Aunt Fan,' said Merve, shoving on. 'Anyway, dolls are daft, and if Overman catches you nursing that on doors he'll tan your arse.'

197

'Ah, ay? He tans my arse and me dad'll see to him—you know my dad?'

'*Heisht*, you!' said Blod, 'bad language, May Harries...!'

'You'll hear worse in Eight-One,' said Ned Tranter. 'We got five-year-olds down there who can singe the beard off Satan.' He looked her over.

'More bugger you for hearing it,' said Blod. 'Don't hold with it—bad language from the childer—mine aren't coming down this Cwmglo—die first, says my Randy.'

'Is he still off?'

'Ay, a month,' said Blod, empty.

They tramped on down the gallery, spreading left and right to the stalls and headings, standing on the gob when the drams went past, some with ponies, some pulled by human horses, mares mostly; and they came from the lower roofs of the four-foot seams, stripped to the waist with their hair sealed on their sooted breasts and their teeth white in their coaled faces as they heaved to the loads, hobnails scraping. The little cage-army rolled on, the men ducking to the roof and the overmen were following, striking up at the plugs to bring down the falls for the clearing gangs coming up behind.

'You there, kids?' cried Ned Tranter, turning, and the ledge candles flickered on his strong, smudged face.

'Comin', sir,' said Merve, giving May another shove.

'You sod!' shouted May, kicking at him, and Merve swerved and her boot went high and he caught it, upending her, and the children danced about her in shrieks as she picked herself up out of the road dusting her doll and he made a noise as he went off and she cried after him in a voice of tears. 'You'm a bastard, Merve Jam, you'm a blutty bastard.'

'Now, now,' said Blod, kneeling. 'Now now, May Harries, do not mind him. And no more swearing or you will not go to heaven.' She kissed her.

'Nor me,' said Ned Tranter over his shoulder. 'Any time you like I got an empty dram for you, little Goldie, an' fill you up, remember.'

'And any time you like my Randy'll see to you,' said Blod. Standing in the road with the door children she watched him disappear with Merve into Stall Eight-One, and there was a fine swagger on him that made her grin, being a chap for the girls, she thought, but not this one: not ever this one, Ned Tranter me beauty, for I got Randy.

'What you looking at, Blod Irish?' asked another, Dafydd Jones, aged seven.

'Nothing,' said Blod, and smoothed back her hair. The wake-lights of the ledges brought her face to a fierce beauty, dancing red in her eyes as she looked after Tranter.

'Get on, get on!' shouted the plug-man jabbing at the roof behind them. 'You want this lot down on your nuts?'

Lifting her skirt Blod pulled out the waistband of her drawers and tucked it deep inside, for the three foot seam was coming up and the air was thicker, for Cwmglo drifted ten stalls from the cage. One by one the children headed off into the ventilating stalls, there to sit by the doors and await the drams coming through from the face.

'You there, Mrs. Goldie?' called a voice.

Blod turned at the entrance to her door. 'Ay, sir?'

The overman wandered up, ducking his head under the roof and the candle flame flung black shadows into his bearded face. 'Just remembered—Ned Tranter's got a free dram—are ye on?'

'Just one day?'

'Could be two weeks—his boy lost a finger.' He hesitated, then added: 'Tranter b'ant every woman's dram, but ye can't pick and choose.'

'You leave him to me, I'll handle Tranter.' She smiled at the overman, for she liked this man. He rarely beat the children for sleeping at the doors and he never took a woman underground, or none that she heard complaint from.

'Why are you on doors, then—a big strong cow like you?'

'Because me man says so.'

'And now you want drams, eh?'

'I told you—me chap's off and I need the money.'

'It's a long haul with Tranter—you carrying?'

'Ach, no, man—only since yesterday.' She pushed out her stomach and he grinned at her, saying:

199

'Report to Tranter, then. You can take his Number Two. If ye yell loud enough you've always got Merve Jam on One.'

'It'll be Tranter yelling, mind,' said Blod.

He winked at her. He thought she was beautiful standing there in the candlelight: he was forty-two and had buried a wife up in Derby a year back, and he wanted a woman for his children. 'I'll book you,' he said, 'Six a week out of Tranter's pay, remember—up to you, girl—stick out for six.'

'You watch me,' said Blod.

She went back up the drift of the gallery to Tranter and Merve Jam in Eight-One. Naked as badgers, the pair of them, with Tranter cutting and Merve filling and coal sweat was painting them up already. Tranter turned at the face and lowered his pick; the muscles of his fine body bulged as he straightened: Merve rested, leaning on the shovel.

'You got a dram, says Overman,' said Blod.

'Now I got a filly to pull it, eh?' said Tranter, and came from the face.

'If ye pay—six, it is.'

'Six shillings for a woman? What do ye take me for?' He turned to Merve. 'Is that full?'

'Ay.'

'Then away with ye!'

Merve hooked up to his towing-belt and leaned to the weight; the dram moved, biting at the grit on the rails; thundering softly, it went down the track to the stall vent-door where May Harries opened up, and through it to the gallery.

'You dram for me and you strip,' said Tranter.

'Six shillings,' said Blod, 'and no odds to that. But don't tell my chap for I'm supposed to be on doors.' She pulled the coarse dress over her head and stuffed her bodice into her belt. Tranter sat down on the gob, his eyes moving over her. Warm air fanned them as the door of Eight-One opened up.

'Shakes alive, girl, with a body like that you're wasted on doors.'

She pulled off the loose string and put it between her teeth, scragging back her hair, and this she tied tightly pulling hard at the knots while Tranter watched the candleflame touching her breasts with leaping shadows of redness.

'Six shillings a week, and you're entitled to the look,' said Blod. 'Where's me belt?' She walked past him, peering into the corners of the stall.

'I'll give ye eight with you thrown in,' said Tranter.

'That's a fine rate for a decent woman—two shilling.' She found the belt and tugged it around her waist, pulling for the hook.

'Will ye?'

'I will not, but you can always try,' said Blod. 'Hand me that shovel and I'll split your skull.'

'I can make it easy, mind—the long haul or the short one —you or Merve. They're not fussed on the turn-out up the line: just as you like.'

'What are ye after, man—a woman or a dram?' Blod faced him, her hands on her hips. She did not want trouble with Tranter. She was starting the way she intended to go on. Soon Merve would be back with the empty dram, for he was on the short haul. It usually happened like this with the new women; she had heard the others talking. It was happening all the time, and often she thought it was astonishing that it did not happen more—men and women working together in the hot confined spaces of the stalls. Once Tranter got used to her it would be all right, and she needed the money, she thought. Also, if it got too bad she could shout for the overman, and he would give him Ned bloody Tranter, for that was one thing this particular overman wouldn't stand for.

Tranter spat on the line and made a face at her. 'Right, you—the long haul and five shillings—take your pick.'

'It's cheap at the price,' said Blod, and spat on the line, too.

With Tranter cutting like a demon, Blod was filling Number Two as Merve came back with his empty dram.

'Right, woman—out of here,' shouted Tranter, gasping. Never had he cut a dram-full so quickly, and he held a grudging admiration for the woman who had filled for him.

'Shall I shackle you up, Mrs. Goldie?' cried Merve, running up. Blod smiled, for he had got trews on.

'I'm shackled,' said Blod. 'And don't tell Randy—I'm on doors, remember.'

'She's good,' shouted Tranter. 'Give her a start.' and Merve knelt behind the dram and levered it with a mandrel as Blod hooked up the towing-chain to her belt, and heaved. Kneeling now, with the chain between her legs, she grunted, and the dram moved up the incline, for here the stall drifted up an inch a yard.

'And again so!' yelled Tranter, and came off the gob and flung his weight against the dram stock. Straining, on all fours, Blod Irish hauled; slowly the coal-dram followed, its heap spilling off as it touched the roof.

'You filled her high, Mr. Tranter,' said Merve.

'Ay, lad—on this stall we thin 'em down, eh, Blod Goldie—left on the turn-out, remember—on the long haul!'

'Hallo, Mrs. Goldie,' said May Harries as she opened the ventilation door to let her through. 'I thought you was on doors, Mrs. Goldie?' She held her doll against the rock as the mare went by.

'So did I,' said Blod.

Wesley's *Heathland* beat out the Methodist, over the large and small, the well-dressed, the ragged the fed, hungry, hypocritical and holy: up in the front row was Petheric, the Cornish agent, and what is that fella doing in Welsh Calvinistic, asked Sun: Miss Thrush, with the coarse hassock pricking through her red stockinged knees, knelt beside Gideon, and moved her lace-frilled wrist an inch for the touch of his homespun sleeve. Mr. Duck Evans, reliving the lash of the house of correction, winced and shuddered while Mrs. Duck smoothed and consoled him. Sid Blump came in and sat beside Sun and she saw with horror that he only possessed thumbs. They flooded in from Black Pins and Dynefor, Aberdare Top and Hafod where the old Brychan died, he who was sired by Anlach the Irish king who brought Christianity to South Wales; they poured into the pews from Dyllas Colliery and the quarries of Pennant, the rock which built Cyfarthfa Ironworks, and from the towering carn of firestone which built the Castle.

They shouldered in from the squat slums of *China* and the ornate little houses of the agents, washed and polished, and they took their seats in the Big Calvinistic and sat with stony faces in the pews of varnished silence while the melody smothered them. And Morgan Howells sat in the Big Seat facing them; with six deacons either side; fearsome in black, he returned their stare.

Deacons who were drunkards, hucksters who were saints stood shoulder to shoulder and raised their faces to the timbers and there burst from them the hymn:

> *Worship, honour, glory, blessing,*
> *Lord, we offer to Thy Name;*
> *Young and old, their praise expressing,*
> *Join Thy goodness to proclaim!*

Colliers, iron-miners, hauliers and puddlers, and the men of a dozen trades in iron: Welsh, Irish and Spaniards from the tumbling cottages of Sulleri with their swarthy wives and dark-skinned children, all swelled their chests and roared their praises in a great harmony of soprano, contralto, soaring tenor and bass, with the children piping treble. And the shout of concord rose above the chapel, soaring above the narrow streets and into the grimy attics where the burned-out colliers of Lefal and Tasker lay; into the swimming cellars of the old, the refuse of the great town: Megsie Lloyd lying beneath the five-foot ceiling of the Crown as far down as Swan Street, she heard it, and shifted, fevered, in the bed. Many heard it who did not hear it, such as those of the Catholic faith. From every corner of the biggest town in Wales there arose the sounds of worship; from the pews of the Baptist up near Fishpond, Bethel Independent and Bethania up in Georgetown, Zoar and Ynysgau, the Adulum Independent and Zion and Ebenezer there came the shout of praise, a harmony that rose above the squalid slums, and dominant above it all was the great melody of Boyce, the beloved *Sharon* of Osler, a doxology coming from six hundred throats, and a thousand more in the cottages around, for family on family was singing:

As the saints in heaven adore Thee,
We would bow before Thy throne;
As Thine angels serve before Thee,
So on earth Thy will be done.

Blind Dick was singing, shaving blind in the window, Shoni Melody was singing the counter descant, flat on his back in his attic in the Star, bare toes wriggling at the end of the blanket: Mamie Goldie was singing, too, dollying the sheets of the Reverend Evan Evans, and mostly out of tune; the night-shift colliers coming from Pit Tasker and the old Abercanaid, the furnacemen around the glowing bases of Cyfarthfa and Ynys were singing amid the clanging of the ladles: bowed in black and fragile, old Iolo Morgan-Rees was praying on the cobbles of Bridge Street. In the Aunty Popi Davey lodgings Molly Caulara was telling her beads, and Old Wag, in her doorway facing the Castle Inn, was knitting to the beat of it, her coal-scarred face leering at the winter sun. Merthyr, for the crucifixion that was hers, was giving praise amid the cradle song that had given birth to Merthyr—the shrilling of whistles, the roaring songs of the drunks and wailing of the beggars, the thunder of the furnaces and the hissing of the molten iron. And Dic Penderyn, raising his face from the hymnal, saw that the eyes of the Reverend Morgan Howells were fixed upon him, and in them he saw the threat. Dic glanced at his sister beside him; she was singing with her face turned up, her eyes closed, oblivious to anything but the glory of her God: but Sun nudged his elbow.

'You see Morgan watching ye, Dic?'

He nodded, returning the minister's owl-like stare.

Kneel and pray, stand and sing, and up into the pulpit went the minister. Dust motes crowded in a sunbeam from a window: Morgan Howells cried:

'May the Lord hear this prayer: let mercy and truth not forsake thee; bind them about thy neck, my people, and write them upon the table of thy hearts, so listen, you.' Gripping the brass-bound book, he cried: 'Today there will be no sermon, for we have a business among the deacons, and the anger shall engulf you. On one matter only will I address you, and I pray to the One Who hearest all that my words shall not lie in the stony ground: "while men slept, his enemy came and sowed tares among the wheat, and went his way..." Matthew 13:25. And the tares have grown high and consumed the wheat ... you hear me?'

His voice rang out, battering off the faded walls, and he shouted, his fist high. 'Neither sermon nor an earthly directive shall you have, but the Word alone, and this shall suffice you; this shall command you before I speak in the name of the head deacon of the Calvanistic Methodist, which is the true faith, and I read from the book of God, Isaiah 59, also 56, so hear this,' and he read, with a fist high: ' "Behold, the Lord's hand is not shortened, that it cannot save; neither his ear heavy, that it cannot hear. But your iniquities have separated between you and your God, and your sins have hid his face from you, that he will not hear." ' His voice rose to a shout:

' "Yea, they are greedy dogs that can never have enough ... and they all look to their own way, every one for his gain from his quarter. Come ye, say they, I will fetch wine, and we will fill ourselves with strong drink; and tomorrow shall be as this day, and much more abundant!" ' He brought down his fist on the pulpit. 'This is the cry of the new Unionists, this is the dogma of the "never have enough". On all sides there is sprung up in the land the banners of the ungodly who oppose the will of those whom God has granted domination over us. Their baying is heard on every street corner, in every inn and tavern where the drink is strong, in every cottage that lacks a bible. From all corners come the lackeys of the new order who propose force; the effeminate ones like Twiss have come down from Ruabon to preach sedition in your hearts, and to these evil men you have turned your ears. Illegal benefit clubs are the springboards of these outlawed Unions, and to these new associations you are paying your pennies in the name of a promised freedom that is the freedom of the gaoler. Illegal oaths are being sworn against the majesty of the King, illegal plans are being made for the overthrow of the legal Government. . . ! Now stand and confess—all Unionists here!'

Up in the gallery a woman was sobbing: Gwen wept, her face lowered from Dic's accusing stare. He said, pushing away Sun's restraining hand: 'You knew about this? You knew?'

'I did not know.'

'You fool,' whispered Sun. 'Of course she did not know! Leave her!'

Men were murmuring in growing anger, the deacons shifting uncomfortably in the Big Seat, children being hushed into silence by astonished mothers. And all heads swung as Gideon rose at the back: Miss Thrush raised a hand to her face. Bringing out his book of membership, the head deacon cried:

'So, we have the first to confess. Your name, please.'

'Gideon Davies.' Gideon felt his way along the row and reached the aisle.

The congregation turned in its seat, in disbelief. The head deacon cried:

'Your name is not familiar. Are you a member of this chapel, properly listed?'

'Head Deacon,' said Gideon, 'I am not a member.'

'Then why stand you?'

'In the name of God.'

The muted voices grew in sound.

'Silence!' Morgan Howells got to his feet. To Gideon he said: 'You affront the name of God, man? Stand to confess or stay silent. You defy the principles for which this house stands.'

'I stand in defiance of those who betray those principles,' answered Gideon. 'Was this house built to defend the rights of master, but not servant?'

'How dare you!'

'I dare because I protest in the name of dignity, Morgan Howells. . . !'

'You will take your place—you will sit, fellow!'

'I shall not sit until I have challenged this injustice, and nor is there any man in here who will remove me. You speak of the scriptures, you quote from the Book, Isaiah fifty-nine, but how do you stand if I quote you fifty-seven?'

206

Morgan Howells drew himself up in starched anger; the head deacon tugged at his sleeve but he shook the hand away: his face glowed and his eyes shone at the prospect of a fight; he shouted:

'So, we have at last exposed the godhead of the evil about us, eh? The nests are flushed, the serpents rise. How dare you defy me when you sustain greed, and I sustain love? When I stand in the light of God and you in the shadow of the devil? Eh? All right, all right, then let me meet you on this ground. "The righteous perisheth," says fifty-seven, but shall I quote you fifty-eight? Does not this define my duty? "Cry aloud, spare not: lift up thy voice like a trumpet, and show the people their transgressions . . ."'

Gideon, smiling, replied: 'Indeed, the works of God are marvellous, but nothing so wonderful as the interpretations of his self-appointed disciples. Is it not also your duty to cry aloud the transgressions of the masters of this town. The people fast, and you do not see; they are afflicted in their souls, and you take no knowledge.'

'I once met a drunkard who knew his bible,' said Morgan Howells, blandly.

'And I a minister of the Church who beat his wife.'

'If you speak slander, fellow, it is of your own Church clergy, I vow: I charge all present to take little heed of it, the criticisms have been ours since the Reformation.'

Even Gideon joined in the laughter. 'Indeed,' continued Howells, 'if you still have complaint on this particular ground I suggest you lay it before your Ecclesiastical Commissioners, since we Nonconformists stopped beating our wives about the time of the divorce.' Unsmiling, Howells plucked his fingers deep in his beard while the laughter and applause beat about him.

Gideon replied: 'Your denigration is correct. The church runs on a system of rank where the bishops plunder the parsons and the parsons plunder the people, with the assent of King and State.'

'Beware your tongue, blind man.'

'Let the sedition stand, if it be sedition, and not Truth.

Because of a system where God was a politician, I took off the cloth that once I wore and considered taking yours . . .'

'I doubt we had a gown to fit you?'

'The heresy did not fit me, neither the hypocrisy, Minister, for I witnessed a casting-out. Not a hundred men of political reasons, but of a child who stood in labour—they watched her beaten through the chapel door with bibles and sticks, in defiance of John chapter eight . . .'

'You contest our laws, yet you are not of us—be silent!'

'I contend that your interpretation of your laws are wrong! Pervert the laws of your God if you will, but leave us the laws of Man. Make nonsense of the thing you call religion but stand aside from the rules by which we live, or these pews will be empty.'

'I command you to leave this house!'

'It is not Nonconformity; it is witchcraft, it is mumbo-jumbo, man.'

And as the deacons leaped up and the tumult grew in the congregation, Gideon shouted: 'Stand, then—stand all who are members of the new Union! Stand, too, all members of the benefit clubs, the Oddfellows and Ivorites—stand, men, and be counted!'

'If they stand they will be cast out!' roared Howells, fist shaking.

'Better than to sit with a crooked conscience in this house of the masters, for it is no longer the house of God.' Gideon felt his way to the door. 'Stand, stand and leave this place!'

And they rose in the pews; first Dic Penderyn and Lewis Lewis, who was at the front, then Randy Goldie, Wil Goff and Joseph Harries, the father of May who worked the Cwmglo doors. Ned Tranter stood, and Sid Blump, though he did not know why he was standing. John Hughes stood, he who had fought at Waterloo and later died in agony before the muskets of the redcoats: the man Hopkin also rose, though his woman pulled at him, saying she would give him hell when she got him home, and the customers of Jump Jackson rose with him, led by the man with the burned face. Belcher and Curly Hayloft got up, though they were not Calvinists, for many had

208

come that day in challenge to Morgan Howells, who was doing what had been done in a chapel at Tredegar. Tom Llewellyn, the respected Cyfarthfa puddler, took the aisle with Abod of Penydarren, who was a Baptist. Many stood who were not even Unionists, but who felt compelled by the courage of those who were: and they thronged the aisles amid shouts and accusations from the deacons while Morgan Howells stood white-faced, and trembling.

'Take their names! Take their names!' and the deacons put their arms across the door and listed every man who passed through. Some went with their wives, who also stood in protest: many, grey-faced and near to tears, left wives who were fuming in the pews, or silent—shamed in the eyes of God. In the street Dic said:

'She knew! Gwen knew! That was why she invited us!'

'Don't be a fool,' said Sun, 'she did not know.'

She took his arm. Empty, unspeaking, they went back home to Ynys.

It was the weekend Dusty Wilkins died of the fever and came to life again, which was right and proper, said Mamie, for we don't usually die of the cholera in January. Quiffed up and polished was Dusty, with the lads from the Cwmglo pit filing past his coffin sniffing and weeping, and up sat Dusty looking around him and what the hell is happening, and you couldn't see colliers for dust. Hopping off the trestles in the front room he went down Bridge Street as bare as an egg, nothing on him but the boiled shirt front flapping and shouting blue murder, and everybody thought him a clay-cold corpse. And they were fanning them and patting the backs of their hands all the way up Glebeland, for the chapels were turning out; Mrs. Stinkin Shenkins, hard at it in labour up by Fishpond Number Three, saw him rise at speed past her window, and she had an assisted delivery, and Sid Blump, coming out of Miners' took a header into the canal.

Blod Irish, however, died in January, but that was because they didn't really know the date, said Billa.

'We was never sure, see?' explained Randy. 'My Blod was queer in that respect—could have been three months away, might have been six...'

'A month or two don't make that much difference, son,' said Mamie.

'Don't you blame me,' cried the overman at the Head. 'D'you think I'd have had her tubbing the heavies if I'd known she was six months gone?'

'Yes,' said Billa.

'Don't talk daft!' Lancashire pits, this one, with a fist on him for stunning mules, and Randy had him a minute after he came up with Blod following on the stretcher board: down he went with blood on his mouth and it took four colliers to heave Randy off.

'They'll blacklist you, mind,' said a collier, 'striking the overman.'

'Oh, Blod,' said Randy, 'oh, my poor little Blod . . .'

'What's happening here?' asked the agent, coming up in his trap, and they stood sullenly, the whole shift, staring down at the body of Randy's wife. Tethering the pony the agent stepped down on to the cinders.

'She birthed at the face,' said one.

'What was she on?'

'Dram-hauling.'

'How far was she gone?'

'Could have been six months,' said Mamie, sobbing, 'could have been four.'

The men moved their feet uncertainly as Randy rocked Blod in his arms and none moved to take her away from him.

'Six or four, make up your mind, woman,' said the agent.

'My Randy don't know.'

'We will have to know it for the inquest. Where was she?' Pert and quick, he turned to the overman.

'Heading Eight, stall one.'

'That were a long haul on a heavy,' said a collier.

'Nobody asked her to haul, remember—she signed herself on.'

'Her man was off, they needed the money, and she was feeding for two,' said Billa Jam with Amos in her arms.

'Randy wasn't eating proper, you see,' said Mamie.

A collier said at the winter sun, 'That Eight-One is nigh two hundred yards in, remember . . .'

'Who was she dramming for?'

'Ned Tranter by here.'

The agent turned. 'Did she complain?'

The collier Tranter said: 'Not a word, sir—she was as strong as a horse. My boy was hurt so she stood in for him.'

Randy was still rocking her, kissing her face; her skirts, from waist to hem, were sodden with blood.

'Where did you find her?' asked the agent, and out with a notebook, official.

'I didn't find her,' said Tranter. 'My Number Two dram was coming up empty, and young Merve Jam got blocked on the line.'

'Where is he?'

'Here, sir,' said Merve.

He was in tatters and smudged with coal, his face impish but streaked with tears.

'How long have you been down Cwmglo, boy?'

'Two months, sir.'

'And you were hauling a second dram for Mr. Tranter.'

'Ay, sir. My mam says . . .'

'And you had taken a dram down to the turn-out and were coming back with it?'

'Ay, sir.'

'And you found this woman's dram blocking the rails?'

'Her name is Mrs. Goldie,' said Mamie, raising her face.

'Where was the woman?'

'She was sitting on the rail, sir.'

'Did she speak?'

'Ay. She said to run down to the stall and fetch Mr. Tranter, sir. She said she had cut her leg, sir.'

'And you fetched Mr. Tranter?'

'Straight away, sir, but when we found her she was dead.'

'The child was half born,' said Billa Jam.

'Did you see to her?'

Mamie said, 'I went down. I saw to her.'

The agent was writing.

Mamie said: 'But she had bled to death before I got there.'

'The cause of death will be established by the surgeon in due course.' Pencil poised, he said: 'What was her name again?'

Randy laid Blod back on the cinders and climbed slowly to his feet. 'You bastard,' he said, 'you bloody bastard!'

212

'Now, now, stop that!'

Tranter was nearest and quick, despite his size, and he got Randy coming in, the other colliers tripped and held him, and in their grip he began to cry, which was best for him, thank God, said Mamie, and they took him into Number Five with the kids, not Number Seven with Dic Penderyn's missus, for she was in there knitting a bellyband for Blod's new baby, which is pretty daft, you stop to think of it, said Sun, since I should be knitting for myself.

'It's a queer old life, though,' said Dic later. 'Blod Goldie, aged seventeen, kicks the bucket and old Dusty Wilkins, nearly seventy, comes back to life.'

'It's the way it goes,' said Sun, and wondered if she ought to tell him about the baby. She decided against it.

'One thing, it has got a couple of Billa's kids into school,' said Dic.

Sun knitted on in the lamplight and the fire was dying in the grate.

'The agent came to see them—Randy was a Benefit member: they're putting up the twopence a week for Billa's Amos and Asa to start with Miss Williams the School next week,' added Dic, looking over *The Cambrian*.

'The Benefit's wasting its time,' said Sun.

Dic said: 'Will you tell me why we plot and plan for a Benefit if the folks won't take the benefits they're offered?'

'Food she wants, says Billa, not education.'

'If we get education we'll have the food, woman. Can't she see that?'

'Billa's only concerned with bellies. Besides, the fairies will have 'em.'

'The what?' he lowered the newspaper.

'When they go to school they have to write their names on paper, don't they?'

'Ay.'

'Right, then—Billa says it's dangerous, and I agree with her.'

'Dangerous?' He removed his pipe, staring.

'Just the same in Ireland, and I agree with her. Bad fairies

213

read those names on paper and God knows what might happen.'

'You don't believe that rubbish?' He was on his feet now.

'Rubbish or not, I've seen it happen. You remember that Bron Babbie who used to live near you in Chinatown? The whole family wiped out. They was as happy as little fleas till her Olwen started school—and Madoc paying, mind. A week after that kid wrote her name on school papers nothing went right.' She knitted on; in, over, through, off; one plain, one purl, her mouth pursed, as if she had said nothing. 'Them's sods, those fairies.'

'Good God,' said Dic, 'heaven forbid that we have any if ye think like that.'

Sun did not reply but smiled in her stomach: her skin these days, she had noticed, possessed a new sheen and beauty, though it could have been imaginaion. Hooking his coat over his shoulders he went to the door: the barges were sailing past the window and the heaped coal was rimed with frost; breath from the horses spurted like smoke in the still, winter air. Sun shivered and pulled her shawl closer about her.

'You off out again?'

'Got a meeting at the Wellington.'

'That Lewis Lewis fella again?'

'Now, don't start all that, for Christ's sake!'

'Ale and Lewis Lewis will lead you to the devil, Dic.'

'So we sit down here and whine!'

'We sit down by here and save what money we can till things get better. You can swill your belly and shout your politics all the time we got money in the house, but what will ye do if they lay you off?'

For answer he spun up a shilling and snatched it in the air. 'Now's the time for Benefits and politics, girl—I'm laid off.'

She saw the dim lights of the Iron Bridge as he opened the door, and got up, dropping the knitting. 'You ... you what?'

'Got laid off Number Two this morning.'

'But you said it was shift-break.'

'Ay. Now I'm saying I'm off. The hauls have stopped to Vaynor.'

Sun raised the tips of her fingers to her face. 'Oh, Jesus!'

'Same as Wil Goff and John Hughes, Luke Pearson, Tom Williams—and he's got six—the Jones brothers and Phelps—all out.'

'And all Union men.'

'It makes no odds.' He looked out on to the misted terrace. 'They say Crawshay's blowing out—if he blows out Ynys, too, everybody will be off, Union or not.'

'But you could get down Cwmglo?'

'Not till they get some safety regulations—not that slaughterhouse.'

'It was good enough for Blod.'

'That's why she's dead,' he said, and went out, slamming the door.

Sun sat down and started knitting again. She would go up and see Gid Davies, she thought: Gid would know what to do. There might be work down Cwmglo getting coal, of course, but she did not want Dic down Cwmglo where week after week the stretchers were coming up. She knitted violently, thinking that it was a scandal. The town was in rags in the depth of winter because of over stock-piling by the masters, yet coal was being called for from abroad and they couldn't see the value of it. Dic was right, she reflected: now was the time to turn to coal—Gid Davies was always shouting this at the meetings. The Cyfarthfa collieries mainly served the iron-works, and, since there was no big profit in them, the coal inspector would not spend money on them, and the safety regulations were almost criminal. Years later, in the first big Gethin explosion forty-nine men were to die and about a hundred and fifty were injured: later still, because ventilation was inadequate, there was a second explosion when thirty were killed and twenty injured. Cwmglo was a pig, Sun re-flected, because of the parsimonious policy; it was legs and arms off because they were skimping the pit funds: rising, she went to the mantle and opened the tea caddy. Carefully, she counted the money; it was two pounds fifteen and eightpence.

She was frightened. In town the day before, five were found dead of exposure and starvation, and they were always fishing out dead Irish from the cellars of *China* and Pontstorehouse. She wondered how the Crawshays could sleep in their beds, but there was one thing about this lot, she thought—they had made their own money. Not so Anthony Bacon of an earlier Merthyr: according to Gid Davies, Bacon had built Merthyr on money from the slave trade: places like Pontypool and Blaenafon, built by money of the big London merchants, had been built on blood: Tredegar and Risca, Aberman and even the great Dowlais whose gigantic slag mountain was reflecting on the kitchen window as she stood there—even Dowlais of the iron Guest was a monument to the vicious Bristol traders who had made their fortunes catching blacks in Africa and shipping them to the American plantations. This, she reflected vaguely, was what Gid Davies always called the 'purity of profit motive'—a motive based on greed. Standing there watching the barges go by in the frost Sun rubbed her face. It was words, words, words, talk, talk and more bloody talk. On one hand the workers were drinking themselves silly in the beer-houses: up the street the parsons and ministers were on their knees in the name of God, and up in Dowlais the masters were living like princes while the towns were full of vagrants and beggars: it didn't make sense to her. All she knew was that Blod Irish, Randy's girl, had miscarried while dram-hauling and that Dic had gone up to Jackson's Bridge for a meeting at the Wellington. Standing there at the window she held her stomach, wondering if she should try to get rid of it. Nobody knew, after all. If things got worse she wouldn't be able to feed it. Perhaps, she reflected, Madoc Williams had been right to kill his four, though it were a pity about that Olwen, for she was a beautiful little kid. They had sent him into the mad-house, she thought, yet perhaps he wasn't as mad as they made out ... One thing she knew, they weren't getting her down Cwmglo: nor Dic—he wasn't going down Cwmglo Pit. She'd see this new one dead first.

A faint tap came on her door, and Sun turned.

Mamie appeared, her face pale, and she was shivering in her shawl.

'Come and see Randy,' she whispered. 'You got a minute, girl?'

'What's wrong?'

'Don't know. He just sits. Can't get him to talk...'

'Ay, wait a bit, then.'

Bending, she put some slack on the fire. Mamie said. 'You ... you could always raise him a smile, Sun. He just stares. Mind, it'll be better when we can get our Blod up to Adulum. The house is at odds with her cold upstairs.'

Sun tightened her shawl around her face.

'Step easy on the ice, girl,' said Mamie. She caught Sun's arm and stared at her with red-rimmed eyes. 'Oh, God,' she said.

'Hush, Mamie.'

'Things would have been all right, see, if they hadn't loved for a baby.'

'Things will still be all right, you see.'

'Like you and your Dic. Got to be cool with a man at a time like this, Sun.'

'Ay.'

'You watch your fella, then.'

It had begun to snow again, painting up Sun's hair, and her eyes glowed at Mamie from the pale beauty of her face, reminding her of Blod when she was living down in Taibach with Mrs. Halloran. Mamie said:

'She was a good little piece, that Blod, ye know.'

'Yes, Mamie.'

'Billa was always on to me, but I loved her, ye know?'

'Of course.'

'I ... I was a bit hard wi' her at first, but that's natural, like. After they was married I treated her like as a daughter, you remember?'

'Ay.'

Mamie gripped the door of the back, suddenly weeping.

'Don't take on so,' said Sun.

217

'I was a damn pig to her. One time I give her nothing but grunts.'

'All that's over, Mamie. Shall we go in now?'

Mamie raised her face. 'She would still be here now if it weren't for that baby. People like us can't afford babies at a time like this, ye know.'

'I'll remember,' said Sun.

They turned to footsteps. Lemuel Samuel, late of the Shop, Taibach, came from the darkness, and in his hand were some winter flowers.

' 'Evening, Mamie Goldie,' said he.

'Why, Lemuel Samuel!' Mamie peered into the rags.

'Just come to pay respects, Mrs. Goldie.' He gave her the periwinkles and snowdrops.

'But come in, man—you're perished, Mr. Samuel, come on in.'

'No thanks. Best to have his own people about him at a time like this; Randy, I mean.' His face was pinched and blue with cold.

'It was kind of you,' said Mamie, simply.

Lemuel sighed. 'Don't miss 'em till they go, do we?' He nodded at the flowers. 'I picked that lot up on the Beacons. Time was I could afford decent flowers—I started on my own, ye know?'

'Ay, we heard...'

'Bloody dog ate the letters—ate the orders as fast as they arrived. Very easy, it is, to fail in business. Did six months in Monmouth for debt—you hear that? I hate dogs now—blutty great woofin' things.'

'Ay.'

The wind of Ynys blustered between them, parting them; Mamie shivered.

'Best you go in, Mamie,' said Sun.

Lemuel said: 'I picked them special for Randy, them flowers. Give them to him from me and my Mavis. She died the same way. I was a sod to my Mavis, Mamie Goldie.'

They stared in the uncertainty of grief. He continued: 'All she wanted was an assisted delivery—cost half a crown, but I wanted it free . . . I wanted everything free, you see?'

There was sleet in the wind. Mamie put the flowers against her face, shivering more. Sun said quietly: 'Goodbye, Lemuel Samuel. Will you take sixpence from me?'

They stood listening to his footsteps echoing down Bridgefield.

'You there, Molly Caulara?'

Molly sat on the end of her bed in the Aunty Popi Davey and listened to the navvies and sale-coal colliers hitting it up in the Iron Bridge public just opposite, and the rumble of the carts on the cobbles outside. Earlier, walking the frosted streets she had eaten at the Quaker soup-urn down Bridge Street, and unless St. Peter's got a high hat on and dressed in Quaker black when I get to the golden gate that's one entrance they can keep, said she. Once, when young in County Mao, she had watched a child spit in the face of the Holy Virgin for a bowl of Protestant soup, and watched her father die in the corner of their cabin because he would not turn his coat, and saw her uncle eat because he did. But the Quaker of Bridge Street only smiled from the bearded gentleness of his face and the gaunt woman beside him filled the steaming bowl.

'Eat, child, eat.'

'You there, Molly Caulara?' called Shoni Crydd. 'I've got me sixpence, mind.'

'God bless you, woman,' she heard the Quaker say as she wandered away up the Taff to the Aunty Popi lodgings. And on the way she saw Dic Penderyn come out of Number Seven Ynysfach; face low in his collar, up to his elbows in his trews was Dic, and his brow like thunder. Vaguely, she had wondered how his life was going with that little Sun woman he had married; vaguely, too, she remembered a summer day and the laughing romp of the haystack up on the Brecon road.

' 'Evening, Dico.'

'Hello, Molly.' He made to move on, but she delayed him with a glance.

'How are ye doing?'

'Not so bad.' With a flourish he gave her one of his pamphlets.

'Are you still on heavy with the Benefits and the Unions?'

He raised his face to hers. 'Somebody has to be.' He waved a cynical hand. 'All this old lot's fit for is begging on their knees. You don't kneel and beg from masters like these, you up and take. The only language they understand is the wrong end of a gun.'

'They'll lead you to hell, you know.' She tightened the shawl about her face and he smiled at her pale beauty. She continued: 'People like that big Pole Zimmerman are chock full o' the gab, but you won't see them for dust when the Military come out. And they'll have you—pastin' up the *Twopenny Trash*.'

'It's the chance we take—look at the place. The town's in rags, half the folks here are starving. You heard about Blod Irish.'

'Ay.' She narrowed her eyes to the wind. 'It were a pity, that—a good little soul was that Blod Irish; how's her Randy doing?'

He wiped his mouth with the back of his hand. 'The man's demented; just sits and stares...' He looked at the sky. 'God alive, what a country.'

'The country's all right, fella, it's the people.' She smiled, touching his arm, and the touch brought her to a sudden warmth. 'Some are lucky—you got a good filly, they tell me.'

He grinned wide. 'Ay, Sun's all right.'

'A jaunty piece, and pretty. But then, you could always pick 'em. Is she with childer?'

'God forbid,' he said.

'Keep her clear o' the childer, Dico—you'm a hot man, but keep her clear till the times get better:'

The wind whistled in from the Taff and the moon beamed over Sulleri where the criss-cross roofs slanted amid a crazy hotchpotch of gables and chimneys; the night bayed with cold,

221

the frost flashed along the fozen road.

'Got to go,' said Dic.

'Ay. Take it slow, Dico—Merthyr's an expert in death.'

'Sufferin' saints,' he said, taking her off. 'You're a happy soul.'

'Just take it slow, especial with the politics. Things'll get better quick when spring comes in and the rate of iron rises ...'

'God's blood, woman!' He turned, glaring at her. 'You're as bad as the rest of them, and I gave you credit for sense. When the rates of iron rise, is it? Are our bellies dependent on the rates of iron when Crawshay sits up there with gold in his bloody castle?'

'He's ... he's got to keep going,' said Molly. 'You rook him now and he'll go bankrupt, and the town will starve. I'm telling ye, Dic ...'

'Christ! When will you people learn?' He flung back to her. 'How the hell did he get the first half million—did he pick it off trees? No—he got it from us, his workers, and now we're wanting some of it back. All right, the world rates of iron are down, but that's not the workers' fault—can't you see that, woman? It's because Crawshay and Guest don't know their business—the fools overstocked. That's what Zimmerman says and he's right. And if they made their piles when times were good they should share it out now times are bad.' His voice rose. 'But mark me, things are changing, and you'll watch them jump. The Union is coming—Gideon says this, and he is right. This is only the beginning. All over the country the Lodges will rise, and branches form in every works. We are only hundreds now, but soon we'll be thousands, even millions —and we'll put a bargain on our labour that will make these buggers dance. The first thing we'll demand is increases ...'

Molly laughed gaily. 'Increases, ye say? Don't be daft, fella!'

'Ay, increases, for we want a share of the profits—God alive, these masters make enough! Yes, it will come—perhaps not in our time, says Zimmerman—nor our children's, but it will come and swamp the country. By God, we'll wring the pockets of these employers! As Zimmerman says—we must cleanse it all, and start again . . .'

'You'm a hot bugger, mind, Dic Penderyn,' said Molly. 'Old Wag reckons she's got a witch fancy about you, so watch out—says you'll dance on a rope.'

'They'll have to move. . . .! Got more suspicions than teeth, that one.'

They smiled at each other: there arose within her a small frenzy of love for him, and she fought it down.

'Good luck now,' she said, and walked away.

And she went back to her Popi Davey lodgings and sat on the bed.

'I've paid me shilling to Old Wag, and I've got your six-pence here, Molly Caulara,' said Shoni Crydd, and he closed and bolted the door.

Raked from the summer kisses of Dic Penderyn, she raised her head.

In the beery, blinkered gasps, the bed of rags, the yorked trews, buckled belt and riot baton of the gigantic Shoni Crydd, special constable, she saw on the stained ceiling a pattern of leaves in June sun: in the bearded scourge, the calloused hands, the floundering monstrosity of a thing called love, she remembered the laughter of that summer loving in a haystack up the Brecon road.

'Aw, to hell, girl, don't start that!' said Shoni Crydd. 'Now, what you crying for, Molly Caulara?'

They were collecting the rents outside the Aunty Popi Davey as well as inside, where Molly Caulara was paying hers. Mr. Steffan Shenkins, beadle in service to Mr. Coffin of the Court of Requests, was in attendance; it being necessary to remove the effects if the rents were not forthcoming, and a very distressing business it can be, mind, turning out folks in the middle of February.

' 'Evening, Miss Thrush,' said Mr. Steffan Shenkins, deacon of the Big Ebenezer, and do not mix me up with that drunken coot of a brother of mine, Mr. Stinkin Shenkins, for we are as different as chalk to cheese.

'Good evening, Mr. Shenkins.' Amid her shelves of jars

223

stood she, shawled and mittened, and her cheeks were full and bitten red with frost. 'Four and sixpence, is it?'

'If you please, Miss Thrush, for the lower premises only.' Out with his little black book then, licking a stub of pencil. 'Are the other occupants available, Ma'am?'

'The other occupants are here,' announced Mrs. Bach Taibach, her arm around Willie. 'One and sixpence for the room above, Mr. Steffan Shenkins.'

'But there are two rooms above, Mrs. Taibach.'

'Only one occupied by me and my son,' replied she, and called up the stairs, 'Mr. Note, the rent man, if you please.'

'Oh, Mam!' whispered Willie.

Mr. Note shambled down the stairs and drooped before the beadle, his face low. With his rags hanging on his shanks and shoulders, he drooped.

'Music don't pay in Merthyr, do it?' said Mrs. Taibach, and Percy Bottom Note raised his head at this, saying:

'The people of Merthyr are very musical, Mr. Beadle.'

'But not prepared to pay for instruction, are they, Mr. Note?' said Mrs. Taibach.

'But you cannot buy music with money, Mr. Beadle,' and Mr. Note smiled.

'I will pay for the room,' said Miss Thrush, fishing in her purse.

Mr. Note straightened. 'Indeed you will not, Miss Thrush.'

They stood together, silenced on the frosted boards.

'It seems we 'ave come to an impasse, so to speak,' and Mr. Steffan Shenkins awkwardly shifted his feet. 'Now, if you was Ebenezer ...'

'I am of no religion, sir,' said Percy Bottom Note.

'Then ... then are there any possessions? As you know, the court is most considerate ... one and sixpence is not a large sum, and ...'

'There are no possessions, Mr. Beadle.'

'Oh, but there is,' interjected Mrs. Bach Taibach. 'There's a silk-faced harmonium upstairs, made in Swansea in 1776.'

'Oh, Mam!' whispered Willie.

'It is not a possession, sir,' said Mr. Note, 'it is a harmonium.'

'Nevertheless of value, you agree?' said Mr. Steffan Shenkins warmly. 'I'm sure Mr. Coffin himself would treat it respectable. Indeed, I heard talk that the deacons up in Adulum are in need of a harmonium...'

'Please let me pay, Mr. Note,' said Milly Thrush.

'Then would you care to vacate...?' asked Mr. Shenkins.

'Yes, indeed, Mr. Beadle.'

At the door Percy Bottom Note bowed to Miss Thrush, saying: 'You have dignity and warmth, Miss Thrush, even in February.'

Hands deep in his pockets he mooched into the snowing street.

It was starlight on Dowlais Top.

Even the cats were in down the deserted streets of Aberpennar ... around the unborn town of Maerdy, later called Little Moscow, the snow was thinner, though the grass was shivering at being out all night: along the lonely, desecrated little valleys the warmest place was down the pit, and the *tylwyth teg* were skating on the ice of the Afan playing *Touch me Last*. Black and deserted were the streets of Taibach; the sheds and smelters of the English Copper Works were empty, the furnaces blown out down Mill Yard Row where Mrs. Halloran lives. Plump as a wheat-pigeon was Mrs. Halloran once, said Blod Irish who lodged there earlier, but now gone to a shadow because of the drop in prices. It is the economics that do beat us, mind, said Mrs. Halloran—when once you've got copper you're bound to 'ave the economics, like the agent said. But I'm quite happy, said Mrs. Halloran, for I've still got the rent. As I always say, love, you can empty the larder, they can cut off the coal, they can take the furniture, they can empty your stomach—nothing matters if you still have the roof. That Mamie Goldie—bless her, too, and I wonder how she's doing up in that Merthyr—she used to say the same: whatever they take, girl, your victuals or your virginity—ye got to keep the slates. It'll be a lot better, though, when we get the workhouse: that's what the agent says. You simply can't have copper without the economics.

'That you, Mr. Halloran?' she called.

With her back against the wall she sat; the moon over Dinas Woods shafted the empty room. Like a sack of coal propped up in a corner she sat, wife to Big Mike Halloran who once smelted for the English Copper in the Taibach casting-house: with her white hair down over her shoulders and a shilling held up between finger and thumb, she waited.

Footsteps echoed on the cobbles outside. She cried:

'That you, my lovely? Dinner's in the oven, Mike. Ach, wash yourself after, fella—you look weary to death.'

Never smelled of ale, mind—not like some I could mention —that Dai End-On, for instance, and that horrid Mr. Jam. Neither hops nor spirit passed his lips—don't hold with it, my Mike used to say. A good day's work for a fair day's pay, that's what he reckoned; big man, mind—topped six foot four: used to knit bed-socks special for him—they was always through the rails.

The door opened and the moon came in, bowing first.

'That you, Mike?'

'It is only me, Mrs. Halloran.'

'Why, it's Mr. Henry Chalk, the school-master! Come you in!'

'Rent collecting spare time, Mrs. Halloran. You got the rent?'

He stood as a blackboard blotting out the moon, his face chalk white, his mittened fingers making rabbits on the moon-lit wall, and he stooped over her, his easel legs astride her in the corner, his eyes flickering red in the etched shadows of his cheeks.

'Ay, I've got nothin' else,' said she, 'but I've got the rent—a shilling?'

'Are you all right, Mrs. Halloran?'

Bright and perky was her face. 'Right as rain, man—waiting for my Mike.'

Still at a stoop, Mr. Chalk wrote with a shivering hand:

'Mill Yard Row. Number Eleven. Mrs. M. Halloran. One shilling.'

And he took the shilling from her frozen fingers.

'I tell you she spoke, she spoke to me!' sobbed Mr. Chalk later.

'Don't be ridiculous,' said the coroner. 'According to medical evidence she'd been dead for a week.'

Mr. Steffan Shenkins knocked on the door of Number One, Ynys: it was opened by Miss Blossom Thomas, daughter to Papa Tomo Thomas who had been in bed over five years with the rheumatics, and I think it's a damned scandal, said Billa Jam; all over the country there's women like her taking care of the old 'uns when they should be sparking with the young 'uns, it's a waste of good human sport.

'She looks pretty fruitful to me,' observed Mamie.

'Courted and lost, so they say,' replied Billa, shaking out the smalls. 'Now all she's left with is Papa and rheumatics.'

'Good morning, Mr. Shenkins,' said Blossom Thomas, curtseying.

'Good morning, Miss Thomas; the rent, if you please?' He adjusted his spectacles and opened his book.

'I am sorry,' said Miss Thomas.

'So am I,' said Mr. Shenkins.

'D'ye want any help down there, woman?' shouted Mamie, her head out of the back of Number Five, and in crackers. 'Shall we pop up and see to him?'

'No, thank you,' said Miss Thomas, 'I can manage.'

'Who is it down there?' shouted Papa Tomo upstairs in bed.

'It's the Church of England parson,' called his daughter.

'Oh, ay? Well, tell him we're Baptist. And it's no good him patting the bloody dog for he only speaks Welsh.' He sang then, a bawdy sea-shanty of his youth, and the men of Ynysfach cocked their ears to listen. Mr. Steffan Shenkins said:

'It is now five weeks, Miss Thomas, and that is eight and ninepence. You have a framed picture of a deer pursued by hounds, I understand.'

'I have a water-colour of a mother feeding her baby,' said Miss Thomas.

'Ah, yes, I have mixed up the addresses: Miss Grieve, for-

227

tunately, will accept either. I will give it to the court collector, Miss Thomas—you will have a chance to redeem it if it is not auctioned by the end of the month.'

'As long as it pays the rent, Mr. Beadle.'

Mr. Shenkins ticked off her name in his book. 'Please fetch it. I will endeavour to persuade Miss Grieve to forfeit eight and ninepence, but she may prove unwilling, you understand?'

'I understand. Thank you, Mr. Shenkins. If I wrap it will you keep it private, Mr. Shenkins?'

'Of course.'

Strangely, he bowed to her before she closed the door.

'You can bugger off out of here for we've paid the rent,' said Mamie, as the gambo and rent cortège went by, and Billa Jam took the opportunity to empty her bucket of suds which sent the bubbles up the beadle's gaiters.

'Dear me,' said Mamie, her hand to her throat. 'Don't tell me they're in trouble in Number Seven...'

But on the door of Number Seven, Ynys, the beadle knocked.

Sun smoothed down her apron and patted her hair, which was now to her shoulders and tied with black ribbon. She opened the door.

'Mrs. Penderyn, I am sorry to have to inform you...' began Mr. Steffan Shenkins.

'Yes, yes. But for God's sake take what you want before he gets back...'

'She's entitled to the bed and the table, remember,' said Mamie Goldie, leaning around the door.

After saying that she went back to Number Five, led Billa and the children after her and shut and bolted the door. And all down Ynysfach the people went inside and bolted the doors and drew the curtains while the Penderyn furniture was carried out to the Court of Requests, for debt.

One thing about the the folks of Merthyr, they can say goodbye to most things, but they are beggars for keeping their pride, said Mamie Goldie.

SPRING came in over the mountains bright and hot and the snows melted on the great Vans Rocks of the Beacons, and the land grew warm under a kinder sun. All over The Top from Abergavenny to Taibach the ice began to melt in rushing streams that began in trickles and grew into cascading torrents of ice-white water. In the glow of spring the land brightened, new tints grew on the trees of Cyfarthfa Park and the black, frozen streets of Merthyr were rutted with slush. As if at a signal of life reborn, the doors of the cottages opened, windows were flung wide to the warm air coming down the valley and a new chatter began: the whole kaleidoscope of sound and colour of the greatest iron town in the world burst anew over the streets in a rainbow of April showers and warmth. The streets were crammed with new immigrants, gay were the colours of the incoming broughams and traps of the gentry. As if at the end of a long hibernation sleep the aged workers of a lost generation tottered out on to the pavements; dutiful wives and daughters placed the kitchen chairs outside the fronts and backs for champing granchers and toothless grans: mufflered children danced the hopscotch down the chalked flags or trailed in viper snakes of lost hope to the penny a week private schools where they were not allowed to speak Welsh by order of England.

But a new hope and urgency was in the air: the whispers of Reform began in the tap-rooms and grew into a buffetting demand in every Lodge and benefit club. Political agitators were everywhere on The Top: tub-thumping in the Square off High, raising platforms outside Ynysgau and fists and banners down Graham and Duke. The Chartists met in the Three Horseshoes and discussed it; the new Unionists, meeting in defiance of the law, paraded their banners around the town led by fife and whistle bands and yelled aloud their songs of glory, Reform or Die with Lord Russell's Bill: the leaders of the new revolution ranted on the street corners their fierce denouncements of Church and State and the new ideology of pie in the sky. And the Church's leaders met the challenge head-on. Pulpit was thumped in verbal reprisals; with beard-trembling indignation the established servants of the Big Seats from the Welsh Wesleyan to Ebenezer opposed Reform in the name of God and the starving poor who would always be with them. This belief was confirmed by a new rush of famished immigrants from Ireland, wandering in from Bristol and the ports of Gower. Bare-footed and in rags, they ate their way like a locust swarm into the hills of Merthyr, went down on their knees in the mud of High Street and begged before the stalls where the groceries were spilling, till beaten away by the special constables. They offered their children for sale before the broughams of Penydarren and their daughters for prostitution before the Castle of Cyfarthfa, and the agents seized them. Turning away all but the fittest, they housed these in the cottages of the evicted Welsh and signed them on at cut rates. A rush of foreigners who were prepared to work for a jug of ale now swarmed into Merthyr and Dowlais and fought at the gates of the Alderman Thompson Works. And this was the new bargaining power of the capitalists who now joined in the shouts for Reform. For them it was a new banner to fly in the faces of the landed aristocracy; the great houses of Beaufort and Tredegar who had never accepted as equals these self-made princes of wealth. So the iron masters flouted their riches before this gentility; drove to church with coaches and fours and liveried postillions, gave banquets for the marriages of their sons and daughters and lavished dowries that vied with eastern potentates: blaming the old aristocratic influences and the heredity system for confining the rights of the working classes. And the new ferment of the working classes, the new demands for democratic ideals at a time of an eight hundred million pound national debt, was projected by the industrialists as a direct result of a corrupt parliamentary system that threatened the sacred rights of capital and property. With a new slogan of Freedom, Justice and Equality the masters moved to the sides of their workers and thundered the cry for a Bill of Reform, blaming the new shopocracy and the old aristocracy for the plight of trade. And Crawshay, foremost in this fight for Reform, nominated a candidate to represent the people in the forthcoming May elections for Brecon. A new leader had appeared on the horizon of the workers' distress and they roamed the streets of Merthyr and Dowlais in torchlight processions, proclaiming that all who opposed Reform should be hanged on the gallows, stoning the houses of the Tories, burning in effigy prominent people who stood in opposition. Crawshay, the new hero of the oppressed, was eulogised and toasted in the name of Reform. His iron-stone miners cheered him in the streets.

He then cut their wages by twenty per cent.

Dic Penderyn came through the door of Number Seven, Ynysfach just as Shoni Crydd, the special constable attending the court beadle, was coming through it with two kitchen chairs, and Crydd went one way and the chairs another.

'What the hell is happening here?'

Sun said quietly: 'They have come for the second time.'

'I paid the rent!'

Mr. Steffan Shenkins said, consulting his book: 'You last paid it on the third of December; eighteen shillings is owing and the Court of Requests is confiscating your furniture both in this sum and a bill for twenty-two and fivepence claimed by Mr. Andrew Marsden, shopkeeper of Merthyr.'

'Oh, my God!'

'That's what I said,' remarked Sun, 'but you still went on swillin' ale with your fine new friend Johns up at the Lewis Lewis Benefit.'

'What are you taking?'

'Two chairs, the blankets received from Mr. Marsden, draper, the chest of drawers from the bedroom, the clock, and

231

the tub and dolly from the kitchen.'

'Take them and get out, it's cheap at the price.'

'And I am to inform you that the court will auction same articles in repayment of the debts unless redeemed within a fortnight from this date.'

'No chance of that,' said Sun, 'the way he's going you'll have the rest of it within the next fortnight.'

'You get inside, you noisy bitch.'

The beadle added: 'Further, Mr. Penderyn, if you lay hands on a constable of the law again, I will have you put in charge.'

'Don't worry,' said Shoni Crydd, brushing himself down. 'One day I will have him for it—me and Mr. Abbott, the barber—and personal.'

Sun slammed the door behind them; empty, they wandered about.

'Now perhaps you're satisfied,' she said, and went to the window. Distantly, she could see the court gambo lumbering over the bridge.

'I'm not breaking my heart over a few sticks of furniture, girl.'

She swung to him, furious. 'But I am! Will you tell me what else I've got? Night after night I'm sitting in here while you're up at the Oddfellows taking the oath—swilling your stomach with Jump beer and spouting your damned politics.' She held her stomach, staring up into his face. 'We've got a baby comin', or don't ye realise it? Nigh two months you've been off—the iron's still coming out—why aren't you working?'

'Because I'm laid off—you just said so!'

'Ay, and for why? Because of the politics. For all his shouting of reforming this and that, Crawshay don't stand for the tub-thumpers, and you know it!'

'Ach, don't talk stupid! Rowlands and Andrews were laid off, too, and they're both Tories—the politics are nothing to do with it.'

'Then are ye getting another job?' He turned away from her wrath but she gripped him and swung him to face her. 'God

232

alive, time was I thought you'd make something of yourself—
even Gid Davies said so. Now all you're fit for is kicking up
the sawdust and laying on the cocks. From the moment you set
eyes on that good-for-nothing Lewis Lewis you've been going
to the devil, and me with you.'

'We've got to have the meetings... !'

'Ay, you've got to have the meetings, I grant ye that. But do
you have to float 'em off on beer? Have ye any money, for
instance, for there's not a bite of bread in the house.'

He laid three shillings on the table and she snatched it up.

'Benefit money?'

'It's as good as any other.'

'It won't be if the parish knows you're drawing it. Dic,
Dic ...!' She clung to him. 'Don't you realise the state we're
in?'

'It will change soon,' he said. 'By God, it will change
soon...'

'And who'll be doing that? You fellas are all the same.
There's young Randy gone off and Mamie's half demented.
Every man in Ynys is roaming the streets and shouting the
politics, but where does it land us women? There's Mrs.
Tranter with six kids to feed and her chap tub-thumping down
Bridge and every agent in town booking down his name.
Cwmglo and Tasker and Lefal are on short time—at Tasker
alone all but three colliers are on parish relief...'

'Aw, stick to your kitchen!' He pushed himself away.
'D'you think I don't know? According to Gid Davies and
Zim, Crawshay's going to sack near ninety puddlers—that'll
be the end of us—and there's good men getting out while the
going's good...'

She shouted, following him round the room, 'And can you
tell me why he's sacking the puddlers? Can the fella do anything right? Look, see sense—would Crawshay be laying off
puddlers if he could afford to keep 'em...?'

'He's laying them off because the trade is down!'

'Of course—can you blame him? Would he be cutting his
own throat if there was profit in keeping them on? You say the
fellas are going—of course—the tradesmen are getting out,

233

and Crawshay knows it. Would he be losing good puddlers to Beaufort and Tredegar...?'

'Oh, woman, shut it!'

'Ay, I will when I've had my say, for I'm not finished.' She pointed to the window. 'There's jobs going out there for hauliers and miners, and there's good men taking them. When anything goes wrong it's poor bloody Crawshay but it's never *you*—isn't it true that Fothergill's paying his colliers five shillings less than William Crawshay.'

'Ay, and we're seeing to that.' He roamed the room, thumping his fist into his hand.

'You're seeing to it, eh? That's a good one!' She laughed, her head back. 'And what will you do when you get there—blow him out? Where will that land the sale-coal people of Aberdare? All ye can think of is blowing people out and marching on this and that—you're not human, man—ye all belong to the jungle!'

'The jungle is the only thing they understand!'

'So you're fighting for it now?'

'Ay, if needs be.'

'Then God help ye all, for the Brecon garrison will cut you to pieces. In heaven's name!' She stared at him. 'Don't you realise that? Don't you understand that they'll bring in the Military? You've got that Tom Llewellyn dancing down the streets shouting about Reform, there's this Twiss fella you're always talking about twisting ye round his finger—but I've told you before—you'll not see the backside of one of them when the guns come out. Look—even Crawshay's backing you on the Bill of Reform—what else do you people want?'

'I've had enough of this, I'm getting out!'

She ran to the door and spread her arms across it. 'But you're not. You're not leaving here till you promise me you're done with that Benefit.' She thumped herself with her fist. 'I've a young 'un in here and I need food. I'm nigh seven months away and I'm having it decent, in by here, not out in the gutter on the parish.'

'We'll have changed things before you have that,' he said quietly.

His tone stilled her. Gasping, she faced him over the bare room. A man stumbled past the window, his hobnailed boots rattling on the cobbles but they did not hear him. A barge glided past with sale-coal for Abercynon, but they did not see it. Sun said, staring at him.

'You're fighting for it, then?'

'Ay, we're having the Request Court down for a start.'

'And then?' She clutched her shawl against her throat.

'Then a go for decent wages.'

'Is Gid Davies in this?'

'Gid Davies stands for a charter, and the Union . . .'

'Mr. Zimmerman?'

'Zimmerman stands for a fight, and he's right. Davies is wrong.'

She whispered, her face pale, 'So you're in with them, then. It's people like Zimmerman and Lewis Lewis and Cobbett's Trash from now, is it?'

He approached the door. 'It is the only way.'

'They'll cut you to pieces.'

'So be it. We're standing it no longer.'

She smiled. 'And this is what ye call Reform? You just go out and take.'

He said evenly: 'We've got London and Manchester people down with us now. We've got the backing of Morgan Williams and Zephaniah of Nantyglo: Cobbett pamphlets are coming in. Lord Russell's Reform Bill won't get through without a fight, and it will take somebody bigger than Crawshay who is only after the protection of property, he doesn't give a damn for the Reform. We beat the shopkeeper Stephens and Bruce the magistrate when they took Tom Llewellyn . . .'

'You call that justice? You broke the windows and threatened an innocent man—you were lucky to keep out of prison—that was the rule of a mob.'

'But we beat them; if the rule of the mob will change things, then it's that rule from now on, says Zimmerman.'

'God in heaven, ye must all be touched.' Raising a hand Sun wiped her sweating face. 'If ye go now, Dic, I won't be here when you come back.'

'I'm getting a shift-job with Lewis Lewis, hauling the timber over in Penderyn—Lewis knows people; he's well in with the Bodwigiad gentry, and he spoke for me.'

'If Lewis Lewis spoke for you I know you're bound for the devil.' The Great Hammer began to crash from Cyfarthfa.

He approached her and she drew herself up. Momentarily, he pitied her shapelessness, the black droop of her shawl, the way her dress lifted in the front, showing her legs. Yet, despite the pallor of her face there was in her eyes a brightness and beauty he had never seen before: vaguely, he wondered if she was about to cry, having lost most of the furniture now ... He remembered then that he had never seen her cry.

'Got to go, Sun,' he said.

She did not reply. A foot the shorter she just gripped her dress and stared up at him.

'But soon I'll be back, and bring you money for the ...' He touched her dress and she moved away, still staring.

'Not Lewis Lewis, Dic,' she said then. 'He'll bring ye to trouble. There's other jobs ye can get—even the parish, breaking on the road, but ... not Lewis Lewis.'

Bending, he kissed her face. 'Goodbye.'

When he had gone Sun leaned against the door and bowed her head.

And Mamie Goldie, standing by the window of Number Five watched him striding up the towpath towards Jackson's.

'And we think we've got trouble,' said Mamie. 'With Blod dead and gone and Randy God knows where ... bless my soul, here's Gid Davies coming ...'

'He'll collect an outing if he goes to Number Seven,' said Billa, stitching, 'for all he's the wonderful Gid Davies. Come away from that window, Mamie, it anna decent watching.'

'You reckon he's calling on Sun?'

'More'n likely.' Billa rose, drawing her away. 'Ye'll get a cold in your eye, woman—come away, now,' and she drew the curtains.

Tap tap on the door, and Mamie was up instantly, flinging the door open.

236

Gideon removed his hat.

'Number Five, is it? I am seeking Mamie Goldie.'

Mamie beamed. 'And you've found her, Gid, lad—come you in, and welcome.'

He sought her hand and the old warmth of friendship leaped between them.

'I've found Randy,' he said simply. 'I was up at Adulum with flowers for Jobina, and I found him with Blod, sitting by the grave.'

Mamie swallowed, her hand to her throat. Then she smiled.

'I'll come up and get him, Gid,' she said.

After Mamie had left for Zimmerman's up in Cross Street, Billa Jam said: 'Can you spare a moment for me, Mr. Davies?'

He nodded, smiling, and she fetched him a chair that faced the window where the light was on his face and she could see him properly.

'We're doing all right, Mamie and me,' said Billa.

'I'm glad.'

'We're ... we're doing fine, really—got plenty of washing despite the times—got plenty of kids about—you heard about my Adam, of course?'

'Yes, I am sorry.'

'And my two lads Merve and Saul, the twins—Saul's starting down Lefal day after tomorrow?'

'They are both a little young for the pit, Mrs. Jam. I was wondering...'

'My pa was down when he was six, and these are gone nine—they eat like mules and we need the money.'

'I see.' Gideon twisted his fingers in his lap. They blamed the masters for the early starts, but half the time it was the working classes. Education was the root of it all, of course. Education, he reflected, looking up at the light, was the only lever that could prise these people out of the vicious habits of years. Education ... If only Crawshay would open a school—a little one for a start—even a penny a week ...

Billa said: 'You remember the three Irish lads who used to

lodge at my place in Taibach?'

'Mike, Tim and Joe? Of course.'

'Well, they're moving into Merthyr next week, and they need two extra drams. Good workers, mind, and fine lads, and they're lodging in by here with us. You remember Mike in particular?'

'The big handsome one, according to Mamie.' Gideon smiled reflectively.

'The one that is sweet on me,' said Billa.

'I ... I didn't know that, Mrs. Jam.' He raised his face.

'You do now.'

He was at a disadvantage, and knew it: women say much with their eyes.

She sighed and wandered the room. 'Don't know much about women, do ye?'

He sat and she walked about and he cursed his blindness. She said as from a distance. 'Disgusting, isn't it—me with ten kids.'

Searching for his pipe he filled and lit it, staring blindly through the smoke. 'You ... you want Mr. Jam back is that it?'

Her feet scurried over the floor and she was on her knees beside him. 'Oh God, Mr. Davies, oh God, I want my Mr. Jam...' She gripped his hands momentarily, then got up again, saying calmly, 'It ... it's for the kids mainly, ye see. Don't ... don't get me wrong, Mr. Davies, it ... it's nothing to do with ... with having a man around, if you get me. Just that it's bad for the kids having no pa, and ...'

'I seem to remember that he came once,' said Gideon.

She did not reply, and he added; 'They tell me he's off the bottle, too.'

'That right?'

'So they tell me. Even goes to chapel—Taibach, they say.'

'Good God, he's taken the oath.' She added: 'Will you ... will you mention it?'

'I'm due down there in a week—of course I'll mention it.'

'He can please himself, of course. I mean, I don't much care

238

if he comes or not—you realise that? It's just that...'

'I understand.'

'And don't mention it to Mamie, will ye, Gid Davies?'

Smiling, he lit the pipe again, shaking his head: a gang of colliers off shift from Cwmglo crowded past the window in good-natured banter and oaths.

'I've always kept myself to myself, ye see,' said Billa.

'That's how it should be.'

'That's what I mean. Thank you, Mr. Davies.' She opened the door. 'Goodbye, Mr. Davies.'

Despite the smoking furnaces of Ynys the spring air seemed suddenly sweet and clean.

When Gideon reached Zimmerman's house in Cross Street he saw Mamie Goldie standing outside, knowing her only by shape, for the sun was bright.

'Haven't you been in yet, then?' he asked.

'Ay, and just coming out, for he's sleeping. The big foreigner said not to wake him ... sleeping like a baby, he is.'

'He'll need good care when you get him back to Number Five, Mamie.'

She said, with a catch in her throat: 'Even while I were standing there he was calling for Blod...'

'It will pass. He is young, and time heals...'

'Gid...' Mamie touched his hand. 'Do you ever get down Taibach these days?'

Gideon lit his pipe, trying not to smile. 'Not often.'

'Never get news of that good-for-nothing Dai of mine?'

'Sometimes I hear a mention.'

'Wouldn't ever have him back, mind—wouldn't give him house room. It's just that I'd like to know how he's getting on, ye see.' She caught his arm. 'Don't seem right to cast him off, as it were—especially if he happens to be in trouble.'

'Trouble?' He was not going to make it easy: according to Dai End-On even spare parts of the mangle had been thrown... Mamie said then:

'Well, ye never know, ye see. Anything could happen—he

239

might even be dead.'

'If he is dead he is beyond assistance.'

Annie Hewers hurried past with averted eyes; people bask-eted and shoved on their way to the market; the hucksters were already quarrelling about the price of the stalls, the boozies searching out the taverns.

Gideon said: 'I'll do my best, Mamie, but I can't promise anything. But if I do bring Dai back I hope there won't be any violence.'

'Violence? Good God—what do ye take me for?'

'Well, last time Dai and Billy came . . .'

'Ay, I know. Well, I'll speak to Billa Jam—sometimes she's not herself, as ye know. She do tend to take the law into her own 'ands, so to speak, but I'll vouch for her.'

'That's generous of you, Mamie.'

'Granted. And I'd be inclined not to mention this . . . this suggestion, if ye understand.'

The sun sworded down over Merthyr, lighting the faces of the cramming, chattering people; ragged urchins were looking for pockets in the crowds and diving under the bellies of the passing drays, for the ale was coming in from Hopkins' Brew-ery.

'I will be the soul of discretion,' said Gideon.

She peered up into his face. 'By the way—you heard about Sun and Dic?'

Gideon was instantly attentive, and Mamie continued: 'Got their furniture restrained again.'

'What!'

'Not an hour ago—Coffin's Court.'

'Did the beadle have a warrant for the distraint?'

'Search me,' said Mamie, 'ye know Steffan Shenkins—he just come up again and took.'

'But I didn't even know Dic Penderyn was off.'

'Ay—weeks—puddler's labourer down at Ynys, and haul-ing. Sun reckons it's because he's marching with them Lodges and things.'

Gideon was already moving away, and at that moment Zimmerman put his head out of Number Eighteen, and called:

'Ah, you have not gone, Mrs. Goldie. Come, your son is awake.'

Sun was standing at the door of her cottage when Gideon approached.

The old yearning for him moved in her again, blinding what should have been anger, and the child moved within her, too, as if stirred from sleep by the emotion.

'You come for me, Gid?'

'Sun!'

Reaching for his hand she drew him within the kitchen, and Mrs. Zeke Solomon in Number Four fell off the chair in the bedroom window and hit her head on the door and what the hell you doing standing on chairs at your age, anyway, said Zeke when he came back from the synagogue after instruction and observances.

'She's always standing on that chair,' said Billa. 'Next time I see her on it I am coming up there and blutty hit her off.'

'Better than the parish register, she is,' said Mamie. 'The very idea—counting up the groceries in the shopping baskets. You know she shaves, don't ye, Billa?' All down the Row the doors were coming open.

'She don't!'

'As sure as me eye—saw her lathering and shaving, didn't I?' she shouted up at the window.

'Oh, Mrs. Goldie ... please, Mrs. Goldie...' protested Mrs. Zeke Solomon.

'Right you, then down off that chair or it's going round the neighbourhood.'

'Who's in there now, then?' asked Billa, interested.

'The blind man—Mr. Gideon Davies, the blind man...' replied Mrs. Solomon.

'Not you—you hop off out of it,' said Billa and softly closed the door.

Gideon said, in Sun's kitchen, 'Mamie has just told me ... the Beadle has been here?'

241

'Why you worrying about me, then?' asked Sun.

'Because I feel responsible.'

'Don't you feel responsible for me, boyo, I can take care of myself.'

'Of course.'

The table was between them. Gideon said: 'May ... may I sit down.'

'Ay, on the floor—they've taken the chairs.'

'I am sorry, Sun.'

'You're sorry—that's a good one. What about me?' She patted her stomach. 'I've got this lot due soon and the fella who put it there is tipping his elbow and shouting about Reform.'

'It's the price we pay for freedom.' He remembered the colour of her hair.

'Freedom, eh? Och, you lot are nothing but hot air. My God, the women of this world would eat a fine stew if we depended on agitators. Before people like you and Twiss and Zimmerman got going my Dic was all right!' She walked about in pent anger. 'We were settling fine, with the baby coming, and all that—you can live in this town, ye know—Crawshay don't eat people alive, for all the slander ye give him!'

'But we need Reform, Sun—even the masters see that. We merely propose ...'

She swung to him. 'Ye propose? Ye propose damn all, ye only bloody talk. Were you at that Lodge meeting up at Tafern Uchaf, Penderyn, when he met Lewis Lewis, the haulier chap?'

'Yes.' Unaccountably, he remembered the road from Taibach, and her nearness.

'Well, it handed down from that night—he came home breathing fire and hops and Lewis Lewis on the brain: the agent heard of it and laid him off, and he hasn't been the same chap since. Oh, God!' She began to cry and he felt his way around the room and held her: the bulge of her carrying was against his loins and she shook with sobs and her tears were wet on his hands.

'Come now, Sun, Sun!' Her nearness was bringing an emotion in him.

'Eh, I wish I was dead!'

'Don't say that.' His throat was dry and he clenched his hands.

'I wish I was back wi' Billy Ugmore!'

'And don't say that, either.'

She raised her face to his, thankful for his blindness. 'I do, I do. *Ow* ... I wish I was back with Billy Ugmore, for life were straight with him!'

'Hush, Sun, the neighbours will hear.' He held her and the child moved against him with a kick, as if in vehement protestation. She wept in tuneless sounds and wetness and there was no dignity in it; presently, she ceased.

'There now,' he said.

'There now me eye,' said she, wiping and sniffing. 'You'll go from here and start the same old thing again, and ye won't be happy till the blood is running in Merthyr, will ye?'

'We will not be happy until we get a Bill of Reform,' said Gideon. 'And this generation might have to suffer so the next ones live decently ...'

It angered her. 'Oh, ay? And it's the likes of us that have the furniture taken for debt, eh?' She clenched her fists before him. 'I told Dico and I'm telling you, Gid—you won't see your secret army for dust when the Military come out—they'll be away, away!'

Gideon said: 'You are wrong. In a fight they will discover their importance, and their courage. The Roman slaves were never numbered lest they discovered their strength and knew their power, and so it is with the workers of Merthyr and Dowlais.' He turned to her and she saw in his face a new light. 'Or are we all to wail, like you, over a few sticks of furniture. Is it the women who are going to hold us back in this town when women start rebellions?' She began to speak but he shouted her down. 'If the army of the government is attacked in these streets it will be for the first time in English history,

243

and the Welsh will show the way. Or are ye content to sit down under the injustices, snivelling to your neighbour while they grind you lower and lower? All right—your man drinks —but don't blame him, blame the masters who take his all and toss him a pittance.' He was walking about now, shouting as if addressing an assembly. 'Reform must come and men and women be prepared to die for it—for it is not only the iron towns we are concerned with, but the nation. Do you realise that in Oxfordshire the farm labourers are on one and two-pence a week? That in Lancashire the children are being kicked from sleep by the slubbers of the machines? And six-year-olds coming home with black eyes and broken noses; dying in their sleep? Being torn to pieces when they fall into the machines?' Finding the table he thumped it with his fist. 'D'you know, Mari Penderyn, how you stand in the fight? You carry a child in your belly—will you sit idly by in five years time and watch him go down Cwmglo Slaughterhouse on two shillings a week to give Dic another dram? God alive, woman —you're a mouse in a world of tigers, and that's how the churches, chapels and masters want you—a bloody mouse. But it's not for us, for things are going to change. And if we can't change them by my way—the recognition of the Union and lawful negotiation, then we'll do it Zimmerman's way, by blood.'

Sun said evenly: 'You will hang for it, ye know—they will find a scapegoat and hang him for it: in 1800, under Richard Crawshay they hanged Sam Hill; in 1816, under this Craw-shay's father they hanged Aaron Williams for riot. And under this Crawshay they'll hang another, mark me ...' She closed her eyes, gripping her hands.

Gideon said impatiently: 'They might hang a hundred of us, but what does it matter? Every year hundreds of us die in one way or another—pits and ironworks, child-fevers, the cholera. If a hundred of us were hanged for town drainage and another hundred for a piped water supply the price in death would be cheap, for the slums in this place are worse than the slums of Asia.' He levelled a finger in her direction. 'There's over thirty thousand people in this town and he hasn't provided a single school out of the profits; the accident rate is as bad as any town of The Top, and we don't enjoy even a hospital—there isn't even a stretcher at Ynys Works—did you know that? If Dic roasts his legs down there they'll cart him home on a board...'

Sun watched him: it was a new Gideon, one of violence, far removed from the gentle creature she had known. Feeling his way to the door, he opened it.

'By God, you've changed,' she said.

'And by God there's less in you than I thought. You're not worth a man like Dic Penderyn; you should have stuck to the likes of Billy Ugmore. Heavens above, woman—a few sticks of furniture...'

For a few moments Sun listened to him tapping his way down Ynys towards the canal bridge, then she ran across the room in sudden anger and slammed the door.

Later, when Billa Jam was putting her children to bed in Number Five, Mamie came up the stairs and there was peace in her face.

'Sun Penderyn's got her things back,' she said quietly. 'Gid must have bailed 'em out of the Court.'

'Ay, and you've got your Randy back. Can you tell me what this town would do without Gid Davies?' Billa smiled at the stars appearing over Merthyr.

'I don't know about that,' Mamie said.

Gideon walked slowly back to Cross. He was trying desperately to quell the emotion that threatened to consume him. It was astonishing, he thought, that on the journey from Taibach this girl had hardly impressed him, other than with an ability to lie. Slim and beautiful—in the coach at Gitos Farm on the night of the drovers—she had been in his arms and he had rejected her. Now another man's wife, shapeless with approaching childbirth, her womanhood called to him, and he hated his weakness. Reaching the door of Eighteen Cross he leaned momentarily on the railings, vainly trying to recapture the sounds of her, the smell of her hair; the memory of the time he saw her face after the onslaught of the Cefn Riders brought him to a trembling joy.

The door opened and Zimmerman appeared, concern on his broad face.

'Are you all right, Gideon?' he asked.

Gideon straightened. 'Of course, of course.'

ON Dowlais Top, violated by Sir John Guest who burned out the town, the wind wails among the slag-heaps like an old hag crying for her lost youth. But in summer the air is gentle in *The Fair Place*, which is the ancient name for Waun Hill, and here the parishes once met in the tap-rooms of the old Full Moon, which is as close to the stars as nearby Bedd y Gwyddel, the grave of the Irish Giant. Once the Ancient Britons lived here; near it the Prince of Brycheinog had his palace. Here, but later, walked Lady Charlotte Guest who translated the *Mabinogion*; she whose agent was the magnificent writer G. T. Clark ... Long, long before the creation of Penydarren, the cinder-pit the Homfrays and Thompsons jammed between Merthyr and Dowlais, there dwelt in these parts the gentle Tydfil who was slain on the spot where her church of glory now stands, once a celtic cross. This was the history, before the coming of the Magnificent Greed, that died under the bloodstained streets of Merthyr Parish : this was the Welsh culture that was sacrificed to hoard the millions of Hensol, Cyfarthfa and Caversham Park; that bought the art treasures of Canford Manor, the millionaire home of the Guests in England.

It was on the last day of May that the workers climbed the tracks and defiles from the crazy streets of Dowlais for the annual Waun Fair held up by the old Full Moon and Trecae Farm, and it is a wonder they had the strength, said Gideon, for even Crawshay said in *The Cambrian* that wages in Merthyr were low and that distress was prevalent among his workers.

'Think yourself lucky, girl,' said Dic, folding up the newspaper. 'Last week Jane Brace, aged twenty-seven, wife to Jem Brace of Epping, was sold in the market, pinioned and haltered, for the sum of two and sixpence by the Poor Law master, and he got sixpence interest.'

'Who bought her?' asked Sun, knitting. She closed her eyes to the pain of early labour.

'Doesn't say,' replied Dic, 'but no prosecution was offered by the Crown against her husband, Jem Brace, because it was discovered later that she was living in sin.'

Sun lowered the needles. 'Who with?'

'The fella who bought her,' said Dic, and got up, stretching and yawning.

'Poor little soul,' said Sun, at nothing.

'Ay—had she been a gentry bitch they would have been charged with slavery, rape and living on immoral earnings—but now you know your value—two and sixpence: you still tell me we don't need Reform?'

'I still say it'll lead ye to the devil. God, I'll make ye rub your heels together if I'm proved right—are ye off, then?'

'Ay.' He was standing by the door, grinning, and she thought that save for Gid Davies she had never seen a man as handsome.

'And you're taking Randy—keep him short o' trouble, now. Keep him away from Lewis and that new fella Will Johns.'

'I will, Sun.'

'He's ill, ye know—anything happens and Mamie'll never forgive you.'

Despite the obesity of her shape he thought she was beautiful; there was about her a new radiance now she had got her furniture back, and he was grateful to Gideon Davies. What with one thing and another he wondered how they had ever managed without Gideon Davies. As if reading him, Sun said:

'Have you heard that Dai End-On and Billy Jam are due back next door but one?' The child roamed within her and she gritted her teeth.

'No!'

'They're a pair of gorgeous old twisters—worse than your Union man from Bolton Lodge—when's he coming?'

'According to the Benefit, next October—staying at the Miners'. Talk is that he is meeting Crawshay for discussion.' He lit his pipe and blew out smoke in a cloud. 'Maybe if we get discussion we won't get riots—good fella that Bill Twiss, mind—got a good tongue.'

'Wouldn't trust him as far as I could heave him.'

'You're wrong, Sun—he's a good Union man.'

'So am I. He'll give ye Twiss by the time he's done with ye—you want to keep that bugger up in Bolton with the Authority Lodge.'

'Maybe so, maybe not—one thing's certain—all credit to Crawshay. Everybody's telling me he's set against a workers' Union, and here he is meeting a delegate.'

She said levelly, 'One day you people will realise that you can get a damned sight worse than the Crawshays though everybody's for skinning them. If you'd lived in Derry, like me, you'd have had the knackers off the Irish landlords.' Sweat suddenly beaded her forehead and she wiped it into her hair. She frowned up at him. 'Just you and Randy, is it ...?'

'Well, no,' Dic said uncertainly, 'we're supposed to be meeting Lewis Lewis at the Wellington.'

'More fool you ...' She thought: Please go, for God's sake go ...

'He got me a job hauling in Penderyn, didn't he?'

Sun nodded. 'All right, but keep Randy off the ale—and if you come back stinking of the stuff you won't hear the end of it.'

'*Whoopo!* Blutty hark at it! Goodbye, girl.' He opened the door.

'Aren't ye going to kiss me, then?'

He turned, grinning. 'And me smelling of ale?'

'Before you do,' she said, and put out her arms to him.

'My lovely,' he said.

'Oh, Dic!' she clung to him. The pain bloomed within her. He whispered: 'When you're back to a reasonable shape, I might even make love to ye.'

'That'll knock back your output.'

He looked at her as she smiled up from the chair. 'I'll pray you an easy time—but Mamie will be with you, won't she?'

'Good old Mamie...'

He kissed her again, and what began as a caress ended in heat and strength.

He winked at her as he went through the door, and she lay back in the chair with clenched eyes; never had she known such a pain. It had been on for the last five hours, now it was growing like an explosion within her, and she was glad Dic had gone. Getting out of the chair she went to the wall and knocked three times to Mrs. Solomon. Mamie Goldie came in moments.

'Are ye away, then?' she asked, her head around the door.

Sun stooped over the chair. 'God in heaven,' she said, 'what a pain!'

'Honeysuckle, you've only just started!' Mamie slapped her on the rump calling, 'Billa Jam, you there?'

'What you want?' the reply came faintly.

'Zeke called me—the Penderyn kid's away. Come on, come on...!'

'Can I help any?' asked Mrs. Zeke Solomon, peeping around the door.

'You've done your job—now get up on your stool again.' Mamie stood before Sun, hands on hips, grinning. 'I suppose you didn't happen to mention it to dear little Dico, did ye?'

'No point in spoiling his day,' said Sun.

'God help ye,' cried Billa, coming in with bowls and sheets. 'Eleven times I've been through this palaver, but Billy Jam is having the next one.'

'I told you to hop it!' cried Mamie, pushing Mrs. Solomon through the door. 'It's midwives we're after, not a blutty congregation.'

Just before midday a woman began to shriek in Ynys and the other women of the cottages, with their menfolk either charity-begging along the streets or attending the big meeting up on Waun Hill, paused to listen. The Spanish woman in

250

Number Ten, for instance, sat down in her kitchen and held her stomach, rocking to and fro. Miss Grieve, passing along Bridgefield Terrace in the pony and trap with Mr. Waxey Evans, heard it, too, and stiffened on the seat, her fingers clutched in her bombazine lap.

'You all right, my precious?' asked Waxey.

'Perfectly.'

Miss Blossom Thomas, daughter of Papa Thomas in Number One heard it as she was laying the table for dinner and gripped the cloth till the knuckles of her hands shone white, and when Sun cried again this woman raised her face, smiling, and said, 'Oh, it is wonderful, wonderful!'

'Can't ye stop that Penderyn wife braying?' shouted Papa Tomo Thomas. 'Worse than donkeys, some of the wives round by 'ere.'

'It is her first, it is her first,' said Blossom, with a light in her eyes.

'There there, me little love—give it hell for me,' said Billa, wiping the sweat from Sun's face.

Mrs. Duck Evans looking in the bins around Dynefor heard it, too. Lemuel Samuel standing in Bridge Street with coloured ribbons heard it also, and remembered Mavis who had died in shrieks that could have been bought for half a crown.

It is said that the new bride called Morvenna Doherty, married that very morning of Waun Fair heard it as well, for Sun is excellent in the vocals said Mamie, and right and proper too, for shouting do assist a birth: Ay, asserted Mrs. Zeke Solomon, these noisy labours may assist the brides, but it sets the fellas back on conjugal rights.

Bang bang on the back of Seven Ynysfach when all was silent.

'What you want, Zeke Solomon?' asked Mamie.

'Can I come in, Mrs. Goldie?' asked Zeke around the bedroom door.

'You're in,' said Billa, 'what can we do for ye?'

'You got that baby yet?' Her eyes were rimmed red in the plaster of her face.

Sun was lying on the bed as drained of blood as a corpse.

251

Billa, exhausted, was slumped in a chair surrounded by bowls and rags and buckets. Mamie, standing at the window, was letting down her hair.

'It's a boy,' said Billa, 'though God knows how. Jesus, I've never seen such a birth.'

'She's lucky to be alive,' said Mamie. 'Now goodbye, Zeke Solomon, we've had enough of ye.'

But Mrs. Zeke Solomon was scratching her ear. 'Queer, mind,' said she, 'how she kept on hollering for Gideon Davies. True, he's a friend of the family, but it's queer . . .'

Mamie approached with business. 'You damned old faggot!' cried she. 'You ought to be ashamed o' yourself, making those insinuings—out, *out*!'

Very fast went Mrs. Zeke Solomon.

'The poor little soul,' said Mamie. The question was in her eyes.

'Don't you dare,' said Billa. 'Don't you dare, it ain't no business of ours, remember. She can shout for who she likes.'

Darkness fell on Waun Hill, and the workers gathered. With the fair over the crowd began to mass: they came from Dowlais, the puddlers and miners of Guest whose company truck shop was twenty per cent higher in prices at a time of depressed trade; they came from Merthyr under Crawshay, the iron-stone miners with their wages cut by forty per cent, the discharged puddlers; and they came from the shambles of Penydarren, the Alderman Thompson. But they did not only come from the three great works, but from Aberdare also, and Penderyn, Hirwaun and Abernant. In their thousands they came as if on a signal, arrowing in black snakes across the mountain tracks to the hill where their ancestors, the Iberian and Brythonic Welsh had met for centuries in debate. They came with black flags that signified their distress and white ones lettered with the words 'Reform in Parliament' and these petitioned their hope. And they gathered in a great mass with the falling of dusk, their numbers swelling as the torches sparked and waved, and there grew upon Waun Hill a glow of redness that was not the spilling of the hearths but the glowing fire of discontent that precedes rebellion. Agents were despatched at once by the masters to attend the meeting; spies for the Government finished their night meals and wandered carelessly from the surrounding inns and stared up at Waun Hill, and the hucksters ran. Gathering the spoils of the Fair Day, the smugglers of brandy and the poachers, the stall thieves, picaroons and pickpockets rove their paths through the oncoming workers and dived for the open plains. They blew out furnaces in Gelligaer to come, ragged and dishevelled; straight from pit and drift the labourers and technicians came in streams of ragged fire to the summit of Waun, their torches blazing; thronging into the stuffed tap-room of the old Full Moon, they hammered the teak for ale, or sat on the steps of the Waun Houses, spilling into the shippon of Trecae Farm. And the moon came out and blazed over the crooked streets of the iron towns far below them. John Petherick, the Cornish agent of Penydarren Works was there, Mr. Steffan Shenkins, the beadle of Coffin's Court was there, as was a young captain from Brecon Barracks, dressed as a collier, and these listened, and did not speak. A silence dropped like a curtain over the massed workers as Gideon climbed a rough platform on the highest point of Waun, and threw up his arms.

'Men of Glamorgan, workers of Monmouthshire, do you hear me?'

'Ay!' Oaths and shouts muttered into silence, and Gideon cried:

'We meet this day in the name of Reform, for it is only by Parliamentary Reform will we gain our just rights...'

Ragged shouts of applause and assent arose and the torches waved, and Gideon shouted in Welsh: 'The alternative is violence, and we do not seek violence, although our cause is just. It is a time of depressed trade and our wages are cut. But were our wages raised by Crawshay's forty per cent when times were good and he was selling at nigh six pounds a ton?'

The men roared encouragement, and he shouted: 'The anti-Truck Act of ten years back forbade the company shops, but Guest still keeps a Shop in Dowlais and charges twenty per cent over the odds for food. Did this employer cut his food

253

prices when the iron market was flourishing sixteen years back and a collier's wage was thirty-five shillings, compared with the twenty he gets now?'

The torches flared, and the men jostled for a better view of the speaker as Gideon raised his fist and yelled: 'They tell me Crawshay has eighty thousand tons of iron mine in stock-pile because of the state of the trade—are we to be penalised for bad management, for if this is management then give me anarchy! Must we live and die by the law of supply and demand? If the fortunes of the masters rise on the flourish, then they must expect to pay out in depression to the makers of their wealth, the people.' Gideon had got them going, and he knew it, stooping, his fist swinging within an inch of the nearest face. 'For the difference between masters and men is clear—depression of trade means for them smaller investment: for us it means food off the table and starvation for our families! How say you?'

They leaped to him. From the packed ranks came a great roar of agreement.

'Let him claim that he is stock-piling through generosity, to keep his men employed, and I will abandon the charge of bad management and substitute the claim that this is our entitlement, for if he stock-piled eight hundred thousand tons of iron he could still afford us decent wages and keep the bulk of the Cyfarthfa fortune intact! But more—he has begun to discharge us—were not eighty-four puddlers sent home six days back? Let the reduction of the wages of the iron-stone miners imposed but a week ago come out of the Stock Exchange investments which we have built. Let Cyfarthfa and Hirwaun be run at a loss, supported by the banking houses where these great fortunes lie, and which we have amassed for the Crawshays since the coming of the truly paternal Granfather Richard!'

They flung up their arms to this, stamping their feet on the mountain turf in a drumming like thunder, and Gideon cried: 'Churchman he might have been, ay, and autocratic—and he bowed his head when they hanged Sam Hill, God forgive him, but he was still one of us. And if he didn't open a school in the place like Sara Hopkins did for Blaenafon, at least he gave us a Sunday one for the good of our souls and bought us corn when times were bad. But where is his absentee son this minute? Up in London—we never bloody see him. And all we get from the grandson in Cyfarthfa is "My Eye".'

They shouted with laughter at this, and Gideon cried: 'But "My Eye" doesn't quell us any more, because we are hungry— he admits we're distressed—read your *Cambrian*. But what does he do about it? He stands aside while the Court of Requests takes our furniture for debt. I advise you now—do not accept an abandoned stall except at an advanced rate—we'll teach him to drop wages. And go on parish relief if you can't get cheaper bread ...!'

'Talk sense!' shouted a miner. 'If we go on parish relief they'll send us back to our own parishes, and that will put us on the roads!'

'You've got to keep the roof!' bawled another.

'What happens come winter, me and six childer?'

Gideon yelled back: 'If you all apply for relief you'll break the shopkeepers by putting up the rates—can't ye see that? And if you squeeze their pockets they'll join you for Reform and not oppose you.'

'Don't shout at me about parish relief, man,' called a collier. 'I've had some, and the officers treated me and mine like dirt ... But Crawshay subscribes to support us—be fair!'

'Are ye with us or against us, blind man?'

'Are ye with this?' yelled Abednigo Jones, a fourteen-year-old five-footer as he climbed up behind Gideon with a flag bigger than himself. 'Can ye read, men, or shall I spell it out? Reform in Parliament, Reform in Parliament! And give three cheers for the House of Lords!'

Boos and groans accompanied this, and Zimmerman climbed up, too, and cried: 'Three cheers for the landed flunkies who sit in idleness in their palaces and watch your children starve—do you know the income of your Sailor King, or shall I tell you?'

'Send him back to Poland!' bawled a man.

'Or Moscow with the Tsar!'

'Give him a hearing!' shouted Lewis Lewis, scrambling up. 'For the people in his country are worse off than you!' Magnificent in brawny strength, his presence silenced them. 'Do you know the income of a belted earl, then? D'ye know the price of a bishop? For if you don't, then now's the chance to learn it, for some are getting more by larceny than Crawshay for making decent iron. Listen! The aristocracy of England derived their wealth from the spoils of the Reformation—and do ye know what the Reformation is, even? You don't, do you, because you're not educated. Do you realise that this man here has the facts and figures from the Black Book of Wade—have you heard of that, even—do you know any bloody thing? The salaries and incomes of the Dukes of Northumberland and Buccleugh and the Marquis of Stafford, Zim!'

'A million pounds a year,' said Zimmerman, and he straightened, pushing back his waving, bright hair. 'Foreigner, you call me? But I know more of your masters than you, you fools. In this year of 1831 there are three hundred members of the royal family—think what they cost you! You've got thirteen thousand nobility—though God only knows who made them noble, for they roister and fornicate away their lives—they cost you six million a year. Four hundred thousand gentry come next at fifty-two million, and up in Cardie the parish poor are getting three and sixpence a week for breaking on the roads.'

The crowd did not move; there was no sound save the hissing of the torches. Zimmerman's accent thickened, and he said: 'God alive, you're all half dead! Don't you care what is going on? Do you know that a lord receives the first hundred thousand of his income free of tax? That he pays no postage rate—nor do his recommended friends?' He drew himself up, dominant with his great size. 'If a peer obtains money by false pretences, can you imprison him? You cannot. Neither can you seize his estates for debt or render him bankrupt, for his property, like his person, is inviolate. But you can be sent to the hulks for a sixpenny fraud! He kills game at will, while you can be transported for treading on a partridge egg. You can be sentenced to the treadmill in the House of Correction for leaving your place of work without permission—the peer can roam at will and never work at all, because you are keeping him. In the year ending last January there was a national revenue of fifty-five millions in tax—and nearly four fifths of this came from the industrial classes—*you*! Do you realise your importance, and power? Yet there is a nine hundred per cent tax on tobacco, but ale is cheaper for they want you drugged. Will you hear more, you stupid mules of Welsh, English and Irish, for if you want it I'll shout all night. Are bishops popular here? Are archbishops favoured by the mob? It would appear so, for you have two you do not need. In France they would receive a thousand pounds a year—in Britain you pay them twenty-seven thousand each. You have twenty-four bishops, you blind fools, who are worth six hundred a year each in Paris and over ten thousand pounds a year here. You have appointed twenty-eight deans, sixty archdeacons, three thousand aristocratic dignitaries of the Church and eight thousand incumbents—at a cost of ten millions. While a bishop I know is worth half a million and slept with Lady Hamilton, Nelson's favourite whore . . .'

Wild laughter broke out at this and Zimmerman raised his fist. 'You laugh, you stupid fools, when you should all be in tears: you drink when you should be sober, and you beg when you should demand! Aristocracy by acquirement is theft, and aristocracy by birth is feudal barbarism. You slave away your lives and beat the women who bore you in the temper of the rapacious thieves who rule you! "Receive the Holy Ghost," says the bishop, and then dresses up in riding habit, drinks a stirrup cup and leaps a five-barred gate. How can such a reveller claim the infallibility of the Holy Scriptures?' His voice rose to a cry. 'Listen! The times have passed when the lord is the despot of his domain—merchant prince or aristocrat—to tax, imprison, torture, rob, maltreat. Borough-English and Child-wit—Christ, but how can you know what these mean? —are monstrous usages of the past—the first night with the bride and a tax on women who gave birth without the squire's permission. Yet does not defilement exist in this town? Your furniture is distrained and you squat on your haunches and watch; in Poland, to which you would send me, that Court of Requests would not stand another twenty-four hours. You are to be soon driven to the polls to vote as you are instructed or go on the black list: you live in slums comparable with Asia, you have no hospitals or schools provided; the beauty of your women is being sullied by labour, the growth of your children stunted. The treatment of the parish poor by appointed officers in Merthyr parish is a public scandal and yet you tolerate it—you tolerate anything, because you are a broken people ...!'

'Mind that tongue, foreigner!' yelled a Welsh collier.

'And you your neck!' bawled Zimmerman, 'before I come down there and break it ...'

'You take us to violence and they'll bring the Military in, remember!'

'Then let them come, and use it to prove your manhood if not your nationality, for the Welsh, in my history, have never gone short on a fight. And do not talk to me of violence, my friend, for violence is the profession of good government. From the start of the slave trade until this day theirs has been the law of the whip and bludgeon—their revenge in Tudor times the bloodstained rack and in modern times the art of hanging, drawing and quartering—do you know they're bringing back the Anatomy Bill? Once more the turrets of London Bridge will be littered with the filth of decomposing limbs to satisfy a royal decree.'

'That is sedition,' said a man.

'And it is I who state it! You are the sheep-led tools who fly from the musket when you should be the liberators of a land born to be free! Lewis Lewis!'

'Ay, Zim.'

'Bring the calf.'

It began to rain then, breezing into the faces of the staring crowd; men previously aware, now seemingly hypnotised by Zimmerman's oratory. And the raindrops hissed on the flaring torches so that a drift of steam arose, rising from the white faces as if they were on fire. The mob jostled for better position as Zimmerman took in his hands a new-born calf and raised it high above his head, and he cried in the silence:

'See here this calf which will soon be sacrificed. And in its blood I will wash my hands; I tell you this, if we do not gain our ends by just means, then you will take to violence, and the white flag of Reform that flies here tonight we will stain red, as it was stained in the *Champ de Mars* massacre of forty years ago.'

All was silent then, save for the hissing of the rain and the faint bellowing, in its struggles, of the new-born calf.

And there came from the crowd then one called Tomos Glyn Cothi; bearded and grizzled with age was he and Lewis Lewis and Dic Penderyn helped him up on to the platform and he cried:

'Know me, you of the Welsh? Let us continue the talk in our tongue lest Cornish agents and London spies be among us. Have I not always charged you to fight against those who oppress us—in the name of God? Did I not sing you revolutionary songs from the bars of Carmarthen gaol? Now I say, take care!' He raised his skinny hands upwards and shouted above the growing clamour. 'Have I not, in company with Taliesin Williams preached the gospels of the great Orator Hunt, the advantages of Free Trade, and begged you to spread your activities among the populations of Lancashire, Yorkshire, Staffordshire and the labourers of the Forest of Dean? You who know me can vouch for my true radicalism. Was it not I who distributed to you the Welsh translations of Cobbett's *Twopenny Trash*? And pinned to your streets the placards of the Rotunda Radicals which denounce oppression and the misery of the poor? Men, it is such as I—so hear me—who, with the Unitarians of Heolgerrig and Georgetown, are the true spiritual advisers of the New Movements which hold the seeds of Moral Force Chartism, your only hope of freedom. You hear me?'

'They can hear you in bloody Swansea, man!' shouted one.

'Take him out of the pulpit, somebody!'

'Blutty past it, he is, and he will have us on our knees!'

The old minister shouted while they pulled at his clothes in laughter, 'You are the greatest force of men alive today, because you have a just cause. But is there Truck in Merthyr? There is not, for the master of that town is serving you in his way. Do not be swayed by any force of argument save the *facts*! In the name of God I beg you not to listen to men of violence, for they will use you to their ends and then depart, and your agony will be that of the Cross . . .'

The torches waved and sparkled and there rose about the old man a growing clamour, but this he pierced with his cry, 'I beg you—stay sober and *think*. Do not act while drunk with ale and power, for the iron masters are not your true enemies —the foreigner here is right!' He swung around, pointing into Zimmerman's face. 'Your enemies are not Guest and Crawshay—harsh these might be, think you, but these are your employers . . . and you do not do them justice!'

Bawls and jeers broke about him, but he shouted: 'This is a world slump in trade—would you break their banking houses? Do this, you fools, and you will starve! No, men—your enemies are the hereditary enemies; the pimps and ponces of the great estates and their hundred thousand wrangling lawyers. They patronise a Church Established, wage unnecessary wars, create employment for useless sons in the army and navy, conquer and retain useless colonies for the high office of half-wits in plumed hats, pay unmerited pensions to relatives in useless posts in the royal household, the Admiralty and the courts of law.' His voice rose to a shriek, and they were silenced by his vehemence. 'They live in a profusion of luxury— maintained by those who live in misery—but would you compare William Crawshay with the likes of these? Crawshay *works*! You hear me?—like you, he works. If you want blood then march on London in the bigger scheme, and tear these parasites from high office, but do not cut the tap-roots of your own employment . . .!' His last words faded into silence as men mounted the platform and pulled the old man down, but still he shouted and again they heard him. 'Moral justice will be served only by moral force. Does not your master support the Bill of Reform? Get your reform first, and afterwards bargain for better wages on the boards of a true democracy . . . If this fails, fight then—and fight like tigers!'

Strangely, hearing this voice coming from a mouth unseen, the men grew to quiet again, and Tomos Glyn Cothi sank down on the steps of the platform and wiped his bearded face with the back of his hand, and before him Dic Penderyn knelt in the crush of men.

'Are you all right, old man?'

'Ay.' The minister sighed and stared at the sky and there was in him a beauty, for his eyes were good despite the years.

'Shall I fetch ye a drink, Minister?'

Cothi smiled and put out his hand, touching Dic's face with the tips of his fingers.

'My God,' said Cothi, 'they are bound for the devil. But think of the challenge!' His fingers moved over Dic's features, resting on his lips. 'Just fancy being young at a time like this.'

And about them the mob was growing in anger; oaths and curses broke from the ranks of swaying men and Abednigo Jones, the boy, leaped on to the platform and raised his white flag which shouted for Reform, and he was joined by another lad, one named Willie Taibach who was shrieking at the sky, and together they chanted:

'Reform, Reform, Reform, Reform ...!'

The word was taken up then, bellowed from thousands of throats and ceased only when Lewis Lewis yelled:

'Ay, Reform, Reform, but first the bloody furniture! Who's with me for Coffin's Court?'

'And burn it to the ground!'

'God help them,' said old Tomos Glyn Cothi.

Dic and Gideon helped the old man to his feet and there beat about them a great tumult, and from this disorder Tom Llewellyn, a Cyfarthfa miner, shouted:

'All who oppose Reform should be hanged on the gallows! And I will be the first man to do the hanging, free of expense, you hear me?'

'Ay ay!'

He scrambled on to the platform. 'Who's for a trip to Aberdare to wring the neck of Fothergill, the master? And loot his bloody truck shop—he who has publicly claimed that Crawshay is paying his men too much?'

They brandished their torches and mandrels, and flocked about him madly.

'By God, we'll hang him if he doesn't retract!' He quietened them with a yell of command, a natural leader risen from the ranks. 'Right you—a thousand men with me and we march on Aberdare—there the workers will join us. Lewis—where's Lewis Lewis?'

'By 'ere, Tom, lad!'

'Tomorrow lead the rest of them and burn Coffin's Court!'

They began to chant, swayed by his vehemence: 'Coffin's Court! Coffin's Court! Coffin's Court!'

And they streamed down the mountainside, with the Llewellyn contingent making west in a red stream for Aberdare. The night grew to quiet. At the platform Gideon pulled Zimmerman aside from a clutch of men.

'It went well,' said he, 'but it was not what I intended—neither is it what the London Association intended. Old Tomos Cothi is right, it is much too early—soon it will become uncontrollable.'

Zimmerman lit his pipe in his cupped hands. 'It is quite excellent.'

Gideon stared in his blindness. 'But they will riot—you have driven them into riot—don't you care what happens to these people?'

'Not particularly,' said Zimmerman.

'Coffin's Court! Coffin's Court!'

The chant thundered in the streets, and people came spilling out of their houses and throwing up the windows to the growing mob.

'What is happening, Blossom?' demanded Papa Tomo Thomas of One Ynys, and he sat up in bed. 'What the blutty hell is happening?'

'God save us!' cried she, tottering, 'it is a riot.'

'If it's a riot then I'm in it—what are they rioting for?'

'God knows!' cried Blossom, quivering. 'God knows!'

He eased himself out of bed. 'Fetch me the crutches, woman, and pull yourself together—heaven preserve me from the apron politicians.' He poked a stick through the window. 'Right you, lads, slow down, I'm coming!'

The sun bathed the June morning in precious smells of agents' simmering bacon. William Crawshay paused at his breakfast in Cyfarthfa Castle and turned his head, listening: Merve Jam opened great dark eyes at the stained ceiling in Number Five; the Spanish woman in the Row was already up, sharpening a knife on the copper. And down the alleys of Georgetown and Williamstown came the miners and colliers, the ladlers and puddlers and ballers, the washerwomen and coal-croppers.

They were spilling over the doorsteps down by St. Tydfil's, banging on pails up Duke and kicking tin cans down Graham, and the mob grew. Led by Lewis Lewis they came in a wave up Bridge Street and met the crowds from Jackson's and Quarry head on.

'What is that, Annie?' asked Megsie Lloyd in the bed in the cellar of the Crown, and Annie Hewers sat closer and wiped the blood from her mouth.

'It is nothing, it is nothing. You are dreaming, my lovely.'

Down Tramroadside came the rabble waving brooms and copper-sticks, and the Irish from Fishpond mostly had pokers, according to Sid Blump who went to earth in the graveyard, and Shan Shonko and Old Wag were going with their skirts up for speed down Swan Street followed by a crowd like the French Revolution.

'*Coffin's Court! Coffin's Court!*'

'Dear me, what is all the noise, Mrs. Taibach?' asked Miss Milly Thrush, coming up into the bedroom, and Mrs. Taibach opened bleary eyes, sat up and put on her wig, and her large breasts faltered under the low-necked night-dress till covered by six pounds of curls like black tallow.

'What's that you say?'

'The Devils of Gehenna are after us!' Miss Thrush gathered her petticoat against her throat as if somebody was down it. 'Listen!'

'*Diawch!*' ejaculated Mrs. Taibach. 'It's a riot,' and she waved out fat legs and went to the window, staring out at the Iron Bridge. '*Diawch!*'

For Mamie Goldie and Billa Jam were going over the Taff like runaway drams with Asa and Amos after them, Merve and Saul, Caleb and Caradoc, Abel and Aaron and Abiah carrying the chamber, and behind them came the Nipper Tandy gang off shift from the Tasker drainage—Belcher and Big Bonce, Skin-Crone and Godiva, top bare as usual, with Blackbird bringing up the rear and yelling for them to stop.

'Upon my soul!' ejaculated Mrs. Taibach. 'A riot it is—thank God the likes of us don't get mixed with the lower classes.'

'Willie isn't in, mind,' said Milly Thrush, and Mrs. Taibach swung to the bed.

'*Uffern Dan!*' She leaped as if lifted by a whip of scorpions, staring at the empty pillow.

'Heard him leave the house before light,' whispered Milly.

Mrs. Taibach sank on to the bed, fanning.

'Pray compose yourself, dear lady,' whispered Miss Thrush.

'I will, my girl, don't you worry! I'll have the skin from his backside if he's mixing with trash!' She sighed. 'Headstrong and wilful as a spring ram, he is!'

'Oh, dear. Perhaps I ought to go and see Gideon...'

'That anarchist? It's the likes of him and that Mr. Note that has got us into this revolutionary state.' She glared, baleful and Miss Thrush shrank. 'I'd gibbet the lot of them if I had my way—drawin' and quartering 'd be too good for 'em. Up the King and down with the labouring classes, I say.' She rocked herself in grief and blunt, surly anger and her great breasts swung to the blasts of a hunting horn coming out of the Popi Davey where Shoni Sgubor Fawr, the informer, was breezing into the sunlit morning with his fighters and molls. The streets were filling with the clamour of the mob, and Merthyr trembled to its thunder. But Blind Dick the singer and Hugh Pughe his friend, the harpist, were going with uplifted smiles for the Abergavenny Eisteddfod on their old pit pony, clip-clopping over Iron Bridge with the sun on their faces, oblivious to the commotion about them. Percy Bottom Note, sheltering in the coke ovens of Cyfarthfa bank, raised red-rimmed eyes to the sun and retreated back to warmth and the choking fumes: Lemuel Samuel beside him slept on under his counterpane of rags, but his fingers were moving in the hair of one called Mavis, who shared his dreams. Molly Caulara stood at the window of her Popi Davey lodgings and looked out on Bridge Street where the crowds were marching, and vainly she searched for Dic Penderyn. Vaguely, she wondered if he was at home with his wife, for whom her loins still ached, for it had been a bad labour—all the previous evening with the men up on Waun Hill she had listened to Sun crying. Now, faintly she heard the wail of a baby, and smiled. Above the snores of the man in the bed she heard this and smiled, wondering if it was Dic's. Now there came from the Taff a dull roar of the mob and she shivered in the early sunlight, drawing her shawl closer about her bare shoulders. Ned Tranter stirred in the bed and opened his eyes.

265

'What you doing, Caulara?'

'Just looking. There's a crowd down Bridge Street, and...'

'You come back in here.'

Dr. William Price was trotting down Pontmorlais in his goat cart, wearing the ceremonial dress of the Druidic Feast, the flowing white robes denoting purity of belief in the great Hu and the fox-skin on his head, tails flying, the elemental blessing of the earth: sunlight flashed on the bardic sword he held high, and Willie Taibach saw him coming while in the act of rifling potatoes from the shop of Evans Grocer and opened his shoulders and got the goat with a swede; his following salvo of potatoes missed the bard by inches. Very fast went the bardic cart round the corner of High Street, pelted by everything throwable since the start of Creation, for we have enough trouble with agents and politicians without having to put up with blutty druids at a time like this. All down Thomas Street and in Market Yard, the shopkeepers were battening down, but some got up too late. Andrew Marsden the draper lost three sets of silken drawers, and fifteen chemises were going like sails down to Gwern and Twynpin, and the conserves and loaves were rolling up Dynefor, while Abbott the barber was shaving and lathering free and Sid Blump lying back with his feet up smoking a cigar. Locked and barred were the doors of the taverns till confiscated by mob contingents in the name of the thirsty poor, and best home-brew was flowing down Plymouth Street in six inch waves, said Jump Jackson in tears. But there was little looting, said Mamie Goldie, only organised deductions, for we do not want the riot to get a bad name. But the Three Horseshoes lost two pins of burgundy and six flasks of gin, and it is a blutty scandal to say Papa Tomo has them under the bed, said Billa, for the old lad hasn't walked in years. The starving were flooding out of the culverts and cellars and the Irish marched down from Pontmorlais in a mob, forcing open the stalls and shops and handing out food, all very orderly, taking from the rich and giving to the poor, and Old Wag was seen going up Duke with two sides of mutton.

'Spots on your belly, my little lovely,' said Papa Tomo in Number One Ynys, and he tipped the bottle at the ceiling.

'Oh, Dada!' sobbed Blossom, in tears, clutching her rag doll.

Annie Hewers ran out of the cellar of the Crown, took two loaves that were lying in the gutter, and dashed back again to Megsie: Mrs. Duck Evans was seen with a new shirt for Mr. E., and down to thirteen collars he is, poor soul, said she: Mrs. Penderyn, the mother of Dic, took six pounds of potatoes off the stall of Mr. Onions in the market, and put down a penny as if it was gold. And Joseph Coffin cried from the window of his house: 'I will not rest until you are under lock and key!'

'Get your head in, you old bastard!' shouted Lewis. 'Dic, you there, mate?' And he led the rioters into the yard of Coffin's Court.

'Ay, man!'

'Run around the back and heave some cinders through the windows—they tell me there isn't a nail in the place, by God it should flare.'

Dic seized Randy's arm. 'Come on, man, come on!' and he towed him through the crowd down Tramroadside. Here he held out a handful of stones, but Randy only stared at them. Dic cried: 'Look, fella—are you in with us or not? Make up your mind ...!'

But Randy did not really see him. He was looking above Dic's head towards Adulum Fields and Blod. Dick shook him, shouting into his face, but Randy's expression did not change.

'Right, lad, sit by here,' said Dic, and took stones and pelted the court windows. Glass tinkled, bringing the mob in the front to momentary silence, then into renewed roaring as the shattering of glass rose to a crescendo in the hail of stones. Running round the front, Dic joined Lewis Lewis and a dozen others with a timber battering ram, charging the heavy doors of the court, staving in the panels first, then bringing up the bolts and hasps in splintering crashes; the doors went flat, and they were sprawling full length. Sticks and cudgels waved as a forest as the colliers streamed in, and the voice of Lewis rose above the shouts of triumph:

'The records first, lads—then the furniture. By God, we'll give him Coffin. In, *in*!' A giant in strength and purpose, he pulled them past him, yelling, 'Wil Goff, Wil Goff, are ye here?'

'Here, Lewis!' shouted Wil, jumping to heighten himself in the mob.

'Have you a list of the people's furniture distrained—the one you read at Tafern Uchaf?'

'I have, man!'

'Then hand back goods to every man who lost them!'

They were fighting to climb the narrow stairs to the loft and their furniture, they were overturning chairs and tables in the storerooms and dragging out beds. Tom Vaughan's *Ascent of Venus* was on its way up Court Street already and Merve Jam, escaped from Billa, was flying away under the *Whipping in the Temple*, and the Irish streaming out of the cellars of Pontmorlais came in especially for mattresses. Robert Jones's bed and kitchen table were carried out in whoops and his grancher's armchair was passed over the heads of the cheering men —special, this armchair, for the old man bought it in Canton when a seaman on the China Run.

'One chest of drawers, a bed, chairs and pictures!' shouted Lewis Lewis above the din. 'And I'm not leaving here till I get them—by God, I'm having the roof off this hell when I do.'

'You'll not find them here, man,' cried Wil Goff, reading from a ledger. 'Auctioned to Williams Grocer, it says ...'

'I know, but have they been carted?' Lewis twisted in the roaring crowd.

'Collected by David Williams yesterday afternoon.'

Lewis fought a path into the yard. 'High Street, then—and collect it off David Williams—who's with me?'

'Lead the way!' A dozen gathered about him; another dozen ran through the yard for the house of Mary Phillips, for the two china dogs belonging to Bob Rees of Islyn. In all directions groups of men were running now, shouted on by Wil Goff who was calling out the names of people who had bought their furniture, and in the hubbub Tom Llewellyn arrived from Aberdare followed by his men, and he waved a paper high, shouting, 'Fothergill retracted, Fothergill signed a statement!' and his voice was drowned in thunderous applause.

Willie Taibach and Merve Jam were carrying out the records and documents and flinging them into the road. The flames leaped up, black smoke began to billow over Merthyr and pages of debts were blowing down the road to Maerdy Garden, pursued by pit-lads and torn to pieces. And at that moment Joseph Coffin put his head out of his window, shouting, 'All right, burn them, burn them! There's another set in here!'

'Is that a fact?' asked Tom Llewellyn, rubbing his chin.

'Well, I never!' said someone.

'Is he light in the head—telling us that?' asked Dick Llaw-Haearn. 'Did ye hear that, Row Thomas?' And Rowland Thomas, who later died, stooped and picked up a stone and Coffin's head disappeared and the window slammed down.

'After him,' said Abednigo, and he shouted for Willie Taibach. 'I say burn his lot, too.'

'One thing's sure,' said Dic, 'you'll always have debts while one set lasts!' and they ran. Led by Tom Llewellyn, they barged down the door, and as they came in the front, Coffin and his family went out of the back and up Court Street in their nightshirts. Storming into Coffin's house they flung out the copies of the debts and these they burned, too, piling out the furniture to add to the flames. And they swept up the stairs in hatred, stripping the paper off the walls, levering off the doors and breaking out the windows, then they set fire to the house. Many things happened which were not recorded, such as two stipendiary magistrates doing bottoms into the Taff and Shoni Crydd, James Abbott and two other special constables going up to Adulum Fields with a mob of Irish behind them; and Betsy Paul, Dick of the Iron Hand's mate, chased Mr. Steffan Shenkins up Bunker's Hill with a pair of scissors, threatening to bring him back two stones lighter, but this kind of behaviour do tend to drop the tone of the place, said Billa, mind, for a man's privates are entitled to respect, especially Mr. Steffan Shenkins'. The Riot Act was read outside the shop of Tom Lewis and the shopkeepers were cramming the entrance to the Talbot and Castle Inns, begging for military protection. The Nipper Tandy gang rigged themselves out in gentry finery, with Lady Godiva prancing back to the culverts in silk and peacock feathers, and Big Bonce and Belcher were done up to the nines in bombazine suits and grey tall hats, doffing them left and right to the neighbours hanging like beans on Iron Bridge. Carts and gambos were cramming the streets as impounded furniture was returned to its original owners. The sun blazed through the smoke of Coffin's house, drifting in a black pall over Merthyr.

Merve Jam, Billa's eldest, went up to the front door of Miss Sara Grieve and hit it with his boot to shift its hinges, and behind him came Abednigo Jones carrying his white flag of Reform and after that a crowd like the barricades of Paris. Nervously, Mr. Waxey Evans peered round the chain.

'Open up, Waxey,' demanded Merve. 'You remember me?'

'Unfortunately, my wife is indisposed...' said Waxey, white.

'No odds to that—do you remember me? I'm the fella you filled with buckshot...'

'It was a dreadful thing to do, mind,' said Abednigo.

'Absolutely blutty dreadful,' said Willie Taibach.

Waxey faltered, his hand to his heart, and Merve cried:

'Ianto House, eh? Doing pretty well marrying Sara Grieve, eh, Waxey? Has she got a picture of a mother and a baby?'

'Why, yes!' Perceptibly, Waxey brightened. 'The baby Jesus?'

'Bring it here,' said Willie Taibach, pushing to the front.

The picture changed hands with alacrity in glares and ingratiating smiles and Merve said: 'Next time you buy from Coffin's auction we'll have this place down, Waxey Evans— never mind blutty pictures—understand?'

'Yes, sir,' said Waxey.

After they had marched away Waxey lay against the door on trembling legs.

'Oh, my God,' he whispered.

From the hall he entered the drawing-room where candles were guttering on the drawn curtains, casting weird images on

270

the coffin of polished oak wherein lay Miss Grieve with closed eyes in a perfumed intonation of death in red roses, and her will, recently read, lay on the table beside her.

'Oh, certainly,' whispered Waxey, 'I will have to get out of Merthyr.'

For, although the drains had been flushed out with caustic soda, the lotions and potions previously destroyed and a death certificate issued without thought of an inquest, it would be an act of God if one was convened by a People's Court, and the body examined for spirits of salts . . .

Bending he kissed her face in all its marble rigidity.

'You shall have Ianto House and I the six thousand—draw it from Brecon Bank first thing in the morning; Australia, Africa—China, even—who knows? And you'll be in good company with Ianto up in Vaynor.'

Bowing, he shut the door.

A mouse watched him from a crack in the skirting as he went upstairs.

'*Caws gyda bara! Caws gyda bara!* Cheese with bread! *Caws gyda bara!*'

The cry for food thundered up from the milling crowds. The cobbles of Merthyr echoed to the boots of tramping men and women, and they went in a long procession around the town with their flags and banners; down High and up Bridge Street and along to the Castle Inn where the shopkeepers were sheltering; armed with picks, they went, with mandrels and rusted scythes, old flint-muskets pulled from the walls, old swords stolen from gentry museums: tramp, tramp, *tramp*.

'Cheese with bread! Cheese with bread!' They flocked down from Dowlais and Penydarren, they came running in from the nearby towns of Tredegar and Hirwaun, they marched in from Abercynon. And Sun Penderyn raised herself in the bed and covered the face of her suckling boy. The door slamed downstairs.

'That you, Dic?' But she knew it was not Dic.

Tap tap on the bedroom door, and she took a deep breath.

'Come in,' she said.

'It's only me,' said Gwen, Dic's sister.

'He isn't back yet,' said Sun.

'Morgan is downstairs, can I bring him up?'

'Do ye have to?'

'Please, Sun, listen to him—it's for Dic's sake. Has he been back?'

'Ay, once—just to see the baby. Now he's away again with the men.'

'Is he in his right senses?' asked Gwen, screwing at her hands.

Marriage to the fire and brimstone Morgan Howells, the big Newport Calvinistic, had done nothing to rob this woman of her beauty, thought Sun. She said, bitterly:

'Are any of them in their right senses? *Caws gyda bara*—one would think the whole place was starving—do you know that not a single man of those Lodge leaders is out of work? There's Lewis mining at Penydarren—eight shillin' a week, true, but at least he's working—Tom Llewellyn is still puddling for Crawshay on top rates ... *Duw Duw*, it makes me sick!'

'We've got to protect him, Sun,' said Gwen, sitting on the bed. 'Won't ye let Morgan come up?'

'Don't bother yourself, he's in.' Sun lowered her eyes from the man in the doorway, and buttoned her nightdress.

'Congratulations on the birth of your son, Mrs. Penderyn,' said Howells, simply.

'Thanks. When he's of age I'll bring him over to Hope for an official casting out. And ye can rave and rant against the Benefits and Unions, though we'll have a dozen of those before he's twenty-one.'

Morgan Howells said simply: 'It is happening as I prophesied, it is all coming to pass. Would ye have me serve a god of greed, as your man?' He drew himself up, as if containing with an effort the burning spirit within him. 'Ye realise he's in danger, don't you?'

'Don't tell me that, man—I've been living with it.'

'His companions will lead him to the fire.' The minister entered the bedroom. 'Were I not Gwen's husband I would now be in Newport caring for my people in Hope Chapel. You know sedition was talked on Waun Hill, at the meeting?'

Sun raised her shadowed eyes to him; she had been stitched by the works surgeon and the pain in her loins was a little fire that blazed with every breath. Gwen stiffened as the door slammed downstairs; heavy boots were coming up the stairs two at a time.

'Here he comes,' said Sun, 'you can explain it to him yourself.'

Dic ran into the room, and paused, eyeing Morgan Howells. 'What's going on?' he demanded.

'The big minister's just explaining about sedition.'

'The consequences of sedition, to be accurate,' said Howells.

'Dic, *please*,' whispered Gwen.

'Ay,' said Howells, 'you can rant your Union talk, you can spout your Benefit politics and threaten the masters of the town. But when you carry talk of Reform to the very gates of St. James's, the King is interested.'

'And about time, isn't it? God, we pay him enough.'

'Petherick's report is already on its way to London, did you know this?'

'Get out, the pair of you.'

Morgan Howells said: 'I beg you to listen, not for me, not even for your sister, but the sake of this woman and the son she has borne you. This riot, Penderyn, will not be contained within the boundaries of this town—it will spread its fingers to every corner of Wales. The Military have already been called out, do you know this? The Brecon Highlanders are on the march. A court has been rifled, its documents burned; the house of Coffin has been put to the torch, magistrates insulted and threatened. The houses of bailiffs have been ransacked, the possessions of decent people carted on exhibition through the town...'

'Decent people! Auction thieves, you mean!'

'I shall not bandy words on it, there is not time. Did not one of your own leaders on Waun Hill warn that Melbourne seeks the opportunity to strike at Unionism—where better than in Wales? The forces of law and order have been destroyed, greed and violence is on the streets. And, mark me, for this a scapegoat will be found, and he will be a leader. I have a position of importance in the community of Newport...'

'And that's the bother of it, eh?' Dic shouted. 'You're here to keep the family respectable, man—you're not worried about the people in the street!'

'That isn't fair, Dic,' said Gwen, softly.

'I have a position of importance,' continued the minister, unperturbed, 'but I have no influence in this town, least of all in support of people who never see the inside of a chapel. If trouble comes, Penderyn, you face it alone.'

Faintly came the chanting of the mob as it marched up Bridge Street.

'Alone,' said Gwen, 'for Sun is coming back with us to Newport. Did you see Mr. Evans downstairs in the trap?'

Slowly, Dic turned and stared at Sun. 'You ... you're leaving?'

'What else do you expect me to do, man—sit here until the Military come for you?'

'It's the chance we take, all of us,' said he.

'Ay, for you, but not for me—I've the baby to think of. You're all mad, mad!'

'By Christ,' said Dic, going to the window, 'a man is best alone than mixing with friends and relations.' He swung round to her. 'Give us another couple of days and this thing will be over—it's only a wage increase we're after, ye know ... we're not killing anybody.'

'Crawshay will grant no wage increases under threat of force, he has already said so,' remarked Howells.

'Help me get me things, Gwen,' said Sun, pushing back the bedclothes.

They did not speak more for the mob had changed direction and was coming up to Georgetown: over the canal bridge it came in a waving of sticks and cudgels, led by Abednigo Jones with his white flag of Reform and Merve Jam blowing on a hunting horn; and they thronged along the towpath and Dynefor Street, making for the Cyfarthfa Works; under the windows of Ynys they went in yells and shouts, with Mamie and Billa in the van and the children dancing around them, and

274

Mrs. Zeke Solomon got off her chair and went under the bed, and they piled into the Three Horseshoes and hammered the counter for ale. In hundreds they came, like a black finger of rags, curving over the Iron Bridge by the Popi Davey and thrusting for Jackson's and Quarry on a visit to the castle where Crawshay was watching from his look-out turret. Dic turned from the window as the stragglers went past.

'What do ye want of me, Sun?'

'Just this, boy,' said Gwen. 'Go with Mr. Evans of Penrhiw; we brought him especially, for he knows Aberdare mountains like his hand—go with him to the mountain for the next three days, until the trouble's settled; his brother's deacon of Seion—remember? This makes it respectable, and it's Morgan's idea ...'

'If I had to choose between respectability and Lewis Lewis, I know who I'd choose.'

'That's not the choice,' said Sun, 'for I've had enough. It's between Lewis Lewis and us, and if you don't want us, we're off.'

Dic ran his fingers through his hair. He was thinking of Zimmerman and Twiss of the Authority Lodge; he remembered the words of Gideon, and the aged Tomos Glyn Cothi. Up at Waun that very moment there was a meeting of a council of war; that day Lewis Lewis had talked of fleshing swords to the hilt and ambushing the Brecon Highlanders, and he did not altogether trust Lewis Lewis: and Tom Llewellyn, the respected, had vanished.

'I've told ye before,' said Sun, shaking out her petticoats, 'and I tell ye again—you won't see 'em for dust when the bayonets come out.' She turned to the minister. 'Would you mind removing yourself while I get meself dressed, your worship?'

'Come, Morgan,' said Gwen, and took him to the door. The baby cried in gusty breath, fists waving.

Dic said: 'Sun, will you wait while I slip up to see Gid Davies?'

'Can't ye think for yourself, then?'

She thought he looked handsome standing there in his blue

coat and trews; it was a sort of ragged strength by which she would remember him.

'Will ye?'

Despite his strength there was in him a weakness, and she pitied him.

'Give ye ten minutes,' said Sun and began to comb her hair.

'And you'll stay if I go with this fella Evans?'

'I will.'

'For three days?'

'Four,' said Sun.

After Dic had gone Gwen came back. Sun lowered the comb. 'You've taken his soul, ye realise that? If he goes with Evans he'll never be able to look at his mates again.'

'But he'll be alive,' said Gwen.

Tap tap on the door of One Ynys, but Miss Blossom Thomas did not hear: sobbing in a disarray of straggling hair and wetness was she, and Papa Tomo well into his third flask of blue ruin and roaring his sea-shanties along the coast of Ushant full forty fathoms deep, and the language coming up was enough to take the varnish off the pews of the Ebenezer.

Tap tap on the back now; scurrying footsteps. Flogged by the cat of Papa's dissipation, keel-hauled and scuppered by tales of Annie Wong Lee of Hong Kong and an opium dream in Malaya, Miss Blossom Thomas peeped around the door of the back in distress, and every neighbour in the Row was either slamming the doors or pushing shut the windows as Papa's profanity blasted up the canal to Dynefor.

Then Blossom Thomas ceased to weep. Kneeling on the doorstep, smiling through her tears, she picked up her picture and rocked it against her; one of a woman tending a baby, and his name was Jesus.

ON the common land of Hirwaun the farms and cottages were being turned into strong-points and the area into an armed camp. Gangs of men were coming in from Breconshire and Glamorgan, bringing with them weapons obtained from raided houses; Black flags were rising on high mounds and hills. Furnaces were blown out in Risca, coal shafts jammed and technicians forced away in Dowlais and Penydarren; the rebel army grew in numbers, the long black columns tramping over the mountains, an army of the respected furnace trades—the ballers and puddlers, shearers and blenders coming to join the colliers and miners of the pits, drifts and levels. They came marching to the beat of a drum or whistle, they came singly and in groups; armed with the trade tools, rusted swords and tappers, ancient pistols and fire-locks, they came from the Top Towns and advanced on Merthyr; they despatched outriders to distant places, they called on their Lodges and Benefits and scarecrow Unions scarcely born. And they gathered at a place north of Aberdare, following their instinct for the mass meeting, soon to be a part of their lives. They came from the darkness of a hidden people, into sunlight; an ancient race stepping over the shadowed threshold into a new and terrible awareness; they did not speak of this, they could not have explained it, but they knew that their history had begun. Flinging off the immaturity of centuries, they gathered, at dusk, on the lonely heath, and on a crag in that silent place a man was standing, and his name, for want of one that day, was John the Racer. In his hand was a knife and at his feet lay a calf tethered for sacrifice. About him were gathered men with great white flags, and one was Abednigo Jones, the boy: young men or boys mainly carried these flags, for another was Willie Taibach and yet another was Mervyn, the son of Billa.

'Bring the flags!'

The boys moved forward from the ranks of men, and these numbered thousands, and their breath was steaming in the stillness.

'Who with the basin?' cried the man, and a child moved forward with one in his hands.

'And one has the loaf of bread to be impaled?'

The wind whispered over the mountain and John the Racer cried, the knife held high, 'Let us announce this martial law! Let this flag fly in the name of the Welsh, as it flew for the French, our comrades in suffering under the 1791 massacre! Let this flag, when stained with blood, rise for the first time in Britain as a signal against authority!' and he knelt with the knife and severed the head of the calf, and the child with the basin caught its blood.

The men sighed as the basin was raised, and they heard him cry, 'Thus I wash my hands in the blood of this animal in token of the blood we will spill this day!' and this he did, raising high his stained hands. Next the flags he washed one by one, and on one standard he impaled the loaf now also red, and this banner he raised high as the moon broke over the hills.

'See this, then! The freedom flags that will strike off the shackles that bind us. Do you swear to follow them until the day is won, as did your comrades of the Bastille? For we have argued long enough, think you? Today, the talk is finished and we are in battle. *Bara neu waed!*'

'*Bara neu waed!*' the Welsh of ancestry echoed his cry.

'*Bara neu waed!*'

It thundered like a shock wave over Hirwaun, reverberating into silence.

'Bread or blood! Bread or blood!' The English among them repeated it.

Then all was still. Silently, as men with a purpose, they split into squads, and commands were whispered. Led by the boys with the blood-stained flags and the one with the impaled loaf in the van, they converged in ten thousand on to the town of Merthyr.

In St. James's the lamps were burning; with couriers from Wales galloping in every hour the King himself was engaged on this affair of State. In Brecon Barracks the 93rd Highlanders were drawing from the armoury their musket-shot and powder, for St. Tydfil herself was under siege. A ring of steel was closing around the hills, but Dai End-On and his mate got through. As Mamie said later, to do a thing like that you'd have to be as daft as Dai and Billy Jam.

'I'll not tell you again,' said Billa, covered in suds.

Here's the old tin bath slopping by the fire and Mam's got the lads into it, and where's the soap, Abiah, and who's got the towel? Auntie Mamie! Scrubbing like a washerwoman and looking twice as healthy, for these kids do give one a glow, mind, Billa was on her knees beside the bath, and will you stop arsing about, Caleb!

'Aw, Mam!'

'Get into that bath or I'll land you one,' said Mamie, handing over Aaron. '*Duw Duw*, woman—did ye have to have nine o' the fiends?'

Rub, rub, rub—got beautiful hair, mind, my Amos—anna you, Amos—got lovely 'air! and Billa upended him and kissed his bottom. 'Anna he got lovely hair, Mame?' Billa sighed. 'Just like his da, mind.'

'Mr. Jam hasn't got any hair!'

'He 'ad once,' said Billa. 'Don't you deny him, now—make two of your old soak any day, remember.' She sang then, her voice like an angel.

'Can I put me boat in, Ma?'

'You can't put your boat in—I want this over by curtains—don't ye know there's a riot on?' She belted Caradoc in passing. 'And stop playing wi' your pinkle. Got another one, Mamie?'

'Coming over!' Mamie stripped the trews off Abel and dropped him into the bath. Shrieks of joy and howls of soap in the eyes, back-slaps and rubs, kisses, threats and cuddles; and Sun Penderyn, with Dic gone to Aberdare mountain, soothed her baby and smiled, listening, for everybody knew up Ynys Row when it was Billa Jam bath night.

'But I do miss my little Adam, though,' said Billa, and lowered her eyes, and instantly they were about her fighting for a place—in her hair, faces against her throat, down the front of her for warmth, and she knelt in wet limbs and kisses. The firelight was flickering on the cups and mugs; bacon was sizzling in the pan, best back straight out of Dai Rees's shop, and serve the beggar right, said Mamie, for he overcharges more than Guest of Dowlais. Borrowed ten pounds of cheese from the Grocery—saw it running down the hill—as God's me judge, Billa, I didn't loot it—it were blutty running, I tell ye.

'You'll get transportation for sure, you're caught—too light-fingered for my liking, you are. Did ye manage any eggs, Mame?'

'Poached half a dozen down the front o' me—nearly hatched out—come on, come on, lads, and not so much noise or you'll have the rebellion in.'

'Or the special constables,' said Billa, getting up. 'They can smell that bacon for miles, remember, and people our class don't eat bacon.'

Shirts on now, hair combed, ears examined and collars for ticks for there's funny people about these days, and up to the table they went, all nine of them, faces soaped and beaming.

'Good old Mame!' Out of the pan came the rashers, eggs for the oldest, dips for the youngest, and don't you bolt it now, Caleb.

'Ain't you having any, Mame?'

'Ach, leave it for the savages—you enjoying that, boys?'

Hoots and shouts and stop licking the jam-pot and look what Asa's doing under the table, Auntie Mamie!

Billa said, 'But I'm worried about my Merve.'

'Let him do the worrying—he's gone ten, ain't he? Probably with my Randy—look, forget 'em,' replied Mamie.

'He's in bad company with that Abednigo Jones. You think

280

I ought to go out looking?'

'You're staying here—it anna decent for virgin women on the Bridge. Coo—did Coffin's Court go up! Dear me, just listen to that old Papa Tomo—going up the yard-arm again— my heart bleeds for that poor little Blossom.'

'Somebody coming, Ma!' shouted Saul, his mouth full of bacon.

'And Dic gone up to Aberdare with the Seion deacon fella from Penrhiw, you heard?'

'Best place for him—I'll have to slip in to see Sun later.'

'People coming round the back, Mam!' shouted Caradoc.

'The Military!' cried Mamie, and peeped around the curtains. 'God save us,' said she, sinking down and patting.

'Who is it?'

'It's my Dai and Mr. Jam.'

'*Diwedd!*' exclaimed Billa, and whispered:

'You, Saul—pull yourself together. Round the back with you and ask them in the front. And do it polite, remember. Tell 'em we'll be down. The rest of you to bed.'

'Oh, Mam!' in chorus.

'Bed or I'll brain ye,' hissed Mamie.

Dai End-On and Mr. Jam sweating it out now, leaping to attention every time a board creaked.

'Treat 'em indifferent, remember,' said Mr. Jam. 'This is the time to keep your head.'

The door came open and Mamie and Billa were in.

Dressed like twins, with perfume behind the ears out of the herbalist in Cross Street; straw hats with wide brims tied under the chin with pink ribbons, black velvet bands around the throat and cameos of the Queen, black taffeta dresses caught at the waist and draped round the buttocks with pink cosey, corsetted at the waist and pushed up in the bust where white lace spread. They entered and sat delicately opposite Dai End-On and Jam.

'Well,' said Dai, 'I will go to my death.'

'You wanted to see us, we understand,' said Billa like ice.

'Well, ye see . . .'

'Well?'

'Gid, you see—that is, Gid Davies, sort of mentioned it last week down in Taibach, and we was thinking...' Mr. Jam faltered, his eyes on Billa. Lavender water swept the nostrils of Dai End-On and he sweated ominously.

'Up to you, of course,' announced Mamie, her nose up.

'Nobody asked you to come, you two—ye realise that, I suppose?'

'Ay, but, you see...'

'I mean to say, we're doing all right,' said Mamie. 'We managed fine these last months—even my Randy don't miss you...'

'I'm off the glass, though,' said Dai, snuffling.

The door moved in a creak, but nobody heard it, and the children peeped through the crack.

'I've done with the Oddfellows, too, see,' said Jam for no reason.

'Got a good rag and bone round now,' asserted Dai. 'Pulls the cart himself, too, having got no moke.' He looked at Billa. 'Very industrious. Somebody lifted his donkey, ye see.'

'Him, too,' said Jam. 'Doin' full shifts down Brombil back in Taibach. Doing good, ain't you, Dai boy?'

'Oh, well,' said Billa with business, 'we will have to think about it, won't we?'

'It's a big step, ye see,' added Mamie. 'When once ye make the break it's ... well, it's sort of tricky starting again, ain't it?' Snared by independence yet muted by habit, they stood, inarticulate, faltering in the gaze of the other until nothing was left to them but flight. Billa said, damp:

'Oh, well, I suppose you'd better be going, then,' and she saw a flash vision of Big Mike the Irish boy and his face was square and strong; years younger ... and the disgust swept her, but still her spirit yearned. Now she heard herself say: 'Ay, Mr. Jam, it was good of ye to call.'

'Goodbye, Missus,' said Mr. Jam, glum.

'Might see you again some time,' said Mamie.

'Ay,' said Dai.

Nothingness enveloped them, and Mr. Jam said, turning

away, 'Sorry about our lad, Billa—our wee Adam.'

'Oh, God!' shrieked Billa, and clung to him.

Mamie raised her eyes. Dai was standing with his arms open to her. The kids skidded round the door, in whoops.

The moon was sliding up the window of Number Five.

Before the moon was high the children of William Crawshay left Cyfarthfa Castle in the company of trusted servants, all disguised as beggars, and took to the hills. They took the mountain tracks, keeping clear of the roads where the men were marching, and by morning reached the town of Monmouth and the safety of the Beaufort Hotel.

Next morning Major Falls of the 93rd Highlanders marched in from Brecon Barracks at the head of his men, and they numbered but sixty-eight; later this rose to eight hundred. They were big men and their kilts and sporrans swung to the beat of their marching-drum; they came with muskets slung, looking neither right nor left at the tumult that lined the way, for cat-calls and jeers beat about them all down the Brecon Road. Here they were halted, joined by William Crawshay, Anthony Hill of the Plymouth Works and Bruce the magistrate carrying his Riot Act, and the workers pressed about them as they went down Tydfil Wells and into High Street. Behind them came an army of workers; those who had washed their hands in blood the previous night. Women were shrieking insults, children prancing along beside the soldiers.

'*Diawl!*' shrieked one, 'they've forgotten their trousers!'

'Ach, no—they've dropped them so they can walk the faster!' And this the Welsh believed because they had never seen Highlanders before. Some said they were Welsh struck dumb, and cried to them in the mother tongue; others called them foreigners. And from the crowds came the chant:

'Bread or blood! Reform in Parliament! Secret vote! No Court of Requests! Bread or blood! Reform in Parliament. Free Trade and cheese with bread!' Many carried weapons; hedge-stakes and shovels, mandrels and hammers. Abod of Penydarren, the giant husband of Liz Treharne who marched beside him, carried half a wheelbarrow. Lewis Lewis was there in the centre of the mob, and Gideon Davies was led by Merve Jam, his friend, who also carried a red banner. Abednigo Jones carried a flag, too, and on it was daubed 'Bread or blood'. Dic Llaw-Haearn also came, with Betsy Paul, his woman of the Nipper Tandy gang. Richard Evans the puddler of Hirwaun was there, too, but Tom Llewellyn, who defected, was not. Dai Hughes fought in Castle Square as well, with John Hughes who died of wounds, and with them were Tom Vaughan and Dan Thomas who were transported for life. John the Racer carried a red flag, and about him were his young sons, also David Richards, who got fourteen years. Among the thousands who pressed about the soldiers that day were some who should have stayed away. Many there were who should have come, but did not, such as William Twiss of the golden oratory and Zimmerman who, but a night before, had inflamed these men to violence, but was never seen again. Some there were, too, whose lives were being fulfilled that day—people like Randy Goldie and Mr. Waxey Evans, Mamie Goldie and Billa Jam, also Mr. Percy Note, all from Taibach, and Annie Hewers who came from Pontypridd.

But Dic Penderyn, who was put to death for being there, was up on Aberdare mountain, it was claimed, with the deacon of Seion as witness to this fact.

Reaching the Castle Inn, Crawshay, Hill and Bruce the magistrate, went within with Major Falls, and therein met Josiah John Guest, the master of Dowlais Works, among others. And the crowd bayed louder and pressed about the soldiers as they took refreshment handed out to them, and the baying grew into shouts of fierce anger as the Highlanders went into the Castle Inn by groups, and came out with bayonets fixed for action. Seeing this, Lewis Lewis climbed up on to the shoulders of his comrades, and shouted above the mob:

'See, we are threatened! We are come to discuss wages and Free Trade, and we are shown bared bayonets. Crawshay, Crawshay, Crawshay!' and the mob took up the name, and that of Guest, but neither of these men came out of the inn;

instead the high sheriff appeared, and, mounting a chair, he addressed the men in English, and read the Riot Act. Because many did not understand this, the magistrate Bruce read it again, in Welsh.

The mob was growing in numbers now, cramming like herrings in a barrel up and down High Street, down Post Office Lane, and over Glebeland behind the inn; they were rammed shoulder to shoulder on the waste land leading to the cindertip, they were forced by the weight of more coming in through the railings of Professional Terrace, and fainting women and children had to be passed over the crowd. And they pressed the Highlanders back to the wall of the inn so that it was impossible for them to use their arms: many joked with the soldiers, speaking to them in Welsh; but many, too, spoke in English, trying to suborn them; hearing this, Major Fall called from a window, ordering his men not to reply. It was half past ten in the morning when the Riot Act was read, and soon after this, the master Anthony Hill came out and stood on a chair, shouting:

'Now hear me out—hear me! You will get nowhere with your arms and threats—indeed, you may shout to bring down the town, but inside there we cannot hear a word. Will you appoint...'

His voice was drowned in fresh roars, but he cried, his hands held high, 'Will you appoint a deputation to lay before the masters your claim? How can we tell your requirements amid this disorder? Send within twelve of your leaders and we will talk with them man to man...'

Now fresh gangs of men were coming down Pontmorlais and over the cinder-tip from Jackson's, and those behind were forced forward so that those in front were jammed against the soldiers, and a voice cried then:

'Get between them and the wall of the inn, you fools—give way, give way—drive them free of the wall!'

Hearing this, the Highlanders outside the inn called to those at the windows above, in panic, and the windows were pulled open and muskets appeared. Gideon Davies, pushed to the entrance by willing hands, stood on the chair and shouted: 'I call twelve men who are of this town—David Hughes, Lewis Lewis and David Richards; Daniel Thomas and Thomas Vaughan, also Dai Solomon and Robert Jones—this is seven. These men come forward and join with five more waiting in the entrance. Declare the aims now, and clearly!'

'Make way for the deputation!' shouted Mr. Bruce, up on the chair, and the soldiers held him while the men pushed past him into the inn.

The shrieking of women was growing among the mob; many of these had come from the brick-fields and cropping on Lefal and Tasker pits, and some were ore-miners come from Abercanaid.

'Mind how you go now, love,' said Mrs. Duck Evans to Mr. E.

For it was a Friday and the day of the poor relief pay, and every week Mr. E. collected the five and eightpence from the office of the parish in Professional Terrace.

'There's rough old things happening in town, my lovely,' said Mrs. Duck Evans, and kissed him, 'so be careful.'

Mr. E. was shivering. Last night while the men were marching he had risen in the bed on the first floor of the Dynefor Doss and a duck had looked through the window. With a head as big as a coal bag, a beak like a shovel and lanterns for eyes, it had smiled as only ducks can smile and quacked to raise the graveyard, while Mr. E. gibbering, buried his face in the breast of his wife. Now, with morning, she went on tip-toe and kissed his gaunt face, saying:

'Now now, there's nothin' to be afraid of,' and she patted and smoothed him. 'Just tell the officer our circumstances haven't changed. You never know, he might shift us out of here after three months on the parish.' She beamed up into his face. 'You lean on me, my beautiful—everything will be all right.' Smiling, chattering, she hurried him through the door.

Deciding not to wake the children until she could buy some food, Mrs. Duck Evans, late of Taibach, went down on her knees by the bed and clasped her hands.

'O, merciful God,' she said. 'O, merciful God...'

Annie Hewers, late of Pontypridd, knelt by the bed in the cellar of the Crown and held the hand of Megsie, and smiled, and Megsie said, her voice bright with joy, 'But I'm better—I've never felt better, Annie ...'

'Ay, ay ...'

'Can I get up today, then?'

'We'll see,' replied Annie. 'Sleep now, is it?'

'Ay, sleep ...'

'Mrs. Ned Tranter brought us a bit of butter and some milk, and I lifted some riot bread. We'll have a feast when you wake up ...' Annie went to the grating, staring up at the boots of men pounding there, and their shouts enwrapped her in the soul of the mob. Vaguely, she began to wonder what she would do when Megsie died; go back to Ponty, more than likely. She would not have stayed as long as this had it not been for the neighbours. And God, what neighbours! Mrs. Ned Tranter, for instance—got a sod of an old man—nothing in skirts was safe with him. And old Shan Shonko—who would have thought she had a heart? And Gid Davies, of course. She wondered what she would have done without Gid Davies over this sickness. The cellar door rasped and Molly Caulara stood on the step.

'You all right, child?'

'Yes, Molly.'

'Your Megsie sleeping, is she?'

Annie smiled brilliantly. 'Don't know why, with all this noise.'

'And you're not frightened, or anything?'

'Not frightened at all, Molly. Not frightened of nothing no more.' Boots were stamping in metallic clashes on the grating.

Molly gestured at the bed. 'She looks better, but you know that, don't ye? They always look better ...'

'Yes, yes, I know.' There was growing in Annie Hewers a fierce choking anger.

After Molly Caulara had gone she sat on the bed and looked at her shaking fingers.

The workers' deputation was coming out of the inn. Silence

curtained the mob; it began at the entrance where Gideon was standing and spread like a paralysis through the ranks of the men, extending up High and over Glebe until there was total silence, and in this silence Josiah John Guest, the Dowlais master, stood on the chair and cried:

'Now listen, and I will report the outcome of the discussion. Your deputation demanded, in your name, certain reforms which include reduction in the price of bread and all such basic items necessary to your daily lives . . .'

'Ay, and about time, master! The price of bread is a bloody scandal!'

Mixed shouts followed this—cat-calls of derision and shouts of applause and Lewis Lewis, climbing a lamp-post, yelled: 'The price of everything is a bloody scandal! What are ye trying to do, Guest—starve us to death? What about your Shop? And where's Crawshay in this—doesn't he vote for Reform?'

Cheers and hurrahs now and the mob stamped its feet. Guest shouted:

'Your deputation has asked for higher wages, too, and I am to tell you this. If you disperse now we will give serious consideration to your complaints—have I not always done this . . .?'

'Ay—with your prices up by twenty per cent!' yelled Philip Jones, the gambo man.

Guest spoke again, but his words were obliterated in a sudden rush for the entrance; the soldiers crossed their muskets; the inn door opened and shut, and within moments Guest appeared at an upstairs window, shouting:

'Now I am to warn you. You are rioting in the face of the King's law. The Riot Act has been read—disperse or take the consequences!'

A young man scrambled on to the back of a comrade and cried: 'If we disperse now you will give us nothing. For my part all I am asking for is a bit more bread . . .'

There was a surge of anger about him, and he was pulled down into the crowd, and Abod, the giant of Penydarren, stiffened in the mob, yelling:

'Ay, well I want something more than bread! And so does my missus. We want cheese with it, and ale, and smokes—by Christ, you lot get enough. I want cheaper rent and no more bloody Courts of Requests, and we've waited too long already.'

A man yelled then: 'We want *everything*!'

The crowd bawled, and as the clamour mounted Crawshay came to the window and shouted: 'For my part I will not treat with anybody under threat of violence. Go home now. Send to me, within a fortnight, a deputation who can speak for you and I will give consideration to any injustices you think you may have ... But, by God, I will not treat with a rabble!'

Groans and moans burst from the men, and one shouted: 'Is this what ye call Reform?' The mob began to chant again: 'Bread or blood, bread or blood ...!'

And as Bruce the magistrate notified them that the hour of the Riot Act had expired, Lewis Lewis shouted from his position on the lamp-post:

'Now, ye see how much you'll get!' and he followed this in Welsh, 'We come here to get an increase in wages and all we get is soldiers set against us. We come here in the name of Reform and all they're prepared to give us is bullets. Now lads, if you're of the same mind as I am, let us begin by taking their arms ...!'

The sun was directly overhead, said Gideon later; the sun burned down, said Mamie, when she heard the firing.

'Come on, lads, into them!' yelled Lewis Lewis, and Gideon cried:

'No, in the name of God, wait, *wait*!'

The men rushed the Highlanders.

'Get behind them!'

'Trip the bastards!'

'Clear them from the wall!' and Lewis Lewis, in the van of the charge, shouted, 'On, on! Get them away from the wall!' And he leaped upon the nearest soldier and seized his musket as Major Falls ran out of the inn to take command, to fall almost immediately, being swung aside by Abod of Penydarren and clubbed down by another, some say Liz Treharne. Soldiers fell, sinking under the crashing mandrels as they

289

fought to use their arms. A worker shrieked and dropped, clutching at a bayonet which was sticking through his body. A boy fell, his head crushed by a musket-butt. Then a volley of stones smashed every window in the inn, and the crowd, forced on by unseen pressures, rammed the Highlanders against the entrance; the door flew open and the soldiers were carried within, sprawling. Women were screaming, men roaring encouragement to their comrades, a baby was crawling among the boots of the men. With a forest of stakes and mandrels heaving, the workers were fighting to get into the inn when a single shot spurted fire from an upper window.

Rumour had it in Tredegar at that time that William Crawshay fired the first shot of the massacre that followed, but none have proof of this. But now, with the order to fire shouted, volley after volley was poured into the massed people, and they slipped down where they stood, in screams. Gideon Davies fell early, being near the entrance, and a soldier clubbed him as he staggered blindly. Now ragged fusillades cracked out from the inn windows, and nearly all the soldiers in the forecourt were wounded and down. One, Private Donald Black, was seen by witnesses to be struggling with a worker; and in the mêlée of arms and legs, amid the swaying, cursing mass, a bayonet was seen to flourish; Private Black fell with the weapon in his thigh. According to the testimony of James Abbott the barber and Shoni Crydd the constable, the man who wounded him was Dic Penderyn...

Meanwhile, Mr. Waxey Evans, having had his trunks sent down to the Posting House, was ready to leave Merthyr. But, being in need of ready cash, he decided to call at the Brecon Bank in High Street opposite Professional Terrace and draw enough to tide him over the immediate future. So, with Sara Grieve safely interred with her Ianto up in Vaynor, Mr. Evans dusted the scurf off the shoulders of his morning coat, brushed up the pile of his grey hat, and with gold-knobbed cane, gloves and carnation made his way briskly down Bridge and up Thomas Street to Professional Square.

'This cheque, please,' said he at the bank counter.

The cashier was nervous, but not of Mr. Evans. With red-rimmed eyes twitching seriously, since he had been up all night in an attic down Post Office Lane, he peered at the door; here six special constables were standing with drawn batons.

'Anything the matter, man?' asked Waxey.

A volley of shots pierced the shrieks and screams. The cashier paid him in guineas, and these Waxey Evans stacked in little bags in his small travelling-case. The young man said: 'I can't think what's got into them. I really cannot think . . .'

Waxey was counting. He normally counted the money when drawing on the account, and it was necessary not to raise the smallest suspicion.

'My condolences on the loss of your wife, sir. It is tragic, absolutely tragic!' the clerk added. 'You will be back, of course? I mean . . . I trust this is but a temporary absence?'

Waxey Evans sniffed, snapped the travelling-case shut and departed, turning into Professional Square with his two hundred sovereigns just as Mr. Duck Evans was coming into High Street with his five and eightpence parish relief. And, as the mob came pell-mell down from the Castle, Corporal Joe McCann of the 93rd sighted down the barrel of his musket and pressed the trigger. He was aiming at the giant figure of Abod of Penydarren, but missed. The ball hit a lamp standard, ricochetted through a roof, cut through a king-post and whined down into the crowd, striking Waxey Evans an inch under the heart: dropping at the feet of Mr. Duck Evans, he died instantly. In the path of the retreating crowd he fell, and the workers leaped over him. When they had passed Mr. Duck Evans noticed the travelling-case; aimlessly, he picked it up, for the events had made but little impression. Vacantly, with the case held against him, he made his way down Thomas, over the Iron Bridge where Molly Caulara was waiting.

'Have you got the time?' asked Molly. 'Ye lovely handsome fella.'

'About midday,' replied Mr. Duck Evans, and raised his hat, and went up Dynefor to the Doss.

'What you got there, my lovely?' asked Mrs. Duck Evans, when he came in.

Giving her the five and eightpence, he wandered away.

'No, that I mean, my beautiful,' said she, and took the case.

Before the Castle Inn twenty-two people lay dead—men, women and children. Scores more were rolling and many were shrieking, and the cobbles were shining with blood. Sid Blump was lucky, for he died quickly. Pushing through the crowd he held a Highlander still with one hand and hit him flat with the other; an officer shot him personally; they were surprised to find that he possessed no fingers. Nearby died one, Mr. Note, who was once a revolutionary. But the spirit of war had surged in him again when he heard the firing, and he remembered in the lost ambitions the last movement of his Gun Symphony that had died in the arms of Mrs. Taibach. He came late to battle, for the mob was retreating even as he arrived with Lemuel Samuel, who fled. And hearing Willie Taibach shrieking in the folds of his blood-stained flag, he had stooped to succour him, and a soldier took him from the back. Percy Bottom Note died in Welsh, which was his father's tongue:

'A gyrraf hefyd y prophwydi ac ysbryd aflendid o'r wlad!' he said.

Amazingly, Curly Hayloft died in the arms of Tilly, who was dead. He had come into town to buy a physic for Mercy Merriman who had drunk Taff water, and had sheltered in the entrance of the King's Head hotel while the volleys of the Highlanders swept the blood-stained streets: then, in a lull of the firing he had run for it, and a musket-ball broke his spine. So he dragged himself along the cobbles of Professional Square like a wounded leveret while the insurgents leaped over him in flight, and here a woman was sheltering with a child. And this woman, who was an iron-stone miner of Hirwaun, gathered him against her, and her hands, which were calloused with labour, scoured his face: therefore, her touch, to him, was the touch of Tilly. She stared in wonder when he took her hand and pressed it against his lips.

Randy Goldie did not die, although he succeeded, with Lewis Lewis, in wresting away a musket from Private Alex

McGregor of Dundee. And with this musket, quite unnoticed, he wandered in a hail of fire, looking for Ned Tranter, who was in charge of Stall One, Heading Eight when Blod Irish died. Based largely on information given to him by Merve Jam, who spoke at the coroner's inquest, Randy's suspicions had flowered into fact. Ned Tranter, it seemed, was with a detachment of rioters sent by Lewis Lewis up to the Brecon Road to guard the northern approach of the town. In this direction Randy walked, climbing the cinder-tip behind *China*, and made his way up Quarry Street. Earlier, he had seen Dic Penderyn go into the Castle Inn as a member of the workers' delegation—or thought he had, and he had waited for Dic to come out, but he never did. Later still, just before the massacre, he was sure he had seen Dic standing by the tap-room wall at the side of the inn, but thought he must have been mistaken because when he reached this spot, Dic was not to be found. Now, with his stolen musket slung on his back and every Highlander in Merthyr beading him in the sights, Randy strolled across the line of fire that later shot down Mrs. Taibach, and the air was filled with the shrieking of the ricochets, for Lewis Lewis and his men on the cinder-pit were now firing with glass marbles. With a bullet hole in his collar, two in his trews and one in his sleeve, Randy wandered aimlessly, thinking about Blod. In summer, he remembered, with flowers in her hair in Dinas Woods, Taibach, she was very pretty.

Gideon Davies was lying against the wall of Abbot the barber's when Miss Thrush the Sweets found him, and he was not dead. Indeed, the blood of his wound was congealing and when she knelt beside him and gathered him into her arms he opened his eyes and smiled, knowing her, it seemed.

'Sun, Sun . . .' he said, and clung to her.

'Oh, God,' said Miss Thrush, 'whatever shall I do?' and she snatched at the legs of men running past her, and one paused, and knelt. A musket-ball struck the stonework of Abbott's shop above them and whined into space. The sight of the blood on Gideon's face held Miss Thrush with rooted force.

'Quick! Get him up!' cried Abednigo Jones.

Therefore, helping to lift Gideon, she did not notice Mrs.

Taibach walk past with Willie in her arms ... going round the corner of the Castle Inn oblivious to the shrieking wounded and the bawled warnings of men, and Willie's face was against hers and his bare arm hanging down her apron. She walked right through the volleys that shot down Rowland Thomas, he who had wandered into the High Street and picked up a soldier's hat. But the rioters were still firing from the cinder-tip behind the inn and she gasped to the smash of the ball and went to her knees, staring into Willie's face, until the next random volley laid her down with her arms about him. Jess Banks, who was English, died beside them, hand-in-hand with his wife, who was seventeen, and the neighbours took the baby, though it cried for two days. Mr. Stinkin Shenkins, the boozey brother of the beadle, he died also, in shrieks, beating his fists against the wall of the Baptist in Maerdy—the shot had taken him low. Shoni Melody, whose business was not riot, was humming a tenor solo from *The Messiah* in the attic of the Star when a ball took the window and struck him in the face, while poor Old Wag, who was knitting in a porch off Post Office Lane, died cleanly with the jersey in her lap, and she hadn't dropped a stitch, said Mamie. Some say Shan Shonko died also, but nobody got the proof of it, for she merely disappeared, while others said the Highlanders had eaten her. There were many who died that were not recorded, dragged into attics and cellars by terrified relatives; many of these died for want of medical attention, and were buried in secret graves. John Hughes, an old soldier who had fought at Waterloo, died in agony, for the ball took him in the back and came out of his navel, and he was concerned with the indignity, said the surgeon who signed his death certificate *Justifiable Homicide*. This verdict he also gave on the body of one, Annie Hewers, who died in tears, rushing on to the bayonets with her fists raised, crying the name of Megsie, her friend.

Some of the soldiers were wounded.

With Lewis Lewis and a small body of rioters firing on the Castle Inn from the cinder-tip behind *China*, the order was given to evacuate the defenders to Penydarren House, Forman's mansion built on the site of a Roman fortification. But the Military were converging on to Merthyr now, coming at the frantic commands of the magistrates' emissaries; the Glamorgan Militia came from Cardiff, the Llantrisant Cavalry galloped in and attacked the snipers on the cinder-pit, and were beaten off by salvos of glass marbles, for the rioters had run out of lead shot. The cavalry escorted the evacuating coaches of the iron masters up the hill to Penydarren.

And Merthyr, under the red flag, fell to the rioters.

'RIGHT, you, missus,' said Abednigo Jones, 'I got him by here, now it's up to you,' and he sprawled Gideon down over the bed in Miss Thrush's room, snatched the musket she had carried and ran downstairs and through the shop.

For many minutes Milly Thrush stood there with her hands to her face listening to the distant guns and Gideon's faint breathing. His head wound had begun to bleed again and was spreading on her pillow in a widening stain. She wanted to be sick. Once, when a child, she had cut her finger, and she was physically sick then; the sight of blood always did this to her. Now she swayed and held on to the bed-rail in a mist of horror, and Gideon groaned in his unconsciousness. Going to the window she looked through the Arches on to a deserted Bridge Street where smoke was drifting; nothing moved in Bridgefield. A sale-coal barge had stopped on the canal, lying askew from bank to bank, and the towing-horse was grazing peaceably nearby. To her right she saw smoke rising from the simmering furnaces of Ynys Works, but the dram-road was stilled, and the doors and windows up and down the Row were shut. It was as if the riot had taken Merthyr by the throat and choked it into death. Then a small figure carrying a red flag walked past Ynysgau Chapel, and Milly recognised it instantly as Merve, Billa Jam's boy; he walked in jerky sentences of pain, and the banner he carried high swayed and ripped in the wind of the Taff. In the middle of the Iron Bridge he fell, then rose, dragging the flag on the ground behind him. In this manner, falling and rising, he reached Ynys Row. The barge horse raised its head and watched him go to the house of Miss Blossom Thomas; there, beside the step he fell, and lay still.

Gideon groaned then, and turned on the bed, and Milly went to him, her hands screwing together, staring down. The wound in his head was bleeding profusely now. She began to bite at her fingers; sweat flooded to her face and she wiped it into her hair. Suddenly, she turned and ran downstairs, returning with a bowl of water and a cloth. With clenched teeth she sat beside him. The blood was on her fingers as she began to wipe it away. The coldness of the water stilled Gideon, and he sighed and did not groan again. Tearing up one of her petticoats, Milly put the soaked cloth over the wound and bound it tightly, flinging away the blood-soaked pillow. Then she heard footsteps on the road outside. Four special constables were marching towards the shop with drawn batons, and one she recognised as Shoni Crydd. Cleaning her hands of blood, she ran downstairs again and was behind the counter as the men entered.

'You been here all this morning, Miss Thrush?' asked Shoni Crydd.

'Ay, thank God.'

'You've had no trouble, then?'

'Only the firing, and the mob . . .'

'You haven't seen a woman with a musket?'

She faltered, but he did not appear to notice. 'A . . . a musket?'

'A woman carrying arms—she was seen on River Side, not more than half an hour back, with a wounded man.'

'God forbid they come in here,' said Milly.

'If they do, you yell, eh?' Crydd wiped his sweating face. 'The town's gone bloody mad. We got sixty specials and about that many Military—and they've gone up to Penydarren. You know Mrs. Taibach and her son are dead, I suppose?'

The shock she showed was real. As the men went through the door she leaned, bowed on the counter; faintly, from above stairs, she heard Gideon call, and she overturned a tin of paste brooches and began to snatch them up. A constable said from the door 'You see that woman with a gun, you call, remember.'

She nodded. 'Yes, of course.'

When they had gone she lifted her skirts and ran upstairs to Gideon and knelt with her hand over his mouth, listening to the retreating footsteps. Then, straightening him on the bed, she began to undress him, and this she did with the utmost care, so that he should not be exposed to her.

It took her an hour to get him under the blanket, but when this was achieved he slept almost immediately, breathing in the rhythm of one at peace.

From the floor beside the bed his little white dog stared up at her: bending, she fondled it, and it licked her hand as if in gratitude.

'You are not allowed in here,' she whispered, and picked it up.

As she went to the door Gideon spoke, and she turned.

'Sun . . . Sun Heron . . .' he said.

She straightened as one with dignity and gripped the door.

'I . . . I am here,' she said.

That evening Randy Goldie climbed to the heights of Cefn, which overlooks the Brecon road. Here a body of rioters under the command of Abod of Penydarren had made their camp, awaiting the passage of an ammunition convoy coming from Brecon Barracks in support of the Highlanders. Of this body of insurgents, which numbered over a thousand, some four hundred were properly armed; the rest were mainly Irish, and these carried bludgeons. Road blocks had been set up across the road to Aberdare now, even mountain tracks were controlled by rebel snipers; nobody was allowed to leave Merthyr; farmers and their families trying to enter the town with goods were turned back. All this Randy saw, but did not find himself concerned. With the musket primed and the flint cocked he searched, in darkness now, for Ned Tranter. And, with returning sense, began to skirt the camp of the rebels up on Cefn Heights, shouting:

'A message for Ned Tranter of Dynefor! A message for Ned Tranter!'

And at ten o'clock, when the moon was high, Tranter heard this cry and came from a mass of men lying on their bellies on

Cefn Heights, and shouted.

'Ay, ay! Here's Ned Tranter!'

'The message this way,' shouted Randy, and retreated.

So it was that he came to a place of bushes which was away from the main body, and there he waited, shouting in the darkness: and Tranter came.

In the light of the moon Ned Tranter saw the face of Randy Goldie, and the musket in his hands, and Randy came to him close and touched him, then pulled him nearer, lowering the musket.

'You remember Blod Irish?' he asked.

And struck, and Tranter, who was big, went backwards, tripped and fell. Randy picked up the musket.

'This is from my girl,' he said, and fired.

When Abod, the Penydarren giant was called, he came with his wife, Liz Treharne, and they pushed through the ring of men where Randy was standing beside Tranter lying dead.

'What happened?' boomed Abod, and a collier replied:

'His name is Randy Goldie and he called from the dark for Tranter, and he went. And Goldie killed him.'

'She miscarried in Cwmglo,' said Liz softly. 'You know Tranter, he were a dog on the women.'

'Dear me,' said Abod, and rubbd his chin, and the moon shone down on the place of justice. Stooping he picked up the musket, cocked the pin and snapped it shut. ' 'Tis a light old trigger, mind. Some of these things do go off easy. Dear me, dear me . . .' he tossed the musket and Randy caught it. 'Now kill Highlanders—get back up there on the top of Cefn.'

At seven o'clock next morning Captain Moggridge of the Cardiff cavalry set out from Penydarren House to escort in the ammunition and baggage convoy coming from Brecon, and on their way through the town were fired on from many houses. And, after they had passed a narrow defile, the rioters came down from Cefn and blocked it with boulders, so that the cavalry and ammunition could not enter Merthyr by that route, but crossed the mountains from a village which was later drowned: this made the ammunition late for the defenders.

With the King both angered and dismayed, troops were now ordered into Merthyr from places as far away as Salisbury and Portsmouth, where the new steam-packet stood waiting to transport them, for it had been conveyed to the Government that the rebels of Merthyr intended to lead the rebels of England; that not only the Midland towns would rise to join the Welsh but London's east end, where the people were starving. Here, with parish relief down to a few shillings a head, the only Kingly assistance was a few tossed coppers to the Spitalfield poor: Reform would extend, said the Welsh, to the palace of St. James's, which was costing the country thousands a month.

At this the King was naturally concerned, and henceforth took more interest in the Merthyr correspondence from people like the Tory squires and the Marquis of Bute, much of which he personally annotated.

The iron masters besieged in Penydarren House were also concerned; for they learned that their ammunition convoy had been ambushed and the force under Captain Moggridge routed: that a hundred more cavalry sent in relief had been beaten off by musket-fire; that a troop of the West Glamorgan yeomanry under Major Penrice had been ambushed, disarmed and sent back to Swansea in disgrace.

What had begun as a riot was now a military operation.

Mrs. Duck Evans, late of Taibach, opened the travelling-case of Mr. Waxey Evans and counted on to the bed two hundred sovereigns. She had never imagined there to be so much money in Merthyr. And as she snapped the case shut and locked it, Mr. E. came into the room and looked out of the window.

'There is two hundred guineas in this travelling-case,' said she. 'Now tell me, Mr. E., where did you get it?'

'Ah,' said he.

'In the name of God, tell me, so I can give it back!'

'Ay,' said Mr. Duck.

'Where, then?' Shrieking this, she seized him and shook him, and he grinned amiably at this new game; from his throat came the sounds of the idiot; from his mouth the saliva ran in streams while her vehemence and panic beat about him.

'You half-wit—*tell me*!' and she struck him in the face. Still he grinned, rocking to and fro on his heels, and she threw herself down on the bed, and wept, saying:

'Holy Father, have you no pity for me?'

After a few moments she raised herself, and said: 'You know what they'll do, don't you, Mr. Duck Evans—you a sidesman in the Ebenezer? Can you think what they'll do for two hundred guineas. They will cut off your hands, perhaps, and dip the stumps in tar, as they once did to the forgers. And they will blind you, and send you back to me.' Her voice rose to a scream, and the neighbours in the Doss raised their white faces, thinking he was beating her. 'Don't you understand— they'll flog you if you take their ducks, but they will kill you if you steal their money, you hear me? You can insult their women, you can shame their daughters, but you must not touch their money—can you imagine what they'll do to you for two hundred guineas? Oh, my love, tell me where you got it!'

'Ay, ay,' said Mr. Duck Evans, and beamed.

Later he left her and she went to the window of the Doss, looking down on to the deserted streets, seeing instantly a tiny figure crossing the Iron Bridge with a flag, and this was Merve, the son of Billa; and the figure fell and rose, and fell again; and rose once more, the flag held high, and disappeared into Ynys Row. And there came to Mrs. Duck Evans a new courage, and she lifted the travelling-case and held it against her. Her mind went back through the bludgeoning years, to the hungers and threats and evictions, the agonising births, the screams of the women trapped underground, and she was with them, aged six. She remembered the yellow pools of excrement outside the doors; the heat of furnace summers, the bitter winters of the rags, her washing burned to holes, her father coughing, the typhoid, the cholera, the rickets of her youth. And she remembered the time she starved a baby to the point of death, then placed a saucer of water near its mouth, and the lizards came tumbling over its lips. She knew again the bright explosions of her youth and the blood-stained stumps, and she saw, in a sudden beam of the afternoon sun the parkland of Cyfarthfa rolling in June green against a sky of strickening light. She put the case under her arm and said through the window at Merthyr:

'The way you've treated me it's cheap at a thousand times that much,' and she went downstairs to her sickly children, kissed Mr. E. on the cheek where she had struck him, and added:

'The parish 'ave paid a bit more this week. Come on, my lovelies, we're moving out of Merthyr.'

Later, she went to the door and looked at the sky, and said:

'I won't forget, and I'm very much obliged.'

In a tumult of exultation Lewis Lewis, commander of the rebel contingent which disarmed the Swansea cavalry, now led his forces south and east over the Taff River, and here, bristling with muskets and sabres captured from Major Penrice, joined forces with those of Abod who had ambushed the ammunition wagons on the Brecon road. And he addressed the massed thousands to repeated cheering.

'Now we are armed, who shall we fear?' He raised high his hands and leaped on to a crag. 'The soldiers are bésieged in Penydarren, and they are few. It is we, the workers, who hold Merthyr for once, not this scum who call themselves masters!'

The rebels roared, stamping their feet; the afternoon was split by muskets fired into the air. Lewis Lewis continued: 'I say we mount an attack on Penydarren and flush them out... !'

'Unless they agree to our terms!' cried Abod.

'And the terms shall be restoration of wage rates at Cyfarthfa and Hirwaun, nothing less. Are ye with me?'

'Ay! Ay!'

It is said that they heard these roared replies as far east as Penydarren, and that one iron master collapsed with a paralytic stroke.

'And abolishment of the black list!'

'No victimisation!'

'Then let us treat with Crawshay, Lewis!' bawled Dai Solomon. 'Let Richard Evans, the puddler, speak for Hirwaun, and you for Cyfarthfa!'

'Wait you, Lewis!'

'Somebody is coming ...'

'A messenger—pull the bugger down!'

'Leave him!' commanded Abod, and shouldered out of the crowd, and men made way for him. And he stood in great size, hands on hips as the emissary from Penydarren, a young yeoman officer galloped up. He was small and fair, and the down of youth was on his face, yet he held himself well and was not afraid.

'I have a message for your leaders,' he said, and dismounted. 'I come from Penydarren. Mr. Guest and Mr. Crawshay, representing the masters, ask you to send a deputation to discuss terms of peace.'

Abod fumbled at this, but Lewis Lewis wandered up, his thumbs in his belt. 'How many more delegations, you think? Are we bloody children? You tell me how the last one fared.'

The young officer stood before him, unsmiling, and Abod said: 'He's a hearty wee cock. Shall we down his trews and check him for inches?'

But Lewis Lewis said: 'How many for this delegation? And what do we discuss?' The young officer said:

'I am only to inform you that you will be received, and treated with respect,' and he put his fists on his hips, like Abod, and looked him up and down.

'By God,' said Abod. 'He'd be rough to take, eh, son?' and he chucked the boy under the chin, and the young soldier said:

'It is not you I am worried about, Welshman, it's the other ten thousand.'

Men shouted with laughter at this, and gathered around him in cheers, and none laughed louder than Abod, who could have broken him with a hand. Lewis Lewis said then: 'Go back, sir. Tell the iron masters that this afternoon six men will come to parley at Penydarren. Touch a hair of their heads and we will tear the place to pieces. Now go.'

After the young officer had galloped away, Lewis Lewis, Abod and Richard Evans formed the insurgents into an order of battle, for the taking of Penydarren House, and there were eight battalions, each of one thousand men, and to them were appointed leaders; men like Thomas Vaughan and Daniel Thomas, John the Racer and David Hughes. And the great army formed up in the manner of soldiers. With Lewis Lewis at their head, led by the red flag in the hands of the boy Abednigo Jones, they marched down the Brecon road to the castle at Cyfarthfa; here they blew out the Crawshay Works, and sent their deputation on to Penydarren, while the rest waited, cleaning their bayonets and polishing their muskets, and many of them, especially the Irish of Pontmorlais, were drunk. Among them were women and children, some being the tattered orphans of the William Davies levels, who had caused the death of Jobina. Other small parties entered deeper into the town, especially to the north and west, and here requisitioned food, powder and shot from tradesmen; the powder chambers of the drifts and pits were also rifled for the muskets, and as far east as Dowlais twenty barrels were taken. Their look-outs, mounted on the horses of the West Glamorgan yeomanry, were galloping the hills from Trefil to Penderyn, north to Garn and south to Abercynon, and fire signals were smoking on the high ground. The encirclement of Merthyr was complete.

Miss Blossom Thomas laid down her doll and ran in a flurry of petticoats to Number Five Ynys Row and hammered the door: Mamie opened it.

'It is young Merve,' she began, white-faced. 'Oh, for God's sake, bring Billa!'

'Merve?' Mamie's expression did not change.

'In my house now, and wounded!'

Mamie shouted: 'Billa, Billa! It is Merve, it is Merve!'

'And near to death,' gasped Blossom. 'Oh, the blood, the blood!'

Billa and Mamie found him on the floor of Papa Tomo's kitchen, and he was lying like a compound accident, his bare arms outflung, and Billa went on her knees beside him, and, weeping without tears, ran her hands up his shirt and down his trews, and the ball had struck him high, taking through the right shoulder in a downward path, and, spent, was lying in his chest. He was dying.

'Sorry, Mam,' he said.

'Quick, ring a surgeon!' cried Blossom, biting at her hands.

'Ay, but no,' said Billa, and she sat on the floor and took his head in her lap and there cooled his face with a rag and water Mamie brought. 'They are not putting him to the knife. I have seen the laudanum, and it does not work.'

'He will die?' whispered Blossom, kneeling.

'He is already dying,' said Mamie.

'Sorry, Mam,' said Merve.

'God,' said Mamie, 'This is no country for children and women,' and she walked Blossom's kitchen, empty. 'And not a word of my Randy...'

'There's me little boy,' said Billa, kissing him. 'There's me fine big Merve—fighting again, is it?'

'Sorry, Mam.'

And there came to Mrs. Billa Jam of Taibach a quiet that turned Mamie's face to her, and Blossom Thomas heard this, for it came after a small gasp from the child, and he shuddered once in Billa's arms, and died. And then she lowered her head and her hair, which was unpinned from a wash, swept over his face; she wept.

Then from the bedroom above came a roaring song, and the window went up and Papa Tomo Thomas hung out for all to see the red flag which Merve had brought, and he waved it at the deserted streets of Bridgefield, crying:

'Right you, come and get it and I'll blast ye into the sea! Roll me down to the Frenchies, me lads, and we'll show 'em what cannons are. Ahoy there, me hearties! By God, if I had decent legs I'd teach ye how to make rebellion! Shoni Crydd, Bill Tobbo and Mike O'Hara—ye call yourself special constables? Ay, well here's a flag of blood, and Papa Tomo is defending it—tell old Crawshay to come and get it!' and he tipped the flask of gin to his lips, belched and pardoned and waved his fist at a passing dog.

Mamie said: 'Blossom Thomas, if you don't get up there and stop that palaver I'll up and murder that old bastard.'

The riot was spreading. All that Saturday groups of men carrying flags and Cobbett's pamphlets journeyed over The Top to the towns of Ebbw Vale, Nantyglo and Tredegar, though Beaufort under the more benevolent duke was ignored, the workmen there being contented. To Blaenafon and Llanelli and Pontypool hundreds of Merthyr and Dowlais men and boys went next morning, seeking support of their demand for Reform. And the tradesmen of the Top Towns answered the call. They came in their hundreds, blowing out their furnaces and throwing down their tools: all that Sunday they travelled, carrying the banners of their secret lodges and infant unions, playing their bands of fifes and drums. And they arrowed like the fingers of a giant hand on to old Waun Hill, spilling down the narrow streets of Dowlais. These were not only the underpaid cutters, hauliers and colliers, but the men of the respected trades who, till now, had never caused disturbance. Their wives came too; armed with sacks to loot food from Guest and Fothergill's hated truck shops, they ran alongside the marching columns of men, adding their shrieks to the bawled threats; with their children on their backs they danced jigs over the mountain grass, tore shift bandages for wounds, spiking the heads of clubs and cutting food. Some there were in Monmouthshire who would not come, and many of these were visited by the dreaded Scotch Cattle, the enforcers of the new Union laws. Dressed in the skins of beasts, their leaders with cow horns strapped to their heads, these roamed the towns, dragging out men for beatings, burning the furniture of the black-legs. And so many travelled to Merthyr that night under threat of force, herded like cattle along the tracks to Waun Hill by men with clubs and trailing ropes that prevented escape. In the morning, a Sunday, a great civilian army therefore converged on the Merthyr parish, and it numbered over ten thousand, according to the *Merlin*. With Merthyr and Dowlais already full of rioters, the deacons, shopkeepers and gentry went under their beds as the great rabble poured on to

Waun and raised its flags of Reform amid wild shouts. Ragged, hungry, unkempt from sleeping out, this new force was joined on the hill by that of Lewis Lewis and Abod of Penydarren, whose delegation to the iron masters had won victory: Crawshay had agreed to restore the wages lately reduced at Hirwaun and Cyfarthfa. And Lewis cried:

'Does not this only land us back where we started?'

'To hell with the wage restoration—we want an increase!'

'Ten per cent all round!'

They waved their arms, shrieking. 'Ten per cent! Ten per cent. What we want is Reform, not prattle! Reform, Reform, Reform!'

'Reform all round and wage increases, or we march on Penydarren House! By God, we'll teach them about old Forman's ready money!' And they prepared for the march. But already their ranks were splitting in dissent, and there came among them men who were not radicals, and these widened the split, dividing them, and one shouted, pulling down Lewis Lewis:

'And if they give you ten per cent after the restoration, what will ye ask for then, you fools? For you're already greedier than your masters! Listen—the Military are coming—we know this: not a few hundred, but thousands, perhaps, and they'll shoot you down like dogs. I say accept the terms, and thank your God, for they might not be offered tomorrow!'

Then this man, too, whose name is not known, was pulled down, yet his words were echoed and cheered by the ragged army on the right, while on the left came jeers and shrieks of derision, and Abod bawled, leaping up:

'And what of the blood they spilled by the Castle Inn? Do they die in vain? What of the children and women who have been murdered, shot down in cold blood? Is this what you sacrifice for wage restorations—your own flesh and blood? Rise here one man who has lost his own—here, Toby Garner, and let him be seen!' and he hauled up beside him a man wizened and small, and he was weeping. 'Does Toby Garner fight for restoration now, or does he cry for revenge for his wife and son?'

The man drooped before them, and they went quiet, remembering the Castle Inn and the bloodstained road, and Abod yelled: 'I say march on Penydarren and take the place by storm. Get signed documents for a ten per cent rise *after* restoration ...!'

'And when you've broken Crawshay's bank—what then, big man?'

Curses, cheers and jeers rose from the mob, which swayed, arms high. And for an hour they stood on Waun and quarrelled, and bitterness grew in the place of comradeship. Spies broke away and ran to inform the iron masters. And at ten o'clock that morning four hundred and fifty soldiers marched up Dowlais Hill with Guest at their head, to make the split wider.

It was on this morning that Gideon's fever subsided, but he was still delirious, and many times called Sun Heron's name. And, sitting there beside him, Miss Thrush knew that sight would have told that she was not beautiful, as Sun Heron was beautiful, she of the red-gold hair. With sight he would have known that her breast was too full, her hips too large; that her hands and feet were not dainty, as Sun Heron's, for it was by this name he continued to call her, not Sun Penderyn, another man's wife. In the onslaught of middle age Miss Thrush had wilted; obesity now was taking charge, and she would have recalled the defiling years only to be winsome, and gay, as the woman Gideon loved. Yet the passion in her grew for him even as she sat there, and his need called to her.

'Sun Heron ... Sun Heron ...'

And there came to Miss Thrush then an awareness of love, and a need that it be fulfilled; this awareness grew and brought to her throat a dryness, and a beating of her heart that no power of will could stifle. And as his hands roamed the blanket in search of Sun Heron, Miss Thrush began to tremble, and the trembling grew from her lips and consumed her.

'Sun ...'

Afterwards, she could die, she thought. After she had offered herself and known acceptance or rejection, she could leave him, and know herself to be defiled, as a stag defiles itself in its pit. Yet she would know the fulfilment of her love, this she reasoned, clutching at her hands. For a minute of her life she would be possessed, though in the name of another and in the bed of a loved one; and would give to this man the relief of love.

'Sun... Sun... !' It was as if his whole being was reaching out for her.

'Gid,' she said.

The sound of her silenced him and his eyes opened full on her face; she shrank away, exposed in the deceit. And then Gideon smiled and there came to his face a radiance she had never seen before; he raised himself in the bed and opened his arms to her. Kneeling, she touched his lips with the tips of her fingers, and the touch momentarily stilled him, as if he disbelieved. Then he grasped her hands and began to kiss them, calling her name, which was not her name but the one for whom his soul and body cried.

'Sun!'

He sought her; his hands moved up her arms and drew her down to him, and his lips swept her face and his fingers were in her hair; there was in him a passion of strength that brought her to momentary terror, for she had never been used before. And then fear left her in the knowledge that she would be his wife, and this brought her to a new, untainted joy. This joy was awakened by his kiss, and her mouth was one with his and there beat about them a great wind of oblivion as he drew her to the bed.

'Wait,' she said, in command, and he quietened at her bidding, as men do.

She did not speak more; indeed, she dared not speak again lest, through the mist of his sickness, he would have knowledge of her subterfuge, and cast her out. For her there was no taking, but giving; later, she thought as she undressed before his blindness, she would renew the laces in his boots, for they were worn, as she had expected. Laces, boots, razors, bodies—one was not more important than the other in the pursuit of his pleasure. And if she should die, broken by his strength—for he was a big man—would not this be justice, because of her betrayal? she reasoned. Her dress ringed her feet, and then her petticoats; looking momentarily beautiful, Miss Thrush unpinned her long hair and waved it down to her waist, and this covered some of her approaching nakedness as she took off her bodice, and she saw, in revulsion, that there was little shape to her breasts, and she was thankful for his blindness, that she had so little to give. This confession of inadequacy chastened her, and she momentarily dropped before him in the window sunlight. But there was upon his face such an expectation of joy that she banished this; the knowledge of his need diluted in measure the sadness that her gift was small. Now she took his hands in hers and held them against her breast, and he closed his eyes and drew aside the blanket that she might enter into his warmth. And in the moment before his arms took her and his lips sought hers in gusty breath, she saw in a sky of astonishing blue the golden outline of the mountain flashing in the sun: the harvest of the world, she saw amid a growing, lovely music. She did not see the stunted trees and violated earth, but a bright river flowing down the sewer of the Taff. The wildness that consumed her then was the breaking out of her long captivity, the loneliness, longings, the fretful tears. He knew well of her, and she knew him as a man contained and strong in will, if unused to women. She worshipped him in whispers and caresses, and Gideon was good to her, because she did not defile them. And when the bright explosions of their union grew in the pace of love he cried aloud, yet did not call a name. Wondering at this cry, she held him, and he said:

'I love you. I love you.'

The words came as an echo in her soul, transcending in their simplicity any lovely sound she had ever heard. Nobody had said this to her before: not the man she remembered as her father: the child who had kissed her in a churchyard outside Wigan, nor the youth who had demanded her in rough-hewn strength, aged seventeen, in springtime on the banks of the Stour. They induced in her refinement amid the outrageous act committed against her; smothering with dignity the impropriety that she should be so invaded. Honour was laid in her husband and his kisses were sweet to her mouth. Vaguely, she wondered if she might bear his child, and in this new-found womanhood drew him down to her, telling in a gust of words that she needed him, too, in truth and love. Then no longer was she in the bed of a lover, but taken to a wild place which she had never known; a land of flowing forests laden with the tangled skeins of primitive flowers. And in this place the man's voice grew louder, louder; it was a command in which she died by conquest, in a strength greater than hers, and she knew that she was one with him, that the union was complete. She was astonished that it was so beautiful, so simple, and she could have cried aloud at this discovery, such was her peace, and joy. Presently Gideon sighed.

'Milly . . .' he said.

In a clubbed silence of disbelief, she held him, listening, but he did not speak again. Until now she had heard him calling for Sun Heron, so it must have been imagination, she thought; indeed, how could it be otherwise? How could this man have called her name when she was but the husk of the woman he was possessing?

Knowing this, she yet held him, cherishing his face with kisses.

Now for the first time the great forces joined; the insurgents came thronging down narrow Dowlais Hill, but they were now without purpose. Having delayed the attack on Penydarren House, divided over whether or not to accept the wages restoration or persist for an increase and other points of Reform, the rioters stumbled on with the most militant in the van, and among these were Lewis Lewis and Richard Evans; but other leaders such as Abod and Dai Solomon, Tom Vaughan and Dan Thomas advised for acceptance of the masters' terms, and these, under their own banners, followed at the rear. Thousands, too, their fire quenched by the dissent, were drifting back to their homes—their great numbers allowing them to defy the Scotch Cattle who guarded the escape routes back to the towns of The Top. The story of lack of union was being retold. The leaders were not the only ones divided: collier was pitted against puddler in the grasp of greed; baller opposed cutter and the behinders and picklers of the Pontypool tinplate shrieked their arguments at the Vaynor hauliers, demanding respect for trade: Union branches squabbled with the Benefit members, Oddfellows challenged the Dowlais Building Society to see bloody sense. And the clamour rose from them as they stumbled, hungry and disorganised, down the cobbles of Dowlais High; and they marched in ragged contempt, distrustful of neighbour and town, trade against trade, rate against rate. In this fashion, with their red and black banners of Reform sagging on their shoulders, they came to a place which was the narrowest on the hill, and before them was a solid block of red and gold, and the shine of bayonet steel. It was the 93rd Highlanders, their vicious enemies of the Castle massacre, and elements of the Militia. Some of these were lying side by side on the road; others were kneeling, a great body was standing; all had bayonets fixed, and their muskets pointed fifty deep. From the windows of the little terraced houses of the Irish projected muskets; around corners and from the grimy alleys the bayonets pointed, flashing in the morning sun. And before the soldiers their commanding officer stood motionless, his sword upraised, waiting to give the command to fire.

The van of the rioters stopped, flinging themselves back as those behind tried to force them on. Lewis Lewis spun to face them, crying:

'Ay, then what ails you? Rush them!'

The mob muttered and shoved; some lowered their faces: none moved forward and a man cried, dancing to the fore: 'Lewis is right—rush, rush! We are thousands, and they are under five hundred!'

'Are ye daft? D'ye want the same as ye got at the Castle?'

Another shouted: 'I say keep them here on guard while we get in the men from the Brecon and Swansea roads—we've got bloody thousands up there doing nothing!'

The soldiers did not move. The commanding officer was like a statue, the sword upraised, and in this presence of courage and training, the mob gibbered, its purpose waned. Still another—a man with one leg—came from the edge of the crowd on a crutch, and waved it, shouting:

'Are ye milk-sops or are ye Welsh? God alive, I come from the north—is this what ye call Glamorgan?'

'Talk sense, man!' bawled a woman. 'Half of your lot are running.'

'And what about the Merthyr workers, then? Where the hell they got to?' This from a Dowlais puddler under Guest, and he was eight pounds ten in debt to the Shop there, and on the black-list. 'Is this a Dowlais fight alone? I'm a Staffordshire man, and proud of it. One bang from a fowling-piece and you damned Welsh are off!'

313

'I say rush and to hell with what comes!' shouted Lewis Lewis.

They fumed, they pushed and muttered threats; they fretted, but they did not rush, and in seconds years were lost; Reform was lost; hopes, ambitions died. And they fell to silence, staring at the bayonets. From behind the soldiers came Josiah John Guest, and he cried, his arms high:

'See, you are betrayed! Most of you are from Dowlais and the towns of Blaenafon and Pontypool, Tredegar and Nantyglo under Crawshay Bailey. Is this a Top Town fight, then? Or is it your fight for the people of Cyfarthfa? For where are the comrades of Merthyr, for whom you have come to fight? Are they attacking Penydarren House? They are not! They have camped in thousands on the road to Brecon!'

'It is a lie!' shouted Lewis Lewis. 'Am I not here?'

'You might be,' said Guest drily, 'but what of the thousands? Are Dowlais men to die for Cyfarthfa?—if so, it is a strange form of riot. And I tell you this—I have come in your cause; for had I not done so these soldiers would have cut you to pieces. Earlier we told your deputation that Mr. Crawshay *might* grant a restoration of wages. Now you want even more, and he withdraws all his offers, for you do not adopt peaceful methods of negotiation. As for you Dowlais men—have I not always listened to your complaints?'

There was a roar of derision, about the last sound they made. Guest shouted: 'Bring all your complaints to me after a return to work, and I will listen again.'

'Ay,' said Lewis Lewis, 'I wonder where I have heard that before?' He swung to the mob. 'I say rush them! They can't kill all of us—rush them, and join the Merthyr men at Cyfarthfa!'

Guest said blandly: 'At Cyfarthfa, man? The last time I heard of them they were retreating along the Brecon Road.' They were not, but anything would do; it was stroke and counter-stroke. Now he turned to Colonel Morgan. 'Right, Commanding Officer, they have been warned, now you may fire when you care, even though they be my own men mostly,' and he stepped through the ranks of the soldiers and went into

314

a house. The officer moved to the side of the road and pressed himself against the wall, the sword held higher. And the men stared into five hundred levelled muskets, then faced down, and broke.

It was Monday the sixth of June, the day of the Guest betrayal.

The soldiers did not move; the mob began to disperse into the hills, but many, braver than the most, crossed to the west and joined the insurgents on the roads to Brecon and Swansea, to help them keep control of the town, and here they underwent much drilling and parades, with a flying of banners, and two great black flags were seen flying on the turnpike road to the north. But, from his high turret in Cyfarthfa Castle, William Crawshay, the iron master, noticed a split in the ranks of even these rioters, for despite the crackle of their muskets and drilling, many were seen to be returning home, and there remained only the hard-core of armed insurgents. Some were seen throwing away their weapons or burying them. Soon, even the parades ceased; the banners were lowered, the red flags burned, the effigies destroyed. And Crawshay, to assist the return to peace, again abandoned the reduction in wages at Cyfarthfa and Hirwaun, or so it was reported: this he later, and publicly, revoked.

Sun Penderyn was sitting on the bed in Seven Ynys, looking out at the dram-road and deserted Bridge Street when Mamie came.

'How's Billa?' asked Sun.

'As well as can be expected, poor girl. God, she pinned her soul on that little Merve.'

'It will be better when old Dai and Mr. Jam come,' said Sun.

'And your Dic,' said Mamie. 'Did I tell ye my Randy's been seen?'

'No!'

Mamie beamed. 'Ay—seen up on Cefn night 'fore last—by old Nell Regan, the Dynefor Irish—ye remember Nell?'

Sun nodded. According to the reports coming in, anyone up

315

on Cefn above the Brecon Road was armed; one of these detachments of rioters had ambushed the 93rd, and the Highlanders were after every one of them: led by Captain Moggridge, the Swansea rebels were being brought home captive in batches: it was said that the new soldiers entering the town had immediately been sent to capture the outlying rebels, and Crawshay himself was preparing to assist in apprehending the ringleaders. Standing there at the window Sun began to wonder what had happened to Gideon. Zimmerman, they said, had fled before the first shot was fired, but it was inconceivable to her that Gideon would run, too: William Twiss, the Unionist she despised, had gone to Aberdare, boldly preaching the need of Unionism, she had heard. The puddler Tom Llewellyn, into whose hands most women would have delivered their lives, had been seen as far east as Pontypool. Turning away she thanked God that Dic was on Aberdare mountain.

'I am thankful to Morgan Howells, mind,' she said to Mamie, who was making the bed.

'Ay, ay, he do good intended,' gasped Mamie, bending. 'Be all right, won't it, when your Dico comes back with that Seion fella.'

Lifting the baby against her, Sun turned again to the window.

The men were crowding in now, made courageous by their very numbers. They thronged down Dynefor and Jackson's, through Dixon and into *China*. Sun saw Philip Lewis, the gambo man, come into Sixteen Ynys, his face blackened, as if he had just returned from a Tasker shift; a few days earlier he had clubbed down a Highlander with one fist and felled a second with a tapper: Blind Dick and Hugh Pughe trotted in on their pony, the harp over its rear—first prize for tenor and accompaniment at the Abergavenny Eisteddfod—and now they were looking for Shoni Melody... Among the men coming in from the Swansea road was Dai Solomon and Tom Vaughan, Dick Llaw-Haearn and Robert Jones, and these went quickly to their sobbing wives, already in earshot of the transportation hulks, yet unable to run because of children... Molly Caulara was on the Iron Bridge again, chatting to the colliers who stayed at home, with the superficial gaiety of a woman lost: the radical Unitarians were flooding down the streets, fearlessly ranting the need of Reform in the face of defeat. Dragoons were galloping the lanes around Merthyr, bringing in the malefactors on their saddle cords, haltered like beasts. Militia squads were marching with the precision of conquerors, their blue and red uniforms a contrast to the ragged droop of the bearded conquered. The Castle and Talbot hotels were being prepared for the arrival of Mr. Evans Thomas of Sully, the chairman of the county quarter sessions; coaches and horses were being requisitioned to convey the accused to the county gaol at Cardiff. Men and women were being snatched from their houses as the pace of retribution grew. Shopkeepers thronged the streets with new-found courage, condemning and accusing, and whole families were examined for the presence of loot. Several of the murdered were claimed by mourning relatives from the coach house of the Castle Inn, and decently buried, but when the relatives returned from the funerals they were examined before the military court for participation in the rising. Therefore, many who died of wounds for want of medical attention were buried secretly, by night, in the open fields or cinder-tips of the works; therefore the total number killed by the soldiers that day has not been recorded. And the gambos and carts began again their endless journeyings, returning the furniture to their previous owners, though Miss Blossom Thomas never lost her picture. Clank clank up to the door of Number Five, Ynys, and Mamie Goldie opened it wide; the young lieutenant said, with soldiers at attention behind him:

'A man died who belonged to this house. I have orders to examine his mother for participation in the riot—Mrs. Jam, I am instructed...'

'Get out, you murdering swines,' said Mamie, 'the man was ten years old,' and she slammed the door in his face.

Strangely, although she did not see this, the young lieutenant bowed.

In her misery, when darkness fell, Merthyr tossed and turned: two inquests were held for scores of dead.

And Dic Penderyn did not come.

Instead, with darkness, Shoni Crydd came with three other special constables. The moon was shining over Merthyr when Sun opened the door. And they spoke no word, but pushed past her into the kitchen, and when she came, demanding, they slammed the door behind her.

'What the hell's the meanin' of this?' She gripped the petticoat against her throat.

'You'll soon know, Missus,' said Shoni Crydd.

The baby began to cry upstairs, but she did not hear it. And when Crydd eased his great bulk into a chair she stood above him, flushed with anger.

'He hasn't been near Merthyr, and you know it!' she breathed, bending to him. 'He's been up on Aberdare mountain, and you know that, too, don't you?'

'Ay, ay, woman,' said Shoni, and lit his pipe.

'Then what are ye doing here?'

Bill Tobbo and Boy O'Hara were Irish, and they leaned against the wall with easy confidence, coming to collect a Welsh; but Mog Morgan was Welsh from Swansea, and there was a sickness in him as he listened to the baby, and his bowels shrank in the knowledge of his perfidy.

Shoni Crydd said: 'There's evidence against him. Sworn statements have been taken from James Abbott, the barber, that your man was in the deputation . . .'

'A deputation—here, in town?'

'At the Castle Inn. Tom Darker confirms it, and he saw him again in the mob some five minutes later.'

'Tom Darker! D'you take the words of a paid Judas now, then?' A panic was growing within her. Soon Dic would come, and they would take him, these men would not be here unless they knew he was coming . . .

Crydd said: 'And the testimony of Jim Drew—this fella swears his life away, woman, an' he'll be hard put to deny it. For Drew says he was in the Castle deputation: that he saw him wrestling with the Highlanders, and stab a private soldier with a bayonet, and that's a hanging crime.'

'But how could he, fella, if he was up on Aberdare?' She gripped her hands and shouted into his face.

'Where your man says he was and where he got to are different things, Mrs. Penderyn. Shall I tell ye something else? I saw him, too.'

'You're a bloody liar, and Dic will prove it!'

'Me and the Private Black. God alive, woman—what else do you want—Guest, Crawshay and the whole army troop?'

She wandered about, holding herself, pausing before Mog Morgan, who turned away his eyes; the chair creaked under the bulk of Shoni Crydd; the two Irish Specials watched her with understanding smiles. To Morgan, Sun said: 'And you, did you see him, too, or didn't they pay you enough?'

'I'm only doing my job, woman.'

'And your job is a stink in the noses of decent Welsh!' She swung to Shoni Crydd. 'Have you sought out Lewis Lewis, for there's no damn mention o' him that I hear of?'

Crydd blew out smoke. 'They're fetchin' him. They're fetching them all, Mrs. Penderyn. And I call on you to tell your man to come quietly, or it'll be the worse for him.'

Sun sat slowly on to a chair, her eyes bright in her bloodless face. 'May God have mercy on ye soul, Shoni Crydd, and Abbot and Drew, and the man Tom Darker, for me chap was up on the mountain, and with a witness to prove it, and I tell you this. The truth will out and you'll be stained with it, you and yours down the generations, and you'll ne'er rub it out. How long are you staying?'

'Until your fella comes.' He grunted on his clay and cocked it up in his heavy face and folded his hands on his stomach.

'Then out and fetch another four,' said she, 'for if my Dic finds the likes of these in here, then God help you.'

Crydd did not reply; reaching out, he lowered the wick in the lamp and the room danced with shadows; upstairs the baby had ceased to cry.

'One shift out of you—one sound, and we floor you, woman —remember it,' said Boy O'Hara, the Irish, and Bill Tobbo, who hailed from County Clare, moved to the sound of running footsteps, and stood pressed behind the door.

319

The special constables ranged as far afield as Pembrokeshire and Carmarthenshire, pulling suspects from their beds and transporting them to Merthyr under escort: the hills from Waun to the Blorenge were combed for escapees; barns were pulled out and haystacks prodded, farmhouses were visited by night, and at ten o'clock David Hughes, Tom Vaughan and Dai Thomas were brought in roped—he who was known by the nick-name Dick Llaw-Haearn, and his woman, Betsy Paul, had to be beaten off by the constables. Then, before midnight came Tom Llewellyn of Cyfarthfa, and he was caught on the mountain of Caerphilly, trying to reach the sea, and the workers lined the roads and jeered when the Military brought him to the Castle Inn, in chains, because he had defected. Broad, handsome, bright in the eye, he came now with shuffling feet, his face low; and men shouted insults into his face, and women, who once adored him, spat on his clothes. Many there were who had not run away, but returned to their homes to await the knock; men like David Richards, whose wife was in labour even as the Specials came, and David Jones who was frightened of his mother, but no man alive: these were haltered by the neck, yet walked with dignity and smiles, despite the humiliation. Some were captured who are not recorded; broken men and boys, ragged and dishevelled, soaked with the dew of sleeping rough; thumped into wakefulness by the batons of the special constables, the ruffians of Merthyr, and many carried bruises, and blood was on their faces: some, too, were wounded, the injuries septic, and they stood in the Castle yard in aimless groups while the surgeons attended them. Joan Jenkins was brought in shackled to her husband and brother, and both these were men terrified while she walked cocky, spitting at the feet of the examining magistrate; these, with others, were taken for looting furniture, but claimed they were looting their own property, then, for it was furniture distrained by Coffin's Court, for debt. Margo Davies of Dynefor came weeping, with her hands over her face, unafraid of the possibility of transportation to the Colonies and the bloodstained sticks, but fearful of the anger of her outraged relatives. Twenty-six rioters were taken to Cardiff gaol by

320

escorted coaches, rumbling out of Merthyr amid the cock-a-hoop Militia, the prancing yeomanry of boy-men on their big farm mares and horses: they went with manacled hands and feet, in the manner of felons, bowed on the juddering seats. Two there were, however, who were uncaptured just before this event, and both were to have their names written in the annals of their country's history; one was Lewis Lewis, and the other was Dic Penderyn.

When the mob broke on Dowlais Hill, Lewis Lewis ran to the village of Penderyn, the place from which Dic had taken his name to avoid confusion with other Lewises. It is said that his wife and family, with their furniture distrained, were living in Brecon; but he ran to Penderyn because it was his home, he was born there; also, at one time earlier he had been employed by Mr. Morgan of Bodwigiad, to whom it has been said that he was related, having been a huntsman on the estate. Indeed, many have claimed that Lewis Lewis was the illegitimate son of one of the local squires who abounded in those parts; some even said he was of noble birth, and that this is why he escaped the rope, but no proof exists of any of this. It has even been assumed that the English government mistook Lewis Lewis, aged thirty-eight, for the younger Richard Lewis called Dic Penderyn, since both men had connections with this village so named. One thing is sure; no man played a greater part in the riots of Merthyr, yet he did not die for this responsibility.

Hiding in the grounds of Bodwigiad, Lewis Lewis was taken on the road in Penderyn, for the special constables had a nose for cook-pots, and two named Eynon Beynon and John Selwyn lay in wait at a place of loneliness beyond small cottages; as he went past in the night mist these men took him from the hedge, and both were mountain fighters. One tripped him and as he sprawled the other held him, but he rose and flung them off; hands clenched, he awaited them, and they came with batons drawn.

'Come quiet, Lewis, or it'll come worse for you!'

And Lewis feinted and caught Beynon with a right to the head, ducked Selwyn's swinging baton and hooked him to the stomach, and as he fell Lewis dived for the open fields, but the man Selwyn, who had once fought with Abod of Penydarren, went full length and caught his heels and pulled him down, and, holding him, awaited the truncheon of Beynon, who beat him. Yet the villagers of Penderyn slept on, for he made no sound, it was said. And they bound him on the road, being men of great strength, and took him to the Lamb Inn, and there detained him; and they sent a child to the Castle Inn to tell of the capture: William Crawshay, the iron master, hearing this, rode personally with Colonel Bush, the commander of the Pensioners, and Lieutenant Franklin with a large body of his yeomen cavalry, and took him from the Lamb Inn. With his hands tied behind him and a halter around his neck, Lewis Lewis came on foot into Merthyr with an escort of cavalry jogging about him and an iron master and a Colonel of the Pensioners leading the way in triumph.

In this manner Lewis Lewis came, and his was the dignity, said the people.

And on his way to the Castle Inn the prisoner passed within sight of Seven Ynys where Shoni Crydd and the other three Specials were lying in wait for his friend and namesake, Dic Penderyn.

Dic parted with his escort, the Seion deacon's son, at a place just south of Cefn Heights where the 93rd Highlanders' ammunition convoy had been ambushed; here, according to his family's belief he had been living in a cave, and did not return to Merthyr until they instructed. Mr. Evans returned to his home in Penrhiw and Dic walked in darkness across the tracks until he came to an inn, and there drank. Other inns presented themselves on the return to home, and at these he stopped and drank also; he was tipsy when he came past the simmering furnaces of Ynys and crossed the dram-road, unseen, and ran down to Number Seven Caradoc and Asa, two of Billa's boys were playing on the slag tumps as he came, and one of these he grasped and tossed high in a gale of laughter, and Shoni Crydd heard this laughter and rose from his chair in Sun's kitchen.

'Watch the woman,' he said, and Bill Tobbo gripped Sun

and twisted her against the wall and put his hand over her mouth. Boy O'Hara, the big Irish, got it first as Dic entered, because he was nearest. Gay with laughter, Dic burst through the door, his arms out for Sun, and he shouted, seeing O'Hara, ducked the baton and swung him hard to the jaw, and the Special slipped down the front of him with a sigh: three now, and Dic wheeled as Shoni Crydd came in, caught the baton and twisted it from his hand and pinned the big man against the wall as Crydd kicked and clubbed, but every blow took him clean, and blood was on Crydd's face as he got clear. Sun turned on Bill Tobbo who still had his hand over her face, and bit him, and when he yelled and got his fingers free she took her nails to him while Dic leaned over her shoulder and caught Tobbo square, and he fell.

'Run for it, Dic!'

'Not till I've done these bastards,' and he backed into Crydd who was rising and sent him floundering, then back-handed O'Hara as he was getting up. Sun was down as Mamie Goldie came through the door with a copper-stick; stooping, she dragged Sun to a corner, then belaboured Shoni Crydd with one hand while she threw the table cups at Mog Morgan, who was standing in a corner doing nothing while Tobbo and O'Hara were bellowing for help. With Crydd on his feet again, Dic attacked, hooking left and right to face and body with smashes to go through him, and the table went over in a crash of crocks, with Crydd between its legs and Billa, who had come through the back, hit Mog Morgan with a chair, and him still doing nothing but shielding himself. And, at that moment the three big Irish lodgers, Tim, Michael and Joe, who were due from Taibach to lodge, wandered along the Row looking for Billa and a bed, and heard the fighting, and a pot came through the back window to make sure of it, so they waded in, leaving their coats outside, which is right and proper, said Mamie after, for you can't let a good fight go by. This brought the neighbours, male mostly, and Mamie and Billa landed Shoni Crydd copper sticks for luck and pulled Sun outside while the men piled in, with more special constables running down from the Popi Davey. They've had some fights up and

323

down the Row, said Mr. Papa Tomo Thomas, waving his red flag, but nothing like the one they had in Seven Ynys when they tried to take Dic Penderyn, for most of the neighbours came out to assist the Specials along Bridgefield with rolling-pins and shillelaghs, and the Miners' Arms turned out, and the roughs came running in from Iron Bridge, and the worshippers got up off their knees in Ynysgau Chapel, for they were just giving thanks for the end of the riot. And then the Military came. The Military came with loaded muskets and bayonets fixed just as Shoni Crydd came out backwards with Mamie and Billa after him, and he tripped and fell at the feet of the sergeant.

'What's happening here?' the sergeant demanded.

Frozen, the Welsh stood, and Crydd said, from the ground: 'It's the man Lewis . . .' and he pointed at Dic who was standing in the doorway with his arms around his wife.

'How many more Lewises,' said the soldier. 'We've got one up at the Castle already.'

'Richard Lewis, this one,' said Crydd, getting up, and blood was on his mouth, 'but he goes by the name of Dic Penderyn.'

'And you are arresting him for riot? I've never seen the man before.' The sergeant was young, his accent broad North Country.

'For riot, on the testimony of James Abbot, Thomas Darker and James Drew.'

'This has not been notified, and he is not on the list,' replied the sergeant, consulting a paper.

'How could he be?' asked Sun. 'He was nowhere near the rioters, he was up on Aberdare mountain these past four days.'

'I saw him in the deputation,' said Crydd. 'James Abbott and I will bear witness—we saw him in the Castle Inn deputation. And William Williams, the tailor, saw him also. James Drew bears witness that he saw him stab your soldier.'

The sergeant's eyes immediately snapped up at this. 'Private Black of the 93rd?' He moved near to Dic and Sun. 'You stabbed one of ours, with a bayonet?'

'I was on Aberdare mountain . . .'

'Oh, God,' whispered Sun.

The young sergeant stepped aside and nodded peremptorily to his men. 'Take him,' he said.

The neighbours stood in silence. Only one voice was heard then—old Papa Tomo down in One Ynys, waving his flag and bawling; then another. Faintly, from the floor above, came the sound of the baby crying.

RANDY GOLDIE came back to Mamie two days after Dic was taken, and these two days after the ending of the riot he had spent up in Adulum Fields, with Blod. Mamie sank down on to a chair and Billa went out, taking the children, as he entered; he was soaked with dew and trembling with the sleeping out, despite it was June.

'Hallo, son,' said Mamie.

'Ay, ay,' he said, and he stood looking at her, not moving.

'Where you been till now, then?'

He shrugged. 'Up with Blod.'

'Anyone see you come in?'

He did not reply, but sat down and looked at his hands. 'You all right, then?' he asked eventually.

'Ay, fine. Old Dai and Billy Jam coming today, you know.' She warmed to him, trying to envelop him in her love, yet nervous to touch him lest the gossamer thread that bound them be broken by clumsiness. And as she moved uncertainly to get food for him, the door opened and Sun came in with her baby, Richard Jay. Her eyes switched from Mamie to Randy, and back.

'Randy's come home,' said Mamie simply.

'Ay, I see.' Sun kissed him in passing. 'You hungry, love?'

Randy nodded. The look in his eyes made her fight for normality.

'The kids will be glad you're back, boy.'

He nodded, his eyes distant, and said: 'I had Ned Tranter, mind—I saw to Ned Tranter.'

'Yes?' said Sun, and Mamie clutched herself at the fireplace.

'Oh, ay,' said Randy. 'I had him right enough—I shot him up on Cefn.'

'You ... you what?' whispered Mamie.

Sun reached out and gripped her arm, saying: 'You shot Ned Tranter because of Blod?'

'Ay, ay.'

There was no sound then but the ticking of the clock. Sun said: 'Have you told anybody else this?'

'Only the fellas—but Abod said it was all right, though. Dic said it didn't matter, neither—he said Tranter deserved it because of Blod.'

'Dic said that? When?'

'A couple o' nights back, up on Cefn. He'd come up from the Castle.'

Mamie was standing with her hands against her face; Sun said: 'You ... you saw Dic up at Cefn?'

'Oh, ay.' He grinned and wiped his mouth.

Sun said evenly: 'Randy, are ye sure it wasn't Lewis Lewis?'

His eyes were steady on hers. 'Lewis Lewis? Don't be daft —it were Dic, I tell ye. D'you think I don't know Dic from Lew Lewis?' Then he turned away and screwed his fist into his palm, saying, 'But I had that Tranter, mind—ay, girl, I had Tranter...'

It was at this time that the iron master, Samuel Homfray, blamed William Crawshay of Cyfarthfa for being the cause of the riots; history relates this; the fact is recorded.

Gideon met Lemuel Samuel in High Street. And it was with a surge of joy that he recognised him from a distance of over twenty feet, for little identified Lemuel, in his rags, from the army of beggars in Merthyr at this time. Gideon was as a man revitalised with the return of his sight; as with the blows of the Cefn Riders a year ago, so the concussion caused by the musket butt had raised a curtain on his blindness, and he had never seen so well since the Taibach accident. Shadow and sun, however, alternatively fluctuated; the streets shimmered brightly, then died into blackness, but he saw Lemuel clearly.

''Morning, Gid Davies!' said Lemuel.

'Good morning, Mr. Samuel.'

'You heard about me, Gid Davies?' Lemuel beamed. 'Got a job in the Star slaughterhouse!' He seemed to have forgotten that Gideon should be blind, and he gabbled amid the press of the people going to market, 'Special on the calves, I am—I remember, I always used to say to my Mavie—get me around the meat an' I'm happy—there's money in meat, ye know. Just give me a good knife and a few fat pigs, and I'm fine.'

'Everyone to his own vocation,' said Gideon, and he saw Lemuel clearly for the first time; the creased folds of a gaunt face that had died, the pin-boned carcass, skewered and trussed on a skeleton draped with rags. The man moved furtively, nudging. 'You heard about that Dic Penderyn, of course— death by hanging?'

'I have,' said Gideon, head bowed.

'But Lewis Lewis got reprieved. Serve him right if he got it, too—don't hold with rioting and stabbing soldiers—only doing their duty.' Lemuel sniffed. 'But it was a pity about Mrs. Taibach and her Willie. Very fond of her, I was. And Percy Bottom Note—old enough to know better—I saw him, mind —you'd never believe it. He just walked on to the guns.'

'A man has his reasons,' said Gideon, blandly.

May Harries, the door-trapper, passed them, looking up at Gideon with large, serene eyes, and she returned his smile, her teeth missing in front: it was a red, gummy smile of milk and a freckled nose upturned, and he thought he had never seen anything more beautiful. Distantly, he heard Lemuel say: 'But Sun Penderyn's chap asked for it, though. I mean, you can't stab a King's soldier with his own bayonet and wound him sore, now can ye...?'

'Is there proof of this?'

'Oh, ay!'

'But how can you be sure?' asked Gideon. 'Do you believe all you are told?'

'Told me eye, Gid Davies. I saw him—I tell ye, I saw the lad at it!'

The street sounds died; for Gideon then sun began to fade, and the people pushed, chattering soundlessly like puppets. He said: 'But how could you have seen him stab the soldier—you weren't even here!'

'Oh, but I was, Gid Davies! I came with Mr. Note. We were sleeping near the beehives for warmth, and heard the firing.' He grinned delightedly. 'But Mr. Note, he stayed longer'n me, though!'

'You actually saw Dic Penderyn stab Private Black, the Highlander?'

'Ay, ay!'

Gideon swallowed down the sickness rising in his throat, and said: 'Are you ... are you quite sure it wasn't Lewis Lewis? No—don't reply at once, be careful. Have you ever seen Lewis Lewis, the haulier?'

'Ay. When Crawshay brought him back as a prisoner.'

'And that was the only time you saw him? Did you see him, for instance, during the rioting outside the Castle Inn?'

'Of course—when he was up on the lamp-post. And I saw Dic Penderyn go in with the deputation after you called for them ... I was at the back.'

'But did you see him come out?'

'Come out...?' Lemuel Samuel scratched his ear, frowning.

'Think, man—it is important. You saw Dic go in, you say. Did you see him come out with the rest of the deputation?'

'No, but Lewis Lewis wi' his hat off, cheering on the mob!'

'Did you? Private Black, who was stabbed, gave evidence that it was Dic out in front with his hat off cheering on the mob.'

'Well, well...' Lemuel Samuel was nonplussed, and Gideon said:

'There was ten thousand people in front of the Castle Inn, and you were at the back. Are you still certain that you saw Dic Penderyn struggling with the soldier, Private Black?'

'Oh, ay—I just said so.'

'What was he wearing?'

'Who?'

'Dic Penderyn—I asked you what he was wearing.'

'A grey smock and duck trews—saw him as clear as me eye. After he stabbed the soldier he fired at a window of the inn and ran off.'

'You are quite sure that the man who stabbed Black was wearing a smock and duck trews?'

'Ay!' Lemuel Samuel stared into Gideon's face.

'And you're prepared to swear this on oath to Mr. Tregelles Price.'

'Ay!' Lemuel grinned. 'I got the right fella, didn't I?'

'You did not. Dic Penderyn was wearing a blue coat and trousers that day, there is proof of this. You be careful, Lemuel Samuel—everybody is talking too much, everybody has seen too much. A man's life is at stake, and the only one who seems to realise it is Private Black, the soldier—even he can't identify the man who stabbed him. You watch that tongue, or somebody might try nipping off the end of it.'

'Dear me,' said Lemuel Samuel.

Merthyr seethed with bitterness and plans for revenge; the cause of Reform, which once unified master and servant, was now destroyed by the rising, said Colonel Brotherton, who gave the best official military account. 'It must be long before, if ever, this bad spirit is allayed,' he wrote; he who, but a few weeks later, met his death in the riots of Bristol.

In riot he was an expert.

The bailiffs came soon after Dic was arrested and evicted Sun and Richard Jay from Number Seven, Ynys, so she moved in with Mamie and Billa, though it's a bit inconvenient with Dai and Mr. Jam coming in, said Billa, to say nothing of Mike McTigue and Joe and Tim, his brothers.

'But Dai and Mr. Jam won't be here permanent for at least a fortnight,' said Mamie.

'I'll find somewhere else,' said Sun on the doorstep.

'You'll do no such thing,' replied Billa. 'Neighbours is neighbours, or so I've been told, and it anna a bad thing—we'll 'ave enough women in the place for a petticoat government. What you say, love?'

'Somebody's coming, Mam!' yelled Saul.

'Somebody's always coming to this house,' said Billa, and she took Sun's arms. 'You go inside, love, and make yourself at home.'

'Gid Davies been asking about you, you heard?' said Mamie.

'I haven't seen him,' replied Sun, and she smoothed her baby's face.

'Called twice, but you was out.'

Somebody took a fist to the door.

'That'll be Randy,' said Mamie, and opened it, and Dai End-On and Billy Jam were standing on the doorstep with beams.

'Good God, it never do rain but it pours,' said Mamie.

''Morning, missus!' said Dai.

'How are ye, Billa?' asked Mr. Jam. Solvent and sober were they, and returning to wives and lovers, eh, me darling, said Mr. Jam, and the two of them bowed with buttonhole posies on their chests big enough for a State funeral. Dai said: 'Come early, see—we know you'll be delighted.'

'It'll be a bit of a squeeze, if you get me,' said Mamie, shepherding them inside. 'We got Mrs. Penderyn staying a bit, see, so it's awkward on the beds, you understand?'

'Dear me,' said Dai, glum.

'I want to sleep with me da,' wailed Asa, jumping on tiptoe.

'The dear little soul,' said Mr. Jam, vicious.

'He's not the only one,' said Billa. 'You'll have Caradoc and Amos and Abiah too. I tell you, we just anna got the beds!'

'And the rest are in with me,' said Mamie.

'*Diawch*,' whispered Dai. 'I was hoping...' he faltered, looking.

Bang bang on the back.

331

'*Diwedd!*' said Mamie, 'I am in rags. Who's that now, then?'

Mike and Tim and Joe on the doorstep, handsome and dark in their Sunday best, and down they went in bows with bunches of Welsh poppies.

'What you lot want, then?' asked Billy Jam, weak.

'Come to lodge, Mr. Jam,' replied Mike, and he straightened his stock.

'Good morning, Mike,' said Billa, and there was a new beauty in her.

'Could ye come back a bit later, lads, while we try to sort something out?' asked Mamie. 'Things are sort of topsy-turvy . . .'

'I'll help you sort it, Mame,' said Mike, and came inside, but Dai End-On pushed him off.

'Away,' said Dai. 'We'll have lodgers when we grant ye, *away*!'

With clasped hands Billa roamed into the front room and stood before the window; she was shivering. Saul and Asa came in behind her, but she ushered them back into the kitchen. She was frightened, not of Mike the big Irishman, but of herself. And even as she stood there clasped within herself, he tapped the glass of the window. His hair was black and shining, she noticed; his teeth were white and even in his smile. She could hear Dai and Mr. Jam tramping down the dram-road, their hobnail boots chinking on the rails, and Mr. Jam was laughing. With trembling fingers she pushed up the window and Mike's hands closed on hers on the sill.

'What about me, then?' he asked. 'Oi Oi, missus, what about me?'

'Oh, God, Mike, leave me alone!'

'He's no good to ye, woman—you know he's no good to you!'

'Ach, please . . .'

'I love you—and I told you 'afore and I'm telling you now. I want ye, Billa.'

'And all me kids?'

'And all your kids. Look, I can have me pick o' the women

332

—I'm on good money and I'm as spright as a spring lamb. I'd work for ye, girl—I'd do late shift for you—say the word and I'll thump him out of it.'

People were passing down the cut; a barge went by and the bargees waved, but she did not raise her face, and Mike said: 'You make pretty men, and I want me own son—but it's got to be from you, Billa.' He emptied his hands at her. 'Now what have ye got in Billy Jam but a randy old drunk?'

At this she lifted her face and said to him: 'You get out of here, Mike McTigue. He's my fella and you've got no right to slander him! I think you're disgusting! Get out, you hear me?'

He straightened, and she held the sill lest she should fling herself against him, and said, with tears in her throat, 'There ought to be a law against it, pestering a decent woman!'

He looked at her. 'Didn't know ye felt like that ... Goodbye, Billa ...' He drifted away.

The door went back on its hinges then and three of the boys rushed in, seeking her in shouts, hauling at her arms. Amos, aged five, got a chair and stood on it and put his arms around her neck, kissing her with a wet mouth. Then Mamie came and stood with her hands on her hips, shouting:

'You know where that pair have gone, do you?—Jackson's —that means the Wellington, and they haven't even taken their boots off!'

Billa nodded. Mike, with his hands deep in his trews was going over the bridge.

'Goodbye, my darling,' she said.

It was a fortnight after Dic's trial.

Gideon said: 'Can you spare a minute, Sun?'

She was shopping in Georgetown with money Mamie had given her, and did not turn when she heard his voice, but stopped and leaned against the wall of the Horseshoes.

'Haven't ye caused us enough grief and bother?'

When she faced him she saw that his eyes held a new expression and colour, and she said, warmer, 'You can see, Gid?' and peered.

'More than a little.'

She smiled. 'Oh, I'm glad, I'm glad!'

'A soldier hit me with a musket butt,' he said simply. 'I have sight now, but it will fade—indeed, it's not so good as it was. How are you?'

Her face was pale, and she was thin. He was worried at her thinness.

'As good as can be expected.'

'And Richard Jay?'

She brightened into life and her eyes shone. 'Och, he's a wee fella! The spit and body of Dico, did ye know?'

'Yes, Mamie told me.'

'But ye never come to see him, Gid.'

He could not explain that he could never bring himself to do this. Not only did he feel responsible, in large measure, for her grief, and was ashamed; but this was Dic Penderyn's child, and the thought that another man had possessed her since the journey from Taibach induced in him an abhorrence. Standing there within reach of her was like reliving a dream: indeed, recently in a vivid dream he had possessed her, and her body had been sweet to his, so that desire and taste seemed to unify his need of her. Time was, he thought bitterly, he could have possessed her with a gesture: she had even offered herself, and he had rejected her. Now, standing before him in her soiled coat and the weariness of a heavy labour, he needed her infinitely more; the shadows were deep under her eyes, her hair was untidy, but he did not see these things; he knew only that he loved her, but she belonged to Dic Penderyn.

The smoke of Cyfarthfa moved between them. She said: 'Dear me, things do change, don't they? Not many of the old friends left save Mamie and Billa, and I don't give tuppence for Randy ...' She shifted the basket on her stomach. 'And it were a pity about old Waxey Evans—I mean, he was a wicked old soak, but he didn't deserve that.'

Gideon nodded. Sun continued, stepping off the rails: 'And Sara Grieve, the poor thing—that were quick, weren't it?'

'Yes.' By moving behind her he could get the scent of the wind; she never lost this strange and lovely smell, and he remembered that it came from her hair. Now he was thinking it strange that in his dream of her this same hair had been long and thick to his fingers, its perfume different. Such, he thought bitterly, was the sad incompetence of dreams; now he smiled, for he preferred her hair short and unkempt, like this.

'That right you are living with Miss Thrush of Taibach?'

'Not, it is not true. She ... she took me in after the riot, and I will never forget her kindness, but I'm back in Cross Street now.'

The furnaces of Cyfarthfa went into blast then, two great valedictory flames roaring into the sky and the old bell-clang of the naked iron beat down Dynefor and consumed them, forbidding speech. Gideon said, when the roar subsided: 'You remember when we came into Merthyr together, Sun?'

'After the Cefn Riders?' She rubbed her face, smiling. 'That were a hundred years back.'

'And now you're married to Dic Penderyn.'

'Ay.'

The silence came again and they lowered their faces and moved their feet. A new and stifling awkwardness was parting them.

Gideon said: 'You ... you've heard of Tregelles Price?'

'The Neath master?'

He nodded, looking at his watch. 'I was just coming down to Mamie's to see you. You've heard he is getting out a petition for Dic, I suppose—he and Taliesin Williams, the schoolmaster, are coming up to my place tonight. Mr. Price would like to meet you ...'

She looked at the sky. 'They are wasting their time.'

'Perhaps, but at least they can try. Listen, it is important that you know this. One petition is based on the fact that after the deputation in the Castle, Dic went out of the back door, not the front...'

Her eyes snapped up at this. 'Don't be ridiculous! He was nowhere near the Castle—you yourself advised him, with Morgan Howells, to go up the mountain with the deacon's son!'

Gideon said levelly: 'He was at the Castle right enough,

335

Sun—best you face this. He might have started on the mountain, but he didn't stay there long. Half a dozen people saw him in the deputation—Abbott, Williams, Darker...'

'That bunch of criminals!'

'Randy himself saw him outside the inn, as well as up on Cefn—remember?'

Recalling this, Sun stiffened, and Gideon added: 'Marsden the draper saw him in the passage. Nancy Evans, William Philip and Ben Davies all attest to seeing him standing by the tap-room before the fighting—even David Abraham, the Special, saw him there and cautioned him not to go into the fighting.'

'So he was not in the fighting ...?' She was suddenly, urgently aware.

Gideon replied: 'Half a dozen testify that he was not, but men like Abbott and the other Specials are swearing his life away. That is why we must have this final petition to send round Wales—we will get thousands of signatures...'

She interjected faintly, as if the knowledge of Abbott's testimony had tamed her, 'And I still say they're wasting their time. The King has been threatened, he will have to hang somebody...' She closed her eyes. 'Oh, what a fool he was to come down from Aberdare...'

'Did you ... did you know Tregelles Price has seen Dic, Sun?'

'Ay. It was more'n they'd do for me—they turned me away.'

He said softly: 'Don't lose hope, I beg you. Because he's sentenced to death it doesn't mean he'll die, you know. Lewis Lewis was reprieved, wasn't he?'

She raised her face, 'But there's a difference, isn't there! There's a difference now they've discovered he's of noble birth —the bastard son of this one or that one ...'

'I beg you not to believe all the things you hear!'

Bitterly, she said: 'Morgan Howells came yesterday. The day before I was fancied up with the Church of England— these are the devils who are hanging him! Pray, pray, pray!' Her voice rose. 'While you're on your knees ye can't get the bloody size of 'em. My God, what a country!'

Gideon said: 'In this I agree—we are faced by a corrupt institution. The King himself has read most of the Merthyr correspondence—some of it he has personally annotated—the facts are clear, the perjury is proved, yet he will not even grant petitions for an interview...'

Sun said softly, her voice vibrant: 'Then the blood of my Dic be on his head.'

'Mr. Price is going to London to see Melbourne, the Secretary of State—don't lose hope, I beg you.'

'I have lost hope,' she said. 'I'll not come up to see Mr. Price, and tell him from me that he's wasting his time. They will have to hang someone.'

Strangely, as she walked away, he heard her gay laughter echoing through the woods of Tir-Phil. Gideon watched until she turned up Chapel Street for the shops in Iron Lane.

'That youngster Dic Penderyn's due for the long drop, then,' said Dai End-On, and he parted his whiskers in the Wellington up by Jackson's and poured in a quart without so much as a swallow.

'First quart to settle the dust,' said Billy Jam. 'Set 'em up again, Mr. Jackson.'

'You living here, you two?' asked Jump Jackson, pouring the ale.

'Just moved in,' answered Dai. 'That fella they're dropping used to live next door but one to us—in fact, his woman's living wi' us now.'

'She's a nice kid is that Sun Penderyn,' said the landlord.

'Mind, it's the least we can do,' said Mr. Jam, and lifted his quart. 'Down the hatch, Dai lad—here's to the next thousand —it's a good local this—very convenient, as the saying goes.'

'Then you'll be interested in what it says here,' said Jump Jackson, bringing out *The Cambrian*. 'But God, they're roasting old Crawshay,' and he squinted over the top of his glasses, and read:

'"In looking at this peaceable conclusion of an unusually dangerous and bloody transaction, we cannot avoid thinking that the patient and forgiving character of the workmen stands painfully contrasted with the despotic and avaricious conduct of the master . . ." '

The landlord folded the newspaper and put it under the counter. 'And that's an extract from the London *Observer*, remember—enough to give the poor old lad a heart attack—I bet his dad won't like it; meself, I don't think it's fair.'

'Drink up, me old darlin',' said Dai End-On. 'We might as well go home the first night wet—I intend to start the way I'm goin' on.'

'I'm with ye in that, me old soak,' replied Mr. Jam, and Jump Jackson said, reflectively:

'But 'tis a bit hard, nevertheless. The lad used to come in here, ye know. He were a bit heavy on the ale, and sharp with his hands on a drunk, as the saying goes, but I'd lay me life on one thing—he'd not take a weapon to a man—there was no need, see—his fists were good enough. Did ye hear what Mr. Sockett said for the defence?'

'Ay—another quart o' that excellent brew, if you please,' said Dai.

' . . . He said it was a cryin' shame to hold the trial in English. Dic Penderyn was Welsh—he'd not know if he was pleading innocent or guilty.'

'Nor me,' said Dai, pushing up his mug.

Jump Jackson continued: 'And Mr. Sockett weren't in full possession of the evidence, mind—and they'll never publish the trial, of course. John Guest of Dowlais don't think Dic did it, and Mr. Dillwyn, the foreman o' the Grand Jury 'as written to Tregelles Price to say he's changed his mind about the verdict of Guilty—think o' that, lads—he's changed his mind!—what the blutty hell's happening, I say? You know what I think?'

'I think it's a beautiful brew,' said Dai, gasping and wiping his whiskers.

'I reckon that Lewis Lewis did it—that's what I think,' said Jump Jackson. 'You know what Squire Morgan of Bodwigiad

338

called him—a devoted victim!'

'That's what they'll call you if I don't get this quart,' said Billy, pushing up his pot. Taking it, the landlord filled it, adding:

'A devoted victim, eh? Ye don't get squires talking like that unless they've had a finger in the pie, so to speak, if ye get me. I reckon Lew Lewis rose off a silk-lined bed.'

'Now you're talking,' said Billy Jam, 'a silk-lined bed—that's what I'm off to—comin', me love, Mrs. Billa Jam Tart!'

The landlord said: 'Don't ye care about a fella dying, then?'

'Ye've got us in tears,' said Dai End-On.

'God help your women, that's all I say.'

'Ay, ay,' said Billy, and lifted his pot. 'Bottoms up, me lovely.'

CARDIFF was like a town of the dead when they hanged Dic Penderyn. Most of the shops were closed on the previous day, curtains were drawn over the windows of cottages, doors were locked and barred. Nothing moved on the deserted streets; the scaffold awaited, its rope dangling.

But at first light a man on horseback galloped in from Worcester, and this was the hangman—a novice who had been found at the last minute since no professional hangman could be induced to undertake the task. And soon after this a great crowd of people began to move like a black finger in procession: first from the valley of the Taff these people came; many from Merthyr and Aberdare; later, in smaller groups came more, dressed in mourning black, and they made no sound, these people, who had come to watch Dic Penderyn die; this, the first Welsh martyr of the working class. Many were Catholic Irish, and these told their beads in whispered incantations; others were English, the Staffordshire specialists; most were Welsh, coming with measured tread, with their brass-bound bibles under their arms, and they went with their faces upturned to the dawn, as if to an early chapel. Sun and Billa walked at the head of the Taff Vale procession, and they were dressed in funeral black, for to attend the hanging of a relative was the custom, to send the last goodbye. Mamie, whose feet were bad, did not come, so she stayed at home with Richard Jay, Dic's baby son: Randy did not come, because, although he had been told, he did not know of this event; and he rose early and went up to Adulum to visit Blod. Gideon walked with Miss Thrush, that she could guide him were his sight again to fail; Dai and Billy Jam did not come since they were drinking in the Wellington. Tim and Joe McTigue, the Irish lodgers of Taibach did not come, but Mike, the eldest, did, in order to be close to Billa at this time. Molly Caulara came, and walked at the back, alone, since she was of the Popi Davey, and people wondered why she wept, since Sun Penderyn was not weeping. Gwen, Dic's sister, did not come because she was confined by illness, nor did his father and mother, because they could not bear it. But the Reverend Morgan Howells had come the previous night, and now with others, was in the condemned cell with Dic, and here he prayed. Miss Blossom Thomas walked in the Vale procession, because old Papa Tomo demanded this, as he would have done from a son; and she walked with her hands screwing in fear, and men had to support her. Abednigo Jones was there, also, hands in his belt, and let's get this lot over and quick. Dr. William Price of Pontypridd came, perhaps in the hope of a body for cremation, for this he later invented. Many were there from the benefit clubs of the Top Towns, and the new leaders of the underground Unions, for whom, in part, Dic was dying. It is said that some travelled from London, and a few from the Bolton Authority Lodge. One whose name was Morfydd Mortymer came with Richard Bennet, and they journeyed over the mountains from Nantyglo, where they lodged. Many early Chartists came, the men of vision who later fought for the Six Points of Decency; John Frost, later the mayor of Newport, was surely present, as would be Zephaniah Williams, and perhaps even Jones the Watchmaker, but history has no proof of this. Many came who did not know who was to be hanged, until they asked; a few arrived to tell of the spectacle; to see a man die was what they sought. And they massed in a black mantle around the scaffold, these people, numbering over five hundred.

And of them only one was staring at the platform lest she missed the first glimpse of Dic Penderyn when he came, and this was Sun.

All over Wales people were praying; the chapels and

341

churches had been filled since dawn; and not only did the Welsh attend the early services, but the Irish, and these were keening in the packed terraces of the Top Towns from Swansea to Blaenafon. Of all nationalities and denominations, the people did not go on shift; but flooded into the pews of Calfaria and Ebenezer, Zion and Salem and a score of others; they packed themselves ten deep standing in the Roman Catholics and the Chapels of Ease: they stood in massed funeral black in the fields and knelt in the roads, furnace areas, smelting sheds and compounds; they stopped the barges on the Old Glamorgan canal and knelt in the fields as the time of death approached; they spragged their drams and tethered the mules and horses and knelt on the line, and many wept, it was said—some not for Dic Penderyn, aged twenty-three who lived in Merthyr, but the things he stood for, and a nation wept because he was Welsh. Wandering preachers, black-clad and trembling with indignation, declaimed the outrage from lonely crags to the empty places, demanding from their God an explanation of the injustice of the King and Melbourne. In the pits and drifts, the levels of coal and the limestone caves the colliers and miners gathered by candlelight, and knelt. On the Iron Bridge in Merthyr Blind Dick and Hugh Pughe sang eulogies of the man from Aberafon who was about to die; in the penny-a-week schools the children listened in pent silence, wondering why.

And so did Dic Penderyn.

In the cell in Cardiff Gaol he was sitting at a table, and about him were four men, and they were dressed in black; Joseph Tregelles Price, the saintly iron master of Neath, the Reverend Edmund Evans of the Merthyr Wesleyan, the Reverend Morgan Howells, Dic's brother-in-law, and the prison chaplain.

'Is it raining?' Dic looked at the high, peep-window.

'Since an hour, perhaps,' said Morgan Howells.

'The crowd down St. Mary's will get wet.'

Distantly thunder boomed and reverberated over The Top, echoing in dull claps and whispering into silence.

'Is the crowd large?'

'Many have come,' said Morgan Howells.

Rising, Dic put his hands in his pockets and stared up at the little square window, and said: 'My God, this is hard measure, but the cause was just. You think there is a chance of a reprieve now, Morgan?'

'There is no sign of it. Melbourne has already delayed it a week. I entreat you to make your peace with your God.'

'*Diwedd!* You don't change much! At the moment I am more concerned with my body than my soul. Is it for the surgeons?'

Edmund Evans said: 'Many care little what happens to the carcass after the soul has fled.'

'I care a great deal.'

'Then write what you will,' said Tregelles Price, 'and I will see that it is carried into effect,' and with this he took his leave; the cell door clanged open and shut, and Dic sat at the table and wrote to Gwen:

'Yr wyf yn deisyf arnat i ddyfod yn ddiatreg i nôl fy nghorff, oherwydd nid oes dim tebygolrwydd am ddim arall yn bresennol. Dos at Philip Lewis a gwna iddo ef ddyfod a chertyn i lawr heno, a chymaint o ddynion a allo, mewn rhyw wedd, i ddyfod gydag ef. Yr wyf yn credu fod yr Arglwydd wedi maddau i fi fy amrywiol bechodau a'm troseddiadau, ond am yr wyf yn cael nghyhuddo nid yr wyf yn euog ac am hynny gennyf achos i fod yn ddiolchgar.'

which, being translated, means:

'I entreat you to come without fail to fetch my body, as there is no likelihood of anything else at present. Go to Philip Lewis and get him to come down somehow tonight with a cart and as many men as he can. I believe the Lord has forgiven me my sins and transgressions, and as for the charge now made against me, I am not guilty, and for that I have reason to be thankful.'

343

This letter he gave to Morgan Howells, and the prison chaplain Jones and the Reverend Edmund Evans read it also, and Dic said:

'Now examine me for the good of my soul, as you put it, and I will tell you the truth of it yet again.'

Edmund Evans of the Wesleyan spoke first, saying: 'Do you continue to deny that you stabbed Private Black with a bayonet?'

'I do. At the time he was wounded I was not in front of the Castle Inn.'

'Yet,' said Chaplain Jones, 'you do not deny that you were one of the deputation of leaders who entered by the front door to meet the iron masters?'

'I do not deny it—I state it. This is in the Petition. I was with Lewis Lewis when the deputation was called for. I entered the inn by the front door and left it by the back entrance—there are witnesses to this.'

'Name them.'

'As I said at the trial—after the meeting I left with Will Johns. Mr. Marsden, the draper, saw us going through the back door; I nodded to him, and he acknowledged me.'

'Mr. Marsden has already testified to this. And then?'

'Then I intended to keep my promise to my wife, and return to Aberdare mountain. But I stood for a while by the tap-wall of the inn, on the Glebe side. There I saw Nancy Evans, who is with child, and her son, Evan Evans . . .'

'Who else?' interjected Morgan Howells.

'David Abraham, the special constable, spoke to me while I was there.'

'What did he say?'

'He warned me not to come round to the front of the inn since trouble was starting—did he bear witness to this?'

'He did. Anything more?'

'Ay. Ben Davies, the navigator, stood with me, and we talked—how many more witnesses do you want?'

'Kindly proceed,' said the chaplain, and Dic said, his voice low:

'I keep on telling this! When the firing started Ben Davies,

344

the Evans boy and I ran down to Iron Bridge. As he went, Philip the Puddler of Two Furnace, shouted to us—he spoke in Welsh at the trial—I heard him swear to this...'

Morgan Howells said bitterly: 'Everybody in Christendom has sworn for you, but the evidence is not heeded. Only the evidence of the liars Abbott, Drew and Darker, appears to have weight ...'

'That is not fair,' said Chaplain Jones, sharply.

'But it is a fact!' Howells turned away. 'God knows we've had our differences, but I am disgusted at the handling of this boy's trial.'

The Reverend Edmund Evans said: 'Anger and bitterness will not help us. Only facts can help us now.' To Dic, he said: 'You speak of this man Will Johns. If he accompanied you through the back entrance he is a key witness. Why has he vanished, if he is your friend?'

'He is a drinking friend,' interjected Morgan Howells, 'there is a difference.' He swung to Dic, his voice raised. 'Had you kept your word to me you would have no need of such people now. I sent you with the son of the deacon... !'

Dic cried: 'What the hell do ye expect of me? You threatened to take away my wife and son. I am an enroller for a Union Lodge. How could I have faced the men again if I had not joined the deputation?' He added, bitterly: 'Best you three face the truth of it. I am a Union man; this is why I am going to die.'

There was a silence. Distantly from the town came the tolling of a bell; then the chaplain said: 'One question more, and we will leave you with your God. If, as you say, you were not at the front of the inn during the fighting, how is it that Private Black—though not identifying you as the man that stabbed him—said he saw you with your hat off and cheering on the mob?'

Dic shrugged. 'I cannot speak for Private Black. Perhaps he mistook me for Lewis Lewis; perhaps he is saying what he has been told to say; I do not know. But find Will Johns of Ynys compound, and he will save me. Even the deacon's son will swear that I left him for but a short time on two occasions—

once when we got news of the deputation, once later, when I went to Cefn Heights and met the son of my neighbour, Mrs. Goldie.'

'Why did you not mention such other meetings at the trial?'

'Because nobody asked me. Was Cefn Coed mentioned? The trial was in English, and the gabble so fast that much I did not understand.'

At this, Morgan Howells turned away. 'Oh, God,' he said. 'Ay, ay, well, thank Him, at least, that they will let me die in Welsh, even if it is for another.'

'Lewis Lewis, the huntsman of Bodwigiad?'

He did not reply.

The chaplain said: 'Let this be known officially to you, so that you may prepare your soul to meet your God, and know that there is no hope of release. The petition of eleven thousand signatures has been rejected: the Quaker master, Tregelles Price, has himself visited Lord Melbourne, the Home Secretary, and later took fresh evidence to London, when he saw Lord Brougham, the Lord Chancellor. The reprieve was rejected then, there is no chance of it arriving at this late hour. Do you still persist in your innocence?'

'I am innocent of the crime for which I am going to be hanged.'

And Morgan Howells said then: 'Let the record stand, that you take it to your grave. Joseph Tregelles Price, when rejected by Lord Melbourne, said these words: "I felt that this young man's blood was on my own head if I did not strive for him in every way. Now I put that burden from my conscience on to yours." '

The chaplain remarked, turning away: 'We are concerned with this man's soul, not the iniquity of the Whigs; let us stay with the subject,' and Howells replied:

'This man is my relative, and he has a right to know: let him know also that I petitioned the King, and that he would not receive me: the Whigs are not alone in sharing the guilt of blood.'

The Reverend Edmund Evans said then: 'I ask you to

swear before God, then, that you did not stab the soldier Private Black, and to state before Him, Whom you are soon to meet, that you are going to hang unjustly.'

Dic said: 'I did not stab the soldier. And I will continue to swear to this with my dying breath.'

Morgan Howells turned away at this and covered his face with his hands, saying:

'I cannot bear this. They are going to kill an innocent man.'

When the hangman came in and pinioned his arms behind him, Dic said:

'The hangmen are younger than I expected. Where do you come from?'

The man tied the knots, saying: 'I come from Bristol, but all last night I travelled from London, and arrived here at three o'clock this morning.'

'It were a pity you did not arrive later, I think.'

Later it was known that the authorities had scoured the neighbouring counties for a hangman without success, and that the professionals in London would not undertake the task. This hangman was a novice, and had undertaken this hanging because of his poverty.

Dic said, before they opened the cell door that led to the gallows:

'Morgan, I do not want to die.'

'We all have to die,' replied Morgan Howells. 'Do you but precede us by a year or two.' In Welsh he said this, which was their mother tongue.

At the door Dic paused, and said: 'You will care for my baby son, and my wife, to whom I have not been good, because of the drinking?'

'She sends to you her love,' said Morgan Howells. 'If this is the punishment for drinking then many stand condemned. Your sister Gwen says that she will be united with you, both now and in death. Your mother and father are in prayer for you; Wales itself is in prayer for you.'

And Dic Penderyn said again: 'My God, for all, and for

347

me, this is a bloody hard measure. Thank God I have had the Sacrament.' With this he turned to Morgan Howells, who had been joined by the sheriff and said: 'I am going out to suffer unjustly. God, Who knows all things, knows it is so.'

With this he walked to the scaffold. The Reverend Edmund Evans walked one side of him, the sheriff walked on the other; behind came Mr. Woods, the prison governor and he was with Morgan Howells; after them came the hangman and a gaoler. Nor did he lose his composure as he mounted the steps to the platform, but looked around the crowd as if seeking friends, while the hangman tied his ankles. It is said, also, that the rain increased and that thunder began to roll in from the sea; many of the people knelt, and bowed their heads. Perhaps he was looking for Sun, perhaps for his sister Gwen, but these he did not see, nor even the face of Molly Caulara, who knelt and prayed alone on the distant street. But, near the scarlet uniforms of the Red-coats on guard against disturbances he saw one face upturned, and it was that of Mistress Morfydd Mortymer, the young agitator of Blaenafon whom he had insulted in the Long Room above the bar of Tavern Uchaf, at the meeting of the Oddfellows Lodge. And he remembered her face with its glowing, dark eyes, and the way she held herself. Suddenly, she clenched her hand and swept back her hair, and as the hangman placed the noose about him, she cried, her voice shrill:

'Die hard, Dic Penderyn. You are dying for Wales. Die hard, Dic Penderyn!'

Legend would have us believe that lightning split the sky and that thunder roared as Dic Penderyn died; it is known only that it was raining, and that, in the moment before the trap was pulled, he cried with his face to the sky:

'*O Arglwydd, dyma gamwedd! O Arglwydd, dyma gamwedd!*'

Which, being translated, means:

'O Lord, what an inquity! O Lord, what an iniquity!'

And the thunder rolled over the town and the people bowed their heads, for they were afraid.

LEWIS LEWIS was heard by a gaoler to be crying in his cell when Dic Penderyn was hanged, and this man went to him, and Lewis said:

'Dic is innocent. I know him not to have been there. I was by the soldier. If I had been sharing the same fate I would have disclosed it on the scaffold.'

The statement has been recorded for history.

Also recorded for history is the letter William Crawshay, the Cyfarthfa iron master, wrote to his father a week later.

'As Bell and the children and Eliza were going to church on Sunday week a bitch of a woman called out from a party of folks who were standing on the path, "There go the devils..."'

Hatred for the iron masters seethed, not only in Merthyr, but the Top Towns. And Colonel Brotherton's prediction of a rift between master and worker that might never be bridged was coming to truth. But William Crawshay was not responsible for the hanging of Dic Penderyn, let history record this, too; for he, like others, had accepted the testimony of Shoni Crydd and Abbot the barber, whom the people of Merthyr ran out of the town.

Crawshay wrote:

'My conduct at all times to my men has been guided by the liberal and humane feeling ... I have ever been the last to reduce and the first to advance the rates of wages...'

This was true, but it would appear that he could afford it.

For, at the wedding of his son a few years later a series of celebration functions took place for hundreds of guests at the Castle Inn, the scene of the rising; the King's Head and the Bush Hotel. And a great wagon shed in Cyfarthfa works was converted into a ballroom of magnificent splendour; draped with shrubs and greenery especially imported, decorated with squares and pennants, it was lighted by huge gas chandeliers and a polished wooden floor was laid for dancing. A banquet in this great hall attended by the ladies of Merthyr provided boars' heads and massive joints of beef, and waiters by the score in evening dress drew wine from casks for the entertainment of the guests. At a later festivity at the Bush Hotel for gentlemen the tables were set for three hundred; the menu began with turtle, soups, turbot, rounds, rumps, ham, tongue, venison haunches and fowl; it was followed by pheasants, woodcocks, partridge and leverets, and the meal, as reported in the *Cardiff and Merthyr Guardian*, was ended with pineapples, grapes, almonds and raisins washed down with port, sherry, claret and champagne.

Three years later, in the summer of 1849, over fifteen hundred men, women and children died in the parish of Merthyr for want of a decent water supply that would have cost the price of these dinners; the details of the cholera being given in the Report of the Local Board of Health under Dr. William Kay, which was read in Merthyr in 1854.

Let posterity judge, said Gideon, and if it be claimed by posterity that such masters were creatures of their time, then let me name others who were also children of their day—Robert Owen, Wilberforce, Lord Shaftesbury, and the iron master of Neath which is close to Merthyr—Joseph Tregelles Price.

Ay, said Gideon, let posterity judge, but let it also be fair; this was a fight for Reform, not against masters.

William Crawshay the Second was not responsible for the death of Dic Penderyn—even if he never raised a finger to oppose it: and no one man was responsible for the Merthyr Riots.

350

Now they took the body of Dic Penderyn back to Aberafon, the parish of his birth, and a great procession of mourning people followed the gambo that carried it through the lanes from Cardiff. Among those who pushed the cart of Philip Lewis, the gambo-man, was Mercy Merriman and Lady Godiva, top covered: those who later carried his coffin were Belcher, Big Bonce and Blackbird, the navvies; also Gideon. And the mourners, who numbered hundreds at Ely grew to thousands within reach of Pyle. Here crowds came to meet it, jamming the roads and flooding over the fields, even coming from the little whitewashed cottage called *Penderyn*, from which he had taken his name. With the Reverend Morgan Howells at the head of the cortège, it called at many churches and chapels on the way, seeking a Christian burial, but none, it is said, would take him in. But the vicar of St. Mary's Church, though Protestant, declared he would receive the body and lay it in consecrated ground, though he was forbidden by the authorities to hold his service within the church, since this, they claimed, was the body of a criminal. So Morgan Howells stood on the churchyard wall and raised his long, thin hands, and cried:

'See here an injustice, see here the coffin of an innocent man! Let it be known, and recorded, that the blood of Dic Penderyn lies on the hands of the Government and the King himself: and if this be sedition, then let this be recorded also, for I have a stake in this affair, I have a knowledge of the outrage... !'

Sun raised her face at this, and Howells cried: 'I have a knowledge of it because he was my relative. It was I who sent him away from Merthyr lest, because of his radical views and tub-thumping, he be branded as a scapegoat before a crime was laid. I have a stake in this affair because I am a Christian, and as a Christian I shall not stand silently while hostages are found and publicly put to death as an example to malefactors. For I tell you this—the malefactors are not here today—let agents present listen and report these words, and I trust they give offence ... the malefactors are those who sit on thrones, the lords and peers who govern, the Church dignitaries who

351

stand aside from responsibility—and to whom the life of a working man is of less value than a partridge egg, when an example is to be made of one to impress the mass. Did not the beloved Tregelles Price have two petitions rejected by the King even in the face of fresh evidence that proved the perjury of James Abbott and Drew? This man Abbott, in particular, has sworn away his life—did he not threaten to be even with him? I ask the people of Merthyr parish to remember this iniquitous man. In the face of this I myself travelled to London and the King refused me an audience! Let it be known that the death of this man is an offence, not only against the laws of the country, but against God . . .'

Sun moved, pushing her way through the crowd, and the people parted, and Billa did not follow her. And it happened that she came to the place on the edge of the crowd where Gideon was standing with Milly Thrush, and she raised her eyes to his face.

'Gid . . .' she said.

Seeing this, Miss Thrush moved away to a quiet place and stood, hands clasped. And Mike McTigue, seeing Billa Jam standing alone, came nearer to her, reaching for her hand. They stood together, listening to the oratory of Morgan Howells. Gideon and Sun also stood together in the drifting rain, and there was no sound but the wind, and the preacher's voice.

And Sun Penderyn saw again in her mind the young strength of the man she loved, and whom she had owned, but whose heart she had never possessed in full measure. She heard again the sounds of his laughter and remembered him in the compound of Liz Treharne, and his arms about her wet body:

'You coming home with me, missus?'

Now Sun smiled. The heat of the furnaces, she remembered, was warm on her arms and shoulders, and his chin was rough against her face.

'Don't ye even care who's kissing you?'

The rain was dripping off the brims of the black hats about her, and she smelled the people in soaked clothes; and she heard again from the bed of Seven Ynys the voice of the night watchman singing bass on the night that Madoc and his four children died.

'Make in me a little one ... a little Dic Penderyn?'

And she closed her eyes and bowed her head.

Molly Caulara, who was standing on the road away from eyes lest she be discovered, did not see this, but came nearer to the gambo and reached out and touched it. She remembered a sunlit field that was a part of her youth and saw the face of Dic Penderyn bending above her and hayseed was in his hair and his teeth were white in the moment before he kissed her: she was sixteen, she recalled; there for the boys to learn on, but he had treated her with respect and dignity. Morgan Howells was still ranting at the sky, his face upturned in the fervour of his emotion; the rain was on her face as she touched the gambo again, for she could not get close enough to touch his coffin.

Miss Milly Thrush, amazingly, was thinking about Percy Bottom Note and Willie Taibach, and she did not see Gideon gripping Sun Penderyn's hands amid the intonations of the St. Mary's vicar. Vaguely, she was wondering what she would do about the harmonium she had saved from the beadle of Coffin's Court, for there wasn't really room for it in the bedroom—especially if Gideon Davies came back with her to the shop ... after all, she reasoned, there was nothing to keep him in Eighteen Cross now that fanatic Zimmerman had gone, and it did seem a waste of rent keeping two establishments. True, he was comforting Sun Penderyn now, but that was right and proper—they were old friends, after all. Not that there had really been anything between them in the past, she thought: how could there have been? Gideon was a man of honour, and Sun was married to Dic Penderyn. And in a fantasy of her own breeding Miss Thrush remembered, too, the sister in Pontypridd and the little shop there; the size nine boots, the laces he called for once a year, which was a lifetime away, now that he belonged to her. After all, she reflected, there was that navvy girl Jobina, or whatever he called her—there was no reason to think he had been anything to her, either. Only to her, Milly Thrush, had he come for love; she straightened amid the crowd, smiling joyously at the recollection, and people standing nearby saw this smile, and were perplexed. It was the fulfilment of all she wished for; for ever safe in his love she could face the world; it was a banishment of loneliness now that she was one with him. She would become his eyes, and in his need of her his love would grow, and there would flower from their union a greater, fuller life. Now he was coming through the crowd, seeking her; he called her name, and seeing her bright expectancy and upraised hand, people guided him. Now Gideon stood before her, his hand outstretched to her.

'Goodbye, Miss Thrush.'

Momentarily, she stared up in astonishment at him, then bowed her head.

Gideon said: 'Or would you care to come back with us in the first trap?'

'No thanks,' said she, recovering herself, 'I can manage, thanks.'

'But you must ride home—please, it was so kind of you to bring me.'

Her eyes were filling with tears now, but she smiled, saying, 'No thanks, Gid Davies—I'd ... I'd rather be alone, thanks. Always been used to seeing to meself, ye see ...'

'As you please.' Gideon bowed to her. 'Goodbye.'

The rain struck her face as she watched him go back into the crowd, and then she heard his dog whining at her feet. Bending, she lifted it against her, pressing its wetness against her cheek, and it was shivering.

'Goodbye,' she said.

She made a mental note to order more size nines and laces ...

'Billa!'

On the very edge of the departing crowd Billa stopped and gripped her hands. Mike McTigue touched her arm, saying over her shoulder:

'Don't go off like that, girl.'

354

'I got to, Mike—ye know I've got to.'

'Not before you hear what I've got to say.'

'Oh, God,' said Billa. 'Won't ye leave me alone? Look, the trap's arrivin'—you know I've got to go with Morgan Howells and the rest of 'em, and . . .'

'You are going with me,' said Mike.

'Are ye mad, fella!' She swung to him. His face was smooth and unlined; his strength seemed to reach out and grip her, forbidding movement; she thought it was disgraceful that she should even be looking at him like this; she was at least ten years older . . . and a horde of kids . . .

'He's a drunk, Billa—you've took him back, but he's at it again up in the Wellington. God alive, girl—will ye never learn?'

'What do ye want of me?' She touched his face. 'In the name of heaven, what do you see in me? I've got nothing to offer you—can't ye see I'm done for?' Desperately, she pushed her wet hair from her face. 'I've had me time, can't you see that? Do you want a rag of a woman when you can take your pick o' the fillies?'

'I love you,' he said, and took her to the lych-gate, ignoring the staring people.

Billa said: 'God help us.'

The rain was sheeting down as they got to the trap. Morgan Howells had already climbed into it, and Mike confronted him. 'Mrs. Jam won't be coming back in this one, Minister,' he said. 'I'll get another from Aber.'

The minister's eyes switched over them both. 'It . . . it has been a tragic business. Are you all right, Mrs. Jam?'

'Ay, sir.'

She was soaked with rain and shivering; her clothes were clinging to her wet body, her hair was down now, stranding her dress. Mike took off his coat and put it around her.

Morgan Howells said: 'I am glad, Mrs. Jam . . .'

Mike led her away, and she turned her wet face to his. 'But me kids . . . me kids!'

'The kids, too—come on, my lovely.'

'You ready, Sun?' asked Gideon.

She nodded. Most of the people had gone now; the Church was deserted save for two labouring figures.

'The minister is waiting,' said Gideon. 'Come.'

'Ay.'

The sky was threatening with thunder clouds. Lacking a brilliant light Gideon could not see her face; only the outline of the bonnet, he saw, and the deep shadows of her eyes; he thought she looked even smaller than usual standing there before him. Suddenly, she said:

'Empty ... empty I am, without my boy ...'

He left her then and went to the grave and placed upon its mound a piece of paper under a stone, and Belcher and Blackbird, who were the diggers stood back, and were careful of it. Returning to her, Gideon said:

'But you have his son. You will always have Richard Jay ... Come. Morgan Howells is waiting.'

Molly Caulara was standing at the lych-gate and she put out her hand to Sun as she passed.

'God be with ye, Mrs. Penderyn.'

They looked at each other.

'Goodbye, now,' said Molly Caulara. She stood watching the trap disappearing along the road to Neath. Behind it, in great blades of gold and crimson, Swansea was making iron; the very ground beneath her feet was trembling to the shot-firing. After the two labourers had gone she went to the spoiled earth and there knelt, picking up the paper Gideon had left, and on it she read:

Ye see me only in my chains, ye see me only in my grave. But behind each forehead, in each heart, is not my place prepared for me? Am I not mankind's ardent breath that endless thirsts for liberty? So, I will rise again, before the people stride. Deliverer, judge, I wait to take the streets: upon your heads, upon your necks, upon your crowns I'll stamp. For this is history's iron law; conceit it is not, threats are none. The day grows hot, how cool your shade, O, willow leaves of Babylon ...

356

Rising, Molly Caulara looked at the sky, for the rain had stopped and from a break in the clouds a golden light began to shine. Then Morriston began to pour from the bungs, and the molten iron flashed its incandescent whiteness on the lowering clouds; Llanelli, too, was stirring in bonds of fire: beneath her feet the ground began to tremble violently to the underground shot-firers of Aberafon; above her the sky was glowing in rainbow colours as the cauldrons were stirred. And, as the clamour of the iron-making grew about her, she remembered Dic's words:

'All over the country the Lodges will rise ... we are only hundreds now, but soon we'll be thousands, even millions ...!'

Hearing his voice as an echo, Molly Caulara stood amid the growing thunder of the Aberafon hammers, seeing in the eye of her mind an army of men sweeping across the fields towards the towns of industry, their fists clenched: and from them came a great shout. The sky became brighter, brighter in her imagination, before shattering into nothingness and brilliant light. She heard Dic say:

'And this is only the beginning. As Zimmerman said, we must cleanse it all and start all over again ...'

Sweat was on Molly's face. Above Aberdare a great, valedictory flame was standing, shafting the Top Towns as with a beacon of hope for the future, and this sight raked her from her dream. Shivering, she replaced the piece of paper on the grave, and smiled.

' 'Bye, Dico,' she said, and took the road that led to a distant glow, and beneath this glow was the town of Merthyr.

THE CONFESSION

IN 1874, forty-three years after Dic Penderyn was hanged at Cardiff on the order of the Home Secretary, the Reverend Evan Evans of Nantyglo was travelling in the United States. He was called to the death-bed of Ieuan Parker, a Welshman of Cwmavon, then living in Pennsylvania. This man confessed to the crime for which Dic Penderyn had been executed.

Historical sources: *The Insurrection at Merthyr Tydfil in 1831* by Professor Gwyn A. Williams, M.A., Ph.D., F.R. Hist.S. (Note: Professor Williams, perhaps the ablest authority, does not state the name of the Welshman who confessed but establishes the confession); *Dic Penderyn* by Islwyn ap Nicholas; *Dic Penderyn and the Merthyr Rising of 1831* by Harri Webb, who states Ieuan Parker's confession: 'It was I who wounded the soldier that Dic Penderyn was hanged for. I got away to America as soon as I could afterwards, but I could never escape from the memory of it. When you go back to Wales tell everybody that Dic Penderyn was innocent.' *The Merthyr Riots of 1831* (The Welsh Historical Review, Vol. 3, Dec. 1966, No. 2) by D. J. V. Jones. This historian states: 'As an explanation of his [Dic Penderyn's] death, it may be that the Government, which was shocked by the seriousness of the Merthyr riots, decided to make an example of this unwilling martyr.' (Neither the Marquis of Bute nor Mr. Justice Bosanquet, who sentenced him, seems to have expected him to be hanged—Home Office Papers 52/16: letter from the Marquis of Bute, 16th July 1831.)

An extract from *The New Newgate Calendar*, the Folio

Society, with an introduction by Lord Justice Birkett—*Riots at Merthyr Tydfil*: 'The soldier could not identify the prisoner [Dic Penderyn] as the party who had used the bayonet ... The prisoner persisted in denying his guilt, and declared that he would do so with his dying breath ... On the night before the execution, the unhappy convict was urged to make a confession of his guilt, but he positively denied ... He continued firm in this declaration up to the time of his death ...' The article concludes with the statement that Lewis Lewis confirmed this assertion, stating that he could have given satisfactory evidence of Dic Penderyn having been altogether absent from the affray.

AUTHOR'S NOTES

NEW EVIDENCE CONCERNING THE
EXECUTION OF
RICHARD LEWIS (DIC PENDERYN)

INFORMATION about Richard Lewis (Dic Penderyn) has been obscured by the mists of time, largely because certain documents such as his trial record, the Tregelles Price petition and letters from the sentencing judge Bosanquet to Lord Melbourne (the then Home Secretary) have been lost to posterity until today. And, as is usual in cases where the historical facts are thin, what was not known about Penderyn's life has been invented by a succession of early historians. The name of Dic Penderyn has been enhanced by national pride and the man himself built up into a hero almost pantomimic in quality. Yet, as one eminent historian has remarked, it is astonishing how popular legend has in this case followed a pattern of sober truth.

Now, however, the curtain has been largely pulled aside by nothing less than a stroke of luck. After two years of research and another year of writing this novel, I received in December 1970 from the Departmental Record Officer of the Home Office a letter which informed me that '... the additional information given in your letter of the 23rd November has led us to the discovery of some papers about Richard Lewis ...

It was the sort of find a writer dreams about. Within a day or two I was at the Record Office examining Bundle Zp 37 of HO 17/128 Part 2, which contained the *Sentence passed upon*

Lewis Lewis and Richard Lewis, a *Transcript of the Evidence for the Prosecution*, *six* letters from the sentencing judge to Melbourne (hitherto it was believed that three were written, none of which survived), *two* petitions in respect of Dic Penderyn and *one* in respect of Lewis Lewis (hitherto it was believed that but one was presented), *one* Petition in respect of Penderyn in the form of a letter from his prison chaplain and surgeon, *two* letters from Tregelles Price to government officials; other miscellaneous documents.

Until this discovery most historians believed Dic Penderyn had taken no active part in the Rising; that, because he had brawled with James Abbott, he had gone into hiding during the riot and had been picked off the street and hanged by Lord Melbourne as an example to the militants and Unionists in Wales. Nothing in the new evidence argues this fact—indeed, his murder is further emphasised. But what is now discovered is that he was not innocuous, as has been claimed by historians. Richard Lewis, alias Dic Penderyn, was not only a workers' leader but one important enough to enter the Castle Inn on the day of the Merthyr Rising and negotiate on behalf of the working force of thousands with men of the calibre of Guest and Crawshay: before the inn that day was massed some ten thousand men, yet he was one of a deputation of twelve. He might not have been a trade union official in the mould of William Twiss of the Bolton Authority, nor a Zephaniah Williams who was being groomed to lead the later Chartists, but he was doubtless a young man of political importance and steeped in the fight for Reform. Indeed, the family from which he sprang must have been head and shoulders above their contemporaries—it is doubtful if the great Welsh preacher Morgan Howells would have tolerated an unintelligent woman for a wife, the elder sister who so influenced Dic's life.

Melbourne, at this time, was thirsting for action against the embryonic unions, as Cole and the Webbs relate—even Peel, at the end of his tenancy, was trying to ferment Union reaction in the North which would sanction the use of government forces to destroy them. The Merthyr riots quite obviously were

362

not government sponsored, but they provided the opportunity for the strength of action Melbourne sought. Dic Penderyn is now seen to deserve the laurels imposed on him by our ancestors' word of mouth; he died, and lives, in the sanctity of sacrifice—the first accepted martyr of the Welsh working class.

TRANSCRIPT OF THE EVIDENCE FOR THE PROSECUTION

(Taken by William Meyrick Esq., lawyer for the Prosecution; July 14th 1831).

James Abbott
'I am a hair-dresser at Merthyr Tydfil—I was sworn in a special constable 3rd March—I saw a crowd first from half-past five to six o'clock in the morning—they were then in the market-place ... by Mr. Jenkins, the druggist ... at first three or four hundred—increased much by ten o'clock—some thousands at the Castle Inn... I saw Lewis Lewis after the men went into the house, the Castle Inn ... I saw some of them return ... I saw Lewis Lewis hanging on to the lamp iron ... he was speaking in Welsh ... addressing the mob—I observed a rush from the mob upon the soldiers—the soldiers were beaten very much—many of the soldiers came in disarmed to the passage of the Inn... I was stationed in the passage of the Inn... *I saw a soldier coming up the steps—saw him struggle with two or three others to keep his musket—which he lost. Richard Lewis was one—and others of the mob. The soldier that had lost his musket was making his way into the Inn, and as he was on the top step or thereabouts Richard Lewis charged him with a bayonet and made an incision in the thick part of the thigh, somewhere above the knee considerably—* The bayonet was fixed on the gun. I took the soldier by the arm directly and led him to the brewhouse—I know the soldier —Donald Black—he is here—I left him in the care of a person dressing him, I saw a large hole bleeding like a pig—I have not the slightest doubt of the person I saw.'

Under cross-examination, Abbot said:

'The ironmasters desired the mob to pick out twelve to fourteen—I heard Mr. Crawshay speaking—ten or twelve persons were to be sent in as a deputation to the ironmasters—I can't say what happened ... Mr. Guest said he would speak to them —treat with them ... the mob was perfectly quiet up to this time—I did not see the ten or twelve go in, but saw them come out again ... when they came out they seemed very dissatisfied ... I suppose some 8,000 to 10,000 workmen were collected—there were at that time soldiers in the Castle (Inn)— they had arms ... there were soldiers outside the Castle (Inn) ... the mob seemed dissatisfied ... Lewis Lewis stood up and attempted to speak after the deputies came out—the first time I saw him was after the deputies came out ... he was higher than the generality of the mob ... a man said ... he stated in the presence of 10,000—he spoke as loud as he was able—I did not hear any threat, he did it respectfully, he said they wanted bread and cheese, that there were many families that had not sufficient ... I did not hear Mr. Guest promise them bread and cheese for their families—the soldiers were one deep, the workmen were close to the soldiers ... I did not see the soldiers do anything till the mob came upon them. They tried to take care of their arms. The soldiers got mixed with the mob ... the bayonets were upright ... some of the workmen seized hold of the muskets—the firing did not take place immediately from the windows. Some person fired ... I saw several (workmen) wounded before the firing took place ... When the firing took place the consequences were very fatal— none of the soldiers had been attacked—that I know ... when they saw their comrades struggling below they fired from above—there were Magistrates with them—Mr. Bruce was downstairs in the passage at the time of the rush, and Mr. Hill at the door. He was not off the first step. Before the wound was given to Donald Black I had not noticed him at all. I saw a flag in the crowd ... I saw three muskets in possession of some of the mob ...'

William Williams

'On Thursday 3rd June I was a special constable—I was stationed with the other special constables, and Mr. Bruce and Mr. Hill in the passage—I saw a mob in front—I saw Lewis Lewis holding the iron of a lamp post raised above the rest of the mob—I heard him address the mob in Welsh "Boys, let me say a word—these are come against us—if every one of you is of the same mind as me we *shall force their arms away from them*, I shall make to so begin"—The other words I did not comprehend—then he got down—there was a rush upon the soldiers by the mob—I saw their bludgeons go up and the people rushed forwards—some of them were holloaing out for bread—"Squeeze closer, on, on"—I was behind some gentleman I assisted the gentleman to take the man in. A man was taken from the crowd that had one of the soldier's fire-arms ...'

Under cross-examination, Williams said:

'...When I heard the words "Squeeze on" there was a great crush in the crowd. I did not get out of the passage into the street. There is a flight of steps from the passage into the street—the foot pavement is beyond that. My duty and occupation prevented me from observing accurately where the soldiers were standing and what they were doing. What further explanation Lewis Lewis may have given I do not know.'

Under re-examination, Williams said:

'A rush took place in about half a minute after I heard the last words. The people at the front had bludgeons up in their arms.'

William Rowland

'I am a constable was on duty at the Castle ... I heard the High Sheriff read a paper. The gentlemen afterwards addressed the mob and requested them to disperse—I heard persons go into the Castle (Inn)—part of the mob and came out again ... I heard several expressions used by the mob—one in particular said "That the soldiers who were come there were no more than a gooseberry in the hands of the mob". This was said opposite to the Castle door loud enough to be heard at a distance—one "that they were determined to be revenged on the constables" and "Particularly would play the devil with the constables" or words to that effect. I saw a flag right opposite the Castle door—they had a great number of very large clubs, and some with small pit wood which they use in the levels ... I saw both prisoners there, I saw Lewis Lewis supporting himself on the lamp iron ... I could have wished to see more men—I thought myself in danger ... There had been a meeting before—a Reform meeting—I saw people passing through Merthyr with a flag on the 30th May ... I did not hear all Lewis Lewis said. He might have qualified ... They attempted to take me into the mob. They were very riotous. They desired to send ten or fourteen men in. The proposal came from the gentlemen. I let them into the room. I was sometimes looking one way and sometimes another—They said there was nothing settled. Everyone wanted to know the result of what the gentlemen had said—They could not be closer ...'

Thomas Darker

'I am a special constable. I was in the passage—I was there when the deputation came out—the mob appeared to be very riotous—armed with large sticks—some as thick as my arm. Nothing particular about them. A great deal of Welsh was spoken that I did not understand—*I saw Richard Lewis first in the passage coming out with the deputation. The first time I saw him after he came out was about five to ten minutes—I saw him in the front of the Castle (Inn) with his hat off he waved his hat and shouted*—I saw a flag—I had seen a Reform procession before—they had a flag then.'

Under cross-examination, Darker said:

'*Richard Lewis was standing by the door with his hat up*— What had been said from the window of the Castle (Inn) just before he *waved his hat* I did not hear.'

366

James Drew
'Special constable—I was at the Inn on 3rd June—I saw both prisoners—*I saw Richard Lewis wrestling with a soldier and one or two more—he pushed the bayonet at his thigh.*'

Under cross-examination, Drew said:

'It was but one struggle—more muskets than one were laid hold of nearly at the same time.'

John Bruce Esq. Magistrate of Glamorganshire
'I act for Merthyr—I remember the soldiers coming... I sent for them in consequence of what had happened the night before... So great a mob Mr. Hill (ironmaster) and I were unable to go the direct road to meet them ... we met them at Pandy ... came down to Merthyr with them to the Castle Inn ... a very large mob before us and following us—made use of many threats as to the paucity of their numbers (the soldiers) —exhorting each other to overpower them ... part of the soldiers went into the house ... the rest stood in the street. I placed the constables in the passage... I stood at the door except when called in to consult with anyone in the Inn ... if the Commanding Officer had understood Welsh no musket would have been seized... Expressions were used, urging one another to "Squeeze close, press upon them, keep between them and the wall ... don't let them have the wall..." The mob was armed with bludgeons—they had a sort of red flag... I did not notice either of the prisoners ... proclamation of the Riot Act (was) read in a loud voice ... I explained the nature of it in Welsh and English ... they seemed to treat it with perfect indifference ... I saw the general scuffle and turmoil ... I saw the wounded soldier brought in bleeding— Major Falls was brought in with his head bleeding...'

Donald Black, Lance-Corporal in the 93rd Regiment (Previously a Private).
'I was one of the detachment that marched from Brecon to Merthyr on 3rd June... I went inside (the Inn) and then turned out again ... the mob made a rush on us and I was

367

wounded—They tried to take my arms from me ... my musket was seized, it was wrested from me. I was wounded in the right hip—I don't know the man that wounded me—*I saw both the prisoners in the crowd*—I did not see them laying hands on anyone—I saw one of the crowd try to break our rank and get in our rear—Captain Sparks came out and turned him back, and Lewis Lewis said he would not do that to him. *Only saw Richard Lewis taking off his hat and cheering but not laying his hands on anyone in the crowd* ... Great confusion among the men when the rush was made on us—it was *before the rush was made that I saw Richard Lewis.* After the rush was made there was so much confusion I could not identify any man—I was so much confused, I do not know who wrested the gun from me—I had a bayonet wound which bled very much—I was taken back into the brew-house—I have seen the man who took me into the brew-house (James Abbott). Saw him at Merthyr, and here ...'

Under cross-examination, Lance-Corporal Black said:

'... I was on the pavement ... we had fixed bayonets ... Some person endeavoured to get into the rear, Captain Sparks laid hold of him—Lewis Lewis did not seem to like seeing one of the workmen to be laid hold of by a soldier. I believe it was in English that Lewis Lewis said "You would not do so to me." ... I did not like Lewis Lewis stand at the rear—we were trying all we could in our power to keep persons from the wall—It was impossible. I do not understand Welsh.'

Under re-examination, Lance-Corporal Black said:

'I was stationed by the door—the crowd was immediately in front—my object was to keep as near the wall as possible—Our guns were not charged.'

DEFENCE

RICHARD LEWIS said on Friday morning this riot began to get up.
LEWIS LEWIS said nothing.

The Jury found RICHARD LEWIS guilty. LEWIS
LEWIS not guilty.

The jury said they thought LEWIS LEWIS guilty of
encouraging the mob to *disarm* the soldiers.

DEFENCE

Author's note

I consider it technically correct here to point out that in the
Second Petition for Richard Lewis (Dic Penderyn)—which follows hereunder—the man William Jones (who heard James
Abbott's evidence read back to him) stated this witness's con-
tradiction of the evidence he had originally given. Abbot
originally stated that he was 'on the steps of the Inn'. He
altered this to 'in the passage of the Inn'. The reader's attention
is drawn to the evidence of Lance-Corporal Black who stated
he was *on the pavement* in front of the Inn, which was on a
lower level than the passage. Clearly, Abbott would have had
to be positioned on the steps to witness the actual wounding.
Joseph Tregelles Price, the Neath Quaker ironmaster, makes
much of this point in the Petition.

THE FIRST PETITION

To: *William the Fourth*   From Joseph T. Price
    King of Great Britain.
              CASE OF RICHARD LEWIS—Condemned
              at the Cardiff Assize July 9 1831
              to suffer the penalty of Death.

Charged upon the oath of James Abbott of Merthyr Tydfil and
others with having (at the Parish of Merthyr Tydfil) with
divers others unknown riotously assembled and with having
feloniously attacked and wounded Donald Black of the 93rd
Regiment with a bayonet whilst the said Donald Black was on
duty.

Donald Black, it is on evidence, was stabbed in the *Front*
Street, opposite the Door, the *front* door—that he was stabbed
by Richard Lewis—and therefore Richard Lewis was con-

victed—no evidence appears to have been given of a contrary kind.

Richard Lewis declares his innocence of this charge, in the full prospect of death—he declares that he freely and fully forgives his accusers from the bottom of his heart, and trusts solely in the mercy of God for pardon for all his sins and in this state of mind states that when he went out of the Castle Inn *as one of the Deputation who waited on their Masters*—he went out at the back door and another man named Johns went out with him—that he did not afterwards go round to the Front door, that he stopped for 15 or 20 minutes on that side of the Castle Inn—that on hearing the first gun-shot he ran off down a street (which is called Glebeland) through an archway over the Iron Bridge towards Kirkhouses' [the agent for W. Crawshay over the miners and colliers]—that Nancy Evans, wife of Evan Evans of Merthyr, saw him standing *there* by the side of the Castle Inn all the time after he came out through the back door, and saw him run away. That Elizabeth Lewis also saw him run away, and many others. On being asked if he had ever had any quarrel or scuffle with Abbott, the principal witness, he said that on the evening of the illuminations on occasion of the Reform question coming out, he had a scuffle in Merthyr Street—that Abbott was there and took part in it—that Abbott at that time said he would be up with him the first chance he had—that Will John David was with him that night and can tell how it was that night.

This simple declaration made to the writer induced him to proceed to Merthyr to ask the parties named questions upon the facts. These, in company with John Thomas, a Constable, without telling the parties what declaration Richard Lewis made to him, he first had the following replies from:

Nancy Evans, wife of Evan Evans.

She was standing with Richard Lewis by the Tap Room window of the Castle Inn for about twenty minutes before the first gun-shot went off (the Tap Room window is on the side of the Castle Inn, not the front) that Richard Lewis was not in the Front Street at the time of the firing (or for twenty minutes before). She saw him run away at the first shot and her boy, Evan Evans, who confirmed it, was along with him—the boy says that Richard Lewis ran faster than him and ran before him through the Arches.

Elizabeth Lewis says she stood opposite the Tap Room window—saw Richard Lewis standing by the Tap Room window a quarter of an hour before the firing commenced, and when the firing commenced he ran away.

William Philip, puddler, works at Cyfarthfa—saw Richard Lewis run off as hard as he could at the same time with him on the first shot going off down the Glebeland to the Arch by the Iron Bridge.

Benjamin Davies, navigator, works at Penydarren—knows Richard Lewis very well—saw him standing by the wall (the Glebeland side of the Castle Inn) about a quarter of an hour before the firing commenced—he heard the firing and then they both ran through the Archway towards the Iron Bridge, and that he (Benjamin Davies) stood, and Richard Lewis went on—had nothing in his hand at the time—he was with him a quarter of an hour till they both ran together towards the Iron Bridge—that Richard Lewis had a *blue* jacket and trousers and waistcoat on at the time. Several others were ready to offer their testimony, but the writer considered it [unnecessary?] to take same; on the point he sought for Johns who is said by Richard Lewis to have gone out with him from the meeting in the Castle Inn of the Deputation and the Masters, but Johns could not be found—he is said to have gone off.

David Abraham, a special constable, was standing near Abbott at the time of the riot, and that though he knew Richard Lewis he did not see him in front of the Castle—he had seen him by the side of the house and cautioned him against going forward, and believes he was not forward in front—in that part of the crowd.

Thomas Cottrell, waiter at the Castle Inn, was looking out of the same (an upper window) saw the soldier who was stabbed in the thigh—saw the act of stabbing—that the man who stabbed the soldier was clothed in a coat of a sort of *drab* colour, *he is quite sure it was not a black or a blue colour*—and that if Richard Lewis had on a blue coloured coat or jacket it could not have been he that stabbed the soldier.

Ann Morgan lives opposite the Castle Inn—saw the soldier of the 93rd who was stabbed in the thigh by a bayonet—*saw the act*. She knows Richard Lewis very well, that it was another man who stabbed him, not Richard Lewis—the man who stabbed him had on a *drab* coloured frock coat and duck trousers, and afterwards he broke a window with the gun and then went up the front street running as fast as he could, and the gun in his hand—she cried murder when she saw the man stabbed—she knows it was the same soldier that Richard Lewis is accused of stabbing.

Richard Lewis was wholly unknown to me till I saw him on the 24th Inst. in Cardiff gaol. I left my home near Neath Abbey that morning on purpose to see the condemned prisoners, Richard Lewis and Lewis Lewis—having heard his narrative I thought it right to ascertain whether it was susceptible on confirmation or not. I found it fully and correctly confirmed as the foregoing statements. I therefore yielded belief to them and determined in consequence to proceed to London to present the case to the proper authority. And now make my appeal to those authorities for the extension of mercy to Richard Lewis.

To William the Fourth
    King of Great Britain.

Joseph T. Price.
Watchets' Hotel. Piccadilly.
27th July 1831

Author's note.

This is the first mention of a quarrel between Richard Lewis (Dic Penderyn) and James Abbott, the principal witness. As a result of this Petition the then Lord Chancellor, Lord Brougham, wrote to Mr. Justice Bosanquet, the sentencing judge, expressing '... a serious doubt whether the credibility of Abbott, a principal witness, was not affected by the fact, if true, of his having entertained personal animosity against the Prisoner ...' Lord Brougham added: '... I deem it right to transmit to you the statement of facts before mentioned and request you to take into your consideration and inform me whether you see any ground for altering your opinion as to the guilt of the Prisoner . . .'

In order to allow the judge to reconsider his verdict in the case, the Lord Chancellor then granted a stay of execution for a fortnight.

Mr. Justice Bosanquet took no positive action—in a letter dated August 1st to Lord Melbourne he dismisses the possibility of animosity on the part of Abbott, and dilutes the prisoner's allegation of a scuffle between himself and Abbott on the grounds that he was *asked* by Mr. Price if there had been one. Here is the judge's letter to Lord Melbourne:

Cardigan.
August 1 1831

My Lord,

I have the honour to send to your Lordship a report of the evidence given in the case of Richard Lewis at Cardiff and also to return Mr. Price's representation—your Lordship will observe that the assertion now made by the Prisoner that he was not in front of the Castle Inn after the Deputation went out, is inconsistent not only with the evidence of James Abbott, but also with that of the two special constables on duty—Thomas Darker and James Drew as well as of Donald Black the wounded soldier. It is very singular that the defence now made for the Prisoner should not have been suggested at the trial in any way, though the Prisoner was very ably defended, and I believe that on referring to the Petitions presented to your Lordship by and on behalf of the Prisoners Richard Lewis and Lewis Lewis, and which were shown to me before they were sent to London, you will not find the ground now taken relied upon.

It is also remarkable that the imputation now made upon the credit of James Abbott on account of a previous scuffle with the Prisoner and words of which were not referred (?) to in the cross examination of that witness, which was long and minute, and should now be remembered by the Prisoner 'on being *asked* by Mr. Price whether he had ever had any quarrel or scuffle with Abbott'. It is very probable that the Prisoner may have been at the back or side of the Castle (Inn) a quarter of an hour or twenty minutes before the firing, and have run away, as many others did, immediately after the firing, and that a person in a coat of drab colour may have been seen from an *upper* window of the Castle Inn stabbing a soldier in the thigh without suffering any part of the evidence for the prosecution to be untrue. I have the honour to be, my Lord,

Your Lordship's faithful and obedient Servant,
J. B. Bosanquet.

The statement of Benjamin Davies as given by J. T. Price is apparently inconsistent with the evidence of the prosecution as given by four of the witnesses.

Author's note

Mr. Justice Bosanquet wrote, in all, six letters to Lord Melbourne in respect of the case—hitherto it was thought that three were written, and that none survived. From this correspondence emerges Bosanquet's apparent determination that Dic Penderyn should die, and much of Melbourne's implacability is thus now explained. Only in his last but one letter—that of August 6th—a week before the execution—does a little of the judge's confidence begin to fail him under the weight of new evidence brought by J. Tregelles Price, and he states:

'... under the circumstances it may be a matter of your Lordship's consideration whether it is advisable that the sentence of death should be carried into execution, there being reason to think that the justice of it will be considered doubtful...'

The unhappy Bosanquet, hoist by his own insistence in rejecting all but Abbott's evidence, wrote:

'... one individual may satisfy the exigency of further justice.'

And, then, finally, in his last letter (August 6th) to the Home Secretary, he said:

'... If upon further consideration your Lordship should be induced to recommend a commutation of the sentence of Death ...'

But Melbourne was already convinced that somebody should die, and it was too late.

However, out of this correspondence arises a strange occurrence that probably will never be adequately explained, and Bosanquet refers to it in the last letter. It appears that one, Henry Morgan, took personally to Melbourne a declaration of guilt on the part of the two prisoners—a document which was apparently presented to them for signature, and which was purported to have emanated from them. Certainly this 'confession' made an adverse impression at the Home Office, as Mr. Price was quick to point out in one of two letters to Lord James Stewart, an official there. The existence of this document angered the people of Merthyr, and the two prisoners, and, as a result of this, Mr. Price immediately forwarded to Melbourne, via Lord James Stewart, the following refutation of the confession presented by officials of Cardiff Prison:

Cardiff.
August 1st 1831

We hereby humbly certify that we have respectively attended Richard Lewis now under sentence of death in the Gaol of this place since his conviction, and that he has uniformly and solemnly denied any participation in or knowledge of the act of wounding, or endeavouring to wound the Soldier, for which offence he, the said Richard Lewis, is condemned to die.

(Signed Daniel Jones (Chaplain to the Gaol)
William Jones (Baptist Minister)
Lewis Powell (Independent Minister)

375

Author's note
Joseph Tregelles Price, now in desperation, made a final attempt to secure the reprieve of Dic Penderyn (Lewis Lewis was reprieved by Melbourne on 3rd August) by sending his Second Petition, which, it is understood, was accompanied by over 11,000 signatures, mainly from the town of Merthyr. It is significant that he did not this time address it to the King.

THE SECOND PETITION

Petition—Glamorgan Assizes

In the case of Richard Lewis, the Prisoner respited until the 13th Inst—I stated before that he admitted that he was engaged in a scuffle in Merthyr Street on the night of the illuminations; that James Abbott, the principal witness took part in that scuffle and that Abbott then declared that he would be up with him the first chance he had, and that Will John David could tell how it was on that occasion.

I have seen this person twice—he states 'that he was present when Abbott the Barber and Dic Lewis quarrelled the night of the illuminations, and heard Abbott then declare "Come thee I will be up with thee again the first opportunity I can get" or words to that effect. 'That he saw him strike Richard Lewis in the street—that he has known Abbott about three quarters of a year.' Will John David mentioned another person who was present—this person was called Edward Mathews, a Pudler, he says he was in Merthyr the night of the illuminations—saw Richard Lewis and others in the street near the Bush Inn—saw Abbott strike Richard Lewis. David Rees also saw this, he is a miner, and he also preaches among the Baptists; he declares that he saw Richard Lewis and Abbott scuffling together—he thinks it was a little past ten o'clock at night—he heard Abbott in parting declare to Richard Lewis that the first opportunity that he should have *he would be up with him.*

I saw Abbott myself and mentioned these statements to him —he declares on the contrary that he did not know Richard Lewis previous to the time he saw him at the Riot by the

Castle Inn—that he never had a quarrel with him on any occasion—produced William Henry James, Adam Newell and George Williams, all of Merthyr, who admitted that they were present at the row in Merthyr on the night of the illuminations when Richard Lewis received blows, and returned them, but that neither of them saw James Abbott there. Adam Newell admitted that he might have been in the street yet not be seen by him.

Richard Lewis stated to me that a man named Johns went out with him through the back door of the Castle Inn after the interview with their Masters—this Johns could not be found. Marsden a respectable linen draper of Merthyr, says that he was in the Castle Inn at that time and *saw Richard Lewis* go out through *the back door*.

Rice, the wife of James Rice lives opposite the Castle Inn, in front of it, was looking out of their house at the time of the fight—*saw Richard Lewis* in the street *dressed in a blue jacket and trousers—before he went in as one of the Deputation—did not see him after*.

Thomas Burnell, a tallow chandler, was in the Castle Inn at the time of the riot—saw the Highlanders engage with the workmen in front of the doors, saw no such person dressed as Richard Lewis was that day stab any soldier—but saw some person in a flannel smock strike one of the soldiers with a bayonet, but from the confusion that occurred he could not take upon himself to swear to him—does not know Richard Lewis.

Henry Jones, a Gentleman residing in Merthyr—was in the Castle Inn at the time of the riot—saw the commencement of the attack and observed Lewis Lewis advance towards the soldiers—saw several others join him, but from the instant the confusion that prevailed was so great that he could not identify any—he did not see anyone clad in blue jacket and trousers as Richard Lewis is described to have been, and he considered it was extremely difficult to distinguish individuals from the confusion which existed—he described it as comparable to the rush and tumult of the waves of the sea.

Thomas James, a miner, works at Penydarren with William

Lewis, Master Miner—was outside the Castle Inn at the time of the riot—saw a man dressed in a *smock frock and trousers* by the front door stab a soldier in the thigh with a bayonet, and then he went off up to the front street.

There were one or two men killed at the time so dressed—killed a few yards from the spot, several persons declared to me they had seen such persons dead or dying. And it does seem probable that under the eyes and fire of the soldiers in the upper windows and below—any man stabbing a soldier would be picked out *as an object for them to shoot and be shot.*

William Jones, fitter of Cyfarthfa Works, was present in W. Meyrick's office on the Thursday before the last quarter sessions. [W. Meyrick was solicitor for the prosecution against the rioters.] James Abbott was there—he heard the evidence read over which he was then considered to have given—and which he would be expected to give in court. It stated that he [Abbott] was on the steps of the front door of the Castle Inn when Donald Black was stabbed; this statement, Abbott then declared to one of Meyrick's clerks named Davis, was *incorrect—that he was in the passage of the Inn at the time,* and William Jones says that he considers that if he was in the passage of the Inn (thronged as it was by soldiers in the front) it would be impossible for him to see so as to distinguish a person stabbing a soldier on the outside of the house at that time.

William Edwards, Master Collier and Miner or undertaker of Job Work in those departments at Penydarren Ironworks, states that he was in the Castle Inn at the time of the Merthyr riots—that he was standing near James Drew who gave evidence in the case of Richard Lewis—that they were within the passage several yards from the front door, that the passage was crowded with soldiers so that it was impossible for *him* and he is *sure* it was also impossible for Drew who was further *in* than he was, to see, outside the door, *who*, in particular, inflicted any wound on any soldier—and he declares that he, Drew the Barber, remained with him from the *commencement* of the scuffle, before the firing of the guns—until several hours *after* the same was over, with the exception of about an hour or

378

rather less—and which absence was stated by him to be for the purpose of assuring his wife of his safety; and he, (William Edwards) further states that Drew did not go from him *until a quarter of an hour or twenty minutes after the firing was over*.

William Edwards further says that as he spent several hours with James Drew that day in a neighbouring public house, it appears to him not a little extraordinary that Drew should not have mentioned to him his having seen Richard Lewis stab the soldier if it was a fact that he did see it, but he declares that Drew did not tell him.

On reviewing the several features of this case, considering that Donald Black could not recognise the man who stabbed him, that though he says he saw Richard Lewis he does not say he saw him *at the time* of the fight—that Richard Lewis passed in from the front as one of the deputation and must have been observed then, that he went through the back door, that it is asserted by several persons that he was *seen* standing by the side of the Inn for 15 or 20 minutes before the firing, and that Richard Lewis was not in the front street consequently during the struggle; that one of these persons, Nancy Evans, the wife of Evan Evans, a woman far advanced in pregnancy, appears to be an unexceptional evidence *quite in point* —that Abbott declares he did not know Richard Lewis *until* he saw him on that day, that he declares he cannot speak to his dress, that he said in the hearing of William Jones that he was within the passage—that the passage was much crowded— that other persons who knew Richard Lewis, some *equally well placed* for seeing—others, particularly those opposite and above, in the windows, *better*, who saw a man dressed in a drab frock stab a soldier in the thigh did not see Richard Lewis stab him—that no other soldier than Donald Black is represented to have been so stabbed, that a man dressed as he is said to have [?] who was seen to stab a soldier in the thigh *was shot near the spot*; that *Drew's evidence is shown by William Edwards to be ill calculated to support Abbott's*; that many lives have already been taken legally by the soldiers at the command of the Magistrate—and that no soldier or peaceable subject lost his life by the hand of the rioters—It is

submitted that there are grounds on which Mercy towards the condemned prisoner Richard Lewis may availingly be asked. I do therefore *humbly and respectfully*—and *earnestly* ask for the extension of *that* benign prerogative of the British Throne *MERCY* for this condemned British Subject, fully believing *also* that its extension in this case will contribute to allay a feeling of irritation, to restore order and maintain tranquility —objects of the sincere desire and prayer of the Petitioner— the King's loyal and affectionate subject,
Dated at Brecon the 5th day
of the 8th Mo (Aug') 1831

> Joseph T. Price of Neath Abbey,
> Glamorganshire

To this document Joseph Price received but Melbourne's official acknowledgment. A now weakened Mr. Justice Bosanquet, however, received the following:

Mr. Justice Bosanquet   Whitehall
                                    9th August 1831

My Lord,
I am directed by Viscount Melbourne to acknowledge receipt of your Lordship's letter of the 6th Inst. upon the case of Richard Lewis, and to inform your Lordship that Lord Melbourne does not feel warranted in taking any course for further suspending the Execution of the Law.

PS. I have to acknowledge the	I am Etc.
receipt of your letter of the 7th	(Signed) S. M. Phillipps
Inst, the Prisoner Lewis Lewis has	
been removed.	

(To transportation—*Au.*)

Author's note
The discovery of the lost Bosanquet letters, the Transcript of Evidence, the three Petitions, the Morgan Petition and the prison chaplain's refutation of it are no less important than Tregelles Price's letters to 'Esteemed friends' in high places. The find makes an important contribution to the personality

and character of Dic Penderyn who has lived in the history and hearts of his countrymen for a century and a half. A little more of the legend has now been stripped away and the bones of irreducible truth exposed, and one fact is stronger now: when the people of Merthyr ran James Abbott out of the town they did it in the name of justice that has weathered the intervening years. Was Ieuan Parker, who forty years later confessed to the crime, the man in the grey frock coat who was seen to stab and run away? Certainly Richard Lewis and Lewis Lewis were not related, this theory has been quite disproved. The legend that Lewis Lewis was of noble birth now seems much less likely; the claim that Dic was an unimportant hostage who hid on Aberdare mountain is now rejected. Perhaps the finding of the trial record which, even as late as a fortnight before Dic's execution the Lord Chancellor himself had not seen—may throw further light ... unless it has been conveniently lost ...? But one thing is sure: as Professor Gwyn A. Williams said in his Cecil-Williams Memorial Lecture in 1965, Dic Penderyn's last words—'*O Arglwydd dyma gamwedd!*' (O Lord, what an iniquity!) have echoed louder and longer than all the muskets of the Highlanders who massacred the Merthyr workers before the Castle Inn in June 1831.

Alexander Cordell

The newly found papers may be inspected at the Public Record Office, Chancery Lane, London, W.C.2.

The permission of H.M. Controller of the Stationery Office to reproduce the above Home Office material is acknowledged with thanks.

For my friends Geoff Thomas, librarian, and
Arthur Morris, teacher.

Book Two

LAND OF MY FATHERS

I am again indebted to the following for making available to me books of research, original documents, letters and maps, some of antiquity:

Mr. G. A. Dart, F.L.A. and Mr. E. Goulden, F.L.A. of Headquarters Central Library, Cardiff; the Departmental Record Office of the Home Office; The National Library of Wales; Mr. J. Bowring, B.A., A.L.A. of Douglas Public Library; Mr. D. G. Edwards, M.P.S.; the Gwynedd Archives Service and Mr. S. C. G. Caffell, B.A., A.L.A. of Gwynedd Library Service, Llangefni; Mr. D. Francis, B.A., A.L.A. and Mr. G. James, B.A., A.L.A. both of Merthyr Public Libraries; Mr. Wilfred Bowden, J.P. of Abercynon; Mr. T. Iowerth late of Bangor Branch Library, and not least to Mr. Geoffrey Thomas the Cultural Services Officer of Libraries, Archives and Museums, Dyfed, to whom this book is dedicated.

Idris Davies's *Gwalia Deserta* is quoted by permission of Mr. Ebenzer Morris and the Estate of the late Idris Davies.

To many others I am also grateful for help, especially to John A. Owen whose *History of Dowlais Iron Works* was a constant companion in the writing, and to Jim Robinson and Deryck Brown for research: also to Ian Stuart for his encouragement, interest and suggestions.

Lastly, my thanks to Mam-gu, my first love, for being of the Rhondda.

In a certain part of the Island there is a people called Welsh, *so bold and ferocious that, when unarmed, they do not fear to encounter an armed forces; being ready to shed their blood in defence of their country, and to sacrifice their lives for renown.*

Gerald of Wales – *c*.1146–1223
– quoting Henry II of England

I stood in the ruins of Dowlais
And sighed for the lovers destroyed
And the landscape of Gwalia stained for all
    times
by the bloody hands of progress.
I saw the ghosts of The Successful Century
Marching on the ridges of the sunset
And wandering among derelict furnaces,
And they had not forgotten their humiliation,
For their mouths were full of curses.
And I cried aloud, O what shall I do for my
    fathers
And the land of my fathers?
But they cursed and cursed and would not
    answer,
For they could not forget their humiliation.

Idris Davies
Gwalia Deserta

One

Anglesey
1831

My tenth birthday, I remember, was one of those early up flying April mornings when even churchyard corpses were dreaming of high-buttoned girls, parasols and kisses.

Certainly it was a day when the clergy from Petter to Wesley Street were sitting ducks.

At six o'clock most mornings the privy ten-holer on Turkey Shore was occupied by bright-faced boyos who always got up first – deacons, the leaders of the community. And here the business of the day would be discussed – as to who would be on what 'bargain' that week, who would be carting, and the quality, or otherwise, of the sermon given by a travelling preacher a week last Sunday.

"First up, first served," said Andy Appledore, my mate who sat next to me with the *copar ledis*, and he lit a rag, dropped it on to a board and floated it down the gully-way of the big ten-holer, and you couldn't see deacons for dust. The language coming up from that privy was enough to singe the tail off Satan, let alone deacons.

Andy went one way, I went another.

It becomes clear to me, said my father at the inquest, that this particular Englishman is a bad example to a well-mannered Welshman, and I didn't sit down for a week.

I ran fast that morning up to Costog Spinney, then down to the beach where old Joe Herring, my friend the black-faced gull, was waiting for his breakfast.

Dear me, I was in love with the world that morning; it was full of sun, wind, birthday greetings, and all the sweetness of

April. Panting on the edge of Ogof Fain I saw the sea below me dancing in spindrift, and he was a marvellous blue with him that week, frothing up his white-topped breakers and smashing them against the harbour wall where the copper carriers spiked the sky with cobwebs of rigging. Far away to the north was Ellan Vannin they call the Isle of Man: to the south was snow-capped Snowdon, and great bedsheet clouds were lumbering across the caverns of the wind.

Ach, I do love the bright springtime days when the mutton chops do handsprings across the meadows. The birds play leap-frog, the lads are all polished and quiffed – putting years on the girls, my mother used to say. Aye, there is something in springtime that gets everyone frisky, and it is a hell of a thing when you're ten years old, to see folks billing and cooing in hedges and knees up in haylofts, and Satan himself in the back pews of Calfaria, looking for clients, according to my father.

Tall and wide-shouldered is Dada, his head higher than any man in Amlwch . . . with our dead mam's hymnal on the pew between us. The most eligible widower in Town, I'd heard say, with fat women fanning themselves in flushes at the sight of him.

"Please keep away from that English Andy Appledore," said he.

"Yes, Dada."

'Rock of Ages' it was then, full blend of soprano, contralto, tenor and bass, with my piping treble coming up beside my father's voice. In shafts of sunlight from the Chapel windows the dust-motes dance; a blue bottle is wheezing among the polished boots and black-stocking knees.

"Never been near that ten-hole privy," said I.

"Accepted," said my father. "And there are a few in Amlwch who may need heating up. In due course all will receive their just deserts, Taliesin, as did Samson for setting fire to the tails of foxes. So take the hiding just to please me, is it?"

"Yes, Dada."

Wasn't me. It was that bloody Appledore.

Sweating, me. In this mood he could rend a lion.

*

On the other side of my father was my Cousin Poll, aged fifteen. All peaches and cream was she under her poke-bonnet, a face all innocence and very flourishing in the breast, being in milk.

It always set the congregation staring when we took my Cousin Poll to Chapel on Sundays, and she always did herself up gay in colours, contrasting the bombazine black, said she, and the women, creaking and corsetted, gave her the eye. A crying scandal it is, said one: with his woman scarce cold in her grave, said another, that Gwyn Roberts brings a harlot in to share a pew with decent people . . . But my father did not appear to hear this. Through the Chapel door he came, standing politely aside while Polly took her seat. Radiant was my Cousin Poll; a primrose in a bed of deadly nightshade.

A bit more about my father and Cousin Poll, while on the subject.

Large was he, as I have said, with thick-muscled arms where the hairs grew like forest trees: Iberian Welsh to the marrow, the people used to say: so tall that he ducked his head under the back of Three Costog, and that was six foot two. In he comes from the Smelter with funnel dirt upon his face, and there, in the kitchen, sits our Poll feeding my little sister Meg, with a wicked little smile . . .

After my mam died, having my sister Meg two months back, my father brought this Polly into our house.

The death of Gwyn Roberts' missus is a tragedy, they said in Town, and he will be a long time getting over it.

O aye? they were saying now.

For about this time my Cousin Poll brought forth, too, and her baby was dead. So my father took the dead baby from Poll's breast and buried it with my mother: then he took our Meg and put her on the breast of Poll. Naturally, the people in Town had opinions on it, and Mr. Dafydd Owen, our deacon, said:

"Your niece's child was born out of wedlock, Gwyn Roberts – how can you bear it – a baggage suckling your child?"

My father went about his business as if he hadn't heard.

"You will show Cousin Poll due respect, Taliesin, you hear me?"

"Yes, Dada."

"Her mother, like yours, is dead; her father is at sea. She is alone and of our blood. It is right and fair that she should come and live with us, you understand?"

"Yes, Dada."

"And do not heed the gossip in the Town."

"No, Dada."

"Your Cousin Polly's milk will taste as sweet as Mam's. If in doubt, ask little Meg."

"Yes, Dada."

"And Poll is in need of us, poor little soul."

Mind you, I was coming a bit sore these days about this 'poor little soul' business, for she do not look so poor to me, this Cousin Poll, and make sure she has an egg for her breakfast every morning while she is on the feed, and no bloody egg for me.

"I know where she'd finish up if she belonged to me," said Mrs. Dahlia Sapphira.

We were at table, I remember. I suppose I could have chosen a better time to raise the subject. Poll was upstairs putting Meg to bed; Dada and me were together after a hard day on Turkey Shore.

"Born out of wedlock, is it?" I asked, getting into bread and jam.

My father blew his tea. "To what are you referring?"

"Poll's baby."

I could never get the hang of this birthing baby stuff, with Andy saying she'd gone swimming among tadpoles.

"And who stated that?" asked my father.

"The *copar ledis* do say so."

Mam's bread board, warped by years, was beside me on the starched, white cloth. She was a noble little thing, my mam, with Welsh-dark hair and the face of a housewife, with little fat hands for cutting bread and butter on her little fat tum. What that big handsome Gwyn Roberts do see in her I do not know, said more than one, but I knew. Gone? Not to us. She walks this house. Now my father said:

"Is that a fact? Then tell these *copar ledis* to stick to chipping copper, or I'll be down to have their tongues out for measuring. It's the good girls who get caught for babies, Tal."

"Old Poll's always at it, mind," I said.

"At what?"

"Don't know, but Andy Appledore do say so."

"One more mention of him and you are straight to bed."

I did not fear him. He rarely laid a hand on me: to strike a child is to assault the child, he used to say, except when blowing up deacons.

"Anyway, we can manage on our own," I said.

My father gave me a queer old look, and a sigh. "We cannot manage on our own, Meg needs her – her milk, I told you."

"We can get milk off Dulcie Brown Cow."

"We cannot. Your sister is not a bull calf. Now, do you think we could have an end to this?"

The kettle was grieving on the hob. My mam used to swing it off with a smile. I wanted to run upstairs and cry on the bed. Ever since Poll had come he had taken less notice of me. Now he said, his hand in my hair:

"Be generous, Tal – she had nobody in the world but us."

Serve her bloody right.

Mind you, there were some happy compensations in having a harlot in the place, and a happy little soul was old Poll, give her credit; coming in, crying, "Morning, Uncle Gwyn, how you doin', Cousin Tal? (she couldn't even speak English, never mind Welsh) Make a good breakfast, both of you, and a bottle for my darling Cousin Meg – steak and kidney one side, rice pudding the other . . . There, there . . ." and she opens the front of her bodice, whispering as mothers do, "Hush you, hush . . . old Poll's got plenty," and our Meg crowed delighted in her tears and clamped herself on like a navvy on to a pint.

My father said, his voice low, "A good boy you are, Tal,

not staring. Ladies are entitled to privacy and respect when feeding babies."

So everybody was happy at such times, including me, for I could see old Poll at it in the cracked mirror of the kitchen. And a good old set she had on her, too, smooth and white, the colour of lotus flowers. Beautiful are women, I think, possessing such lovely things.

"She is taking it, Polly?" my father asked his pipe.

"Yes, Uncle Gwyn."

"She is a lusty baby. You have no pain?"

"No, Uncle Gwyn."

Mind, this was the daughter my father always wanted, for once I heard him talking about this to my mam. "A son for you and a daughter for me, eh, Peg? A little poke-bonnet in the house, woman, and I'll be doubly blessed . . ."

Now he said, "If pain comes, Poll, you'll tell me, yeh?"

"Doin' fine, Uncle Gwyn, really, Uncle Gwyn."

Dear me, Uncle Gwyn.

I still say we could have got it off Dulcie Brown Cow.

About this time I received a lesson in the sweet mystery of life, as Dada called it: trust my mate Andy Appledore not to be behind the curtain, either, when Cousin Poll was handing out religious instruction, though the way she was acting now butter wouldn't have melted in her mouth. And my father would have had fits with his legs up if he'd seen the way she behaved in our barn on Saturday Fair Night, the week after Easter.

Mind you, it's on summer nights mostly when grown-ups start getting frisky, I find, when the moon sits smiling on the sea and warm winds come fanning in from Snowdon. The animals are at it, too, I've noticed, with Bill, my ferret, knocking hell out of Milly, and Ben Rooster, our cockerel, rousting up his women, to say nothing of the lads in Town.

About the hottest male in Amlwch that year was my mate Appledore. Rising sixteen was he, with ambitions to do his utmost for Welsh womanhood, said the *copar ledis*, who spent most of the day fighting him off, and these days he was breathing down the neck of my Cousin Poll.

"Your night in, Tal, Poll's night out – and don't forget to shut up the hens, there's foxes about," said my father, on his way out for his Oddfellows pint.

"And don't have any women in, mind," added Poll. Done up in her Fair Night braveries was she, all pink and flouncy, and she fluttered an eye at me.

"And where might you be off to, Madam?" asked Dada.

"Band of Hope."

"A good girl you are," said he, kissing her. "Here's a penny for the South African missionaries. Back at half-past nine, remember."

"In bed by nine, Uncle Gwyn, if that suits you better."

"And keep away from that Andy Appledore."

It appalled her. "O, shame and damnation on you, Uncle Gwyn, for such a suggestion!" and she wriggled and went coy, melting him.

O aye? I thought. If that penny lands in the Fund for Missionaries I'd be mistaken; more likely a couple of gin tots for her and Andy Appledore, for I knew they were on the booze, and turn our barn near Three Costog into an abode of love.

No wonder our hens were off the lay; such things can have a bad effect on chickens.

When I went out that night to lock up the henhouse I found our Ben Rooster and his wife Betsy absent. So I went into the barn to look for them. And in there came Cousin Poll hand in hand with Andy Appledore, and what happened then took the shine off cassocks. I just lay there in the shadows, sweating cobs, my hair standing on end and breaking my neck for a closer look. Faint, I crept out of that barn and came face to face with Dada.

"Well I never!" said he. "I thought you were abed. I was just coming to find Ben Rooster and lock up the henhouse."

"Just done that, Dada," I lied.

"And Cousin Poll? Where's she?"

"Came home half an hour back."

He would have asked more, I think, but did not; behind the barn door old Poll giggled in the dark, but I don't think Dada heard. Instead, he did a strange thing: reaching out, he held me against him, saying:

"A good little lad you are, Tal. Home then, the two of us?"

It is funny, I think, that grown-ups don't catch on so quick.

Everybody in Town knew what old Poll was up to, but I suppose that's difficult to understand when you're hoping she's your daughter.

"Come," said Dada, and took my hand; together we climbed the little hill back to Three Costog. So everybody was happy, including old Poll: two hours later she came through my bedroom window like a witch on a broomstick.

That night a fox knocked off poor old Ben Rooster, who was supposed to be locked up in the henhouse, yet my father never even mentioned it.

Strange, really, come to think of it.

Two years later, when our Meg was two, I was still working with the *copar ledis* on the tables along Turkey Shore.

There is a size for you are some of these copper ladies! – and enough gas in them to light the flares come market. Six to a table we were, women and girls one side, kids like me opposite, and it was *chink chink chink*, the little hammers rising and falling; twelve hours a day, six days a week – chipping the rock away from the copper vein before it went into the Smelter.

The miners dug out the 'bargains' up on Parys Mountain, the carters brought it down to the harbour and tipped it close to us. And then we were at it, chinking, chinking, chinking, and you've never heard such a gabbling since they raised the Tower of Babel: girls and women in their home-spun tunics and red scarves, with spotted yellow handkerchiefs on their heads – chattering like magpies, leg-pulling and shrieking laughter.

But that was in summer, with the sea calm and blue and the gulls soaring in the harbour wind above us.

Come winter it was different.

Then the wind would tear in from the sea and bite us to the bone, and the copper ladies under the tent roof were tied up like bales of rags for warmth, with their blue noses sticking out of their mufflers and their fingers like claws of ice. But still the copper ore would pour down from Parys Mountain and still the hammers would chink away in the dark, with children as young as six years old dancing to broken fingers. Then snow would come and frost the land and our breath would smoke in the tent, and the moment the overman's back was turned we would dash in twos and threes for the warmth of the Smelter where my father worked.

Pretty quiet were our *copar ledis* in winter, but they were sitting newspapers when a new spring came sweeping over the earth.

Wonderful it is to get a whiff of the scandal when you are twelve years old: as to how Dora Jewels, the Jew girl, has had the Sailor's Farewell off Mr. Ifor Bach, the skipper of the *Mona Queen*, and if Ida Promise, the ugliest woman in Amlwch, isn't inching up Shoni Bob-Ochr, the Welsh Dutchman, they were very much mistaken: but musical, too, as well – singing Welsh folk-songs in full harmony – beating time with their hammers. And the sound of their voices would drift over the sea in a sulphretting musical scarf; the sailors coming into Amlwch harbour cocking an ear above the thunder of the rigging.

The following year, when I was thirteen, two things happened to change my life. I got promotion and was sent up to the Precipitation pits; also, I fell in love.

In love with Miss Prudence Ichabod, aged sixteen, and to hell with copper ladies.

Dark and slim was Pru Ichabod, with eyes as big as saucers, dark-lashed and flecked with green, and her cheeks were high in her small-boned face; white were her teeth in the curved, red smile of her lips. And she walked with a pretty swing to her hips that drove me damned demented.

Aye! The moment I set eyes on this Pru Ichabod in the Welsh Wesleyan she drove me spare; three months she sat on my bolster back home in Three Costog and it took me a year to get her off. We used to sit behind her in Chapel, and the perfume of her fluttered me down to my socks. See her now, coming out of Chapel with the sun on her face; summer, full and splendid, was into us.

"Well, well! Good morning, Tal Roberts. Fancy seeing you!"

Dear me, she smelled even sweeter outside in the sun.

Most women, I find, smell as sweet as nutcake, even old

Dahlia Sapphira with lavender water under the arms, but none smelled like Pru Ichabod that Sunday morning after Chapel.

"Ay ay," said I, moochy, for off comes my father's cap and he bows deep, sweeping up the pavement:

"Good morning, Miss Ichabod! A fine June day it is going to be, I'm bound."

Why can't I talk like that?

"Lovely indeed, Mr. Roberts," says she, silky.

"Did you enjoy the sermon? Mr. Owen at his best today?"

"Aye, Mr. Roberts – a marvellous tonality, mind."

"But sincerity, too, Miss Ichabod – sincerity is the essence," and he elbowed me to keep me upright.

The congregation, glum, pressed about us in smells of moth balls and whiffs of polished mahogany, God now being on his way to St. Eleath, Church of England.

"And how is little Meg, and Poll?" Pru dimpled a smile at me. "Taliesin in long trews, too – working the Precipitation, is it?"

God help her if she hadn't noticed. I stood on tiptoe with my hair quiffed up and the crutch of my new trews cutting my throat.

"Two men in the family now," said my father, and he touched my head. "But old before his time, this one." Which was the standard joke about my pure white hair, and I hated him.

"Grown inches since I see you last, Taliesin," said Pru.

Two months she had been ill with the chest, poor soul – two months of agony for me: wandering around Brickpool hoping for a sight of her, stealing up to her window in Sixteen Methusalem. And every time Dr. Griffiths Thomas Davies of Bryn-y-fryd came out I examined him for news. His smile would send me off with daylight under my boots; his frown of worry painted pictures of crow-clad funeral directors in serge and dubbined boots: love in its purest form I held for Pru Ichabod.

"Are you managing better these days, Mr. Roberts?"

My father replied, "Perfectly now, Miss Ichabod."

"If Poll wears badly, do not be afraid to ask, mind, for I

am better now."

"You would be the first I would come to for help, Ma'am." Down she goes again and her dress spreads wide in her curtsey: up with her then and a fluttering wink at me; it is good to know when you've made an impression on a female.

"Come, Tal," whispers my father, replacing his cap. "Quick!"

For Mr. Dafyyd Owen, the head deacon, is approaching with the Book under his arm, and he is afflicted with bodily odour, poor man, says my father. Away with the pair of us up Smelter Hill to Three Costog, our cottage.

Those were the early weeks I spent working at the Precipitation pits, and received seven shillings a week, the wages of a man.

Marvellous are the works of humans to take red water from a mountain and turn it into copper.

See them digging the new shaft on Parys – red-core Parys that is riddled with copper – working as did the Romans. Down, down goes the shaft into the bowels of the mountain: fill the shaft with water and leave it for nine months: then pump it out into Precipitation.

In come the ships carrying scrap iron for the stew.

Aye, this is the stew of copper – old bedsteads, old engines, wheels and nails – scrap of all description from the iron industry of the North comes surging into Amlwch on the ships. The carters unload it and carry it to the pits: and in it goes, iron scrap into the sulphate stew, the blood of Parys. And we, the stirrers, worked the brew with wooden poles – wooden ones, since metal ones would melt in the acid – even copper nails in our boots. Stir, stir, stir – nine months it took to melt the iron into a liquid. And the sludge that dropped to the bottom of the pits was copper. Break this up cold and cart it like biscuits down to the maw of the Smelter for refining.

This was the process; a job for men, not boys.

"You are growing up, Tal," said my father one Sunday morning after Chapel. "Thirteen years old, is it? You're the height and width of a man."

I did not reply, knowing that my father had something under his waistcoat that was bound to come out.

"You are aware, I suppose, that Miss Prudence Ichabod is a beautiful woman?"

"She's all right," I said, chewing at a straw.

"Also, that she is pledged to marry Mr. Dick Evans, the landlord of the Oddfellows, Market Place?"

This stopped me in my tracks. Dick Evans? God, I'll kill him.

"A bit of a surprise for you, is it?" My father glanced at me as we walked together over the short mountain grass.

"Her business," I replied, dying inside.

At this, he stopped and slipped easily to the ground; crossed his thick arms around his knees and stared at the harbour. I thought: Tonight, at high tide, I will get up in my nightshirt and walk into the sea. My father said:

"You know something peculiar – something almost unbelievable? When I was about your age I fell in love with a girl called Prudence – an English girl – as fair as Pru Ichabod is dark."

I thought: And when the tide goes out they will find my body on the sand. Already I could hear the tolling of the bells, the congregation sniffing and wiping; me boxed in cedar and brass handles.

"She was twenty-two and I was thirteen," said my father. "She married a butcher, I remember." He turned, gripping my arm. "Look, look, Tal, there is little that happens to you that has not already happened to me. And little you do that I have not already done . . . no, do not turn away, son – men face each other in difficult conversations."

His eyes, I remember, were blue in his strong, square face, and he continued:

"Women are weaker than us, Tal; true love protects. Pru Ichabod is frail. Further, she is in love with Dick Evans, the landlord of the Oddfellows. Do not make it difficult for her. The choice between the two of you is hard enough as it is . . ."

Oh God, let me die . . .

"You are fast growing up, Tal. All in Town speak of

it – Taliesin Roberts, who is a man at thirteen years. But when your body moves in manhood, do not always trust it, for bodies can betray."

A strange time to talk of such things, I thought, and on a Sunday.

Hot to set alight I sat there, my eyes lowered before his steady gaze. He added, "Let Pru Ichabod be, Tal. To pursue her at this time would be to put her into an impossible situation. Be generous."

We sat together in silence. The wind whispered and I smelled the salt tang of the sea.

My father said:

"Home now, is it, and see what Cousin Poll has for dinner?"

3

Saint Peter was in a perky old mood when he fashioned my Cousin Polly. My father said he was getting his own back on the Roman hordes who used to play hell with the Welsh. She is one of the beautiful Goidels who kept the centurions tossing and turning around 50 B.C., said he.

I don't know about Romans, but she started to have a terrible effect on me, especially after Pru Ichabod betrayed me with Dick Evans of the Oddfellows. And when my father was on night-shift at the Smelter, I got it worst of all.

It is the good girls who get into trouble, Tal, mark me, said Dada.

Generosity, like wisdom, can be the biggest fool of all.

"You all right, Cousin Tal?" asked Poll.

The night was black with him, the wind doing doh-ray-me in the chimney and only me and Poll in the kitchen. I was shivering to have my teeth out. It was the week of my fourteenth birthday, and the way Poll was behaving it looked like being my last.

I'd just got in from the Precipitation and walked the three miles down from Parys. My trews were soaked with sulphate water and I was anxious to get them off.

Being a stirrer (Shallow Enders, we were called) we used to wear a rum barrel on each leg above the clogs, to save us from the splashes – but now I could feel the copper water heating up my shins.

It was only when I found the tin bath steaming hot by the fire that I remembered about Dada being on night-shift, and by the look on Poll's face I had only ten minutes to live.

The sight of that tin bath do bring back memories!

Time was, when I was a nip, Dada and me used to bathe by the copper out the back. Marvellous, it is, to share a bath with your father. In with him first, rubbing for bubbles, and I can see him now – shoulders on him like Barney's bull: down goes his head; come up blowing like a whale: up on his feet now, eight feet tall, rubbing for a glow with the towel, his fists thudding against the packed muscles of his stomach. "Here we go, *cariad*!" he shouts to my mam, and reaches out and hooks me in, aged six.

"Right you, Tal!"

But it was different now I was growing up.

Give Poll credit, mind, she didn't come in while I was bathing by the fire. I left my trews to soak and put on others she'd laid out ready.

"A pretty boy you are, though," said she, coming downstairs from Meg, and taking the lobscouse off the hob.

"Aye, woman, let's have it," said I, and waited, staring at the starched white cloth while she ladled from the saucepan. Mutton stew she smells of, and a pink petticoat sweetness. And I sat there with my knees knocking.

"How old are you, Tal Roberts?"

"Fourteen, Missus."

"Gawd! Ye'll be eight feet up by the time you're twenty." And she put the saucepan back on the hob and came back and stroked my hair. "And such lovely hair you do have, too. But fourteen's too young for a decent dinner, or I'd eat you with spuds and cow cabbage."

I got into the stew, packing the bread in after it and wishing her to the devil.

"Never mind, small acorns do grow into very large oaks," said she. "You marry me, Cousin Tal, when you grow up?"

"I'm not particular, Cousin Poll."

"Meanwhile, while I'm waiting, I'll take a snip o' that lovely white hair for me locket," and she made big eyes and pulled it up the front of her.

"Ach, lay off!"

Snip, snip went the scissors.

Judges 16, verse 19. Try having your hair cut while you're

eating lobscouse. Samson got himself into the same predicament.

But real trouble started coming in the spring I was fifteen.

I suppose, thinking back, it had started long before that. My mam (before she died) owed Greathead's Truck Shop for a couple of pounds of candles, they reckoned. And five years she had been gone before the debt was discovered. So they put it on my father's debit when he came for his six weeks' pay.

"Two pounds of what?" he asked.

"Two pounds of candles, Mr. Roberts."

"Not for us, Tasker, we burn oil."

"Here's the entry, Mr. Roberts. In your wife's name."

"And the woman dead these past five years? Talk sense!"

"Don't know about that, Mr. Roberts."

"I do," said my father, "give it here," and the clerk of Greathead's Shop gave Dada the account and he tore it into pieces.

"Debt paid," said he.

But you don't so easily get rid of a debt to Greathead's.

Every six weeks' pay night it was the same now – the Robertses still owe for two pounds of candles.

"I'll tell you what I will do," said my father. "I'll buy another two dozen candles and push them up the agent."

Now, you do not talk like that about the agent of the Marquis.

"They'll have you for it, Mr. Roberts," said Mr. Dafydd Owen.

"I am not paying a debt my wife did not incur," said my father.

I ran fast that spring morning to feed Joe Herring, my friend the black-faced gull, then dropped to my knees and scrambled to the cliff edge: and I saw, a hundred feet below me, the mighty swirl of the sea. There, standing on one leg awaiting me, was Joe, his beady eyes winking in the sun. Clearly, I heard a voice, my mother's voice, calling me above the wave-crash in the plaintive wailing of the gulls:

27

"Taliesin!"

Aye! As clear as day I heard her voice whenever I climbed down the cliff to feed old Joe; but knew that it was the daft old wind playing his flutes in the thickets above, and the crying of the oyster-catchers from the sea. Down, down, down I went, toes and fingers scrabbling for a hold, down the hundred feet to the beach, and dropped the last two yards.

"Night-shift," I said to the bird. "You hungry?"

I had been feeding him since my mam died. Once, wandering, loosened with tears, I had seen him flapping in the bay below me hooked like a fish on the breast of the sea. And I had stripped off my clothes and dived in naked, swum to him, cut the line, and dragged him ashore, breaking his wing.

I had taken him home to my father, who fashioned a feather quill and prised out the hook in his throat; then we fed him on sprats and oil.

His broken wing he reckoned was my fault, and he'd had me on toast ever since.

So every third evening, winter, summer, wet or fine, I would come down to the beach after shift and fetch him out a mackerel. He was awaiting it now, and I pulled in the line with a flounder wriggling on the end of it, and Joe had him down without showing which way he went.

"Greedy old bugger!"

He just watched me, his breast feathers ruffling in the wind.

Another, another. God knows where he put them.

It was on this particular evening that I saw my father coming along the sand towards me.

Very strange, this, since he was supposed to be at work.

Stranger still was the heliograph signal flashing out at sea.

True, as a lead-refiner under the Smelter boss, Mr. Edward Rees, my father came and went almost as he pleased. Even as I stared at his approach I heard the whine of the Smelter and saw its yellow smoke gathering above the harbour. The heliograph message stopped winking, obliterated. Then the prow of a cutter made shape, and a shark's-fin sail cut the smoke. The cutter appeared, shaking herself like a terrier and I saw her mains'l bellying in the slanting wind. Now, in a confusion of jumbled water she came inshore, her prow spraying water . . . making directly to the beach where my father was standing.

Looking back, my father was sailing pretty close to the wind in more ways than one about then. He made no bones about who he spoke his mind to. And I'll always remember the night we collected our six weeks' pay.

The copper agents always paid out in the ale-houses, a different house for every trade: the tutworkers who worked the bargains got theirs in the Old Glastonbury; the halvaners who dug the waste were paid at the Blue Bell in Amlwch Port (fourteen ale houses within three hundred yards down by there). Dressers received theirs at the Farmer's Arms, Smiths at the Two Frigates and Carpenters at the Windmill, School Lane.

Dada and I pocketed ours at the Oddfellows where old Dick Evans, now the husband of my dearly beloved Pru Ichabod, held court.

A queer old lad was this Dick Evans, with a body like a lath and the face of a thrashed dog, and God knows what my Pru saw in him; but he be privately endowed, see, said Bill Bopper, the tasker of Greathead's Truck Shop; as plump as a market pig was this Bill Bopper, with an expression to match.

This came out as my father and I were going into the public.

"What does he mean?" I asked.

Dada glanced at the debt collector and thumped the bar for ale. "Pass such eloquence unheeding, my son. It is an intellectual leap for some to lift a pint," and he smiled at Pru, who came up to the bar. "A quart for me, Ma'am, a half for Taliesin."

I could have wept.

Where had gone the bloom that I had loved?

Two years now Dick Evans had been at her, the bed and the tub: twins first, now she was carrying again. But she smiled at me and I saw in that smile the woman she might have been. My father glanced at the pair of us, then lifted his pewter and blew off the froth: like most good Welshmen, he liked his ale. "Drink deep, Tal, but never drink drunk," he used to say. "Hops, like love-making, is a pastoral activity of the Celtic mind."

"You all right, Pru?" I whispered amid the thunder of shouts and chinking glasses.

"Doing fine, Tal!" and she mopped up the bar.

"Come on, come on, woman!" shouted her husband, and I stiffened.

"Easy, lad," said my father.

Oh God, I thought, one day I will flatten Dick Evans and take you from here. And, as if reading me, he raised his bloodhound eyes to mine.

"Very obedient, isn't she, mun!"

After a couple of pints I forgot about Pru Ichabod.

Dandy it is to be drinking ale with your father. Don't swallow – just open the gullet and pour it down. Everybody in the public was at it; parting their whiskers and tipping up quarts; quarrelling, soothing, paying debts with promises, grumbling about wives. And in every voice lay the eternal threat – to empty Amlwch of Cornishmen. Always it is the same – a couple of glasses and they're marching on Plas Newydd, my father used to say – then back home to the grouses of their half-starved wives.

Men drowned themselves in the fumes of ale that pay night: the drained sulphretted faces of the smelters I saw, their lips cracked by the poison that ate their lungs.

Copper beat everything flat with its production: laying waste the country, killing animals and humans. Rees the cripple was there, I noticed, a man spawned on the farms, but now a tributor who had dug out his heart on unfair 'bargains'. Gory Blood, too – he who mined the shafts up on Mona; his mate, Alfie Cromwell, was beside him, a man of warts and a vacuous sense of humour; also Old Cog Costog, the tiny husband of Betsy, who lived next door to us up above Brickhill. She used to hit Hell out of him when he came home plaiting his legs; a rancid disposition had Betsy; no kind of wife for a scholar like Old Cog, who worked the engines up on Mona.

"Wales, O Wales," he would cry after a whiff of the hops, "'Thou who hast the fatal gift of beauty . . .'"

"Get the poet right," my father used to say. "'*Italia! Italia!*' it is, and he was down the Po Valley, not up bloody Snowdon."

"Is this an inference that I do not know my Byron?"

"It is. Next we'll be having Shakespeare for Plato."

"Died in the Greek war of independence, I heard," said Old Cog.

"Dear God!" groaned my father.

Very happy I was to have this straightened out, having assumed that he got an arrow in the eye at Agincourt.

"Who?"

"Plato."

"Another quart, and quick," said Dada.

"I hear that you and your father are going into the carting business, young man," said Old Cog.

A travelling newspaper, this one, and your business was all around Town.

"Are we?" I asked.

"Aye, and if I had a son six feet up, I'd loosen me engines and start carting – money there, mind."

The pay was chinking now, and the babble was like a Muldoon picnic. I saw Pru watching me from the bar as Bill Bopper, the tasker, pushed his way to the front.

"Is it true ye have shop debts, lad?" Old Cog jerked his thumb at my father who, eyes closed, appeared lost in a dream.

"Our business," I said.

"Your father has a bone of contention in this respect, I understand . . . ?" His pink eyes, those of a rat, inspected me.

"Has he?" I'd always been doubtful about bones of contention, and Cog said:

"And, what is more, I understand he is airing his grievance tonight."

"Is that a fact?"

"It is, and I take issue with it. If the debt has been incurred the family pays."

"If my mother incurred it."

"And, in taking on Tasker Bopper by refusing to pay, he is also taking on the Marquis of Anglesey."

"That doesn't bother my father much," I said.

He regarded me, head on one side. "We don't get a lot out of you, do we, Taliesin?"

"Not a lot, Mr. Costog."

"Pray silence!" roared Bill Bopper, then. "In the name of the Marquis," though God knows what he had to do with it. Yet, as always, it silenced them. There was no sound now but breathing and the chinking of paymasters' money.

"Joe Oldfield!" bawled Bopper, and poor old Workhouse Joe came up, his clothes burned to holes by copper water.

A Bradford man, he had a missus and five kids in the House of Industry down Narbeth, the first workhouse in the country, and he had tramped North into copper to bail them out. Bopper slapped down money.

"*Jesus!*" whispered Joe, staring at it. "Is that all?"

"How is that made up?" called my father.

"Oldfield's business, man – stick to yours!"

"How?" Dada came to the bar, and the tasker said, sighing:

"Forty-two-day period at six shillings a week less shovel hire time and candles; less fourpence for the doctor and ten shillings shop debt – draws twenty-four shillings."

"Proof of shop debt?"

"Sure, Holy God, would ye audit the account personally, Gwyn Roberts?"

Bad Irish, this one. The only thing we had against the Irish in Amlwch was their stomachs, it was the Cornish we wanted out, but Tasker Bopper was the dregs.

"Leave it, Mr. Roberts," whispered Joe Oldfield, in the silence. "I need the loot."

"Any more palaver and he'll be out on his arse," said Bopper. "Next!"

"Have a sight of it each week, Mr. Oldfield," said Dada, "before you sign your six weeks' cross."

The names were called. One by one the men went up for their pay, and this day, for some reason or other, we were mixed in the trades, with deductions for the Truck Shops, fuses, candles, gunpowder, hire of tools, and often rent. And the tutworkers and tributors on the 'bargains' got it worst that pay night, I recall.

These were the men who worked in teams of four, who got a face of copper and rock on an auctioning system called 'bargains'.

In St. Eleath's square these 'bargains' were struck, and the team-leaders bid against each other to the agent, who would strike with a pebble the leader who won. And so, with their income tuned to the rate of copper per ton of rock shifted, their stomachs were dependent on the luck of the 'bargain'. The standard was five per cent copper; if less than that, their pay was lowered; if more, it was raised. I have known tributors work for a week on an auctioned 'bargain' and draw no wages at all, so God was very popular with the teams – every dig up on Parys Mountain being dependent upon the Deity. Keep Him sweet, was the cry, or the agent will drop the rate. Down on their knees morning, noon and night, these 'bargain' workers, in the name of Jesus.

And the Cornish agents of the Marquis – men like Jimmy Liar and Billy Spy – also made a profit out of us on the mine stores – a practice they had brought from the Cornish mines. They'd buy candles and powder in bulk when times were bad and sell them to us when times were good.

A deputation to the Marquis? somebody suggested. The place is in rags, folks are starving – a deputation, for *God's* sake – go over the heads of these pilfering agents.

Blame the Marquis, said my father, also the rotten Welsh gentry; not only those who rule us now, remember, but those who sold Glyndŵr to an English king. If I had my way, said he, I would hang these parasites from a Parys whimsey – death by ritual strangulation.

I had gathered the impression that my father didn't think much of the Marquis of Anglesey.

"Gwyn Roberts!" bellowed Bill Bopper, the tasker.

My father stood before him, and I groaned, sensing trouble.

"Last pay day, eh, Mr. Roberts?" called a man.

"Aye," replied Dada. "This time next week we'll be carting."

"Thirty-one-day week," said Bopper. "Four shillings a day, agreed?"

"Agreed."

"And no stoppages?"

"Correct."

"But a little matter of eightpence for two pounds of candles."

"Oh yes, I forgot – can I see the bill?"

Bopper showed it and my father took it and tore it into pieces. "Debt discharged," said he, again.

"You know what this means, don't you, Gwyn Roberts?" asked one of the paymasters, handing over his pay.

"I do. The Marquis will be eightpence short."

"You'll regret it."

"No, he will. The loss is his. Come, Tal," and he put his arm around my shoulders.

The stars were big; donkeys and horses stood statuesque in the moonlight of Pritchard's fields, and I remembered their begging eyes when under the whip.

I said, "There's going to be trouble, isn't there?"

"Of course," came the reply. "Eightpence to the Marquis is the difference between life and death: he was born with the ethics of a vulture."

We walked on. The copper-dusted trees were night hags brooding on the starved earth: two skeletons who called themselves mules were grazing on the garlic-tasting grass.

"The men thought you ought to pay. I could see it in their faces."

Said he, "The men there tonight sickened me – eternal gratitude possesses no pride."

We took the old path that went over the bridge by the Old Brewery. The night glittered with cold air and light. And, at that moment, a man stepped out of the shadows. It was Skipper Rowlands, the captain of the *Amlwch Queen*.

This was a man I had often seen with my father. Big and heavily-booted was he, wearing a blue jersey and yellow neck scarf. Talk had it that he was bad company; up to his neck in running rum and guns to Ireland.

"A word, if you please, Gwyn Roberts?"

I left them together, glancing back as I reached the cottage gate: they were no longer there. It was as if they had disappeared into the night.

Poll was asleep by the grate with Meg in her arms. I went back outside. A light was dancing on the waves inshore.

4

That summer my father retired from the Smelting and I gave up the dirty old Precipitation pits. We went into carting.

This was before the coming of the railway, and carters were in demand. With Parys Mountain three miles distant from the harbour, everything dug up there – ore, ochre and brimstone – had to be horse-pulled down to the harbour. Smelter coal had to come from even more distant places.

Carters contracting under Mr. Hughes were paid by him at a shilling a ton; we hired the cart, but were expected to buy our own horse, and for this my father had been saving.

So now there was five of us in Three Costog Cottages – my father, Cousin Poll, Meg my baby sister, me, and Dobie.

Lovely was this Welsh cob, Dobie, bought at Llangefni Fair. Great in strength, standing fifteen hands with big brown muscles down his back and thews; his hooves were as large as dinner plates, all ragged with white hair; his mouth was as soft as the inside of a thigh.

He was a grandad and often bad-tempered; his teeth said he was nearly as old as me, but lithe and gay was he that summer day we walked him back from Llangefni, with the hired cart grinding along behind. Done up in our Sunday braveries, my father and I were up front with the reins; Poll, with Meg on her knee, sat on sacks behind.

And, as we came down Llaneilian Road, the doors came open and curtains went back. But my father looked neither right nor left as we came through the sulphur-ridden country of Brickpool: the evening sun was setting, the sea lay before us like a corpse stained with blood.

*

My little sister Meg was growing up.

Aged five now, her wrist bangles were disappearing with her bubbles and coos: nobody could have brought her up as fresh and clean as did our Poll. And now Poll said when we'd done our first shift at carting:

"Old man Greathead's agent came today, Uncle Gwyn."

My father was kicking off boots. "O, aye?"

"About the debt."

"What debt?"

"The eightpence for the two pounds of candles."

His expression did not change. "What did you tell this agent?"

"To get about his business, like you said; that the last thing he'd get off us was two pounds of candles."

"Well done, Poll; a good girl you are," which was a change; lately he had been cool with her.

That first day had been hot on the brimstone, with all the sounds of summer as we came down from Parys. It was a tough old business, this carting.

The loading was done mainly by immigrant labour; a ragged army of men, women and children swarming like red ants. But since we were expected to lend a pound it was shovel, shovel, shovel into the bowels of the mountain, with buckets from overhanging whimsies swaying high, tipping into the waiting carts. And the air was filled with the bawled commands of overmen and tutworkers, the neighing of horses, grinding wheels, and the ragged labour yelling wild Irish oaths.

We ate in a deathly silence that night, with a threat of an eightpenny debt in everybody's heart.

"What did the agent say to that?" I asked, blowing at my tea.

Poll took a breath. "That the Robertses wanted to watch out, so they did; that there was more than one way to skin Welsh rabbits."

We ate in a silence of tinkling knives and forks: currant cake for afters; no wife in Amlwch could turn out currant cake like Poll.

After supper I went out the back to the tub for a real wash; pulling off my shirt it ripped at the seams.

Nothing could be kept decent, working in copper: skin chafes, blisters, sore eyes, burned clothes. Most of the working population of Amlwch was in rags – the clothes they wore, once they'd been in copper, were never worn decent again. So, the streets of our town were filled with tattered, broken-booted folks, a rag-tag, bob-tailed army of gaunt neighbours full of burns and chafes; half naked in summer and muffled up in holes come winter.

These were largely the immigrants from the Irish and Black Country hungers. Flooding into Anglesey at a time when we could scarcely feed our own (copper was dying on world markets) they ate their way like locusts across the turnip and potato fields, at the mercy of the Guardians of the Poor.

I looked up at the sky that night.

Moonlight, they say, is the sunshine of the dead.

"How much did the agent ask for, Poll?" I came in and sat at the table again. My father was smoking his pipe in a holy quiet; there was no sound but the singing of the kettle.

"Eightpence, of course."

"Best pay it." I put eightpence on the table, but Dada reached out and swept it on to the floor, saying:

"Listen to me, Tal, I will not pay it. It is not your mother's debt or I would have known of it. She and I starved together; we knew the date of every coin in the house, we wrapped up every crust of bread. I will not pay it, neither will you, or you are not your father's son," which was a bit of a speech for him, and I didn't forget it. I replied:

"But the debt is written. If necessary they will whip it out of us at the Quarter Sessions."

He got up noisily. "They're welcome to try."

God Almighty, I said to myself, and went down to the barn for a look at Dobie, for he was sweating badly: after a while I returned. My father was still smoking in his chair by the fire, his herb tobacco a perfume in the air. Poll was clumping around the kitchen, Dada was white-faced, and I knew they'd been having words in my absence.

It is sad, I think, when loved ones fall out of love. Time was, when Poll first came to us, she was his darling, a goofey for sitting on his knee. But lately she had grown into a woman and perhaps he had lost the daughter he had longed for. With Andy Appledore still in the offing, perhaps Dada was wondering what else she might bring home.

Summer was into us, warm and green; another June Fair came up, with Poll all frills and fancies, being her night off.

"And where might you be off to?" asked Dada.

"Band of Hope," said Poll, sarcastically.

"Very funny. But you'll be back and abed by ten o'clock, girl, or you'll have me to account to."

"To Hell! D'ye think I'm a child? I'm turned eighteen!"

"Act like a child and I'll treat you like one. And keep away from that Andy Appledore!"

They had forgotten, I think, that I was there; getting up from the table I mooched out to the back, and heard Poll reply:

"Christ! There's some dirty old minds round by 'ere I'm thinking . . ."

"Yes, and more than one," shouted my father. "So bring home another and you can find somewhere else to live."

"Perhaps I'll do that anyway," said Poll.

I think I knew then that the rift between them was too wide to be healed, and that no good would come of it.

5

About the time I was rising sixteen I was coming a little warm with me about women, with queer things happening around the lumbar regions. And it was clear that this new comrade possessed something more than an academic interest in girls. So, most hours off, I used to limp with him into the Cemaes woods in the hope of showing him off, since a few stockinged legs had started wandering, with garters of bright ribbons. These, it appeared, possessed for him the same common interest, and it is only right and fair, Andy Appledore used to say, that you should share your manhood with the world.

Here, above the sea, the beech trees stood firm and strong to the wind, a heritage of greenness contrasting Amlwch and its stinks of sulphur garlic.

Nature luxuriated here. Lying beneath a bush with a halfpenny bag of Slip-down ju-jubes I used to contemplate the world, and if Siân Fi-Fi, aged fifteen, happened by I contemplated her in tempestuous breathing. She was the cushiest little fourpenny this side of the market, the lads said: her thighs were of silk, her breasts tipped with honey, and she'd come pretty pliable for a penn'orth of ju-jubes. And I can see her now through the mist of years, lying there in the refuse of the autumns, her face patterned with sunlight. She said, Irish:

"You'm a terrible fella, you, Tal Roberts," for she was as murphy as a spud, though named with the Welsh.

"Hold your hat on, Siân Fi-Fi," said I, "I'm only just started."

"Put me in the family way as sure as Fate, you will."

This appeared to be the general hope, for she was a great talker on the *copar* table where she was employed. And I soon got a name for a sort of Lothario, with sheaves of females following me in the hope of similar treatment. To this day I do not know why I never fathered six out of Siân Fi-Fi (and why she was called this nobody seemed to know) for she married Joey Belcher, the cobbler, at the age of eighteen and in seven months had premature twins.

Sometimes, when the weather was cooler, we used to gather *gwymon*, which the English call flat wrack, from the rocks – a sort of seaweed – and take it up to poor old Erfyl, aged ninety, her great-grandad, for rubbing into his rheumatics. Rub rub rub – hours we were at it, with Siân on his left shoulder and me on his rear, for it do not seem decent for ladies to see the genitals, he used to croak, turning over. He needn't have bothered for Siân had seen most. And, while we were rubbing he used to tell us tales of his youth; of how he was handed an empty sack by his dad and told not to return home till it was full of sheep wool. It took him a week to fill the sack, he said, poor old Erfyl, and he lived off the land, begging his food, sleeping like a tramp, aged five. "And that, I reckon," he used to say, "is why I got the screws today." But he still lived to a hundred and two, which is more than you will, said Andy Appledore, if you keep giving ju-jubes to Siân Fi-Fi.

But there was more to her than garters.

My memories of her are hand-in-hand roamings; chewing, with her, the *delysg*, a weed we found on the shore; eating the leaves of the hawthorne in spring, gasping to the bitter tang of sorrel. Bumbledores we caught between thumb and forefinger, too, extracting, with barbaric joy, the sacs of golden honey.

Down to the fair we'd go. Sailors from the West Indies danced the hornpipe to whooping roundabouts and blasting German Bands; organ-grinders cranked for dancing bears and monkeys. The flares hissed, the caulking hammers rat-tatted from the shipyards on the quay. Blacksmiths struck their anvils, carpenters sawed, riggers climbed like cluster flies against the sun-shot sky.

And best of all was watching the ships coming in and the sailors flooding ashore with ships in bottles, sea shells, fabulous coral, love-spoons, the shrunken heads of cannibals, love-birds, love-fruit, beribboned guitars and mandolins.

All the wealth of the Orient came leaping into Amlwch these days; mulattos with cockatoos and parrots on their shoulders, looking for ale and women, and most Saturday nights there was a blow-up down Town, with men like Bob Butt and Dico Canaan in the thick of it with their pointed clogs and fists. And then a race along the shore to Cemaes to get the garters off old Siân; a midnight bathe, or just a solitary laze in moonlight.

Here, according to my father, had trod the early Celtic saints: here had camped the Roman legions under Suetonius and King Egbert the Saxon, eight centuries later; also the Normans under the banner of Lupus and the Earl of Chester. And I would lie on my belly on the soft, brown breast of Mona, and press my face deep into this mother and draw from her tales of her past.

Diawl! Lie on your back in the glades of Cemaes; watch the tracery of black branches cobwebbing the sky. Touch the ancient oaks, feel beneath your fingers the vibration of centuries – the chanting, the lutes, the harps! How many lovers have lain like this and seen this same Welsh sky?

Here the first bluebells, the first wild daffodil! Llaneilian and Porthwen, Dulas, Moelfre! These are the magic names of Anglesey, old when Europe was young. *Ogof Sant*, the cave of holy men; Ffynnon Bwstri, its waters a cure for blindness . . . the sparkling brook of Safn Ci tumbling down to the sea! Here the court of Caswallon Law-Hir, the northern prince my father revered: there the nest of the linnet.

Sometimes I used to sit naked above Porthwen, seeing the Skerries to the west and Ellan Vannin to the north. Sea-pink and golden gorse decorated the summers; Welsh catchfly and sea lavender, lady-trees and moonwort grew in profusion in the woods of Cemmaes.

Lie still. Do not lift a finger. Here comes old Brock Badger, poking at the earth for nuts. He knows I'm here, of course; and he bawled down his set, no doubt, informing his wife and family that here comes this white-haired Welshie from Amlwch, the boy with the old man's hair.

Not the least interested in badgers, me.

I lay on my back watching the stars doing handsprings over the branches, and spare time squinting around to see what this old wood-pig was up to; snuffle-snuffle, snort-snort.

He was old, this friend. Once his teeth were white and strong, now they were but rotting stumps in still vice-like jaws – he could sever a terrier's paw or wrench the spade from the hunter's hand. Give a cudgel to a badger, my father used to say, and you wouldn't see red stockings for dust: give a fox a gun and you wouldn't coax the cowards into donning red coats.

"You'm a greedy old badger," I said, as he licked the last of the sugar off my hand, and I got up.

It was then that I saw my father walking along the edge of the wood.

6

Now, sitting in the wood within a few yards of him, I saw my father lift a telescope and look out to sea. In the moonlight I saw a little boat with a slanting jib-sail tacking for the shore. She came fiercely, with foam on her prow; her keel scraped sand and a man jumped out – instantly I recognised him – Skipper Rowlands of the *Amlwch Queen*. Turning, he put out his hand to another man standing in the prow and helped him into the shallows while my father caught the boat's painter and dragged it to a shore anchor.

Rowlands led the third man up the beach to a sandy track. I watched, and saw my father join them: suddenly the lighthouse beam swept the sea, brightening the world. Although they were now in shadows I saw Rowlands and Dada help the man up the track and then they disappeared from my view. That he should need assistance was in itself strange, for the man they were helping was possessed of a fine athleticism.

Without knowing why, I found myself following them.

The three of them – Rowlands leading the way and my father following with his hand on the big man's shoulder – took field tracks up to Parys Mountain, they did not keep to the carting road. At a discreet distance I followed, always keeping out of sight, for Dada kept turning, almost as if he suspected they were being watched. Past the loading bays of Parys Mountain we went and down the lane to the Precipitation pits, where I once worked. Then, turning abruptly into the shelter of trees, the three of them descended into a hollow that led to the farm of old Iorri Ifan, a ramshackle building being reclaimed by Nature. At the entrance to the farmhouse gate Rowlands turned and deliberately looked about him while the stranger and my father went forward into the house. Sinking lower in the undergrowth, I watched until he, too, turned and followed his companions.

Indecisive, I sat down in the bushes: the silence of the wood, the very loneliness of the place was filling me with a portent of coming disaster.

This was not mere smuggling: none of these men had been carrying anything and the strange behaviour towards the incoming stranger intrigued and frightened me; it was almost as if they were protecting him, and would do so even at the cost of their lives. It was sheer curiosity that took me onward, stealthily towards the entrance to the derelict building, and from its kitchen I heard muffled voices. The entrance door, however, was stout, as if recently repaired: as I approached it down the path night-cobwebs blew across my face; involuntarily I shivered, not with fear but with anticipation, and rose from my crouched position. From the darkness of surrounding trees came a man. He was broad and squat and had the shambling gait of an ape: upon his head he wore a cockade hat and about his shoulders a heavy rug, and in his hand was a pistol; the hammer, clicking back, halted me before him.

"Right you, boyo – inside!"

Through the muffling scarf that half covered his face I recognised the valley sing-song of the Southern Welsh; a long way North, this one, I thought. Then his fist came out and he struck me in the back, forcing me on. Through the door I went with the pistol in my back and through another door into a dimly lighted room of covered windows.

Here some twenty men stood or lounged on the broken floor: at a little table my father and the stranger I had seen were standing; all heads turned as I stumbled in with the sentry behind me.

"For God's sake!" My father's voice broke the stunned silence. "Tal!"

"Who's this?" demanded the stranger.

He was a big man and younger than my father. His brown

hair hung in shining waves to his shoulders, over these was thrown a black travelling cloak, and this enhanced his size. He sat as he asked the question and thrust out long legs, his big hands folded on to a hickory stick, one curved at the top like a shepherd's crook; he appeared suddenly like a giant raven perched upon a bough, and his eyes, bright blue, seemed to burn into mine. My father said softly:

"It is my son."

"But uninvited."

"I apologise to you, Gideon." My father approached me, saying softly, "What the Hell's the meaning of this?"

I took off my cap and screwed it in my hands; the men moved awkwardly in soft-breathing attitudes of disassociation.

"You followed us?"

The sentry said, "Found him skulking outside, Gid Davies," and the other said curtly:

"Bring him to me, Gwyn."

My father, his eyes furious, jerked his head and I stood before the table as the man behind it raised his face to mine. His eyes, I noticed for the first time, were strangely opaque, the pupils fixed and dilated; then I recognised the whiteness of his stick. Blind. He said, and his voice was deep and tuneful:

"How old are you, Taliesin?"

"Sixteen, Sir."

"Then you are no longer a child. You followed us, did you not?"

Earlier, he had spoken in English, but now it was Welsh. "Why?"

"I . . . I was afraid."

He leaned forward, smiling up. "Of me, you mean?"

I looked at my father. "Of the smuggling."

The men chuckled behind me, some whispering. The blind man said, "Oh come! What is a little bottle of brandy between friends? Or an ounce or two of tobacco – the quality's good, is it not?" He laughed bassly, lifting a hand to an attentive audience. "Everybody's at it, are they not? Even the Bishop, they tell me, is a connoisseur when it comes to

Irish port!" He beamed around the room. "My young friend Taliesin, if you are as sensible as your father claims, you'll see small harm in a little bit of swag on the side when half the county's queueing up behind the rummy gentlemen!"

"But it is not smuggling," I said.

It silenced them: had a mouse run the floor I would have heard it. The man before me rubbed his chin, his smile dying, then said:

"You deal with this, Gwyn, he is certainly not a child."

My father came closer.

"I'll be responsible for him, Gideon." To me he added, "Take a seat at the back, Tal, and grow a few years older."

Obeying, I sat on the floor at the back of the kitchen: the men whispered among themselves, disturbed, casting glances at me over their shoulders.

Joe Oldfield was there, his skinny arms projecting through the rents in his coat; Ikey and Alby Sapphira, the Jewish twins, and Mr. Appledore, the father of Andy, also Mr. Ifor Owen, a sidesman in the Wesleyan, the brother of the Elder and Mr. Ichabod, the father of my Pru. Others were there whom I knew also, but not by name, and several more whom I had never seen before – men from as far south as Menai, some said – Southern men, too, the followers of Gideon Davies who had settled in the North for other reasons than work. Now Gideon was speaking, his deep voice quiet and purposeful, and I had to strain my ears to hear him:

"As I said," he continued, "the Southern towns are going on fire, and it is only a question of time. Plans are being laid up and down the country from Liverpool to London; the industrial towns and cities plan for war. And war it will be unless these robber barons share their wealth with us, the makers of that wealth. But they will not share despite all the threats, since they had never shared before. Can ye hear me, you at the back?"

We called assent, and he said, "For a thousand years we have lived in servitude – in earlier times in abject slavery under the English. But it is not only the English who exploit us now, it is our own, remember. The wealth of the industrial aristocracy is derived from the labour of factory children –

aye, ours and yours, you who are English here. It is on their blood that float the great estates!" He rose, his voice growing stronger, and he stared down at us with his sightless eyes. "So force will be met with force, we have begged enough. And it will be a struggle to the death with our allies, the down-trodden of the London slums and the labourers of the Forest of Dean. It is a crime, and it will stop."

The audience mumbled aggressively, staring around in dull anger, and Gideon rose to his full height.

"But would you leave it all to your Southern cousins? When the first blow is struck a million men will be under arms in the Chartist cause. Will it be said, when victory is gained, that you in the North sat on your backsides while other Welshmen fought for the Charter – so listen to its aims. Secret ballot at the polls, the right of every man to vote, equal electoral areas – for the boundaries are being rigged – no property qualifications for M.P.'s, and paid Members, too, ones we can kick out annually if they don't suit us. Listen to me!" and he leaned down, swinging his fist before them. "I repeat – will you be under the bed when the time for retribution comes, and still call yourselves Welsh? For we will sweep them down in a thunderstroke, and up here you could be part of our victory!" He was breathing heavily. Not bad for a blind man, I thought; Hell would blow up were he sighted.

"Gwyn!" he called.

"Aye, Gid." My father touched his arm.

"When is the printing press due up from Dinorwig?"

"There's always talk of it but the bloody thing never arrives."

"I will try to hasten it." He unrolled a bundle of literature. "Get these pamphlets out within a week. Pin them on the lodges, on the Works' gates, on trees – nail them to the door of Plas Newydd itself. Let them have fair warning that the North is taking to arms."

The meeting closed soon after this, the men dispersing silently into the night; I was standing at the kitchen door, waiting for Dada when the blind man called, "Taliesin!"

He was seated now and I stood before him. He said,

"Draw closer, lad, that I may touch you," and he beckoned: stretching out his hand he touched my face, then ran his fingers over my features: I shivered, for his fingers, though long and slender, were at the tips curiously deformed; the thumbscrew; the nails were missing. Now these fingers were in my hair.

"The colour?" he asked, staring up at my father.

"White."

"Albino?"

My father said, "Peg, you remember, was Iberian dark – a blackbird's wing, it was said: Taliesin, in her line, is a throw-back in the lineage."

Gideon Davies grunted. "Ah, I remember – Dafydd ap Owain!" He gripped my hand. "That is a glorious line – can you tell of him historically?" He turned his face up to mine.

I said carefully. "It . . . it was he who laid waste the province of Tegeingl before the armies of Flanders attacked us in the hills of Llangollen."

"Excellent! And the year?" Arms folded, he surveyed me blindly.

I replied, "It was the twelfth century, Sir, but I do not know the year."

He rose, pressing on my shoulder. "And now we fight again, eh? It is our Welsh curse, always to be fighting. See that you serve your father well and your country better. And die for her if needs be, eh, Gwyn?"

My father said, "Oh come, Gid, he is still a lad."

The reply was instant. "If he is sixteen he is a man. The responsibility for freedom is ours, his, and all who come after, and he is old enough to know it."

If this one had his way I'd got about another fortnight to live, by the sound of it.

Strange is God's behaviour, I think, that he makes mountains of iron, ochre, brimstone and gold; then says: "Now sort that out. Fight over it, dig it, stamp misery on the faces of the poor with it, make the rich richer . . . and put it back into the soil again."

So it was with the copper of Parys Mountain; Welsh copper for minting the head of a foreign queen; copper for sheathing ships' hulls the better to ply the slave trade; copper for tears.

But all Parys Mountain provided for us, the workers, was God's water, as Amlwch called it. In the bubbling red springs that scampered down the hills were gifts of Nature: a detergent, excellent for leg ulcers, a cure for the itch, mange in animals, a killer of worms in sheep and children; good for dropsy, internal bleeding, and the bowels. A cup of Parys Mountain water was as good as a physic from the bal doctors if your tubes went tight.

Not that the bowels were tight that winter, with my father down on the beach every weekend with Skipper Rowlands and still refusing to pay the bill for eightpence claimed by Greathead as a debt for candles.

Eightpence, eightpence, *eightpence*.

The winter went by, though, with scarcely a nudge of trouble in our house, though some were not so lucky. The *copar ledis*, now under a tent, chipped away with their hammers, their hair and eyebrows mantled with frost. Mr. Small, a tutworker, was killed in a fall on Mona Mine and four others with him; we didn't know their names, since they were only Irish. I remember seeing poor Mrs. Small, her black-stockinged legs skinny in the wind, weeping in a feast of indigo.

Andy Appledore, my English mate, got the molten copper over his arms and legs in the Smelter; learning the trade was he, and never rightly got the hang of it, and his Lancashire mam and dad used to carry him round town on a board. Yet he was as handsome as a young lion the previous summer, showing it to the girls. Mrs. Ida Promise went into the family way under Shoni Bob-Ochr, the Dutch Welshman, and Dora Jewels lost her second with a mismanagement.

Also, my little Pru Ichabod died of the chest, and was laid in the warm earth of April; put there by Seth Morgan. Wheedling, nobbly-knuckled and sparse was old Seth, his staff like a flock of carrion crows, and for God's sake get her under quick.

But it wasn't all mine falls, copper burns, politics and undertakers.

There were nights when Dada had the three of us in the kitchen with firelight on our faces while he told us, in Welsh, the four branches of the great *Mabinogi* and other tales from the Red Book of Hergest.

I can see old Poll now, shivering, enwrapped in the weirdies and ghosties, while the night winds sang soprano and hammered in the chimney.

My father's voice was deep, his thick, strong hands held out to us, the fingers curled up into claws. But it was his *eyes*. Like bright jewels they shone in the masked darkness of his cheeks. He said:

"Towards a valley rode Peredur where great pines stood, and saw, on one bank of a rushing river a flock of black sheep, and on the other bank a flock of white sheep nearby. From its roots to its highest branches, a tree was on fire, one half glowing red with tongues of flame, the other half bright green with summer leaves. And, even as Peredur watched, he heard a white sheep bleat, and a black sheep crossed the river and turned white. Then a black sheep bleated and a white sheep crossed and turned black. And Peredur, fearful because this was magic, saw an exhausted deer plunge into the river beside the burning tree, pursued by hounds. And the hounds pulled it down, tearing it, and the whiteness of the river turned to the colour of blood . . ."

"*Diawch*," whispered Poll, shivering more.

I said, "But this we have heard before, Dada. Tell us, instead, 'The Tale of Delwyn'."

"We," said he then, "are direct descendants from bards who sang from the book of Taliesin," and he touched me. "This is why you are so named."

"From Iolo Goch, the bard of Glyndŵr."

"From him, a direct line in my blood, he who told of Delwyn, the tale which I read now."

Taking a tin box he drew from it a little book in manuscript, adding:

"When I am no more, preserve this in our line, Tal, giving it to your son and your son's son, as it was handed down to me by my father, and to him by his father before that, and before that also. Cherish it. But if no son springs from you, then bury it in the soil of Wales, for it is hers, and no foreigner has claim to it." My father then opened a yellowing parchment with care, and read:

" 'Listen. When first King Maelgŵn was crowned, the gods tested him, sending across the Irish Sea waves of hated Goidels, hairy monsters sunk to the level of beasts . . .' " he stared at our intent faces. Meg stirred in sleep. Above the hissing of the kettle I heard wave-crash from Costog beach and the wailing of gulls. My father continued:

" 'Until now kept in check by the Romans, these Goidels came in swarms of coracles, to ravage the fair land of Gwynedd; but Maelgŵn sent a billow of fire over the ocean, and the sands of Deganwy were littered with charred corpses. But twelve Goidels remained alive, and King Maelgŵn, being merciful, set them free to roam at will, first cutting out their tongues so that they would not corrupt the Celtic speech.' Are you listening?"

Later, he replaced the manuscript in its tin box.

The debt is eightpence, for two pounds of candles in your wife's name. Please settle it at once, or you will hear of this further.

Once a week now this note from Greathead's Truck Shop came regular; as regular as clockwork my father tore it up.

"Would it not be best to pay it, Mr. Roberts?" suggested Mrs. Dahlia Sapphira, now teaching music spare time and putting years on herself at the very sight of him. "No point in asking for trouble, *bach* . . ."

Young Dahlia, her figure returned since her chap flew south, was suffering, her mind kicking up its heels now it was spring again: ravished by erotic dreams was she, promising her fancies to get Dada behind the sofa or under the piano by Christmas, and the very sight of her hovering around Three Costog worried me to death, never mind him.

The debt has been outstanding for over six years now, said the final Greathead note. Legal action will be taken unless it is settled at once.

"Oh, God," I said, tossing it on to the table, "Pay it and have done with it."

Dada did not reply, and I pushed away my plate, disgusted. Haricot bean soup, it was, worse than donkey's brains, though Poll did what she could.

The slump of 1838 was upon us now and things were getting skinny. Ore production from the Mona Mine up on Parys was down to seven hundred and fifty tons that year, less than half what it was five years earlier: the 'bargains' were getting poorer, and so were the workers, and Mr. Treweek, our manager, was sending his Cornishmen over the hill, never mind the Welsh; the Marquis of Anglesey, dining off silver plate down in Menai, was losing weight.

"I'll give him bloody Marquis," said my father. "Pining to death, is he, for a few pounds of candles?" Rising, he added, "Ah well, let's get on shift," and he tightened the big belt at his waist. "Coming, Tal?"

We always worked night-shift at weekends, but Dada insisted on doing the final run up to Parys and back alone, and I knew why.

But we didn't go on shift that night. Bang bang on the back, and I opened it. Jacki Scog, the pig murderer, stood there.

"What the Hell do you want?" I demanded, for I hated him.

"Dear me," said he. "Long trews, big balls, is it? It is your father I am interviewing; kindly send him."

Dada pushed me aside. "Yes?"

Jacki Scog said, "Mr. John Hughes, contractor, do send me. Kind of you to report to him at once, Mr. Roberts," and he pulled off the black cap he wore for pig-killing and screwed it in his hands.

"No notion what he wants, Mr. Scog?"

"Just come, and quick, yeh?"

John Hughes the Carter was the darling of our Cornish masters and the ripest Welsh saint in Amlwch, with twice to Chapel every Sunday and beating his wife on Saturdays. A bull of a man was he; bald as an egg and bellowing bass in the Psalms, he had a chin on him like a navvy's arse. Talk had it that his mam saw faerie marks on the butter an hour before she had him.

Five feet up, filling his doorway, he eyed us with intent to kill.

"You asked us to call," asked my father, quiet.

"O, aye!" Mr. Hughes clutched the velveteen lapels of his smoking jacket, staring up. "You enjoy carting for me, Gwyn Roberts?" He had a voice like a cinder under a door.

"Passably."

"Then pay Mr. Greathead his eightpence."

"And what has a Shop debt to do with carting, Mr. Hughes?"

"Nothing. But pay it just the same, or you're out on your arse."

"In the situation in which we find ourselves, it will be a pleasure, Mr. Hughes."

"Right. Now bugger off."

On our way down the garden path of the big house, I asked:

"Who won that round, Dada? Did we have our backsides kicked, or am I mistaken?"

There was an ash beard on the bars of the fire when I got home that night. My father had said he had another engagement, and was not yet back. An ash beard, the old ones said, betokened the coming of a stranger.

With Meg upstairs in bed, Cousin Poll looked washed and perky with a spirited coquettishness, and the Devil himself, I reckon, was down in the cellar trying on pink-lace spacers.

"You like my dress, my lovely?" asked she, her fingers pinching out its scarlet skirt, and she pirouetted around the kitchen. Weeks now, she'd been making this old thing.

"It's all right," I said.

"All right, is it? Is that all? Eh, Lover, you do send me all goofey!" She pouted red lips.

"Look at the grate," I said, changing the subject.

She obeyed, her hands creeping slowly to her face. "*Diawch!*" she whispered, "Bad strangers comin'!"

"Any time now."

The ash beard grew longer as we watched.

"Where's Uncle Gwyn?" asked Poll, fearfully.

"God knows. The whole damned world's lop-codded."

"The world's all right, it's the people living in it," said Poll.

Never having heard her speak wisdom, I sat down and stared at her in the firelight. Most beautiful she looked standing there with her black hair down her back. Of Latin blood was she that night, her eyes sparkling, her cheeks high in her small-boned face.

Until then I do not think I had recognised her beauty: she was in full bloom.

Smiling down at me, she clutched her hands, saying softly, "You think anything about me ever, Tal Roberts?"

"O, ah!"

"I don't mean cooking and washing, an' all that. I mean, like walking me out Sundays for others in Town to see, and have us over – you know – proper goofers."

"Sparkin'?"

"Well yes, really speaking."

"Never given it a thought, *cariad*."

"Dear me," said she, and held herself, "the way you say that do send me shivery. A lovely voice you do 'ave, Tal. I'm too weak now to carry a clek."

I got up. I was worried about my father and she was a pester to me.

"You're a good old girl you are, Cousin Poll," I replied, "but I am too young for women."

"You'd fill a bed though." Dark and sultry she said this, like Cleopatra when the light went out, and she was getting me into a sweat, with shivers under the armpits. She whispered, coming closer:

"Ach, Lover, looking at you I feel like last week's rhubarb. You'm a fine set-up chap, my darlin', my mopsy, my pearl. You do send me all love-sick and spooney," and she reached out and drew me into her arms. "Come to bed for two minutes and I'll show ye which end up ye are."

I thought of my father fine and upright, now perched tranquilly on a pint, while I broke the ropes of Hell by frolicking with a blood relation. I said, desperately:

"Hey up! You've got other chaps on the go, for I've seen 'em . . . there's that Tom Merv Williams and Dai Mount . . ."

"Ach, come on, Lover!" cried she, and pulled me, skidding my boots on the floor. "The other chaps don't mind as long as they don't miss it. Be a Rodney, Tal, shiver up ye shanks."

Bang went the garden gate as I was halfway through the door for the stairs. It was my father, thank God. She'd nearly had me.

Entering with happy gusto, Dada stared at us with mild surprise. "Ay ay!" said he. "The trouble with virtue is that it never knows when it's coming or going. Those who suffer, conquer – remember that." Saying this, he tossed sixpence and two coppers on to the table, adding, "Take that to Greathead's in the morning, Poll, and settle up for these," and he pulled out of his pocket a bunch of candles. "You, Tal, put them up in Nellie's room behind the clock," which meant that I was to hide them.

I said, "What have you been up to?"

"Thrice blessed am I with children who do what they're told – get rid of them, I said."

Clutching the candles, I took them upstairs and put them under Meg's bed and stood there in the moonlight, watching her sleeping face: her eyelids flickered a couple of times, but I was certain she was asleep.

The strangers, not one, but two, came to the house a little earlier than we expected.

Special Constable Mostyn Morris was a six-foot scowl of a man and going up in the world, said the people of Amlwch, for he wore high heels to raise his stature in life. Advertising for a female companion, he got a reply from his wife, so we called him Casanova.

But Morris was no joke on the night he came to Three Costog as Arresting Officer. We eyed each other on the doorstep, Morris and me, cats of a different breed.

"Grown some for sixteen aren't we, Tal Roberts?"

"Gone seventeen now," I said.

"Aye? Well, I'm after the organ-grinder, not the bloody monkey, yeh?" and this he said in Welsh.

"Who is it?" called my father from the kitchen.

"Casanova."

"Ask him in. I've always wanted to see him with his trousers on."

There was no point in taking it seriously.

Like me, I think my father knew that the die was cast.

It was close to midnight. I shut the door on a night of stars and the stink of an acrid, bitter land.

Dada nodded towards a chair and Morris sat. His great bulk in constable blue seemed to obliterate the room.

"You come at a convenient time," said my father. "Say your piece and go."

"I will, Gwyn Roberts." The policeman took out a book and opened it on his knee. "Where were you between the hours of nine o'clock tonight and now?"

"Do I account to you for my movements?"

"You do now. You called, with your son here, on John Hughes Carter at six o'clock, did you not?"

"You're well informed."

"Aye, mun. It's my job. Then you went to the Oddfellows?"

"I did."

"And drank there for an hour?"

"God bless Dick Evans."

"And left there at ten, he says." Morris consulted his notebook. "What did you do after that?"

"What's all this about?" I asked.

Poll opened the door to the stairs, peered around it, and went out again. Morris rose, throwing wide. "Oh no, girl, come you in! Let the family know what's happening," and Poll entered, made large eyes at me, and sat down. Morris said:

"You arrived back here at eleven, did you not, Gwyn Roberts?"

With the air of an Old Testament prophet, my father said, "I did, and to save you asking, I walked down to the harbour for an hour before that. Is there a law against taking a walk?"

"There is about breaking and entering."

"Breaking and entering where?"

"Greathead's shop."

"What kind of fool do you take me for?" My father rose. "I who've had a quarrel with Greathead's for a debt I did not owe?"

There was a silence, then Morris said, "A fool who will break and enter for a couple of pounds of candles."

"And you hope to find them here?" I asked. "We use oil. There's not a candle in the house."

"You're welcome to search, yeh?" said Poll, but her face was pale.

"No, he is not," said Dada, and opened the back door.

The stars walked in with the moonlight; never will I forget the beauty of that night. My father shouted, "Come on, *out*! We've had enough of you. Arrest me if you have the evidence, if not, shift!"

The door of the stairs came open then and Meg stood

58

there, her eyes gummed with sleep.

"The quarrelling awoke me," said she drowsily. "Is some-body wanting candles?" and she put them into my hands.

Then the second stranger, Red Bracer the gaoler, came to arrest my father, and he and Morris took him away.

8

Ten minutes after my father was in gaol the Guardians of the Poor Committee arrived in the interests of morality; they hooked Poll and Meg out of our house, and put them next door.

"The chapel Elders have suggested it, Taliesin Roberts."

"Of course," I replied.

"It is no reflection upon your integrity, you understand?"

"Perfectly."

"Will I be back when Dada returns, Tal?" Meg, her hand in Poll's, shot a grieving look at me as she went next door to Old Cog Costog and Betsy.

Bending, I kissed her. "The moment he is home. Do not cry, my precious."

I had been three weeks on night-shift since my father was taken: now I awoke to an afternoon girt with light, for summer was in the hedges with a shine of blackbirds, and oyster-catchers and curlews were shouting demented. I was in the barn with Dobie when Poll came visiting.

Old Dobie was sick and wounded. A whimsey bucket up on Mona Mine had caught him in its swing, and his side was red raw and congealed with blood. Morning and night I had to bathe and bandage him, which meant putting a twitch on him – a cord twisted with a stick on his upper lip to quieten him – for he was as touchy as a housewife owing rent. Then I'd cleanse him with carbolic and soapy water and put on Horses' Ointment, also a cure for breast ulcers.

I glanced up as Poll entered the barn. "Mind his rear," I

60

said, for he'd flatten a rhino if it came within range, a trick my father had taught him.

I knew Poll had something up her apron the moment I saw her.

"I got a letter," said she, and preened.

"O, aye?" I went on bandaging.

"Come last night while you was on shift." She raised her face with a strange, infantile assurance. Fishing down the front of her she fetched the thing up.

"What's the odds?" I spoke lightly, but I was worried. "For Dada, is it?"

"Same letter as always comes month end, Tal. What you goin' to do?"

"Take it to him in Beaumaris."

"To the prison? Don't be daft! Perhaps he's adventurin'."

"And perhaps you're right." I took the envelope.

"You go to Beaumaris, likely I'll come, too?"

"Ach no, woman. You stay and mind Meg."

She raised her chin in opposition. "O, aye? That be my job in life, ain't it – minding your old Meg! Well, now your pa's gone I'm afinishin' wi' that, Tal Roberts. Likely I'll cut loose and find meself a fella." She sent me a wink. "I could do better'n here, ye know, for you're throwin' stones at it, when I ought to be up an' sparkin'."

"Who will care for Meg, then?"

"Likely you. I got me own life to live, Tal Roberts, so I'm not bothered hot."

"She is of your blood."

She did not reply, but put herself jaunty, and there grew in me a great sickness for my father. Had Poll and Meg not been weighing on my shoulders I'd have left this place that moment.

Not a lot can be had talking of it, but I was hollow with his going. Upon the little cottage rooms had fallen a mantle of grief that I could touch, and I used to stand by his empty bed, fighting tears.

Meanwhile, Poll was stepping it jaunty around the barn, picking things up and putting them down. Now, pouting in a piece of broken mirror, she said at nothing:

"Your Meg anna my business, Tal Roberts, I didn't born her, yeh? She do come from another womb. Moreso, trouble's on its way, and I reckon to be gone before it arrives."

"Trouble?"

It turned her. "Don't you come so stiffin' coy, you know what I mean. Every night I dream it, cold as a witch's hand."

"You're mad."

"Mad, is it? I'm the only sane chap in Three Costog. What with you goin' mooney over badgers an' your dada out nights with rum gentlemen . . ."

"Rum gentlemen?"

"Smugglin' fellas – come on, Tal Roberts, I weren't born yesterday."

I was relieved. For a moment I'd wondered if Poll knew more than was good for her; if so, she'd have put it around Town.

Finishing off poor old Dobie, I left her without a word and walked down to the harbour across Turkey Shore where the *copar ledis* were belting it out and the Smelter rolling her sulphurous smoke over the blue-tinted sea. The sun was hot, the wind kind, and I knew comfort in the bedlam of the quay unloadings; in it one could bury the sense of loss and biting fears.

The scrap-iron tramps were in; cranes were swinging, carts and horses thronging in hoarse commands, chain-clatter, wheel-grinding, whip-cracks: iron for melting into the sulphate Precipitation pits up near Mona, where I once worked.

But more than scrap iron was coming into Amlwch that morning, for it was on that day that I saw Rhiannon for the first time.

The mail packet from Ireland was in harbour, too: a little wide-beamed sloop with brass ventilators and binnacle, snow-white decks and a touch of class.

I straightened, watching, because from her rail gentry were coming ashore.

Every so often we got the gentry in, mainly the Quality from County Cork and Ellan Vannin: coming to do us over here, my father used to say, after skinning the poor Irish of their wit and turnips over there.

Walking daintily in their summer dresses and big hats, the ladies came first, handed down the gangplank by a chap in blue and gold: with their skirts held up and their heads inclining politely to the ragged Welsh workers, they were followed by their gentlemen in morning coats, top hats, and airs of authority: bound for the tour down to the South, I thought, after a couple of days rest at Dinorben Hotel, recovering from the voyage.

Mr. Treweek and his two drunken sons were there to greet them; also Sanderson, the agent of the Marquis. And all around them, as this retinue proceeded, the mob of scorched and tattered copper workers doffed their moleskin hats or tugged their Welsh forelocks.

What has happened to my country? I wondered. Gideon Davies was surely right.

Time was, sprung from princes, we raided English castles and burned the English occupations: at the time of Cunedda and Maelgŵn we laid full strong against the Romans and fought from Carlisle to Chester, along Sarn Helen to Neath. Now, hundreds of years later, we were a people in thrall, bowing and scraping to an invading aristocracy put here by the Church, our old Traitoress, and apologies for Welshmen who despised their heritage.

God help us. Our nationality had gone out like a smoking candle.

Rhiannon de Vere walked alone.

She approached where I was standing like an acolyte in white; her long, lace-trimmed gown, well bustled, reached to her feet; a pink, summer hat was lying on her shoulders.

No Cousin Poll was this one; no Pru Ichabod matched her: she was like an Iberian princess bred of a distant age, and moved within my racing thoughts.

Nearer, nearer she came.

I was standing on the cobbles of the Britannia public,

unaware of the waiting chaise and its two white mares stamping before me.

Nearer; now on the arm of an elderly gentleman, she approached, and delayed in mounting the steps of the chaise as her eyes found mine: dark-lashed in her Celtic face, they drifted over me in quiet assessment.

How to tell of her smile, with only words to use?

I was still staring as the chaise drove off; Rhiannon raised a hand to me, but I did not make reply, for she had taken my legs with her.

A quick half pint at the Britannia and I got news of her.

Her people, the landlord said, were up from Dowlais in South Wales, where they were in trade – iron, he thought: her mother was Welsh, her father Irish, and they had property in County Clare.

Let loose a captive butterfly and it will mate with a rare species, I thought.

Dowlais, eh? That's where my Aunt Mellie Williams lived . . .

As fresh as a little girl's pinny, I went back to Three Costog in a world changed from despair to expectation. And in this mood I opened the letter again – the one Poll had brought me – and read:

Rendevous for scrap iron. Menai Ferry.
Midnight. June 10th.

If this kind of thing continued, I thought, I'd never see the skies over Dowlais . . .

9

I thought I'd find Skipper Rowlands, my father's accomplice, in the Oddfellows that night, and I did.

I also found Dick Evans, who had buried my Pru Ichabod and had now come up with another.

She was a perky piece, this new barmaid they called Alicia, with the face of a schoolgirl and a bust full of erotic problems; a splash of crimson was she, serving up the jugs to the beery men. I slapped down money and she poured a pint.

"You got the same colour hair all over, my charmer?" she asked, pouting over the bar.

"Not under the arms." I sank my teeth into the amber flood and stared around the room, I had scant respect for her, having known Alicia since she was aniseed balls, all-sorts and weenies.

"Oho, upperty-upperty are we now, Tal Roberts?" It was like a raven's squawk.

I turned away, and Dick Evans cried above the hubbub, "Tell him you don't give a monkey's arse, girl, including the monkey. Don't you fret, my beauty."

It was said of Dick Evans that he never allowed a virgin in the place and I believed it.

She shouted more, but I didn't hear her words; pushing my way through the men I stared back at Skipper Rowlands who was perched on his pint like a big, jerseyed raven. He nodded almost imperceptibly; I nodded back, and the banter of the pay night beat about us in foul language and curses. Yes, I thought, Gid Davies was right – it was a hell of a place, this copper town, and it needed cleaning up.

Ale was most of the trouble in Amlwch these days.

With a population of some seven thousand, there were over sixty beer houses in Town. And the women took the rub for it, as usual, with black eyes and broken noses most nights, and Saturday a Roman holiday when it came to wife-beating, one of the local sports.

Aye, they took it hard in Amlwch, like in most industrial towns. Skinning the pennies to make ends meet, they were chained at home with children, wading to the shops in a foot of filth and washing raw sewage off the kids. Typhoid and cholera snatched at their children, pigs and goats wandered at will. Never did I hear women cry like I heard them cry in Amlwch, rocking themselves in their windows, surrounded by their tattered, howling kids.

Don't blame the men, said my father; blame Treweek, the manager, and his tipsy sons; blame Sanderson, the Plas Newydd agent, blame the Marquis, but do not blame the men: if St. Peter himself was a tutworker in Amlwch he'd be on the tipple.

I'd got my own views on that: nobody pours ale down a working man's gullet.

We were lucky up on Costog, but down Town rats were scuttling over sleeping babies.

Years after I left, the Education Commissioners said that Amlwch was the poorest place and with the lowest morality in the whole of Anglesey. No hospital existed; most doctors who called themselves surgeons were habitual drunkards who didn't know a scalpel from a saw. The dregs of the Cornish medics, they drew their fourpence per week per Welsh worker under false pretences. One of them, Dan Sleep-Late, they called him, was doffing up the whisky in the Oddfellows even as I watched.

Skipper Rowlands raised his face and flickered an eye. Sinking my pint, I followed him out into the night.

Wider than me, this one, with a strong, square face burned brown by sea-wind; the moment he opened his mouth I knew him for Irish.

"It strikes me you've had a letter, me boy," said he.

"Aye."

Taking it from me he held it up to the moon, whispering, "Honour to their houses, the sweet souls, but they'll get us bloody hung."

"Who's sending these? My father gets one regular."

"Ye don't know?"

"I do not."

"Then keep it that way, so they can't beat it out of ye in Beaumaris."

I said, bitterly, "As they are doing to my father?"

"Ach, lad, you cotton on quick. Somebody talked, d'ye see?"

"Who?"

He stared about him. The harbour lights of the port were glimmering glow-worms in the rising night mist: the lighthouse at Lynas was dousing the blossoming stars. Rowlands said:

"Would I be tellin' even if I knew, ye numbskull? But there's a donkey travelling the area putting all the mares in the family way, and it's either him or Dick Evans." He stared up at me. "Is that enough, or do I write it down?"

"Are you certain?"

"Jesus, I'm not! But in this game there's always a bloody conjuror with his hand in the till and the trick is to find the rabbit."

"And my father? Please tell me."

He smiled at me and his eyes were good. "You'd best know, son, so you can see what you're into. Two whippings on the frame so far, a fortnight on the treadmill, another whipping round Town soon, then seven years transportation."

I bowed my head. "God, what for?"

He laughed softly. "Formally arraigned, formally sentenced. For breaking and entering Greathead's shop and stealing blutty candles."

I breathed a filthy word.

"Aye, so call it names, lad, but it's our current justice. He won't open his mouth so they've got to have him for something."

I raised my face. "An appeal . . . to the Marquis?"

"Appeal to him? Don't make me laugh. Now this letter. It's about a printing press. They call it scrap iron for security reasons, but the lads need it for the pamphlets and posters. Just meet it at Menai and wheel it up to Iorri Ifan's farm, yeh? I'll do the rest."

The night wind was suddenly cold. I was thinking about Meg. Rowlands said, "Christ, mun, they'll not bloody hang ye if you're found wi' it, you know. A month or two on the treadmill at most. Anyway, it'll be crated – how should you know what's in the box?"

I nodded.

"Ye'll do it, son?" He clapped me on the shoulder. "God speed ye, Tal. Roots are there to hold on to in a stiff breeze, you're the son o' your father."

He'd had a few, by the look of him. I stood watching as he rolled off down to Town. Funny, for although my father dealt with him, I never really trusted Skipper Rowlands.

I got old Dobie out into the night-shift carters and began, with them, the long sleepy procession up to the loading compounds. The stars were big above Parys Mountain and the naphtha flares were dousing the moon: instead of waiting my turn for the loading, I went straight on as if heading for Precipitation, and nobody appeared to notice me.

Soon I was alone in the summer night with Dobie: the activity of the mountain died behind me.

An hour or so later, taking east, I went through Talwrn. The wayside cottages were toads ready to spring, their blinkered eyes watching, their roofs shining quicksilver in a weird grandeur. A baby cried faintly; someone loved in a squeak of bedsprings.

Through Llangefni I went, and here Dobie snorted and looked over his shoulder at me, as if recognising his home; on to Brynsiecyn on the back road for safety and I reached the gate that led down to Foel ferry by Menai Inn, which I assumed was the rendezvous: here I got down off the cart and stood at Dobie's head watching the ferries coming and going from the Caernarfon side and listened to clocks chiming midnight. After that I didn't wait long. Not a sound I heard, not a whisper, but a man suddenly leaped from the dark, spinning me sideways into the berm, and the point of a knife pricked my throat.

"Who are you?" A whisper.

Only a professional works this way. Lying in his arms, I whispered back, "Taliesin Roberts, the son of Gwyn."

Another loomed above me. "Where is your father?"

"Beaumaris gaol."

"*Christ!* When?"

"Weeks back."

"Who sent you, then?"

"I've had a letter."

"Your father's letter. You opened it?"

"With Skipper Rowlands, my father's friend."

"Beaumaris, you say?" The man gripping me relaxed. Rising, he pulled me up beside him. "On what charge?"

I told him.

The moon blazed and I could see them clearly now.

One was tall and slim, a man of education and good breeding; his companion was short and squat, his voice high and thin, like a mountain fighter's. I said:

"My father has been taken, so I have come in his place."

"What for?"

"A printing press."

I saw them exchange glances and one sighed with relief, saying, "How old are you?"

"Seventeen."

"You know the punishment for this – printing pamphlets?"

I stared back at them. The other said, "Hanging, drawing and quartering our gracious Queen reserves for treason, lad, and you are pretty near it. Your age will not save you, remember. Skipper Rowlands knows of this, you say?"

"It was he who sent me."

The bigger man shrugged. "Up to you, but die, if need be, to save anyone getting this printing press, my son," and he went to nearby bushes and pulled out a trolley and on the trolley stood a packing case.

"It weighs a ton, or nigh it. Give us a hand, boy."

I did so, and we lifted the case and trolley on to the back of Dobie's cart, and covered it with brushwood from the berm. They faced me.

"Now where to, tell us?"

I replied, "The old farm behind the Precipitation."

"And who is to receive this printing press?"

"Skipper Rowlands."

"He will be there to receive it, because you need help unloading."

"He will be there."

The smaller man groaned. "God help us, they will be snatching them from the cradle soon." Reaching out, he gripped my shoulder. "Go in God."

The other said, turning away, "He'll get a lot of bloody help in that direction – away with it, lad, and get it under cover."

I reined Dobie in and he strained to the greater load; some printing press, I thought; big enough to print *The Trumpet of Wales*.

Dawn was fingering the sky with hope when I got back to Parys Mountain; the ramshackle farmhouse of Iorri Ifan raked burned rafters at the paling stars.

At the farm entrance two men were waiting in the shadows. They started forward when they saw the cart: one was Skipper Rowlands, the other Joe Oldfield.

"You're late," said Rowlands. "Quick, give a hand," and Joe took one end and we carried the case into the kitchen and laid it on the floor. I made to go but Rowlands stopped me.

"No, see this," said he, and prised open the lid of the box.

Muskets, pistols, sabres and two-piece pikes: arms of every description – the things I'd seen in gentry museums: bags of shot were there, too, even mining black powder. I stared at it: beneath it was a little printing press.

"Best you know, Tal Roberts," said Rowlands. "Now you're in this up to your neck."

Next morning I saw Old Cog Costog and his Betsy in Town: he was sporting the black eye she'd handed him for tippling it with Alfie Cromwell, the English: she'd warned him a couple of times about his doubtful friendships but Old Cog, the rebel, never took heed of it. "I'm the man of the house," he used to say, "I snap my fingers and she jumps six feet. Aye, a good wife should be on her knees to her husband – 'come out and fight, you bloody little coward,' and she's there on all fours raking under the table."

One thing about Old Cog; like most Welsh poets he was light in the attic, but he never lost his sense of humour.

With them, outside Greathead's shop that morning, was my little sister Meg.

Good neighbours were these two, mark me: since I could remember we'd lived next door to each other and never a dull or ditchwater word over the wall between us. Just the usual popping in and out for caddy tea or a bit of lard for rubbing on someone's chest or liniment for rheumatics; otherwise we kept our distance, like good neighbours should. And she kept quite a good table, too, did Betsy, for Cog earned good money on the engines, though he put a lot of it up against the wall, too, said Dada.

I was up to my elbows in my trews, mooching over the Square when I heard Meg's little shriek of delight and her face was bright with sun and her head fair curls.

"Your Poll's gone, Tal," said Betsy, flat.

"Walked out without a word," added Cog.

"*Gone?*" I couldn't believe it.

Down Market Street that morning the carts were end to end, with stalls going up in St. Eleath's square and gentry carriages queueing at the bank. Beggars were crying for alms, mostly the riff-raff refuse of the South Wales ironworks; legs off, arms off, many soldiers from the Napoleonic wars. And they raised their drum-stick limbs to us as we stood there talking. Meg sidled up and put her hand in mine.

"Aye, Tal, Cousin Poll has made off," said she.

"When?" I asked Betsy, and she eyed me.

"Dirt to dirt, anna it, Tal Roberts? Never did like her, never approved of her. Told ye so, didn't I, Cog? Best off without her."

"God!" I raised my eyes to the sky. It was one thing after another. Betsy added:

"Gone for some fancy chap, more'n likely; very hot under the tails the likes of that Poll, beggin' ye pardon."

"Took one-and-fourpence from the tea caddy, mind," said Old Cog, glum. "Saving it for the rent, we was, wasn't we, Mam? And two china dogs and the bread board."

"*Heisht* you, darlin'," whispered Betsy, elbowing him, "he anna got that kind o' money."

"I'll pay, though," I replied. "But what about Meg?"

"O, loveliest of children!" cried Old Cog, his arms wide to the sun. "'And on that cheek, and o'er that brow, so soft, so calm, yet eloquent . . .'" Bending, he kissed Meg's face.

"Quiet, you!" said Betsy. "Greathead's it is this mornin', not Byron," and she smiled into the sun. "Can't mind her, see, son? Things are tight now with my Cog up on the Mona engines, so I'm due out scrubbing."

"You mean you can't have Meg now Poll's gone?"

"Sorry, Tal Roberts."

We stood in the confusion of Amlwch's sun and wind, the scurrying people, their shouted greetings, the scrape of hobnails, the clopping horses; everybody was in Town that morning, I reckon: racked, undecided, we stared at each other. And Meg's eyes were filling with tears.

"Especially with your dada in Beaumaris, an' all that . . ." added Betsy.

I said, lifting Meg against me:

"We've got an aunt and uncle down Dowlais way . . . I've written them a letter."

"O, aye! We forgot! Aunt Mellie, *Boppa* Williams, isn't it? Sister on your dada's side?" Betsy mopped and flourished, being on the change, and Old Cog shouted at nothing, eyes closed:

"'A mind at peace with all below, a heart whose love is innocence. She walks in beauty, like the night . . .'" and he reached out, stroking Meg's cheek. His missus said:

"Sorry in my heart I am, Tal Roberts. But folks 'ave to eat, see, that's the trouble," and she eased her great fat legs along the pavement, giving Old Cog one in the ribs. "Home, you," said she. "Faggots and peas it is this morning, not Welsh poets."

I stood watching as they went into Greathead's.

Farther down Market Street, in a raven-black clutch of Chapel worshippers, I bumped into Mr. Dafydd Owen, our Wesleyan Elder.

Parsimony in frugality was he, with a brass-bound Bible under one arm and under the other the books of the Slaughterhouse. Seeing Meg and me, he raised his eyes to Heaven and gathered us against him in grievous pain.

"Oh, Taliesin!"

"You ill, Mr. Owen?"

"Sick to my heart, lad. This morning your father was brought back from the prison at Beaumaris; he is incarcerated now in the gaol in Wesley Street."

"For the whipping around Town tomorrow? Yes, I heard, Mr. Owen."

"Have you yet seen him?"

"Red Bracer, the gaoler, would not let me in."

"May God grant you strength." He wrung his withered hands.

I raised my face. "They did the same to Jesus."

"Oh, no!" Censure, deep and pure, lay on his ancient face.

I said, "After my father has gone, we're going from here, too, Mr. Owen. Down south to Dowlais, likely. We have an aunt . . ."

The happy crowds pushed and shoved us in the sun's nonchalant brightness: I thought of my father . . . the third whipping in a month; this time before his own people, and said, with an effort. "No . . . no point in us staying . . ."

"I understand. And that little harlot, Cousin Poll, she has also deserted you, I understand?"

"Her business, Mr. Owen. She's been good to us till now."

Megan sneezed at the sun and I wiped her nose. "No place for her here, either – Poll, I mean."

But he was not listening. Racking his brains for memory, he said:

"I have a brother in Dowlais, you know – a deacon in the Welsh Wesleyan – he serves in the same Chapel as Mr. John Guest, the ironmaster, whose wife is Lady Charlotte, the best blood in England. My brother tells me that they are looking for an assistant schoolmaster there . . ."

"Kind of you, Mr. Owen, but my English is peasant."

"Perhaps so, but you are beautifully educated in the Welsh classics. Would you like a letter of introduction?"

"Thank you very much, Mr. Owen."

I said it to get rid of him, for the mouth often says one thing and the heart another.

It do beat me how Chapel deacons are appointed: this one managed the Amlwch Slaughterhouse, and six carcasses of veal pumped up for the Dinorben gentry come Sunday, plus fifteen ox-tails.

Passing Pritchard's fields the doe eyes of the little calves always raked me; one day we will pay for this, said my father. Mr. Owen's question tore me from my thoughts:

"When will you be going, you say, Taliesin?"

"When my father leaves Amlwch."

"So you will be walking in the whipping procession?"

"Of course. Mrs. Costog's having Meg."

"Then we will walk together, you and me, and I will give you the letter I promised you then. Meanwhile, remember, I beg you, we Welsh should grovel for crumbs from no employer, least of all to the tenant of Plas Newydd. How old are you, Taliesin?"

"Seventeen, sir."

"May I speak personally?"

I nodded, and he said:

"If you believe that your father is being whipped for the theft of a few candles, you're a larger fool than I took you for."

I nudged Meg and down she went in her little bobbed curtsey, while I bowed.

Patriots were all over the place, I thought; one never knew where they'd turn up next. And Mr. Owen bowed back, a man of impeccable loyalty, religion and tolerance: God knows how he ever got mixed up with a slaughterhouse.

They brought my father out of the gaol in Wesley Street and tied his wrists to the back of our cart, his arms outspread; starched blood was still upon his shirt from the earlier whippings in Beaumaris, and he moved like a man still on the treadmill. He looked for me among the crowd and I raised a hand to him. Red Bracer, the Amlwch gaoler, after fixing a scold's bridle over my father's face, turned Dobie, our horse, and the whip, moving fast, slashed down.

Walking next to me in the procession behind the cart was Mr. Dafydd Owen, and he said:

"You are worthy of your father, Taliesin. For one so young it is an ordeal, walking behind the cart of a relative's punishment. You consider the punishment unjust, I take it?"

"For the theft of a few candles? Of course."

"Have you considered – I asked you this before – that a greater charge might be involved?"

I did not reply to this.

Outside the Dinorben Hotel were standing the Quality; English mainly, but with a sprinkling of Welsh gentry. These were the people I had seen disembarking from the Irish mail sloop a week or so before. And all about them stood the smelters, carters, tributors and tutworkers; the miners, spraggers, coalers and hewers, also a score or so *copar ledis,* with whom I once worked. And Mrs. Dahlia Sapphira, who once had designs on my father, raised a fat fist as the cart went by, and shrieked:

"Stick it, Gwyn Roberts. Stick it, mun!"

Rhiannon was not on the street.

She was standing by a leaded window of the hotel, with her hands over her face.

Most felons were whipped or put in the stocks on Fair Days. It was a change of entertainment from the bull and badger-baiting, cock-throwing, wife-beating and endless pitch and toss. Also, it instructed incoming paupers of the inadvisability of staying too long in Amlwch, and informed the Quality of our Welsh respectability.

Social conditions were going from bad to worse around then, in 1838. With the ore running out on Parys Mountain, the copper boom was over, yet still the immigrants flooded into Amlwch.

With them came the starvers from Ireland and the North Country, bringing in their ranks the blacklisted workers of the rioting southern towns.

After the Bread or Blood riots of Merthyr seven years back, hundreds of wanted men escaped to North Wales. Under assumed names they had streamed with their families into the copper trades, running from the Usk House of Correction. Undercutting Welsh copper wages, the immigrants would crowd the pavements to see the whipping carts go by, cat-calling, whistling, jeering, the blind fools.

"Go on, Bracer lad – give 'im a penn'orth!"

"That's right, make the bugger dance, my lovely!"

"Put one on his shanks for me, old lad!"

But not today.

Today they were silent.

Irish, North-country men, Midlanders, even Cornishmen, stood with downcast faces; their eyes switching at those around them, the hostile, fuming Welsh.

Returning past St. Eleath's gate I saw the Church of England clergy, black-gowned and twittering like rooks at a conference.

Here the cortège halted because the mail coach from Bangor was coming through. Red Bracer, tiring, gave the whip to Cross-Cut Jack, once an old Landore mountain-fighter, with shoulders on him like a barn ox and a face for chopping firewood.

On our way up to Quay Street my father fell to his knees, finding it difficult to breathe. So Red Bracer removed the scold's bridle from his mouth and gave him a spell.

The sun burned down. There was no sound in my ears but my father's gasping and the cracking of the whip. And in a sudden silence a man bawled with a voice like a siren:

"Is this the best ye can do, Dafydd Owen? Ye bum-faced bloody Pharisee! Is this in the name of the Welsh Wesleyans?" and Mr. Owen, beside me, cried back:

"What can I do? Have I a monopoly on the law?"

"What about a monopoly on God, ye boot-faced, bloody puritan? We'd ne'er stand for it in the Catholics!" Irish was Jobie Quarts, the landlord of the Red Bull in Pig Market. "Ye're luxuriatin' in pastures of devotion while a decent man is whipped for nothin'! Do your job, mun, shout your authority, or we'll come in there an' take it from ye!"

"When the law is the authority the Chapel has none – be reasonable!" The Elder beside me shook with anger.

"Ay ay? Mind, ye did the same thing two thousand years ago, did you not? Anointment don't come in half pints, Deacon, it's penitence or nothin'."

Another bawled, "Hold hard there, Owen, and I'll fetch ye water to wash your hands . . ."

Standing bowed at the cart my father raised his head at this, saying:

"Be silent, Jobie! The Elders can do nothing. The trial was fair, the punishment just."

Halfway up Machine Street, on the way to the harbour, Mr. Owen questioned me on this:

"You heard what your father said?"

"Yes."

"And what have you to say to it?"

"I have nothing to say, Mr. Owen."

"There is more in this than meets the eye, isn't there . . . ?"

I closed my eyes.

The sun stood still.

I was walking on splashes of my father's blood.

A woman broke from the ranks of the people along Machine Street and lay down in the road in front of Dobie;

others joined her, legs kicking, petticoats flying as the gaolers tried to pull them away.

Soon the road was filled with kicking, shrieking women; grandmas, rosy-cheeked girls in poke-bonnets, old hags, the Fair pickpockets; large-hipped worker-women, too, the *copar ledis*, tougher and more courageous than their men. If Robespierre had done the knitting and left the Revolution to Madame Lefarge, said my father, the chances are he'd have kept his head.

Amid shouts and shrieks, they cut my father free of the cart and bore him away, but he fought them and was standing alone when policemen came running to the assistance of Red Bracer: from Turkey Shore they came, men of Beaumaris Prison, and among them was Special Constable Mostyn Morris of Amlwch. With their big hobnails stamping on the cobbles and their hardwood truncheons stuck out before them, they came in a phalanx, scattering the people with short, sharp blows. Retying Dada to the cart, they positioned themselves about it and the whipping continued, until we reached the harbour.

Here they loosened him and he stood bloodstained and swaying. I went to him.

"No, Tal, leave me."

"Dada . . . !"

"*Leave me!*"

Those who had brought a cutter began to escort my father aboard, but Mr. Dafydd Owen cried:

"*Wait!*" and climbed upon a bollard. "It is the entitlement of a felon to address the town before transportation, and I would hear what this man has to say. I myself am dissatisfied with the justice of his sentence."

After much nodding and whispering among the crowd, this was agreed.

My father said then, leaning against the cart:

"Earlier, I asked you if you were patriots, and got no answer. Now I ask if you call yourself Welsh?"

He wiped blood from his face. "Listen! We have the misfortune to be sitting on copper, and it is needed for the

English trades. So our gentry bring in Cornish experts to teach us how to dig it; how to mint it with Victoria's stamp – the Royal Pimp who feeds her penal settlements with our Welsh heroes and makes whores of Welsh women. And we, whose copper this is, have known no profit from the greed save hunger.

"Where goes the Welshman mutilated on a whimsey – home to his wife and children – treated by Cornish doctors I wouldn't let near a horse. Where goes the refiner with molten copper over his shoulders? To the earth floor of his hut – and not a sovereign, mark you, from the Marquis in Plas Newydd."

The crowd thicker, massed before him now; the constables moved uncertainly; Red Bracer fingered his scold, and my father cried:

"Think ye that Anglesey's pensions are adequate? He who makes more out of larceny than Dick Turpin? Silas Bach of Petter Street lies blinded by copper sulphate – a shilling a week after twenty years up on Parys. Cornelius Solomon, now eighty, breaks stones along Machine Street on parish relief!" He raised a fist. "Out of a hundred and five petitions from the halt and maimed, his lordship has granted six pensions, and from these the Guardians have stopped the parish shilling! Are ye standing for all this, or are you fighting for it, like me?"

They made no answer: disconsolate, they hung their heads.

"All right!" Dada shouted. "Whine for alms, then, you apologies for men, but you'll get nothing from Treweek or his ale-soaked sons. You'll get nothing from Sanderson, unless you take it!"

Insulted now, they grumbled among themselves like bulls at a manger, and Dada cried:

"You're being swindled at the 'bargains' and diddled in the Truck Shops – the agents run hand in hand with their master – yet you'll sit on your backsides after I'm gone, because you're a broken people." He levelled a finger. "Have you forgotten Hywel Dda and the hundred tribes? Upon the head of Llewelyn a new body grows in English dust and he'll come and take the streets if you start being Welsh! Can't you see the ploy, for God's sake? The way to kill a people is not to drive them into slaughterhouses, but make them forget who they are!"

He glared around.

After they had taken him to the prison in Beaumaris, I stood there until darkness, looking at the sea. Then I collected Meg from Betsy and took her into our cottage, fed her, and put her to bed.

"Our Dada is gone, has he, Tal?" she asked.

"Aye – natural, isn't it, being his birthday?"

"His birthday, is it?"

"Yes."

"Do folks go off on birthdays?"

"Grown-ups, usually."

"Well I never," said she at her fingers. "Coming back soon, is he, like our Poll?"

"Just as soon as his party is over," I said. "Our Poll's got one on the go as well."

"Will I go off when me birthday comes round?"

"You and me going off soon."

She wept and I held her. Strange are children. She was only seven years old, but I wondered who was kidding who.

After I'd got her abed I went into Dada's room and collected up the things he had left; papers, chiefly; some love-letters from my mother tied with scarlet thread.

Strangely, the little tin box in which he kept 'The Tale of Delwyn' had vanished: I presumed that he had taken this with him, the only real treasure he possessed.

"Goodbye, Dada," I said at the door.

There was growing within me a cold, shivering anger.

Two

Dowlais
1831

A hunter's moon, fat-bellied after a banquet of summer, rolled his backside along the rim of the Brecon Beacons when Meg and me, jogging on Dobie, clip-clopped up from the plains of Brecknock, heading South.

Above us flashed the cosmic fires of chaos; Pleiades of red and silver; the Milky Way streamed tails across the Universe.

For the last five days we had been at it. From Amlwch town, over the ferry at Menai we had reined old Dobie; down, down south through the forests of Penllyn and Dyfnant we had come, Meg dozing in the saddle before me. Then through ancient Rhayader to snoozy Builth, where the great Howell Harris preached: sleeping in wayside barns and thickets, working our passage on the tin whistle: Meg dancing, me telling the tales of the folk-lore *Mabinogi*, that my father had passed on to us.

At every little market-place we rested I'd tell the *Mabinogi*.

Beginning on the tin whistle to raise a crowd, Meg would dance; then, with her sitting cross-legged at my feet, I'd give them the folk-lore of King Arthur.

Hunched together, squatting on their hunkers, they would listen, and it took them back to the bedtime stories of their childhood.

I told these stories by declaration, striding before them as my father had done in Three Costog, my fist swinging an inch from their faces.

When I'd finished, Meg would go round with my cap.

Thus we worked our way through sleepy old Brecon. On

to Libanus then, and a climb through the pine forests of Tal-y-Bont, along the Redcoat Road, past the Drovers' Arms, through Coed Taff to Garn.

Here stood the cottage of Aunt Mellie Williams, my father's sister; married to a woodsman on The Top rough shooting, was she, and ten years past his grave was her husband, Sam, though still fit and able.

Sitting with his boots up on the settle in the kitchen he regarded me from under shaggy brows.

"You're not the first to come, ye know, Taliesin. Your Cousin Poll was here a while back."

"But she didn't stay," interjected Aunt Mellie, cold.

"And if she had, it's me guess we'd have seen her off by now," said Sam, and he ran his fingers through his mop-gold hair; for a man of eighty he looked fifty.

"No better'n she should be, mind," explained Aunt Mell, "though we be open-minded, b'ain't we, Sam? Down with the Rodneys in China, we heard tell, an' ye know about them!"

I said I did not, and held Meg closer against me in the mild hostility.

Sam stared at me in the flickering fire-light: gin-traps and snares of poaching were stamped upon his face, the cruel lines of pegged crows: I'd like to have known what my father thought of him, and said:

"I'm sorry Cousin Poll's been a bother."

"No bother, but ye've got political trouble up at Anglesey, I heard tell, and we're not askin' for more."

"Ach, lad," said Mellie, plump and motherly, "our Tal's too young for the politics, anna you, son?"

"Cousin Poll was too young for gentlemen, but she collected a few," said Sam.

"Dear me, Husband, mind the little one," whispered my aunt.

To break the silence, I said desperately, "You . . . you got my letter, Uncle Sam?"

"Aye. But the police'd been into it; ripped and torn, it was."

"They're intercepting mail?"

"Aye, so learned about your pa, didn't they! Breakin' and entering?"

"That was the charge, Uncle Sam, but there's more to it than that."

"I bet there was."

Rising, he tapped out his Turk's Head pipe on the grate and I saw the full size of him; a man of great dignity and sinewy strength. Age had left its mark on his riven features yet granted him an extraordinary presence. Turning from the fire, he said:

"Listen. Blood to blood, it is, and relatives are welcome under this roof. But we've enough trouble in Merthyr without begging for more. You heard about the Bread or Blood?"

"The Merthyr riots seven years back?"

"Aye, but still not over, lad. Spies are everywhere. The Chartists are gathering in every iron town on The Top between here and Blaenafon. Trouble's comin' and we can do without scruffs and felons. So let me say this – stay in Dowlais, if you must, but keep out of bother. The pot-houses and taverns are packed full of unionists, socialists and tub-thumping anarchists."

"I'm not staying," I replied. "I am only asking you to care for Meg for a while."

It stilled him and he moved uncertainly: his wife said, swiftly, "There now, Sam – 'tis only the little one, see? Dear me! Wonderful it will be to have a little bonnet in the house again. Soften ye'self, is it?"

Sam moved his hobnailed boots uncertainly. "How long?"

"I'll be back for her as soon as I can."

"You're certain sure o' that?"

"Aye, just hold her for me till I get a start. I . . . I've got a letter."

"You'm stack full o' blutty letters, son!"

"From Mr. Owen, our Elder, to John Guest, the ironmaster."

It raised his grizzled face. "For employment? In what capacity?"

"Assistant to the headmaster at the Stable Free School," I said.

"A Free School, is it? D'ye hear that, Mell? Free my arse! Listen, you! Guest builds a school, all right? Then he stops fourpence in the pound from his workers' wages if he's got no children – single men, remember! If a man's got kids he pays more – twopence a week each child. Education, ye call it? For a couple of hundred in a working population of thousands? Let's get this bloody benevolence right, nincompoop! So there's a profit, isn't there – and where does that go? – on sick relief, since they're too bloody mean to build a hospital." He was sweating and breathing hard.

It was an astonishing outburst.

"Sam," pleaded Aunt Mell, "*let it be?*"

"Aye, let it be! Everywhere I hear talk of Guest benevolence! Nothing is free in Dowlais, son, take my word for it. Burn off a leg at the furnace and they trim the stump on your kitchen table; it'll be another twenty years before we get a hospital. They soak iron scalds with whisky here, and take us home on boards!"

Aunt Mellie said, with plump homely charm, "A scholar we have in the house now, is it, just like your da?" A diplomat, this one.

"Good on the Welsh poetry, mind," added Meg, warmly.

"And a situation with the Guests might make a difference, eh, Sam?" said Aunt Mell, slyly.

Sam was rubbing his chin; his mood had changed with astonishing speed.

"Aye, and well it might, Missus. I never gave that a thought . . ."

There was a smell of *cawl mamgu* on the hob; afterwards, whenever I thought of Sam and Mellie, I smelled granny's broth, and now their blood called to me, the unpretentious kinship of true relatives, and Mellie said, suddenly examining Meg's cheeks:

"This child, ye know, has a suspicion of agnes. I'll have to clear that up."

"Acne," said Uncle Sam, at his pipe.

"Agnes," said Mellie. "You think I don't know agnes

when I see it? I've been clearin' it up all my life."

"I am sorry. I apologise to you," said Uncle Sam, and raised fierce, shaggy eyes at me. "Meanwhile, the small one stays, agnes and all, but the big one goes."

And Mellie said, "And now, get Meg to bed, Tal. I want to hear about my brother . . ."

- It was the look that her husband gave me then; a strange look of triumph mixed with pride: one thing was sure, this one wasn't exactly what he appeared . . .

A couple of days later I saddled up Dobie, left Meg in the care of Mellie, and rode past Grawane Houses into the crazy, criss-crossed roofs of Quarry and the clanking of the Cyfarthfa ironworks; taking this road to escape the cluttering cottages of Tydfil's Wells and Fishpond.

I regretted the decision because the road grew narrower immediately, the cottages thicker. And here, as if barring my approach, a cinder tip behind a brook rose up before me, a sulphretting mass emitting plumes of acrid flame: worse than Amlwch at its best, this; a Devil's paradise of windowless habitations from which peered faces through the smoke. Wan and ill, these; human refuse dropped out of the rectum of the sky into a labyrinth of alleys and filth.

Whispering to give Dobie confidence, I reined him on through the narrow streets and unpaved courts, past whole families clustered together on broken doorsteps, getting occasional glimpses of sticks of furniture and unmade beds.

From these rooms new smells arose to challenge the stink of Crawshay's Works: the scent of newly baked bread, boiling fish, lobscouse. It was an appropriation by the owning rich of poor men's decency: the penury and deprivation of Cyfarthfa stood as a monument to a man defiled.

Bully boys and pickpockets eyed me from the dark corners, the Rodneys of a town bleeding to death: tarts sidled along the slushy roadway, or sold their wares shrilly from top windows. This, I learned later, was the running sore which some called Pont-Storehouse and others called China. Only the dissolute – thieves, vagrants and prostitutes – called it home.

Merthyr was not alone in this disgrace: the rich Sodoms and Gomorrahs of Birmingham, Liverpool, Nottingham and London challenged each other for new depths of degradation in which to plunge the labouring classes. Park's Cellars, known to the Welsh in Merthyr as Sulleri, related the abyss of total greed; the inhumanity of its ironmaster – a crime on the body of Mankind from which the town will take a century to recover.

Yet quite early, with the sun just setting, it was nevertheless dark, as if a mantle of pestilence had fallen upon the town. I saw eyes watching me as through a sun-glass hazed with smoke, soot and acrid air. And now came a roar from the nearby Cyfarthfa ironworks. A furnace went into blast, the ground beneath me trembling and scything into the rhythm of ceaseless hammers. Simultaneously, a nearer furnace was tapped, its molten iron flowing in incandescent flashes – a fizgig of light, gorgeous in variegated colours of red and gold. This blaze lit the world, illuminating squalid places, sending light shafts into the fog, etching into shape the topsy-turvy town.

China, in those seconds of scintillation, was written indelibly upon my mind.

As Dobie plodded on in a foot of filth, beggars, maimed and ill, called to me. Skeleton children waylaid me, shrieking from wizened faces. A relay of drunks now, reeling four abreast along the decaying walls, bawled unintelligibly; one pausing to dance to a drunken Irish tune on a whistle, his hobnails clattering. And, as the sparks of the furnace tapping flew above him, I heard the blasting engines shriek; the clanking of chains, the whirring of the Big Wheel.

Alongside the canal now, its murky waters reflecting the glow, I saw a girl watching me from the tumbled entrance to a court.

Bent nearly double, she was about fifteen, but a cripple aged seven by the size of her, and her eyes, bright in the hollows of her starved face, stared up into mine. Bare-footed, in rags, she was supporting herself on a ladle. And in that radiant moment of furnace glare we saw each other, before our world again subsided into darkness. It was as if she had been plucked out of my sight, but I knew, with a strange certainty, that I would see her again; that our futures were linked.

Now a tattered procession of people were following me: thugs and layabouts hastened out of doors; roughs were shaking their fists. And, as I spurred Dobie, some ran alongside, trying to grip my stirrups: another, braver than the rest, flung himself at the reins, but Dobie shook him off. Ploughing forward, flinging up mud, we galloped now, scattering a band of men who had linked a human chain across our path. Followed by threats and stones, we skidded along the bank of the canal, turned left down Jackson's and over the bridge to the Morlais tram-road, where trucks, heaped high with glowing slag, were being hauled down from Pen-y-darren.

Sounds of pursuit died behind us. It was the first and last time I would go into China, I promised myself, but the face of the girl told me that this would not be so.

And, as I rode away I thought of the ditty about copper-making which my father used to tell, when I was young:

> It came to pass in days of yore,
> The Devil chanced upon Landore.
> Quoth he, 'By all the fume and stink
> I can't be far from home, I think.'

I don't know about Landore down Swansea way, but this old doggerel certainly applied to Cyfarthfa.

It was dusk; the stars had killed the sun by the time I reached Dowlais market, and the moon, wondrous in the heavens, banished the hissing naphtha flares above the stalls.

These, stretched with canvas, were end to end across the square in front of Dowlais stables; a sea of billowing roofs decked with flags.

I slowed Dobie to a halt and tied him in a hollow beside the road.

Wool merchants were here, auctioning their bales; packmen from Pontypool and Swansea opened their black boxes and displaying their wares – silk from Gascony, embroidery from Flanders, ivory from the East. Tanners and saddlers were here, throwing up their musty smells: coopers making barrels worked like demons, their hammers rising and falling in piercing clouts. There were necklaces and beads, amber, sharks'-teeth bangles, bracelets of beaten gold: black men, brown men, Orientals with eyes like cobras', brayed and postured, their hands clutching ornaments of marvellous colours. Chickeners had come, slapping up the small, cold carcasses.

After gathering a crowd at the entrance, playing on my tin whistle, I began to give them part of 'The Lady of the Fountain', for anything to do with King Arthur always entertained them. And I'd just got to where Luned, Owain's lover, was about to be cast into the flames when there was a disturbance at the market entrance.

A lady had alighted from her carriage on the road behind

me. Seeing her arrival, the people hushed. Tall and straight, the lady walked. It was her dignity that encompassed me, not her beauty; yet she was heavy with child.

In a long, white dress, smiling under her broad-rimmed hat, she came, and the crowd parted. A man ran up with a chair.

The lady sat.

"Pray continue," said she, politely, smiling up.

With an effort, I said, ". . . And when Owain came to a forest clearing he saw a bonfire blazing there, also two young men who were leading a maiden towards it, to cast her into the flames, and Owain cried, 'What charge have you laid against this one, that she should die?' and the men replied, 'Owain has failed her. Therefore, under the law, we are taking her to be burned.' But Owain commanded, 'This shall not be so. Let me stand in her champion's place and I will do battle with you both for her.' And the young men, hearing this, left the maiden and attacked Owain, shouting, 'By the one who fashioned us, we will kill thee, too,' and Owain was hard pressed . . ."

I stared around their faces; gentry, roughnecks, drunks. And in front of them, quite composed, was the lady. She said:

"You tell a fine tale, White Hair, but why not in English? Come, I do not comprehend all your beautiful Welsh."

"There is no English version, Ma'am." I took off my cap.

"Why not? Such a classic?"

"Being primitive prose, it is not easily translatable."

"Who says this?"

"My father. He was a bard."

"And he taught you well, for that is correct. Do you know other tales?"

"I know eleven, Ma'am."

"But there are twelve!" Her chin went up.

"Twelve with the 'Tale of Delwyn', but few know of this."

"'The Story of Taliesin', you surely mean?" She peered, frowning. "How informed you are! Come, let us test you in the classics," and the people laughed softly. "What law, for instance, governed Luned's punishment in 'The Lady of the Fountain'? – can you answer that?"

I said carefully, "Under Hierosolym's Law a woman shall be burned and her champion hanged, if he be defeated in combat."

She opened her hands in a gesture of disbelief, saying softly, "Did . . . did your bardic father also instruct you in this – these are annotations."

I nodded.

"A Welsh law, was it not?" It was a trap. I said:

"No, Lady, it was the law of Europe."

"And burnings outraged Cobbett – you know of him also, I suspect!"

"No, Ma'am."

"Shame to Christianity! Shame to chivalry! Shame to England!" She laughed gaily then, and the people took up her laughter. I remember the hissing of the flares and the laughter of the people, and the lady said:

"Well done, White Hair! You are truly blessed. I have need of Welsh scholars, and would certainly like to meet your father."

"He is dead."

"Then to his son I say this – love Wales and she will repay you. One thing's sure – you've made a good start – but love learning better. You are passing through Dowlais?" She peered at me.

"I have come for work, Ma'am."

"Then work you shall have, for there's labour in plenty here, is there not?" She smiled around the faces about her.

Activity in the market appeared to have ceased; the coopers had stopped their hammering: pack men, their wares clutched against them, had drifted in from the stalls, and I wondered who this lady was. She said, turning to Dobie:

"This one is your friend?"

"Yes."

"Like you, he looks in need of a feed. What is your name?"

"Taliesin Roberts."

"And your father's bardic name?"

"Gwyn Mynydd."

"White Mountain!" It delighted her and she rolled it around her tongue. "There now! I knew you for a Taliesin or

94

a Delwyn because of your hair, Radiant Brow." She pointed. "Over there are stables. Take your horse to the ostlers, feed and bed him. And if you yourself have no pillow tonight, go to Dowlais House and say I sent you!"

"What name shall I say, Ma'am?"

"Lady Charlotte Guest."

Autumn faded into winter and the Top Town cobbles were glazed with ice: back-door snows were ten feet high, heaped around the clustered terraces leaning shoulder to shoulder against the cold. East winds howled Irish banshees down the alleys of the Dowlais poor. Then spring, elbowing winter out of it, came dancing over the Beacons. Bright and hot came she with cowslip bracelets in her hair and bluebells on her feet; her thighs were cloths of gold, her hair of swansdown cloud.

I love this Wales when she dresses up for springtime! In winter she's frizzed and sad, an old hag wailing among the sodden branches; summer sees her as a garlanded woman, desiring, desirable. But Wales, in springtime, is a maid all dancing, red lipped, with skirts of green rushes and a bodice of blossom.

What place can compare, in spring, with my beautiful country?

The sun was high; warm winds fanned the mountain grasses as I reined old Dobie along the hedgerows of Dowlais Top, talking him towards Pontsticill, and up to Dolygaer.

Here the forest firs and pines formed a block as solid as Napoleon infantry, their tops speared with blinding light. Little waterfalls squirmished in the rock outcrops, spraying arms of joyous water. It was a sun-burst morning of dew wetness, every leaf sparkling from night downpourings of rain. We went slowly, Dobie and me, savouring the scents of spring; bob-tailed rabbits scampered before us, curlews shouted curses up in the blue.

I was at peace, save for memories of my father.

Never had a job come so readily, nor was so easy: six shillings a week all found (and two for Dobie's feed): a little fat cook in a kitchen to feed me on a table corner, a little room over Dowlais House stables, and five Welsh cobs to look after – that was all. Oh, and part-time help to Old Joe Hitherto, the Dowlais warden. One night-shift at the Company stables I did, too; this was no hardship.

Two hundred horses they kept in the Dowlais Stables off Market Square. Hereford shires, these mostly; they dwarfed my cob Dobie, big though he was: horse-power for the ironworking loads on the tram-roads, coal up from Gethin to the furnaces, clay from the brickfields, finished iron and ingots down to the Cyfarthfa canal wharf, all bound for Cardiff and the ports of the world.

John Guest, the ironmaster, hadn't given my letter from Mr. Owen a second glance; things were all cut and dried by Lady Charlotte, by the look of it.

"Name?"

"Taliesin Roberts, Sir."

His agent, Mr. Clark, hovered nearby, but the ironmaster saw to this himself; something he always did, apparently, with a house employee.

"Where from did you say?"

His speech had the right intonation; no trouble with his phonetics, this one: rub him down with a Welshcake and he'd have been a Taff. I answered:

"Amlwch, Sir, up Anglesey way."

He nodded and his eyes were blue in his brown, square face. Handsome beggar; I think he knew it.

I liked him, but not much. He said. "My neighbour, Sir Richard de Vere, knows it well; I do not. Where are your people?"

"My parents are dead." I told him about Meg and work in copper, and he nodded, attentive, saying:

"Right, then, Roberts. Industry will be paid for with money, laziness or dishonesty with discharge. You understand? And if your horse eats too much, he's out – tell him that."

Nearly thirty years older than Lady Charlotte, John Guest was the grandson of a Shropshire yeoman farmer who emigrated to Wales and, with partners, rented land from Lord and Lady Windsor. Useless land, thought they, so they charged him thirty pounds a year. A century later the owners raised this rental to twenty-five thousand guineas, such was its mineral wealth. And even at that figure they were out of their minds, said the locals where I took a pint.

Now the owner of the biggest ironworks in the world – bigger, even, than the nearby Crawshay empire – John Guest the Younger married into gentility; taking the hand of Lady Charlotte Bertie, who claimed she was of the finest blood in England. Soon she brought forth his first-born, a son.

But all was not as clean as it looked concerning Guest, I'd heard. Dai Tomorrow, landlord of the Vulcan and Friendship in Market Square, reckoned that he was like the rest of the ironmasters when it came to wages. He had seen him, he said, with his hands full of sovereigns, holding them under the noses of starving Welsh. Even William Crawshay, his competitor, had claimed that Guest's Truck Shop in Dowlais gave him a ten per cent advantage in trade, for the prices there had gone up as iron went down. "Give me Crawshay," said Dai Tomorrow (who would never do today what could be done next week) "you know where you stand with him."

But the best blood in Wales that fine spring morning was up on Dolygaer, I reckoned: this, the battlefield where gallons had been spilled in the name of Welsh freedom. With bone-cold fingers I reined in Dobie and looked about me.

Here was the country of Tydfil the Saint; there the grass-covered palace of the Prince of Brycheiniog. All Wales seemed alive to me at that moment – Cunedda and Maelgŵn – heroes who had fought the barbarians of Bedd y Gwyddel, the Irish giant who had come from the sea, and been flung back to Ireland by the stubborn Welsh.

The honour of my country rose in me as I stood in that

bloodstained place.

It was then that I saw a horse and rider coming towards me out of the forest:

" 'Morning," said I, and removed my moleskin hat.

Tell me that God and Fate are not in service to lovers! *It was Rhiannon.*

So still she sat on the white mare, staring: then recognition came and she smiled.

"We've met before, haven't we?" she said in Welsh.

It was a celebration of love just to sit there looking.

Dobie nuzzled her white mare, quicker than me on the uptake. I said falteringly. "You . . . you live here?"

She gestured with her whip. "Kierton Manor. Between Pontsticill and Vaynor, but you're a long way south, aren't you?"

"You remember me?"

"Of course. Last autumn, up in Amlwch!"

The hubbub of the Amlwch unloading clattered in the ear of my memory. I saw her again, coming off the packet from Ireland; beautiful then, the year had flourished in her, bringing her to a new womanly shape and dignity. I made to pass, reining Dobie up, for he was becoming too intent on her mare, but she delayed me.

"What's your name?"

"Tal Roberts."

"Tal?" Her eyes questioned, laughing.

"Taliesin."

"How beautiful! Fair brow? Radiant brow?"

"Reckon I was white-haired at birth. Started off aged sixty."

She laughed softly, regarding me. "I remember your hair." The mare tossed, and she steadied it, coming closer. "You work down here now?"

"Aye." I screwed my hat, feeling unequal, dying to be gone: dry in the mouth and wordless now that she was near. "For . . . for John Guest – well, Lady Charlotte, really speaking."

"Good gracious, she's my aunt!"

"Good God," I said, faint.

"Well, not an aunt, exactly. I'm a cousin to Mary Pegus, Lady Charlotte's half-sister. She's sixteen, a year younger than me. I stay at Dowlais House with her, when she comes from London." She raised her olive-textured face. "Where are you going now?"

"To the shooting lodge. You know it?"

"Only from the parties given by the Guests. Can I come?"

Above her a hawk was flying in a stormy pentecostal sky; the sun had vanished over the tree-fringe of the forest. Earth smells arose in a sudden coldness. It was as if a hand had placed between us in a mosaic of peering eyes. But Rhiannon, unconcerned, wheeled the mare expertly, smiling over her shoulder.

"Come," I said, and reined Dobie in; and she followed me along the track that led to the lodge.

Rhiannon left early on, but I stayed with Old Joe Hitherto, the Dowlais warden, cleaning guns till dusk, and then took home back to Dowlais, with the pale moon rising up from a savagery of pines.

At a ford in the bottom of Dolygaer forest a man was standing, barring my way: waiting apart, but a little way off, were three more.

"Down off that nag, Tal Roberts," said a voice, and I recognised it instantly. It was Sam Williams, Aunt Mellie's husband.

He looked younger in the red light of coming dark. His tattered shirt was open to the waist; around his mop-gold head was a bright red scarf and his scarlet sash betokened Union affiliation. On high buckled shoes he sauntered towards me, a fine arrogance for one so old, and tipped back his head at a marvellous angle of conceit.

He said, and it was a surprise, "We meet again. Your Meg sends love to you, but I do not, for this is business. Now prove who's best, nephew, you or our fighter, by here."

I got down off Dobie. "What are you up to, for God's sake?" and for answer he pushed up one of his comrades, who complained:

"Christ, Sam, he's your nephew?"

"Yes, so do 'im quick and 'ave done wi' it, Knocker," said Sam, adding confidentially to me, "He'll just bust ye beak, son—it's in the line o' business, so to speak—no offence intended. We want to see if you're made like your da."

"I'm obliged," I said.

"So we can enrol ye official, understand?"

"Enrol me?"

"That's it." He turned to his fighter, "Empty him and have done with it, Knocker, like I said, I'm starvin' for supper."

I weighed the man before me for size; with his bunched fists cocked up and his slits of eyes peering from a ring-battered face, he circled me flat-footed in the graceless stance of the old Mendoza.

"Come on, Knocker," shouted a man from the trees. "He's only a lad, ye know—don't take all day," and the fighter spat on his hands and said:

"God help me. It's the first time I ever served knuckle pie to a nip," and rushed.

I had a left in his eye when he swung at me and a right hook over his shoulder as he blinked: then side-stepped like my father had taught me, as he rushed again, blindly hitting air. But it couldn't last, of course. I knew that if he caught me with one of his swings I'd be waving goodbye with my boots. Over his crouching form I saw Dobie glance over his shoulder at the combat, so I circled the fighter again.

"Right, Dobie," I called, as I got him in range, and the old cob's hind legs shot out and caught the boxer square in his moleskins. Somersaulting past me, he hit the ground at the feet of Sam Williams, bawled unintelligibly, and lay still.

"Christ!" said someone as I went back to Dobie, who was now grazing like a spring lamb.

Sam Williams, holding his stomach, was bellowing laughter, and he spluttered, "Well done, Nephew!", and waved high his hat. "The workingman's union had need of your pa, and now has need of you. You've passed the test with flyin' colours."

"Thanks very much," I said.

"You got the job with the Guests, I hear, and spare time

hobnobbin' it with the daughter of Sir Richard de Vere! It couldn't work better." He slapped me on the back. "Bad cess if you let the grass grow under your feet!"

I thought, my God, who could you trust? and said, "What do you want of me?"

"The testing of ye, like now, for good strong brothers are needed for the fight. All good Welsh are in it, mind – your father, Skipper Rowlands, and the most unlikely people, like me. But you're in the hub of it." He flung wide his arms. "Dear God, it's more than we expected to have an ear in Dowlais House!"

"A spy? The Guests have been good to me."

"Good to ye? Christ!" He stared into my face. "What about the rest of the working population? If ye talk of Guest and his woman, then give me Crawshay! Have ye any idea at all about the larceny of profit, mun?"

"The Guests are more concerned with literature, talk sense!"

"Talk sense, is it? You cheeky young bugger! She's more concerned with chandelier Balls while folks are starvin'!" His face was white with anger. "Jesus, can't you smell the hypocrisy? She's tossing pennies into benevolent funds while children are caught in drop-hammers. She's touring the continent while cholera sends down three kids in five!"

He swung back to face me, his face furious. "Do you believe in the Sacrament, Roberts?"

"Aye."

"Then would ye believe that the Reverend Jones refused it to her ladyship, and that the Rector of Dowlais backed him?"

I didn't reply.

"Listen, lad," he breathed. "In the Bread or Blood riots of Merthyr Town, Sir John – the man you're working for – played an active part in selling out the workers. Guest and his missus, like the Crawshays, tipped up their noses when Dic Penderyn hanged, though Guest said he was innocent, mind you – and all turned their faces from the Swansea transportations." He paused, staring at me. "Did your pa ever make mention of a man called Gideon Davies?"

I held my tongue, not knowing what was involved.

"He's our leader, the Chartist organiser in the South. And the military have hold of him and are beating Hell out of him while we're standing here."

Men came up, pestering at his elbow, but old Sam shook them off, saying, "Gid's the only one among us with knowledge of the Chartist plans, and the Redcoats want them badly."

I asked, "And how can I help him, for God's sake?"

"If he talks it's the end of us, for Napier's Hell-bent on breakin' us before a shot is fired." A pulse in his forehead was beating violently. "So we're after springing him, understand? They've got him around here somewhere, probably up in Penywern, and they'll be movin' him to Brecon Barracks any time now. But, it's the date, ye see . . . ?"

"You want the date when he'll be moved."

"Ay ay, we need the date, the route they'll take to Brecon, the number of guards – and the sweet country will be in debt to ye, for if Gid talks it'll spill the blood of a thousand Welshmen."

"And if we get him out?" I asked.

"Then we'll shift him out o' the place. He's blind, did I mention – he's blind, ill, and he knows too much."

The forest glittered with stars and cold air; brandy snaps of cauldron light were playing red on the pine tops.

"Are ye on, son?"

I nodded. "I know Gideon Davies, the blind one, he is my father's friend. Say what you want of me."

Knocker, the mountain-fighter, was now on his feet again, walking unsteadily towards us, and Sam cried huskily:

"Away, Knocker, away!"

"Away ye'self, Sam Williams!" cried the man. "I'm downing that white-haired bastard and having the bones from his back."

"Ach, hop it," said Sam, "while you're still standin'. Amlwch sent us a good one. You were lucky, mun, you only fought the horse."

15

Summer came flying in over the Brecon Beacons and the brooks sprayed and shouted down to the valleys. The days were of blinding brightness, I remember, and Rhiannon and I walked on beds of autumn gold. Our trysts in Dolygaer forest were a delight to me and yet a treason of the mind, because I knew it could not continue.

Watch this for summer madness.

Galloping Dobie up the tracks from Tarn, I took him full pelt along the bridle path leading to the waterfalls, shouting aloud above his thundering hooves: and I saw, in a duck of overhanging branches, Penny, Rhiannon's mare, a statue against white, racing water.

Seeing me coming, Rhiannon dropped her riding-crop and flew towards me, one hand holding on her hat, the other hitching up her skirt: shouting and stumbling she came, and I leaped off Dobie and she staggered into my arms: flinging her down into leaves of patterned sunlight, I kissed her, and her hat fell off and her skirt went up, showing her white, silk pantaloons. Again and again I kissed her until we were gasping for breath and then we rolled down to the bank of the brook where I nearly ate her alive.

Personally, on reflection, I'll be glad when I'm past this ridiculous caper, for it puts years on you. For those early days of making love to Rhiannon de Vere were a physic of madness. I'm old now, my youth gone, but I'll always remember that year of hare-brained celebration, when the hills abounded with blossom, the brooks sang to the rocks and the earth flung up sweet perfumes. It was a passion of togetherness that put out the sun.

"Soon I'm telling them," cried Rhiannon, sitting up. "We can't go on like this!"

One moment a lady, next a village girl; this was her charm. Her lips moved over my face, my hair. I did not speak. It was enough just to lie like this in her warmth, and her breast was soft under my head. She said, leaning above me:

"I am, Tal, I'm telling them. What matter where you come from, or I? I'm shouting this love to the world."

I replied, "Yes, then I'll land in gaol and you in a French convent."

I held her against me. There was no sound on the forest air but the songs of blackbirds.

"I don't care. I'm telling them!" And she suddenly pushed herself up and stared down into my eyes.

"No," I said, turning away.

A silence came between us; even the blackbirds cocked up ears, I reckon.

"No, Rhia," I said, trying to sit up, but she pushed me back.

"Please, Tal . . . ?"

I fought the tumult, for there was a stiffness in my loins and great wish to be one with her, my body saying one thing and my good sense another.

Nothing that had happened to me before had been like this: no Siân Fi-Fi could invade this pure longing; there was a dryness in my throat and a forging of my loins in heat and strength, and Rhia knew of it.

"Please love me, Tal . . . please? Nobody will know."

Somewhere amid the tempest of our breathing I heard a twig snap and the echo died in my head without recognition. Footsteps crunching forest leaves I heard next above the cascading music of the falls, yet still did not heed the warning. Instead, I heard myself say faintly:

"No, Rhia . . . *no!*"

Her hands moved over me.

"*Tal!*"

I thought: I'm taking this one away: she is right, this can't continue. I'll take her to where only time and space exists, under the indifference of a foreign sky . . . somewhere away from class and convention I will take her.

I thought, too: it is my fault, this: I had ensnared her with the poetry of love; I had opened my heart to her, and now she had entered, I was rejecting her. Opening my eyes I stared at the tangleweed of branches above us, seeking escape in light shafts filtering down through the growing dusk: again I heard the approaching footsteps, and again rejected them.

"You all right, Miss de Vere?" asked Old Joe Hitherto, sod him, his boots two inches from my head.

Five feet up, worn with age and care, Old Joe drooped in his moleskin jacket before us, and thank God we were decent. With a pair of conies swinging at his belt, he stared down, then pulled off his cap, and grinned, exposing broken, yellow teeth.

"You restin', you two?" asked he. "I reckon you both look fair done up . . ."

Rhiannon came first to her senses and stood, brushing leaves from her skirt.

"Not resting, old Joe. We were making love – kissin' sweet – like Maypole dancing, you know? – Tal Roberts and me."

"*Rhia!*" I whispered.

"Dear me, that anna right, lady!" He wagged a disapproving finger. "You must 'ave made a mistake, I fancy. You be gentry, he be any ole boot leather."

But she bent closer, for him to get the sense of it, and whispered secretly, "Kissing, Joe, *real kissin'*. Tal Roberts is my chap, boot leather or not. You understand?"

"Well, damn my backside," said Old Joe, scratching it, and stared from one to the other of us.

"Rhia, for God's sake . . . !"

She replied, cool. "Best they know, and the sooner the better. You see, Mr. Hitherto . . ." and she gave him village girl talk so that he would understand the better, "I fancy I'm marryin' ole Tal Roberts, an' going to live wi' him in the ostlers' loft, him on the horses, me doin' the hens."

"*Dammo di,*" whispered Joe, and got going.

I said, "What's wrong with you, for God's sake? Are you mad?"

"Saner than you." She picked up her crop and swung herself side-saddle on the mare, smiling down.

"Maybe you're not havin' me, chap, but I'm havin' you. I anna milking babies on the wrong side o' the blanket."

I stood watching as the mare picked a path through the forest.

Ostling nags being a thirsty old business, I used to polish a pint or so some nights down the Vulcan and Friendship in Market Square and listen to the political speeches, like hanging Queen Victoria and bombs under Parliament, all Members present. And I was just killing a quart one dusk when Fanny, our new maid in Dowlais House, came rushing into the tap, telling me I was wanted up there right away.

"Who by?" I asked.

"Her ladyship," said she, screwing up her pinny, and it is astonishing to me how a pair of trousers and a wink have an effect upon them. Lavish in the buttocks, smelling of lavender was Fanny, and blushing red. She added:

"Brainy it do look, mind – Welsh bards and a Justice of the Peace – rather you than me, Tal Roberts."

In the hall of the big house Maria, aged four, came up with Ivor and Katherine in the pram, and I kissed them one by one, Maria being the image of Lady Charlotte.

"Roberts 'as come, your ladyship," announced Fanny, and pushed me in.

Entering the large, ornate drawing-room with its chandeliers and palms, I bowed to three gentlemen sitting before me, and Lady Charlotte said:

"Roberts, this is Mr. Justice Bosanquet, the Reverend John Jones, Fellow of Jesus College, and the Reverend Thomas Price."

Stiff as ramrods they sat, the Judge in the middle.

Mr. Jones I had seen before, the Oxford don famous for his Welsh scholarship, whose bardic name was Tegid: for this man my father had shown the greatest respect. The Judge raised his paunched, sallow face to mine.

But a few years back, at the trial of the Merthyr rioters, this one had sentenced an innocent Dic Penderyn to die, and I reckon he had an eye for a Welsh patriot. Over his shoulder I noticed Sir John Guest and Clark, his agent, poring over books, disinterested.

"You would like to sit, Taliesin?" Milady sometimes called me this.

"Rather stand, Ma'am."

She spread wide her black gown, smiling up at me. "I expect you're wondering why I've sent for you? To learn more of the 'Tale of Delwyn' – does this surprise you?" She warmed to me. "Remember we once discussed it?"

I nodded.

"Tegid and Mr. Price are my Welsh teachers, and naturally interested."

The two bards gave me kindly nods: Justice Bosanquet was staring at me like a ferret at prey. Standing there in my moleskin trews and muddy boots I felt insecure and unequal, and was dying to be away. But more, there was an inexplicable knowledge growing within me . . . that my destiny was linked with the magistrate. Lady Charlotte continued:

"We are planning to publish an English translation of the *Mabinogi* and other stories from the Red Book of Hergest – you know of this, of course."

I nodded.

"These gentlemen will translate it, and I will help – I'm still receiving Welsh lessons, as you know – but we will have a beautiful production. Now, Tal, Mr. Jones here thinks that you are confusing your 'Tale of Delwyn' with the 'History of Taliesin' . . ."

Mr. Price, the younger of the bards, smiled at me. "It's a reasonable mistake; Taliesin meaning Radiant Brow, Delwyn meaning Fair Brow."

"Oh no, Sir," I answered. "They are quite different manuscripts."

"And from where have you heard of such a manuscript? A modern tale, you mean?" The Judge asked this, his manner bored.

"No, Sir. Fourteenth-century."

"Come, lad, don't be ridiculous!" He clapped his hands together in disbelief. "You are close to the era of the *Mabinogi*. Had there been such a manuscript we would know of it!"

I said, "It exists. My father owns it."

It sat them up. Even John Guest and his agent raised their heads, and the former said sardonically, "A few more years, my love, and this one will give performances – like your French scholar Vicomte de la Villemarqué; he also makes up that which he does not know."

But his wife didn't appear to hear this. Staring at me, she said softly, "Your father possesses a fourteenth-century manuscript?"

"Yes, Milady."

"You have seen it?"

"Oh yes."

"How came he by it?"

"It was handed down through our family."

"It is in modern writing – a transcript, you mean?"

"No. It is in the original Celtic script."

Bosanquet rose to his feet. "I do not believe this. Like Villemarqué's *Chevalier au Lion* it will be a copy, and of some modern yarn, I vow. How would we not possibly know of it?" He swung to John Jones. "What say you to this nonsense, Tegid?"

The clergyman was deep in thought. "It is possible."

"But highly improbable," added Mr. Price.

They were momentarily silenced. Beyond the window that faced the Works a furnace was going into blast: pygmy workers danced against a pulsating redness as the bungs were poured: the sudden beating of drop-hammers forbade coherent thought: Sir John was first to speak. "It becomes astonishing, gentlemen, when we have to approach the lower orders of the Welsh *Literati* to discover original manuscripts. Take my tip and send him back to grooming."

Bosanquet added, picking up his hat and stick, "Like the *Mabinogi* itself, I suggest, there's a happy application of wishful thinking in all this." With mock servility he bowed, adding to me, "I take it that we can see this mysterious document?"

"Perhaps," I replied. "I do not know."

"He does not know," the magistrate repeated, and turned to go. "It is in your father's possession, you said?"

"Yes, Sir."

"And where is your father now?"

I took a breath. "In Van Diemen's Land."

All but Bosanquet appeared shocked; he asked, "Where your father at present resides, I assume?" A small, cynical smile was playing on his thin mouth.

I nodded.

"He emigrated?" asked Mr. Clark, the agent. "You . . . you mean that he has obtained a post in Australia?"

I didn't reply immediately and the Judge smoothed his foot on the carpet, saying quietly, "You'd be wise to look a little deeper into this, Sir John . . ."

"You mean he was transported, don't you?" said Lady Charlotte.

"Yes, Ma'am."

"For what crime?"

"For stealing candles."

"Really, and for how long?"

"Seven years." I added. "I have since heard that he has died."

"How many candles, for God's sake?" asked Mr. Clark.

"About two pounds."

They looked at one another. Justice Bosanquet said blandly, "For stealing a couple of pounds of candles he is transported for seven years to the Colonies, taking with him a fourteenth-century manuscript! We are now in the realms of airy nonsense!"

John Jones rose to his feet. "No wait – this is of literary importance and I want some answers."

"So do I," said Bosanquet, and the clergyman turned to me.

"The reason why your father went to Van Diemen's Land is immaterial to me. But this . . . this fourteenth-century manuscript – he took it with him?"

"I believe so, it was not among the things he left behind."

"And this . . . this 'Tale of Delwyn' – do you know it in detail?"

"Oh yes," I said. "My father often read it to us."

"Will you tell it to us now?" asked Lady Charlotte.

"If you wish."

Reluctantly, the Judge resumed his seat: the other five sat on the scarlet-cushioned chairs, staring up at me. I will always remember them sitting there, waiting in a sort of resignation to a coming disbelief.

"Please sit, Taliesin," said Lady Charlotte.

I shook my head, and began:

"Once, long ago, in the castle of Deganwy, Maelgŵn, King of Gwynedd, held a banquet. And while his guests tore venison and swilled it down with mead, one of his bards, after extolling the greatness of his king, told this story, which is the 'Tale of Delwyn'."

My mind reached back to the winter fires of Three Costog: I heard again my father's voice and saw his eyes shadowed in the lamplight.

I continued, "When Maelgŵn was crowned, said this bard, the gods tested him, sending across the Irish Sea waves of Goidels to ravage Gwynedd. But Maelgŵn sent a billow of fire and the sands were littered with charred corpses: only twelve Goidels remained alive, and the king, being merciful, set these free, first cutting out their tongues that they should not corrupt the Celtic speech."

Lady Charlotte gasped, and I said:

"But all this was untrue; the bard was lying. Maelgŵn, of Roman blood, was a despot, and the true Welsh beyond his borders were planning his downfall: the chief plotter was one, Prince Arfon, and Maelgŵn, seizing him, imprisoned him without food in a dungeon after blinding him under torture to reveal the names of his accomplices. Prince Arfon would have died had not bees, hiving near, swarmed through his prison bars and fed him with their honey."

The furnaces simmered beyond the windows; red light glowed within the room. I said:

"Now, among the leaders of the prince's followers were

the bard White Mountain and Delwyn, his son, who was white-haired at birth, hence his name. Travelling to Deganwy, Delwyn entered the court of King Maelgŵn and obtained his favour, for the king had an eye for a pretty youth, as had Marged, his sister, who, seeing Delwyn enter as a page, immediately fell in love with him.

"Because of his white hair the Princess Marged called him *'Fy Machgen Gwyn'*, and the two became lovers."

Fanny entered, bringing tea; nobody served it. I said: "As a spy within Maelgŵn's court, Delwyn learned of Prince Arfon's removal to Deganwy town for public execution, and he and his father and other patriots rescued him from his captors and brought him back to his own people; even Princess Marged helped to secure his release.

"Then the bards, once men of peace and now led by White Mountain, attacked the kingdom of Maelgŵn, to bring it down and restore to Gwynedd the rule of justice, but the rebellion failed. The bards were routed and White Mountain killed: and Delwyn was brought before King Maelgŵn who smote him with an axe, disfiguring him and banishing him to a foreign land for twenty years."

There was a long silence, then Lady Charlotte said, "It is a sad and terrible story. What of the Princess Marged?"

I replied, "To expiate her brother's cruelty she fled to a lowly place, there to work among the villagers, who were suffering from the Yellow Pestilence."

"And her end?" asked Mr. Price.

"She caught the plague, and died. But first gave birth to Delwyn's daughter."

Mr. Jones observed, quietly, "It is a good story and it rings of the truth, were it not for its contrived ending." He stared with large, serious eyes at the window.

"Your opinion?" asked Lady Charlotte of Mr. Price, whose bardic name was Carnhuanawc: he shrugged. "It is typical of the period, bloodthirsty and dramatic, but I doubt its authenticity."

Justice Bosanquet reached again for his hat and stick. "For my part I'd heard enough halfway through it. White-haired boy; it appeared to me that you might have been foretelling your own fate. I am much more interested in the identity of your father's crime. Meanwhile, you should not be employed by the gentle people of this house."

Lady Charlotte waved a dismissive hand.

The long-pay furnace men were coming off day-shift as I left Dowlais stables that dusk – the red-eyed ballers, puddlers and rodders who ran their own furnaces and did their own accounts; more, they employed their own labour. If these dropped tools the Dowlais production stopped. Crawshay and Guest were in constant competition for world markets, but also for men like these, and the workers knew it.

Things were becoming skinny in the iron trade about now, and with the lease of Dowlais running out, talk had it that there was trouble between John Guest and Lady Charlotte. I'd heard rumours, but discounted them, that he had cut her out of his Will, and the speculation in Town was why? So many of these specialist tradesmen were leaving Merthyr for Rhymney, where employment seemed more secure. Jake Kilrain, the six-foot seven-inch puddler was one of these, and he gave me a wink as he passed me down High: behind him mooched his labourer, Knocker, who was fighting twenty rounds that night with Borer Deal over in Pontypridd, and was due for a shellacking if he didn't keep off the gin.

"Hey, Tal – old Sam wants you!" he shouted.

"What for? I'm just off out."

The men pushed and shoved along the pavement, their iron-tipped boots clattering; shouting their banter up at the windows where buxom wives leaned out, and getting as good as they got. Children came running down the streets to greet them. Knocker said:

"It's important, son, get going. The Guests won't thank ye for tuning up their gentry virgins, ye know, they keep their pigs in styes. Good news, lad – you'll be better off with Sam – and take that apology of a horse, for ye'll need him."

I gripped his arm. "Good news?"

"You'll find Sam waiting in the yard of The Welsh Oak, and for God's sake don't mention that he's found your blood relation." His battered face puckered up into a smile.

"Who?" I got him by the coat and shook him to rattle. "Who, Knocker?"

"If I tell ye that, son, you'll be as wise as me," and he shook me off. "Meanwhile, if she asks ye to the Ball, send me an invitation?"

The stars were big over Dowlais Top as I wheeled old Dobie over Market Square and trotted him up Charlotte Street to the Oak. Sam was there astride his old Welsh cob, once a barge horse. I cried:

"Knocker said you've found one of my relatives!"

"Bide yersel', wee Tal." He reined up and trotted off, me after him.

"Sam, please! Who?"

"Jesus, mun, would ye have me spill it all over Town? That Knocker's got too much jaw, and the chances are young Borer Deal, the English Terror, will ease it for him."

"Poll, do you mean?"

"Learn to wait and cure impatience. Grief, you're a hot-blood!"

"My father, then?" I was desperate to know.

"Now, how in Hell can your pa rise from the grave in Australia?"

I sat there fuming. "You're a wicked old sod," I said.

"That's putting it mildly," said Sam.

Here, approaching Llangynidr Mountain the land was like the lunar country of the stars, and Sam knew the sheep tracks like the veins in his arm, leading us over broad escarpments and down defiles. Heather abounded, and hunchback trees crippled by the winter gales: nothing moved save the occasional scampering of hares and rabbits, but fierce things were shrieking in the dark, right music for a funeral cortège.

I think I knew where Sam was taking me; whispers had it that renegades and wanted men were hidden in these parts. The moon came out, resplendent and full, lighting the dull forbidding panorama.

"I'm takin' ye to your father, me son. Now then, what d'ye think o' that? Rose from the grave in Van Diemen's Land!"

I reached out and caught his bridle, pulling us to a stop.

"Dada? You're mad!"

"Unless it's a mistake, but I doubt it. The age of miracles, young Tal, is not past – come shake off."

Reaching a cave entrance, one half-submerged in earth and shadow, Sam halted as a sentry came out of the ground like a black apparition; I heard the click of a musket cock.

"Who's there?"

"Sam Williams, and the Roberts lad," whispered Sam.

"Down off those nags, the lads'll take them," and we followed the sentry down an incline into the cave entrance. Here was a light-lock, because, although I could hear distant voices, no light emerged. The man dropped to all fours and called down a hole, "Ifor, are ye on?"

"Aye, Shanco!" came a faint reply.

"Throw the rope in, I'll send the lad first, and there's an old 'un coming after. He'll need a tie in case he gets stuck."

Three men were now standing about us, their features distorted in a faint, wavering light; then a rope snaked from nowhere and struck my legs. The sentry said, "Now listen, you – ceiling to floor is thirteen inches high – are ye a collier?"

"No," I replied.

"Then ye aren't going to like it. Lead with ye arm and the boys'll pull you through, and if the roof grips your arse, don't panic. If you panic and fight it you'll swell, understand?"

I nodded and went full length: my eyes, growing more accustomed to the intense darkness, were fixed upon a distant faint glow of light. As I inched forward I heard the sentry say, "And you anna going at all, old man; we've had younger than you die in there."

"You try and bloody stop me," said Sam.

The men behind me chuckled gutturally: the hole, over three feet wide, gripped my buttocks as I squirmed forward; momentarily stuck, I held my breath, and then a hand gripped my wrist and hauled me through into a cave of blazing light. On my knees I looked about me, shading my eyes, and my father came forward from a group of men and took me into his arms. Unspeaking, he just held me, then said softly:

"No, Tal, no – men are watching."

He was older: the months of his absence had stripped him of his fine presence; he was somehow diminished, his features gaunt, his cheeks haggard. But his eyes still shone with the old substantial fire. Nor had his strength deserted him, though his rags of clothing drooped, and his wrists and ankles, I noticed, were still chafed raw by the manacles and leg irons.

Many men were there, standing in respectful silence or talking together in an air of disassociation.

"But how long have you been here?" I gasped eventually.

"Only a week – I got word to Sam as soon as I could. How's Meg, and Poll?"

Sam, easing through the light-lock, got to his feet and said, "Meg's with us, Gwyn – your Poll's doin' fine – aye, fine – got housework down Pen-y-darren." They spoke more but I did not hear them: the knowledge that he was safe swept over me in waves of intensity. I cried, "But how, Dada, how?"

He told me that he had never been shipped to Van Diemen's Land: of how, after months in Beaumaris, he had escaped along the road to the Swansea Bridewell, where he was to await the prison ship: the Redcoat guard, he said, had been attacked and overwhelmed by Top Town unionists and they had pulled him out of the prisoners' cart and smuggled him up and into the Rhondda through Pontypridd; there, in hiding, they had brought in a blacksmith to strike off his fetters – he and five others, one a woman, he said – and then walked them by night over the hills and into the caves of Llangattock: two days there, and then to Mynydd Llangynidr.

Behind my father, as he talked, I saw a dozen or so men sitting at tables in the cavern; stripped to the belts, they were silently working; balling shot, pouching black powder: two more, a little distance off, were machining pistol barrels – gunsmiths – North-country men by their speech, brought down for the trades. Sam interjected:

"Christ, if Brecon Barracks comes in here they'll swing the lot of us – is there any other way out?"

"Several," said Dada, "providing you know where." He asked me:

"Are you working in Merthyr, Tal?"

I explained about the ostling.

"And he's not mixed up with this lot, Sam?" he asked next.

There was a silence. My father said, "So he is, eh? Sam, where's the sense in it? I've no woman – one for the rebellion, the other for work – that's the rule – or the rest of the family starves . . ." he stared at us, one to the other. Sam said:

"Ach, come, Gwyn, see sense! Did ye expect the boy to sit on his arse when his father's gone to transportation? He told me what Gideon said, and Gid was right."

"And Gideon's been taken now, they tell me."

"Aye, poor Gid – these months back. They say he's up in Penywern, but I've got me doubts. One thing's sure, they'll be hitting lumps off of him." Sam added, "He left for the Forest of Dean and the English picked him up on the road."

A black-maned giant with a fist like a ham came up and barged between us, saying, "Ay ay, perish the privileged orders, death to the bloody aristocracy. Now will you lot put a pin in the arse and let's get back to work?"

"Who the Hell are you?" whispered Sam, pushing Dada aside.

"I'm the foreman of this lot and it isn't a vicarage tea-party – out, old man, and take the lad with ye!" and Sam cried:

"And may I ask who ye think you're talking to?" He jerked a thumb at Dada. "You might be foreman o' this bloody stye, but you're standin' in the presence of the North-ern representative – this is Gwyn Roberts, mun, next in line to Gideon Davies."

"If he don't bloody say, I don't bloody know, do I?" The big man nodded at my father. "You should talk more, Mr. Roberts. I'll fetch ye some decent clothes."

"It's the autocracy of the working classes," said Sam, and gripped my shoulder. "I'll send ye the time and place so you can chair the next meeting, Gwyn. Come on, you," and he turned me. "Are we hanging around here all day?"

My father did a strange thing then; he kissed me.

The night wind was cold on my face. I was glad it was raining.

We hadn't got twenty yards on the horses when a voice called:

"Iestyn! Hurry, they're leaving . . .!"

Sam reined in his cob as we heard running footsteps in the heather, and there came from the dark a young man; broad and tall was he, and in the rain his hair was comically tufted. "Are you happening down Nantylgo way?" he asked Sam.

"We're not, we are Dowlais," replied Sam, regarding him. And then he saw the envelope clutched in the young man's hand. "But, if it's a letter for a dearly beloved, we'll get it through – runners are comin' and going, ye see."

He took the letter and put it in his pocket. The young man said, "Give it to my sister, Morfydd Mortymer, she's with my wife and my mam in the Bailey Houses down Furnace Row – but don't say where it comes from, mind."

"Leave it to us, son," said Sam, and we rode away without a backward look.

But on a ridge I reined in Dobie and glanced back.

The young man was still standing there, watching us in the rain.

The afternoon I had off was cold, as if autumn had blown an arctic breath over the mountains, and amazingly, the hills of Dowlais Top were white and beautiful in the mornings like Church of England brides.

I sat on Dobie in the cobwebbed whiteness of Dolygaer, waiting, and he raised his head and neighed, seeing Rhiannon coming on her mare against brilliant light; the sun had melted the morning frosts.

My excitement increased when I saw her coming and I was dying to tell her that my father was safe, but dared not. Side-saddle, she joined me and we rode side by side, unspeaking in an affinity of silence. But after a bit, she said:

"You're lost to me. What's wrong?"

I was thinking of Dada, but said, "I was wondering if you'd be going to the Dowlais House Ball tonight."

"Of course. Would you turn up if I got you an invitation?"

"Not my line, going to parties."

"Good grief, Tal, you're an old stick in the mud. I suppose you don't approve of gallivanting."

I shrugged. "The Rector of Dowlais doesn't – at least, not the parties Lady Charlotte gives."

"That's because he's an old God-botherer. Mary Pegus doesn't worry about him, either, so we'll be going together."

"When did she arrive?"

"Yesterday afternoon, from Uffington; the rest of her family are coming tomorrow." Her mood was suddenly frizzed and her chin went up and she was pert with me. Dobie was making up to her mare and doing a damn sight better than I was. Rhiannon said, "You can be a stuck up old thing, you know, Tal Roberts. It's a sort of inverted snobbery, you realise that?"

"There's no snobs like those in the working class, mind."

"Now you're being impossible."

"Anyway," I added, "you won't lack for company. You can have the pick of the Brecon infantry and the yeoman farmers."

"I'll give it thought," said she. "What's wrong with you? You've been as dull as an old turnip ever since I arrived."

My mood was vacillating between despair for the future and joy for the present. More than ever before, now my father was in the fight again, I was hopelessly committed, and the love affair with Rhiannon was complicating all my plans. I wondered how she would accept it when the time came to leave her; when the decision had to be made to cut myself off, and I cursed my ineptitude for getting myself into an impossible predicament: in many ways I was beginning to hope that our love would be officially discovered . . . an automatic end to it before her outraged father.

God knows what would happen to us, I thought, if Rhiannon had a baby.

"Aren't we speaking now, then?" she asked.

"Sorry."

She said softly, "I reckon you're getting tired of me . . ."

"God, no!" I reached out and she gripped my hand, her mood changing at the touch; in all but size she was bigger than me.

Now she said, "You're sure, Tal Roberts – quite sure?"

I might have known; her eyes were sparkling; sin and mischief were in her face. Half out of the saddle, leaning down, I kissed her.

"Then take me to the shooting lodge," said she.

I shivered. "It's too damned cold, and you know it!"

"It won't be so cold making love." She made a begging face.

I said, "Honestly, Rhiannon, you're worse than me – you'll get us bloody hung."

"Don't swear, please don't swear."

"But we can't go on like this, it's dangerous." And Dobie looked over his shoulder at me as if I was light in the head.

"Dangerous?"

"Look, love, what if you have a child?"

"Your baby? Oh Tal, Tal!" She closed her eyes and turned up her face in expressive delight.

"Be serious, for God's sake – people are talking . . ."

"Talking?" She was instantly aware, and intent. "Who's talking?"

"Oh come, it's all over Dowlais, and you know it!"

She reined in her horse, suddenly angry. "If it is, I've heard nothing. And anyway, who cares? I don't, because I love you."

"Rhiannon, come on, come on – we've got to face it. We just can't carry on like this."

Her eyes were suddenly bright. We were still now, the horses grazing. "You don't want me, do you?" she said softly.

"I want you and I love you, *cariad*, but we simply cannot carry on in this way. What kind of a chap would I be if I let people tittle-tattle, but how can I deny it?"

"Who's tittle-tattling?"

I shrugged, empty. "Oh, in the pubs – down the Vulcan and Friendship, for a start." I raised my face to hers.

"You talk about me in that dirty old place?"

I retorted, "Now be fair. I didn't say I talked about you. I'm only saying that it's common knowledge."

"And you want to put an end to it, is that it?"

"I didn't say that, either. Just that I think we should be more careful."

"O aye?" She was taking me off. "And that's the difference between us, isn't it? I don't care, and you do – when lovers start being careful they're falling out of love. Oh God," and she wept.

I was off the horse in seconds and lifted her down into my arms; once I'd got her I tried to lever her off because she was bringing me into a sweat. I wanted to talk calmly and reasonably, but it had become emotional, as I'd expected.

"Let's go away, Tal!" Suddenly she held me away, her

eyes searching mine. "Nobody would know – we'd just go. We're both old enough to know our own minds, and . . ."

"They'd bring us back, Rhiannon."

I saw beyond the smooth, sharp curve of her cheek the radiance of the forest; sun-shafts, beaming through the elms, made sovereigns of gold on the leaves of past autumns; wild strawberry and tamarisk, growing in profusion among the tree roots; the wind moved between us bringing scents of the forest and threats of greater cold from the distant mountains.

"No hope for us, is there?" said Rhiannon, flat, and I kissed her, whispering:

"There's every hope. Just that we've got to be cool about it, darling. If anything went wrong, what would we do for money?"

"I've got money."

"Oh, Rhiannon, won't you try to understand?"

She was smiling in tears, as women do, looking up into my face.

"I'll try – if you take me to Old Joe's shooting lodge . . ."

I said, "You just don't care about anything, do you?"

She shook her head. "No, I don't. I told you before – I love you. And I don't care about anything else. *Please?*"

Earlier, I'd heard the rustle of branches; earlier still the clattering panic of disturbed birds, and had buried my fears in Rhiannon's kisses. But now I heard the heavy breathing of a horse and its dull, thumping hoof-beats, and raised my head.

To my astonishment, Lady Charlotte was sitting on her big black horse no more than twenty yards away: seeing us, she approached slowly, reining in: Rhiannon, feeling me tense, turned.

"Good afternoon, Milady," said she, and bobbed a curt-sey.

It was as if she had known of her presence all the time. The lady said, her face frozen:

"Good afternoon, Rhiannon, I thought I'd find you here. I'll see you in Dowlais House within the hour. Do you think you might manage that?" and the look she sent withered us. Then she spurred the horse and trotted away.

We stood together, Rhiannon and I, hand in hand. She said, "All right, so it's out officially – why look so glum? We love each other and it's time the whole world knew – her included."

"But your father . . . ?"

"And him."

I said, "They'll skin us alive."

"All right, so they'll skin us – but not in the next half hour," and her arms went about me hard and strong.

We hadn't got time to go to the shooting lodge, but when it comes to what happened next there's not a lot to choose between the workers and the aristocracy.

The gourmets of the county didn't go short at a Dowlais Ball; Sir John and Lady Charlotte competed with the Crawshays for splendour when it came to entertainment: they dined off lamb and pheasants' tongues, boar's head and pork rumps, venison, stuffed quails and beef and honeyed hams, and washed this down with port, sherry, champagne and the finest wines mulled and spiced with cinnamon.

And while the Guests vied with Crawshay at table, Maisie Lumpkin reckoned she could make a sheep's head (a penny a time at the back door of the Shambles) do for six. People like us, said Maisie, have an expectation of life of twenty years, and four years less when the cholera comes to town: the disease that could have been prevented had our employers spent a thousand pounds on providing more water than they stole for the Works.

I couldn't settle that night after Rhiannon and I had been caught, and was stupidly jealous that, at the Ball that night, she'd be in another man's arms when she belonged to me. So I found myself wandering around Town: I mooched along High Street towards Pen-y-darren.

Ill-clad children were playing outside their doors, their bare feet stained with the excrement that flooded down the gully-ways: ancient faces peered down from upper windows, a long-since discarded human slag. The slums, row after row of decaying houses, put up in John Guest's early time, had become a sink-pit of deprivation and despair. These children, I reflected, as Maisie had said, would be lucky to reach the age of sixteen while Guest's sons and daughters lived in luxury. Long, long before these privileged few reached adolescence, those I saw now would suffer lientery, small-pox, typhus or consumption; many would die of scrofula and the general wasting of acute malnutrition. On that walk through Dowlais and Pen-y-darren that night I saw the full horror to which these ironmasters had condemned the earners of their fortunes.

Returning to Dowlais House I heard the music of the Ball, so after bedding old Dobie down for the night, I wandered round to the front of the house and stood in the shadows of the bushes beyond the wide lawn, hoping for a sight of Rhiannon through the windows.

All the young bloods of the county must have been there that night, for a legion of horses and traps were waiting; stallions, too, with all the trappings of the Brecon military. Tables lining the walls, white-clothed, were laden with the food and wine; beneath the chandeliers were people I recog-nised – the Vicomte de la Villemarqué, glass in hand, was amiably chatting to Thomas Price, one of Lady Charlotte's *Mabinogi* translators: Mr. Justice Bosanquet was there, Stephens, the Dowlais engineer and John Evans, his mana-ger: Henry Bruce, the magistrate, I saw talking avidly with Mrs. Wyndham Lewis, the friend of Disraeli; William Crawshay was sitting by the window, removed from the others, apparently contemplating the scene before him.

The majority present, however, were not industrialists but the young and dashing former yeomanry, the part-time de-fenders of aristocratic privilege, as my father once described them – ready to gallop their sabres to the nearest workers' disorder: and upon their uniformed arms danced the gowned beauties of Glamorgan.

It was then, at the height of the music, that Rhiannon, hands clasped, moved into the light. And then, as I peered from my hiding-place, she deliberately went to the french doors and stared out on to the garden in my direction.

It was as if she had been called by some unspoken tryst. Had I moved, she would surely have seen me; never have I felt more at one with her; never have I known such a longing for her presence.

"Rhiannon . . ." My lips formed her name.

Motionless, she stood in a long white dress that reached to the floor: upon her head a little tiara flashed its jewels, enhancing her dark, spectacular beauty. I wanted to race across the lawn, fling wide the doors, and take her into my arms.

Suddenly, to my amazement, she opened the doors, closed them carefully behind her and stepped out on to the gravel path. Nobody appeared to notice her departure and I found myself standing on the edge of the lawn.

"Tal!" She called to me as if assured that I would be waiting, and I ran from the shadows and into the light. "Tal, are you there?"

We met in the middle of the lawn, a senseless, stupid act born of desperation; in the light, in such a place, scores in the room could have seen us. Now she was in my arms and I kissed her lips, her face, her hair: but hours before I had actually possessed her; the act had enhanced the magnetism of her presence, not diminished it.

"Oh God," she whispered. "Tal, Tal . . ."

That we would be seen was inevitable. Had we planned it, it could not have been more absolute. The tall figure of Sir John was striding over the lawn towards us: behind him I saw the open door of the crowded room; a group of stilled guests were looking in our direction.

"Rhiannon!"

We were standing hand in hand when Guest reached us. He said:

"Twice now. This is becoming a habit." He touched Rhiannon's arm. "Your parents are looking for you – return to the house." He jerked his head at me. "You – go to the library – I want a word with you. Such behaviour; I'm outraged and appalled."

Rhiannon smiled at me, and said over her shoulder as she went, "I love you, Tal. Don't look so glum! Everything will be all right now, it's far better that everybody knows."

*

As instructed, I went to the library, going through the back door of the house.

The room was wraithlike, ghostly with its great shelves of gilt-edged books; there came to me both the scent of perfume and the odorous tang of decaying paper. Nothing moved. Faintly, I heard the music of the ball, a chinking of glasses, the indeterminate mumbling of voices.

And then another voice made words behind me, and I turned to a man's soft laughter and a woman's soprano protest.

A red velvet curtain moved almost imperceptibly behind me.

I realised that I was trapped, an unwilling eavesdropper.

"Come on, Karen, who is to know . . . ?" said a voice.

"Darling, be reasonable! This is Sir John's library – anybody might come!"

"We've never been caught before, my poppet!"

"But here, dearest, of all places . . . ? Look – I could have sworn I heard footsteps a minute back . . ."

"Somebody passing in the hall . . ."

"Honestly, Johnny, your regiment could come in here and you'd not hear it. *Please* . . . ?"

"Right, when?"

The girl said, hesitantly, "I . . . I could meet you at the inn next Wednesday?"

"God, that's nearly a week!"

"I know. But Jules is taking me on the circuit tomorrow, and I won't be back till Wednesday next."

"On circuit with a judge! And I'm on leave!" He cursed effectively. "Anyway, I'm escorting a prisoner from the police station on Wednesday. Damn these Chartists!"

The girl said, apprehensively, "Is there going to be trouble?"

"There will be if we don't see to this one, he's important. Oh, come on! If I have to go to Brecon as escort commander I won't be back for a month – be a sport, get them off."

I heard the swift inrush of their breathing, the rustling of a dress. The girl whispered, "No, Johnny, oh *no*! This is Lady Charlotte's house . . ." she broke off, and I heard her add, in panic, "*Listen!*"

Footsteps had echoed in the hall. Then the library door came open and Sir John Guest came in, slamming it behind him. Confronting me, he asked in anger:

"For heaven's sake! What's wrong with the pair of you? What are you trying to achieve?"

From behind the curtain I heard more pent breathing. It astonished me that Sir John hadn't heard it, too. He continued, "It's disgraceful! Needless to say, Rhiannon's father is furious, and I feel responsible. His daughter and a groom! For God's sake, how long has it been going on?"

I didn't reply, and he added, "You'll have to go, of course. Frankly, I blame Rhiannon more than you, but you can't stay here now."

He was clearly trying to hold on to his sense of outrage; I liked him better.

"Milady saw you in Dolygaer woods only this afternoon. How far has this gone, Roberts?"

I said, "I'm sorry."

"You will be if Sir Richard gets his hands on you, so you'd best clear out as soon as you can." He hesitated, adding, "Not . . . not necessarily out of my employ – Lady Charlotte doesn't want this – but certainly out of Dowlais House." He was now plainly conciliatory, and I wondered why. "I . . . I'm told that Old Shenks, our tally-man down at Pont-Storehouse, is getting past it. Until you find somewhere else to work, you can share his night-shifts and his pay."

Sir John glanced at his watch. "But before you go there's another matter which Mr. Justice Bosanquet wishes to deal with. Wait." He pulled a bell-cord.

Fanny the parlourmaid entered.

"Give Mr. Justice Bosanquet my compliments, Fanny, and ask him to spare me a moment in the library."

Fanny made big eyes at me, bobbed a curtsey, and went out.

Sir John said, "It is about your father, Roberts. All in all, you're becoming a little intriguing. You'd be advised to answer his questions truthfully and accurately or you'll find yourself in even deeper trouble."

The curtains beside me moved almost imperceptibly; vaguely I wondered what would be the scene if they were pulled; the humour of it touched me, despite the situation.

Within minutes the Judge came, seated himself on a chaise longue and fixed me with his small, sharp eyes.

"You remember me, Roberts?"

"Yes, Sir."

"I'll come to the point. You'll recall, at our last meeting, that you said your father was dead?"

"Yes."

"And that he died in Van Diemen's Land?"

I nodded, my mind desperately searching for answers.

"How came you by this knowledge?"

I said, carefully, "A convict, returning to Amlwch from Australia, said he had seen his grave." This lie was all I could think of.

"Where in Australia?" He was persistent.

"In the Macquarie Penal Settlement."

He and Sir John exchanged glances. "I see. The name Gwyn Roberts – your father's name – is not an uncommon one, you'd agree?"

"Yes."

"Therefore, there's a possibility that the grave the convict saw was not your father's?"

"It's possible."

They were both watching me carefully, I noticed; then the magistrate said, "You tell us that your father was transported for stealing candles – to the value of eightpence."

"Yes, Sir."

His small face peered up. "Seven years in a penal settlement for a couple of pounds of candles? You consider that just?"

"It was unjust."

He nodded kindly. "Unless, of course, there was a greater crime involved – treason, say?"

"Had there been I would have known of it."

"No, not necessarily. For reasons of national security the law sometimes leans on a minor indictment, suppressing the real reason for a heavier sentence."

"I do not understand what you mean."

"I have an idea that you do, Roberts." He smiled. "I am suggesting that your father was transported, not for the theft of candles at all, but for being the Northern representative of these damned Chartists."

Sir John interjected, "Is that indictable? Merthyr's full of Chartists."

"But moral force members, not the advocates of physical violence, or we would put them behind bars." He turned his attention to me again. "What say you to this, Roberts – that your father, while working as a refiner under Mr. Edwards at the Amlwch Smelter – was involved in organising a revolutionary lodge in Anglesey and bringing in arms that would put its violent aims into practice?"

I did not reply to this.

"You heard what I said?"

"Yes."

"Have you no comment?"

I answered, "If that was so, I'd have known about that, too."

"Yet one other person in your family knew of your father's political activities, did she not? I refer to the cousin your father brought into the house after your mother's death."

I prayed for outward calm; within, I was sick at heart and frightened. Clearly, the man before me had unravelled every fact of my father's movements in the North. Soon he would confront me less subtly with the fact – that Dada had never sailed for Van Diemen's Land, that he had been free since his escape. It was like an intricate stage-play that was slowly unfolding my fate: soon, I thought, a bell will ring for another act and I will be confronted with inescapable facts which could only be countered by bare-faced lying, and I was no good at lying. Bosanquet said, quietly, "You knew of his political plans in the North?"

I shook my head.

"And you know, too, that your father never sailed for Australia, don't you – that he escaped on his way to Swansea Bridewell."

I enclosed my eyes to escape the intensity of their stares.

Bosanquet's eyes were almost hypnotic beneath their bushy brows. He cried, "You know that, don't you?"

"I did not know."

"Indeed, your father has been in contact with you, has he not? Every thief and murderer in Wales take to the mountains in the face of arrest. If he has not been to you, then you have been to him?" He rose from his chair, shouting, "Answer me!"

I said, unevenly, "None of this is true. My father is dead. His friend in Amlwch saw his grave."

"And I am telling you that he's very much alive." Coming around a table between us he stood before me, lowering his voice to a whisper. "Listen to me, Roberts. Your father has been found guilty of treason, and for that he was sentenced to be banished from the land. His judge was lenient, but if you come before me for the same crime, I will not prove so. Do you know the punishment for taking arms against the Queen? It is this – and the law has never been rescinded – that you be hanged by the neck until life is almost extinct, then cut down, disembowelled, your entrails burned before your eyes and your body quartered." He shook a finger before my face. "I am warning you, Roberts, lies, either here or in the courtroom, will not save you, nor will your youth. I give you one last chance. Have you, since you last saw your father in Amlwch, been in touch with him in any way?"

"No."

"Had you heard of his escape from custody?"

"No."

"Your cousin – the one who betrayed him – do you know her whereabouts?"

"I do not."

"You swear to this?"

"I swear to it all."

"Before God – if I bring a Bible?"

"I swear it – on a Bible if you like." I was trembling; the trembling grew, spreading to my hands, and he saw it. Sir John said, quietly, "Shall I bring one, Mr. Bosanquet?"

There was a long silence, then the Judge walked past me, touching my shoulder as he went, saying:

"Not necessary. He is telling the truth, aren't you, Roberts? Keep him away from Miss Rhiannon, of course, preferably under your eye, but the lad is perfectly innocent of his father's whereabouts."

He knew I'd been lying, of course; I could see it in his face.

I had to get to Sam Williams at once, to report what I had heard from the other side of the library curtain. It might not be Gideon Davies the hidden man had been speaking of, but there was a very good chance that it might be. Anyway, after the interview with Justice Bosanquet I intended to put a distance between me and Dowlais House.

Meg, hearing the garden gate open at the Garn cottage, came running out to meet me.

What chemistry lies in the tie of blood? I hadn't seen my little sister for months, and there was a new maturity in her talk. I saw my father's face in her face, and the closeness of her, hot from the fire, brought to me a oneness: I kissed her.

"You comin' back for good now, Tal?" she asked.

I nodded, my arm around her shoulders, and we went together into the kitchen and its crying kettle.

"Where's Aunt Mell?" I asked.

"Next door borrowing tea," sang Meg, and smiled her rhubarb smile at me, her teeth missing in front.

Aye, I thought, she had changed; Dada would scarcely know her, with her puppy fat and big knees. Her voice now held the sing-song intonation of the valleys, my mother's people.

"Our Poll's down Town, ye know," she said.

"Poll? Our Cousin Poll? *No!*"

"O ah! Often we do see her on the chat, down Merthyr market, twice last week."

"Did . . . did you speak to her?"

"Aye, but she put her nose so high she tightened her garters. Too good for us now, I reckon." She added. "She were with one of the beehive boys."

"Beehive boy?"

She made a face, shrugging, "He were thimble-rigging and Poll were tacklin' up the gents, said Aunt Mell. Whee!

She were done up fine in frills and fancies!"

"Thimble-rigging?"

"Aye, like they cheat at the fairs, you know. Don't let the magistrate see her, said Aunt Mellie, and Uncle Sam do say she's a Rodney."

It was the infant speaking with a woman's tongue; I changed the subject. A Rodney could mean anything—gambler, prostitute, thief.

"Where's Uncle Sam now, then?" I asked.

"In by 'ere." She opened the parlour door to the front room.

"Why didn't you say?"

Sam, boots up and into *The Cambrian*, had his spectacles on top of his head, dozing: I waited until Meg was out of earshot, and said:

"It's next Wednesday."

"You're sure?" He rose instantly.

"Only that a Chartist is being shifted down to Brecon."

"Any details?"

"The escort's a troop, probably mounted, and they'll be leaving from the police station."

"There's never been soldiers billeted at the police station!" He was adamant. "They're up at Penywern Barrack Row."

"There's some at the police station!"

Sam put down the newspaper and walked to the window. "If that's so, then they'll shift him by night. Gid Davies is too important to move him in the light: these days they wouldn't get a prisoner fifteen yards up High Street without a fight, and they know it." He squinted his eyes at his pipe. "Well, maybe it's Gid Davies and maybe it's not, but he's a Chartist prisoner, an' that's good enough for me." He raised a heavy face. "And how did ye come by this, for God's sake?"

I explained, omitting to mention Bosanquet's interrogation of me; if Sam Williams began to think me a dangerous liability he'd relegate me to some unimportant job behind the Chartist lines. Now he said, with businesslike intent:

"Well done. I were beginnin' to think we'd get nothing out of ye being in the Dowlais stables—that you were keener on sparking with that gentry piece than fighting for the country."

"That's over now," I replied.

"Jesus Christ, am I delighted to hear it!" He lit his pipe, blowing out huge clouds of smoke. "Listen. Be at The Patriot up High Street tomorrow dusk, I'll be gettin' some people together." He rubbed his bristled chin reflectively. "Let me see – a Redcoat troop is four plus one for prisoner escort, usually – we'll jump the bastards before they're clear of the town." He evinced the air of one who has said nothing in particular.

As I went out the back Meg put her hand in mine, saying, "Have you heard when Dada's coming back off the ship, Tal?"

I held her against me in the scullery. Aunt Mell's teeth were in a cup on the window sill, I remember, next to a bowl of floating senna pods, and I knew a small, quietening air of peace and domesticity.

Kissing Meg goodbye, I said, "Don't you worry, Meg Roberts. He'll be coming home soon now – sooner, perhaps, than you think."

God knows what would happen to her if things went wrong, I thought.

Shenkin Powell, the retiring checker on the barge canal in 'China,' had all his buttons about him, said Sam.

As old as undertaking was Old Shenks and a confusion of a man if ever there was one.

Foreman on the thirty-eight per cent ironstone, he was lavender water behind the ears on pay day. Of mincing gait and knitting on the side (one plain, two purl, girls – I'm doin' meself a bodice) he once dropped a horse with a left hook for a pint: the right hook he saved for the bruisers, and every pug in Town was frightened to death of him.

No wickedness in Old Shenks who knew his Bible backwards; twice to Church on Sunday, the children loved him (he used to kneel in the street and stroke their faces upwards). Women respected him, though the only one he'd slept with was his mam: three times a week he visited her grave in Pant.

"So you're takin' over me nights, lad?" said he soprano.

"Yes, Mr. Powell. Sorry, Mr. Powell." I stood before him in the canal tally-hut. Behind his wide shoulders I saw the swim of the canal and the night-shift barges moving out of Dowlais wharf.

"Ach," said he, sad. "Jeremiah eight, verse twenty-two. 'Is there no balm in Gilead?' . . ."

The big shire horses strained to commands: bargees, the morning-shift just come on, laboured in swirling mist; casual child labour, their eyes gummed with sleep in the frosted compounds, stood in shivering groups, waiting to be taken on.

The ironmasters, glutted with labour, worked on a nucleus of the specialist trades, depending on migrant workers for unskilled work. These came in starving, ragged streams across the mountains of The Top, crowding the streets, begging on the pavements; jamming up the cobbles of the taverns and ale-houses.

With no public lavatories, they defecated in the open, these people, exposing themselves along the Taff. And down at the China Wharf, the confluence of export and import of pig, finished iron, limestone, coal, the human misery was at its worst – a rectum of despair that called itself China.

Old Shenks now, powdering his broken nose in a bit of mirror, said:

"Ye've got to keep 'em out, mind, or they'll be in an' eat ye whole, especially when the cholera's around; can't take risks with the old effluvia."

"Right, Mr. Shenks."

"And don't invite the women in – pity do extend to fornicatin', mainly speakin', and the reverend gents don't hold wi' it. The poor old molls come begging at night – it's the cold do get 'em, see?"

I pledged celibacy.

He could remember as far back as 1758, he said, when the iron first came to Dowlais; he saw the first furnace built at Cyfarthfa seven years later: he watched the Iron Bridge go across the Taff and the first, second and third Merthyr riots; he was present when a lad was killed by a cannon on the night Nelson came to Merthyr, and at the race between the Trevithick engine and the horses down to Abercynon.

I marvelled at him. "You saw the first Trevithick?"

"Ay ay, but I didn't hold wi' it, see? Horses breathe, engines fart." He jabbed his finger on the table.

"You collect the tallies off the barges, understand? – and the clerks do enter them in their books. Now I'm best off, you're the night-shift."

"Thanks, Mr. Shenks. If I get it round me neck I'll call at your house."

"You do that, son. Number Three Beehive along the British Tip; I'm digging a hole for me hip with our Jen. Knock twice and ask for Shenks."

"Our Jen?"

"Don't come in wi'out a knock or she'll 'ave ye with the bloody ladle." I gave him twopence and he spat on the coppers. "Ach," said he, "here comes a feed. These days I'm tightenin' me stays."

Poor old lad, I thought. Munching his iced whiskers, he hauled off into night-shift retirement on half pay – sleeping in a hole; yet he had given fifty years to iron. In his prime he had also given an outing to Dai Benyon, Champion, over thirty rounds, who complained about scent in the clinches.

Shenks left behind him a faint fragrance of toilet water.

There was another human commodity abroad around the canal; this was the Rodneys. These were mainly the un-wanted or orphans; their parents having been killed in the mines or furnaces, or having just deserted them.

The Rodneys were the lowest of the social order, many of them living in the disused 'hives' that ran the length of the British Tip – decaying coke ovens still warmed by the inter-nal fires of the great cinder mound. Burrowing like moles, the children had formed small networks of underground tunnels into the warm mass; within these burrows the air was sulphurous from the burning tip, the earth floors filthy and puddled with human faeces. The nearest pure water meant a walk of two miles, and every night long queues of women gathered at the wells, centres of gossip and fierce quarrelling. Talk had it that they were also the centres of riotous assemblies, with orgies of drinking and fornication; the respectable inextricably mixed with the disreputable. Virginity and life could be lost at the well heads, it was said, but the journeying was necessary, the four great Works taking the abundance of water coming down from the Beacons.

It was in one of the hives – Number Three Beehive Row – that old Shenks lived, he said; the only adult I knew of being granted the privilege of a beehive guard.

It was Saturday night, I remember: though officially on duty in the tally-hut, I had booked in all the barges: those due out on Monday dawn were tied against the wharf, their horses at feed and the bargees, another isolated community, out on the town with their women.

Locking the door (earlier I had knocked up a wooden bed) I went out into the shivering cold, making for The Patriot Inn up in High.

The Patriot, next door to the Colliers, was but one of a couple of hundred taverns in Merthyr then, conveniently situated close to the police station. Indeed, it was possible, from a window upstairs in its Long Bar, to observe the comings and goings of the law-enforcers, a vital activity during revolutionary Chartism. But watchfulness was not without its sense of humour. On the wall above Sam's head (I saw him the moment I entered) was an inscription which read:

Sweet smiling village, loveliest of lawns,
Thy sports are fled and all thy charms withdrawn.
Amid thy bowers the policemen's hats are seen,
Now desolation reigns where once our joys have been.

"Come you in, Tal," called Sam, and I took my seat at the table among some twenty others.

Colliers, ironstone miners, furnace men and ostlers, Chartists all, they were straight from shift. Two puddlers, their red eyes blinking in their scorched faces, particularly looked me over, then stared ahead in a predetermined eloquence of silence.

They had come, these workers, from the coal workings of Penyard Pit, the Nantyglo Level and Trecatti; one at least was from the Brewhouse Coal and two from the Rhas-Las Drift, they said. Six were from Dowlais Ten, in the middle of the Works, the furnace Brewhouse served, and two came from beyond The Walnut public where the great new Ivor Works was being built. Another claimed he was a roller on the Gardner Big Mill, the pride of Dowlais.

From what was now the greatest iron town in the world they had sent half a million tons of finished iron down the Glamorganshire Canal to Cardiff, and were justly boastful of the achievement.

Within their Merthyr home of thirty thousand people, they valued parenthood and beat their wives but rarely. They worshipped with gusto, in the ale-houses and the Chapels, singing in choirs with a preference for Oratorio.

They fought bare-knuckle for honour, because they loved a fight: but only recently had they discovered the inequality of their existence. Even Mr. Clark, John Guest's agent – but not Lady Charlotte or her husband – conceded that 'Dirty Dowlais' was as bad as the slums of Bombay, the brightest jewel in Victoria's crown.

They had also learned, these workers, that the Dowlais directors were annually banking two hundred thousand pounds while they were burying their children for want of a decent water supply. So now they had joined the national ranks of the Chartists: the employers weren't prepared to give, so they would take: and Chartist leaders like Frost and Henry Vincent, knowing their anger, would put them in the battle's van.

Sam Williams said, "Are all representatives here?" and looked around the room; I was looking for my father; this was to be his first Dowlais meeting, and I was nervous for him: Bosanquet had only to lift a finger and the whole of Brecon garrison would be out on the streets. Some twenty representatives of Merthyr's Chartist lodges were in the room; it needed but one to be a defector – and Napier's spies were everywhere – for the inn to be surrounded. Knocker was reading from a roll, the men answering their names, and Sam said, when this was finished:

"This is a special meeting called at a moment's notice, and I'll tell ye why. We know where Gid Davies is, we think. More'n that, he's being shifted from the police station to Brecon barracks next Wednesday."

There was a hubbub of suppressed excitement; a man called from the back, "Penywern you mean, Sam?"

"I do not – the police station across the road."

"Ye mean he's been there months and we never knowed of it?"

"Christ! What kind of organisation is this?"

"Let's fetch the lads and hook him out of it!" Their anger grew.

Sam cried, "Now easy, easy!" He glared about him. "Would ye have us announce our intentions by the rule of the mob? All right, they've made bloody fools of us, but we're here now to get the fine man back." He looked at his waistcoat watch. "And there's more on the go than Gid Davies tonight, lads. We've Gwyn Roberts, the Northern representative, comin' to address us, an' I pledge ye to the deepest security: Gwyn's wanted as much as Gid Davies, his friend these twenty years – more, perhaps – and if he goes down we all go down."

"Don't tell me there's a union spirit in the North, Sam!" This from an Irish giant with a face like a bunch of laughs.

"Aye, I will! Good shamrock country up there, too – for Welshmen are the same as Irish, Shamus, when it comes to a fight."

"Ach, balls to ye, Sam," said a Welsh voice. "When ye get above Rhayader they don't know bloody Guy Fawkes."

Sam said, and it silenced them, "This fella does. He's just jumped transportation for runnin' guns up in Anglesey, and I'll trouble ye to mind your mouths, for his son's sitting among ye."

The room door came open and Dada came in.

He looked older; compared with the faint light of the Llangynidr cave, this lamp was pitiless. Seeing me, he winked as he took his place at the head of the table.

"Next Wednesday, eh?" he asked Sam, after the introductions.

"Aye, but we can handle it from here – you stay down."

"God no, it's Gid, and I'll be here. But are you sure it's him?" and I replied:

"We can't be sure, but think it is. Sam says all interrogations go on up in Barrack Row, Penywern. This man's held in the police station, just across the road from here. It's a civil crime, and the police are holding him."

"Police?"

"The Specials – the usual; with military backing."

Sam said at nothing, "Months he's been there, perhaps he

anna worth having."

There was a silence, and my father rose, saying, "Listen, dead or alive, every Union man is worth having. And if he's a Chartist, too, then more so. For this is a movement that's spreading its fingers on the throat of the country, and we won't rest until we rid ourselves of this damned autocracy that rules our lives and watches our children die."

The men stared up, shocked, as I was, by his sudden vehemence, and I saw him again, in my mind, standing on the quay at Amlwch. He cried:

"Ay, tub-thumping you may call it, any name you like, but it is time we thumped, not sat on our backsides and waited for the rule of law." His voice rose. "For there is no law in this land save the law that suits the knight, the peer, the Church and the industrial robbers! The Angleseys and Penrhyns up in the North, the Guests, Crawshays and Hills down here."

"Christ, mun, go an' tell 'em that up in bloody Amlwch – one bang up there and the buggers'll be off!"

It rocked them; they shouted laughter, and my father cried, cutting them into silence, "Aye? Sweet Jesus, you have to come down South for scholars and education! Is there anyone here who can count up to five? Do you know your Welsh history?"

"Mind ye tongue," said a voice.

"And you your talk," said Sam, "for it was you who started this, Daio. The man's a guest, so give him a hearing."

Dada said, "It's the old two-nation story, is it not? Well, we up North have a version of that, too – the North for the Welsh, we say, and the South for the Taffs. And all the Welsh are in this fight, not just Merthyr. God Almighty, are you the only ones exploited, then? I've watched families starve to death in copper while you lot were drawing face-work rates and puddler's pay. And we've had the Cornish copper agents on our backs since the slave trade and the Romans before that, before you knew there was iron in Merthyr." He was breathing heavily, now haggard in the face.

"Listen, the moment I stepped foot in this room I knew the hostility. What's more, I expected it, and it is wrong: it's wrong because it divides us at a time when it is unity in manhood we need – Welshman, Northerner and Southerner, Irishman, Spaniard, Scotsman and Hunky. By this time next year two million men and women will be under arms in Britain, and we will call for help from the French, if needs be, to pull these parasites down. It is a call to arms in the name of decency, irrespective of race or creed."

It did nothing for them; we sat among them, Dada and I, but as people alone, save for Sam and a couple of others. And I think I knew then the tragedy of my country; we had allowed greedy foreigners to ravish the land and drive between us an unfathomable wedge.

So we sat, North and South, within an unspoken disharmony, and Sam, knowing it, said:

"Now to the main items of the evening. Meanwhile I say this – one day you'll know the debt ye owe this man. I'm Irish, an' I've no part in the enmity, but I look upon ye all with some disfavour."

Old Nana, the mother of Irish Joe Dido, the shot-firer, who kept The Patriot, came up from downstairs to bring the ale: she was a little scrag of a woman with an air of dislike for men, us in particular.

"Are ye finished puttin' the world to rights now?" She had a tray of pewters in one hand and a big ginger tomcat under her arm.

"Och, Nana," said Sam, "don't you bloody start."

She put down the tray and then came back with the ale.

"Is it right the dear fella's languishin' in the station over there, Joe?" she asked her son.

"He is, Nana," said Joe Dido. "Now will you sod off?"

Sam said, "There's a dozen or so publics on the route the escort will take, see – which will be up High from the station and along Charlotte to the new Ivor Works. After we snatch him we can bed him down in any one of 'em."

Knocker said, "Lest they lift him through Dowlais gardens up to the Gwern?"

"Don't talk stupid," came a reply. This was from the landlord of The Welsh Oak; a revolutionary to his fingertips, his face was parched white from a furnace blow-back and one eye peered from his scalded cheek. "Would they haul him through the gardens in the middle of the town? They'll get him into the open, I say, and meet a troop from Brecon – that's the usual when they go from Penywern."

They considered this, and Old Nana said, stroking her cat:

"Have ye got the wind up, you lot, then?"

"Oh Nana, bugger off!"

"I were only askin', see? Because back in the Wexford Ninety-eight we'd 'ave had the sods on pitchforks, and that were before tea."

"If we snatch him through the gardens, he'll likely end up in the New Inn. That's close," said my father.

"If he's that close he'll end up here, in The Patriot," said Nana. "Meanwhile, you lot sit here sinking quarts and polishin' your arses. When's the revolution, for God's sake?"

"And then?" asked somebody, ignoring her.

"A day or two, then we ship Gid down to China," said Sam.

"Who gets him then?"

"I do," I answered, standing up. "By tomorrow I'll be down on Canal Wharf, tallying."

"You, Tal?" My father looked perturbed.

"Why not?" asked Sam. "He's already up to his neck."

"China?" asked Joe Dido, "that's the first place they'll look."

"Not so. Five go in down there and four come out, Joe, leave it to your betters," said Nana.

The others, I noticed, looked me over with faint approbation, and the old woman said, "And once you've got him, son, he's yours – yours until you get him down to Cardiff docks and aboard the ship to America, understand?"

I nodded.

"That's a tricky sample, Missus," said Dai Tomorrow. "He's only a kid, mind."

"Then now he can grow into a man," came the reply. "We'll spring Gid Davies, house him, mend him – if it be Gid Davies – and carry him down to Dowlais Wharf: the rest is up to you." She clapped her hands. "Right, then – Wednesday dusk, remember, and all report to me downstairs – Old Nana. Socks and pick-handles and hit to kill."

"*Iechyd da i bob Cymro. Twll din i bob Sais*," added Knocker, lifting his pint. One eye was filled up, blood was down his muffler.

"Aye, son – arseholes to all Englishmen," added Nana.

Long after they had all gone I sat there talking to Dada: then Sam returned.

"Time to leave, Gwyn," said he. "By the way, d'ye recall that Mortymer lad working with the gunsmiths? Tell him I delivered the letter he gave me."

Smiling, Dada nodded.

"And tell him that his sister Morfydd's playin' Hell about him being away from home; his young wife, too – they want him back."

I couldn't account for it, but I knew I would see Iestyn Mortymer again.

Dai Tomorrow, the five-foot landlord of the Vulcan and Friendship, was doing well these days.

Since he had obtained the Brew Contract for the Dowlais stables, the ostlers, farriers and muckers-out were not only paid out by him in his pub, but were provided with the Allsops upon which to spend it; thus Dai got a two-way cut, though he wouldn't do today what could be done tomorrow.

I don't remember what took me into the Vulcan that night, and as I came in, Fanny, the Guest parlourmaid, went out of the jug and bottle.

"And what have you been up to, you randy old soak?" asked Dai, his face over the counter.

"Don't believe all you hear from her," I replied, and pushed him money.

"Don't sell Fanny short. She's got the feel of things in Dowlais House, and her and your Rhiannon are as thick as thieves, I hear."

"I doubt it."

"Aye? Well, I tell you this. Sam Williams thinks high of Fanny; there's not much goin' on round these parts that she don't know about, he says."

"He's welcome to her."

It was strange, I thought: I despised Fanny for spying on the Guests, yet I'd done exactly the same thing myself.

"Well, a pint on the house, son," said Dai. "We can drink together, can't we, since we're going to die together?"

"If Sam Williams has his way."

*

The stable men came in for their six weeks' pay, and I remembered how my father and I used to get paid at the Oddfellows up in Amlwch. It was the same old greed and corruption, North or South: doubtless, the Guests had shares in the Vulcan and Friendship.

"Been blottin' ye copybook again, I hear," said Dai, and he smiled me a leprechaun smile: Irish was he, with shamrocks in his mouth, but the Taffs liked him and gave him a nickname – proof of local acceptance.

"Just pour the pints, mun, it's all you're fit for."

Over Dai's shoulder, perched like an undertaker's rook on the skew seat by the fire, was Eli Firmament: potent on a hassock and the metrical psalter was he; just out from Correction, having done six months – interfering with children. Talk had it that he popped his false teeth for ale on Monday and got them back on Friday.

"Watch your tongue, Dai." I nodded towards Eli.

"Yes, he's been seen up in Penywern recent," and Dai went on polishing. Barrack Row being the place where the Guests housed their soldiers for putting down the Welsh.

Upstairs they were fighting a couple of terriers later, and the dogs were now on the leash, snapping and snarling at each other. What with them and the shouting you couldn't hear yourself think. And Eli was watching me, a man of evil intent.

Jake Kilrain, the giant puddler, came in, handling people aside.

I shut myself off, thinking of Rhiannon: without her I seemed to be standing within a vacuum of solitude; the bar noise beat unheard about me.

"Go up there and fetch her, then," said Dai, as if reading my thoughts.

He poured glasses for two farriers, big men of furrowed brows and tired eyes, and they brought with them odours of crushed oats and urine: from the furnacemen came stinks of soot and fire, from colliers stale tea and tommy-boxes. You could tell their trades by smells.

"I said go up there and fetch her," repeated Dai. "Hell, mun, imbecility's your greatest talent, so it is; the poor lass must be pinin' to death."

I drank, not answering.

"D'ye love the sweet child?"

Sod him, I thought, he was touching raw spots.

"How ye doin', son?" suddenly bawled Jake from across the room.

"*Dando!*" I gave him some rough Welsh.

"Is it right Sir John has eased ye out?"

"Right and fair, Jake."

"And you're taking old Shenks's tally nights down the canal?"

"Sharing shifts."

"Aye? Well, I'm a second-class fella, too, though I were just tellin' Eli here, temperance is a sacred virtue all the time you're sober."

"Watch him," breathed Dai, swabbing the bar.

"Jake's all right," I said softly.

"Ay ay, but he had a few before he come."

The men were well informed, I thought. Then I remembered Fanny.

Half an hour later the room was full. Jammed against the bar by the night-shift rollers coming off, I was into my third glass and seeing Dai Tomorrow yesterday, for I wasn't used to Allsops. A man beside me whispered into my ear, "I've a darlin' wee Kathleen back home in me cot, and I'm celebratin' for a hooley, so I am." He hammered the bar for ale. "She's a decent piece, my missus, ye know."

The customers roared, and it hit between us. He shouted:

"I said she's a decent little piece. Mind, I wifed and chapelled her proper, oh aye! But I've not seen her in the light since the altar, now would ye believe that?" He drank deep and gasped. "Six bloody weeks I've been down Penyard, I never seen the sun." Turning, he dropped money into Dai's hand, who said:

"Stop bumming up your missus, Mick – Mother o' God!"

"Ach, away to Hell!" The Irishman shoved him, asking me, "Do you know the Rhondda?"

"No," I said.

"She comes from Porth. Tidy folks, ye know, me place is like a new pin, but I've forgotten what she looks like . . ."

"She'll have flat feet, though," said Dai, swabbing up the counter. "They get those in the Rhondda, walkin' up the hills."

The Irishman ignored it. "You got a woman, lad?"

Dai said, "Go easy, Mick – he don't know if it's slated or thatched."

"I asked if ye had a woman. Ignore this dirty bastard."

"No."

"That's a tremendous pity, Taff." His rheumy eyes glistened above his glass. "It's a fine poise woman like mine ye need; she walks around that bedroom like an African queen."

"Ay ay," added Dai, "with the jerry on her head."

"Will you give up, ye palsied wee pixie!" The Irishman swung to him. "I'm raisin' the womanly race, can't ye see?"

"Ach, buzz off!" said Dai, polishing. "He's got his own troubles, ain't you, Tal? – he don't want more from a randy old drunk."

I heard an old man say, "I live wi' me daughter since my Ellie died – her chap's foreman down the Garn. But I can't come downstairs wi' the kids, of course, I 'ave to stay in me room."

A man with a silky red voice like a Bolshevik declared noisily, "Aye, she's narrow-faced and as dry as tinder, mun – lift her skirt and ye'd find a bird's nest – don't you fret, my beauty, she'll be here any minute to see where I am." I swung around, but he was gone as if evaporated.

"Where's your Alfie got to, Joe?"

"Ain't you heard? Killed down Gethin."

"But he were only ten!"

The room fell into a conspiracy of silence, as if conjurors in black were crawling under the tables.

"Holy Jesus, look at that," whispered a man, and I turned to the door.

The babble died; even the dogs upstairs stopped barking.

Rhiannon, in a white cloak, with her long black hair tumbling over her shoulders, was standing there. Seeing me among the men, she raised her face higher, and smiled.

"Hallo, Tal."

It was snowing outside; the market hall, just built, was clad in white; early winter having pulled a bedsheet over the world.

Afterwards, they told me, Jake Kilrain, the big puddler, got Eli Firmament by the coat and lifted him out of his skew seat by the fire.

"You saw nought, remember, Eli? *Nought*, you hear me? If you did, it was the Allsops, understand? A word of what you saw in here and I'll swab the bar with ye."

Dobie was tethered outside. Going to him, Rhiannon said:

"Fanny told me you were down here, Tal. I . . . I just had to see you. Take me up to Dolygaer . . . ?"

"In this weather? God no!"

"Please, Tal, please take me."

Her face was powdered with snow, her eyebrows flecked with it: she looked like a snow maiden come from the forests of Grimm. I looked around; the market square was deserted; the walls of the stables leered down, imprisoning us. When I drew her against me she was trembling, and the trembling came into me also, bringing us to a sudden, intimate warmth. Her lips were scarlet against the wind-bitten redness of her cheeks, her eyes were shining.

I kissed her. What began in kindness ended in snatched breathing, and she tore herself away.

"Oh, God," she whispered.

"Come," I said, and took Dobie's bridle. Together in the saddle, we took the road that led to the lodge.

Joe Hitherto used the shooting lodge mainly for cleaning guns before the Twelfth, having his own tied cottage in the grounds of Dowlais House. And since the Guests only used it when the game was in flight, the stone lodge stood isolated and alone, mantled with snow.

It was dark within the lodge.

Rhiannon tidied the flowered curtains against chinks; I lit the single lamp, and a warm, yellow glow searched the corners of the room.

Outside in the snow I gathered loose timber and piled it under the chimney: a fire was soon leaping in the open hearth, painting in redness the four small bunks, the piled rugs, the gun-racks, the sheepskins on the floor. Rhiannon knelt beside me and I blew the wood into a forge-glow; we sat there.

Amazingly, now that she was here beside me, I had no physical need for her; my father's predicament was invading the inner tenement of my mind, stealing desire.

Nevertheless, it was enchantment to sit there with Rhia's hand in mine. Her eyes were bright, as if with unshed tears, her lips bitten scarlet by frost, and the shadows of her high-boned face were deepened by the red light. This beauty enhanced the intimacy of utter quiet ... wind-sigh, the crackle of the logs. Also, and I recall this so well through the years, there was a lovely smell of tansy and woodruff, which old Joe used to keep the moths away.

The years have gone on a rush of tears, but I will always remember the perfumes of that room, where I made love to

Rhiannon.

"Wait!" I exclaimed. "Poor old Dobie!" and I went outside and put him in the stable, with a bag of oats to keep him warm; returning, I stamped the snow off my feet.

"God," I said, "they'd comb the meat out of us if they found us here. Our tracks in the snow are six inches deep."

It appeared to startle Rhia. She said, making big eyes, "Comb the meat out of us? What an expression!"

"That's what will happen, like it or not." I beat myself for warmth and sat down beside her.

"Would you use such a phrase in Dowlais House?"

"Probably not." I spread my hands to the blaze. "Why, what's up?"

"There you go again," said she, and she stared at the fire with a sloe-eyed indifference, as if she had said nothing.

"What's the odds?"

She shrugged, saying, "You know, I heard you talking to the ostlers once . . ." Uncertain, she hesitated.

"Continue, do not spare me." I grinned at her, kissing her face.

"You . . . you sounded as rough as them – you were actually swearing."

"*Damnia a'i chwythu!*" I said, "is that a fact?"

"But, then you spoke to Lady Charlotte – and sounded very, very different!"

"You don't speak Chinese to a Hindu."

Ignoring this, she said, "Actually, Lady Charlotte mentioned it, also. But she knew why. Welshmen, said she, possess a trick of the soul – one speech for the bawd, another for the bard."

"That sounds exactly like Lady Charlotte."

"Dual identity."

"Aye, the English gentry bring out the best in Welsh beggars."

She should have laughed, but did not. "Don't trifle with me, Tal."

"*Diawch!* This sounds important!"

"Lady Charlotte said you were an enigma."

"Her opinion isn't confined to me – she is, too."

Rhia smiled at the fire. "But I am not. I am uncomplicated. Everybody knows where they stand with me. I tell you that I love you, Tal, and this is true. If I told you that I would die for you, that would be true, also."

I put my arm around her. "And now you are doubting if I love you?"

"Do you?" Her eyes beseeched.

"Of course, with everything in me I possess."

"You'd die for me?"

"Dying would be the easiest part."

"Then why do you keep leaving me?"

The flames were red in her face, her eyes bright. It seemed impossible, but I thought she was about to cry.

"Leaving you?"

"As I said—you keep leaving me. Just when I think I've got you, you've gone."

I dared not tell her about my father. Her possession of such knowledge was unfair to her. She said, in the crackle of the fire:

"Then, if you love me, take me away?"

"How can I, woman? I haven't five guineas to call my own."

"Money isn't the reason—I've got money . . ."

"You expect me to live off you?"

"And that's not the reason, either!" She was abrupt.

I got up, wandering about. Rhia said, "There's something bigger than me going on, isn't there? Nobody has told me, but I know. And you're here in Dowlais because of that, not because you love me."

"That isn't true!"

"And when the right time comes, you will leave for good."

I did not reply.

She added, staring at me with lost, forlorn eyes: "It's to do with the Chartists, isn't it?"

"It has nothing at all to do with the Chartists—why do you imagine such things?"

"Fanny told me."

"Who?" But I knew whom she meant.

"Fanny, the parlourmaid. You're up to your neck in it, she

said. 'You'd best keep off that Tal Roberts,' she said, 'or you'll be landing in politics.'"

I came back to the fire. Beside her now, I took her hands in mine. "Listen, what Fanny doesn't know she makes up. Yes . . . all right, I am involved, but . . ."

She interjected, her arms going about me, "Then why won't you let me help you? Anything to do with you is to do with me."

"You cannot."

"I'm frightened, Tal – please tell me what's going on?" She was crying now. "I'd . . . I'd go anywhere with you. Please give it up and take me away?"

"You'd never survive it."

She became haughty and distant. "That's like a speech you've prepared."

"It isn't; it's a sermon on stones, a genesis of hatred written for the poor, and you know it's true."

"And that's made up, too."

I emptied my hands at her. "You're used to fine things – life comes easily for you; you snap your fingers and everything happens. How can you ask me to take you into poverty?"

She got up, flouncing about, brushing at her tears in disdain. "I'm much stronger than you think, and you know it!" Then she clasped her hands and turned back to me. "Oh God, this is dreadful, we're actually quarrelling . . ."

I held her and there was wetness on my lips when I kissed her: she said, as one holding back a grief:

"Make love to me, Tal, please make love to me?" She stared about her like something trapped. "Let's forget the world, if only for a minute?"

It was a madness, a thriving impulse that we had never known before; it banished all sense, obliterated consciousness. The pillows of the bunk were cold to our faces; it was a celebration of warmth within a world of ice; a cosy play within an uncosy act of dying.

Rhiannon, beneath me, turned away her face and the redness flew to her cheeks.

Her lashes were dark, her lips scarlet with my kisses; her

mouth possessed a subtlety I had never known before. The coldness of my fingers took her breath and she clung to me as something lost, when one with me. With Rhiannon it was as if our bodies had come from twin moulds, fashioned by hands of silk. In the depth of her I knew an exultant strength; she spoke, though at first I did not understand her.

"Gently, Tal, gently . . . ?"

Motionless we lay then, the act consecrated by silence save for our breathing: unified, discontented with movement, Rhiannon stilled me with her whispers. To have moved a finger would have sullied the moments. The stillness of the room, now our pent breath, was like a sacrament; even the night beyond the window was still, a white-furred world awaiting our gasps, the spy: an owl called and it momentarily shocked us, the screech echoing in the frost-laiden air.

"Do not move, darling, please do not move!"

She held me, as one forged into immobility, scarcely breathing.

It was an unmoving joy that transcended anything I have known: by word, touch or glance, I could never express it; it was an impetus unresolved and lost in time.

"Lie still, Tal?"

I obeyed and there was no sound but the beating of our hearts, heart-beats that seemed to fill the room, enveloping us; now moving slowly into a rhythm where one heart only could be heard.

I am old now; I have known many women, but never has this happened, save with Rhiannon: even our breathing was unified, from gasps to small, unvapouring breaths.

I saw beneath me the waves of her black hair on the pillow: the sharp curve of her cheek I saw, and I raised my face and looked around that room, taking in every detail, listening for every sound. Yes, other women I have known, for woman, to a man, is need as well as love. In the business of my plundering manhood, they have made shape as undifferentiated pieces of malleable clay; some noble, others unrefined. But none were such as this, whom I joined to me on that winter night in Dolygaer.

"Please . . . Just hold me?" The request was urgent. We lay together in a sad, fierce oneness, and I lowered my lips to Rhiannon, consummated, with her, in unmoving peace.

Later, again by the fire, Rhiannon said:

"There is a difference between us, Tal; this is why we are apart, although one. I look at you with the eyes of a wife, you look at me with the eyes of a lover. But thank you for that love-making."

She drew from me then, rose, and went to the window, saying:

"It's snowing again. Our footprints are gone. They will never find us now." Then she came back, took my hands and drew me up beside her. "Whatever happens, Tal, you will always be mine, remember?"

"Whatever happens," I replied.

"This . . . this thing between us, whatever it is, will take you away from me, but we will always be one, Tal. Never forget tonight?"

Such was the unusualness of her voice that I held her away, searching her eyes, and she said then:

"Thank you for being gentle with me. And . . . and forgive my stupid apprehension, but . . ." She was smiling. "I'm with child."

Mae'r Siartwyr yn dod! (The Chartists are coming!)

This was the new clarion call echoing over the land. Sick of it, the Welsh of the valleys gathered for rebellion, and in the counties of England an army was being formed.

On the night before our attack on the military to free our prisoner, seven hundred Chartists marched around Merthyr in gay colours, with brass bands and the banners of their lodges and benefit clubs; planning, they said, to meet again in a vast rally on Christmas Day, on Heol Cerrig Hill.

The ironmasters, from Dowlais to Cyfarthfa and Pen-y-darren to Plymouth Works, panicked. With the Merthyr riots on their conscience, they alerted Brecon garrison, begging its commander to send a force at a moment's notice.

But we in Dowlais had more important things on to consider: first we will get Gid Davies out of Redcoat hands, said my father, who, despite the initial hostility to a Northern leader, had now taken command in Gideon's absence.

You couldn't see across the bar for steam in The Patriot public, Irish Joe Dido's place, for the wet-pit colliers from the Race Lace Level were in there playing dominoes. Soaked to the skin, they were drying themselves off before Old Nana's hearth fire, which she kept especially for wet colliers, and now the steam from their clothes was smoking up the lamps. Old Nana herself was squatting on a skew seat, warming bed-bricks in the oven. Big Tom, her ginger cat, watched every move.

As skinny as a quarryman's haft was Old Nana, aged ninety, come up from County Antrim these seventy years back. Joe Dido's mother, she ruled the ale-house with a hand of iron, and Big Tom ruled her, sticking his claws into loitering customers. Now, for some unknown reason, he was yelling his head off.

. "What's wrong with him?" I asked, coming to the fire.

"He wants me abed," said Old Nana, and raised her ancient face to mine. A revolutionary, this one, since the years of the Irish famines – pull the garters off bishops and strangle the Queen.

"You know about Gid Davies?" I asked her quietly, glancing around.

"I do," said Nana.

"For God's sake stop that bloody cat!" bawled a collier.

"You try stopping him," cried she, and turned her bed-bricks in the oven, saying, "Half-past ten Sam wants you on the job, son. The military convoy leaves with the prisoner fifteen minutes later."

I nodded.

The colliers guffawed, dry-swimming the dominoes. "Can ye hear me above this bloody palaver?" asked Nana.

"I hear you."

"Right. Now, there's a tunnel leading from the cellar downstairs to the grounds of Dowlais House – an old working. And the convoy is taking the lane through Dowlais gardens up to the Gwern Road, we've heard – do ye know the grave of Tancy the Dog?"

"I do."

"Ten yards behind it in the coppice is a brattice cloth entrance to the working – Mark, Mary, Joseph, I've shivered me bones on the face down there in me childhood for the Guests, I know every inch . . ."

"And my job?"

"Get into the tunnel from our cellar, and you'll meet Joe Dido halfway through: help him place the powder charges, for after they fetch Gid Davies through we're bringing that tunnel down – on soldiers, if needs be. Are ye listenin'?"

"Yes."

"Clear the brattice entrance where the tunnel comes out in the orchard, then help Knocker carry Gid Davies back into here."

"Is that all?"

"No, here's the easy bit. Go back into the tunnel and fire the fuse, once my son, the last man through, is back in the cellar. And check that he's brought his powder box back, or he'll have this public down on top of us. He's the best shot-firer in the business, is Joe, but he's as addled as a Chinese egg."

"I fire the fuse," I said.

"You fire the fuse when Joe's clear, then run."

"It's risky, mind."

"It's a bloody sight more risky being ninety." She lit her pipe.

I got up. "What are you drinking, lady?" Talk had it that she could put most colliers under the table.

"Well now," said she, "since I'm communin' with the spirits soon, I'll sink a wee drop o' the hard stuff – raw gin preferably. And then I'm away to me bed, I don't trust meself with six-foot handsome fellas. What about this for a knee?" and she lifted her skirt.

"Easy, Nana, it's hard enough as it is."

"It put the skids under County Clare, I tell ye. Can you spare five minutes?"

"Ach, I'd love to, girl, but we haven't the time."

She fanned me away. "You're more useless than this bloody tomcat. He has me in bed at half-past eight to warm it up, but he don't come up till nine."

I slapped down twopence for her gin, kissed her, and went to the door.

"Don't forget the matches," called Nana.

It was cold on the streets; the night was sparkling with frost. I walked aimlessly, to waste time, thinking of Rhiannon and the dangers encompassing my father.

Nobody was in the yard of The Patriot, and the door of the entrance to the brewer's cellar was unlocked.

Finding a lanthorne on a peg I lit it and went down steps

into the dark; soon I came to the old working Nana told of. Bent double, following the drift for about two hundred yards, I stopped to listen to the traffic of Market Street drumming above me.

Farther on I struck pit-water, but breathed fresher air as the drift shallowed, then the old brattice cloth halted me and through its decaying chinks I saw the moon.

Here the drift sloped sharply upward; I set the lanthorne on the gob and worked swiftly, clearing the entrance of fallen stones. Cold air and moonlight struck my face as I crawled up into the Dowlais orchard, and the coppice where the grave of Tancy the Dog stood was white with frost.

Crippled trees of winter enveloped me with icy arms. Nothing moved. The lane the Redcoats would take sparkled in silence.

For perhaps an hour I sat there shivering, listening to the activity of Dowlais stables; the clattering of hooves, Shire snorts and the shrill commands of ostlers. From Jones's Court, just across the road from the garden wall, came the wailing of babies; a man and woman were quarrelling in a cottage behind the Chandlery: faint music came from the windows of Dowlais House. Another Ball? I wondered. And, if so, would Rhiannon be there, dancing with the cavalry beaux . . . ?

I thought: when this is all over, I am leaving Wales. Once my father is safe, I will go from here and take Rhiannon with me. On the road to tell the tales? – I did not know: nor did I know how it would happen, or when, but we would travel together – away from anything that savoured of Dirty Dowlais. The very night, with its shivering cold, seemed part of the resolve.

As I got to my feet and beat myself for warmth, a man's head and shoulders rose up before me, fracturing the moon.

"That you, Tal Roberts?"

I clenched my hands. "Who is it?"

The head came closer, spurting breath. "Irish Joe Dido – did ye see Old Nana?"

I nodded.

"And is the brattice entrance clear?"

"It is, where the Hell have you been, and what about the mining?"

"All done, son – nothin' left to do but light the fuse."

"How many are we?" I asked, thinking of my father.

"If there's five mad Welshmen in this orchard there's fifty, and they're all three feet between the eyes. God help the English. Listen!" and he put his finger up for silence.

A little hay cart was coming: flanked on both sides by marching soldiers, it was drawn by a white dray and preceded by an officer on horseback.

Now we could see the little procession clearly – four Redcoats and their officer. As we watched, it entered the shelter of the grave coppice, and the trees about it moved, suddenly becoming men. A small army of black figures darted out with raised pick-helves, clubbing, clubbing, and the soldiers went down. All in seconds; there was no sound save the shrieks of the floundering horse as its officer was pulled off and silenced.

Running, Joe Dido and I reached the ambush: red-coated soldiers lay everywhere, their limbs moving stiffly, and colliers were going round them to make sure, tapping the semi-conscious. Knocker was already lowering the tailboard of the hay cart. In the light of the moon I saw the astonishment upon his face.

"Hey, Sam, is this Gid Davies?" He was staring down at the man on the litter.

"Just get him out," commanded Dada, coming up.

With Knocker on one end of the stretcher and me on the other, we doubled back through the brattice cloth and into the old working where Joe Dido was putting the percussion cap into the charge. Running past him in the light of the lanthorne we reached the cellar and clattered through it: men were waiting at the top of the steps and hands reached down, hoisting the stretcher up into the yard.

Men were running up behind us and I flattened myself in the tunnel now, holding high the lanthorne; my father paused to peer into the light.

"Tal?"

"Aye, Dada – get clear, for God's sake, we're pulling down

the roof."

His eyes were steady in the slanting light, and he flattened his body against the wall, like me. "Did ye see Gid's face?" His voice broke.

"Get clear!"

I pushed him aside and ran back into the dark. Joe Dido was scarfing the fuse and we lit the end of it, kneeling, watching it hissing and spluttering sparks.

"Right," said Joe, "*away!*"

We were going up the steps into the Patriot yard when there came a dull thump, and a rumbling as the roof came down.

Men were standing around the stretcher as we reached it; my father was upon his knees beside it. I looked down into a reddened, bruised mask that was no longer a face: the opaque eyes moved slowly in Gideon's swollen cheeks. His lips were split, his shirt tattered and starched with blood.

"But you didn't tell them, Gid? You didn't tell them?"

Sam Williams bent to him; tears were in his eyes, I noticed, but not in my father's: there was upon his face an anguish and hatred that I had never seen before. And I think I knew, in that moment, that I would never wean him from the task in hand; that he would never rest until the task was finished.

Gideon Davies spoke then and we bent to hear him.

"No," he said, "I didn't tell them."

"Right," said Nana, "get him inside quick, before he dies on us."

Never will I forget my father's face as they lifted his friend. And when the stretcher had gone into the house he went to a lonely place in the yard and stood there, and I did not go to him.

I was in the checking-office a week or so later, tally-carding the barges, when Old Shenks came in.

"We've got Gideon Davies," said he. "Come," and I followed him along the canal and over the Taff to Jackson's at the bottom of the British Tip.

Here among the rickety courts and alleys was the Pen-y-darren to Abercynon tram-road that skirted the Morlais Brook, and a line of trams I'd checked earlier on were coming down to the wharf: sheet fire from the nearby Cyfarthfa furnaces was playing on the topsy-turvy roofs of the cottages, the threatening glow before the roaring blast: the iron was due for tapping; drop-hammers were beating on the rain-washed air. Splashing along side by side in the filth of Morlais, ignoring the begging children of Beehive Row, we arrived at the very foot of the tip: Number Three in the Row was Shenks's home, he said, and knocked on the door; a battened window swung back and a face appeared.

"Our Jen," said the old man, and stood aside and the door came open.

I recognised the girl before me. She was the tattered child I had seen in Cyfarthfa over a year before, when I first came South. Now about seventeen years old, still bent nearly double, she supported herself on the same cranked ladle, her drum-stick arms projecting through rents in her dress: her eyes, as before, held me; they burned as with fever in her sallow face. Old Shenks said:

"You got a lodger, Jen."

"Ah." She was looking me over. "Who's he, then?"

"Now come on, I told ye he was comin'."

"Ain't he got a tongue?"

She stood aside as we entered, walking on the cinders of the old oven. A broken lantern hung from a semi-circular roof, casting a faint glow through the shadows beyond: along the curved walls were laid filthy straw mattresses. In the middle of the oven was a big black cauldron; a charcoal fire licked up flames, and the air was acrid with smoke.

"Where's Gideon?" I asked.

"Hold hard, son," said Shenks, "ye've got to bargain."

"Have you got honey?" asked the girl, coming closer.

"Money, she means," whispered Shenks, nudging me.

"We don't keep no one free." The girl's small, peaked face stared up. "Everyone pays the Rods, don't they, Shenks Boxer?"

"How much?" I asked.

"Four shilling a week." She smiled at me with broken, yellow teeth. "Even old Peg-Leg paid, didn't he? And Big Buzz and Waspie, they all pays Our Jen—even you pays, don't ye, Shenks?"

"I pays regular. You don't have no trouble with me."

"Four shillin', then," and the girl held out a small, grimy hand, stamping her clogs in a circle about me. "It was our Queen, really speakin'."

"Your Queen?" I asked.

"Well, it was our Queen's idea, see? 'I'll take the old man in,' says Queen, but she had to get me to agree, because it ain't Queen's hive. Understand?" Her small, peaked face peered up at me.

"No," I replied.

The girl said, "Well, Queen reckoned she owed this chap one, 'cause once his friend were good to her."

I nodded. "She lives here too, your queen?"

"O ah! She been here two year come spring Fair Day, and Sam Williams comes down, see, an' gives her a talk."

"She knows Sam Williams?"

"Aye! She's good on all the gents, is Queen."

Old Shenks asked, "Who brought Gideon Davies here?"

"Knocker and old Sam—on the dram-road from Dowlais

Top. He's blind as a bat, this fella, ye realise."

"Take us to him, please."

Reaching up with her ladle, Jen hooked down the lantern and led us deeper into the darkness beyond the coke-oven walls; shadows flung by the wavering light danced her hunchback form grotesquely on the sooted ceiling.

Here, deeper in the stomach of the tip, the air, strangely, was purer: two outlet pipes, shafting upward through the roof, mirrored the stars: beneath each pipe were two wall niches, each holding a palliasse and a bolster: at the head of one such cell hung petticoats and dresses.

"Queen's cell," said Jen, in explanation.

In the opposite cell, lying motionless on his litter, was Gideon Davies, his face upturned. I thought him dead.

His hand was cold in mine, as cold as death.

"He's alive, mind," said Jen, "though I dunna give much hope for him."

"Mr. Davies . . ." I whispered, my face close to his, but he made no reply: clearly a doctor had attended him for the swellings of his cheeks were reduced; one eye was still bandaged, but the other, wide open and opaque, stared defiantly back at me.

"Mind," said the girl, "Queen saw to him before she went out on shift, ye know – gave him milk an' a wash all over."

"He drank milk?"

She grinned at me with a broken mouth. "Yes. Big Buzz slipped over to Creigiau Farm and milked one o' the buggers."

To my astonishment Old Shenks said to her, "This fella, Jen, he's sort of special. You won't kill him, like you did Peg-Leg?"

"Christ, no!"

"Because, if ye put this one in the Taff, like you did him, the queen might fly off."

She considered this, scratching.

"Then the hive would go cold. Besides, he's worth more alive than dead, Jen – how much?"

"Four shillings – now come on, Boxer, I just bloody told ye."

The old man said, "She wants four shillings a week."

I took out the silver and dropped it into her hand, saying:

"And you'll keep Big Buzz and Waspie and the others off him?"

The girl smiled, shaking her ladle. "Anyone tries at him gets this."

Old Shenks said, while I stared at them both, "Ye know, Jen, it could be your pa come back – you thought of that?"

"Jesus, no!" She pushed back her hair. "Can't be. This bugger's got two legs, Pa only had one," and she raised Gideon's blanket.

Outside in the Row I said to the old man, "God, she's mad!"

"Maybe. She ain't alone round these parts."

"Who was this Peg-Leg you spoke of?"

"The children took him in because, like Jen's father, he only had one leg. But he became their bully man, their boss: he sent the boys out thieving and made the girls prostitutes. One night, while he slept, they unscrewed his wooden leg and beat him to death with it."

Old Shenks lit his pipe and its fragrance momentarily banished the stinks of Morlais. "Mad, you say? Not as mad as she makes out – it keeps grown-ups away if they think she's a lunatic, an' she's got quite a bit tucked under the mattress, has Our Jen."

"But is Gideon safe with her?"

"Safe as a bank – you and the queen-bee being related, so to speak."

"Related?" I stared at him.

"Ay ay – Sam Williams reckons you've got a lot in common – she being your Cousin Poll."

The early winter snows had gone. Gentle October winds were into us, and it was a fortnight or so before I dared to approach Jen's hive again, for China was alive with searching Redcoats.

With Chartism growing in the land, unrest was up and down the valleys; men stopped work and defied the blacklist, furnaces were blown out and production stopped: the Scotch Cattle, gangs of roving unionists wearing animal skins and cow-horns, were beating men who worked on when the Union said stop, or hoisting the guilty ones to the top of pit-heads.

Hillside meetings became a nightly occurrence; with bands playing and flags of their clubs and lodges waving, the Chartists proclaimed the New Ideal, Lovett's Six Points of Parliamentary reform. On every other street corner, new Demostheneses ranted and raved. And the ironmasters, sworn to banish all unions, formed their own – The Association of Employers.

As fast as the prisons filled, new leaders arose to replace those banished to transportation: the treadmills of Usk, Beaumaris and a dozen other towns were never out of use, the cries at the whipping frames never silent. *Agents provocateurs* sent into Wales never arrived, spies among the workers disappeared. The aristocracy and shopocracy were lampooned openly: attacks on the military grew as patriots were smuggled out of cellars and attics to freedom abroad.

But still the transportation ships sailed from the Welsh ports with chained insurgents. Welsh womanhood being among them – sent to the brothels of the Colonies by order of Victoria, now publicly proclaimed by Welsh and Irish as The Royal Pimp. Barracks were built in Welsh towns, English soldiers pounded our streets, and General Napier, on Melbourne's instructions, set up a counter-espionage movement to '. . . examine the state of the districts . . .'

Whispers of Chartism and revolution sent bishops to the country and curates under beds – 'More pigs and less parsons' was now the labourer's toast. The rich lodged their jewels in bank vaults and spent more time in Church: the Archbishop of Canterbury undertook a continental tour in the name of a capricious Almighty, who, until now, had always voted Tory; the Queen herself was indisposed.

All was not well with the Guests, either, according to reports. With a home by the sea in Sully and a London house, they felt the need of something more propitious than Dowlais Manor, and set aside three hundred thousand pounds for its purchase (they eventually settled on Canford Manor, Sussex). Further, Sir John was planning to form the Works into a joint stock company with assets of a million, so they were immersed in a new theology of profit, and that meant keeping wages down. Meanwhile, they were preparing for flight to Grosvenor Square, their haven of escape from the cholera.

Rhiannon, however, was concerned on another account. She begged me, "Please, Tal, please – let me help with your father's friend!"

Fanny, the maid, had been at it again, I thought.

"Darling, no," I replied. "It's far too dangerous."

"Then, at least let me bring him some nourishing food?"

"I don't want you mixed up in this!"

She glared at me, snatching herself away in anger.

"What kind of a woman do you think I am?"

Beside Rhiannon, I had Our Jen to contend with; she was even trickier.

When I took to the hive the food Rhiannon had given me, Jen was sitting in the middle of the floor like a witch on a broom, cross-legged, the ladle across her knees.

"Hello, my lovely," said she.

I said, "I've brought food for Mr. Davies."

"Food?" Reaching up, she snatched down the bundle as I went past. "I does the food."

Hands on hips, I glared down at her, and she smiled up.

"You think I'm mad, don't ye?"

I did not reply.

"You're the mad one to bring that fella here." She jerked her thumb at Gideon. "He's bloody near dead, ye know. Any time now the Lord'll be moppin' his brow. I seen liver ones floatin' down the Taff." She got up. "You'll never ride 'im down to Cardiff, son, the soldiers'll see to him long before that."

I met her eyes, and she winked, adding, "Ye see, lad, I know these parts, an' what comes an' goes. I'm saner than you, really speaking. Just that it suits ole Jen for people to think she's addled." She gestured around the walls and the children's straw mattresses.

"Now, you take this lot – they're only kids, see. So I brings 'em in from the streets and puts 'em in this hive and tell 'em they're bees: I make the bee noises, they make 'em back, and out they go for honey and bring it back to Jen . . ."

I interjected. "Where's Poll?"

"Ach, dear me! Poll, is it? You and her related, eh? These last few nights she don't sleep much, our Poll – just talkin' about you."

I said, "I brought this food for Gideon, not you, and I'm going to see that he gets it," and I strode past her, deeper into the cave. Catching my arm, she hauled me back, the ladle up.

"Listen," she whispered. "I'm boss here, son. Everything's shared, crust an' crumb. Old Poll might be the queen, like the kids say, but I'm in charge, 'cause I got the ladle."

Footsteps sounded outside the door and Jen swung round, saying, "Christ, here they come – Big Buzz first, as usual – with his honey."

Big Buzz, as she called him, was a tall, rangy lad of about

fifteen; there was about him a sinewy strength. Until Old Shenks came to the hive, Buzz was its guard, he told me, eating while the rest went short. Now he was one of a dozen workers; a thimble-rigger by day, a pickpocket by night.

I watched Buzz enter. Seeing Jen approaching, he stood nervously before the cauldron, screwing at his hands. And Jen, with the aplomb of an ancient princess, squatted on the floor beside it, gripping the ladle, saying:

"Hallo, my charmer, what you got for me?"

Excitement struck his thin face. "I got twopence, Jen!" Fishing into his rags he dropped the money into her lap.

"More," said she.

"Got no more, Jen." He was shivering.

"Turn out, Buzz, there's a good boy."

Bemused, he was staring down at her, and she shrieked, the ladle up.

"Turn out!" And then, by way of explanation to me, added, "He's a good lad is Buzz, but sometimes he do tamper wi' it – like thief bees." She made a faint humming noise.

"You been eating it?"

"I only got twopence!"

Rising, Jen struck out with the ladle, the spoon caught the boy's shoulder and he danced about, howling: and she, stooping and straightening, thumped blow after blow into his body. As I leaped to intervene, Jen stepped back, saying:

"He's a thief bee, ain't you, Buzz?" and then she quietened, adding confidentially to me, "He's bigger'n me, see. I 'ave to lather him much more'n the others."

Gideon was asleep, so I sat by his mattress and watched the children come home; bringing their earnings.

There was a bantam hen from Waspie, a shrew-like child with an impish stare: chicken giblets from Song, a tattered urchin with a ready smile: half a rabbit from Hare, a gnome of a child with a deformed lip, aged eight: six sausages stolen from Butcher Heppo's stall in Merthyr market came next, a grubby, evil-looking, half-man-half-child called Doss being the donor: then two duck's feet from Hummer, aged twelve, filched out of the bins of the Lamb Row public, and a loaf of bread from Shrinky, who, cranked-back like Jen from work in the lower levels, was only four feet high. One other worker brought money—a shilling from Fly, who held the horses' heads outside the Castle Inn.

It was then that Poll came in.

Everything ceased.

This was not the Cousin Poll I had known; the harlotry of powder and rouge had painted out the smile that I once knew, and her eyes, once alive with sin and mischief, held the false brightness of mascara: even her voice, when she spoke, had changed: two years on the pave had taken their toll. Seeing her coming, the children rose; even Jen, pinned on the ladle, struggled up.

Unlike them all, Poll was well fed. Dressed in a long, grey skirt, wearing a broad-rimmed hat, she entered with the self-assurance of one who took obeisance as her due. And the children stood silently, their switching eyes alternating between Poll and the cauldron: Shrinky, crying, was silenced by the upraised ladle. Fingering it, Jen asked softly:

"How did ye do today, my precious?"

Poll didn't appear to hear this, but opened a purse and dropped a sovereign; the children squirmished for it on the floor. Biting on it, Jen said:

"You'll 'ave your supper now, Missus? You got someone visitin', look," and she nodded towards me.

Not replying, Poll walked past her, and past me, too, into her cell.

I greeted her, but she ignored me, lying full length on the bed, eyes closed, her hands folded behind her head. And Jen, beating away the begging hands of the children, filled a bowl with choicest pieces from the pot, saying amiably:

"Take ye time, kids, take ye time! You got to feed the Queen, ye know." She approached Poll with the bowl of food.

"Get rid of him," said Poll, her eyes still closed.

"Well now, ain't you two happy to see each other, and you born relatives?"

I said, at the cell door, "Thank you for taking care of Dada's friend, Poll."

"Get rid of him," she repeated.

"Bugger you," exclaimed Jen, "you've upset the Queen." She gathered the children about her, adding, "Best he gets goin', eh, kids, 'afore he gets stung?"

They encircled me, following me to the door. I looked back before I went through it.

Poll was standing with her hands over her face.

Within a week of Gideon arriving in the hive, a squad of Redcoats under a Captain Wetton came down to Canal Wharf and started going through the cottages, throwing out people's possessions, poking under beds. And they hooked me out of the tally-hut to take them into the stacking areas and round the moored barges.

They went through the warehouse with a tooth-comb, burrowing like moles into the stacked pig ingots, emptying waiting trams of fish-plates and spikes. Wetton was watching me closely, but did not speak; he was the new English commander of the Penywern garrison, Old Shenks told me, and it was clear to me that he was on a concentrated search for Gideon, their lost prisoner. The last I saw of the soldiers was them marching off towards Morlais brook and Beehive Row.

"Don't worry," said Old Shenks, coming on shift, "if they go into the hives it'll be the first time ever. Adults, not kids, hide wanted people around these parts."

An Irish bargee called O'Reilly came in for his tally-card for his Cardiff run, and Old Shenks waited until he had gone. Then:

"Your dada wants you up at Llangynidr," said he.

"Llangynidr? What for? I was just going to get my head down."

"Reckon ye'll get no sleep today, old son. Knocker says it's important. The boys up there are running a dram load of rough stuff down to Abercynon."

"Rough stuff?"

"Don't ask me, son – that's what he told me." It was the way he looked at me that made me ask:

"Arms?"

"Don't call it names, for God's sake."

I'd heard the term, of course; up and down the valleys arms were being made in small quantities and smuggled down from remote places like Llangynidr into the towns.

"What for, Shenks?" I asked, but he lit his pipe and turned away, not answering. I said:

"All right, there's a revolution coming – but where, and how?"

The old man shrugged. "You ask your betters, lad, not me. Getting patriots out of the country's one thing, a revolution's another. I'm too old for sense, but I reckon Wellington will cut fanatics to pieces, and there's more than one fanatic around."

"Men like my father, you mean?" and he shrugged empty, and waved me down, replying:

"Ay ay, if ye want it straight. But there's hotter heads than him. Best you get up there to Llangynidr, then ye might see what I mean."

He sat at his table and began to write out tally-cards; it was an indication that the conversation was finished, so I stood by the window for a bit and watched the barges moving off; the man O'Reilly, waiting on the tow-path, made a brief signal. I saw Old Shenks nod.

Old men, I have found, often speak with two tongues; one for practicality, another for wisdom. I began to wonder if this old man was up to something he didn't want to share with me.

It was dusk when I went up Dowlais Top on my way to Llangynidr, and it was dark and the stars were like Chinese lanterns as I reached the cave on Dobie. A man was standing on guard at the cave mouth, and although he recognised me, he told me later, he called:

"You – the password!"

"Beanswell," I called back.

"Who do you seek?"

He approached me with his musket at the ready and peered at me and Dobie, and his eyes were sunken in the caverns of his face and his clothes were ragged. I replied:

"Gwyn Roberts. I am his son."

"Ach, dear me! The Captain himself, is it?" He winked, presenting arms. "Shanco Blackbird Mathews I am, honour to ye name, lad. For there's a hundred or more comin' and goin', but if I blew this bloody musket the sods'd vanish. Shall I accompany ye?"

"You can hold the horse," I said, and went past him into the cave.

"Will you tell me when the revolution's starting, so I can get back to Nanty for me supper?" This he called after me, and I went flat and crawled through the light-lock, and an unknown helper seized my arm and dragged me through.

My father disengaged himself from a clutch of men.

"Ah, Tal, good lad. Later we'll be needing you. Meanwhile you're just in time to hear The Watchmaker."

Other men surrounded us; one was Iestyn Mortymer, the lad whose letter Sam Williams had delivered to Nantyglo, the town at the top of Black Rock; he greeted me with a curt nod – not a great deal to say, this one: the others were talkative, and the black-maned giant whom I had seen before suddenly put up his hand for silence, saying, "Listen!"

A low knocking came on the rock door and the big man knelt, listening, and a faint voice called:

"Mr. Edwards?" It was the sentry outside.

"Aye, Shanco!"

"'Tis the revolution committee, Mr. Edwards. Shall I send 'em in or shoot 'em?"

The man Edwards said, "Christ, we can do without comedians – send them in, Shanco!"

There was a pause; whispered consultation behind the light-lock; the men about me stirred uneasily, their faces gaunt and careworn, grotesquely shadowed in the yellow light.

As my eyes became more accustomed to the glow I saw above me the vaulted roof of the cave, and beyond the searching fingers of the lamp a gulf of blackness. The tables I had seen before had vanished.

About a hundred men were in the cave, sprawled in various attitudes upon the earth floor or lying back against the rocky walls; in one corner pikes were roped in bundles like firewood, their rough iron heads dully gleaming: beside these were packing cases, some ten or more, and upon these other men were sitting. Now there was a scuffling at the light-lock.

"Here he comes," whispered Dada beside me, and knelt beside Edwards.

I watched fascinated as a hand and then an arm came through into the light; elegantly decorated at the wrist with lace, the hand waved, disembodied, seeking assistance, and my father gripped it and hauled and the arm became a shoulder and the shoulder a man; they pulled him through unceremoniously into the light, and he stood there, this man, in a fine velveteen frock coat and trews, then bent, beating the dust from his shoulders.

"The Captain?" he asked.

"This is our captain," said Edwards, and indicated my father.

I weighed the man before me.

He was of medium height, and slim; extraordinarily handsome, his dark eyes moved slowly around the scene before him. My father offered his hand in friendship, but the stranger did not take it.

"Your name?" he asked faintly, in English.

"Gwyn Roberts," said my father. "Welcome to Llangynidr," and this he said in Welsh.

The man snapped, "Talk English, man, for God's sake. The Irish are with us one to one; Scots are here, even Spaniards, and the rebellion is more English than Welsh, for it is nationwide. Are you the leader here?"

My father replied quietly, "No man is leader. None here stands an inch above another, Mr. Jones. But I am the captain of the Merthyr contingent, for Gid Davies is blind."

"But safe now, I hear?"

This was William Jones whom men called The Watchmaker, one of the three leaders of the Welsh Chartists, of whom John Frost was its chief and Zephaniah Williams of Coalbrookvale its second-in-command.

Many said that Jones the Watchmaker was the most fervent and fanatical of the three, with his fiery talk of shifting Victoria off the throne and fleshing swords to the hilt in a victorious battle that would fling off the English yoke. Certainly there was an arrogance in his attitude to my father, and the way he held himself was, for me, foppish.

"Yes," said Dada. "Gid is safe, and we will get him out of the country."

"Did he talk?" asked Jones.

"Had he done so, we would not be here."

The man glanced about him, then jumped lightly on to a packing-case.

"I will address the men," said he, and faced them, his feet astride, his hands upon his hips.

"There's a bloody pansy for a half-pint revolutionary," said a voice beside me, and I turned. Iestyn Mortymer sat on his hunkers and I joined him, whispering, "You don't think much of him?"

"God help us if we're dependent on the likes of him to lead us," came the reply. "I've got a sister back home who'd take him while she poured the tea."

"Hush you," growled the big man, Edwards, and gave us a look to kill. Raising high his hands, he said, "Listen, you, listen all. The time has come to hear the plans, and Mr. Jones is travelling round to give it to the Pontypool contingent, of which we mostly are a part. Can you hear me at the back?"

"They can hear ye in Brecon barracks, Ed," called a man.

"Then peg back your ears and give the leader a hearing, for you'll not be hearing it twice," and he gestured to William Jones, who cried, his voice highly pitched:

"In the past ten days I have spoken in Pontypridd and Aberfan; from Crickhowell to Usk and east to the labourers of the Forest of Dean, I have travelled to rally our comrades in the cause of Chartism." He raised a small fist. "And if men of Beaufort and Merthyr march in my Pontypool column, they are welcome. I greet you all."

He paused, breathing heavily.

"The time has come to put these valleys to the torch! No longer will we workers tolerate the ever downward trend of wages when the iron trades are down, for we do not get rises when times are good. No longer will we accept the filthy housing of places like Merthyr's China, or Dirty Dowlais under the benevolence of the scrounging Guests.

"Listen again. I will not keep you long, for I am not here to inflame a rabble, but if we lie down in the face of this exploitation our masters will sink your hopes for another ten generations." He flung up his arms. "So we will tear the crown from the tyrant's head! We will trample their banners in the dust! We'll build a new Jerusalem out of the ashes of the old!"

"Wait," said my father, and came to the fore.

William Jones lowered his hands and there was no sound but his breathing; slowly, he turned.

"God! You dare to interrupt me?"

"Aye," said Dada. "Because, with respect, we've had enough of rampaging speeches about tyranny. We've had enough, too, of words and hotness, for words are cosy old things when they advocate the business of dying, which can't be easy if you're stuck by a Redcoat bayonet."

Jones the Watchmaker shouted, "Mr. Edwards, I am here by invitation. Can you stand by and see your speaker insulted?"

"Ay ay, he can," said Dada, "for I'm the captain here. And it's a bloody sight more insulting, I vow, to sit chained in a cart, for I've had some. So temper your tongue, Mr. Jones, or we'll send for John Frost, the spiritual leader of this mad-cap expedition. Can ye hear me at the back?"

They rose to him, on their feet now in simmering excitement, and Dada said:

"Listen – bad cess, as say the Irish, to any man with no respect for Chartist leaders, but we'll flesh swords to the hilt on our own account. Merthyr has its own contingent – we're miles away from Pontypool: let Mr. Jones poach his marchers from Brecon and Abergavenny, and Blaenafon, the town of mountain-fighters. We in Merthyr will make our own run to Newport, and we don't need salty old talk to send us on our way. What say you?"

They shouted in chorus until Shanco Mathews banged on the light-lock for quiet and Edwards silenced them by bawled commands. My father said:

"Lest Mr. Jones forgets the reason for his invitation, I will tell you it. For, if you are prepared to die in this fight you have a right to know the plans and dispositions. The scheme is this. To invest and capture the town of Newport and to stop the mail coach to Cardiff. The failure of other mails to arrive will alert scores of other towns and cities from here to London. For two million men are under arms in Britain, awaiting the signal to rise in rebellion, and we, the Welsh, have been chosen to be in the van."

"When do we go, Welshman?" shouted a foreigner from the back, in darkness. "Lead the way, and we'll follow!"

My father said, "We move on Sunday, November the third. We march in three separate columns – the first under John Frost, the western men from Blackwood; the centre column under Zephaniah Williams from Ebbw Vale district; the third under Mr. Jones here, driving out of Pontypool: all three columns join forces at Cefn, between Risca and Newport; then they will descend in a body and take the town."

"And after that, mun?"

"After that, comrade, we march on London," shouted William Jones, and he quoted, "'We'll rend their veil, we scorn their steel, we shrink not, nor dissemble. By every burning wrong we feel, cold tyrants, ye shall tremble!'" and he seized a sword nearby and brandished it above his head. "These are the words of our Chartist poet Ernest Jones. If they are good enough for him and our beloved Henry Vincent now in gaol, they should be good enough for us!"

"Aye," said my father, and reached up and took the sword away from him. "But words will not be enough when Wellington brings out the troops that beat the French. Cool heads may win, but men like that will cut the fanatics into pieces." He tossed the sword into a corner. "Listen again, men – more plans and less poetry."

It silenced them.

"Merthyr, it is decided, will supply three contingents, and their task will be this: One squad will be stationed on the heights above Garn on the Brecon Road, and cut the road to Brecon barracks: a second will ambush any troops coming up the road from Swansea: a third, under my command will be astride the road at Llanhennock to repel all military reinforcements aiding Newport from Monmouth. This contingent, swelled by numbers after Newport has been taken, will then march on Cold Bath Fields prison and release the hero Vincent. Before that week is out, my friends, the government of Wales will be run from the tap-room of the Coach and Horses, John Frost's pub in Blackwood!"

I stared at my father as the men rose about him in shouts of exultation, for there was a light in his face I had never seen before: little to choose between him and Jones, I was thinking; both possessed a frightening, tub-thumping eloquence. Iestyn Mortymer, squatting beside me, said above the hubbub:

"A good old boy your da, I'm thinking. I had one like him once; they'd spark a bit if they could get together."

I gave him a glance in the yellow light. His eyes were good, this one, like shining orbs in his square, handsome face. I said back:

"Never seen him like this, though: another couple of minutes and he'd set himself alight."

"The whole business stinks, mind."

"It's a stink, and it must stop," I said.

He rubbed his fingers through his dark hair. "Aye, and perhaps we need such leaders – a pack of whirling dervishes, to get some spirit into the mass."

He surprised me; I had never heard one speak like that.

"You approve of Jones and my father?"

He raised his face to mine. "Jones, no. People don't trust him. Rumour has it that his Pontypool column will never see the skies over Newport. But your father, aye, he's all right, but I tell you this – he'll sell his words with blood." He rose in the babble and shove of the men. "I lost my dada to the furnaces, you will lose yours in this rebellion. Men like him go home in coffins."

Dada, freeing himself from the others, came to us, saying: "Dobie's outside, is he, Tal?"

"Aye."

He gripped Mortymer's shoulder. "Listen, I want the pair of you on this," and he jerked his thumb at the packing cases. "This lot have to be delivered to Turnout Six on the Pen-y-darren tram-road at midnight – two hours time."

"Turnout Six, the tram-road," I repeated.

"Aye. And Sam Williams and Old Shenks will be waiting and fix the load – under three tons of dog-spikes going down to Canal Wharf. A bargee called O'Reilly will be hauling them down to Abercynon in the morning. If you're still on duty then, make sure they're tally-carded through, understand?"

"Yes," I said.

"And Tal . . ." He drew me to one side. "What's this I hear about a girl . . ."

"What about her?"

"A gentry?"

I faced him. "Aye, well?"

"You realise the danger, I suppose?"

"It's not important, Dada."

"But at a time like this?"

The men were pulling at him, invading the affinity with questions; Edwards was trying to turn him into a goodbye with William Jones. I said softly, "I'll tell you when there's time, Dada. Meanwhile, forget it."

"Aye, and meanwhile don't trust her. The daughter of Richard de Vere? You're a worker, Tal, you'll never stand on her side of the chandeliers."

I whispered. "Go easy. Who wants to?"

He nodded. "All right, but if anything slips out you'll be the first under suspicion, remember. This lot wouldn't think twice about tearing you to pieces."

We slid the long, thin packing cases through the light-lock, Iestyn Mortymer and me, and straddled them, three each side on Dobie, who was watching me with an evil eye because he was on overtime, and meantime shifting his rear to get Mortymer into range.

"Watch his hind legs," I said, in passing.

"It's the fillies on two legs you've got to watch," said he at the moon.

"O aye? What does that mean?"

"Your dada's right, boyo. I heard what he said. It's common knowledge, did you put it in *The Cambrian*?"

"What's it to you, then?" I came around the horse, and he said with a dark, lazy smile:

"I heard it in the Vulcan and Friendship. Once Old Joe Hitherto climbs on, everybody knows. Ye need your head read, sparking a gentry at a time like this." He nodded towards the cave mouth. "They'll have your balls for Spanish castanets." He took a final tug on Dobie's saddle rope, tightening up the boxes. "Do you love the maid?"

There was an easy strength about him; a manner that dispelled anger, and he was older than me. The moon suddenly blazed and I saw him more clearly.

"Aye," I said.

"How old are you?"

"Eighteen."

"Your first girl?"

"No."

"Good for you, but why the English?"

"Who said she was English?"

"Good God," came the reply. "Don't tell me you're sparking gentry Welsh – she'll sell ye down the river soon as bloody look at you."

This angered me and I fancied a go at him, yet his careless, easy charm again placated me. Now he said, as I took Dobie's bridle and we went along side by side:

"Do you love her, Tal?"

"Aye." I warmed to him because he had used my name.

"And she loves you?"

"Her business."

He made a face at the misted moon, for clouds of rain had come up. The air was needle crisp and suddenly cold, the heather flattening in quick buffets of the wind. "Dear God," said he, "you're a tight old boy when it comes to romance – are they all like you up North?"

We walked on side by side with Dobie between us hating every minute, and the sky over Dowlais Top was suddenly a strickening red as the furnaces were tapped: the clouds, fat-bellied with pulsating light, poured down a radiance over the earth.

"What's your wife's name?" I asked.

"Mari."

"Where's she now, then?" and he said, as if to himself:

"Over at Nantyglo in one of the Bailey houses with my mother and sister."

"What are ye doing up here, then?"

"Working for the Chartists – over suspension. We get furnace rates, mind, just to see us over, until we get the Charter."

"You think we'll get it?"

"God, yes. Or why would I be here?"

"When did you see your wife last?"

"Six weeks ago. You know the sentry back by there? Old Shanco Mathews? He slips over to Nanty from time to time to take her money."

"Why don't you go yourself?" I asked, and he stopped, pulling up Dobie short.

"Because if I go, I'll stay the night, and if I do that they might get me. That means four go to transportation, not just one: Shanco's got no family."

The fizz-gig light of the furnace tapping died: we heard the drop-hammers forging the soul into the iron, and Dobie's eyes were bright under the moon. Then rain fell, sweeping over the boulder-stricken country, and I wondered about Rhiannon. Every step now was bringing me closer to her and I knew a small, comforting warmth. Above Garn Caws, at seventeen hundred feet, the stars seemed even brighter, and I imagined her asleep in the bed at Kierton with this same moonlight on her window, this same rain pattering on the glass.

"What's her name?" asked Iestyn suddenly.

"Rhiannon."

"Is she beautiful, as Rhiannon of the *Mabinogi*?"

"I've only got words to use," I said, and it delighted him, for he replied, quoting in Welsh:

"'I welcome you,' said Pwyll, 'for it seemed to him that the beauty of every girl and woman he had ever met was as nothing compared with the beauty of this lady . . .'"

"You know the *Mabinogi*?"

"It is the Welsh soul – who does not?"

Trefil came up on the moors and we saw the lights of Beaufort in the sky. And I knew with this new friend an understanding and nearness I had felt for no man save my father.

A furnace whistle from the valley told us that it was midnight, and we made our way now with greater care, coming to Dowlais Top where the Guest trains were tipping their loads of muck: leading Dobie down a fire-break in the forest, we came to a road facing the railway line.

Here the new locomotive 'Perseverance' was steaming on the wide track, and behind her was a line of trams stacked with dog-spikes for Spain – I knew these tallies now like the back of my hand.

"Wait here with Dobie," I said to Mortymer, and whistled my way down the line, hands deep in my trews: and I saw against a roseate sky two men rise up from the waggons like brooding hulks, and one I recognised as Knocker. I wandered up to him, still whistling.

"Got rough stuff, Knock," I said. "Where's Sam?"

Sam's face then appeared above the side of the same tram; ridged with bumps and bruises, it seemed, fashioned by the strange red light.

I said, glancing around, "Is it safe?"

"Be your age, lad," said Sam. "Is it safe anywhere? With bloody Wetton plunderin' down on Canal Wharf, waiting to knock up our kneecaps? Who's he?" and he indicated Iestyn, who had led Dobie to us. I explained, and Knocker said happily:

"O aye, I remember – the love-letter lad. I delivered it personally, mind – and you got a right old varmint for a sister – she threatened me with the poker, she did."

"That's the least will happen if you get mixed up with her," said Iestyn. "Are we staying here all day, Mr. Williams?"

"Aye, load up," said Sam. "Is this the lot?"

"It isn't. Another load coming down before dawn."

So we loaded the tram and the engine puffed off, down to Canal Wharf where Old Shenks and Bargee O'Reilly were waiting. And we got off back, Iestyn Mortymer and me – he to the arms cave and me down to Dowlais along the Pen-y-darren road, and I knew again, more strongly, that our destinies, his and mine, were linked.

I did not know then that it would be under a hail of Redcoat bullets along the road to Monmouth.

The night before the big Chartist demonstration in Merthyr, Poll tapped the window of the tally-hut, just as I was getting my head down. Getting out of bed, I let her in. Rain was splashing down the window.

"Hallo, Tal," said she.

"Ay ay, Poll."

In the lamp-light of the hut, I could see her better than in the dimly-lit hive; she looked even older, and the rain had washed the mascara off her eyes on to her cheeks, giving her a strangely haunted look.

She said, her head low, "Don't think a lot of me now, Tal, do ye?"

"You're all right. You'll always be good old Poll."

"Oh yes?" She raised her face. "Always been good old Poll, hasn't it! But if you'd sparked proper instead of lagged, I'd still be on me feet."

"Somewhere down the line it went wrong," I said.

She shrugged, empty. "Perhaps I just made the mistake of wantin' to be alive." She rummaged under her coat and brought out something I instantly recognised. "I only come to give you this, Lover," she said. "Our pa used to read to us from it, remember?" and she gave me the manuscript of 'The Tale of Delwyn'.

I held it joyfully against me. It was impossible to believe that I had got it back, and said, "I . . . I thought Dada took it when he was arrested . . ."

"No, I took it, 'cause it was his. But then I tried to sell it. Nobody wanted it – only a book, see?"

Dry of words we stood there like strangers.

She added, "So you'd best 'ave it, and keep it for Pa."

I waited. There was more to come, made evident by the twisting of her fingers. I said, "Sit down, Poll," and drew up a chair.

"No, not staying," came the reply. "I'm off directly," and Poll raised her painted face. "It . . . it was me who told old Casanova, too."

"Mostyn Morris – the constable – about Dada?" I peered, perplexed because I was now hearing it from her own lips.

"Aye, Tal, it were me." She stared vacantly around the hut.

"But why, Poll? Why?"

She emptied her hands at me. "Pa were . . . well, he were sharp on me, remember? Over that Andy Appledore. After Meg was on her feet he don't need Poll no more, I reckon, and . . ."

"That's not true, and you know it!"

"And . . . and you, too. You slid up garters wi' anyone but me, you realise?" She held herself. "I boiled for you, Tal, deep in 'ere. A sort of motherin' and frolics, all rolled in one. But nobody cared much for me in them old days."

A silence of awkwardness came between us. She continued, "You think anything much about me now, Tal?"

I had no words for her and she came closer, her hand shaking on mine. "I'd go straight for you, *cariad*, eh, ye sweet thing. I'd go straight, ye know – I'd give up the pave." Then her expression became alight with a sudden radiance and for a moment she was Poll again, in bloom. "Honest I would, Tal, I'd go decent. Say the word an' I'll start again. I ain't ill, ye know – they say I am, but I ain't. I'd keep your place brushed and tidy for you, and I'd wash all over, mornin' and night." She opened her arms to me. "And I'm a steady old boafer, like the lads say – I'd be worth the rent. You listenin'?"

I nodded, and she added, "Be a sport, Lover, give us a chance?"

My mind flew back to the kitchen of Three Costog. We stood in silence, reading thoughts, while the rain poured down, and I lowered my head. Poll said:

"Because of that gentry piece, isn't it?"

I nodded.

"I saw her the other day, an' she's all right, but she's only got the same equipment as me, an' anythin' she can do, I can do better."

I looked at her: head on one side, she added, "Go on, Tal."

I thought: one wrong word here and we are all dead. She had betrayed once, she could do it again. I said, quietly, "Gid Davies first, Poll, isn't it? It's got to be Gideon Davies first, if you want to make up, you see?"

Her eyes narrowed; she was fighting for comprehension. I said, "No good talking about us till we get him out of Beehive Row and down to Abercynon."

"Ay ay, well Old Shenks do come talking last night about that . . ."

"About what?"

"About getting him down to Abercynon. On Rally Day, he said – Saturday, ain't it? On the barges wi' the Chartist bands playin' on their way to Cefn Fair, and banners and flags, an' all that . . ."

I said, "You'll help?"

"Jesus, yes, what d'ye think I am?"

"It's dangerous."

"I don't care none about that."

I took a breath. "First to Abercynon with him, then, and after that to Cardiff. Then we'll talk about us, is it?"

Her eyes became alive. "You promise?"

"No! Can't promise. Who can promise? Perhaps I'll stop a bullet, perhaps you . . . First we get Gid down to Abercynon."

We stood together within our indecision; the rain beat down, drumming on our world, and Poll said, her eyes bright:

"Give us a kiss, Tal?"

I caught a glimpse of the purity of Rhiannon's face: even a kiss, I thought, could mean acquiescence . . .

"Just a kiss, Lover? You won't catch nothin'."

I put my arms around her and kissed her, and she clung to

me gasping and sobbing, like a woman drowning. I said, holding her away, "Poll, you'd best go. The military have been round once tonight, perhaps they'll come again."

She said, "Gawd, I feel clean now! Ain't that wonderful?"

She looked at me within the icy silence of her loneliness. Time was that Poll had a fancy-free piquant charm; in Chapel, a nobility and grace even; but now this had gone. She said:

"The runt of the litter, ain't I?"

"Ach, no! You'll always be good old Poll."

"What . . . what happened? I wonder." She smiled, empty, "I suppose I grew up, is that it?"

Then she collected herself with the little fussy movements women employ before leaving, and said, looking away. "Sorry I hooked out of Amlwch and left you flat wi' Meg, Tal."

I didn't answer, and she added, going to the door. "After I'd done it – gone to Mostyn Morris, I mean, I had to go: I just couldn't bear to see him whipped." Suddenly she began to cry. "God, I couldn't bear to see 'im whipped . . ."

Opening the door she went out into the night: holding the blind aside, I watched her running through the rain to Beehive Row.

Shenks Boxer came into the tally-hut a few moments after Poll left.

"Young Poll was that?" He beat rain from his shoulders.

"Yes."

"What she want?"

"It doesn't matter, Shenks."

"I told you before about havin' the molls in 'ere, mind."

"It isn't what you think."

He grimaced. "Your business. She'll likely do her bit, that one, so no odds to that."

I nodded. "Let's hope so. But it's a pity we have to trust the others," and he replied philosophically, screwing plug tobacco into his pipe:

"Aye, but when the queen bee flies, the hive swarms, don't it? They'll 'ave to come. Mind, Sam Williams don't worry about that, the more the merrier on Fair Days, he says."

"Have you seen the Union lads?"

Shenks nodded. "They ain't runnin' this Chartist Rally for a half-dead blind chap – it's county-wide. But we're getting a few extra banners stitched up, the wives are at it now – 'We Want a Hospital', 'We Want Doctors', 'We Want Stretchers'. Just about every lodge and Benefit Club will be carrying invalids – stretchers and corpses will be end to end."

"I hope to God it works."

"Ach, you're mooney for a funeral, of course it'll work! When poor old Gideon comes out o' Beehive Row, he'll just be an extra body."

"What happens if they lift the blanket?"

The old fighter lit his pipe; the match flared, banishing the shadows and lighting his disfigured face. "Then Gid's a gonner, ain't he? So it's up to us to see no squaddies get near 'im." He licked his knuckles and struck his fist into his palm.

"It's a risk."

He shrugged. "All right, it's a risk. Can you think of anything better? It ain't so healthy in Beehive Row, come to that."

Over a hundred million people crossed the Atlantic that century, and most of them must have visited Merthyr's Chartist rally before they went, said Dada: the town was jammed like herrings in a barrel. Political rallies, like annual Fairs, being the essence of corruption, most people took their morals out of pawn in the morning and sold them back at night: there was bull-baiting, pitch and toss, cock-fighting and thimble-rigging, but one thing was certain: for a rally that was heralding a coming national rebellion against the State, things were circumspect.

The theme for this Chartist march being the need for hospitals in Merthyr, it was the organisers' intention to move the stony hearts of their employers to grant medical facilities: the attempt failed – we didn't get a wheeled stretcher in Dowlais, Cyfarthfa, Plymouth or Pen-y-darren until the 'forties, and the first hospital in Dowlais came ten years later. But the Merthyr Chartists, though a mere two thousand strong, were increased to an army by the valley contingents coming in from all corners of the town.

They came with the insignias of their lodges and the costumes of their Benefit Clubs: they came marching in from all points with flags and streamers waving and banners strung across the roads. In ranks of six abreast they marched, chanting their aims in unison, the need for reform. From Nantyglo and Brynmawr they came, from the Chartist lodges of Blaenafon, Abertillery, Bedlinog, Pontypool, Bargoed and a dozen other iron towns. Some had been marching for days, sheltering on the treeless mountains, crouching soaked in caves and quarries. With hope and aims for fulfilment they marched, shouting their defiance of military authority and employer domination.

They came not with arms, but with music and the poetry of Ernest Jones, now in custody for sedition. In company with their comrades of Sheffield, they had as their slogan, 'March, Death or Glory'. They knew the history of the Plug Plot disturbances of Preston, and by heart the speeches of Rayner Stephens, the attacker of the New Poor Law. 'Let the child take the needle, the housewife her scissors and the men to the knife,' said he, 'aye, and the firebrand, too, if all else fails.'

Rayner's cry was on their lips as they marched to Cefn Fair in Merthyr, the centre of the cauldron that day. And banners they carried proclaimed:

EVERYMAN FOR SECRET VOTE: PAID M.P.'S, NO LANDED ONES: EQUAL VOTING DISTRICTS AND ANNUAL PARLIAMENTS!

They thronged in their thousands, dressed in the colours of their clubs and Societies; the Oddfellows, Ivorites, True Britons and a score of other lodges and Benefits: weavers and bleachers of the North Country, deputations from the woodsmen of the Forest of Dean.

Gentlemen puddlers were there in grey suits and stove-pipe hats, the cream of the trade of iron: Irish luggers and trimmers were drunk at seven in the morning. Waving their beer notes, they flooded into every pub in Merthyr, from the old Dowlais Inn to The Colliers, hammering the counters.

Their women came too; tipsy Irish arming it around with Spaniards, and pinafored Dowlais ironwork girls in their brown woollen stockings and quarter boots. With their black straw hats and brightly coloured kerchiefs on their heads, these marched in hundreds, bold-eyed, picturesque in their black shawls and coloured earrings. And they waved aloft their calloused hands and bawled their bawdy songs, a strident contrast to the official music . . . Buxom, wide-hipped, armoured against weather by their lusty thirteen-hour shifts of piling sheared iron or moulding furnace bricks up Penyard for five shillings a week before deductions . . . they were a part of the official labour market, said a visitor to Dowlais, 'Among whom the young masters played the role of many dingy sultans . . . with promises of shorter hours and higher pay'.

As far as I knew, not many succumbed: these, the 'lower orders' as Lady Charlotte called them, but the beating heart of Dowlais labour, the fulcrum of her obscene fortune.

Quakers and priests abounded in funeral-black procession, chanting from brass-bound Bibles; touts, toughs; medicine men and quacks slapped up their bottles of cures from mange to toothache and ointments for piles. A fat Hereford bull, contentedly munching, was being led to the baiting ring for the sport that would make him tender . . . followed by snarling bull-terriers straining on the leash.

And then, as the column, ten abreast, rounded Canal Wharf, I saw the Beehive Row contingent led by Jen. With her hair hanging down, she was dancing a crippled fandango, using her ladle as a crutch: prancing here and there in her rags, waving to the crowd, her gap-toothed mouth leering into the sun.

Waspie I saw, also Song: Hare of the deformed mouth was there hand in hand with Fly, the horse-holder aged twelve; Shrinky, in her crippledom, was riding a flying-angel on the shoulders of Doss. But Poll was not there, neither was Big

Buzz. The band marched past, the combs and gazooters shrill to the deep-throated trombones and ophicleides. Our Jen cavorted and spun, her spindly legs kicking up. Seeing me, she momentarily paused, then swung the ladle around her head in new grotesque contortions. The sun shone down. The music blasted the calm clear air.

Thumping reverberations were approaching from the other side of the river, for, with the head of the march in China, its tail was still in High Street. Shift-workers of Cyfarthfa dropped their tools to watch: the furnaces simmered in threat. Sprag-men on the long-haul wagons to Abercynon Basin on the rack-and-pinion railway leaped down from the engine footplate; 'Perseverance' steamed and shunted in protest at the stop, clanking her loads: her firebox sparkled and belched relief. As I stood there the first Hospital Column came around the bend of the wharf.

Packed together by the narrowing street, the people came in growing disorder, quarrelling and pushing for room, shouldering each other aside with their stretchers and placards. It was well-constituted chaos, I thought; typical of Sam's organisation. Above the marchers were slung banners proclaiming:

WE WANT A HOSPITAL, ONE FOR EACH TOWN.
WE WANTS WHEELED STRETCHERS.
WE WANT PAID SURGEONS.

Children were running among the crowd, distributing leaflets by Ernest Jones, the Chartist poet; taking one, I read:

The Song Of The Day Labourers
Sharpen the sickle! How full the ears!
Our children are crying for bread!
And the fields have been watered by orphans' tears,
And enriched by their fathers' dead;
And hopes that are buried and hearts that broke
Lie deep 'neath the treasuring sod,
So sweep down the grain with a thunderstroke,
In the name of humanity's God.

Ernest Jones

Minor placards announced demands for drugs, not whisky-dousing, and first-aid centres for accidents. And suddenly, to my astonishment, I saw Fanny, the Dowlais parlourmaid, dressed as a nurse within the crush. About her thronged the litters and stretchers, each carried by two giant colliers, the hewers of the steam-coal faces from Bedlinog No. 1 to the Old Black Vein. Stripped to the waist these stretcher-bearers came, coal-grimed, straight off shift. And on their stretchers and litters bounced the blood-stained actors, among them the 'corpses' of those who had apparently 'expired' on route, for black-gowned priests were giving 'last rites', one of these being Dai Tomorrow.

And then I saw Old Shenks and Big Buzz of the hive: on the stretcher they carried, his face covered with his blanket, was Gid Davies. The marchers spilled over on to the wharf itself, close to a line of moored barges I had just tallied in for Abercynon, and the bargees, furious at the interference, raised whips and foul language: the usual antagonism between bargees and ironworkers.

I watched the anger and disorder. The procession pushed on, the stretcher-bearers now engaged the bargees in wild altercation. Fists were raised, oaths and threats were flung; and when the column reached me – not twenty yards from the tally-hut – Old Shenks, Big Buzz and Gid's stretcher had disappeared.

"*Well!*" said a voice behind me. "Would ye believe that? I wonder where they got to," and I turned to find Sam Williams and Knocker.

"I didn't even see the going of them," I said, softly. "Are the bargees in on this?"

Sam raised his face to mine: as old as a dead crow he looked in that morning sunlight.

"To a man," replied he. "Give it six hours and Gid Davies'll be in Abercynon. You listening?"

I nodded, and he moved closer. "Then listen again. You're being watched, you realise that?"

Sam continued, "By Old Eli over there, probably others." He nodded through the ranks of the procession which had now surrounded us in music and chanting. "Which is all to the good, is it not? For while they're watching you, they're missing Gid."

Leaning on a bollard on the other side of the road was Eli Firmament who used to drink in the Vulcan and Friendship, and the hate in his eyes must have liquified his brain. Not ten yards from him, lounging disinterested, was Jake Kilrain, the giant puddler, and Sam said:

"As I say, there'll be others, but leave that one to Jake. Can you hear me above this racket?"

"Yes."

"Right, now jump one of the 'Perseverance' wagons to Navigation House, Abercynon: she's due down there in three hours, her footplate tells me. Gideon won't arrive on the barge run till well after dark, and the lads'll take him to the stables of the Swan. Understand?"

"The Swan."

"That's it. The landlord's name is Maginty, and he's one of us. Just make yourself known to him—say 'The Devil a monk would be', and he'll get things moving. He's teetotal, but ye can trust him . . ."

"'The Devil a monk would be'?" I repeated.

"That's it. The rest is up to you. Old Shenks will help you handle the run down to Cardiff Sea Lock, it's too bloody dangerous for ninnies like us. All right?"

"Yes, Sam."

"It's not! I lay ye ten to one none of you make it, even with Maginty's help. There's renegade military searching the canal between Abercynon and Cardiff."

"Renegade?"

"Deserters, and they're tougher than the real thing."

"That's pleasant," I said, eyeing him.

"Aye, and make sure Old Eli sees ye hop the Abercynon Wagon, *Number Fifteen*. The wagon number's important because he'll pass it on to the military, and that'll take the pressure off the barge."

Knocker said, "He being a dear devoted comrade of your mate, Captain Wetton."

"Captain Wetton!"

"It could be poetic justice, done properly," said Sam, rubbing his chin. "Don't you owe that one a couple?"

"*Iechyd da i bob Cymro. Twll din i bob Sais,*" said Knocker.

"No odds to that, Knock," I replied, "will you do a good turn for a Welshman?"

"If he's from the South."

"Will you take my old cob Dobie up to Kierton Manor in Pontsticill and hand him over to Miss Rhiannon de Vere?"

"I'll do that," interjected Sam. "Likely he'd hit Hell out of him on the way. Any message?"

"Just say that I've left Merthyr, and I can't afford to feed him."

I did this with a heavy heart, not bearing to say goodbye.

"About time, too," observed Knocker.

I lay on my back and shut my eyes to the morning sun thrusting down darting rays.

Hidden in a chamber of the stacked ingots on Number Fifteen wagon, I lurched and bumped down the old dram-road route, my world obliterated by the puffing, hissing 'Perseverance'.

Not half a century ago the Dowlais Company built the first railway to Morlais Castle for limestone: the second, Overton's Rack-Assisted from Pontmorlais, linked the Works to the terminus at Pont-Storehouse, where I had my tally-hut. But this, Overton's third ('Ten Mile') railway, from Carno Mill to the Navigation at Abercynon, was the prideful boast of Dowlais.

One horse hauling twelve wagons forty years back was replaced, through the genius of Richard Trevethick in 1804, by the first locomotive to run on rails. You can forget George Stephenson and his half-hinged 'Rocket', my father used to say, *his* first engine arrived ten years later: trust poor Wales to take a back seat in an English roll of honour.

Never before had I done this run by rail: when necessary to make a tally-check at the Navigation, I'd travelled by barge along the route Gid Davies, Poll, Big Buzz and Old Shenks were taking now, which was risky. The twenty-five mile Glamorganshire canal, from Dowlais to Cardiff Lock, worked through nearly fifty locks, all time-wasters; ideal check-points for Captain Wetton and his Redcoats.

I prayed now that, tipped off by Eli Firmament, Wetton would follow me instead of Old Shenks's barge . . . in the hope that I'd lead them to his prisoner. Clearly the military believed that the railway or the barges would be Gideon's method of escape to the sea.

Is there a sadder sound in the world, I wonder, than the *rat-tap-tap*, *rat-tap-tap* of a train taking you away from the one you love? Or to stand on an empty road and watch a coach entice your lover? Your lips move, but make no sound; you see and hear, but you are not alive.

The sun made love to the earth that morning; the hills of Glyn-dyrys shimmered; a hawk, I remember as we rattled along, was flying against a stormy, pentecostal sky; all was blinding warmth and colour. Yet nothing absolved me from my inner grief at losing Rhiannon.

Perhaps, I thought, one's tenement of clay was bought and paid for at birth; that the dreams we foster are but the dusty myths of tomorrow that never become today; that love, like patriotism, is the hole men crawl into when they are afraid.

The wagons bumped and lurched in a cacophony of shrieks and clanks; down, ever down from The Top. Farm women, high-breasted and robust, straightened from milk churns as we rushed by, their faces astonished by the noise and action; pensive children, drooping in rags, gave sullen stares of greeting, too shy to wave: the stalwart birches of Waunwyllt stood black against the clouds.

Bumping along in the rattling, swaying tram my thoughts were now all of Rhiannon, the turmoil of revolution forgotten. I saw her in my mind against the white cloth of Dolygaer's winter, the place where we made love: I saw her swinging her gaitered boots through its lanes, her cheeks bitten red with frost. In the keen and beautiful air of autumn I saw her eyes large and startled as I kissed her, and heard her say:

"Oh come on, Tal – why delay if we love each other?" and her hands moved over me, making her the lover.

And now she was having my child: the thought both censured and excited me, but what would be the end of it I dared not think.

"What's the time, Tal?" Again I heard Rhiannon's voice.

"Must be midnight."

"A full moon, is it," and she raised herself and looked at the window.

"Not for another hour or so, unless Lady Charlotte's changed it lately."

"O hush, you, the silly old politics. Love me again, my precious?"

But it was not supposed to end like that, with her coming for a baby . . .

She is gone now, my Rhiannon, but I will always remember her.

Then my dream was shattered, for the brakes of the 'Perseverance' went on with a crash, sliding me down the length of the tram: the wheels skidded, sparks flew, and the day exploded into reality.

The face of Captain Wetton stared into mine during a two-hour interrogation: they checked and counter-checked every tally-card and invoice I carried before they let me go.

But, and God be praised, they stopped the search half an hour after the barge carrying Gideon was due at Abercynon.

The Abercynon basin had to be seen to be believed. .

Strategically placed as a signpost from the Top Towns to Cardiff port, it carried to the industrial towns like Merthyr, Aberdare, and Quakers' Yard the mineral wealth of the country – limestone, coal and iron ore from Spain for the manufacture of iron; then carried down the finished products from the Top Town furnaces to Cardiff.

The Basin itself was at the confluence of the Aberdare and Glamorganshire canals, roads and tram-roads. Here the River Cynon made a fork with the Taff, vying with it for dirt and disease, both now being mere sewers. Time was, said Old Shenks, when both ran bright and clear through the bluebell woods of places like Mountain Ash. Wild daffodils bloomed along their banks; ragwort and foxglove decorated the halcyon days, with the mountains waving green and the brooks and streams that clean you could drink from them with cupped hands.

But all that had gone with the coming of the iron and coalmasters. Abercynon, once the home of the roe and hart, the haven of wild birds, was now a blackened monument to industrial greed; and the big silver fish that had fought up to the spawning grounds had long gasped out their lives on sands of ash.

· The hive of the army of artisans and labourers who worked here in the basin was Navigation House, now the beating pulse of the Welsh Industrial Revolution: standing at the confluence of drovers' tracks, the railways and the canals leading south, it had so far sent this year to Cardiff docks (and 1839 was not yet out) a quarter of a million tons of coal and finished iron, at a penny a ton per mile.

Here on their high stools, bent over their ledgers, were the clerks and tally-men of the Canal Company formed by the ironmasters; the accountants and book-keepers with their plumes scratching, recording the up and down traffic – iron ore from Spain sent up to the furnaces of Merthyr and other iron towns; bearing-plates, fish-plates, dog-spikes and rails bound for India and Argentina, Africa and Peru.

This was the courthouse where legal disputes were settled and summary whippings carried out: here the stone-masons' areas, the wood-yard, dry dock and repair channels: here the smiths hammered and clanked and the '*Quack Quack*' bargees (who mainly lived in Nantgarw) poled and laboured in a forest of swinging cranes.

The Basin, once known as Junction, was a smooth flat sheen of water, a pond where loaded barges were navigated into line for the journeys up to the Top Towns or down to Cardiff port.

Swan Cottages, two lines of single and double-storey homes, served the clerks and resident bargees: the Swan and Boat inns, the Traveller's Rest and Junction served them ale, a few painted ladies thrown in for good measure served them pleasure. You couldn't go wrong if you knocked three times on the door of the Swan, for instance, and asked for Nellie.

I entered the inn after my confrontation with Captain Wetton with an unconcern I didn't feel.

" 'Evenin'," said the landlord.

I nodded him greeting and looked around the room.

The place was full of the hotch-pot trades of transport; bargees, raucous and foul-mouthed, spraggers and plate-layers straight from lifting and packing on the lines, engine drivers and mule-skinning gipsies from the old pack-horse trails, remnants of a dying breed.

Swarthy Spaniards were there, and dark-skinned men from the Mediterranean ports; North-country navvies and West-country men from the hills of China Clay. And with them were their women, most in gay colours, their quarrelling shrieks piercing the fug of ale and tobacco. In a far corner, near the door, sat Eli Firmament, his small, red eyes watching me over the top of his porter: we stared momentarily, then I turned away.

The landlord was pouring pints. Behind him, polishing glasses with dying lethargy, his wife moved within the elephantine slowness of almost total obesity, one eye blinking from the fatted layers of her face. I said to the landlord:

"A pint," and looked past him, adding, "The Devil a monk would be . . ."

He pushed a glass towards me. "O aye? So the Devil's troubled. What troubles you – Captain Wetton?"

I drank, watching him, and he added, "Make mine a quart."

I eyed him. "They told me you were dry."

"Roberts, I were, but you try bein' a teetotaller in Wales. Besides, look what I've got behind me," and he jerked his thumb. "She were a good ride once, mind, but the brewers 'ave a lot to answer for. It were the bloody Allsops – in Paris, of all places." He grimaced. "Got a face like a nun in a movement of cantabile."

"No odds to that." I didn't like him, and he knew it.

"Yes, you're right. Down to business, then – Gid Davies is here, but so's Eli Firmament."

"Aye, I saw him now just."

He went on pouring glasses as if he'd said nothing in particular, then:

"Perhaps he'll 'ave to go for a walk, I don't know. I'll speak to the lads . . . meanwhile, take the second door on the right, it's where the nobs hang out. Poison Ivy will be with ye right away."

I drained my glass and left him. When I looked again for Eli his chair was empty.

A few ancient colliers were champing their whiskers and eating their lungs, and some of them peered over their pints at me as I left. As I reached the darkness of the night outside the back door a light began to dance, supported by an unseen hand. I waited. The light began to dance eerily towards me and I came face to face with the landlord's wife.

Never will I forget that face: grotesquely masked by the wavering light of the lantern she carried, it was monstrously disproportioned, bloated and discoloured; yet her contralto voice was cultured: her accent was French.

"Monsieur . . . ?"

I took off my cap. She said, "You 'ave come down on the railway, I understand."

I nodded assent, and she said, "The great man your comrades have sent – Gideon Davies – is safe, and his companions, the old man and the girl are with him. Their names, if you please."

"Old Shenks and Poll."

"And yours?"

"Taliesin Roberts."

"Excellent. One must be careful, as you know, but we have been expecting you. Do the two with Gideon Davies know about the arms?"

"Old Shenks does, he arranged it, but the girl does not know."

"She can be trusted?"

I suppose I hesitated, for she added, "All must be trusted in this business, Mr. Roberts. One word in the wrong place and all our heads will fall."

"She can be trusted."

"*Voila!*" She made an expressive gesture. "Then all appears simple, but great care is needed, as I said. All day long the soldiers have been searching for arms in the Basin;

they have turned out all the rooms in our inn, and known informers are actually sitting within our tap. Now, if you are ready, I will take you to your people; see to Gideon Davies, and leave the arms to me, understand?"

"I understand."

She raised her lantern higher, saying, "Ah, now I see your beautiful white hair more clearly; how stupid of me to doubt."

She opened a door and I saw beyond her the broad sheen of faintly moonlit water, the Basin, and beyond that to the squat shapes of moored barges. Following her from the Swan, I went along the tow-path of the pond to the front door of Navigation House. Here, in the porch a light burned faintly. Leading the way, the woman entered a hall, and then descended twelve winding stone steps to a cellar, tapping on a door hidden behind stacked furniture.

Old Shenks opened the door, a cudgel in his hand; the landlord's wife raised her lantern.

"Monsieur?"

"Aye, Missus," said Old Shenks, and I pushed forward into the little room. Poll, on her knees beside Gid's litter, smiled up.

"Hallo, Tal," she said.

Before the woman left, I said, "Thank you, Madame. We begin to know our friends. But is it safe here?"

She emptied her hands in an expressive gesture of nothingness. "What better place?"

"But in Navigation House, the canal office? Under their noses?"

She patted me. "But is that not where people rarely look? And what is Fate? *Le Nez de Cléopâtre*, for instance? Had that nose been longer the history of the world might 'ave been different. Long noses we also cut off in Abercynon, as we did at the barricades. And gentry noses mostly.

"Listen more. South of the treble locks before Pentyrch is the lock cottage of Tom Ostler the bargee; he is your last lock resting house before the final run to Cardiff. The emigration ship is the *Erin's Hope*. She clears the Lock on the morning of the fifteenth; eight days' time. At barge speed you will get there early; this is bad. Once in the Sea Lock area there is no escape, you understand?"

"Yes, Madame."

"So rest your passenger with Ostler and his good wife; they will be expecting you and have food and clothes if you need them: he can bring a doctor if necessary, and will serve you well."

I asked, "When do we leave here?"

"When men come for you; another barge and a fresh horse are being made ready. Do not ask more, leave it at that."

"Yes, Madame."

At the door she paused, smiling. "*Bon voyage*, and good luck." Hesitating, she then said:

"Ah yes, but one thing more. A gentry nose was smelling around the Basin yesterday. 'Is one called Taliesin living here?' this nose asked my husband at the Swan."

I did not reply, and she added, no longer smiling, "A beautiful nose, but I sent it on its way to smell elsewhere. Everything in its place, *n'est-ce pas*? Gideon Davies first, this nose later. You will attend to that?"

"Yes, Madame," I said, and contemplated Rhiannon. Had she been near enough to be upbraided, her face, as always, would have been sanctified by its usual radiant innocence. But Poll, in tune with a world of substance and cruelty, said, after the woman had gone:

"By God, if she comes sniffing around on this trip to Cardiff, I'll not be responsible!"

It was a night of storm.

For three days we had held Gid in the cellar of Navigation House, hiding by day, coming out for food at night. Now thunder rolled over the roof in reverberating crashes and lightning lit the mountains.

Poll said, "We need water."

Old Shenks was over in the Swan. Gideon lay as still as death on the litter. Earlier, he had tried to talk, his words fumbling on his mouth as if after a stroke, every sense urging him to speak, but he could not. Eventually, exhausted by the effort, he lay back. I said to him:

"Gid, listen. We are taking you south to Cardiff. It is the network, do you remember? It is sending you to the sea for the ship to America, do you understand?"

Poll knelt beside me. "He is dead," she whispered. "Jen was right, he breathes, but he is dead."

"Quiet, he understands every word."

She rose, holding her ragged dress together at her throat. "What's the point of all this if he's going to die on us?"

"He will not die, and if you want to make it up to Dada, this is his friend." I added:

"Look, he has soiled his clothes. When Old Shenks comes back I'll change him . . ." and she cried:

"No, please go, Tal. I want to do him." She was agitated now. Her moods were sliding between expectation of joy and deep despair, and as we faced each other over the litter, I was uncertain of her, and becoming afraid.

For there was a strange light in Poll's face, something akin to madness, as if there was a tapping in the hall of her mind. Perhaps, I thought, once alone with Gideon Davies, she might kill him. Her remorse at betraying Dada had brought to her despair; had my father been the man lying on the litter she could have expiated the pain she had brought him. But the helpless one before her was not my father, and her reaction to him might be different. But through all my fears I knew I had to trust her. Between here and Cardiff she would have a dozen opportunities to do Gideon harm if she intended it.

Outside on the Pool the barges were sliding up and down, their squat hulks alive with dancing, silhouetted figures; earlier, coming from the Swan and Mrs Maginty I'd watched the bargees getting them into line: somewhere among them, I thought, was the man O'Reilly and his family with the cache of arms Iestyn and I had brought from Llangynidr.

Footsteps sounded below the trap-door of the yard then: I heard the scrape of boots in a lull of the thunder, and pushed up the boarded flap: the head of Old Shenks was framed against the flying stars. He lowered a steaming bucket and tossed me a towel. To Poll he gave a small basket of food.

"I'll give a hand," said he, and lowered himself down.

"No," I replied, "We're off back to the Swan, you and me."

His eyes switched from me to Poll and then moved to Gideon on the floor. The question in his face was plain. Poll said, smiling with sudden brilliance:

"My job, Old Shenks. I'm his nurse, ain't I? I got to do 'im."

Gideon's blind eyes, wide open, were staring fixedly at me as I looked down from the trap-door.

It must have been midnight before I left the Swan. I saw Madame and Maginty behind the bar, but spoke no words to them. There was a brawl between a Welsh collier and an Irish bargee whom he called a 'Quack Quack', something guaranteed to start a fight even before opening time, let alone stop-tap.

"You're taking a chance, aren't ye?" Old Shenks had said. I knew what he meant. He added:

"She's puggled. Ye can see it in her face."

The noise of the bar enveloped us; a gaggle of Irish bargees were dancing to the music of a fiddle, their clogs stamping the time, and their women were arming them around in shrieks, and Old Shenks watched them with a cat-like stare of imperturbability; senility, said he, being the last refuge of the old; one thing was certain, it hadn't touched his brain. A harpy with a red mouth like a letter box came dancing up, snapping her fingers and dancing a fandango in front of us, and the bargees roared, and Old Shenks said:

"I don't trust her, that one. If the mood struck her she'd put a knife in poor old Gid, you realise?"

"Ach, you've a shrivelled soul, Shenks, give her a chance."

"A chance is all she wants, I reckon." He stared moodily into his ale. "I reckon you ought to kick her out, mun."

I said, "She'll do it for my father. Poll's all right, I tell you — you didn't know her in the old days, beside, we need her."

"Not as much as all that, and if that gentry piece of yours turns up, anything could happen — that Poll's mad for ye, you realise?" He grunted. "Anyway, how did your fancy piece know where we were?"

I knew but did not tell him — Fanny, the Dowlais parlourmaid; her tongue was inches too long.

Shenks said, with finality, "Ach well, I'm off to bed. But we can do without your well-meaning friend, you know, while Captain Wetton's sniffin' around, remember."

"Wetton? He couldn't track an elephant in the snow." I replied carelessly, thinking about Rhiannon.

"Don't be too sure."

I followed the old fighter to the stairs and he went up to his room.

As I pushed my way out into the darkness I saw the faces of Maginty and the French woman, and they were expressionless.

*

That winter was into us with sweeping rain, but the tow-path around the Navigation pond was still covered with autumn's dross of gold. It was a black pig of a night with the wind in a festivity of temper, charging head down across the valley: one of the Swan characters called Dai-Come-Home-Via-Railings was dancing a jig against the scurrying moon and by the time I'd got rid of him there was rising within me an intuitive sense of disaster, and I cursed myself for my foolishness for leaving Poll alone with Gideon. I actually ran the last few yards to the trap-door, and knelt, levering it open.

The tiny room was empty. Dropping into it, I stared around, whispering, "*Poll!*"

Nothing stirred except the lantern, swinging gently from its big hook in the ceiling.

Suddenly, in a little buffet of the wind, I heard voices.

Opening the cellar door I looked around the stacked furniture into darkness, seeing nothing. Moving silently into the main cellar, I looked up the winding stone steps to the floor above.

"*Poll . . .!*"

Suddenly realising that the voices were coming from another cellar room, not from upstairs, I crept towards the sounds in the darkness, seeing almost instantly a chink of light beneath a door. The voices grew louder, but were indistinct against the background of the storm; I could not identify meaning. Then suddenly there was a scuffle and a shrill outcry; a man's high-pitched shriek now, muffled as with masking hands; I heard the noise of a chair overturning, deep-throated oaths. Then a man shouted, and I heard this clearly:

"Tie him, for God's sake. We'll settle this palaver!"

More scuffles now, a faint whimpering; this grew to a sobbing that echoed around my hiding-place, an eerie accompaniment to the sounds of storm which now appeared directly over the Basin. Now more determinate noises came: a man being bound. I heard the victim's protests grow fainter, dying into suffocating groans as he was gagged. Hobnails scraped the stone flags of the cellar and I immediately retreated to the winding staircase. A door burst open. A beam of light splayed the floor. Two men burst out of the room, dragging between them a prisoner, and his boots trailed the flags, kicking and clattering wildly; behind these came other men, but I saw only their legs as they pressed on in whispering commands, to the very cellar in which, but a few hours earlier, we had been hiding Gid Davies. Descending one step, I peered around the corner into the cellar area, seeing in the framing doorway a man's hand go up and a rope snake high over a bacon hook. The bound man struggled furiously, shrieking behind his gag: the cellar was filled with his animal panic. Men heaved. I saw their straining bodies, the taut rope, the condemned man rise, his tied legs bucking violently.

In the slanting rays of the cell lantern I momentarily saw the victim's face, bulbous, scarlet; eyes dilated with terror, suffused with blood.

Silence.

No sound now but men's breathing and the obscene noises of ritual strangulation. The rope trembled, taut. The body, arching and bucking, slowly pivoted. The rain sleeted down, crashing in gusty squalls against upstairs windows; thunder boomed and cracked, dying into the rim of the world. Slowly the dying man swung, in gasps . . . into inactivity: his legs moved slowly now, pathetically twitching; the feet amazingly jerking up and down, his bound hands spasmodically twitching, fingers clawing . . .

"Right you," said a voice. "*Out!* Back in half an hour and cut him down."

"What time are the clerks due back?"

"Night-shift comes on after supper – half an hour; tallies first, the bosses don't come on 'till six."

"Aye, well I want him six foot down long before then. Dump him anywhere between here and Nantgarw, he's got the whole county to sleep under, the bastard. I'll be gone now just, so I will."

A man said, and his voice was as bitter as dregs, "He were a cough-drop, mind, that one."

"Aye, less diabolical intervention, he'll be playin' dolly

stories wi' St. Peter."

"Poor little scratch, there were nothin' of him, mind . . ."

"Thinner'n Handel's lute."

"Ach, save ye pity! Got a gab on him bigger'n a baby's bum, an' there's only one place for him."

Taking advantage of their hesitation, I descended the stone steps and flattened myself along the cellar wall, waiting there in pent breathing, in darkness. I heard the creak of the trap-door as they climbed out into the night; a careful sound as they closed it from above. For at least a minute I stayed, listening to the noises of the house and the gentle, rhythmic creaking of the hanged man's rope.

The storm had ceased; only whispering booms now were clattering over The Top, and the rain was falling on the roof as if in quiet balm to the night's activity.

Feeling in my pockets I lit a match; it flared in my hand, banishing shadows, and I crept forward with the subconscious urge not to awaken the dead.

The open cell door made shape, framing its slowly revolving burden. The match burned my fingers and I dropped it, momentarily standing in blackness before lighting another.

Raising it, I looked up into the face of the hanged man, seeing the bloated cheeks, the protruding tongue, the bulging eyes. And despite the malefaction of that countenance, I knew it instantly.

Eli Firmament.

"God Almighty!"

As if hearing this, and called by Deity's significant command, there came from the gaping mouth a last strangling gurgle. I stared up. Eli Firmament stared down, and in his dead look I saw his condemnation.

Suddenly the trap-door went back and above me the head and shoulders of Old Shenks appeared, framed against the rain-washed stars like a departing soul. He called softly:

"You down there, Tal? The lads awakened me. Maginty says we're moving early . . . that you, Tal . . . ?"

I could not answer him. I was still staring up into the dead eyes of Eli Firmament.

Poll said, "They came soon after you left, Tal—Sam Williams, Knocker and six more waitin' in the cellar with Big Jake Kilrain, and with them was Eli Firmament and he were squealing for a pig-sticking till they shut him quiet. They waited till I'd finished doin' Mr. Davies, then they took up his litter and carried him down the tow-path to this barge."

"Getting Gid away a trifle earlier, they told her," added Shenks.

Poll said, brightly, "I asked what they was up to—just leavin' early, they said, because of the military pokin' around—besides, said Sam, we want the bacon hook."

"To hang a pig," said Old Shenks, softly.

"Funny old time to hang bacon, I said," continued Poll, "and I didn't see any old pig either, except Eli Firmament, and he didn't 'ave no apple in his mouth." She laughed and I saw her eyes in the dim light of the barge aft cabin. Now she stopped and whispered to Gideon like a mother speaks to a child:

"Don't you worry, Mr. Davies, I've got you. First light tomorrow and we're off directly down to Cardiff wi' you. Don't you worry about hanging old pigs."

And Gideon smiled and moved his body. I would have spoken to him then, but I felt the long-boat swing into the wind as the bargees poled her, and they took us along the bank of the turn-pool and out into running water through Isaf Lock into the lower canal, south for Cardiff. The young barge horse took the strain, and with Old Shenks walking at its head, we were away in the first cold redness of a watery dawn.

A cool old lad was Shenks; neither frost nor frenzy in him. I couldn't have done better at a time like this, and got proof of it in the miles to come.

It was a beautiful November morning after the night of storm, with rushes waving at us from the canal banks, and from the fields the great moon-like eyes of cows watched us with stares of bovine queens as we clip-clopped past: gold-crests and tits flew about us, chirping into the watery sun: mallard were flying clear of the staining Industry: a mother coot with a well-grown brood behind her paddled defiantly across our prow, then shepherded them into a feeder-creek to watch us pass, and Poll, sitting on the stern within sight of Gideon's litter in the aft cabin, tossed them bread.

Before us, when the canal lined out, we saw the earlier barges, filled to the gunwales with finished iron; behind us were others. At every one of the forty-nine locks and all through the nearly six-hundred-foot drop between Merthyr and Cardiff, we passed scores more going up, their twenty-ton holds heaped high with iron ore from Spain or limestone from quarries like Llangattock.

Astonishingly, I knew no apprehension now; it was as if my fears had died with Eli Firmament, which was ridiculous because there was more than one informer lying in wait. And I could tell, by the cautious looks and guarded greetings of oncoming bargees, that our presence was no longer a secret. With a casualness that betokened duplicity, all barges gave way to us; every man leaped to the assistance of the lock-keepers to see us through, their women and children cautiously peering from cabins.

The Nantgarw community of bargees, conservative in the extreme, who kept their own customs and resented the in-fluence of strangers, now opened its arms to undercover escapees from Merthyr. It was also clear, from their little gifts to us, that they knew that sickness was aboard . . . a packet of sugar, a can of milk, freshly cooked bread from the wayside ovens.

Always will I remember that journey from Abercynon to

Cardiff: Wales arose, independent, purified.

Women with colliers' caps on, sitting outside their doors, waved gaily as we went down: children ran along the banks pestering to lead the horse. No more were we accused of coming South with Northern airs and graces; we were as one with them, the Southern Welsh, unified in a common task, to get a Welsh hero down to Cardiff.

Down through the bright country we went along the cut. It was as if we had left all our cares behind us north of Abercynon: no sign of military patrols, no talk (from barges going up) of the independent loafers and armed deserters who were the scourge of the valleys. We just floated calmly on for mile after mile: first past the head of Sir Charles Smith's tramroad that served Gelligaer and Quakers' Yard, down, down through the locks with the old Taff, sulking and broody, mooching along beside us with her filth of The Top.

Now past the Dinas and Hafod tram-road, then east of busy Pontypridd with her distant gay market and lines of coloured washing, the home of the mad Dr. Price; along the stretch called The Doctor's Canal, past Treforest collieries and the pits and drifts of Dynea where the canal lapped up to the mouths of the coal levels.

Women, stripped to the waist in the keen sunlit air, swarmed like flies over the waiting barges, carrying head-baskets of coal like Egyptian aristocracy. It was a journey of sun and wind under the open, blue vault of a cloudless sky.

Squatting at the tiller, I stared into the sunset. And saw on a humped bridge over the cut about two hundred yards before us a figure astride a horse: against the red sunset I clearly saw horse and rider. Motionless they were as if carved from black stone, etched against the redness.

I glanced down at the barge horse and Old Shenks on the tow-path; they were marching with the weariness of the day's trudge, heads low, feet dragging. And, when I looked again, both horse and rider had disappeared. Even as I watched, the sun sank into oblivion, its last shimmering rays fingering the empty bridge.

"Did you see that?" I called down to Shenks.

"See what?"

"It doesn't matter."

Night fell. The moon came out, lighting a dull, forbidding country, a world changed. How strange it is that the land smiles in sunlight, and darkness brings threats and shadows waiting to spring. I was filled with sudden apprehension.

The horsed rider I had seen looked surprisingly like Rhiannon, even from a distance.

By midnight Nantgarw itself was behind us, and the great treble locks before Pentyrch coming up. And Poll, who was now at the horse's bridle, called from the towpath:

"You there, Tal?"

Old Shenks, asleep on the floor beside Gideon's litter, did not stir: climbing out on to deck, I called softly, "What's up?"

"Trouble coming, I think," said Poll, and slowed the horse: the barge swam on weigh through overhanging alders where the moon made no light, and I saw her face in that blue light: strangely shadowed, that face beneath the tight scrag of her shawl . . .

"I'll come down," I said, and moved to the gunwale.

"Not yet!" commanded Poll.

Two men had emerged from the hedge of an adjoining field in moonlight; wandering in single file towards Poll, and their arrogance matched their tattered clothes and mud stains.

Their feet were bare, their red pantaloons tied at the shins. Upon their heads they wore French cockade hats; over their shoulders were slung Army muskets. Even from the barge I got the stink of them. Feet splayed in the mud, legs wide, the first, a man of gaunt height, pushed back his hat and examined Poll with an impudent stare, and the second cried:

"Manna from heaven, Ben Stripe! Look, a wagger!" and he gripped Poll's arm, while his companion snatched at the other. And they walked her along the tow-path while she led the horse, bantering, swaggering as she fought to push them off.

Renegades.

These were the dregs that hung on to the legs of the Brecon military; gouge-fighters, kick-fighters, the riff-raff deserters from the old French wars. In batches they had come ashore from hired Breton schooners, trained and battle-worn, owing allegiance to neither queen nor country. Taking to the mountains first, they then scavenged in roving gangs, moving into the industrial towns for theft, haunting the highways, tram-roads and canals with robbery and violence. A glimpse of a cockade hat or a pair of French pantaloons and the military shot on sight, but where was Captain Wetton when he was needed? I wondered.

"*Tal!*"

Now one had pinioned Poll's arms behind her back; the other had her skirts above her waist, and in the struggle they were nearly under the horse, which reared up, hooves skidding in the tow-path mud. The smaller of the two came clear, not expecting me, as I leaped off the barge, and I caught him with a right that laid him flat: the other, the bigger, flung Poll aside and came at me low, head down for the butt. I stepped aside and he ran past me, yelling as he toppled into the cut. The barge slid up on the weigh, running him under. I caught a glimpse of him flailing in the rushes: his oaths and curses followed us into the night.

"Jesus," whispered Poll, "did you fix them!"

"Perhaps," I said, snapping up the horse into a trot. "But it's two more worries we could have done without, for they won't forget. I'll take a spell, you get back aboard with Gideon."

Poll was sparkling like a new pin that night, as we slid the barge alongside Tom Ostler's lock cottage: it was a night for dormice and owls and hooting things, with thickets waving to unseen hands, and the moon beamed down from rents in the clouds like sun-shafts.

Earlier, we had passed a race of 'coal-holes' – black openings in the hillsides where narrow feeders entered, lapping at the entrances.

Here, by the light of the naphtha flares women and girls were working long convoys of lilliputian iron barges, linking them into trains of six and hauling and heaving them into the entrances: here unseen colliers, less covered than they in nakedness, laboured at the seams. And, as they worked, the women were chanting a bawdy song in Welsh, wagging their bottoms to the rhythm and kicking up their legs in sinuous, provocative gestures and antics that delighted me and shocked Old Shenks, who was knitting off duty.

Poll, hearing the singing, came clambering out of the aft cabin (I was with the horse) and, with clapping spoons in her hands began to dance audaciously, bucking her body in gay vitality. And the other women, seeing her, clapped the time with hilarious joy.

I can see Poll even as I write this, with her skirts up to her thighs and dancing to a tattered audience of coal-grimed, bare-breasted women, young and old, who jigged and jogged on the lips of their man-made pandemonium.

Now we slid away into darkness amid the fire-fly lights of following barges, until the tumbledown outline of Tom

Ostler's lock cottage by Treble Locks made shape in moonlight; a twisted edifice of phallic chimneys and Tudor gables: a mute amen, it appeared, to the obscene chorus of the women of Gehenna.

Tom Ostler, the lock-keeper, was a one-armed chap with good Welshness in his face. "He had two arms once," said his missus, "till he had the gate accident – jumped into the lock to save a child, and the gates closed and gripped him – so I hopped in and sawed it off."

"You did what?" I asked, astonished.

"Wouldn't be here now if it weren't for my Jasmine, mind," said Tom, all six foot and sixty years of him.

"She actually cut off your arm?" I stared at him.

"Ay ay – the water were comin' up, see?"

"More'n he'd get from that Dolly Oh-no," said his wife from Wigan, hanging her smalls on the fender.

"Dolly Oh-no?" asked Poll. "Who's she?"

"The fancy piece he were courting. Couldn't slice funeral ham, that one, never said no in 'er life."

"Ach, give it a rest, girl, that were forty year back," said Tom.

"She sawed off your arm?" I repeated in disbelief.

"Made a good job too!" Tom unpinned his empty sleeve, jerking the stump up and down with rhythmic precision.

"Mind, I'd rolled and boned a few legs o' pork 'afore then," said his wife, "being a butcher's daughter. Same job really, though they makes a lot of less fuss and palaver."

"Some woman," said Old Shenks.

"O ah!" exclaimed Tom. "She don't take nothin' lying down, she's after me legs now," which put everyone into stitches, of course.

"Some arm, ye mean," said Jasmine. "It took some sawing. The military wouldn't believe it, neither."

"The military?" I asked, looking up.

"That Captain Wetton from Dowlais Penywern."

"Does he get as far south as this?"

"Aye, on patrol after deserters mainly, but don't worry: you and the girl in the barge, Mr. Davies and Old Shenks in the house, to make an early start."

I looked at Poll and she looked at me, and Mrs. Ostler added, "Mind, likely little Poll could share a bed wi' me . . .?"

"That would be best," said Poll, which surprised me.

Earlier, following Tom Ostler's instructions, we had poled the barge into a pool lay-by beside his cottage, and Jasmine, his missus, had helped carry our things from the cabin; she was a lively, bright-eyed woman of candid stock, as dark as sin and big-bosomed, and her mutton stew she ladled boiling hot from the saucepan; we ate like people famished.

Just like a wedding in Amlwch, it was; sitting there in the kitchen while the kettle sang and the cat washed its face by the hob. And Poll's eyes, dark-lashed in her pale face, were rising and lowering at me across the table; I knew she had something under her apron that would come out later by the look on her face. Tom Ostler said:

"I've worked out that if one of ye gets a lift down to Cardiff port tonight he could be there Thursday and arrange with the *Erin's Hope* to take Mr. Davies aboard on Saturday."

"Ye'll need to give the skipper a bit o' notice, natural," said his wife.

"And since it's a three-day barge run down to the Bute Ship Canal, it'll give you a clear four days to deliver Mr. Davies," added Tom.

"Can you keep us hanging around here without some suspicion?"

Tom Ostler shrugged. "A few hours won't rupture us. Who's going south, have ye made up your minds?"

"To Cardiff?" I nodded at Old Shenks. "You'd best; you know that new sea-lock like the back of your hand."

"Then take this wi' you," said Tom, and handed Old Shenks an envelope. "Give this to Skipper O'Shea, and for God's sake don't mention the name o' Tom Ostler or we'll all swing together."

"Do you handle this sort of thing often?"

"Official, you're the only candidates, arrived by chance: unofficial, we run about ten or twelve like you a month . . . to Bilbao in Spain, then cleared to America."

"All Sam Williams's people?"

"Mostly Sam Williams's people, but others are startin' now . . ."

"Coming thick and heavy these days," said his wife. "God, what a country!"

I thought it astonishing that such domesticated people, their children married and gone, should be members of an organisation running escape routes to the sea. Yet it was their household's very normality that lent it strength.

According to Tom Ostler's placid conversation, it appeared a usual occurrence for Captain Wetton to drop in for refreshment while escapees were hiding below stairs. Wetton, it appeared, was a regular visitor when on patrol.

The courage of such people was commonplace at the time: half Wales was at it in one way or another. With the transportation hulks crammed with patriot convicts, families like the Ostlers were getting hunted men to America via Spain by the score.

And leaders of espionage groups, men like Sam Williams of the Union, put their lives in the hands of such as these, for Napier's counter-espionage didn't stop at torture when it came to confessions: one craven down the line could hang a score within the chain's command. And this chain, to my own knowledge, stretched from North to South in Wales. Loyalists like Skipper Rowlands were dependent on the sense and fortitude of the Ostlers, though a hundred miles away: Sam Williams's life hung on the thread of Old Shenks's integrity.

It was a chapter of Welsh history that has never been defined because of the individual secrecy; sacrifices of those who ran the routes, snatching patriots from the gaols of England. It was built on the courage of Welsh men and women: those who broke the rules, like Eli Firmament, paid the price, patriot or traitor.

In the ensuing silence Tom said, getting up, "Best to bed; it'll be a different kettle o' fish in the mornin', and we've got to get Mr. Shenks away."

I think I knew that Poll would come that night. Her passive acceptance of Mrs. Ostler's offer for her to sleep within the house was as much a ruse as my acceptance.

Rhiannon's absence, the uncertainty of the future, was building within me an intemperate demand for escape, both from this nightmare journey and my own male need.

Nothing mattered save the wish to possess Rhiannon.

After Old Shenks had left for Cardiff port, I lay in the cabin and listened to the lapping of water: barge after barge, in a singing of ropes and tumbling water, slipped up and down the cut. A baby cried, strangled by darkness; men's guttural voices I heard, women's gentler replies. And the moon, shafting through the port-hole windows drew etchings of water-silver upon the ceiling. I lay stiffly, every nerve tensed, and my longing for Rhiannon bore down upon me, forbidding sleep until well after midnight.

I sensed rather than saw the white form of Poll standing beside my bunk, and was not surprised.

"Tal . . ."

I opened my eyes.

It was not Poll the street-walker, the wanton of China. Fashioned by need she stood before me then in frail sisterhood; no immodesty touched her, no carnality stained me. Instead, I remembered her as the one who raised Meg; who had come to us in Amlwch at a time of greatest need; washed, cleaned for us, suckled my sister. Who to know? I thought. And who to judge, since life had thrown us so violently together? Was one a cockatrice to snatch at moments of oblivion within the senseless fight?

In that blue light, half-clothed, Poll looked seraphic.

Her breasts were of alabaster whiteness, her hair of deepest black upon her shoulders: serenely beautiful she looked in her tattered petticoat, and her feet were bare.

"Tal . . . !" Again she called, and touched my hand.

I reached for Poll, all guilt abandoned in a senseless urgency; my body moved for her, not Rhiannon. Yet desiring was not desire, nor lusting lust: it was a crisis of the head built upon companionship: a wish to melt in her: to be reborn in dark-sweet-dark or golden girl, her age or shape or colour undefined.

"Please love me, Tal. Nobody's ever loved me, they only took."

I opened my arms to her.

"Listen!" whispered Poll, and drew from my lips, her head inclined towards the door.

"What is it?"

I listened, too, hearing nothing but wind-sigh down the canal, and the creak of overhanging branches.

"It's nothing!" I kissed away her breath.

Now that she was with me it seemed that she had been there all my life; in part or total service, always Poll, a play in my existence. I smelled again the wild thyme she pinned upon her clothes in Amlwch, saw her smiles, and her aggression: all became the whole. Harlot, trull, strumpet? She was none of these. She was a honeycomb woman and her mouth was sweet to me.

"*Listen!* Tal," she rose beside me, her face chalk white.

Her fear snatched at me like a contracting muscle: listening, I heard a low, distant buzzing. A fly around a lamp? Then the strange sound rose to a louder note, rising and falling on the wind.

Now it appeared to be within the cabin.

A captive bee?

Poll's hands made claws of her fingers and she put them in her hair and screamed with all the facial contortions of a scream, but made no sound.

"What is it, for God's sake?" I gripped her shoulders and shook her to rattle. "*Poll!*"

The bee-song grew louder still, now coming from the cabin roof. I raised my eyes to the ceiling. Slithering feet I heard then; the unmistakable clamour of naked feet on wood . . . now falsetto consultations came from the night, then silence.

And in that silence the cabin door crashed back and Big Buzz burst in with Jen behind him. They stood motionless. The hive children crowded in behind them until the cabin was filled: the bee-sound they were making died away.

Our Jen said, saluting with her ladle:

"Well well! I never did. Just look at this, my charmers – the things they get up to!" and she reached out, seized Poll's wrist and twisted her out on to the floor.

Clutching her torn petticoat, Poll shivered before her.

"No clothes, neither? Dear me!"

It was the same old Jen, purposeful, articulate. I leaped off the bunk and pulled Poll aside.

"Get out!" I whispered. "Get out, all of you!"

"Oh no, my lovely," said Jen. "We ain't goin' without our Poll, are we Buzz?"

The children pressed about her.

Waspie I saw, and Doss: Shrinky was there at the back, also the three child cripples, their eyes like saucers. To fight would mean fighting children. Jen said, serenely:

"Mind, we nearly 'ad rag babies, didn't we, Buzz, when we thought you wasn't comin' back, Our Pol. But I've been in this game, girl, since your arse were a thimble. Once you're with Our Jen, there ain't no pissin' off."

She grinned at us, her teeth gapped and discoloured. Poll stood staring, as one mesmerised.

"So now you're comin' home, my honey-pot, ain't ye? Ye see, these little drones an' workers need the loot, and you're their queen."

I took a step, but Big Buzz barred the way, and in the hands of the children were knives.

Poll gasped, "Tal, I'll go. She'll kill us, else; I got to go."

"Ay ay," added Jen, "more'n likely, precious, so make yourself decent. And charge him sixpence for seein' your petticoat. Really, in all my life, I ain't never seen such goin's on, 'ave you, Buzz?" She elbowed him and he chuckled inanely, spit dripping from his mouth.

There was a silence, and then she shrieked:

"*Sixpence!*" and raised her ladle high.

I dropped the silver into her hand.

"Right you, and any more foolin' around wi' Poll and I'll move me backside lively – up to Penywern and the military, and to hell wi' your old Gid Davies."

Snatching Poll's wrist she pulled her towards the cabin door, but before she went through it, Poll said:

"I loves you, Tal. I've always done, remember?"

"Come on, come on!" said Jen.

I stood on the stern of the barge and watched Poll being prodded along the road that led to China.

"She's gone, you say?" Tom Ostler peered in disbelief. "That was sudden. Why?"

His wife added, "At a time like this, for heaven's sake?"

I said, "With Old Shenks gone, too, I can't handle the barge now."

We stood in silent perplexity, wondering what to do: if they had any suspicions, they didn't make them apparent. Then Tom said:

"Aye well, son, ye canna stay here. At latest, the military will be round the day after tomorrow and we're done for if they find Mr. Davies here."

"What about the old Star Inn, near the Cow and Snuffers, Tom?" asked Jasmine. "It's the nearest lock with a lay-pool, an' he could hang out there till the old man got back."

"The Cow and what?" I asked.

"The Cow and Snuffers," said she. "Disraeli meets his Mary Ann there, but we ain't supposed to know."

One thing, they hadn't lost their sense of humour. "But how do I get there?" I asked. "I'll need a tow-lad, won't I?"

"No. I can get you that far."

"Right. I'll handle it after that."

"You must," replied Tom. "I got to be back here to handle Wetton."

Jasmine helped us to get Gideon back aboard the barge, then we slipped it down through the trebles with six others coming down behind us and two more going up: with me at the nag's head and Tom on the tiller we rode her down to

Melingriffith and the old Star Inn, a mile or so south.

And the last I saw of Jasmine Ostler was her waving goodbye with a little lace handkerchief in the dawn.

Later, I learned they committed her for treason at Cardiff Assizes; fettered her at the Bridewell in Swansea to Mary Ann Brewer, a prostitute, and sailed her on the *Tory* in October 1844 for seventeen years in Van Diemen's Land. She died six months later in a punishment cell in the old gaol at Paramatta, which, spare time, was used as a brothel: typical of Jasmine, I thought; as old Tom said, being Lancashire she took nothing lying down.

A dumpy, ruined place was this Star Inn; an old pub built beside the ancient pack-horse trails when the iron came down on the backs of animals; the days of the fierce drovers who slashed their live animals for black puddings, and fought each other, Hell-bent for right of way. Some queer old boys Wales has spawned in her time, said Tom Ostler.

Aye, dirty old lads, these drovers: romancers have built them into legends, but they were evil; heartless to their animals.

"You'd be best in here, mind," he added, and opened the iron door of a little lock-up attached to the inn. "Time was they put the drover drunks in here," said he. "What better, mun, for a Welsh hero?"

I did not answer, being sick to death that Gid Davies had come down to this.

After Tom had helped me carry him and our belongings the hundred yards or so from the barge pool into the Star Inn's gaol, he took his leave of me, to return to Treble Locks, saying:

"It shouldn't be too long, Tal. Old Shenks'll be with you soon. I'll send word down to him tonight."

"Tell him to bring more food," I called, and waved him off.

It was the last time I saw Tom Ostler: talk was that they hanged him after Jasmine went, but I never got proof of it.

*

After seeing to Gideon, and with the sun high, I walked around the ramshackle rooms of the old public.

In the middle of the shattered tap-room I tried to imagine its activity when droving was at its height in the Vale of Glamorgan; the bull- and bear-baiting, the cock- and fist-fighting: the navigators' randies which, as they pushed the canal through to Cardiff nearly fifty years ago, put every spare woman to flight or in the family way.

And soon, I thought, now that Trevethick and Stephenson were inventing railways, men like Brunel would push the lines all over the country, and the eternal boardroom squabbling, the same old tap-room conflicts would start again: a new era of industry; a score more towns like Merthyr, another fifty Amlwchs. Was there no end to the violation and carnage?

I noticed unwashed plates and mugs on the splintered bar counter; filthy rags in a corner, the remnants of a mattress. Clearly the place had been recently used, probably by tramps.

Strangely, I did not give a thought to deserters . . .

Lighting the barge lamp, I hung it from the lock-up ceiling when dusk fell: Gideon was asleep in a holy quiet; twice I bent to the litter, listening for his breathing . . . but his heart was still thumping with its old defiance.

Before darkness I lit a fire and upon it cooked oatmeal and toasted bread; mixing this with milk I propped Gideon up and fed him.

Feeding him brought us our only small affinity, perhaps because he was in my arms. He swallowed automatically, a man swallowing chaff; he drank clumsily, spilling it down the front of him like an untaught child. His eyes were still upon me when, the bowl empty, I laid him back.

For the first time I noticed a phenomenon.

His eyes, large and blue in his haunted face, seemed opaque, and fixed; unmoving when I moved, unlike the eyes of a portrait. The blank stare of those pale eyes searched me, and I shivered, saying involuntarily:

"Come on, here's a treat, Gid," and I took from my pocket

the tin box holding 'The Tale of Delwyn'. "I'll read a bit from this – things my father used to read to old Poll and me, when we were up at Amlwch," and opening the manuscript at random, I read aloud:

"'Now solve this riddle, Welshman . . .

"'There was living in the land at that time a woman of honey fashioned by bees. Her body was of wax, her head pollen, her face was of bee-bread, and her hands and feet made of larvae, the stuff of queens: she was a delight to men, this woman; her lips were sweet, nectar was upon her tongue. But it was she, the honeycomb woman, who betrayed Prince Arfon to King Maelgŵn as a traitor; and Maelgŵn put out Arfon's eyes and imprisoned and starved him in Castell Deganwy. Later, relenting, she entered the dungeon on wings with her swarm, and fed Prince Arfon. The honey she fed him was her blood, the wax she fed him was her flesh, being in love with Delwyn, his son, by whom she had been rejected . . .' "

I looked up at Gideon in the light of the flickering lamp and knew the fixed stare of his eyes. I read on:

"'But the bees prevailed upon the honeycomb woman to return to them, saying, "You are the prisoner of the hive. Without you we will die. Let us seek a mortal woman whose body is of flesh and whose veins run with blood, and she will serve your Prince." And so, bidden by the woman, a princess came to Delwyn and stood before him, and said, "A honeycomb woman bade me come to serve your father, and I am not of honey, I am real: I stand before you in flesh, not a sweetness that melts in the sun." This the mortal woman said, not knowing that her testing time would come; that soon, at the hands of a priest and a foreigner, she, in her prince's service, would suffer outrage.

"'This is the riddle. Who, then, was the honeycomb woman? And who the mortal who did not melt in the sun? Solve this, Welshman, and you have solved 'The Tale of Delwyn'.'"

When I had finished reading this I shivered, closing the book; for I still could feel old Gid's eyes upon me in the dark.

*

I awoke within minutes of falling asleep, aware of a change in the room. The lamp, flickering low, suddenly dimmed almost to blackness, and, as my eyes grew more accustomed to the faint glow I saw a great black shape looming above me, and I stiffened on the floor. Then I realised that the black shape leaning over me was Gideon; that his form was obliterating the lamp. Sweat broke out upon my face as I stared up into his blind eyes, and he stared back at me in his blindness as if mesmerised by my nearness. A sudden panic seized me and I would have reached up and thrown him off, but he spoke.

"Taliesin!"

His voice broke the spell and I reached up and wiped the sweat of my face into my hair, gripped him by the shoulders and gently forced him away.

"What is it, Gideon? What is it?"

"Go back," said Gideon, in a whisper.

The lamp suddenly flared up and I saw his eyes large and full upon me, and it was impossible to believe that this man was blind, as sightless as Prince Arfon, who had been blinded by his enemies.

Now Gideon gripped my hands, and astonishingly, as I rose, so he rose with me, staring into my face.

"In the name of God, Tal – leave me. *Go back*."

With the knowledge of his strength had come relief and I could have wept for joy that he was recovering; yet, strangely, the sense of foreboding deepened within me; but I cajoled him, whispering to him encouragement as I helped him back to his litter, and he lay there, exhausted by his effort, and I knelt beside him, stroking his hair. Gideon spoke again, and his voice was firm and strong:

"There is evil here, Taliesin. We blind ones are given other senses. Leave me . . . you are too young . . ."

A low tapping came on the cell door and he turned his head to it, saying, "Don't open it, Taliesin."

Going to the door I whispered, "Who is it?"

Rhiannon said, "Tal, is that you . . . ?"

I opened the door and let her in and she said, her finger to her lips, whispering:

"I waited until dark in case somebody saw me come. This morning a girl called Poll came to Kierton with Fanny, the housemaid from Dowlais House – she begged me to come to you, this girl: 'Go to Treble Locks on the canal,' she said, 'and the lock-keeper will tell you where Tal is,' and I did so, and Mrs. Ostler sent me here."

"Oh God," I said.

But Rhiannon didn't appear to hear this, adding, "There is a light in the windows of the inn next door – do you know that two men are in there?"

"Two men?" I stared at her, and I heard Gideon ease his big body on the litter, listening, and Rhiannon whispered excitedly:

"One is a priest. Surely he would help us – he is a man of God, Tal, you'd only have to ask," and she looked at Gideon on the floor.

I kissed her face and drew her within the tiny room, knowing that 'The Tale of Delwyn' was being fulfilled by prophecy, step by step, and that, like me, she would have to suffer it.

Leaving Gid with Rhiannon, I crept out of the cell door, shut it quietly behind me and went on all fours through the tangled undergrowth of the gaol forecourt to the nearest window of the Star Inn next door.

Raising my head, I peered through the cracked, mud-stained glass.

Two men were sprawled over a trap-door in the middle of the decaying floor of the tap-room; they were eating from newspapers and drinking, turning up their bottles.

One man was small. Of evil countenance, he was dressed as a priest in black. The second I recognised as the one I had thrown into the cut. Bearded, of great height, he dwarfed his companion and now said bassly, with a fine French accent:

"Ah yes, I remember her! The wife at Treble Locks? But she is fat and fifty if she's a day." He spat. "Come! Keep your English! I tell you this – it is to my village in France that you should go for beautiful women . . ."

I drew back into the shadows, realisation dawning.

Priest and foreigner!

These were the two of whom the Tale had warned; men who would make an outrage . . .

The little priest said, "We cannot pick and choose. I am a man of God, as you know, but that woman walking the barge horse took my eye . . ."

Said the Frenchman, "I have seen her before, she is a Rodney of China! Lovelier than the Woman of Samaria, is she, yet a shilling would buy her! Oh, to have her within reach of a nudge," and the little priest raised his blue-veined hands upwards, crying:

"Judge not the wild oats of my youth, O Zion! Pester me with her kisses red as wine! Had it not been for that white-haired bastard I would have died for her on all fours."

"Don't worry, Priest," came the reply. "Nobody ever went to Hell on his knees. How old is she, you think?"

"The bargee bride? No more'n twenty, but these water folk come brutal if you lift their women!"

"Yes indeed," replied the other. "Look at my fine red pantaloons, they are ruined. When I meet that one, you can have his female; I will entertain myself by pulling bones from his back." He turned, looking straight towards me, and I drew away instantly. "What time is it?"

The little priest said dreamily, "Eleven o'clock, by the size of the moon. Where did they get to, Frenchy? She could not have travelled far. He called her 'Poll', remember?"

The big man wandered about, drinking from his bottle. "Around these parts, she is, no doubt. There is a loose barge up in the pool—what about that one?"

"Nobody aboard. I looked through the window."

"My poor friend, you are in a bad way," said the French-man. "But it is not laying a woman that brings bad dreams, it is thinking about it that knocks your brains loose. Would you recognise this bargee Rodney?"

"In the dark."

They spoke more, but I could not hear them. On my way back to the cell I knelt upon a ring-bolt, the forecourt barrel access to the cellar, and I nearly shouted with the pain of it.

It was raining now and the wet undergrowth fastened into my clothes, soaking them as I shook myself free. Mud and wetness was on my face when Rhiannon opened the door to me. To my astonishment, Gid was on his feet again, feeling his way around the walls, assessing the room. Rhiannon asked:

"They'll help us, Tal?"

"No. We'll have to get away." I went to Gideon and he leaned against the wall, gasping. I said, "Save your strength, Gid, we've got to get away from here."

It was not the presence of the men which was bringing me to panic; it was the inevitability that Rhiannon, without even being aware of the reason, might be sacrificed in the name of Poll.

With Gideon staggering between us we got out into the night without detection: the rain splashed down, soaking us yet assisting escape. Reaching the barge, we helped Gid into the aft cabin, and there he lay down gratefully, his face sheet-white; he did not speak even when Rhiannon questioned him.

Leaving them together, I poled the barge out of the lay-pool into the cut, and there, to my astonishment, I saw Dobie tethered beside the barge horse, happily grazing nearby and he raised his head and gave me an evil look and a snort. He followed happily behind the barge horse as we pulled off down the cut, his apprehension diminished now he hadn't got to work.

His presence brought to me a warm, undeniable comfort. For if Dobie had brought Rhiannon as far as this, the chances are, if he hung around, he could take her home again . . .

The rain had stopped and the stars looked down, but I remembered again the words of 'The Tale of Delwyn' as we slid along through the night:

'. . . This the mortal woman said, not knowing that her testing time would come; that soon, at the hands of a priest and a foreigner, she, in her prince's service, would suffer outrage . . .'

When, later, with the dawn coming up, I looked down into

232

the aft cabin, Rhiannon was kneeling by Gideon's bunk, holding his hand: she had washed and fed him, and was speaking to him as if he were her own.

A bright new optimism came with the arrival of Rhiannon: it coincided, for me, with Gideon's sudden recovery of his strength. She seemed to radiate vitality and the joy of our reunion quenched my original fears. Her confidence and gaiety transmitted itself to Gideon, who, now that he was upon his feet, appeared revived. Though still weak from his beatings, he was now getting around the barge; sometimes, at night, sitting in his cloak on the prow, bird-listening, as he called it, returning the called greetings of passing bargees.

And Rhiannon astonished me; no pampered gentility, this one, now she was given the chance to prove her worth: she handled Gideon's dressings like a nurse, cooked and cleaned the cabin, and walked the horse with laughing pleasure. She was dressed like a boy in a sheepskin jacket and wearing a narrow home-spun skirt down to her calves: the incongruity of her appearance enhanced by the little moleskin cap she perched on her braided hair. And old Dobie, in possession of a newly-found mistress, clip-clopped patiently along behind the official barge horse, ignoring me.

Earlier, Rhiannon had said, while Gideon conveniently slept:

"Look – I'm over four months now," and she opened her jacket and groaned to the grip of her skirt, her hat on one side. "Here's an old mule-kicker comin' for the Roberts family."

I asked, quietly, "Have you told your people about the baby?"

"No!" She was affirmative, content to leave it like that.

"Why not? They're entitled."

"Not until I show, and that isn't yet."

"Oh come on, love, they've got to know some time."

"Of course, and when they do, I'll be a long, long way from here."

"Perhaps you won't," I said.

"Oh yes I will, Tal, because you'll take me – you promised, remember? That is why I've come."

A lot had happened, I thought, since I promised her that.

Now, smiling into my face, she said, "You said you'd take me to a place where time did not exist, remember?"

"Yes, I will, but it can't be yet, darling. One's got to be practical – you can see what my responsibilities are. Rhiannon, what did you tell your people?"

She was clearly perplexed. I added, "About you coming down here on this mad caper."

She emptied her hands. "I told them I was going to stay with Mary Pegus."

"In those clothes?"

"Ah!" She was trifling with me. "I looked a lot different when I left."

"There's going to be trouble, you realise that?"

"Of course, I'm not a mental case."

"There'll be fighting. A lot of people are going to get hurt, even killed."

She groaned. "Oh God, why can't we all live in peace?"

"Because there's two worlds, love – yours and mine, and mine isn't doing so good. For God's sake, can't you see what's happening under your nose? The cruelty and the injustice?"

"That's why I want to be with you," she replied. "You think I'm a pampered fool, don't you? You think I haven't given a thought to what goes on, and that if I do, I don't seem to care. But I do care and I hate the inequalities; I hate to see children going to the mines in Dowlais, and women hauling trams; I hate the brickfields and the lime kilns, the rioting, the strikes, yes and the hunger on every side in the middle of wealth." Her voice rose and I noticed Gideon open his eyes. There was a brief silence of wave-lap and the sigh of the wind, and in that silence, Gideon said:

"She shouldn't have to explain, Taliesin. If your father was here he'd say you weren't worth her, and if you've promised you'll take her with you, now's the time to do so."

"In the middle of a revolution, man?" I shouted this. "Talk sense!"

"Aye, most of all in the middle of a revolution, for women make revolutions, fight in them, die in them and put an end to them when they've had enough."

He was breathing heavily. Through the window behind him I saw a woman, one of the bargees' wives: gaily dressed was she, laughing in the cold sunlight. And in a flash vision, the delusion of her face and symmetry called to me, and I thought she was Poll. God, I thought; it would be different if Poll were here, and not Rhiannon. Gideon's voice raked me from my thoughts; he said:

"Listen, Tal, better she takes her chance and stays than go back home with her tail between her legs, because she'll never forgive you for that."

"You realise, don't you, that she's going to have a baby?"

"Yes, I heard, and that's one of the reasons why she ought to stay. Because it is not for this generation that we're fighting, remember, but the next, and the one after that. And if she's going to end as a working man's wife, isn't it right that she could have her say in the outcome of this business?"

"So what do you expect me to do – put her in the attack on Newport?"

"No, but she can tend the broken heads, as she has tended me. She can reload muskets, bring up powder with the boys, run errands – aye, and fight if needs be, as her sisters fought on the barricades of Paris and up the steps of the Bastille. Do ye know, Taliesin, that the men wilted in the fight long before the women? That the first in to free the Bastille prisoners were women? That the French Battalions were more afraid of them than men?" He waved me down. "Ach, read your history! From Ernest Jones to Plato the same tale is told. It's the likes of her who fashion the course of history."

I listened. I was persuaded, and it was a mistake. Much better had I closed my ears to them and sent Rhiannon home to Pontsticill, where she belonged.

Now the winter country ahead came up with cloudy threats of rain and the land seemed subdued, crouching under the threats of deluge.

Once I had seen this land in summer, and it was milk and honey country; of hazel, cherry, blackthorne and dogwood. Birch and elder had grown in profusion here since the Ice Age; fast-growing spruce and pines crowned the western hills. It was ecclesiastical country, the distant environs of Llandaff, and it had escaped the axe of earlier centuries: now it lay flat and fearful under the setting sun in calm, monastic seclusion.

Rhiannon said, "How long are we staying here in the lay-by, Tal?" Miles away in my thoughts, I did not reply.

We were alone now, walking down the deserted cut; Gideon was busying himself about the barge cabin. Earlier he had gathered rushes by pulling them from the thwarts and these he had plaited into intricate patterns and designs, his flattened fingers amazingly dexterous as he bound them into shape with sap-grass Rhiannon had discovered in the water; small, quaint dolls he made, and now was fashioning imitation love-spoons, one for Rhiannon to wear, said he; another, a smaller one, for her baby. We could see him by the door.

"He's better," said Rhiannon, walking beside me in the cold; the evening was arriving with promises of ice; rain was falling over distant Llandaff in faint, thundering booms.

"Overnight," I said. "His strength is astonishing – and it's mainly since you arrived."

"That's the effect I have on people!" She added:

"I asked you how long we're staying here?"

"Until my father comes, this is a rendezvous."

"What will he say about me being here, I wonder?"

"God knows. I don't think he'll agree with Gideon."

"When is your father due?"

"Midnight."

She questioned more: unlike Poll, she had to be in the heart of everything. I replied, "All right, I'll tell you, then perhaps you'll realise why I want you away from all this. Arms are stored in the barge. It's a floating arsenal. The dog-spike load I'm carrying is only there to cover the boxes – cases of muskets, pistols, bayonets and pikes – shot and powder, for distribution among the valley contingents. Men will come with my father and they'll load it out. And whoever is found in possession of such stuff will end in transportation, you included."

"Right. If that's the end of it, so be it. So long as we're together."

"And I shouldn't bank on that."

There was a need in me to hurt her, if, by this means, I could force her to leave. It was not necessary that she should play a role in this; she was not equipped for it, neither was she required. For this was a working-class struggle in which her kind would be rejected, and I resented her presence. Also, I did not trust myself. I loved her, and love could turn a man to cowardice. Yet, had Poll been still with me I would have snatched at her for support, let her run with me, if necessary, into battle. Rhiannon's very femininity, her inability to understand the extent and danger of the struggle ahead, gripped me with growing apprehension, but there was more to my fears than this: there was gnawing at me a timeless, senseless dread I could not shake away, one beyond all reason and comprehension, and it sickened me.

"Perhaps now you know why I want you out of this," I said.

Rhiannon didn't appear to hear this. She said, with a smile, pointing, "Tal – how handsome Gideon looks, plaiting his rushes . . ."

Later, I pulled the curtains of the barge, took the key out of the aft cabin door and gave it to Rhiannon, saying:

"We're nearly out of food, and Old Shenks may be overdue. The village is only a couple of hundred yards away."

"Why can't I go?" she asked.

"You'll be safer here – look I'll be back in half an hour." And I kissed her. Gideon, still busy with his rushes, didn't look up as I left them. "Don't open the door to anyone," I said.

It was a ridiculous decision; almost as if I had been commanded to leave her unprotected. I gave no thought to more than average danger: the moon was coming up, barges were constantly coming and going past the lay-pool. She would only have to shout and a score of men would come.

And so, unknown to me, the Tale was being fulfilled.

As Old Shenks moved north from Cardiff, as arranged, I hurried west to the village. And, with neither of us more than minutes away from the moored barge, the irony became complete.

The priest and the foreigner, the two men from the Star Inn, tramped south in search of Poll.

How many times since, I wonder, have I cursed myself for my tragic stupidity. And yet, I repeat, it was as if my absence had been commanded.

When I returned from the village I found a great activity around the barge, and ran with my provisions: the moon, beaming down, lit the scene; the stern was crowded with jabbering women and children; groups of people were on the tow-path and around the lay-pool, chattering and gesticulating, and the barges were snubbed nose to stern along the canal.

I ran, and plunged into the crowd by the aft cabin door, and the people fell to silence as I entered.

Old Shenks was sitting on the floor with Rhiannon in his arms and a barge woman was attending her. The body of Gideon, viciously stabbed, was crouched in a corner half under a bunk. And Rhiannon was half naked, her clothes ripped from her body; blood was upon her face.

"Rhiannon!" In growing horror, I knelt, pushed the bargee aside and took Rhiannon into my arms.

All around were signs of a violent struggle and blood from Gideon's wounds was everywhere; the bargees crowded in now, their mute faces staring at the wild disorder. Old Shenks said:

"Christ, man, where were you when you was needed?"

I didn't get the sense of him; Rhiannon's heart was thudding against me and her breathing was laboured. The barge woman said:

"Hey up, lad; leave her!" She looked up at her man standing above us, "O'Reilly, get hot water from our stove, and towels, quick." She called to a man bending over Gideon. "Leave him," she commanded, "that one's dead—

O'Reilly! Will ye get these people out of here?"

I said, "Oh God, woman, what happened?" but I knew what had happened, and Old Shenks replied, kissing Rhiannon's face:

"Two men. They kicked the door down. Somebody saw them runnin'."

"I saw 'em!" called a lad from the back. "It were Priest and Frenchy, I reckon – I saw 'em!"

I said to the bargee. "She . . . she's having a baby, nigh four months gone."

She was businesslike, this woman, fat and grimy, her black hair tousled in the fashion of the Irish; she replied, "Aye, I know, but she'll likely hold it, she's young," and Rhiannon, as if hearing this, opened her eyes, saw me, and said:

"Tal!"

"I'm here, love."

Old Shenks bowed his head, whispering, "Oh Christ, bloody murder I'll do for this . . ."

"Don't worry none," said the man O'Reilly. "If it's Priest an' Frenchy the bargees will have 'em down to the third generation, so they will, aye!" and he made a fist of his hand.

"I'll have them long before that," I said, and rose. "Lie still, girl, lie still . . ." for Rhiannon was twisting and shuddering in Old Shenks's arms. She said then:

"They . . . they were the men at the inn, remember?"

I nodded, kneeling now, holding her hands, and I bent to kiss her, saying, "Look, close your eyes . . ."

"They knocked and we wouldn't let them in, so they broke down the door. Oh, the way Gideon fought! But the little one had a knife. He couldn't see . . . and the big one hit him from behind." She began to cry in stuttering panic, her hands making a cage over her mouth. I said:

"Rhiannon!" and held her, pushing Old Shenks away; I was with her at the start of Time, kissing her lips, her face, her hair.

"And . . . and while they were doing it they kept calling me Poll. 'Lie still, Poll,' they said, 'Keep quiet, Poll . . .'"

The barge woman got up, rolling up her sleeves, crying, "Ay ay, now out of here everyone, come on, come on, it's no place for men. Have you got that bloody water, O'Reilly?"

I went to Gideon. His body was covered in knife wounds, one thrust being through his heart.

"And I want two men," called the woman. "Come on, don't stand there gaping, get this poor fella out of here." She glanced at me. "You, too, mun – out," and she helped Old Shenks to his feet and steered him through the door.

"Don't go, Tal," called Rhiannon, raising herself on the floor.

"I'll be back," I said.

On deck now, Mrs. O'Reilly said, "She's not the first woman, and she won't be the last, do not look so holy. But she's bleeding a bit, and might need a doctor. O'Reilly and me are on the way back up, so we'll take her. You her chap?"

"Sort of," I replied.

She clapped me on the back and grinned wide. "Canal Wharf, then, and I'll try to get Sam Williams. What's her name?"

I told her.

"Holy Mother," she exclaimed. "Gentry, is it? Aye well, she'll be just the same as us when it comes down to the essentials, son – it's the business of being a woman round these parts, see? She'll likely pull out of it."

"Will she lose the baby, Mrs. O'Reilly?" and she threw back her head and cackled at the moon.

"Dear God, no son!" cried she. "Not if the O'Reillys have a hand in it, so to speak. For I've midwifed more down this Glamorgan cut than they've birthed in the cabins of County Cork."

"God bless you, Mrs. O'Reilly," I said.

"Ach, and He will that – she births now, you have the next one."

She was still cackling as I made my way to the prow and went down into the dog-spike load. There I broke open a case and took a pistol, loaded and primed its flintlock; then I pulled a ten-pound bag of quarrying powder and a set of lucifers, which were match-heads and sandpaper. I had just tied the gunpowder around my neck when Old Shenks came in search of me, calling down the hatch:

"Are ye down there, Tal?"

I crouched low in the darkness lest he saw me.

Later, when I was certain he had gone, I left the barge and took along the tow-path towards the Star Inn, to kill the men.

The old inn was nearly a tumbledown now, I thought as it came up through night-mist: it wouldn't need a lot to flatten it, and I found the cellar access trap-door and lifted it, watching the tap-room through its smashed windows, but the place was empty. Perhaps they would not return, I thought; whether they did or not, I was determined to destroy what was left of the inn; it stood as a monument to my own defilement, and I hated every brick and stone of it. But there was also a good chance that the priest and foreigner would come back, for I saw their twin mattresses on the floor, their scattered bottles and tins of food; on a rail above the bar two blanket coats moved lazily in the wind like hanging corpses. Next moment I was in pitch darkness as I closed the trap-door above my head.

Mice scuttled away as I crept through the cellar; cracks in the floorboards above me afforded thin, moonbeam light; broken barrels, the riotous relics of a past age of gluttony, barred my way; from within these came the incessant squeaking of rats in colonies.

I hadn't been in the cellar for more than minutes, fixing the concussion charge, when I stopped work to the heavy tramping of boots overhead; the priest and Frenchman were returning.

At first they spoke only in grunts and whispers, as if the night's work of rape and murder had partly satiated them; then I heard the Frenchman say, his voice raised:

"Was it necessary, Priest, to kill the blind one?"

"What the Hell, mun!" came the reply. "He had me by the bloody throat, and you not lendin' a hand, for ye were doin' the woman."

Irish. It was the first time I'd noticed it.

"But it was not the bargee Poll, my friend, for I heard her making protest. She protested, did she not? But sometimes, I

242

think, in Welsh, for I did not understand."

"Ach, fella, they always protest when their hearts aren't in it, but did you enjoy her? That's more to the point."

"She was like eating honey."

"And me, I can tell ye! Och, while I'm up and breathin' – where do they spawn such women?"

"Some women are chickens, Small One, others are like swans. And this one was a cygnet. But do not swans, in this country, belong to the Queen?"

"Holy Mary, what's the odds?"

"Because any time now the *cuirassiers* will come and cut us to pieces; the girl was a noble."

I heard the little cleric laugh. "Aw Frenchy, to Hell! Swans or chickens, women are ten a penny down the cut, nobles included. Here, sink this an' ye'll feel better in the morning'," and he tossed the Frenchman a bottle, who missed it, and it went clattering over the floor above my head.

I was in a dilemma.

Hatred of the two men above me had built in me a seething anger I could not resolve by reason or plain sense. I had come to dispose of them: the charge was suspended, the fuse path laid: all I had to do was run the powder in a trail to the outside trap-door and strike the match. Then would follow the snaking blaze and the final detonation that would obliterate the tumbling inn and the two rapists above me; no pain, no expectation, no fear for them: just the instant decimation of the brain by skull splinters. My task would then be over, the revenge for Rhiannon's outrage fulfilled. But I could not strike the match. And I think I knew, crouched there in the cellar, that their deaths in such a manner would accomplish nothing: the sin against my girl could never be erased by so easy a path. She was demanding more – that a personal violence be involved; that these two would know the reason why they were dying, as criminals know when being led to execution.

They were talking again now, their banter mingling with their obscene laughter; I heard her name called – Poll they called her for want of another – and I crawled away from the suspended charge, fighting for calmness amid an inner fury. Reaching the trap-door, I threw down the powder bag that had made the fuse, and pushed up – up and out into the night with the pistol in my hand. Running around to the front door of the inn I burst through it. The men on the floor rose up on their mattresses in the moonlight, their faces astonished by the speed of my entry, their hands reaching for their weapons, and the priest found one, a knife. This he threw, and I ducked, hearing it whistle above me and bury itself, quivering, in the door behind me.

"Right," I said, approaching them. "Up!" and I levelled the pistol.

But I had come too close to them and was standing on the edge of a mattress, and they were professionals. Climbing slowly to his feet, the smaller one suddenly flung himself backwards, pulled at the mattress and tripped me; I fell headlong, the pistol clattering out of my hand.

Immediately the Frenchman was upon me, but I flung him off and rose, hooking him hard to the face as he lumbered in for a hold; and as he staggered I seized a broken chair and smashed it down over the back of the priest as he dived for the pistol on the far side of the tap-room. The big man was at me again on the moment I turned to face him; shouting hoarsely, he caught me in a bear-hug, raising me off my feet. And as he turned me I saw the priest painfully crawling towards the pistol, leaving behind him a trail of blood.

Somehow I hooked my right leg around the knee of the foreigner and we spun, momentarily tottering together in an embrace, before falling with a thud, me uppermost. I saw a flash vision of the man's bearded face, his white teeth behind his hairy lips, and his red tongue lolling as I gripped his throat. But, with astonishing strength he forced my hands away and rose, to face me, stooping, his breath coming in gasps, and I suddenly realised that he was twice my age. Spittle and froth gurgled over his beard as he gasped for breath, and I dived at him head first, catching him in the midriff and pumping out his lungs: grasping his chest, he turned, staggering away like a wounded animal, but I was upon him again, now infuriated by the heat of the fight. In my blind rage I could see nothing before me but the blood-stained face of Rhiannon and the knifed body of Gideon. I struck again and again, thudding my fists into the big man's body, and he slid along the wall of the tap, his knees sagging to the attack. I heard the shrill cry of the priest on the other side of the room, but ignored it; I was intent now on one thing only, the death of the man staggering before me. And then I heard the priest shout again, and turned in the Frenchman's strengthless arms. And I saw, on the other side of the room the little man sight the pistol; instinctively I dropped to all fours as the pistol blazed, and the ball, meant for me, struck the Frenchman in the chest. The impact of the half-inch round flung him back against the wall, and he lay momentarily flattened against it like a crucified doll, before pitching head first across the floor, his big body rolling sideways across the mattress.

"Now you," I said, and turned, and the priest let out a small, wild shriek of fear and lurched towards the door, but I reached it first and slammed it shut.

Cornered against the bar, the man flung the pistol, but I ducked; catching him with one hand, I spun him round to face me and struck with the other fist, and he groaned, and his eyes rolled, then he sank down the front of me, to lay senseless across the dead body of his companion.

I raised my bleeding hands to my face and stood there, staring around the shattered room; at the dead body of the Frenchman, and the unconscious man in black. Yet, despite the sense of victory and the vindication, I felt besmirched by the very essence of the place: all its bawdy past seemed to surround me as I stood there, making me one with its iniquity.

Slowly, painfully, I walked across the broken floor and out into the moonlight. Soon, I thought, my father and his men would come, so I would have to get back: more importantly, I had to get back to Rhiannon and Old Shenks, who would be hunting for me.

So it was but a small surprise to me when I heard him coming; the dust had got Old Shenks and his lungs were

245

bagpipes.

Kneeling, I fired the powder-trail and a little blue flame spurted up, then disappeared under the cellar trap-door.

"Tal, where've you been?" gasped Old Shenks, hurrying up.

"Looking for those two swines, but no sign of them," I said.

"Then come back to Rhiannon, the child's askin' for ye and the O'Reillys are just off up to Merthyr with her."

"Yes," I said, and hurried along beside him.

We hadn't got a hundred yards when the world about us glowed with strickening light: canal, tow-path, forest and hills were instantly illuminated; and all hung in the pulsating light that slowly, reluctantly died into blackness, then the night was split by a clattering roar; the ground beneath us shook.

"Good God," breathed Old Shenks, gripping me. "What the Hell was that?"

"No idea."

Old Shenks peered at me, then wiped his whiskers with the back of his hand.

"Queer old time of night to be quarrying."

Passing the Cow and Snuffers public, we took the towpath south, through Llandaff Yard.

It was nearly midnight according to Old Shenks's watch, and I was worried. In my anger I had forgotten the outcome of such an explosion; a blast like that, I now realised, would pull in every Redcoat patrol for miles, and according to the Ostlers, Captain Wetton was already in the vicinity.

So now it was a race against time.

I sat on the bunk where Rhiannon lay in the O'Reilly barge and listened to the lapping of water as the bargee got his horse going along the cut; there was a mystic splendour about the night that belied the coming of a storm. I said to Rhiannon:

"I've got to go, *cariad*, but you'll be all right with these people."

Earlier, I'd got a bottle of laudanum we had used on Gideon, and its effect on Rhiannon was now apparent; she was hovering within the vacuum of consciousness and sleep, but her grip on my hand was strong.

"Can you hear me still?" I asked, and she nodded.

"I can't stay, for there's things to be done, understand? Go back to your people, tell them all that has happened. Up at Treble Locks the Ostlers will fetch a doctor. Do what he says, and as soon as I can, I will come back to you."

Her lips moved. "Don't go, Tal."

"Got to go, love, there's nothing else for it. If a military patrol stops the barge, leave it all to O'Reilly; just tell them that you remember nothing until the bargees found you on the tow-path – nothing, understand, Rhiannon. Our lives are in your hands."

At first I thought she was sleeping, then she said, and her voice was strong, "You're going to fight?" Her eyes were now wide open.

"Aye, girl. Got to fight, see? No alternative."

She didn't reply, so I added, "For you, for me – aye, and for the baby. To make things decent; we can't go on as we are."

In Welsh, she said, before she closed her eyes:

"*Mi ddoi di yn ôl ataf. Wyt ti'n gaddo?*"

"Yes, Rhiannon. I promise. I will come back to you."

Mrs. O'Reilly came up then with business, a bowl of water and a bedsheet rolled up under her chin. "Away out of it, lad, the girl's still bleeding."

"Yes," I said.

"Holy God, what's the likes of her doin' mixed up wi' the likes of you?"

"Don't know," I said.

"Have ye spoken to her pa?" Her calloused hands were stilled and her black eyes switched over me.

"No."

"Would it be askin' too much to know when you might?"

"When I get back from the march, Mrs. O'Reilly."

"O aye!" Fists on hips now, and she swept stray hairs from her sweating face. "After the march on London, is it?" She glared at me. "After you've put the world to rights, eh – like my big oaf, O'Reilly! Sure, you're a marvellous set o' fellas, so ye are, for swilling ye ale and hammering pikes for a revolution, but you're better at side-stepping your bloody responsibilities." She nodded at Rhiannon's sleeping face. "This one here, for instance. Ye put her in the family way and then post her back to her ma. You know what they'll do to her, I suppose? I know that gentry lot. They'd show more sympathy for a mongrel bitch."

I met her eyes. "Got no alternative, Mrs. O'Reilly."

She was wandering about in pent anger now, picking things up and smacking them down, and she said, over her shoulder, "Right then, go, and good riddance to ye, one an' all. For I'm a woman an' I've got no time for strikes and blow-outs and Union marches. You men are addled, the lot

248

of ye; you've got no chance and it'll only end one way – with your heads on Parliament Square and the rest of you in bloody strips. Now away out of it for I've got a woman to attend to."

The aft cabin door came open and O'Reilly, her husband, came in.

He said, screwing at his cap, "Bengie's on the tiller, Ma, Alice is leadin' the horse. I'm away now, so I am."

"Are ye? Is that a fact?" She approached us, her eyes blazing. "And how am I supposed to handle a barge, five kids and an ailin' woman, for God's sake? Bad cess to ye, Michael O'Reilly, for fetching me out o' Galway into this stink of a country. All right!" She waved her arms and flung the bedsheet at us. "Away with ye and fight the revolution, an' I hope ye never come back, d'ye hear me?"

O'Reilly lowered his head. "Goodbye, Ma," he said.

I closed the door behind us. The stars were big over the moon-lit land. I heard her shout:

"O'Reilly!"

"Holy Mother, what now?" said he, and opened the door again.

His wife was standing beside Rhiannon's bunk with her apron up to her face, but she was not crying.

"Ye'll come back to us, Mick, like this one keeps sayin'?"

"Aye, Missus. I promise. I'll be back."

"Then get goin', for God's sake? Why are ye hanging about?"

But he didn't go back to her.

They got him through the head with the first volley from the Redcoat carts, along the road to Monmouth.

My father had come with his contingent of twenty men, when O'Reilly and I got back to my barge, and Old Shenks was already handing out the arms. It was speedy work, with the hammers rising and falling and the wooden cases splitting under the levers. Look-outs had been posted as the muskets, pistols, pikes and powder were distributed. I found Dada in the aft cabin, and he faced me as I entered.

His eyes were bright.

"Gid . . . they tell me," he said, simply.

"Aye, Dada."

"But how, Tal? For God's sake how?"

O'Reilly fidgeted, restless, and said, "Mister, it weren't his fault. We was waitin' in the cut, and . . ."

"You shut it, I'm asking him!"

I said, "I . . . I sent Old Shenks to arrange things in Cardiff. He wasn't back and we needed food. So I went to the village . . ."

"And left them alone?" He came nearer and his face was sheet-white. "You left a blind man and a slip of a girl alone at a time like this? The bloody barge is full of arms . . ."

"Leave it, Dada," I said.

"Leave it? Gideon's dead, and you say leave it?"

I pushed past him. He shouted, "My friend's dead and your girl's been raped and you say leave it?"

I shouted back, "Aye, so leave it in the name of God!"

"Jesus," he said, and pushed me aside as he went through the door. "Just dish out the arms and get yourself back to Merthyr with your woman, it's all you're fit for!"

Later, my father said, before he and his men moved off:

"Earlier I asked you how it happened, Tal. Now I'm asking why. Can you answer that? Why, why?"

For answer I took from my pocket the tin box containing the manuscript of the 'Tale of Delwyn'.

After my father and his men had gone, Old Shenks and I gathered up the wreckage of the packing cases and buried them on the fringe of a nearby wood, next to the place where the bargees had buried Gideon in an unmarked grave. And I stood for a bit looking down at the newly turned earth, and there was a coldness in me akin to the coldness of death, I think.

"You all right?" asked Old Shenks, coming up.

"Aye."

"Good old boy, mind, that Gid Davies."

I nodded.

"Got plenty o' guts. Blind, see, but not so blind, really speakin' – he knew the time o' day. Your pa's mate, you say?"

"Friends all their lives," I replied.

"Aye, well that's it, ain't it? It do come rough, ye know, when you're on the same toffee-apple. Boys, see, then young men – on the piss together. It's a love, in a manner o' speaking, specially if ye happen to be sparkin' the same women." I didn't reply.

He looked at the moon and whispered as Mick O'Reilly came up, "A man comes sore, ye see Tal, when a love like that goes down. It . . . it's the best sort o' love." He thumbed his face and looked at the moon. "I know, see. In my time I lost a lot o' good mates."

I did not reply.

"That's why your pa said things he don't mean. You understand?"

O'Reilly said, "When are we movin' off, Tal Roberts?"

"Now," I said, and was thankful he had come.

"I'll make ready," said Old Shenks, but I put out my hand to him.

"Not you, Shenks. You go back to the Ostlers, then to Canal Wharf. My father said . . ."

"Did he now!" The old man bristled. "Then you and your pa can get stuffed wi' oat-cake both ends up, you in particular. Not comin', am I? And let a decent fight go by?"

We left the rendezvous lay-by with faint threats of dawn in the sky. O'Reilly had a musket, I had the pistol and Old Shenks carried a pike, and he sat on Dobie like St. George after the dragon. And we hadn't got fifty yards when the rain pelted down: the heavens opened and the clouds shot stair-rods, a cloudburst that soaked us in minutes and sent Dobie curvetting at the onslaught.

"Jesus!" exclaimed O'Reilly, looking around Dobie's bridle with a cold, dishevelled face. "What the Hell's happening?"

"It's revolution day," said Old Shenks. "As usual, God's backing up the Whigs and Tories."

We cut across country from Whitchurch to Lisvane in vicious downpourings of rain which I have never forgotten, and all the time we travelled the sky darkened. The wind rose, tearing hay out of the wayside barns, bringing down roofs and trees, blocking the roads with debris. Brooks and streams, already flooded by November rains, overflowed their banks and swamped the fields: the rivers raged, tossing on their breasts the wreckage of isolated farms. By midday, when we were east of Castleton, thunder and lightning added to the chaos of our lives: soaked to the skin, bedraggled, with our clothes chafing with every step O'Reilly and I led Dobie on, and Old Shenks, mute with misery, sat in the saddle like some ancient patriarch, with his pike spiking the sky, a lightning rod, said O'Reilly.

We struck north after leaving Castleton, making for Llantarnum on the Newport to Abergavenny road, and here the Afon Lwyd had burst its banks and had flooded the fields; the land was one great lake. And it was here, wading up to our knees in water, that we struck Jones the Watchmaker's Pontypool column, and they were marching on Newport, so they said.

Earlier, John Frost's column pouring down from his headquarters, the Coach and Horses at Blackwood, had waited for hours at the Welsh Oak Inn at Cefn for Zephaniah Williams's army coming south from Nantyglo, Newbridge and Abercarn. Now, we heard later, both these columns were waiting again for the one which we struck now, the William Jones's: and long they'd wait, cried O'Reilly above the lashing rain, for these didn't look like getting south of Malpas.

"Have ye ever in your born days seen such a mob?" cried Shenks, lurching in the saddle.

"God help the revolution," I shouted back, "if this is all it can muster."

A man was sitting by the side of the road, clear of the tramping boots: and he gave not a sign that he noticed them, this ragged, dripping army of men and boys: out of step, splashing along in the flood, their lodge and Benefit Club banners hung like dish-rags on their poles. And then he raised his head and looked up as we came abreast, this man, so I stopped at Dobie's head, and asked:

"How many are you?"

He was old and his face was ravaged with work and hunger, his accent, when he spoke, was North Country. "How many, ye ask? Aye, well ye may! There's not more'n six hundred here, marrer, and they promised us thousands."

"And where's William Jones – have you seen him?" bawled O'Reilly.

"Ach, indeed – back in The Green House, sinking doubles and wavin' a sword."

"Not since?"

"Once since, when we stopped at the Abbey for a parley wi' Boxer, the old M.P., who told him the error o' his ways." He wiped water from his sunken eyes. "I come on this outin' for my missus. Leave it to us, I told her, after this you'll live decent, you and the kids. We'll strangle bloody ironmasters."

"What now? Are you going on?"

"Aye," said he, getting up. "To strangle bloody Chartists. What the Hell is a grown man doin' on this mad caper to Newport?"

"They'll be there, though," cried O'Reilly, now beside me, and he shoved away a drunken man staggering against him in the mob. "The spalpeens might be drinkin' now, but come the firing, they'll march on London."

"Look out!" cried Old Shenks, and wheeled the horse. "There's more coming!"

Eight abreast now, they flooded down the road, a mob of mudstained weary men, their ranks a hedgehog of pikes and mandrels. They came in a tattered army, surging along. And, as they marched they were shouting drunken songs and waving two-stick banners. But one man, a leader, I saw marched alone. Inches taller than the rest, he stepped out in regimental style, his military bearing evident, and on his shoulder he carried a musket. Bare-headed in the pouring rain he went, ignoring the banter and jeers of his companions; a ramrod of soldiering, this one, his right arm swinging to his regulation pace. And there arose from the reeling, roaring mob a discordant shout: a hymn of rough voices within the drunken caterwauling, and this came from a group of disciplined men behind their fine leader. I heard the words of Ernest Jones:

> We're low, we're low, we're very very low,
> And yet, when the trumpets ring,
> The thrust of a poor man's arm will go
> Through the heart of the proudest king!

They were abreast of us now, these few soldiers, and I knew then what this attack on a town could have been, had people like Sam Williams, Gideon and my father had their say. But now, said Old Shenks from the saddle, we're being led by a watchmaker, the landlord of the Royal Oak up in Coalbrookvale, and Frost, the draper mayor. God help the town, added O'Reilly, if the men who had fought Napoleon could be here, instead of ballers, colliers, labourers and drunks.

We knew the truth of this when the shutters of the Westgate Inn went back, and showed us professionals.

"Aye, God help us," said the man on the road. "The military will chop us up as they did at Peterloo; what price our wives and children then?"

"Yes, but one thing you've forgot!" exclaimed O'Reilly. "The soldiers are with us, see? Starvation pay and floggings is all they get from their gentry officers."

Aye?

We know better now.

The rain poured down in a roar that sprayed white arms of water over us; the wind tore at our soaked clothes, stung our flesh with the pain of needles.

Cutting through the marching ranks the three of us took east across the flooded fields for Ponthir and Llanhennock to the rendezvous on the Monmouth Road where my father and his men were waiting in ambush. Wearily we marched, and Old Shenks, though riding, was becoming exhausted. Thunder battered the sky in drum rolls, and Dobie was prancing around in terror. From Barry north to Chester the storm raged all that day we heard later: from Shrewsbury to Snowdonia the land was swamped under a turmoil of water.

"I was right," said Old Shenks, "Jehovah ain't voting for the workers no more."

"Ay ay," answered O'Reilly. "The old chap always changes sides when the chips are down."

I did not reply. We were now confronted by the River Usk, a cauldron of rust-coloured water foaming in full spate, shouting at us, reaching up arms as if to drag us down. Above its roar I yelled at O'Reilly through cupped hands:

"Follow this north and we come to Llanhennock."

"Lead the way, lad," he shouted back. "You're young, it's your revolution!"

35

I knew the land around this part of Gwent. Time was, when I was a nip, my father would take me to Chepstow to visit his father; and I remembered now one particular May when the place was all blossom, hitting up for a bun-eared cow-pat of a summer; with coloured birds flying over the Usk and coots and crakes playing leap-frog with spring in a most disgraceful manner.

But now the countryside was forbidding and dull as we came along the Monmouth Road into Llanhennock and the cottages and terraced houses stood shoulder to shoulder in the gloom, locked and barred against strangers, because of the attack on nearby Newport.

"Listen!" said O'Reilly, and we stood on the deserted road. Faintly came the unmistakable crack of muskets.

"The lads are into them," said Old Shenks. "What now?"

"To find my father and his men."

"Did he say what part of the village?"

I shook my head. "This is his rendezvous, but he doesn't even know I'm coming."

"Reinforcement, are we?" asked Old Shenks, who was fading; time and time again I'd told him on the march, why we were coming.

"Well," said O'Reilly, beating water from his hat. "I hope he don't expect a lot from me. The only thing this old musket's good for now is knocking heads in. Look at me powder," and he held up his flask.

"Yes," I answered. "My pistol's the same. Everything's soaked."

"What we want is a housewife's oven, to dry it out," said Shenks.

"Ease up. Have ye brains gone soft?"

"It's true, I tell you — it's an old collier trick."

We laughed, but it was half-hearted, for the rain was lashing us.

Moving south, we were only a mile from Newport, searching for Dada when O'Reilly said, "Heisht! What's that? Listen."

A premature darkness had fallen over the land so we did not immediately see him — a lad of about twelve lying in the roadside ditch, and we carefully lifted him out on to the verge. Shenks asked:

"What you doin' here, lad, for God's sake?" and the boy replied:

"William Jones stopped the lads at Cross-ye-Legs, but a few of us come on . . ."

"You walked from Groes-y-ceilog?" I asked, astonished, for the ball had taken him across the stomach and cut him wide, and the bones of his ribs were stark white and smeared with blood where he clutched himself.

"No, Mister. When the lads come down Stow Hill, George Shell and me went in with them, against the Westgate: George stopped it in the passage and I caught it going up the steps. Christ, mun, you never seen such a mess."

"When was that?"

He was broad and fair, looking more like a man, and he said, "Coupla hours back, or so. Redcoats everywhere — come down from the Workhouse. They was waitin' for us, I reckon. There was dead lads all over the street." He sighed like a child. "You know Tom Callister?"

"No."

"He's another o' my Llanhennock mates. You get back home to your mam, Ianto, he tells me. And the military were there tying the lads up and sending for carts. They'll be comin' by here now just, to the prison in Monmouth."

"Christ," whispered O'Reilly. "The attack's over . . ."

"O aye, Mister. There ain't any fightin' in Newport now."

I closed my eyes, wondering where Dada was.

Old Shenks said, lifting the boy, "No odds to that. We're getting you back home to your mam. Where's your place?"

Ianto pointed. "Over by there – second cottage, but I can't go home in this state, can I?"

"But you can't lie here, either," I said.

"Ay ay, I can – till the rain cleans me up, see? She's got two kids at home, and they're both younger'n me . . ." He looked at the sky and the rain beat fast upon his face; down was upon his cheeks and his lips were red. "Jesus . . ." he whispered. "Ain't it gettin' dark . . ." and he closed his eyes.

"He's away," whispered Shenks, and screwed up his hand.

We knelt in silence. Then O'Reilly said:

"Listen!" He had ears for brown mice, this one.

Across the fields behind us men were coming – twenty, I counted, and my father was at their head; I knew him by his gait. Beside him was the black-maned giant Edwards, the man I had met up at Llangynidr cave. We left the boy and went to greet them.

"It's bad, have you heard?" Dada asked.

We told him about Ianto.

"Yes, the lad's right. William Jones's column never arrived; every gun the lads carried had soaked powder. Under cover, with dry powder, the soldiers mowed them down from the Westgate windows. And the army reinforcements never came through this way. It's my guess they brought in troops from Brecon."

"From Newport workhouse," I replied. "They were holding them in reserve up Stow Hill, according to this boy. Do you know anything more?"

My father replied, "Only that everything's lost. A deserter came through half an hour back, going like the wind, but we collared him. He said that all the columns were late getting in – the weather, apparently. And Jones's lot never got south of Malpas."

A man beside him said, "People like Frost couldn't plan a vicarage tea-party, mun – and Jones wi' his big talk of wading in blood!"

"What happens now, then?" I asked, and Dada replied:
."Chartist prisoners will be taken. Soon the carts will be coming through." He jerked his thumb. "Edwards knows this place backwards. He's found us a headquarters in the wood over there, a quarry. We can lie low in it and make an attack on the road and free the lads."

"Is there a roof to the quarry?" asked O'Reilly. "My gun's useless, we need dry powder."

"So will the Redcoats, butty."

A man spoke at Old Shenks's shoulder: he was a Cornishman by his accent and his face was a pudding of laughs. He cried, "Maister, I'm prayin' they get me first time out. My old Biddy'll kick my arse for comin' on this outing." The men laughed. The wind howled about us; water was running out of my boots, I remember.

"It's the bloody pastor I'm afeared of, son – he be a real Bible-punchin' vandal – and he'll have me out the front . . ."

My father cut them short. "Back to the quarry then, all of us, and wait for the prison carts coming through. If the lads make a run for it they'll still stand a chance. Where's that boy?"

"Here," said O'Reilly, and lifted Ianto.

"Bring him along, we can't leave him here. What about his mother?"

"I know her," said Edwards, and took Ianto from O'Reilly. "I'll take him home."

We stood, all of us, in disconsolate, silent groups, watching Edwards as he carried the boy down the road to the cottages of Llanhennock.

"You," commanded my father, and ordered a man nearby. "Stay and act as sentry," and he glanced at his watch. "Any time now the carts will be through – your mates, remember, so make no mistake about it. Any sign of movement – carts, soldiers – run over the field and shout into the wood, understand?"

"Aye, Captain."

Dada raised his arm. "Right, follow me, all of you," and he led us across the soaked field adjoining the Monmouth Road to the tree-fringe that hid his headquarters, the quarry.

As we squelched along I stole a look at my father.

He was wearing a buckskin jacket and trews of some quality; these I had not seen before. Bare-headed, despite the wind and rain, he walked like a knight from Aneirin's *Gododdin*. This is how I had always seen my father; not with his arms outstretched, bowed behind the whipping cart of Amlwch. Inches taller than any man there that day, save Edwards, he walked with dignity, his head up. Yet soon, I thought – and it was a sudden and terrible vision – that tunic would be stained. And he who was beside me now would leave me an empty shell to venerate. In defeat and death, I thought, he would be one with those who had preceded him; and returning to the courts of his people.

I could have reached out and touched my father then, and the strange thought struck me that, had I done so, I would have touched a myth; one already dead in service to his country.

As we entered the wood my father smiled at me. "Come, Tal – such a face? Smile, for God's sake. What we do today we do for Wales."

I counted twenty men within the open quarry cave.

Stripping off our soaked clothes, we were instantly twenty naked men, hopping and shivering in the November cold; wringing out our shirts, emptying water from our boots, we gasped and slapped our flesh to bring back the circulation.

Edwards returned, unspeaking. My father asked:

"You found his mother?"

"Aye, Captain. Do not speak of it."

A man said, "God, what a country, eh? Nigh twelve he was, no more. Wales is forgotten, mun. The devils o' Gehenna are with us."

My father, trying to dry his powder, glanced up. "They are not. At last we're fighting back. This is the best day the country's had since Suetonius, for God's sake."

"Jesus," murmured a man beside me. "Who the Hell's Suetonius?"

I wanted to smile. How often, before and since, I have wondered if my father, so much with the people, was truly of the people? His learning, his nobility of character often removed him, I thought, from the common run. Yet they followed him; this was certain. They followed him loyally, all men who knew him; blindly obeying, without demur. Was this, I wondered, a fault of the Celts? This unquestioning, unswerving obedience to anything savouring of birth and distinction?

Soon, I thought, the sentry will shout and all here will go out to make war. And then they will know, these men, the cost of such obedience. Yet, being Welshmen, they would not hesitate, for it was in their blood.

And then, as if bringing to a conscious end the drama of my mind, we heard the sentry shout, and scrambled into our clothes.

"Steady," said my father. "Do not rush it. Don't begrudge them a little more time to live!" and hands on hips, he grinned around him. "Your powder's wet, but so is theirs. Musket butts and fists, then. Free your mates, but do not hit to kill, remember."

We trooped in single file back to the Monmouth Road and lowered our bodies into the water-filled ditches either side of it.

"Look," cried the sentry, and pointed.

They were coming. Despite the rain we could see them clearly, about ten carts in line, horse- or mule-drawn, and flanked with marching soldiers. And in the carts the prisoners were crammed like herrings in barrels, too tight to fall out.

They were half a mile away, coming around a bend in the road, and we heard their iron-tipped boots ringing in a steady, tramping rhythm and the grating of iron-ringed wheels. Amazingly, from the column of marching men, pent prisoners and heaving animals, a rainbow mist arose of steaming breath and sweating bodies.

"How many are they?" asked Old Shenks on one side of me, and O'Reilly, on the other, replied:

"Some hundred prisoners, I reckon – perhaps more . . ."

"Double that," I said. "Twenty to a cart. And about a hundred soldiers."

"Dear me," said a voice, and I had to smile, "I'd rather be back home in bed wi' my missus – this lot will cripple us."

"Och, Benny," came a reply, "you're no bloody good in there either, mun, she told me."

"I tell ye one thing, son, I could do with a pint."

They bantered, chuckled, laid wagers on their lot. And then my father called down the lines:

"Listen. Let them pass, understand? Lie low in the water and let them go by, then come out when I shout and take them in the middle – the middle, remember, then fan out either side. It's confusion we want, the lads in the carts'll do the rest."

I watched their rain-washed faces as they stared with hunted eyes towards the oncoming convoy guarded by trained soldiers.

They were not trained fighters, these; they were artisans and labourers. Aye, over twenty rounds up on the Blorenge punch-bowl of a Sunday morning for sport – all right, but not to the death.

Yes, they fought: they'd been fighting all their lives, but mainly to keep their children fed, or their wives out of debt to the Truck Shops run by the Guests or Homfray. A few had heard of their Celtic past – of the ancient tribes who had fought the might of Rome long after England had been bludgeoned into submission – but most didn't care a jot about it. The hope was not conquest, but to try to keep off the blacklist, out of the House of Correction at Usk if they were caught paying pennies to the outlawed Union.

Now they stared with vacant faces at the oncoming Redcoats, and no leader of that time, including John Frost, could have commanded a more disconsolate army. The convoy came on, nearer, nearer. The ammunition boots of the soldiers were now thumping the road with cold, military precision.

The head of the column, led by an officer on horseback, was no less than fifty yards away: peering through the roadside grasses I could see the prisoners clearly: many were wounded, their bloodstained bandages fluttering in the wind. And then, above the pouring rain I heard a faint, discordant sound, and realised that they were singing. In Welsh they sang, mostly, which was their mother tongue, but more were shouting the words of Ernest Jones, our Chartist poet, in English:

> Then rouse my boys and fight the foe;
> Your weapons are truth and reason.
> We'll let the Whigs and Tories know
> That thinking is not treason.
> Ye lords, oppose us as you can.

Your own doom ye seek after.
With or without you, we will stand
Until we gain the Charter!

And there arose from the carts then a battering cry in unison:
"The Charter! The Charter! *The Charter!*"

Now they came abreast of us. I saw the horsed officer stare
down at the ditches either side of him, and my father, seeing
him draw his sword, yelled:

"Right, lads! Into them! Get into them!"

Instantly, it was pandemonium.

As we stormed across the road towards the carts, the
soldiers fought to unsling their muskets, and the prisoners,
leaping down on to the road, stopped to fight or fled in all
directions, in wild disorder. I saw the astonished face of a
Redcoat as we met; holding the advantage of surprise, I
hooked him hard to the chin and he fell against me, clutching
me and pulling me down. And out of the corners of my eyes I
saw a levelled pistol; exploding in a shaft of fire, its ball took
O'Reilly through the head, blowing out his brains.

Now, within a mêlée of struggling, cursing men I struggled up, butted one soldier and struck down another, then
stooped to haul one off my back, and Old Shenks came up,
steadied himself and hit the man flat. Edwards, the giant, was
nearby, lifting soldiers off their feet and clubbing them down
like dolls: beyond him my father was fighting with almost
methodical grace, pulling prisoners out of the jumble of men
and animals, striking away those who opposed him. Men
were shrieking, bawling from bloodstained faces within the
struggling mass; some horses were down, their hooves clattering about, carts were overturning. And from the heaving
bodies a wild clamour arose in the fierce downpouring rain.
Locked together, men were rolling about, punching, kicking,
clawing at each other within a howling in English and
Welsh.

And then, floating on a sea of bobbing heads, I saw a face I
knew – Irish Joe Dido, Old Nana's son. And he was shouting
some bawdy song of the Wexford '98 Rebellion and waving
an Irish flag: Knocker, I saw next, climbing down the back of

a cart, his head bandaged and his clothes in tatters, and he shouted something incomprehensible as he leaped the road-side ditch in escape.

Now a man gripped me, shouting into my face, "You Welsh bastard!" and he swung me over his hip so that we crashed down together into a forest of stamping boots and legs: astride me, with his red tunic in rags, the soldier was bawling, bawling, and I struck up at his crimson face, missed him and hit another. I covered my head as a fist swung down. The soldier shrieked to the pain of his smashed knuckles as I ducked and his fist hit the road. And I saw, in a gap of the battle a man swaying along the verge. It was Sam Williams; like a drunken man he went, before suddenly collapsing, going head first into the ditch. Fighting myself upright, I butted through the mass of bodies in his direction; in time to see my father fling up his arms. And I saw a soldier's bayonet plunge through his chest and slide, blood-red, through his buckskin tunic at the back, impaling him.

"Dada!" I was upon him, hauling the soldier away, and my father stood for a moment, surprise upon his face. Pulling out the bayonet I gripped him around the waist and hauled him away to the side of the road. And I knelt above him while the tide of the fight ebbed about us.

My father's eyes were closed and blood was bubbling down his jacket. And, as I bent to get him over my shoulders to lift him, I heard a voice I recognised.

"Here – you take his legs!"

It was Iestyn Mortymer, the young man I had run arms with, up at Llangynidr, and with him was a man of width and strength; Iestyn cried:

"No, better – get him over Big Rhys's back!" And Iestyn stooped; with his right arm in a sling and heavily splinted, he lifted with me and the big man bent to take the weight at the moment a bright light exploded in my eyes, and I fell across the body of my father.

Later, they told me, the counter-attack had formed a pattern.

Having absorbed the initial impact of our attack, the

Redcoats took command. For these were not the comparatively untrained recruits who had fought so well at the Westgate, but others of the 45th: a hundred and fifteen of Napier's most experienced troops held in reserve for such an eventuality. They were the veterans of Waterloo who had scattered the cavalry at Quatre Bras and shot up the French Imperial Guard under Ney at La Haye Sainte: men whose comrades, with the French, had laid fifty thousand graves in two square miles of country.

Aye, indeed; they had little to fear from us – a bunch of untrained colliers and ironworkers; theirs was a trade of blood and violence.

I opened my eyes to a jolting, searing pain in the back of my head where a soldier's rifle butt had struck me. Green trees and overhanging branches tore at my face and hands as I danced in a dream through the forest. And the man who had carried me laid me down in the same quarry we had left but fifteen minutes earlier to attack the convoy. Others were there; wounded men; men panting from bloody faces; men rocking themselves to the pain of unseen wounds. They were all about me, these, like a pack of gasping, hunted animals. And I saw the face of Iestyn bending over me.

"You all right?"

"*Duw!*" I whispered, and sat up, feeling my head.

"Aye, did he hit you. But Big Rhys got him for it, the bugger."

Realisation struck me.

"Where's my father?"

"Beside you," said Iestyn.

Dada was lying where the man, Big Rhys, had dropped him, and he was dying.

The bayonet had taken him low, up through the midriff muscles and high into his chest, piercing a lung before slanting out through his shoulderblades. But he was still conscious, though his face was death-white; a premature corpse.

"Dada . . ." I said, bending over him.

"You all right, Tal?"

I nodded. Blood welled into his mouth and he swallowed it down.

"Got me this time, didn't they, the sods!"

It was one of the few times I heard him swear.

Iestyn, kneeling beside me, said, "Not likely, Captain. This time tomorrow you'll be back home," but my father did not appear to hear this, for he said, softly:

"Tal . . . the book."

Iestyn whispered, "What . . . what did he say?"

But I knew, and ran my hands over his tunic, and found it, the tin box that held 'The Tale of Delwyn'; I drew it out and held it up in the dim light.

"That . . . that girl you've got – Rhiannon, isn't it . . . ?" His voice was faint and I had to bend to his mouth to hear it.

"Aye, Dada – Rhiannon."

"Give it . . . if she has a son?"

I closed my eyes. "If she has a son, I will give it to him."

There was a silence broken only by his breathing; the men were listening. Then:

"Watch out for Poll, eh?"

I nodded, fighting tears.

"Aye, don't forget her – and Meg?"

A bright crimson stain suddenly widened on his white shirt. He said, his voice so faint now that I scarcely heard:

"'The coming hope, the future day, when Wrong to Right shall bow . . . And hearts that have the courage . . . to make that future now.'"

Then he sighed, turned away his face, and slipped easily into death.

I held him. Even after he had ceased to breathe, I held him.

After a few minutes Iestyn Mortymer came over the floor to me, drew my arms away, and laid my father on to the earth.

"Hush, Tal," said he. "You cannot kiss him back."

Empty I felt, without my father.

The quarry cave was open to the forest. For hours – almost up to midnight we could hear the soldiers beating through the trees and the rasp of their bayonets as they thrust into the undergrowth. But after midnight the sounds of their search died away. So we listened for the iron-shod wheels of their carts, the signal that they had continued their march to Cold Bath Fields, the prison, but no such sounds came to us.

"They're still there, boys," said a man. "They'm only waiting for daylight."

"Then they'll bait us like rats in a trap," said his companion.

Easing over away from Big Rhys, who was sleeping, I took my father into my arms, and held him; cold, cold that body against mine.

Moonlight filtered down through the tree-tops: the men slept, snoring; some groaned to the pain of their wounds. They bandaged each other with strips of shirt, comforting one another with a rough, vulgar badinage; you don't need women for nurses, I've discovered, when comrades are around.

Iestyn Mortymer was sitting opposite to me, his head bowed over his broken arm, and he smiled once, opening his eyes to mine.

"Why are you fighting, Mortymer?" I asked him.

He shrugged, but I persisted, to take my mind from grief.

"For my son, and against Cwm Crachen," said he at length, and smiled. "That's the second time today I've been asked that."

"Cwm Crachen?" asked a man nearby. His accent was faintly Scottish.

Iestyn nodded. His hair, I noticed, was as black as mine was white in that dim, eerie light.

"You didn't say you had a son," said I.

"I didn't have one when I saw you last, Tal Roberts."

"What's his name?"

"Jonathan."

"Cwm Crachen?" asked the man again, and Iestyn turned to him:

"The Hollow of the Scab," he replied. "The place where my son was born. Do not ask more, man, leave it at that."

Outside in the forest the rain poured down; the wind was blustering among the little crags and crevices. A man said from the dark in a fine cultured voice:

"They said the Church and Chapels would be with us. They said the soldiers were on our side. The gentry were our friends, they told us. Yet here we are alone."

"Ach, give over, Sol, for God's sake. The Church, did ye say? The Old Testament backsliders? Ranting and ravin' in their pulpits, they're all in it together."

"They piss in the same pot, mun."

"Receive the Holy Ghost, eh? Then they drink a gin and leap a five-barred gate. Don't talk to me about the Church."

Another said, plaintively, "Frost, Williams and bloody Jones the Watchmaker! March on London, is it? They couldn't march on my Aunt Fanny."

There was a silence; then:

"So where did Jones's column get to?"

"Get to? Malpas, no further! A schoolgirl outing, it were — half a mile o' tit in half-inch strips. They were pissin' it up in the Green House, I tell ye, while I was into the Westgate Inn with hatchets."

The wind whispered in the quarry; the brown walls shone with running water. A man said, ruefully, "Mind, they'll make us jump this time for sure. They hung Dic Penderyn for somethin' he never did. Christ knows what they'll do to us."

"Don't talk like that, Paddy, there's dead folks in here,

mind."

"Apologies to their souls, mate, call them bloody lucky."

The night went on, and Iestyn said, "Rhiannon is a lovely name, Tal Roberts."

I held my father closer, for rain was driving in.

"Aye, and your wife's, Mari. There's Welsh in that."

"Yes, but she's English." His eyes were strangely shining, for there was little light. A man deep in the cave said:

"It'll be transportation, mind. High Treason, see?"

"Och, give over, Taff," said a North-Country voice.

"You lot would be wise if you got to sleep," said Iestyn, and rose, and the new leader was born. "You're sitting here with more yap than a pack of women. Are we proud of ourselves, for God's sake? Take it how it comes. The least we can do is keep our dignity," and he knelt beside me and took my father in the crook of his arm, saying:

"Sleep, Tal—lie back and sleep. I will hold him till the soldiers come."

"Is there no chance to get away?"

"No, they're all around us. Sleep, is it?" and he pushed me back on to the rock floor.

"Aye, he's right," said a man. "Sleep," and the place was quiet save for the pattering rain and doleful dripping of the forest.

Near to dawn somebody went around the quarry cave kicking the sleepers into wakefulness.

"What's up?"

"What the Hell's happening?" and Iestyn, standing in the middle of the floor, said:

"Right. Get up, all of you, we're making a break. I want the unwounded in front with me, the old men in the middle and the walking wounded at the back. Crawl, if you like, but we're going out. We're not sitting here like bloody mice."

"Ye askin' for it, ye mad young spalpeen!"

"They're waiting for that—just dying to blast us!"

"Stay if you like, Irish, you're not bound to come," said Iestyn. "Follow me, the rest of you."

With the leader in front we made a break for it, dodging and swerving through the trees, and ran into a half-circle of gleaming bayonets. The sergeant's voice cut through the rain:

"Come on, come on, then, you bloody Taffs. We're just dyin' to let you have it – come on!"

They ringed us with steel, cuffed and prodded us through the forest, and out to the carts waiting on the road for the march to Monmouth.

They thumped us through the forest with their musket butts; they prodded us up into the carts where our comrades, recaptured earlier, were waiting in the rain. I was up first and I pulled up Iestyn after me, then the man who was his friend, Big Rhys. Old Shenks had to be lifted in because the cold had got him, being over eighty. Irish Joe Dido, the son of Old Nana, was at the back of our cart, which was third in the line of ten: and he shouted, when they threw him into it:

"Be Jesus – call ye'self lucky. If my Old Nana were here she'd 'ave the bloody lot of ye!

"Easy on me, ye big English oaf!" And he began to sing up at the rain, an Irish revolution song about the hanging of Father John Murphy at Wexford.

The convoy had moved a bit and was now outside some Llanhennock cottages, and the old men and women came out and stood on their doorsteps, staring up with white, furious faces: hatred was in them for the English. And the men bared their heads; the women pulling their shawls over their faces, and we did not look at them, being ashamed.

Gradually they rounded us all up; little groups of shivering, dejected men and boys, uncomplaining under the prods and thumps. Many of them I knew by sight; a few of their faces I had seen in The Patriot meetings or on cock-fight nights in the Vulcan and Friendship.

Standing near me in the cart was Big Rhys, the boxer. And he turned his face to me, this man, and weeping, said:

"O, fy mab, fy machgen bach dewr!"

A man behind me asked, "What's wrong with him, for God's sake?" and pushed a bit in the standing crush. "Something up, Fighter?"

Iestyn said quietly, "Shut it – you asked that before. His son is dead; no more of it."

The big man wept on, biting at his fingers.

I was trying to keep Old Shenks upon his feet. The carts had halted again, but he kept slipping down the front of me. A sergeant went by, his pigeon chest ablaze with medals; grizzled and bucolic, this one, and get these bloody Taffs down to Monmouth quick. I called over the side of the cart:

"Sergeant, this old boy's gone eighty, and he keeps fainting. Can't you give us room to lay him down?"

"Hand him down here and I'll lay him out." He glared up, his moustache bristling. "You bastards!"

"Don't waste your time," said Iestyn to me. "You'll get nothing from them, Tal."

"He ain't fainted, mun," said a voice behind me. "The poor old bugger's dead." And he reached out and turned up Shenks's eyelids.

Jake Kilrain died, I heard later; the giant puddler who had seen to Eli Firmament, who deserved to die. Sam Williams died, too, but later, apparently, and I don't know where. But Knocker did not die; he escaped to Cardiff and took a ship to Brazil, so the tale went; if he did he was lucky, for Zephaniah Williams tried that and they picked him up aboard.

Zephaniah, like John Frost, the Chartist leader – they captured him in the house of Partridge, the printer in Newport – they both went to trial with William Jones and six others for High Treason, which carried Victoria's sentence of hanging, drawing and quartering, the filthy death that every felon feared.

There were some on the attack I never saw again – like Dai Tomorrow, who put off capture until fifteen years later, according to reports, and married a widow with a public in Abercarn, then moved to Maerdy, which they later called Little Moscow.

There was a rumour, too, that Old Cog Costog didn't die in bed, but came South with Skipper Rowlands and a boat-load of Anglesey lads, to fight for the Charter. And they were taken into custody ten minutes after landing in Bute Lock, and went to transportation. God knows why he finished up in Norfolk Island, but he was still quoting poetry, I heard, when they put the noose around his neck.

But Old Shenks, my friend of Canal Wharf, he who had served me, Gideon, and my father so well, died standing up; and I held him.

"Right, whip up the horses!"

The convoy started off again along the road to Monmouth. In the jolting, swaying cart, I held Old Shenks against me, and suddenly the wheels skidded to a stop. The officer on horseback came galloping up, and when he shouted I recognised his voice:

"Roberts, father and son. Are the Roberts pair here?"

It was Lieutenant Wetton, who once was a captain, and I knew instantly that I had heard that voice before – behind red curtains in Dowlais House library.

Recognising me, Wetton reined closer, crying:

"Out, Roberts – down on to the road!"

Big Rhys turned in the crush. "Give him me," he said, and took Old Shenks into his arms. I fought my way to the side of the cart and vaulted down.

"Ah yes!" Wetton smiled down. The rain, blustering in the wind, swept along the road between us. "We meet, I hope for the last time, Roberts. Your father is dead, I understand?"

I did not reply and his mare clattered around me as Wetton drew his sabre. He cried, his voice high-pitched with anger:

"So we're getting some justice at last, are we? You damned Northerners are worse than the Taffs. So far you've got off scot free, haven't you? So take this to remember me by," and he slashed down with the sabre and sliced my face from eye to chin.

'. . . and smote Delwyn, disfiguring him, and sent him to a foreign land, and it was twenty years before he returned to his own country.'

The lads tore the sleeves out of their shirts and tied me up a bit and the carts started off again. And, strangely, after those two days of tempest, the sun came out and the land smiled about us. And it seemed to me, although it could have been a fever, that it was shining for us; because in a break in the lowering clouds a beam of light shone down as if from the Heavens. I raised my face, like the others, for it was dazzling in its intensity. In its rainbow colours I seemed to hear my father's words:

> The coming hope, the future day
> When Wrong to Right shall bow.
> And hearts that have the courage
> To make that future now.

The carts rumbled on, along the road to Monmouth.

Three

Tal-y-Bont
1861

I returned from the convict settlement in Australia in the summer of my fortieth birthday, and owning nothing save the rags I stood in, made my way from Swansea Docks into a smiling land.

At Tonna, outside Neath, following the canal there out of habit, I worked two days harvesting on a farm for a barn bed and meals, a man who gave a helping hand to returning convicts, paying them half agricultural rates, fivepence a day. I snared rabbits in Rheola Forest and killed a sheep outside Hirwaun, where I worked with Crawshay's iron-stone miners; pathetic, half-starved men, women and children who laboured exposed, in bitter winters, under the spray-shot cannons of a dynasty's benevolence . . . until they discovered my identity, and I was discharged.

From Hirwaun I took up over Mynydd Aberdare, and along the ridge to Dowlais Top; to the cottage where Sam Williams and Aunt Mellie had lived.

A child of about five was standing at the cottage gate; neatly dressed was she, in a home-spun frock, a white pinafore, and clogs; and I knew by her white hair that she was of Gwyn Roberts' blood; also the eyes of Meg were in her face. But she shrieked when I greeted her, and ran, this child, and my sister Meg came to the cottage door, her hands white with flour.

"Tal . . . !" she said, and closed her eyes.

We stood in the silence of indecision, friends but strangers, and she said then, holding the little one against her:

"You're back . . . ?"

I nodded. "Aye, Meg."

I saw her not as a prim housewife, the cygnet who had become a swan (for she was tall, fair and beautifully possessed) but like the daughter she now clasped against her: with bright curls, and small fists waving, I saw her, her tiny rosebud of a mouth slobbering upon Poll's breast.

"You . . . you didn't write, Meg?"

She raised her chin. "Not really – Old Sam advised against it, and my man, too. Dunna get mixed up wi' it, he said – he's foreman at Race Level now, mind; we're doin' all right." She frowned, peering at me. "Where did ye get that terrible scar?"

"It doesn't matter," I said. The child looked over her shoulder at me and hid her face again. "Sam and Mellie both gone, are they?"

"O ah!" She brightened, but she was not the Meg I knew: "Old Sam died . . . let me see – about 'Fifty – near ten years back, and Auntie six months later . . . left me the cottage. Sam's friend, Knocker, got killed, ye know?"

"Killed?"

"Shot down Cardiff way, but I ain't sure, really speaking, for some say he got away." She lowered her eyes. "You heard about Dada, of course . . ."

I nodded.

"They buried him up at St. Woolos, you know . . . justifiable somethin' or other they called it."

"Justifiable homicide"

"Aye, that's it." She sniffed and wiped on a little lace handkerchief. "Mind, I do go up sometimes and put flowers on 'is grave. But . . ."

"But what, Meg?"

I fought the longing to take her into my arms.

"Well, my chap don't hold with it. Got the children to think about, he says." She brightened. "He . . . he's foreman at the . . ."

"Children, Meg?"

She held the little girl against her. "This one and another couple inside."

"I'm glad."

The wind moved, bringing between us the old Dowlais stinks, and Meg said faintly, lifting the child. "We ... we gotta go, *cariad*? Got to get Dada's dinner, 'aven't we?" She peered past me. "He ... he'll be back off shift any minute."

There came from the kitchen behind her a scent of granny's broth; my stomach, smelling it, too, rumbled for pounce thunder.

"Goodbye," I said.

For all my love of her childhood, it seemed inadequate.

"Goodbye, Tal. Any ... anything you want you just ask for, mind. You was always good to me, Tal." She waved the child's hand, dying to be gone. "Say goodbye to the nice gentleman, Ceri."

I had got no more than fifty yards when I heard her shriek like a woman scalded.

"*Tal!*" But I didn't look back.

Around Dowlais market the hucksters were at it – bargain boots at sixpence a foot; meat stalls, bread stalls, potatoes for a penny a pound, eggs five shillings a hundred. Macassar oil was being sold by quacks, music sheets and *The News of the World*.

Navvies were in from the outlying railways dressed in their moleskins and gaudy scarves, tipsy already, although the day was young; brawny, insolent, barging the women about with their brightly-coloured waistcoats. The thronging crowds were buying Liver Pills for Biliousness and Dr. Clee's ointment for Skin Eruptions, Rheumatics and Intestinal Worms: dentists were fitting teeth, barbers cutting and shaving outside cheese and butter stalls.

And on the fringe of the crowds sat the derelicts of the gullies – the filthy dilapidated houses, the overcrowded ill-ventilated rooms surrounded by collections of filth. And among these squatted the diseased and maimed; the puddlers, ballers and fillers who would work no more. In line after line they squatted; legless, armless, many with no feet (molten iron had got into their boots) and many blinded: starving, they rattled their begging tins along the walls of the Vulcan and Friendship and the Holywell Hotel, crying hoarsely from their burned faces; they who bought, with their blood, the millionaire pomp of Cyfarthfa Castle and Dowlais House.

It was the same old Dowlais that I had known two decades ago, and I remembered the words of Edward Davies, a Merthyr surgeon: 'There are more wooden legs in this town than any in the country with four times Merthyr's population; our streets are thronging with the maimed and the mutilated.'

If anything, I thought, it was worse than the 1830's.

In such company I could lose myself; in such a concourse of humanity, I was not alone. Nobody even glanced at my disfigured face, the legacy of Captain Wetton.

Now, standing outside the Vulcan and Friendship, I remembered Rhiannon: of how, an age before, I had taken her on Dobie in the snow, and made love to her in Dolygaer forest . . . the memory of her, the place itself, suddenly called me with obliterating force.

Making my way through the crowds in bright sunlight, I hitched up my bundle and took the bridle path I knew so well, up to Hitherto's lodge.

On Dowlais Top I stopped and looked back, seeing below me for the last time the dirty, straggling town amid its sprawling, barren mountains; like a bundle of dirty rags spread out in faintest hope of their bleaching, with belching furnaces and black table-lands of rubbish all around.

Aye, I thought, so leave this pit of greed and sorrow and go where it is clean . . . to the place where you made love to Rhiannon.

I walked through the bowers of Dolygaer forest under a bright green shuffle of leaves; above me a kestrel hawk soared in vaporous air-space. Here, I remembered, hand in hand with Rhiannon, I had seen the trailing sword of Orion and the flashing of Sirius amid a wilderness of blossom.

Here sang the robins of winter; there soared young larks in the rafters of heaven; in the hazel wands, where I passed, were the petulant protestations of a redbreast. All was alive with the flame of summer; a reed-warbler chattered to its young: amid languorous blooms of convolvulus, silver-bubbled streams meandered down to the Falls, where danced a sea of dandelion and willow-herb. All was born anew within the seething anguish of our parting.

Following the track that led to the shooting lodge, I walked more slowly, and with care, lest I disturbed Joe Hitherto; were he alive he must surely be eighty, I reflected. And saw him all of a sudden, outlined head and shoulders in the plover field beyond his gate; turning, he cried:

"Well, dang my arse! If it anna Tal Roberts!"

I stood before him gripping my bundle.

He was as old as a dead stoat, with bags under his eyes like the toss-pots of the Casbah; but his brain was up and lively and in his eyes was a wicked gleam.

"You remember me?" I asked.

Closer now, he surveyed me, his faded eyes peering.

"Well sod me! Where you been? – what you been up to?"

"No odds to that, Joe," I answered. "Just passing, and I'm on my way."

A bird whispered sorrowfully, the cadence of its voice rising and falling on the soft, clear air.

He said, out of context, "That girl died, ye know . . ."

"Rhiannon? Yes, I know."

"And Sir John, too – these six year back, an' more. It were jist 'afore goldfinch time, as I recall . . ."

I envied him his articulate sense of time, measuring all by the seasons. He added, screwing at his moleskin cap. "But Lady Charlotte's still goin' strong – married that Schreiber chap, did ye know?"

"I did not know."

His presence, despite its nostalgic sweetness, was also a transgression: I desperately wanted to be alone amid this glowing richness. Joe added:

"Mind, it were a pity about that little de Vere piece, weren't it?" He grinned with broken, yellow teeth. "You were real soft on her, if I remember."

"Yes," I said quietly.

"Went to India, got married, left 'im, came home, and died. Nursing the Old Cholera down in China, she were."

In trackless words, sunless, airless, we stood, just looking. I said, "Joe . . . I've got to go . . ."

"But not directly?" A pathetic eagerness struck his lined face. "You just sod around for a bit, and welcome, eh?" He pushed past me like a man exorcising wickedness, lifting his cap and crying, "Go into the lodge, mun – make yesel' a cup o' tea, I'll be back this minute."

"Thank you."

Alone in the lodge I stood listening to a ring-dove sobbing, a ravishing sweetness on the forest air.

This place, indeed, this room, I thought, was almost exactly as Rhiannon had left it.

Beyond the window where we had watched the snow, March helleborine arose in scents of wild thyme, and the glades were hazed with celandine: within the room were the same, now bald, sheepskin rugs, the faded pictures on the walls; the same, but now faded chintz curtains. And in the silence of the chattering forest, in the mellow-sweet drone of bees, I heard her voice:

"Make love to me, Tal? Please make love to me . . .?"

The room abounded with her presence, and I knelt in the place where she had lain, and knew sounds that were echoes of reality. It was as if, for one undefined moment, I was holding her in my arms and deep within her body, and I raised my face and called her name:

"Rhiannon!"

The forest sounds stopped, listening to a stranger's voice.

"*Rhiannon!*"

It was a heresy of self-deceit: a warped notion of romantic nonsense; I turned to leave, embarrassed by my own behaviour.

A girl was standing in the open doorway, as the kettle boiled.

She surely must have heard me.

"Mr. Roberts?" and she came into the room, smiling. If she noticed my disfigured face, she made no sign of it.

I bowed.

She said, "My name is Marged. Old Joe sent a keeper to the house, and I came straight away. You knew my mother, he says."

Beyond the door stood a little dappled mare; the girl was dressed in brown riding-habit: her face, her form . . . was the epitome of Rhiannon.

In my silence, she asked: "Did . . . did you know her, Mr. Roberts?"

"Yes."

"My . . . my mother is dead. You knew that, too?"

"Yes."

I could not drag my eyes from her face. It was like the crystallising of a hypnotic dream; as if Rhiannon had returned: even the voice possessed the same cadent quality, a dark contralto sound.

"Did . . . did you know her well?" the girl asked.

"Not well."

Her eyes had lowered to my hands and the wrists wasted by the manacles, and I put them behind my back. She said, unmoving:

"She died when I was six years old," her eyes drifted

around the room and she faintly smiled. "She . . . she used to come here a lot when she was young, she told me. She loved Dolygaer forest, this old lodge especially. Old Joe says she was always here, before she married . . ."

"Married?"

"Her people went to India and she married there. My father died out there when I was two, so she came home again, to Wales."

"I see."

"He was an army officer." She raised her eyes and looked at me, then moved with delicate grace, bending to peer through the window. I said quickly:

"You live up at Kierton now?"

"With my grandfather, Sir Richard. There are paintings of my mother all over the house, but none of my father. I'm always trying to find out things about my people – which is natural, I suppose, but nobody seems to know anything. That's why I jumped on old Penny, and came down here."

"Penny?"

She smiled brilliantly. "My mother had a mare called Penny."

We stood as strangers, talking with the inanimate falseness that impedes strangers.

"Yes, I remember," I said, and returned her smile.

It didn't traduce her; her task was discovery, and she was possessed of the woman's subterfuge; later, if this was unsuccessful, she would resort to chicanery; I would have to guard my tongue.

This secret was Rhiannon's, bound by the girl's illegitimacy.

"You used to meet here a lot, Old Joe said." Marged laughed gaily, looking beautiful; like the Princess Marged in the 'Tale of Delwyn' I thought vaguely.

"Joe's a romantic old fool," I replied.

She examined me with the academic interest one reserves for a child, and asked, "Did you ever meet my father, Mr. Roberts?"

"*Diawch*, no! He was an army officer, I was an ostler!"

"But an educated man, nevertheless, aren't you!"

I added, "Anyway . . . your father was in India."

She opened dark, rebellious eyes, replying, "Yes, you're the same as all of them, aren't you! The more I question the tighter you get."

I walked past her. "You shouldn't be questioning me. You should be asking these things of your own people."

It quietened her; she swiftly turned away, and I thought she was going to cry, saying regretfully:

"After my father died in Johore, my mother sailed home, they tell me, and went into Merthyr's slums to nurse the poor. She caught the cholera, and was ill for only two days, my grandfather told me." She groaned. "God knows what she was doing down in that dreadful place!"

I replied, "I am sorry. Now you are telling me things that I do not know. I know only that your mother was beautiful – everybody was in love with her."

She raised her face. "And you, Mr. Roberts?"

"I was a servant."

To my astonishment she approached me, and, putting out her hand, she touched the scar of my face with the tips of her fingers, saying:

"But one beloved, too, unless I'm mistaken. She called you '*fy Machgen Gwyn*', my White-haired boy, did she not? Your hair is white now, but for another reason . . ." and she lowered her hand and stood there, smiling.

I had no words for her. She asked, "And this is where you used to meet, you two?" She looked about the room.

I went past her to the door. "Goodbye, Miss de Vere."

"Why do you call me that?" She raised an eyebrow in admonishment: she and her mother, like the cockatrice, could kill with a glance.

"Because I do not know the name of your father."

Since my rejection by Meg, so total and complete, there was born within me a hunger greater than desire: it was the need to be more than of myself, but part of another; isolation brought an inexpressible sadness. There is a demand in humans to know an affinity with one beloved, and with Rhiannon dead and my father, Poll, and even Old Shenks gone, there was none to whom I could turn for this solace.

And now, standing there in the doorway, I fought the temptation to snatch my daughter into my arms.

She was of Rhiannon's womb, flesh of her flesh, and therefore mine.

"Goodbye," I said.

"My . . . my mother never went to India. You know that, too, don't you, *fy Machgen Gwyn?*"

We stood looking at each other.

"I'll go further. She never even married. You see, she only loved one man."

Every inch of her; her dignity, her beauty, even her admonishment; she was, at that moment, totally Rhiannon.

I bowed to her.

"Goodbye," I repeated, and turning, left her, taking the track past the Falls to the peaks of Gwaun that rose in strickening sunlight.

And I took the road that led to Brecon; turning my face to Amlwch.

And, as I walked, the words of the Tale rose up before me: '. . . and the Princess worked among the villagers of Deganwy, they who were suffering from the Yellow Pestilence; and she caught the plague, and died: first giving birth to Delwyn's daughter, for they had been lovers.'

Four

Amlwch

I was a week on the road before the weather-cock of Amlwch came shouting through the dusk; a fractured opal moon was rising over the earth.

Tramping over the top of Parys Mountain all was quiet, as if the Devil had cleaned his tools and put them away for night-shift: the whole red land, silent, opened its arms to me . . . in welcome to one returned via Golgotha.

Memories of Dada, Poll and Meg flooded back on that walk down to the harbour, and the nostalgic clip-clop of old Dobie's shoes beat within me a silent rhythm of peace: the deep bass of my father's voice I heard then, Pru Ichabod's soprano incantation in Chapel, Meg chuckling, her tiny fists begging for Poll; the hoarse, howling protests of Andy Appledore as the molten copper bit him . . . and the sultry whispers of Siân Fi-Fi with her drawers down in Cemaes wood.

Nothing stirred in Amlwch; it was as if the Marquis had forbidden human activity between the hours of dawn and dusk. But soon, I knew, the publics would swing wide their doors and the drunks flood in, and the night would be filled with bawling men and the shrill protests of women: the same old Amlwch of drunken ill-repute, yet filled with the sweetness and neighbourly goodness that gave the lie to official historians.

Outside Fifteen Quay Street on my way to the harbour I saw Ida Promise scrubbing out the back, and no sign of Shoni Bob-Ochr, the Flying Dutchman: bent and scrawny was Ida now, pining for him, her only love.

Dora Jewels was sitting in the bay window of The Crown,

weighing up a Guinness, and Dahlia Sapphira, busty and in full song, was giving 'Rescue the Perishing' a going over in the tap-room of the Adelphi, with Tasker Bopper on the accordion, and every dog in Town must have been making for the hills.

Seth Morgan, still alive, which astonished me, went by, dozing on a cloud of Beneficiary Wills; Jacki Scog, still pig-killing, passed with a leer, his brain sharpening knives. And, as if to crown it all, I bumped into Siân Fi-Fi. Wide-hipped and prolific was Siân, done up in vanity flounces, with a floppy hat bouncing on her shoulders and a retinue of followers bouncing along behind.

Vaguely I wondered if any were mine.

She looked right into my face, did Siân . . . and passed me by.

On the cobbles outside the Britannia, I paused, for this was the place where I had first met Rhiannon.

I approached Three Costog, our old cottage above Brickhill, with care, lest people who knew me had taken over. A light in the kitchen window stilled me, and I gripped the fence near Dobie's barn, looking in. A woman (in another age it could have been my mother) was busy in the kitchen, and I wondered if it was old Betsy Costog; then realised that she must long be dead. She raised her face to the window once, this woman, and I drew back into the shadows.

Now, walking along the cliff top, I made my way to Cemaes wood . . . with one last duty to perform. I was hungry, but knew no hunger: tired, yet knew no weariness. For there was burning within me an urgency to achieve one last and solitary task, not only in the name of my father, who had commanded it, but in Rhiannon's name, and Poll's; in Meg's name, and Sam Williams's, Knocker's, Old Shenks's, Aunt Mellie and Old Nana — aye, Lady Charlotte and Sir John, the bards Price and John Jones — even Justice Bosanquet . . . the score or more who had taken their roles and played them in the 'Tale of Delwyn'.

For are we not, as my father once said, mere phantoms in a game? '. . . puppets moving hither and thither, irresponsibly, unknowingly within a play of pawns? And to whom is to be apportioned Saint or Devil?'

I came to the wood where old Brock Badger used to play, and there knelt, looking at the stars. All the sounds of the night were about me; the *chit chit chit* of a bird, the indefinable whispers of things that crawl: far below me I heard the waves crashing on Costog beach.

Finding a piece of elm I fashioned it into a tool and began to dig.

The hole I dug was circular, no wider than the span of my hand, but so deep that, when I had finished I was lying on my side with my arm deep in the earth.

Opening my bundle I took out the manuscript of 'The Tale of Delwyn', wrapped it in oilskin and put it into the hole, carefully replacing and stamping flat the injured ground; upon this I placed a rock.

Thus, as my father commanded (I possessed no son), the manuscript was returned to the Welsh heart whence it came ... safe from those who would corrupt it into a foreign tongue.

Sitting with my back to the bole of a tree, I slept.

Perhaps I dreamed; I do not know. The night was warm and still, given to dreaming.

In my reverie I saw a tree make shape beside a river; on each bank of the river sheep were bleating: on the near bank the sheep were white; on the far bank the sheep were black. And the tree itself was of the *Mabinogi*; one half being alive with summer leaves, the other half being on fire.

So it is with Wales.

Between cockshut time and twilight my country smiles; her sighs are stilled, her scars erased. In springtime she is beautiful in her white hawthorn, like a Church of England bride.

Spring in my land takes me back to the dandelion days of my youth; the honey-sheen of sun on the sapless rushes; the noonday music of melting ice.

But, come summer, Wales is Welsh best; a mother clad in green finery. The sheepland pastures are her body, the wheat her Brythonic hair. The little streams are my mother's veins, the Teify, Towey, Usk and Wye her arteries, the mountains of Plinlimmon her breasts. She is at once Iberian-dark, prideful, fiercely Celtic.

In her womb she holds the little terraced cottages, in her hands her generations: her right eye is the sun, her left eye the moon, her voice is the wind.

Kneeling there in Cemaes wood the spirit of this mother moved, enfolding me ... within her arms she holds her exiles.

O, my beloved country, who has raised her sword to the fire of her invaders and brandished her honour in the face of shame! I can see from here the white beam of Lynas, I hear the brooks tumbling through the heather in Dolygaer. Are the black cattle still lowing from the upland farms of Cad-waladr? Does Parys Mountain of Amlwch run with Celtic blood? And is the starlight on Dowlais Top still as bright as when I made love to Rhiannon?

How great my country! Conqueror of the Jute, the Pict, Anglian, Scot, Irish, Dane and Romans—they who came with fire and laid their bones upon the altars of Cader Idris. Cunedda Wledig; Iago the son of Rhun, who fell at Chester; Arthur and Urien, the Splendid Blood of the North; and Owain, the son of Urien!—these are the magic names, the line of my deathless Welsh princes.

This, then, was the part of the tree that waved in beauty.

The other half I saw was the part on fire: the branches that flame between twilight and cockshut time, when the world is dark.

This is when my country burns with the catalysis of an artificial sun, her nights alight with radiant ovens—the tigers of predatory iron that feed on flesh.

Shedding her seasons, she pulls on blackened rags, shovels coal, heaves ropes, digs coke, bakes bricks, becomes illumin-ary; a mother at the stake, afire with lambent flame. Her hands stir molten iron, her bowels spurt smoke, her eyes calcine. And the summer song within her throat becomes a siren-shriek.

Then she is one with the white-hot chains that bind her; a blackened hag, defiled.

Now the burning tree glowed within its cindering depths, and I saw, as a watching child sees in a grate, the emblem of its carnage.

The stunted fields of my country I saw, the impaled breasts of tortured mountains. And from the pain of the lances in her womb the land cried out as the tree cried now, hissing and cracking in the mutilation.

And in that consuming of tree and land, I heard the protests of my people; the groans and breathlessness of worked-out colliers, the shrieks of entombed children, the screams of women trapped in machines.

Now, as the higher branches caught in scintillating brightness, there arose beams of variegated light that polarised the sun: conspiring to explode into final detonation. The soil heaved up, mushrooms of rock spewed out, and there arose black monuments to my generation.

And over this charred, lunar wilderness stole the smells of Cyfarthfa and Pen-y-darren; of Nantyglo, Risca, Bargoed, Tredegar and a hundred other graveyards . . . and the stink of Dirty Dowlais covered all – putrescent, as a corpse lies putrefying.

Damn you!

My country and my people have been carried off, outraged by you.

Damn you England!

I rose in the moon-filled wood and listened to the wave-lap of Costog beach below; the beach where I once saw my father, Skipper Rowlands, and the boat. And the sounds seemed to call me, as a seafarer is called home.

I went down to the beach.

And I saw, on the emblazoned sea, a white bird struggling in the waves . . . and remembered the days of my youth, and Joe Herring, the gull . . . And even as I watched the frantic efforts of the bird, I heard a voice like the voice I heard thirty years before, in the cry of the circling gulls.

"*Taliesin* . . . !"

But this time it was not my mother's voice.

I waited, listening, wondering if it was a trick of the wind, but it was not: so clearly was it Rhiannon's voice. And I remembered the last words of the 'Tale of Delwyn': 'And after twenty years in the hostile country, Delwyn, whose face was afflicted by his captors, returned to his own land. And there was a white bird struggling on the breast of the sea, calling his name. The bird was the soul of the Princess Marged, so Delwyn went into the sea to become one with her, but the honeycomb woman who served his father stretched out her hand to him.'

"*Taliesin!*"

The struggles of the captive bird became weaker. I started forward and was wading through the shallows when a hand caught mine and drew me back.

Poll said: "They told me you was coming, Tal – folks saw ye in Town: then you watched me in the kitchen window, and I followed you here."

I was looking at the white bird. She said, peering: "What they done to ye?" She added:

"Gawd, you look proper ill. Are you all right?"

"Yes," I said.

"What you starin' at, then?"

I said, "There's a white bird dying in the sea."

Poll peered through the moonlight. "There anna! You're seein' things."

I looked into her eyes.

She was older; the matron of her suffering had lined up her face for fifty . . . until she smiled, and then she was Poll. She said:

"Been waitin' all these years. Gone clean, like I said – understand? Take me on, is it? If ye can't 'ave that gentry piece, I'm still around. I'd wash and mend an' be decent, mind – good old Poll, remember?" She hesitated. "I . . . I got some granny's broth on the stove, and . . ."

"Yes," I said.

"Dear me, that skinny and tired ye are . . . Give us a try, Tal? Just a week or so – I won't bother ye none . . . and . . . and see how I get on?"

I looked at the sea. The white bird had gone.

She said, faintly. "Always loved ye, Tal . . ."

I put out my hand to her. For reply she kissed my face; the moonlight was bright yet she made no mention of my affliction.

Together, we walked up the beach, to Three Costog.

FURTHER READING

Public Order in the age of the Chartists, F. C. Mather, Manchester University Press

Dowlais Iron Company Letters 1782–1860, County Records Committee of the Glamorgan Quarter Sessions & County Council and Guest Keen Iron and Steel Company Limited, 1960

The Monmouthshire Chartists, Newport Museum and Art Gallery Publication

The Miners of South Wales, E. W. Evans, University of Wales Press

'In Search of the Celestial Empire', Keith Strange, *Llafur*, Vol. 3, No. 1, 1980, University College, Swansea

'Report to the Board of Health The town of Merthyr Tydfil, 1850', T. W. Rammel, HMSO

'Sanitary Conditions of Merthyr Tydfil', *Cardiff and Merthyr Guardian*, 1847–1855

'Crime in an Industrial Community 1842–1864: the Conquering of China', David Jones and Alan Bainbridge, *Llafur*, Vol. 2, No. 4

The History of Dowlais, Rev. J. Hathren Davies, Trans. Tom Lewis

'A Visit to the Ironworks and Environs of Merthyr Tydfil in 1852, Edwin F. Roberts, William E. Painter, London, Merthyr Public Library

'The Merthyr Ironworker (Toiling & Moiling)', Pamphlet, Merthyr Public Library

'Poor Law Administration in Merthyr Tydfil Union, 1834–1894', Tydfil Davies Jones, Merthyr Public Library

'State of Education in Wales', Merthyr Tydfil Library

Directory of Bristol, Newport and Welsh Towns 1848 – Merthyr Tydfil, and neighbourhood, Merthyr Public Library

'Cholera in Nineteenth Century Merthyr (The Flail of the Lord . . . ?)' Pamphlet, Merthyr Tydfil Library

History of Merthyr, 1867, Wilkins (Subscribers' History (Au.))

South Wales, Thorough Guide Series, 1888, C. S. Ward, M.A., Dulau and Co., London

Copper Mountain, John Rowlands, Anglesey Antiquarian Society

The Industrial Development of South Wales, 1750–1850, A. H. John, B.Sc. (Econ), Ph.D, University of Wales Press, 1950

South Wales Ironworks, 1760–1840: an Early History (from original documents), J. Lloyd, Bedford Press, London, 1906

Guest Keen Iron and Steel Co. Ltd., The Dowlais Story, 1759–1959, Cardiff Public Library

'A Study of some of the social and economic changes in the town and parish of Amlwch 1750–1850', John Rowlands, dissertation submitted for the degree of Magister in Artibus of the University of Wales, 1960, Gwynedd Library

John Frost, a study in Chartism, David Williams, Cardiff, 1939

The Trial of John Frost, shorthand notes

The Diaries of Lady Charlotte Guest (including letters from collaborator John Jones – the Mabinogion translation, and Bessborough Papers) original manuscripts, National Library of Wales

A History of Modern Wales, David Williams, John Murray, 1950

Children Working Underground, R. Meurig Evans, National Museum of Wales

Children in the Mines, 1840–1842, R. Meurig Evans, National Museum of Wales

Official Guide to Monmouth and District, Monmouth Chamber of Trade, 1928

'Public Houses, Inns, Taverns & Beer Shops of Dowlais', Pamphlet – B. F. Donelon of Merthyr Tydfil

Merthyr Historian Vol. III, Merthyr Tydfil Historical and Civic Society, 1980

The Industrial Revolution in South Wales, Ness Edwards, London, 1924

Home Office Papers. Bundle Zp 37 of H.O. 17/128 Part 2, Departmental Record Office, Home Office

South Wales Miners, R. Page Arnot, Allen & Unwin, 1967

Welsh Folk Customs, Trefor M. Owen, National Museum of
Wales, 1959

Children in the Iron Industry 1840–1842, R. Meurig Evans,
National Museum of Wales

The Condition of the Working-Class in England, Engels, Progress
Publishers

Hospitals in Merthyr Tydfil (1850–1974), Joseph Gross

The Mabinogion, Lady Charlotte Guest* – a facsimile repro-
duction of the complete 1877 edition, John Jones Cardiff
Ltd.

* Posterity has ascribed to Lady Charlotte Guest the first translation into English
of the Welsh *Mabinogi* and other tales from the Red Book of Hergest. In the 1877
edition of her book, which she describes as 'My Mabinogion' she states '. . . for
the accurate copy I used [the Welsh from which she translated, Au.] I was
indebted to John Jones, Fellow of Jesus College, Oxford . . .'

This statement relegates the bard to the role of a copyist, yet in her diaries,
which, presumably, she did not expect to be published, she states that 'John
Jones had begun a translation'. Further, 'Taliesin Williams gave me a correct
translation to appear in my series.' Further still, she states that 'Mr. Justice
Bosanquet translated' and that the Comte de la Villemarqué (an eminent French
scholar) gave her a translation into French of the 'first three parts of the
Mabinogion'. On her own account she states that the Frenchman claimed that 'I
did not write my book myself.'

The Rev. Thomas Price also assisted her, and John Jones was actually
teaching her Welsh at the time the translations were first published.

In the light of her own statements, her decision not to share official credit with
her many collaborators was unfair and illegal; today, it would be actionable. (It is
to be wondered what role Lady Charlotte Guest actually played in the work: the
writer believes that her majority contribution was that of Producer.)

For Ernest Roberts of Bangor, in the North, and
Don Griffiths of Tonypandy, in the South, and
the men who got the slate and coal, from
Bethesda to the Rhondda.

Book Three

THIS SWEET AND BITTER EARTH

I am grateful to many librarians, also to the old gentlemen of Industry – sought out in homes for the aged, their little front rooms, in the street and on park benches; in their way they compare with the respected historians – people like Mr. R. Page Arnot, to whom all miners are indebted.

Without the aid of such men this book could not have been written.

One

1900

CHAPTER ONE

Six days ago, when the workhouse cart left Wrexham, there
had been eight of us, but the Crowther lads had hopped off
at Denbigh and the Rhubarb Twins left us in Conway. And
so, when we came to Bethesda, there was only me and Ma
Bron left. With my legs swinging on the footboard I was
watching the stars above the Glyders when she asked:

'Where you off to, then?'

Bluenose, our workhouse driver, was hunched black
against the moon, and his old mare, knowing he was drunk,
clip-clopped along the summer road as if she knew the place
like the back of her hoof.

'You deaf, or something?'

'I'm going to Padarn,' I replied, wanting to be rid of her.

'You got people there?'

'Sort of.' I shrugged her off.

'What you mean – sort of? Either you got people, mate, or
not.'

'Got a grandpa, if he's people.'

'You'm lucky,' said she. 'I only got aunts.'

'Do they live in Bethesda?'

'Pesda, they say.'

'Same place.'

She spoke again but I let her ride, for she was a fancy
piece, this one, and she'd got a six inch nose on her since
leaving Wrexham workhouse, and my mam always said you
shouldn't let too many into your pantry, which applied to
sixteen-year-old Welsh bits. It was a gorgeous April night, I
remember, with the moon as big as a Dutch cheese, sitting
on the top of the Flights of Penrhyn, and the Ogwen River
was strangling the fields with a quicksilver flood.

'You raised in these parts, Toby Davies?'

Down to christian names now. 'Sort of,' I said again,
pretty civil.

She fluffed up her bright hair, looking like a great fair

9

dove on the footboard and peered at me, her eyes dark smudges in the pallor of her cheeks. 'You know,' said she, 'you're a stitched up fella, ain't you? – down south in Porth they'd open you up with a razor.'

For all her talk, I've never seen a woman at sixteen as pretty as this Taff from the south; there were some flighty bits turned up all the years I was in the workhouse, and some of them had babies, but I never did see a girl there to hold a candle to her, with her bright, laughing eyes and tumbling gold hair. She was a warm piece, even for the Rhondda, I heard the Master say; sure as fate someone will turn her into two, and some folks reckoned he did.

There was no sound but the wind and the clopping of the hooves, and Ma Bron sighed like the well of life going dry, took a deep breath and opened the buttons of her bodice; the baby in her arms hammered and sucked.

'How old are you, Toby Davies?'

'Sixteen, same as you.'

'You Welsh speaking?'

'Aye.'

'I'm not.' She smoothed her baby's face. 'I was raised down south, but we only talked English – I suppose I'm half and half.' She smiled at me. 'Will you be my friend when we get to Pesda?'

'Ay ay,' I said, making a note to cut and run for it, for I once had an aunt in the back pews of Pesda's Jerusalem, and I know what she'd have done to people arriving with black sin babies. We looked at each other, Ma Bron and me, and then at the baby, and she said, raising her face:

'You like my little Bibbs?'

'She's all right.'

'She's mine proper, ye know – she ain't just a foundling.'

'Who's her father?'

We glared at each other.

'You've a dirty mind on ye, Toby Davies,' said she, 'just like the rest of 'em.' She fondled her baby's face. 'Hasn't he, Bibbs? He's a dirty old bugger, ain't he?'

The cart left Nant Ffrancon Pass behind us; the chimneys of Bethesda began to steeple the moon. The baby slept. Ma

Bron and me swayed and juddered together on the foot-board; she said:

'I liked your ma before she died.'

I bowed my head and salt was on my lips.

'She were helpful to me when my baby came.'

I did not reply.

She said, 'You only stayed on, really, 'cause your mam was ill, didn't you?'

I nodded.

'Best for you to be out and about, now your mam's gone.'

Aye, best, I thought, when once your mam's away in the box.

Bron sighed at the moon. 'Mind, you're a big boy, ye know – soon you'll be gettin' across the women. And your grandad's going to have fits with his legs up when he sees you in the nose-bag.' She stared about her at the cottages of Caerberllan. 'Is this Bethesda?'

'Coming up now,' I said.

'You know these parts?'

I nodded.

'You heard of Pentir, where my aunts live?'

I didn't tell her that this was my land in childhood; that this big country was my history. All my memories were of Bethesda, Deiniolen and Tregarth, when my parents brought me up from the south on visits that lasted months: now I remembered the Sunday teas, the day of rest from the quarry, with people sitting around in starched black, waiting for chapel. Welsh cakes were on my tongue; in my head was the thunder of the sea at Port Penrhyn where the great ships came in, and the sound of the quarry hooter echoing in the valleys. It was slate country, hard and daunting, yet I loved it, and the mountains rearing up about me brought again the old, unfathomable excitement.

'How d'ye say that again?' asked Ma Bron, staring back at the cottages.

'*Caer-ber-llan*,' I said.

Once, when young, my mother lived in Twelve Caerberllan.

'Pity about your mam dyin' so sudden,' said Ma Bron at

the moon. 'She were a nice little thing. Had a hard time at the end, didn't she?'

I stared at the road.

Bluenose took us up into Capel Bethesda, along the town's night-deserted road; the taverns and cottages of the quarrymen squatted like bull-frogs in the moonlight, awaiting a spring. 'Where does your grandpa work, you say?'

'Black Hill Quarry,' I replied.

'A labouring fella, is he?'

It stirred me. I said, 'He drives the engines *Rough Pup* and *King of the Scarlets*. He takes the trains out of Gilfach and along the lake to Bethel, and the sea.'

'Is he an owner?'

'*Diawch*, no!' I warmed to the subject. 'But he's Number Two driver to Assheton-Smith, and . . .'

'Who the hell's Assheton-Smith?' She made large eyes above her baby's face.

'And . . . and he says that if I settle with him, he'll get me down to Port Dinorwic on the incline-loading, or even work me as a *rybelwr*.'

'What's that?'

'Special trade – slate labourer – you're a girl, you wouldn't understand.'

'Is there money in it?'

'Aye, woman. And if I cart the rubbish clean I can split all sizes – for money on me own!'

She didn't reply to this. I made a fist of my hand and struck my knee. 'Aye, damn!' I said fiercely.

Suddenly, the dawn was uncertain in a red fleece of a day, and amid moon-darkness the sun was driving the world before him, shepherding the night clouds like sheep over the rim of the mountains. I stood up, turning on the footboard, crying: 'You see that big hole?'

Standing, too, Ma Bron nodded; the caverns of the biggest man-made hole in the world had made shape. I cried, as the cart slowed, 'If you buried all the people in the world in that hole, and all the people dead already, and all the people going to die, you'd never fill it, Ma Bron, you hear me?'

'They can hear you over in blutty Wrexham.'

'That hole's so big it would never fill with people, missus! You could just go on piling the bodies in, an' you'd never get to the top – you realise?'

'It's an interesting thought.'

'And this is the biggest slate town in the world! Welsh slate's the best, you know.'

'Well, I never did,' said she.

Sitting down on the footboard I screwed my fingers, hating her.

But all would happen as I had planned it, I thought. Already I could feel the bite of the rope around my thigh and the rock face danced in wetness above a hundred foot drop. In the eye of my mind I saw the stone splitting its face to a gunpowder flash, and white smoke pouring from the riven mountain. I heard the shouts of men as the drills stuck fast in the greystone vein, which my mother had said was richer than gold: I was aboard the *Cackler* and the old *George B* again, rumbling and swaying along the line to Lake Padarn, as I had done with my grandfather in childhood, up from Tonypandy on a visit. *Velinheli* and *Cloister*, Bethesda and Llanberis – these were the magic names! I would work the two and four foot gauges to the giant L.N.W.R., for my grandpa had driven them all. And I could see him now in that coming dawn, a giant in strength and purpose, his big hands on the engine brass as we clattered down to Bethel for the port-incline, and the song of it danced in my brain.

We had stopped outside the Waterloo public now: the only one watching us was an urchin with his finger up his nose.

'Where's Pentir, then?' asked Bron, easing herself down off the boards, and rubbing her rear. '*Diawch*, mun – eight hours up by there, it's a wonder I ain't split me difference.'

The urchin bawled, in Welsh, '*Y ffordd orau i Bentir ydy drwy'r caeau!*' and Ma Bron said, staring at him:

'Chinese, is he?'

I answered, 'He says it's over the fields to Pentir – I'll take ye, shall I?' and I picked up her bundle.

'Oh, no you don't,' said she, 'you put it down.'

The dawn sea-wind whispered and was cold on our faces.

13

'Don't trust you,' said she, and pulled the shawl higher about her baby's face. 'Don't trust anybody, do we Bibbs? – you bugger off, Toby Davies.'

The cart had gone. Uncertain, we stood looking at Bethesda, then she hoisted her bundle higher and strode off down the road to Bangor.

'Might see you some time, yeh?' I called after her.

'Not if I see you first,' cried Bron.

CHAPTER TWO

The cockerels were knocking their heads off by the time I reached Deiniolen, and there was a smell of bacon on the wind as I trudged up to Black Hill Quarry, where somebody told me Grandpa was working.

Here thick wedges of quarrymen were pouring out of the cottages, and I joined them: silently they marched in the thin sunlight like men raked from dreams and few gave me more than a glance. Behind and below us, as we marched upwards, the sun spread disclosing patterns of gold over the fields of the upland farmers.

All about me in that upward climb there grew a black desecration. The fields began to tremble to concussive shot-firing and quarry bugles sang. Rounding a bend in the road I came upon whining mill machinery, wagons and locomotives: trucks, harnessed in threes, were climbing and descending slate inclines. The men about me tramped with a quickened pace, as if the quarry working had injected them with a new fervour. Here, the mountain seemed to have exploded, and from the gaping mouths of caverns, relays of clanking wagons emerged. At the quarry gate a foreman said to me:

'You after rubbishing, son?' This in Welsh, and in Welsh I answered:

'I seek Ezra Davies, sir.'

'There's half a hundred Ezra Davieses.'

'Grandpa of Tabernacle Street – he's expecting a grand-son,' said a man in passing.

North or south, the Welsh don't miss a lot.

The foreman pointed. 'Down the incline to the barracks.' He asked, 'You wanting work in slate?'

'Aye, sir.' I stood decent for him.

'God alive, you're madder than Grandpa.'

As I began the descent to the barracks I saw the Anglesey men coming out of them for the shift; these, like Grandpa, apparently, lived in the little cabins that dotted the mountainside: they greeted me as I approached them; tough men, cast in the same womb-mould, mainly clean in the mouth. One said, nodding at my bundle, 'Just starting, lad?'

I looked him over for trouble but his eyes were kind.

'What's your name, boy?' he asked.

'Toby Davies.'

'Where from?' His ears, I noticed, were thin and bloodless; criss-crossed with tiny, broken blood-vessels; the hallmark of the quarryman, bought with cold.

'Tonypandy – my dad was in coal.'

'O, aye!' He spat slate dust. 'I was Rhondda once, God knows how I landed here – a woman's eyes, perhaps.' He grinned wide. 'But I'm back there first opportunity, it's best down south.'

I said, 'D'ye know where I can find Ezra Davies's cabin?'

He smiled at the sun. I said, 'The driver of *The King of the Scarlets* – Grandpa Davies.'

'We got a Grandpa Ez as an orderly in *Caban* Two, but he don't drive.'

Just then I saw my grandfather open the door of this cabin and come out with a broom.

So much for dreams.

Through ten years I remembered him, seeing him then – right back to when we visited him from Tonypandy, down south. He was a fine, fierce old grandpa then, northern Welsh to the marrow, but he had a thick ear on him from mountain fighting I'd have sold my soul to possess, and he'd given me a course of boxing lessons, I recall. But that was years ago. Now the Clock of Time had got its hands on Grandpa; change, constant and enduring, was upon his face as he patted his chest for dust, leaned on the broom and peered at me in the sunlight.

'Well, well,' said he, 'if it isn't my little Toby!'

Taking off my hat I screwed it before him, and I saw one who had earlier towered above me; in the lined parchment of his face I glimpsed the jumping footplate as we went through Bethel with slate, and I heard again the clicking of the valves and the *shee-shaa, shee-shaa* of the *Cackler*'s pistons come alive in wounds of spurting steam. Grandpa said, as if reading me:

'Don't drive no more, Toby boy – you come for engines?'

'It don't matter, *Taid*, I come to be with you.'

The slate labour beat about us and there was nobody in the world for us then, save ghosts. But I still always remember that fine April morning when all Nature was painting up for a beautiful summer, and the face of my grandfather as he leaned on the broom, gasping, for slate-smoke had got him proper. Seeing him was like being with my mother again, for she was of his features.

On those visits years back we would start out together, my mam and me, for the wayside halts, to meet my grandpa bringing trains down to the port. Hand in hand with her, stretching my legs to match the stride of her laced-up boots, we went together, and her head was high, her skirt billowing, bonnet-streamers flying.

'How did she go, Toby? I never got word of it,' Grandpa asked.

'The heart took her.'

'Wrexham workhouse, was it?'

'Aye, I stayed on working there, to see her through.'

'Dear me,' he said at his fingers.

Men were coming out of the *caban* and they shouldered Grandpa aside; it filled me with a sudden anger, and I pushed one back.

'Hey – easy!' I said.

The men glared, their humour changed. Behind my grandfather's thin shoulders I saw the cabin bright and clean.

He said, wearily, 'Now you come for a job?'

I took him inside and sat him on his bed. Some off-shift quarrymen called in earthy banter.

He said to me, staring up. 'It's . . . it's me chest, ye see – I got dust.'

I looked around the cabin that soon would be my home; for a time anyway, I thought, until I could get money enough to take Grandpa south and get into coal, my father's trade. Coal was all right, the Coal Owners said – being vegetation, it did no damage to the lungs; in fact, to breathe a

bit of coal-dust was healthy for a man, they reckoned ...
though later I learned the truth of this. But this slate dust,
the smoke of granite, had changed my grandfather into a
walking wheeze; since he had been on engines when I left
him, I wondered how it had happened.

'When they took me off the locos, they had me in the mill,'
he explained.

I sat beside him on the bed, wondering if slate-masters
found it difficult to breathe.

'We got to get south, Grandpa!'

'First you get the fare,' answered a man nearby, and wandered towards me; his Welsh was pure and he had a set of
bull shoulders on him.

'Tom Inspector,' said Grandpa. 'This is Tobias, me grandson.'

'You the foreman?' I asked.

The men in the cabin laughed with boisterous humour.
One cried, 'That's his ambition – he's a rubbisher.'

'Got the wrong politics, eh, Tom?' said Grandpa.

The man said, 'And religion denomination. What are you,
boy?'

'Congregational.'

'You'll change; the foreman's a Calvinistic Methodist, but
jobs come ten a penny, if you've got a pound.'

'You got to bribe 'em,' said Grandpa.

I thought, desperately, I've got to get south, *south* ...

The men gathered about us. One nudged me, nodding at
Grandpa. 'His lungs are gone; it's harsh up here for the old
'uns.'

I gripped the few pence in my pocket, and looked slowly
around the rough cabin walls.

These cabins – built mainly for single men working away
from home – were dotted all over the quarries of Caernarfonshire; they were halls of richness when it came to oratory,
with a Lloyd George under every bed, said Grandpa.

The men in this one were mainly large: enjoying a surly
strength, their speech was the high sing-song of the Lleyn
peninsula; their wit sparkled under the low, slate roof: politics, unionism and theology flourished; the need for a

Workers' Combination against the twin masters, Lord Penrhyn and Assheton-Smith, dominated all discussion.

There was Dick Patagonia, who was always going to emigrate; Yorri Jones, who had bad feet. Sam Demolition was a shot-firer; Dico Bargoed, an old southern mountain-fighter come north to die, was the cook in this *caban*; my grandpa was its cleaner. But the man I remembered best of all arrived after the others, while I was settling me down in a bed beside Grandpa: the twenty men in the *caban* stared up in expectation as Ben O'Hara opened the door.

I think I knew, in the moment he set eyes on me, that his destiny was linked with mine.

'Somebody signed on?' He was tall, handsome, and with a brogue on him like the bogs of Connemara.

'Grandpa's kid,' said Tom Inspector.

'One thing's sure, he's got Grandpa's chin.' O'Hara beat his hat against his thigh for dust. 'What's ye name, wee fella?'

If I was wee it was only in the shoulders, for I nearly matched his height. Getting up, I faced him, and smelled the drink from yards.

He strolled closer with arrogant grace, shouting, 'What ails ye, Grandpa? Must you feed him to the dust? Isn't one enough in the family?'

'I got no option,' said Grandpa, moodily, 'the lad insisted.'

In the middle of the room O'Hara pulled out a flask, swigging it deep. 'And if he had any sense he'd up and go. Thought you was too old a cat to be messed about wi' kittens.'

'Mind your business, Ben, and I'll mind mine.'

'How old is he?'

'Sixteen,' I said.

'And didn't we say in the Combination that we'd keep down the rate of lads? The rubbishers are starving to death under Assheton already – what's he going on?'

'Port Dinorwic, if I can get him,' said Grandpa, coughing.

'You'll do him a good turn there on his bollocks.'

'I aren't having him in the dust!'

'Damned old fool – can't you talk him into the farms?'

'No,' I said, getting up.

It turned him, flask in hand; his great, dark eyes switched over me. '*Arrah!*' he said, softly, 'the mite speaks for itself.'

'And Grandpa now,' I replied.

He smiled. 'That's fair and decent. What's your name?'

'Tobias,' and he retorted:

'I'm talking to men, lad; when I talk to boys they get the back o' me hand.' He swung away from me, facing my grandfather. 'They're yellin' for farm hands down in Peris, why cough him up on dust in this forsaken place?'

'He won't get dust at the port, that's the idea,' said Tom Inspector.

'The foreman down there's a bastard, an' he'll work his tabs off – now come on, Granfer, come on!'

Grandpa hunched his shoulders, saying at his hands, 'He's a Davies boy, and them's coal or slate; I'm not havin' him on the land.' He raised his face defiantly. 'You're always on the talk about Combinations, aren't you? Now you sign him on! When I come up here first I tasted the earth and the water, and it was good. I cleared the scrub up here in my time, when Penrhyn stole Llandegai; we dug and ploughed and sowed, and all we growed was loneliness.'

Ben O'Hara said, with a fine Irish lilt, 'Are you speakin' to me or to God, fella?'

A silence fell on the room; the men shifted with uneasy application, their hands untidy, stitching and lacing; mending boots and holes. Ben O'Hara dropped his coat behind him and stripped off his shirt: there was a rough-hewn strength about him that the ill-fitting quarryman's clothes hadn't concealed; black hair was on his chest and forearms as he wandered to the cook-stove where the old Rhondda mountain-fighter was bending, half asleep.

'What's eating, Dico, me son – lobscows?'

The old man didn't reply, but rose, wandering away from the simmering pot with the catlike grace of the athlete in age; in his burned out brain, contused with blood, were the spattered memories of three hundred fights, they said. Ben O'Hara grinned after him, then spooned the broth to his lips and whistled at the steam.

'Dico'll have you, tasting the supper,' said a man.

'He couldn't hit a hole in a wet echo.'

'Go easy, Big Ben,' said Tom Inspector, 'this was his trade.'

And Grandpa roared, 'Are you taking him or not, ye bloody Irish yob?'

Over his shoulder, O'Hara said, 'He's on the farms, me old son; I'll not be recommending him, neither for the quarry nor the port.' He flung down the spoon.

Grandpa said, holding his chest, 'And this is why we drop our pennies to Parry's blutty Combination!'

O'Hara replied, 'Come off it, Grandpa. If you'd had Parry's Combination thirty years back, ye wouldn't be eatin' dust today.'

I cried, 'You can count me out of the Combination, whatever you call it, Mr. O'Hara – I'll get a job on me own.'

'It's a free country, son, you can try, but you'd be happier on the land, d'ye see?' Hands on hips, he surveyed me, grinning wide, the handsome bugger. 'If ye insist, then, here's the bribe – you can pay it back at a shilling a week.' He offered me a sovereign.

'I'll do it on me own,' but I took it later, to please Grandpa, who said with moody discontent, 'One never knows where they are with you, Ben O'Hara. I wonder how Nanwen puts up with it.'

Vaguely, I wondered who Nanwen was.

CHAPTER THREE

My grandpa might not have been driving the trains any more, but he had a pull with the drivers, and next morning we went down to the loco sheds for a puffer that would get me to the port. The shunt moved on a string-chain and we lay together with our boots cocked up and slid down on a slate-haul into the station of the valley.

Lying there beside my old grandpa, with the cold kiss of slate under my head, I listened to the singing of larks above the grinding wheels, and through narrowed eyes watched gulls soaring in the enamelled blue of the sky like handfuls of feathers flung to the wind.

How wonderful, I thought, is the gift of sight; God must have pondered the treasure long before breathing eyes into the heads of people. The whole world was a song of sight on that bright summer morning: the sparkle of the diamond dew of the mountain, the creeping legions of sheep; the contrasting colours of lane, field and hedgerow glowing in the sun; the waving poplars, oaks and elms. Momentarily, I closed my eyes, and in the suffused lightness of blood and sun, the blindness that came in dreams shouted from redness. But, when I opened them again, the country smiled, bringing me to peace.

All about me on that downward slide was the song of summer; framed between my hobnails were the twin lakes of Padarn and Peris; rearing up to my left was the 'Lady of Snowdon'. And in that swaying, bucking run on the wagon there was a sense of freedom greater than I had known: it spelt release from the bondage of Wrexham workhouse, it cleansed the loss of my mother. I felt a new, wild hope for the future, and this hope grew into a stuttering excitement when the slide ended in the valley and I helped Grandpa out. Slapping ourselves for dust we went together down the platform where a little engine was puffing and farting, impatient to be off to Port Dinorwic, and Grandpa shouted up to the driver:

'You take my grandson to the Incline, Will'um?'

Beefy red was the driver. 'This herring in boots? *Diawch,* man, it'll be a disaster on his crutch. Lifting and stacking, is he?'

'Ay,' I said. 'Are ye taking me, or not?'

'If ye shove,' said the driver, and I was up and behind him, with the fire-box open and the coal going in. He added:

'Don't make it the biggest thing in your life, lad – just steam her,' and he dropped a handle and we were away, with his gold hunter watch out and two hoots on the whistle, and I never saw Grandpa go.

Out of the station we went, rattling and bonking in a hissing of steam and soot explosions, with twelve wagons behind us bucking to come off in the sun-struck, verdant country.

'You got a good old grandpa, mind,' yelled the driver.

To hell with Grandpa, it was the engine I was after.

On, on, whistling and hooting, stuttering along in a clanking thunder, with Lake Padarn flashing silver at us one side and the mountains lying on their shoulders winking at the sun: sheep fled in panic, cows scampered, for here comes that little black bugger again, good God — thumping over the level crossings, with the peasants standing obediently, faces lowered to *The King of the Scarlets* all black and gold and red, and I wouldn't have changed places with the King of France. Before us stretched the rolling hills of Wales; behind us, curtseying, the parasite wagons carried the black gold of the earth, and all in a *click-clack, woosha-woosha,* thundering through Penllyn where the horse was killed, to Bethel, Pensarn and the sea. Open with the fire-box door again and heat and flame struck out in search of me as dust woofed up, and I slammed it shut with my foot.

Approaching Dinorwic, he slowed us and the brakes screamed in pain.

In a thunder of silence we stood while steam wisped up.

Harsh commands now at the top of the incline, the drop to the port.

'Turn-table! Where the hell are ye?'

'Come on — come on!'

Men running; shackles clanked; disengaged, the little engine swung.

Marvellous is the ingenuity of Man, using the pull of the earth to Man's advantage. Fascinated, I watched. Four wagons on the parasite slid down the incline; full to the brim with slates for the world, they crept down the rails into the maws of Port Dinorwic. The beefy driver said:

'Right you — off, me son. Off! This isn't an annual outing.'

I walked down the track-incline into the port.

I'd have given my soul to have stayed on that engine.

Here, either side of the great sea-locks, was a vast store-house of slate; enough to cover the thatched roofs of Europe. Along a network of narrow gauge railways half a dozen little engines were fussing and fuming and wagons clanking from one pile to another; down the tunnel incline, through which I had come, the wealth of Llanberis was pouring; the finished slate from the bowels of the mountain, undisturbed, until now, since the world was made; split, fashioned and squared by the craftsmen of ages.

The dock itself was a network of spars, sails and steaming funnels — the new era of steam, the great eighty and a hundred tonners: sloops and ketches, square-rigged schooners; little barges from the Thames estuary, Holland and Spain had thronged through the gates of Port Dinorwic; even bigger ships were standing off nearby Port Penrhyn, awaiting their turn for loading. Whistles were blowing, mule-whips cracking, commands bellowed by bully overseers; cranes were swinging in belching steam, ghosts of grey dust were labouring in hundreds, heaving the slate cargo aboard the decks in hundred pound stacks — the Mottles and Greens, the Wrinkles and Reds, they told me later — slates of different size and colour; the imperishable roofing that neither laminates nor cracks in Arctic snow nor Sahara sun.

I took a deep breath and strode into the yard and the first ominous thing I saw was the port foreman: very powerful on his knees, this one, according to Grandpa; doing the breast stroke along the back pews of Calfaria, with fornication punishable by stoning, and what the hell do you want?

'Come for work, Foreman,' I said.

'South, are you?'

'Me mam was Bethesda.'

'Ye look a string-bean to me. Where do you lodge?'

'Black Hill Quarry.'

'Then why not vote for Assheton-Smith by there?'

'My grandpa's got dust,' I said.

He saw the sense of it, which surprised me, for most Welsh foremen were only half human: dumpy and fat was this one, and a watch-chain across his belly like the chains round Pentonville. Through puffy cheeks he regarded me.

'Name?'

'Tobias Davies.'

'Age?'

'Sixteen.'

I dropped the sovereign Ben O'Hara had lent me, and he picked it up and bit it in his teeth. 'Where you from, you say?'

'Wrexham workhouse.'

'When did ye get in?'

'Yesterday.'

'What you wanting?'

'Loading and stacking, Foreman — give us a start?'

'Shilling in the pound for me — first twelve weeks?'

I sighed. 'Aye, God willing.'

He watched me, his little eyes switching. 'Are you a religious boy?'

I shone with anticipation. 'Oh, yes!'

'Denomination?'

'Congregational.'

'Bugger off,' said the foreman, and gave me back my sovereign.

I mooched back over the fields to the cabin in Black Hill Quarry.

Grandpa said at the door, 'Mind, they're always changing the blutty foreman at Dinorwic. A week last Sunday he was a Church of England.'

25

'You made a right cock o' that between ye,' said Ben O'Hara.

'Mind you,' said Ben later, 'I could get him over to Blaenau.'

I ate that night in the *caban* at Black Hill quarry amid the banter of their horse-play, one victim after another selected for their bawdy humour. In the company of men, with Grandpa eating beside me, I spooned up the delicious lob-scows, which seemed a standard fare, and packed in thick wedges of black bread behind it, gasping at the steam. Everybody talked at once, it appeared, and none took offence, despite the difficulty of language, for there were men of the southern Welsh counties there, and the Welsh was different: a man from Lancashire, thin and wiry from the pits, was arguing with another from Tyneside; Ben O'Hara feeding them to a quarrel with Gaelic interjections which nobody understood. A few were silent; tongue-tied men, cabin-riven, who had never known a home; others, like Joe Dispute, were engaged in fierce verbal combat upon the benefits and disadvantages of the new workers' Combination everybody was talking about. Dai Half-Soak was giving a sermon up in a corner in his night-shirt. Dick Patagonia was explaining the merits of mass emigration, and Sam Demo-lition, at the end of the table, was tying up explosive charges. Ben O'Hara ate with untidy relish, his dark eyes shining at me over the table. He said:

'Hard luck, Tobias, but your luck might change over in Llechwedd.'

'Llechwedd?' I asked.

'Llechwedd is an underground slate quarry in Blaenau Ffestiniog, owned by the Greaves,' explained Grandpa. He munched his white whiskers on the food; I could tell by his switching eyes that he didn't like Ben O'Hara. He added, 'if the lad works away he lodges away, an' that costs money.'

'Nanwen might have him,' said Ben.

The men went silent at her name.

'Your missus?'

'Why not?'

'Because people will talk,' said Grandpa.

'Ach, come off it, Grandpa,' said Tom Inspector, 'he's only a kid.'

'I could ask her,' said Ben.

'He'd keep his tabs that way, mind,' said a man. 'Those loads at Port Dinorwic are for men, not boys.'

There was little sound but the whisper of the wind in the eaves and the metallic tinkle of spoons. Grandpa said, 'What trade?'

Ben said, 'Rubbisher, for a start – they're always shouting for *rybelwrs* over in Llechwedd – they get big waste.'

'He can ruin his tabs just as easy on rubbishing,' grumbled Grandpa. He patted me with benevolent understanding. 'Ye got to watch ye tabs, ye see, Toby lad. It don't sound decent to talk of it, but you got to keep your tabs right in slate, or you're in trouble.'

I looked at him. 'Rupture, son,' said Tom Inspector. 'Slate's queer on the lift, for your feet are loose. If your boot slips on a hundredweight load, ye tab comes down, and you get no wages. And if the slate slides on the lift, you've got no blutty feet.'

'What about your missus, then?' asked Grandpa, and Ben lit his pipe.

'He could try her. I'm not promising her – nobody promises for Nan.'

'Would she take him?'

I said, 'I'd rather stay here with you . . .'

'I asked if she'd take him,' said Grandpa. 'He's my grandson, you know.'

'She'd show the cobbles to the Prince of Wales, if she didn't fancy him,' said Ben. 'I'll give him a letter for her – leave it at that.'

Tom Inspector said, 'The pay's good, son, and the Greaves are better masters than the Asshetons and Penrhyns.'

'The lad's got brain, ain't he?' called another. 'Finish up in the office, perhaps.'

'He'll have to get on the right side of Jesus.'

'You take Llechwedd, lad,' said Ben O'Hara. 'Here, you'll not make enough money to fill a virgin's lamp.'

Grandpa said, 'That's fixed, then – you go in the morning.

27

And you treat Mrs. O'Hara with respect, remember.'

'I take that for granted, or I wouldn't be sending him,' said Ben O'Hara, and his searching, dark eyes were steady on my face.

CHAPTER FOUR

The hedgerows were swiping about and the trees waving me good-bye as I took the road to Blaenau next morning. Though sad at leaving Grandpa, there was a large excitement in me at the thought of going to work in Llechwedd, which men said were the biggest slate caverns in the world! So big were they that the candles of the quarrymen were like glow-worms in the dark, and men lived and died in them without ever knowing their size.

Through Nant Peris pass I went and struck over the mountain to Roman Halt while the pale moon was thinking of breakfast. In the Land of the Eagles I walked with the summit of Snowdon piercing the clouds to the west and Moel Penamnen to the east was spearing at the sky like a hunter.

Things were happening fast, I reflected; within two days I was out of Wrexham workhouse, in and out of Port Dinorwic and on my way to Blaenau with sixpence in my pocket, a letter to Ben's wife, and a tin of Grannie Ointment in my bundle, which was a cure for chilblains, breast ulcers and sore feet.

God, I was in love with the world that morning!

The curlews were shouting to me from the marshes, the larks going demented, and the late April blossoms were streaming wind-alive around me. Striding out for the Crimea Pass now and through the Lledr Valley, I was helloing right and left to strangers in passing carts. For people were up and doing, and I gave the eye to a couple of young ones – (maidservants in Elen's Castle) putting years on themselves as they milked the doorsteps. All that day I walked, taking short cuts along the river to watch the otters at play: at dusk I slept, to awake ravenous, and bathe naked in the shallows, splashing around with the morning trout, and picking my shirt free of quarrymen's fleas. With the old sun soaring overhead, I reached the top of the mountain and stood there, gasping, looking down on Blaenau Ffestiniog.

It was Bethesda all over again; a slate town sprawling and slicing itself to death: mountain after mountain of slate slag gleamed dawn wetness in the morning sunlight; the ravaged land festooned with tramways and ropeways.

I took a deep breath and went down into the valley, shouting in Welsh to a passing man, 'You know Lord Street, Bodafon, mate?'

'Near Uncorn – look for Tabernacle.' He limped past me, gasping, broken by slate.

Coming to One Bodafon, which was Ben O'Hara's house, I opened the little gate and clanked up the path.

Awkward I feel when meeting strangers: stand on the slate step, sideways in your jacket and with your trews on backwards; knock like a mouse: half the curtains in the street go back and women rush out with arms full of washing.

The door comes open; Nan O'Hara stands there, smiling.

How am I supposed to tell of her, with only words to use?

The sack apron she wore enhanced her beauty; there played on her mouth the smile a woman uses to a boy, but if she made seventeen I doubt it, a year older than me. And Ben O'Hara nigh twice her age was the truth of it.

My fingers shook as I gave her his letter; tearing the envelope, she read swiftly, and her eyes danced at me: black was her hair, I remember; her lips were red.

'Well now,' she cried, 'come in, Tobias Davies!'

I tiptoed in my bulls-blooded boots over the slate flags and there was daylight under me and the hall floor: now a shining, black grate and a red-toothed fire. On the doorstep she'd been my height; in the kitchen I leaned above her.

'You're a valley Welsh, Ben says – that right?' She was cracking herself to put me at my ease.

'Aye, missus,' I replied, rolling my cap. 'Rhondda, really.'

Her voice had the sing of the north in it. 'But you speak Welsh?'

'A bit – me mam was Gerlan, so she said.'

'Bethesda way? I might have known her.'

'Not now. She's dead.'

A silence stole between us and she fussed up and patted herself to see if she was still there, saying, 'Ah, well – you think you'll be staying here for a bit – working Llechwedd, like Ben says?'

'If it's all right with you,' I said, falsetto, which was happening from time to time; one moment soprano, next a double bass; she didn't appear to notice.

'I got good neighbours, remember,' said she, severe. 'Decent chapel people – no drinkers. We don't like drinkers.'

'Nor me,' I said, dying for a pint, for it was thirsty work coming over Roman Halt.

'You don't drink, Tobias?'

'*Dammo di*, no, the filthy stuff.'

Nanwen put the kettle on the hob, smiling at its tears, looking demure and beautiful perched on a chair, and I sat, too, fidgety. I raised my eyes to hers when she said, 'You ... you prefer to work for the Greaves instead of old Penrhyn over in Bethesda?'

'O, aye! The Greaves pay over the odds; Penrhyn skins it and bottles his water.'

She did some coughing at this: something gone down the wrong way.

'Didn't ... didn't your grandpa work in Bethesda once?'

'Christ, aye – years back. But then he was Assheton's driver – he got no truck with Pharo Penrhyn now.'

'You're lucky to be able to choose. Ben and I are off to Bethesda soon.'

'Off to Bethesda?' I rose. 'He's leaving Deiniolen area? He didn't say!'

'It's the Combination, you see.'

'But I've only just come!'

'The moment he gets a cottage we'll go – Ben's a Parry man, the quarryman's champion, and he's in Bethesda – that's where the Combination's needed.'

'Nobody mentioned it,' I said, dully.

Rising, she swept the kettle off the hob and the tea died in hisses and scalds. 'Ben's not a man to splash his business over Town.'

Beyond her smooth profile, as she sipped her tea, I saw through the window the slate tip, dark and threatening; one day, I thought, it would do the slide and come down with its razors: it appeared obscene that she should be here, I thought, instead of walking in a sunlit field. Also, it seemed impossible that she belonged to Irish Ben O'Hara, he of the muscled, hairy body. Outside in the street a herring woman was shouting her wares, and Nanwen glanced up, sadly smiling; there was about her a submissive calm mingling with a young, capricious mischief; she said:

'Such a stare, Tobias . . . why such a stare?'

'You call me Toby, missus?'

Rising, she put her cup on the table and took mine from my hands.

'Will five shillings a week kill you? I can keep you on that.'

'For sure!'

'Ben comes home some week-ends, you know. Will you give me a hand to shift the boxes out of the back bedroom?'

It stilled me. I had forgotten about Ben coming home.

We stared uncertainly at each other. Then:

'A good breakfast before you go to Llechwedd, morning shift – you think Mr. Morgan will take you on?' she asked brightly.

'Mr. Morgan?'

'The overseer – he's a good man – Ben knows him; many of our friends like him are moving to Bethesda soon, so make a friend of him.'

'That's the man I've got a letter for, I think,' and I took it out of my pocket.

We stood looking at each other. 'Two letters! Ben's done you well, Toby – a place to live, a job . . .'

'Aye, he's all right.'

Up in the back bedroom, shifting the boxes, I said, 'If you call me Toby, shall I call you Nanwen, then?'

'Oh no,' said she, going to the door. 'You call me Mrs. O'Hara.'

And down the stairs she went with her sack pinny held out before her like the Queen of Sheba. She didn't part with a lot, this one, by the look of things.

'A good dinner when you get back from shift – you making off for Mr. Morgan now?' she called up the stairs.

'Yes,' I said, sober, for she was slipping away from me.

At the door later, I said, 'I just call ye missus – that suit ye?'

'Of course.'

And the moment I was out in the street she shut the door.

Dull as ditchwater, in love with Nan O'Hara, who didn't give a damn for me, I lounged along to Llechwedd.

CHAPTER FIVE

After checking in at the entrance to the galleries I walked the tram-road looking for Mr. Morgan, the overseer, and the first one I came across was Sam Jones: he was standing near the Mill with a ring of other apprentices around him and I could tell by their faces that they were looking for trouble.

'Well, well!' said Sam, expansively. 'Is this one a pansy?'

'Drop your coat and you'll know,' I said.

'Dear me,' said he, sad. 'A valley man? Shall I do him now, or after?'

They ringed me in a giggle of girls, but they had no real wickedness. Most were *rybelwrs*, the labourers of the teams; some, like Sam Jones, were apprentices working with the grizzlers, the old slate craftsmen who could split a razor. Now real men were shoving past us, crunching up the road to the caverns of darkness and Sam and his mates followed on, hawking and spitting in the swirling dust, and a few rubbishers were pushing some wagons before them.

In the candle-light where the galleries yawned either side of us, men were already forming into teams: horses were snorting in the dust-laden air: winches shrieked here, wire ropes whined in stiffening bars down the inclines; rank on rank, below and above us, were formed the slate pillars that supported the mountain. The air was freezing, a sub-terranean arctic; I was shivering by the time I reached the big Victoria by the passing loop.

'In there,' said Sam Jones.

'Gang overseer I'm after, remember.'

'And got him – Mr. Morgan – in there, I say.'

'What's his religion?' I asked.

'Got none, he's a Christian.'

In the cavern three candles burned in the blackness like the jaundiced eyes of disembodied ghosts, each in a radiance of swirling dust, the lung silica. One swaying candle approached me, grotesquely hewing out the face of a devil; the lowering shadows of brow and mouth I saw first, then teeth; the caverned sockets of his eyes; the devil spoke, and its voice was kind.

'New apprentice, lad?' The candle went higher.

'His name's Toby Davies, Mr. Morgan,' said Sam Jones, still at my elbow.

'I got a letter,' I said, fishing it out.

The foreman read it in squints, his weak eyes puckered up. 'Ben O'Hara, eh? Sober for once? There's a sample of a Combination secretary!' He smiled at me. 'I'll take you, but you got to work, son.'

'He'll work,' said Sam, 'or he'll have my boot up his jack.'

He didn't look much in the dark, this Sam Jones; I decided to try him in the light. 'Stay here with us,' said Mr. Morgan, 'we're a rubbisher down on the team; we'll see how you get on. Here's your candle-tack and matches.' He pointed into blackness. 'Over there's a wagon – fill it, push it out through the loop, empty it and bring it back. When the whistle goes up there, Harri Ogmore's blasting, so duck – understand?'

'You duck into the blast shelters,' added Sam. 'You'll learn, after a couple on your nut.'

'You'd best get along, Sam Jones,' said Mr. Morgan.

I took my saucer with the candle on it and walked into darkness.

All the time I worked in Victoria cavern at Llechwedd, and I never saw it. Some said it were just a little hole in Blaenau; others reckoned it was like the dome of St. Paul's. For my world, from the time I entered it, was the world of the individual miner – the five foot radius of my own guttering candle, the candle of Mr. Morgan, the team foreman, Harri Ogmore's candle eighty feet up in the roof (he was our rockman) and that of the splitter, a man called Tom Booker. On that first shift the rock waste boulders seemed screwed to the floor as I heaved them up; the wagon was ice-cold to my bruised fingers: I moved by commands of sound and sense and the iron wheels grating before me on the push in blackness, with the patter of little feet running before me, the rats.

'Mind our little friends,' said Harri Ogmore once, come

35

down from the roof, and he flung a piece of bread into the darkness.

'Our dear little four-footed comrades, what would we do without them?'

Nobody killed a rat in Llechwedd. With no other place to do it, except on the floor . . . somebody had to clean it up.

'No lavatories, see?' Sam Jones explained. 'We tried big tins once, but people fell over 'em in the dark.'

The shift hours, they told me, were six to six: after five hours of collecting slate rubbish I wondered if I'd last it.

At midday a bugle sang, and the foreman cleared us out of the cavern while Harri Ogmore, high up in the roof, having drilled a hole in the rock with his *jumper* and tamped in gunpowder wads, lit the fuse: the mountain shuddered. Crouching in the blast shelter, my world of darkness was riven by bright, orange flashes as the rocks cascaded down. Candles waved in the suffused light amid choking dust; men stumbled about, tripping over the fall: from the loop came the clip-clopping hooves of the great farm horses who toiled along the inclines, hauling wagons from the seven floors to the turn-out and the downward runs to Porthmadog, and the sea.

The splitter and I returned to the Victoria to find Harri Ogmore staring up into the darkness.

'I split her on the whole face of the bargain,' said he, and he did not cough: neither he, the splitter, nor Mr. Morgan: only I was coughing, retching my heart up beside them.

'A bit or two o' silica don't hurt nobody,' said Harri, his hand on my back, patting. 'Cough on, me son, you'll get used to it.'

'It's new lungs, you see,' explained Mr. Morgan. 'Wait till you start breathing on one, like me.'

'Then you only cough in winter sunlight,' said Harri Ogmore.

But there were consolations to exchange for dust, and one of them was Nan O'Hara. After the first week working in Llechwedd I couldn't believe my luck.

The old larks were at it again when I finished that first week's work, the air out of the cavern was sweet and clean and the sun caressed my aching body as I walked sprightly down the High, knocking up my cap to people left and right, especially women between nine and ninety, for you never know what's cooking. And there, waiting for me in One Bodafon, was Nan O'Hara, polishing a plate for my dinner and a smell of lobscows half-way up Lord Street to greet me, and here I bumped into Mr. Dan Morgan, who had taken me on.

'You all right, young 'un?' In daylight he was a happy, fat little man with a cherubic, jovial face.

I assented, standing respectable.

'Are you warm for chapel come Sunday?'

'Aye, sir!'

'Denomination?' His eyes wrinkled with kindness.

'Same as you,' I replied, carefully.

'Congregational, eh?'

There's a bit of luck. I'd have been a Passover Methodist to be allowed to stay on with Nan O'Hara.

Sam Jones, whom I saw a few days later in Lord Street, lived a few yards short of Bethania Chapel, but this didn't have a holy effect on him: his hobby being to get the Blaenau girls into positions where their parents couldn't assist.

A year older than me, he was a big-shouldered lad; fierce dark with hair on his chest and quick to quarrel. We walked together down High Street, Sam and me, and I sensed the strength in him.

'Where you lodging, then?' This he asked in Welsh.

'One Bodafon.'

It stopped him, mouth open. 'Ben O'Hara's missus?'

'Aye, what's wrong wi' that?'

'You're a lucky old bugger, mind.'

He said no more then, but I knew what he was thinking, and there descended upon us an awed silence broken only by our boots, then he said:

'Big Ben Irish send you?'

I nodded, eyeing him.

He joined the gangs down the line.

'She's a pretty little piece, man, but you watch old Ben;

he's got her signed for, sealed, and ready to be delivered.'

'What's wrong with that?'

'She's not much older'n you.'

The men off shift caught us up in banter, and suddenly, above their clamorous voices there grew a wild, discordant sound, the accident bugle. I heard Dan Morgan shout:

'Right – everybody off the line – *everybody*! Accidents are coming up from Five.'

A man near me yelled:

'Back, lad – back to the mill turnout. They'll be needing the likes of you.'

I joined the groups of running men in the race back to the mill; as we neared it the accident bugle changed its single, clarion note to a gasping, broken calling. From below ground there came concussive blasting, the shot-firing of the new shift but I also felt on the soles of my feet the strident panic of uncontrolled explosions. Sirens began faintly to whine from the cavern entrances as the crush of workers pushed up to the turnout; here was a sea of waving candles and the breathless bawling of frightened men: above them all, ringing out, was the voice of Mr. Morgan.

'All right, all right – it's Number Five road; six accidents on the wagons, watch your feet.'

I stood with the quarrymen on the edge of the line and peered into the darkness of the tunnel; the ranks of waiting rescuers were coughing in the dust-filled air after the exertion of the run: in the flickering light I saw their taut limbs; red-eyed men, their faces wavering like ghosts as the wagons began the outward clatter from Lefal tunnel. And, as the accident train crawled nearer in its metallic thunder, the candle-tacks went up one by one; men leaned over the line.

'Aye, it's Number Five, all right, like Morgan said.'

'A rockman ran out of rope?'

'Don't be stupid, man, it must be an explosive pack gone up – there's six wagons comin'.'

'My mate's on Two, and he just said . . .'

'Sod your mate – it's a premature – must be – a team and a half are hit.'

'Is Oakeley hospital told?'

'Aye, Tom Evans went down.'

'They got the beds?'

A man said, with deep authority, 'Ned O'Leary's one – the Irish. He lit the fuse before the bugle and collected his mates in the fall.'

'Where?'

'In Clough, they say.'

'End of the line?'

'The end of the line for some, lad.'

I noticed, with growing surprise, that apprentices were pushing through the crush to the entrance down at the Mill. A man called, 'Hold it, lads, don't panic – wait, you!'

'Here comes the Apprentice Stakes!'

'One bang and they're off – I told you to *wait*!'

'Grab those boys,' cried Mr. Morgan, and men scuffled and tried to hold them, but the boys ducked down and ran in head swerves for the light. I said to Sam beside me:

'Where're they off to?'

'You'll soon find out.' He pulled himself clear of me and we stood momentarily, checked in silence; there was no sound in the tunnel now but the heavy breathing of men. Then, above the grating advance of wagon wheels, I heard a faint, unholy sighing.

'What's that?'

'That's the halt and lame,' said Sam, and he was off: I watched the men about me staggering for balance as he shoved his way down the line. Mr. Morgan said, close by:

'You stay, Tobias – it's decent to stay. You may be needed.'

The wagons slid into the lights of the candles. Pushed by volunteers, they stopped before us and from their boxes came the sighing of pain.

In the trolley box before me was a mess of blood; I saw a face, stark white, a smashed arm and leg where the splintered bones pushed up through soaked red rags of clothing; amazingly, the face smiled at me.

'Who is it?' asked somebody.

'Ned O'Leary.'

'The other five?'

'Happy Travers, the English – his team, and Bill Williams's men. But poor old Ned's worst hit.'

'What happened?' asked Mr. Morgan. Men kneeling now, their rough hands spreading into the trucks, easing limbs, finding new positions, their voices consoling. A man said:

'It were a premature; two rockmen came down, and the rest were caught in the slides.'

'God Almighty. Get them over to hospital, this one's bleeding to death.'

'Ned don't need the Oakeley, mister, he needs a priest.'

'He's a good Catholic, mind.'

'You going to shift him?'

'If I can get an apprentice.'

'There's one by 'ere,' said a voice beside me, pulling me forward.

'Lift him, then.'

The maimed quarryman rose miraculously out of the wagon; willing hands momentarily held him above the boards.

'Right you.' A man elbowed me. 'Get you in.'

I stared at their wet faces. Mr. Morgan said, 'He got some chance if he don't get pneumonia, young 'un. Your young body will keep him warm for the run to Oakeley – just get in and lie, and we'll lower him into your arms.'

I stared at Ned O'Leary's now unconscious face. Eyes wide open in his dying pallor, he stared back, snoring defiantly. A man commanded, 'Go on, get goin'. We can't hold 'im up all night!'

I saw the ring of their shadowed faces, the humped cheeks, the sparkle of their eyes in the candlelight. Shivering, I slid over the rim of the wagon and laid down in the warmth of Ned O'Leary's blood. I heard a man say:

'Ye wasn't sharp enough by half, Tobias. Your mate, Sam Jones, be half-way up Bethania now.'

Another said, 'When the accident bugles go ye don't see apprentices for dust.'

They laughed in a sort of doomed banter: somebody pulled a blanket over us both. One thing about Ned O'Leary, I thought – he had to come to Wales to die, but he did it snug. With him in my arms I lay in blackness, listening to the trickling of his blood.

Ten minutes later, in the forecourt of Oakeley Hospital, they lifted him off me.

'He's dead,' said a nurse.

I could have told her that half a mile back.

Nanwen was waiting at the door as if expecting me; the accident bugle had its own particular message; I left a trail of blood over her hall; in the kitchen by the fire she had a bath filled with steaming water.

'They told you?' I asked.

'Get your clothes off.'

I said, 'It . . . it isn't decent, Mrs. O'Hara; nobody but you and me in by here.'

'Don't be daft,' said she.

So I took them off and there was a shyness in me and a great business of covering the front of me, since nobody but my mam had seen it before, but to my surprise she wasn't the least bit interested.

But I soon forgot about Ned O'Leary. I'd got my hands full with Nan O'Hara now, to say nothing of my new mate, Sam Jones. And I could think of worse people than Sam to get drunk with on a Saturday night in Blaenau, which had twenty publics for ale and more chapels for confessing sins next day. I found Sam in the spit and sawdust of the Queen's, and I was just about to kill a pint when the door opened and Bando Jeremiah Williams came in; this, apparently, was the local beer bully and pew polisher, with God sitting on his shoulder, in search of harlots; a ·crush on Nanwen had he, and God bless Queen Victoria. Seeing me now, his hands spread on his stomach, he said expansively:

'Damme, boys, what have we here, eh? Nan O'Hara's lodger?'

The Gospel according to St. Sam, apparently, was to hit them as they lifted their glass, but this one topped six feet.

In the slant of my ale I saw Nanwen's eyes . . .

'A good cook, is she, Toby? Down to christian names, aren't we?' said Bando, putting his stomach against the teak bar.

'He's a man, remember!' whispered Sam, lifting his pewter.

The room went silent; men with their heads together, whispering about Nan O'Hara: Bando Jeremiah, all seventeen stones of him, weighed me for size.

'Leave it Tobe, let it slide,' said Sam quiet, which was pretty good advice with Bando Jeremiah the terror of the neighbourhood. 'We'll 'ave him presently, not to disappoint him,' and pure and sweet he smiled his widest smile at Bando and elbowed us both to the room next door.

After our third pint, coming past the gold clock on our way out of the Queens, Sam said, 'You got a shine for Nan O'Hara, have ye?'

'My business.'

'Ye know,' said he at the moon, 'if I got a shine for a woman I'd be telling you about it, but that's the difference between us, I expect, you comin' from the south.'

'North or south makes no difference.'

'Like my gran used to say before she kicked it – Welsh brain, Welsh tongue, Welsh heart – north or south, all the same – we both come from caves.'

I nodded, seeing him with affection in the heady swim of the hops. 'Aye, that's true, boyo.'

'Though up here in the north, mind, we 'ad carpets in ours.'

CHAPTER SIX

Come Sunday week I was there beside Nan in Chapel, all spit and polished up, with my new hobnailed boots sparking and my Emporium collar under my chops, and I walked her into the back pews with pride; Nanwen O'Hara and her new lodger. All about us, as the harmonium got going, were thronged the quarrymen in their Sunday best with their virgin daughters and comely wives, for people fed pretty well under the Greaves, give them credit. And there was beating in my ears a glorious harmony of tenors and contraltos, basses and sopranos, the Quarryman's Hymn:

> *'O! Arglwydd Ddww rhagluniaeth*
> *Ac iachawdwriaeth dyn,*
> *Tydi sy'n llywodraethu*
> *Y byd a'r nef dy hun;*
> *Yn wyneb pob caledi . . . pob caledi . . .*
> *Y sydd, neu eto ddaw,*
> *Dod gadarn gymorth imi*
> *I lechu yn dy law.'*

I sang hesitantly, watching Nan's mouth for the words, for while I was rapidly getting back into the northern lilt, I was remembering it from my mother's knee. And I could not fathom that this was a part of Nan O'Hara I could not comprehend: this, a secret language locked within herself, she shared with nobody but her country. She was instantly the very breath of Wales, singing joyfully, leaving me empty and bereft of friendship, but with an undying consolation: Irish Ben O'Hara wouldn't have understood a word of it.

The great hymn, *The Eternal Refuge*, rolled on, and I felt a sudden sense of pride that though my father was of the south, I was becoming a part of these northern people, who were ancient when the world was young. And Nanwen, as if guessing the emotion within me, bent towards me, mouthing the Welsh, making me her pupil.

People around us were watching, I noticed – Bando Jeremiah Williams the rent-collector, for one. Sam Jones, captured by his mam and dad, gave me a silent groan across the aisle.

Next week-end it wasn't the same; no longer did I have her to myself.

Ben came home.

Sit chewing with your elbows on the cloth in Number One Bodafon, and watch them at it.

Eat with your eyes cast down in their presence; pretend that you are not there, for they do not really want you: nothing is real in the presence of lovers, and you are alone.

He was a handsome beggar, give him that: at Black Hill Quarry, with the immensity of everything about me, I hadn't realised the size of him. She, so small and slender beside him . . . I feared that he might crush her if he moved. Her dark eyes moved swiftly in her flushed cheeks as she served the meal – a rabbit that had committed suicide as I walked over the mountain; even the way she cooked rabbit made me fall in love with Nanwen.

'You all right, Toby?' Her eyes flashed up, concerned; which was reasonable, the way I was behaving. Ben said, bassly:

'Nan tells me you're settling in at Llechwedd, lad.'

I nodded. His arms, bare to the elbows, were crawling with black hair; his chest, with his white shirt open to the waist, was matted with it: Nanwen's arms were smooth and white. Compared with her sensitivity, he was drunk with strength. More, his age and the bottle were touching his face; the skin taut and tanned by the quarrying wind; stubbled with the beard of a man who should shave twice a day, a class of ape. He said:

'I met Dan Morgan coming in tonight.'

'Dan Morgan?' My voice went falsetto, and he smiled tolerantly, as men do with boys.

'Your foreman. He reckons you're working good on the bargain, so he does.'

The bread was dry on my throat. He spooned up the rabbit broth, 'Got you on the Cathedral, he says.'

'Ay ay.'

'Don't you look at people when you talk to them?'

I raised my face to his. Nanwen said, instantly, 'Oh, come, Ben – you hardly know each other – shy, aren't you, Toby?'

I wanted to die, I was so ashamed. I thought, let him talk, he won't get much; why the hell couldn't he have stayed in Black Hill, with Grandpa? Nanwen cried, coming from the grate, 'We went to Chapel together last Sunday, didn't we, Toby?'

'So I heard.' Ben broke the bread with large hands; his nails were dirty, I noticed: it was sickening to have to eat with people who didn't wash their hands before eating: vaguely, I wondered if Nanwen noticed it.

'Who preached?' he asked.

'Mr. John Trevelyn from Pentir – remember, Toby?'

Distantly, my mind asked me where Ma Bron was: I wondered if she was having as bad a time as me, with her aunts in Pentir; straight-laced and pure, most of these aunts, especially the maiden variety.

'A few caught it at Llechwedd recent, they tell me,' Ben observed.

I nodded.

'And they had you for a mattress?'

'Under Ned O'Leary, but he died.'

His hand scurred on his stubbled chin. 'Dan Morgan said you did right by him; ach, I knew the fella – as Irish as a bog: if you had him on your belly, you did the Micks a turn.'

Nanwen beamed, saying, 'Mrs O'Leary wrote you a letter, didn't she, Toby?'

I was thinking of Ned O'Leary. Up in the cemetery they kept an open grave planked and strutted, ready for the next one down, and poor old Ned filled it, for he bled to death in my arms. The Oakeley hospital was a good run away from Llechwedd; this meant that injured men had to be trucked or stretchered down the roads and over rough country. Dan Morgan reckoned that you could trace the route by the bloodstains, so Ned and I must have followed the trail like bloodhounds.

'I'm glad she wrote to you,' said Ben.

It was becoming a stupid conversation: steamed dry of

things to say, we were sitting like upright mummies in wraps of self-consciousness, talking nonsense, while in my mind Ned O'Leary bled to death. And we ate in fits and starts in a white tablecloth silence of colly-wobbles, the nerves of unspoken questions – Ben challenging, me on the defensive. I'd have liked him stronger still: why the devil couldn't he say 'I meant to be alone with my wife, so lodgers must get to hell out of it'? Instead:

'Grandpa had a turn, day before yesterday.'

'What happened?' asked Nanwen, concerned.

'The dust took him coughing; I thought he'd never stop.' Ben drank the beer Nanwen had given him (she didn't give me any) and said:

'You know he wants to get back to Bethesda?'

'No.' I replied.

'Aye, it seems he worked for Penrhyn once and left him for Assheton-Smith on an exchange.'

I nodded. 'To get the locos – he wanted the driving, see?'

Ben said, 'Well, it appears he sub-let a cottage in Bethesda in those days – one of the Caerberllan Row – to a fella moving in, and it's still in Grandpa's name.'

'Yes,' I said. 'Number Twelve. My mother lived there when she was a girl; years back she used to take me there for holidays.'

Nanwen said eagerly, 'And he wants Toby to go back there to live with him?'

'If I can fix him a job in Bethesda – Mr. Parry may manage it, he's still got a pull.'

Her eyes shone and she momentarily gripped my hand. 'My, that would be fine, wouldn't it, Toby?'

Yes, I thought, and you would be rid of me.

'But there's more to it than that,' said Ben. 'Grandpa wants us to live there with him, too.'

'All four of us in Bethesda?'

'Why not? The Combination wants me over there – we'd have to find a place, anyway, and I can't see Lord Penrhyn's agent handing over cottages to Union men like me. Grandpa's different – he was once on the Penrhyn books.'

'When's the tenant moving out?'

'Next week. Grandpa said he don't want it standing

vacant – if it's empty, questions'll be asked.' He added, 'Dan Morgan is moving over, too.'

I said, 'To Bethesda? Why the rush?'

His eyes gleamed and he rose, thumping his fist into his palm. 'Because this is where we're having the fight – God alive, this place is bad enough, but it's a bitch to nothing compared to Bethesda. Besides, once Pharo's pulled down, people like the Greaves and Asshetons will naturally fall, it's in the law of things.'

Nanwen said, 'You think they'll agree to a Union man in occupation?'

'I'm not in occupation, am I? – Grandpa'll pay the rent. That's the idea.'

'And if Grandpa goes, what then?'

'We'll meet that when we come to it,' said Ben. 'Penrhyn's already agreed to the exchange.'

'The exchange?'

'Of the bargain teams – a switch of men between Black Hill and Bethesda – according to the slate-masters' Union that meets in Caernarfon ...' he narrowed his eyes at me '... they disperse the troublemakers by switching us around.' He drained his glass and gasped. 'This time they've done it in the right direction. Not so intelligent, are they?'

I gave him a grin. 'And Pharo don't know what he's getting in Bethesda!'

'Ach, now you're talking!' He laughed, pointing at Nanwen. 'Did ye hear that, woman? The babies are from long clothes at last. Aye, we'll give 'em lock-outs and reductions in wages!'

Something hit the door to have it off its hinges and Sam Jones stood there polished and quiffed, with creases to cut his throat and a posy in his buttonhole big enough for a wake; it was Saturday; he was after lowering ale and lifting the birth-rate.

'No drinking now, remember!' said Nanwen, her finger up. She tightened my coat and smoothed my hair with her fingers.

'*Diaw*!' exclaimed Sam, 'd'ye think we're heathens, Mrs. O'Hara?'

'Near enough,' said Ben.

47

'Have a good time and keep off the women,' said Nanwen.
'Don't hurry back,' said Ben.

The house was silent when I got back with quarts aboard; back teeth awash, I took off my boots at the bottom of the stairs and crept within the cosy smell of the kitchen. All about me were signs of Ben O'Hara: yesterday, it was only in magic that he even existed; now he was here in the bed upstairs, hat and coat on the kitchen door; his clay pipe, in the hearth, was still warm to my fingers. In a fug of ale I stared at the cracked face of the alarm clock ticking on the mantel.

Up the stairs in my socks now like a wraith out of the churchyard: slipping into my room, I began to undress. Naked, the blankets gave me rough kisses. With my hands behind my head I watched the moon rolling tipsy over the slate mountain; echoing footsteps died into silence outside Tabernacle where the dead were whispering with dusty lips; down in Lord Street a baby was strangling its cries.

Blaenau slept, mostly: but lovers were awake.

Ben O'Hara and Nanwen O'Hara, for a start.

I heard his bass whispers and Nan's replies. And she laughed softly once, a high breath of a laugh that ended in a sigh: after this the house talked to itself, as houses do at night; the careless bed, ever betraying, complained.

On my wedding night, I thought, I shall have mountain grass beneath me and the sky for a blanket: I shall take my woman to some quiet place and make no sounds to pester another's loneliness.

To be needed is the heart of yearning: the love sounds of two, the intimacy of the pair, brings to the hearer a most solitary sadness, yet, because I loved her, I was happy for her joy: I could even sanctify her pleasure and cherish her relief ... but I could have killed the one who was bringing her this unity.

To insist that Ben was her husband, that my thoughts were adulterous, brought no consolation. Lying there, it seemed to me that every man in Blaenau was loving his woman; that only I was lying alone.

The bed told the rhythm of their love-making and I

turned my face into the pillows and pressed my fingers into my ears, seeing in the portals of my mind the smile of Nanwen's face.

'Oh, Ben, *Ben* . . .!'

This is what makes for the hollowness.

Next morning she was up and doing, dashing about with secret smiles, fetching tea, making ready for Chapel; pink, flushed and gorgeous – never have I seen her more beautiful. And, by the innocence of her face, she hadn't been up to anything.

Her lips were red, still blooming under his mouth.

I preferred her husband; he was dazed, grumpy and normal.

From the red-barred grate, as she fried the bacon, she shot glances of affection at me over her shoulder, and her hair was black and tumbling about her face. I saw in her shining eyes her love of her man. He had again possessed her; it was the water on her throat, this certainty of his love.

'You all right, Toby?'

I stared at my plate.

'Sleep well, did you?'

I could not meet her eyes.

'Oh, come, *bach*!' she cried, dancing up to me. 'There's another one outside like you – all grumps. With such bears around, how do you think I feel?'

Soft, I thought.

Leave her to her chap. Away out of this, me.

Find Sam Jones again: you want decency, you've got to seek men.

'Oh, Toby, what's *wrong*?' She begged with her hands, her face full of concern.

Away!

CHAPTER SEVEN

Trouble was coming, said Sam Jones, who wasn't overloaded with intelligence; but even he could see it.

'If we move to Bethesda we'll walk right into it,' said Nanwen.

'Then why go?'

She looked at me. 'Because my husband says so.'

Earlier, I'd caught a big spit-gob spider for her, knocked him off and ground him into a bowl of onions; the idea of this was to make a hot poultice to put on the chest of one of the Emma Hoppy sisters next door but three. The delicate one was Emma, and twice a week Nanwen rubbed her in oils. The other Hoppy was called Angharad, and I'd have rubbed her chest any time she'd liked. I never did discover why they were called the Hoppys.

'You agree with the Combination business, then?' I asked, and Nanwen said, 'Will you tell me when women's advice is asked on anything?' and her eyes, like saucers, threatened to drop from her face.

'Ben's right,' I said, 'that Penrhyn's an old bugger.'

'Do you have to swear?'

But he was, and the rest of the owners weren't much better. The Slate-Masters' Union was meeting every month to sink champagne and sing God Bless The English Prince of Wales, while their agents were busy dismissing quarrymen who even breathed about a Union: the Bethesda agents were employing tale-bearers and scabs to work among the teams, according to Ben, and they informed on the workers: son against father, brother against brother – a pound a tale they called it in Tregarth. Get across Mr. Young, Lord Penrhyn's agent, and he would telephone Black Hill Quarry, in case you thought of slipping over there; back-chat Assheton's agent and you'd have to crawl on your belly to the Oakeleys of Blaunau.

'But I give it to the Greaves, though,' said Mr. Morgan, our team foreman, 'we do get a good eisteddfod.'

'Another twopence on the bargain and they can keep their eisteddfod,' answered Tom Booker, lighting his candle. 'Eighteen shilling a week? Give it to me hat and coat, I told the agent – they don't have to eat. The sod, he whistles me up, you know, like I wasn't human.'

'Go flat on your belly again when that agent whistles, mun, and ye'll be right down the road, remember,' said Mr. Morgan.

Tom said, 'If he whistles me like a dog I'm behaving like a dog.' He hawked and spat. 'Same as that bugger over at Oakeley – "Ye can afford to smoke, eh, Booker?" said he. "Ay ay," said I, "at threepence a week," and the psalm-singing yob, d'ye know what he said? – "If God had intended ye to smoke, Booker, he'd 'ave put a chimney on your head." "Is that right?" I asked him. "And now I'm pulling this blutty truck – why didn't he put a hook on me arse?"'

'God'll 'ave you one day, talking like that, Tom Booker,' said Harri Ogmore.

'Meanwhile I keep me independence,' said Tom, and cupped his hands to his mouth, shouting up to me, 'What the hell you doing up there, young Tobias?'

'Trying out the chain,' I yelled down from twenty feet up the rock.

'Then bloody come down, laddo – I'm rockman on this bargain,' and Harri Ogmore spat on his hands for the climb.

'Are you climbing today, lad?' asked Dan Morgan, our foreman, and I took him by the sound of his voice in the dark, for his candle was out.

'Aye, sir.'

'And you watch it, yeh? Or I'll be answering to Nan O'Hara.'

This he spoke into my face, in blackness; I didn't see Mr. Morgan's face, but he saw me. Like a cat for the dark was he, said his missus, who was a Scot. 'An' this come from bathin' his eyes wi' water – his piss-water, d'ye see son, an' it has to be his own, ye understand, not mine, not his feyther's. Every night that man bathes his eyes wi' his water straight from the pot.' Now the eyes of Dan Morgan, unseen in the darkness, burned into my face.

'Harri Ogmore's mad – be careful, yeh?'

'Yes, Mr. Morgan.' I liked my foreman. Jesus sat on his shoulder. Standing near to him, waiting for Harri, I listened to his dust-filled lungs going like harmonium bellows.

'I'll take up,' said Harri, and I heard his boots scrabbling. Mr. Morgan said:

'How do you like that for a musical chest, lad?'

'Is it bad with you, sir?'

'It anna as good as me eyes, though I'm near blind in daylight.'

'Will you get a pension, Mr. Morgan?' and Tom Booker heard it.

'A pension?' cried he. Skinny as a lathe was Tom, with a face on him like Lazarus before revival. Now he cackled, 'A pension? A quarter of a million that Penrhy paid for his slate castle at Llandegai, and they think him benevolent when he lays out for pauper's coffins.'

'Leave it, Tom,' said Mr. Morgan. 'Toby's going up,' and he gazed at the darkness above us.

'He'll break his blutty neck.'

'He'll have to risk it some time.'

Faintly the voice of Harri, our rockman, floating down; tiny gleamed his candle-tack from the caverned sky above us, sixty feet up.

'Climb careful,' said Mr. Morgan.

Our team in Victoria was much like any other.

Dan Morgan was our foreman, and he argued the 'bargain' with the agent, which was the amount of yardage we had to cover at a time: Tom Booker was the splitter – he cut the slate to handable sizes after Harri, the best rockman in Llechwedd, dropped them down from the bargain. And he had an eye like an eagle, did Harri, hanging on by his eyebrows up in the roof. In the guttering light of his candle you could see his 'jumper' tool gleaming as he bored for the explosive charges, chug-chug-chug, *bump, bump, bump,* then in with the gunpowder, and he'd take that rock down the vein as neat as a curlew's whistle. Once down, Tom would get at it, driving holes for his plugs and feathers, hitting them in to the metallic ringing of his hammer; and he'd run them apart with the accuracy of a knife – just small enough for a block and tackle lift on to the wagon. Down the line to the turn-out I'd push the wagon then, with my arms as stiff as black bars; on to the turn-out for the mill, where our two dressers were waiting: known as countess and duchess, ladies and standards, all sizes would come out, cut as clean as box-wood and ready for the roofs of Europe: half the Continent would have died of pneumonia long since, said Dan Morgan, if it hadn't been for us. And the best reward in the world was in the mill shed with the engines going: the very best brand of silicosis for the very best slates: ten years in the mill shed is where Dan Morgan caught it. "Give me Bethesda and the Great Hole any time," he used to say. "You dangle in fresh air, summer sun and winter cold. But rockmen don't get the dust so bad, and a hundred foot drop to the lower galleries is a decent death compared wi' the choking. For slate is razors: clean amputations, a decent way to die!'

'Remember what the old fella said,' Harri had said. 'Get on the face – you be a rockman.'

'Ay ay!' I cried, delighted.

'Right, you, come up and show me your guts. You scared of heights?'

'Don't know.'

'You climb, *bach*, you'll soon find out.'

He was queer, was Harri, for he was never happier than with his feet off the ground and nothing below him, in darkness. I've seen him with the rope half-hitched around one thigh – the standard rockman hold – and the rest of him in space, eating his dinner. But Mrs. Ogmore said, 'There ain't no sense to it, Toby Davies.' (She was a London cockney.) 'The man's just a flower. Two years now I needed my chimney pointing, and the fella's too frit to climb the roof, ain't you, Ogmore?'

'But I'll do it after dark, missus,' cried Harri. 'I could break me neck from ten feet up, in daylight.'

'Ye daft ha'porth – how can ye point a chimney in the dark?' and she had emptied her hands at me.

'But that's the trick of it,' explained Dan Morgan, 'anything goes in the dark – no head for heights, see?'

I stared up at Harri's candle swinging like a glow-worm in the roof of the Big Victoria. 'You goin', son?' asked the foreman.

'Aye,' I said.

It is eerie to be rising from the ground, in darkness. It is as if the night is enveloping you in prayer-book arms: before you your candle-tack on your hat flickers blood on the rocks, the slate is cold and wet-slippery to your fingers. Up, up, hobnails scraping for a hold, don't look down for God's sake, says Mr. Morgan, lest you see a candle; fingers slither for loose places, rubble falls in little avalanches: and Harri Ogmore, swinging in space with his candle, the show-off, comes nearer, nearer: the dust is in your eyes, your mouth, your blood; sweat trickles its ice down the middle of your back.

'Come on, come on, what's bloody holdin' ye?' yells Harri in the dome of roof.

In the pity of Jesus . . .

'Don't look down, Toby!' This from Mr. Morgan, the unseen pygmy on the ground.

This, they tell, is when the man is made: he either rises or falls. All men look the same when they fall on slate: I sensed the terrifying desire to let go with my hands, to enjoy a brief sensation of hissing space, the impacting smash of flesh and bones. Already I had seen a man fall from forty feet in Lefal; I saw again the shapeless limbs grotesquely akimbo, the live, red bones thrusting up through the rags. I paused, flattened against the face, gasping.

'Come on, lad, don't make a meal of it.'

Whimpering with fear, I climbed higher, hands seeking a hold.

Now, within reach of him, I tore away one hand and reached up for Harri's boot. 'Oh, God, I'm going to fall!' I yelled.

'Bugger me, I wouldn't do that,' said Harri, cool, and pulled his boot away. 'You climb and like it, son.'

The air was cleaner here, fifty feet up, for the dust had

lain; and I heard an elemental song of freedom that diminished my terror. I looked down for the first time, seeing below me two pin-points of flickering redness, and these were the candles of Tom Booker and Dan Morgan: above me, swinging on a chain from the domed roof of the Victoria was the spider body of Harri Ogmore, and he was rodding out a bore-hole with his auger and whistling.

'There's me lad,' he cried, grinning down in the light of my candle. 'Come up 'ere and be a rockman.'

There was a ledge in the rock; on to this a short length of steel rail had been laid, buried under stones; around this rail Harri had linked his thigh-chain; from this he swung, making his web; I got my hand around it like a drowning man.

'Now, *come off it!*' protested Harri, 'that's my blutty chain.'

Through the sweat of my eyes I saw his face square and strong above me, floating disembodied against the roof of the cavern; nothing but that candle-lit face moved in my world of fear; below me was the echoing voices of the team in blackness. I gasped, '*Arglwydd!* Give us a hand mate.'

'Balls to you,' said he. 'We got to think o' the bargain – we haven't got all day. Look,' and he swung on his chain towards me. 'Here's your rail and here's your rope, and don't you drop 'em or you'll crown the blutty foreman.'

I flattened myself against the rock face in horror.

I don't know how I took it and I don't remember burying that rail on the ledge.

Harri said, swinging away to his borehole. 'Right, you – now tie your rope to the rail and half hitch the running end around your thigh.'

This I managed to do, clawing with bleeding fingers.

'Right,' said he, 'now swing out into space – go on, let go of that rock and swing out.'

Shivering, with the rope around my thigh, I clung to the face of the drop, and he cried, 'Swing out, or I'll give ye one,' and he struck out at me.

Eyes clenched, I clung there as if stitched to it.

'Let go, what's stopping ye?' Grabbing me, he braced his

feet against the roof and hauled me off the rock by sheer force. Drifting out we swung like twin pendulums in the darkness while velvet voices thudded in my ears: legs thrust out, Harri pushed again, and we swung out again in wide arcs, clasped together in the hissing blackness. Round and round we went, dangling from the Victoria roof, as generations of rockmen had done before us.

'So you want to be a rockman, yeh?' cried Harri.

Fear convulsed my throat; I clung to him.

'Then get off my chain and swing on your rope.'

He prised me away from him, levering off my clutching hands. I was slipping down the front of him to the length of my rope; it was the first sensation of the total drop. I yelled; no sound came forth; I fought him, but he had the greater strength.

'Go on, get *off*!' and he thrust me away.

Isolated, held by my own rope for the first time, I began the circular, pendulum swing from the roof. The very action of the swinging I interpreted as dropping, and awaited, my nerves clutched tight within me, for the smashing blow of the floor. But, when I dared to open my eyes, there was nothing of violence; there was no sensation save that of absolute freedom; weightless, I was swinging like a star in an arc of darkness, with Harri's candle circling above me, the moon of my night. The pendulum slowed; gravity brought us together in a succession of gentle bumps.

'Good, man – now climb.'

With him beside me, I did this, and reached the ledge upon which he was working. 'Now this,' said Harri instructively, 'is the bore-hole. Get the right charge in here and we've got half the bargain down, yeh? You drill just the same as for splitting, understand?' His grimed face went up and he grinned at me, a handsome devil in that eerie light.

'Just you, me and two candles – sixty foot up – yeh?'

'Aye!'

There was growing within me a large sense of pride.

'You like it up here?'

'Ach, indeed!'

He laughed bassly and bawled down between his feet:

'Got another rockman, Mr. Morgan!'

Three happy months I spent with Nanwen in Blaenau: looking back, I reckon they were just about the best of my life to date, for it was fair working with Dan Morgan's team under the Greaves – barring some week-ends, that was, when Ben came home and messed things up. May smiled at June, and she was a right one that year – setting the old currant bun ablaze over the mountains, filling our world of showering blossom with a new radiance. Sometimes, on the weekends when Ben didn't come, I'd give Sam Jones the shove and spend the day in the country with Nanwen: she'd even bring a little picnic out – real plum cake which I loved, and bottled tea. And we would walk clear of slate country to places like the Roman Halt and sit together on the short mountain grass, listening to the curlews; seeing the kingfishers flashing their colours over the brooks. On times like this I'd sit windward of her, so as to get her perfume, for sweet as a nut she smelled to me when the wind was right; but with queer glances in my direction at times, as if she suspected I was weak in the head.

If ever a chap nearly set alight with passion – this was me that following July. Mad, mad in love was I: got her on my mind all day in Llechwedd; had her on my pillow half the night.

It is the very devil, mind, to be living with the one you love, yet dare not lift a finger. So perhaps it was for the best – for my sanity, anyway, when a letter came from Ben towards the end of that month, saying that he and Grandpa had moved into Twelve Caerberllan, and asking me to help Nanwen pack for the journey over.

'A letter from Ben!' cried she.

I groaned deep in my soul.

She lowered the note-paper and smiled at me, her eyes alive. 'Oh, Toby, we're going! They've actually moved in! And they want us to join them just as soon as we can arrange it – isn't it wonderful?'

Marvellous, I thought.

The letter had built a little gravestone over all my sweetest dreams.

CHAPTER EIGHT

And so, after three months together, Nanwen and I left Number One Bodafon, and I was sad.

She was a feast of the mind that July day, in her pink Sunday Outing dress down to her ankles (with real grandmother lace at throat and sleeves) and her white poke-bonnet with streamers.

Very proud was I, taking her between the lines of neighbours; all down Lord Street the people were out watching the furniture cart, the quarrymen hiding their pints behind their backs, the Blaenau urchins skipping along beside the rumbling wheels, and Sam Jones sweating like a dray in the shafts.

There were others going to Bethesda on the 'exchange of workers' but none as grand as we. People took note of it as we entered the station terrace; with porters and suchlike hitting their caps off, I reckon they thought we were some of the high class Greaves. People were taking note of the furniture, too, elbowing and nudging each other, for I'd got all the privates like chambers and chinas well underneath and all the teak and marble conspicuous on top, there being an art in carting in public.

'And where might you be going?' asked the ticket man in the booking office.

'Why, the damn cheek of it!' whispered Sam, shocked.

'Oh, no you don't,' I answered, for half Lord Street was in the office and most of Llechwedd breaking their necks for news. And I was just writing it down when Nanwen came up.

'Two singles to Bethesda,' said she, and paid four shillings.

Four shillings for two singles and a load of furniture to Bethesda!

'Bloody highway robbery,' breathed Sam.

'Husband and wife tickets do count cheaper, Mrs. O'Hara, remember,' said a voice, and from the crowd came Bando

Jeremiah Williams, and he leered at me from a crimson, whiskered mouth, and swept his hat low at Nanwen's feet.

'My husband is not travelling, sir,' said she. 'He is meeting me at Bethesda.'

'Happy am I to hear it,' said Bando, straightening his stomach. 'And relieved I am to know that you will enter your new home out of the company of drunkards and lechers,' and he gave me a look to kill.

Crowds of people now, pushing and shoving in gay humour, for everybody off shift came to see the trains come and go, but a few tears, too, for young husbands and old lovers travelling south for the coalfields of the Rhondda, to get out of slate. Sam and I were like labouring blacks getting Nan's furniture on to the railway flat when the train gave a whistle and people scrambled aboard.

Bando Jeremiah Williams I saw again then, and his eyebrows shot up in mute surprise when I tapped his shoulder, turning him to me.

My first man; I was in the service of Nanwen

'Here's one to remember from the drunkards and lechers,' I said, and hooked him square and his shoulders went back and his boots shot up.

'Oh, what a dreadful thing to do,' I heard Sam say as he helped Bando to his feet and began to brush him down. And he straightened him with a left and hit him flat again with the right.

'See you over in Bethesda, mate!' I yelled as the train puffed away, but he didn't see the going of me, since he was top speeding in the opposite direction.

It's good to be knocking around with people like Sam Jones – drink together, fight together – and we don't understand each other, really – he being from the north and me from the south.

But we make rugs out of gorillas when it comes to slandering Nanwen.

CHAPTER NINE

It was a few weeks before the Big Strike that we all moved into Number Twelve Caerberllan – Nanwen, Ben, Grandpa and me, and it was two up and two down, with Grandpa in the next best bedroom and me downstairs in the kitchen under the table. Going under the table in these times made it easy for the others doing shifts, but it weren't so good when they came down to breakfast, with people's boots on your chest.

Bethesda wasn't much of a place about now. With some three thousand quarrymen employed by Lord Sholto Douglas, and mostly at his throat; the town had gone to the dogs, according to Grandpa. The old generation was beating its breast and thanking God for being poor, the new generation of slate-workers were meeting in secret up on the mountains or sitting on the ten-holer latrine in Port Penrhyn (where foremen were forbidden to enter) trying to form a Union.

Time was when the Penrhyns were honoured in the land, and no real need for a Combination of Workers, the old ones told us. I used to lie under the table in those early days in Twelve Caerberllan: off-shift, weary as a lame dog, I'd listen to Grandpa and Ben going at it hammer and tongs; it gave us a life of it, Nan and me, wondering who was right.

Said Grandpa, 'You got to be fair, son – the Penrhyns built a school for education over at Llandegai, for instance . . .'

'Aye – *be* fair, then,' retorted Ben, always spoiling for a fight. 'To be a scholar there you've got to be Church of England!'

'And they got a real accident trolley now – never had one in my time.' Grandpa munched contentedly on his bread and cheese.

'An accident trolley! Is that what your generation calls progress? You accept the dust, the typhoid, the black list?'

'Got to be reasonable,' said Grandpa, calmly, and munched on. 'We're workers, they're gentry.'

I never saw a chap eat as good as my grandpa with no teeth; I couldn't take my eyes off him, with his pruney old chin slapping up and his shaggy white eyebrows coming down: God knows what was going on inside those chops, but on purple gums Grandpa could shift more lobscows in fifteen minutes than a squad of Welsh Guards.

'Reasonable?' shouted Ben, taking the bait. 'Would ye be mythering about a man like Pharo, and giving him the credit, when he's maiming more good men than the Crimean war? The first hospital they had here, man, was in Bangor, and they'd carry a man wi'out legs for three miles on a litter, ye daft old faggot!'

'Enough of it, show some respect!' cried Nanwen.

'Respect? The old bugger's soaked in it – three times to chapel and God bless the owners for starving us?'

'You got to have God, son,' said Grandpa, vacant. 'That's the trouble with you and your Combinations – you'm forgetting about God.'

And Grandpa chewed on, oblivious to anything. I lifted my eyes from my plate and caught Nanwen's glance as she soothed Ben.

Sixteen stones, and weak – I'd met others like him. Hair on their chests, tears in their eyes; Grandpa had his measure, and Grandpa knew it.

But, of the two of them, Ben was right; this young Lord Penrhyn, with his pay stoppages for the smallest offence, was bringing his workers to the point of mutiny. Indiscipline brought instant discharge; the quarrymen's families were cutting the bread thin and scraping on butter, while he was turning over a hundred thousand a year; he was taking all and giving nothing, except to chosen favourites.

Lovely places like Tregarth were being turned into hotbeds of men who could be bribed. Chapel congregations were being split apart; enmity existed where once was harmony.

As the Old Lord was loved by Bethesda people, so his son was hated.

Fifty years ago the Old Lord was feted when he married

Lady Fitzroy; the people of the town decorated it with flags and pennants; bonfires had been lit at Garth Point, guns discharged by loyal subjects.

But now, with the son, whom the quarrymen named Pharo, in Penrhyn Castle, the people of Bethesda had the ashes of a despot in their mouths. The slave-owners who had taken Government compensation for the emancipation of the plantation slaves, were back, the quarrymen said; and making new profits from slavery in Bethesda.

But I wasn't much interested in the Pharos that fine, hot summer evening; there was a rising sap in me for a bit of a romp around and a cock at anything spare, and there wasn't much doing round Caerberllan, it appeared.

The summer moon was riding on a thousand sheep of gold as I went out to find Sam Jones, recently come from Blaenau, I'd heard. All over Pesda were posters asking good men to come and die for Queen Victoria, because there was a war going on somewhere, apparently, and I thought it might be a good idea to go and die if I couldn't get a job next day. And, damn me, the very first person I came across down High Street was Ma Bron, and I don't know who was the more delighted of the pair of us.

She being the quickest death Bethesda offered at the moment.

'Good heavens,' said she, looking glorious, 'fancy seeing you so soon – Sam Jones said you'd come over to Bethesda.'

'You know Sam Jones?' I asked, astonished, for the beggar hadn't been here more than a day or so.

'O, aye,' said Bron, fluffing up her bright, fair hair. 'I know Sam Jones all right,' and she made no eyes to speak of. 'What you doing here, then – milking old Pharo?'

'Been doing errands and things round Town,' I replied. 'Trying Pharo for a permanent job tomorrow morning, Ma Bron,' I said, denting my bowler. Luckily, I was dressed pretty decent that night for woman-killing; in my new double-breasted jacket and my home-spun trews washed out pale and creased and ironed by Nanwen.

I don't know why, but I was shy of her now; so fair and beautiful and got up was she as the people scurried about us:

bonnet on her bright curls, peacock feathers, purple cape and high-buttoned boots; with her skirt on the ground she looked like something out of a Paris salon like Nanwen talked of, never mind Wrexham workhouse.

Stepping back, she glowed at me. 'My, ain't you growed big, Toby Davies! In three months I say you've growed blutty feet. Me baby died, ye know.'

'Your Bibbs? Sorry about that, Ma Bron.'

'Got the Penrhyn fever – they can't do much on the fever. What time is it?'

'Pretty late,' I said.

'I got to go,' said she.

She was a woman: in weeks, she had grown older than Nanwen, and the sight of her sent me palpitating, for she was a well set-up figure with the carriage of a queen and splendid breasts, unusual for Bethesda, where schoolgirls used a quart pot to shape a pair of thimbles. And the wind was taking her hair, blowing it about her shoulders in gold abandon, yet there was little gaiety in Ma Bron. Indeed, there was about her face a pale, famished beauty; as if the artist of youth had stripped her cheeks of flesh and blood and laid upon them the sheen of white jade: no life was in her, although she was young.

Her red lips moved against the whiteness of her teeth, saying:

'I be kept, ye know – terrible, ain't it?' And the old Bron momentarily came back, and winked. 'I got a posh gent in Bangor – I'm back there now just, but I'm coming home soon to Bethesda.' She sighed, looking sad of a sudden. 'I ain't been any too good, neither – I had the fever, too – you had the fever, Toby Davies?'

I shook my head, watching her sad beauty. 'You coming back here, you say?'

The chance that she might walk a lane or two with me filled me with an inner, expectant hope, drying my throat. Indeed, there was growing in me a curious wish for her that was beyond desire; it was a strange and inexplicable movement of love, something protecting: she was usually so gay; I could have wept for her sadness.

'Aye,' said she. 'Besides,' and she suddenly clapped her

63

hands together with a little delight, 'I met Sam Jones!'

It seemed to explain everything. 'But best be kept, meanwhile,' said she, 'with the strike comin', and all that – best to have a roof.' She looked wistful. 'Besides, he's such a lonely old soul, an' I wanted to make him happy – good to keep people happy ain't it?'

She was lost to me.

It was as if she had loosened my kiss on her mouth and moved out of my arms.

Perhaps I was staring at her, for she said, smiling, her head on one side:

'You all right, matey?'

'Never been better.'

Her eyes were suddenly alive. 'If you come across Sam Jones, will you do something for me?'

I nodded, and she said, 'Tell him I'm comin' back, eh? Tell him I'll turn up that gent in Bangor if he'll take me on, eh?' She fluffed up and patted her hair. 'Barmaid at the Waterloo, if I'm lucky – may be next week!'

'Sam'll like that.'

She gripped my arm. 'He's a queer cuss, though – never knows where you are wi' him. Ask him to pop over and see Bron again soon, is it?'

'You got better equipment than me, mind.'

'Tell him?' Her eyes begged.

Never in my life have I known a chap like Sam Jones for getting on the right side of a woman's particulars.

'I promise, Bron,' I said.

Bethesda leered at us. She said, as if agitated by his very name, 'Now he knows I'm a loose, he don't come to me, understand . . .?'

'You're all right,' I said.

Reaching out, she smiled and touched my face. 'Goodbye, my lovely.'

There was an emptiness in me after she had gone.

The first chap I saw in the Waterloo after that was Sam Jones.

'Ma Bron's looking for you,' I said, getting an elbow in among the quarrymen of the bar.

They were off shift from the Big Hole and the talk was

64

mainly of Pharo and Young, his English agent; over in a corner a man was preaching the benefits of W. J. Parry's workers' Combination. Sam didn't reply to me, so I said:

'I come here with her first, you know.'

'Have her if you like, mun.'

The landlord slid my glass towards me. I drank, watching Sam. 'Don't want her, but she's had it bad – keep it decent, eh? She's gone on you.'

'The way they all fall for me, sometimes it frightens me,' said Sam. He drank and wiped his mouth: fine and handsome he looked, his shoulders filling out for a man. 'What's she to you, then?'

'Nothing. Just treat her good or I'll float you out of Bethesda.'

It pleased him; his dark eyes shone. The noise of the quarrymen beat about us. He said, 'You got your hands full in Caerberllan they say.'

'Watch your mouth.'

'No offence. Just that there's talk.'

'About who?'

'You at the moment – they're scared of Ben O'Hara. But he can't hit his way out of a paper bag . . . you'd be safer with Ma Bron.'

'Let them bloody talk,' I said, and gripped my glass, staring at the ale. A few men were looking my way, I noticed. Sam said, 'They got to talk about somebody, mind. You signing on tomorrow?'

I nodded.

'Got your sovereign for the foreman?'

'See you down there,' I said, and turned for the door.

'That was quick.'

The men were staring at me. Sam said, 'Sod 'em all, Toby – you stay.' He grinned. 'Next they'll be talking about Grandpa.'

The moon was shining over the slate mountains as I took back home to Caerberllan.

Quite a few people I saw that night on my way home – little Eddie Jones, for one, aged six, and he shouted through the grime of his urchin face:

'*Gwell Bantu na hwntwr!* Toby Davies? *Gwell Bantu na*

hwntwr!' (Better be a Bantu than a South Walian) so I yelled back the standard Welsh reply:

'Gwell wog na gog, Eddie Jones!' (Better be a wog than a North Walian).

He shrieked with delight and ran off into the dark. Some said he lived in the workhouse at Bangor, but he was always around Bethesda quarries.

Mrs. Pru Natal, the midwife I saw next, hurrying along to Bodforris where somebody was confined. Responsible for the next generation of quarrymen was she, with her threatening bedside manner and box of ground pepper for difficult cases, and I knew a surge of joyous expectancy; I sometimes worried about this, wondering if I was normal, for the very sight of a midwife always switched me on, while I could pass a pair of lace-trimmed spacers on a wash-line without the bat of an eye.

Nanwen was standing outside Number Twelve like a goddess in white with an apron, looking at the moon; her face was pale, the shadows deep in her cheeks.

She leaned towards me, smelling my breath and she was warm from the fire and comforting to the senses. Had there been any justice in the world I would have swept her into my arms and away to a place of loving a hundred miles from Bethesda, for a wedding in white.

'You been drinking, Toby Davies?'

'Damn me,' I said, 'what do you expect?'

There was in her an impression of expectancy, even anxiety in her moments of waiting, and I drew closer.

'I love you,' I said, but nobody heard; she was gazing towards the road now, her hand to her mouth; never had she looked so beautiful.

'Ben's late,' she said.

CHAPTER TEN

In the middle of a hot July, I signed on at the Big Hole to work for Pharo Penrhyn.

Everybody in Twelve was up at dawn, Nanwen cutting the tommy boxes and filling tea-bottles, patting and smoothing Grandpa, as if sending him off with Ben and me was the most normal thing in the world, but I knew she was worrying in case he wouldn't get a shift.

'Pharo gave ye the cottage, didn't he?' said Ben at breakfast.

'Aye, but I got me doubts about Young, his works agent,' said Grandpa. 'When we gets to the quarry things may come different.'

'Don't be daft, man. If you're on the Penrhyn books you're on the books.'

'The left hand don't know what the right hand's doin',' said Grandpa.

'The land agent who ticked us for this cottage isn't the works agent, mind. They give me the cottage but there was no talk of a job.'

'Meet it when we get up there,' I said.

We chewed away in silence amid Nanwen's bustling smiles of encouragement; I watched her slim fingers sweeping the kettle off the hob; she filled the cups with nervous, anxious hands; then:

'There ... there's always a place for a good craftsman, isn't there, Ben! From splitting and dressing to locos, Grandpa knows it all – got to have instructors, haven't we?'

'Not over seventy, with bad dust,' said Grandpa.

'You're special,' I said. 'That's why you got this place.'

'Aye, well, I was sweeping the cabins for Assheton and I can sweep again; we'll see, won't we? – 'cause I say the rent man's made a mistake. We shouldn't be here in Caerberllan.'

'Cheer up, cheer up!' cried Nanwen. 'First day working at Bethesda, and you're as miserable as black coffins.'

Ben chewed on, ignoring her, tearing at the bread with his huge, hairy hands.

Now along the Row we went; doors were coming open, brass being polished, slate steps being milked. Out on the road to Betws-y-Coed the quarrymen were flooding out of Bethesda: they were coming from Gerlan and Rachub, Sling and Tregarth – some from as far afield as Bangor and Pentir – a six mile walk for many; men and boys, the rockmen and agents, wending a path through the marching army on penny-farthing bikes, the latest craze. And the drumming of hobnails on the flinted tracks grew to a thunder.

And the Penrhyn hooter, the call to work, shouted over the mountains.

'Here's a fighting force, if ever the Combination wants it,' growled Ben.

Mr. Morgan, my old foreman (just arrived over from Llechwedd on the exchange), was walking in front of Ben, Grandpa and me with Guto Livingstone who wasn't quite a full pound up top (being a dreamer of distant places ever since he stopped a boulder on the nut, according to Sam). 'My cross,' his poor old missus used to say, but he was still the best rubbisher in Bethesda, being great in the shoulders, if brainless. Also there was Mr. Albert Arse, a neighbour of ours in Caerberllan, mainly thus called because folks will insist on dropping their blutty haitches, said his missus, Annie, who was a London cockney. Very partial to the Arses, I was, he being one of the finest rockmen Penrhyn had, according to reports, and Annie the best mother in Bethesda according to Nanwen, cockney English or not. And what went for Nanwen was always right with me.

'Give old Penrhyn hell, Toby, lad!' yelled a voice in Welsh, and down the ranks I saw Sam, bright-faced and quiffed, with his trews as white as a cricketer's flannels, despite his mam being ill, folks said.

'Ay ay!' I shouted back, seeing beside Sam his dada for the very first time: a cock-sure little five-foot preener, this one, with a face like a hen's arse.

'Sam's father,' I said, elbowing Ben, and he growled bassly:

'Aye,' he grumbled, 'small and evil – in God's humour he sired that big fine lad – Sam takes after his ma, sure enough. A fine woman she is – dying slow of an illness, folks say, but she labours herself to the bone for them.'

'Is Mr. Jones in the Combination?'

'Would a fussy apology like him be in the Combination – talk sense!'

'Combination or not,' said Grandpa, wheezing at the pace. 'Don't you trust him – he ain't Congregational ye know – they reckon she 'as to chloroform him to get her weekly wages, poor soul, and her with a cough like death's trumpet.'

'We've got 'em, mind,' said Ben, dourly. 'Christ, we've got 'em.'

The army swelled to a thousand tramping boots up the pitch to the Big Hole.

They came from the cottages that once their forebears owned, these quarrymen – nearly a thousand of such cottages existed on the Penrhyn estate alone, each with its tidy little patch of vegetables. They marched from the scores of tiny smallholdings that dotted Llandegai mountain; from the inns, taverns and the *cabans* where they lodged (earning about six pounds a month) – men born in the language of slate, mostly, but also English and Scots, and Irishmen who had taken Welsh wives. Isolated by language, the foreigners kept to their own sects. Yet they lived and worked together in mutual respect and harmony, bound by the same ideals – the Combination of Workers they were trying to forge, and their fierce dislike of the young Lord Penrhyn.

In the surly countenances of the men going to work on that first morning I sensed a sullen anger: none spoke, after initial greetings, to others joining the ranks: apart from the thundering boots, the breathless lungs, the silence was as great as the temple of Solomon.

Trouble was coming: it stank on the wind.

As we neared the Head I saw a cluster of men waiting by the check-in: those already employed went to the right; we, applying for jobs, marched left. I remarked, 'I hope Sam Jones, my mate, gets in,' and Ben grumbled reply:

69

'Don't bother yourself – they'll love Sam Jones with that sort of a father.'

'Because Mr. Jones is against the Combination?'

'Aye, and because he's known for a blackleg.'

'Then what hope have you got?'

'I got recommendations of a different sort, me boy.'

'And Grandpa.'

'See to yourself, young 'un – never mind about Grandpa.'

I had come across a few agents and foremen since I'd been in slate, but never one like this. Rolling fat was he, Irish born and Irish temper, and sure to God don't you come from the same county as me? asked Ben, grinning wide.

'Name?' asked the man.

'Ben O'Hara – ye can count me in for a special recommendation, sir? – me name's on the books already.'

'Benjamin O'Hara of Limerick? This the one?' He examined his list.

'Ay ay, man, and strong for the Roman Catholic.'

'Save it for Black Hill, it don't count here.' Out with a notebook, very official and thumbing it with grubby fingers. 'Have you got the letter of recommendation, then?'

'Mark, Mary and Joseph, I nigh forgot!' and Ben passed him an envelope: the man took it, crinkling it for money.

'Also me young friend here, Tobias Davies – Welsh speaking, remember.'

'That won't help him.'

New men pressed about us, faces stretched out, yearning for work.

I watched. The agent put the envelope into his pocket.

'Are we in, then?' asked Ben.

The man nodded heavily, eyes switching around the questioning faces.

'Splinters, dressers and rockmen I want particular,' said he. 'Rubbishers are ten a penny.'

'Then here's the best slate-dresser in the business – me grandfather,' said Ben, and pushed Grandpa up in front of him. The old man braced back his thin shoulders. The agent peered.

'Do I know you, Grandad?'

'Should do, Mr. Agent,' replied Grandpa brightly. 'The Old Lord and Mr. Assheton-Smith – fifty years I served 'em, man and boy.'

'Age?'

'Sixty-five.'

'Dust?' He listened on Grandpa's waistcoat.

'The bellows aren't what they used to be, but they don't affect me,' answered Grandpa, and his chest was howling.

The agent said to Ben, 'Grandads I can't do – not with that chest – he goes home.'

We stared at each other; the men shifted like nervous sheep, dying for their turn.

'You and the lad,' said the agent to Ben, 'take it or leave it.'

'Don't Pharo get old too, then?' asked Grandpa.

'Now, now, none o' that!'

Bully State of Maine, the pugilist, shouted nearby, 'He be a bloody expert, Mr. Agent. I know'd him good – he tells the trades to boys. Perhaps he don't have to breathe, but the poor old sod's got to eat, ye know.'

'Come on, move along, move along!' Big men behind the agent began to threaten. We moved aside, Grandpa with us: empty, we stood, with the crag winds blustering about us at the height: I heard the commands of the team foremen as the rockmen lowered themselves down the faces of the galleries.

Grandpa said, 'I done it all – rock face, splitting, dressing – I even done *rybelwr* at the start, and drove the engines: then I'm sweeping cabins, now I'm off.' He stared about him. 'Yeh?'

'Lose yourself, old man,' said the agent.

I said, 'You was here in case you was wanted, *Taid.*'

The Welshness pleased him. Grandpa smiled.

Standing with Ben I watched him going down the pitch back to Caerberllan, and Nanwen.

Every night when we got home, Ben and me, we'd find Grandpa sitting humped in his chair by the grate while Nanwen prepared the evening meal. I can see him now, staring at nothing; remembering the days when he was young, perhaps, though he never said much about it. And up and down the little Caerbellan Row of cottages came the sounds of men returning home from work.

Say what you like, there's nothing like living in a community – one big family, with all the family's fights and loves and grief and happiness. Children yelling, plates clattering as daughters laid the tables, cups of tea being poured, and come on off the settee, you lot – make room for your da. Steam from a dozen kettles spurting up, grates being poked, babies crying at being put to bed in daylight, chairs scraping flags as people sat up to table; the bass voice replies to wifely questions, shrieked threats to chirping children. And smells better than the spices of India are wafting down that Row: lobscows and steak and kidney, the basted corpses of suicide hares and rabbits, fried trout out of the Ogwen, tickled out by experts on the way back from the Great Hole.

I've lived in a few places since then, but nothing ever came up to those autumn days in Caerberllan, before the Big Strike and the following Big Hunger.

'Toby, stop dreaming,' said Nanwen. 'Sit up at table.'

'Lest Grandpa eats off your plate,' added Ben, and put his fist under Grandpa's chin to lighten him, poor old dab.

But still I listened to the song of Caerberllan.

Once, all these cottages were built and owned by the men who arrived there seeking work. Deciding to mine for slate, each immigrant selected a little bit of common ground; together they built this row, for instance, and named it Caerberllan. All over Llandegai mountain this happened, and scores of tiny slate caverns were opened by the peasant investors. But then Lord Penrhyn arrived. Under the Land Enclosure Act he seized the whole of Llandegai mountain for a start, laid out roads and fenced it in.

'He stole it,' said Ben now. 'It was common land, and on this common land the people built their homes; but since the cottages belonged to the land he enclosed, Penrhyn stole those, too.'

'And what are you doing about it?' asked Grandpa.

Ben said, 'He owned the whole community. If an employee argued about wages, he was sacked and blacklisted with other slate employers: once sacked, he could be evicted from the very cottage he built, because it was now a tithe dwelling.'

Nanwen said, 'It's a scandal. In their time the owners of these places starved and were then evicted. And they could no more rent out their cottages than eat them.'

'That's one in the eye for the Old Lord,' said I. 'The way you've been talking, you've made him out a saint.'

'He is, compared with young Pharo, his son,' said Ben. 'But don't you worry, me son, the Combination will see to him.'

'O, aye?' asked Grandpa, innocent. 'Your fine Mr. Parry's got a deal of things to see to before he gets down to halting tithe rent – fifty years from now these cottages will still belong to the Penrhyns – and take it from me, ye Irish mare, young Pharo will take care of your blutty Combination.'

Bedlam then, with me and Nanwen jumping in to act as referees.

Mind, I reckon old Grandpa only did it to bait Ben, the old criminal.

CHAPTER ELEVEN

'The fact remains,' said Nanwen, 'now Grandpa's laid off we shouldn't really be here. Now he's stopped work, the bailiffs will evict us.'

'The land agent can shift us from under this roof whenever he pleases,' I said.

'Meet it when we come to it,' growled Ben, 'we have trouble enough for now.'

The autumn faded: the country grew into a deeper gold.

The 'bargains' were getting tighter, the hours shorter, the pay thinner.

'Three shillings a yard suit you, Mr. Morgan?' asked the overseer.

Ferrety thin and crippled was this Penrhyn agent; a blue, peaked dewdrop of a nose in the late autumn cold and a face as lined as Crewe Junction.

'How many yards?' asked our Mr. Morgan, smooth.

'Eight yards opening over nine days.' He tipped back his hat. 'Yeh?'

Our foreman pondered it. 'It's thin.'

'Thinner where there's none – take it or leave it.'

'What about roofing?'

'I'll gift ye a pound for the roofing,' said the agent.

'And drilling by "jumper"? God, man, you'll kill us.'

The agent sighed deep. 'Look – you can poke holes in it with your fingers.'

'Then you bloody try,' said our Mr. Morgan.

'Enough of that, Mr. Morgan,' said the agent.

Ben stood silently, watching, his eyes brooding with a cold violence.

He said, taking a chance, 'Before you came, we had old Dan Shenkins on the bargains, and he were fair with us. If he saw you figure out a bargain like that he'd turn in his grave, he would.'

74

'He'd do more,' said Grandpa, coming up, 'he'd do a blutty handspring.'

Strange about Grandpa these days. He came to work with us, he came back home off shift with us; sitting around all day on the tumps, pretending he was needed. Many old men did this in Bethesda.

'You're not dealing with Softy Shenkins now,' said the agent, 'this is me.' And he limped off, leaving us with slavery. Mr. Morgan said:

'Reckon I'd do better to find a widow with a bad cough.' He scowled.

'When he goes for burial I'll dance on his grave,' added Ben.

'They should bury buggers like him when they're alive,' said Albert Arse.

This was unusual for Mr. Arse; for a quiet man with an aristocratic name, he was sometimes very revolutionary.

For my part I wasn't very interested in the bargains our foreman got, so long as I drew my pay – eight shillings a week now, five to Nanwen, three to me. And, now that the nights were drawing even colder, I was away by moonlight most Saturdays, coat collar turned up against the wind of the mountains, down to the Waterloo to meet Sam Jones, with Ma Bron, the barmaid, in the offing.

There was a brass band playing along High Street, trying to get the blood warm on martial music, for some people called Boers were playing hell with the Army over in China, or some such place.

'Africa,' said Sam.

'How d'ye know?'

'Dai Forceps told me.'

'There's a mine of information,' said Ben.

It was cold, even for October, as I went up the Row for town and Mr. Roberts, the deacon of the big Ebenezer, was standing in his window looking out on to a frosted world. As I went past I pulled off my bowler to him, he being respected in Caerberllan; a quiet man of God was Mr. Roberts, and keeping a diary of all the Ebenezer events, such as who preached, and when; and on his mantelshelf he kept a picture of Jesus framed in sea-shells.

One day, I thought, I would present myself before such a man as this; with Nanwen beside me, I would stand in the Ebenezer with the congregation putting up a harmony of tenor and soprano, and mud on the boots of the big bass quarrymen. And then home to tea and ham; everybody fussing about with happy congratulations. And I would take her away to a far corner of the earth where she'd forget she had ever set eyes on Ben O'Hara.

I coveted her.

For less love than mine, some men would have put Ben to bed with a shovel. I could not rid my mind of dreams. After all, as Grandpa said, none of us is perfect: take all the sinners away from the saints, and all you've got left is Moses and his Tablets.

Mr. Sudden Death, the Co-op insurance man, was coming round the corner of Bodforris, so I pulled up my collar and coughed myself blue in the face, and went up to town to kill a pint with Sam.

Get mixed up with the Co-op on a Saturday pay night and they'd have a policy on your life and a bottle of your water before you could bat an eye.

The bargain crews were huddled against the cold under the naphtha flares of the stalls, and the cockle and mussel women were shouting their wares. Hugh Fish, a wisp of skin and bone on his cart, was waving his herrings under passing noses, shouting, 'Fresh out of the bay, with bellies like gentry. Buy, buy!' and old Marged at her crockery stall was holding up chamber pots and shouting, 'Friends for life, remember – not a word of what they see, never mention what they hear.' And then I remembered, when I saw the stalls thickening more, that this was also market day. The team foremen were tiptoeing over the holy marble of the bank, drawing the long-pay sovereigns (I'd had mine earlier) and one of the first with a fist-full of silver I came across was Sam Jones:

'Did you hear what happened at the Ffridd Gallery today?'

'No?'

'You remember the teams there ran the contractors out of the quarry a week or so back?'

'Ay ay!'

'They did it again today – and stoned 'em.'

'That means trouble – Penrhyn won't stand for that!'

Together we pushed our way into the bar of the Waterloo and there behind it was Ma Bron, her face powdered, her hair curled, and showing enough bosom to kill the Pope.

'Well, well, look who we have here,' said she, pouring jugs.

'A couple of pints and a little less tongue,' said Sam, and leaned to me. 'Young, the agent's dancing mad, and Penrhyn's after the men who did it.'

'You can't stone contractors,' said a voice, and there stood Deacon Tossle with his pew duster in one hand and a pint in the other – having just slipped in from cleaning out Jerusalem: very popular was Deacon Tossle for liking ale as well as God; even Jesus was not averse to a little nose-varnish, given the right occasion, said he. For months, to my certain knowledge, Deacon Tossle drank in the taps before his mates discovered it, and then he cleared the Big Seat by a foot; most of the drinking being done in the vestries.

'Aye, but we got to cut out this new contracting system,' said a rubbisher, leaning over. 'A bargain's a bargain – we worked it that way with the Old Lord. Why the hell do we have to put up with Pharo's middlemen?'

'Treat us like pigs they do, mind,' said Albert Arse, solemn, and how he got in there at twopence a pint beat us, with his army back home to feed.

The roars and banter beat about us, and a drunk yelled, 'Aye, me lovely girls, you should 'ave seen 'em go – like the clappers wi' bricks behind 'em.'

'The victory is yours now, perhaps, but you'll rue it in the end, mark me,' said Deacon Tossle.

The cockle women were coming in with baskets; smooth-faced matrons dressed like nuns, and their soprano cries mingled with the clash of glasses and argument.

'D'you stand for Penrhyn, then?' asked Bully State of Maine, belligerent.

'I stand with you, fighter, because I'm a good quarryman,' came the reply. 'But violence on the works doesn't serve Mr. Parry, your leader, since he condemns violence.'

'Don't we get violence all the year round from Pharo?'

'In violence you are breaking the law,' Tossle insisted. 'Is there a man here who can justify it to Mr. Parry face to face?'

The second mention of W. J. Parry stilled them; uncertain, they growled about them like bulls at a manger. For Parry was their champion, their hope for justice.

'What we going to do, then?' I asked. 'Just sit down under it while the contractors take middleman cuts? It lessens the bargain pay-out, remember.'

'Ah, yes.' Tossle looked me over. 'Toby Davies – Grandpa's lad, isn't it?'

'Aye.'

'And how old are you?'

'Knocking seventeen.'

'Right – ten years from now you'll see the sense of arbitration, for which Mr. Parry stands. The young are bringing us to violence, and it is the young who will suffer. Bribery, swindling at the face, corruption in the galleries, this is our lot. You will never change it by bricks or gunpowder, but by civilised argument.'

I asked soberly, 'What d'you reckon will come of it, Deacon?'

Mr. Tossle drained his pint. 'Ask Colonel Ruck, the Chief Constable, when Penrhyn calls in the military.'

'Right, mun, let 'em come,' yelled Dai Forceps, mate to Bully, 'we'll give 'em soldiers – this is a peaceful town!'

'It used to be,' said One-pint Tossle.

A silence fell upon us after he had gone, and Bully cupped his chin in his hands and smiled at Ma Bron, who was filling the tankards with professional flourishes.

'Ye know,' said he, 'I'd rather watch her than listen to deacons. She serves that ale, does our little Bron, like a woman with a divine right.'

'She's got a divine left, too,' said Sam.

Together, as mates, we pushed our way through the sawdust into the lamp-flaring street.

Bron followed Sam with her eyes, her hands pausing on the jugs. I winked at her, but she ignored me, watching Sam. Got it bad.

Sam didn't spare her a glance.

Ugly Dic, the police sergeant, was abroad in High Street that market night, and with good reason, for the Romanys were coming in from the mountains at dusk with their gay clothes and banter, followed by their dancing wives: bright were the trinkets and paste diamonds of the stalls.

Mr. Price of Cloth Hall, with his mauve shawl over his shoulders, was measuring cloth; Joe Bec, the Gerlan baker, was throwing up crisp, brown loaves in competition with the English Bakehouse, and people were slicing it off and plastering it with wedges of farmhouse butter.

There were fortune-tellers, a strong man from Caernarfon, and a woman doing a ballet, dressed as a dying swan; sheep were thronging in with neat little cobs, for auctioning. Benny the Brave from Rachub was already in tears as he held up his coloured umbrellas, crying, 'If I don't clear this lot, what will Marged say?' Bill Brunt (whose brother died on Snowdon rescuing Pharo's stupid gentry) was in a different sort of tears, wandering the gutter, half-minded, in search of his relation. And the mountain farmers were also coming into market — the men who tore down Penrhyn's fences as fast as his bailiffs put them up — stern-faced and in rags they came. Fiddles, in contrast to their savagery, were shrieking about them, street urchins picking pockets. And then, right in the middle of it, a pony and trap appeared, and in it was sitting Mr. Parry, the quarryman's leader: severe and unforgiving was his square, handsome face.

Sam, excited, was yelling, 'Mr. Parry, Mr. Parry — *look*!'

This was the unpaid solicitor who was head and shoulders above all leaders in Caernarfonshire, and that included Lloyd George, men said.

'I bet he's off to give old Pharo hell!' yelled Dai Forceps behind me.

In the event Pharo gave hell to us in Bethesda.

Down the middle of High Street, pushing aside the

79

hawkers and urchins, a little mob of quarrymen were coming, and I recognised men of the Crimea galleries, the Agor Boni and Ffridd; those who had stoned Pharo's contractors. Laughing, cheering, they surrounded Mr. Parry's trap and marched beside it with a military bearing, holding their arms like men carrying guns. Guto Livingstone I saw in the ranks, who didn't know if he was in Bethesda or Bolivia; and there on the flank was Albert Arse holding up old Dick Jones, the miser who bottled his water: nine sheets in the wind, most of them, too; I saw the disgust on Mr. Parry's face. And behind all this lot came the recruiting brass band giving us *Rule Britannia,* and I don't know who was making more noise, the band or the rowdies. But others were thronging in, too – decent quarrymen of sober habits – people like Mr. Roberts, for instance, who never touched a drop. These stood fifteen deep, watching.

'We going in, mate?' asked Sam.

'You bet.' And we doubled through the ranks of men and got close to the carriage, giving it a pull, and we didn't stop until we had turned it in the street and come back to the Public Hall.

Silence as Mr. Parry rose to his feet in the trap, smiling around the intent faces; come to beard Pharo in his slate temple; removing his hat, he said:

'All right, men, it's pay night, and market day. It's right that you should celebrate. But your spirits are running as high as the ale – no trouble with the police, remember!'

Clasping his hands before him, he continued, 'Aye, not a spot of bother with police, so oblige me, for we've trouble enough on our hands – with the hotheads who ran the contractors off the gallery for the second time in a month.'

The men eased their shoulders, staring about them in search of scapegoats. Mr. Parry said:

'Understand this – trouble is coming. Yet you keep tying my hands. You are not dealing with the Old Lord, remember – indeed, you are not answering to anybody: you leave that to me – to face the Honourable Sholto Douglas, not the easiest of men – on your behalf, and for a quarryman's wages: I am scarcely an overpaid solicitor on thirty shillings a week.' He lifted a finger and swept it over the silent faces.

'So mark me now, if you didn't do so before – in the town, in your homes, on the gallery faces. I am your elected spokesman. Don't take my legs away if you want me to make a stand. Unruly behaviour in Bethesda tonight, and the police will be here in force from Bangor: violence in the galleries will bring in the military from Caernarfon.' He waited, watching them; we stood like men hypnotised, and he added, 'The first man at fault accounts to me.'

It was so quiet that I heard the hissing of the naphtha lamps.

Then ragged cheering began, swelling to thunder, and those still left in the inns and publics came racing out, slopping their tankards. We pressed about the trap, shouting his name, but Mr Parry didn't appear to hear us.

He stood apart, the lonelist man in Bethesda.

Then he reined up his pony and the trap clattered over the cobbles towards Bangor, and Penrhyn Castle.

Sam and I bought faggots and peas and went on a tour of the Bethesda publics.

CHAPTER TWELVE

Nanwen looked prettier still a few weeks later.

Smooth and pale was her face as she sat at her sewing, and her dark hair, shining in the table lamp-light, lay in flowing waves over her shoulders.

I loved her hair. Sometimes she would tie it with coloured ribbons, and this would make her into a girl again; then she would let it hang loose, and this turned her into a woman. Now she lifted her eyes in a whimsical little stare and her hands paused on the needle.

She always did this when I was watching her; her smile greeted, yet her eyes admonished. Sometimes I wondered if she knew of my love for her.

Ben said, grumpy, drunk with strength, 'You heard about Penrhyn summoning those twenty-six men of the gallery for stoning his contractors?'

'Here we go,' said Grandpa.

'You think this is the start of trouble?'

'You bet your boots.'

'I 'aven't got any boots,' said Grandpa.

I said, 'Mr. Young the agent's up in Great Yarmouth, they say – people reckon Penrhyn's moving too fast.'

'Will there be a strike?' asked Nanwen, quietly.

'There's going to be a protest,' rumbled Ben, getting up. Fisting his face he wandered the kitchen. 'Would we be decent if we sat on our backsides and watched friends go to gaol?'

'Will it come to that?'

'They won't go free, woman – Penrhyn's got the magistrates sewn up neat in a bag.'

'It's a scandal. He waters their wages and then summons them for protesting,' said Nanwen, and I was a little surprised. The skin of her face was stretched tightly over her highboned cheeks, her voice was strained.

Often I had wondered about her having a baby; the

thought brought me to an inner sickness. Up and down the Row and round the corner in Tangadlas, the women were knocking them out; the washing lines waving full of napkins, belly-bands and comforters; it was more like a sprog farm than a slate town, and the hammering and squalling going on turned the mind of a lonely bachelor. I tried to get a peek at what Nanwen was sewing, but I couldn't make a head or tail of it. I didn't want her to have a baby, unless it could be mine.

Bang, bang on the back and I got up and opened it. Mr. Morgan stood there with slate dust on his face. He peered:

' 'Evening, Mrs. O'Hara – you there, Ben, lad?'

'Dear me, come in!' cried Nanwen, delighted, sweeping him in with her skirts.

'Can't stop – the missus is waiting – I haven't been home. Up at the Hole there's talk of the summoning, you heard?'

'I have, and he'll never get away wi' it,' observed Ben grimly.

'He's done more, man, he's sacked all twenty-six.'

'No!' Ben roamed the room like a tiger caged, but I was looking at Nanwen.

One day, I thought, I will take you from here, away from this worry and his disregard. One day I will build a house on a hill for you where a little river runs, with servants to wait upon you and there will be nothing for you to do all day but walk under a parasol. And there will be an end to the sack apron, the slate dust, the eternal confrontations. A strike was coming, and a fight with Penrhyn would be a fight to the death. Everybody would suffer, most of all the women.

People nearly starved to death in earlier strikes. The dismissal of eighty quarrymen in 1870, because they had tried to form a Combination, had disgraced the name of Penrhyn. Then, four years back, in a fight for fair wages, a lock-out came, and Bethesda went thin for a year.

Ben said, 'He's sacked twenty-six men before the court finds 'em guilty? – the fella's ravin' mad, so he is!'

'You're not dealing with an ordinary employer,' said Mr. Morgan, and Grandpa raised his hands to the ceiling and cried in a cracked voice:

' "Go in, go in, speak unto Pharaoh, that he let the

83

children of Egypt go out of his land!" – Exodus 6:11 – what d'ye think of that, boys – "And say unto him that if you refuse to let them go, I will smite all thy borders with frogs!" '

'Quiet, Grandpa,' I said.

Ben shouted, 'Get some sense into this – what does Mr. Parry say?'

'I came in to ask you that,' answered Mr. Morgan, 'you're the Combination man. It's serious, you know. If the men walk out now they won't go back for years,' and he left us.

Nobody realised how right he was.

It was strange, in the light of what happened afterwards, that Sam should bring us the final news.

'Anybody there?' he asked, knocking and opening the door.

It was near midnight, and we were yawning for bed. Sam was a stuttering rush of words:

'Word's just come that Pharo will suspend quarry working if the men march on the Bangor magistrates, Mr. O'Hara!'

'And who says they'll march on Bangor?'

'Mr. Parry, not an hour ago, yeh?'

'Parry said that? – talk sense!'

'Come in, come in!' called Nanwen, and Sam entered, tearing his hat to bits.

'It all just happened – Mr. Parry says to the devil with Pharo – that we're entitled to make a peaceful demonstration. And he will lead the march on Bangor.'

'When?' I asked.

'Tomorrow – Parry's sending people round with the news – I'm one. Everybody to be in High Street by eight o'clock in the morning – going to close Port Penrhyn, stop the ships, and march on the magistrates!'

'God help us,' whispered Nanwen.

I got up. 'Better to starve than live crooked.'

'He'll suspend the town for this,' said Grandpa, spitting in the fire.

'Let him,' said Ben. 'He can suspend us, even sack us – he can't eat us alive.'

'Damn near, according to my da,' said Sam, uneasily.

'Luckily, your father doesn't represent the opinion of this town – will you be there tomorrow, Sam?'

84

'If me da is, Mr. O'Hara.'

Ben nodded, turning away. 'That means you won't, because your father's spread on the Penrhyn blanket.'

'I'm coming, I tell ye, Mr. O'Hara – I'll be there, won't I, Toby?'

I did not reply.

Already the doubts were starting, and the strike hadn't even begun.

There was fine talk that Lloyd George himself would march at the head of the strikers in the morning.

'A politician?' asked Nanwen, innocent.

'He'll watch which way the wind blows first,' said Ben.

He must have done.

Next day he was still tucked up safe in Caernarfon.

In the morning the sky was cold and grey and the town was filled with the clatter of boots; to High Street went the men, summoned by their leaders, to march on Bangor in protest at the summoning.

'You don't go,' said Ben.

I stared at him. 'Why not?'

'Neither you, nor Grandpa. The house is in his name, and when he is gone it falls to you; we need the roof.'

'It's sense,' said Grandpa.

'God alive!'

'Please,' said Nanwen, begging with her hands. 'We daren't risk eviction.'

Only that morning I had awoken to the sounds of her stifled retching of sickness, and knew that she was with child.

I had confirmed my inner fears.

So I left them, sick at heart, and mooched up High Street, where the men were assembling; they were a brave sight with their bantering and threats and a Lodge band forming up to march at their head. One of the first people I saw was Ben, up on a barrel, swinging his fist into the faces of a crowd.

'This is a peaceful demonstration of strength, remember!' he cried. 'We will surround the court house and await the sentences. If our comrades are gaoled, we'll tear the place down.'

They leaped to him, lustily cheering.

'But, sure to God, will any magistrate dare to sentence a single one, with three thousand quarrymen waiting outside? Now we'll know the stronger – the Workers' Combination, or Pharo!'

The town trembled to the cheering. It was the first time I had seen Ben as a Combination man, and I was strangely proud. He cried:

'We are peaceful men seeking justice, but force will be met with force. Even Mr. Parry is behind this official protest – are ye with him now?'

They bawled their assent, and he shouted, 'Right then, form up decent and march like soldiers – let Pharo suspend the town if he wills – tonight we will return to Bethesda with our twenty-six comrades!'

'*Cythril!*' ejaculated a man behind me in the crowd, and I turned to see the little wizened face of Sam's father. 'The Devil himself is in that Irish pig.'

'He speaks for the town,' I said, 'be fair!'

'He'll have the lot of ye out of Caerberllan in time for Christmas – d'ye realise?'

'Our business.'

'It'll be yours in the end – and Grandpa's, mark me. Harbouring that madman, you've less brains between ye than a chocolate mouse. The town's not all for Parry, remember – a lot of us are for Penrhyn. Ye don't shoot all the dogs because a few 'ave fleas.'

I tore myself away from him and mingled with the crowd to lose him. I looked for Sam among the marchers, but could not find him.

A sudden desolation gripped me: I was aware of approaching disaster; it was more potent in its threat than anything I had experienced before.

'Come snow, the five of ye will be on the road,' said Sam's father, tugging at my sleeve. 'With O'Hara loose, man, you'll be beggin' for bread.'

I ran, to save myself the sin of murder.

Sickened, I wandered the empty street after the men had gone.

Nanwen was going to have a baby; the least she could

have done was to tell me. In the midst of this fear, it was like an adultery. I knew a great and awful emptiness.

So I was glad to find Ma Bron sitting on the steps of the Waterloo, with her arms folded on her chest and her skirt six inches above her ankles.

Enough to send any normal chap raving mad.

' 'Morning, Toby Davies,' said she. 'Good looking people around town these days, ain't there?'

I knocked up my bowler at her, standing sideways in my trews, which was the effect Bron always had on me: it took a Sam Jones to handle her.

'Seen Sam this morning?' she asked.

'Gone with the marchers, I expect.'

'Oh, no he ain't – he's widowing up in Rachub. Never mind, mate, you'll do. Like a cup o' tea?'

The sun was warm on her bright, flowered dress; winter forgot it was November: all about us the deserted balconies frowned their chapel allegations.

Ma Bron jerked her thumb. 'Nobody in 'ere, gone on the march, ye see, even the blutty landlord.' And she preened and flounced her beauty at the morning. 'Alter all, Toby Davies, we're sort of workhouse mates, ain't we?'

It seemed fair enough in the face of Nanwen's defection.

I followed Ma Bron into the tap-room with its smell of stale beer, my hobnails hammering the saw-dust.

'You like to see my room, son?'

Unaccountably, I was remembering Randy Andy, aged eight in Wrexham workhouse, who, orphaned, fell in love with the tailor's dummy. One day they missed him and found him down in the cellar among the coal; standing with a candle in one hand and his arm around its waist: nothing but a knob for a face, a canvas bust and moulded mahogany where her legs should have been.

People got to love something, said Randy.

Being in love with Nanwen was rather like this, I thought.

They had a hedgehog in the kitchen of the Waterloo to eat the crickets; Ma Bron's room was next door to this, warm and snug from the grate where stew was simmering: the brass-knobbed little bed with black stockings draped over the rail, a hint of perfume, and Ma Bron's white eyes in the darkness of the corner moved like a dance of the senses.

'Has Sam Jones been in here?' I whispered.

'O, aye,' said Bron. 'Some I favour, Sam especially.'

The clouds sank over the window in bleak understanding; the room was in false twilight: I saw Bron only by the whiteness of her face now, and her hands that floated, disembodied.

'You like me, Toby?'

'Ay ay.'

I heard the rustling of Ma Bron's skirts, saw the brightly flowered dress mystically rise, and heard her gusty breathing. Parched in the throat and trembling, I watched: it was like an evaporation of the soul.

'Would you like to make love to me, Toby Davies? – I called you in special, ye know – Sam being absent.'

'The deacons'll have us,' I gasped.

'The deacons never got Sam Jones,' said she.

We stood apart; the world died in our breathing. My loins knew the old, stifling sensations; as iron is forged to heat and shape, and my hair was standing on end.

'You ever done this before?' She approached me, a wraith of wickedness in flouncing petticoats. My heart thumped in my throat, as she added, 'After we've finished up here I'll take ye downstairs for a bowl of custard an' apricots. You like apricots?'

'*Diawch*,' I said, 'I go daft over custard and apricots.'

'Dear me,' said she, 'this is going to be a blutty tricky one.'

There was a place of childhood that I remembered, and here the harvest stooks had been set; on the evening I came to watch the mad hares dancing.

There was a man and a girl, laughing in the wheatfield, and I watched, aged nine, on a day's outing from the workhouse. The bodies of these two matched the gold of the autumn; the man was big, his shoulders naked, muscular from reaping: the girl's arms were round and smooth, her skin as lustrous as ironed satin, as was Ma Bron's under my hands, in that sunlight.

Never before had I touched a woman's breasts; it was a sweet and awful ecstasy.

And so, as my two lovers mated, the girl's hair became entwined about the body of the man in lovely wreaths of shape, even as Bron's hair, fallen about her, became a richness in my hands.

Later, the man and girl rose and walked away. Examining the stubbled wheat where they had lain, I could trace the outline of their bodies; the fulfilment, for me, of all things beautiful. I was spent, almost by the contemplation of such beauty, for the man had made love to his girl with singular respect: and she had been gentle with him, undemanding and quiet. Later I touched the ground, and it was still warm as if vibrant with life.

Ma Bron's loving was not like this; it was tempestuous, like people gasping.

Suddenly she twisted herself out of my arms and flung herself away on the bed; in that light her eyes were green, the shadows deep in her breast.

'Jakes alive, fella!' she gasped, 'you don't give much away, do ye?'

Hating myself for my inadequacy, I sat there, head bowed.

'You're tighter than old Dick Jones, mun, and he bottles his water.'

If only she would be quiet, I thought desperately, I could imagine, in this dim light, that she was Nanwen.

'You ain't a patch on Sam Jones, ye know – pays his respects to me, do Sam, and proper.'

I raised my face. It was sad and vulgar to sit there half dressed and half a man. Bron said softly:

'You'm just a little boy, ain't you, Toby Davies? – you'm damn useless to a girl, so be off!' Rising, she flung my clothes at me. 'You ain't grown up yet – go on, blutty hop it!'

And I didn't get my custard and apricots.

The town was deserted of decent people as I went home.

Yet, I thought, I had known her, my first woman: it brought to me a sweet, sad sense of pride.

She might, in dreams, almost have been Nanwen.

Yet, amazingly, for all my first love's failure, I knew a strange and secret contentment – that it had been with Bron ...

CHAPTER THIRTEEN

The winter sky was jewelled like a crown above Llanberis Pass. Heaped with snow drifts, the galleries of slate howled their desolation. January swept out February 1901 in icy blasts; March came in with her soprano arias.

The town froze. Icicles hung gleaming over the Ogwen river; the trees creaked their scarecrowed branches under frosted moons. Silent was the Big Hole, a refuse heap of ghosts. The little cottages were barred against the cold, but the turrets of Penrhyn Castle glowed with light, its lawns sparkled to the great occasions, now the military were in Town. Elegant were the scarlet uniforms of the Hussar officers; beautiful were the coloured dresses of their ladies.

Despite the dirty old strike, Nanwen was very pretty about now, being peaches and cream and dainty in the front, as women generally are when carrying. Sometimes, when she was stretching up for the washing-line, there was a fullness in her. Not that Ben appeared to notice, since he was busy drawing up Combination meetings and writing his political speeches for the Public Hall. Very simple it was for me to pretend that the baby was mine, so I became careful with her lifting and carrying, and mind you don't fall, *fach*, in case you damage the brain, and more than once Grandpa raised an eye and Nanwen herself looked at me very old-fashioned.

A lot of funny things were happening in Bethesda about now.

Grandpa, for one, was acting queerer than most.

'Ah well,' said he, after breakfast, 'time I was off.' And he smarmed down what was left of his hair in the mirror and put his teeth in.

Off to work, was Grandpa: with the town on strike and the Big Hole deserted, he was off on shift; it had been this way with him for the past fortnight.

Fear was in Nanwen's trembling hands, as she glanced at Ben.

'Leave him,' said he, doing his Union books.

'But it isn't sane!'

'Leave him, I say!'

I got up from the table. A cold winter mist was swirling down the Row; most of the strikers were still abed, their doors shut tight against the wind. Above the slate tumps the Glyders were suffocated in cloud; hoar frost from the night sparkled like diadems on the walls. Making a big occasion of polishing my boots, I asked:

'Shall I come, too, *Taid*?'

The old name stilled him as usual; I rarely called him this.

'Ach, no, son – it's an old 'uns parade. The agent wants advice on the Sebastopol gallery, ye see?'

'Are they having trouble there, then?' asked Ben, writing.

'Well, the face has stopped dead,' explained Grandpa. 'The thirty-five slope changed to forty-eight a month back – more'n ten degrees – the vein ended.'

'A lamination fault?'

'Dan Morgan knows about it, for it's been hitting the bargains.' He chuckled. 'Yeh?'

'And they've called you in to help?' asked Nanwen, her eyes bright.

'Aye, well, we old stagers know, don't us?'

At the door he stared about him. 'Anyone seen me other boot?'

'You'd go better with both of them on, old china,' called Ben.

For weeks now he'd been boning his new boots with ox-blood paste, making them shine: it had set us back, but he had to have a new pair; the old ones were snapping at the furniture. Nanwen said now, kneeling:

'It must be under the table.'

'If it was I'd have seen it,' I said, for this was my bedroom.

Ben said, 'Now come on, Grandpa, you can't lose something as big as a boot!'

But Grandpa could, and I was the one who found it.

It was on the top shelf of the dresser, hidden behind the photograph of Grandma.

'Poor little man,' said Nanwen.

Guto Livingstone, in Seven Caerberllan, due for a belly full of Accumulation Pie (this being Saturday night) finished off his bread and dripping and sat with his little dump of a missus by the grate: warming their hands to a fire not there.

' 'Evenin', Guto,' said Ben and I coming in with the Union funds.

Pinched and pale, these two, taking the strike bad, people said, and I'd give him bloody Penrhyn if I could lay me hands on him, said Mrs Livingstone, whose English name was Bid.

'Now now, my South Sea island beauty,' whispered Guto, light in the head, and she sniffed her disgust and heaved up her rags like a nag in a bone-yard.

'Soon I will take you away from here,' said Guto, 'to a lovely place on the rim of the world.'

'Risca would do,' she replied, 'though it ain't the end of the earth – anywhere away from this bugger up in Penrhyn Castle.'

We entered on tiptoe, Ben and I, so as not to fan her wrath. 'Things not goin' so good, Mrs Guto?' asked Ben, and she upped and flounced about.

'Well, it's indecent, ain't it? Once he promised me the earth, but I didn't get farther than blutty Bethesda.'

'One day, my lovely,' whispered Guto, looking at his maps. 'Venezuela don't appear so bad, ye know, my little concubine?'

'Likely he'll land me in Blaenau Ffestiniog, the daft nit,' said she. 'Dreams, all dreams – what you doing there, Irish?'

Ben and I were counting out the Union money.

'Three and tenpence, missus,' I said.

'Three and tenpence – the Union dues? What the hell can a woman do on three and tenpence?'

'The fare to Boston has dropped to three pounds, mind,' said Guto. 'Oh, to see the sun rise on the Allegheny in Pittsburgh!'

'With this idiot here and the children crying upstairs?'

'It's all the Union can afford, woman,' said Ben.

Mrs. Guto Livingstone lowered her head and fought her tears, saying, 'Down south it were better'n this – God Almighty!'

'Mind, they don't get strikes in Italy, people say,' mumbled Guto. 'The Pope's in charge of the Union.'

I said, touching her, 'Perhaps it will end soon, Mrs Guto.'

She raised her tear-stained face. 'Life, you mean?'

'Don't cry,' said Ben, 'it anna fair – not with people here.'

She was from the south; talk had it that women didn't cry north of Corris; leastwise, not in company. Now she said:

'All my life I been on strike for something or other. What for now?'

'Guto will explain it,' said Ben.

'Guto? Half the time he ain't even here!'

'May our enemies never be as happy as us, I say,' said Guto. 'You ever been to Spain, Ben O'Hara?'

His wife said, 'There's fine slate for the taking and the quarry stands empty. In the Eastern Valley it were the same – business wanting coal an' the seams gone wet.'

Said Ben. 'Now listen to me, woman – whether ye know why he's out or not, it doesn't matter, sure to God. What matters is that he can't go in. So will you stick it, eh?'

'By God, Irishman, ye ask a lot,' said she, hands screwing. 'I got two kids upstairs, remember.'

'Some women have six. Now answer me – on three and tenpence a week, will ye stand for the Union? A week, a month, a year? I need it for this book.'

And Guto said, smiling into her face, 'You only got to ask, girl – I got the whole world waiting for ye. Now, wouldn't I look a dandy wi' a fez on me head in Persia? Ach – with you beside me, my little belly dancer, I'd sail on a board to Alaska, or on a catamaran across the China sea. Now then!'

She said, 'Do ye hear that? Dear God, I got trouble!'

'But will ye stand, woman? – that's the point. You're sane, so answer me – will you stand if the Union calls?' asked Ben.

Sighing deep, she put the pencil into Guto's hand.

Pity, I was finding, is something you don't expect from God.

'Is this for the tickets?' asked Guto, vague.

'That's right,' said she. 'We're away on elephants to Africa, and I'm as addled as you – sign your name.'

Ben's distribution area of strike money, I discovered, was generally Bethesda South: thus, with fifty or so sub-treasurers doling out the money, nobody could abscond with a fortune. We even had a couple of Union clients in Tre-garth – one, of course, just had to be in the cottage next door to Sam, and out came his father and reviled us as loafers and layabouts: I saw Sam's mother grieving her breast by the fire, but no sign of Sam, thank God. Next, it was our privi-lege to call on the great Mr. Parry – he who could have earned thousands a year in London, shared every humility with his quarrymen, and carefully signed for his few strike shillings. It was then that we remembered our own strike pay, and that of the Arses in Number Two Caerberllan, so we made back home damned frozen.

Bang bang on the door of Number Two and it opened an inch on a chain and there was Albert Arse peeping through the crack as bare as an egg.

'*Diawch!*' said he with his lovely valley accent, 'it's the Combination man, get your socks on, Annie.'

'Six shillings from the Union,' said Ben, and I followed him into their kitchen, and there was the tin bath by a shin-ing grate and Tommy and Rosie Arse, aged six, splashing within it, also the triplets, Miriam, Dan and Agnes, and not a stitch between them; with Mrs. Annie Arse swilling them through the suds as fast as she could catch them, and them playing 'touch me last' in shrieks, and I've never heard such a commotion since the Ladies' Guild got into Handel last Easter.

'You got a penny for me, Uncle Toby?' This from Agnes, climbing up my trews.

'Sherbert dabs, mind – you promised,' cried Miriam, and she dripped through my lace-holes.

'Ain't they lovely?' shouted Mrs. Arse, hugging Rosie. 'A pity, ain't it, that they 'awe to grow up into people?'

'Tom's doin' it in the bath again, Mam,' yelled Rosie, and

I saw in her child's breasts the woman she was going to be as she splashed and screamed.

'How much did ye say?' asked Annie, belting Tom.

'Six shillings,' I replied, and she laughed, her head back.

'Six shillings to feed this lot? Reckon old Pharo spends more on snuff.' She pushed back her hair from her shining face and steadied Miriam; whipped the towel off the fire guard, and hugged her into it, eyeing us. 'That right we've got traitors going back to work already, Ben O'Hara?'

Ben raised his great dark eyes at her. 'Not true.'

She nodded. 'Only wondered, see, 'cause when the kids get skinny the *bradwrs* come out, ye know.'

We stared at her, and she smiled, adding, 'And when the traitors come out you can count on me . . .'

Albert said, appalled, 'Annie, you can't mean that! *Break strike?*'

'Aye.' Tom fought to be free of her now, and she tucked him under her arm. 'I've had nothing but trouble since you landed me up in Bethesda, remember? – and I don't need more.' She swung to us on her knees. 'My chap here don't drink nor smoke nor chew, yet we don't own a penny piece to bless us, and all I hear about is you and your damned Combination.'

'Please don't swear, Annie,' said Albert.

Now she rose, hands on hips. 'Don't swear, eh? You're dreamers, you men – the bloody lot of ye, so now I'm tellin' you something. Before my kids go on the starve I'm on me knees to Penrhyn or share an agent's bed.'

'Annie!' Albert covered his face.

Lifting the strike money she slammed it down on the table. 'Pinch and scrape and beg? Not me, mate – I'm a Bow Bells cockney. I don't fight for Wales, Bert – I don't even speak the lingo.'

Albert was instantly beside her, patting and smoothing her while the children wallowed and plunged, but she pushed him off and said:

'Sod you for bringing me here, Albert!'

As struck in the face, he stared at her: then, uncertain, he stroked her arm, cajoling her:

'It will be all right, Annie, me love. Things'll change, you see. Only yesterday Lloyd George said . . .'

'And sod him, too.'

Silence in a dripping of water. The children, bereaved, gaped up.

We waited within the indecision of her troubles, and Ben, shifting uneasily, said, 'The point is this, Annie, we need the women: sure as faith, we'll win if the women stand . . . just put your name in this book . . .

'Count us out, O'Hara, I'm signing nothin'!'

We turned to Albert; in the silence of pent breathing, he almost hid his face.

'Well,' asked Ben, the pencil towards him.

'It . . . it's what my woman says, really . . .' said Albert.

They were still apart when we left them. The naked children, scared at the rift, stood like white aborigine statues about them.

Outside in the Row, I said to Ben, 'That's one family we've lost. You've got two good traitors there when Penrhyn offers bribes.'

'Don't you believe it,' said he, and ticked Albert's name. 'She's a Londoner – she's had all this before. When those kids get hungry she'll give him bloody Penrhyn.'

CHAPTER FOURTEEN

People suffered a lot during that first winter of the Strike; few realised that there would be two more strike winters to come.

The place was freezing solid now, with ice outside and hunger within; some, like poor old Tam Dickie, the road-sweeper, froze all through. Yet the snow-drops brought to the mountains a tiny hint of spring.

'Is that you, Tobias?' asked Tam, leaning on his broom that dull old day.

'Christ,' I whispered, and made to slope off, for I knew he was going to tell me about his missus leaving him again.

'Aye, it's me, Tam,' I said, stamping for warmth and steaming.

'My missus 'ave left me, ye know?'

He'd told me eight times already, poor old sod, but I steadied him in the High Street to the blustering shoves of the wind. With his moleskin hat and long black coat he could have put the broom through his knees and gone round chimneys. A vixen shrieked from the hills; I thought it was a witch.

'Sorry in my heart I am, Tam,' I said.

He snuffled at me. 'Roadsweepers anna good enough for some people.'

Nothing to do with road sweeping, I thought: his missus, half his age, got up one morning and put on black stockings: she had a run in the left leg. When she came home that afternoon she had the run in the right leg, and there was at least one randy baker up in Sling.

I waited upon his suffering. 'You never see her now, then?'

'Gone three weeks – she entertains gents, ye know.'

It was his second wife; rumour had it that she was living in Manchester; that Tam paid her like the others – five shillings a visit.

He turned his grizzled face to the pale stars; they were cold enough that dusk to faint right out of the sky. 'She's a good girl, really, ye know – I know her, see – she anna doin' nothing wrong, though she's up in Manchester.' He munched his iced whiskers at me. 'Just that she married a bit young, eh? It were my fault, really.'

'Tam,' I said, 'I got to go.'

'Dear me,' he said at the snow. 'There's empty I am without my girl.'

I was tiring of him. Youth has scant respect for troubled age.

'You've still got your daughter, though.'

He brightened, wiping his eyes. 'Ay ay, I still got my Elida. She's at Llandegai School now, ye know – one of the Penrhyn's scholars.'

'Aye,' I said, dull.

Because he was a roadsweeper she used to pass him in High Street on her way home from school.

I took off my hat to him.

The children were singing in the High Street near the police station, baiting Ugly Dic: the broken-teeth urchins of the terraced rows thronging outside the shop of Mr. Clark the Photograph, and in his window I saw the notice:

'The people whose photographs appear below owe me money.'

Distantly, behind me now, the children began to chant:

'*Mae'r ffordd yn rhydd i ni*
Mae'r ffordd yn rhydd i ni
Waeth be ddywedo'r plesmon
Mae'r ffordd yn rhydd i ni.'

(The way is clear to us. No matter what the policeman says. The way is clear to us.)

It was a funny life, I thought: the Queen's cavalry prancing down empty streets while the people starved behind their battened windows; the Bethesda police threatening us with their batons while the deacons were powerful on their knees in chapels; and Madam Good Thing had a notice over her bed saying *Thy Will Be Done*.

Everything was upside down in Bethesda about now, I reckoned. With the place still on strike, Nanwen had her baby; even that, being a breech birth, didn't come out right.

'What's wrong with you, then?' asked Ben O'Hara.

'Nanwen's crying,' I said.

Never have I heard a woman cry in labour like Nanwen.

Grandpa said, after the third day, 'They're a sight longer than most in getting that baby, mind.'

Dour and glum, Ben worked on his Union ledgers, and there was no sound but the wind wolf-howling in the eaves of Caerberllan, and Nanwen's crying in the room upstairs.

'It's a first baby – sure to Jesus, it's bound to be difficult, the sweet mite,' said Ben.

I was tortured by inner fears; every sound of her wracked me. Once I had looked through the door of the bedroom where the midwife and the neighbours had gathered around the bed like assassins over a bomb, and I heard Nanwen calling for her mother.

'Can't you do something for her, Ben?'

He emptied hands at me. 'What? It's women's business.'

'It's yours,' I said.

'One day you'll have your own woman, then you'll know.'

Aye, I thought, and I'll treat her better than this.

Presently Nanwen stopped her crying, and another began to cry, and the house was stilled. I slept, and the crying of this new one did not disturb me; in the morning, when I came out from under the table, they told me it was a girl.

Later, the women brought it down the stairs, billing and cooing and handing the thing around. It had a red face, a behind like a prune, and bags under its eyes like the flesh-pots of Jerusalem; I couldn't bear to look at it, for the pain it had given Nanwen.

At night they took me in to see her, and she was feeding it; I turned away my face; I could not bear to see her breast in that predicament.

'Isn't she lovely, Toby? See now, she's the spit and image

of Ben!' and she humped the thing around her shoulder to bring its wind up.

Away out of this: up through Tregarth and away for a walk up the mountain to clean places, me.

The sly contagion of my love could not have touched my face, for Nanwen didn't appear to see it: better things were afoot to please her mind – Ben O'Hara and her baby, Ceinwen.

Spring sped away in skimpy feet; people grew thin. Summer came, fanning live along the hedgerows, bringing June, and it was Traitors' Day.

Like flocks of birds wheeling and cawing over the valley, the people were on the march, to watch the scabs come in. Grandpa, preparing for his shift that never was, rushed out down the Row, and back again.

'Ben, there's hundreds coming!'

Like a bear at feed Ben lurched into the Row.

'So Penrhyn was right, then,' said Nanwen, rocking Ceinwen.

'He give us fair warning,' said Grandpa, 'he pinned it up on the gates. He said he'd break the strike.'

'If he pays scabs to work, there'll be a bloody riot,' growled Ben.

'Five hundred and fifty starting today,' I said.

'You know, and I don't?'

'Sam Jones told me.'

'And wouldn't he be the first to know? The fella's a scab like his feyther, ye realise that, I suppose?'

'He is not!'

'God Almighty, Toby – do ye want it down in writing? He's a scab, I tell you – only the night before last I saw him in the public, listening to Young, the agent.'

'That doesn't mean he's a scab!'

Nanwen said, 'Leave it, for God's sake,' and she sighed.

'Aw, well,' said Grandpa, 'I'd better be off.'

I followed him down to the gate of the Row, to see the Old Loyals coming in to break the strike.

'Dear me, Toby,' said he, patting his chest, 'if only people didn't 'ave to breathe.'

I restrained him. 'With the blacklegs going in, is there need for you today?'

'*Duw Duw*,' he wheezed, 'your grandad was behind the door when Jesus handed out breath.'

'Then stay in today, *Taid*.'

'*Diawch*, no! I got to earn me money, man – Penrhyn's paying us over the odds as it is.'

I watched him going through the gate and over the river to the quarry.

The road to Betws was clattering to boots.

They were coming from Rachub and Gerlan, from as far afield as Llanberis and Dinorwic, from Llandegai Mountain and Pentir: the Penrhyn quarrymen, as if summoned by a distress rocket – on strike for better wages – all came down to the Big Hole, to watch the scabs go in

The *Daily News* had it, so did *The Clarion*: Young, the agent we hated, was handing out papers, and it was pinned up on the Works gate – the strike was broken and the men were going back, he claimed. To enforce the lie, Colonel Ruck's special constables were marching three deep along the Bethesda pavements, batons at the ready; a phalanx of blue ready for battle.

The cavalry of the military, straight from the stables of Penrhyn Castle, jingled along High Street; sunlight flashed off the scarlet coats and drawn cutlasses. But the Workers' Combination was out on the streets, too, flourishing their banners of the Benefit Clubs and Lodges, marching in step to the beating of drums: Bethesda was crammed like a netful of shrimps that day; every quarryman for miles had come in, their moleskin and corduroy coats and trousers scrubbed white for the occasion.

By midday they were heading for the bridge of Ty'n-Twr over the Ogwen, yelling the scab song at the top of their lungs, taunting the five hundred who had come to break the strike. Flanked by the prancing Queen's Bays they came, lining the route where the scabs had to pass, with urchin children doing cartwheels in the gutters and wives shrieking encouragement.

'I'm coming, too,' said Nanwen. 'I'll get Ceinie.'

'You're staying here, woman,' commanded Ben.

'I'm coming, I say – I'm in this as much as anyone.'

At the bottom of the Row the sounds of the men grew louder. Insults were bawled in Welsh and English, as Young, the agent, arrived. Men were chanting, 'Pharo, Pharo, *Pharo!*'

Ben said, 'I've got to go. Mr. Parry'll be needing me, sure he will – look, will you stay with her, Toby? She's a mad woman in this mood.'

Slamming the door behind him he ran down the Row.

Leaning against the door, I faced Nan, barring the way. 'It's safer here.'

'Pharo's splitting the town into two,' she said at nothing.

'That's the way slate-masters work.'

'Aye, well, I can forgive him for closing his works because they belong to him, but now he's dividing the town, I'm behind Ben.'

'That's how it should be.'

She approached me; never had I been so close to her, and she would be in my arms. Faintly, I heard the sounds of the mob, the marching boots, the cheering. With her eyes on my face, Nanwen pressed the latch; the door opened, struck my shoulders and slammed shut again: automatically my arms went about her and my lips were on her face.

It was as if I had struck her. Leaning away, her eyes opened wide.

'Toby!' she whispered.

I kissed her lips: gasping she twisted her face this way and that, fighting to breathe, then pushed me away, to stand staring, in disbelief.

'Toby, for God's sake!'

Beautiful she looked standing there with her hand to her mouth and the redness flying to her cheeks.

'I . . . I am sorry.'

'And I should think so!' She was trembling, searching for lost words. 'Upon my soul, I'd never have believed it!'

The sounds of the road beat between us.

I said, 'Couldn't help it, Nan. I love you.'

It was out. Her eyes, wide and beautiful, searched my face.

'It's the truth,' I said. 'I do ... I love you.'

'Aye, well ...' she turned away, her fingers twisting together in panic 'Sometimes you don't say things ...' Her eyes were hostile now. 'Not fair on Ben, is it?'

'I want you,' I said.

'And don't say that, either! – d'you hear me? You start talking that way and perhaps you'd better go from here.'

Coldness came between us like frost on a rail, yet my craving grew for her: the desire for Ma Bron compared with this had been as nothing.

I replied, 'Perhaps I'll go, like you say, but it won't change things. I'll always love you and you'll always know it.'

She was trembling. I sensed, within her anguish, something more than an affront; there was in her a growing indecision, and she was knowing its agony. Instantly I wondered if she was suffering the eternal longing that I had grown to live with, and suddenly, without reason, I knew her wish for me: it lay in her eyes, wide open, fixed upon my face.

'Nan!' I caught her hand, but she snatched it away.

'Oh, God, no ...!' She began to tremble.

Still staring at me, she moved away, leaning against the wall, and she was trembling more. I had scarcely touched her, yet it was as if I had possessed her.

Distantly, a whisper in the room, came the chanting of the mob.

'One day,' I said. 'You see – one day.'

'Toby, go – please go now, eh?'

I turned my back on her, not trusting myself. The shouting of the people beat about me as I leaned against the door, outside in the loneliness.

I was up at the railway line when the scuffling broke out: either side of the line was packed ten deep with quarrymen when the Penrhyn coach came through with Pharo's engine pulling. And Ugly Dic was there with the dragoons in mounted groups, their eyes like needles. The sun burned down on a turbulence of swaying men, threats and cries.

Pushing my way to the line, I saw the end of the coach come open: Lord Penrhyn appeared, resplendent in his morning coat and top hat. Hands on hips, with Young, his agent, beside him, he calmly surveyed the scene about him. A cool bugger this one, give him that. As if in recognition of this, the mob grew quiet.

And in this quiet another group of men, the strike-breakers, marched two abreast up the railway track towards Penrhyn.

The crowd grew to silence; even the trees stooped, listening. The traitors approached; at the steps of the coach, they stopped. And Lord Penrhyn deliberately counted silver and put it into the hand of the first traitor.

And, as the man took it a voice yelled from the crowd:

'*Bradwr!*' – meaning *traitor*.

The name was taken up by the mob. '*Judas!*'

One by one the strike-breakers came up to Pharo to receive the bribe, and, as each one took it, the cry echoed around the valley:

'Judas! *Judas!*'

And then I heard Ben's voice and saw him standing on a crag. With his arms up he shouted, 'Repeat their names, men – record their names!'

With bowed faces the *bradwrs* went up to Penrhyn for their bribes, and as each man held out his hand, his name was bawled by the quarrymen:

'John Job Williams!'

'Judas!'

'Will Evans!'

'Judas!'

'George Shenkins!'

'*Judas Iscariot!*'

'Silas Jones and Samuel Jones!'

I pushed men away, peering through the craning heads. Sam Jones and his father took their bribe side by side, and I yelled with the mob, 'Judas, Judas Iscariot!'

Other men I knew, respected men, were coming for the money.

The mob was pressing around the little train now, jeering and threatening Penrhyn and his agent: more and more men came up to receive money: he was dividing the town. Over five hundred men took bribes; two thousand more refused them.

Men I respected came up to Pharo, their hands out, their faces low. Dick Patagonia was one (recently come to the Hole). But I didn't expect to see Harri Ogmore. I didn't even know he was here.

Leaning against the Ogwen bridge, I said, 'Bloody hell, Harri – *you*, of all people!'

'I got two kids, mind!'

'Albert Arse has five. Christ, you make me sick!'

He slouched away. Others went by in groups to prevent attack, followed by jeering workers: Silas Jones and Sam, my mate, stopped and faced me.

'They paid thirty bob for Jesus, Sam – remember?'

'My mam ...' The quarrymen pushed and shoved about him, shouting into his face.

'Your mam would rather die first, and you know it,' I said.

I saw the hurt in his face. Turning away, Sam followed his father.

By nightfall the quarrymen were painting it on trees, stretching it in banners across the lanes, writing it on walls:

TRAITORS' DAY – 11TH JUNE 1901. *REMEMBER.*

Five hundred and ninety-four workers broke strike that day – among them 242 quarrymen, 82 labourers, 68 mechanics and 117 old men and boys, but Grandpa, although he went to work that day, wasn't among them.

'Time he was back, eh?' said Ben that tea-time. 'Any minute now,' I said at the clock.

But my grandpa did not come, even with darkness.

The Row was quiet, as if ashamed; the wind played his soprano song in the eaves, like a sobbing child.

'Bethesda will regret this day,' said Ben, fist on the table.

'What do you expect of folks?' asked Nan. 'Hasn't the strike been on long enough when the children begin to starve?' Drawn and pale was she, her eyes raising in accusation at me over the starched, white cloth.

And then, racing footsteps: a pail went clattering down the Row. A man's cry, and somebody calling my name:

'Toby Davies, *Toby Davies!*'

They brought Grandpa in on a board and I raised the white sheet that covered his face.

'Dead?'

'Aye, dead,' said Mr. Morgan, and turned away.

'Bring him in,' said Ben.

The men moved, looking from one to the other of us with searching apprehension. One said, 'He's in a bad state, man, it was six hundred feet . . .'

I said, 'He should have died easy, ripe with years . . .'

Nan began to cry, softly at first, then almost hysterically, her hands over her face.

I asked, clutching Grandpa's hand. 'But what happened? How . . . how did it happen?'

'Folks saw him on the edge of the drop,' replied a man. 'One moment he was there, next moment gone. He isn't the first to jump, because he got no wages.'

'Bring him in,' repeated Ben, but Nanwen cried:

'No, please! Not inside, I couldn't bear it.' Lifting Ceinie she turned away horrified. Ben said, his voice rising:

'Would ye lay him out in a field then?'

'Oh, God, this dreadful place!' Nan whispered, and turned to us, her eyes wild. 'Take him somewhere else . . . please!'

'Take him where, woman?' Ben stared at her.

'Leave it,' I said.

'Indeed I will not!' Ben turned Nan to face him. 'Ye'll act like any other woman. The dear man'll come in and you'll lay him out, so ye will.' He peered at her. 'This is his home. What's wrong with you, in the name of God?'

Nan was sobbing. Annie Arse coming closer, said:

'It isn't given to everyone, Mr. O'Hara, so don't expect it.' She stroked Grandpa's face. 'I'll lay you posh, won't I, little man?' She nodded, and the men took Grandpa in.

Later, we took him over to Coetmor and laid him in the

grave they kept open for the next Big Hole accident, and he don't have to breathe down there, said Albert Arse.

I was a bit surprised about Nanwen.

The women I'd become used to took their share of death.

CHAPTER FIFTEEN

That summer Ma Bron was prettier still, and to hell with the dirty old strike, said she, I ain't lowering the birth rate for anyone, and she went up High Street past the Public Hall with her skirt billowing and bonnet streamers fluttering, very prominent in the breast, and flourishing in the stomach.

Diawch, I thought, that was a close one. I wonder who got her like that?

Having missed it by inches in one way or another, there was a rising sap in me for anything in skirts about now, and Ma Bron had a wink on her that was more like a promise. And since I was still in love with Nanwen but so far getting nowhere, I'd settle for a smile from her and a romp with Bron, given the chance. Now Bron stopped before me, all dimples and peaches and cream, looking gorgeous, but it was clear, even to one in my need, that she wasn't in the running.

'How gets?' said she, taking off the boys, and I stood my decent act for her, but wary, for ladies in this predicament are usually after husbands.

'Dear me,' she added contralto, and patted her stomach, 'you're a pretty lad and no mistake, Toby Davies, 'cause I've gone off old Sam Jones now, the blutty *bradwr*.'

Her talk was different from Nanwen's. Nan's speech was cultured, like her nature — the close-knit texture of the biblical Welsh, and with the high lilt of the Lleyn Peninsula, said Grandad once. Bron's was rough, tainted with the voices of the valley immigrants of the south — English accent, Irish, too, troubling the true Welshness.

'Do not call Sam that,' I said.

'Why not?' The smell of her perfumed the wind and fluttered me down to my lace-holes. 'Taking the Pharo bribes, ain't he?'

'His mam's ill,' I said.

'Needing an operation, poor soul, they say,' and she patted her stomach again. 'Dear me, don't we all? Ah well, as long as I can stand near enough to the tap to draw the Waterloo best brew. Sam's the father, ye know — or maybe that gent in Bangor — or even you — I'm not real certain. Got to take it as it comes, don't we?' Head on one side, she smiled prettily.

Does spunk lie in the burly redcoats who had faced the Boers? Or did it lie in Ma Bron, who laughed her way through trouble? I wondered.

'You like to marry me, Toby Davies?'

'*Diawch*, mun, I'm not particular.'

'That's what I thought.' She sighed deep and addressed the front of her. 'Oh, well, me lovely, we'll 'ave to make the best of it, won't we? Goodbye, *bach*.'

'Goodbye,' I said.

Mooching around, without the price of a drink, I watched the dragoons for a bit, until I saw them watching me; then I walked on, leaning into the wind, and the sunset was playing *paint me up in blood* with the trees; there was in me an emptiness for Sam Jones, and I reckon he was empty for me, now his mam had cancer.

Men were on the streets as I returned from Tregarth, the *Village of Traitors*, and here the little houses had screwed tight their doors and windows, as if in shame: a few loungers were on the walls, dangling their boots and eyeing me, for not many Bethesda folks hit Tregarth these days. Slowing me down outside the cottage where Sam Jones lived, I saw, through a chink in the curtains his mam in her rocking chair and his da at the table getting into his Bible. I hung around for a bit, hoping Sam would come out, but he didn't.

Later, I went back to Caerberllan, for it was rushing in thunder under the Ogwen bridge and I was frit to death of flying vipers: terrible things are these and funny what they get hold of. So I went over the river like something scalded and the first one I saw near the kissing gate of Caerberllan was Ben O'Hara, and he, like me, was going up to Town with the devil behind him. And then I remembered that it was the Long-Pay night (even if nobody got any) and that W.J. Parry, the strike leader, would be addressing us all in the Public Hall, so I leaned into the wind up to High. There, standing on the kerb to make him higher, was Dai Love

Jenkins, and Mave, his missus, smarming down his hair with spit, and I'd never yet seen her with her teeth in.

' 'Evening,' I said.

No answer: lost were they. The Iron Duke himself couldn't have shifted them, and I heard Mavis say, 'There there, my lovely, don't be long now, staying away from Mave. Just do the old Combination and back home to me, is it?'

'Mr. Parry is speaking tonight, mind,' I said.

'Got to be presentable, haven't we, *cariad*?' and she smiled her rhubarb smile. 'Chest out now, stomach in by 'ere,' and she tapped it. 'You do know where the fruitful lie, don't you, my precious,' and she patted his cheek.

Like a man to the scaffold was Dai, eyes staring.

'Smile, mun,' said she, 'your Mave 'as got you.'

Funny thing about Dai Love Jenkins, he was the best splitter in the trade, especially when vertical, but he seemed lower by an inch every time I saw him.

Outside the Public Hall, Dico Bargoed, the old mountain fighter, now as blind as a bat, felt for my face in his darkness. Sam Demolition, leading him, smiled.

'That you, young Toby?' asked Dico.

'Aye.'

Husky and light was his voice; too many throat punches. 'You heard I went blind?'

'Yes, Dico Bargoed, and very sorry I am.'

The men pushed and barged us and I could have struck their faces.

He said, 'You heard about my lad as well?'

'*Dammo*, yes — doing good, isn't he?'

His battered old face shone. 'Foreman up at Scunthorpe now, you know,' said he. 'Only rising thirty — rolling mill foreman in a couple of years. Good stuff in him, see?' He leaned, confidential. 'You ever got a minute, lad, considering the strike?'

'We've all got spare minutes, sir.'

'Then slip down to Pen-y-Wen and read his letters to me, eh? They come Monday mornings regular,' and he gripped my shoulder with a fist of iron. 'Got to choose who shares ye business, ye see — don't need to be all over Town, do it?'

'Leave it to me, Dico,' and behind me Mr. Albert Arse and Guto Livingstone were pushing up my shoulder blades. 'You attending Union meetings at last?' I asked them.

'Aye, well, my Annie has sent me,' said Albert. 'Wants to know what's going on, and Guto wants to book on the Isle of Man ferry, poor old dab.'

Thronging into the big hall the air was bee-hum with expectancy. Mr. Morgan, my old team foreman, called over the chair, 'Ben O'Hara speaking, Toby?'

'He didn't say, mister.'

His bright blue eyes burned in his cherubic face. 'Let's hope he's sober, eh? What's wrong with him these days, Toby?'

'Up to him, Mr. Morgan.'

He eyed me. 'We don't get a lot out of you, do we, lad?'

One-Pint Tossle was there with his yellow pew duster, as usual; this time thoughtful: rumour had it that one of his sidesmen had defected and become a *bradwr*, because he had a dying child — a dreadful thing to do, with God on the side of the Workers' Combination.

We pushed down the aisle for seats, me guiding Dico Bargoed; I sat down next to an old rubbisher, and he said, as grave as sin:

'Sorry in my stomach I am about Sam Jones.'

'His business,' I said.

'And Harri Ogmore — God, I'd never have believed it — *traitors*! And I'd 'ave put me last bob on Harri, I would.'

'All right, then,' I said, 'but leave Sam out of it,' and Mr. Morgan said, politely:

'Learn the facts before you criticise, man — you call them traitors. I prefer to know them as the men who cannot stand.'

'And Penrhyn's turned Tregarth into an armed camp,' cried another. 'You heard they attacked Agent Young while he was cycling?'

'He'll pedal sharper, the bastard,' whispered a third.

'And the blacklegs 'ave got real guns for protection now, you heard?'

And they'll need them before this strike is over.'

The conversation stopped when Mr. Parry mounted the stage; always this silence for the Quarrymen's Champion. I looked around the sea of eager faces; lined faces, many wasted by the dust disease, but all bore in their eyes the nobility of men at peace with themselves.

Reserved men, they were unlike their comrades of the south. Raised in Nonconformity, they lived by the fierce chapel creed bestowed on them by their fathers: few raised their fists to enemies, fewer splayed their boots on Saturday nights. But they were tough men, disciplined; worthy of the Combination.

'Nigh a thousand here, mind,' whispered Dan Morgan, beside me, squinting around him, but I didn't really hear him.

They did not bet, these mountain men; they rarely quarrelled, nor did they mountain-fight; they were resentful, though – mainly of the English, whom they didn't understand – and of the Penrhyns in particular. They claimed, and justly, that the getting of coal down south was a Sunday outing compared with the winning of slate; but it was cleaner to die on a quarry face when the rope ran out, than gasp out your life under a fall. They sang with national fervour, and with the same joy as their southern cousins, but their melodies were more in a minor key; they laughed with the same gusty banter: their humour was bitter, tinged with irony.

Everything these men did politically, was governed by the command of W. J. Parry, the man of Bethesda. I straightened in my seat as he came to the front of the stage and raised his hand.

'Can you hear me at the back?' he called, and men bawled assent. 'Then let me greet you.' He paused. 'Eight months we've been out now – time the strike was over, some say? Time Lord Penrhyn saw sense, say I, for people do not elect to starve for nothing. First, the decision, so keep cool heads – does the strike continue?'

Silence. A forest of arms rose all over the hall: there was no sound save the coughing of the slate refuse. Parry cried:

'Time was, you know, when this town was happy under the Penrhyns – aye – believe it, you younger ones. Aristocrat of wealth the Old Lord might have been, but he was a gentleman. Paternalistic, you say? Aye, but approachable.' He emptied big hands at us. 'True, he was as opposed to organised labour as his son, our New Lord. "He's an obstinate young man," said he, when introducing us years ago, "try not to cross him." And the reply from Sholto Douglas with whom we are locked in battle now? "Let him try it, and watch out." '

He waited for the laughter to subside. 'So I think I knew, all those years ago, that we would one day enter the dark valley which engulfs us now. But, could the Old Lord return this evening to his castle, I vouch we'd be back at work tomorrow!'

I looked around the hall. Ben, I saw, his eyes glowing, his fist clenched on his knee, aching for a fight: near him sat Mr. Roberts, the Ebenezer deacon who lived in Caerberllan, his hands clutched together, as if in prayer: sinners and saints sat side by side in the Public Hall at these strike meetings.

In the quiet of starched minds Parry shuffled his papers, smiling down at us; great in strength and purpose he looked then, his fist up. 'But we are not without fault, remember! Your honour was diminished when you chased the contractors out of Ffridd Gallery, and injured one with stones. It diminished further when you threatened the magistrates of Bangor. *I tell you this*,' and he levelled his finger at us. 'Had Edwards died – and he nearly did – men in this hall would have been hanged at Caernarfon. I command you again – no violence! This is just what the agents want; all the police are dying for an excuse to break your heads.'

In the following silence came the sound of military cavalry passing on the road.

'And so,' cried Parry, 'what now? On strike for months, we are becoming experts in the art of the starve. In turn though, Lord Penrhyn's profits are growing pretty thin. Indeed, it is hoped that the noble lord is going to a shadow – he'll be down, for instance, about a hundred thousand pounds for every strike year. Our children have started to die, but so has Penrhyn's soul. And if the spectre of death is only around Bethesda's corners, the mark of national disdain is on her so-called aristocracy. From all parts of Britain the subscriptions to our cause flow in: the *Daily News* is behind us, and so, now, is the London *Daily Chronicle*. And if the pittance be small when divided up into Union Relief – and I myself am not too proud to receive it – we will not cease this strike until we have gained our just objectives, and here I name them once again – a minimum of 4s. 4d. a day, reduction of the contract system of working, an end to bullying, reduction of Works fines, an annual holiday and democratic Benefit Clubs.'

Cheers at this, and he cried fiercely above the roar:

'We must not lower our banner now! It must be a fight to the death with this tyrant, who can congratulate himself on the rise of the death rate here already, so there is no need for him to thin us out with the military, unless, of course, he is dissatisfied with the rise . . .'

It inflamed them. They leaped to him, waving their fists, and cheering hoarsely; chairs and tables overturned in the rush to reach the stage, and Mr. Morgan shouted above the din:

'Slander now! By God, old Pharo will make him pay for that!'

'But it is the truth,' I cried.

'The truth won't save him, lad – not from Pharo!'

Now a harmonium was playing, and the noise died into its chords; we sang again the hymn of old, in full harmony:

'O, God our refuge, our salvation,
Hear this prayer in time of trouble.
Fold Thy healing wings above us,
Turn Thy face from our iniquities . . .
Rise, O rise, Thou God of all creation . . .'

I hadn't seen anything of Sam Jones for weeks; although I had called a couple of times at the Penrala Bakehouse (which belonged to his uncle) I dared not call at his house. The rules had it that you couldn't talk direct to a *bradwr;* this meant finding a go-between who wasn't in the slate trade.

I was sorry for Sam, thinking about his mam.

'They tell me there's a casting out next Sunday over in

Tregarth,' said One-Pint Tossle, the deacon, just come out of the Ebenezer, dusting pews.

I made a guess. 'Ma Bron?' I knew she belonged to the Tregarth Shiloh, because of her aunts.

'The barmaid of the Waterloo,' said he.

'Bit late, isn't it? The damage is done.' Poor old Bron, I thought.

'Not all is lost,' replied he. 'Her virtue can be recovered by a public confession; the man responsible for her sinful condition will be publicly denounced as a warning to others.' He sighed. 'Then, after a week or so they'll be accepted back into the congregation. It is an admonishment, not a punishment, remember.'

'They'll still do it, Deacon Tossle.'

'That is a lewd remark.'

'It may be, but they'll still get up to it – they've been at it for a million years.'

He drew himself up in his black alpaca. 'I agree with the Shiloh elders!'

'Sam Jones, is it?'

This was usually an official secret; it maintained the virtue of surprise.

'You know?' he asked, affronted.

I looked at the stricken trees and longed for summer. 'It'll kill his mam,' I said.

'He should have thought of that before.'

If animals had souls I'd be interested in their God.

CHAPTER SIXTEEN

The quickest way to empty a Bethesda pub or chapel, these days, was to bring a *bradwr* in; therefore I was surprised that nobody lifted an eye on the night I, a striker, took my seat in Shiloh, the chapel in Tregarth.

It was a big affair in Wales about now, this casting out; the important·thing, said Mr. Morgan (now nearly blind), was to fornicate abroad like some town dignïtaries, who mainly performed in Manchester or Liverpool: the biggest sin, apparently, was being found out, and, since it is usually the good girls who get into trouble, said Nan, it became a plunder of the innocents.

In the case of this particular casting out – Ma Bron and Sam – neither had cause for complaint: the pair of them should have cleared the Big Pew by inches long since.

For my part I found it astonishing how willingly the rebels comply with the rules. There sat Sam between his mam and dad, stiff-backed and pale before the Big Seat up front, with his hair combed to a quiff, his face polished with soap, and his tall, starched white collar cutting his throat.

Diminutive and furious sat Silas, on his right: on his left his mother was bowed to the agony of her cancer.

Ma Bron, on the other hand, was flourishing; even her dowdy black dress enhanced her loveliness; her comely shape sweetened her beauty. But tears were in her eyes as she turned once, and seeing me there, whispered a smile at me – immediately to be elbowed by the maiden aunts either side of her, a pair of brooms in stays.

The chapel was a box of living mahogany and black, aus-tere· stares of conviction; line by line, suffocated by the shame of the event, the people clattered into the·pews: in moaning boots and funeral black the deacons entered from left and right, with the head deacon taking the Big Seat. The great room quietened in its emptiness: no sound but the coughing of the Penrhyn tubercular.

Expectant, the congregation awaited its last important member in vain.

Minutes ticked by, to no avail.

Hate, I thought, is the web we spin; nothing saves us from the snares we weave. Dai Signficant on the other side of the aisle (the Englishman who felt insignificant without a Welsh nickname) stared at me in sudden realisation – that I shouldn't have been there.

Silence still; the dust-motes danced in yellow lamp-light.

I thought; aye, you are waiting for God, and He hasn't come.

In the winter night of this casting-out chapel, recently built for glory, I thought of lovely things in which to hide myself; things like Nanwen, and Fair Day in the morning.

In this black silence, with people agonised by mock virtue, I lived in a dream of sun, in Pesda's *Ffair Llan*.

I heard the happy cries of the rock vendors whose stalls, where the bright-faced children gathered, were end to end. Here, too, were the crockery salesmen shouting their wares, clanging plates together, juggling with gravy boats and moustache cups, running saucers up and down their arms in a medley of laughter: urchins ran in the lanes of my mind as I sat there, yelling their shrill insults; queueing at Mother Hughes's sweet stalls for gob-stoppers and aniseed balls, spraying the girls spare time with itching-powder and taunting them with squeak feathers and lady-teasers.

There was a merry-go-round with statue horses going up and down chased by gigantic cockerels with feathered plumes and outspread wings; circling madly in blasts of martial music, and a miniature conductor beating time. And, in the middle of the commotion I saw Ma Bron in pink with a farm yokel on one arm and a slate boy on the other, alight with the joy of the fair day.

I love the day of *Ffair Llan*, the twenty-ninth of October, and all its fun and gaiety; running breathless through the crowds with a girl in your hand is better, I think, than being lonely in Shiloh Chapel, among these unhappy people.

The dream was over. The service ended. The head deacon rose, and read:

'Deuteronomy 22:13, "If any man take a wife, and go into her, and hate her, and give occasion of speech against her, and bring up an evil name upon her, and say, "I took this woman, and when I came to her, I found her not a maid". Then shall the father of the damsel, and her mother, take and bring forth the tokens of the damsel's virginity unto the elders of the city in the gate." '

The deacon straightened and gazed about the congregation. Pent and stiffened, they returned his stare.

The head deacon paused, lowering the Book.

'Rise and face me, the girl Bronwen, who is with child.'

Ma Bron rose to her feet, with head erect, and the deacon raised the Book, and read:

' "But if this thing be true, and tokens of virginity be not found for the damsel: then they shall bring out the damsel to the door of her father's house, and the men of her city shall stone her with stones that she die; because she has wrought folly in Israel, to play the whore in her father's house: so shalt thou put away evil from among you." '

Silence again, save for the crying of the summer wind down the lanes of Tregarth, and the head deacon said:

'For a second time this girl is brought to child; and on this second occasion the man, Samuel Jones, the son of Silas, has admitted to being a partner in her guilt.'

The deacon looked about him. 'I quote also John, Chapter Four, recalling to you the occasion when Jesus came to the city of Sychar, resting by Jacob's well. There, you will remember, he met a woman of Samaria, and said unto her, "Go, call thy husband, and come hither," and the woman answered, saying, "I have no husband." And Jesus said, "Thou hast said well, I have no husband, for thous hast had five husbands; and he whom thou now hast is not thy husband ..." '

In pent silence, the congregation held its breath, and the deacon added, 'Look well upon this woman whom we are casting out. Is not she also a woman of Samaria, a paramour who will despoil herself with any man? And would not Jesus chide her also, were he present in this chapel tonight?' He looked down at Sam. 'Who represents this man who was tempted, and fell?'

Silas, Sam's father, rose.

'And who represents this woman?'

One of the aunts rose, and the deacon said:

'You will escort this man and woman out of our chapel. Only when they are married will they be accepted back into this congregation.'

Outside the Penrala Bakehouse (near the grocer's shop of the brothers from Patagonia), the people stood together; in the windows the curtains fidgeted and faces watched: unseen eyes moved in the road to Glasinfryn as Ma Bron and Sam Jones went up to Sling, to the house of his mother's brother. And, following them, I called to Ma Bron.

They waited, standing apart, as strangers.

The wind hit between the three of us in the light of the summer moon.

I said, 'I am sorry. Nanwen O'Hara said it could happen to anyone.' This I said to Bron, since I could not speak to Sam direct, he being a *bradwr*.

And Sam said, 'Tell him to bugger off; we don't need no one,' and Ma Bron said:

'O, Sam, do not pester him. You do good to come, don't you, Toby?' and she leaned towards me and her warmth touched me.

I said to Bron, 'Tell him I have money — two shilling saved, if he is going south, to the Rhondda,' for this I had heard.

'Toby got two shilling saved, for us — you want it, Sam?'

'Tell him balls,' said Sam. 'I wouldn't have his two shilling if he were the last one living,' and Ma Bron said:

'Oh, my precious, do not be like that.'

'Tell him balls,' said Sam.

'We got a baby comin', remember?' Pinched and urgent was her face.

'You got a baby coming, not me.'

'Say I'm sorry about his mam,' I said.

'Toby says he is sorry about our mam,' said Bron.

'She's not your mam,' said Sam, 'she's mine.'

'You stop behaving like a bloody kid,' said I, 'and I'll talk to you direct, Sam Jones.'

Bron said, looking at the stars, 'D'you know something, lads? My baby moved. Sometimes, she's so sad wi' her that I think her dead, but right then, she moved again,' and she held her stomach.

Fishing into my pocket I brought out the florin and offered it to her.

'Cross your baby's palm with silver, Bron. Take it, eh?'

But Sam pushed her aside and brought down his hand and the florin ran in a circle on the road between us. Bron stooped and picked it up.

'I'll have it, Toby. I'll keep it for my Bibbs-Two,' said she.

'Oh, Christ,' said Sam, and covered his face. Bron held him.

'I got to go,' I said.

'Right, then – you go – don't you stand there watching my Sam, go on, piss off,' said Bron.

I took the back road through Tregarth, and I heard her saying while she patted and smoothed him, 'All right, mun, he's gone. Now now, Sam ... there there ... Don't you cry, my lovely.'

Tregarth had something to answer for, I reckon, between the pair of them.

CHAPTER SEVENTEEN

Many of the southerners, people born with warm blood, began to drift south again during the spring of 1902 – back to coal, boyo, they were saying, where things are easier. At least it's dry underground, they'd say – no more hanging soaked to the skin down a rock face or hammering slate in the dark with nothing but the light of a candle: no more "dressing" the stuff in sheds full of swirling dust. Compared with slate-smoke, the killer of the lungs, a little bit of Rhondda coal dust is good for the chest, so say the coal-masters' doctors.

O, aye? I'd heard that one before somewhere, too.

But I will say this – I didn't know it then, but the getting of coal, I discovered later, was a Sunday School outing compared with the getting of slate; given the choice I'd take any pit in the country rather than work in places like Llanberis or the Great Hole. And I'd take any master thrown at me in exchange for the likes of the new Lord Penrhyn.

Summer passed; autumn came; Bethesda and her villages starved down the gold-dusted lanes. The Penrhyn quarries, unworked save for the *bradwrs*, were practically empty of men. Over two thousand quarrymen starved with their families while Penrhyn waited for hunger to beat them. By the beginning of that second winter of the Big Strike the snow was feet deep around the cottages and stamped into ice by the hooves of the patrolling dragoons, ordered into town to keep us behaving. The chapels were crammed to the doors. As with the southern cholera chapels, God, in the midst of the people's misery, was very popular.

'Mind,' commented Nanwen that November, 'I'll miss the southern people a lot – I've become quite fond of folks from places like Tonypandy,' and she gave me a heaven of a smile.

'Don't make too much of it,' said Ben, writing on the table, as usual.

'Different people, mind,' said I. 'Chalk and cheese, north and south, but all good Welsh.'

Doing his eternal books, making the figures match, Ben raised his face. '*Arrah!* Here ye go again, you damned foreigner!'

'Is a South Walian a foreigner, then?' I asked.

'No, but it's typical of a foreigner to make a gap where none exists?' His great dark eyes smouldered at us; his white teeth appeared in his unshaven face. The coming of Ceinie had changed Ben O'Hara, for the worse.

Where he gets the money for drinking, I don't know, said Nanwen.

I could have told her: Union funds. It would have needed an accountant to balance Ben O'Hara's books.

Now he cried in his thick bog Irish, 'Nationalism is splitting the world – what we want is internationalism.'

'I only said that I liked the people from the south,' said Nanwen, sewing. Though calm, her face was white.

He swung to me. 'Different people, ye say, youngster? How different? Where?'

'North Wales, South Wales. Different blood, different cultures.'

'Mark, Mary and Joseph – fancy words now! The lads are out of their drawers!'

'Ben, now mind . . .' said Nanwen, but, he went on:

'*Ach*, come on, son – we'll mend you in the great debate and shame the illiterate among us, eh?' His black eyes danced and he reached out and thumped me with his fist. '*Culture*, eh? Barriers, d'ye mean?'

'Language, for one,' I said.

'O, ay ay – any more?' He was set on trouble.

I added, 'Geography and time – even the soil is different: limestone in the south, a softer people. Granite up here.'

'*Ach*, be Jesus, geology, now, is it? But I'm a beggar for the education, ye know, Toby – give us some more.'

I fought to keep cool, saying, 'The southern people have the strangers in their blood – French, Spanish, even Italian folks, coming from the east.'

'Would it be a sociological question you're raising, perhaps?'

'Leave it,' said Nanwen, lowering her sewing.

'I'm not leaving it, woman, I'm just getting started. Sociological?' he peered at me.

'I . . . I don't know what that means,' I said.

'Do ye not, now? Isn't that the greatest pity, or I'd be pledged to listen to the wisdom of the street. Couldn't you explain to me – in the simplest of terms, ye understand – what the intellectuals consider the main and basic difference between the Welsh in the north and the Welsh in the south?' He grinned at me over the table.

The room tingled with silence; there was no sound but our breathing and the ticking of the clock. I hated him; I hated his smooth-tongued ability, his arrogance, his cruelty.

Nanwen, as if reading my brain, raised her face to me like a woman baptised, and said:

'In the south a woman will say, "Come in, love, and have a cup of tea." Here, we'd say, "Would you like a cup of tea?" But the tea's the same, and so is the heart. Is that what you mean, Toby?'

I closed my eyes. 'Aye.'

Ben rose, smiling down at me, but I saw his trembling hands: and he knuckled his fingers as he moved around the table, like I have seen the old Cornish grandfathers do – they who got the tin and China clay, a generation of men who walked on their hands. At the door, Ben said:

'You're lucky to have a woman speak for ye, son. By Jesus, I'd give a lot to have one speak for me.'

After Ben had gone, Nanwen said, 'Where does he do his drinking, Toby?'

'Drinking?'

She was instantly impatient. 'Yes, drinking – he's even been at it earlier tonight. And where's he getting the money for it?'

I got up and went to the window. No woman in the world is having the man out of me. Setting her needlework firm in her lap, she raised her voice. 'Now listen, Toby – you men know, so answer me!'

123

I turned, facing her. 'Your chap – you see to him!'

Momentarily, we glared at each other.

Earlier, coming down the Row I'd seen Ben shuffling home, swaying in the wind, and he'd had his Combination accounts under his arm; not my business what he was up to. Then little Ceinie, tottering on the doorstep, had seen me coming, and ran towards me, arms flailing for balance, and I'd knelt, beckoning to her.

'Come to me while I pick you up!'

More like my kid than Ben's, for he scarcely noticed her these days. She was the image of Nanwen with her fine black hair and red lips. Anyway, I'd come to think of her as mine, since Nan and I starved to keep her fed.

The child put her arms up to me again now, and I lifted her against me and wandered around the kitchen. There was a shivering of hunger in me, and I was grateful for the warmth of her. On her knees now, with a great air of independence, Nan said, 'He's spending Union money, isn't he?' She furiously poked at the fire.

'You'd best ask him.'

She covered her face. 'Oh, God, what will happen if he is?'

'If he is they'll near kill him.'

'He . . . he must be mad,' she said, as if unhearing.

I put Ceinie down. 'Ach, he's as weak as piss!'

'*Toby!*'

'Well, he is! Where the hell did you get him from? – couldn't you have waited a bit before lumbering yourself with a big, hairy oaf without the guts of a louse?'

She rose, white-faced. 'He's my husband, so mind!'

'And you're bloody entitled to him!'

Ceinie, staring up between us, began to whimper; hail swept the window in a sudden bluster of the wind. As if defeated, Nan turned away, sinking down into the chair. Head bowed, she said, gathering Ceinie against her, 'Oh, God, I . . . I don't know what to do.'

Like a woman in mourning she looked, sitting there; even her hair was lifeless: it took a Ben O'Hara to kindle in Nanwen her youth's vitality. Raising her face, she said, 'Are you hungry, Toby?'

124

All evening there had been a sickness in me for food; we'd all had breakfast, but it was scant enough.

'No,' I said.

Heavy-eyed, she stared at the lamp. 'Another month or two of this and the town will be six feet under. Old Joe Bec, the Gerlan baker, has had to close down – you heard?'

It was a brave attempt to change the subject; she would do anything, this one, to switch the guilt away from Ben. I shrugged, empty. Joe Bec was only one of dozens. Grocers had been giving away their stocks; bakers baked away their savings, milkmen left milk free for sickly children. When St. Peter tots it all up he'll give good marks to the shopkeepers of Bethesda and the villages round about.

Suddenly, Nan said, 'Oh, God . . . I've . . . I've got to tell someone . . .!'

I turned back to her and she raised her eyes above Ceinie's now sleeping face, saying softly, 'Do . . . d'you know Mr. Fellows, the Union man?'

'Aye – Assistant Treasurer in the Combination?'

'He came to see us the night before last.'

I stiffened. 'What did he want?'

'He asked to see Ben's pay books. Ben . . . Ben told him that he had to cast them up, or something.'

I nodded. 'Did he accept that?'

'Of course – he was very polite. But . . . he wants Ben to bring the books to his house for checking tomorrow night. Toby, what will happen . . .?'

I said, 'You'd best face it, Nan. If he's down on his money they'll sell you up.'

In horror, she whispered, 'The furniture, you mean?'

'Of course. These are decent men, but they'll have no alternative. It's public money, not theirs, and they're responsible to the Combination – they'll just have to take it back.'

She closed her eyes as if in prayer, then whispered, 'Oh, Toby, please . . . please help me.'

I wandered around, staring down at her. I didn't know what to do. Pity and anger were intermingled with a fierce and growing hatred for Ben O'Hara and everything he stood for. Also, I felt disdain for Nanwen's hopeless, blind loyalty for someone who didn't give a damn either for her or her child.

I said, as evenly as I could, 'I'll help all I can, you know that. But you'd best face up to it – all of it. It'll mean eviction too, you know.'

She protested, 'But . . . but the house is nothing to do with it. Grandpa's name's in the rent book, and when he died it passed to you!'

For a long time I'd been worried about eviction. With Ben ranting on street corners I wondered how we'd lasted as long as this: the land agent was using any excuse these days to shift out strikers and get their traitors in. And the evictions were beginning in earnest now: day after day people were being turned out into the streets. Most families just walked off. Pawning their valuables, they bought train tickets for places like the Rhondda – arriving there like immigrant Irish in the clothes they stood up in: others returned to the farmlands of the Lleyn Peninsula and Anglesey. Slowly, Bethesda was emptying. Heaven help Nanwen and Ceinie, I thought, if they found themselves homeless in the middle of winter. Now Nanwen repeated:

'Surely I'm right, Toby – they can't turn us out!'

'And me harbouring a Union throw-out under the roof?' I sighed. 'That's a good situation – we'll see what Penrhyn's land agent makes of that one.' Bending, I caught her hands. 'I tell you, Nan – face it! The trouble becomes that much smaller if only you'll stop hoping, *and face it.*'

She wept.

With Ceinie between us, I held her.

Later, when night came and Ceinie was abed, we sat together, Nan and I, and she said, empty:

'Sometimes I don't know about this place, Toby; all my life I've been in trouble with Bethesda.'

Although I could not even see her face in that light, her nearness, the sweet intimacy of her presence was having an electric effect upon me.

She said, 'When I was little, I remember my father going off to work at dawn – we lived Port Dinorwic then, for he was of the sea. Then he went into slate – being a ship's rigger he made a good rockman – and Assheton-Smith took him on, but he was soon transferred to Bethesda, on an exchange.'

Soon, I thought, I will go from here, and all I will have left will be your voice. These are the precious moments, I thought, yet you talk, talk, when I could be making love to you. She continued.

'So he had a five-mile walk to the Hole in the morning and the same walk home at night; my mam was always at the gate to send him off, or greet him.' She laughed softly. 'I can see her now – she was a pretty little thing – a girl, really; she married young, like me.' Her voice failed.

'Tell me,' I said. There was a dryness on my throat; I was hearing her words only as echoes in the mounting intensity of my need for her. Nan said:

'Aye, well cometimes he would go off in the snow, and my mother would kneel on the kitchen floor and pray for the snow to stop; unless it did he'd get no time in, and be sent home; this meant no pay. It was a *smit* day – you heard of this?'

'No,' I said. I *had* heard of it of course; *smit*, the essence of a people's misfortune, was a common word in Caernarfonshire.

'They don't use it much today,' said she. 'He couldn't work the quarry face in snow because of slips, though the men used to beg to do so, because they needed the money. The agents said they'd have to *submit* to the will of God. It changed to *smit*.'

I thought, desperately; who would know, except us, if we did make love?

The wind was singing his Jenny Jones down the Row, hitting up the doors and windows in fury; in the faint light of the window moon now, I saw Nan's shadowed face and the ragged dress at her throat. She smiled wanly, saying, 'It was a bad winter when I was four years old. We starved thin, like now. And when we saw my father coming with the men, we'd shawl our heads and join the other women at the gates, to greet them. They'd be soaked through, and shivering, and always the same old *smit, smit smit* . . . The women weren't suppose to cry, but my mother did, because she was young, and my father was ashamed of her, I remember. "Not in front of the others, Nell," he used to say. Then one month we hadn't a bite of bread in the house and went on the Parish and Quaker soup – and all it did was snow. Day after day Dada would go off, and come back with nothing. Then, one day, when he'd been to see the workhouse clerk, he came home with the others, and he was crying.' She stared at me, wide-eyed. 'If you'd known my father you'd have known what that meant. In front of everybody, even his mates, he was crying. My mother took him indoors and got the towel and wiped his face and said it was the rain, but he couldn't stop crying.'

I closed my eyes. Nanwen said, 'I was hungry. It was a terrible winter, that one – fifty *smits* on the run.'

I didn't reply. She added, 'Mind, my mother never cried again – not after that.'

We sat in silence, listening to the wind. Eventually, she said:

'It's worse this time – a two-year strike. Where would we be without the *Daily News* and the choir subscriptions?'

I thought; one day, I will take you from here, and there will be no more hunger.

'You gone to sleep, Toby?'

'No.'

'Terrible about Annie Arse and her little lot, isn't it?' she hugged herself with cold.

'First little Agnes and now Miriam. Do you think I ought to go up and see her again?'

'Leave her for a day or two, she's taking it sore,' I said.

I had been in myself when Agnes died – she went the same way as most of the babies we lost – a chill: without decent food they couldn't stand the winters.

Albert had put her white coffin on the kitchen table; very pretty Agnes looked in her little white dress with snowdrops in her hands: like a tiny sacrificial virgin, said Mr. Roberts, the Ebenezer deacon, who came to pay respects.

We all stood around her, I remember, in our black suits and creaking boots, empty of words while the women wept.

But Annie, her mother, did not weep: there was no sound but the fury of her eyes; louder than words spoke those eyes.

Now, three weeks later – Miriam, the second of the triplets – was being buried tomorrow. Albert said, empty:

'Maybe it's best that they don't grow up into people, like Annie says.'

I had touched Annie's hand. 'Sorry in my heart, missus.'

No reply. Trembling, Annie stood, staring down at Miriam.

'Don't seem fair really, do it – two in a month?' said Albert.

The sound of Nanwen brought me back to the actuality of the present.

'It's cold down here,' she said, rising. 'Best go to bed?'

I knew a wild sense of expectancy as I followed her up the narrow stairs.

On the landing, Nan turned to me; astonishingly, I was beset by a strange, heady humour. We were making so much of the pretence of living, yet folks like Sam Jones and Ma Bron just took as they pleased. People like Mrs. Knock-Twice over in Betws, for instance – kept her door unlocked for her man to come back; you only had to tap it and call yourself Fred, yet here we were revering the business of love-making like a biblical text.

'Come in with me, Nan,' I said, touching her. 'Just for a bit?'

There was in her face, in that dim light, an untroubled innocence.

'Who's to know?' I asked.

'I shall know.'

I said, 'Do you know something? You're like a little girl with a rag doll. You keep pulling me apart and stitching me up again.'

'Not here, Toby.' She kissed my face. 'Tomorrow? Up on the mountain?'

'In two feet of snow?' We laughed together, softly, for fear of waking Ceinie, and our laughter died into uncertainty.

'Go to bed now, is it?' she said. '*Soon . . . ?*'

I entered my room. The moon, iced to the ears, was rolling drunk over the rickety roofs of Bethesda, shining her frost on the toppling desecration of Penrhyn's refuse. Undressing, I slipped into the icy sheets and lay there, staring at the yellow searchlight of a moon crossing the boards.

CHAPTER EIGHTEEN

A few days later, bored to death with having no work, I took myself over the fields to Bangor in a foot of snow. Strangely, my mind was filled with thoughts of Sam Jones and Bron, especially Bron, and I wondered how they were doing down south. I missed them; their friendship, I thought, was as hopeless as my love for Nanwen.

The night was as black as a raven's squawk as I passed Bodforris on my way home, and I knew something was wrong in Caerberllan when I heard all the commotion. So I broke into a run when I got through the kiss-gate till Mr. Morgan grabbed me in passing and swung me to him, and his face, in the lamplight of his door, was that of a timid nun.

'Don't go down, Toby – it's being seen to – don't go down!'

'What's happened?' I shook myself free of him.

'It's Ben O'Hara,' said Albert Arse, coming up. 'But the Combination men are seeing to it.'

'Bring him in with us,' said Annie, arms out to me, her hair in crackers.

'*Nanwen!*' I said, staring down the Row.

'It anna anything really speaking,' said Mrs. Morgan, 'an' it's nothing to do with us – come back to bed, husband.'

I flung them aside and went down the Row at a run, and the first one I come across outside Number Twelve was Ugly Dic, the policeman, who, usually a man of dash and style, was now vacant and shivering. Guto Livingstone and his missus were there, also Bully State of Maine, who happened to be passing.

'What is it?' I cried, pushing in.

'It's the mad O'Hara,' said Bully. 'He's in there and bolted the door.'

'Been screaming mad, she has,' said Ugly Dic. 'Don't you fret, Mrs. O'Hara, I'll soon 'ave you out, my beauty!' and he hammered the door, shouting for entry.

I pushed him away. My first shoulder charge splintered a panel, my next took the lock, and the frame split up; Nanwen shrieked my name as I ran at it again; the door went down, and I was in. And, as I rose, Ben came at me.

I ducked as he charged into me, overbalancing in bawling anger: his face, twisted and white, was not the face of a drunk, but a drunken madman. As I rose, his fist caught me on the shoulder, and I saw, in the moment before I squared to him, the form of Nanwen lying against the table, her arms protectively around Ceine. People were thronging in now, women shrieking, men shouting commands. Ben came again, fists swinging, but I was up; steadier, I hooked him square with a right; it staggered him, but he shook it off and rushed again in the confined space, tripped over a fallen chair and fell headlong into me. People were pressing into the kitchen now; faintly, above their warning shouts I heard the baby screaming. Guto, with more sense than he owned, tripped Ben and held his legs, but he kicked and fought like a mad thing as I pinned his arms. Then Bully State of Maine hauled people out and knelt, adding his great strength to mine: I saw, in a flurry of arms and fists, the pale outline of Nanwen's face through the cage of her fingers as she slowly sat up against the wall: bruised and shining with sweat, I watched it uncover in the pale light of the lamp; her hands were stained with blood.

Blind fury struck me. Scrambling up, I took Ben with me. My first punch spun him against the wall, free of Bully's outstretched hands: and, as he gathered his failing strength and lurched towards me, I stiffened my legs and hit short: taking it full, he hit the floor like a sack.

Instantly, Nanwen was beside him, kneeling. Her bruised face stared up from the floor as she turned him into her arms.

'Enough – he's drunk! Sober, he'd kill you!'

In a ring we stood; Bully State of Maine, Guto, Albert, Ugly Dic, and me. Ceinie ran to me and I lifted her into my arms. Our breathing filled the room; around the corner of the broken door Tommy and Rosie Arse, fingers in their mouths, peered in childlike contemplation.

'You all right, Mrs O'Hara?' asked the policeman.

Nanwen nodded.

'And your husband?' he knelt.

Ben stirred in her arms, coming round. This is the trouble with drunks, they never go out though you hit them with a seven-pound hammer.

'He will be all right now. Thank you for your help. Go, please.'

'You got a bad face there, missus – you want to prefer charges?'

'I tell you I'm all right,' said Nanwen. 'He just ... just went mad. He wasn't hitting us.'

She got up from the floor and took Ceinie from me, leaving Ben to amble up as best he could: sitting on the edge of a chair he stared at the boards in a glaze of hops, and I hated him. I hated all he stood for and all he ever was: it was all I could do to stand there and impotently watch him. He raised his swollen face to Nanwen and stupidly rubbed his chin.

'Ach, I'm sorry, me sweet colleen. Did I hurt anyone?'

She, with her face averted, said to all there, 'We'll be all right. Go now – how many more times do I have to tell you?'

The policeman said, wagging a finger:

'All right, O'Hara, I'm going now, and for this ye can thank your missus. But any more rumpus and I'll 'ave you inside – it's a breach of the peace, ye know?'

After they had gone I fastened the door as best I could, and said:

'And understand this too. You're a mad drunk and you might have killed somebody. You hurt either of these two, and I'll have the liver out of ye.'

'And you understand this,' cried Nanwen. 'It's only the drink – he'd die before he'd hurt us.'

She was holding Ben now, her arms protectively about him.

'What the hell do you want of me?' I shouted.

'Now listen.' She crossed the room to me. 'This is my fight, not yours, and it's my responsibility, so leave it. Any damned lecturing will be done by me, too, and if you don't like it, you can go!'

Ben slumped down into a chair, grinned stupidly.

'Strikes me that'd be best,' I said.

'Well, that's it, then, isn't it!' She glared at me.

In her temper, on the edge of tears, she still maintained her engaging honesty; I knew her better then, I think. Sometimes we reach our greatest understanding in the middle of our greatest loss.

Ben, vacant still, mumbled, 'Jesus, me sweet man – what have I done to deserve all that thumpin'? I must have killed the Pope.'

'It's all right, darling, I'm here,' said Nanwen, stroking his face.

'That chap there comes storming in and belts me right and left. For God's sake, what for?'

I thought: as a man, O'Hara, you're about as useful as a fart in a breeze. What the hell did she see in you?

'Woman,' said he, 'what happened?'

'It's all right, Ben. I tell you, it's all right.'

I left them to it.

It was freezing in the street; putting up my coat collar, I mooched aimlessly over the Ogwen and up to the Hole. The chasms and galleries yawned at me in the light of a fleeting moon; it was cold coming back, but the air, though sprinkled with icy points of pain, was like a cleansing solace to my loneliness. When I got in they had all gone to bed, and I sat in the empty kitchen for a bit, staring into the dead fire, thinking of Ma Bron and Sam Jones, and what a time it had been for them as well.

By the time I went to bed I knew what to do.

We weren't in step, Nanwen and me; we were hearing different drummers.

Best to go, before it ended in trouble.

I didn't bargain for the actions of the Quarrymen's Combination.

They came in black severity; these, the leaders of the Union.

Late in the afternoon of the next day, they came – Henry Jones and Griffith Edwards, also Peter Roberts of Carneddi: William Evans came, he who had been dismissed by Lord Penrhyn for representing the men, also Robert Davies, the chairman of the 1896 Workers' Delegation. These, reserved and quiet, filed into the kitchen of Twelve Caerberllan.

And Ben sat before them, and would not meet their eyes.

They were ordinary workers like us, claiming neither rank nor privilege. But representing thousands, they had the right to order and dismiss; to complain and censure.

'Is it wise for you to stay for this, Mrs. O'Hara?' asked one.

Nanwen said, sitting beside Ben, 'I want to be with my husband.'

'And you?' The eyes of the committee turned to me; another said:

'There is a request that Tobias Davies be present; if necessary, as a material witness.'

'You'll get nothing out of me,' I answered.

'Let him stay,' said Ben, cynically. 'Can't ye see he's part of the family?'

They frowned up from the pages of the Combination books, and Henry Jones, the Strike Committee chairman, said:

'These accounts, entrusted to you, O'Hara, for the payment of relief to members of the Combination show a deficit of over fifteen pounds. The entries have been examined by the Strike Committee; all here are agreed upon the amount – do you admit the shortage?'

Ben nodded, his eyes lowered.

'And you cannot replace the money?'

Nanwen said, 'We can sell the furniture, Mr. Jones, but it won't make fifteen pounds.'

The shame of it had struck her in the face; she had the look of someone old.

'How much, then?'

Ben gestured emptily. 'Say half?'

Silence. They rustled papers, glancing at one another; I hated the cruelty of it, but recognised the justice. People were on the starve; they couldn't let it pass. Mr. Jones asked:

'Has there been illness in this house?'

'None,' said Nanwen. 'The money went on beer.'

'You knew this, Mrs. O'Hara?'

'She did not,' said Ben.

I heard footsteps in the Row outside; the bass questions

and replies of gathering men. Its money had been stolen; the Union demanded justice.

Mr. Jones said, 'Then you admit to converting Combination strike money to your own use?'

'I stole it, man,' said Ben, 'is that what you want?' He grinned, rubbing his unshaven face.

I stared at Nanwen. You, I thought, will have to share your life with this. Sweat sprang to her forehead and she wiped it into her hair.

We waited. Outside the cottage door the hobnailed boots of men were growing louder, impatient for justice.

They assessed the furniture's value at seven pounds; the sum outstanding was eight pounds one and fourpence.

'In terms of ethics, it could have been a thousand pounds, you realise that,' said the man Edwards. 'At the time of the men's greatest need, you stole from them.'

'Christ, get on with it, man,' said Ben, sighing.

'They no longer need you in this community.'

Nanwen's face was white, her hands clutched together in her lap.

Another said, 'It would be in the interests of your safety if you left here . . .'

'Ireland,' said Ben. 'Out of this God-forsaken country.'

'It is not God-forsaken,' said Mr. Jones, 'but it has been forsaken by the likes of you.' He shut the accounts. 'Right, then, let the Irish have you. A single fare for the two of you.'

'Three tickets,' said Nanwen, wearily, 'I've a child asleep upstairs.'

'Ah yes.'

They looked at each other with questioned finality.

One said, rising, 'Leave everything as it is, Mrs. O'Hara. Take only what food you have and the clothes you stand up in. Be prepared to go this afternoon – the Committee is concerned with your husband's safety.'

In the afternoon three men came and stamped their feet for warmth in the snow outside, waiting.

After helping Ben tie their bundles, I came down to the kitchen. Nanwen was standing there.

'You coming, too, Uncle Toby?' asked Ceinie, and I lifted her against me.

We moved awkwardly, contained by silence, Nanwen and me; words had vanished between us. The bruise on her cheek held me with relentless force. Above us Ben's boots were stamping the boards; the men outside were beating themselves for warmth.

'The Rhondda, is it?' asked Nanwen, empty.

'Aye,' I said. 'More'n likely.'

'Best you go back to your father's country, eh?'

'Good people – Tonypandy,' I said.

She smiled at me; her teeth were even and white against the pale curve of her lips. I said, *'Nan . . .'*

Head on one side, she smiled at me, and I knew a sudden sense of wild joy, a strange and intimate knowledge that one day, despite all this, she would be mine: this hope, ever with me, had an uncanny will to survive.

I said, 'One day I'll find you. One day, wherever you are, you'll be with me.'

It was a sort of self-unity just to stand there within reach of her.

'You'll do all right, Toby.'

'Aye, I expect.'

'More than one you'll lead up the gospel path down the Rhondda. You go south and forget about Nan, eh?' She laughed with her eyes. 'Poor old dab, like Grandad would say. Remember how he went with his trews half-mast?'

I thought desperately: *Come with me . . .!*

'Got to go,' she said, taking Ceinie.

Empty of her, I stood while Ben came clumping down the stairs, and I closed my eyes to her nearness; when I opened them, hers were full on my face.

'Good-bye, my darling,' she said.

I stood by the kiss-gate of Caerberllan, watching the three of them, with the Committee escorts either side, plodding through the snow to the station.

Ceinie, in Nanwen's arms, turned once to wave, but I could not wave back.

The wind was cold on my face, as I turned past Bodforris down the road to Betws, south, for the Rhondda.

Two

The Rhondda

CHAPTER NINETEEN

If I'd had the railway fare, like others getting out of the north about then, I'd have landed in the Rhondda down in South Wales that much earlier. But, after leaving Caerberllan, and losing Nanwen, there didn't seem much point in going anywhere at speed, so I took the road to Betws and Swallow Falls at my leisure, sleeping in barns. Llechwedd called me, probably because it was there that I had first met Nan, and I stood in the snow outside One Bodafon looking at the windows, until I saw Bando Jeremiah Williams eyeing me from Uncorn, so I turned up my collar and tramped back down to High.

As the days passed into weeks I came to know myself better. A good day's tramp along an empty, winter highway, I was finding, did much to dispel my sense of loss.

I worked for a farmer for a month's lodging that saw out December; I jugged out ale in a little public on the slopes of Moel Llyfant to the collarless labourers of the old Welsh farms; listening in the candle-lit tap to tales of poaching and trespass. I wouldn't have changed them for gold, these haughty old Welsh crows of the land with their gravy-stained waistcoats and drooping whiskers.

Come next April I was there in the tap, eyeing up the landlord's daughter and forking manure spare time, and there was a farm girl over in Dolgellau with plump round arms and hayseed on her breasts. She talked all through it about the coming Spring Outing; had she been quiet I could have imagined she was Nanwen.

The hawthorn was a shower of white blossom, I remember; and the heather blowing green waves in the wind as I took the road south again with the promise of the Rhondda and its coal slowly being forgotten in the fine comradeship of the cottage families, as I went from farm to farm, hiring out my labour.

This period of my life was like a peasant dance compared with the slog of Bethesda slate: the money was poor, the fare frugal, but my body thrived. I stayed a year in the Dolgellau country, taking labour and love where I found it, and life was off again, this time south-west to Aberdovey; late winter found me with the coastal fishermen.

What is there in the sea, I wonder, that brings such a pull to the blood?

Looking back, I reckon my years between the ages of twenty-three and twenty-five, spent on the sea, were about the happiest of my life: on reflection, I've often wondered why I changed the sea for coal.

These were flounder fishermen, the sailors of the little gunter-rigged smacks that wallowed in the Dovey estuary, and, if the tide was running right, braved it east into Cardigan Bay, coming back with loaded nets and gunwales awash if the shoals were about – mackerel, herring and the little cousins of the big flat-fish – the dainty gold-backed wrigglers of the sandy inlets.

During the summer of 1909, after a year of wandering the quays as a longshoreman, I heard the shout of the Rhondda again, as if something deeper than the sea was stirring, my own people; and I kicked off my sea-boots and put on hob-nails again, striking out through the narrow streets of lovely Aberdovey and up the sheep tracks of Cader Idris, the Mountain Chair of the Clouds.

Here, where the Roman legions formed after savaging Plinlimmon, I trudged in a new and marvellous loneliness, and washed myself in the tumbling brooks, the source of the Wye River; from its summit I saw the misted estuary and square-rigged schooners in the bay, where the barques and barges with slate from Portmadoc and coal from Barry lumbered into Tremadoc. South again I went, and into lovely Rhayader. Here, on a late June evening, I chopped firewood and swept out the stables of an old coaching station public on the road to Builith. It was rolling, lush farmland of fat sheep and buttocky cattle lowing for milking, and bright-faced young girls, pert and buxom. The landlord, I remember, was an old soldier from the Boer War; his missus thrived on cheek and customers – a boiling joint, if ever there was one, with a wicked eye on her and cherub lips.

It was here that I met the Wraith Girl of Rhayader: as this I still remember her.

There was a little room off the tap, and the woman was sitting on a chair in the middle of the floor. So still she sat that I wondered if she breathed; nor did she stir as I came closer with my tankard.

'You work here?' I asked; she did not reply.

She was no longer young; her face was pale, her gaze averted; I wondered if she were alive.

The sounds of the tap-room next door beat about us as I slowly circled her: amid the bass booming of men and the shrill laughter of women, this one sat as still as a fallen hand.

'You ill, missus?'

She was motionless, but I heard her breathing; a quick inrush of breath from one apparently transfixed.

I put down my ale.

She did not move even when I bent above her, gripping the back of her chair.

Her hands were clasped together on the coarse sack apron that covered her knees; her peasant's boots were cracked and broken. And then, suddenly, in the lights of a passing trap I saw her eyes fixed upon me. I had known a few women since my days with Nanwen, but none had asked me with her eyes, like this.

We fought in a passion of breath and kisses, and I drew her to her feet so that we were like writhing statues locked in the middle of darkness.

'You sleep upstairs?' I whispered.

She did not answer, but I saw her eyes, large and startled in the glow of the window moon, and again they spoke.

'Later, then?'

For answer, she loosened her hair of its clasps and let it fall over her shoulders. Later, I saw a light go on in a room over the barn.

I tell of this woman in detail since she is often in my mind.

Later still, I helped the landlord and his blowsy wife ease out the drunks

He, stunted by ale, moved like a motivated corpse, while she, with her great bare bosom pushed up like a whale in harness, winked at me coy. Her baggy obesity and painted eyes made the ghost of a woman who had died: pretty good pair, I reflected; strange housemates for the lonely little peasant.

In the cheeping of mice I left my bed and tiptoed down the corridors. The house was as still as an undertaker's. The peasant girl was awaiting me, her arms out to me from the bed.

In all truth, I never in my life had another night like it, but next morning I remembered little of it because of the Rhayader ale.

She never saw the going of me as I cocked up my boots along the road to Builth.

In a Builth Wells yard, taking the waters, I chanced upon a five-foot dwarf with a face like a navvy's arm-pit, a cupboard of obscenities, and he hadn't a decent leg under him: sporting leggings and a dandy's yellow waistcoat was he, with a walking stick made from the penis of a bull; he begged tobacco off me, but stole the lot, for his clay had a hole in it.

'How're ye faring, me darlin'?' he asked.

'Come down from North Wales,' I said.

'Through the city of Rhayader, was it?' and I knew him for bog Irish, with the same tunes in him as Ben O'Hara.

'Ay ay – last night,' and I started to get going.

'Then ye likely stayed at the inn, did ye not?'

Tiring of him, I was on my way when he called, 'You enjoyed the services of the deaf mute ghost, be chance, the Wraith Woman?'

It halted and turned me. Said he, 'Ach, t'is a legend round these parts – she gives of her favours if you happen to be under thirty and six foot up – like you, me boyo. She's a bright lass for the fellas, be God.'

I stared at him and he rolled tipsy, adding, 'Like a lover she once had, they say – a fine young sapling.' He blew out smoke at me. 'I've waited on her a bit meself, for she gives fine joys to a man, I heard say. But with me knocking sixty and five-foot-two, I've seen neither hide nor hair of her.'

'I have,' I replied, starting off again, 'and she was flesh and blood.'

The dwarf waved his stick at me. 'There's nobody living there save the old Boer War soldier and his painted missus – think again, son!' He glared at me

'As real as you, don't be daft,' I said.

'O, aye?' and he spat. 'Then I'll tell ye something – I'll lay ye twenty to one that ye've laid wi' the Wraith Girl of Rhayader, and the stain of it will lay upon ye soul. Now then!'

He crossed himself.

I went pretty fast along the road to the south.

In ancient Brecon, that still echoes to the clash of alien swords, I found employment, first with a wheelwright and then as a striker with a blacksmith in The Struet, and I stayed with him and his four-foot-high missus until the October Fair in the Bulwark. It was here that I laid out a pugilist from Swansea in the boxing booth, and collected a golden sovereign.

With this in my pocket and my hands still blistered from the anvil striking, I struck out over the mountains up to Merthyr, taking the old Roman road, Sarn Helen.

Snow was falling as I reached the Storey Arms, the half-way house of the drovers, and the tap was full when I entered, with the pugilist I had laid out there well into his cups before me, and a blind clergyman drinking deep of a brandy flask, with his guide dog lying by the fire.

Here the drovers were arguing in the bedlam of the tap-room: fine fierce oaths they used, sinking their ale in shouted banter, with an Irish melodeon blasting and Merthyr gipsy women kicking up their heels in the sawdust while the clergyman beat the time.

Outside, staining the snow, were thousands of sheep being driven up to the high valleys of the Aberdare and Merthyr; a maggoty, moving mass bleating for food.

What went on in the old Drovers' Arms that night was

nobody's business, for the place was rent with the squeals of women and the shouts of men. Come dawn, all was quiet. I never saw the going of them, save for the snow beaten into ice by countless tiny feet.

The clergyman, dozing by a cold fire, raised dead eyes at me from the folds of a fire-scarred face. That afternoon he was seen going down the old road to Brecon, which was the country of his fathers he had told me; later, he was found in the snow near Tregarth, with the guide dog strangled beside him.

A month later, while working as a haulier in the iron town of Merthyr, I saw a placard offering twenty pounds reward for the pugilist I had beaten at Brecon Fair, since he was wanted for the murder of the old blind clergyman, but I never heard of the end of it.

Unaccountably, during that month of labouring in Merthyr, I knew a clear and vibrant affinity with Nanwen; she appeared to be with me every hour. Such was the sense of her nearness, that I expected to see her around every corner, during my morning tramp from Abercanaid to Merthyr, where I worked. Later, I knew the reason for this.

I have never since neglected an inexplicable premonition.

I worked as a collier in Blaenafon, at the head of the Eastern Valley, as an ostler in Cwmglo, and a farrier over in Nanty; I lodged with a widow woman in Abertillery.

These were the great industrial valleys that ran over The Top to the land of iron and copper and the great rolling sulphur clouds; you could read a newspaper in the flashing of the furnace bungs.

Here worked the cosmopolitan communities that had flooded in during the earlier century; Europeans, and the endless columns of starving Irish who found their homes and graves in the iron towns where the beds, shift on, shift off, never grew cold. They were a bold people, their bodies hardened and enriched by intermingled blood – the dark-skinned Spanish, the gay Italians who courted the Celtic Irish, their folk-lore merging with the Welsh culture.

Spring had come to the land, and the Rhondda, when I

entered it that sunny afternoon in April 1910, was as bright as a young girl out in her Easter clothes, with the wild flowers of the mountains a madness of colour in the sun. Dandy wet-a-beds grew in yellow carpets along the lanes; bluebells waved their heads off in the woodland as I strode into the Coal Country. And I thought, as I walked alone down from the mountain, of the generations of men who had come in before me, seeking new lives in the valleys of the Coal Rush.

I thought of my father; of how he had come here with a pack on his back, as I, to settle in the pits of Tonypandy. After a year or so, he had told me, he had hungered for a wife, so he took himself to Gilfach Goch where the women were known to be extra decent. Here, at the Fair, he had sought out my mother; sweeping his bowler in the gutter, she related, while she curtsied back, but my wicked old Grandad showed him the door because she was Congregational and my father was Church of England.

But next morning he missed a shift, did my father, and was straight back over to Gilfach Goch, and what with Grandad shouting on the doorstep and my mother howling, it was a choice bit for the relatives, he said, with neighbours chipping in and children swinging on the gate. And up and down Glamorgan Terrace (they lived in Number Six) people were scandalised, apparently, because my Grandad was proving an awkward old sod. But, after a while my grandfather repented, and my father, done up posh in his new suit and funeral bowler, called and asked officially for her hand, but he had to go to Congregational.

Within a month my mother had been pledged, banned and bedded in Tonypandy, and since my father never did things by halves, nine months to the day she brought forth me.

I sighed, smiling at my thoughts as I plodded down the mountain sheep track into Gilfach Goch. And I stopped for a bit outside Number Six, Glamorgan Terrace, and touched the gate that my people's hands had touched, until I saw curtains move.

Then, I was away to Penygraig, and along the valley road to Tonypandy.

God must have been in a good humour when He fashioned the towns of the Rhondda, and had a great time inventing some of the names.

He must, I think, have made a fork of two fingers and laid them on the land, pressing them into the rich soil so that the big dividing ridges of Maerdy and Tynewydd rose up in between. The mountains, upon which He breathed in His labours, grew green; the land of His touch became fertile. One valley He called Rhondda Fach, the other Rhondda Fawr, and down each green belt He ran a foaming river.

It was a big country, like its granite sister-land up north; in the rounded hills lay unbounded wealth – timber, limestone, coal, and Man smelled its riches from afar.

The Coal Rush of the nineteenth century began.

Begging for food and money, the immigrants flooded in. Speculation mushroomed, leader-barons rose, and the twin valleys, divided communities of alien habits and customs, began to prosper. In the lust for wealth, pit after pit was sunk by imported navvies called sinkers. Little townships sprang up haphazardly around individual pits, often named after their engineers or owners – roughly a town to the mile by the year 1900, some overlapping; all joined in the south by a common road; here was the confluence of the two rivers, Fach and the Fawr. Communities like Maerdy and Ferndale rose in the Rhondda Fach; Treherbert, Treorchy and Trealaw darkened the sky of Rhondda Fawr.

Tonypandy, the town of my birth, lay near the end of the river confluence at Porth.

Now, with my bundle over my shoulder and whistling to have my teeth out, I strode through the Rhondda, past the two big Naval Pits and over the Adare Incline and on to Tonypandy square.

It was a gorgeous April afternoon and a Saturday long-pay day, too, and the place was crowded with people going about their business; broughams and traps, pony and dog-carts coming and going; melodeons playing in the gutters. Ragged tramps tugged at my sleeve for alms; wizened Irish, the refuse of the old Eastern Valley ironworks trudged in melancholy discontent among the poshed up, bowlered gentlemen bowing this way and that to hoop-skirted ladies: coloured parasols flourished, for the spring day was hot.

It was obvious to a stranger that the Rhondda, in the spring of 1910, despite its labour troubles, was doing well. With Glamorgan county sitting on a crock of gold, this was the end of the rainbow: over ten million tons of coal and coke were exported from Barry Docks alone that year, and most of it came from the Rhondda pits.

On I went, pushing my way through the crowded pavements – seeking lodgings first, then a job, and there was a new delight in me at being back among my father's people.

Most of the talk about me was English and the high lilt of the Irish; the Welsh I heard had a different song to the North in it, and I listened to a cheeky gaggle of women waiting on their doorsteps for the collier husbands. Sitting on backless chairs were they or leaning in doorways, their caps ready for their long-pay sovereigns. One of the younger ones, bright-eyed and generous in the breast, gave me a wink, and cried in a thick Irish brogue:

'*Arrah!* he looks a handy one. Irish, is it?'

'God, no Mary! – look at his nose – Welsh, for sure!'

'Wrong, missus,' and I joined their banter, for God help you if you didn't. 'I'm an Oriental Jew – where's Adams Street up by here?'

'Keep going – who're ye after, mun?'

'I tell you I'm after lodgings, Blod, and you'll be wiser than me!'

They shrieked at this, waving me down, and one shouted, 'I can fit ye in, mind, if me old man turns over!' and she shouted laughter, slapping her plump thigh. 'Lodgings, is it? Then keep off the Irish.'

'What about it now?' I asked, meaning business.

They pondered this, their crackered heads nodding in secret whispers. 'Ye could try Mrs. Smith up in Court Street?' said one.

'English?' said another. 'Come winter she'd be sliding his dinners under the door. You'd be best off with us, son. Welsh doors are always open to hospitality.'

'That's only so the blutty sheep can get out,' cried the young Irish.

'You try Mrs. Best at Number One, Chapel Street – she'll feed ye, if ye pay. She always buys the best, she says. Most round here'll play a harp on your ribs.'

'Or there's Angie No-Knickers, if ye aren't all that keen about eating!'

'*Diawch*, I haven't the strength.'

They sent me down to Chapel Street with their shrill voices, and I wouldn't have changed them for gold; their men were lucky – girls to hang on to in a stiff breeze.

When the mother of God arrives again, she'll likely come in a Welsh shawl.

Mrs. Best was scrubbing the front doorstep of her Number One as I came down Chapel Street, and she was of a different ilk to the women I had left. Wiping her little plump hands on her apron, she peered up at me from a warm cherub face.

'Bethesda, did ye say?'

'Some years back, mind,' and she gabbled, delighted. 'Come in, come in – there's always room for a likely lad.' But in the kitchen she saddened at me. 'But I can't 'ave ye long, because the Company's taking the roof off me – I lost me chap, ye know. Lancashire born and bred, he were.'

'I'm sorry,' I said.

'Aye, well, that's the way of it. The chest took him. Gone to a better home, hasn't he? Now they want the house, so I'm renting a cheaper one for lodgers over in Senghenydd – you know it?'

'Senghenydd? No.'

'Over in the Aber valley – good men there, too – easy lodgers. Welsh chaps who like the best. I never buy ought but the best, ye know.'

We grieved together, both for her loss and the imminence of our parting.

'But I can give ye a week or so if you fancy?'

'It'll tide me over, missus,' I said.

'Will ten shilling a week kill ye? You see, son, you got to pay for good stuff – in fact, I've just come back from Town with a pound of best neck from the Co-op – the divvie's handy, eh? I always sees to me gentlemen proper, you understand – Church of England, is it?' She peered at me with anxious eyes.

'Congregational.'

She patted herself for breath. 'Ah well, can't have everything. I'll get up and air your bed, son – I gave the place a good do through when me fella died.'

'Much obliged,' I said, and pulled my cap at her and went past the Square and along Dunraven, made a few enquiries along the way, and got myself signed on at the big Ely Pit; sixteen shillings a week starting next Monday morning day shift at six o'clock.

The Rhondda was paved with coal, right enough. It was all so easy that I couldn't believe it.

After settling myself in with Mrs. Best in Chapel Street, it was getting on for evening and with four shillings in my pocket I reckoned I deserved a pint on success, so I washed, shaved, brushed up and took me across the Square for a pint at the nearest public, the Pandy Inn.

The place was filling up with day shift colliers coming out of the two Naval Pits and the big Glamorgan colliery up at Llwynypia.

I had to shoulder my way into the big tap-room to get to the bar.

And the first woman I saw in there was Ma Bron, serving jugs behind the counter.

'Good God,' I whispered.

But she hadn't yet seen me, and she tripped into the room with a pint in her hand and the other one out to a collier, and he turned her in a circle while his mates clapped a jig.

The same old Bron, I thought, making the most of life; a dream of a woman now; older, mature.

In a world that was changing all the time, she was constant. And then I remembered that, when I'd last seen her and Sam after the casting out, they'd intended to make south for the Rhondda.

Vaguely, I wondered if Sam was still with her.

Laughing, her head back, Bron pushed her way back to the counter. Time died in her eyes when she saw me.

'Ay ay, Ma Bron,' I said.

I had the better of her. 'You're surprised?' I asked.

'*Toby Davies!*' she gasped. 'What you doing here?'

'Came in late today!'

'My, you've growed!' She looked me up and down in wonderment.

'That's what you always say.'

'But . . . I can't believe it. You're a man!' She snatched at my hands, pressing them in her joy. 'But it's eight years, mate – it must be – where you been?'

'Looking for you.' I landed her a wink.

'I bet! Scotching up that old Nan O'Hara, the Irishman's wife, more'n likely! But what ye doin' here?' Her face was alive, her whole being consuming me; people were watching her joy.

'Where's Sam, then?' I asked.

'Why are you interested?' She went cool on me.

'He was my mate,' I said.

'And mine, once.' She poured a jug, adding bitterly. 'But you didn't bed with Sam Jones, Toby, you only knew him.'

'You've left him?

'No woman leaves Sam – he left me.'

'Another skirt?' I asked, and she drew a long breath like the well of life going dry.

'What d'you expect?'

'But you stayed as bright and clean as a wash-day!'

She smiled, but not with her eyes. 'I ain't gone short.'

'Don't change, do you?' I said, and there was a sudden warmth in us. But the customers were becoming impatient, pushing and shoving.

'Can't talk now,' said she. 'See you tomorrow. I'm off all day tomorrow – Sunday.'

'Where?' I looked at the hostile faces around me and wondered if I was holding up their ale or imposing on their woman.

'On the Square by the fountain – two o'clock?'

'Are ye sure you're free?' I gave her a wry smile as she handed me a pint, and I sank it, watching her as she poured another.

'Now you're here,' she said.

I pushed my way out of the Pandy and into the clear April day.

The stars were shining over the mountains; life was suddenly incredibly beautiful, and full again.

Yet even the act of meeting Bron again had revived in me my longing for Nanwen.

I stood outside the Pandy, rubbing my chin reflectively.

'Well, I'm damned,' I said.

CHAPTER TWENTY

I lodged that night with Mrs. Best; next day at two o'clock I was waiting on the Square as decent as my tramping clothes allowed; in my cracked boots and faded coat and trews I scarcely matched Ma Bron's magnificence. Done up fine was she in a white blouse and a long black skirt, with her fair hair shining under her pink spring hat. Spinning her bright parasol over her shoulder, she looked like gentry. We went together as old friends should – arm in arm – turning every head as we passed: the Pandy barmaid courted by a tramp, no doubt, but the least to care was Bron.

Past the Rink we went and over the Taff Vale Railway line, and behind the Glamorgan colliery we climbed Mynydd Trealaw, taking the sheep tracks up Tyn-tyle mountain to the slopes of Penrhys and St. Mary's Well.

We didn't talk much; it was enough to be alone in this newly discovered friendship, and the mountain grass was flashing greenness in the warm sunlight with the promise of May: scitterbags of sheep, stained black with coal-dust, roamed about us in baa-ing contentment.

Below us the Sunday Rhondda simmered and chattered on the still, cool air.

Below the Holy Well we sat, and there was a warmth in us; I sought Bron's hand, and we laid together, eyes clenched to the red-blooded brilliance of the sun; strangely, I again remembered Nanwen.

'Life's queer, isn't it?' said Bron, invading my mind.

I sighed, resting on my elbow above her, tracing each feature of her face.

Her fair beauty had flowered. Neither time nor Sam Jones had begun to denounce the flawless quality of her skin; the girl had gone, leaving behind a woman.

'Good to be back with friends, I mean.'

'God, you're beautiful,' I said.

'That's what all the chaps say.'

'And all the chaps are right – what's wrong with Sam Jones – what does he want from life?'

It stirred her and she came up beside me. 'I know what he wants, and if I were a chap I'd blutty give it to him. All the time he was with me he was pickin' and choosing like a broody stallion, one skirt after another. There's no satisfying the fella.'

'He needs his head read.'

'That's why I took Bibbs-Two back up north to her aunt. She was born in Porth, bless her – down the road from here.' Bron lowered her eyes, playing with her fingers.

'Sam was all right for a bit, after Bibbs-Two was born, ye know; he came off the beer, he even used to dig the garden – we had a company house then, till he put one on the foreman's whiskers and got himself blacklisted in coal for six months – then he went labouring.' She sighed, 'We had it tough, I can tell ye. I used to take in washing to make ends meet – scrubbed me hands into holes, and the first money he earned he'd sink a pint and chase a barmaid.'

'When did you last hear of him?'

'Nine months back.' She stared at me. 'I haven't seen Bibbs for over two years you know – you can't keep a child in a house of bickering – she's coming up for eight now, would you believe it?'

She shook her head dolefully, adding, 'I was like some little rag doll. One day, he'd be all over me, next moment giving me a thumping – mind,' and her eyes flashed, 'he didn't get that all his own way, neither.' Quieter, she said, 'And so it went on, one year after another – job after job, back into coal one minute, on the blacklist the next – pit after pit – Treorchy, Wattstown, Treherbert – you name it, we'd been there; fighting it out and making it up – drinking, whoring – I never met such a man.'

'And then?'

She emptied her hands at me. 'He just vanished nine months back.' Picking a dandelion, she held its beauty up to the sun. Faintly, amid the soft bleating of the sheep, came the sound of traffic down on the Tyn-tyle Road, and

Mynydd-y-Gelli, on the other side of the valley, was stricken with swords of the sun. 'Aye, plain vanished. I had a letter ...'

'A letter?'

'From a woman in Porth at the end of the valley. Some kind soul – she didn't sign it. It was just after I started at the Pandy – a month or so after Sam left me final. It seems he was living with a Spanish piece in Hannah Street, near the station. I was over there like a rabbit, but the birds had flown. It was true enough, the neighbours told me.'

'He likes a change, does Sam.' I sighed.

'You know,' said she. 'I reckon he got hold of the only Spanish piece this side of Spain – I only ever heard of two in the Rhondda.'

'And you?'

'You know about me.'

'Tell me.'

'I've been around.' She glanced away.

'You'd be a fool if you hadn't.'

'And what about you, then? What about Tobias?' She playfully tripped my elbow from under me and we lay together but apart, laughing at the sky. 'I suppose you're the same old monk I rolled in the sheets in the Waterloo back bedroom?' She laughed gaily.

'Try me,' I said.

She cupped her chin in her hands and lay on her stomach. 'Ay ay – what about that old Nanwen, eh? That weren't so innocent.'

'You don't know Nanwen.'

'You ever think of her?'

'Of course, but she's in another age.' I sighed. 'Now I'm tucked up with Mrs. Best over in Chapel Street, and butter won't melt in my mouth; least, not till I see an opportunity.'

'Well, here's one coming up, and you can take it or leave it – there's room in my place!'

A silence grew within the day; the song of the birds was stilled; even the sheep listened.

Our smiles died and we faced each other, severe within the moment of decision.

'You really mean that?' I asked.

'It depends.'

'On what?'

'On what you want from it. You've just come in, haven't you? I've got one of the Sinkers huts behind the Pandy – it runs with the job. Time was that Sam was there with me – now I'm alone.' She paused, seeking words. 'But perhaps you'd like to look around – one thing's sure, you'd eat better with Mrs. Best.'

There was in her face such a tale of expectancy that I drew closer. It was the same magical Bron; the girl of Bethesda again. Of a sudden, I held her against me.

'Oh, God, Tobe – you come, eh? I got to put my arms round someone decent.'

I heard her words as an echo. We did not kiss. I just held her. Later, we rose and went down into the valley.

We wandered as people uncaring, lost in the renewed friendship, and there was a fine glory in the day, with the wind blowing wild and free about us, promising summer, and this warmth was in the pair of us.

'It's been a lonely old time, eh?' said Bron, after I'd told her my history.

'It's been all right,' I said. 'Like Grandpa used to say – there's only one way to take life, and that's by the scruff of the neck – you haven't had it so easy, either.'

'But easier than you; at least I had Sam for a bit.' She nudged me secretly, screwing up her eyes and wrinkling her nose at the sun. 'Dear me, now you've come me mind's as bright as a little girl's pinny.'

'The deacons'll have us,' I said, uneasily. 'They can be pretty stiff in the Rhondda.'

'And I'll have the deacons, down to the third generation. It's in the name of common humanity – a little bit of love and three square meals a day?'

'You were right the first time,' I said.

She turned me to face her and I saw the old Bron, abandoned and carefree, as if the Sunday had touched her with a naughty finger; the wind, suddenly rising, had got her hair, blowing it out behind her like a wand of gold; her eyes were alight with the old mischievous way. There was a fine wickedness in her; part of the earth that seemed to beat about us in all its simple beauty, diminishing loss; bringing to us a oneness I had never known before. A curtain had dropped over the past and brought our lives together.

It seemed natural that I should kiss her.

'Diawch, no!' said she, pushing and shoving. 'It's Sunday. But I'll make it up to ye back in the Sinkers, maybe.'

'I'll keep you up to that.'

We stood in each other's arms momentarily.

'One thing, though,' said she, softly. 'Come and go the best of 'em – and there's been a few – there'll always be Sam, ye know. I mean, he's my legal husband ain't he? If he lifts a finger, I go, mind.'

'You're mad.'

'Perhaps, but a woman can hope and I do me best to be honest.'

I'd have lived with her had she offered nothing but cooking.

'We'll handle Sam Jones when he arrives.'

'He'll arrive, he always does,' said Bron.

Such was the quietness between us then that I imagined I heard, like distant music, the old rivers Fach and Fawr, the beating hearts of the Rhondda, boasting and laughing their way over the crags to the sea.

CHAPTER TWENTY-ONE

And so, three weeks later, on the morning Mrs. Best was moving over to Senghenydd in the Aber Valley, I packed my bundle, left Chapel Street, and moved in with Bron at Number Six the Sinkers Huts on the other side of the Square.

'She'll lodge you well, son – a good soul is that Pandy barmaid – don't touch a drop, ye know – though she works among it.' Mrs. Best patted and smoothed me and straightened my collar like a mother. 'Don't forget now, if ever you want a change and come to the Aber Valley, you can count on me – pay for the best, you're entitled to it.' She bit on the sovereign I'd given her and slipped it under her apron, and I heaved up my bundle and took it over to the Sinkers, built years back for the navvies sinking the Scotch, the Glamorgan pit up the road in Llwynypia.

A lot asked me why I hadn't signed on at the Scotch, which was nearer, but I didn't fancy it. D. A. Thomas, who owned the Ely, wasn't the best of owners in the Rhondda, but he was a saint when it came to some. And in the three weeks I'd been on the Ely shift, I'd made good friends – people like Heinie Goldberg and Mattie Kelly.

The May morning I moved in with Bron was gay with sun; and even at that time of the morning the town was flourishing with people.

Every woman in sight seemed to be up and doing, scrubbing their fingers on the wash-boards, swilling out the tubs, cleaning windows, with happy good mornings right and left, and smells of frying bacon swept like perfume from the open doors of the terraces.

The Sinkers was alive with activity; biffs and howls coming out of the kitchens where children were being made ready for school; and the open drain down the back of the Huts was foaming with suds.

Already some of the older children were about – rushing

around with their great iron hoops; urchins were fighting or playing Dolly Stones; black-stockinged little girls in white pinafores sucking gob-stoppers and hopscotching on the Square. Ancient grandpas and grandmas, pale with Rhondda early hungers, were arranging backless chairs outside their doors; birds sang, cats arched to yapping dogs; the sun struck down from the mountains.

'Ay ay, missus,' I said, coming through the door of Number Six, and there was Bron with the bed made and going round with a duster like a woman demented.

'Not so much of the missus,' said she. 'You're a lodger, remember.'

I put my arms around her waist from the back and kissed her hair.

'*Jawch*, mun – one thing at a time,' she said, elbowing me off. 'How did you sleep?'

'Like a top if it hadn't been for Mrs. Best snoring.'

'Remember how your old Grandad used to snore, you said?'

'*Ach i fi* – don't remind me!'

'By the way – talking about Bethesda – did I mention the Arses?'

'Who?'

'The Arses – come on, you remember Albert and Annie and the kids who lived in old Caerberllan. They're in Tony-pandy. And the Livingstones ... Guto and his missus – I met them in Porth – poor soul – she's got a cross, Guto's still addled.'

She was at the sink now, tying back her hair.

'What takes you to Porth these days, then?' I asked.

'Is there a law against it?'

I said testily, 'I only asked you what takes you to Porth?'

'What takes anybody anywhere? – go where I like, can't I.'

'Because Sam is in Porth?'

Going to the table she began to cut my tommy box, sawing at the cottage loaf as if she had a coal owner roped to the table. 'Bread and dripping suit you?' she asked, ignoring me.

160

'Aye, fine – I've just had egg and bacon with Mrs. Best – it's a higher standard.'

'The standard's likely to drop,' said she, 'but I'll be waiting for you in the Pandy, when you come off shift.'

'I'll slip in for a couple of pints,' I said. 'One to settle the dust, the other to settle you.'

'That'd be the day. Best you go, or the lads'll be off without you.' She heaved aside my bundle. 'I'll wash this lot through and have it ironed by the time you're home.'

I kissed her like a man going to work; it seemed the most natural thing to do, and she looked at me strangely.

'You act as like you've been here years, you do,' she said.

'If I'd had any sense, I would have been.' I went out to the front and leaned on the railings beyond the gate, awaiting the coming of the colliers for shift.

If there was one woman hanging around outside I bet there was ten.

Mrs. Rachel Odd from next door, I saw first, and knocked up my cap to her. Fat and wheezy was Mrs. Odd, a boiling joint, with her old man's cap on top of her head and her sack apron pinned up on her stomach.

'How are you?' said she. 'Just off on shift, is it?' and the other women edged closer to get an ear in.

'Aye, missus,' I said, wary.

'I didn't get your name, really.'

'Toby Davies.'

'Just moved in, 'ave you?'

'Aye.'

'Down the Scotch, is it?'

'Ely,' I said.

She gazed sightlessly at the clouds, saying, 'I lost a brother down the Ely – lodging with Ma Bron now, are ye?'

'That's right.'

'She's a generous soul, but the stomach don't come first with some of the young ones, ye know.' She approached and patted me benevolently. 'Still, I expect she do come up with other exciting things.'

'I was just mentioning,' cried a woman, 'he's a real lovely fella.'

'Do he play a brass instrument?' asked Mrs. Primrose

Culpepper, coming up from Number Seven, and she was as hard to look at as the midday sun. 'My old man's in the band, actually, and he's looking for recruits, horn players mainly.'

I shook my head.

'That's a blessing, I say – got to be thankful for small mercies, haven't we? We got Will Parry Trumpet down in Number Eleven, for instance,' and she belched and pardoned. 'He can keep ye awake any shift – like up in Adare Terrace – remember that musician up there Rachel? Nine till five, six days a week we used to get the horn whether we wanted it or not. Ah well,' and she heaved up her stomach and set aside her broom. 'Got to go and get a little bit of fish for my chap – good luck, I say. Tell your Bron I'll be bringin' her a bit of custard tart directly. You like custard tart?'

She talked more, but I didn't take much notice since I was looking out for the colliers coming on to the Square; every woman was out that morning, I should think, waiting for the shift going on, including Bron.

'Thank God you've come,' I said, 'I've been having a hell of a time.'

'That's all right,' said she, handing me my tommy box. 'They dish it out, you hand it back – that's the way they expect it. Now you watch it, eh?' she gave me my tea bottle. 'The Ely, I mean.'

'Ach, forget it.'

'I mean it Tobe – she's a bitch – watch it.'

Every weekday shift the pit gangs collected; coming from different parts of Tonypandy and the valley towns beyond; each man aimed in his own direction, gathering mates on the way. On that first morning when I moved in with Bron, I was awaiting a gang from Trealaw; it picked up the Pandy men and was met by scores from Penygraig, on their way to the Glamorgan.

Near the Pandy it was joined by Heinie Goldberg and Mattie Kelly, the two mates I had got to know down the Ely.

'Here they come,' said Bron. 'You got everything?'

'Everything except you,' I said.

I heard Primrose say as she nudged Rachel Odd, 'But he's a well set-up fella, mind, and it anna any business of mine if folks ain't legally wed.'

Expectations of twins had Mrs. Odd, by the size of her; imminent.

'You're right, missus,' said Bron. 'It ain't.'

'Easy,' I said. 'Let them talk.'

'As long as I don't hear,' said Bron. 'She needs a clean up, that Primrose Culpepper, her mind especially.'

'See you later, lovely boy,' said Rachel Odd, dainty.

Four abreast, the Ely colliers, my gang, came marching along De Winton, their numbers swelling as others joined the column.

Doors were coming open like magic all round the square; files of men ran out of Church Street, Pandy Terrace and Cwrt to shouted good-byes.

'*Bore da' chwi!*' shouted Heinie Goldberg, my stall mate, and Mattie Kelly, an inch higher than Heinie's five foot, waved greeting beside him.

I took my place between them.

'Don't waste a lot of time, do ye, *bach*? I thought you was keeping Mrs. Best happy?'

'*Cythril!* Do you get around?' cried Mattie, his little cherubic face cocked up.

I ignored them, enveloped in the din of tramping boots and banter, and marched on, grinning.

'Barmaid at the Pandy, ain't she?' asked a third. '*Daw*, I'd rather have five minutes with her than the Chinese Strangler.'

'She even kissed him good-bye!'

I made a mental note to see it didn't happen again.

You had to take it; if you didn't they'd give you a hell of a day.

'But how do you handle a piece like that?'

'He handles it, if I know him,' said Heinie Goldberg.

'Reckon you'd be best down the Scotch,' growled Ben Block, all seventeen stones of him thumping along in front of me. 'Being nearer, ye could keep an eye on her.'

'It'd need my missus to get me down the Scotch,' said Mattie Kelly. 'I wouldn't take a stall down there if they paid me a fortune, eh, Heinie?'

Heinie shrugged, 'Mabon do think well of it, though.'

'O, aye?' shouted another, turning in the ranks. 'He wants to work it. Mabon himself's turning out to be a fraud, never mind coal owners.'

'All I hear around these parts is talk of this chap Mabon,' I said, happy at the change of subject.

This was the leader of the big Miners' Federation that was fighting to get better working conditions and pay for colliers. His true name was William Abraham, but he was better known by his Bardic title of Mabon. Member of Parliament for the Rhondda, he was the biggest thing that had happened to Welsh coal for a century, according to Heinie.

'Don't talk balls, Jew boy,' said Mattie Kelly, now. 'Mabon's like the rest of 'em – they start out all right but end in the pockets of the bosses.'

'Aye,' said a man nearby, and his face was that of a hawk, coal-grimed still, despite the bath; his eyes, black-laced, shone fiercely from his scarred cheeks. 'Big in the stomach now, and that is all. Time was that Mabon was all for the colliers; now he's in bed in the south of France with a coal owner either side.'

'I wish I was,' said Mattie, 'especially with a couple of their daughters, instead of going down the blutty Ely.'

'You don't treat folks fair,' said Heinie, bitterly. 'When you negotiate, you've got to hunt a bit with the hare as well as the hounds, stands to reason.'

I chanced a look at Heinie as we marched on towards the Ely. Fact was, I'd seen little enough of him, save for his little bald head popping up and down as we worked the stall in the light of the lamps. He looked to me more like an outsize gnome than a collier, with his little bits of cauliflowered ears attached to his skull, and his nose was as flat as a Japanese wrestler's, the Rhondda being a spawning ground for the Noble Art.

Gone was Heinie's first flush of youth, but he could fill a tram faster than any man on the five foot Bute seam, the new face causing all the trouble. Nigh forty years old, was Heinie, with the criss-cross tell-tales of hewing and fighting white above his cheeks. In his time he had held the great Shoni Engineer to a ten round draw at Scarrott's, but that was when he was young. When he was old he had taken on a lad called The Tylorstown Terror, a shin-bone wisp of a boy called Wilde: and the lad had laid one on Heinie's chin within seconds, knocking his eyes as crossed as Alfie Tit's in the Tonypandy Co-op. Down the stalls you had to watch him, too, since he'd eat out of other people's tins: once he had a wife, a slim-boned girl who died: Heinie hadn't eaten properly since, said Mattie.

'What was her name?' I asked early on, turning to face him under the eighteen inch roof.

'Leave me what I got of her,' said Heinie.

Now the cage door slammed behind us and we were going down the Ely: she was a treacly mess of engine oil from the workings, and water fifty feet deep, had a sump at the bottom, and it always chilled me. One day the brake will slide on the drum, I thought, and we'll be down, down, past the Bute landing road and into that sump; oil, water, coal-dust. Sometimes, in dreams, I heard Heinie choking and Mattie Kelly gasping as the winding gear snapped and we dropped down, down, *down*.

In years of it, I never got used to the cage, least of all the Ely.

'One day it won't stop, ye know.'

'Don't talk daft,' said Heinie.

He was a philosopher when it came to consolations; perhaps life meant less to him than me, now I had found Ma Bron.

Stripped to the belts, we laboured; cutting the coal and bunging it back with our feet in the stall – Heinie, Mattie Kelly, Ben Block and me, and every time you lifted your nut you hit the top of the five foot seam, which was more like two-foot-six.

'You shift your backside like that again and I'll have this pick up it,' said Ben, double bass; heavy in the chest he was, and sweating like a Spanish bull. Strong for his God was Ben, with drinking and fornication a long way down his list.

'I'm coming round,' I said, twisting sideways under the roof of coal, and I thought of sunlight a couple of thousand feet up, and Bron, her bright hair shining, pegging out her washing.

'Get the muck back,' said Mattie, working beside me. 'Ben Block's by 'ere and he keeps filling my tram.'

'You should worry,' said Heinie.

'His eyes are going,' said Mr. Duck Evans, a new man, crawling up with his curling box (with this he scooped up our coal and emptied it into our tram) and I thought of my old foreman, Dan Morgan, of Blaenau, whose eyes, I supposed, had long since gone.

'Ben ain't what he used to be,' said Heinie, packing the gob, and I could hear the rats squealing inside as he hammered the rubbish under the roof to support it, replacing the coal we had taken out; forget to pack up the gob and the roof came down. 'You heard what happened last week?'

I shook my head, pondering the roof for cracks. Heinie said, 'Somebody down at the landing put a dead rat up the sleeve of Ben's coat, and he took it home to his missus for a kitten.'

'Poor old sod,' said Mattie. 'His brain's gone, too – like yours, Heinie.'

'More than likely,' replied Heinie, grinning. 'Last month – before you come in, Toby, the fireman sent Ben and me up to the junction to give the lads a hand; he was in one stall, and I was next door in the other. "You in there, Heinie, lad?" he shouts. "Ay ay, Ben, it's me," I called back, and he yells, "Then just swing us a bit o' your chalk over the wall, mun, I want to mark up for the foreman," and I puts my head over to see what was happening and the sod clouts it with his shovel. "That was my head, ye silly old bugger," I told him, and I slid down the wall my side with a lump on me head as big as a duck's egg, and he comes over the wall and hits me with his shovel again, shouting, "Half o' that will do, boyo – I don't need a bit as big as ye head, ye know," and he still didn't get any chalk.'

'Mind, your bald head, when shining, do look like chalk,

166

Heinie,' said Mattie Kelly, grave, and just then Ben Block sat back on his hunkers and said, 'We'd best mark up for the foreman, Heinie – you got a bit o' chalk down by 'ere?'

'Christ,' said Heinie, and got out and sat under the belly of Lark, our horse.

Really, she was only down for a lark, this old mare, that's why Mr. Duck Evans, the Stall Ten haulier, called her that. And it was a caution to hear him talking to her. 'Now come on, Lark, my girl,' he used to say, very educated, 'put your best hoof forward; you are such a lazy old mare, you shouldn't really be with decent horses, should you?' and he would feed her what was left of his tommy box or even give her a drink from his jack.

Everybody used to bring down scraps for the horses, and we were lucky with Lark since she was a canny old devil. We didn't do a lot of ripping the roof (making a wide groove to get the horse's head into the stall) because Lark used to bend her knees for us if the roof got low, and a mare like this is worth a few apple cores, instead of the whips, like some of the hauliers hand out underground. One down the Scotch used to hit his horse with a sprag. 'That horse'll bloody have you one day,' Heinie told him.

'Hit that mare with the nearest thing handy, he would,' said Duck, 'and the old horse just awaited his time. And one night shift, when there was nobody about, he got that damned chap in a narrow place and squeezed the blutty life out of him.'

'Killed him?' I asked.

'You try breathing, with a horse leaning on ye,' said Duck. 'I always treats my animals respectably, don't I, Lark?' he cried, and threw his mare a piece of his cheese, but a rat scuttled out of the gob and took it before it stopped rolling.

I noticed that the lamps were going a bit dim as we settled in the stall with our tommy boxes. 'You got much gas here?' I asked.

'Now and then,' said Heinie, lying back with his boots cocked up. 'The big Universal over at Senghenydd is the place for gas if you want it; down here in the Ely it's mainly roof falls and water.'

'Mind, Lark will tell ye about the roof,' said Mattie, biting into his bait. 'Horses are better at detecting a roof fall chance than canaries are on gas.'

'She turns up her eyes,' said Duck, proudly. 'I've seen my old Lark going down the road wi' a journey of trams behind her like an express train, and the chap'd be a fool who didn't get after her. Twice in two years she's saved me on falls.'

'And water?' I asked.

'The Ely's a wet bitch, some places,' said Ben Block, heavily, and he bit out a great wedge of cheese and packed his mouth with bread. 'I had water twice down by 'ere.'

'You never said,' mentioned Heinie.

'He never had it,' said Mattie, 'he's thinking o' somewhere else – now come on, Ben, come on!'

'Down this pit, I tell you – 'fore you lot kissed a collier's arse,' grumbled Ben, wheezing fat. 'I was getting out the pookings – working wi' an old slate Johnny North – and the face went down while he was picking, poor old bugger. He hadn't got a lot of breath as it were, and with water over our mouths he breathed less. I got him out, but he died. I was fourteen, I remember.' He sighed deep and we chewed silently, thinking of the old collier who drowned. 'Next morning, when I come up with his body, the agent stopped me tenpence for lost chalk. I used to get eight bob a week, those days, and had to keep me ma and two sisters. Christ, times was bad.'

'They're not much better now,' said Heinie, 'on the old Sliding Scale.' He sighed. 'And we got trouble coming soon, sure enough.'

I was just about to ask what the Sliding Scale was when Mr. Richard Jones came up and ducked his head into our stall.

'Trouble's just arrived,' said Mattie.

Mr. Richard Jones, the Ely Lodge chairman, had a face of undertaker grey, a lanky figure to match, and tired eyes in his battered cheeks where years of coal had cut their lace; nobody spoke as he sat by the gob, opened his tommy box and took out his grub.

'You lot on a Roman holiday, then?' His voice was a surprise, being bass and beautiful.

'We was just working out who's pinched the Union funds,' said Heinie. 'How's Mabon?'

The Union man ate daintily, and his hands were clean; age had wearied him, but in him I sensed was a latent fire.

'Mabon is doing reasonably well for you ungrateful people,' said he. 'The fact that I don't think he's got our real interests at heart these days don't say anything for the old days – he was good in '77 when we elected him Miners' Leader.'

'That was in 1877,' said Ben Block. 'I'd decapitate the bugger if I had him down by 'ere today.'

I said, 'I'm new, Mr. Jones, so I can't talk much, but it strikes me that what we want is more Union representatives and less Members of Parliament.'

His eyes raised to mine.

'Nobody seems to think a lot of Mabon,' I added.

'That's because few of us take the trouble to discover what he's trying to do.' He sighed. 'Paid Members of Parliament was one of the old Chartist aims, eh? – now you've got parliamentary representation, don't you want it?'

'We've got Lloyd George,' said Mattie, 'but we're still in trouble.' He cursed silently. 'Also, we've got abnormal places down 'ere, too. People like Mabon and Mainwaring want to try shovelling some of this lot.'

This Bute Seam down the Ely Pit was the cause of most of the colliers' complaints, I was finding. Wherever you went in the Rhondda these days, there was talk of it, and argument was hot.

Mr. Thomas, owner of the big Cambrian Combine, had offered us a rate of one-and-nine a ton, and the Union was after two-and-sixpence, on the grounds that within the seam were abnormal places – rock and shale interspersed with the coal. Also, Mr. Thomas would only pay for large coal left on the screen; this was unfair: to get at the coal in abnormal places you had to break it up. 'Two-and-sixpence is a living wage, Mr. Jones,' said Mattie now, 'it ain't asking much. One-and-nine means starvation.'

'You know what'll happen,' said Heinie. 'We'll come out.'

'Strike? And what about the Conciliation Board that's

169

sitting now?' asked Mr. Jones politely, 'Won't you give them a chance to bridge the gap?'

'Sod the Conciliation Board,' said Ben, 'all they do is talk – I got kids at home, an' they need feeding.'

'It ain't fair, and you know it, Mr. Jones,' cried Heinie. 'From the time this five foot was opened, she's been abnormal.'

'It is what has been agreed. Don't blame me,' the old man said, 'blame the Board.' He raised his eyes to mine. 'I've seen you before, son – have we got your Union contribution?'

'Contribution?' cried Mattie. 'Up north in the Workers' Combination, he kept the funds, didn't you, Tobe?'

'I helped collect subscriptions,' I said, 'nothing more.'

'The O'Hara business was it?' asked Mr. Jones, and it surprised me.

'You heard of that down here?' I asked, and he replied:

'Not much misses the Federation. Unless we keep a national blacklist, they shift their roots and try it again somewhere else – brothers in need, God help us – we've just got rid of one.' He sighed. 'So we're needing a new Lodge treasurer – would you care to give a hand?'

'He's an able scholar, aren't you, Tobe?' said Mattie, warmly.

I got up and wandered away down the heading and hoped that was the end of it.

That night, after my Ely shift, Bron and I came home from the Pandy hand in hand. Dusk was settling over the mountain, polishing the stars, and her room in the Sinkers looked pretty, save for its dividing blanket down the middle, which she was pleased to call the Walls of Jericho – nuns one side, said she, monks on the other.

Bron had rearranged the furniture too, apparently. On her side of the blanket – the larger room – were the chairs and table; a wash-stand, dolly and tub in the corner, and, of course, the grate for cooking – plus, of course, the double bed she had once shared with Sam. On the monk's side of the drape was the bed that had once belonged to Bibbs-Two – a narrow old cronk of a thing knocked up by Sam, and this bed of pain was now mine. So Bron was in feathers and I was on boards – and all protests were dismissed with an airy wave of her hand. Earlier, she had climbed the mountain and returned with wild flowers, decorating both rooms; they were as pretty as anyone could make a hut that was built to house navvies; even on the room door she had hung flowers, and her doorstep was scrubbled whiter than Mrs. Rachel Odd's next door, which was saying something.

'Good smell,' I said, 'What have we got?'

'Irish stew – they can keep their lobscows up North.'

'I'd rather eat you,' I said, but she moved neatly out of my arms and began to lay the table.

I thought she looked beautiful as I sat by the grate and filled my clay.

'Don't smoke now, Tobe – we're just going to eat,' she said.

There was about her a grace that approached elegance: I had noticed this before.

She was not a small woman, and her red and white gingham dress enhanced her fine figure, which she made the best of in the right places, being Bron. She had done her hair in a different way, too; it hung in fair ringlets either side of her face. And suddenly, unaccountably, it seemed that she was Nanwen; she of the dark Iberian beauty that so contrasted Bron's.

It was incredible: as if Nan, smaller, dark, had entered the room and slipped into Bron's dress: that it was she laying the table as a ghost of the past. It was a phenomena I never explained.

Then the woman at the table turned and smiled, and she was Bron again.

'You're quiet for a change.'

'One thing at a time – get your feet in first, eh?'

A silence came; you could have touched it. She added, going to the grate and stirring the pot. 'You seen Nan O'Hara since you left Pesda?'

'No.'

'Ever think of her?' she tasted the stew, gasping at the steam.

'Of course.'

'You still love her?'

'Queer time to ask that – tasting stew.'

'Come on, you've had my life story.'

I got up and wandered about. 'Aye.'

'I'll say one thing, you were always honest.' She sighed, ladling the stew into bowls. 'God, we're a queer lot, ain't we? Sometimes I do think the human race is mad – you in here and in love with Nan O'Hara; me cooking you stew and dreaming of Sam.'

'That's the way it goes. Got to make the best of it.'

'You known any other women since you left up North?'

I brought a bowl to the table while she cut the bread. 'You're looking at one of the original virgins.'

'I bet!' She giggled like the old Bron, wrinkling her nose. 'Dear me, you take me right back to Bethesda!'

'I used to throw stones at it then, but it won't happen again,' I said. 'Now tell me the truth and shame the devil – all that has happened to you these years.'

We sat down and I faced her over her white tablecloth; it was going at the creases, I noticed, but no woman I ever met washed whiter than Bron.

'My business,' she replied.

'One law for me and another for you, I suppose.'

'Keep 'em dancing!'

'That one of your rules?'

The smile died on her mouth. 'It is now.'

'What do you mean by that?'

'Sam put me up on the shelf, but I'm not coming off it for anyone just like that – least of all you.'

We ate in silence. The noises of the town were dying: mouse-dreaming, an owl shrieked from the trees as if awakened from slumber. Somebody was emptying a tin bath down the gullyway – a man off shift, probably a farrier; they kept queer times.

'It's Sam, isn't it?' I said. 'We'll never be without the sod.'

'Don't call him that! Sam's all right. It's just, well ... just that he's a wicked old bugger. He can't help that.'

'Why the devil did you take me in then?'

She raised her face. 'Because I'm not having you lodging with anyone – I want to know you're kept decently, eating proper...' She faltered, looking close to tears.

'A sort of dogs' home then, is it?'

'You mean more to me than you think.'

'It sounds like it.'

She seemed to be slipping away from me for a ghost who didn't give a damn for her.

Parting the window curtains, I saw a few urchins lounging around the lamp-light; a man was sitting in the road close to the Pandy singing a faint, drunken song.

From the bosh, Bron said, 'It's custard and apricots for afters, mind.'

A faint memory whispered to me out of the past: I remembered the bedroom in the Waterloo at Bethesda, a love-making gone wrong. Trust her to humour the situation.

'Strikes me it isn't any more successful this time,' I said.

Deliberately, she crossed the room and stood before me, then reached up slowly and put her arms about my neck. 'I tell you what, Tobe – I can't explain why, but sometimes you mean more to me than Sam.'

I made to turn away, but she held me, her eyes moving over my face.

'Damned women,' I said, 'it sounds like it.'

Later, I said in the darkness, 'You asleep, Bron?'

Etched against faint moonlight, like marble, was her face; her lashes dark on her cheeks. Strange about Ma Bron; her hair was like gold, her lashes black.

'Toby, go back to bed.' She sighed in half sleep.

'Go on – shift over, so I can come in, is it? You said that to me once, remember.'

'Up half the night? – you'll miss the morning shift.'

'To the devil with the shift – come on, Bron, be a sport.'

'*Arglwydd!* Go *home!*'

A pattern of moonlight crossed the floor as I lay in the narrow bed and listened to Ma Bron's soft breathing – on the other side of the blanket.

I dreamed, I remember, of colliers and love-making. And, beneath my pillow the plaintive earth heaved; the mountain groaning to the lances in her side as the roof falls bellowed down the old workings and the water swirled two thousand feet below: colliers I dreamed of first, Bron later:

'There's gas about, lads – look at this lamp fading . . .'

'Slip up to the lamp room and fetch a blutty canary.'

'Aw, come off it, you're bleeding all over me knees.'

'He tells a good tale, though – reckons he was in the 1901 Senghenydd!'

'He do say that little boys burn blue – blue as the sky those little fellas burned down Senghy, according to Joe – about eighty caught.'

'And a hundred and forty-six died at Risca, a hundred and fourteen at Cymmer, an' a hundred and seventy-six over at Llanerch, remember?'

I heard them talking; the colliers of the past. In my sweating dreams, when I should have been in the arms of Bron, I lived again my inner fears of the Ely sump; and the ghosts of a lost generation spoke softly:

'Two hundred and sixty-eight dead at Abercarn, remember – sixty at Ferndale – Christ, the Rhondda's had her share in her time – and the water'll come in down that blutty Ely one day for sure, you watch . . .'

'Where did you collect it, Daio?' and the wraith of an answer, falsetto, came:

'I catched it down the Albion in 1894, with another two hundred and eighty-nine – and I'm still blutty down there – charred as the cinders of Hell.'

'Christ Almighty!' I exclaimed, and sat up in the bed.

'You all right, Tobe?' Bron this time, from the other side of the blanket; the living, not the dead.

'Aye,' I said, sweating. 'Just having a nightmare.'

'Can ye have it quieter?'

I dreamed again; this time of happier things:

'Come on, Bron!'

'All the girls have got it and all the girls hang on to it,' said Heinie Goldberg in that dream.

And the voice of Bron from behind the blanket again, 'Now stop it, Toby, go to sleep.'

Up and down Tonypandy, over to Gilfach Goch, via Pentre, into the Trealaw Ward, I cursed Sam Jones.

The morning shouted his promise of summer. Stripped to the belt, I went out the back to the pump. The mountains were lying on their backs, rubbing their eyes and yawning at

the sun: earlier, I had heard the early shift ostlers and farriers (being with horses they were always first on) going up to
the Cambrian and Scotch. The two Navals were beginning
to thump and whine their pit engines from the Adare Incline; trucks and railwaymen were clanking and shunting,
and the statue of Archibald Hood still pointed the way to his
colliery. If I had my way I'd turn that bugger round, said
Heinie once. And Bron, looking gay and lovely in a summer
dress, came out of the little privy down the back, and her
hair was lying on her shoulders. Her fair, Brythonic beauty,
fair as an angel, flowered before me.

Later, while I was whistling and blowing, diving my head
under the pump, Bron began to comb out her long, bright
hair in the sun.

'Have a good night, my lovely?'

'I had the wedding night of a Franciscan friar.'

'But don't ye feel marvellous, now you've managed it?'

'Sure as Fate I'll have you one day, missus,' I said, and
tossed my towel across my shoulders and opened the door of
the back.

All up and down the Row men were washing, bubbling
and gasping; Moses Culpepper was in his tin bath on his
cabbage patch, with his missus shrieking for a pig-sticking
and throwing buckets at him while he bawled and hollered.
It was a sight for sore eyes, said Bron, seeing Moses in the
bath, and I prefer him in bulrushes.

'Just been talking to Wendy Fourpence over at the De
Winton,' said she.

'Oh, yes?' I tried to ignore her.

'Got an eye for you, she has – "Who's that big handsome
collier you're living with, Bron?" she asked – the damned
cheek of it!'

'A few more days of this and I'll be trying Wendy Fourpence,' I said.

'You run Wendy Fourpence and you're not coming back
here alive!' said Bron, her eyes flashing.

'Good for the goose, good for the gander,' I said. 'You
have Sam, I'll spend fourpence.'

'*Toby!*'

I ran for it, chuckling.

CHAPTER TWENTY-TWO

Things were getting tighter in the Rhondda a few weeks later; it looked as if I had dropped right into it; but not so tight that I couldn't take Bron out (even though I'd just been laid off for a fortnight) – this being Fair Day and her Saturday night off from the Pandy.

Heinie said now, lowering his glass at the bar. 'Wages were all right on the Sliding Scale till they signed the Boer War peace.'

'Come on,' I said to Bron as she served the jugs, 'don't get into politics!'

'Wages was all right till the Boer War started,' said Mattie. 'Now we can't afford the price of a pint.'

'You killed that one all right,' said Bron, taking his glass for polishing. 'And most of you seem to have the price of a drink when you come in here.' She was done up to the nines in a bright, pink frock, and I was eager to get her to myself. A man cried, 'Stick to pouring ale, woman, and leave the wages to ye betters – it's worse'n being back home wi' my missus.'

'Aye, and God help your missus, I say,' countered Bron. 'You don't go short, Billy Price, with your kids out working and your mother-in-law on the parish.'

'Mind,' said Mattie, chewing, 'there's still good money to be had in the valleys.'

'But not getting coal.' An old ironworker from Tredegar, this one, with one blue eye shining in his scalded face where the other had been plucked out by fire. 'Owners like Thomas should be gelded, I say – lest they start paying for small coal, the Rhondda's heading for trouble.'

Bron smacked down a glass on the counter and put her hat on. 'You hang down a rock face up north with Lord Penrhyn, laddo, and you'd go thinner in the belly on slate. Ready, Tobe? – this lot don't know when they're lucky.'

'We'll vote you in on the Miners Federation,' called

Mattie. 'With views like that you ought to be in bed wi' Mabon.'

'If I work things right I ain't in bed with anyone,' said Bron. 'Where's my flower?' and she took my arm.

Very spruce and done up, me, that Fair night; boots to shave in, bowler polished like a real Heath hat; alpaca suit buttoned down the front, a wing collar cutting my throat, hair smarmed down with water. And Ma Bron, ankle deep in that ravishing pink, looking as exotic as an orchid with her hair piled high and diamanté earrings, and she treated me that night like I was the only man alive. Along De Winton we went arm in arm, turning every head on the street.

'You don't get any older,' I said. 'It's not fair on the others.'

'Some people grow old inside,' said she, bowing to people.

'Still got Sam with us, have we?'

'Many don't have a lot to show for their mistakes, Tobe; now I've got you.'

'And what have I got that Sam Jones hasn't?'

'You're here,' said she.

Because it was Fair night the Scarrott boxing marquee was in the fairground behind the Pandy, and was packed with people come in from the valley. De Winton itself was a jabber of foreign tongues, too – Welsh and English, French and Italian thrown in, and half the thick-eared fraternity from Bristol and Cardiff seemed to be there, queuing outside the chemist's for cobwebs and leeches for cuts. Some of the local boys like Snookey Boxer, Martin Fury and Dai Rush I recognised, also the ageing Shoni Engineer who had hit Heinie about, and talk was that Jimmy Wilde himself was in Town for an exhibition.

Beer parties were over from Gilfach Goch and Porth – even the dead rose in the cemetery, folks said, to hear the Salvation Army playing *Washed in the blood of Jesus* outside the Pandy Inn. Drunks were already on the streets; fancy folk from the big houses strolling with their parasols and canes, the gentry big hats going round at the sight of Bron's beauty, and Bound and Wilkins the milliners, were doing a brisk trade with the farm women down from the hills.

Patsy Pearl, leading light of the Vale harlots, gave Bron a slow, sad smile outside the De Winton jug and bottle.

'How you doing, Patsy?' asked Bron, stopping.

'Passable.'

'Don't see you much down the Pandy these nights.'

'I used to come a lot before, though,' said Patsy, pale.

'That chap still drinks there, you know?'

They smiled at each other. It was women's business; I looked away. There was in Patsy's face a light; later, Bron told me that she was in love.

'But she does better than a Turkish harem,' I protested.

'Men don't understand.'

Next door to the De Winton, in the little market place, the stalls of the home-produce women were end to end, for this was Fair night and everything was open, including the mortuary.

Cockle women were here in their black, nun-like habit, crying their wares: fat butterpat women, with red, chubby hands, the market wives of the mountains, and their language was pure Welsh: duffing up the great mounds of butter and slapping it into pats, shouting their banter at the passing people: here were the sweet stalls, the bawdy Irish confectioners with their bugs whiskers, bullseyes, gobstoppers; Everlasting Toffee and Toffee Rex tins of gorgeous creamy mints, with liquorice by the yard.

Mrs. 'Catty' Ledoux was there on her meat stall, skewing up the horse-meat with wheedling flourishes of her claw-like fingers; Mrs. Mia Bellini was selling her ice-cream, yelling its quality in her shrill Italian. May Plain and Dora Dobie, the washer-women, were selling starch and hunks of conservancy soap. There was black pudding, faggots and peas and bright, red polonys sizzling and bubbling in savoury pans, and the smell sent my mouth watering.

'My God, there's style for ye,' cried Mrs. O'Leary, pointing her ladle at Bron. 'Where did ye get that rig-out, love?'

'Over at Wilkins, do ye like it?' Bron pirouetted, arms out.

'Sufferin' God, all you want is a man, me girl! Like me!

My fella's out drinking, and me working me fingers to the bone!'

We bought steaming faggots and peas from her, watching her ladling it into the bowls. 'Are you pledged to him, Bron? *Ach*, stay single, girl – he'll bed ye and land ye with six like mine – honest to God, t'is only me chap's drinking, ye see – he takes no comfort in other women, like some I could mention.'

'Is that a fact?' demanded Mrs. Shanklyn, on the faggots.

The peas plopped and steamed and we got our teeth into them, jostled and bustled on the pavement, screwing up our faces to the scald of it, blowing to cool it, and Mrs. O'Leary whispered confidentially, 'Don't ye know it, Bron – the Shanklyn chap's up to his knees in strange women – anna that right, Shanklyn?' and she slapped her mate on the shoulder. 'Patsy Pearl, ye say? My fella, ye say? Sure to God if Patsy took him to bed it'd need me over in Clydach to come and switch him on,' and she bellowed laughter, her great breasts shaking.

With the faggots and peas down us, we bought a string of polonys, and Tonypandy, endlessly gay and endlessly in grief, flooded past us on the pavements.

Gangs of rowdies were pushing in and out of the crowds, and the language they were using took the skin off Satan: in droves came the children, the ragged, muffled new generation following the Salvationist band, ear-deafening in its blasts of trombones and tubers. The Temperance Legion was out again, always on Saturdays, coming in single file along Dunraven and De Winton, holding high their banners of sobriety despite the catcalls of following urchins: feigning drunkenness came others, a tatterdemalion riff-raff, a thriving element of the Rhondda's soul: from the lodging and dosshouses came these, whole families; rickety children, some as bandy as hoops, paraded in shouting, jostling columns of the Rhondda; they knew no trade. This was the human refuse that hangs on to the coat of Industry; living amid squalor in the slums, a livelihood of horse-minding, begging and stealing small coal from the patches; sheep-killing, when the opportunity presented.

'*Scarlet* woman,' said a man, and handed Bron a copy of

The Trumpet of Temperance. 'Are you not the female who serves alcohol behind the counter of the Pandy?'

His age was saving him, but his battered elegance stilled us; education in any form commands respect.

'Get on your way, old man,' I said, but he faced me with resolution, bracing back his thin shoulders. Speechless, I spluttered at him while Mrs Shanklyn and Mrs. O'Leary shook with mirth as the band thundered past. Bron handled it better; opening the paper she read it steadily, then folded it and gave it back to the man.

'You know,' said she, 'every time a Welshman lifts a pint he looks around for John Wesley. The trouble with piety, old man, is that those who spout it are usually sods.'

It quelled him: fuming, he snatched the paper from her and ran after the banners.

Strange, I thought, this mercurial ability of Bron to change; one moment she had the language of the educated; next, that of the gutter.

In a peculiar way it added to her charms.

Now, amid the yelling, joyful crowd we danced to the music of the merry-go-round; were caught up in the strident orchestra of the Rink steam engine with its ten feet iron wheels and boiler belching sparks; a harmonic pandemonium of sounds. Pickpockets were active, slouching through the packed bodies with sullen intent; rowdies out of the Pandy were trying to pick fights: there were coconut shies, target shooting: chairoplanes and swingboats.

It was Tonypandy Fair, where pallid children wandered in search of dropped bread while fat buckeroos of men tumbled bank notes in total disregard. Here went the street hawkers, rock vendors and stall criers, the cat-meat men, muffin men, medicine quacks; every one knowing many reasons why this was the greatest town on earth, except Porth, if you came from Porth, or Maerdy if you came from Little Moscow, as it was later called.

Mrs Annie Arse and Albert we came upon by the stalls, with Tommy and Rosie, the children. 'Remember, I told you that the Arses were in town?' cried Bron.

'Well, I never!' I shook Albert's hand and Annie patted and softened at me, and it was good to meet old friends. But the years, if they had grown the children, had sullied Albert and Annie: poverty was written on their clothes. Tommy, now knocking fourteen, was a man before his time: dark handsome, independent and ragged, his fists were on his hips. Rosie was big in all the right places, her young face expectant with its inner joys.

'And Tommy growing up, Toby Davies – you noticed?' asked Annie, thin as a lathe. 'Things haven't been too good with us, you know – skinny on the parish, but we managed to feed him, eh?'

'They're both a credit to you,' I said.

'Take a bit of handling, mind – don't they Albert? – our Rosie especially – a caution, ain't you, Rosie?'

'She's a good girl, though,' said Albert, meek.

'You heard from the O'Haras since they went to Ireland?' asked Annie of me, with a nervous glance at Bron.

'Not a sign, missus.'

'Just wondered.' Her face was vacant. 'Things ain't what they were, though, are they? But Albert's going down the Ely soon – bit o' luck and we'll get Number Two at the Sinkers – that's near where you live, ain't it, Ma Bron? – where you lodging then, Toby?'

'With me,' said Bron. 'In Number Six.'

'Living together, are you?' asked Rosie, delighted.

'Dear me,' said Albert, flushed.

'Ah, well,' said Annie, awkward, 'we got to get going.'

I said, 'I'm down the Ely – might be seeing you, Albert?'

'You'll both have to come round to Number Two, when we move in.' Annie faltered, looking sad. 'Nothing like the old times, is there – and old friends?'

Rosie, with a faint smile on her rosebud mouth, looked me over as I took off my hat, and Albert added, 'You'll 'ave to take us as you find us, though.'

'When they move in to the Sinkers you ain't going out without a pass,' said Bron afterwards. 'I've sized that Rosie.'

I laughed. 'She's only a kid!'

'She'd handle you, mate.'

'What you looking at?' demanded Bron, later.

'You're a touchful woman,' I said.

'Half a crown would fetch you Patsy Pearl, you know.'

'Half a crown when I got free ones begging me?'

'Mind, you're a cheeky old beggar, Toby Davies – what's wrong with you?'

'Give me two minutes and you'll see.'

'Ay, ay. You lay a finger on me, Samson, and I'll howl back home for a pig-sticking, and the pugs'll come in and show you the four corners of the room.'

'I'll handle the pugs, missus, and you after,' I said.

'What's happened to you, Toby Davies?' Her eyes swept over me; an urchin, chewing rock from a dribbling mouth, stared up in astonishment at her beauty.

'I've growed up, like you said, girl, hang on to your drawers.'

'That's something to look forward to. Time was you knew where it was but didn't know what is was there for.'

You couldn't better her. Hands on hips, she regarded me, and the fairground beat about us.

'No trouble from you, Toby Davies – you're in my place on terms. I'll open the window, mind, and yell for Snookey Boxer.'

'And I'll have him, too.'

'I believe you would – saucy old boy!'

'Now that Sam has gone.'

It changed her; the spell was torn.

'Let's get back home.'

That much cooler (with Sam like a ghost between us) we were going for the Sinkers when we bumped right into Guto and Mrs. Livingstone: it wasn't unreasonable – as Bron said later, for she had seen them in Porth earlier: the Rhondda being a homing ground for immigrants from the north, ever since the Big Strike (it was on for years) sent the quarrymen down to coal in thousands.

'Well, well, *well*!' cried Mr. Guto, 'it's just like being up north – Toby Davies, of all people!' and she smoothed and fussed me while Guto tugged at my sleeve for attention.

The fair crowds pushed about us. Bron, I remember, looked a gilded lily of a woman in that garish light.

Outside a meat pie stall the Livingstone's were standing; starved they looked, but Guto was normal.

'You ever been to China?' asked he as the crowds pushed about us.

'Away there for a weekend soon, my love,' said Bron, holding his hand. 'You ain't the only beggar off abroad, ye know. How're you doing, missus?'

'It be pretty dry for us, in a manner o' speaking,' said Mrs. Guto, and her hands and arms were chapped with the suds. 'But things'll get better, never fear.' The people shoved us all together, knocking Bron's hat off, and she cursed and swiped at the offender: then she looked at the pies and at the Gutos. 'You fancy a pair of them? Me and Toby was just having some, weren't we?' She gave me an elbow, brightening me up.

'Four, and make 'em big ones, I'm starved,' she shouted, and the pie-man, white-coated and beefy, served them up with flourishes.

'It's his birthday Wednesday, isn't it, Guto?' said his wife.

'It's his birthday tonight – hot pies, indeed!' Bron paid the money.

'It ain't that we haven't got the price of things,' said Mrs. Guto, taking her bowl. 'Just a bit short, eh, Guto – getting our divvy from the Co-op Monday, see?'

Eager-faced urchins danced about us, making faces of agony at the savoury smell of it: broad-faced peasant women from the hills shrieked lustily from under their big hats, hitting off their men's bowlers; the organ music rose, discounting thought. Mrs. Guto yelled, nudging Bron, 'Send him a card, Wednesday, if you think of it, love. He always looks for birthday cards, poor old dab. Mind,' she explained blowing at her bowl, 'I always manage to send him some – his old Gran up in Pesda, for instance – she's been dead years, of course – then his cousin down in Wrexham and his brother in Glasinfryn. None of 'em write to him, but he do look forward to cards.'

I pitied her.

Snookey Boxer went by with Orphan Effie, the girl the Salvation Army had recently saved, and Snookey rose his bowler, very polite.

'We got to go,' said Mrs. Guto, her thin face pinched up. 'Very good of ye, I'm sure. Our treat next, remember?'

'That's all right, missus,' I said.

'Oh, Christ,' said Bron, after they'd gone.

'What about home, then?'

The Rhondda sleeps: the fairground is silent, only the dying naphtha flares, like the wands of drowsy fairies, send beams of skittering light over the debris of the Rink.

The red-nostrilled stallions of the merry-go-round are stilled; stray cats, ever the scavengers of the Rhondda nights, pad the trampled mud in search of dismembered polonys and lick the savoury-sweet fish batter on truant fish wrappers; Mrs. 'Catty' Ledoux, the Frenchwoman who eats cats, is stroking a pet persian. High goes the moon, shedding silver on the roofs, where a handful of gravel against the stars would patter on slate under which Johnny Norths were sleeping: dreaming, making love in the fidgety, nerveless fits and starts of all the Rhondda loving.

The towns, huddled in the narrow gorges and gulches, link hands in the moonlight; the old urinal near the Empire, ancient then, guggles and gushes, mistaking shadows for customers; the unwashed quarts and pewters of the pubs, from the New Inn over in Blaenrhondda to the Pandy in Tonypandy, stand in sightless emptiness. Above ground all is dead; below ground the hearts of the towns are beating.

'Goodnight,' said Bron.

CHAPTER TWENTY-THREE

The year of the Riots gave us a glorious summer.

June had come and gone in all her verdant clothes, painting up the hedgerows, decorating the fields, and the children back from Sunday School made daisy rings and piss-a-bed chains.

July sent cool winds softly over the mountains, and the country clear of the industry was honeyed and golden; the Twin Rivers, Fach and Fawr, bubbled and leaped down to the plains.

August, far from cooling us off with threats of things about to die, packed her bag of mid-summer sun and heaved it over the mountains, and we simmered and broiled in the blazing days, with people like Ricardo Bellini making a fortune on ice-cream, and spending a lot of it on Patsy Pearl when he should have been laying it up for Maria, beloved wife.

'You can't blame Patsy, mind,' said Bron now, 'that's her trade. It's the men I blame, every time,' and she went round the hut like something demented, as usual, hitting the dust from one place to another.

'I know who'll blame little Patsy if Maria catches her,' I said over the top of the book.

'What are you reading?' asked Bron.

'Edgar Allan Poe.'

'Good God!'

I liked to read; I had always done it. 'Read, Toby, read,' my mother used to say, 'everything you can get your hands on,' and, after starting, I could never get enough. Archibald Hood, once the owner of the Scotch Colliery, had done his colliers well in this respect; opening his Miners' Library, where you could borrow anything from *Coal Owners – Guardians of Poor* to *The Decline and Fall of the Roman Empire*.

'I think I'll bake today, being Sunday,' said Bron, 'you fancy a rhubarb tart?'

'I fancy you,' I replied.

'It's Moses Culpepper's rhubarb, mind.'

I didn't go a lot on Moses's rhubarb, especially since he used to water his garden night and morning, contending, as he did so, that this was good for rhubarb. The tricky bit about eating the Culpepper rhubarb was trying to forget about the watering can.

'I feel in a special light mood,' said Bron, and she tripped happily around the hut. Mood, according to one of her relatives, played a large part in successful baking; the duller the woman the heavier the pastry, apparently – a sign that the Devil was in the house. Bron actually used to sing to hers, weaving her hands lightly in the air above it – mainly, *The Lass with the Delicate Air*. It was a bit of a palaver, really, getting hold of a rhubarb tart.

'He lost his glass eye last night, you heard?' she asked, sprinkling flour.

'Who?' I lowered my book.

'Moses – and his false teeth, too, according to Rachel Odd. Got himself filled up at The Golden Age; came back here, sneezed 'em over the Square, and lost his glass eye, the silly old faggot.'

'I don't go a lot on the ale in The Golden Age,' I said.

'He's going home, I reckon, is Moses. Last week he took his lad to the Sports ground to see the county cricketers – white flannels, see? They finished up among the new cemetery gravestones.'

'He'd better keep his eyesight away from the Ely agent, Ben Block does – he'll get his ticket for sure, otherwise.'

Tap tap at the door, the gentlest of knocks; Bron opened it, and Mr. Richard Jones, the Ely Lodge chairman, stood there.

'Why, there's a surprise!' said Bron, and bobbed a curtsy to his bow.

'Come you in, Mr. Jones.' She wiped the flour from her hands. 'I was just off next door, directly.'

'Busy, is it? I can come back again, mind!'

'Ach, no sir, make yourself at home.' She softly closed the door behind her.

I was wishing him to the devil; Bron, too. I knew what he had come for.

Gaunt and grey, Mr. Jones perched on the edge of a chair and peered at me with his red-rimmed eyes; his face was like dust, and dust was in his chest but not his big, bass voice. 'You've given some thought to what I spoke of, Toby Davies?'

'Lodge treasurer?' I shook my head. 'No.'

'Good brothers are needed for the coming fight – stand or fall together, see? It is something to be offered the trust of the Union, lad.'

'Didn't you say you knew what happened to me up in Bethesda?' I asked.

'Questions have been asked, and answered – O'Hara's dishonesty in the Quarryman's Union was nothing to do with you.' Mr. Jones smiled faintly.

I saw beyond his ashen face the dim outline of the Pandy.

Dusk was falling. People, long from Chapel, were standing in little groups, the women with hymn books, the men laden with their big coloured bibles.

'A coming fight, you say?' I asked.

'To the death, if needs be.' His voice raised. 'The old Sliding Scale was once the miner's friend, now it's his enemy. The Boer War lifted prices on the Scale by seventy-five per cent; but, when the peace was signed eight years back, the cost of living cut take home pay by half. The Cambrian Combine's in trouble unless they raise to two-and-six a ton.' He nodded sagely at me. 'God will be on the side of the Federation in this, mark me.'

'Strikes me that God's on the Cambrian's Board of Directors,' I replied. 'They deny us a united protest? You'll have to shift the county police before you shift the Cambrian Combine.'

'You suggest force?'

'You want a rise in wages, Mr. Jones, that's how you'll have to get it. The blacklist, spies within the Union, intimidation, bribes – the owners use force six days a week. Now they've got our agents in their pockets, force is all they recognise.'

187

'They're grave charges,' said he, his hands folding together.

'But true, and the Miners' Federation knows it. You won't get anything without a strike.' I got up. 'But the valleys are still doing well enough, aren't they? I've no complaints.'

'Aye, but it is not today we're fighting for lad, it's tomorrow; not for this generation, but the next. We've got to get rid of the Sliding Scale; get payment for Small Coal and retention of House Coal at five shillings a ton.'

'They'll call in the military before they'll sign to that, Mr. Jones.'

'But you'll help, son? – new blood is needed. Thirty years I've worked for the Union, man and boy. Sometimes I feel as old as Methuselah. Tell me you'll serve!'

'If you think I can,' I said, sighing.

'God bless you.' The old man rose. 'I'll bring the books round tomorrow. In my day we thought it a privilege to hold the Union's books. Honesty is the basis of unionism; men of honesty are hard to find and scallywags abound. They're kicked out of one place and turn up in another – men like Nairn, who disappeared with the Rochdale funds; Needham, who stole from Bridgend – these two went north – the Union rarely prosecutes, you know. The northerners come south, of course. Ben O'Hara, for one.'

'Ben O'Hara?' I stared at him.

'He's settled up Merthyr way – Abercanaid, I think.'

Realisation brought the old, obliterating emotion. I was fighting for the sense of it. 'They ... they've left Ireland, then? – *Abercanaid*, you say?'

The old man nodded, his eyes questioning my reaction. 'The Federation checks the move of every scallywag – the quarrymen wrote that he moved to South Wales within the last year or so.'

I reflected, bitterly, that Nan and Ben must actually have been in the Merthyr area at the same time as me; they could have easily been living in Nightingale Street. It was a bitter twist of Fate, the place being so small, that we had not met. I had a sudden and nearly overwhelming urge to walk through the door in search of her.

Bron entered, saying:

'One day women'll have a Union, you know. Then it'll be ten to five, and no baking Sundays.'

After the old man had gone, she said, looking at me strangely, 'What's happened to you, Tobe? Seen a ghost?'

Since I was on night shift that Monday, I went shopping with Bron in Town.

Mrs. Mia Bellini, the wife of the ice-cream man, we met on the steps of Paddy Ginty, the grocer; I hit up my cap to her, Bron bowed.

Dark and flashing was Mrs. Bellini, heaving bosom and hoop earrings.

'Seen my Ricardo, 'ave you?'

A direct descendant of a Corsian bandit was she, according to Ricardo, her husband, and God help me if she ever finds me with Patsy Pearl, he used to say.

'In the Scotch library,' I replied.

'The library?' cried Mia. 'What for the library? The fool cannot read!'

'Just seen him there, Mrs. Bellini.'

She hit her forehead with her fist. '*Mama Maria!* When I catch him I kill him! The library, you say? – you men, you are all the same – dirty boots, dirty minds – all the time it is women, women!' and she swept down the street.

'She's not far wrong,' said Bron. 'Is he in the library?'

'In Patsy Pearl,' I said. 'Number Eight, River Row. Monday's his afternoon off.'

'You know her address?'

'I've heard talk of it,' I said.

'And I bet Patsy's heard talk of you.'

'That's a dreadful thing to say!'

'That's a dreadful thing to do,' said she. 'I tell you what, six-foot-three; if I ever catch you up River View, Corsican bandits won't come into it.'

Despite the street criers and clattering trams the day was suddenly quiet.

'You're conquered territory, Bron,' I said. 'You belong to Sam, so why can't I get off?'

'Get it right. I belong to nobody now.'

'That makes me free.'

'Oh, no it doesn't – you belong to me.'

'That's unfair.'

'Of course.' She glared at me.

Cooler, with sheet-ice like a window between us, we went into Ginty's.

A small dark, woman passed by on the other side of the street; it could have been Nanwen.

It was good enough for a Band of Hope meeting in Ginty's grocery shop that afternoon. And Paddy Ginty, as Irish as peat, was going like a steam-hammer behind the counter, while his missus, thin as a Galway ghost, watched the customers with her large, haggard eyes.

'I was just telling Mrs. Culpepper, if I never move from here,' said Ginty, 'it's the economics of the Rhondda's all adrift, sure to God. Don't ye agree, Toby Davies?'

'We've got no economics,' I replied.

'That's right. If it wasn't for the Board of Guardians and the Quakers, the place'd be flat on its face. And if the Co-op carried the debts I do, it'd be in blutty liquidation,' and he smacked up the butter pats. 'Still, sure to God, we're all God's creatures.'

'There's a heaven for ye somewhere, Ginty,' said Bron, 'though I doubt if it's in the Rhondda.'

'One slice of bacon, please,' said Primrose Culpepper, 'and a little less old tongue with it, Ginty.'

'There now – see what I mean?' asked Ginty. 'A slice of bacon – all me clients are pantry blutty clients.'

'Got to live from hand to mouth, haven't we?' said Mrs. Shanklyn. 'It's just the same in the trotter and faggot trade – bowl to stomach, isn't it?'

'*Arrah!* Now ye've got it,' said Ginty. 'The place has got no larders – like India, if ye get me – nothing in reserve.'

'No reserve for Union strikes, you mean?' said Bron.

'Exactly!' Ginty raised a boney finger. 'You're all threatening strikes, but the town can't stand a strike. The time's wrong for it, your Union's not ready for it. You've got people like Ablett, Rees and Hopla in disagreement, the Naval Pit at the throat of the Pandy Committee and Nantgwyn knocking out the teeth of both. I'm tellin' ye – fight now, and you'll all lose blood.'

'Mind,' said Rachel Odd, 'if there's going to be trouble, count me in. Six kids I got, and one in by 'ere,' and she patted her stomach. 'The way things're going I'll be breast-feeding this one through the school railings.'

Bron said, 'A cottage loaf and two ounces of liver, for God's sake, Ginty.'

They spoke more, but I didn't really hear them, for I knew that Ginty was right. A dark cloud of threat was grow-ing over the valleys: the old sufferings were about to return, and folks knew it. It was part of the inevitable cycle of Rhondda life.

Bron's elbow jogged me back to reality. 'Come on, forget it, mate – it's far too beautiful a day.'

Outside on the pavement the off-shift colliers and their wives thronged four abreast amid the clanging trams and strident voices of the street-criers; fiddles were screeching, concertinas going, and Tonypandy was golden with summer. Patsy Pearl we met, and Bron paused; then the new overman at my pit sought a path between us, and Patsy, I noticed, caught his eyes, and smiled. He was a man and a half, this new Englishman, John Haley, and the Scarrott heavyweights were trying him for size. Returning Patsy's smile, he pushed on.

'You all right, Patsy?' asked Bron, who never passed her without a word.

'A bit tight, you know – it's a hell of a time about now, really,' Patsy answered.

Aye, and you must have got rid of Ricardo pretty sharp, I reflected.

'Did you see Mr. Haley just then?'

I looked away in disassociation; not my business, women's gabbling.

I heard Patsy say, 'Do he come into the Pandy still, then?'

'Aye,' said Bron. 'A lot.'

'I'd go decent for him – you know.'

'You'd best try it, girl,' said Bron, 'you never know your luck.'

Up came Rosie Arse. Summerful and chesty was Rosie,

191

her eyes alight with vitality, like a tiger hunting. 'Seen my mam have you, Ma Bron?'

'Not today, Rosie.'

'Changing me name, ye know?' She perked and pouted, looking gorgeous.

'I don't blame you, with a name like that,' I said, and bright eyes switched over me; there was talk of boys and darkness whispers beyond the light of the fountain in Pandy Square; at fourteen she looked two years older. It was astonishing to me how Albert had fathered such beautiful children.

'Seeing one of the councillors about it, I am.' Her beauty was comely, her puppy fat disappearing; soon, I thought, you will have shadows in your cheeks and jewels for eyes, and the colliers will see a woman. 'Deed done, or something,' she added. 'Me name's Harse, really, see? Trouble is these Rhondda yobs can't pronounce their blutty haitches.'

'Deed Poll?' said I, and spelled it into her questioning face.

'Dear me, legal profession now?' said Bron.

'Give her a year or so and she'll set this place alight,' I said, after Rosie had gone.

'She's not doing so bad now,' said Bron, eyeing me for shock. Turning, she switched on a smile for Sarah Bosom and Dozie Dinah who passed us, arm in arm, and I hit up my bowler.

'Funny pair they are,' I said. 'You know, come to think of it, they're a queer old lot living in the Rhondda.'

'I was just considering that,' she replied, giving me an eye. We walked through the crowds.

Heinie Goldberg, we saw, alone as usual, with a little bag for groceries; Jimmy Wilde and his missus went past, all eyes turning to the pale shadow of a man who was knocking them flat all over the valleys – eighteen men in one night, at Scarrotts' booth, over in Trebanog: never more than nine stone, he took on men six stones larger; as much a phenomenon as the Rhondda itself.

'*Diawch*, I'm dry,' I said, 'you'd have to prime me to spit.'

'I'm going on, then,' said Bron. 'I'll get the liver on.'

'A glass of milk might soothe me,' I said outside the dairy. 'Got a cold coming, I think.'

'You've a plaster for every sore, 'aven't you?' She put two-pence into my hand. 'Go on, I'll treat ye.'

I kissed her, and passing people frowned, worried.

'Go on with you,' said she, pushing, 'get off,' so I took her twopence and went into the De Winton.

Moses Culpepper was standing at the bar, parting his whiskers and killing a quart; most of the old-timers drank quarts, those days; the younger generation, being delicate, sipped pints.

'Old and mild,' I said, and the landlord nodded: beefy and red was he, a change to Moses, who looked pale and drawn despite his eighteen stones. What with one thing and another, Moses had been having a bad time of late.

'Any news of your eye, yet?' I asked, and he shook his head, doleful.

'It's the marble season, mind,' said he. 'Anything could have happened to it. Now I've hit up me ampton – it never rains but it pours.'

I said, 'You poor soul. That's a tragedy.'

'It'll teach him not to rub his knees with horse liniment,' said the landlord, and I slid him twopence for the pint.

'But he's got my sympathy, sure to God,' said an Irishman. 'I'd not wish that on a duck.'

Said Moses, glum, 'Me missus thought the cork was in and poured it over me privates.' So I'd heard; the whole of Pandy must have heard, with Moses charging around shouting murder.

The time went on and I ordered another pint. The talk was of horse racing and bets, and when the pits would come out; of Mabon, Bill Brace and Tom Richards, the Members of Parliament. Suddenly, the landlord said, 'Hey, by the way, Toby, did you see that chap who were asking for you?'

'What chap?' I wiped my mouth and set down the glass.

'He was in here some time back,' said Moses, writing a betting slip.

'Asking for me?'

'Well,' said the landlord; 'after Ma Bron, really, weren't he?'

A silence sparked within the din.

Both surveyed the room as if they had said nothing. It was crammed with noisy colliers, settling Tonypandy before they raised the dust.

'A chap asking for Bron?' I asked.

Moses, realising the error, shifted uneasily; the landlord adopted an air of studious absence.

'Made a right cock of that now, didn't ye?' said Moses, and the landlord said, uncertainly:

'Well, he'd been over to your place, see, and he couldn't find Bron in the Pandy . . .'

'What did he look like?' I could feel my heart thudding in my chest and heard the clash of glasses, the hoarse shouts, as echoes. An Irishman cried, 'Dark and tough, a great lump of a fella, so he was.'

'Nothing to it, Tobe – a man's got a right to ask,' said the landlord, plaintively, and I got him by his buttons.

'*When?*'

'Half an hour or so – come on, come on, hold your bloody horses!'

'What did you tell him?'

'I sent him back to the Pandy, that's what!' He shoved me away, brushing himself down. 'Jesus, I ain't a home for lost dogs, ye know.'

'You've got less brains than a horse's arse,' said Moses. 'Look, he hasn't even finished his ale.'

I went over the Square and into the Pandy like a man out of a gun, and pushed the door back on to its hinges. I glared around, but Sam wasn't there. Something greater than intuition told me it was him.

'Just kick it open,' said the landlord, 'don't bother.'

'A chap asking for Bron? Where is he?'

'You ask Bron, mister, no business of ours.'

But I could see by his expression that somebody had been asking, so I shoved my way through the gaping customers and ran to the Huts, and there was Bron standing before the mirror, preening and fluffing up, and she didn't spare me a glance. Slowly, I entered.

'Where is he?'

'Who're you after mate, the Pope?'

'Sam's been in here, hasn't he?'

'If he has he's been pretty sharp,' she replied, 'I've only just come in myself. Turning to me, she added, 'Anyway, he's got the right, hasn't he? He's my husband, and this is my place.'

It came as news to me; lately she had seemed so completely mine.

But it was the same old Bron, I reflected; Sam had only to wink an eye and she came running.

'Back in Porth, is he?'

She walked past me to the sink and began to fill a bowl. 'At this rate you're going to miss shift – I haven't even got the tea on.'

'Answer me!' I caught her by the wrist and swung her against me.

'You leave go of me or you'll get the frying-pan,' she said softly, her eyes alight.

Tense, fighting to control myself, I released her, and she said, turning away. 'According to you, he's in Tonypandy.'

'You can't run the two of us, Bron.'

'Right then – you sod off.'

'Don't swear!'

'Jealous, stupid beggar! – you're enough to singe a saint.' In the middle of the room she swung to face me, saying, 'Dear me, you've a reckless imagination, haven't you? Honest to God, you're the one chap I know who can make a monkey's tit out of nothing.'

She was close to tears; only Sam Jones could make Bron cry, I remembered.

'You swear he hasn't been here?'

She walked back to the grate and poked it into a blaze.

'I'm swearing nothing, son – you'll have to take my word for it.'

I didn't know what to do; how to handle her. Had Sam been there, it would have been easy – I hit my fist into the palm of my hand.

At the window, I bowed my head.

'Don't be unhappy, Tobe,' said Bron, at the bosh.

I didn't reply; I hated the thought that she was lying to me, and said so.

'I didn't lie,' she said, wiping her hands, and turned me into her arms like a woman cajoles a child, but I pushed her away.

'I can't stick this,' I said.

'You'll have to, mun – there'll always be Sam.'

'No man can bear being second best.'

She held me away. 'And what about me? – it cuts both ways, you know – what about Nanwen?'

'*Eight years* ago, woman? She's out of my life, and you know it!'

She made a face. 'I'd be a larger fool than you take me for if I believed that.'

Empty, we stood apart.

CHAPTER TWENTY-FOUR

Trouble was coming.

It was breathed on the mountain air, at the lodge meetings, and guzzled through ale in the publics. Acrimony over "abnormal places" was developing between the colliers and the Owners. There was even talk that, if we didn't stop claiming the extra ninepence a ton and payment for small coal, the Ely management would lock us out of the Bute seam.

'That don't seem likely,' said Heinie. 'Cut their own throats? That isn't capitalism.'

'It would make us an example to the rest of the Union, though,' I said.

'You should worry, Toby – you've got it good,' said Ben Block. 'You, Heinie and Mattie – I've got six mouths to feed.'

As a single man, I wasn't doing so bad in the Bute seam.

Even without payment for small coal, I was taking home nearly thirty shillings a week after stoppages, and Bron's twelve bob a week at the Pandy helped us to skin it out, for the rent at the Sinkers was only five shillings. In fact, we had six sovereigns saved in the tea-caddy.

But people like Ben Block, with a houseful of kids, were not so fortunate. Twice this spring Ben had been laid off for a fortnight, and gone on short time once; a couple of rejected trams a week – when the checkweigher refused to accept them because of shale content or small coal – and Ben Block and his like were in trouble.

Even at the height of the Rhondda prosperity, some colliers – especially those with big families – were going on the Parish.

Take Albert Arse. Since coming to the valleys five years back, Albert had worked in practically every pit in Rhondda Fach, and, with a family of four, had known hunger when laid off.

The coal owners weren't particular about colliers; a cut in manpower meant a rise in profits. In the last seven years, with coal output steady at about two hundred and fifty million tons yearly, the value of exported coal had risen by three shillings a ton 'free on board' at the docks. But the colliers of South Wales saw little of this prosperity. The age-old jingle survived, but it was still only a colliers' dream:

> Eight hours to work
> Eight hours of freedom
> Eight hours of sleep
> And eight shillings a day.

At Mabon's rate of progress, men said, we'd likely get such a Utopia round about a hundred years hence.

Go-slows began in the pits by disgruntled colliers, who, working in 'abnormal places', and faced with the loss of small coal (also threats of the loss of their concessionary coal), begged in vain through the Conciliation Boards for a rise in wages to meet the leaping cost of living. The managements reacted by laying men off, and the old spectre of destitution began to stalk the valleys. Emigration began again, something that had not happened since the beginning of the Coal Rush fifty years back. Whole families could be seen trudging the road to the west – back to the farms and the promise of sun. As in the Welsh iron era, the industries of Pennsylvania and Pittsburgh called, and people were spending their last savings on passages to America.

The Rhondda, once bulging with humanity, began to thin its streets; accommodation came vacant. What was once a landlord's paradise was ceasing to exist. Albert and Annie Arse, Rosie and Tommy, were a case in point.

At the beginning of September they moved in down the Row to Number Two, the Sinkers. Albert was prepared to work for a pittance on the top – carting rubbish for two shillings a day; then, with the prospect of Tommy beginning work, the family fortunes changed. At ten shillings a week the management put a premium on boys, making no indiscreet enquiries about their proper ages. But, despite all this, few colliers, and certainly not the Miners Federation, were seriously thinking about a South Wales strike to get conditions improved.

Indeed, on that bright, autumn morning when young Tommy started work, most people seemed more concerned about Moses Culpepper.

'He found his teeth, ye know, Ma Bron?' shouted Rachel from her wash-line.

'Who, Moses?' Bron, too, was pegging out, being a Monday.

The women gathered as usual; the Welsh being experts for a gossip over the wall.

'Last night a mongrel looked through the window of the Crown, and it was wearing 'em!'

'Wearing what?' shouted Etta McCarthy, leaning on her gate.

'Culpepper's teeth.'

'*Gawd!*' shrieked Etta, 'I don't believe it!'

'It were, I tell ye!' shouted Dai Parcel, the postman, at the gate of Number One; coming back down the Ely today, was Dai, an old collier; now moved in there with his mates Gwilym and Owen, all widowers. 'Saw it myself, but he hadn't got his eye, mind.'

'Very funny, I must say,' said Primrose Culpepper, easing Moses off his chair with her broom. 'Kindly raise your backside so I can sweep out. You can handle this blutty lot, I'm not stooping to pick up rubbish.'

'It's me eye I'm after chiefly, though,' said Moses, heaving up his stomach. 'I'm not the same on the women, mind, with me eye absent.'

'Lost your love life, Moses?' This from Dano McCarthy stripped for washing, while his six sons were bubbling and towelling over their buckets on the patch.

'He'll never be the same,' said Primrose Culpepper. 'Any spare chaps going loose round your way, Bron?'

'Not that I know of,' said Bron, giving me a shove.

The cackling and banter went on all down the Row.

When I came out with my bait tin and jack, Tommy Arse was waiting at the gate, and Annie, his ma beside him, her hair in rags.

Bagged and belted was Tommy, nigh fourteen. In a pair of Albert's cut-down trews, he was quiffed and poshed up, ready for the Ely.

'*Daw*, couldn't you spare him another year, Annie?' asked Bron.

'His pa's on short, and we need the money,' said Annie, thinly anxious.

'Does the new overman know he's under age? He's English and tough, they say.'

'Got Willie Shanklyn's birth certificate,' I said, 'so he's fourteen and two months.'

Bron said, turning away, 'One wonders who's luckiest – Tommy or Mrs. Shanklyn's idiot – one thing's sure, the pit'll never get Willie.'

'Got no option,' said Annie, screwing her hands. 'He's eatin' for a regiment, ain't you, Tom?' and Bron knelt and took the boy's hand in hers.

'And how does Tommy feel about it?'

'Christ, missus,' said he, and his face became alive. 'Down the Ely with Uncle Toby, I am, and coming for a farrier lad with horses, for the pay's good, and bring home money for ma!' I never again heard him say so much.

'God help you,' said Bron, and tried to kiss him, but he pushed her away and came to me.

She wandered inside. Listening for the coming of the lads, I followed her.

'He could have been ours, Toby – you realise?' There was the strangest expression upon her face.

'Sam's, more likely.'

But her smile, slow and sad, did not fade. 'Well, he could have been, couldn't he? – ours, I mean. Like Bibbs-Two – she could have been yours – you ever realised?'

'One thing's sure, we'll never have one at this rate.'

The knowledge that Nanwen was in the south was bringing to me a new and vital independence; as if I had shed the cloak of my necessity, making Bron of less importance.

'You've changed the last week or so, Tobe.'

'Isn't that natural?'

'Do we have to share a bed, just because we live together?'

'Not necessarily, there's a lot more fish in the sea.'

200

'You're getting bitter.'

'What d'you expect?'

There was a pause; the chatter of the women outside invaded our privacy.

Bron said, looking at her hands, 'Suppose I fell for a baby?'

'Wouldn't that be natural, too?'

'I'm married, ye know – I got to think about babies. Not fair on a kid, is it – taking its pick of a father.'

'If you loved me and not Sam Jones, you wouldn't even think of that.'

Her voice rose, 'And if you loved me you wouldn't be giving me such hell about it – can't you wait till I'm free?'

'Free of Sam?' I laughed in her face. 'You'll never be free of him! In the last four months I've had him for breakfast, dinner and tea. One day he'll come, give you a wink, and you'll be straight through the window.'

She wandered about, fists clenched. 'I'd rather be yoked to a pig!'

'Come on, be honest – lies never suited you.'

'I would – I . . . I wouldn't give him house room. Life with Sam again?' She strode about. 'The beggar charms the honey out of the hive, then skips off with the first queen bee – it wouldn't last five minutes!'

She was nearly crying; I wondered if it was for Sam, or me. I tried to turn her into my arms, but she shrugged me away and went to the table, gripping it, head bowed.

'What a damned good start for a Monday wash-day!'

'I'm sorry,' I said.

'What for? You're right, aren't you?'

And Tommy burst into the room, forgetting manners, yelling, 'The colliers are comin', Uncle Toby, the colliers are coming!'

Bron turned her wrought face to mine. 'You bring that boy back in one piece, mind, or you'll never hear the end of it.'

'That's better,' I smiled at her and she dashed a hand at her face.

'Good-bye,' I said, though I'd have liked to kiss her.

She was right, I supposed, as I hauled Tommy off to the

morning shift. Bibbs-Two could have been mine, come to think of it.

All the Row was out to see Tommy Arse start work that early September day, which was the custom with a new lad starting, and a shout went up as the Ely shift wheeled into the Square, and there was Primose Culpepper hugging Tommy to the ample breast, more dangerous on breathing than being down the pit: Rachel Odd ran after us, patting and blessing him, and watch yourself in the trams, lad. Will Parry Trumpet, always pushed but never late, galloped out of Number Eleven, and damn me, we're going to have that bloody bugle again, said Heinie, flies open as usual, when we joined him and Mattie.

Marching next door to me was big John Haley, the new Ely overman; handsome and aloof, he had about him the air of a man who wouldn't be tampered with. Patsy Pearl, I noticed, was standing with her baby Madog in her shawl as we marched past the chemist's: got it bad, had Patsy, her eyes, like saucers. But the English foreman, a widower, rumour said, didn't appear to notice her. Instead, he leaned across me in the ranks and put his fist on Tommy's shoulder. 'New lad, eh?'

'Yes, sir,' said Tommy, rigid.

'Easy,' I said, 'nobody's going to eat you.'

'Name?' asked the foreman.

'Tommy,' I said.

'Just Tommy?'

'Tommy Arse.'

The foreman didn't bat an eye. 'You're blessed with an original name, son – are you blessed with years?'

'Fourteen and two months,' I said.

'The boy speaks for himself. Age?' He leaned over to Tommy.

'Got my birth certificate to prove it sir,' said Tommy, stretching his thighs to keep our stride, 'though Willie Shanklyn's name's on it, mind.'

I groaned, closing my eyes.

'That's buggered that,' said Heinie, and the foreman said:

'Once I had a son the same size as you, Tommy Arse.'

I glanced at the man. I bettered six-foot-three, and he gave me inches. 'You lost him, Foreman?'

He moved me over and marched with Tommy.

Past the Gethin we went and into the lamp room, and Tommy was all eyes as he got his first lamp and watched the lamp man light it.

'Right, you,' said John Haley, the overman. 'I'll have him,' and he gripped Tommy's shoulder with a ham-like hand. 'First time underground?'

'Yes, sir.'

The coal-starched shoulders of the morning shift were all about us as we filed into the cage; the gate clanged shut. Near me, his head against the overman's stomach, Tommy's brown eyes stared with his inner fears. The cage dropped; the foreman's hand went out.

'Knees bent, stand limp. Don't fight it.' Tommy came off his feet then, but Mr. Haley held him down.

'Jesus,' said Tommy.

At the Bute landing, John Haley said to me, 'Did you make his application?'

'Aye, Foreman,' and he said to Tommy, gripping him still:

'Properly introduced, officially taken on, eh? All in order. Now then, this business of the names – are you Tommy Arse or Willie Shanklyn – the owner of the Cambrian Combine has written in asking this personally – all the way from France.'

'I'm Tommy Arse, really,' said Tommy. 'Shanklyn's only the fiddle, like Uncle Toby told me.'

I made a face, turning away. Haley said to me, 'They need the money?'

'As poor as ragged mice, Foreman,' I answered.

'God, what a country!' To Tommy, he added, 'Arse, you know isn't the best of surnames – how does Tommy Shanklyn suit you? – t'is a bit of both.'

Bright and pleasured was Tommy's face.

'Or even Tom Shanklyn?' The foreman regarded the roof deep in thought; it was a matter of tremendous importance. 'You see, you being a man now, you might even forget about the Tommy . . .?'

Tommy rose to his full height of four-foot-ten. 'Aye, sir – Tom Shanklyn.'

'Right,' said Haley, and winked at me. 'Get going with your butty and start loading – Mr. Goldberg'll issue you with your curling box. And lift with your knees together, remember?'

'I've told him,' I said.

'Get going, then – are you hanging round all day?'

'There's water down here again,' said Mattie, splashing around in the dark, and I brought our lamps up, and the water, six inches deep, swirled its oily blackness into our boots.

'There's always water in this stall,' said Heinie.

I said, wading about, 'What the devil was the night shift doing? Did they slacken off the pumps?'

'Pumps still going, I can hear 'em,' said Mattie.

I didn't like it. In a warmer stall it wasn't so bad, but getting out big stuff under wet, cold conditions like this was worth a pound a ton, never mind one-and-ninepence. I stripped off my shirt, hung it on the roof and lay down in the stall. The water flooded over my arm, bringing icy fingers to my neck and throat.

I hewed and cut, kicking the coal back with my feet, and Mattie hauled it away with the curling box, emptying it into the tram. It was a hard seam, this Bute – five feet at its highest; above two feet high at the point where I was cutting. Beyond the face rats were scuttling; they'd scuttle faster, I thought, when Mattie packed the gob.

I had got used to the rats. Time was when the very sight of one would make me feel sick, but Llechwedd's Victoria cavern had broken me in: they were moving around more than usual that morning, and I mentioned it to Mattie.

'Taking over the Ely,' said he.

In the silence of the face, when I was not breathing, I could hear distant shot-firers in other headings, raking the bowels of the mountain; the clanging beats of the sledge-hammers as they hit up the pit-props, and sometimes, I fancied, even voices in far away galleries; the ghosts of lost generations, perhaps, talking out of the past?

Did unknown fish swim, perhaps, in the acres of static water? I wondered. Did the rocks three thousand feet under my elbow thunder to underground rivers? In the window of my mind I again saw Bron walking the shining face of Glamorgan; and us lying here, digging out coal for the fires of people to whom our deaths would mean nothing.

I brought up my knees to ease my aching back; sprawling around under the roof, searching for the seam.

'There's a dignified position for the new lodge treasurer,' said Mattie.

'In this position I've given some of my best performances.'

'Ay ay, well shift your arse over so I can come in.'

I saw Lark, Duck's horse, turn up her eyes at the roof. The rats were squealing louder still.

'You are not chasing rats today, my lovely,' said Duck, and he hitched her to the tram by dropping in the pin and gave her a slap, but Lark didn't move. Duck nodded and brought out his watch, peering at it in the lamp-light. 'Just as I thought – snap, eh? This old mare can tell the time, you know?' and he opened his tommy box, eating delicately.

'Who's this coming?' growled Ben Block, squatting down on the gob.

'It's only me, lads,' said Tommy. 'Ay ay boys!' Black-faced and happy was he, coming with his curling box for loading.

'Ay ay boys, indeed!' said Mattie. 'Cheeky little bugger. I thought you was down on Three Road with the new foreman?'

'I were,' said Tommy, opening his bait box, 'but he sent me down to be with Heinie.'

'Mr. Goldberg to you,' I said, crawling out.

'Is there going to a strike, mun?' asked Tommy.

'If there is, you won't be in it – you're not a paid up member.'

Tommy looked suddenly close to tears. 'A strike? But I've only just started!'

'Don't you worry, my flower,' said Heinie. 'You sit by 'ere with Uncle Heinie.'

'Don't you call me a flower,' said Tommy.

205

'Unofficial?' A prop trembled beside me; dust showered down from the roof.

'Unofficial strike? Talk sense, mun!'

'It could happen,' I said. 'People like Mabon will have to make up their minds.'

'They would lock us out first, these owners,' said Duck, biting into his bread and cheese. 'But all the Cambrian and Glamorgan lodges would come out, too, they say. And we're twelve thousand strong in the Cambrian alone.'

'Count in Maesteg, the Western Valley and you've got two and a half times as much,' said Mattie, chewing, and he drank from his jack, eyes clenched against the sweat, and gasped. 'Take the whole of South Wales and Monmouthshire and you're better'n a quarter of a million.'

'They'd bring in the police if we start violence.'

'And the military!'

'They shot the colliers down in Featherstone, remember?'

'Who's Home Secretary now, for God's sake?'

'Winston Churchill.'

'He'll give you Featherstone,' said Mattie. 'Those blutty Suffragettes want to watch out with him about, an' all.'

'Christ,' said Ben Block, looking at his cheese. 'She must have got this out of the blutty mousetrap.'

'We'll be doing the breast stroke down here soon,' I said.

'I'm reporting this pit to the agent,' said Mattie.

'Poor little scratch, you'll frighten the arse off him.'

'Or try Haley, the new foreman?'

'That's more reasonable,' I replied. 'Up north, we'd have seen to it long since.'

'Are you talkin' of the North Wales Quarrymen's Combination?' asked Duck, polite, and I answered:

'Men like Mabon aren't a patch on people like the Parrys.' I nodded around. 'If we'd had W. J. Parry heading this Union, we wouldn't be wet-working.'

'Give it a rest, Tobe,' cried Heinie. 'Sitting around on a tenholer privy with their shirt-tails out — just to duck the agent?'

'It do sound a pretty strange quorum — I'd like to have heard the speeches,' said Ben Block, chuckling, and Mattie said:

'Success has gone to ye head, Tobe,' and he stooped for his pick. 'I'm prepared to bare me breast, mind, but not even for a quart of Allsops would I bare me arse.' He got up, groaning.

'Can I have a quart, Uncle Toby?' This from Tommy, his eyes shining in the lamps.

'When we get up, son,' said Heinie, cuffing him. 'First smell o' the barmaid's apron, eh?' Fists on his hips, he surveyed Tommy. 'Unions, Federations, Combinations? – it don't mean a lot to you, now, does it?'

'First quart, eh? Damn me!' said Tommy.

There came a silence of dripping water and a crescendo squealing of the rats.

'They're making an awful lot of noise these days,' I said.

'Better than *Judas Maccabaeus*. You heard the tenors in Upper Trebanog?'

'They ain't paid up members, you know? They got no right to squeal without permission,' grumbled Mattie.

'You bitter old sod,' said Heinie.

CHAPTER TWENTY-FIVE

I wanted to take Bron with me to the Rocking Stone meeting at Pontypridd that coming Saturday night, largely on the suggestion of Heinie Goldberg, who was an expert in certain matters, he claimed.

'You're quite sure that there's nothing wrong with you, then?' he had asked. 'I mean biological – that's the word for it – biological.'

'Not that I'm aware of.'

'You live with her, but sleep apart?'

'That's the size of it.'

'It's an awful waste,' said Heinie, sadly.

It was three days later, and we were on our way home from the Ely shift.

'It . . . it's just that she's in love with this Sam Jones fella?' he asked.

'That's it.' And he answered, surprisingly:

'Every woman's a virgin, Tobe, when she's in love.' An amazing philosophy, coming from Heinie.

It was food for thought. Damned women! I thought; you can never get to the bottom of them.

'That's one way of putting it,' said Heinie. 'Look, *bach*, wheel her up to that Rocking Stone next Saturday, sit her on it, then stand by to fight her off.'

I replied, 'I can't – she says she won't come – she's not interested in politics. Anyway, that yarn about the Rocking Stone trick is an old wives' tale.'

'Bet you a pint on it,' said Heinie. 'Do you fancy one now to settle the dust?'

'We'll set 'em up at the Pandy.'

'And cast an eye on the sacrificial lamb,' said Heinie.

We went up to the bar and hit it for ale, and Bron served us, looking gorgeous in her pink dress, but she had a face as long as a kite.

'You had much experience with women?' asked Heinie, quiet.

'Not a lot.'

He drank steadily, watching Bron serving the customers; certainly, she wasn't her usual self that night.

'Have you ever run a woman that this one knows about?' he asked, reflectively.

I thought of Nanwen, and gave it a shrug. 'Aye, once – but it was a long, long time ago.'

'That makes no odds,' Heinie grinned at Bron and gave her a wink; for reply, she put her nose up.

'That could be the trouble,' said he.

In my desperation I'd landed among the witch-doctors.

I didn't stay long. Bron had got them on her, this was sure, and I wasn't in the mood to cajole her. It had been a harder shift than usual that day, with the engineers poking around the stall trying to find where the water was coming in, and I was soaked with sweat and oil. Bron wasn't off until midnight, so I had my bath and was towelling myself down when she arrived in the middle of it.

'Good God, there's a sight!'

'Keep the door closed, it'll upset the Welsh matrons,' I said.

'One thing's sure, mate, it don't upset me.'

'You make that clear. What are you doing?' I tied the towel around my waist.

'Pinning this clear a bit.' She was standing before her little mirror on the chest of drawers with pins in her mouth, pinning up the front of her dress.

'You're too late, the colliers are half-way down it.'

She turned her head, raising one eyebrow at me in disdain. Gone was the girl in Clayton workhouse; vanished was her immature prettiness. Life had moulded her into a vital womanhood; no wonder she drew the Pandy trade.

'Isn't good enough, Bron, you're setting the chaps alight.'

'You had your chance and you didn't take it.'

'We were kids then. Why can't it happen again?' I

approached her and put my arms around her waist, but she moved quickly away.

'Because Ma Bron, in the old days, didn't have the sense to keep her legs crossed.'

'You can be vulgar, too, can't you?'

She crossed the room, and I watched her.

'Women face facts – that's what you want me for, isn't it?'

'I want you because I love you.'

She swung to me. 'And you broody about that Nan O'Hara all these years?'

'She's past history and you know it!'

I have often since wondered how easily a woman reads a man.

'*Ach*,' she said, disdainfully, 'you've still got her on your mind!'

'Wouldn't it be fair? It's the same with you and Sam.'

She went to the bosh and began wringing out the dish-cloth, her whole being agitated, and I wondered at her sudden show of temperament; it wasn't like her. She was volatile and changeable, but rarely ill-tempered. 'Upper class, wasn't she, eh?' She flung down the cloth. 'Too high and bloody mighty to give a nod to the likes of me.'

'Don't swear, Bron.'

'There's a few of her kind round here, too – they think they piss port wine. And she was too good for poor old O'Hara, too, wasn't she? No wonder he went on the ale.'

'Now, come on ... *come on* ...' I was becoming angry.

She was flushed, and suddenly furious. 'Rushing around like a pig in a fit, dancing her attention!'

'Suffering God,' I whispered, 'where did you find this sort of mood?'

'When you start gassin' about that Nan O'Hara!'

I shouted. 'I never even mentioned her!'

'But you're broody about her, ain't you? An' that's just the same!' Suddenly, she paused before me, her fingers twisting together. 'It ain't fair, Toby. I'm doing me best to be decent about Sam ...'

'What isn't fair?' I put out my arms to her, approaching again, but she turned and ran to the door and stood there momentarily, her head bowed. Then she said, 'if you don't know, then you get on with it!' The door slammed behind her.

But, a night or two before the big meeting at Pontypridd, Bron's mood had changed.

'Didn't I tell you?' said Heinie, in the Pandy that night, 'she's jealous. Jealousy makes 'em awkward. Though the cheese is usually that much sweeter when nibbled by another mouse. Next thing you'll know it's love and marriage?'

'You old faggot,' said Mattie, joining us at the bar. 'What d'you know about love and marriage?'

'He knows about sex,' said Dai Parcel, coming up with Owen and Gwilym, his mates. 'He hasn't the time to keep his flies done up,' and he shouted at Bron for ale.

Gwilym said, his glasses on the end of his ring-scarred face. 'Everybody's at it. What we want is a religious revival.'

'Remember the Evan Roberts Revival, Dai?' asked Duck, leaning over.

'Remember it? He led it,' said Heinie.

The day shift from the Scotch was coming in; bull-chested colliers as black as negro slaves were shoving to the bar, and Ma Bron was going demented with the foaming jugs in a thunder of coughing, for the lads were settling the gob.

I noticed John Haley, the Ely overman, sitting alone with a pint in a corner; nearby, Patsy Pearl, her eyes like stars, was giving him the come-hither, but he didn't appear to notice. And Evan Evans, the temporary landlord of the Pandy, beaming bucolic above his outsize brewer's goitre, opened his arms in blessing as the colliers flooded in. Ed Masumbala, the big Negro, had Precious, his baby son, on his shoulder; Albert Arse, on the other side of the room, was buying Tommy a pint. Beside him leaned Red Rubbler, the Irish mountain fighter from Porth; very interested in Bron, by the look of him and after trouble, too, by the cut of him; leaning over the bar, trying to weigh up her legs.

'Shall I ease him off gentle?' asked Heinie, anxious.

I shook my head. 'Leave him, she can handle it.'

'He's a groper, mind – done time twice.'

'Up to her.' I turned away.

Her pink dress was pretty, I thought, but I'd have liked it a bit higher in the front. Perhaps the pins had come out again, and Bron hadn't noticed. Also, it was well above her ankles, which was asking for it in a place like this.

'Ay ay, Toby!' shouted Bill Odd, from the crowd, and I gave him a nod; more than a nod would have cost me a pint. Coming in the door, Will Parry Trumpet was giving us the bugle; an ear-splitting, blasting sound, bringing yelled protests.

'Time was, the valleys were swept with a mass hysteria,' said Gwilym, tugging at my sleeve. 'It were Gabriel's horn all over again, just like that.'

I sipped my ale, watching the fighter. I heard a man say, 'Bron's got more up there tonight than the Nutcracker Suite,' but Owen was after me again, commanding attention.

'It was the cholera chapels repeated, ye know?' said he. 'The pubs was empty – it was a mortal sin to drink. Grown men were refusing to ride in the cages together – Non-conformists versus the Church of England – half the Rhondda was on its knees!'

'I'd rather chase her through the daisies than go down the Scotch,' said somebody.

'A Baptist wouldn't share a stall with a Roman Catholic.'

'Methodists wouldn't ride in the cages with Congregationlaists.'

'And if the cage-winder weren't Chapel, he'd give ye a blutty ride!'

'Processions were the order of the day,' said Mattie. Over his head I saw Red Rubbler grinning vacantly at Bron.

'Drunkards were dressed in white, the lodges closed for lack of funds – everything was going into the offertory boxes.'

'Pit ponies stopped pulling because hauliers stopped cursing.'

'God was very popular,' said Owen, dully.

'I prefer that barmaid to organised religion, though.'

'The beer's gone up shocking since she appeared in the Pandy.'

I was suddenly angry; not with the men, but with Bron.

'A good pair do have an effect on trade,' said another. 'She weren't behind the dairy door when bottles was handed out.'

'You randy old soak, Billy!'

'Mind, my woman's chest do take a lot o' beating, but I'm a leg man meself, personally speaking.'

'Don't know what you're all on about,' cried a third, falsetto. 'I put my women up on a pedestal, I do.'

'That's only so ye can see up their skirts, mun!'

I saw Heinie frowning at me. 'You ready for off, Tobe?' he asked softly.

'No,' I said.

I was watching Red Rubbler on the other side of the bar.

'Let him be, he's a professional,' said Mattie. 'He'd kill you.'

'I'll see to it,' said Heinie, and pushed through the crowd.

'A head taller than you? He's mine.' I pulled Heinie aside.

The boxer was leaning over the counter, holding Bron's dress. She, with her back to him, wouldn't know what he was up to until she moved. Dano McCarthy and his six big sons had come in, shouting, and the sudden commotion had riveted Bron's attention. Now the jugs slopped as she moved, and her skirt went at the seam.

Instantly, she turned, pouring the ale over Red Rubbler's head.

In seconds, it was uproar. Drenched, the boxer wiped beer out of his eyes, gasping, then lunged at her.

'You bloody *bitch*!'

Bron hit him with a jug.

Bedlam. Colliers bawling, loving it, and the landlord shouting for order.

Reaching the boxer, I swung him to face me and hit him with a right. He was big, and it didn't floor him; instead, he staggered against the bar, then grinned, wiping his unshaven face.

'Ay ay,' he said, and rushed. I side-stepped him and he barged into the men, slipped and fell; rising, he swung them aside for room.

'You big, Welsh bastard!' he said.

I got him with another right as he came lumbering in; it straightened him momentarily, and I saw his chin cocked up and begging as I ducked his swing and hit out with the left. Taking it full, he dropped.

'Christ,' said Heinie.

'And I thought he didn't know a left hook from a coat-hanger,' said Mattie.

'Come on, you,' I said, and reached over the counter.

'All right, don't be rough!' cried Bron.

John Galey lifted an eyebrow at me as I steered her through the door.

Tonypandy slept. Furious, I lay in my bed on the other side of the Walls of Jericho and stared at the pattern of moonlight crossing the ceiling.

'I don't blame Red, I blame you!' I said.

'I thought I'd have the fault for it,' said Bron. 'But, it was a good punch though – never seen a chap done better.'

'He's a poor, ignorant oaf! What do you expect from a man like that? You set the Devil alight – low and behold in that dress!'

'They're mine, I can do what I like with 'em.' I heard her sit up in bed. 'What's wrong with you, anyway – you taken the cloth? That Nan O'Hara got some too, if you're in luck.'

'You leave her out of this!'

'She's in here every day, mate – what's the odds?'

I was about to shout something back; strangely, my conscience stopped me.

The thought that Nan was close now – as near as a few hour's walk – was bringing me to a new if uncertain warmth.

Earlier, I had gone out to the back, believing Bron to be already in bed. But she was still undressing; her fair-skinned beauty had caught my breath.

Now I lit the candle behind the Walls of Jericho and started to work on the lodge accounts. They had been kept meticulously by Richard Jones; every payment entry made in his copper plate hand-writing. I smiled, thinking of his fanatical dedication to the Union. Perhaps, I reflected, it needed men such as he and Parry – the unpaid slaves of ideals – to make the industrial world go round.

Later, in bed, I listened to Bron's breathing.

Strangely, at such quiet times, my thoughts invariably

turned to Nanwen; she, the epitome of all my dreams, I thought, could never be replaced by one like Bron.

Vaguely, I wondered if this was a true love; if my desire for Bron was purely physical. Certainly, I'd have killed Red Rubbler if he had laid hands on Nanwen . . .

'Toby . . .' Bron now, from the other side of the blanket.

'Yes?'

'Did you hit out that boxer because of me?'

'I'd have done it for anyone.'

She giggled. 'Didn't know ye had it in ye – fisticuffs, eh?'

'Aye, and you want to watch it, or I'll be starting next on you.'

The room went silent; an owl was crying faintly from Mynydd-y-Gelli.

'Toby . . .'

'What now?' I suitably humped and heaved, to discourage her.

'I've changed me mind about next Saturday – I'm coming with you to the political Meeting.' She sighed in half sleep. 'What's it all about, anyway?'

'I'll come over there and explain in detail.'

'You come over here and you'll get more than you handed Red Rubbler.'

'Good night, then.' I turned back again.

'Best to know where you get to these days, perhaps,' said she. 'Lest you end up in places like Abercanaid.'

'Abercanaid?' I cocked an ear to the blanket between us.

'Merthyr way, isn't it – or ain't you never heard?'

Somebody had told her about Nanwen being there, of course. I'd half expected it – nothing much missed Bron.

'Nice having your Nanny around again, is it?'

It angered me.

'You might have mentioned it, you rotten bugger,' said she.

As I said to Heinie later, I couldn't make head or tail or her.

'So if I catch you up in Abercanaid, you won't know what hit you – d'you hear that?'

I smiled to myself: Bron fell to silence.

The night went on. All down the Row the huts were whispering to each other in the dark; faint snores and groans came from the sleepers of Tonypandy.

'Good night, lovely boy,' said she.

CHAPTER TWENTY-SIX

We were a lot warmer together, Bron and me, when I took her off that Saturday to the political meeting. The fact that I hadn't mentioned about the O'Haras being up Merthyr way and she holding out on me about Sam, seemed to even things up between us.

'Was it Sam who came that day?' I'd asked her.

'You'll never know, will you, ye poor soul,' said she.

And so, the difference put on the side of our plate, so to speak, I was trying another tack, for the Walls of Jericho were still firmly up in the Sinkers.

'You'll likely find that golden bugle under the Rocking Stone at Pontypridd,' said Heinie, 'that's where they sit the barren wives, you know.'

'Come off it!'

'Then you ask Rachel Odd. Dry as a desert was Rachel, before Bill took her up to Ponty. He sat her on that Rocking Stone and she brought forth sprightly.'

'Triplets,' said Mattie. 'Nine months to the day.'

'Bill got her home by a fast train.'

'I don't believe it!' I said.

'Put a little Welsh bakestone in her oven.'

'Don't be disgusting,' said Mattie.

So I made great preparations for this political meeting. Taking out my Sunday suit I ironed the creases to cut my throat: I got Dora Dobi, the washer-woman, secretly to starch me up a collar, with Reckitt's Blue on the shirt and lavender water under its arms. I took half a sovereign out of the tea caddy – sixpence for flowers, sixpence for tea in Ponty, twopence for a buttonhole as big as a bride's bouquet, and five shillings to hire a pony and trap. Doing it proper – I'd even invested money in it.

'She won't know what hit her, poor little dab,' said Heinie.

The autumn smiled on the valleys that gorgeous Saturday evening.

It set the neighbours back a bit to see that pony and trap outside the Sinkers, and folks were pretty forlorn: standing around with never a word while I handed Bron up and climbed in beside her, for it's not often you get gentry behaviour round Tonypandy square.

Most of the hard cases came out of the Pandy Inn too, standing with their quarts respectfully under their bowlers, and I was proud indeed to be stepping out official with the prettiest barmaid in Town. And, as we clip-clopped that little nag over Trealaw bridge and past the station, we set every head turning.

Hundreds of the lads were here, catching the train to Pontypridd, and Heinie cupped his hands and bawled, 'Good luck, Tobe!'

'What does he mean – good luck?' asked Bron.

She eyed me, but I made myself busy with the reins. Then, suddenly, she began to sing, hands clasped before her, looking as lovely as a picture under her broad-rimmed, summer hat. Bron sang, the pony clopped along and I gave Sam Jones a thought as we entered Porth, and was anxious there, for Bron was silent.

'You still around?' I asked her.

For reply she reached out and silently gripped my hand; Sam and Nanwen, for once, were pale, unsubstantial ghosts.

'I'd work for you, girl,' I said.

No reply; just held her face up, smiling at the sun.

'Will you come away with me then – to some new place? And forget about everyone except us?'

She'd gone so quiet I thought she'd dropped off.

'Two pints, please,' I said, and it opened her eyes, and she laughed gaily so that people waved and urchins cheered from the gutters as we took the valley road to Ponty.

'London, even – I'd dig the roads for ye,' I said.

When the cottages thinned a bit after leaving Porth, I stopped the pony and tried to kiss her, and her hat fell off and her hair came down and she was pushing and smacking as gay as a virgin maid: very sweet, it was, trying to kiss Ma Bron on the road to Ponty. Birds sang, the hedgerows flourished in the wind; the corn in the fields was so golden that you could have pinned up angels' plaits with it.

I thought desperately, in my wish for her: I'll settle the dust under this one for good. If she wants Tonypandy, she'll have it. I'll wed her, bed her and bring out sons, but not for the pit, oh no! No boys of mine are ever going down the Ely. Tell you what, I told her – I'll buy me a job on the local council from eight till six every day except Sundays, with a black stock and a wing collar – macassar oil on my hair and powder under me arms – flavoured sweet as a nut.

She laughed all through this, hitting me about. 'You're as daft as a brush, Toby Davies! Don't you know I like you as a big, sweaty collier?'

In that ride after leaving Porth, where Sam had once lived (and lived even now, perhaps, I reflected) a new gaiety and charm came between us, like a blessing from the sun.

The market was in full swing as I reined the pony into the narrow streets of Pontypridd, and urchins were hanging like sheaves on the arched bridge, waving us greeting.

Every collier in South Wales must have been in Ponty that evening, for the trains were shunting in from the Great Western and Taff Vale Railway like strings of centipedes, and the lads were pouring out into the streets, raving for the publics.

They came by canal barge, too, and three to a dray; in brewers' wagons, dog carts, and they climbed the hill to the Druids' Circle that overlooked the town, and surrounded the famous Rocking Stone in thick wedges of black.

'There's a lot of police around,' said Bron, as I tossed a penny to an ostler lad to mind the pony.

'Yes,' I answered, 'and they're watching every move.'

In the market the stalls were end to end, with everything man can buy since the Creation.

There were poultry stalls with feathered necks swinging and ducks and geese being executed in squawks: pig-stickers were at work on the cobbles, carcasses being swilled in boiling vats. There were button and silk mercer stalls, quacks up on boxes selling potions for constipation, cauliflower ears and womb disorders.

'God!' exclaimed Bron, 'I've never seen anything like it!'

Drunks were already on the streets in rolling gangs, arms linked and roaring their bawdies; here went the riff-raff of the old iron-works and the worked out refuse of the Coal Rush; in pacing groups, hands cupped to their ears for harmony, went the collier choirs, their sweet-sounding hymns ignored in the rush and tear that was forever Pontypridd. Snookey Boxer, still wearing his boxing boots passed us, holding Effie's hand, and by the expression on their faces there wasn't a brain between them. Looking for the boxing booth and a quick guinea was he, and Effie well stuck up with a toffee apple.

'Can you see the Rocking Stone?' I shouted to Bron, and pointed upwards to the mountain.

'Is that where we're off to later, then?'

'Give it till dusk.'

'For the Union meeting, is it?'

'Got to be dark, see.'

'To sit me on the Rocking Stone?'

'*Diawl!*' I exclaimed. 'Who told you that?'

'Mun – do ye think I'm daft? It was me who put old Rachel up to it!'

'I'll skin that Heinie Goldberg,,' I said.

She kissed my cheek. 'You change my mind about Sam Jones, Toby Davies, an' I won't need rocking!'

'Right, then, we'll see, for you're a devil of a woman for promises.' I took her arm and hurried her through the crowd. 'What I can't get down the Sinkers, I'm trying for under the stars.'

'You'll be lucky,' said Bron.

Mabon had already delivered his Union speech, apparently, when we had climbed the hill to the Rocking Stone.

Here were the big-wigs of the Union; chairs and tables were set within the Druid's Circle about the Stone, with rank on rank of colliers a hundred deep. And Mabon, great in stature, was standing on the Stone, head and shoulders above everybody, his thick arms flung out to the crowd, for his usual biblical text before departing, and he cried:

' "I will go before thee," said the Lord, "and make the crooked places straight" – Aye, men! Isaiah 45 – remember, you who know the Book? "I will break in pieces the gates of brass, and cut in sunder the bars of iron. And I will give thee the treasures of darkness ..." ' and he flung upwards his great hands to the lowering sky, 'Come men, come – you know the Word – quote it with me!' and a great murmur came from the men as they spoke:

' "... And hidden riches of secret places that thou mayest know that I, the Lord, which call thee by name, am the God of Israel!" '

A silence grew on the mountain, as if the town itself was listening.

This was William Abraham the bard, now nearing seventy years old; time could not taint his marvellous presence. He stilled his colliers now as he had done in 1877 – thirty-three years ago, when they first elected him as a miners' agent. For a third of a century he had represented them in Parliament, bringing to the Chamber his marvellous gift of oratory.

Possessed of astonishing *hwyl*, the unusual Welsh eloquence, he could hold a thousand men on the tips of his fingers.

But these days, Mabon's influence with the Miners' Federation was on the wane. His domination of wage negotiation had gradually evaporated, as had the miners' confidence in his integrity. Lodge leaders now openly complained that he had become an 'employers' man; one unfit to lead the new younger legions who were bent on social and economic reform.

The miners' distrust had now extended from the coal owners to Mabon, who was once revered, and one cried hoarsely, his hands cupped to his mouth, 'Now we've had the biblical, Mabon, what about a rise?'

The colliers began to chant and stamp their feet.

'How further can I serve you, then?' shouted Mabon, his arms opening to us in astonishment.

'By telling the Conciliation Board that we'll never make the Bute seam pay!' cried a voice, and I recognised Mr. Jones, my lodge chairman.

'Isn't it up to the Bute colliers to prove it can be made to pay?'

I left Bron and ran to the edge of the crowd, calling, 'Let D. A. Thomas strip down the Ely, and try.'

Men turning now, craning to find the speaker. I shouted, 'Four months now I've been working the Bute. Give me a wife and kid and I'd be on the Parish.'

'Come nearer,' called Mabon, and I did so, pushing through the men, shouting:

'Isn't it roundabouts and swings, Mabon? One pit is a loss, another's a gain. Hang us all on what can be earned down the Bute, and they'll crucify the coalfields.'

Applause clapped into silence, and Mabon said, 'See the Union's position, young man! The Owners claim you're going slow on the Bute. Unless we come to some agreement, they'll lock you out.'

'Lock out the Bute colliers and the Combine pits down tools,' cried Mr. Jones, now beside me.

'Pledge your best efforts to make the Bute seam pay, and nobody will be locked out,' replied Mabon. 'Weeks back this threat was made. Come autumn, unless output improves, they'll shut the Ely gates.' Hands on hips, he surveyed me. 'You speak for yourself, collier?'

'He speaks for the Ely,' shouted Mr. Jones.

Mabon raised his hands for silence as the commotion grew.

I yelled, 'There's not a married collier who can live on Bute wages, and the Owners know it. That's why they want the Cambrian pits based on this seam. Betray us now, and you'll have a strike on your hands that will break the Federation.'

I never expected what ensued. The men recoiled like pent springs, roaring assent.

Torches began to spark and wave in the crowd. Men were being hoisted up on to the shoulders of comrades, yelling their individual complaints. And Mabon, as if in answer put a chair on to the Rocking Stone and clambered upon it, his hands again upraised. Within the thunder of shouts and boos, his lips began to move soundlessly; the crowd ebbed into silence, and a collier shouted:

'Christ, lads, here it comes – the tonic solfa!'

Strangely, nobody laughed. Not a sound they made, once Mabon began to sing.

Pure and beautiful, his bass voice echoed in the dusk. Arms wide, he sang, softly at first, to command attention. The mountain whispered; the flickering torches bathed red and black in skittering shadows, the faces of the listening men. Resonant and powerful was that voice that had for forty years commanded silence. When all else failed, Mabon sang: we listened now to *David of the White Rock,* in Welsh.

'Tell me what you want from me, and I will serve you,' cried Mabon, after the song.

Arms flung up, his great beard trembling in the red light, he looked as Moses must have looked before the people of Israel.

Sick of him, I turned and went back to Bron.

'Is there going to be trouble?' she asked.

'If there is, you won't be in it. I didn't bring you up here to listen to the politics,' and at that moment Heinie, Mattie and Mr. Duck came up.

Four sheets in the wind was Heinie, and Mattie not much better, with Duck holding them up, and the pair of them stinking of Allsops to dry the mud on a navvy; Heinie with his flies undone, as usual.

'Watch it, Heinie, there's ducks about,' said Bron.

'We're just off,' I said.

'Come on, come on,' said Duck, and he staggered, holding up his mates. 'This is the Union at work, my beautiful,' and he tipped Bron under the chin.

'I've seen enough of the Union to last me a fortnight,' Bron replied. 'Arguing, threatening — why does everybody want strikes and lock-outs?'

'Striking against a lockout is the only thing we know,' said Heinie, rolling.

'The trouble with Mabon,' said Duck, indicating the Stone where Mabon was still speaking, 'is that he's too damned old. Young blood like yours is what we want, Toby,' and he clapped me on the shoulder.

'I'll be that much older if I hang around here,' said Bron, testily.

'O, aye?' and Duck fixed her with his eye. 'Stay and improve your mind. Women will benefit, too, you know — political freedom.'

'I don't want political freedom,' said Bron.

'Easy, Duck,' I said, and eased him aside, but he swung me away, with just enough ale in him to make him quarrelsome. 'Doesn't she know that we're fighting for her most of all, then? Let her speak for herself! If we don't get paid for small coal now, she'll starve in her kitchen on big stuff tomorrow!'

'I'll starve, too, if me missus catches me in this state,' said Mattie.

'You're riding a greasy pig, Duck,' said Bron, 'leave me be – I don't understand the politics,' and she shook him off.

'She's right,' cried Heinie, falsetto. 'Keep the women out of it. It's a sad old house when the cock's silent and the hen does all the crowing.'

'To hell with the lot of ye, I'm off,' said Bron.

Darkness had fallen over the mountains.

The meeting ended, the hill of the Druids was empty save for discarded political pamphlets and sandwich wrappers blowing in the wind.

Standing together on the Rocking Stone where Mabon had stood, Bron and I looked down at the blaze of Pontypridd below us, where the market, despite the late hour, was still in full swing.

'Best get down there,' said Bron, 'before somebody walks off with that pony and trap.'

'No hurry,' I said. 'Sit,' and I drew her down on to the Stone, and we rocked together, looking at the moon.

'If this puts me in the pudding, there'll be the Devil to pay rent to in the Sinkers, you realise?'

'You don't get puddings just by sitting on a stone.' I drew her against me. 'Other things have got to happen, too – your ma never mentioned it?'

'I read about it somewhere, I think,' said Bron.

There was a new sweetness in her face for me as we rocked together, like statues in that moonlight.

'I'll read it to you again, if you're interested.'

Her eyes were incredibly bright, like a woman in tears, but she was smiling. 'Spring heather can do queer things, they say, if ye get it up your garters.'

'Don't you fret, missus, I take good care of my women.'

'*Arglwydd!*' And she looked at me very old-fashioned. 'Cocky old boy, aren't ye?'

It was the strange, lilting look in her face that took me; she was the Bron of Bethesda again. Head on one side, smiling; hands on swaying hips. 'You know, Toby Davies, I'm getting a shine for you. Now ain't that strange? Last one down the hill is poleaxed,' she cried, and pulled up her skirts and ran demented, with me after her.

I caught her near the bottom of the hill.

Flushed and breathless was she, and I kissed her in the thickets where the moon had hidden. Nearby were the ashes of a dying fire where Irish gipsies had camped for the market. Sitting in its glow was a woman feeding a child, so we up and walked again.

She disdained to cover herself as we passed, this woman; when I bowed to her, her chin went higher; the baby hammered her and sucked.

Later, perhaps, when the market was over, those of her tribe with young children would return and spark up the bonfire, and the men would bring out the wine, and there'd be dancing to the guitars and castanets. Heinie Goldberg reckoned he'd had a night with one of these girls and he'd never known such an outing, but there was always a palaver if one of them came full, with Pedro this and Mario that rushing around the Rhondda, sorting out the father.

There was a place of moonlight nearby where the wind blew soft and here we sat in an arbour of the bushes, Bron and me, and she must have known what I intended since I'd done my best to make it clear. Yet here she was acting the virgin surprise.

This women do, I find, when they're keener than most.

'Dear me, no,' said Bron.

'Just remember that old Rocking Stone, my precious,' I said.

Amazingly, I think we both knew strange shyness, which was difficult to explain, since we'd shared a room for months. But we were closer here, in this foreign place, than at any time with the Walls of Jericho between us; or was it that the business of making love (which begins with the eyes and passing the cheese) had all been done before?

Now there grew between Bron and me a bond that fused us tight; and, gypsy bonfire sparks started blowing up between us.

I came nearer; Bron lowered her face.

'Best not, Tobe.'

Which is only really a woman's way of calling you on.

'We'll be sorry tomorrow, mind,' said she.

The breath of the wind is like a swig of gin; time suddenly paused and pushed us through its door.

There is a freedom in the wild places that does not spring from beds, and little rivers are running in your head and flowers make the hot, anxious perfumes. It was being like children again, lying there holding hands in the heather, and my heart was thumping as I bent above her.

'Do not make it hard, precious,' said Bron, and I saw the moon in her hair and her eyes were narrowed as she turned away her face. So big that moon, triumphant brilliance – having a good look at me kissing Bron, and now I touched her breast.

'Hop it, Tobe.'

The shock of my coldness took her breath.

A lifetime back it had come to this. I remembered the heart-thumps of the lad in the Waterloo bedroom; the crumpled dress, the moonlit window, Bron's whispers.

Now I heard her voice again, the voice of a woman, the soprano turned contralto:

'You need me that much?'

'*Diawch,*' I whispered, 'I'm in a terrible blutty state.'

She giggled, being Bron, and I needed her more. 'Easy, mun, ye've got to let 'em breathe. Careful with me, is it? – I ain't usual, you know.'

I did not reply, for this business of loving is an obliterating chord of sound in the breast. 'Dear me,' said she, 'what's happening . . .?'

Bron was warm and soft beneath me and now willing. There grew in me a giant need of her; a forging of heat and strength.

No sound then but the rushing of the wind and a gasping of kisses, which is a stillness when the world ceases.

It was love come alive in the body, a tumult of chaotic movement; bringing to me expression, in word and deed, beyond my understanding.

Light flows here, in the darkness of clenched eyes; a fusing of the mind and heart. And, as my strength tightened about her, there came a breathlessness of kisses I had never known before.

The wearing of that love was like a garment. At first there was no compulsion. Locked in the womb of her arms I knew an ecstatic oneness.

Transported from the present, I no longer laid with Bron on the mountain above Ponty, but in some strange place amid a galaxy of stars. And I saw, in the voice of her eyes, the message that lovers understand. Others I had taken, and enjoyed, like the Wraith Woman of Rhayader, but even Bron's merriment was beguiling; bringing to the ridiculous posturing a purity. No pillows lurked here, no formal bed seduced it and her breast was white under the moon. And even as she became one with me in that fragmented second of time, there was a yet a newness in its joy; lithe and quick was Bron beneath me, in the dance of life.

In a passion of coolness, the moment transported me to another distant lover ... a sudden betrayal I did not understand.

'How did all that happen, then?' asked Bron, opening her eyes.

'Largely done by mirrors,' I said, 'and bits of red paper held up to the light.'

I spoke again, yet did not hear my words: Bron replied, her voice clear, yet I did not hear her.

I heard only one voice, suddenly, beyond the flax of the dream, and this was the voice of Nanwen.

So clearly I heard her voice, as if she were beside me; it came out of the night, from nowhere, a counterfeit.

But Bron had not heard it, and she twisted her body so that, locked together, we rolled slowly down the slope as one, while the night stepped over the petticoats and lace-trimmed drawers and trews in all its stumbling breath.

'Oh, that were gorgeous!' Bron whispered against me. 'Do it again?'

The moon dropped her Sunday dress over the night, hiding us from gipsies.

So I loved Bron again, seeing before me Nanwen's face; even feeling on my mouth Nanwen's breath.

CHAPTER TWENTY-SEVEN

And so, towards the end of August, when the painting was gold on the trees of the mountain, I took myself down the Sinkers Row and fished out Will Parry Trumpet.

'You got your trumpet?' I asked.

'Aye, and ready,' said he, wonderingly.

'Then bring it along here,' and I positioned Will outside the window of Number Six where Bron was washing up and singing like an angel. 'Sixpence,' I said to Will, 'for six good blasts.'

He stared at me, rocking in the wind, being as thin as a starved ferret. Six good blasts, I thought, could be the end of him.

'On this trumpet?'

'On this trumpet,' I said.

'T''is right good payment,' said Will. 'I reckon they don't get more in the Household Cavalry. When do I start?'

'This minute,' I said, and the neighbours gathered in anxious concern and the night shift colliers put their heads out of their windows, cursing flashes, as Will Parry Trumpet gave them six blasts of his trumpet, and I paid him sixpence.

When I got back inside the kitchen Ma Bron was at the bosh, pretty glum, but the Walls of Jericho were removed.

That room looked as palatial as a Victorian mansion with its tattered old blanket down.

'You won't lose by it,' I said, and put my arms around her waist and kissed her bare back above her chemise. 'The matrons of Wales would give a lot to be in the position you're in now.'

'And I won't gain a lot; ought to have me head examined.'

'We'll see about your head later,' I replied.

Moses Culpepper put his face through our kitchen window, shouting, 'What's all this trumpeting, then?'

'Has Will Parry got his sixpence?' cried Bron from the bosh.

'Ay ay missus,' sang Moses.

'Then kindly remove your chops from my window-sill or you'll end up in blutty hospital.'

'No offence, mind,' called Moses.

'None intended,' said Bron. 'Now go to hell from here.' She pushed past me, looking gorgeous, her hair tousled with sleep. 'The damned cheek of it – give you an inch and you take a yard.'

I was combing my hair and gave her a grin.

'Walls of Jericho, indeed!' she said at nothing.

'Took them down, didn't you?'

'Some people think they own the place, too.'

'Possession's nine points of the law.' As she passed again I got her and tried to kiss her, but she slapped me away.

'Just because you pop something into the pawnbroker's it don't mean he bought it – I told you before, I don't belong to anyone.'

'*Duw!* Where did you find this sort of a mood?'

She ran to me; I held her and we did not speak.

It's a strange old business, trying to understand women.

'You all right?' I asked at length.

'Aye.' She was hard against me, her face hidden, sniffing and wiping, and I knew she was remembering Sam.

Scratch scratch at the door then. With a glance at me, Bron opened it, and a little sheep stood there. It did more to change the subject than I could.

'Well, I never did!' Bron ejaculated. 'If it isn't our little Arabella!' Her mood vanished, she bobbed a curtsy and opened the door wider, and the thing walked in daintily.

'Toby Davies,' said Bron, 'this is Arabella, friend of the Culpepper's. But you've got the wrong house, Arabella! – Primrose lives next door!' Bending, she untied her red hair ribbon and put it around the little ewe's neck. 'There now, go to see them pretty. Out, out . . .!' and she swept it through the door with her apron, saying:

'She's Primrose's really. She's known her since she was a lamb. On her way to the slaughter-house, she roamed away from the flock, and just popped in. Primrose pays the farmer a penny a week to keep her out of the abbattoir.'

I wasn't really listening. Through the kitchen window I

could see the town hemming in the dusk, and the misted, roving shapes of off-shift colliers.

'It took a sheep to cheer you up,' I said.

Bron sighed. 'Well, I always reckoned that animals were better'n humans.'

The coming of Arabella had broken a sad, empty spell.

Ever since the Rocking Stone meeting some eighty of us had been laid off from the Bute seam – over a week now, because the sea-coal demand had gone down at Cardiff, or something; I never did get to the bottom of this supply and demand, neither did the Union.

'I've got to hurry,' said Bron. 'Will ye be calling in to the Pandy for a pint?'

'I haven't the necessary.'

'You can rob the tea-caddie.' She opened her purse. 'Tell ye what, I'll stand you?'

'I'll earn my own money,' I said, and she sighed at the ceiling. 'Oh, for God's sake, don't start that! We share, don't we?'

'I'll have an early night. Besides, I've got Lodge books to do.'

'Please yourself.'

I lay on the bed and watched her at the mirror.

She was doing a bit of pruning and preening, I thought, for somebody off to serve ale to colliers. Wearing a white blouse and long, black skirt pulled in as tight at the waist as a Church of England dog-collar, she looked lovely smart; it was sad to think that only part of her belonged to me.

'Don't take any old buck off anyone, remember – if Red Rubbler's around, you shout,' I said.

Making faces in the mirror above the bosh, she said:

'Expect you'll be asleep when I come back, then – don't forget your supper. Lobscows, remember.' She pouted and painted, a woman absent, her expression as changeable as her mood.

'I can smell it,' I replied automatically.

Strange how I knew that Sam Jones was in the offing.

Now she began to comb her hair and I watched its tumbling waves in the faint light from the Square.

I could sit for hours watching a woman do her hair, seeing the business of the fingers, hearing the scurr of the comb, the gentle tearing of the brush.

'What's happening at the Ely, then?' she asked, hairpins in her mouth. Earlier, I had found one of these in the bed; part of a feminine sweetness that seemed to speak of a bond between us.

'Difficult to say,' I answered.

'Voted on to the Union committee now, aren't you? – don't you know if there'll be a strike?'

'Nobody wants a strike, but we'll likely come to it.' I sighed. 'The Owners reckon we're going slow.'

'And are you?' She was brushing down her dress now, trying to see the back of her skirt in the mirror, I replied:

'You go slow down the Bute seam and you draw no wages, mate. It's wet, it's abnormal, it's full of rock and shale. And they're trying to force the rates for the Bute on all the pits in the Combine. It won't wash.'

'So what next?'

'We're trying to get the backing of all the Welsh pits.'

'And will you?'

'Miners have always stuck together; I expect they'll do it again.' I sighed at my books on the table before me. 'Half the trouble is that the Owners won't arbitrate.'

'*Diawch!*' She was walking about and patting herself with finality. 'There's new words cropping up every minute.'

'Accept an independent decision,' I said.

But she wasn't listening, and I sensed in her a private anticipation she was trying to suppress.

Bron's inborn honesty always betrayed her; she was no actress.

The Sinkers was waking up for the evening; the colliers of the Scotch were making ready for the night shift; children were bawling – always a palaver as they were threatened into bed. Pablo, the Mexican parrot belonging to Bill and Rachel Odd gave his usual cheeky whistle, a sign that Rachel was getting into the bath, and it's very disturbing, mind, Rachel used to say. But it was enough to make anybody whistle, said Bill, her husband, for it takes me five minutes to get her in and ten to get her out, when she's expecting.

'He's a cheeky old bugger, that parrot,' said Bron.

'Got red ticks on him, too – unhealthy for children.'

There was growing between us a new barrier of coldness fed by words of nothingness.

It was like the siege of Jerusalem going on next door now, with a lot of swishing and swoshing and the kids shouting; Bill Odd booming bass while Rachel shrieked soprano. Farther down the Row the McCarthys were at it again, Etta throwing the pot of aspidistras at Dano and giving him stick in her rich, Connemara brogue, and nine times out of ten, one of the family caught it. Will Parry Trumpet was practising for the brass band – giving Handel the cornet, and I know where that cornet would end up if he was mine, Primrose Culpepper used to say, for it's the children of Israel sighing for reason of their bondage, Exodus 2: 23 – a great one for the biblical was Mrs. Culpepper.

'She's a bloody cough-drop, that one,' said Bron. 'Her pa was a Seventh Day Adventurer, ye know.'

'Adventist,' I said.

'Aye, she's a good one though – got a lot of love – that's what's wrong with this place – not enough love!'

She was ready to go, standing by the door.

'Here?' I raised my pen. 'Don't be daft – the valleys are built on love.'

'Still?'

'Of course – the *people* are the valleys. Folks don't change.'

'Hope you're right.' She came to me at the table and bent to my lips; her perfume drifted over me. I said:

'We might be in trouble with the Owners again, but the people will stand together; they're changeless.' I looked at her. 'Like us?'

She smiled into my face, her eyes dancing. 'Dear me, poetry now, is it?'

'When I look at you.'

She brushed my mouth with hers; it was scarcely a kiss. 'Don't wait up. I'm late shift tonight, you know – Mrs. Evans is off, so I shouldn't hang by the neck waiting up.'

233

Momentarily, she was the old capricious Bron, and I liked her better.

Pouting a kiss at me, she closed the door.

Through the kitchen window I watched her running towards the Pandy.

I did the books for a while; made mental notes that people like John Haley, the Englishman, and Albert Arse, both new members, hadn't paid their subscriptions, then packed the ledger away, had my supper and lay reading on the bed.

When I got up to light my pipe I found that Bron had left an ounce of tobacco on the mantel as a gift for me.

All down the Row the night was strangely quiet, and there grew within me, in the noisy loneliness of the darkening room, an elation mingled with an unaccountable dread. Bron wouldn't be back for hours, of course, but her nearness, I reflected, never failed to banish my insecurity. Her almost masculine air of self-sufficiency served to strengthen the bond between us: living with Bron made a man two against the world. Now she was gone I felt empty and uncertain.

Normally, this richness of belief served to dispel my nagging worry of Rhondda's approaching disasters; it needed no crystal ball to foretell that trouble was coming.

With the issues at my own pit, the Ely, unresolved, the confrontation between the Union and the Cambrian Combine management was widening to a chasm; this could have been the root cause of my enveloping depression.

Also, in the uncertainty of Bron's absence, my visions of Nanwen returned; even while in Bron's body, this was happening with stunning insistence.

I lay on the bed and listened to the trams going down De Winton. Had I been in the money, I'd have been out there forgetting it all with people like Mattie and Ben Block; sinking a pint up at The Golden Age; perhaps giving the wink to Annie Gay, the barmaid there (whom I fancied) or listening to Heinie's boasting talk of being a ring professional when the legendary Shoni Engineer was knocking them cold.

Yet tonight this only battered on the outer portals of my mind.

I was lying as a fake on the bed; a man removed.

234

At last, after eight years of loss, I had been given news of Nanwen. Now that I'd heard she was near me, my need of her was rising like a panic within me, despite my love of Bron. Sometimes a wraith of myself discarded the rough cast living in Tonypandy and sailed to Abercanaid.

Bron and Sam Jones, I thought; Nanwen and me ... It was a concourse of lost loves, make-believe, and snatched joys, the living of lies; and I cursed myself for my own responsibility in the scheme of it.

If I really faced the situation, I'd know the truth, I reflected.

Sam lived as much in the Sinkers as did Nanwen: he always had, from the moment I'd entered here. A lover might hold Bron in his arms, but she was as unsubstantial as a cloud; never could I capture her wayward, roving soul; this part of her still belonged to her husband.

Four of us living in the hut.

Bron, Sam, Nan, and me.

I must have dropped off because the mantel ticker said midnight when I awoke and put out my hand for Bron. Then I realised that I was still fully dressed, and rose.

Going out into the Square I saw that the Pandy had closed; the late drinkers of this and other publics were wending homewards amid the usual bawdy choirs. A great autumn moon lit the criss-cross, crazy roofs of the town and men stood in clutches around the fountain lamp, arguing rapaciously: others slouched in shadows like prospective footpads.

I tried the back of the Pandy, but it was locked, and I was just going round to the front when Evan Evans, the landlord, seeing out the last customers, came to the side door accompanied by Fang, his outsize Alsatian. Fang, normally as gentle as a spring lamb, became like a dog afflicted with rabies when once Time was called: setting about the clients until the bar was cleared, since his supper depended on it.

He was loping in my direction when the landlord called him off.

'Where's Bron?' I asked him.

'Search me, I haven't seen her.' He turned to go but I

gripped him and swung him to face me; the dog snarled deep in its throat.

'When did she leave?'

'Leave, ye ask? I've been managing on me own – she didn't even arrive.'

I said, lamely, releasing him, 'She ... she said she was on late duty ...'

He shook himself free of me. 'Not here, she's not.'

'Sorry, Mr. Evans.'

'You'd best be. This is the second time you've been here causing trouble. Now away with ye, before I whistle up Fang and he lifts the seat of your arse.'

It was fair. I pushed past him through the door and strode off down De Winton.

It was as if the Rhondda, sensing privation, was having its last fling of pleasure before the coming of hunger.

Rowdies, arm in arm, raked the streets, clamouring at the beerhouses as landlords fought them off; harlots stood in corners, surveying the prospects of payment; wives were collecting husbands, ragged children pulling at fathers. Among the roughs went the more respectable; the home-going visitors of the little terraces after the Victorian evenings of tea and song. With their Bibles under their arms, the God-fearing closed the chapel doors.

Sarah Bosom, the persian cat-breeder, went by with Dozey Dinah, her mate, on her arm, and Dozey, half asleep, gave me a wink. They kept house together in One Church Street, these two, with Sarah breeding and Dozey on her needle. Kept to themselves, too, though nobody got to the bottom of what kept them together, for they were as different as chalk from cheese. I touched my hair to them as they passed with bowls of faggots and peas.

All the Rhondda was coming alive in the individual, passing faces. Mrs. O'Leary and Mrs. Shanklyn I saw then, packing up their stall, and O'Leary waved to me with a fat, bare arm.

'Seen Bron?' I asked her.

'*Gawd*, what a life,' said she, sweating, 'I haven't had time for a scratch. Me old man sinks the profit, you know

236

– but he's good otherwise.' She turned to Patsy Pearl who was standing nearby with Madog, her baby. 'Seen Bron, pet?'

Shanklyn, I saw, was adopting an air of distinguished absence, washing up with gusto.

I knocked up my cap to Patsy, and she said innocently, over her bowl of faggots, 'Come off the last tram, a few minutes back, she has – you've just missed her.'

The women exchanged glances, I noticed, and I didn't want to appear too put out, so I hung around talking to Patsy for a bit.

The Penny Bazaar was closing down; cockle-women, as straight as Amazons with their baskets on their heads, were homeward bound with a marvellous dignity. The jug-and-bottle customers were thinning out around the side entrance of the De Winton; pale-faced children, the sacrifice to ale, waited in line of their parents' night-caps, clutching jugs covered with bead-trimmed muslin. Solly Friedman Pawnbroker tiptoed past us, raising his bowler to Patsy, his smile wider than a barmaid's bum: little Annie Gay stepped by with a fine independent air and a cheeky swing to her hips – recently she'd moved to lodgings opposite the Glamorgan colliery, and I'd made a mental note of it, since it's a good idea to have something in reserve.

'She's a good 'un, mind,' said Patsy, lowering her bowl, and she shifted Madog more comfortably in his shawl on her back.

'Annie Gay?'

'Your Bron. She'll love you when you've got pennies on your eyes, remember, Toby Davies.'

'I hope so.'

'So you treat her decent, eh. Try to understand?'

I looked at her. Madog had his thumb in his rosebud mouth, slobbering, and he gave me a toothless smile. 'Understand what?' I asked.

'Nothing – just treat her decent. She's the best you'll ever dig up.'

'Don't lose sleep, she gets treated all right.'

'You seen the Three Road Overman?' she asked. There was about her face a wan, anxious loveliness.

'John Haley? Not the last ten days – the Bute seam shifts are laid off, aren't they?'

She shrugged, empty. 'Just wondered – no sign of him in the Pandy again tonight?'

'No sign of Bron in there, either.'

'Course not – it's her night off.'

'Is it?' I smiled at my thoughts. 'Both gone short, haven't we, Patsy!'

I heard Mrs. O'Leary say to Mrs. Shanklyn as I strode away, 'Oh, Gawd, now she's blutty done it.'

Everybody appeared to know what was happening, except me.

I met the Livingstones on the edge of the Square. Dribbling, Guto was staring at the moon, and his wife said, 'Out late, aren't we? We've just been down for a little bit of fish – he do like a little bit o' fish, don't you, mun?' She nudged me confidentially. 'You heard the O'Haras are down in these parts, Toby?'

'Ben O'Hara?' I didn't believe her. Nor was she having me as easily as that. Mrs. Guto was all right, but she'd got a handy tongue. I said, 'Last we heard he was somewhere up Merthyr way.'

'Didn't Bron know, either?'

'She will by now,' I said.

'Just arrived in the Aber valley – he's working down the Universal. Funny you ain't heard.'

'When . . . when did that happen?' I tried to keep calm.

'Last week, according to Albert Arse – he met 'em in Senghenydd.'

The full implication of the news had now taken my breath. She added, 'Albert was over there shift-hunting – the Bute seam's stopped temporary – but then, you'd know. Poor Albert, he'd only just started – and Tommy off as well.' She sighed at the moon. 'Bumped into the O'Haras, did Albert – they was out shopping.'

The knowledge that Nan was now only a few miles away was having an astonishing effect on me; I cursed the brightness of the moon.

'Thought you'd be interested,' said Mrs. Guto, with a wink.

It was a drama of irony that was slowly being played.

As Nanwen moved nearer, Bron seemed to be moving away.

I knew where she'd been that night, of course.

The last tram into Tonypandy came in from Porth.

The lamp was on in the kitchen when I got back; it was plainly one of those things – as I'd gone out Bron had come in.

Her face was pale in the lamp-light as she glanced up from the stove. 'Ay ay, Tobe!'

'Aye, mun.' I tried to sound normal.

'Thought you'd be abed – been cooking the Union books again?'

I sat down at the table with the *Labour Weekly*, watching as she filled the kettle and poked the grate into a blaze. She had taken off her hat and her hair hung in tight ringlets down her back; there was in her an unconcealed weariness.

'God, I'm tired,' she said. 'What you been up to?'

'Been asleep. Put my head down and just dropped off. Had a hard night at the bar?'

It was unfair, but I couldn't help it.

'Never damn stopped from the moment I got in,' she said.

'Is there that much money about?'

She made a wry face in the mirror as she waited for the kettle. 'Mainly the Scotch colliers, now the Ely's locked out and a lot down from Clydach.' She smiled. 'Patsy Pearl was in again – looking for John Haley.'

'O aye?' I was surprised to hear her complementing the lie.

My tone evoked a glance from her; she said quickly, 'Like a cup of tea?'

I nodded. 'Working to this hour, they ought to pay you overtime.'

She turned; her hands were clasped together, the knuckles white.

'I haven't been working in the Pandy tonight, Toby.'

'I know you haven't.'

'If you knew, then why the *hell* didn't you say so?' She swung to me, furious.

'And why the hell did you have to lie about it?' I got up and flung the paper down. 'What's more, I know where you've been!'

'That makes it easier,' she said, empty.

'Sam again, isn't it?'

'If you know, why trouble to ask?'

'Christ, what a bloody great fool I am!'

The kettle was singing. Going to it she stood staring down at it. 'I'm the fool,' she said.

'But why? *Why?*' Crossing the room I turned her to face me. 'Aren't I enough?'

Her lips were bright, as if fevered; her cheeks were blooming red, and faintly scratched, scurred by a man's beard. She looked drained of vitality.

'Can't help it, Tobe,' she said, faintly.

'Is that all you can say? Woman — what's wrong with you? I thought we were doing all right!'

For answer she shook her head; she was beaten; I had never seen her in this state. Moving lethargically to the window she drew the curtains, looking out into the night.

'For pity's sake, Bron! You go straight to him from me. Is that fair?'

She bowed her head. 'No.'

'He's back in Porth, isn't he?'

She nodded.

'But not with that woman?'

'No.'

'She's gone, so he's after another skirt — he snaps his fingers and you come running. For God's sake, where's your pride?'

She turned her face to mine. 'I lost that a long time back.'

I said, desperately, pacing about, 'Well, we can't go on like this can we?'

'I'll . . . I'll go if you like?' she said.

Amazingly, the thought that I would lose her brought me fear; a frightening sense of impending loss, and I could not bear it. Bron was looking at me, as if awaiting my agreement. We faced each other over the room. The kettle was boiling its brains out, as if crying for the pair of us. I didn't know what to do. I wanted first to hit her and then comfort her, and I was terrified that she would start to cry. If she started that, I thought, the farce now being enacted would turn into reality and the parting would have to be faced.

She said, 'Do . . . do ye want me to go, Tobe?'

I crossed the room and took the kettle off the hob, seeking escape in practicality.

To break the tension more (for she still hadn't moved from the window) I clattered cups and saucers about and made a great play of finding the milk.

Coming slowly, she joined me at the table; her hands were shaking; there was upon her face an incredible sadness. Softly, as I poured the tea, she said:

'My Gawd, Tobe – he ain't like you. He can be a bugger.' She twisted her hands together. 'I ain't never known such a man like Sam Jones.'

I didn't reply. I dared not trust my voice. There was burning within me a mounting hatred of everything he stood for.

'I suppose you went to bed with him?'

She took the cup and saucer from the table and turned her back upon me.

'*Did you?*' I yelled at her.

'My husband, ain't he?'

'And where do I come in on this?'

She smiled sadly. 'You don't, Tobe – I've always told ye that – not while Sam's about.'

'God almighty!' I put down the cup.

Outside on the Square a drunk was singing, a faint, high-pitched song of shouts and grunts; it seemed the only sound that Tonypandy had to offer.

'You . . . you'll have to make up your mind then, won't you,' I said gently.

The kindness seemed to revive her. 'You need me here?'

I nodded. 'Of course I need you!'

'Because you love me?'

'God knows why!'

Her face became suddenly agitated. 'Then say it – say it now?' She came to me and caught my arms, gripping hard. 'Go on, say you love me?'

'I love you,' I said.

241

She stroked my face. 'Good old Tobe – such a pity, isn't it – getting hooked up on me?'

'But I'm not sharing you – it's Sam or me from now on.'

I wanted to kiss her, but could not. It didn't seem right to put my lips on hers.

So, there was an emptiness between us as we undressed that could not be bridged by words; we moved as strangers in the moonlight of the window, together, yet alone.

With only her petticoat upon her, Bron went to the bosh and poured out the hot water left in the kettle. There, stripping to the waist, her back turned to me, she began to wash herself.

After a minute or two I became aware that she was scrubbing herself with an almost desperate vigour. I looked from the bed. Red and blue patches stained the fair sheen of her skin. Like a woman possessed, she was scrubbing at her body, as if hating it.

Getting out, I crossed the floor and turned her to face me.

'What's all this?' I said, touching her and I pulled it away. Half naked, she stood before me, her face low.

'Who the hell did that?' I asked, and touched the bruises of her arms and shoulders, even her breast.

'Ach, Tobe, it's nothing!' She turned away, discounting it.

I knew a chain-reaction of anger; it contained me, forbidding speech. I snatched at her wrist and twisted her nearer while she clutched at the towel in a vain attempt to hide herself.

'Was it him?'

'Aw, forget it – he don't mean any harm!' But she was uncertain; furtive in her fear of me, and I pulled down her sheltering hands.

'Look at you – just look at you!' I swung her around; her shoulders were swollen by clutching fingers.

'God in Heaven, woman – is this what you want?' I stared into her face.

She said, cajolingly, 'But ... he's always been like that, Tobe – doesn't know his own strength, see? He don't mean it, honest ...'

'I'll kill him,' I said. 'You go to Porth again, and I'll make

you a widow – d'you hear me?' I turned from her, trembling.
'The bastard!'

'Don't say that, Tobe.'

'Well, he is – a bloody bastard. Do you call that love?'

When I turned back to her again she was standing with
her hands by her sides; there was upon her face an expression of infinite understanding. 'But he doesn't love me, I
know that. Sam'll never love anybody, as long as he lives.'

'Yet you waste love on him? – a man who treats you worse
than a whore?'

She nodded.

'Then you make the best of it, I'm going to bed.'

'Put your arms round me, Tobe,' she said.

'Go to hell.'

'Please?'

I got into the bed and turned my back upon her.

I was acting like a child, but it was the best I could do. It
was sickening to find her so weak – he'd taken everything off
her – self respect, pride – she no longer seemed like Bron.

'If I wash myself all over again Tobe – will ye?' There was
in her face a contrite beauty.

'Oh, Christ, come on,' I said, and got out of the bed and
held her.

'He ain't so bad really,' she said. 'Honest, Tobe – not when
you get to know him.'

For a long time Bron sat at the table by the grate, her face
in her hands. The night went on.

'Come on, come in here,' I said, pulling aside the blankets.

She did so; we lay apart in the bed as strangers. She
said:

'Expect I'll get a letter from Bibbs in the morning.'

'Look, it's late ...'

'She usually writes every month, ye know. It's really the
aunt, of course.'

'Go to sleep. It'll be a different kettle of fish in the morning.'

'Why? I'm not on till afternoon and you ain't going anywhere.'

Her change of mood, her sudden, almost flippant attitude

243

to what had happened angered me, and forced upon me new thoughts of Nanwen.

Lying there, I reflected that I had always been Bron's second string: she loved Sam, she'd never made any bones about it.

I chanced a look at her in the room moonlight. She was **lying with her eyes wide open, her hands clasped before her,** as one in prayer, and I pitied the conflicting emotions with her, knowing in my heart that even this apparent flippancy was an attempt to normalise our relationship. The dishonesty of the situation was grieving her: she was in love with Sam but in bed with me; the immorality would never bother Bron, the betrayal did: everything she did was naively fair.

I began to wonder how I could relieve her. If leaving her would give the balm, then I would go. Yet this could only bring her to more loneliness. A month or two with Sam, and she'd be back on her own again.

'What is it now?'

'She'd think a lot of a proper father you know – my Bibbs, I mean.'

'Not my kid,' I said.

'Sam don't care about her.'

'Whether he does or not, it's him she'll want, not me.'

'Don't say that,' she said.

'Bron – look, for God's sake go to sleep?' I heaved over in the bed and turned my back upon her to widen the chasm between us.

Softly then, she began to cry, stifling the sobs in the pillow. This brought me near to panic, but I did not turn to her.

I thought, desperately: if I went to Porth, found Sam and reasoned with him, he might, perhaps take her back permanently. Or better, I'd get out and he could return here, to the hut. He wasn't living with anybody now, according to Bron, and the hope that I might be able to smooth things over between them – perhaps get Bibbs down from the north to renew a bond – brought me relief. It was inconceivable that even Sam would exchange Bron for some fancy woman on a permanent basis.

And then, without apparent cause, fear swept over me at

the thought of losing her. It was a ridiculous situation. I was suddenly furious. Had Sam appeared in the doorway then I'd have had the pair of them with the same fist.

'Toby . . .?'

'Will you go to *sleep?*' Up on an elbow I thumped my fist into the pillow.

She touched my shoulder with the tips of her fingers, whispering:

'You . . . you remember that day in the Waterloo? You know, when the landlord was away, the men were on the march, and you came in . . .?'

The room grieved within its silence. I'd hurt her, and was glad.

'Nanwen's over in the Aber Valley,' she said then, softly.

It was as if all she'd been saying had been leading up to this, such was the finality of her voice.

'Yes, I know – Senghenydd.' I answered curtly. I wanted her to shut up and leave me to my despoiling loneliness; a hatred of Sam Jones and everything he stood for was searing me.

'You knew she'd come recent?'

'Yes.'

'Then it would be fair, wouldn't it, if you saw Nanwen again?'

Conscience, I reflected, uses strange concoctions in the art of human healing. I'd have preferred her stronger. Why the hell couldn't she be as honest as she was supposed to be, and call herself a whore? All she was doing now was offloading some of her responsibility.

After a bit, because she was crying again, I took her into my arms.

Within moments, she was asleep.

She'd had me up half the night.

Trying to obliterate thoughts of her love-making with Sam, I held her, watching a pattern of moonlight cross the boards.

If only she were happy, I reasoned, there could even be a small, if sad sublimity in the loneliness . . .

CHAPTER TWENTY-EIGHT

The day before the Cambrian Combine management locked out nearly a thousand of us from the Ely Pit, I took myself over to the Aber Valley, about ten miles away, to try to see Nanwen.

It was about a week after Bron had been over to Porth to see Sam, so I had no conscience about going. Like as not, I reflected, Bron would take the opportunity to go to Porth again in my absence, for now a chasm that could not be bridged by words had come between us.

It was ironic, I thought, that, at the very moment of possessing Bron, I had entirely lost her; as if the action had made her spirit free.

'Off, then, are you?' she had asked, when I got up early.

'Aye, for a few hours.'

'Going to Senghenydd?'

'Why not? I'm not much wanted round here.' It was childish and ineffective, but I could not help it. 'Good chance for you to kick over the traces again isn't it?'

'You want me to go?'

'Please yourself.'

At the hut door she said, with a whimisical smile, 'Give her my love.'

I said evenly:

'Pity, isn't it, Bron – we were doing all right.'

'We could still do all right, mate – it's you who're making an elephant's cock out of a pig's ear.'

'I don't share my women.'

It was pious, and I regretted it.

'Tell that to Ben O'Hara.'

She always managed to better me when it came to words.

For the first time since I had come to live in the Sinkers I felt I had truly lost her, but brushed the emotion aside, being filled with an expectant joy now, at the prospect of seeing Nanwen.

These were the days when I'd go to the Athletic Ground and lose myself in rugby; soon after I'd arrived in Town I'd joined the local club, the Ystrad Stars, and there was a fine comradeship of knocks and lads of an afternoon off shift, and knocks mostly, for my rugby was like my cricket – what I couldn't get my bat to I got my head to.

But today I took the early tram to Porth and got a lift on a brewer's cart to Caerphilly; sitting with my back to the ale casks, dozing in the sun.

I walked from Caerphilly and got into Senghy, which was the local name for Senghenydd, before midday. Even the bleached trees of the mountain, tortured to death by the rubbish of the tips, seemed to beckon me with leaf and flower as I strode into the village. In the Square I asked for Ben O'Hara and got sent to a nearby pub the Gwern.

'Big Irish fella with a thirst like a desert?' asked the five-foot landlord, peering over the bar like a stoat at a rabbit.

I sank my half a pint, all I could afford. 'That's right. Just come in, they say – got a wife and little girl.'

'Try Four Windsor Place,' said he, and wiped his whiskers. 'You his butty?'

'Sort of.'

'Then settle his slate – he already owes me.'

By the look of things I'd got the right O'Hara.

Number Four had a front I would have expected of Nanwen, and she always kept a marvellous upstairs.

Ceinwen, aged nine, was standing near as I knocked on the door; she regarded me with unspoilt eyes; long plaits, ink on her fingers and school books had she.

'Senghenydd Board School?' I asked her, and she nodded, shy.

'Don't remember me, do you?' and she shook her head.

I'd have known her among marching thousands; Nan's serenity and dark-Welsh beauty, in miniature. The door opened and Ben stood there, filling it.

'Sufferin' God!' he ejaculated. 'Is there wind of ye?'

'I told nobody,' I said, and he reached out and hauled me into the narrow hall, crying:

'Devil take me!' And he shouted to Ceinie. 'D'ye know who this is, me lovely? It's your fine big Uncle Toby, that's what! Hey, Nan – come on her – it's the lad from Bethesda!' He shouted bass laughter. 'It's ye sweet fella!'

She arrived with flour on her hands, wonderment on her face.

'Toby!'

The sight of her stopped my breath. With Ben bellowing nonsense between us, we stood and stared, and it was wrong that I could not take her into my arms.

There was no change in her, save a gentleness of years, and then she smiled, and beauty, as always, flew to her face.

'Christ!' roared Ben, pulling me through the narrow hall. 'You're a man wi' a weak nut, for sure. Didn't I hear tell you were over in the Rhondda?' He thumped my back. 'Why the hell didn't ye come before?'

'Hallo, Nanwen,' I said.

The girl came in behind us and we went into the kitchen to a smell of baking and warmth, and Nan took off her apron with agitated fingers and patted and smoothed her hair and there was talk of a cup of tea, though as Ben went past me I smelled his ale.

There was about him now a brutal strength, and a coarseness born of drink.

Later, we sat at the kitchen table and talked of Bethesda.

'So Mrs. Livingstone told you we were here – she gets all the latest news, that one!' laughed Nanwen.

Ben roared, 'Albert Arse must have told her – we met him out shopping, down the village. Talk about tom-toms. Is that right they're living down the same Row as you now?'

'The Sinkers,' I replied, 'moved in recent. You should see young Tommy – he's working, you know – coming on in leaps and bounds – handy with 'em, too.'

'And young Rosie's a jewel of a girl, too, Albert says,' shouted Ben. 'When she was toddling she was coming for a caution! Remember the Love-Jenkins?'

'Aren't they round here somewhere – in the Aber Valley?' I asked.

The words were flying now.

'Not come across them yet,' said Nanwen, and lowered her eyes as they met mine. From a corner of the room Ceinie watched me with an unquiet stare.

Despite Ben's occasional surly silence, Nan and I chattered on about Dan Morgan, my old Llechwedd foreman, who had now gone blind; of Grandpa with his trousers half-mast and Sam's mother, who had died. We talked of Sam Dickie, whose wife never came back to him – all this according to the Livingstones; we laughed together, remembering old Dick Jones, the miser who bottled his water.

'He wouldn't give a bit of cheese to a starving navvy,' shouted Ben, thumping the table with his fist, but I sensed that the atmosphere of renewed friendship was dying between us, despite the old memories.

'Tom Booker died, you know,' said Nanwen, softly. 'Tom Inspector, too – killed in a fall at Penrhyn Quarry.'

It quietened my thoughts, bringing life into perspective. A young woman hurried past the kitchen window with her basket; she was greeting somebody I couldn't see; her hair was fair, her smile beautiful; she was vibrantly alive, unlike this forced and artificial conversation; strangely, I remembered Bron.

'And Dick Patagonia – remember Dick? And Harri Ogmore, too – they all caught it,' growled Ben.

'All four?' I gasped. 'God! Poor old Harri taught me to fly on the chain!'

'He's flying with a harp now, me son!' Ben rubbed his stubbled chin like a man needing ale. 'Shot-firing – the usual. No warning. Sam Jones's father was on the fuse – he took all four of 'em.' He settled his elbows on the table and grinned at me. 'Don't you see Sam Jones these days, then?' Taking a hip flask from his pocket, he swigged deep from it, eyes clenched at the ceiling.

Nanwen's movements quickened, and I realised that Albert must also have told them about Bron and me. I realised, too, that Ben was tipsy. Meeting his eyes, I shook my head, and he grunted deep, pushing himself up from the table to knock out his pipe. 'Ach, what the hell – does it matter – any of 'em? Every man jack o' them were bloody *bradwrs.'*

'But they didn't deserve to die,' Nanwen added, quietly.

At the grate, with his arm around Ceinie's shoulders, Ben said:

'So ye say ye haven't come across your mate, Sam Jones?'

Nan said, 'another cup of tea, Toby?' and she flashed a warning glance at her husband.

'No,' I answered, replying to Ben.

'Which is a wonder, considering you're living wi' his missus, according to Albert Arse.'

'People need to nurse their own troubles,' said Nan, angrily. She poured the tea and handed me the cup. 'Not our business, is it?'

'It's simple enough – Sam didn't want her,' I replied.

'How's Bron's little Bibbs, Toby?' Nan asked, quickly.

I laughed. 'Growing up, like Ceinie. She's up north in Caernarfonshire with her aunt. The aunt writes occasionally.'

Ben said, 'She's out of the way, so to speak?'

'Ask Sam Jones, mate, not me.' I met his eyes.

'So you ringed up with Bron after Sam left her?'

I said, 'Bron needed a friend – that's how these things start,' and Ben replied:

'Ach, stop coddin' us along, lad – t'is a pretty romantic business, ye know, and I always approve of love. You had a fair glance for Ma Bron when she was up in Pesda, for she's a well set-up lass.' Stooping, he knocked out his pipe in the grate and said into Ceinie's face, 'Which goes to prove that you have to watch the opposite sex, me sweet child, since ye never know where ye are with 'em – on your backside or your elbow.'

Ceinie did not move. She was staring at her mother. Nanwen's face was pale. I drank the tea, inwardly cursing myself for coming.

'Are ye marrying the wee soul?' Ben asked, filling his pipe and grinning aimlessly in my direction.

'Ben, please,' said Nan.

'Dear God, I forgot – she's married already! Does it set ye fair, Toby, me son – lyin' wi' another's man wife?'

There was no time for reply because two colliers came and hammered on the window; codifiers of Welsh ale by the look of their stomachs, and Ben shouted:

'I'll be with ye directly, my darlins'.' He turned to me. 'I'm away on shift, ye young skut, so I am. D'ye fancy a light pint with the lads before making your way back to the Rhondda?'

I shook my head, watching him. The shame of it was in Nanwen's face, and I hated him.

'Your tommy-tin's in the back,' said Nanwen, cold.

Laughing, he waved to the window, got the box and his bottle and crossed the room to Ceinie. Taking her hands in his, he stage-whispered:

'Now, hearken, treasure. The fella in here is after ye ma, understand? So you keep an eye on him for the sake of your pa, is it? And, if they step anywhere together, it's up to the pit and three pulls on the hooter.'

Nanwen said, 'Ben, how dare you!'

'Aye, woman, I do.' He straightened, no longer smiling. 'Because, with one man's wife in the cupboard, he's bound in this direction now.'

'You watch your mouth,' I said.

'And you yours, me son, lest this time I shut it. How many women do ye want?' He pushed past me to the door, pulling it open. 'Give him a piece o' your cake for the journey, missus, and send him on his way, for I'll have the balls off the bugger if he's here when I get back.'

Nan gasped, 'Ben, for God's sake, Ceinie's listening!'

'Let her hear! A man never knows where he is with you two from minute to minute – damned Welsh! When she mixes the Godly with the ungodly, she'll have a stew to feed the world.' He stared at us. 'What the hell do you two see in each other?'

'Nothing that you'd understand,' said Nanwen, and I flashed a glance at her. 'You'd best go, Toby.'

'Out, ye big lanky bastard,' whispered Ben, and pushed wide the door. 'And don't come back, my lovely boyo.'

But he feared me; I saw it in his face.

His two mates, awaiting him on the road, watched us with beery apprehension: tipsy on shift, I reflected, and these would never set foot down the Universal where drunks weren't needed to raise the danger.

Joining them, Ben marched off, swaying. All his movements, like his lust for ale, had become misshapen by the years.

Ceinie went back inside the house, but I noticed her watching us through the window.

'Got to get her dinner,' said Nan, and waved to her, calling, 'I'll be in directly.'

And then she turned to me. 'Oh, *Toby*,' she said.

I moved to the gate. 'I shouldn't have come.'

'I'm glad you did.' She was close to tears and I wanted to put my arms around her. All down the street the curtains were moving, doors coming open; women greeting each other.

I said, 'After all these years, we're still in the same mess, aren't we?'

She made a gesture of emptiness. 'But you're happy with Bron, surely?'

The big Universal, the distant Windsor pit, whispered between us in smoke, brought on the mountain wind.

'I love you, Nan,' I said.

She looked at me. 'And I love you, Toby. It's like being alive again, seeing you.'

I said, 'You need me, you send for me, remember?'

'Aye.' She had upon her face a beautiful expression.

'Goodbye, then.'

Strangely, Ceinie waved from the window as I went.

Bron was still at the Pandy when I got back home.

Dusk was falling, for I'd walked the whole ten miles, stopping for a few pints in Caerphilly, trying to sort out my thoughts.

Perhaps it would be best to go from the valley and start a new life, I considered; there were other jobs, other places for a man without attachments.

I wandered into the empty hut. Bron's hand was everywhere; the ironed washing on the fireguard, the grate like polished ebony, and not a speck of dust. The bed was neatly made, the blankets meticulously folded; bacon was in the frying-pan, an egg on the side.

And in the middle of the kitchen table was a little vase of wild flowers; beside it was a note.

'I love you,' it read.

Damned women.

Didn't know what to make of them.

Nor men either, come to think of it . . .

CHAPTER TWENTY-NINE

'We're locked out,' said Heinie, as we reached the gate of the Ely, reporting for shift the following month.

The colliers crowded up behind us, bawling unanswered questions at the locked colliery gate, trying to read the notice that the management had posted up. For a month now the Owners had been promising this; now they'd done it.

'Read it out, Heinie!' yelled a man from the back.

They fought for room as the crowd increased, swinging their comrades aside, and Heinie shouted, 'We're bloody locked out – can't you see the gates?'

Silence while he read the notice. High above the motionless pit wheels of the Ely, a lark sang, his voice cadent in the still September air; the morning sun bathed the valley in a golden radiance.

Nearly a thousand men waited, pent.

Heinie cried, 'You're out, I say! All eight hundred and eighty of ye – they've shut the Ely,' and a voice cried:

'You blind fool, read it again – give him his glasses! *Eighty*, you mean – the Bute Five Foot teams – that's what the argument's about, not the whole shift!'

'You're out, it says – every man jack – every Ely collier – underground and on the top!'

'They can't do that!'

'They've bloody done it,' said Ben Block.

They cursed in a rising tumult of threats, and Tommy Arse, standing near me, shouted:

'But I'm starting a new stall today – I anna anywhere near the Bute seam, sir!'

'You're out just the same, young 'un,' said Moses Culpepper.

I saw Tommy's stained face; the only collier I had seen shed tears.

'Now there'll be trouble,' this from Bill Odd, and he

gripped the gate with his big fists and rattled it. 'Nine hundred out, eh? And over one seam?'

'It'll bring out the whole of the Cambrian!'

'And the Scotch Glamorgan, too – Christ, we'll show 'em.'

'We'll have that Mabon for this – him and Mainwaring,' cried Dai Parcel.

'Don't blame the Union representatives!' shouted Richard Jones, and he stood on a plinth. 'Calm, now men – keep calm!'

'They lock us out – nine hundred men and boys – and you say keep calm!' Boos and insults rose; the colliers heaved; the gates clattered, but held.

'Break down the gates!'

And there arose in the crowd a man of good height; the sight of him standing with Richard Jones on the plinth momentarily stilled the mob.

'Break down these gates,' said John Haley, the English overman, 'and they'll bring in the Glamorgan police to crack your skulls: take a single cage down the Ely by force, and they'll send in the troops – remember what happened up in Featherstone? Now then – easy, and *cool* ... Richard Jones here is right,' and he put his hands on his hips and grinned about him. 'Can't you reason why the owners lock out nine hundred men, with only eighty of the Bute Seam in dispute? To bring the place to violence!' They stared up at him, muttering like bulls at feed, and he said, in the silence, 'Go home. They want us out, they shall have us out. But, by God, when we're back it will be on our terms!'

The colliers rose to this, cheering and shouting. The door of the Gethin went back and they flooded into it, stamping for ale, while every spare skirt the landlord could muster went round with jugs.

'Dear me,' cried Annie Gay, with a saucy eye at me, 'what a lot of lovely men!' and she clapped her hands. 'Gets right up my nose when folks run 'em down.'

'*Daw*, look at them,' said Mattie. 'I like a pint, but not at eight o'clock in the morning!' He pinched Annie's bottom. 'You come down from your pub special to see me?'

We clustered together, penned by the mob at the gates. Trams were clanging their bells for passage; tradesmen standing up in their carts, cursing and cracking whips. Dano McCarthy cried in his thick Irish, 'Go home and fret, is it? *Ach*, the skuts! St. Paul himself never thought so wrong,' and he crossed himself. 'And I come from Ireland to get a fair deal from Wales?'

'This place is mad daft, Pa,' said Shaun, his youngest. 'We'd be best back home in Galway.'

'Suffering' God!' cried Dano, lanky and thin, 'that's where Etta will land me in the Sinkers, for she don't approve of the striking.'

'Do any of us?' asked Mattie Kelly.

'Me, for one,' I said. 'If they want a lock-out, let them have a lock-out. The owners have the money, but we've the strength. All for one, is it? Aye, then – one for all – they'll think again when the Nantgwyn and Pandy drop tools.'

'And the Aberdare and Ogmore lot, remember – us first, them later,' said Moses Culpepper, soprano. 'I said it before – strength in numbers – two hundred thousand colliers in South Wales, remember!'

'You got to ask your missus first, though,' said Mattie.

'Aye, but he's right,' said Ed Masumbala, the black man, and men went quiet, for he rarely spoke; much respected was he, like Beli, his black missus. 'Strength is right; we got to stick together.'

'Tell that to Mabon,' said Heinie Goldberg, and he shouldered a path into the free. 'We pay our money in the Miners' Federation, don't we? Conciliation boards and half-cock committees, is it? Now we can watch them earn their wages.'

I looked at John Haley the new overman. He was standing with Tommy beside him, wrapped in thought, as in a leaden shroud.

I crossed the road and pushed through the men to him. His fine blue eyes, ringed with coal, moved slowly over me; no wonder Patsy Pearl was curdling Madog's milk.

'Haley, Haley?' I asked. 'There's not much Welsh in that.' I gave him a grin.

'Is it a crime?'

'*Diawl*, no mun – we'll sign a Chinee into the Union.'

'No Unions for me, mate.' He looked beyond me, a man removed.

'You don't believe in collective bargaining?'

'I do not.'

'But you take the Union's rises and stick to Union's rules? You can't have it all ways.'

'I take what's coming. The stewards don't force pay awards, Welshman, the colliers do – the power lies at the coal face. There's too much money and career prospect in the Union, that's why you're lumbered with people like Mabon. Negotiate with this Owner? They crawl under stones better than him.'

'What will come of it?'

He looked at the sky for words and said: 'Trouble.'

'Real trouble?'

'The place is going to starve.'

Snookey Boxer, bulky, flat-faced, came up and pestered me, pulling at my sleeve, making incoherent sounds; night-time, on the steps of the Empire, he cut out dolls with scissors and brown paper. I shook him away, but he came at me again, rolling on his heels. I said to the over-man:

'We'll fight, then?'

He looked me over, sighing, as if he had never seen me before. 'God Almighty,' he whispered, 'won't you people ever learn? We've got to fight, there's no alternative.'

'The business is getting them all to fight,' I replied.

'God help you if they don't.'

I watched him going up Dunraven with his hand on Tommy's shoulder.

Unless I was mistaken, I thought, we were going to see more of John Haley.

So the whole of the Ely Pit (not just the Bute Seam) was locked out – nearly a thousand colliers; it was an act of violence that was uncalled for and unnecessary, and the Management refused arbitration on the price of coal per ton. Four days later, the Nantgwyn and Pandy, two other Combine pits stopped work in sympathy with us in the Ely, and the fingers of hatred for D. A. Thomas spread outwards through the Rhondda like the fingers of a hand. As grievances against other Owners were aired, more pits dropped tools – the Lower Duffryn in Mountain Ash and the Lletty-Shenkin in Aberaman – when the police stopped colliers taking home waste wood for their fires – a custom long accepted by managements.

One by one the shutters went up in the tradesmen's windows, for lack of custom; the doors of the little terraced houses were shut tight to keep in the warmth. Aye, said Bron, the doors are closing against hunger like the slamming of coffin lids.

Within weeks, because we were all pantry clients, like Ginty said, the children began to cry for food – while Mr. D. A. Thomas – Mabon's mate, the colliers said – was tucked up fed and warm in the south of France.

'This place is going mad,' said Bron, at the hob.

'Well, what d'you expect?'

'I expect some blutty sense!'

'The Ely didn't strike, you know – it was locked out,' I retorted.

'The Ely isn't Nantgwyn, the Pandy Pit, Lower Duffryn and Lletty-Shenkin!'

'We stand together or fall together.'

'Folks'll be on the starve.' She swung to me. 'Where's the sense of striking when you could negotiate? That's what you've got men like Mabon for, isn't it?'

'But the Owners won't negotiate, woman!' I sat on the bed. 'What the hell can you do with Owners like Thomas who lock their workers out? We were in the middle of negotiations for fair rates for work and they slam the door and go off home – how do you handle people like that?'

'And what are the women of this town going to do, eh?' White-faced, she bent towards me, making points with her saucepan; she had never looked so fiercely beautiful. 'It's all right for you lot, you know – it's the women and kids that do the scratching. You men are a lot of bloody kids – like an Irish parliament – everybody talking, nobody listening; shouting your heads off in the publics – you should hear them in the Pandy – will that bring negotiation?'

'You've got to have two for a negotiation!' I was getting angry. 'What the hell can we do if Thomas won't talk?'

'Ach, come off it, ye bugger – you've been hitting up for a strike for months. And now you've got one, it's the Owners' fault.'

'Because families can't live on one-and-nine a ton!'

A silence came; there was no sound but Bron's breathing. At the grate, she said over her shoulder, 'You'll go back, you know.'

'Aye, and on our terms!'

'On masters' terms – with your tails between your legs. Union or no Union, that's how it's always been.'

'Don't talk rubbish, woman – we'd be half dead by now if it hadn't been for the Union. And that's what's happening now – the Owners are trying to break it.' I strode about. 'The trouble with you is you've been reading too many newspapers.'

'Does nobody tell the truth except the Union?' she cried. 'What about the pits flooding out if there's nobody down there to man the pumps? What about the ponies?' I was too sick of this newspaper bogey even to reply to it.

I said, 'Tom Mann's got an article coming out soon. Class solidarity in the face of oppression is what's wanted now, he says. So let the capitalists look after their own property or let it go to hell, and he's right.' I went to the door. 'If you want the truth you should read the Union pamphlets – the newspapers are run by the Owners.'

'Who's Tom Mann when he's home?'

'God Almighty!' I said.

I put on my coat and muffler: the night was star-lit cold in the window, an early raw, even for the Rhondda, God being a Tory and working for the masters. I said, 'If you don't know who Tom Mann is, there's no sense in continuing this stupid conversation.'

'Now you're off, I suppose!'

'Aye.'

'Got money for beer, have you? Ten bob a week strike pay? You'll find your mates in there. What the hell would happen if women went on strike?'

I closed the door and leaned against it, facing her. 'What's wrong with us? We've had trouble before, haven't we?'

She said, with cold practicality, 'Same as is happening all

259

over Town. Colliers fighting Owners; wives fighting husbands.'

'Not true. The women are behind us – why not you?'

'*Listen*, I'm like the rest of the women if I think there's chance. But you haven't got one. I've seen all this before – in Clayton workhouse, in the mill country – I've seen it in Bethesda. Later, when there's big Union money behind you, you can fight. But the Owners have a union of millionaires! Unless you sink your pride, you'll pull this town into the gutter.'

'You've missed your vocation,' I said. 'They'll call you to the bar.'

I slammed the door behind me.

Sad was my town that October.

Silent, deserted, were the streets of Tonypandy; the empty trams rumbled through a place of loafers; the front and backs were shut tight to the world. Shawled, mufflered and cosseted, huddled over their dead fires or bedded in groups for warmth, the people began to starve in earnest.

No longer the Salvation Army pumped and blasted on the Square in Pandy; Will Parry's trumpet was put in cold storage. Instead, the trundling soup kitchens of the Quakers appeared; gentry people, too, served us, and they will be remembered. Up on the hillsides the old levels were opened in secret; on the "patches" small coal was scrabbled; men and boys working like blacks; women and girls dragging it down in sacks, watching for the police patrols. Pickets were posted: magistrates threatened with anonymous letters.

And, as up in Bethesda in the strike against Penrhyn, out came the blacklegs.

'Every community's got them,' said Mattie Kelly.

'The dregs of a community,' I said.

'Oh, aye?' said Heinie. Thin and pale he looked already. 'Men with sick wives, more'n likely.'

'Bollocks to 'em,' said Moses Culpepper. 'We stand or fall in sickness or health.'

'Even the chapels are against us.'

This wasn't unusual. The chapels and the Church of England had vested interests in the south of France, people said;

when it came to economics, God went out of the window. Yet we all clung on to God in our hearts.

'If I had a starving child, I'd kill that bloody D. A. Thomas,' cried Mr. Richard Jones. Things were changing when he talked like that about the Owners.

'They won't let the Quakers serve soup in the vestries.'

'Who won't?'

'The Elders.'

'I'll give 'em head deacons when this strike is over – the toe of my boot in the arse.'

'And Jesus fed the five thousand? Is it Christian?'

'Changing my religion to agnostic, I am.'

'Mind, starving kids do weaken a man,' said Bill Odd. 'Mine cry in their sleep, you know.'

'No more peaky than my lot,' said Moses, 'you seen 'em?'

'At her wit's end, is my missus.'

'And my little Willie needing special food, and all?' said Mrs. Shanklyn.

'When there's no more faggots, feed 'im on the peas, love,' said Mrs. Leary.

'Sod these coal owners.'

'It will end,' said Patsy Pearl. 'Nobody's wanting love.'

'I'll give ye a tanner for it,' said Solly Friedman, pawnbroker.

'And Dozey, Sarah's mate, goin' to a shadow?'

'Oh Lord, my God, hearken to our call,' they sang in the chapels.

'Thou who watches the sparrow fall,' rang out from the Church of England.

'You get more religion in the inns and publics,' said Bron.

'Mrs. Catty Ledoux seen up in Penygraig yesterday, you heard?'

'And she ain't the only blutty cat consumer. Got slanted eyes, you noticed?'

'Gives me the shivers, she do,' said Bron.

'Mind,' said Primrose, 'French, ain't she? – I never did trust the French, not since the Battle of Waterloo. But fair's fair to Ledoux, I say – got mouths to feed, ain't she? Though Sarah Bosom's persian were worth a fortune; she ought to restrict herself to tabbies, I think.'

At night, if the wind was right, we could hear little Madog crying up near River View, Patsy coming thin in the milk with her, according to reports.

'They eat rats in China, you know, when things get skinny.'

'*Ach y fi!*'

'You can say that again,' said Bron, and shuddered. 'I've got to be a lot more hungry before I drop to cats.'

'They dropped to rats once, up in the Eastern Valley,' said Richard Jones. 'In Dowlais they cooked them on shovels and quarrelled over the gravy.'

'Ten bob a week strike pay?' cried a woman in the De Winton. 'Six mouths to feed? If I had starving kids I'd feed 'em Ginty, never mind cats.'

The world, I thought, holds no better teacher than adversity.

In places like Caerphilly and Senghenydd, and down the Rhymney Valley, the pits still worked, being out of the Cambrian Combine, for this was not yet a National strike. But, in our part of the Rhondda, the Cambrian, the strike was total.

'You fools, you're playing right into the Owners' hands,' cried Bron. 'They're after breaking your hearts. And you'll be back on their terms, as I said before.'

'We'll die first.'

She glared at me. 'Probably.'

The strike went on.

In the pinch-pale, coal-stained witch of a night; in the sparkling air of Tonypandy with her glinting roofs of frost: under the eaves of Court Street, Ely Street, Adare Terrace and Church Street; in the empty pantries, the bare front rooms, the foodless kitchens, the bellies rumbled as I went on my rounds, with Union strike pay – as I had done with Ben O'Hara years back.

They had stomach trouble in Number Two, the Sinkers, for a start, but it wasn't much to do with the lockout.

'Oh, *Duw*,' whispered Rosie Arse, twisting on the sofa in the kitchen. 'I got a pain and a half in my tum.'

'Come in, come in,' Albert greeted me, and sat me at the table.

'It's strike pay,' I said. 'If Rosie's that bad I'll come back later, if you like.' I opened my ledger on the table. 'How long's she been like that, then?'

'She'll get worse, I reckon, before she gets better,' said Annie, coming in from the back. ' 'Evening, Toby.'

'Is it something she's eaten?'

'Oh, *Arglwydd!*' groaned Rosie, holding her middle.

'She ain't eaten at all – that could be the trouble,' said Albert, worried. 'Or what you think, Annie? Perhaps we got another woman in the house, really speaking?'

'She's a woman these past two years,' said Annie.

'Is she going to die?' asked Tommy, her brother. He was getting bigger every day, shaving, a man before his time.

'They don't usually,' said Annie. 'What can we do for ye, Tobe?'

'Ten bob, missus, sign here – strike pay,' and I slid them the silver.

'Strike pay, is it? – you always was an angel,' said Annie.

'Shall I fetch the doctor?' asked Tommy, dark-eyed and serious.

We got no money for doctors,' said Albert, and knelt by the sofa, soothing Rosie's head. 'Where does it hurt, my precious?'

'Cor, love us,' whispered Rosie, going cockney. 'I am 'aving a turn,' and she moved her great dark eyes to mine.

I looked around the bare room. Everything had already gone into pop; there was nothing left but the table and chairs, the couch and the crockery.

'Anything I can do?' I asked, getting up.

'Nothing I can't handle,' said Annie.

'Shall I go and fetch Farrier George?' asked Tommy, his eyes like saucers. 'He's good when horses have pains ...'

'She's my daughter,' said Albert, flushed. 'She ain't a mare, ye know.'

'She's a mare, all right,' said Annie.

The wind was howling for a Wake as I plodded up to

263

Court. Will Shanklyn was out looking for firewood, according to Mrs. Shanklyn, so my baby won't die of the cold.

'He won't die of the cold, ye understand, Toby Davies?' said she. 'All the time there's an Owner's mansion with teak on the stairs, says my Will, my Willie's dying warm.'

I followed her into the front room where her idiot son was lying; cold as charity he looked, with his little white face pinched up.

'Isn't fair, really, you think of it, Toby Davies?'

The lad snuffled in sleep; I held her against me while she wept.

'I got the strike pay – ten bob, missus.'

'We don't like the charity,' said Mrs. Shanklyn, blowing her nose.

'Strike pay isn't charity.'

'My Will reckons it is. He don't mind the five bob Benefit Club money, you understand – he pays twopence a week for that, see – but he won't take strike pay.'

'But it's an entitlement – and you need it for Willie.'

Her obesity was thinning out. The flesh hung on the pin-bones of her gaunt face, her breasts sagged on her stomach. She wept in blueness and shivering, the tears running down between her fingers. 'Oh, God in grief, what am I going to do? Mrs. Change, the midwife, reckons he's dying. Ye see, Toby, Willie needs special food. Milk, mainly – he never could keep down solids.'

'Then the ten bob will help you, Mrs. Shanklyn – please take it?' and I pressed it against her, but she pushed me away.

'Will would go mad,' she said.

'He'll go worse if Willie dies, girl. Where's the sense in it?'

She said at the window, 'There's milk in the Co-op and eggs and butter. We could make a go of it when I ran the faggot and peas. But now there's no money about. That's how we kept our lad alive – milk and eggs. They builds him up fine, you know – he's big for fifteen, actual.'

I thought of Tommy Arse, vibrant with health and muscular; I thought of Willie Shanklyn, born lop-sided, who had been dying since birth.

I said to her, 'Need Will know, girl? All you've got to do is to sign your name.'

'He'll kill me,' she said at nothing.

I knocked on the back next door to us and Rachel Odd appeared at the window in her night-cap, at three o'clock in the afternoon, and all the kids about her, standing with their fingers in their mouths, all six except the last two, being twins, recently delivered.

'Hallo, my son,' said Pablo, the parrot.

'Strike pay, is it?' asked Bill, and he eased his greasy bulk into the kitchen where Mrs. Odd was cooking with a candle.

'That all you've got to cook on – candles?' I asked.

'Just till tonight, when Bill gets back with small coal from the "patches".'

'The police are up there – you mind you don't get caught,' I said to him and put the strike money on the table. 'Sign here, Bill,' and he did so with a flourish.

'Stay for bread and dip, will ye, Tobe?'

'No thanks, Rachel – got to get back to Bron directly.'

'She at the Pandy? I thought she was stopped.'

'She still goes, but custom's small – no money about.'

Mrs. Odd, watched by the children with spit on their mouths, carefully laid a slice of cottage loaf in the lid of a biscuit tin and held it over the candle; fat spluttered. The aroma coming up from that bacon dip never smelled so sweet in the Café de Paris.

'Christ, mama, hurry up,' said Ianto, aged nine. 'I'm first, being eldest.'

'Any news?' asked Bill at the table.

It was as cold as a workhouse yard in that kitchen; blue-faced, pinched, the children shivered in their bare feet on the boards. I shook my head. 'None. The Federation's doing it's best to bring the Owners to talks, but they'll have nothing of it.'

Bill hugged himself against the cold. 'They're mad! Nobody struck, ye know? – even on the one-and-nine a ton. What are they trying to do to us, for God's sake?'

'Beat us to our knees.'

'That'll be the day,' said Rachel. 'Who's next, my charmers?'

'Me,' cried Blodwen, aged eight, and she grinned at me with her teeth missing in front; hands cupped, she received the bacon dip like a woman at communion.

'I'll be up to that Owner's mansion first,' said Bill, bassly. 'My kids starving and bloody D. A. Thomas on steak and chips?' He thumped the table with a fist. 'The Union's big now, me lad, and the Union'll handle him. I say stay out.'

'And you with eight kids?'

'Who can break strike if we stay out, eh? Next?' cried Rachel, the bread and dip held high.

'Me,' said Olwen, aged seven, and her tiny blue feet slithered on the floor. She ate delicately, for all her hunger, kittenishly, her green eyes watching me.

'Eat it slow,' said Rachel. 'Thirty-two chews, remember – make it last. They haven't shut down in the whole of the Rhondda yet, I notice . . .'

'It'll spread.' Bill picked up Ruth, aged three, and put her on his knee. 'And serve them right! Look, I only want to feed my lot, nothing else. They can keep their ale, their smokes, their chews – I just want enough to keep a table – for Rachel and the kids – not much to ask, is it?'

'It's too much for the share-holders. They've got to have profits.'

'And Thomas a millionaire? What else does he want?'

'My wedding ring,' said Rachel, 'and I'm putting it in pop tomorrow. Growing kids can't live on bacon dip.' Suddenly angry, she busied herself about, picking things up and hitting them down again, and Bill said, 'Ach, don't be daft, woman, there's no bloody need for that.'

'Married to you, there is!' said Rachel. 'Or this blutty Pablo will 'ave to go; plucked and feathered, he'd make a dinner.'

'What you going to do for decency, then?' asked Bill, and they had suddenly forgotten me.

'All we're worth is a damned old curtain ring, anyway,' said Rachel, and in passing, kissed him.

It seemed wrong to stay longer. The children were watching them with deep apprehension.

'That's right, you sod off,' said Pablo the parrot.

Mr. Richard Jones breathed frosted air at me when he opened the door of Number Fifteen, Court.

' 'Evening, Mr. Jones,' I said. 'The Union hand-out's arrived.'

'We don't need it,' said he, and his watery eyes regarded me. His missus came then, peering over his boney shoulder. 'Who is it, love?'

'Toby Davies,' I said, 'come with the funds. Ten bob for spending – the Union's compliments. What will you have, sir, a flitch of bacon or a hamper from Ginty's?'

Hand in hand, they smiled at me. 'How're the lad's doing?' he asked.

'They're alive.'

I saw the kitchen behind them, the bare room, the dead fire.

'You need it, too,' I replied.

'Children need it more. Take it down to Mrs. Ledoux.' Mrs. Jones clasped her mittened hands together. 'Breaks my heart to see those little mites, it do. Her husband's left her, you know.'

'The Brittany onion-sellers aren't very dependable,' said Richard, archly.

I closed my ledger. 'You're a good one.'

'How's Bron?' he asked.

'Middling.'

They shrugged; hunger was helping age to give them the pallor of workhouse ghosts.

I took off my hat to them and went down the street to see 'Catty' Ledoux.

There were enough cat skins curing in the scullery of Mrs. Ledoux to make fur coats for the matrons of the Rhondda.

Through the cracked window of the kitchen I saw the children – all seven – up at the table and banging their spoons, with a brown, sizzling corpse that could have been mistaken for a rabbit, and Mrs. Ledoux was basting it with ceremonial flourishes.

Nobody got the proof of it, for dead pussies tell no tales,

but there was a distinct shortage of pets in Tonypandy at the time, especially in the vicinity of Court Street where the mice were getting away with murder.

I gave Mrs. Ledoux the ten shillings and she took it in a purring gratitude of French and feline grace. And I saw through that window, the caterwauling children, amber-eyed and bewhiskered, their spoons clutched in their paws, tails erect in a chorus of mewing.

Mrs. Ledoux, with a clawed hand, clutched the silver against the furry front of her.

Her iris eyes glinted at me in the dusk.

'*Entrez, s'il vous plaît, monsieur?*' she purred at me.

I got going, and didn't stop till I reached the end of Court Street.

There I bumped into Sarah Bosom and Dozey Dinah: lanky and thin was Dozey; Sarah was the short of it, lavish in the hips and breast, and in tears.

'We had our Timmy this morning,' grizzled Dozey. 'True, she were out all night, but she came in for her breakfast,' and Sarah wept openly into a tiny lace handkerchief.

'We'll 'ave to slip down to Church Street and ask Mr. Goldberg about it – he'll know what to do.'

'Seen to us individually, if ye understand,' said Dozey, 'in times gone by.'

'Has he, now?' I said. I knew Heinie had a past but I was doubtful if he'd got a future.

'Meanwhile,' sobbed Sarah, 'if you see a lovely big white persian, you'll let us know immediate?'

I bowed to them.

Bron wasn't in the Pandy when I called for her; the land-lord raised a flushed, heavy face to me as I came in; the bar, once full of the shouting, rollicking shifts from the Big Glamorgan, was as bare as an Eskimo burial ground and twice as chilly.

Even the Square was empty. It was as if the strike had come in with winter brooms and swept up the refuse called people.

Bron wasn't home, either.

I threw down the ledger, counted the money I had left,

and lay on the bed; later, I undressed and got in properly. After a bit, I slept.

Bron came home near to the dawn: she did not light the lamp. I saw her but dimly, as a man lying within a husk of dead love.

CHAPTER THIRTY

Some, who were wrong, said that the Rhondda blew up when Winston Churchill, then Home Secretary, sent soldiers into the valley: others who were right, claimed that the violence really began when police, under the leadership of the hated Captain Lindsay, their Chief, began to beat up our coalfield picketers, who were acting peacefully and within the law.

'You know,' said Heinie, after this, 'all the Cambrian management has to do is to make its own laws, see the police carry them out, and sit on its backsides until the colliers' children begin to fail.'

They failed all right.

Up to now, they were children confined to the Ely colliers. But, on the sixty-third day of the Ely Lock-out (when we weren't allowed to work though we wanted to) the Miners' Federation made its call to the rest of the Cambrian colliers. These, after a mass meeting of assent, came out in sympathy with us of the Ely.

More than a dozen pit wheels in the two valleys stopped turning.

The battle was on. And, according to Bron we were on a hiding to nothing. As things turned out, she wasn't far wrong.

Poverty, deep and true, stalked the valleys.

Famished in the little bare bedrooms in an icy bitch called November, the children died, and the little white coffins, always the first, began their drab processions to the mountain cemeteries.

Later, though toughened by earlier privations, the old ones began to falter: the poor, the ailing; women with consumption, men with miner's asthma. Then the big yellow coffins with shining brass handles, beautiful with flowers, passed the curtained windows in a clattering of black-plumed horses, and the Hibernian band played *The Dead March in Saul.*

But, according to the popular newspapers, these did not die of starvation: they died, it was said, of a score of diseases from tuberculosis to scarlet fever, 'flu to whooping cough, croup to pneumonia. Few took account of the truth that the Rhondda was starving. Our constant applications to the Owners to recommence work at the Ely and put the Bute Seam to new arbitration, was met with rejection: unless the colliers accepted one-and-ninepence a ton, said the Management, the Ely would stay shut.

And so, one by one, with the pumps silent, underground workings began to flood. Engine-house fires were put out in Tonypandy, which brought Mr. D. A. Thomas back from the south of France.

'God help us,' said Bron. 'The strike will be total.'

'It'll only be total when the blacklegs are dealt with,' I said. 'That's up to us, it has nothing to do with God.'

'You know,' laughed Heinie, 'when you talk that way, you sound like a communist.'

'He's in good company,' said Dai Parcel, come over to visit us. 'Jesus was the first.'

'I wish you lot wouldn't talk like that,' said Bron. 'We're in need of God now, that's certain sure.'

We were in despair.

The Combine management had brought in outside labour; these joined with scabs to keep wheels of some pits turning, and our attempts to picket the colliery entrances were again broken up by the police and strong-arm volunteers working for the Owners.

The colliery up at Clydach was a case in point; they were still taking out coal and running it in trains past our noses. And Chief Constable Lindsay, known as 'The Roman Centurion', had taken more pit ponies underground; then he gave newspaper interviews telling of the heartless attitude of the colliers to their animals, who were in danger of drowning now the pumps had stopped.

'He's been taking ponies underground every day this week,' said Mattie Kelly. 'If there's one horse down the Scotch there must be four hundred.'

'Why do they want ponies down the pit if there's no work

for 'em?' asked Rachel Odd, come in to borrow bread.
'Wake up, woman,' I said.

'For the sake of public opinion,' explained Heinie. 'One drowned pony and the whole country'll be against us.'

'King George is losing sleep already,' said Mattie. 'If pit ponies drown they reckon he'll abdicate.'

'What about us – won't he abdicate for us?' asked Bron.

'You're not important compared to a pit pony,' said John Haley, who had joined the Union now and come with Richard Jones. 'Keir Hardie'll be in trouble, the way he's talking – anti-patriot, they'll call him now – criticising the King.'

'Christ, what a world,' said Rachel. 'You heard about the Shanklyn boy?'

'The doctor gives him a couple of days, at most.'

'The Shanklyns'll give 'em pit ponies if that boy dies, including God save the Prince of Wales.'

'And that's been tried before! Remember the Chartists?'

'So what's the Union doing about it?' asked Haley. 'What's our weak-kneed Federation got in mind, now the kids are dying and everybody hates us?'

'The Federation's been more active than you think,' said Mr. Jones. 'So listen, and spread this to every Ely lodge member. The Union has called for a mass meeting and demonstration of strength tomorrow. All of you – get the buglers out at dawn and rouse people up. All committees and stewards are to be responsible for turning out in force.'

'Just a demonstration?' asked Heinie, innocent.

'An official Federation mass meeting, man – everybody up at the Athletic Ground by seven o'clock. Discussion first; the total strike resolution repeated, and then a march to Clydach to drown the engine-room fires. We're to shut down every pit still working with blackleg labour.'

'Now you're talking,' said John Haley. 'But what about *positive* action?'

'Isn't drowning fires and closing pits positive action?' asked Richard Jones. 'What more do you want?'

'Drive out the Metropolitan police, for a start. Attack the newspaper offices – run out the lies!'

'Cool heads will win, Overman,' I said.

'Violence will win – it's the only way!'

'With Captain Lindsay spoiling for a fight and a hundred and fifty Metropolitan police billeted in Town? – talk sense!'

'You fight now,' said Haley, softly, 'or you might just as well let this generation die, wipe the slate clean, and start all over again.'

'Every time I fought outside me weight I got a hiding,' said Heinie. 'We're featherweights compared with the London government.'

'And even if we drove out the police, they'd bring in the military – do ye want another Merthyr?' asked Richard Jones. 'Sixty shot dead and hundreds wounded?'

'God alive, man, that was eighty years ago; come up to date!

'It could happen again,' I said. 'The Owners can call in the military at the drop of a hat.'

'You've got the right Home Secretary in Winston Churchill, that's for sure,' said Richard Jones. 'Right now he's getting practice in by beating up London suffragettes.'

'Who are they when they're home?' asked Bron, making tea.

'Women rebels trying to get the vote for women.'

'They must be pixilated,' said Rachel. 'I'd beat 'em up meself.'

'One of them died, did you hear that?' asked Haley. He took the tea Bron offered him and warmed his hands on the mug.

'Winston Churchill knocked her off?'

'Same thing,' said Heinie. 'The London police again, the big brutal swines, but Churchill gave the orders. Give them a hard time, he says. That's nothing to what the bugger'll give us.'

'The all-time enemy of the working class,' said Haley, staring out of the window.

'Rosie Arse has fallen for a baby – you heard?' asked Primrose Culpepper, just come in.

'Don't change the subject!'

'A boy, ain't it?' asked Rachel from her corner, sipping her tea. 'Grand little bouncer – ain't it romantic?'

'It is when you know the father.'

'And changed her name to Rosie Jenkins. Rosie Arse weren't good enough for her, I suppose – Arse was good enough for Annie.'

'Rosie Arse-Jenkins it'll be for sure, and she's called the kid Llewellyn.'

'Llewellyn Arse-Jenkins,' said Mattie reflectively.

'Send her dada soft, it will – doted on her, he did, poor old Albert.'

John Haley rose and put down the mug. 'Well, I'll see you all tomorrow. Got to do something, haven't we? Best do it quick.'

'The Federation's calling this mass meeting, not you, Overman,' said Richard Jones, 'let's have that one straight.'

'As long as they act,' replied Haley. 'When the Owners start importing blackleg labour, we've got to move – with or without your bloody Federation.'

'You damned rabble-rouser!' said Bron.

He bowed to her, smiling, as he went through the door.

'He'll cause trouble before he's finished, that one,' said she.

'He won't if you all follow the Union's lead,' said Richard Jones. 'Only unity will help us now – independent action by anyone tomorrow and the police will come in.'

'So you're starting trouble in the morning, are you?' asked Bron, undressing. 'You start easing out scabs and blacklegs and the police'll be in – or have you forgotten all about Bethesda?'

There had come between us a sense of isolation. She was going to Porth now with growing regularity; I had almost accepted it. We did not discuss it; it was as if it had become an unspoken agreement between us – she went to Sam; I could go to Nanwen.

We no longer made love. Had I made approaches to her, I suppose she would have acceded; offering me the husk of a woman out of pity. But, although my need of her was great, I could never have used her as a mere receptacle: possibly, I thought, lying there in the dim lamplight, this was a proof of love.

Try as I may, I could not isolate this emotion: it was hating and loving simultaneously. I said, answering her:

274

'If trouble comes, mun, you won't be in it.'

She made no attempt to cover herself while undressing, and across the shivering room, I briefly saw her nakedness. The sight brought to me the old, parching need. And perhaps some telepathy flashed between us, for she turned holding her nightdress against her.

Strange, I thought, the sudden warmth in all that coldness; smiling, head on one side, she stared at me over the ocean of the bed.

'Poor old Tobe,' she said, 'poor old lad.'

The winter night seemed to beat about us; the moon in the hut window was sighing with the cold: frost was on the Square, icicles hung spiked glass from the eaves.

'You need me?'

It seemed like weakness to take her offering of second best. I thought of Sam wanting her over in Porth; also, I thought of Nanwen in Senghenydd, wanting me.

'Not particularly,' I replied.

'Not particularly, eh? Dear me – *hoity toity!*' She made a face at me. 'Ah, well, perhaps it's best, since you've got to be up in the morning. *Damn* men!' She got in beside me and thumped the pillow, like I'd have thumped Sam Jones if I'd had him then. 'Right you are, boyo – you chase off to your fancy Nanwen, though you'll find she ain't got nothing better'n me, though she might have bells on it.'

I awoke once in the night because I thought I could hear her crying, but it was probably the wind.

CHAPTER THIRTY-ONE

To make sure he was early, I knocked Will Parry Trumpet out of bed next dawn, and, while Will was tuning up his bugle down the gullyway at the back of the Huts, I ran over the Square to Heinie's room in Church Street, behind the Pandy.

'Come on, come on!' I cried, hammering his door, and he up and opened it and scurried around in his combs, shouting:

'Sound the alarm! Strike up the trumpet – give it hell, Will Parry – D. A. Thomas'll hear that Angel Gabriel!'

Meanwhile, the town was beginning to wake for the earliest shift in months. Peal after peal of that bugle echoed over the Square; answering bugles were sounding in every corner of the valley.

This was the morning of the Federation's mass meeting; the Rhondda was responding as to a call to arms.

Tonypandy spun into life like a whipped top. Colliers, enginemen, farriers and ostlers, top workers and face workers poured in black streams from the doors of the terraced houses, many dressing as they went.

'Get a move on! We've got to get Richard Jones up on the platform,' I yelled at Heinie, and he ruptured himself into his trews, bare feet hopping on the boards, and waved his arms into his shirt: slop water into a basin, down with his face to come up streaming: in front of the mirror now, roaring with pain to the scur of the razor.

'You're undone in the trews again,' I said, and the moon put her fingers through the window and did up his flies for him.

The bugle blasted on while I waited for Heinie; Will Parry making a meal of it. Dogs were howling to kicks as we eventually made our way up to Court where Richard lived, cats slamming down the alleyways, children being scolded for wetting the beds.

The old people, the tortured refuse of the old generation, opened their eyes to a misted dawn. Babies were being potted, vests lifted for furious mouths, aunts shaking uncles, lovers covering their ears to the blasts of Will Parry's bugle, and 'the daft nit wants to get hold of himself, raising Cain at this time of the mornin',' cried Mrs. Change, the Pandy mid-wife, with her night-cap bobble out of her bedroom window. 'Stuff up that blutty bugle, Will Parry, or I'll tell on ye!'

'You stuff up, missus,' yelled Will, blasting away. 'I'm waking the town by orders o' the Federation, that right, Toby Davies?'

'Just go on bugling, *bach*,' I commanded, passing him with Heinie.

'It do surprise me where he gets his breath from, mind,' as Mrs. Change told Bron later. 'I'm the medic round these parts generally, and one good rallentando ought to have him over. And he's impotent too – though I don't make it public – medical etiquette, and all that. Anyway, I don't go a lot on this conjugal palaver myself. Come on, come on, get back,' and she eased a relative away from the window in his night-shirt.

'*Jawch*, what a life it is,' cried Primrose Culpepper from her door. 'Out to make trouble, are you? Come to a bad end, you will, as God's me judge,' and the mob swept past her, cheering and hullabalooing.

'No, not you, my lovely, you can't go,' said Mrs. Liv-ingstone, her arm round Guto. 'You got to be sane for this one, boyo – I keep telling him, eh, Toby?' and I knocked up my cap at her.

'Where are you off to?' I cried, gripping Tommy Arse as he dashed past me, for everything seemed to be happening at once now.

'Not to Union meetings,' cried he, pushing me off. 'Not, leastwise, till I've 'ad him . . .'

'Had who, mate? Who's for it now?' asked Heinie, bright-eyed.

'That Shaun McCarthy, the swine!' Tight-fisted was Tommy, looking for a murder. For weeks now, they'd been trying to get the father out of Rosie.

'One of Dano's lads?' I asked. 'You're bonkers, Tom!'

'Our Rosie just told us – he anna getting away wi' it mind – laying my sister.'

'Don't be daft,' called Heinie, swinging him back into the crush of men. 'All the McCarthy boys are virgins, Ma Etta sees to that.'

'Not Shaun, the young one – took Rosie's advantage, he did – she just told us.'

'Won't it wait for the revolution?'

'It won't,' shouted Tommy, and went.

'God help us,' said Heinie.

Like packs of starving dogs the men of the town were pouring over the Square now, making for the Athletic Ground beside the Incline, as Heinie and I fought our way up to Court for Richard Jones. And still the bugles were calling, calling.

Bron we met next, confronting us as we organised the stragglers. Her black shawl was scragged tight over her hair, her face pinched with cold.

'I'm coming, too,' she gasped, lifting her skirts.

'You're not, mate – this is no place for women!'

She tried to catch my arm, but I shook her off.

'Haven't women got rights, too, then?'

'Now, come on! You don't agree with all this – you said so!' I shouted.

'And now I've changed me mind, haven't I?'

'Since when?' asked Heinie, wryly.

'Since the blacklegs came in, you said, and the police started beating up our pickets.'

I strode off, but she followed me, picking and pestering, and she nearly fell once as the men surged about her. 'What happens to you happens to me, Tobe,' she shouted, one fist up.

'O, aye? That's a new one. A few days back we were rabble-rousers – remember?'

'Not now. There's nothing left to do but fight, I realise.'

'Go and tell it to that fella in Porth.' I pushed her away.

'Keep your moss on and your hands off me!' The men

closed about her. I swung people aside for a path, and Heinie followed.

'And what was all that about?' he shouted.

Furious, I didn't reply.

'I thought you two were mates!'

'We were.'

'And now she isn't good enough? That it?'

I glared at him. 'Our business, Heinie.'

'And mine.' Stopping me, he hauled me back to face him, his little flat face glowering up into mine. 'She's a good one, and she's my mate, too, so try shoving me!'

'*Ach*, she knows what she can do.'

'Right, then, but don't you rough her up.'

The men were swaying about us: Lodge leaders were being hoisted on to the shoulders of others: the colliers thronged in a great black wedge of humanity towards the dias where Federation officials were waiting to address them. I shouted at Heinie. 'You'd have roughed her long before this – if she were yours.'

'Well, she's not mine, worse luck.' He grimaced. 'The way you're behaving, you just ain't fit to clean her boots.'

We glared at each other.

Saddened at the first rift between Bron and me, I waited with Heinie on the doorstep of Richard Jones's house while he took leave of his wife. All down Court the doors were coming open and colliers rushing out with flung good-byes.

'So you're going to put out the engine room fires?' asked Mrs. Jones and it seemed as if, in her misery, she was unaware of us.

Thinner and paler than Ginty's colleen was she; and worried about her husband's breathing.

In Welsh she spoke to him, thinking I did not understand.

'Give us a couple of hours, woman, don't make a meal of it,' said Richard.

'Do you really have to go? What about the young ones?'

He said, looking past me, 'I'm on the Standing Committee. Mainwaring and Rees will expect me. I'm down to speak first for the Ely Lodge.'

'They expect too much,' she replied. 'They always have. Give it all up soon, will you *bach*?'

'*Ach*, missus, see sense. The Union's my life.'

He did not resist when she tied his muffler, for he was looking at the sky, where a clutch of ravens were flying.

His wife said, 'All our lives it's been like this – married to the Union, aren't you, in a manner of speaking. Besides ...' and she stroked his arm. 'You aren't fit to go, *bach* – you should be under the doctor.'

He fought for breath, saying huskily, 'Talk properly, woman – even at a time like this – Dr. Lyon's tops eighteen stones,' so, in English she said, warmly:

'I think a lot of you, Richard ...' and she leaned against him.

He stared anxiously around. 'Ay ay, but loose me, girl – not in front of people.'

And, as if the cue to a drama in coal was given, he coughed, eyes closed, to inner soundless explosions.

'I got to go,' he said in wheezes. 'Young Toby's waiting.'

I behaved as one disinterested. 'You ready, Mr. Jones?'

'Aye, son,' and he turned to his wife.

They looked at each other, smiling, with empty resignation.

'*Yn iach! Ffarwel ...!*'

Strangely, he kissed her.

With Heinie on one side of him and me on the other, we fought a path for him through the packed ranks of roaring colliers, and took him up to the platform where the members of the Workmen's committee were waiting. The chairman, William John, spoke first, ending with the words:

'We will not lower our banner now! This committee will strain every nerve to bring the fight to a successful issue, and it is our intention to stop any man from working on in the collieries now the Federation has said stop. With your help, our pickets will prevent any official – including our much respected Chief Constable Lindsay – from entering the colliery yards ...!'

His speech ended in thunderous cheering, and he added, his arms high, 'Now I ask Richard Jones, the chairman of the Ely Lodge, which spear-heads this fight, to address you,' and Heinie and I helped old Richard up the steps of the platform.

Thin and pale he looked standing there surrounded by the big-wigs of the Federation committee, but the very sight of him brought the men to instant silence: his fine voice rang out:

'Well, we are come to it! On this day, the sixty-third of the lock-out at the Ely, we are joined by the strength of the Miners' Federation! Think of it – all you who have starved with your women to keep your children fed! The whole of the Cambrian pits have struck in sympathy. Count in Aberdare, Maesteg and pits in Monmouthshire, some thirty thousand men have laid down tools against tyranny!'

Not a murmur. The wind, ruffling his thin hair, was the only sound of the morning, and he continued:

'So, as William John says, we must not lower our banners now – it must be a fight to the death with this tyrant – we quote W.J. Parry, the great Union leader up in Bethesda. Today we will begin by drowning out the fires up at Clydach, which is still working on, though the Federation has said stop!' He raised his voice. 'By this time tomorrow every pit in the Combine will be idle – not by our wish, mark me, but by the decree of a management which has locked out a thousand colliers on a whim.'

They bawled mass assent at this, but he conducted them into silence. 'And by this time next week the Winding Engineers' Union, the Stokers, Enginemen and Surface Craftsmen's Union will have joined hands with us in this fight against evil. *For we did not call this strike*, remember – we were locked out of a pit which was exploiting us, yet one we were still prepared to work!'

They roared, waving a forest of arms. Richard cried:

'But one thing I beg of you – no violence! Let the violence shown by this vicious management never be matched by ours! Unionism is negotiations, conciliations, argument – violence is the business of employers! What you do in the next few days will be known to history, remember. Unions, federations of workers all over the world are watching. Picketing has begun at all the Combine collieries – let it be

281

peaceful, despite police beatings. Let the blacklegs and imported labour be persuaded against working, in an orderly manner . . .!'

A man yelled from the crowd, '*Persuaded*? Persuade bloody blacklegs? Aye, Richard Jones, we'll persuade 'em!'

Another shouted, 'And you talk of a fight to the death? What is this, a Sunday school outing?'

'Men, *men* . . .!'

They jostled about him, raising fists as he cajoled them:

'I beg you to stop and think,' he cried. 'The police are here in force. And not all Welsh police, but the London Metropolitan drafted in . . .'

'And we'll bloody show them!'

'Get him down!'

'The ailing old fool – take him off the committee!'

And Richard shouted, his voice piercing their bass lowing, 'The Ely men – my own Lodge – are already starving. Do you prefer to starve in gaol?'

'Talk sense, they can't gaol all of us!'

'Give us a pint o' your blood, Dick Jones, I want to water me garden!'

Laughter mingled with the jeers; I could have wept for the old collier. Then a man cried, 'You're talking Owners' language, mun – we're talking colliers' talk, and we've been meek too long!'

'Negotiations within the law . . .'

'Sod you Dick Jones and sod your negotiations! We've had enough!'

'Then blood will be spilled on these mountains!'

'Not yours, old man, that's certain. What the hell do you want of us, you and your committee? We've got William Abraham who calls himself Mabon, Vernon Hartshorn and D. Watts Morgan and biblical buggers like you left right and centre – when are we goin' to get some Toms, Dicks and Harrys – men at the face?'

'No violence, you say? I'm up to me ears in pawn!'

'I've got five kids starving – ain't that violence?'

'Mabon says . . .' Richard tried to quieten them.

'To hell with you! Does Mabon starve?'

'Stop talking, mun, and get us up to Clydach Vale – we'll give 'em blacklegs.'

Hoots and catcalls drowned out words and sense. They jostled about the platform and, with Heinie beside me, I worked my way closer to the steps, climbed up, and brought Richard down.

Little and old he looked, as if the mob had touched him.

We held him between us while he fought for breath.

It took the authority of Noah Rees, the secretary of the Cambrian Lodge, to regain order.

'God help them,' said Richard, leaning against me. 'They'll take you to the devil, d'you realise?'

'Empty bellies raise tempers, old man,' said Heinie.

'But why vote me in if they don't do what I say?' He stared about him, gasping. 'Listen to them! Hundreds have died to build the Union . . .'

'They're tired of words, Mr. Jones,' I said, and he turned his ashen face to mine, saying:

'It'll come to words in the end, it always does. Too young you are to see good sense, but you'll understand when the police come out. Have you seen the big Metropolitans with the batons up in front? Have you heard their stamping?'

'Time enough when it comes.'

'No time at all. Too late then,' he said.

'Best get him home?'

Slowly, clearing a way through the mob of howling men we took him back up to Court Street and gave him to his missus.

The colliers were organised by the time we got back.

Columns were being formed by the Federation stewards; tempers were regained. They even raised a cheer for us as we took our place in the Ely Lodge ranks.

Urchins and pit boys were handing out Tom Mann pamphlets and colliers' newspapers like *Justice* and *Labour Leader*; a brass band came from nowhere and formed up at our head.

Women and children were running out of their doors, pent with excitement, the wives black-shawled and capped, hopping about us like frock-coated undertakers. Bang, bang, on a big bass drum, and we were off up the hill to Clydach. And we were but one such mass meeting.

All over the Rhondda the colliers were answering the Union's call; snake after snake of men marching in the mountain towns in search of blacklegs and imported labour – the old, old stick which was used to thrash miners.

Up past River View we went to the colliery, bringing families to their doors, waving to Patsy Pearl who was feeding her Madog on her doorstep (and I saw Ricardo, the ice-cream man, fashioned on the bedroom window) and on to the colliery where we chased out the blacklegs and hosed out the engine fires, stopping the cage.

One blackleg we caught, wrapped him in a bedsheet, and marched him like a ghost at the head of the band; another we hoisted to the top of the pit-head, leaving him swinging there, yelling for a pig-sticking.

Down the valley road then, and along the railway to the Nantgwyn Naval colliery; here we did the same, then marched on to the hated Ely through Penygraig, making sure it was shut. Back down Amos Hill we went, singing and cheering, with half the population following us now, some said twelve thousand. To the two Pandy pits and the Anthony we went – all of the Cambrian Combine, with whom we were in dispute. Here we gave the blacklegs a run, sending the women and children after them, and Primrose Culpepper and Rachel Odd in the van, had a field day, hitting the daylight out of them.

It was nearing dusk and we were tired by the time we got back to Pandy Square, leaving behind us a trail of wet fires and halted cages; the wheels of shunting engines jammed, trucks derailed.

The police, mainly Glamorgan Constabulary, watched at the entrances to colliery offices or agents' houses, arms folded, and did not move against us.

'What of the country police now, then?' called someone.

'And what of the big Metropolitans?' asked somebody else. 'Skulking behind the curtains of the Thistle Hotel, are they?'

'They'll stop skulking when we go down there tomorrow,' I replied. 'Big trouble will arrive when we tackle the Scotch.'

'You can say that again,' said Bron, when I got back to the Hut.

'Well,' said she now, 'have ye had a good day setting the world aright?'

I kicked off my boots and lay back on the bed. 'One thing's sure – you didn't contribute.'

The meetings and demonstrations weren't really over, but I'd returned early because I was worried about her. Now she said, caustically:

'I tried to help and nearly got me eye filled up.'

I had to grin. She was at her best in this mood; her mercurial ability to change disallowed any vendetta; she never sulked. When something went wrong between us she behaved, in minutes, as if it hadn't happened.

Now she was ironing, with a blanket on the table. Nothing interfered with Bron's ironing – weekday, strike day, it had to go on, and she reckoned she had the whitest washing in Tonypandy, never mind the blutty Sinkers. She even lent me a wink as she held up her drawers; lace-trimmed were these but with a rip across the rear, and she flapped them at me and made draughty noises and big eyes.

'That'll tickle your fancy,' I said.

'Chance'd be a fine thing!'

'*Ach*, go on with you,' I said. 'There's nothing in them.'

'You never know your luck,' and she pouted prettily. 'I know a few who'd be interested.'

'So do I.' It was meant to hurt her and it stilled her hands momentarily, then she smiled. 'Ah, well, back to the convent. Meanwhile, you've drowned the fires, stopped the pumps and settled the blacklegs, is it?'

'Aye, in all pits but one.'

'What about the Llwynypia Scotch? Why does she get off?'

'She doesn't. We're down there first thing tomorrow.'

'Ah, well, I suppose that's progress.'

'Don't you agree?'

She spat on the iron and whistled at the steam. 'I didn't once, but I do now. We've a right to peaceful picketing – that's the law. When the police change that law, I'm with ye.' She ironed vigorously. 'But I tell you this, you'll be in

285

trouble tomorrow when you tackle the Glamorgan pit.'

'We know all about that.'

I was hungry; with it came the usual irritability. She seemed so composed. Getting up, I went to the tea caddie; it was empty.

'I took the last eightpence to Ginty. Bread and mousetrap suit you?' she asked.

'I'd prefer roast chicken.'

'That's the main course – didn't you eat at the soup kitchen? I did.'

'Too busy chasing blacklegs.'

'Aw, me poor sweet boy!' Smiling, she wandered towards me at the grate, her arms out to me.

I didn't know how to handle her. Every time I looked at her these days I saw Sam Jones. She walked into my arms and there was a kindness in her against me. I held her; we did not speak. Then:

'Hell of a time we're having, ain't we, Tobe?'

I did not reply.

'Thank Gawd little Bibbs ain't here, eh?'

I nodded against her. She said, 'It . . . it's the people with kids that get me. If a kid started to cry – one of mine, I mean – I'd go mad.'

'It'll pass. Bron . . .'

She looked up into my face. I said, 'Don't go to Porth again – not till we get through this bad patch, anyway.'

Perplexed, she held me away, staring. 'Christ, man, what do ye take me for?' She searched my face.

'Well . . .'

'Listen,' she said, 'if you've got trouble, I'm in it, too. Bugger Sam Jones.'

'For better or worse, you mean?'

She made uncertain gestures. 'Well, not that. It's just . . . well, it wouldn't be decent if I walked out on you now, would it?' She lowered her face. 'Anyway, Sam don't want me.'

We stood apart. 'Any more than that Nanwen really wants you,' she added.

'You don't know that.'

'I got a fair idea, or she'd be over here to get you. I would.'

She shook her head at me as one does to a wayward child. 'Dear me! You're a regular cuckoo in the nest, ain't you? Like me, you're a loser.'

I nodded, sighing, and she said:

'You poor old sod. I just don't know what I'm goin' to do with you, I don't. Come on, come by 'ere.' She put her arms around me and smiled capriciously up into my face. 'Look, if you can't have that old Nanwen, would it ease ye any if you tumbled me on the bed?'

I said, 'You just don't understand, do you, Bron?'

'You're a man, and I've been up against a few in my time, but mate, you take the biscuit.' She stood away, opening her hands at me. 'Oh well, if you ain't all that keen on me, would some bread and Ginty cheese warm ye?'

'Now that's talking!'

She ran to the biscuit tin and brought out the food, spreading it with relish on a corner of the table. 'There now! I got that special for my old Tobe!' She cut me a hunk of bread and a wedge of cheese and I attacked it, a man famished.

'Come on,' I said, my mouth full. 'Where's yours?'

'I'm all right,' she said. 'I ate on the Quakers. I told ye.'

Smiling, she watched me bolting it.

'You sure you don't want me after?' she asked, head on one side. 'Like a sort of second course?'

I was well into the bread and cheese. 'Quite sure.'

Her eyes narrowed with suppressed delight and she reached out and squeezed my hand. 'That's all right, then! The way to the heart's through the stomach, they say — friends again now Tobe, ain't we?'

For a long time that night (for we were abed by nine) I lay half dreaming of Nanwen. I wanted her; she wanted me, yet she had to live a life with a drunken Ben O'Hara. It was an impossible situation, I thought, to be so close to her, yet so distant.

'What you thinking about?' asked Bron.

'Nothing much.'

'About how the lads are going to do the Scotch tomorrow?'

'No.'

'What. then?' But I didn't reply.

She was up on an elbow; the cold of the room swept into us and I pushed her down. Frost was on the window; icicles hung from the downspouts and gutters.

'Thinking about that Nan O'Hara, is it?'

Her eyes were large and beautiful in the soft light of the window.

'Yes.'

'You in love with her, Tobe?' She leaned above me, looking into my face. 'Really, truly in love, I mean – like dying?'

I did not reply. There was no point in hurting her.

With finality, she said at the ceiling, 'Always loved her really, haven't you?'

'It's just the same with you – you've always loved Sam Jones.'

'Hell,' she said, softly. 'A woman just can't help loving Sam Jones. He's a bad bugger, I know, but ye can't help lovin' him.' Rolling over to me, she said, 'But what you going to do about it? Loving that Nanwen, I mean?'

'I don't know.'

'You could always knock off Ben O'Hara!'

'Don't be ridiculous.'

We lay in silence, then she said, 'Love's a very funny business, you know, Tobe. You take these policemen beating up our pickets – somebody loves 'em, I suppose.' Distantly, I heard the sounds of a gathering mob. Sleep was claiming me after the exhaustion of the day.

'Bron, go to sleep. Why d'you always wake up at this time of night?'

'And then old Richard Jones – he's half dead, poor soul. And his fat old missus waddles around like a ram with footrot, yet he loves her, don't he?'

'Good night,' I said.

'Aye,' and she sighed deeply. 'Love's a funny old thing, you come to think of it.' She touched me gently. 'Like me loving you, for instance.'

I listened, and she said, 'Mind, I do love Sam – I just said so, didn't I? But I love you, too – all at the same time. Anybody hurt you, mate, I'd better 'em.'

'You'll have to make up your mind then, won't you?' I replied. 'Sam or me.'

'Like you with that Nanwen.' She kissed my cheek. 'But you'll always be friends with me, won't ye, Tobe? Even if you start poodle-faking wi' her?'

We lay together, her hand in mine, and I listened to the sounds of the night. The mob noises were pulsating on quick flushes of the wind, but I tried to ignore them. Memories of Nanwen's dark beauty was invading me with persistent force.

When this lot was over, I thought, I'd go over to Senghenydd and bring things to a head; it would be Ben O'Hara, or me. Life was just a mess of conflicting emotions and frustration, continuing like this.

'Good night, son,' said Bron, and kissed my face, and I remembered the perfume of Nanwen's hair. 'You all right, are ye?'

'Aye.'

She whistled against my ear. 'Don't take it all so ripe, mun – that's your trouble, ye know – you take it all so serious, and cupids ain't like that – they're just, well . . . little old dancing chaps with flowers behind their ears . . . you listening?'

I breathed so steadily for her that I nearly dropped off.

'Eh, my, you're a sweet thing, Tobe – just like a little lad you are – come on now, cootch up to me, is it? And anything you fancy in the night, mate, you just give aunty the elbow . . .?'

CHAPTER THIRTY-TWO

We had been asleep for about an hour, I suppose, when I was aware of a gathering of people in the Square. Bron awoke, too, sitting up beside me. 'What's happening?'

'It's the Glamorgan pit – hell's setting alight.'

'But you're drowning the Scotch fires in the morning!'

'Earlier, it seems,' I said, getting out on to the boards and peering through the frosted window.

Men were thronging to and fro on the Square under the light of the fountain; I heard bass shouts and the high voices of women. And just then the door nearly came off its hinges under Heinie's fist. He entered on a rush of words:

'The Cambrian management have taken over the Scotch,' he cried. 'Word's just come out.'

'But what about our pickets?'

'Flung out by the police. There's three outside with split heads one's a hospital case.'

'And Lindsay's occupied the colliery?'

'That's it,' said Heinie. 'And Llewellyn, the Combine manager, has gone underground with eighty blacklegs.'

'We'll soon dig them out.'

'But there's a hundred policemen guarding the top – they're all over the yard, and in the power station.'

I was dressing hastily. 'If there is there'll be trouble!'

'There's trouble already – it never really stopped. A lot of the lads are at Llwynypia now. And another fifty Cardiff bobbies have come in overnight to the Thistle Hotel.'

'So they're making the Glamorgan Scotch a show-down, eh?'

'That's the size of it,' said Heinie. 'A gang of our boys tried to talk to the blacklegs, but the police drove them off.'

'I'm comin', too,' said Bron. She was pulling on her drawers, unconcerned about Heinie.

'You're not. You're staying here,' I said.

Heinie said, 'The Management's taken the scabs underground, they say, to save the ponies.'

'Yet they took those horses down themselves especially?'

'But it works,' cried Mattie, appearing at the door. 'Now there'll be talk about the brutal miners, though Manager Llewellyn don't give a sod if all four hundred ponies drown.'

'You're dealing wi' some lovely people,' said Bron.

'If he isn't careful he'll drown his eighty blacklegs,' and I flung open the door.

Bugles were blowing in strident blasts as I ran out on to the Square.

Word had gone around like a prairie fire blazing. The Combine Management had got control of the Big Glamorgan colliery, known at the Scotch. Blacklegs were working the engines underground. Chief Constable Lindsay had thrown out our pickets and a force of constables were now guarding the colliery pits.

The colliers were infuriated.

Out of their beds rolled the children, out of the doors poured the men, grabbing their tools as they went – mandrels, axe-handles, shovel hafts, brooms.

Followed by their shrieking women, they came pell-mell on to Pandy Square, raising the roof, and even the dear departed in the cemetery must have cocked their dusty ears to listen, said Bron.

From Court Street to Chapel Street they came; up from afar as The Golden Age in Williamstown; rushing in streams from Gilfach, Maddox, Primrose and the Bush, and they packed the Square – the centre of all Town activity – like sprats in a cask.

Moses Culpepper and his Primrose were there, also Rachel and her Bill. The McCarthys came in force, led by Etta, wielding a poker and shrieking like a Sioux Indian. All the Arses came, save Rosie and child; I saw Dai Parcel, Gwilym and Owen; also John Haley and Will Shanklyn with the O'Learys. Diving into the mêlée of the swaying mob, they joined the chorus of yells and threats, for the Town was maddened by the management's occupation of the Scotch.

Where, earlier, there had been organisation and purpose, now it was anarchy, without a Union leader in sight. All the thick-eared fraternity turned out this time, too, with famous people like Tom Thomas and Martin Fury crowding in with the likes of Dai Rush and Snookey Boxer, their blood up at the prospect of battle.

Mr. Duck, lately returned from exchange work over in Senghenydd, fought his way into the crowd beside me.

'Toby, this is madness!' he cried, cultured.

'Try telling them that,' I shouted back.

'Where's Mabon at a time like this?'

'Or Noah Rees, Mainwaring – Watts Morgan – where's anyone?'

The men were swaying in a body, shoulder to shoulder, across the length and breadth of the Square, chanting, amid cat-calls, 'The Scotch, the Scotch, the *Scotch!*'

I yelled to Mattie and Heinie, 'Raise me, get me up!' and they swung me high on their shoulders, turning me in the crush of men.

I shouted, my hands flung up, 'Listen, *listen!* Don't act like a mob. Wait for Mabon?'

A man yelled above the rest, 'We're always waiting for bloody Mabon – we don't need the Union to dig out bloody Llewellyn.'

'Pelt out the scabs – run them out of Town!'

I shouted, 'The police are waiting for us, remember?'

'Bloody bad luck for them!'

From my swaying perch, I saw the face of Bron among the infuriated men, with John Haley beside her, barging and shoving for room, trying to protect her.

'*Bron!*' I fought myself down and ploughed through the men towards her, but the sheer weight of their numbers swept me away.

'Bron, *go back!*'

The falling of a leaf will start an avalanche.

In hundreds we started the march on Llwynypia. Meeting other columns coming down from Clydach Vale, Dinas, Penygraig and Trealaw, we marched up the Llwynypia Road and on to the Big Glamorgan colliery. Some lit torches, and from these other firebrands blazed. The pale moon was rolling on billowy, wash-day clouds, her light dimmed with the redness of the waving torches.

Now that we were committed to drown out the Scotch by force, there came upon the marching men an unearthly quiet.

'My gran's milk,' said Heinie, beside me, 'I've never heard colliers as quiet as this.'

Doors were coming open along the road; whole families standing there, their faces pale with apprehension. The torch-light shot shadows into the eyes of the women. This move spelled more hunger: some, like the Ely people, had been eating skint for three months already; their bellies gnawed.

'How are you, Toby?' asked John Haley, pushing into the ranks with Tommy Arse.

'No better for asking,' I answered. 'This business stinks.'

'But time we stopped the Scotch isn't it? She's on the list.'

'We should have done it this morning, before the police made it into a fortress.'

'Time comes when you've got to fight, man,' said he, tersely, and his eyes were shining. 'Like loving when you've got to love.'

'Ye don't usually get your skull fractured, just for loving,' said Duck behind me.

'The women don't hold with it,' said Mattie. 'My wife's playin' Hamlet, first act.'

'She ain't usual,' replied Ben Block. 'My missus is behind us – she says give 'em hell.'

'Time'll come when we'll be behind the women,' grumbled Dai Parcel, over to my left. 'Under their skirts, me, when the batons come out – Toby's right, this business stinks.'

'Then why are ye here?' shouted Tommy Arse, and I chanced a look at him in the tramping of the boots; big and handsome he looked, a boy made into a man.

'Because colliers stick together,' I replied.

'And fall together likewise,' said Heinie. 'It won't be the first time I've had a baton on me nut.'

Lock and Company, the grocers, had barricaded their

doors and windows to protect their hams, for the best money hangs from ceilings. Studley's Fruit Shop, in the process of getting out the apples and pears, hung a drape over the photograph of the late lamented Queen Victoria, since loyal subjects appeared few and far between. Watkins the Flannel had got his bales inside; the Monument Chemist slammed shut, with Tailor Jones going demented to save his Union boss frock coats, and the roars that came up from the Square that night eased the slates off the workhouse roof, according to Solly Freedman, the pawnbroker, raising dust up Zion Hill with his trunk on wheels.

We marched on.

There grew an accompaniment to the stamping thunder; a low chanting in the ranks, like cattle lowing; by the time we neared the Big Glamorgan we numbered thousands.

We of the Ely were in the van. Behind us, I saw a massive column now, snaking back to Tonypandy, a great wedge of torchlight. The chanting rose higher as we spilled along the railings of the Scotch.

Many women had joined us, their faces wild, their shawls scragged back over their hair; many armed with pokers, for women fight to kill.

Urchins were darting through the ranks of men, their shrill cries sparking the growing of shouts and bawls.

Before us the road lamps were bright; the pit-wheels of the six pits of the Big Glamorgan stood black against the stars.

A man in the crowd yelled, 'Pull up the railings as weapons. If we get the power house we'll stop the Scotch!' and the men about me spilling out of the ranks and began to tear up the wooden fencing surrounding the colliery. Stone-throwing began; glass clashed and tinkled as windows shattered. Then came quiet.

Before us on the road the police began to mass. Led by a mounted figure, Chief Constable Lindsay, the 'Roman Centurion' they formed up out of the shadows silently, without command; no sound came but the clattering hooves of the horses and their slithering hobnails.

And they stood like a black barrier between us and the power station.

Big bastards, these; we feared them. They might have been ordinary Welsh policemen, but they were hand-picked in anti-riot, from Cardiff and Swansea mainly, and no bloody truck with the black-faced yobs of the Rhondda.

The silence grew in strength and power.

Stock still these policemen stood, and it was clever. Even Lindsay's horse was motionless, with Lindsay astride him, his sabre stiffly upward.

As black marble statues, they were motionless: the night was as shifty as a monastery in Lent.

'Christ,' said Heinie beside me, 'now we're goin' to blutty 'ave it.'

We hesitated.

From within the colliery came shouted commands. More police poured out, breaking the tension; others were forming up on the east of the colliery, also behind us, boots clattering in the eerie silence.

Then a new leader swept to the fore of us, John Haley, and he shouted, wielding a fencing post, 'Right, follow me! Come on – get the power house, stop the pumps!'

Bedlam came loose in a chorus of cat-calls and shouts; men lacking courage.

'Dig out the manager!'

'Beat up the blacklegs!'

'Bring up the ponies!'

A new chanting began, '*Scabs, scabs, scabs!*'

Stones began whistling overhead; the windows of the power house clashed as urchins got the range. Ed Masumbala I saw, his black face shining with sweat, as the rush at the police began. Hair down, fighting to be free of men who tried to hold her, Rachel Odd was like a mad thing, swinging her fire-tongs; behind her came Primrose Culpepper and half her brood, darting forward from the crush, baiting the wedge of policemen barring our way.

But, though I joined John Haley and reviled them, the mass of the colliers did not shift.

'Wait till they charge, then,' I shouted. 'And pull out these damned women!'

Stones were hissing over us now; empty windows, stab-toothed, were grinning at the moon, truck buffers ringing as the stones pelted down. The grass slope above the road was thronged with children and ruffians, but the police, so far, were out of their range.

Men hauled the women and children out of it: the road was clear for a charge.

But the police charged first.

I have never seen anything like it.

They came in a solid box of blue. Tense, gripping our weapons, we awaited them.

They came in a phalanx, the centurion attack of another age; stamping upright, like automatons, faces lifted, expressionless; knees bobbing up, with mechanical precision; approaching slowly, their short, hardwood truncheons held upright at their belts, big fists gripping white. Wide-shouldered and burly, their domed helmets made them gigantic.

Their pace quickened to a rasped command as the distance closed.

Seventy yards.

A collier bawled. 'Come on, then, Bobbies, and God help ye!'

Fifty yards.

'Christ!' whispered a man beside me.

In the front rank, I crouched, waiting. Mattie was one side of me, Heinie on the other.

Twenty yards.

I could see their big faces now; jaws thrust out; some split wide in joyful anticipation. Some of these Bristol bastards were just delighted by the Welsh.

Ten yards.

Gleaming red, on a command, the batons flew up.

'*Charge!*'

In dervish yells, they leaped at us.

Our front ranks bulged upward to the impact: the mandrels went high, the truncheons smashed down.

Instantly, as pole-axed, men fell sprawling; the colliers stayed down, but all the policemen rose, as if commanded.

And their truncheons rose and fell again and again in smashes of pain.

Men about me were howling, clutching their red faces; others were crawling among the stamping boots, yelling from bloody mouths. Heinie was down, pulling a policeman with him; Mattie was flailing away at bobbing heads. Helmets were being tipped off, chin-straps torn away; amid a sea of struggling, cursing colliers and policemen, the palings and batons, mandrels and axe-handles rose and fell in flailing, crunching thuds.

Men with broken limbs reeled out of the fight with disjointed cries. A face loomed up before me as John Haley struck out; I elbowed him for room and hit blindly, and the punch caught a policeman square. Instantly, he slipped down the front of me and I lowered him to the ground; next moment the bugger was on my legs. Dull blows were thudding all over me now as my companions thinned out around me; two policemen at me, now three, and the weapons were thudding down on my arms, an old trick of the anti-riot: a baton actually splintered on my shoulder as I ducked and brought down my fencing post on to an unprotected head, which disappeared, as if by magic. It was a bawling mëlée of a fight: Tommy Arse leaped to my side, hooking with his fists and shouting madly, and I had to fight to save him from a six-foot Bobby; then Haley grabbed his collar and dragged him out, a moment after somebody felled the boy from behind.

'Get him out!'

We fought for room in a chorus of yells and screams, taking the stabbing blows on the fleshy parts of our bodies, blows that brought a numbing pain.

I saw the furious, snarling faces, yet knew no anger.

Strangely, I fought in a comradeship that embraced even the police. The agony of it all seemed to stitch us together; it was neither my fight, nor theirs. Removed in time and space, in reality I was not there. Amid the cries, the blood, there was an astonishing cleanness ... until I saw the truncheon come down that felled Moses Culpepper. On top of Sam Rays he fell, soundlessly: men trampling on the mounding bodies now.

I saw another baton coming and hooked my fist into the

body of a constable; he grunted and doubled up; I felt my knuckles crack on the big buckle of his belt. Another baton descended, a weapon in slow motion; step by step towards Heinie's unprotected face it came. I saw it, but could do nothing: it hit Heinie on the cheek, breaking the bone, spinning him sideways.

'Collar him!' shouted Mattie.

'Haul him out,' I gasped, and barged into them with Mattie Kelly and Bill Odd beside me.

One-handed, shouting to the pain of my broken hand, my desperation drove them before me.

Will Parry was near me: there was Albert Arse, Shanklyn, O'Leary. Ed Masumbala was with us, pulling policemen aside, clubbing them down with his fist; there was Dai Parcel, Gwilym, Owen, and Duck; also Snookey Boxer and Ben Block, gasping fat, but fighting like a demon beside the McCarthy lads (though Dano was down). Moses was on his feet again, his face a mask of blood. And then somebody bellowed:

'Look out, lads – look out, behind you!' and we swung to a new enemy.

Rhondda policemen were coming over the Taff Railway at our rear. They came in a tearing, swaying clutch, arms reaching for us – their capes streaming out behind them like flying witches.

'These sods are real Welsh mind,' yelled Mattie, and head down, clutching his face, he bolted.

I paused in my flight to grab Tommy with my good hand while John Haley helped me; together, dragging him between us, we ran, while Ben Block, Albert Arse and Bill Odd fought off the police like a rear party.

'Somebody will pay for this,' said Bron.

She bathed Tommy's head while Annie and Albert, nearby, screwed their hands, and watched, weeping.

'The skull's split – God, I can see his brain,' said Bron.

Said Heinie, 'That's unusual – brains in the Arse family? He'll pull through.'

'Can I help, missus?' asked Patsy Pearl, at the door with Madog shawled.

'If you're cool on blood,' said Bron. 'Where's Primrose?' and she indicated Moses lying half-conscious at the door. 'Christ,' she added, 'it's worse than blutty Inkerman.'

'Primrose coming now just,' answered Rachel, and Mrs. Kelly, Mattie's bulldog wife cried:

'*Diawch!* Wait till I get my hands on that Mattie – I'll give him riot!'

'God bless the King, is it?' asked Bron. 'Don't be daft, woman. He was doing what he had to do.'

The bulldog face went up. 'Mad dogs, I say – nothing but a contaminated set of ruffians. I don't know how I'll face the vicar next Sunday.'

'You've changed your tune, 'aven't you?' asked Annie Arse, kneeling beside her Tommy. 'A week or so back, Kelly, you were all for castrating D. A. Thomas.'

They argued, groaned, commiserated with each other in the pain of it; they fought the battle all over again, but I did not take part in it. I saw Bron's eyes raising and lowering at me from across the room as she bandaged and bathed and comforted.

'Can you stick it for a bit, Tobe?'

I nodded, but could have wept with the pain of my broken hand; my other cuts and truncheon bruises were as nothing compared to this searing pain where the knuckles were vanishing in swelling blueness.

'I'll be with ye directly, mun,' she said, and she stiffened beside Moses, I noticed, as Patsy Pearl came over to me, carrying a bowl. Madog, used to men, examined me with his great blue eyes from the confines of his shawl.

'I'll see to you, Toby,' said Patsy, and with her small, deliberate fingers, she bathed my hand with care.

'You've made some enemies tonight – Chief Constable Lindsay for one,' said Mrs. Kelly. 'Remember that!'

'He's not an enemy, he's an enema,' said Bron, watching Patsy.

'But he'll be awful high down with us after this, God help us,' said Mrs. Shanklyn.

Patsy, as she bandaged, was watching me with her mind.

I knew what she wanted, and she wasn't having me easy; none of my business where John Haley had got to.

'You seen 'im, Toby Davies?'

'On the palings by the Scotch, but not recent,' I said, cool.

'All right, was he?'

'Got young Tommy through, didn't he?'

Quietly, now, Patsy said, 'I got a budding for him, Toby.' She smiled wanly. 'Mad, ain't it?'

'Likely he's married,' I answered.

People talked in the room, and she bent closer, whispering, her eyes like offering plates.

'No, not married – his woman's dead, don't ye know?'

'In the heart still,' I said.

She looked at the window where torches were glowing from the Square. 'He's a well set up chap; I come warm inside when I sees him in the Pandy.'

'You got it bad.'

'I tell you, Toby Davies, I ain't a pearl no more for anybody now but that John Haley.'

I protested, 'But you're still at it, woman. You're still on the game!'

'Aye, I know, mun, but me heart ain't really in it, if you get me.'

'Good God,' I said.

It was like a Turkish battlefield, with bodies lying round and women crouched over them with scissors and knives.

'I'll have that hand over by 'ere, if you don't mind,' said Bron now, with business. Blood never sorted Bron out; they could have done with her over at Rorke's Drift. Patsy Pearl said, as I left her:

'You'll speak for me, Tobe?'

'Likely so.'

'Just for old times, is it?'

'*Heisht*, you, for God's sake,' I breathed.

'One good turn deserves another, remember. And you never paid, ye know?'

I left her pretty smart, for Bron had ears to hear brown grass growing.

Now Bron took my hand with her usual couldn't care. '*Ach y fi!*' she explained. 'What happened to the Bobby on the end of this one?'

300

The noise of the misery beat about us, but we did not hear it; my pain seemed to sanctify us, and she made large eyes at me saying:

'Don't let the Patsy touch you again, you understand?'

'Just . . . just an old friend,' I said. 'No harm in it.'

'So I gather, but I'll shuffle you off this mortal coil if I find you white-mooning with anyone, all right?'

'But that doesn't apply to you, does it? – you just do what the hell you like, don't you?' I glared down at her as she retied the bandage.

'That's right. The fella in Porth's a relative, or don't you remember?' Eyes flashing suddenly, she glowered at Patsy and weighed me up for size. She'd got fierce bangle earrings on her; give her a pair of castanets and she'd have gone round a bonfire: even Moses was watching her, and he was semi-conscious.

'This hurt?' she gave me back my hand.

'Like hell,' I said.

She got up. 'Go on, get on with ye.'

Mattie came bursting into the room then; blood down his muffler, and red in the face with him.

'And where might you 'ave been?' cried his bulldog missus.

'Murder's being done,' cried Mattie. 'There's bodies all over the road from here to Llwynypia. And the police are beating up folks in their houses!'

'I'll believe that when it's signed for,' said Bron. 'Even Lindsay isn't as bad as that.'

'Aye, well, I'm tellin' ye!' shouted Mattie. 'Just now they're clearing the Square again, and stone-throwing down De Winton and Dunraven – smashing shop windows.'

'Tonypandy folks?'

'Tonypandy people!' cried Mattie.

'Go and buy yourself a tin of Toffee Rex,' said Heinie, coming to.

'I tell ye, I saw it! Running wild and busting windows, hitting out the lamps and stoning Bobbies.'

'Must be the Irish again,' said Dai Parcel, sitting up. 'Or those rough clods over in Porth, eh, Moses?'

'More'n likely.' Pensive was Moses, with goose egg building up behind his ear, and sparking.

'I hope they keep away from the Co-op,' said Mrs. Shanklyn. 'We're shareholders – sure as fate it'll affect the divvy.'

'What's happening now, then?'

'We're after 'em again, that's what,' I said, getting to my feet.

Bron said, pale with anger, 'You'll risk your lives again for payment for soft muck?'

'It's more than that, and you know it,' I replied. 'I was more tired going to work than rioting, and the pay's the same – we'll end it once and for all. Who's coming?'

'Ay ay,' said Moses, 'let's finish it,' and those who had legs, got up and trooped to the door, and Bron said, backed by the other women:

'Of all the idiot men! Your brains are in your arse!'

'Likely so,' said Bill Odd. 'You coming, Dai?'

'My brains must be misplaced,' said Heinie, 'or I wouldn't have worked the Ely in the first place.'

And, as we opened the door to go out, the London police flung it back on its hinges, and came in.

They did us then as they did the Morgan house later, over in John Street, Penygraig.

Tonypandy will never forget it, said Keir Hardie later, and neither did we.

'Blood,' said Winston Churchill, in Parliament, later still, 'may be shed, though most of it will be from the nose, which can be subsequently replaced.'

'If we'd had the bugger down here in Tonypandy,' said Bron, 'he'd have seen some blood, and not from his nose.'

With mounted policemen clattering up and down the Row, they came into our place like men demented – six London constables with their batons flailing, and the first to stop one was Bill Odd.

Dai Parcel ducked the next baton, and Bron, turning, took it full on the side of the face, and dropped.

Keir Hardie said, in Parliament, that he possessed factual,

eye-witness accounts of the bludgeoning of solitary individuals on the streets; of the police knocking them down and kicking them, and he called for an enquiry into police brutality.

They tripped over Tommy as they barged their way in; they hauled Annie out of it and got Albert in a corner, hammering him with their batons and fists until his face was covered with blood.

Churchill said, officially, 'The people of South Wales owe a great debt of gratitude to the police.'

With my good hand I got the leading policeman: as he stumbled in, striking with his baton, I hooked him to the jaw; the second policeman, in his onward rush, fell sprawling over this man's body, and I got him as well, as he rose, staggering him; Rachel hit him with a chair, the first thing handy. Two down, four left, and one of these punched Mrs. Kelly in the face, sending her flying.

'You bastard!' I shouted, and rushed, with Bill Odd one side of me and Dai Parcel on the other.

Keir Hardie wrote later, 'Mrs. Morgan, of 45 John Street, Penygraig, has had her house forcibly entered by the police when the whole family were indoors. A most brutal and savage assault was committed on two young men. One of the policemen broke his truncheon, half of which is in possession of Mrs. Morgan.'

Churchill said, 'As Home Secretary, I have been greatly blamed for my conduct in this matter, but I am quite ready to defend my action ... If disorder does arise, it will be repressed by the police, if they can possibly do so.'

It was repressed all right; they were at it now.

Old Dai Parcel was down from a baton across his shoulders, a favourite target; and while he was down they started to kick him in the fork, the idea, they said, being to lower the birth-rate: and the kicking went on while Gwilym and I, penned by five of them (for more had come through the door) fought in a chorus of women's screams.

They were big men, and handy; we hadn't a chance. Out of the corners of my eyes I saw Patsy Pearl hanging on to a boot with another policeman kicking her off; Primrose was lying over her Moses, protecting him; Mattie, with Tommy in his arms, was backing away through the door.

But Bron lay still: white-faced, she lay, like a woman dead.

'Bron! Christ Almighty, *Bron!*' I cried, ducking the truncheons on one side and taking them on the other; the lamplight swam as Gwilym staggered against me. Moses was calling faintly, but I didn't hear what he said. I remember only hooking my good hand to a policeman's chin in the second before I was dropped.

'I claim a public enquiry,' said Hardie, in Parliament.

'On what grounds?' asked Winston Churchill.

'On the grounds of the charges against the police,' said Hardie. 'Charges of having ill-used women and other unoffending persons, not during a baton charge against a mob, but under circumstances in which revenge could be the only motive.'

'But, be fair,' said Heinie, when he came to again. 'Nobody can say we're unoffending persons – after all, we're Welsh.'

'Are ye?' asked Mattie. 'I thought you was with Moses when the sea divided off Porthcawl.'

'I'm Welsh,' interjected Dai Parcel, smiling through split lips. 'And right now I feel a bit anti-English.'

John Haley said, 'Count ourselves lucky – so far we've had it easy. If Lindsay keeps pestering Churchill, he'll send in the military.'

'I anna waving to brass bands any more,' said Bill Odd, while his wife bathed his face; black and blue was he from truncheons – mainly those Metropolitan swines, said he – and if it hadn't been for his boots I'd never have known him, poor old dab, said she; but I'll have them, mind – knocking my fella about.

Kneeling beside Bron's still body the minute my senses returned to me, I tried to get my good arm under her to raise her against me.

'*Diawch!*' ejaculated Pru Natal, hurrying over the kitchen floor. 'Put her down, man, we think she's cracked a rib.'

I screwed up my good hand and put it against my face, and said. 'I'll kill someone for this!'

'I got the one who did it, though,' said Heinie, sitting up against the wall. 'He's got a different nose to when he came in, the bugger.'

'Get her on the bed!'

People moving about, urgently whispering; the palaver of the accident.

I staggered about, trying to help.

'Sit down, Tobe – you're only in the way,' said Primrose.

They gathered up Bron's still body and I could have screamed and flung them away; all I wanted was to hold her.

She shrieked the moment they lifted her.

'Bastards, bastards, *bastards!*' I said, my hands over my face.

'There, there,' said Patsy Pearl, 'that'll do you a world of good. They're gone, Tobe – that's the main thing.'

Bron started to cry like a little girl. It was more than I could bear.

'But beating up women!'

Patsy and Mrs. O'Leary held me away from her.

'Bron asked for it, mind,' said Dai Parcel. 'Two she got with the handle of the mangle.'

They laid her on the bed and she groaned, twisting herself to the pain of her body, and hatred, deeper and purer than anything I had known, ran like a flame in me. I bent over her trying to kiss her face, but they pulled me away again.

'Now look, Tobe – hop it. Leave her *alone!*'

I went to a quiet place of the room, and wept, my good hand over my eyes.

'Well, I suppose we all asked for it,' said somebody, while the women undressed Bron and got her into the bed.

305

'I only asked for two-and-six a ton,' said Heinie.

Along Dunraven and De Winton, they collected broken heads; also in Pandy Square, strikers and police; the massacre of the batons and shovels. From Gifach to Hughes, the side streets had been torn up for the Irish confetti; three hundred staves were brought to Llwynypia to replace those broken on colliers' skulls; this was official, according to the Coal Owners.

'Mind, we could have got into that power station if we'd a mind to,' commented Ben Block. 'We let 'em off light, sort of.'

Rumours, like scandal, can outrun a prairie fire.

'Somebody saw Winston Churchill riding a horse up Court Street, you heard?'

'You saw him yourself?'

'Aye, well not personal, but he were seen all right. As certain as me name's Kelly – riding with Chief Lindsay, he was.'

In the darkened sawdust of the four-ale tap, they crouch like conspirators over fires, manufacturing rumours.

'Where did ye hear that, then?'

'I tell you, I saw him – with these two eyes.'

'Who?'

'Winston Churchill.'

'In Tonypandy?'

'In Tonypandy – I swear it!'

'Man, you're nothing but a blutty gas leak.'

'I tell you, I saw him – riding along on a horse with Captain Lindsay.'

'Holy Mother of God, is that true?' gasped Mrs. O'Reilly. 'The devil of Gehenna's among us!'

'*Ach*, stop coddin' us along, Pat. Tell us the Pope's truth, now!'

'But I am, ye blitherer! As large as life, he was – frock coat, top hat, just like ye see in Parliament, be God – and with a truncheon five foot long in his hands, cracking Welsh heads.'

'Aye, well, I'm all for that meself, d'ye see, being Irish.'

'But ye don't believe me, do ye? Jesus, you've more suspicions than teeth, man — I'll swear it on the Holy Water!'

'Och, give him a wee drop of the hard stuff, Mike, for the fella's started seeing things.'

'And he was holding the English rose aloft in his hand, an' all! Are ye off now, Paddy?'

'That I am.'

'You're going, so you are, eh? – then tell me when you're gone.'

'Holdin' up an English rose, indeed,' said Mrs. O'Reilly, in disgust. 'The bugger wants brainin' with a Welsh leek.' And I had flash visions of the entire Rhondda population bowed in sniffing grief.

The rioting went on. All down the main street most of the shop windows were out, excluding Ginty's. I was in there begging for Bron, having run out of strike money.

'Sure,' said Ginty, 'if this goes on I'll be scratching a beggar's arse, so I will. Half the population's on the soup kitchens and the other half's on tick. And now the military are on their way to set fire to the place.'

'Not true, Ginty,' said his missus; thinner than a plasterer's lathe she was, and worried about the hunger. I saw Ginty's eyes then, and read his mind.

He saw her face as that of a cemetery ghost, and remembered her then as she was when young; in summer, wearing a cotton bonnet on a hill near Galway.

'*Ach*,' said Ginty. 'What with one thing and another I'd be best knocking timber out in pit time, and take the narrow squeaks; I used to rip it from underneath, ye know. *Arrah!* I was a foine collier.'

'You're too old for coal now, Ginty,' I said.

'And too daft to be a grocer. There's money in sweets, you know – Big Whiskers and Everlasting Strip, liquorice and dolly mixture – who's this comin'?'

'Mrs. Shanklyn, with her Willie?'

'Can't be – he's dying.'

A loaf of bread, a pound of marge, two cold faggots and a basin of drip.

'On the slate, Mrs. Shanklyn?' says Ginty. 'God, woman, not again!'

'Nigh four hundred horses starving down the Scotch — terrible, isn't it?' whispered Sarah Bosom.

'Bugger the horses,' said Ginty.

'They say the King's worried about 'em, too,' said Dozey Dinah, sad.

'And bugger the King,' said Ginty.

'Ludlow the Sweep do say the soldiers are comin',' remarked Sarah, vacant.

'All got our little crosses, haven't we?' says Mrs. Shanklyn. 'The poor always help the poor, I always say — thank God my Will ain't here no more. Prosperity do always discover our little vices, don't it?'

Frost is on the cobbles; the wind is howling down Dunraven; even the corpses are chattering.

'Just this once, Ginty? I'm flat broke,' I said. 'And Bron's that ill . . .'

Up to his elbows in his trews, huddled against the wind, a collier mooched down Dunraven, and I thought it was me.

Ancient faces, too old to die, watched from cracked windows.

'Please,' I said, waiting.

'Jesus, man . . .' whispered Ginty. 'Would ye break me?'

Uncertain, he looked about him for escape.

'Give it him,' said Mrs. Ginty, *Mark, Mary* and *Joseph!*'

'Three saints,' I said, 'and you're the fourth.'

'Who's this arriving?'

Guto Livingstone, it is, going like the wind. Tattered and defrauded, he goes, with his hollows of eyes black in the light of the moon; knapsacked and bundled is he, with urgent looks over his shoulder for Mrs. Guto: the skeleton had found the key to his cupboard, and unobserved, crept out.

In the witch-howling night he goes, making for Penygraig, to catch the inland steamer.

'You seen my Guto, Ginty?' asked Mrs. Guto, coming into Ginty's, hair awry and breathless.

'Just gone by, this minute, girl,' I replied.

'Got away from me, see?' said Mrs. Guto. 'Off to Santa Rosa in British Honduras — he's got relatives there, he says, poor little soul.'

Shocked, Mrs. Ginty waited, telling her beads.

'You spare a bite for me, Missus?' asked Mrs. Guto.

'No,' said Ginty, coming to the door.

'Being spare in the attic, my chap do get hungry ... I don't eat meself actually.'

'Oh, *God alive,*' said Ginty, barring the door. 'We got to live too, remember?'

'I beg you – look, I'm begging ye.' She pleaded with her hands.

And a cheese got up on its hind legs and walked out to meet her, assisted by Mrs. Ginty. Said Ginty. 'Where's the sense to you, woman?' and he elbowed his wife. 'I'll be as skint as me brother Shamus, and he's got his bum in the county jail.'

'But folks are starving, bless 'em,' said Mrs. Ginty.

'A month more of this and you can bless me, too, Pope and cardinals included. Bad cess to ye, woman – send the sods to the Co-op.'

'You don't get much out of boards of directors, mind,' said Mrs. Shanklyn. 'But you always was a good soul, Ginty. Got a spare tin of pilchards, 'ave you?'

'*Ach,* dear God, she's tryin' me for the miracle of the fishes,' and Ginty crossed himself.

'I won't forget this,' I said, hugging the top of a cottage loaf against me.

'Neither will I,' replied Ginty. 'Now bugger off.'

As I said to Bron when I got home, folks varied at a time like this: Mrs. Ginty was all right, but her old man didn't give a lot away.

'Sam's the one for generosity, though,' she replied. 'He never denied anyone. He was always giving away little bits of himself, especially to the women.'

I cut thin bread for her, with a scraping of marge, worried about her mentioning Sam.

The man was a walking blemish.

Even in a joke, I didn't want him here.

CHAPTER THIRTY-THREE

With eighty policemen injured, some seriously, and more than five hundred strikers wounded (according to an official Glamorgan Police report) Winston Churchill, the Home Secretary, after a lot of palaver about not wanting to, sent the troops into the Rhondda.

'It's because he loves us,' said Dai Parcel, bathing his cuts, 'that's why he doesn't really want to.'

'He don't really want to because he's got a General Election coming,' interjected Heinie, while Primrose put a new plaster on his skull. 'And soldiers are bad for politics. They start shooting people down here like "Featherstone Asquith" told 'em to up north, and we're likely to call him "Tonypandy Churchill"!'

'But did he really send them in – the soldiers, I mean? Didn't he order them to stand by at Pontypridd?' This from Richard Jones.

'The Secretary of State for War, Mr. Haldane, halted 'em at Pontypridd, after he'd heard Churchill had sent them,' I said. 'Let's get it straight.'

'Does he need to send soldiers?' grumbled Ben Block, bandaging his shins. 'Sent the London Metropolitan Police, didn't he? – them's worse than soldiers.'

'And didn't he tell the squaddies to "mow the Welsh buggers down"? – what about that?' asked Heinie.

'Lies,' I said. 'He said no such thing.'

Lies, rumours, apologies, white-wash.

And mainly white-wash, as history will relate.

'One day,' said Richard Jones, 'the tame historians will start their bleating, you watch. By the time they're finished he'll be the hero of the Rhondda.'

Nobody replied. But one thing was sure.

The name of Winston Churchill, then, and later, stank in our valleys.

It was the middle of November. The town steamed with mist in its uneasy truce, while policemen were carted to hospital and colliers were carted away: away to anywhere, their relatives said, before the courts begin to sit. People with bandaged limbs were moving very sprightly around the Rhondda about now – slipped on the ice outside the Pandy, I did: mending one of the windows, I fell off a chair, these were the general excuses. And it was more than your life was worth to send for a doctor.

The big London policemen, marching in squads, were all eyes; hammering on doors for searches at two o'clock in the morning, beating up people they found in the street.

Within a week of the riots starting, the soldiers came marching in.

I was sitting at the table in the Hut, days after the Llywnypia riot, getting the Union strike pay ready, when they marched across the Square.

Bron heard the tramping boots, the clattering hooves of the cavalry and turned her white face to me from the bed.

'That the English soldiers?'

I got up and pulled a curtain aside. 'Aye, they've arrived.'

'Criminals, ain't we?' She sighed. 'God, what a life!'

Splendidly, they came, the pride of the Army.

With fluttering pennants they marched, preceded by Captain Lindsay and his foot constables. Sitting astride their chargers, in full uniform to impress the rebel Welsh, they went in a hoof-clattering, jingling of harness fit to raise Egyptian mummies.

Finger-sucking urchins stared in awe at the fine authority of the English. In a tarantella of head-tossing plumes, they went, a spectacle of brilliance and power in the midst of our indignity.

A few black-clad women were on the Square by the fountain, in hen-clutches and whispers, shawl-scragged against the wind. I heard one shout, her shrill voice piercing the day:

'Bugger off back to England, where you come from, ye rubbish!'

311

It seemed to sum it up for us. I went to Bron on the bed, smiling down.

'How do you feel?'

'Better when I'm up and at that lot.'

'You've done rioting for a bit.'

The baton had taken her across the face; one eye was still shut tight; the other shone brilliantly from the fevered flush of her cheek. Worse, though, was the rib she had damaged. The police, for what they had achieved down Sinkers Row (for others had been beaten up, too) studiously kept away.

Dr. Walker had said it was a greenstick fracture, and bandaged her, but I had my doubts.

Sometimes, in a fit of coughing, Bron was in agony.

Mrs. Change, who reckoned she'd broken ribs on bad deliveries, was worried about her catching cold, and I wondered, since I had it up in Clayton once, if she had pleurisy.

'You ought to have the doctor again,' I said, touching Bron's damaged face.

'Can't afford him twice.'

Her beauty had gone; I cherished her the more when her face wore this parched, anxious frown of pain and hunger.

'You see to the face, I'll see to her stomach directly,' said Primrose Culpepper, coming in to visit. 'Just saying to that old Rachel, I was, how I'll fry up a nice bit of sirloin for that copper-fighter lying next door,' and she beamed down at Bron. 'You could do with a bit of raw meat on that eye, mind.'

'Chicken, if ye can manage it,' answered Bron. 'I've gone off sirloin.'

'By the way, my Moses's set fair for a good feed when I've got the makings. Don't expect he'll get his glass eye back till the end of the marble season, though.' Waddling to the door, she hitched up her sack apron and winked at me, so I followed.

'What's up?' I asked.

'We're sheep-killing tonight in Rachel's,' said she, looking around for listeners. 'We're doing it down the Row – there's no real danger knocking the beggars off, ye know – it's transporting 'em home where you hit the police.'

'I agree.'

'Will you help, Tobe?'

'I'll do my best,' I said, holding up my bandaged hand.

'What was that all about?' asked Bron, when I got back to her.

'Been invited to dine out.'

She turned her face away and closed her eye.

'Sheep enticing, eh? Six months if you're caught, remember?'

'Aye, but we won't be caught, will we?' Hunger was making me as edgy as her.

Even while looking at Bron's wan face, I wondered how Nanwen was getting on over at Senghy, and knew a fullness of relief that the Aber valley wasn't on strike in sympathy with the Rhondda – least of all, not to date.

Somehow, I couldn't have borne the knowledge of Nanwen starving.

They were risky times for sheep these days; every ewe and ram on the mountains had minor strokes when the colliers came out on strike, for the Rhondda Welsh weren't tardy about a bit of mutton on their Sunday plates when times were thin, like now. And the sheep themselves didn't help a lot, putting temptation in the paths of Christian people. These days there were more sheep window-shopping than shoppers: shoving their noses into women's baskets, whipping carrots and bananas off the stall; generally getting above themselves.

So the anarchists were abroad that night when I stole next door into the Odd's hut, and a few other criminals were already present, such as Bill and Rachel; Duck (who was partial to lamb and green peas) Heinie and Mattie, and Ben Block, who was once vegetarian before he became the Camarthen slaughterer. All were sporting head bumps, black eyes or sticking-plaster cuts from their battle with the police.

Primrose closed the door behind me like a nun in a catacomb and peered at me with her shadowed eyes.

'Police are about, mind,' she breathed. 'Blutty Glamorgans, too.'

She brightened the lamp the moment I was in.

Everything was ready to execute the crime; saucepans were bubbling on the fire and Primrose, pale as death, was standing over them like a witch with a brew, stirring big spoons with her hair hanging down. Moses was sharpening knives; Rachel stitching up sheets to hide the dismembered corpse.

'I've got me da's Irish shillelagh,' said Mattie, bringing it out from under his waistcoat. 'Used to pay the rent wi' it back home in Connemara.'

'Now it will pay a little fat ewe,' said Heinie, who possessed no soul.

'Six months if we're caught, mind,' said Ben Block, wheezing. 'Fifty years back they'd have hanged us down the well of the stairs.'

'The Bobbies don't go short on much,' said Bill Odd. 'Least of all these bloody Glamorgans. I expect a hiding from the Londoners, but not me own Welsh.'

'The Bobbies don't go short on anything, ask me,' replied Rachel. 'Over in New Inn, Ponty, the police and colliery officials are putting it down with champagne while our kids starve. Agents and owners are sinking food like Roman emperors; any legs o' mutton walk up my way tonight, I'm going to clout 'em.'

'Like I'm clouting you if you miss,' said Bill.

'Where are all the kids?' I asked.

'In Primrose's place, out of the way. You think they'll catch us? The military's on patrol now, ye know. Talk is that they flog ye first, before prison. That so?'

'Not true,' I said. 'Compared with the police, the military are all right.'

Duck asked, 'Bron still poorly, Tobe?'

'Be another week or so – she's got pain with breathing, mainly.'

'I'd crack a few ribs, half a chance – beating up women,' growled Ben Block.

'Reckon you should have had the doctor again.'

'What do I do for money?'

'Lot of things we should have had,' interjected Primrose. 'Never mind, a cut or two off a shoulder should cheer her up no end, eh? How's those saucepans doing, Rachel?'

314

'Better for a bit of meat in them, lest we'll have to boil the ornaments.'

I said, 'I reckon we ought to be doing this up the mountain. If folks see sheep walking in here it's bound to rouse suspicions.'

'One's thing's sure,' chuckled Ben Block, bass. 'They won't see the buggers walking out.'

Primrose prodded Heinie at the window. 'See any coming? Their time's about now, every night regular – scavenging, ye know, upper-cutting the dust-bin lids – poor beggers are hungrier than us.'

'There's a fat one feeding on the doorstep of Dano's place right now,' whispered Heinie, and we all went peering through the curtains behind his ears.

'Put the oat pan out on the step.'

Porridge oats for sheep; I could have eaten it myself.

'Is she still down on Dano's door, then?'

'Aye,' said Heinie, peeping through the chink. 'The biggest blutty ewe I've seen.'

'Whistle it down by 'ere.'

'That animal's nearly ninety,' added Duck, at the other window.

'Here she comes,' whispered Heinie.

'Turn out the lamp!'

In darkness we crouched, gripping weapons, and there came from the flags outside the patter of little feet.

Mattie and Duck were either side of the door with mandrels gripped; Heinie was standing above them, his Irish shillelagh swung up both hands.

'Right you, Tobe,' whispered Primrose. 'You're the youngest – when the door comes open, look lively and haul one in.'

Outside in the night the oatmeal basin scraped the flags.

'Ready?' I saw Rachel's big eyes in the window moonlight while Bill peered out.

'Right,' said Bill. 'Fetch her!'

The door went back; I grabbed the sheep by the ears, hauling it in. And the way Heinie clouted with his shillelagh should have settled the thing for a fortnight, but this one went demented.

Getting between Primrose's legs, it brought her down on top of Heinie, and these two floundered about in the dark, cursing and hitting out solid. People were bawling, Rachel begging everyone to mind her furnishings, and next time I saw her she was legs up waving, with the sheep in her skirts. Ben Block went down, taking people with him, and Duck caught Bill Odd one behind the ear with his mandrel, sending him howling. *Bedlam.* Everybody was shouting and the animal baa-ing and rushing blue murder.

'What the hell have we collected?' yelled Heinie, staggering up, but the thing was like a raging tiger, and it butted him flat again. Lights were going on along the Sinkers, and what the hell's happening in Rachel Odds? Over the kitchen floor raged that sheep, head down, barging everything in sight – chairs, table, the Welsh dresser, Grandma's chiffonier, and mainly Primrose, by the sound of her; taking it bad was she, halfway over the mangle.

'Get the devil out!' yelled Moses, coming to.

'Light the lamp!'

'Christ' exclaimed Duck. 'It's a ram!'

'Serves you right,' said Mrs. Etta McCarthy, opening the door. 'Sheep killing, indeed! Common thieves now, are we, Culpepper?'

Half the population of the Rhondda present now, peering through the door at us, but they scattered when that ram came out berserk, butting everything, including the door, which we managed to shut, and Ben and Moses slammed the table against it, lying back exhausted.

'Ought to be ashamed of yourselves, all of you!' cried Etta, knocking on the window. And neighbours were banging and threatening, fists up, red-eyed.

'You piss off,' shouted Primrose, 'or I'll come out there and cut the throats of the lot of you!' Hands on hips, she glared around the kitchen. 'Now, what prize idiot picked the ram?'

'It were dark, mind,' said Heinie, sheepish.

'Sorry,' I said, my head going down.

Silence after the damned fools and recriminations were over.

We sat in a monk quiet at the table – Rachel and Bill,

Primrose and Moses, Ben and Mattie, Duck, Heinie and me, and thought of roast mutton, mint sauce and gravy.

Then, suddenly, Primrose giggled; Rachel started next, hands clapped over her mouth; Mattie Kelly wheedled soprano: this set Duck off, then Moses and Bill, and me and Ben Block came last, he booming bass, and he had a laugh from his belly to raise roof tiles.

Sitting round that table, we thumped and roared, and the lights started going on up and down the row again and it's that daft lot in Rachel's place again – when are we going to get some sleep? And folks were wandering around in nightshirts and sleeping bobbles, scratching their ears and what the hell's happening.

Then, when we quietened, Rachel said, 'Mind, I'm against eating flesh myself – it ain't natural, really, is it? – eating our comrades, you come to think of it.'

'A good slice off the shanks do go down good, though,' enjoined Moses. 'I could do with a pint or two just now, a loaf, and a pound or so of leg.'

We rumbled in unison, thinking of spring lamb, roast potatoes and gravy, with bread to polish the plates.

'The old Greeks used to sacrifice a hundred bullocks – I read somewhere,' said Ben Block. 'Just imagine that. That must have raised a sizzling.'

'It is in accord with the laws of Nature,' replied Duck, educated. 'The little innocents have to die, so that we can live . . .'

'But, it's wrong,' I said. 'If I had any strength of character, I'd never eat meat.'

'Says it's all right in the Bible, though?' suggested Rachel.

'We shouldn't have done it, biblical or not,' whispered Primrose, damp. 'Cannibals, ain't we? You come to think of it, we acted like blutty savages. Old Etta McCarthy were right.'

'I'm ashamed of myself, really,' added Rachel. 'I'm not eating flesh again, not after that palaver. Shameful, that's the word for it.' She glared at Bill. 'And you put me up to it in the first place, remember.'

We sat in a new silence, enveloped by shame, and from the door came a little sound; louder now, louder.

Scratch, scratch ...

Ben got up and opened the door.

Arabella stood there with her little forefeet together and Bron's red hair ribbon tied around her neck, and I reckon she was smiling in the light of the lamp.

Arabella, arrived for her weekly oats.

Up with Duck then, in his best courtly manner. Removing his bowler, he bowed low before her. 'My little four-footed friend, pray enter,' said he.

'Oh, *Gawd*,' breathed Primrose, and hid her face. 'Not *Arabella!*'

‐ Many sheep went to their ancestors about now, for the colliers were quick with knives and buckets: and pigs, many devoted family friends, fared little better: nor did colliers, come to that. For the crime of being caught, scores went to prison; Will Shanklyn, for instance. He wouldn't take strike pay, considering it charity, but he took the life of a ewe up on Mynydd-y-Gelli, and, while he was in Cardiff gaol, his son Willie died.

Sad in my heart I was for Mrs. Shanklyn, losing two at a stroke, as it were. 'Anything we can do to help her?' asked Bron.

'You tell me,' I said.

It was thin.

In our hut, with Bron lying ill with suspected pleurisy now (according to Mrs. Change) things were thinner than most. She had been off from the Pandy since the riots, so there was no money coming from there. All I had was the ten bob a week strike pay, and this didn't go far on milk and eggs.

It was strange indeed, going to the bank every Friday night and drawing strike-pay money from the Union funds; about five hundred pounds me and Mr. Richard Jones collected weekly, with Heinie, Mattie and Ed Masumbala as bodyguards, yet we hadn't the price of a pint between us. And we would go the rounds of the Ely Lodge members, doling it out to the half starved colliers, with their wan, pale wives and children peeping round the doors.

I was worried about Bron.

She had been in bed a fortnight now – ever since the police had beaten us up.

The only medic I had now was Mrs. Change, the midwife at sixpence a time, and she was scarcely welcome.

'You keep the old hag away from me,' said Bron. 'There's talk about her, ye know.'

She was rapidly losing weight, but her spirit burned with the same old fire.

'Talk?'

'I've known women handled by midwives 'ave conceived that moment.'

'That can't be the midwife's fault.'

'O, aye? You think again – take that Effie over in Cynon, for instance. Just a common cold she had, till Mrs. Change handled her – now she's in the basket.'

'Don't be *twp*,' I answered. 'Snookey Boxer had a finger in Effie's pie, they reckoned. He's been activating her for months.'

'Snookey was over in Gilfach, picketing – now, come on!'

'So the beggar sneaked back, didn't he?' I slammed the ledgers shut.

'He didn't – he was away six weeks an' she was only one month gone, you ask Effie. Mrs. Change of Life, it were.'

I got up. 'Don't be daft, it's an old wives' tale.'

'All right, then, but you keep her away – she's not selling me puddings.'

I had to smile; I liked her best in this mood. When low, or in pain, Bron reverted to her peasant roots; a contrast, I reflected, to Nanwen's warm practicality.

It was difficult, at times, to say whom I preferred.

But there was growing in me a burning need to see Nanwen again; it was a sort of clean necessity that seemed divorced from the dirty old strike.

I used to change my ten shilling Union pay into pennies and spend it like gold on a daily dole-out: with the rent five shillings a week, this cut me in half before I began the budget, for you've got to keep the slates, like my old man says, said Rachel Odd; lose the slates come winter and you're on a hiding.

Like the O'Learys, for instance, up in Court Street; they were evicted after losing their stall, and Mrs. Shanklyn, with whom they went to live, was right on the edge of it herself, with Will in prison. No messing, as Heinie said – just bloody *out*. The Management didn't give sympathy to striking colliers.

It's amazing what you can do on five bob a week when you come to it.

I only begged once in those first four months, and that was off Ginty.

Reading was free, so I used to read. Tolstoy's *War and Peace*, Engel's *The Condition of the Working Class in England*, and everything written by Hilaire Belloc I could get my hands on; I used to read and re-read his *Path to Rome*. *The Girondin* came out in the year of the strike, but they couldn't get it up at the Scotch library, though I read about it in *Labour Leader*, in which Keir Hardie used to write, telling us how much Winston Churchill hated the Welsh, and what a sod he was for sending the troops into the Rhondda. Belloc must have agreed with Keir Hardie at the time, because later he called Churchill a 'Yankee careerist'.

'The soldier boys are all right,' said Bron from the bed. 'It's the police are the trouble. And Welsh police, too, remember?'

The Rhondda will remember the Glamorgan Police for a century.

'The London police are bad enough,' said Bron, 'we expect rough stuff off them. But if ye want a real good hiding you can bank on your fine Welsh brothers.'

For my part, I blamed Churchill for sending the Metropolitan Police, not for sending soldiers.

They were empty old days, just sitting reading, or doing the Union books.

The Rhondda was as deserted as a bankrupt workhouse. Little happened on the frosted streets. The colliers lounged on the pneumonia corners; the walls of corner houses were stained black with their coal-starched shoulders.

Sometimes they would sit on their hunkers, playing Fives, or fight with their mates just to keep warm. The police were everywhere; in the colliery offices, guarding the pit-heads, wandering the Taff Vale lines.

Not a lot happened, really, especially in those early weeks after the Riots.

Rosie Arse-Jenkins's baby died on the day that Noah. Ablett and Tom Smith first demanded a South Wales strike. So far, only the Cambrian Combine Pits were out – about 12,000 men. Elsewhere, such as in the Aberdare and Western valley of Monmouthshire, a further 20,000 were idle either in sympathy or go-slow and lockout, for longer or shorter periods, for some men had drifted back to work. But had a South Wales Strike been called and the Minimum Wage demanded as a body, then nearly a quarter of a million colliers would have downed tools.

But the Miners' Federation of Great Britain wouldn't support us; the Cambrian Dispute, they said, was a local affair – settle it locally.

'The truth is that the British Federation don't give a sod for us,' said Heinie. 'You can prate all you like about the Union, but we'll never have a Union worth calling a Union, unless it stands together. Now we come off Irish stew and begin to eat the leek.'

We ate the leek all right, and only in dreams did I taste Irish stew.

Hunger, I find, is something you can't get used to.

First come the billious attacks, then the gnawing pains, then the heady swims that blind you into collisions; last, the dangerous time, comes apathy, a listless emptiness.

'The Management's offered us two-and-a-penny a ton, remember,' I said. 'It was in last week's *Labour Weekly.*'

Said Richard Jones, 'But the issue's greater now. The South Wales Federation wants a minimum wage of 6s. 9d. a day for all colliers, never mind the Ely.'

'They'll never get it.'

'There's new men coming on to the Executive,' said Richard. 'Strong, firm men like Noah Ablett, the Maerdy checkweigher – and Tom Smith. These are new leaders who are ousting Mabon. Now you'll see sparks.'

'All I want is a good Sunday dinner,' said Bron. 'You

know, Tobe – a good round of beef, baked potatoes and cabbage? You reckon such dinners still exist?'

She had been in bed a fortnight now and was sweating badly, as usual; I didn't know what to do for her.

'You got trouble here,' said Heinie. 'She's ill.'

'She's starving – do you have to tell me that?' I paced about.

He stood by the bed screwing his cap.

'Aye, she's just plain hungry, that's all,' said Rachel. 'Rachel's here, my little love.'

'If I give her solid food she only brings it up,' I said.

'Then she'll have to have more milk and eggs, won't she?' said Primrose Culpepper. 'We'll just have to share more.'

'Share what?' asked Moses.

The children of the Culpeppers and Odds stood around Bron's bed in a ragged disconsolation, their grimed faces staring.

'Get the kids out of it, Primrose?' I said, gently.

'Aye. Hop it, you varmints!'

'You tried the Parish?' asked Rachel, and she bent above Bron. 'Have you pain, my cherub?'

'Of course I've tried the Parish and of course she's got pain!' I whispered.

'She's declining – you're goin' to lose her, lest she eats.'

It was Heinie who had the answer after the others had gone

He entered the kitchen like a ghost with a purpose, on tiptoe, lest he should awaken Bron, but I knew she wasn't asleep.

'The oven door's open again, Goldberg,' she said from the pillow.

'Sorry, missus,' said Heinie, and did up the front of him. 'How you doin'?'

But Bron didn't reply.

Later, when we were sure she'd dropped off, he said, softly, 'You got to do something, Tobe.'

He stared around the kitchen. 'Anything else you can pop?'

In the past month most of the furniture had gone into the Three Balls. All we had left was the bed, the table and chairs.

'I'm popping nothing else,' I answered. 'Now I'll have it coming in.'

'That's the idea.' He sat down in wheezes and grunts. 'She's worth it, isn't she? Mine was, too, you know. Did I mention her?'

'No,' I answered.

'Died of T.B.' He grimaced. 'It were about eight years back. I was twice her age – she were only a kid, really. The Ocean Coal Company strikers marched over and fetched us out for a rise of twenty per cent – there wasn't a hope in hell of getting it. We struck for a month, and starved – me mostly, for my girl was delicate.' He made a wry face. 'We went back, of course.'

'Got nothing out of it?'

'Nothing at all – like now – a blutty waste of time.'

There was no sound but Bron's hoarse breathing.

Heinie said, with hopeless dejection, 'People were good, but she were too far gone in the chest, and she needed good food.' He looked at me. 'They killed her, ye know, like they'll kill your Bron.'

I stared back at him. He said, 'If they'd come in and knifed her – the coal owners, I mean, they couldn't have done her better.'

'I'm sorry,' I said.

Heinie smiled, empty. 'One's enough between us – you see your girl don't end up the same? You need money for her, you go and fetch it. I did for mine.'

'Steal?'

'Why not? I remember Isaac Evans, one of the Committee at the time my Hannah died – saying that Mabon was taking employers' bribes. Him drinking wine and smoking cigars – getting his son a job in the coal office – and my girl dying. Pretty good, eh? So I hoofed it down to Swansea and stole a fob watch for food.'

'You got away with it?'

'No, I got six months – but it were right, wasn't it? Property's theft, anyway – it says so in the *Labour Weekly*.'

Later, Patsy Pearl called in, wanting to come with me up to John Haley's place, for the story had it that he'd been batoned in fresh rioting over at Cynon recently, and I promised to meet her later.

But first I saw to Bron.

Mostly, when her fever was high with the pleurisy, Primrose or Rachel would come in and sponge her down for me, but tonight I wanted to do it myself.

'You'd make a good nurse,' said she, her good eye dancing at me.

'It isn't the only thing I'm good at, woman.'

I noticed that she was thinner, and her weakness had increased: probably, I reasoned, the fortnight in bed had done that; get some good food into her and she'd be up and about again, giving everybody hell.

Bron began to cough when I restrapped the bandage the doctor had put around her ribs, and I noticed some tiny blood flecks on her pillow.

'What do you want for supper?' I asked.

'Keep it down to steak and onions.'

I bent to her, drawing the bandage tighter; she must have been in agony, but made no sign of it.

'You're a good one,' she said.

'That's what I keep telling you.'

'Sam wouldn't nurse his grandma.'

'I'll nurse the bugger if he comes round here. Doesn't he know you're poorly?'

'I expect so. News gets around.'

I washed her face and combed her hair, and she said, 'You're on the wrong horse, you realise that, Tobe?'

'More than likely.' I was at the stove now, making her bread and milk.

'I mean – you'd best know – I'll be up and away to Sam for sport, the moment you get me on my feet.'

'That's nice to know.'

'You don't mind?'

I was stirring in the bread and sugar. 'Up to you, isn't it?'

The night was silent beyond the kitchen window; faintly I heard the rumbling of a tram; empty, mostly, they came and went up and down the valley in illuminated discontent and with ghostly precision.

'You'd be best off with that Nanwen, really speaking.'

I poured the steaming bread and milk into a bowl. 'Chance would be a fine thing.'

'I'd do the same for you, mind . . . nursing, I mean, if you was ill.'

'That's all right, then.'

Sitting on the bed, I raised her on the pillow, then spooned the food to her lips, blowing on it first.

'You make me feel a bitch,' she said, swallowing, her face turned away.

'That's good.'

'Perhaps if you hit me around sometimes, like Sam does, I'd treat you better.'

'I'm trying that next.'

She swallowed like a woman swallowing chaff, and said, 'I . . . I can't help it, Tobe. It's . . . like being mad.'

'You're the one who keeps on about it.'

Her single eye suddenly blazed 'And why are you so blutty pure and holy? Given the chance you'd climb all over that Nanwen!'

'Of course.'

'Then what do you stay here for?' She made a fist of a hand and thumped the bed, instantly groaning with pain. 'Christ, I hurt. Somebody's been gnawing at me with gum-boils.'

'Then don't get yourself so excited.'

She lay silent. Tears filled her good eye.

'Oh, hell,' I said, 'don't start that!'

'Cootch me up a bit, Tobe.'

'Finish your bread and milk . . .'

'Come on, be a sport. Hold me?'

Sighing, I did so, bending over the bed.

'Don't you fret, my beauty,' she said, 'I'll make it up to ye.' She gripped me, whispering, 'That blutty Sam Jones – he's bound to know I'm ill, but he don't come. He was always the same – wouldn't spit in me eye if I were on fire. Do . . . d'you think he knows about me, Tobe?'

'Of course he doesn't, or he'd be here on the next tram,' I said.

It placated her, and she slept.

325

It was cold in the room and I thought about getting in with her to keep her warm, but blackness was on the window when I finished reading. The clock said eight, and I was due to meet Patsy outside John Haley's room at half-past.

Meanwhile, Bron was asleep and breathing at peace, if noisily.

I wanted to kiss her, but thought it might wake her up.

She'd have given birth to a set of jugs had she known I was going to meet Patsy, so I made sure she was really sleeping before I left her with Primrose sitting guard.

I walked slowly down De Winton to the Gelli Road, and the house on the corner where Haley had a room. Rumour had it that he entertained women there, which I doubted: a pint, a smoke, and John Haley seemed at peace.

Others were not at peace, though they were sleeping; young Shaun McCarthy, for one.

Shaun, once the beloved and youngest son of Etta and Dano, had been thrown out into lodgings for taking the starch out of Rose Arse-Jenkins's bloomers, but nobody (including Tommy, who handed Shaun a hiding) had the proof, for Shaun denied it. I paused at the window where he dozed in his lonely room like a boy embalmed. Dreaming of Rosie, perhaps, with whom he was in love, they said: and properly in love, I reckoned. I watched, pitying him, for he was a regular good Catholic lad: behind him the flickering candlelight on the wall made shadows of fornicating rabbits.

'Dirty old thing, ain't he now?' said Sarah Bosom, going past.

'Ought to be put away,' said Dozey Dinah, holding her arm. 'Regular sex maniac. Etta won't 'ave him back, ye know. How's Heinie?'

This was the scandal at its noblest and best – farted round corners, bubbled through beer. I pitied young Shaun, in lodgings, when he wanted to be back home with Etta and his brothers.

'Good night,' I said.

It was a pity I'd met Sarah and Dozey; later, it wouldn't be possible to testify that all that night I'd been sitting in with Bron ...

Life, at best, I thought, was a savage hunger for food and love, of one kind or another.

On the way up De Winton I met a gang of English soldiers coming down: a boisterous, laughing lot were they, their bodies muscular under their grey-backs, and I liked their cheek and banter; they were towing a cart of coal from the Ely, and one was riding the donkey.

All down De Winton the doors and windows were barred to them.

English soldiers on Welsh streets; the Welsh didn't like it.

'Ay ay, Taff!' cried one, taking me off.

'Ay ay, rough stuff,' I said.

Coal carts like this one were travelling up and down the Rhondda about now, by special orders of General Macready, the English Officer Commanding, a man the colliers respected, even if the Irish rightly hated him later for commanding the Black and Tans.

Starting full at a colliery, these carts would arrive nearly empty at the barracks, and there was never any official inquiries as to how the coal got lost. So on they'd go, spilling coal with such carelessness that the valley children could sneak out and collect it up in bags: the police might send you down for a month for stealing coal off the tips which belonged officially to the Owners, but nobody got sent down by Macready for stealing off the Army.

'You got a fire at home, mate?' called one.

'Don't need it, boyo; got a warm missus.'

I walked on. I respected them, but I didn't want a lot of chat with them.

But you got to give them credit, said Heinie.

The Lancashire and West Riding men gave concerts during the Cambrian Strike; they organised food kitchens in defiance of the Owners, shared their rations with the children, beat us at football, took hidings at rugby. In the early days of their coming, a Welsh girl seen out with a squaddie would likely get her head shaved. But now a few soldiers were being invited home, and, when they had the money,

327

would drink in the pubs. One or two actually married Welsh girls and stayed on as colliers.

Not so the police. The sight of blue instead of khaki was enough to send a Rhondda Welshman raving mad.

Churchill's stupidity in sending in the troops, said Richard Jones, was only matched by General Macready's integrity; he was firm, but kind. He didn't hob-nob with the coal owners; he put his officers under canvas, away from the clutches of the local squires. With the police at large in the valleys, it could have ended with another blood bath like the old Merthyr Riots; Churchill had used a sledge-hammer to crack a nut, people said, and his orders to the police will be remembered by the Rhondda. Blood from the nose, indeed? Blood from the brain, and Macready cooled things down. But it was the indignity of having soldiers in the Rhondda – this is what we hated, not their presence.

They were singing some tuneless song of home, these soldiers, as they went down to Pandy Square.

Mr. Winkle, the cockle man, went along Dunraven with his tray on his head, bawling his wares. His lava bread, they said was the best in the valleys, though Bron reckoned he grew it under the bed. And even the official cockle women come up from Port Talbot couldn't match the plump, delicious cockles he stored in his two gallon china; peeing over them in winter to keep the beggars warm, said she, for cockles, being cold-blooded, enjoy a warm environment.

'You fancy a pint, Toby Davies?' asked he, stopping.

'Not cockles,' I said, and turned down Gelli.

Patsy was waiting in the hall of Number Thirty-Nine, just down from the Empire.

'Hallo, Tobe,' said she, faintly.

John Haley's next door neighbour was standing in the doorway, a broom with elbows, and she turned her wasted face to Patsy, saying, 'Mind, his landlady weren't all that good – went off with the other lodger, she did – always a fancy man round the corner, isn't there?'

'He's in there?' I asked. 'Mr. Haley, I mean.'

'Ay ay,' said the neighbour, barring the way. 'Wait till his friends come, I said to my Girt – we've been doing what we could for him. She were the peak of low taste, his landlady ye know – ye could skate to Trebanog on her dish-cloth. Do you know she used her old man's bottom set to mark the edge of her tarts?'

'Can we go in?' I asked, taking Patsy's arm.

'Didn't even feed him; got no maritals, some people. D'you know she cooked his Christmas pudding down the leg of his long-john? He's been used to a lot better, I'd say.' She stared at Patsy. 'Ain't I seen you before?'

'Come,' I said, and led Patsy into the hall.

Somebody said that the police had batoned John Haley; it looked like the entire Glamorgan constabulary had been at him, with the London Metropolitans thrown in.

'Oh, God,' whispered Patsy, and went to her knees.

'They just come in here after him and did him up,' said the woman from next door. 'Six of 'em – day before yester-day.'

It was a tiny room; a bed, a table, a chair; on the mantel was a fading photograph of a dark-haired woman with a child. And John Haley, his face a dramline of cuts and bruises, was lying in the bed.

Patsy wept.

'That won't help. Get up,' I said. Then, to Haley:

'John, I've come with the strike pay,' and he opened the slit of one eye at me. 'And Patsy's come to feed you.'

The blood-shot eye drifted to Patsy, and closed: he looked like a twin to Bron.

I put the ten shillings into Patsy's hand and she rose, a woman with a new demeanour.

Before Patsy went to Ginty's for food, Haley drank warm milk from the cup she held to his split lips; thirstily, he drank, demanding more.

'What's good enough for Madog ought to be good enough for anyone,' said Patsy. 'It stands to reason, don't it?'

'She fed him breast milk – I tell ye, I saw her through the window,' said the woman next door. 'If I hadn't seen it with my own eyes . . .'

'It was the best drink a man ever had,' said Haley, and put out his hand to her.

One thing was sure – it was all Patsy had.

For my part I was off to the New Inn, Pontypridd a few nights later, but not for ale, it being after closing hours. Once last year, at a Rocking Stone meeting, I had killed a pint in there with Heinie.

This is where the colliery officials caroused: roast chicken and stuffed pork dinners, with wine to wash it down.

Ponty was in a midnight darkness by the time I got there. The town snored behind its shuttered windows, and the full-drunk moon was courting her tipsy stars above the slated roofs down High.

Nobody about save me and a few stray cats in the streets and alleys, enough to feed the Rhondda, for Pontypridd wasn't on strike.

I walked slowly through the town with my eye out for policemen, then vaulted the wall at the back of the New Inn, which was shut.

The cold, bare yard stared up; blank windows awakened, fluttering winks at me and the moon. I stood for a bit listening to the sleeping house.

With the banks shut after the Saturday festivities, like as not the till would be full ...

Deeper in the town, a dog dismally barked: close to me, tiptoeing on bottle glass, two cats eyed each other on a wall, jet shadows of hate against spindrift clouds.

A window facing the yard slid up with a wheeze to the lever of my chisel; I swung a leg over the sill and stood within the warm, sweet smells of a kitchen; red bars grinned at me from the grate: somebody had left a kettle on and it sang a tearful song of hope to me. Come morning, the bottom would be burned out of it, so I took it off the fire.

Through the kitchen door now and over the hall like a wraith, till I came to the tap. My heart was thudding away at my shirt as I stepped silently over the sawdust and ducked under the counter flap, but the till was gone.

In window moonbeams I stood listening to the beetled, mouse-scuttling talk of the house. Smiling, I uncorked a bottle of gin from the rack and drank deep for courage: I drank again until I realised that I hadn't eaten all day. Later

I reflected, I would search the kitchen for food, and take some home for Bron.

Standing there, I saw her face with astonishing clarity.

Back through the tap-room now, and into the hall. At the bottom of the stairs a black cat was sitting. Purring, unafraid, she arched her back as I stroked her, her amber eyes addressing me with night prowling, friendly regard; her very presence brought normality and allayed my apprehension.

Now up the stairs I went. On a landing, I listened again, followed by the cat.

Soft-carpeted, the bedrooms growled and grunted the insensitivity of humans, and I saw, in the eye of my mind, florid-faced agents lying flat on their backs in colly-wobbling, steak and kidney dreams of bubbly and naked barmaids. A door ajar; it magically swung wide to my touch, exposing the room within like a touch from a fairy wand.

A woman was lying in the bed.

Her white face upturned to the ceiling, her hair lay in staining waves over the snow-white pillow: the moon from a skylight immediately died, bringing darkness to her face, which possessed the sheen of jaded alabaster.

I came closer to the bed, staring down at her, as one does at a corpse. Outside, the town was striking the hour; one o'clock, two, I did not count.

So still this woman lay that she intrigued me; the shadowed eyes, the paling crimson of her mouth: she could truly have been dead.

On the table beside her was earrings, a little graven necklace and rings. Of these, I took the necklace, which was of gold. In a flash of the moon, I saw it, but the room was dark again when I turned to the woman in the bed.

Her eyes were wide open.

It was as if she had watched me in the act of theft.

Watching her for movement, I turned to a dressing-table.

Drawing the curtain, I peered down on to the blackness of the flagstoned yard. Money, gold and silver, was scattered on the table; silently, I gathered it up. The room swam suddenly, like a drunken dancer pirouetting, and I held on to the table, cursing myself.

When I turned, with the money in my hands, the woman

was no longer in the bed. And the moon, as if in answer to my question, swung over the skylight, bringing the room into sudden shape.

She was standing in front of the door, and I knew her instantly. As a statue of white, she stood in her long nightdress, her hands held out to me in greeting. Clearly, I saw her; as clear as on a sunlit day.

I could have shouted with fear: it was the Wraith Woman of Rhayader.

Some money spilled from my damaged hand as I tore aside the curtain.

Throwing up the casement window, I swung over the sill and dropped down into the yard.

Here, a man was standing; a groom by the size and smell of him, a misshapen gnome of a man. As I went passed him he waved his stick at me, which I knew was the dried penis of a bull, and he cried in his thin, Irish falsetto:

'Bad cess to ye, me lad! And wicked cess indeed for turning her down! Ye'll be travelling faster than Barney Kerrigan's bull, sure to God, before ye're rid of her this time,' and he cackled laughter, stamping around in the yard. 'She'll be laying her curse on your fifth generation.'

It was the man I had met on the road to Builth, years back, on my way to the Rhondda.

The street was awaking; lamps were glowing in windows, curtains going back, doors coming open.

With my hobnails sparking on the cobbled road, I went pretty fast up the road out of Ponty, cursing myself for drinking raw gin on an empty stomach, as the laughter of the Irishman echoed in my ears.

Mind, said Heinie later, it's happened to me a couple o'times as well, for raw gin from the bottle plays hell with the constitution – 'mine's mainly pink elephants.'

O, aye?

Something was telling me that I'd pay dearly for that trip to Ponty, if the woman of Rhayader had anything to do with it.

Clear – as clear as day I saw her that night again, as I can see her now.

CHAPTER THIRTY-FOUR

It was Christmas, 1910

As an undertaker's cloak, the old anxious sighing for food dropped over the valleys.

No longer the sounds of children echoed down the gully-ways and alleys; rain erased the chalkings of the hopscotch flags; the running chimes of the hoop and iron, whip-lash and spinning tops died in memories of bountiful summers.

All down the coal-grimed streets, where once black-shawled women chattered, the doors were locked; the windows barred to the black intruder Starve.

The High Street shops gazed their brown-papered windows at the frosted streets; the Empire was shut, so was the little Market in Tonypandy: the publics were gated or on short time: dogs, too thin to howl, dozed on wet Sunday afternoons.

Weary old people, the grandparent rubbish of earlier generations, turned their sallow faces to the Rhondda sky and wondered where God had got to; the present generation, the mufflered, moody, still volatile Welsh, turned their eyes from the god called Mabon and the Union, which, they said, had betrayed them.

But the masters, Chapel deacons and the Church of England pastors were still eating, as Heinie mentioned, though larders, like bellies, were empty. And the old people, without asking permission, as usual, began to die.

In the grip of a bitch of a winter, up to their knees in snow, the little black processions, dew-dropped, in creaking boots (a sure sign they weren't paid for) and Sunday alpaca, began the old bible-hugging journeys. Hymns were sung outside blind windows and at gravesides.

In ragged, dejected columns or in white breath before the trundling soup kitchens of Lady This and That, the scant-thin families waited, bowls in blue fingers. Scitterbags of women, once capped and noisily defiant, now stood in dejected lines before the Quakers boilers with their babies on their backs, and did not speak: or crept out under the diadem, Rhondda nights to thieve coal off the tips under the noses of the big Metropolitans.

The children sickened, the youngest first, as always.

Blood on coal, said Mattie; now you Rhondda fools, try licking off the blood in the name of Mr. D. A. Thomas.

Slowly, the workhouse filled.

All down Sinkers Row the babies had ceased their crying; up Court Street, down Eleanor Street, Charles and the Bush Houses it was the same: no babies crying: always a bad sign, said Primrose – it were the same in the Ocean Coal strike – remember, Rachel?

'Things are serious, mind, when the babies stop crying,' said Patsy. 'Will Bron be all right now, you reckon?'

I looked at Bron's thin face on the pillow.

'Aye, and thanks for coming,' I replied.

'Feels more settled, she do, after a blanket bath, see?'

I nodded. At the hut door, Patsy said, 'Don't take it hard, Tobe. She don' know who's washing her – except that it's a woman . . .'

'Yes,' I said.

'And it's only when she's dreaming that she calls for that Sam.' She smiled at me. 'You've always got to reverse your dreams, you know – it's you she means.'

'Of course.'

'Good night now.' Patsy humped up Madog and gathered her shawl about her. 'I'm away up to Mr. Haley, then.'

I gave her a penny for Madog's supper.

'Happy Christmas, Tobe. You want anything, you send for me, is it?'

I nodded. 'Happy Christmas, Patsy.'

For a long time I sat at the table, watching Bron's pale face.

It was over six weeks now since the police had batoned her; after the pleurisy came pneumonia. With the help of the women, and the money I had stolen from New Inn, Pontypridd, I'd managed to keep her alive.

It was Christmas Eve, 1910.

Earlier, I had torn up pages of the *Labour Leader* and

334

painted them in various colours, making paper-chains, and these I'd suspended across the hut: I'd whipped a Christmas tree off one of the estates and had put it in a pot beside the bed with a candle on top, decorated like a fairy. There wasn't a lot to celebrate, but I'd got hold of a bit of under-belly pork, and this, after Patsy had gone, I was roasting for a treat; it was no bigger than two fingers, but it smelled sweeter than the hanging gardens of Lebanon. The idea was to surprise Bron when she woke up; it had cost me half our capital, but I wasn't letting Christmas go by without tickling her fancy.

I was just getting it out of the oven when she stirred in the bed and opened her eyes at the ceiling, and I got the joint out in the pan, still basting it and wafted it to give her the smell of it, but I reckon she wasn't ready for Christmas Eve joint and paper-chains.

'Sam,' she said, 'you there?'

I closed the oven door.

'Aye, I'm here,' I said, and sat back on my heels.

Christ, I could have done with a pint.

At the turn of the year Bron was still very ill.

Normally, every New Year's Eve, folks came in throngs from up and down the valley to see the New Year in, and there would be dancing and drinking, and a gay old time, with the publics spilling out of the doors. And Tonypandy Square would be packed with revellers making the best of it. At near midnight, with the old year dying, people would dance in rings of joy, hands clasped, singing *Old Lang Syne* at the top of their lungs, old and young all mixed up to-gether. And then, on the stroke of midnight, every colliery hooter in the Rhondda would blast out its message of good-will, howling stridently down the valleys – the distant ones echoing over the frosted mountains, making the Rhondda, in all its neighbourliness, one with itself in love.

But this year, standing beside the window, I saw but a few straggling people hugging themselves against the wind: no singing, no laughter sounded from the Square; indeed, there was no sound at all but Bron's quiet breathing.

And then, as if in defiance to strikers, a siren sounded from the Scotch; then another from up Clydach way, then another, a growing chorus of discord wailing and sighing around the empty streets.

I screwed up my hand and put it against my face. Bron stirred in sleep and I knelt by the bed, holding her. Coal owners, I thought, had a marvellous sense of humour.

'What's that, love?' she asked faintly.

I could have gone down to the engine fires and taken the steam cocks to their faces; a hatred, deeper and purer than I have ever known, surged within me.

'*Heisht,* you, it's nothing,' I whispered.

As if brought back to life and reasoning, Bron smiled then; a woman coming out of a dream of death, and whispered something incoherent.

'What's that . . .?' I bent closer to her lips, listening.

'Happy New Year, Tobe,' she repeated.

The sirens wailed on tunelessly while I knelt there, holding her.

What with one thing and another, between coal owners and strikers, the Rhondda had something to answer for, I reckoned.

For the first month or so of the Cambrian strike I'd done little else but read; now I was can-making, something more constructive. It appeared a sort of intellectual chicanery to improve one's mind in the face of people starving. Empty milk tins, refashioned, polished, made good drinking mugs in the absence of crockery, and I sold them down in Porth at twopence a time, my eye constantly out for Sam Jones, but I never came across him. Had I done so, I'd have taken him by the scruff and hauled him up to Bron.

Now, with February chasing out January, and Bron sitting up in bed, I was still at it – the finest can-maker in the Sinkers, self advertised.

'Give you a bangle earring and a fiddle and you'd make a good tinker, Six-foot-three,' said Bron.

'Got an eye for the fellas again, eh? Sure sign you're better,' I said, polishing.

But it was the ghost of Bron, sitting there in the bed.

Her hair, regaining its old flashing lustre, was tied back at the neck with a bright red ribbon – stolen from my old gran's wedding box, said Patsy: over her thin shoulders she was wearing a babywool turnover, knitted by Primrose for Rachel's last confinement. And there was about her an air of wistful contentment; no life was in her, although she was young. The skin was stretched tightly over her high-boned face in a Dresden china beauty; her eyes, once sparkling, were large orbs in the shadowed darkness of her cheeks; as if the merriment of the old Bron had flown away on wings. Left behind was the winter counterfeit of the summer Bron I knew.

'What's all this about Senghenydd, then?' she asked.

Her curiosity, however, hadn't diminished.

I put down a can. 'Heinie suggested it – I can tackle it now you're better. According to Mattie, he knows a chap who has a pull with the foreman of the Downcast; we'll try for signing on.'

'At the Senghy big Universal?'

'Why not – there's nothing doing here?'

'Isn't the Universal on strike, then?'

'Of course not – she isn't in the Combine.'

Pick pick pick went her fingers on the blanket, always a sign of trouble.

'And that's the only reason why you're shovelling over to Senghenydd?

'Would there be another?' I got up and put the kettle on the grate.

'You know what I mean – come off it, Tobe!'

'Nanwen, you mean? Ben's got her barred, shuttered and chained, don't you worry.'

'But if you had half a chance – I know ye!' She was watching me.

'Stuck it out here so far, haven't I!'

A squad of Glamorgan police were marching across the Square; their tramping boots beat between us. Most of the soldiers had gone now, but the police remained to deal with the uneasy peace.

'Don't like you going down the Universal,' said Bron. 'She's like Mrs. Change – a gassy old bitch.'

Gas had never worried me; only water, and a distended

337

death in bubbling suffocation disturbed my sleep; talk did have it, too, that there was water down the Universal ...

'Didn't they have a gas flow down there recent?'

'Coal isn't a fancy parlour job, you know – one has to take some risks.'

She turned away her face like the old Bron, saying flatly, 'You're blutty toop, the lot of you – they'd never get women down a pit.'

'Years back, they did.'

'Now they've got more sense, I reckon. When you trying Senghenydd, then?'

'Give it a week or so; Mattie's going to fix it.' I got up again and made the tea. 'You'll be all right – Primrose and Rachel will slip in from time to time.' I held a brightly polished can up to the lamp. 'Now then, what d'you think of that?'

'You're the best gipsy can-tinker this side o' Maerdy.'

'And this?'

I danced about to happy her, one hand on my hip, a can held high, snapping my fingers.

'Oh, Tobe,' she said in tears, and put out her arms to me.

'Don't be daft,' I said. 'Drink your tea.'

It was over four months in all before Bron was back on her feet, and Mattie landed us the big Universal jobs.

April was into us, after eight months of the Ely lockout; the actual Combine strike being in its twenty-fourth week.

I was in the bath by the fire when the urchin called, handing out what the police called subversive literature. Bron picked up the pamphlet from behind the door.

I sat in the bath with the soap tufting up my hair while Bron read falteringly, sitting on the bed:

> 'Through all the long dark night of years
> The people's cry ascendeth.
> The earth is wet with blood and tears,
> But our meek sufferance endeth.
> The few shall not for ever sway
> The many who toil in sorrow.

The powers of Hell are strong today
Our kingdom comes tomorrow.'

'Is that in the *Labour Weekly*?'

'Aye,' she replied. 'Part of the Cambrian Strike Manifesto, it says. What's a manifesto?'

'Just keep reading,' I replied, and she held the newspaper up to the lamp.

'It says here that Noah Ablett, John Hopla and Noah Rees wouldn't take part in agreeing to a return to work on Management's terms; they said that the colliers had been jockeyed and sold . . .'

'That sounds like Noah Ablett right enough.'

'Listen to this,' said Bron, 'he says,' and she read: ' "We have been deliberately and foully misrepresented by a large section of the public press. We have been bludgeoned by the police . . ." ' She glanced up. 'Well, I can tell 'em that . . .' She continued, ' "One of our comrades lost his life, two committed suicide, many have suffered imprisonment — some are even now in prison. If we could tabulate even a part of the suffering and misery endured by our women and children, we would say that our suffering has been too great already for us to be handed over to the mercy of D. A. Thomas, who is one of the greatest despots these valleys have known." '

'Good stuff,' I said.

'What does it mean?'

'That the Strike goes on.' I stood up in the bath, towelling myself down. 'And it should go on, until the South Wales Federation gets either a guaranteed Minimum Wage for colliers, or calls for a national stoppage.'

'Meanwhile the valley starves?'

I got out on to the floor. 'We've no option.'

Now that the riots were over, we were beginning to see the baliffs for the rabbits, as Heinie put it. The only man to come out of it all with clean hands so far was General Macready. He had left the Rhondda now after a job well done; soon, more of the soldiers would follow him, and their names would ever be respected by the Welsh. But not that of

Winston Churchill, the man who sent them in, despite the efforts of Haldane, the Secretary of State for War, who insisted to him that they be held in reserve at Pontypridd.

For a century Churchill would be remembered, also, for sending in the Metropolitan Police, over whom he held sole control. Their brutality (he consistently refused to allow an official inquiry into police behaviour) was matched by that of the hated Glamorgans, our own constables. The importation of blackleg labour, the free rein given to the despised Chief Constable Lindsay who hated the Welsh; all contributed, in measure, to the Tonypandy Riots.

And the Rhondda will remember.

'When that Churchill bugger goes down,' said Bron now, 'we'll dance in the streets.'

'Dear me, Tobe,' said she now, coming nearer the bath, 'you've got shoulders like a barn door and a waist like an Egyptian queen.' She kissed the top of my head. 'And another hair on your chest. *Fawch!* I haven't seen this one before – must have grown while I've been away.'

'Hop it, you're supposed to be ill.'

'Old Rachel's ill, I reckon. You noticed her lately? Dropped stones, she has — a lazy wind would go right through her.' She sat on a chair beside the bath. 'Fancy your back washed?'

I took the towel from her. 'Sure sign you're up and about.'

'Tell you what, son — cross me pillow with silver and I might let ye make love to me.' She praised me with her eyes.

'Ach, I'm not much good at night, girl.'

'And not that much better in the morning. Hark, what's that?'

It was the Odds next door, singing, 'As pants the hart for cooling streams ...' What they got to sing about?' asked Bron.

'Bill's not doing so bad, remember,' I said. 'Things got better for them after he went to the brickfields.'

We all had little bits of jobs about now to stretch the Union money. Moses Culpepper, who was once a chippy, was making coffins for Dai Up and Down, the undertaker, and was going around measuring up his friends, for old Dai always made his money in advance, so to speak. Ginty, who had closed his shop, had also gone back to the tools and was knocking up emigration chests for families sailing off to America and Patagonia, the new craze. Albert and Tommy Arse had been hauling for the Army; Dano McCarthy had returned to his trade of slaughterer and Mattie and Dai Parcel had jobs as spare-time postmen.

Bron said, civil, 'you've been pretty good to me, mind, since I been ill.'

'You'd have done the same for me.'

'Wasn't your job really, though, was it?'

She was sitting in front of the grate now, her hands held out to the glow. I'd always managed to keep a bit of a fire for her; it was only a week or so in the jug if you got sent down for stealing coal off the tips, and it was worth it. I towelled down and pulled on my clothes. 'Of course it was my job. We live together, don't we?'

'It was Sam's.'

'Oh, God, do you have to bring him up?'

She frowned at her fingers, looking like a sickening child, sitting there with the glow of the fire on her thin features. 'I ... I expect he didn't hear about me being ill — that's why he didn't come, eh?'

'I suppose so.' I was tying my boots.

'Perhaps he was away — he's a hell of a chap for going off somewhere, you know.'

I grunted reply, and she said, turning:

'What you got dressed for? Time for bed, isn't it?'

'Got to go out.'

'This time of night?'

'There's a duchess told me to report to her bedside over in Maerdy — I'll be in with her directly.'

'Don't be daft!' It didn't amuse her.

'I've got to see Solly Freedman, Three Balls,' I said.

'He's closed.'

'Not to me, he isn't.'

She rose. 'What are you popping that's so special?'

'If I tell you, you'll be as wise as me,' and I kissed her. But she stood, unmoving when I reached the door.

'Don't get us into trouble, Tobe.'

341

I gave her a wink to discourage her curiosity; buttoning me up against the cold, for it was a night to make monks out of brass monkeys. Crossing the Square, I went down De Winton to the back of Solly Friedman Pawnbroker.

The little golden necklace I had stolen from the New Inn, Ponty, gleamed like molten brass in the palm of my hand.

I got eight sovereigns off Solly for that necklace, which astonished me, but he agreed that it was solid gold. One thing about Solly, he never asked questions.

It would have been better for everybody, including Solly, if I'd stayed at home and starved it out with Bron.

A new spring came dancing down the slopes of Mynydd-y-Gelli and Penygraig — come over from the Brecon Beacons, folks said, with sunlit hair, dandelions behind her ears and white crocuses on her feet. And the twin valleys, thumped into white iron by the fists of winter, grew warm and soft to the touch.

Snow-drops, sleeping since Christmas, put their noses out of the frosted ground and yawned at the sun; the primrose (always shy of humans) hid her face lest she saw a drunkard, and Primula, her shameful cousin, rose from the rich, warm earth to peep up passing skirts.

Feather-duster winds came greeting down the valley, kissing the dereliction of the unquiet dawns: motionless stood the pit-heads against billowy wash-day clouds. And the twin rivers, Fawr and Fach, stretched their quicksilver radiance through the greening country.

Sometimes, that early season, when Bron was still sleeping, I would climb to the top of Mynydd Trealaw and look down on to Tonypandy.

Of all the valleys, this, I thought, was surely Welsh best. Where exists such loveliness as my Rhondda in springtime? The mountains are sylvan here, the country gold; the hills, bracken-crested, are hot cottage buns, the rivers milk, the sky honey. God knows why exile Welshmen search the ends of the earth when Heaven is on their doorstep.

Sometimes that April, sitting up on Mynydd Trealaw, I would listen to the sounds of spring, and wonder about God and His profoundly bitter humour. Anger assailed me, so that, even had He confronted me, I would have remonstrated: 'But why build cottages on vineyard slopes to desecrate them with fire? Why cast limbs of strength and beauty for mutilation? Why sculp lovely faces merely to chastise them into ugliness? Why, most of all, create in my lovely Wales a vision fairer than belief, just to ravage it with pitheads and strikes?' And why, indeed, I thought, sitting there, build a love as great as mine for Nanwen O'Hara, and then bemuse it with a fierce emotion . . . the one I held for Bron?

Strange, the conflict on that April day. Even while bargaining my soul for a moment in the arms of Nan, I suddenly remembered it was nearly five; that Bron would be awake and looking for her tea.

If I didn't get moving, Rachel would come and make it, and she hated Rachel's tea. And, on the way back, I would try for a seedycake from the Co-op – with the money I'd got from the necklace, we'd celebrate, I decided.

After I'd got her on to her feet proper, I thought, I'd take a trip to Porth, find Sam Jones and try to get them together for good – this would settle everything: she'd have Sam and I'd be free to make a run at Nanwen – to hell with Ben O'Hara.

Rising, I went down into the valley.

After walking for a bit, I imagined I could hear Bron calling me; and then the thought struck me that Sam Jones might have come in the moment my back was turned and removed her, so I ran.

And I didn't stop, except for the cake, until I reached the Sinkers.

Throwing open the door, I stood staring down at the bed.

'Hallo, my lovely,' said Bron, and opened an eye at me.

Kneeling, I kissed her. She was plainly surprised; I didn't kiss her a lot these days.

'Hey, get off!' she said, gasping to breathe. 'Tea, is it?' She stared at me, wide-eyed, holding me at arms' length. 'Gawd! Seedy-cake!'

'God knows why I'm back,' I said. 'I was doing all right with that duchess.'

Mattie reckoned that he'd heard of the Senghenydd jobs

from Dinny Gnatshead, one of the drinkers in the Pandy before the Strike. Turning an honest penny, Dinny called it, with his cap sitting on his ears and the peak down over his eyes. He used to buy a side of bacon and sell it to his wife by the slice; steal coal from his neighbour's bin and sell it back to him at fourpence a bucket: tighter than a duck's arse was Dinny, according to Mattie, who paid him a week's strike pay to get wind of our jobs.

These jobs turned up in the middle of April.

'So you're off to Senghenydd at last, then?' asked Bron, that afternoon when I came in from coal stealing.

'Aye, meeting Heinie on the Square.'

'Will you be back tomorrow?'

'Yes, if I don't get the job.'

'And if you do?'

'Back at the week-end,' I said.

I couldn't manage my collar stud, so Bron dried her hands at the sink and came and fixed it, and I sensed her ill-ease.

'Think you can manage by yourself now?' I asked.

'Ay ay – Rachel and Primrose'll be in from time to time.'

Ever since we'd got up, words had evaporated between us, as if our lives, like the Rhondda, were gathering to a climax of doubts and fears.

Over her shoulder I saw the bare hut: the town, like us, seemed to be dying, too, for nothing moved on the empty square. People were starving properly now. Some over in Trealaw were selling their insurance policies for nine bob in the pound, and the money-baggers, as always, were moving in: the slick city boys with polished shoes and double-breasted waistcoats, while half a million British miners watched our agony from the touchlines.

'What will you do with yourself all week while I'm away?' I asked.

Her smile, as she stood before me, was like a small celebration of love.

'Hang around till Saturday night and you come home.'

I turned from her, going about my business of packing things in my brown paper bag. Bron said:

'What will you both do for lodgings in Senghy?'

'I'm tackling Mrs. Best – I don't know what Heinie's up

to. Can't go wrong with her, she always buys the best.'

We laughed together, but it was forced. If she had cried a bit, it might have made things easier.

Solly Friedman Pawnbroker went past the window; in his black astrakan coat he looked like an avenging angel. Bron said – out of context:

'You heard about that copper up the valley?'

I shook my head. She said, 'Rachel reckons they tied him to a lamp post and poured chamber pots over his head. And him in his best suit, too, and his missus done up in her Sunday braveries.'

'Serve him bloody right.'

'We ain't finished with it yet, ye know, Tobe. Trouble, I mean.'

'Yes we are, it is ending.'

I opened the door of the back and looked at the sky. Rooks were cawing at the April afternoon, circling like burned ashes – carrying in their beaks, like carrion crows, I thought, the poor, sad dead of the Rhondda. Leaving Bron at that moment seemed like a part of this dynasty of death: all down the Sinkers doors were slammed shut as if to keep in the poverty and allow things to die.

I made a mental note to hand the Union books over to old Richard Jones before I left the valley.

'I got to go,' I said, finally, picking them up.

'Why can't I come?' Bron stood apart from me, looking lost.

'If I can settle on a place for us, I'll come back for you later, eh? Besides . . . you've got to work it out – Sam Jones or me, isn't it?'

She lowered her face. 'Like you, with that Nanwen, really speaking?'

'Come Saturday night I'm back by 'ere with you,' I said, 'if you're still around.'

'Don't you worry!' She straightened before me as the sun came through the door, curtseying our shadows. Bron, as usual, had an uncanny will to survive. 'You don't chuck me over that easy, you'll see!'

'So you won't hop over to Porth the moment my back's turned?'

345

Although it was early, the rag-and-bone man was coming, singing his rag-and-bone call; his missus was having a baby; it would be a little rag doll for sure, folks said, so I mentioned it.

'I reckon we're all rag dolls, sort of,' said Bron, empty.

'Good-bye, then,' I said.

The world came through the door and stood between us.

'There's a pain in me for you, Tobe.'

'That's good, hang on to it,' and I kissed her.

I think we both realised that the time had come to part.

Bowlered and polished up, boots creaking for a funeral procession, Heinie came like a man to his bride, with buttonholes either side, stocked and waxed, creases to cut his shins and buttoned up in the flies.

'You losing Bron, Toby?' Heinie always had possessed an unfathomable ability to read my thoughts.

'Likely she's lost me.'

'You leaving her alone won't help, mind.'

'So we'll have to sort that out, won't we? I got her up and about again, didn't I? Now it's up to her.'

'She's a sweet swansdown woman, ye know, you'll not find the likes of her.'

'Aye, well, perhaps there's too many people around; Sam Jones, for instance.' Together we strode down De Winton. 'What about you?'

'Me, son?' Heinie turned his little flat face up to mine, his crossed eyes twinkling. 'I come simpler. New job, new place! All I want now is a little plump widow with a weakness for whiskers and a guaranteed minimum wage. I've always wanted a daughter, ye know.'

'At your age?'

'Ay ay – you start new, Heinie, I said. Good ale and wicked girls – I'm a primitive methodist when I've got me clothes off. But I'd treat a woman good – I did my little Hannah, you know? Two I want, a son to keep me, a daughter to bounce on me knee.'

'You've got to make up your mind,' I answered. 'A good time, or a family, you can't handle both.'

'The good time first. I'll have the family after.'

He spoke more as we strode on, but I wasn't really listening.

'Dear me, I hope old Mattie's cooled those jobs,' said he. 'I don't trust Dinny Gnatshead, really.'

'One thing at a time.'

Dusk and bats were dropping over the Aber Valley when we got into Senghenydd, and there was an excitement growing in me again at the chance of catching a glimpse of Nanwen. Instead, the first women we saw was Sarah Bosom; plumper than ever was she; faster to jump over her than walk round her, with Dozey Dinah on her arm as skinny as adversity.

'Well, I never,' said Sarah, contralto, and she patted her chest for shock. 'Look who's here – that Heinie Goldberg gentleman who helped us!' and she dropped a curtsy low, with Dozey down beside her: pretty it looked.

Down with Heinie, too, hitting his bowler on the kerb; up with him then, expansive. 'I heard you was over here, though,' said he.

'Just visiting, actual,' said Dozey, thinly. 'Come to open a lodging house in Senghy – you working here?'

'Expecting to,' I answered.

'Good clean beds at ten bob a week, all found,' said Sarah, comely. She sniffed and wiped daintily, smiling at Heinie. 'Though kind offers of lodgings are often misrepresented, if you get me?'

Heinie, in a trance of joy, was gazing up at her, a man with fearful ambitions.

'You're welcome, remember – both of you,' said Dozey. 'There'd only be the four of us to start with, see?' and she tightened her gloved fingers and fidgeted her hips at me.

'I'm fixed with Mrs. Best, more than likely,' I replied.

'And you, Mr. Goldberg?' asked Sarah.

Delusions of grandeur were Heinie's; Sarah, in turn, was weighing him with a honeying touch; Dozey pierced me with eyes like phials of poison. She said, 'Lodging with Mrs.

347

Best, eh? Now that Ben O'Hara's out of the way, so to speak, I'd have thought to see you honouring his missus.'

I lifted my eyes to hers.

'Well, Mrs Guto Livingstone mentioned the connection, if I may call it that.' She beamed at me. 'Likely you'd manage to give her some comfort . . . at a time like this?'

'Why?' I asked. 'Has he left her, or something?'

'He's left her, all right, mister – permanent. He's dead.'

The publics were filling; the colliers strolling in arguing, dismal groups in the moonlight and the wind had April shivers in him. I saw the faces of the women before me as white, embalming masks.

'Dead? Ben O'Hara?' I stared at her.

'Ain't you heard? A journey of drams hit him underground . . .'

'*When?*' whispered Heinie.

'About a week back.'

'While we was over here negotiating for the lodgings,' said Dozey.

Gladys Bad Fairy, locally known in the amateur dramatics, I learned later, went past us with her feet at ten-to-two and a bottle of blue ruin tipped up against the stars. Sarah said, 'Jones the Death had him last week, poor soul. Good on the Irish, he is – all burials executed with great deference and respect.'

'Mind, I only met him once, but he weren't my cup of tea exactly.'

Others spoke, but I didn't hear them.

I ached for Nanwen.

'You mind if I go, then?' asked Heinie, tugging at my sleeve.

'Where?'

'With Sarah for lodgings?'

'Aye, of course,' I answered. Realisation was sweeping over me in waves of increasing intensity. I thought, *Nanwen!*

'See you later down the Universal public for a pint?' asked Heinie.

It seemed impossible that Ben could be dead: the wheel of Fate, it appeared, had turned full circle: in fact, as I discovered it later, it had only just begun to move.

'Yes,' I said, looking at the sky.

'Coming, my lovelies,' cried Heinie rubbing his hands, and went.

The curtains of the terraced house in Windsor Place were drawn for mourning, but a dim lamp was burning on the glass of the door: knocking gently, I waited.

It was difficult to believe that, such a short time back, Ben had opened this door to me. Now I expected it to swing back again, exposing him as a wraith in all the mutilation of his accident: I expected to see, in his bloodstained face, the same accusation as I had known in Bethesda.

Instead, when the door opened, Nan stood there.

We stared momentarily, unspeaking.

Her brow was high and pale. Deep shadows embraced the once brightness of her eyes, which looked sick of tears. It seemed as if, in Ben's death, there was bequeathed to her a new countenance; one that left her empty, bereft of life. And then, as realisation grew, she smiled, and she was Nan again.

'*Toby!*'

But she did not move to me. Beaten, she lifted vain hands to me in futile explanation.

I nodded, words being useless.

'I've lost him.'

'Aye, Nan, I heard.'

We stood contained by the embarrassment of her grief.

Ceinie appeared soundlessly beside her from the kitchen darkness of the hall. The child's dark eyes moved swiftly over me in woman-like assessment. Nanwen said, softly. 'It ... it's Uncle Toby – you remember Uncle Toby?'

Ceinie did not speak, except with eyes. Nan said, touching me, 'I knew you'd come. I told Ceinie you'd come, didn't I?' She caught my hand and drew me within.

'I ... I'd have come to the funeral if I'd known before,' I said.

The three of us stood in the kitchen with its smells of human warmth and cooking. She'd got pretty women's things on the table and the iron was heating on the grate; Ben's slippers were on the fender; on the hearth lay his pipe, as he had left it. Over Nan's shoulder, in the scullery, I saw

349

his shaving things neatly laid out on the copper. It was an abysmal ritual of life in death, I reflected; why the hell couldn't she let him die? Perhaps Nan noticed the emotion of my face, for she said:

'Can't get used to it, see?' She gestured, adding vacantly. 'He was here such a little time ago . . .'

'It was quick,' I said softly, and gripped her hand. 'Be thankful.'

Ceinie's eyes were bright with unshed tears. When her lips trembled, I released Nanwen, and turned away.

'Best I got going,' I said. 'I'll come back later, if you like.'

'Oh, no, please stay! Look, I'll make a cup of tea. We can't let Uncle Toby go without a cup of tea, can we?'

Nan bustled about, flashing me looks of tearful apology.

'Come on now, sit you down.'

The activity of the tea-making, the very tears of the kettle, the cup-rattling, seemed to sustain us; I have often thought since that the therapy of making tea surpasses its quality of enjoyment.

And Nanwen was smiling at me over the brim of her cup; that smile took me right back to the white starched cloth on the table in Caerberllan; to Ben, the Union books, and to Grandpa.

'Good to have friends about one at a time like this, isn't it?'

For the first time, Nanwen wept.

Going to her chair I stood above her, holding her while she sobbed. She put out her hand to Ceinie, who did not come; instead, her child's eyes, as startled as a faun's, held mine from the other side of the room.

Ben might be dead, I reflected, but there would always be Ceinwen.

Later, at the bar of the Universal, the pub next door to the pit and named after it, I called to Heinie as he came through the door, entering the throng of working colliers.

A Union meeting was going on upstairs, they told me; a cock-fight was squabbling in a corner of the tap-room. Harpies and harridans, the usual refuse of coal, were shrieking to pumping blasts of an Irish melodeon and an old navvy, the aged, human dross of the Universal pit-sinking, did a Connemara clog dance to a thunderous beating of time. Pushing aggressively up to me, Heinie thumped the counter for ale.

'Two pints, boyo,' said he: blowing off the froth, he killed his alive, then elbowed me. 'How did it go?'

'The usual funeral parlour – what about you?'

'I'm in,' said he. 'Supper tonight and feather-down bedding – ten bob a week, all found.'

I said, 'If they dropped you into a piss-pot, you'd swim out smelling of ashes of roses. I'm off back, bugger the job.'

'What d'ye mean, mun – Mattie's got it fixed!'

Heinie's voice was the only sound in a sudden, intense silence; the music, dancing, clash of glasses and shouting had snapped off the world like the slam of a hand. I lowered my ale.

Two policemen, Metropolitans by the size of them, were standing at the door. The pit-head lights gleamed momentarily in the moment before it closed behind them, then they moved over to the counter.

'Anybody here by the name of Davies? Tobias Davies?'

The landlord repeated, raucously, 'Is a Tobias Davies in here?'

I pushed past Heinie. 'That's me,' I called.

The constables approached me, gently handling Heinie aside.

'You're Tobias Davies, lately of the Hood Huts, Tonypandy?'

'Aye, the Sinkers,' I replied.

One said, looking at his mate, 'As big as a door? A collier? – this is him.' To me, he said, 'Tobias Davies, I am arresting you on a charge of feloniously entering premises known as the New Inn, Pontypridd, on the night of December the 3rd, 1910, and stealing money to the value of eight pounds two shillings, and this . . .' He opened his hand. The little golden necklace I had pawned with Solly Freedman glowed dully in the lamp-light. 'You recognise this article?'

'Yes,' I replied.

'You were silly to pawn it, weren't you – unprofessional, eh?'

They spoke more, cautioning me, but I was thinking about Nanwen and what she would do if I didn't return, as I'd promised: also of Bron, if she didn't have any money. I said to Heinie:

'See to Bron for me, eh?'

'Christ . . .!' whispered he.

'Get moving,' said somebody, pushing me.

I said, 'Heinie! Please . . .?'

'Are you coming?' asked one of the constables, 'or do we have to carry you?'

'If you take your hands off me,' I said, shoving him away, 'or you won't get me as far as the bloody door.'

The bar went silent; people were crouched about us, like animals about to spring. Vaguely, I wondered what would happen to Solly Freedman: it was scarcely his fault . . .

Heinie came outside with us; the April night was cold.

'Good-bye,' I said. 'Remember Bron . . .?' I gripped him. *'Please . . .?'*

'Aye, mun.'

I pulled up my coat collar against the wind.

Three

The Aber Valley

CHAPTER THIRTY-FIVE

During my two year sentence for the theft of less than thirty pounds, I didn't see a lot of the next two summers, except when out with prison working parties in the Rhymney valley; a far call from my beloved Rhondda.

But the spring of 1913 beckoned with promise of an early release. I recall (dressed in gaol grey and my head shaved as clean as a billiard ball) leaning on my shovel with the rest of the convicts, listening to the birds going mad with joy. It was a good spring too, green and fruitful; one far removed from the coming threat of war. And I saw, in the shovel-clatter of the working party around me, daffies and tulips waving their heads off in the nearby gardens while we trenched and ploughed the fields.

All the earth on that bright morning seemed to brim with beauty, and the distant mountains, lying on their backs under the sun, waved their heather, green and gold, in great, rushing swathes of the wind.

'All right, Davies, get on with it,' cried a warder, and I tore my eyes from the sky beyond the mountain, where Nanwen lived.

A lot had happened during my two years in Cardiff gaol.

Peace had at last come to the coalfields: the national strike for a Minimum Wage had ended by last year's spring and the Cambrian dispute of the Rhondda Valley had been settled six months before that: a return to the pits on Management terms.

With starvation facing them, they had no alternative.

'A year of idleness since the Ely locked us out,' said Heinie, on one of his monthly visits – 'you had it easy in gaol, mate – you worked it good.'

Heinie came to visit me with expected regularity.

'And then back on D. A. Thomas's terms, eh?' cried

Mattie, who had come with him that day. 'What the hell did the Rhondda die for?'

'The Rhondda's been dying since they first discovered coal in the valley,' I replied. 'Tell me something I don't know – is there still no news of Bron?'

'Still over at Porth – far as I know,' said Heinie.

'She knows where I am, and she knows why – the least she could do is drop a bloody card.'

A week after I'd been sentenced at the Cardiff Assizes, Sam Jones had come over to the Sinkers and collected her, according to reports.

'Never see hide nor hair of her since,' added Mattie.

'But your Nan O'Hara's still activating,' said Heinie. 'I see her most nights when I come off day shift from the Universal. They ain't never had a prettier mistress at that old Board School.'

It was difficult to talk privately in the prison meeting hall, with the other prisoners and their relatives chattering about us.

Mattie whispered, 'Keeps to herself, she does. though. A tuneful little piece, she is – no followers – give her credit. And you can't say as much for some.' He looked at me.

'Just her and the girl,' said Heinie. 'You reckon to settle down with them when you get out, Tobe? You could do worse, mun.'

I didn't reply. Perhaps, I reasoned, my own sense of insecurity was being shared with Nanwen. She had written every week for two years with astonishing punctuality; every Saturday morning her letter would arrive, telling of the happenings in Senghenydd, and in Windsor Place in particular; the comings and goings of people; of her work as a mistress in the Board School where Ceinie attended. Her composition flowed with the serenity of her nature, uncompromising, kindly; constantly looking to the future and our new life together. And yet I sensed, within the lines, her innate fear of the future, an apprehension that was a part of myself. It was not that I doubted our ability to find a new happiness; it was as if some act of Fate would sully such happiness: Nanwen appeared to sense this, too.

It was a complication fed by absence; letters, at best, can be awkward things, she wrote.

Bron, for her part, sought no such complications; she didn't write at all.

And yet, despite the knowledge that she was now completely lost to me, the Rhondda, that old, dark mistress of coal, black-faced, was calling me with a vibrous, fiery impetus; it was impelling, forcing itself into my being, and I wondered why. Mattie said, 'Mind, some are doing all right in Senghenydd. They can keep the old Rhondda, I say. I'm on me jack with Mrs. Best, perhaps, but some 'ave nice warm feet, don't they, Heinie?' He nudged him. 'Any happy events comin'?'

Glum, looked Heinie. Things in the Sarah-Dozey establishment hadn't turned out exactly as expected, apparently.

'Why don't you marry the girl?' I asked. 'One of 'em at least.'

'That's what I say,' interjected Mattie. 'He could do worse, I reckon. Or even living together in sort of marital accord. Sarah's a well set-up piece – I'd rather be in her than in the Glamorgan Constabulary.'

'She ain't what she looks though,' muttered Heinie, sad. 'Her legs are botherin' her.'

'They don't seem to bother nobody else,' said Mattie. 'You want to get moving, son.'

I said, 'Well, if there was one chap I thought I didn't have to worry about while I was inside, it was my poor old mate, Heinie Goldberg.'

'Aye, but lodging with Sarah and Dozey ain't all it looks,' Heinie answered. 'They'd get no promotion in a harem – it's like a resolution of virgins – they're very fond of each other, you know.'

'Oh dear.'

'You poor little soul,' said Mattie, patting him. 'I thought you was gettin' dozens. But it's not doin' it that does the damage, it's thinking about it that knocks your brains out.'

We sat in a holy silence, grieving about Heinie's conjugal complications.

'Oh well,' I said.

We all got up. 'Next Saturday, then?'

'Two o'clock, outside the main gate – and don't be late.'

'That's unlikely.'

'And straight over to Senghy?' asked Heinie, hopeful.

'Straight over to the Rhondda,' I said. 'Come on, it's a prisoner's request. I want a quart at the Pandy.'

'With that beautiful Nan O'Hara awaiting ye in Windsor Place?' Mattie sighed. 'Don't be daft, mun – start the way you're intending.'

'Tell her Sunday,' I said. 'Lads, I've just *got* to see old Tonypandy?'

I stared at them, and Mattie came up and put his fist under my chin, saying:

'Saturday night, then, and we'll give it Hamlet, like my old girl used to say.' He sighed. 'Six pints of Allsops embalming fluid!'

'She were a good one, mind – Mattie's wife, I mean,' said Heinie, glancing at me meanfully.

'The best,' I said. So far we hadn't discussed the death of Mattie's wife.

Mattie moved awkwardly, grimacing. 'She was all right. Just that she didn't make the best of herself with folks, that's all. Also, I kept her to myself a lot, so to speak – I was never one for bumming a woman up to me mates. She made very good gravy, ye know. Mind, I still got me pigeons.'

'His Milly's in the family way again,' announced Heinie. 'And got third prize in the Pandy to Gelli race, didn't she, Matt?'

'Ay ay – lucky, isn't it?' Dried of words, he stared, vacant.

The cacophony of the room, the relatives' chatter beat about us, bringing us loneliness in the face of Mattie's loss. He said, pulling his cap to bits:

'Come to think of it – us lot are all widowers really, in a manner of speaking.'

'We'll give 'em widowers next Saturday night,' said Heinie.

'We'll give 'em hell in the Pandy!'

'Then straight over to Senghenydd, last train?'

I nodded. 'Anywhere you like – after I've seen the Rhondda.'

' 'Cause that little woman'll be waiting – Nan O'Hara,

358

remember,' said Mattie, persistent. 'Mrs. Best told me to remind ye . . .'

The following Saturday I was standing outside the main gates of Cardiff prison, looking out on to the sunlit city and the traffic clattering along the cobbled road before me. The sun was hot, and grey-faced rooks (You got Cardiff, you got to have rooks, said Heinie) were shouting their heads off in nearby elms. And starlings, a great perplexity of numbers that spring, were rushing in black swarms across the caverns of the sky as if in haste to mate on the rich, warm earth. And, as the clocks struck midday and I waited with my brown paper parcel of belongings, the people I expected got off a tram and started piling over the road towards me – Mattie and Heinie, Mr. Duck and Ben Block, with Dai Parcel, Gwilym and Owen bringing up the rear. Noisy and purposeful were they, swilled with enough ale already to refloat the lost *Titanic*; if I'd been released an hour later they wouldn't have had a leg between them.

Men for comrades; women for kitchens and beds, said Grandpa once; Grandpa was right.

'*Toby!*'

They nearly hoisted me off my feet in the rush, and we finished up off the tram down the back streets of Tiger Bay with our back teeth awash and pledges of eternal friendship, till Mattie started to cry. Back on the tram then and off to the station, Rhondda colliers setting Cardiff alight; dusk found us coming off the train and thronging along De Winton, in Tonypandy.

It was all I had dreamed about, the town at its best.

Poshed up and pretty were the little shop windows, like peacocks come alive after a long, winter sleep. And the pavements were thronging with black-faced colliers and wives; the children at it again bowling iron rings, and whipping tops and bawling. Great brown drays clog-stepped along in a flash of painted wheels; dog-carts trotted, gay little cobs showed sprightly heels; arched glances from painted ladies, lifting their needless parasols; blushing glances from girls growing into women. Ginty's shop was open under new management, for Ginty, like hundreds of others, had shifted to the Aber Valley during the Strike. And the muddy little market, where once Shanklyn and O'Leary had their stall, was alive again and steaming its pigs' trotters, black puddings and faggots and peas. Arm in arm with Heinie and Mattie, I strode on, remembering the old nights when I made love to Bron, and thought I saw the sway of her amid the coloured dresses.

The visions came stronger when once I was in the Pandy.

The Scotch colliers were in there, cramming it to the doors; Red Rubbler, the mountain fighter, eyed me as I pushed to the bar; Annie Gay was serving the jugs, and I reckoned I could see three of her. But John Haley wasn't in his usual corner, neither was Patsy opposite, watching him.

'You go to Senghy sober, mate – we've booked you in with Mrs. Best, and she's respectable,' said Heinie.

'So am I, you're sleepin' with me, God help you,' said Mattie, five sheets in the wind.

I was seeing Annie Gay now through the hop-reeking haze of old and mild.

'You want to watch him, he's bowlered,' said Red Rubbler. 'Last time I saw him he was a fuzzy-wuz – now he's a blutty baldikin.'

'So will you be lest you stop pattin' the top of his bald head,' said Heinie. 'You ain't lost your punch just because you lost your hair, 'ave you, Samson. Beside, you're still sober, ain't you, Tobe?'

'Sober enough to take you, Red,' I said, and saw in Annie's youth and gaiety the smile of Bron: fair hair replaced Annie's Welsh darkness; blue-green eyes lowered admonishingly from Annie's oval face, and, when she spoke, she made the sounds of Bron.

'You sober up, Toby Davies, and I'll be off duty directly,' whispered Annie, filling my pewter.

'He won't be sober this side of Easter,' said Red Rubbler, and caught my arm, but I pushed him aside.

'God knows how he's standing,' said someone, and I think it was Mattie.

'Tell him to take his eyes off my woman or he won't be standing no more,' said Red Rubbler.

'Bron . . .?' I said to Annie.

I heard somebody say, 'Abraham Lincoln had a soft spot for the Welsh, too, did you know?'

'Bugger Abraham Lincoln,' I said, and reached for Annie. '*Bron . . .?*'

Red Rubbler swung me to face him. His large, bald eyes, heaped with old cuts and bruises, regarded me as he drew back his fist. Everything seemed to be dying about me. Even the daffodils on the shelf behind Annie looked as if they'd been out all night.

'Christ,' I said.

I heard Heinie say as he dragged Red Rubbler away, 'Touch him, and I'll kill ye, Red – I'm givin' fair warning.'

'But she's got a husband – that Bron,' said Annie. 'It just ain't good enough, really speaking, Toby Davies. Time you left her off, ain't it!'

'You seen her?' I tried to focus her, and failed.

'I don't know, rightly . . .' said Annie. A man was saying into my face, and God knows who he was, 'Things are never what they seem, ye see, son? Even some stars ain't there really – the light still shines, though they was burned out longer than a million years.'

'Blutty remarkable,' said Mattie, weeping.

'He'll see stars if he don't loose my woman,' said Red Rubbler.

'Two pints of skull attack,' said a voice, and it was Dano McCarthy with Shaun, his son.

'Mind, I'm glad Etta's goin' to take him back in,' said Ben Block, wheezing up.

'Och, don't be daft,' said another. 'God only listens to saints.'

'Bron . . .'

'I tell ye again, me name's not Bron,' said Annie Gay, and Dano cried:

'And I says to him, sure to God, I says, "D'ye call that religion, do ye?" Ach, the fella had a face like a bunch of laughs, and I never trusted him – if a boy's face shines, examine his knees.'

' "Will ye come to communion, Patrick?" asks me wife. "Aye, I will," I said. "And if you loved Jesus as much as I do," I told her, "when it came to the communion wine, ye'd sink the lot." Aren't ye drinking, Shaun?'

'Aye, Pa,' said Shaun, and drank. 'You all right, Mr. Davies?' His young, fresh face smiled at me, and I wondered about Rosie.

'Best you're away, lad,' said Red Rubbler, "cause there's going to be trouble.'

'She'll find her own level, that Rosie Arse, never fear,' said Dano, 'forget her, son. Is it good being out of clink, Tobe?'

'If he don't let go of my Annie's hand he'll be out on his backside,' said Red Rubbler.

People were pressing about me, Red was pulling at my coat. Aunty Boppa Hughes, the new Pandy landlady, said into my face, 'Ain't you met my old man then – Exalted Ifor? His ma used to wash the dishes in the lodger's po, but she were good otherwise, mind. Eh, she were a card! "To my beloved husband I leave the back rent," she says in her will, but then, all lovers die broke, don't they? Used to live round here, did ye?' Her powdered face stared up into mine. Very urgent was this Aunty Boppa's need, apparently, but I never got to the bottom of it.

'God Almighty, Bron . . .' I said. 'Where you got to?'

'Right you,' said Red Rubbler, 'you're off.'

And I was. I don't remember making a raw suggestion to Annie Gay, but I suppose I must have done, for next moment I was sailing through the air of the tap room with Heinie close behind me and Mattie following rapidly. And we hit the cobbles smartly, all three of us, outside the front door of the Pandy, with Ben Block and Dai Parcel arriving shortly afterwards, and Red Rubbler brushing himself down, after he'd tossed out Duck.

'All right, we can take a hint,' said Heinie, sitting up, and he grabbed me as I moved. 'Where you off to?'

'I'm going over to the Sinkers to look for Bron,' I said.

'You're going to Senghenydd, mate,' said Mattie.

I but vaguely remember the train ride back to Senghenydd, and I was vaguer still about the walk down to Woodland and Mrs. Best in Number Ten. But she greeted

362

ne like a long lost lover, ushering me in with matronly chat-
er, despite the hour.

'There's been certain enquiries made, mind,' said she, lips
pursed.

'Enquiries?' It had been a good night, but with sobriety
came remorse, mainly alcoholic. I sat down in the best
kitchen in Senghenydd and held my head.

'It's the prison, mainly,' said Mattie, fearing repercussions.
'After two years it's natural – he ain't himself.'

'Feminine enquiries,' said Mrs. Best roundly. She wasn't
going to make it easy.

'Nan O'Hara?' I asked.

'Mrs. O'Hara, the widow of Windsor Place. She had
supper prepared for you tonight, especially.'

'God,' I said, repentant.

'I'd just slipped out for a best bit o' scrag end and bumped
right into her. You was due there tea-time. Flowers with
beauty, that one, when she's got something under her apron.
Wouldn't be in your shoes. Twelve bob a week suit you?'

Mrs. Best was a woman of economy where economics
were concerned.

'Yes, ma'am.'

'And you've been fighting, too, just look at that eye! Dear
me, Toby Davies – stealing, prison, fighting – ye've been on
the slide since last I saw ye, so ye have.'

'They knocked him about something cruel in prison,
though,' said Mattie.

'I'll believe ye – thousands wouldn't – see you in the morning – sharp to table, money on the nail, and no camp followers, remember.'

I bowed as I went past her in the kitchen, granting her a
grudging, reluctant respect. I even tried to kiss her hand,
said Heinie, in bed. 'Get the pair of us blutty shot, you will,
ye drunken bugger.'

'Go on, get on wi' you,' said Mrs. Best.

Sod women, I thought, and Ma Bron in particular. I'd
have been drunk, even if she'd come to meet me. Two years
in jug and not a single letter . . .

Side by side with Heinie on the white, starched pillows I
listened to his raucous, belly-raking snores, and watched a

wild salacious moon lifting her petticoats over the lush Abe
Valley: yet even this beauty failed to move me; I *longed* fo
the Rhondda.

As Mattie put it (he was simple-minded but in no way ;
simpleton) being here was like worshipping at some lovel
foreign shrine.

But for me, Senghenydd had an overriding compensation.

Nan was here, and at last was mine. This is where the
value lay – *sod Ma Bron*.

It was gone midnight when I awoke.

Getting out of bed, I looked out on to a sleeping village.

Faintly, I heard the old familiar sounds of the shot-firin;
from a thousand feet below, as the Universal night shift go
going. Standing there, sober, I knew a sudden and intens
desire to see Nanwen.

Dressing silently, I tiptoed downstairs to the kitchen anc
through it out into the silver night.

Woodland was blank and deserted under the baleful glar
of the April moon; a stray cat watched me from the shadow;
as I went down the hill past the glimmering lights of the pit
head; here wagons were shunting to a hiss of escaping stean
and commands. On through the Square I went into Windso
Place; slowing to a stroll, head down and up to my elbows ir
my pockets, I came opposite the door of Nanwen's house.

It seemed another life since Ben had opened that door t(
me.

I don't know to this day what took me there at that tim(
of night, save an overwhelming necessity to belong. My life
at that moment, seemed to have made a full circle: i
Nanwen rejected me now, I decided, I'd turn my face fron
the valley, walkout and never return.

It was nearly one o'clock in the morning; a neighbour':
clock chimed the three-quarter hour. Silently opening the
gate, I went up to the door, and quietly knocked.

I waited, tense; a faint light glimmered in the hall, ther
brighter. Brighter, brighter it grew, then spent itself in ex
ploding brilliance upon the glass of the door.

'Who's there?'

'It's Toby, Nan.'

She made a faint, inarticulate sound. I heard the door chain fiercely rattling in her fumbling hands, then she pulled the door open.

She was youth and beauty, vividly aware, stepped out of a grave with a lamp of life; like one of the original virgins, dressed in white, and her hair was tumbling over her shoulders. She was just as I had imagined her in dreams.

'*Toby . . .!*'

Here was nothing of uncertainty, and I despised myself for doubting our ability to love. Her arms were instantly about me, her lips reaching up for mine.

She swiftly drew me within, closed the door and set the lamp down, whispering abstractedly:

'Oh, God, I've waited *all day!* – I thought you weren't coming! I nearly died!' Her eyes searched mine with lovely ever-changing expressions; she was laughing and crying with pent joy; never had she looked so beautiful.

'And Ceinie?' I glanced towards the empty stairs.

'Ceinie isn't here, my love! She's staying in Brecon. See how I planned it?' She held me at arms length. 'Oh, come, let me look at you again.' She showed mischievous astonishment, a hand clapped to her mouth. 'But where's your *hair?*'

We laughed together, softly, so as not to awaken neighbours.

It was a destiny fulfilled; Bethesda, Tonypandy, all the long years of waiting, the doubts, the anxious fears, were magically swept aside. We stood together, enwrapped, and there was no sound but the torment of our breathing.

'Oh, Toby, it has been so long – so *long!*' she gasped against my face.

And, even as we stood there, the siren of the Universal wailed faintly for an accident, the sound eerie, crying on the wind like a witch in tears. Nanwen stiffened in my arms. I could almost feel her reliving the loss of Ben. 'Listen, there it is again!' she said.

I did not reply; my arms went about her hard and strong, drawing her against me.

It was enough, at that moment, to be needed.

The siren faltered, and stopped.

'Come,' she said, and drew me within the hall.

I hesitated, knowing unaccountably in the gain, a sweet, sad sense of loss.

'Nothing can part us now,' Nan whispered.

'*Come ...*?'

CHAPTER THIRTY-SIX

Lie back in the pillows, eyes half closed. It's amazing what
comes to pass when you pretend you are sleeping. And there
can appear before you, in an actuality removed from dreams,
a vision of loveliness in pantomime – the palaver of a woman
getting up in the morning.

Here's a curtain-raiser if ever there was one.

'You still sleeping, Toby?'

Bron's face, but an inch from mine.

Breathe on steadily, like something dead: open one eye
the moment she's away.

Watch!

One leg out now, carfeul not to wake you; up she
stretches, yawning, in the middle of the floor; like a young
faun, bare arms waving (and shivering chilly, April being
late this year). Off with her nightie, and she's bare as an egg.
A glance around for confidence, then a bit of a scratch
(mainly where the elastic catches) looking ecstatic; a lift to
the breasts, to give them a start for the day. Hitch up the
bloomers, knees akimbo; on with the stays, pushing up the
front like a little French countess. Now, here's a per-
formance (doing up the laces at the back now) – wandering,
stooping, like a mare with a load on; down on to a chair to
pull on black stockings; carefully examine each shapely leg:
upright again and on with three petticoats, the last one
flannel; flop out her hair and drape it down her back. Faces
in the mirror now, this way and that, looking for blemishes,
and over her shoulder she cries:

'Tobe! Now come on – time to get up!'

Breathe on, deep in sleep.

'I won't tell you again, mind!'

I watched her, one eye open, and she saw me in the
mirror, swinging round.

'You've been awake all the time! *Diawl!* You rotten
thing!'

367

'And got an eyeful!'

Turning, she dived full length on top of me, fingers scrabbling, searching for tickles while I yelled and shrieked; and I caught her round the waist and rolled her, and her legs went up and so did her petticoats, till we slipped off the bed and bumped on the floor, me on top, entangled in her long, bright hair.

There upside down, I kissed her in a sudden, quiet communion of lovers: no sound but our breathing. And Bron's eyes moved over my face.

'I love you, Tobe.'

God, I thought, I'd very nearly believed her. A couple of weeks later, after I'd gone to prison, Sam gave her the eye and she was off again to Porth.

But did I love her? I wondered. Had I ever loved Bron in the face of my worship of Nanwen? Infatuation, perhaps? I didn't really know then; perhaps because I didn't know a lot about love, which takes a lot of schooling.

One thing was sure; it all seemed to have happened fifty years ago.

But this was a very different business – Nanwen getting dressed on the morning after the night before, after I came out of Cardiff gaol.

Here she was, peeping around the bed-rail when I opened that eye.

'Oh, no, Toby – that's *unfair!*' Her eyes admonished; the redness flew to her cheeks.

'Does it matter?' I asked. 'Don't you belong to me now?'

'Why, yes, darling, but I'm entitled to privacy.'

I closed my eyes at the ceiling. And the room where I first made love to Nanwen, the crucible of former dreams, was painted on my mind.

I saw the little casement window that overlooked the road; the night of a fractured, opal moon, brilliant on his sea-scrape of blue-bagged clouds. The little wash-stand in the corner I saw, its marble top, the ingrained figure of the little white mouse: the wardrobe frowning down at people making love, as wardrobes do, being celibate; the Bible on the table by the bed, and *God is Love* on the wall above it.

Strange, I thought, that in this bare place should be consumated a love I had held so long in chains: and such an unerring formality, too, after the fierce midnights I had planned in youth

And Nanwen? I wondered. What had it meant to her? Hers it appeared, was but a resigned communication, when I wanted so badly that I should bear her gifts of pleasure.

Hours back, she had lain as a woman removed; a fraud of death: a still, vague counterfeit of my manhood's joy: stifling her breath when I forged with her as one: an animal trapped.

Thus had we lain until the night sounds intervened; the barking of a dog, the thumping of the Windsor pit's engines. Compared with the sweet, unchaste wooing of Ma Bron, this was a dowdy immolation.

'Toby . . .' Nanwen stirred faintly on the pillows.

The moonlight, flooding through the casement, seemed to chain her.

'I . . . I'm sorry,' she said.

'That's all right, love, we've plenty of time.'

She whispered, 'It . . . well, I suppose it's because we're not married, isn't it?'

'We've been married since I met you; in the heart.'

'Will you never understand?'

'Only that I love you. Don't you love me?'

It sat her up. 'Oh, God!' she said miserably. 'I knew you'd say that.'

Getting out of bed she drew a sheet about her and went to the window, looking like some wandering goddess of a lost mythology, of whom I once had read.

Somewhere down the street, a baby was crying.

'Look, it's all right, Nan – come back and sleep.'

'Do you think it could be because of Ceinie?' She turned from the window and faced me.

'What's she to do with it?'

'Well, you know – snatching at this behind her back, as it were.'

'We'll ask her tomorrow, and see if she approves.'

She didn't reply, but wandered back and sat on the bed. 'I can't help it – I know it's ridiculous, but I really can't, Toby.

I love you, and I want you, but ... well, it's the way I've been brought up, I suppose. Do you understand?'

'To some extent. But God is love – it's up there on the wall.'

Her eyes, her whole being, beseeched me.

'Yes, I know, but there are certain conditions, Toby, certain rules ...'

'You don't have to explain.'

She stroked my face. 'If we were married, it would be so different.' She stared around the room. 'This ... this seems so *wrong* ...!'

Amazingly, it induced within me a growing humour. I thought of Bron and the first night of love we had spent in the Sinkers. At this stage of the proceedings, she'd done a fan dance with her nightie, and put me into stitches.

Perhaps there is a difference, I thought, between a lover and a wife.

Strangely, I recalled, I'd always looked upon Nan as being my wife ...

'Nan, it's *all right*, I tell you,' and I put my arms about her.

Off shift next Sunday, a May morning, we knew, Nan and I, the advent of summer.

Hand in hand above the scar of the big Universal Pit, there came to us a peace that, I thought, could never be bought by coal.

And it had the promise of a pot-bellied summer, this one, with the first corn thick and green in the valley and the back gardens of the colliers ripe with young plants; everybody digging and hoeing and the spring flowers waving their hands to the warming winds of the mountains.

Time and loss had brought to Nanwen a mature loveliness: as Bron had turned the heads of Tonypandy, so Nanwen did in Senghy: grief seemed to have transmuted all his haggard ills to her advantage. But her beauty that Sunday morning when we walked together, was not as Bron's: in Bron lay freedom and youth, being a girl. The sway of her dress, the provocative cut of her, shouted of vitality. Nanwen possessed the elegance of a woman.

She was wearing a dark brown dress that day, as if still remembering Ben (while, Bron in or out of mourning, would likely have been in pink). The early May was hot; the old sun glowing his contentment as being over Wales so early. Great cumulus clouds towered vertically above us like smoke from the pillage of distant cities, and I mentioned it.

'You're a poet these days, Toby,' Nan said, smiling.

'When I look at you.'

'Indeed,' said she, 'you think as a poet, I notice. Everything you read, you quote. If you'd had a decent education, you'd never have been a collier.'

'Make the most of it, girl, that's all I'll ever be.'

'Oh, come, you're not yet thirty! – there's always time to improve yourself. Besides, you're very well read – Voltaire, Belloc ...!' She laughed softly as we sat together on the mountain grass above the village, and kissed my face.

Laughter, I think, is a signpost: Nan's was a smile in sound, Bron's like a mating cry. Sitting there, all the spectres of our past misunderstandings appeared to vanish, yet I knew the chill of a slight reserve; a small chasm existed between us which, somehow, I could never cross. For the past three weeks (I had been lodging with Mattie at Mrs. Best's in Woodland, but visiting Nan almost daily) since we had been together I had but once enjoyed the fiery excitement of a new lover; but I could not help doubting if Nan found much satisfaction in me. Indeed, I wondered if Ben had discovered also that the possessing of Nanwen's body did not ordain the possession of her spirit.

Now she said, with a laugh:

'Of course you could improve yourself if you tried, Toby. Come, you're far too modest. With very little effort you could become a good teacher, for instance.'

'Ben didn't make much of an attempt, yet you seemed happy enough with him.'

'But Ben was limited, bless him – you have the potential. Why are you so unsure of yourself? Don't you want to get on?' She smiled, her head on one side.

She was wearing the same, broad-brimmed, summer hat she'd worn when I helped her to move from Blaenau, and I thought she looked beautiful. 'Besides,' she added, flatly. 'You are here, and Ben has gone.'

I was a little surprised.

'Has he?' I plucked a blade of grass and lay back, eyes closed to the glory of the sky.

She was peremptory. 'Of course.'

I said, from the grass, 'And dead two years, Nan, so only old crows should still be wearing black.'

'It isn't black!' she examined her dress with obvious concern.

'It's as near widow's weeds as doesn't matter. Are you still going to Ponty market tomorrow?'

'Aye, if Ceinie doesn't arrive.'

'I thought your friend was bringing her back on Tuesday?'

'Could be a day earlier. Her last letter said she was just dying to come home.'

Faintly, I wondered what it would be like with Ceinie, now aged thirteen, pottering about us, and said, 'Well, buy a new dress when you can – pink, perhaps?'

'Bron used to wear pink, didn't she?'

'Not that I remember.'

'I do. I'll buy blue – I'm not in competition.'

I smiled admonishment. 'Oh, come on, that's not like you – it's just that you can't keep paying bills of mortality. I read that somewhere, too.' I gave her a wink.

Her eyes didn't falter on my face. 'Like you, perhaps, Toby, I need more time to lay the ghosts.'

We lay in silence, still hand in hand.

I have often wondered at the power of humans to be perfectly in love, simultaneously, with two people. Love is a sister to pity: pity could be the basis of my love for Bron, I reasoned, but the love I held for Nan was as commanding now as in its callow youthfulness. And yet, why was it that even these few sacred moments with Nan had been invaded by Bron? – the sound of her instant in the quiet day. And I think I understood better Bron's love of Sam Jones – a transgression of the noblest moments of her love for me.

Bending above Nan, I kissed her lips, her face, her hair.

372

'Do we have to talk about it?' I whispered. 'Bron's a life and a thousand miles away.'

'Face facts, Toby — it's this life and a few miles away — she's living in Tredegar.'

I raised my face from hers. 'That's wrong! — she left the south.'

'Aye, but now she's back.'

'When?'

'About the time you came out of prison.'

'You're sure?' I sat up.

'Of course. School teachers get all the news — we're walking newspapers.'

'Funny the lads didn't mention it,' I said, reflectively.

'Perhaps the lads didn't know.'

'They know, all right.' I sat up, staring around.

High above us in the cloudless blue a lark was teaching the world to sing. Intent, we listened, and Nan said, watching me:

'Bron's married to Sam, Toby — you must accept it?'

'I've always accepted it.'

'Is that completely true?'

I laughed. 'Now you're being ridiculous! Come on, don't spoil it! We've got our lives to start anew.'

'And preferably back up North?'

'Up North? Why there, for God's sake?'

'Because that's where we *belong* — it's your home as much as mine!'

'You'll always be a Johnny North, won't you?'

'Of course,' she said simply, 'and so will you.'

'I won't, you know — me pa was Tonypandy.' We laughed, but the laughter died.

By some strange trick of refracted light, the sky was suddenly overcast, and from its billowing cloud-darkness, immediately overhead, two beams of light began to form, a strange configuration. Brighter, brighter this grew in the noontide glare, then shut off with searchlight rapidity. It was startling in its suddenness; it left us silent.

Nan spoke first, her face against me, but I did not hear her words.

In a gap in the rim of the distant mountain, where, but a

moment ago, these twin beams had burned, I saw a sphere of blueness stretching away to infinity, as beyond the daylight stars. And, in an instant, my mind went back to my meeting with Grandpa up in Deiniolen; when he and I, lying in the tram-bucket, slid down the slate Incline into the valley of Llanberis. I knew now, as then, a marvellous affinity with the world through the joy of sight; it transcended all other values with its power. Sight, limited in the dark sequestered places of the mind, could be confined within the walls of coal; shut off in the choked galleries a thousand feet underground; shaded in approaching age, obliterated by death. But here, on this mountain, it was unencompassed, save by the orbit of the meteoric stars.

'You still with me, Toby?'

It was as if, quite suddenly, a chill wind blowing over a blind man's grave, had touched me with an icy finger.

I got up, brushing myself down. Always, in the face of visual beauty, this terror of blindness engulfed me.

Down in the valley the fields, chequered patterns of green and gold flashed their sovereign brilliance under the midday sun. Nan said, 'Best we start back, anyway, if we're going to get any dinner. I've got Sunday School at three o'clock – feel like coming?'

It was suddenly imperative that I should not be alone. I said:

'Couldn't you give it a miss this Sunday?'

'But the children are expecting me! Tell you what,' Nan said, secretly. 'You go back to Mrs. Best for dinner, then come up to the house for Sunday tea, is it?' We began the journey back to the village.

'And after?'

Her eyes held a charming, whimsical expression. 'Now come, darling – I'm a respectable widow!'

'Isn't it respectable, being in love?'

We walked in silence, contained by thought.

I thought of Bron and her capricious wantonness; it possessed in all its abandonment, the virtue of a perfect gift. Perhaps Nan read my mind.

'We're not living together, Toby, and I'm not Bron, remember.'

'There was nothing wrong with Bron!'

I wasn't handling it well, but one thing was sure; I wasn't begging off any woman. Now, approaching the streets, we lowered our voices.

'Oh, dear, do try to understand!' She would have touched me, but people, severe in Sunday clothes, were passing with sidelong glances or short bows of greeting. We stood together, lost, while Senghenydd watched us in a timorous silence.

Nan said, apologetically, 'Well, it ... it's just that you simply can't expect to begin again with me where you left off with her, that's all.'

'That wasn't my intention.'

'Oh, God ...' She looked around her as if for escape. 'This is all so cold.'

'Come away with me, then.'

'Where?'

'Anywhere, as long as we're together.' I added: 'Marry me, then. Now?'

'*Cariad annwyl!* Give me time, Toby. We've been through all this before!'

'*Duw*, missus,' I said with a grin, 'you don't give much away.'

'But my position's different from yours – I've got Ceinie to think of?'

'And I don't count?'

'Of course you do – don't make things difficult, love.'

Suddenly, incredibly, she sounded like Bron; I liked her better.

'At this rate of debauchery I'll be as celibate as a monk,' I said.

Her eyes, her whole being, begged of me. 'Just for a bit longer, darling – wait for me?' Glancing furtively about her, she gripped my hand. 'Look, I live in Ben's house, but it isn't mine. The agent only let me stay because I teach at the Board School. The Board of Guardians ...'

'Do you think the Board of Guardians might let us marry in a couple of months?'

'Now you're being impossible!' She was chin up, angry.

I sighed. 'All right. When do we meet again?'

375

It turned her, instantly warm. 'Come to tea, eh? As I said? I'll make a cake after I've had dinner. You always did like a caraway cake.'

'Caraway cake?'

'You know – a seedy cake.'

I shook my head. 'No, not seedy cake.' I was thinking of Ma Bron.

'But why not? You used to love them. Can't I do anything to please you?'

I was being churlish and inept; I wanted to put my arms around her, and here I was teetering on the edge of a quarrel.

She said, 'Toby, I really must go if I'm to be on time for Sunday School – and I've got loads of books to mark. But promise you'll come for tea?'

'Yes, of course.'

I stood properly for her, taking off my cap.

'And if we're in luck, Ceinie might come home – I'll make a fire and we'll have it on trays – just the three of us!'

In the confrontation, I had almost forgotten Ceinie.

I bowed to her, watching as she made her way with a marvellous grace, inclining her head this way and that to neighbours.

Vaguely, I wondered how I'd have handled it with Bron.

CHAPTER THIRTY-SEVEN

The Aber Valley, about nine miles from Tonypandy as the hawk goes, was as different from it as stout is to cider. The Rhondda towns were black-faced, the terraced houses stained. And even the mountains framing them had to rub coal-dust out of their eyes before waking every morning, for coal dust was in the air, the mouth, the throat.

But the Aber Valley was green-gold; the twin pits of Senghenydd and Windsor being but small, mutilated fingers in a fair land of mountains and tiny tenant farms.

Here the little rivers and brooks, sparkling and bright, were filled to the banks with speckled trout. But the sad fish of the Rhondda, fighting their way up to the spawning grounds, were thin, poisoned by old furnace washings; and the great salmon of the Fach and Fawr had long since gasped out their lives on beaches of coal.

In this valley, the Windsor pit, being lower down the mountain, was comparatively free of gas; it spewed its fumes up the subterranean crevices and these filled the higher, bigger Universal chock-a-block with gas. As late as three years back she'd had a gas flow that closed her down for nearly a week. Nine years before that she'd closed down eighty men's lives in one gigantic flash, instantaneously igniting down her miles of galleries.

But colliers never learn, said Mattie – they still poured in from nearby Cardiff and Ponty to work the giant Universal: and managements never bloody learn, neither, said Heinie – least of all coal owners like Lord Merthyr, who owned the gassy bitch: few of the safety precautions recommended by the Mines Commission had been implemented since the 1901 explosion. The profits were good, the seams were full, the shareholders happy, so Lord Merthyr let it lie.

I'd been down the Universal for the two months since coming to Mrs. Best's in Woodland Terrace, Senghenydd:

now, on this hot, early July day, I was downing tools off shift with Heinie and Mattie.

The cage of the upcast clanged back, and we filed out, Snookey Boxer leading.

'Where did you spring from?' demanded Mattie. 'I thought you was down the Windsor – Christ, we got rough stuff comin' in again.'

'Signed me on yesterday,' said Snookey. 'To hell with the Rhondda, and to the devil with the Windsor pit, says me Effie, ye'll be happier back with the lads. Ay ay, Tobe!' Marriage to Effie had improved Snookey; he was actually coherent.

I gave him a nod.

Mattie said, 'He was with Duck down the Scotch when Lark, Duck's mare, was killed. Duck reckoned Snookey did all right – mind, losing Lark has broke up old Duck something cruel – he ain't the same fella.'

We tramped on in silence, streaming coal dust; red-lipped, red-eyed, grieving for Lark.

'One day I'm getting out of blutty coal,' said Heinie, at my elbow, 'before everything's killed. I'm goin' to sit me on a South Sea island beach with six buxom beauties and to hell with you black-faced sambos.'

'You be content with Sarah and Dozey, ye maniac,' said Mattie.

We shoved and elbowed our way towards the lamp room and the pit wheels of the York Upshaft whirred in sunlight, bringing up the shift: the new shift were waiting at the Lancaster downcast as the cage went back; dour-faced men of wan features, the pale cosmetic of the collier: and they were free of their classical humour, coal's birth-right, for they were going down on shift, not coming up, like us.

'Right, lads, make a start,' cried old Dai Parcel, coming on shift. 'Dig deep for Baron Senghenydd, my sons – Gwilym, Owen and me'll be with you directly,' and he said to me as I came along with Heinie and Mattie, 'How's your hair doing, Tobe? That twopenny cut ain't quite the same as lovely, flowin' locks.'

'The mice 'ave been at him,' commented Gwilym, joining us.

'What stall you lot in, then?' demanded Dai.

'Forty.' I looked round the tap; new men were coming in every day.

'We're the same road as you, ye blind old bat,' called Heinie, 'Bottanic. We see you going past every other shift, but you're too stuck up for a wave.'

'Perhaps, but I'll drink with anyone, if they pay.'

'You old faggot,' cried Mattie. 'All three of you – you're supposed to be going on shift – now come on, get going!'

'A pint going down is worth two comin' up,' said Dai. 'You drinking, my lovelies? And where's little Heinie?'

'He'll buy the second,' I said. 'They weren't all born in Jerusalem, and I've heard his money rattling.'

'Then I'm away to tickle trout – you fancy coming, Mattie?' asked Heinie.

'He fancies Mrs. Best, if I know him,' said Dai.

'I do not, it's all platonic,' protested Mattie as we handed in our lamps and pushed into the Universal tap-room. 'Right now I'm shovelling in a ton of compassionate coal for me landlady, then I'm getting my head down.'

'Who with?' asked Heinie, and Dai called for the pints.

'With Bestie,' said Dai. 'I heard all about it. Between now and Easter she's buying him silk pyjamas.'

'You're a blutty rotten lot, all of you,' said Mattie.

The banter went on as the old shift flooded into the room, and I gave a thought to the day, over two years back, when I had left that tap for Cardiff Assizes; it seemed like another age, but I saw Bron's face in the amber slant of the ale, and closed my eyes, Mattie was still getting some stick; the lads were still pumping me for news of the happy event; sharing lodgings with Mattie in Number Ten Woodland was landing me with responsibility, but I never let on, even though I could see a pretty romance flourishing.

Very billing and cooing, it was between them, bless them, and if ever Bestie broke an egg in the pan, it always landed on me.

'But ye'll have to make your mind up between Mrs. Best and your pigeons, won't you, son?'

Sweet it is, when older people fall in love. And the suitor as usual, was getting the thin edge of it. 'Ignoramuses, all of you,' said Mattie.

'Mind, he could do worse,' said Heinie once. 'I'd like to see him settled – before I depart this mortal life.'

'Very clever,' said Mattie. 'Meanwhile, mind your own blutty business. Proper gentlemen wouldn't mention a lady's name, they wouldn't.'

'No offence intended.'

'None taken,' said Mattie. 'Now lay off. All right, ain't she, Tobe?'

'One of the best is Mrs. Best,' I said.

'So when are you two taking the plunge?' asked Heinie. 'It's your souls I'm bothered about – feel responsible, I do.'

'Listen to who's talking!' cried Mattie. 'And him in the middle of Sarah Bosom and Dozey.'

'When's your happy event, Tobe?' asked Owen, and Mattie said:

'He wants to know when you're marryin'. And that Nan O'Hara blooming like a Welsh rose – come on!'

'She'll keep. She's healthy enough.'

It was going on a long time: usually, they'd forget your business when once they smelled the ale.

'Time you wed the lady, talking serious,' said Heinie.

I didn't reply. You let folks in slow when it comes to deep intentions. It was something I had learned from Grandpa.

The shift swarmed in after us, kicking up the sawdust. Ed Masumbala, the big Texas Negro came in; most respected was Ed, living with Beli, his wife, and baby son up in Fifteen Woodland, just above us. Kept to himself, mostly, but every man in the village accepted him. This was the joy of the Welsh valleys. You could be a Chinese compradore or a Sioux Indian as long as you behaved yourself, and Ed and Beli did just that: he worked the next stall to ours down Bottanic; and always read a verse or two of his bible during snap. Now his white teeth appeared magically in his black face as he lowered his glass and grinned at me.

Strange how I knew in that moment a faint affinity with him, for we rarely exchanged more than a glance.

Heinie called, 'Six pints, landlord – never let it be said I don't pay me whack with you ungrateful buggers,' and the landlord jugged them out while Heinie fished in his pockets.

'*Diawch!*' exclaimed he. 'Me wallet's dropped out!'

Hoots and jeers at this, with Mattie shouting, 'Here we go – the chosen race is at it again!'

'Damn me,' whispered Heinie, searching himself. 'I got important things in that wallet . . .'

'You've really lost it?' I asked, beside him.

'Aye,' he answered, his little face worried.

'Caught again,' cried Mattie, and slapped down the cost, and Dai Parcel cried:

'You're lucky to have the money for pints – poor old beggars like Gwilym, Owen and me are licking halves, eh, mates?'

'God knows why we rioted in the Rhondda,' added Owen.

'And God knows why we're down here at all,' said Gwilym, his battered old face turned up. 'Ought to be pensioned off and living retirement while you young 'uns here buy the drinks. Me chest's bad, ye know,' and he coughed, thumping it. 'The gas do get me. This blutty pit wants reporting to the Mines Commission.'

'So does God,' said Dai Parcel, 'But he'd still get away with it.'

'Can't think what's happened to that wallet,' said Heinie, still searching.

'*Ach,* forget it – mention it to the shift foreman and the lads'll keep an eye out – you're not going down again, for God's sake?'

'You can get your legs chopped off too, mind – you don't need a chest full of gas – remember Ben O'Hara?'

The name stilled me. I drained my glass and pushed my way out through the door followed by Heinie and Mattie; the clear July sunlight nearly blinded us; the air of the mountains was like wine after the fug of the Universal bar.

'Ay ay, then – be seeing you,' said Heinie.

'Reckon I'll just slip back for another to settle me stomach,' said Mattie. 'Tell little old Bestie that I won't be long, Tobe?'

'I'll tell her she's got no future with you,' I replied. 'I'll do more – I'll tell her you're a drunken old bugger.'

'I'll 'ave your blutty head off,' said Mattie.

'One thing's sure,' said Heinie, 'I ain't beholden to anybody, and I don't explain to nobody. Being virgo intacta, as the sayin' goes, I just go fishing. The pair I live with 'ave got ears like Navy mops.'

'You poor little scratch,' I said. 'I'm right sorry for you,' and was off, giving a wave to Dai Parcel, Gwilym and Owen as they went down on shift.

Leaving Heinie to his poaching and Mattie to his debauchery, I whistled me along in the sunshine up the pitch to Woodland. Just the same as down the Sinkers, the old folks were sitting out of doors in the sun; cranked old grandpas like the one I buried up in Coetmor: wizened old crones, who once were lithe and gay in beauty, greeted me with their lovely gummy smiles. But Jaundice Evans, so named for his pallor, was there, too; off sick from the Universal for backing the milkman's cart over his size thirteens, and I didn't go a lot on Jaundice, he being the local gas-bag. Being human, though, I still commiserated on his toes.

'Well, I never did!' cried a voice from the upstairs window of Number Four, 'Just look who's arriving!' and Mrs. Menna Price (the part-time midwife known locally as Mrs. Menna Pause) put her bosom on the window sill and beamed down at me. 'What you doing down there, Toby Davies?'

Very romantic by nature, she was the mother of Woodland, and she was good for the place. Brass shining knocker had she, snowwhite doorstep. I shouted up to her, 'Looking at Jaundy's toes – I've never seen toes done better.'

All down the street the colliers, off shift, were going into doors, greeting children, shouting to neighbours: white-aproned wives with anxious faces were awaiting those delayed in the publics.

'And I've never seen Mattie done better – dished up, done brown and basted – you reckon they're marrying – him and Mrs. Best?'

'You rotten old faggot,' I cried up. 'There's always someone getting it in the neck!' and out of next door came Gladys Bad Fairy, her neighbour, as thin as a shin-bone, crying:

'Mind, she got him through the stomach, didn't she? I'll

give her that – old Bestie do turn up a very fair dinner. I saw her hand him one last Sunday – kangaroos couldn't 'ave jumped it. How does she do for you, Tobe?'

'She slides 'em under the door,' I said.

Menna now, 'You hungry then, Toby lad?'

'Blutty starved,' I said. 'I've lost two stone – look at me.'

'Then you slip in with me, son, and I'll feed you tripe and onions – ye can have me old man's.'

'If I slip up there, missus, I'll want more than tripe and onions,' I shouted, and this put them into stitches, of course.

'Mind, I'll tell you one thing interesting ...' began Menna, and Jaundy Evans interjected with a smirk:

'I thought you was only hungry for that barmaid over in Pandy – I could go for her myself ...'

I got him by the shirt and his toes left the ground. 'Mouth almighty,' I whispered, 'you get your blutty toes straight!'

'Put Jaundy down,' commanded Menna. 'He isn't very fit, you know.'

Gladys Bad Fairy and others around me now; women smoothing and patting me and Jaundy didn't mean it, did you, Jaundy?

Ten years younger and I'd have had the rest of his bloody toes.

My temper diminished as I went up Woodland, for there was Aunty Mari forking hay over the road, saving an old spragman in Number Twelve the agony of the wheels – concussion, two months back: some folks said he'd never make it. I knocked up my cap to her and went into Number Ten, and there was Mrs. Best as plump and mirthful as ever, bustling about the kitchen, red in the face from the fire, and she looked around for Mattie.

I stood in the doorway and watched her. In her presence, as always, I knew the old nostalgia: she was of my beloved Tonypandy; she had cooked my first meals when coming to the Rhondda; she had sent me washed and clean and fed, with my old clothes brushed and pressed, to Bron.

Now she said, 'Where's Mattie?'

'Caught late by the Overman – just coming,' I answered, and she stood back, hands on her hips, her face cherubic. 'My, ain't you some man, Toby Davies! Bend your head under the door, lovely boy. *Ach,* even under the coal dust you're a fine handsome fella.' She linked her hands across her apron and examined me benignly. 'If me old man was still livin' I'd turn meself into a widow for ye!'

'If your old man was alive, girl, you'd be lying in the middle. Come on here, you gorgeous old thing, you're handier than Menna,' and I tried to kiss her, but she smacked me away, shrieking.

'Where's my dinner, then?'

'Oh, go on with you, you've got to wait for Mattie!' She gasped and fanned herself, one of her flushes. I asked:

'And d'you know where Mattie is? – sinking his wages down the pub!'

'You've no cause to criticise – now then!' She wagged a spoon. 'A collier's entitled to a pint off shift, remember.'

'A pint? The fella's shifting quarts!'

'A very fine man is that Mattie Kelly, I'll have you know, so let's have no more of it.' She hit me sideways. 'Anyway, you said he was with the Overman.'

'Can't put a foot wrong, can he? But you marry Mattie Kelly, missus, and you'll have to put up with his pigeons – ticky old things.' I pinched her under her stays and they heard her half-way up Graig.

Later, I bathed in the tin bath by the fire while she laid the table, and, when Mattie arrived with a bunch of flowers and half a pound of stilton as a bribe, I was poshed up, buttonholed, and away with me down to Windsor Place to Nanwen and Ceinie.

One thing was becoming clear to me: after that first loving welcome on the night I came home, there would always be Ceinie ...

But the house was empty when I got there, and a neighbour told me that Nan and Ceinie had taken their dinner to school, so I got *Kilvert's Diaries* out of the library and then wandered aimlessly around the town, mingling with the shoppers.

Schoolboys were playing rugby on the Recreation Ground. There was a young prop forward there I'd have given ten years to and ten yards, in splints. I watched them from a distance, listening to their shrill cries. It was a morning of sun and warm winds, and the old Waun Deilad, where Heinie had gone fishing, was doing its best to paint up the day with its rolling vales and plaintive bleating of sheep. I should really have been in bed, for the shift had been hard, but I didn't feel like bed; I wanted places and people.

In a corner of Commercial Street I bumped into Ginty, of all folks, and his little scrag of a missus, and I don't know who was more surprised.

'Well!' exclaimed he, ''tis big Toby Davies, the collier chap, I'll be buggered! I was sayin' to my missus here, let's take a train ride to Senghenydd – we've a niece in Brook Street, ye know.' Ginty slapped his thigh, delighted, while his wife, as grey as a churchyard ghost, ate him with haggard eyes. 'I'm back to the tools, did ye hear? – timberman.'

'Aye, Heinie told me. He and Mattie are with me down the Universal.'

'We're still living in Tonypandy, of course – I'm down the Ely – not the Bute, mind – I'm too old for the face.' He grimaced. '*Ach,* they were good days, indeed, and I miss me customers.'

His wife said in her lovely, Connemara brogue, 'He's off the groceries, d'ye understand, but still in the trade – even asleep, he's still slicing bacon. "Pass me the butter, me darlin'," he says, and I hand it over the sheets in the dark. "I'll see to the York ham now, Pet," says he, and I give him one of the pillows.' She peered at him from a stricken face. 'You'll always be in groceries, even in the Upper Palace, won't ye, Ginty?'

The midday shoppers barged between us. Uncertainly, Ginty said:

'Have you had a sight of your Bron since comin' out, Toby?'

'*Heisht,* Ginty,' whispered his wife, elbowing.

I shook my head. 'Two years now.'

'Did you hear she was back with her husband, then?'

'More or less.'

'They lived for a bit in Porth; recent, I heard tell they were in Tredegar.'

'Sam always got around,' I said.

'Holy Mother, she was a rare beauty, that one!'

'You was both a handsome pair, if I might say,' said Mrs. Ginty, weakly.

'Talk had it that they were not getting on, though,' said her husband. 'Not that you'd be interested?'

Ginty was all right, but there was always more tongue-pie in his shop than sides of bacon. His wife said quietly, 'Enough now, not our business, is it?'

We moved uncertainly; I didn't want to hear more of it.

'Is it true you're marrying, son?'

'Could be.'

'You could do worse, be God. I've seen the O'Hara widow a couple of times, and she's a feast o' the mind – *Arrah!* May I always be young enough to worship at the shrine of a lovely woman.'

I did not reply.

'Ginty, we got to go,' said his wife, worried at the silence.

An urchin with a lollipop in his gob was staring up into my face and I wished him to the devil; I wished them all to the devil, Ginty especially – single fare.

And there was a strange, new emptiness in me as I wandered up to Bryn-hyfryd where Heinie lodged with Sarah and Dozey, recently removed. And then I recalled that he wasn't in; having gone poaching up the Bryn, so I came back down to the Square, thinking of Bron and where she had got to; wondering, as always, why I had never heard from her. In the crush of the people along High Street I saw a bright head and knew a momentary, ridiculous excitement. Tredegar, did Ginty say? Mattie and Heinie, I reflected, had been forgetful on that particular point, even if it were true.

With an hour or so to spare before going back to Mrs. Best for dinner and a sleep, I left the road and took a track up the hillside, making for Glan Nant, and Heinie. After climbing the mountain for a bit, I sat down where Nan and I used to sit on Sundays, and looked down on to the Universal Pit.

The mist of the fields, shimmering in the midday heat, brought weird shapes to the giant structures of the pit-head; forming, before my shielded eyes, a tormented edifice of trestles and wires crowned by the refracted light of whirring wheels. And the more I stared at the phenomena in the valley, the greater the illusion of instability, so that the towers and smoke-shot chimneys of the Universal, rearing skywards, rocked and swayed, as in a dance of death.

Lying back, I closed my eyes to the red-set brilliance of the sun; feeling against my shoulders the very earth trembling as a leaf wind-trembles, to the shot-firing of the galleries two thousand feet below.

When I looked again the whole imagery of the pit industry made shape; the snaking railway-lines, clanking wagons, shunting locomotives with their belching funnels, all combining into an orchestral roar of metallic hammering.

With such, I thought, men forge the sacrifice for coal; sink their hopes within dark galleries. Eyes are put out here, sleeves tied with string; entombed, men die in fire-damp gas and flood-water. And yet, in the tally of the cost, there lived, within the boundaries of coal's Black Kingdom, a knowledge of achievement that accompanied no other industry.

Below the bright fields of Nature's decoration lay the rich seams of prehistoric forests: here was the stored sunlight of ancient centuries, a source of energy more valuable than gold. We were the first country to mine coal; we were now its biggest producer – seven million tons of it exported from Barry alone this year so far – mainly from the rich seams of the Rhondda, Aberdare and Aber Valleys. And I knew a strange sense of pride that I was having a hand in it.

What lure lies in coal, I wondered, that brings such pride to the heart?

Despite its hazards, the labour, the blood of it, coal fashioned in its stalls a comradeship of men and a kinship with beasts. Down the clanging galleries, under the roof-creaks, there existed a weird, perverted love; it was an affinity of hatred and devotion that erected, beyond the bloody stretchers, a monumental satisfaction that no other trade designed – ship-building, slate, the iron trades, wool – I have talked to men in these; you name it, said Mattie, and the answer was the same – the call was strongest from Old King Coal.

I got to my feet, looking down into the valley, seeing the huddled houses, the strings of coloured washing blowing on the lines. The voices of street-criers drifted up to me – rag-and-bone man, a knife-grinder; cat's meat man and muffin man, cries of children – all combined to build within me an elation, because I was a part of this industry, and its people. And I think I knew, at that moment, that I could never leave them.

And even as I stood there, I heard, in quick flushes of the wind, the thin, wailing siren – an accident. It commanded me as it commanded every collier in Aber. It was persistent, calling, *calling*.

I ran down into the valley.

There was a lot of men around the Lancaster downcast by the time I got there, but I heard the agent shout:

'Bottanic men – I only want people who know the district.'

I yelled from the back, 'I'm working Bottanic, mister.'

'Face men, mind.'

'I'm a face man.'

The overman called, 'Is that Davies of Woodland?'

'Ay ay.'

'Bring him.'

I shoved my way to the front. 'What's happened?'

'It's a fall down the Lewis Morgan road, and I want six reliefs. When did you come off?'

'Eight o'clock, but I've slept.'

'Good man, get your things,' so I ran to the lamp room; another five men were crowding into the Lancaster downcast cage when I got back. The York upcast shaft was bringing up the first rescue shift. Hustling into the cage, I asked:

'If it's the Lewis Morgan area, why do you want Bottanic people?'

He was sour-faced and grimy, this agent, having just come up from the fall. 'Because there's a fresh air shaft in Ladysmith, in between, and perhaps we can use it.'

I looked at the men about me; a couple I knew – the rest I'd never seen before: full shift working, there could be a thousand colliers down the Universal at any one time. Alby Churchill was there (they say he never got over it) who was

Dai Parcel's mate, also Taliesin Roberts, whose mother was Irish, and I knew him through Heinie.

The downcast cage was dropping like a bolt; the winder was giving us a hell of a ride. I shouted to Alby, through his snow-white whiskers, 'Dai Parcel, Gwilym and Owen, are down the Bottanic, I think – you heard?'

'Ay ay! – day-shift clerks.'

'Are they in this?'

'So says the overman – them and three others we're relieving, I suppose.'

'With Dai Parcel in this, it'll be a bloody pantomime,' said Taliesin, in Welsh, being his father's tongue.

At the bottom of the shaft a horse and dram were awaiting us, and we made good time on a clear run, to back up the first rescue shift. An overman said:

'I checked the fall between Bottanic and Ladysmith – looks like six yards – but it'll take some moving because it's right across the width inside.'

'Gas?' I asked, as the horse stopped at the turnout.

'There's always gas.'

'Casualties?'

'Four, they tell – it must have caught all Forty Stall.'

'Forty Stall?' We were clanking down the road beside him now. 'That's mine. I work Forty Stall.'

'That's why you're here, butty – must be old Dai Parcel and two of his mates.'

'Christ,' I whispered. 'And the fourth?'

'The fourth we can't trace – he don't belong.'

'Could be anyone,' said Taliesin.

'A journeyman between here and Ladysmith?' asked Alby, and the overman said:

'Just get 'em out, Winston Churchill, and quick. It don't matter who they are.' He made a strange, lamenting sound, as one speaking with his soul.

But Dai Parcel wasn't buried; neither was Gwilym; this was the way of it – rumour. 'They'd box you in cedar and brass handles if you went for a slash round the corner down here,' said Dai, when we reached the fall.

'Owen's caught it?'

'Owen at least,' said Gwilym, near to tears.

'It don't mean he's dead,' said Dai shovelling. 'It'll take more than a roof fall to kill that old bugger. Are you the relief?'

'Yes,' I said, coming up with the others.

'Then get stuck into it – where's the canary?'

'You don't need a canary, mate, you've got your Davy lamp.'

'Sod the Davy – I want a canary.' He wheezed; a man with Death's trumpet.

'You've got me instead, you miserable thing,' I said, 'shift over.'

'I'll leave you to it, I'm going back to the telephone,' said the overman.

Stripped to the belts, we picked and shovelled into the fall; it was a high one, but the stuff was big – easy to get out. Alby worked one side of me, Taliesin on the other, singing in Welsh, a fine, pure tenor. It was dry, thank God, and the floor was firm; Gwilym, supposed to be resting, went away for the horse; backed up by the others – three working, three resting – we were four yards into it after an hour and a half, propping as we went. There was a plug above my head; this is what brings the falls.

'Watch that bugger,' said Dai, poking up at the roof.

Plugs were the trouble. Usually of ironstone, they were heavier than the surrounding coal; through endless centuries they'd work themselves through the strata on gravity, cutting vertical shafts. Once in the apex of the roof, it needed but a touch to bring them down.

'Come on, move over,' commanded Dai.

'I'm all right,' I said, 'fetch old Alby out of it.'

'Now you'll have to work, me son,' said Dai, ' 'cause I'm coming in.'

Stripped to the waist, sweating and gasping, we hacked and shovelled in silence in the glow of the Davys: listening, at times, for knocking from the entombed, but didn't hear a sound.

'*Diawch*,' gasped Dai, 'I'm gettin' too old for this bloody caper – does any of you young ones really need me here?'

'Lay out,' said a man, pushing Dai aside, 'ye can't stand the pace now, can you – ought to be pensioned off.'

'He's a poor old sod, really, ain't you, Dai?' said another.

'Trouble was he walked his tabs off for the blutty G.P.O. – as a collier, my flower, I wouldn't pay you in washers.'

'Thank God for that,' said Dai, easing out on his belly. 'The aged and infirm – nobody wants us, do they, Gwilym?'

'His daughter-in-law don't, that's certain,' gasped Gwilym, trying to forget about Owen, his butty. 'Owen told me this morning – his daughter-in-law got one on him – ain't she, Dai?'

'Now now, you wicked old bugger,' said Dai, sitting by the gob and fanning.

'Started wetting the bed, mate – 'aven't you?'

Gwilym looked as if he was crying for Owen, but perhaps it was sweat.

They were a caution, these two old colliers, Gwilym and Owen, Dai's two mates. People used to say that they were the pugilists and Dai the referee.

Head bumps and collier's tattoos had cut their design on Owen, who was knocking sixty-three in private: a good pug in his time, he was walking on his heels now, his speech slurred through head punches, and Gwilym cared for him like a mother.

Years back, according to Dai Parcel, they'd box their way up one valley and down another for a couple of sovereigns, taking on the best – the best trial horses who ever trod canvas. And these days, if you saw them in Town, they might be walking arm in arm, like sisters.

Often in the pits there was talk of queer chaps and fancy trews, but this didn't apply to Gwilym and Owen. A love existed between these two old fighting colliers that was undefiled. They ate together, slept together; in their prime, they'd shared the same woman. Sometimes, just for the fun of it, they hit hell out of each other.

Now Gwilym cried falsetto, baiting Dai Parcel:

'She's chucking you out, ain't she, Dai?'

'Just for bed-wetting?' I asked. 'That ain't fair, we're all at it.'

'She's never been fair, that daughter-in-law of mine,' said

Dai, moodily. 'Don't know what my lad sees in 'er – she wouldn't give ye a nod if she were on a blutty rocking horse.'

'It's a sign of age that, though,' said someone. 'What's come over you, Dai Parcel – back to your childhood, is it?'

'Probably wet working,' interjected Taliesin, grinning into my face in the tunnel. 'The sound of water do have a bladder effect, some say – the nurse turned a tap on once, to make me do a sample.'

We stopped working, listening for knocking. Silence. Then Dai said, 'Mind, I don't make a habit of it – bedwetting ain't my particular, really – I'm a paid up member of the Miners' Library.'

'Perhaps you ain't permanently deformed, though, you poor old soak,' said Gwilym. 'Me and my mate Owen worked a stall wi' a farrier chap once, I recall . . .' He gasped, and swung, burying his pick in the fall. 'Peg Pride was his name, and he claimed wet working. But the Overman cut him fifty per cent because he had a wooden leg.'

'That were the Stone Age, though,' commented Alby Churchill. 'Now we've got the Miners' Federation.'

'And me daughter-in-law don't approve of that, neither,' called Dai from the gob. 'Are you lot through there yet? What's taking you so long?'

'Damned near it,' I said, shovelling out, for the fall was getting light. 'Watch, it, lads, she's going down . . .'

And she went as I said it; the coal cascaded, there was a rush of air. I put an arm through the hole, waving at nothing. Gwilym sat on his hunkers beside me and peered over the wall.

'Oh, Jesus,' he whispered, 'poor little Owen.'

Owen was dead when they brought him out. I crawled in, with Gwilym and Dai Parcel following.

'Just the one, is it?' called the overman.

'No,' I shouted back, 'there's another in here.'

He was lying where the fall had thrown him, heaped in a corner with his chin on his chest. I knew him instantly, and held the lamp higher.

'Jesus,' whispered Dai, 'it's poor little Heinie.'

Instantly, I was beside Heinie, but I knew it was too late;

I straightened him out, and pulled the boulders off his legs: not a heart-beat, not a sigh. And there wasn't a mark on him.

'*Duw*, I remember!' whispered Dai, now kneeling beside me. 'He came down an hour after we started shift. He came looking for that wallet.'

'He came looking for this,' I said, and took from Heinie's cold hand the photograph of his wife.

'His missus?' asked Dai.

'Who's this one, then?' asked the overman, crawling in.

He peered from me to Heinie.

I couldn't see him for tears.

My whole being was numb as I walked from the pit, in all the grime of the working, down to Windsor Place, and Nanwen. As in a dream, I remembered that I was due there for tea; now it was nearer eight in the evening.

We had brought Heinie's body out after Owen's, and there was a great hush among the groups of waiting people. Somebody had told Mattie, and he was there, with others of Heinie's mates. He still had the photo of Hannah in his hand when they took him away, but nobody mentioned it.

Although the evening sun was warm, the world was colder than a landlord's heart as I walked down to Windsor Place, and knocked. Nanwen opened it.

'Heinie Goldberg? Oh, Toby, I'm so sorry!'

I nodded.

'Come in, come in,' she whispered, looking around at the watching neighbours.

'No, not in this state. I'll take back home first, and wash.'

The panic was in her face; she was probably remembering how Ben had died.

'Look, please come in, darling – don't stand there on the doorstep – Ceinie isn't here . . .'

'Best not. I . . I only wanted to tell you . . .'

In the silence of lost words, she said, desperately, 'Oh, Toby, please – let's get away from this dreadful place . . .!'

CHAPTER THIRTY-EIGHT

The summer of warm, pattering rain shone through that July. August came, the brown-haired matron of sprinkled gold. With the Strike behind them, the people of the Rhondda, their larders no longer empty, began to lay in stores of wood and concessionary coal for the old hag Winter, for the valleys – Fach, Fawr, and Aber were just about the coldest place on earth.

Come late September, with the trees beginning to creak rheumatic, I was kiss-courting Nan O'Hara strong, but not averse to a wilder romance on the side (wives and lovers being happiest apart). Annie Gay, once of The Golden Age, now serving in the Pandy Inn since Bron departed there, had pretty legs, I discovered, mainly above the knee. After a pint or two in the Pandy tap (with Red Rubbler safe on shift and Nan reluctant) they came prettier every minute.

Sometimes, when I was over in the old beloved haunts, I'd wander around the doors of the Sinkers, trying for a peep into Number Six. There was a distinct danger in doing this, of course: being captured by either Primrose or Rachel, who seemed always on the prowl, meant spending the evening listening to the moanings of Moses and Bill about trying to get a living out of the Bute, down the Ely; a frugal supper, and the kids crawling all over you.

There were a lot of people on the street, but I didn't see anyone I knew as I wandered aimlessly along Court. I could have called in to see old Richard Jones and his missus and scrounged a cup of tea – there were dozens of families who would have welcomed me – but I wanted to be alone. Passing the neat little doors, the whitened steps, I stole glances at the rooms within. Streets like these – Thomas Street, Charles, Jones, Maddox and Railway Terrace – were the beating heart of Tonypandy, yet they clustered about me now as strangers: I had never really known them. Now they seemed to reach out welcoming arms: sunshine gleaming on brass, the samplers on the walls, the china dogs and little Horns of Plenty; some front doors were open and I knocked up my cap to women sweeping out: children, huddled together on the pavements or swinging on front garden gates, regarded me with toffee-stuck mouths and curious stares; cats arched their backs on pillars, expecting attention, dogs sniffed at my heels. It was the very normality that riveted me; in my race for love and reading, the pull of Union matters (the call of the ale at the Pandy and elsewhere) I had lost sight, I reflected, of the town's *respectability* – the everyday lives of the everyday people. It came as a shock to me that, within the rank on rank of terraced streets lived an army of ordinary folk who didn't agitate for reform, who did not riot, who went to church or chapel on Sundays; there were countless women who were home-makers and men who did not drink. It was a different Tonypandy to the one I had accepted as the norm.

Possibly, it was sheer habit that took me back to the Square. And then I recalled Heinie saying how he used to wander around the streets of a Sunday evening, listening outside the chapels and churches to the services in English and Welsh. Great choirs were here, as he said: the soaring tenors and mud-caked basses, their tonsils liquid with Allsops, all joining in massive shouts of praise. Sometimes Heinie used to sing at the face, I remembered – aye, Jew-boy, he used to say, but a Welsh Jew-boy, with songs in my belly.

Especially, he used to love the breathy, adenoidal singing of the children.

Where is he now, I wondered – he who faced the might of the great Shoni Engineer?

On this occasion, to my joy and astonishment, Number Six, the Sinkers, where I had lived with Bron, was actually empty.

The door, ajar to the next tenants about to move in, opened to my touch.

The room, by some strange trick of imagination, though bare of furniture, appeared exactly as we had left it. I saw

395

the table and chairs, the bright gate and its red-toothed fire: the bed with the knitted counterpane, the bosh in the corner. And there even pervaded the smell of Bron's cooking; the stews, fried bread, the flapjacks and bakestones. Standing there in the middle of it all the memory of her filled me with increasing intensity, so that, when I closed my eyes, I even heard her voice. Here was where she hung her clothes; here she put her shoes – two pairs (one patent leather) and her high-buttoned boots – very, very particular about her shoes was Bron. Here, on the line above the grate, hung the long, black stockings. The place breathed of her, coming to life, by some strange phenomenon, with astonishing clarity so that, had she appeared in the doorway at that moment in time, I would merely have accepted her as part of the day. I wandered to the mantel, touching its iron coldness; here it was, in jam jars, that she kept her flowers: flowers to Bron were as books to me; she could not live without them.

'Bron,' I said, unaccountably.

The very sound I had made accentuated my need of her. Turning in the empty room, I called again:

'*Bron!*'

The room echoed its coldness; the open door creaked in the wind. I regretted, bitterly, that I was always promising to oil it, but never did ...

After a bit I thought it was bloody silly to be in there looking for things that were passed: peering carefully for a sight of the Odds's and Culpeppers, I went out into the summer sunshine.

Heinie, without a doubt, would have approved of Ceinwen's voice, especially when she sang in Welsh.

Sunlight streamed into the little front room in Windsor Place, Senghenydd, when first I heard her sing:

> '*Nant y mynydd groyw loyw*
> *Yn ymdroelli tua'r pant*
> *Rhwng y brwyn yn sisial ganu*
> *O na bawn i fel y nant ...*'

Her eyes, while she sang to Nan's playing, never moved from my face.

'There now, what do you think of that, Uncle Toby?' Nanwen closed the piano – another of her accomplishments, and I didn't know the difference between Beethoven and Handel. 'Aunty Etta will be here any minute,' she added.

'Etta McCarthy?' I asked.

'Aye, she's taking Ceinie up to the cemetery. She visits one Sunday in the month – fond of Aunty Etta, aren't you, darling?' she said to Ceinie.

No reply. Only Ceinwen's eyes, a copy of Nan's, moving like lights in her pale, oval face.

'Taking flowers to your dad's grave?' I asked.

No answer; Nan interjected:

'Ben's buried in the next grave to one of Etta's – she lost her first, you know – a girl. She and Dano were married in Senghenydd then moved to Pandy.'

'And had six lads afterwards – that was bitter.'

'It's life,' said she, and sprang up from the piano as Mrs. McCarthy knocked.

The young and the old, I thought, bearing flowers; in their black dresses, black bonnets and boots, it was a rendezvous with death.

Now they stood hand in hand, Etta and Ceinwen, two black crows, in search of buried love.

I often wondered if Mrs. McCarthy approved of me: she was a deeply religious woman in her rough, Irish way: Dano and his six sons had pestered her in the breast and womb; males, to Etta, were like life's necessities – there to be tolerated.

' 'Afternoon, Mr. Davies,' she said, looking past me.

I bowed to her. It was reasonable; I wasn't an angel, and not a lot missed Etta McCarthy.

Tall, angular was she; waisted and bustled, like a spectre from an Irish famine. Nan said, dying to please:

'You've heard about us marrying at the end of the year, Etta?'

'Not official, if ye get me, but rumour has it. And not down here, either, they say?'

I'd rarely heard Etta speak so much.

'Well, Toby wants to stay down here, but I'm longing to go north.'

'Ye could do worse in the south, mind – it's been my hearth and home these years.'

'And mine, in many ways,' I added.

'So I know,' said Etta, archly, and I knew she was referring to my life with Bron. '*Ach*, what does it matter, eh? North or South, the young should be together. Ye can't grieve a life-time, Mrs. O'Hara, and ye've a fine set-up fella here, so ye have, though a bit of Church or Chapel might improve him.'

I gave her a grin.

The sun was striking shafts of gold into the room; dust-motes danced within a holy silence. Nan said, with an effort, 'Ah well, away with you! Will you be back for tea?'

'Wonderful words,' cried Etta, leading Ceinwen out. 'Time was, at her age, I used to go home to see if there was any tea. But don't ye worry about us, missus, we'll be having tea – and likely supper, too, with Shaun.'

Hand in hand (to give something to the neighbours) Nan and I watched them walk to the end of the road; curtains were fluttering around captive aspidistras as we closed the front door.

'Nan,' I said, and took her into my arms.

The old, stifling need of her swept over me.

'Oh, not now!' She pushed me away.

'Come on, girl – they won't be back till dark!'

I cajoled her, whispering things into her ear enough to drive a woman demented.

'*Toby!*' She was outraged.

'I love you,' I said. 'Why not?'

'Darling, it's Sunday.' She hauled out her new dress to change the subject. 'You like it?'

'Great. I like the colour.'

'Blue, you see – it'll help you to know your women apart.' She laughed impishly. 'Define them, might be better?'

I gave her a sigh.

'Anyway, blue suits me,' she added.

'Anything suits you. Did you get it in Ponty market?'

'And cheap – but I usually make my own.' She put the

dress away. 'Remember I used to sew in Caerberllan, when Grandad was alive?'

She settled in a chair on the other side of the fire; it was cold in the room, despite the sunny day; as if a chill wind was already putting his fingers on the soul of the town.

Every day, in one way or another, Senghenydd took its toll; a death here, a maiming there. Only the night before last the Universal siren had gone for a fall – a man up in Parc Terrace – a father of three: his back was broken when they got him out. Ironically, for all the heart-ache the old Rhondda Ely had caused us, she was comparatively free of accidents; but Nan had lost Ben and I'd lost Heinie in Senghenydd.

I began to wonder at the wisdom of making a run for it, before the Universal got me.

Nan said, stitching at her sampler, 'Face it, darling – it isn't as if there's much to keep you here now – Heinie's gone, Mattie's got Mrs. Best, and all your other friends are married.' She raised her face to mine. 'You've worked with slate before – wouldn't they take you on as a rockman?'

'The slate trade's dead, Nan.'

'How many times have I heard that!'

'But it is now. Fourteen hundred people left Bethesda after the Big Strike, and over three hundred cottages were left empty.'

'Where did you hear that?'

'Through the Union pamphlets – Penrhyn killed the industry.'

'Really? I thought the quarrymen had a hand in it.'

It surprised me, and she knew it. I said, 'Ben wouldn't have been happy to hear that. He fought against the injustice of Penrhyn.'

She looked about her casually. I said, in the silence, 'Anyway, whoever was to blame, there's an old, old adage – never go back.'

Nanwen was engaged in thought; I knew the signs – a silent contemplation; a communion that forbade entry.

Now she smiled at me over her needle, and rising, made the tea; there was suddenly a sweet sense of home and belonging; the kettle sang on the hob, the teapot was under its cosy; firelight played on the cups.

'You realise, of course, that we've got Ceinie to consider?'

'Later, Nan ...'

'I mean, well ... she .. she doesn't belong here, does she? These aren't her people.'

'Southerners? Down here, you mean?' I lit my pipe, watching her through the flame. 'All Welsh, aren't they? – but we've been through all this before.'

She emptied her hands. 'You just don't try to understand, do you?'

I answered drearily, 'Now we're getting back to Ben and his theories about nationalism. The older I get the more I agree with him.'

'But it isn't our *home* here. I'll still be a Johnny North if I lived here a life-time.' She stitched vigorously at a sampler. I replied:

'That's because you are making differences where none exist. You can be a Chinese Turk in this place for all the locals care.'

'But half of them don't even speak Welsh!'

'Oh, God! – is that important?'

She sought another tack.

'You don't care about Ceinie, do you?'

'That's childish, Nan – of course I care.'

'She'd get a better education back up north, and you know it.'

'All the scholars aren't up north.'

She was tight-lipped, almost peevish.

'If ... if we returned to Bethesda, I might even get her into Llandegai.'

'Penrhyn's Girls' School? You'd even change her religion?'

'That's an old, old story!'

'And to think you invited me to Congregational Sunday School!'

Her face went up. 'Listen, I'm only trying to do what's best for my child – God knows it's hard enough, what with one thing and another.' She stared about her. 'I hate this black-faced place – I hated the valleys from the moment I

400

arrived here. It's ... it's where I lost Ben ...' She got up from the fire and wandered about. 'Slate was bad enough up north, but this place ...! Rows and rows of terraces, every one waiting for the next roof fall or explosion.'

'Slate wasn't much better – Bethesda was a slaughter-house.'

'Perhaps, but it was clean. I've ... lost one man to the pits and I'm not losing another. If you love me, we'll marry up north.'

I sighed. There wasn't much point in arguing about it. For my part, now I had lost Heinie, there was a vacuum that nothing down here could fill. Nan was speaking again, but I wasn't very attentive. She said, 'Darling, I'm talking to you.'

'Sorry.'

'Look, I've already asked for a week off school – starting the middle of next month – October the twelfth, actually ...'

'What for?'

'To go up north and look around – visit all the old places, the old haunts. There's empty cottages for the asking, you say?'

'A week off? I'd get the push.'

'And suppose you did? I'm sure you'd get another job up there.'

She was excited, wholly expectant; I hesitated.

'What about Ceinie?'

'Oh, she'd come, too.' She took my hands. 'Look, I know you'd love it again, once you were there – we could even stay at Caerberllan – I bet we'd find a host of old friends.'

'It'd cost money.'

'I've got the money.' She yearned at the ceiling. 'Oh, God – I'd give so much just to see the sea again – somewhere clean, away from this land-locked place.'

I shrugged. 'All right, if you're so set on it.'

'And then ...?' Her expression teased.

'Then what?'

'A December bride?' She added, hastily, 'I mean, if we could find a place to live, and you got a job ...'

Heinie used to say that women had only got one brain

401

between the lot of them, but I was rapidly finding that Heinie was wrong.

She was better than Bron for dangling a man, this one.

In the tiny kitchen, pervaded with memories of Ben (though she had at last put away his slippers and pipe), we were washing up when I turned Nan into my arms.

Time had done much to dispel her grief, yet its mark had touched her features with a new, enticing beauty. What is there in grief that beautifies? I wonder. Still as a cat, her hands paused in the bosh; she was looking through the window at the world, and I watched.

Her brow was high and pale, the shadows deep around her eyes, which were large and bright in the high-boned dark texture of her face. And her hair, once so black, was painting itself silver at the temples, the hallmark of widowhood.

The loss of Ben had brought her to a new and delightful fragility: it seemed impossible that she was mine. And there came to me then all the love I had borne her through the years: her eyes grew wide with surprise when I kissed her.

Perhaps, I thought, this was the end of the coldness: we fought in a small hunger of kisses that momentarily obliterated the pair of us. Moments only, those kisses, till I felt the touch of a warning finger, and turned.

Ceinie was standing in the kitchen doorway, watching.

So still she stood that I wondered if she was alive; in a frigid indifference, she watched, motionless. Nan was instantly aware, patting her hair, smoothing her dress. Slowly, I moved away.

'Why *cariad*, you're back early,' said Nan.

Ceinwen raised her hands and clapped them to her face. Crying tunelessly, she turned and raced upstairs. A door slammed.

'Oh, God,' whispered Nan in panic, and followed her.

With my back to the front door, I pulled up my coat collar against the wind and looked at the pale stars. Faintly, from the bedroom window above me, I could hear Ceinie crying, and Nan's consoling replies.

High in the sky a glow was burning: it wasn't far enough

away for Pontypridd or Aberdare, I reflected, so like as not, it was my old, beloved Rhondda.

I watched it for a bit, listening to Ceinie crying, then, hands deep in my pockets, I strode through the gate and along the empty street.

The Universal was simmering like a witch's cauldron as I walked aimlessly up to Woodland. Despite the knowledge that Nan was soon to be my wife, I knew an emptiness that nothing could fill.

CHAPTER THIRTY NINE

A very important day it was, come early October, when Tonypandy played Pontypridd in the Challenge Cup.

People were up and doing at dawn, children yanked out of bed, faces skinned with the rag for the sixpenny newspaper round; grandmas and grandpas were allowed to sleep on, to be out of the way while doorsteps were scrubbed and brass thresholds polished. Best suits were brought out of moth balls, best shirts ironed for creases; boots polished, bowlers brushed, and every man in the valleys shaving extra close; tea caddies were peeped into for saving, wives actually kissed.

Those off duty were thankful, those on duty heartbroken, and the agent down the Universal had a heart attack: half the colliers of the Aber Valley were sick, lame or halt.

The valleys were like a set of fighting bulls every time there was a game in the championship; it only needed a cock-snoot from a Pontypridd fly half to send a Tonypandy Welshman raving mad; rival wives turned up their noses at each other in the market; rival urchins fought in the streets. So very hostile looked Mattie that cold, crisp Saturday when Ponty played Pandy; his stock arched proudly, his wing collar up to his ears; whiskers waxed and his sideburns brilliantined. And Mrs. Best, stayed and bulging in her new astrakan, was beaming, expectant.

'Christ, mate,' I whispered to Mattie, 'you're not taking Bestie.'

'Ay ay — dearly beloved, and all that. Getting married, remember?' said he.

'So am I, come December, but I'm not going beserk. This is rugby, mate — you can't bring blutty women.'

And Mrs. Best cried, 'And he anna leavin' me behind, neither — with my old man the best prop forward in the business?'

'He never was!' Confounded, I started with a new and vital respect.

'Up in Lancashire, mate. Compared with the North, this lot don't know rugby from postman's knock.'

So I danced her in a circle and her hat fell off and she cursed flashes as Mattie and I high-stepped her in the middle of us down Woodland, with all the neighbours cheering. Snookey Boxer had arrived with Dai Parcel and Gwilym and a crate of Old and Mild, Ed Masumbala and his Beli were dressed posh for the charabanc; even Jaundy Evans's toes were better for the rugby excursion to see Ponty play Pandy.

Dear me, how I remember the days when I first came to the Rhondda! — courting Bron spare time and getting fit for it in shorts and jersey on a bitter winter's day, sleet sweeping over the ground and the wind with knives in him.

What woman can understand the joy of it? The gasps and heaves of sweating bodies in the scrum; and the *chang chang chang* of a rugby ball on grass? We used to hit hell out of each other in the ruck on the blind side of the ref; elbows coming up, fists driving in. And I used to love the talk about the big games at Arms Park; the inquests, the pints, the bloody noses and the thick ears. And they can spout all they like about their pansy kick and rush. Give me an up and under and trying to make a mark with a couple of tons of rugby flesh roaring out of the sun; or some bastard in the boiler house handing you a thumping.

Ay ay – Heinie and me used to love the Challenge Cup.

These days, knocking thirty, I used to watch the kids at it down at the Rec, but it wasn't the same as the old boots and pints: or a charabanc bumping along the valley roads, a little barrel of ale, rugby fanatics, and bawdy rugby songs.

Tonypandy, host to the Pontrypridd fifteen, was packed to the walls that sunlit morning before the big match. Everybody sporting favours, everybody talking thirteen to the dozen, with the publics open and drinking on the pavements. Down at the station the excursions were streaming in, broughams and traps swaying in from the mountains, the black streams of colliers already thronging into the Mid-Rhondda Athletic.

Mattie handed out Mrs. Best when our charabanc arrived

on the Square by the fountain, and damn me, there outside the Pandy Inn, where Bron used to serve, were a dozen or so of my old mates from down the Ely. The commotion that went up then nearly lifted the slates.

'Ay ay, Tobe!'

'What the hell you doing here? Aren't you Aber these days?'

'Pandy now,' I shouted. 'Come to see Ponty crucified.'

The charabanc contingent piled and Annie Gay was going demented with her jugs; Scotch farriers and ostlers off midday shift clumped up in their coal-dust; top workers from Clydach and engine-men from the Navals. Dano and his five sons were there (Etta kept Shaun at home, still in disgrace) Ed Masumbala the black man, also Albert Arse, and I was just getting my teeth into a quart when Ben Block came in with Bill Odd and Moses, also Red Rubbler, eyeing me for good behaviour with Annie. It was like the old days, except that I hadn't got Heinie and Bron, with people bawling unanswered questions and backs being thumped in joyous greeting. And yet, withal, there was growing within me a nagging wish for a solitary walk, somewhere away from all these happy, noisy people: it was singular and unaccountable, in the midst of such companionship.

It was as if some distant voice was calling me.

'Hell, Tobe — where are you off to?'

Annie Gay, vivacious and dark, flashed me a petticoat look from the bar.

'I'll be back,' I said.

'You'd best not,' said Red Rubbler, barring the way as I shouldered to the door, and I shoved him aside.

'Go and fly your kite, son — this time I'm sober.'

'*Toby*, where're ye off?'

It was Mattie in the middle of them, slopping his pint.

'It's a call of nature,' I said, and went. It was a call of nature right enough: a baying of the moon, as the wild moose hears, in rut.

I never explained it, but I went commanded.

Halfway along Dunraven, I met her, and wasn't the least surprised.

Bron!

'Good God!' said she, flushed, 'if it ain't old six foot three!'
She had a couple of laughing buck navvies on her arms, both
two sheets in the wind, and I don't know who was more
astonished of the four of us. She waved them off, gently
pushing them away.

'*Why, Tobe!* Would you believe it!' Head on one side, she
eyed me like Delilah before the roof came down. 'My! Ain't
you growed!'

'That's what you always say!'

The people barged us, knocking us together, but she stood
back again in mock awe. 'Can you get under a door, mate?
What's she feedin' you on? And d' you know somethin?
Your hair's gone lighter'n the old days.'

Aye, I thought, perhaps my heart was lighter then.

But now I looked at her, smiling.

Life might have short-counted me on times, but never on
beautiful women; passing wives perked up their noses,
hurrying their chaps along. Bron had a big black straw hat
on with an apple-pie affair and grapes on top, tied under her
chin with black crepe, like you see in the London magazines:
her blouse was snow-white, wrinkled in agony over the fine
stretch of her breasts, the buttons gleaming pridefully. She
looked taller, somehow, and willowy, sure in her beauty, her
eyes switching with the old sly wickedness. I'd possessed
other women since I left her in the Sinkers, but no woman
I'd come across made so scarlet in my being.

'You finished?' Eyes slanting at me now, an admonishing
regard.

'Just about,' I said.

'Can I put me clothes back on?'

I gave her a grin.

It was the way of her that got you, I thought; you never
knew the pain of her: Sam Jones was a sod; he'd hooked her
young and played her like a fish. But, on that sunny October
day, she looked cast in a mould for nobody but me.

Seeing my black arm-band, she said, 'Sorry in my heart, I
am, about your Heinie.'

I nodded.

'Made me cry, it did — *nice* little fella.' She sighed. 'All
the good people die — that's why I'm flourishin'.'

407

'You're all right, mun.'

She went on tiptoe, vividly alive with pleasure. 'You always used to say that, didn't ye? Just all right, am I? Hey — what's this about old Mattie and Mrs. Best!'

'Aye, it's true — next month some time, I believe.'

'Everyone's splicing — it's a disease — how about you?'

I shuffled my boots at her, grinning sheepish. 'Wedding come December, God willing.'

'Gawd help you, son! – being wed down here?'

'No – up north – Bethesda, more than likely.' I added, into her waiting, expectant face, 'We're ... Nan and me, I mean – we're going up there Wednesday week – to have a look around.'

The people pushed us about on the pavement; we stood unsurely, eyes rising and lowering. Bron said, 'I'm glad, Tobe – she's right for you, really speakin', that Nanwen ...'

'O, aye,' I said with sureness.

'I mean, ye'll always be, well .... sort of safe, if you know what I mean.'

She smiled, but not with her eyes.

The people hit between us again, glum-faced with us, because we'd blocked the pavement, and Bron said, brightly, 'My old beggar's off again, you know.'

'Sam?'

'Who else? We was settled fine in Tredegar – he'd lifted most of the young skirt up there, I thought – now to settle down to an ever-loving family – kids?' Her eyes searched my face. 'I'm very fond of children you know. Now I'm up there and he's down here.'

'In Tonypandy, you mean? He's here?'

'No Senghenydd – he was at the Windsor pit first, but he's transferring to the Universal, they say, I wonder you ain't seen him.'

'Not a sign.'

She raised her face and smiled. 'He's a bugger, ain't he? They tell me he's living there with Rosie Arse-Jenkins now. Always fancied her, he did. But if it weren't little Rosie it'd be someone else. What's wrong with him, Tobe?'

'He's a polygamist.'

'Christ, I wouldn't call a dog that – what's it mean?'

'Half a dozen women still wouldn't be enough.'

She stroked me warmly with her mind, saying, 'My, you're wonderful with words, ain't you? I just never met a fella in all my life like you for words – where d'you get them all from?'

'Books.'

'What you reading now, then?' She was trifling with me.

'Now? – *The Ancient Mariner* – Taylor Coleridge.'

'A love story is it?'

'No.'

My mind was fumbling at her, becoming merged into her being, while she, self-possessed, regarded me with a sort of warm, maternal pride. Flicking dust off me, she said:

'I had a letter from my little Bibbs-Two yesterday.'

Passing men were staring into her face. She continued, 'She's ten now – don't time fly? She ... she writes a better letter'n me.'

'Is she still with the aunt?'

'Ay ay – Tyddyn Llewelyn up in Waen Wen – you remember?' She paused, thinking. 'That Nanwen's girl's about three years older, ain't she?' She smiled brilliantly. 'You ... you'll have a daughter ready made, so to speak.'

I thought it was ridiculous that we should be standing here talking in the midst of people. A sudden, urgent necessity gripped me – that I should seize her hand and run with her away from all the complications of new and lost loves. She shrugged.

'Ah, well, I suppose I'd best go and look for the bugger – more'n likely he's come over for the rugby, see? But talk has it that he's got little Rosie in Hendre Road. Where's that in Senghy?'

'Opposite end to Woodland, where I lodge.'

'I'm sorry for Rosie, really, 'cause she's only a kid. But if I catch her with him she'll bloody evaporate.'

I made a mental note to have a word with Annie and Albert, Rosie's parents, over in the Sinkers.

We were walking back slowly along Dunraven now. Sarah Bosom and Dozey Dinah went past on the other side of the road, still in weeds for Heinie. Earlier, while talking, I'd seen the Livingstones – Guto carrying a travel poster about Bavaria. Mrs. Ledoux was stroking a little marmalade cat a the end of Gilfach Road: the Salvation Army band wa playing *Nearer My God to Thee.*

Bron stopped us along De Winton. 'Where you bound fo now then, you old soak?'

'The Pandy – fancy a port wine?'

She said, 'What I got to tell you, Tobe, can't be said in a pub ...' She added, 'I ... I got somethin' to show you, really speaking ..'

I retorted, coldly:

'You could have said a lot to me once, mun, but you didn' even try.'

She lowered her face. 'It ... it were for the best.'

'It wasn't, and you know it. Two years I waited.' I glared at her, steering her across the road, and we nearly got run over.

'Aye – two years!' I said. 'And you didn't care if I lived o died.'

Her eyes moved over mine, in frowns; it was a pity for I preferred her smiling. She said, 'Tobe, it were best, truly – see it my way? She's good for you that Nanwen – she's educated – a teacher, ain't she? Gawd, if I'd got what she's go we might 'ave made a go of it.'

I said, bitterly, 'While I was in gaol you never even sent a word with Heinie or Mattie.'

'And you were perfect, weren't ye?' she returned. 'When are ye going to walk on water? That Nanwen was a bother to us, you know.'

We looked at each other, then smiled. Chuckling together, first, then laughing aloud so that people looked, apprehensive.

I said, 'What did ye want to show me just now, then?'

She was pulling on her gloves. Don't matter now, do it?'

'Aw, come on, don't start that!'

She looked at me. 'No – another time, perhaps.'

'It can't be that important.'

'I got to go,' she said.

I wanted her to stay. She was fussing with her fingers. 'Lawful wedded husband, and all that. And if he's got Rosie

Arse with him, rugby tackles won't come into it. Goodbye, Uncle Tobe.'

A flower-seller was sitting on the corner of Post Office Row so I bought her a bunch of Christmas roses: she swallowed hard and I thought she was going to cry.

Duck and Dai Parcel arrived, halloing, from the crowd then, slapping our backs and waltzing Bron in circles, and her hat fell off and she shrieked, and passing colliers fought for her gloves, sparring up in fun.

'And what might you be up to, woman?' demanded Duck. 'Don't you know this man's spoken for?'

'She's lost her chance,' I said.

And Dai smiled into Bron's face, saying, '*Duw*, you're a rare beauty indeed, missus. Never have I seen the like, and I've courted some. I'd give a finger from each hand for a minute of joy in ye.'

'She's a rose of a woman,' said Duck. Bron glanced nervously about her. I thought, *please stay . . .?*

'I got to go,' she said, and I took off my cap to her. We all looked awkward at each other, as people do before parting.

'Don't . . . don't let 'em get you down,' I said.

There grew about her a new and spirited coquettishness. 'Don't you worry, mun, they're very small pop.'

'Good-bye.'

'Remember me, Tobe?' Head on one side, she regarded me.

I nodded.

The three of us stood watching her as she went along De Winton. The flower-seller said to me, in Welsh:

'Where did you grow her, mister? I've got nothing like it in this old basket.'

CHAPTER FORTY

Some say, who were awake early on Tuesday the thirteenth of October in the Aber Valley, that an angel appeared in the sky above the Bryn: the same chap, said Tommy Arse, that he saw later standing in the sky above Mons, when he was fighting for the King of England, and not King Coal. But little exceptional happened so far as I was concerned, for my thoughts were full of what was happening next day – Nan, Ceinie and I catching the night train up north to Bethesda to scout around for a job and a cottage to go with it.

'We'll not miss ye,' said Mattie. 'Be nice to 'ave a bit of peace, won't it, Bestie?'

'Aye, but he'll be back, mark me,' she replied, and looked up and down Woodland in her curlers. 'Once the South always the South they say. Mind, I'll be at the station tomorrow to see you off – very romantic it is. I'll do meself up posh for you.'

She needn't have bothered.

The whistle went for the change of shift.

Mattie drained his cup. 'Get your skates on,' said he.

We had face colliers like Mattie and me, we had top men; spragmen and banksmen – hauliers, ostlers, farriers and timbermen – and a score of others – all getting through their breakfasts, leaving their wives with kisses or scowls (as they went upstairs to make the beds) – or chucking them under the chin, as I did Mrs. Best, but Mattie, strangely, kissed her goodbye; the first time he'd done it.

'Oh, go on with you,' said she, very pretty with her, despite her curlers.

'Good-bye, Petal,' said Mattie.

And we all went to the pit in a thundering of boots along Woodland.

The day shift was going down, the night shift was coming

up. Nine hundred and thirty-five men were down the Universal pit at ten-past-eight that morning.

Some of my mates from down the Ely were there, too – people like Mattie, of course, old Dai Parcel and Gwilym who worked with the ghost of Owen. Snookey Boxer was in the next stall to Forty, as was big Ed Masumbala, the Negro who lived a few doors up from me in Woodland. Then there were a couple of butties I'd made – Bert Jebb, Welsh speaking, who was married with six kids in Number Eight, Cenydd Terrace, and Softy Jones who was lodging up in Brook Street, near the school where he was once a master, teaching English: very educated was Softy, though he could get out coal as good as the rest of them; in the event he'd have done better, I reckon, to stick to teaching English.

'Plus another Jones you'll be interested in,' mentioned Mattie as we all clanked along for the morning shift, 'and this one ain't a softy.'

I turned to him; he had adopted an air of studious indifference.

'Who?' I asked, but I reckon I knew before I asked.

'Sam Jones,' said Mattie, 'but don't look now.'

I wasn't too surprised. Bron had told me at the rugby outing that Sam was being transferred from the Windsor to the Universal: meeting him on or off a shift was only a question of time.

I wiped my mouth with the back of my hand, and Mattie said, elbowing me, 'Now, come on, Tobe, it ain't the end of the world.'

I was glaring at Sam on the other side of the road; he hadn't yet seen me, and Mattie added, 'And don't start that, neither – there's room down the Universal for the pair of you.'

I doubted it.

And hand in hand with Sam was Rosie Arse-Jenkins – come to see him off, apparently, and she's a caution, said Mattie, marching with the colliers.

Bright and early was she, up with the colliers – off scrubbing at an agent's house farther down the valley, I learned later, and her hair was tossing in the wind and her eyes were alive: waist for a dog-collar, hips on the sway, and her young

413

breasts cavorting and gallivanting in her blouse like a pair of cooking apples. I reckon she stopped more than one leak in the Mineworkers' Federation that morning, and she stopped me up the slope in the press of the men, for I was remembering Bron.

As for Sam Jones beside her, it fascinated me to see him in boots. For years, to me, he'd been the ghost in Bron's face. Mattie said now, as the pair of them approached, 'He's a swine, isn't he, doin' that to Ma Bron.'

'He's never been any good,' I replied.

The men drifted either side of us, but Sam and Rosie paused.

'Ay ay,' said he. Hands deep in his trews, he looked me over.

The years had savoured his dark, handsome looks, and broadened him; he was a hunk of a man, wider than me, if shorter, and I'd have liked to try him for size, for Bron. Rosie, as spry as a virgin maid, raised her cheeky little face to mine, and said, coyly:

'Well, well, Toby Davies, just fancy seeing you! What you want?'

'A word in your ear before you get a flea in it.'

'Tell him to bugger off,' said Sam, bored.

'Don't you two love-birds talk direct to each other, then?' asked Mattie, innocent.

'Not to a *bradwr*,' said I.

'A what?

I was weighing Sam for size, and he said, droll:

'You'd best make off, Toby Davies, before I tan your backside.' This he said in Welsh, his dark eyes smiling. In English, he added, 'Ay ay, *cariad* – you first, and your little hoppo after.'

'After when?' asked Mattie. 'Is he threatening violence?'

'After shift?' I said to Sam.

'After shift; or now, down the Bottanic – when you like.'

'God help you,' said Mattie.

Because of Bron there was burning in me a sullen anger

now Sam was there in the flesh. He made bonfires of people's hopes and warmed his behind on them. I said:

'You're a dirty bugger, aren't you, doing this to Bron.'

'I've told you before and I'll tell you again, son – she's yours, on a plate.'

I indicated Rosie. 'This bit of crumpet for a woman like her? You must be toop.'

'You'd best go, boyo, lest I have you now,' he said, and took his hands out of his pockets.

'Not here,' said Mattie, and towed me along.

Being late queue for the cage, we got to the Lancaster downcast shaft nearer eight o'clock than six, the time the shift started. The cage slammed shut. Mattie, Bert Jebb, Softly and me were first in; Sam was last, and we glared at each other over the heads of the others.

'There's high rise gas this mornin',' said somebody as the cage rattled down in flashing lights. Strangely, I remembered that Nan was taking Ceinie to Caerphilly market that evening, on the train, and mentioned it. I was trying desperately to canalise my thoughts away from Sam.

'There's no market in 'Philly today,' said Mattie.

'*Diawch*, this winder's giving us a ride again.'

'Aye, I can smell gas, too,' I said. 'But not enough to kill a 'flu canary.'

'A fox can always smell his own hole,' said Sam.

'I can't smell it,' said somebody, 'but then, I get gas day and night from my missus.'

'I'd put this engine-winder on a merry-go-round,' said Ed Masumbala, and I realised he was with us.

'He ain't in the Union, ye know?'

'Likely a peer in the House of Lords – he must hate colliers.'

The cage dropped faster. Eight hundred feet, a thousand feet, fifteen hundred, two thousand feet, then it slowed. Lights began to flood the cage, flashing slower on the brattice. The floor of the Lancaster level made shape. As the cage door clanged back and we all trooped out, I said to Sam, in Welsh:

'You grow a tail on Rosie, mate, and Tommy, her brother'll have you for dinner.'

'I'll grow a tail on you, when we hit Forty Stall – never mind Tommy.'

'Must you two talk Chinese? – can't you speak English?' asked Mattie as we shouldered down the underground road.

'He won't know English from Chinese five minutes from now,' answered Sam. 'Nobody – least of all him – is telling me what to do with my missus.' He scowled at me. 'Didn't miss a trick, did you? – bedded her first opportunity.'

'It wasn't like that.'

'So now you can keep her.'

'God,' I said, 'you're not fit to clean her Monday boots.'

Somewhere, far away, I heard a faint alarm bell ringing.

Mattie cried, breaking it up, 'Here we comes, lads – work hard for the Consolidated Collieries – Lord Merthyr's giving me a wedding present, you heard? Is anyone here giving me a wedding present?' He was leaking the news at last.

'Sod Lord Merthyr and the Consolidated Collieries, butty, you included.'

'Don't be like that,' said Mattie.

As we passed the engine house the dynamos were sparking and the belts slapping good enough for Pandy merry-go-round.

I looked at my watch as we got to the lamp room; to this day I don't know why. It was six minutes past eight. The lamp man checked us and we drew tools.

A journey of coal drams was coming, towed by Nellie, an old mare Heinie had loved – he usually had a bit of something for her, so I gave her the apple out of my bait tin.

'You won't be needing it, anyway,' said Sam, clanking along beside me.

'Dear God,' said Bert Jebb, glancing over his shoulder. 'I don't know who you are son, or what's up, but you're just begging for an outing.'

'And he'll get it,' said Ed Masumbala. 'If you ain't Forty Stall, stranger, why're you coming?'

'I'm thirty-two stall, black man,' replied Sam. 'But I've got a big appointment eight stalls up.'

'The overman'll suspend the pair of you, if you are found fighting,' said Mattie, apprehensively.

'And I'll have the overman – you, as well,' said Sam.

'He don't give a monkey's bum for anybody, do he, Tobe, includin' the monkey,' said Snookey.

'Certainly there's a hint of carelessness in his manner,' said Softy.

'It do make the imagination lurch,' commented Dai Parcel, joining us along the road. 'But he's got the whole county to sleep under after, so he'll rest snug.'

'Don't be too sure,' I said, 'this isn't Red Rubbler.'

I looked at my watch again. It was ten-past-eight.

As I put it back into my pocket the Universal blew up.

According to talk later, the Lancaster downcast exploded with a roar that brought down ceilings, sending a shaft of flame a hundred feet into the air, and billowing smoke: it blew the top of the pit shaft to pieces, it blew off the head of Joe Moggridge, a banksman.

Two thousand feet lower, where the night shift was coming off and the day shift going on, it did rather more.

Snookey Boxer, one of the first of the four hundred and thirty-nine men to die, died in Welsh, his mother tongue.

The roof came down at the intersection of Lancaster and Number One North – all of us but Snookey had got round the corner: it pinned him from buttocks to shoulders, and the press, slowly subsiding, made him one with coal.

The blast blew me flat, with Ed Masumbala on top of me, and we scrambled up and attacked the fall, heaving on Snookey's feet, which were projecting from the burning mass shock waves of fire were blasting up and down the Lancaster knocking us over.

We could hear the flames roaring behind the fall as we hauled and sweated, but all we got was Snookey's boots – boxing boots – they came off in my hands as I fell backwards.

'Jesus, man, get out!' shouted Ed, for flames were now spurting at us through the rubbish of the fall. Later, we heard that the heat vacuum following the explosion had

417

sucked back, rushing from the engine house down the level like cordite through a gun, incinerating most of the day shift, men and horses. And even as we fled I heard Snookey's voice crying above the flames:

'*Does ond y chwi a mi y byd. Effie – chwi a mi . . .!*'

'Run for it!' yelled Masumbala, and the roof started to go down like dropping sticks behind us; the walls about us bulged, the floor caved and bucked. Heat fanned about us as new explosions rocked the pit, blowing up individual stalls and headings. Boulders were dropping out of the roof; I ducked some but ran into one that knocked me flat. Everything seemed to be flashing light and sound as Masumbala dragged me upright.

'Run! *Run!*' Towing me after him, he staggered through the debris, scrambling over falls. And suddenly Mattie's face appeared before me in the gloom of the road, a lamp waving beside it. The face gasped and spluttered, an astral countenance lacking a body, crying:

'You all right, Tobe?'

'Aye.' I fell against Masumbala again, and he held me.

'Then come on! The Bottanic, the *Bottanic!*'

With Mattie one side and the black man on the other, I floundered on, half-conscious to the stunning blow on the back of my head: reaching the Bottanic corner, we leaped into it, and dived flat, seconds before the roof went down in Number One North.

'You all right?' Mattie gripped me, turning my face to his in the shine of his lamp.

I rubbed my head. My fingers were red with blood.

There were several men sheltering in the Bottanic roadway, including Ed Masumbala, Mattie, Bert Jebb and Softy.

'Where's Dai Parcel and Gwilym?' I got up, raising my Davy.

'No sign of 'em.'

'Sam Jones?' I asked, steadying myself; distantly came the reverberation of deeper explosions; the confining walls of the chamber trembled.

'He went ahead of us,' said someone.

Strangers were in the chamber; men I had not seen

before. There was young Ben Davies of Commercial Street, crying aloud to the pain of a burned hand, his right; and he held up his left hand, which was untouched, and he was weeping, a mere child. Tom Lewis I knew an old collier who used to work the Windsor, and I said to him:

'Which way did you lot come in?'

'Same way as you.' He rose to his feet and pushed his grizzled face near to mine. 'All lamps out except mine, lads – we'll need the oil.'

'What are the chances?' I asked him, soft.

'Practically none,' replied Mattie, who had ears like mice.

Someone said from the dark. 'The bloody place has gone up, that's what. Sounds to me like the Lancaster Level, from Kimberley to the Downcast.'

'You're likely right,' said the old collier. 'But it won't do no good thinking about it – we've got to get out.'

'Take it slow for a bit, eh? Till I get me breath back,' said Bert Jebb, and lay down by the gob beside Softy.

'What we done to deserve this – burned alive?' asked a man.

Because we're bad buggers, that's what,' said Mattie. 'And my Bestie'll play hell if I'm late home for dinner.'

We sat in silence, saving breath, looking at the old collier's lamp in the middle of the floor, and I thought of the rolling hills of the county above us in sunlight, and the ash, the willows and the young spruce garlanding themselves with the tints of winter. Vaguely, I wondered if I would see them again.

'Mind,' said Softy, stretching out his skinny little legs, 'we can't be entirely alone – there'll be lots of people on top by now – Mr. Hutchinson, for instance, the new agent – now, they say he's a genius on safety in the mines.'

'And Mr. Shaw, the manager?' asked Masumbala, his white eyes rolling in the dark.

'Ay ay,' answered Mattie, 'he's bound to be there, like old Evan Owen of the Miners' Provident.'

'But Baron Senghenydd, who owns this hell, won't be out of bed yet.'

They groused and grumbled; they hawked, spat and

coughed; Old Tom Lewis had a chest that sounded like Miner's Asthma.

'Save your breath,' I said, leaning back on the gob.

A man said, bass, like a voice from a crypt, 'I'd like to get my shovel up that fuggin' Inspector of Mines, though.'

'Me first,' said Mattie.

Most of this I heard in a vague, red dream; my balance was unsteady, my head still spinning: the shape of old Tom Lewis's face made strange gyrations in the dusty light from the middle of the floor.

We rested in silence, save for roof trickles and faint subterranean hammerings: and with such a languid ease that I suspected gas. But the Davy was still burning brightly after an hour of it. The old collier said:

'Anyone got a watch?'

'Half-past-nine.'

I was thinking of Bron, wondering, amid the coughing and spluttering if they'd heard about the explosion in Tredegar and what she'd do if Sam had been killed. Then I remembered Nanwen, and, with a little shock, wondered what would happen about our week up north. I watched, a man detached, as Tom, the old collier, examined the fall that blocked us to Mafeking.

'Mind, there's some fresh air coming in somewhere,' he called.

'Perhaps there's an air shaft,' suggested Mattie.

'Crawl through that, mun, and we're all set for the walk home. My woman's got Irish stew for me tonight, she promised,' said Ed, bassly.

Tom Lewis, the old one, as inscrutable as a Chinese god, sat against the fall; beside him was Billy Eldridge, the lad, seemingly half asleep.

I looked at the other men around us.

Two were impossibly young for this kind of death – Billy Eldridge, for instance – probably fifteen. I wondered how they'd behave when things got worse. You could never know. I'd had some narrow squeaks underground and still couldn't judge what a man might do. I've seen boxers crying like children and urchins playing Dolly Stones.

So far, however, the new men with us were adopting the

usual listless attitude of colliers trapped underground; it was a convenient pose. Only time would tell how any of us would handle it.

'You think we'll get out?' asked Billy Eldridge, suddenly.

'Any time now, son,' replied Tom Lewis.

'Then why aren't we moving?'

'Just resting – slow, steady, easy does it . . .'

'Those are burying words – I want to go up.'

'All in good time.'

Boots in a circle, we sat listlessly, sweating cobs, for the air was coming in hotter still, so we stripped to our belts.

'I'm done this side,' said Softy, 'will someone turn me over?'

More smoke was drifting through the broken-faced slope of the fall; people began to cough again.

'Best make up,' I said, and rose. 'It's cooler farther down.'

'It's firing behind there, isn't it?' said Mattie, softly, nodding at the roof fall.

'Of course not!'

'Well, somebody's stoking us – must be the Devil.'

'Beyond the blockage – in Number One North? Remember the timber was alight when we first come in?'

'Perhaps,' I whispered, 'but lower your voice.'

'It'll be the fire-damp next, that'll cook us for sure.'

This was the after-explosion gas; the death was reasonable.

'Look,' said the old collier, wheezing. 'Keep your death to yourself. We're goin' to be all right, aren't we, Billy Eldridge?' and he patted the boy's knee. 'I got a lad up there same age as you.'

'God 'elp him,' said a voice.

I was sweating badly. The Davy on the floor was lower. *Gas.* The other men undoubtedly noticed it, but nobody said anything because of the boy . . .

Later, they found eighty bodies in the Mafeking area, and the heading was choked with fire-damp. Everything east of the engine house at the shaft bottom was alight. No wonder it was hot.

'Well,' said Tom Lewis, getting a pick. 'We'd best start digging.'

'Which end – Number One North, or Mafeking?' asked Ben Davies. I admired his guts. His hand was dreadfully burned; there was nothing we could do for it.

'Take your choice.'

Men rose lethargically, raising their tools; the flickering light of the solitary Davy cast weird shadows on their sweating, dust-stained bodies. Tom said to Billy Eldridge. 'You stay here with Ben Davies, son . . . The rest of us make shifts. We'll poke a hole in this blutty lot. God helps those who help themselves.'

Nobody spoke for a time. Ed and Bert Jebb, great in the shoulders, began picking at the fall that blocked the road to Mafeking. The confined space began to swirl with dust again. I said to Tom Lewis:

'You stopped to think, that Ladysmith runs across Bottanic? If her roof's down as well we'll be digging for years.'

'But the air's cleaner, mun. It's the chance we take.'

After four hours of digging, with exhaustion claiming us, we lay back, sweating against the cavern walls.

'Likely we're wasting our time,' said Ed Masumbala.

I looked at my watch, carefully winding it. It was one o'clock. The air was filthy and it was difficult to breathe.

Somebody said there was a band of iron around his chest and that he thought he was going to die, but nobody answered.

'Right,' said the old collier, with command, 'we'll dig the other way.'

'Make up your bloody mind,' said Mattie.

Deeply in the bowels of the county came muted reverberations; the thunder of the old workings (probably lamination faults revived by the major explosion). Smoke and dust trickled down from our roof. There was no sound save Ben Davies groaning.

'Listen!'

Somebody, standing, slipped on stones.

'*Heisht,* for God's sake! *Listen!*'

We heard distant crackling, like things on fire; a sudden explosive air moved in the chamber, bringing waves of heat.

'You feel that?' asked Softy.

'What?'

'Hot air came in from somewhere.'

'You're imagining it.'

The old collier rose and went to the fall that blocked the road to Number One North, listening.

I looked at the men about me.

After only five hours or so they were listless. In prostrate shapes their half naked bodies made it a charnel house. Their movements were the slow-motion of the drugged entombed. Had the chamber been smaller, we all would have died, but air, amazingly, was somehow getting in through the rubbish of the fall from Number One North.

After an interminable wait, somebody said:

'What's the time, Toby?'

'Don't keep asking the damned time,' said Softy.

'Why not?'

'It's a variable element,' replied he. 'Precisely in accordance with the attention one pays it, it shortens or lengthens.'

'Educated bastard!'

'I assure you I am right,' said Softy. 'It possesses variable factors – I've read about it. God invented Time, it was Man who tried to measure it.'

'Half-past two,' I put back my watch.

'Is that all?' cried Billy, sitting up. 'I've been down here days.'

'That's what I mean,' said Softy.

I was more worried about Bron.

If Sam Jones was dead, and this seemed likely, she'd be lost, like most women who yearned for such fancy old footers, the bad lads.

I was thinking, too, about the fires beyond the blocked roadways that isolated us; the long galleries of smashed timbers, twisted brattic; a debris of men, animals and steel, all blazing, for I knew the effect of such a thunderous detonation.

As long ago as thirty years back scientists had discovered the source of such explosions – it was the mantling coal dust that needed but a spark. But schemes for neutralising it with

stone dust had been abandoned by Owner after Owner o
grounds of cost. Nearly three hundred dead down the ol
Albion nineteen years back; a hundred and seventy-six dow
Llanerch pit four years before – eight thousand miners kille
in the past sixty years.

Contravention of the laws of the Mines Commission an
the findings of its enquiries; slip-shod safety precautions, th
push for higher profits, all combined to turn the coalfield
into a gigantic slaughter-house. And we in Wales, producing
but an eighth of the total British output, yet suffered a thir
of Britain's disasters.

'I hope old Bessie feeds my pigeons, though,' said Mattie.

Yes if Sam died, I thought, Bron would probably wande
from one place to another, in search of nothing. I'd read
about a woman who did that once – just wandered; sitting a
the tables where she had sat with her lover, sleeping in th
same beds: for nothing, it seemed, could replace Sam Jone
in Bron's heart. Softly, sitting near me, said to somebody:

'Aye, well that happened to me, too. I was driving a head
ing down Windsor, I remember, and there was a little hole i
the rock; in the middle was a little stone – onyx, I think
with the grain of a leaf in it. Before I could stop myself, I'o
picked it up. It must have been the first time that little thing
had been moved since God made the world. It quite upse
me.'

'Dear me,' rumbled Bert. 'Bloody listen to it.'

Nan, on the other hand, would be all right, I thought; sh
was contained, self-possessed: also, she was armed with kin
memories of Ben: Bron would have no such memories o
Sam. It was a maligancy without a cure; she would b
finished.

'We'll be all right as long as this air's coming in,' remarked
Tom Lewis, the old collier.

Strangely, I knew no pestering sense of urgency about it.

I imagined the scene on top, the wailing sirens, the stolid
wet-faced relatives.

There were some good men over at Porth Rescue Station
too, excellent engineers.

Bert Jebb said to me:

'*Nid oes bradwr yn y ty hwn*, eh?' and it turned me: it was good Welsh, and I was surprised, saying:

'Where did you get that from?'

'What does it mean?' asked the old collier.

I translated, ' "There is no traitor in this house." '

'What you on about?'

The lad said, 'An old Johnny North I knew told it me – they used to put it in the windows up Bethesda way, during the Big Strike. That right?'

'There'll be a bigger blutty strike down Senghenydd way when I get out of here,' said someone.

'If you get out,' growled Mattie, and Bert added:

'He reckoned you had forty publics in Bethesda alone, that right? *Iechyd da!*' He drank from his jack.

'You should have seen the barmaids!'

'*Duw*,' breathed little Billy Eldridge, 'just look what's arrivin'!'

We followed his pointing fingers. In the glow of the Davy lamp black pats were streaming over the floor.

'So what?' asked Masumbala. 'Ain't you seen those little fellas before?'

Nobody replied, because they hadn't seen so many. They were beetles of the hard-backed variety that infested most mines: big as the top of a man's thumb, they were entering the chamber in swarms. Old Tom said softly:

'They're escaping from the fire – it must be hot out there.'

'It's hot all right,' I answered.

'Mind, a pound or two of these'd make a good meal, pushed to it,' said Mattie, sweeping beetles up into his palm. 'D'you know they pick the bones of a horse cleaner than a coat o' whitewash?'

'But they don't touch humans,' I interjected.

'Oh, no – course not.' Ed glanced at Billy Eldridge. 'They never been known to touch the likes of folk – but they nip a bit, though.' He shook his hand, sucking a finger.

Softy said, cultured, 'When I go up I'll take some with me and train them to bite my creditors.'

I must have slept. I was grateful for this for I had an

425

appalling headache. Yet it was a hypnotic, almost langui[e]
sense of security I experienced in lying there, watching th[e]
Davy.

Over in the corner by the fall, Ben Davies was snoring
asleep with the pain. Earlier, we'd tried and failed to brin[g]
him round. Suddenly, old Tom said, crawling into the light:

'Listen, lads, we're doing' all right, see?' I saw his fac[e]
clearly for the first time. Time had ravaged it, but it was sti[ll]
square and strong; the sweat of his chest made livid the raw[s]
and burns of his escape from the fire, but he showed no sig[n]
of pain. 'I know this old pit backwards, and I reckon th[e]
bottom of the downcast's blocked – most ways right up th[e]
Lancaster Level, too, and this has sealed us off. But th[e]
lads'll be at it, you know – O, aye – you can imagine? They'[ll]
'ave even told the King.'

'Bugger the King, you stupid old goat,' said Bert.

'Ay ay, but ye know what I mean – they'll be lifting
Heaven and Earth, like. The Federation . . .'

'And bugger the Federation.'

'Look, see sense, boys.' Tom Lewis stared about him wit[h]
red-rimmed eyes. Playing with pieces of coal, they watche[d]
him bitterly. 'It's only a question of numbers – but they'[ve]
got to collect the rescue teams, and the equipment, see[?]
This'll take a day.' He suddenly wrung his hands like a ma[n]
hunted, and I wondered if he'd be the first to crack. The
young ones were doing all right, I thought, so why the devi[l]
all this talk?

'It's you making the fuss about it, old 'un,' said Billy Eldridge.

'I bet Baron Senghenydd's playing Hamlet up on top.'
The old man chuckled. 'I mean . . .'

'He'd play Hamlet if I had him down by 'ere.'

'They say he's all right, though – sent my missus a bottle
o' wine once – first labour.'

'Did she survive it? The wine, I mean,' said Softy.

'Got his purse up his bloomers.'

'A couple of hundred spent on mine precautions, mate,
and we wouldn't be here.' A man swore violently. 'What a
bloody place to die.'

'Nobody's going to die,' I said. 'That's right, Softy?'

'I certainly don't intend to.' He was cleaning his finger-nails.

'And you, Mattie?' I knew this was safe ground.

'I'm dying for a pint of Liverpool Milk, that's all,' said he. 'Has anyone got a chew?'

'Got some rough cut – Bulwark?'

'Don't chew down here,' I said.

'At best, it's a filthy habit,' said Softy.

A man was whispering softly from the dark, '*Uffern dan, Uffern dan!*'

It sounded like Heinie, but I remembered that he wasn't with us, and then we heard it ... slowly, silently, men sat upright, listening.

The chamber was silent save for scurrying beetles.

'Start praying, lads,' said somebody. 'Nobody ever went to Hell on his knees.'

'*Listen!*'

The old collier began to chuckle softly; sitting on his hunkers, he was holding his sides. A man shouted, gripping him:

'Will you shut up, stupid old man?'

Again, we listened. It was no tapping. It was a faint but unmistakable dull thumping of picks and the treble shrieks of a shovel.

'What did I tell ye? Now then!' cried old Tom. 'The lads are coming!'

'*They're coming!*' shrieked Billy Eldridge, leaping up.

Frantic, we ran to the fall, hauling away boulders. Warm air was blowing in waves through the fall: we gasped at it, flinging out our arms to it, men revived; it was a wondrous, life-giving nectar. Soon the middle of the fall collapsed and a pick came through, then a hand, yanking away coal.

In the middle of the floor, I raised the Davy. Men were shouting, joyously dancing about.

'Porth Rescue – it's the lads!'

Billy Eldridge was crying with relief. 'Will my mam be up top, you think?'

'And all your relatives – you'll be a hero!' I snatched him against me.

The hole became wider; somebody was bawling through

it an unintelligible greeting, and we yelled replies: now we
crowded around the ever-larger hole, expectant, till a head
appeared and a cheeky face perked up.

It was Dai Parcel.

'Are you the rescue party?' cried Mattie.

'Christ, no, mun – we're in the next hole down and need
the company.'

Empty of hope, we watched as Sam Jones, Gwilym and
Dai crawled through into our chamber.

'Mind, we aren't entirely alone,' said Sam as a rat jumped
past him.

'Aye, that's better,' said Dai and straightened, peering at
the chamber about him. 'We had the air, of course, but yours
is an improvement – ours was so low you couldn't stand up.
How you doing, my lovelies?'

At nine o'clock that night, after thirteen hours of being
walled up, Ben Davies, awake again, said, 'Can anybody tell
me what we're waiting for?'

'The fire to die down,' I replied.

'And then we break through?'

'Aye, into the air shaft, if we can.'

'It leads to Mafeking?'

'It likely leads to Number One North,' said the old collier.
'Leastwise, if the gallery's still alight, it'll turn us into hell.'

'Now you see why we're waiting,' added Softy.

'Meanwhile, tighten your yorks,' interjected Bert tightening the straps below his knees. 'Our little mates are
coming,' and he threw a stone at a rat that had suddenly
appeared. 'Comfort they're after, ye know. They'll be sharp
up your shins and sleepin' on your fannies.'

One by one they came, scuttling through the fall holes in
whiskering enquiry, escaping from the fire, noses sniffing the
ventilation air of the cavern, eyes beady bright in the lamp-
light like people requesting permission.

'Come in, lads,' said old Tom Lewis, sweeting with
his lips, 'You're entitled – hot work up along Lancaster,
is it?'

Now they arrived in twos and threes, darting from behind
fallen stones, peek-a-booing at humans, who usually gave

hem boots for welcome, and Billy Eldridge began to cry. A
ew of them, crawling about, were methodically eating black
oats.

'After they're gone they'll start on us,' said Billy, brokenly.

'Don't you believe it,' said Bert, patting him. 'I know a
blind woman in Pontmorlais and she fed a rat she thought
was a kitten – used to take the bread from her fingers.'

'Is that a fact?' asked Billy, hopeful.

'Of course. They're friendly things, really.' Softy
reckoned the rats to come to him. 'Brothers in adversity,
aren't we, little people?'

His cavalier attitude was infectious, though there was
nothing of him. Sam, however, was shivering badly: everybody is afraid of something.

'You're a madman,' he said, 'talking to rats like that.'

'That's why I'm cooped up with you down here,' said
Softy.

My headache was getting worse. It was bringing a sickness
that reached my throat. I felt the back of my head; the pain
was crystallising there in short, vicious stabs. I consoled
myself that I was better off than most – young Ben Davies,
for instance, with his burned hand.

Dai Parcel put his head through the hole in the fall. 'The
air's getting cooler,' he said. 'The lads must have been fire-
fighting. Give us an hour and we'll start looking for that air
shaft.'

'It runs east,' said Tom the old collier, 'but I can't remember what side.' He started chuckling again, and it was the
last thing I heard as sleep claimed me. When I awoke Sam
Jones was bending over me.

'You all right, then?'

'No better for asking.'

'Lucky it was your head,' he said. 'It could have been
vital.'

'You're the one weak in the nut, chasing up that Rosie
with a real woman back home.' I spoke softly, aware of
listeners.

'Don't give up, do you?'

'Not where's Bron's concerned.'

'You had your share.' He spat on the gob.

'And hung on to her, if I could.'

'Lawful wedded wife. She always come back to Sam.'

I said bitterly, 'She can't be a full pound up top, puttin[
up with you. But you'll move her too far one day, mate, an[
she'll land you with the likes of Rosie.'

Sam sighed like a man after Sunday dinner. 'Ach, you tak[
them and leave them, boyo – you always were too serious. [
thump or two – they always come back for more.'

'So it's Rosie Arse-Jenkins now, is it?'

'Rose Harse, if you please – it's a slander. You Rhondd[
lot down here never did pronounce your aitches.'

'She'll drop some aitches if Bron gets at her.'

He grinned wide. 'It's worth the risk – sweet sixteen, she'[
got it going in all the right places.'

He had raised his voice and men were looking in our di[
rection. Gossip comes as naturally trapped underground, th[
old ones say, as swimming the River Jordan in the chape[
pews on Sunday. I whispered:

'You're so damned good, Sam. Celtic blood is it? Wels[
princes? Bron's got the breeding and you're as common a[
dirt.'

'Mind, I agree with that,' said Mattie, leaning towards us[
'Most of these randy sods 'ave classical backgrounds – [
knew one who reckoned his people was in the ark with
Noah.'

'This bugger had his own boat,' I said.

'Talking about romantic stuff, I had a woman once,' sai[
Dai, 'though she weren't so special. She used to wash up i[
me bath water and send me a heliograph message when sh[
was ready for love.' He sighed. 'Always went to bed with he[
hat on. She didn't give a lot away – second Sunday afte[
Lent, it were usually.'

Gwilym said, 'They do come in very strange varieties
Owen, my mate, had one who wore wire wool drawers, h[
reckoned.' He grinned reflectively, thinking of Owen, wh[
died. 'He was a regular Casanova, ye know, before we me[
up. I told him – he ought to be bloody well hung.'

'He was, if I remember correctly,' said Softy.

'And did I have an idle one!' Gwilym warmed to his mem-

430

ries. 'Always 'aving one of her turns, she was. And hang on
o it! I said to her once, "What you saving it for, Minnie,
vidow's memories?"'

'Aye, but she were a girl, remember,' said Mattie. 'It
lidn't do a lot for her.'

'Never again,' said Gwilym.

'Aw, come off it,' said Dai, 'I told you before – woman are
ll right.' He shook his head nostalgically. 'And mine were
ll right, too, come to think of it. When she died it were the
graveyard of my dreams. I knew her when she wore orange
oox rope for garters; a tiny little thing she was, and her
maiden name was Cule, so I called her Molly.'

It was the last thing said before we heard singing. By some
strange trick of hot air and echo, we heard the sound of a
choir.

'*Heisht!*' commanded the old collier, and stopped his
chuckling.

'It's the Treorchy Male Voice,' said Bert.

'My crutch, will you shut it?' whispered Dai.

'It's chaps singing – poor buggers entombed, same as us.'

Hushed, we listened to faint voices rising and falling in the
flushes of warm air.

'There's a fella down there with pernicious anaemia,' said
Sam.

'Tenor, by the sound of him.'

'And all the basses 'ave strangled hernias. Who's the conductor?'

'The poor sods are buried alive, man – what do you
expect, the Hallelujah Chorus?' asked Ed Masumbala.

We strained our ears, but the voices died.

Afterwards, I wondered if any of us had really heard it.

'The lamp's gone out,' I said.

'The lamp's still alight, son,' said Dai Parcel.

'I tell you it's gone out.'

Somebody moved in my pitch blackness; Sam said, his
face near mine. 'The lamp's alight. Can't you see it?'

I shook my head.

He raised it; I felt the heat of it and a redness grew in my
eyes. 'Can you see that?' he asked.

431

'No.'

'Christ.'

Dai Parcel moved over and squatted between my legs, moving his hand in front of my eyes; I felt his fingers touch me.

'That'll make a pension – five bob a week,' said somebody.

'You'll be all right, lad,' said the old collier.

I gripped my hands.

Later, I heard them working at the fall, tunnelling in, looking for the air shaft. The rescue teams must have got the fans going again, for cooler air was blasting through now, chilling us; all Dai Parcel had to do was follow the fans.

'Likely we're crawling straight into the fire?' asked someone, Ben Davies I think.

'Not at this temperature.'

I don't know who led the tunnel dig to get to the shaft – I think it was Sam Jones, being the strongest, and they pushed me in after Mattie.

I worked, too; blindness was no disadvantage, for only the lead men had Davys. The rats were delighted, running over us in their efforts to get to pure air: with the roof no more than six inches from my nose and with just enough room to move my arms, I elbowed and kicked back the muck to the next man down.

Soon I heard voices growing in the air tunnel; next ten minutes I was into the air shaft with the rest of them.

'We've done it, lads,' said Billy Eldridge, but nobody else said anything.

Most of those walled up got clear, but the tunnel, temporarily arched, went down with a roar before the last four reached the shaft, and Glamorgan county came down on top of them.

'God Almighty,' said Mattie, beside me.

Dust spouted out of the air shaft like smoke from a gun muzzle.

There was no time to grieve, and somebody shouted, 'Look, there's lamps coming! There's lamps coming down between the fires.'

Coughing, spluttering in the smoke of burning timbers, we picked our way down Number One North, over dead men and horses, under smashed props, over journeys of drams and roof falls, working down the left of the double parting. And the rescue party picked us up as they fought a way through to Bottanic.

As the cage was wound up the York Upcast, I said to the man next to me:

'Who are you?'

'Billy Eldridge,' said he.

'There now, didn't I tell you we'd get out?'

'Aye, butty,' said he.

'And your mam'll be waiting, too!'

'More'n likely.' He was not so forthcoming now, being a man. Cold air kissed our faces: the cage began to slow.

'Tell me when we're in daylight, is it?' I asked him.

The cage was bucking and dancing like a merry-go-round, the ropes clanging in the York Upcast.

'You're in daylight now, mister. Leastwise, it's about two o'clock in the mornin'.'

I stared up, looking vainly for the stars.

The music of the pit, the whining of ambulances, fire engines; the wailing of relatives and the barked commands of police and rescuers beat about me.

Bert Jebb (and he had six kids), Ed Masumbala, Gwilym, and poor old Dai Parcel.

Later, they told me . . .

'Come,' said Mattie, and took my arm.

CHAPTER FORTY-ONE

Is Heinie gone to his girl wife? Dai Parcel, Gwilym, Owe
and big Ed Masumbala? Somewhere in the darkness, a
I sat in a corner with Mattie, I heard a woman's voice
And Bert Jebb's wife, seeing me, came then, clutching at m
hands.

'Oh, Gawd – isn't there a chance?'

'Not one, missus,' said Mattie. 'But it were quick; h
didn't take a breath.'

Beli came now, Ed Masumbala's girl, with Precious, thei
son – so black, people said, that you couldn't see them befor
dawn, but nobody mourned for Dai or Gwilym.

Near me, George Waldron, the banksman who escaped
was telling *Echo* reporters how his mate Moggridge wa
blown to pieces: the Salvation Army was handing out foo
and drinks; nurses from Cardiff were attending to the in
jured, said Mattie, and men down the East Side were bein
brought up; so were the dead. Bells were clanging amid th
shrill crying of children; they were already making coffins i
the carpenter's stop. Dead horses and smashed drams wer
being hauled up the York Upcast; fire hoses being run down
volunteers organised for pumping.

I turned my face to the sky.

'What's wrong with him?' asked a cultured voice.

'He's blind, Dr. Thomas,' said Mattie.

'Toby Davies of Woodland, isn't it?' the doctor asked.

'Aye,' I said.

His cool, smooth hands moved over my face and eyes.

In one swipe the Universal had taken my friends, th
gassy bitch, and their only crime was to labour in coal.

Where was George Smales? I wondered, whom I used to
see out shopping with his son – one of the best prop forward
in the game. And Taliesin Roberts of High Street, Aber, who
plagued the Scarrott professionals when short of a guinea,
but preferred to dig his patch? And Dai Davies, the haulier

434

who called himself Dai Rhymney, cousin to Georgie Hallet, aged fifteen, who worshipped Joe Choynski?

'Down Number Two South, weren't he?' asked Mattie.

'Aye,' I said.

'His mother's pestering me to death,' said Dr. Thomas. 'You say you haven't been near the fire?'

'No,' I answered, and he sighed.

'There's a few who have, God help them.' He said to Mattie, 'Best get him home – old Best has lost one already, she's a mine expert.'

Where was old Bob Roche, I wondered, when the roof came down?

'You seen him, mister?'

Effie came, wife to Snookey; married but unchurched.

I put out my hand to her.

'We got his boots,' I said.

Ed Masumbala gave them to Mattie, it turned out. A pair of boxing boots for Effie.

'Mind, he liked to wear his boxing boots,' said she, and took them.

I began to wonder where Nan had got to – Bron, too, come to that. It was funny she hadn't come looking for Sam.

It was raining; I hadn't realised it. Mattie said dolefully, 'Come on home, Tobe – we're all getting wet, you know.'

'Get him under cover while I see to this head,' said a nurse, and helped me to my feet.

Her hands were rough but she served me well.

'You've got a bad cut here,' she said, and bandaged. 'What did the doctor say?'

'Not much.'

She brought the bandage over my eyes; it was like the end of the world.

'He won't come home, you know?' said Mattie, hopefully.

'It's the shock,' said the nurse. 'You'll go home now, won't you Mr. Davies?'

I pushed them aside. Near me, a clergyman – the Rev. Rees, I think it was, was giving last rites. The rain was enhancing the smells of death. Someone said that the bodies were falling apart on the stretchers: relatives fainting at the identifications. All around us people were vomiting, for a

435

blown up horse had been hauled out of the Upcast. I began to wonder, sitting there in the rain, what would happen to the Masumbalas, now Ed had gone; they wouldn't keep blacks on the rates when he ceased to be a dead coal hero.

'Will you go home now, then?' asked the nurse.

'No,' I said.

A neighbour whispered, 'I reckon he's waiting for someone.' She bent to me. 'You waiting for somebody, Mr. Davies?'

'Ay ay,' said Sam, coming up, jaunty. 'Well, I never – how's the old man doin'?'

'He's just about your size now, butty,' said Mattie. 'You piss off.'

'Sorry, Tobe,' said Sam.

'Piss off just the same,' said Mattie.

I heard the voice of Rosie Arse-Jenkins calling above the clamouring sounds; I heard Sam's reply.

'Ah, well, be seeing you,' he said, and went.

Strangely, above the bell-clanging, the grating of wheels on rails, escaping steam, the panic of it all, I could hear Heinie's voice and a woman's soft replies.

A man nearby said, 'This'll turn Senghenydd into a town of widows and orphans – Christ, there's nigh five hundred men still down there, and only eighteen got out of Lancaster East Side.'

'Owner's compensation . . .'

'From Lord Merthyr? Make me laugh!'

'But Keir Hardie's here, too – give somebody credit.'

'*Keir Hardie!* God! Where's my son?'

Mattie said warmly, 'You ready to come now, Tobe?'

It was raining harder. 'No,' I replied, 'I want to stay here.'

'You waiting for Nan O'Hara?' a man asked gently, into my face: I never discovered who he was.

'Blood on coal, you say?' asked a woman. 'He's blind, isn't he?'

Mrs. Best arrived and put a shawl around my shoulders. Her softness touched me, as coming warm from a fire. 'Come home now, son? Look, I got a bit of lobscows on the hob, and . . .'

436

I gently pushed her away. I wanted to stay, to listen to Senghenydd; to know its chaos, agony and grief, so that I would never forget it.

It seemed impossible that Nanwen hadn't come. Every woman in the Aber Valley with feet must have been there, waiting for their men; husbands, fathers, brothers, lovers. Bron? Well, Bron, I reasoned, was up in Tredegar; she'd likely take some time to get down to Aber . . .

Softy said, arriving, 'Toby, how very good to see you safe and well!'

'He's safe, but he's not so well,' said Mattie. Other people came, some I didn't know. Then Mattie, speaking to Softy, said, 'Look butty – find that Nan O'Hara, for God's sake – we can't shift the fella, and we want him home.'

'Is she about?' whispered Softy portentously.

'I don't care if she's about – just find her – she lives down Windsor – turn her out if needs be.'

'Do your poor old eyes pain you, then?' asked Mrs. Best.

'No,' I answered.

'Thats' a good thing, then – be thankful for small mercies. Dear me,' she added, 'we'll soon build you up. I'll give ye an egg for your breakfast every morning. And after that – carrots – good for the eyes.'

I nodded against her.

'Mind, blind or not, you're among friends, ain't you?' She warmed to me, cuddling up. 'When my time comes I'd like to have friends put pennies on my lids.'

'You'd best move before she has you buried,' said Mattie.

'Here comes Widow O'Hara and her girl,' said Mattie. 'Thanks for fetching 'em. Now, perhaps, we'll get this boyo home.'

I could hear Nanwen calling me above the din of rescue, and Ceinwen's higher, plaintive voice. Next moment they were beside me and Nan seized my hands. 'Darling, your eyes are bandaged!'

'Aye, well . . .'

'Oh, God – your eyes . . .?'

Mattie said, calmly, 'Look, missus, it may be nothing, but . . .'

437

'Can't you see?' Nan gripped my arms, calling about her: 'What's wrong with him? For God's sake somebody tell me.'

Softy said, 'Aye, well he's blind, isn't he? But he'll likely see like the rest of us when that bandage comes off.'

'The fire? Was it the fire?'

'A bump on the head,' I replied.

Nan was shivering. She was alternately enwrapping me in her arms and staring at my bandaged face, said Mattie later: then she begn to cry, softly at first.

I imagined Ceinwen standing alone, watching me with her usual half-veiled disregard. Nan put her head against me and began to sob uncontrollably, and I recalled, with a little shock of realisation, her temperamental show of panic and grief years back, when Grandpa died.

'Nan, get hold of yourself,' I whispered.

People were watching, those who might one day be neighbours; I was a bit ashamed that folks I knew as friends should see her in this predicament.

A passing nurse said, 'You shouldn't distress yourself, Mrs. O'Hara. He's comparatively unhurt compared with others – it's probably only a temporary thing . . .'

It did not avail her. Nan wept on. Vaguely, I wondered how she had reacted when she'd heard that Ben had died. Perhaps, I reflected, this was her trouble. The pit-head scenes, the stretchers, the bandages – all might be serving to revive the spectacle of the casualty, and her loss, and then she said, brokenly:

'Oh, God, I hate this black-faced place and everything it stands for!' She was weeping aloud now. 'And to think, in another few hours, we'd have been going north, out of coal.'

'Easy, missus,' said Mattie, touching her, but she shook him off, saying:

'Well, it's true! I've lost one man to the pit, and now this! How much more does coal want?' She held me in a vice. 'Oh, Toby!'

'You ready for home now, son?' asked Mrs. Best, softly.

I did not reply, for Mattie said, 'Mrs. O'Hara, your girl's gone off, you know?'

'Gone off. What do you mean?' Nanwen swung in my arms.

'She's really upset,' said Softy. 'After all, she's a bit young for all this . . .'

'Oh, God, I hadn't realised!' Nan rose, calling, 'Ceinie!' She waited. '*Ceinie!*'

People took up the name.

'Probably running back home,' interjected Mattie.

'You shouldn't have brought her,' I said. 'This is no place for a child.'

'Oh, Toby, what shall I do?' Distraught, she hung on to me again.

'Go after her,' I said. 'That's all you can do.'

In truth, I was hoping she would go. Her panic was foreign in this place where women waited with the stoicism born to coal. Nor had her presence served me, for I was already enduring the dread of permanent blindness, something I had always feared: now it was assailing me with the nausea of a bilious attack and I wanted to be sick; this in itself, in the company of neighbours, would be an appalling degradation.

'Toby . . .' her tone begged of me. 'Say you'll be all right!'

'Give me a day or so and I'll see better than you.'

'And you don't mind if I go now? I'll come and see you later . . .'

'He's going home, anyway, aren't you, *bach*,' said Mattie.

I listened to Nanwen's departing; it was fraught with the same apprehension of her arrival, and her voice was filled with dismay as she called:

'Ceinie, *Ceinie!*'

Yes, I thought, there would always be Ceinie.

'She's got it bad,' said Mattie.

Softy said, 'Right, me lad, will you go now?'

'Not yet,' I replied.

I heard Mrs. Best say, 'Matt, don't look now . . .'

I didn't hear his reply, but someone said, 'He's got a female following, all right – look who's arriving.'

Nanwen must have actually run past Bron in her flight after Ceinwen: it was only a matter of seconds before Bron knelt beside me.

'God pity us! What the hell 'ave you been up to now?'

'He can't see,' said Mattie. 'He's got a hit on the head.'

'I know.' Bron put her arm around me. 'They've just told me. Are you swinging it, Tobe? – your head's your strongest point.'

She was soaked with rain and there was a smell of smoke and chloroform in her wet, straggling hair.

'The trouble is getting him home,' protested Mattie. 'Bestie and me'll catch our deaths waiting out by here . . .'

'I've just seen Nan O'Hara going like the wind,' said Bron. 'Is she coming back?'

'She's gone after Ceinie,' I replied.

'Aye, but is she comin' back?'

'I suppose so.'

'You seen the doctor?'

'Yes, and he says I'll be all right. So don't you blutty start.'

'What's she yellin' about, then?'

'Look, girl,' said Mattie. 'Whistle up a stretcher and we'll take him home in style – wounded hero, and all that.'

'He don't need a stretcher, do ye, son?' She thrust her arm under mine. 'Come on – you're making too much of it, as usual. You've collected more from me – heave him up, Mattie.'

'Watch it, I'm delicate,' I said.

'I'll give ye delicate. I bet you'd see if I lifted me skirt.' She got me upright. 'Now arm me down Woodland and give the neighbours a treat.'

I went.

'Damn me,' said Mattie, 'he wouldn't shift for me.'

Bron left us outside the door of Bestie's house. 'One thing's sure,' she said, 'you ain't catching any night trains to Bethesda.'

I gave her a grin. 'You remembered?'

'Not much misses me.' She elbowed me in the ribs. 'You get yourself into bed, and if I've nothing better to do I might slip down later.'

Gladys Bad Fairy, who saw her going up Woodland though, reckoned she was crying.

CHAPTER FORTY-TWO

The nurse came again later, replaced the bandage over my eyes, then left. Now I sat propped up on pillows in Mrs. Best's front bedroom facing the window overlooking the street. Earlier, I had slept. Awaking, I listened to the sounds coming down from the pit-head.

It was like lying amid a concourse of the living but unable to communicate, save with the dead. The dawn was breaking, I think, for I heard distant hooters calling men to early shift.

Contained within this coffined isolation, I tuned my ears to every sound, a trick of the blind; the slightest noise being vital to my existence.

Women were chattering in isolated groups down Woodland on this, the next morning after the explosion – the day on which Nanwen, Ceinie and I were due to travel north. Chairs scraped the flags – grandmas and grandpas sat there, I imagined, locked in the sallow grieving of the aged in a town of widows. A kettle was whistling; the methodical tramping of boots – the stretcher-bearers who had been at it all night; the faint crying of children – all this beat upon me as I lay there thinking of Nanwen.

Her reaction to my blindness had been astonishing, even allowing for her dismay for her future. Her fear seemed something more than the horror of injury; this can terrorise some; it was inherent in her demand for Ceinie's well-being.

I wondered how she would behave if I proved to be permanently blind ...

Earlier – about an hour back (when the nurse had changed the bandage) I had seen the world in pastel shades of green and grey; the window, framed as it was with the rescue lighting, had burned on my eyes as a dull, phosphorescent glow.

Now I longed for Nan to arrive and share my hope.

I was a little surprised that she had not come to date. It

441

was hard to accept that her plans for Ceinie's future and her own longing to return north could deeply influence her love of me.

Outside in the back Mattie's pigeons were coo-cooing to the dawn; a soft, throbbing note; a weak chorus of birds began their song, while up at the pit-head the tempo of the rescue was increasing. An alarm bell was incessantly ringing: as if signalled by the coming light, sirens and hooters all over the mountains began a quiet staccato chorus. I thought of the rescue underground at the Universal; the timbering, burning in creosote flares, made vivid mental pictures: I heard, as echoes, the machine-gun barking of the props as the roof came down, the glowing of gas-pockets, the crying of chained horses.

I supposed Mattie had gone down again. It would be hell down there, I thought; a mangled web of ropes, men, horses and brattice. I could hear the *hee-haa hee-haa* of the fire-engine pumps and the whining of the York Upcast as the lads were brought up.

After a while, I slept.

Bron came. It was then evening, she told me.

'How you doing?' She sat down, gasping, on the bedside chair.

'Bloody terrible – I need the sympathy.'

'I reckon you're putting it on,' said she, and rose.

I was prompted to tell her how I had seen the window lights, but did not. It was a position of advantage, I was discovering, to let people make their own assessment.

Her voice came from the window when she said, 'Dear God, what will become of the town? There's hardly any men left . . .'

'How many have they got up?'

She came back and sat on the bed. 'Most of the night shift. But there's about three hundred and fifty unaccounted for and nigh a hundred more thought dead.'

'But Sam got out.'

'Sam got out, mun, but that's about all.' She sighed.

'What do you mean by that?'

'He's back in his lodgings with Rosie Arse-Jenkins – can

you believe it? He's been nowhere near the pit-head? They're bringing in colliers from Cardiff for rescue. Volunteers are marching in from the west – you know colliers. But no Sam Jones.'

'God, he's slipped,' I said. 'What's wrong with him?'

'The bottom's dropped out of him – I think he's disgusting. D'you know, Tobe – this has had more effect on me than anything he's done to date . . .'

'You've been a glutton for punishment.'

'I can forgive him chasing skirt, that's the way Sam's made. But I'll never forgive him for dumping his mates.'

'Don't worry,' I said, 'you'll come to it.'

'Aye? Then you sit round and damn well see!'

The room was silent save for our breathing. Bron added, limply, 'And it's so unlike him – he just loves to impress. A devil in the house and a saint in public.'

I began to wonder whether or not she meant it and I cursed myself for not being able to see. Then, gradually, the realisation dawned that she was enduring an inner fury: this matched the fierce loyalty of her nature. It was ironic, I reflected, that at the time Bron had come to her senses, it was too late for me to grasp the opportunity. I said, softly:

'You mean it this time, don't you?'

She said, 'I swear to God I'll never have him back. If he came crawling now on his hands and knees . . .'

'Give him time.'

'So now, son, I'm on me jack,' she said, with finality, and rose again, leaning on the bed-rail facing me. 'And, while I'm on the subject, you are, too.'

'What do you mean?' I raised myself on the pillows.

'That Nanwen – she's away.'

'Away? What're you talking about?'

'She's off – scarpered, vamoosed – you might as well know it now as later.'

I sat bolt upright now. 'She's *gone*? I don't believe it.'

'You'd better, mate – I've just seen her off.'

'At the station – on the train?'

'Five ten sharp – you might as well have it on the chin. All the way to Bethesda – her and Ceinie – baggaged and ticketed, single fare.'

My voice rose. 'Without even saying good-bye?'

'She couldn't say good-bye, could she?'

I said, weakly, 'You mean this, don't you? It's true!'

Bron replied, sitting on the bed beside me, 'I met Mattie up at the head when I got back from the station, and he said hold it till your eyes improve, if ever. But this is for your ears. Best you learn now, if she can't stand the thought of living with the blind.'

'Did she tell you that?'

'Aye!'

'Isn't she jumping to some quick conclusions?'

Bron sighed. 'I don't know – one's got to be fair, Tobe. Some folks can't stand the thought of blindness, you know – me, for instance. You'd need one good eye in your head before I'd take ye on. I told her that.'

'What the hell were you doing poking in your nose . . .?'

'God, be reasonable, mun – you've got to be represented! So I took myself along to Windsor Place. I only had your interests at heart.'

'I bet!'

'And there they were packing up, the pair of them, and crying. Well, I had to help 'em, didn't I? Mind, she's got the daughter to consider as well, you know.'

'So you both had a long, interesting talk!'

'Aye, well, not a lot, really speaking – she cried and I patted – woman to woman, and all that – you know, about you being blind. And like I told her, it may be all right now, but you're a passionate chap – you sow a few more kids in her when you're up and about, and she's got problems, ain't she?'

'Tell me more,' I said, faintly.

'Well, that's it, really – I mean, I wouldn't want you to think I interfered, or anything. Up to folks to sort out their own troubles, I always say.'

I cried, 'She was all set to come here when you put your oar in!'

'But she weren't – that's the point – and she was worried to death about what would happen to you, being blind. Mind, she cheered up no end when I showed her the photograph . . .'

I turned my face to hers. 'Photograph? What photograph?'

'One of Bibbs-Two.'

'Bibbs-Two – what's she got to do with it?'

'Our daughter – come on, son, wake up. It's news, ain't it?'

'What the hell are you talking about?' I sat upright.

She took a deep breath. 'Aye, well I realise it's a bit late in the day, but I tried to tell ye once, you know – remember the Rugby Outing when we met over in Pandy? I'd just got the photo that morning, actual – the aunt sent it ... here, hold on. I've got it here ...'

She hesitated, then added softly, 'Oh, I forgot, of course – ye can't see it, can you ...? Never mind, keep it just the same,' and she put the photograph into my hand.

'Bibbs-Two ...?' There was growing in me an unknown emotion.

'Ay ay – and she's the blutty spit and image of you, Tobe, just like Nanwen said. I suppose I should have told you earlier, and I was coming round to it, ye know. Can't ... can't rush these things, can we, until we're sensible sure.'

'Good God,' I whispered.

Now she added joyfully. 'Think of it, Tobe – *you're a father!*'

I said, wearily, after a bit, 'so you worked it your way, as usual. You gave them a shove in the right direction.'

'Don't put it like that – it sounds terrible!'

'And you'll take on a blind man? I thought you wouldn't – you just said ...'

She cuddled up to me on the pillow. 'Aw, forget it! I just told Nanwen that for comfort. For better or worse, ain't it?' She kissed my cheek. 'Besides, you always was mine when Sam weren't about. Oh, and I nearly forgot. That Nanwen's sending our Bibbs down on the very next train.'

'*Dear me,*' I whispered.

There was a long pause, and she said, in a voice of tears, 'Rotten lot, ain't I, Tobe?'

But I wasn't really listening.

The street was awakening again to a new and vibrant

445

activity. Somewhere among the strident sounds I thought I heard the voice of Heinie . . .

Lifting the bottom of the bandage, I looked at the window where the sky was flaring. Raising the photograph, I saw it unmistakably against the lightness, and the dim outline of a child made shape.

'Can you see her, Tobe?'

'No,' I lied.

'Ah, well,' said Bron. 'We'll 'ave to make the best of it – you and me, eh?'

'If that's how you want it,' I said.

She was so quiet then that I thought she had moved away, so I reached for her and found her hand.

Softly, she said, 'Mattie's still down on rescue, ye know – don't expect he'll be up for hours . . .'

I nodded, thinking of Mattie.

'And . . . and I asked old Bestie to be a sport, and hop it. Was . . . was that all right?'

'Strikes me the arrangements are best left to you,' I replied.

'That's what I thought. Good old Tobe, I always say. Shift you over a bit, so I can come in . . .?'